CLEAN ALISTAIR MACLEAN ALISTAIR MACLEAN
EAN ALISTAIR MACLEAN AL
CLEAN ALISTAIR MACLEAN
EAN ALISTAIR MACLEAN ALISTAIR MACLEAN AL
CLEAN ALISTAIR MACLEAN ALISTAIR MACLEAN
EAN ALISTAIR MACLEAN ALISTAIR MACLEAN AL
CLEAN ALISTAIR MACLEAN ALISTAIR MACLEAN
EAN ALISTAIR MACLEAN ALISTAIR MACLEAN AL
CLEAN ALISTAIR MACLEAN ALISTAIR MACLEAN
EAN ALISTAIR MACLEAN ALISTAIR MACLEAN AL
CLEAN ALISTAIR MACLEAN ALISTAIR MACLEAN
EAN ALISTAIR MACLEAN ALISTAIR MACLEAN AL
CLEAN ALISTAIR MACLEAN ALISTAIR MACLEAN
EAN ALISTAIR MACLEAN ALISTAIR MACLEAN AL
CLEAN ALISTAIR MACLEAN ALISTAIR MACLEAN
EAN ALISTAIR MACLEAN ALISTAIR MACLEAN AL
CLEAN ALISTAIR MACLEAN ALISTAIR MACLEAN
EAN ALISTAIR MACLEAN ALISTAIR MACLEAN AL
CLEAN ALISTAIR MACLEAN ALISTAIR MACLEAN
EAN ALISTAIR MACLEAN ALISTAIR MACLEAN AL
CLEAN ALISTAIR MACLEAN ALISTAIR MACLEAN
EAN ALISTAIR MACLEAN ALISTAIR MACLEAN AL
CLEAN ALISTAIR MACLEAN ALISTAIR MACLEAN
EAN ALISTAIR MACLEAN ALISTAIR MACLEAN AL
CLEAN ALISTAIR MACLEAN ALISTAIR MACLEAN
EAN ALISTAIR MACLEAN ALISTAIR MACLEAN AL
CLEAN ALISTAIR MACLEAN ALISTAIR MACLEAN
EAN ALISTAIR MACLEAN ALISTAIR MACLEAN AL
CLEAN ALISTAIR MACLEAN ALISTAIR MACLEAN
EAN ALISTAIR MACLEAN ALISTAIR MACLEAN AL
CLEAN ALISTAIR MACLEAN ALISTAIR MACLEAN
EAN ALISTAIR MACLEAN ALISTAIR MACLEAN AL
CLEAN ALISTAIR MACLEAN ALISTAIR MACLEAN
EAN ALISTAIR MA ALISTAIR MACLEAN AL
CLEAN ALISTAIR MACLEAN ALISTAIR MACLEAN
EAN ALISTAIR MACLEAN ALISTAIR MACLEAN AL
CLEAN ALISTAIR MACLEAN ALISTAIR MACLEAN
EAN ALISTAIR MACLEAN ALISTAIR MACLEAN AL

ALISTAIR MACLEAN

WHERE EAGLES DARE

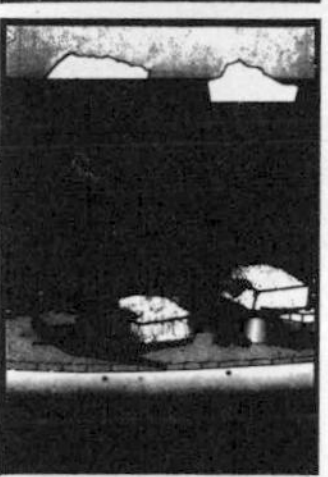

H.M.S. ULYSSES

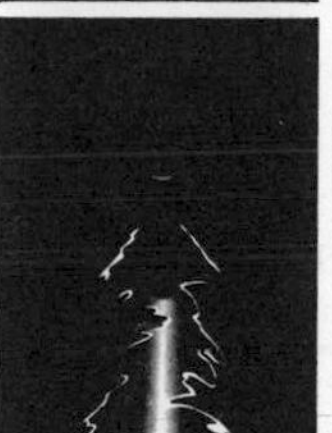

ICE STATION ZEBRA

THE GUNS OF NAVARONE

Where Eagles Dare was first published in the United States by Doubleday & Company, Inc
in 1967; in Great Britain by William Collins Sons & Co Ltd in 1967
H.M.S. Ulysses was first published in the United States by Doubleday & Company, Inc
in 1956; in Great Britain by William Collins Sons & Co Ltd in 1955
Ice Station Zebra was first published in the United States by Doubleday & Company, Inc
in 1963; in Great Britain by William Collins Sons & Co Ltd in 1963
When Eight Bells Toll was first published in the United States by Doubleday & Company, Inc
in 1966; in Great Britain by William Collins Sons & Co Ltd in 1966
The Guns of Navarone was first published in the United States by Doubleday & Company, Inc
in 1957; in Great Britain by William Collins Sons & Co Ltd in 1957

This edition first published in the United States of America
by arrangement with Doubleday & Company, Inc
in 1980 jointly by

William Heinemann Inc
450 Park Avenue, New York, NY 10022

and

Octopus Books Inc
747 Third Avenue, New York, NY 10017

ISBN 0 905712 49 8

Printed in the United States of America
by R. R. Donnelley & Sons Company

CONTENTS

WHERE
EAGLES
DARE

Where Eagles Dare

To Geoff and Gina

Chapter One

The vibrating clangour from the four great piston engines set teeth on edge and made an intolerable assault on cringing eardrums. The decibel-level, Smith calculated, must have been about that found in a boiler factory, and one, moreover, that was working on overtime rates, while the shaking cold in that cramped, instrument-crowded flight-deck was positively Siberian. On balance, he reflected, he would have gone for the Siberian boiler factory any time because, whatever its drawbacks, it wasn't liable to fall out of the sky or crash into a mountain-side which, in its present circumstances, seemed a likely enough, if not imminent contingency for all that the pilot of their Lancaster bomber appeared to care to the contrary. Smith looked away from the darkly opaque world beyond the windscreens where the wipers fought a useless battle with the driving snow and looked again at the man in the left-hand captain's seat.

Wing Commander Cecil Carpenter was as completely at home in his environment as the most contented oyster in his shell in Whitstable Bay. Any comparison with a Siberian boiler factory he would have regarded as the ravings of an unhinged mind. Quite clearly, he found the shuddering vibration as soothing as the ministrations of the gentlest of masseurs, the roar of the engines positively soporific and the ambient temperature just right for a man of his leisured literary tastes. Before him, at a comfortable reading distance, a book rested on a hinged contraption which he had swung out from the cabin's side. From what little Smith could occasionally see of the lurid cover, depicting a blood-stained knife plunged into the back of a girl who didn't seem to have any clothes on, the Wing Commander held the more serious contemporary novelists in a fine contempt. He turned a page.

'Magnificent,' he said admiringly. He puffed deeply on an ancient briar that smelt like a fumigating plant. 'By heavens, this feller can write. Banned, of course, young Tremayne' – this to the fresh-faced youngster in the co-pilot's seat – 'so I can't let you have it till you grow up.' He broke off, fanned the smoke-laden air to improve the visibility, and peered accusingly at his co-pilot. 'Flying Officer Tremayne, you have that look of pained apprehension on your face again.'

'Yes, sir. That's to say, no, sir.'

'Part of the malaise of our time,' Carpenter said sorrowfully. 'The young lack so many things, like appreciation of a fine pipe tobacco or faith in their commanding officers.' He sighed heavily, carefully marked the place in his book, folded the rest away and straightened in his seat. 'You'd think a man would be entitled to some peace and quiet on his own flight-deck.'

He slid open his side screen. An icy gust of snow-laden wind blew into the flight-deck, carrying with it the suddenly deepened roar from the engines.

Carpenter grimaced and thrust his head outside, shielding his eyes with a gauntleted right hand. Five seconds later he shook his head dispiritedly, screwed his eyes shut as he winced in what appeared to be considerable pain, withdrew his head, closed the screen, brushed the snow away from his flaming red hair and magnificent handlebar moustache, and twisted round to look at Smith.

'It is no small thing, Major, to be lost in a blizzard in the night skies over war-torn Europe.'

'Not again, sir,' Tremayne said protestingly.

'No man is infallible, my son.'

Smith smiled politely. 'You mean you don't know where we are, sir?'

'How should I?' Carpenter slid down in his seat, half-closed his eyes and yawned vastly. 'I'm only the driver. We have a navigator and the navigator has a radar set and I've no faith in either of them.'

'Well, well.' Smith shook his head. 'To think that they lied to me at the Air Ministry. They told me you'd flown some three hundred missions and knew the continent better than any taxi driver knows his London.'

'A foul *canard* put about by unfriendly elements who are trying to prevent me from getting a nice safe job behind a desk in London.' Carpenter glanced at his watch. 'I'll give you exactly thirty minutes' warning before we shove you out over the dropping zone.' A second glance at his watch and a heavy frown. 'Flying Officer Tremayne, your gross dereliction of duty is endangering the entire mission.'

'Sir?' An even deeper apprehension in Tremayne's face.

'I should have had my coffee exactly three minutes ago.'

'Yes, sir. Right away, sir.'

Smith smiled again, straightened from his cramped position behind the pilots' seats, left the flight-deck and moved aft into the Lancaster's fuselage. Here in this cold, bleak and forbidding compartment, which resembled nothing so much as an iron tomb, the impression of the Siberian boiler factory was redoubled. The noise level was so high as to be almost intolerable, the cold was intense and metal-ribbed metal walls, dripping with condensation, made no concessions whatsoever to creature comfort. Nor did the six metal-framed canvas seats bolted to the floor, functionalism gone mad. Any attempt to introduce those sadistically designed instruments of torture in HM penitentiaries would have caused a national outcry.

Huddled in those six chairs sat six men, probably, Smith reflected, the six most miserable men he'd ever seen. Like himself, each of the six was dressed in the uniform of the German Alpine Corps. Like himself, each man wore two parachutes. All were shivering constantly, stamping their feet and beating their arms, and their frozen breath hung heavy in the ice-chill air. Facing them, along the upper starboard side of the fuselage, ran a taut metal wire which passed over the top of the doorway. On to this wire were clipped snap-catches, wires from which led down to folded parachutes resting on top of an assortment of variously shaped bundles, the contents of only one of which could be identified by the protruding ends of several pairs of skis.

The nearest parachutist, a dark intense man with Latin features, looked up at Smith's arrival. He had never, Smith thought, seen Edward Carraciola look quite so unhappy.

'Well?' Carraciola's voice was just as unhappy as his face. 'I'll bet he's no more bloody idea where we are than I have.'

'He does seem to navigate his way across Europe by opening his window and sniffing the air from time to time,' Smith admitted. 'But I wouldn't worry—'

He broke off as a sergeant air-gunner entered from the rear, carrying a can of steaming coffee and enamel mugs.

'Neither would I, sir.' The sergeant smiled tolerantly. 'The Wing Commander has his little ways. Coffee, gentlemen? Back at the base he claims that he reads detective novels all the time and depends upon one of the gunners telling him from time to time where we are.'

Smith cradled frozen hands round the coffee mug. 'Do *you* know where we are?'

'Of course, sir.' He seemed genuinely surprised, then nodded to the metal rungs leading to the upper machine-gun turret. 'Just nip up there, sir, and look down to your right.'

Smith lifted an enquiring eyebrow, handed over his mug, climbed the ladder and peered down to his right through the Perspex dome of the turret cupola. For a few seconds only the darkness filled his eyes then gradually, far below and seen dimly through the driving snow, he could make out a ghostly luminescence in the night, a luminescence which gradually resolved itself into a criss-cross pattern of illuminated streets. For a brief moment only Smith's face registered total disbelief then quickly returned to its normal dark stillness.

'Well, well.' He retrieved his coffee. 'Somebody should tell them down there. The lights are supposed to be out all over Europe.'

'Not in Switzerland, sir,' the sergeant explained patiently. 'That's Basle.'

'Basle?' Smith stared at him. 'Basle! Good God, he's gone seventy or eighty miles off course. The flight plan routed us north of Strasbourg.'

'Yes, sir.' The sergeant air-gunner was unabashed. 'The Wing Commander says he doesn't understand flight plans.' He grinned, half apologetically. 'To tell the truth, sir, this is our milk-run into the Vorarlberg. We fly east along the Swiss frontier, then south of Schaffhausen—'

'But that's over Swiss territory!'

'Is it? On a clear night you can see the lights of Zurich. They say Wing Commander Carpenter has a room permanently reserved for him there in the Baur-au-Lac.'

'What?'

'He says if it's a choice between a prisoner-of-war camp in Germany and internment in Switzerland he knows which side of the frontier he's coming down on . . . After that we fly down the Swiss side of Lake Constance, turn east at Lindau, climb to eight thousand to clear the mountains and it's only a hop, skip and jump to the Weissspitze.'

'I see,' Smith said weakly. 'But – don't the Swiss object?'

'Frequently, sir. Their complaints always seem to coincide with the nights we're around those parts. Wing Commander Carpenter claims it's some ill-intentioned Luftwaffe pilot trying to discredit him.'

'What else?' Smith asked, but the sergeant was already on his way to the flight-deck. The Lancaster lurched as it hit an infrequent air pocket, Smith grabbed a rail to steady himself and Lieutenant Morris Schaffer, of the American Office of Strategic Services and Smith's second-in-command, cursed fluently as the better part of a cup of scalding coffee emptied itself over his thigh.

'That's all I need,' he said bitterly. 'I've no morale left. I wish to God we *would* crash-land in Switzerland. Think of all those lovely Wienerschnitzels and Apfelstrudels. After a couple of years living among you Limeys, Spam and powdered eggs and an ounce of margarine a day, that's what Mama Schaffer's little boy requires. Building up.'

'You'd also live a damn' sight longer, friend,' Carraciola observed morosely. He transferred his gaze to Smith, gave him a long considering look. 'The whole set-up stinks, Major.'

'I don't think I understand,' Smith said quietly.

'Suicidal, is what I mean. What a bunch. Just look at us.' He gestured to the three men sitting nearest to him on his left: Olaf Christiansen, a flaxen-haired first cousin of Leif Ericsson, Lee Thomas, a short dark Welshman – both those men seemed slightly amused – and Torrance-Smythe, as languidly aristocratic-looking as any ci-devant French count that ever rode a tumbrel, a doleful ex-Oxford don who clearly wished he were back among the University cloisters. 'Christiansen, Thomas, old Smithy and myself. We're just a bunch of civil servants, filing clerks—'

'I know very well what you are,' Smith said quietly.

'Or yourself.' In the de-synchronized thunder of the engines the soft-voiced interruption had gone unnoticed. 'A major in the Black Watch. No doubt you cut quite a dash playing the bagpipes at El Alamein, but why the hell *you* to command us? No offence. But this is no more in your line than it is ours. Or Lieutenant Schaffer here. An airborne cowboy—'

'I hate horses,' Schaffer said loudly. 'That's why I had to leave Montana.'

'Or take George here.' Carraciola jerked a thumb in the direction of the last member of the party, George Harrod, a stocky army sergeant radio-operator with an expression of profound resignation on his face. 'I'll bet he's never as much as made a parachute jump in his life before.'

'I have news for you,' Harrod said stoically. 'I've never even been in a plane before.'

'He's never even been in a plane before,' Carraciola said despairingly. 'My God, what a bunch of no-hopers! All we need is a team composed of specialist Alpinists, Commandos, mountaineeers and safe-breakers and what do we have?' He shook his head slowly. 'We have us.'

Smith said gently: 'We were all the Colonel could get. Be fair. He told us yesterday that the one thing in the world that he didn't have was time.'

Carraciola made no reply, none of the others spoke, but Smith didn't have to be any clairvoyant to know what was in the minds of all of them. They were thinking what he was thinking, like himself they were back several hours in time and several hundred miles in space in that Admiralty Operations Room in London where Vice-Admiral Rolland, ostensibly Assistant Director of Naval Operations but in fact the long-serving head of MI6, the counter-espionage branch of the British Secret Service, and his deputy, Colonel Wyatt-Turner, had gravely and reluctantly briefed them on what they had as gravely and reluctantly admitted to be a mission born from the sheerest desperation.

'Deucedly sorry and all that, chaps, but time is of the essence.' Wyatt-Turner, a big, red-faced, heavily moustached colonel, tapped his cane against a wall-map of Germany, pointing to a spot just north of the Austrian border and a little west of Garmisch-Partenkirchen. 'Our man was brought down here at 2 a.m. this morning but SHAEF, in their all-knowing wisdom, didn't let us know until 10 a.m. Damned idiots! Damned idiots for not letting us know until so late and double-damned idiots for ignoring our advice in the first place. Gad, will they never learn to listen to us?' He shook his head in anger, tapped the map again. 'Anyway, he's here. Schloss Adler. The castle of the eagle. Believe me, it's well named, only an eagle could get there. Our job—'

Smith said: 'How are you so sure he's there, sir?'

'We're sure. Mosquito he was in crash-landed only ten miles away. The pilot got off a radio message just before a German patrol closed in.' He paused, smiled grimly, continued: 'Schloss Adler, Major Smith, is the combined HQ of the German Secret Service and the Gestapo in South Germany. Where else would they take him?'

'Where indeed? How was he brought down, sir?'

'Through the most damnable ill-luck. We carried out a saturation raid on Nürnberg last night and there shouldn't have been a German fighter within a hundred miles of the Austrian border. But a wandering Messerschmidtt patrol got him. That's unimportant. What's important is getting him out before he talks.'

'He'll talk,' Thomas said sombrely. 'They all do. *Why* did they disregard our advice, sir? We told them two days ago.'

'The whys don't matter,' Wyatt-Turner said tiredly. 'Not any more. The fact that he'll talk does. So we get him out. *You* get him out.'

Torrance-Smythe cleared his throat delicately. 'There are paratroops, sir.'

'Scared, Smithy?'

'Naturally, sir.'

'The Schloss Adler is inaccessible and impregnable. It would require a battalion of paratroops to take it.'

'Of course,' Christiansen said, 'the fact that there's no time to mount a massed paratroop attack has no bearing on the matter.' Christiansen appeared positively cheerful, the proposed operation obviously appealed vastly to him.

Wyatt-Turner gave him the benefit of his icy blue stare then decided to ignore him.

'Secrecy and stealth are the only hope,' he went on. 'And you gentlemen are – I trust – secretive and stealthy. You are experts at that and experts at survival behind enemy lines where all of you have spent considerable periods of time, Major Smith, Lieutenant Schaffer and Sergeant Harrod here in their professional capacities, the rest of you in – um – other duties. With the—'

'That was a damned long time ago, sir,' Carraciola interrupted. 'At least for Smithy, Thomas, Christiansen and myself. We're out of touch now. We don't know the latest developments in weapons and combat techniques. And God only knows we're out of training. After a couple of years behind a desk it takes me all my time to run fifty yards after a bus.'

'You'll have to get fit fast, won't you?' Wyatt-Turner said coldly. 'Besides, what matters most is, that with the exception of Major Smith, you all have an extensive knowledge of Western Europe. You all speak fluent German. You'll find your combat training – on the level you'll be engaged in – as relevant today as it was five years ago. You are men with exceptional records of resourcefulness, ability and ingenuity. If anyone has a chance, you have. You're all volunteers, of course.'

'Of course,' Carraciola echoed, his face carefully deadpan. Then he looked speculatively at Wyatt-Turner. 'There is, of course, another way, sir.' He paused, then went on very quietly indeed. 'A way with a hundred per cent guarantee of success.'

'Neither Admiral Rolland nor I claim to be infallible,' Wyatt-Turner said slowly. 'We have missed an alternative? You have the answer to our problems?'

'Yes. Whistle up a Pathfinder squadron of Lancasters with 10-ton block-buster bombs. Do *you* think *anyone* in the Schloss Adler would ever talk again?'

'I don't think so.' Admiral Rolland spoke gently and for the first time, moving from the wall-map to join the group. Admiral Rolland always spoke gently. When you wielded the almost incredible range of power that he did, you didn't have to talk loudly to make yourself heard. He was a short, grey-haired man, with a deeply trenched face and an air of immense authority. 'No,' he repeated, 'I don't think so. Nor do I think that your grasp of the realities of the situation is any match for your total ruthlessness. The captured man, Lieutenant General Carnaby, is an American. If we were to destroy him General Eisenhower would probably launch his Second Front against us instead of against the Germans.' He smiled deprecatingly, as though to remove rebuke from his voice. 'There are certain – um – niceties to be observed in our relationship with our Allies. Wouldn't you agree?'

Carraciola didn't agree or disagree. He had, apparently, nothing to say. Neither did anyone else. Colonel Wyatt-Turner cleared his throat.

'That's it then, gentlemen. Ten o'clock tonight at the airfield. No more questions, I take it?'

'Yes, sir, there bloody well is, begging the Colonel's pardon, sir.' Sergeant George Harrod not only sounded heated, he looked it, too. 'What's all this about? Why's this geezer so bloody important? Why the hell do we have to risk our necks—'

'That'll do, Sergeant.' Wyatt-Turner's voice was sharp, authoritative. 'You know all you require to know—'

'If we're sending a man to what may be his death, Colonel, I think he has the right to know why,' Admiral Rolland interrupted gently, almost apologetically. 'The rest know. He should too. It's painfully simple, Sergeant. General Carnaby is the overall co-ordinator of planning for the exercise known as Operation Overlord – the Second Front. It would be absolutely true to say that he knows more about the Allied preparations for the Second Front than any man alive.

'He set off last night to meet his opposite numbers in the Middle East, Russia and the Italian Front to co-ordinate final plans for the invasion of Europe. The rendezvous was in Crete – the only meeting point the Russians would accept. They haven't a plane fast enough to out-run the German fighters. The British Mosquito can – but it didn't last night.'

Silence lay heavy in the austere operations room. Harrod rubbed his hand across his eyes, then shook his head slowly, as if to clear it. When he spoke again all the truculence, all the anger had vanished from his voice. His words came very slowly.

'And if the General talks—'

'He'll talk,' Rolland said. The voice was soft, but it carried total conviction.

'As Mr Thomas has just said, they all talk. He won't be able to help himself. A mixture of mescalin and scopolamine.'

'And he'll tell them all the plans for the Second Front.' The words came as from a man in a dream. 'When, where, how – Good God, sir, we'll have to call the whole thing off!'

'Precisely. We call it off. No Second Front this year. Another nine months on the war, another million lives needlessly lost. You understand the urgency, Sergeant, the sheer desperate urgency of it all?'

'I understand, sir. Now I understand.' Harrod turned to Wyatt-Turner. 'Sorry I spoke like that, sir. I'm afraid – well, I'm a bit edgy, sir.'

'We're all a bit edgy, Sergeant. Well, the airfield at ten o'clock and we'll check the equipment.' He smiled without humour. 'I'm afraid the uniforms may not fit too well. This is early closing day in Savile Row.'

Sergeant Harrod huddled more closely into his bucket seat, beat freezing hands against freezing shoulders, morosely surveyed his uniform, wrinkled like an elephant's legs and about three sizes too big for him, then raised his voice above the clamour of the Lancaster's engines.

'Well,' he said bitterly, 'he was right about the bloody uniforms, anyway.'

'And wrong about everything else,' Carraciola said heavily. 'I still say we should have sent in the Lancasters.'

Smith, still standing against the starboard fuselage, lit a cigarette and eyed him speculatively. He opened his mouth to speak when it occurred to him that he had seen men in more receptive mood. He looked away without saying anything.

In the flight-deck, now slid so impossibly far forward in his seat that the back of his head rested on the back of his seat, Wing Commander Carpenter was still deeply and contentedly preoccupied with pipe, coffee and literature. Beside him, Flying Officer Tremayne was obviously failing to share his mood of pleasurable relaxation. He was, in fact, keeping a most anxious watch, his eyes constantly shifting from the instrument panel to the opaque darkness beyond the windscreen to the recumbent figure of his superior officer who appeared to be in danger of dropping off to sleep at any moment. Suddenly Tremayne sat far forward in his seat, stared for long seconds through the windscreen ahead of him then turned excitedly to Carpenter.

'There's Schaffhausen down there, sir!'

Carpenter groaned heavily, closed his book, swung back the hinged book-rest, finished his coffee, levered himself upright with another groan, slid open his side-screen and made an elaborate pretence of examining the loom of light far below, without, however, actually going to the lengths of exposing his face to the wind and the driving snow outside. He closed the screen and looked at Tremayne.

'By heavens,' he said admiringly, 'I believe you're right. It's a great comfort to have you along, my boy, a great comfort.' He switched on the intercom while Tremayne looked suitably abashed. 'Major Smith? Yes. Thirty minutes to go.' He switched off and turned again to Tremayne. 'Right. South-east down the old Bodensee. And for God's sake keep to the Swiss side.

Smith hung up the headphones and looked quizzically at the six seated men.

'That's it, then. Half an hour. Let's hope it's warmer down there than it is up here.'

No one had any comment to make on that. No one seemed to have any hope either. Soundlessly, wordlessly, they looked without expression at one another, then pulled themselves stiffly to their frozen feet. Then very slowly, very awkwardly, their numbed hands and cramped conditions making things almost impossibly awkward for them, they prepared themselves for the drop. They helped each other strap loads on their backs, beneath the high-mounted parachutes, then struggled into their white waterproof snow trousers. Sergeant Harrod went one better. He pulled a voluminous snow-smock over his head, zipped it up with difficulty and drew the hood over his head. He turned round questioningly as a hand tapped the hummocked outline below his white smock.

'I hardly like to say this,' Schaffer said diffidently, 'but I really don't reckon your radio is going to stand the shock of landing, Sergeant.'

'Why not?' Harrod looked more lugubrious than ever. 'It's been done before.'

'Not by you, it hasn't. By my reckoning you're going to hit the ground with a terminal velocity of a hundred and eighty miles an hour. Not to put too fine a point on it, I think you're going to experience some difficulty in opening your chute.'

Harrod looked at him, looked at his other five smockless companions, then nodded slowly and touched his own smock.

'You mean I put this on *after* we reach the ground?'

'Well,' Schaffer said consideringly, 'I really think it would help.' He grinned at Harrod, who grinned back almost cheerfully. Even Carraciola's lips twitched in the beginnings of a smile. The release of tension within that frozen fuselage was almost palpable.

'Well, well, time I earned my wing-commander's pay while you stripling pilots sit and gaze in rapt admiration.' Carpenter studied his watch. 'Two fifteen. Time we changed places.'

Both men unhooked their safety belts and awkwardly changed over. Carpenter fastidiously adjusted the right-hand seat's back rest until it was exactly right for him, manoeuvred his parachute to its position of maximum comfort, fastened his seat-belt, unhooked and adjusted on his head a combined earphones and microphone set and made a switch.

'Sergeant Johnson?' Carpenter never bothered with the regulation call-up formalities. 'Are you awake?'

Back in the navigator's tiny and extremely uncomfortable recess, Sergeant Johnson was very much awake. He had been awake for hours. He was bent over a glowing greenish radar screen, his eyes leaving it only to make rapid reference to the charts, an Ordnance map, a picture and a duplicate compass, altimeter and air-speed indicator. He reached for the switch by his side.

'I'm awake, sir.'

'If you fly us into the side of the Weissspitze,' Carpenter said threateningly, 'I'll have you reduced to aircraftman. Aircraftman second class, Johnson.'

'I wouldn't like that. I make it nine minutes, sir.'

'For once we're agreed on something. So do I.' Carpenter switched off, slid open the starboard screen and peered out. Although there was just the faintest wash of moonlight in the night sky, visibility might as well have been zero. It was a greyly opaque world, a blind world, with nothing to be seen but the thinly driving snow. He withdrew his head, brushed away the snow from his huge moustache, closed the screen, looked regretfully at his pipe and carefully put it away in his pocket.

For Tremayne, the stowage of the pipe was the final proof that the Wing Commander was clearing the decks for action. He said unhappily: 'A bit dicey, isn't it, sir? Locating the Weissspitze in this lot, I mean?'

'Dicey?' Carpenter sounded almost jovial. 'Dicey? I don't see why? It's as big as a mountain. In fact, it *is* a mountain. We can't miss it, my dear boy.'

'That's what I mean.' He paused, a pause with more meaning in it. 'And this plateau on the Weissspitze that we have to drop them on. Only three hundred yards wide, sir. Mountain above it, cliff below it. And those adiabatic mountain winds, or whatever you call them, blowing in any old unpredictable direction. A fraction to the south and we'll hit the mountain, a fraction to the north and they'll fall down that whacking great cliff and like as not all break their necks. Three hundred yards!'

'What do you want?' Carpenter demanded expansively. 'Heathrow Airport? Three hundred yards? All the room in the world, my boy. We land this old crate on runways a tenth of that width.'

'Yes, sir. I've always found runway landing lights a great help, sir. At seven thousand feet up the side of the Weissspitze—'

He broke off as a buzzer rang. Carpenter made a switch.

'Johnson?'

'Yes, sir.' Johnson was huddled more closely than ever over his radar screen where the revolving scanner-line had picked up a white spot immediately to the right of centre of the screen. 'I have it, sir. Right where it should be.' He looked away from the screen and made a quick check on the compass. 'Course oh-nine-three, sir.'

'Good lad.' Carpenter smiled at Tremayne, made a tiny course alteration and began to whistle softly to himself. 'Have a look out your window, laddie. My moustache is beginning to get all waterlogged.'

Tremayne opened his window, strained his head as far as possible, but still there was only this grey and featureless opacity. He withdrew his head, silently shook it.

'No matter. It must be there somewhere,' Carpenter said reasonably. He spoke into the intercom. 'Sergeant? Five minutes. Hook up.'

'Hook up!' The sergeant air-gunner repeated the order to the seven men standing in a line along the starboard side of the fuselage. 'Five minutes.'

Silently they clipped their parachute snap catches on to the overhead wire, the sergeant air-gunner carefully checking each catch. Nearest the door and first man to jump was Sergeant Harrod. Behind him stood Lieutenant Schaffer whose experience with the OSS had made him by far the most experienced parachutist of the group and whose unenviable task it was to keep an eye on Harrod. He was followed by Carraciola, then Smith – as leader he preferred to be in the middle of the group – then Christiansen, Thomas and Torrance-Smythe. Behind Torrance-Smythe two young aircraftmen stood ready to slide packaged equipment and parachutes along the wire and heave them out as swiftly as possible after the last man had jumped. The sergeant air-gunner took up position by the door. The tension was back in the air again.

Twenty-five feet forward of where they were standing, Carpenter slid open his side screen for the fifth time in as many minutes. The now downward drooping moustache had lost much of its splendid panache but the Wing Commander had obviously decided that there were more urgent considerations in life than waterlogged moustaches. He was wearing goggles now, continuously brushing away snow and moisture with a chamois leather, but the view ahead – or lack of view – remained obstinately the same, still that greyly driving snow looming out of and vanishing into that greyly impenetrable opacity, still nothingness. He closed the screen.

A call-up buzzer rang. Carpenter made a switch, listened, nodded.

'Three minutes,' he said to Tremayne. 'Oh-nine-two.'

Tremayne made the necessary minute course adjustment. He no longer looked through the side-screen, he no longer even looked at the screen ahead of him. His whole being was concentrated upon flying that big bomber, his all-exclusive attention, his total concentration, on three things only: the compass, the altimeter, and Carpenter. A degree too far to the south and the Lancaster would crash into the side of the Weissspitze: a couple of hundred feet too low and the same thing would happen: a missed signal from Carpenter and the mission was over before it had begun. The young, the absurdly young face was expressionless, the body immobile as he piloted the Lancaster with a hair-trigger precision that he had never before achieved. Only his eyes moved, in a regular, rhythmic, unvarying pattern: the compass, the altimeter, Carpenter, the compass, the altimeter, Carpenter: and never longer than a second on each.

Again Carpenter slid open his side-screen and peered out. Again he had the same reward, the opacity, the grey nothingness. With his head still outside he lifted his left hand, palm downwards, and made a forward motion. Instantly Tremayne's hand fell on the throttle levers and eased them forward. The roar of the big engines died away to a more muted thunder.

Carpenter withdrew his head. If he was concerned, no trace of it showed in his face. He resumed his soft whistling, calmly, almost leisurely, scanned the instrument panel, then turned his head to Tremayne. He said conversationally:

'When you were in flying school, ever hear tell of a strange phenomenon known as stalling speed?'

Tremayne started, glanced hurriedly at the instrument panel and quickly gave a fraction more power to the engines. Carpenter smiled, looked at his watch and pressed a buzzer twice.

The bell rang above the head of the sergeant air-gunner standing by the fuselage door. He looked at the tense, expectant faces before him and nodded.

'Two minutes, gentlemen.'

He eased the door a few inches to test whether it was moving freely. With the door only fractionally open the suddenly deepened roar from the engines was startling but nowhere nearly as dismaying as the snow-laden gust of icy wind that whistled into the fuselage. The parachutists exchanged carefully expressionless glances, glances correctly interpreted by the sergeant who closed the door and nodded again.

'I agree, gentlemen. No night for man nor beast.'

Wing Commander Carpenter, his head once again poked through the side-screen, didn't think so either. Five seconds' exposure to that arctic wind and driving snow and your face was full of porcupine quills: fifteen seconds and the totally numbed skin conveyed no sensation at all, it was when you withdrew your head and waited for the exquisite pain of returning circulation that the fun really started: but this time Carpenter was determined not to withdraw his head until he had complete justification for doing so: and the only justification would be the sighting of the Weissspitze. Mechanically, industriously, he rubbed the chamois leather across his goggles, stared unblinkingly into the greyly swirling gloom and hoped that he saw the Weissspitze before the Weissspitze saw him.

Inside, Tremayne's eyes continued on their rhythmic, unvarying pattern of movement: the compass, the altimeter, Carpenter, the compass, the altimeter, Carpenter. But now his gaze was resting fractionally longer on Carpenter each time, waiting for the sudden signal that would galvanize him into throwing the big Lancaster into a violent bank to port, the only avoiding action they could possibly take. Carpenter's left hand was moving, but he wasn't giving any signal, the fingers of his left hand were drumming gently on his knee. This, Tremayne suddenly and incredulously realized, was probably the highest state of excitement that Carpenter was capable of achieving.

Ten seconds passed. Five. And another five. Tremayne was conscious that, even in that ice-cold cabin, the sweat was pouring down his face. The urge to pull the bomber away to the left, to avoid the shattering, annihilating collision that could be only seconds away now, was almost overpowering. He was aware of a fear, a fear bordering on a reason-abdicating panic, such as he had never previously guessed at, let alone experienced. And then he became aware of something else. The drumming of Carpenter's left fingers had abruptly ceased.

Carpenter had it now. It was more imagined than real, more guessed at than seen, but he had it now. Then gradually, almost imperceptibly, ahead and a little to the right of the direction of flight, he became aware of something more solidly tangible than wishful thinking beginning to materialize out of the nothingness. And then, suddenly, it wasn't materializing any more, it was solidly, unmistakably there, the smooth, unbroken side of an almost vertically towering mountain soaring up at a dizzy 80° until it vanished in the grey darkness above. Carpenter withdrew his head, leaving the screen open this time, and pressed his head-switch.

'Sergeant Johnson?' The words came out stiffly, mechanically, not because of any crisis of emotion that the Wing Commander was passing through but because his entire face, lips included, was so frozen that he could no longer articulate properly.

'Sir?' Johnson's voice over the intercom was disembodied, empty, but even the metallic impersonality of that single word could not disguise the bow-taut tension behind it.

Carpenter said: 'I think Flying Officer Johnson a much nicer name.'

'Sir?'

'Relax. I have it. You can go back to sleep.' He switched off, took a quick look through the side-screen, reached up and touched an overhead switch.

Above the starboard door in the fuselage, a red light came on. The sergeant air-gunner laid his hand on the door.

'One minute, gentlemen.' He jerked the door wide open, securing it on its standing latch, and a miniature blizzard howled into the belly of the Lancaster. 'When the red light turns green—'

He left the sentence unfinished, partly because those few words were crystal clear in themselves, partly because he had to shout so loudly to make himself heard over the combined roar of wind and engines that any superfluity of words was only that much wasted effort.

No one else said anything, mainly because of the near impossibility of making oneself heard. In any event, the parachutists' silently exchanged glances conveyed more eloquently than words the very obvious thought that was in the minds of all of them: if it was like that inside, what the hell was it like outside? At a gesture from the sergeant, they moved up in line to the open door. Sergeant Harrod in the lead. On his face was the expression of a Christian martyr meeting his first and last lion.

The Lancaster, like some great black pterodactyl from out of the primeval past, roared on through the driving snow alongside the smoothly precipitous side of the Weissspitze. That sheer wall of ice-encrusted rock seemed very close indeed. Tremayne was convinced that it was impossibly close. He stared through the still open screen by Carpenter's head and would have sworn that the starboard wing-tip must be brushing the side of the mountain. Tremayne could still feel the sweat that bathed his face but his lips were as dry as ashes. He licked them, surreptitiously, so that Carpenter would not see him, but it didn't do any good at all: as dry as ashes they remained.

Sergeant Harrod's lips weren't dry, but that was only because his face was taking the full brunt of the horizontally driving snowstorm that lashed along the bomber's fuselage. Otherwise, he shared Tremayne's sentiments and apprehensions to a very marked degree. He stood in the doorway, gripping the fuselage on each side to hold him in position against the gale of wind, his storm-lashed face showing no fear, just a peculiarly resigned expression. His eyes were turned to the left, looking forward with an almost hypnotized fixity at that point in space where it seemed that at any second now the starboard wing-tip must strike against the Weissspitze.

Inside the fuselage, the red lamp still burned. The sergeant air-gunner's hand fell on Harrod's shoulder in an encouraging gesture. It took Harrod all of three seconds to free himself from his thrall-like fixation with that starboard wing-tip and take a half step back inside. He reached up and firmly removed the sergeant's hand.

'Don't shove, mate.' He had to shout to make himself heard. 'If I'm to commit suicide, let me do it in the old-fashioned way. By my own hand.' He again took up position by the open door.

At the same instant Carpenter took a last quick look through the side-screen and made the gesture that Tremayne had been waiting for, been praying for, a slight turning motion of the left hand. Quickly Tremayne banked the big bomber, as quickly straightened up again.

Slowly, the mountain-side fell away. The mountain-brushing episode had been no mere bravado or folly, Carpenter had been deliberately lining up for his pre-determined course across the narrow plateau. Once again, and for the last time, he had his head outside, while his left hand slowly – interminably slowly, it seemed to Tremayne – reached up for the button on the bulkhead above the screen, located it, paused, then pressed it.

Sergeant Harrod, head craned back at a neck-straining angle, saw the red light turn to green, brought his head down, screwed shut his eyes and, with a convulsive jerk of his arms, launched himself out into the snow and the darkness, not a very expert launching, for instead of jumping out he had stepped out and was already twisting in mid-air as the parachute opened. Schaffer was the next to go, smoothly, cleanly, feet and knees together, then Carraciola followed by Smith.

Smith glanced down below him and his lips tightened. Just dimly visible in the greyness beneath, Harrod, a very erratic human pendulum, was swinging wildly across the sky. The parachute cords were already badly twisted and his clumsily desperate attempts to untwist them resulted only in their becoming more entangled than ever. His left-hand cords were pulled too far down, air was spilling from the parachute, and, still swaying madly, he was side-slipping to his left faster than any man Smith had ever seen side-slip a parachute before. Smith stared after the rapidly disappearing figure and hoped to God that he didn't side-slip his way right over the edge of the precipice.

Grim-faced, he stared upwards to see how the others had fared. Thank God, there was no worry there. Christiansen, Thomas and Smithy all there, so close as to be almost touching, all making perfectly normal descents.

Even before the last of the parachutists, Torrance-Smythe, had cleared the doorway, the sergeant air-gunner was running towards the after end of the fuselage. Swiftly he flung aside a packing-case, dragging a tarpaulin away, reached down and pulled a huddled figure upright. A girl, quite small, with wide dark eyes and delicate features. One would have looked for the figure below to be as petite as the features, but it was enveloped in bulky clothes over which had been drawn a snow-suit. Over the snow-suit she wore a parachute. She was almost numb with cold and cramp but the sergeant had his orders.

'Come on, Miss Ellison.' His arm round her waist, he moved quickly towards the doorway. 'Not a second to lose.'

He half led, half carried her there, where an aircraftman was just heaving the second last parachute and container through the doorway. The sergeant snapped the parachute catch on to the wire. Mary Ellison half-turned as if to speak to him, then turned away abruptly and dropped into the darkness. The last parachute and container followed at once.

For a long moment the sergeant stared down into the darkness. Then he rubbed his chin with the palm of his hand, shook his head in disbelief, stepped back and pulled the heavy door to. The Lancaster, its four engines still on reduced power, droned on into the snow and the night. Almost immediately, it was lost to sight and, bare seconds later, the last faint throb of its engines died away in the darkness.

Chapter Two

Smith reached his hands far up into the parachute shrouds, hauled himself sharply upwards and made a perfect knees-bent, feet-together landing in about two feet of snow. The wind tugged fiercely at his parachute. He struck the quick release harness clasp, collapsed the parachute, pulled it in, rolled it up and pressed it deeply into the snow, using for weight the pack he had just shrugged off his shoulders.

Down there at ground level – if seven thousand feet up on the Weissspitze could be called ground level – the snowfall was comparatively slight compared to that blizzard they'd experienced jumping from the Lancaster but, even so, visibility was almost as bad as it had been up above, for there was a twenty-knot wind blowing and the dry powdery snow was drifting quite heavily. Smith made a swift 360° sweep of his horizon but there was nothing to be seen, nobody to be seen.

With fumbling frozen hands he clumsily extracted a torch and whistle from his tunic. Facing alternately east and west, he bleeped on the whistle and flashed his torch. The first to appear was Thomas, then Schaffer, then, within two minutes altogether, all of the others with the exception of Sergeant Harrod.

'Pile your chutes there and weight them,' Smith ordered. 'Yes, bed them deep. Anyone seen Sergeant Harrod?' A shaking of heads. 'Nobody? No sight of him at all?'

'Last I saw of him,' Schaffer said, 'he was going across my bows like a destroyer in a heavy sea.'

'I saw a bit of that,' Smith nodded. 'The shrouds were twisted?'

'Put a corkscrew to shame. But I'd have said there was no danger of the chute collapsing. Not enough time. We were almost on the ground before I lost sight of him.'

'Any idea where he landed, then?'

'Roughly. He'll be all right, Major. A twisted ankle, a bump on the head. Not to worry.'

'Use your torches,' Smith said abruptly. 'Spread out. Find him.'

With two men on one side of him, three on the other, all within interlocking distance of their torch beams, Smith searched through the snow, his flash-light raking the ground ahead of him. If he shared Schaffer's optimism about Harrod, his face didn't show it. It was set and grim. Three minutes passed and then came a faint shout from the right. Smith broke into a run.

Carraciola it was who had called and was now standing at the farther edge of a wind-swept outcrop of bare rock, his torch shining downwards and slightly ahead. Beyond the rock the ground fell away abruptly to a depth of several feet and in this lee a deep drift had formed. Half-buried in its white depths, Sergeant Harrod lay spread-eagled on his back, his feet almost touching the rock, his face upturned to the falling snow, his eyes open. He did not seem to notice the snow falling on his eyes.

They were all there now, staring down at the motionless man. Smith jumped down into the drift, dropped to his knees, slid an arm under Harrod's shoulders and began to lift him to a sitting position. Harrod's head lolled back like that of a broken rag doll. Smith lowered him back into the snow and felt for the pulse in the throat. Still kneeling, Smith straightened, paused for a moment with bent head then climbed wearily to his feet.

'Dead?' Carraciola asked.

'He's dead. His neck is broken.' Smith's face was without expression. 'He must have got caught up in the shrouds and made a bad landing.'

'It happens,' Schaffer said. 'I've known it happen.' A long pause, then: 'Shall I take the radio, sir?'

Smith nodded. Schaffer dropped to his knees and began to fumble for the buckle of the strap securing the radio to Harrod's back.

Smith said: 'Sorry, no, not that way. There's a key around his neck, under his tunic. It fits the lock under the flap of the breast buckle.'

Schaffer located the key, unlocked the buckle after some difficulty, eased the straps off the dead man's shoulders and finally managed to work the radio clear. He rose to his feet, the radio dangling from his hand, and looked at Smith.

'Second thoughts, what's the point. Any fall hard enough to break his neck wouldn't have done the innards of this radio any good.'

Wordlessly, Smith took the radio, set it on the rock, extended the antenna, set the switch to 'Transmit', and cranked the call-up handle. The red telltale glowed, showing the transmission circuit to be in order. Smith turned the switch to receive, turned up the volume, moved the tuning knob, listened briefly to some static-laden music, closed up the radio set and handed it back to Schaffer.

'It made a better landing than Sergeant Harrod,' Smith said briefly. 'Come on.'

'We bury him, Major?' Carraciola asked.

'No need.' Smith shook his head and gestured with his torch at the drifting snow. 'He'll be buried within the hour. Let's find the supplies.'

'Now, for God's sake don't lose your grip!' Thomas said urgently.

'That's the trouble with you Celts,' Schaffer said reprovingly. 'No faith in anyone. There is no cause for alarm. Your life is in the safe hands of Schaffer and Christiansen. Not to worry.'

'What else do you think I'm worrying about?'

'If we all start sliding,' Schaffer said encouragingly, 'we won't let you go until the last possible minute.'

Thomas gave a last baleful glance over his shoulder and then began to edge himself out over the black lip of the precipice. Schaffer and Christiansen had an ankle apiece, and they in turn were anchored by the others. As far as the beam of Thomas's torch could reach, the cliff stretching down into the darkness was absolutely vertical, black naked rock with the only fissures in sight blocked with ice and with otherwise never a hand- or foot-hold.

'I've seen all I want to,' he said over his shoulder. They pulled him back and he edged his way carefully up to their supply pile before getting to his feet. He prodded the pack with the skis protruding from one end.

'Very handy,' he said morosely. 'Oh, very handy for this lot indeed.'

'As steep as that?' Smith asked.

'Vertical. Smooth as glass and you can't see the bottom. How deep do you reckon it is, Major?'

'Who knows?' Smith shrugged. 'We're seven thousand feet up. Maps never give details at this altitude. Break out that nylon.'

The proper supply pack was located and the nylon produced, one thousand feet of it coiled inside a canvas bag as it had come from the makers. It had very little more diameter than a clothes line but its wire core made it immensely strong and every yard of it had been fully tested to its rated breaking strain – its actual breaking strain was much higher – before leaving the factory. Smith tied a hammer to one end, and with two of the men holding him securely, paid it out over the edge, counting his arm spans as he let it go. Several times the hammer snagged on some unseen obstruction but each time Smith managed to swing it free. Finally the rope went completely slack and, despite all Smith's efforts, it remained that way.

'Well.' Smith moved back from the edge. 'That seems to be about it.'

'And if it isn't, hey?' Christiansen asked. 'If it's caught on a teensy-weensy ledge a thousand feet above damn all?'

'I'll let you know,' Smith said shortly.

'You measured it off,' Carraciola said. 'How deep?'

'Two hundred feet.'

'Eight hundred feet left, eh?' Thomas grinned. 'We'll need it all to tie up the garrison of the Schloss Adler.'

No one was amused. Smith said: 'I'll need a piton and two walkie-talkies.'

Fifteen feet back from the edge of the cliff they cleared away the snow and hammered an angled piton securely into the bare rock. Smith made a double bowline at one end of the nylon, slipped his legs through the loops, unclasped his belt then fastened it tightly round both himself and the rope and slipped a walkie-talkie over his shoulder. The rope was then passed round the piton and three men, backs to the cliff, wrapped it round their hands and prepared to take the weight. Schaffer stood by with the other walkie-talkie.

Smith checked that there were no sharp or abrasive edges on the cliff-top, wriggled cautiously over and gave the signal to be lowered. The descent itself was simple. As Thomas had said, it was a vertical drop and all he had to do was to fend himself off from the face as the men above paid out the rope. Once only, passing an overhang, he spun wildly in space, but within ten seconds regained contact with the rock face again. Mountaineering made easy, Smith thought. Or it seemed easy: perhaps, he thought wryly, it was as well that he couldn't see what stretched beneath him.

His feet passed through eighteen inches of snow and rested on solid ground. He flashed his torch in a semi-circle, from cliff wall to cliff wall. If it was a ledge, it was a very big one for, as far as his eye and torch could reach, it appeared to be a smooth plateau sloping gently outwards from the cliff. The cliff wall itself was smooth, unbroken, except for one shallow fissure, a few feet wide, close by to where he stood. He climbed out of the double bowline and made the switch on the walkie-talkie.

'OK so far. Haul up the rope. Supplies first, then yourselves.'

The rope snaked upwards into the darkness. Within five minutes all the equipment had been lowered in two separate loads. Christiansen appeared soon afterwards.

'What's all the fuss about this Alpine stuff, then?' he asked cheerfully. 'My grandmother could do it.'

'Maybe we should have brought your grandmother along instead,' Smith said sourly. 'We're not down yet. Take your torch and find out how big this ledge is and the best way down and for God's sake don't go falling over any precipices.'

Christiansen grinned and moved off. Life was for the living and Christiansen gave the impression of a man thoroughly enjoying himself. While he was away reconnoitring, all the others came down in turn until only Schaffer was left. His plaintive voice came over the walkie-talkie.

'And how am I supposed to get down? Hand over hand for two hundred feet? Frozen hand over frozen hand for two hundred feet on a rope this size? You'd better stand clear. Somebody should have thought of this.'

'Somebody did,' Smith said patiently. 'Make sure the rope is still round the piton then kick the other eight hundred feet over the edge.'

'There's always an answer.' Schaffer sounded relieved.

They had just lowered him to the ground when Christiansen returned.

'It's not so bad,' he reported. 'There's another cliff ahead of us, maybe fifty yards away, curving around to the east. At least I think it's a cliff. I didn't try to find out how deep or how steep. I'm married. But the plateau falls away gently to the west there. Seems it might go on a fair way. Trees, too. I followed the line of them for two hundred yards.'

'Trees? At this altitude?'

'Well, no masts for a tall ship. Scrub pine. They'll give shelter, hiding.'

'Fair enough,' Smith nodded. 'We'll bivouac there.'

'So close?' The surprised tone in Schaffer's voice showed that he didn't think much of the idea. 'Shouldn't we get as far down this mountain as possible tonight, Major?'

'No need. If we start at first light we'll be well below the main tree line by dawn.'

'I agree with Schaffer,' Carraciola said reasonably. 'Let's get as much as we can behind us. What do you think, Olaf?' This to Christiansen.

'It doesn't matter what Christiansen thinks.' Smith's voice was quiet but cold as the mountain air itself. 'Nor you, Carraciola. This isn't a round-table seminar, it's a military operation. Military operations have leaders. Like it or not, Admiral Rolland put me in charge. We stay here tonight. Get the stuff across.'

The five men looked speculatively at one another, then stooped to lift the supplies. There was no longer any question as to who was in charge.

'We pitch the tents right away, boss?' Schaffer asked.

'Yes.' In Schaffer's book, Smith reflected, 'boss' was probably a higher mark of respect than either 'Major' or 'sir'. 'Then hot food, hot coffee and a try for London on the radio. Haul that rope down, Christiansen. Come the dawn, we don't want to start giving heart attacks to any binocular-toting characters in the Schloss Adler.'

Christiansen nodded, began to haul on the rope. As the free end rose into the air, Smith gave a shout, jumped towards Christiansen and caught his arm. Christiansen, startled, stopped pulling and looked round.

'Jesus!' Smith drew the back of his hand across his forehead. 'That was a close one.'

'What's up?' Schaffer asked quickly.

'Two of you. Hoist me up. Quickly! Before that damn rope disappears.'

Two of them hoisted him into the air. Smith reached up and caught the dangling end of the rope, dropped to earth, taking the rope with him and then very carefully, very securely, tied it to the other end of the rope.

'Now that you've *quite* finished—' Torrance-Smythe said politely.

'The radio.' Smith let out a long sigh of relief. 'There's only one list of frequencies, call signs and code. Security. And that one list is inside Sergeant Harrod's tunic.'

'Mind if I mop my brow, too, boss?' Schaffer enquired.

'I'll go get it for you if you like,' Christiansen enquired.

'Thanks. But it's my fault and I'll get it. Besides, I'm the only person here who's done any climbing – or so I believe from Colonel Wyatt-Turner – and I think you'd find that cliff rather more awkward to climb than descend. No hurry. Let's bivouac and eat first.'

'If you can't do better than this, Smithy,' Schaffer said to Torrance-Smythe, 'you can have a week's notice. Starting from a week ago.' He scraped the bottom of his metal plate and shuddered. 'I was brought up in a Christian home, so I won't tell you what this reminds me of.'

'It's not my fault,' Torrance-Smythe complained. 'They packed the wrong size tin-openers.' He stirred the indeterminate-looking goulash in the pot on top of the butane stove and looked hopefully at the men seated in a rough semi-circle in the dimly-lit tent. 'Anyone for any more?'

'That's not funny,' Schaffer said severely.

'Wait till you try his coffee,' Smith advised, 'and you'll be wondering what you were complaining about.' He rose, poked his head through the door to take a look at the weather, looked inside again. 'May take me an hour. But if it's been drifting up there . . .'

The seated men, suddenly serious, nodded. If it had been drifting up there it might take Smith a very long time indeed to locate Sergeant Harrod.

'It's a bad night,' Schaffer said. 'I'll come and give you a hand.'

'Thanks. No need. I'll haul myself up and lower myself down. A rope round a piton is no elevator, but it'll get me there and back and two are no better than one for that job. But I'll tell you what you can do.' He moved out and reappeared shortly afterwards carrying the radio which he placed in front of Schaffer. 'I don't want to go all the way up there to get the codebook just to find that some hob-nailed idiot has fallen over this and given it a heart attack. Guard it with your life, Lieutenant Schaffer.'

'Aye, aye, sir,' Schaffer said solemnly.

With a hammer and a couple of spare pitons hanging from his waist, Smith secured himself to the rope, with double bowline and belt as before, grabbed the free end of the rope and began to haul himself up. Smith's statement to the others that this was a job for a mountaineer seemed hardly accurate for the amount of mountaineering skill required was minimal. It was gruelling physical labour, no more. Most of the time, with his legs almost at right angles to his body, he walked up the vertical cliff face: on the stretch of the overhang, with no assistance for his arms, he twice had to take a turn of the free end of the rope and rest until the strength came back to aching shoulder and forearm muscles: and by the time he finally dragged himself, gasping painfully and sweating like a man in a sauna bath, over the edge of the cliff, exhaustion was very close indeed. He had overlooked the crippling effect of altitude to a man unaccustomed to it.

He lay face down for several minutes until breathing and pulse returned to something like normal – or what was normal for seven thousand feet – rose and examined the piton round which the nylon passed. It seemed firm enough but, for good measure, he gave it another few heavy blows with the hammer, undid the double bowline round his legs and secured the end of the rope to the piton with a round turn and two half-hitches, hauling on the rope until the knot locked tight.

He moved a few feet farther away from the cliff edge, cleared away the snow and lightly hammered in one of the spare pitons he had brought with him. He tested it with his hand to see if it broke clear easily. It did. He tapped it in lightly a second time and led round it the part of the rope that was secured to the firmly anchored first piton. Then he walked away, moving up the gently sloping plateau, whistling 'Lorelei'. It was, as Smith himself would have been the first to admit, a far from tuneful whistle, but recognizable for all that. A figure appeared out of the night and came running towards him, stumbling and slipping in the deep snow. It was Mary Ellison. She stopped short a yard away and put her hands on her hips.

'Well!' He could hear her teeth chattering uncontrollably with the cold. 'You took your time about it, didn't you?'

'Never wasted a minute,' Smith said defensively. 'I had to have a hot meal and coffee first.'

'You had to have – you beast, you selfish beast!' She took a quick step forward and flung her arms around his neck. 'I hate you.'

'I know.' He pulled off a gauntlet and gently touched her disengaged cheek. 'You're frozen.'

'You're frozen, he says! Of course I'm frozen. I almost *died* in that plane. Why couldn't you have supplied some hot water bottles – or – or an electrically heated suit or – or something? I thought you loved me!'

'I can't help what you think,' Smith said kindly, patting her on the back. 'Where's your gear?'

'Fifty yards. And *stop* patting me in that – that avuncular fashion.'

'Language, language,' Smith said. 'Come on, let's fetch it.'

They trudged upwards through the deep snow, Mary holding his arm tightly. She said curiously: 'What on earth excuse did you give for coming back up here? Lost a cuff-link?'

'There was something I had to come for, something apart from you, although I gave a song-and-dance act of having forgotten about it until the last moment, until it was almost too late. The radio code-book inside Sergeant Harrod's tunic.'

'He – he lost it? He dropped it? How – how could he have been so criminally careless!' She stopped, puzzled. 'Besides, it's chained—'

'It's still inside Sergeant Harrod's tunic,' Smith said sombrely. 'He's up here, dead.'

'Dead?' She stopped and clutched him by the arms. After a long pause, she repeated: 'He's dead! That – that nice man. I heard him saying he'd never jumped before. A bad landing?'

'So it seems.'

They located the kit-bag in silence and Smith carried it back to the edge of the cliff. Mary said: 'And now? The code-book?'

'Let's wait a minute. I want to watch this rope.'

'Why the rope?'

'Why not?'

'Don't tell me,' Mary said resignedly. 'I'm only a little girl. I suppose you know what you're doing.'

'I wish to God I did,' Smith said feelingly.

They waited, again in silence, side by side on the kit-bag. Both stared at the rope in solemn concentration as if nylon ropes at seven thousand feet had taken on a special meaningfulness denied nylon ropes elsewhere. Twice Smith tried to light a cigarette and twice it sputtered to extinction in the drifting snow. The minutes passed, three, maybe four: they felt more like thirty or forty. He became conscious that the girl beside him was shivering violently – he guessed that she had her teeth clamped tight to prevent their chattering – and was even more acutely conscious that his entire left side – he was trying to shelter her from the wind and snow – was becoming numb. He rose to leave when suddenly the rope gave a violent jerk and the piton farther from the cliff edge was torn free. The loop of the rope slid quickly down past the piton to which it was anchored and kept on going till it was brought up short by its anchor. Whatever pressure was on the rope increased until the nylon bit deeply into the fresh snow on the cliff-edge. Smith moved across and tested the pressure on the rope, at first gingerly and tentatively then with all his strength. The rope was bar-taut and remained bar-taut. But the piton held.

'What – what on earth—' Mary began, then broke off. Her voice was an unconscious whisper.

'Charming, charming,' Smith murmured. 'Someone down there doesn't like me. Surprised?'

'If – if that spike hadn't held we'd never have got down again.' The tremor in her voice wasn't all due to the cold.

'It's a fair old jump,' Smith conceded.

He took her arm and they moved off. The snow was heavier now and even with the aid of their torches visibility was no more than six feet, but, by using the rocky out-crop as a bearing, it took Smith no more than two minutes to locate Sergeant Harrod, now no more than a featureless mound buried in the depths of the snow-drift. Smith brushed aside the covering shroud of white, undid the dead man's tunic, recovered the code-book, hung the chain round his neck and buttoned the book securely inside his own Alpenkorps uniform.

Then came the task of turning Sergeant Harrod over on his side. Unpleasant Smith had expected it to be, and it was: impossible he hadn't expected it to be, and it wasn't – not quite. But the effort all but defeated him, the dead man was stiff as a board, literally frozen solid into the arms outflung position into which he had fallen. For a second time that night Smith could feel the sweat mingling with the melted snow on his face. But by and by he had him over, the frozen right arm pointing up into the snow-filled sky. Smith knelt, brought his torch close and carefully examined the back of the dead man's head.

'What are you trying to do?' Mary asked. 'What are you looking for?' Again her voice was a whisper.

'His neck is broken. I want to find out just *how* it was broken.' He glanced up at the girl. 'You don't have to look.'

'Don't worry.' She turned away. 'I'm not going to.'

The clothes, like the man, were frozen stiff. The hood covering Harrod's head crackled and splintered in Smith's gauntleted hands as he pulled it down, exposing the back of the head and neck. Finally, just below the collar of the snow smock, Smith found what he was searching for – a red mark at the base of the neck where the skin was broken. He rose, caught the dead man's ankles and dragged him a foot or two down the slope.

'What now?' In spite of herself Mary was watching again, in reluctant and horrified fascination. 'What are you looking for now?'

'A rock,' Smith said briefly. There was a cold edge to the words and although Mary knew it wasn't intended for her, it was an effective discouragement to any further questioning.

Smith cleared the snow for two feet around where Harrod's head had lain. With hand and eyes he examined the ground with meticulous care, rose slowly to his feet, took Mary's arm and began to walk away. After a few steps he hesitated, stopped, turned back to the dead man and turned him over again so that the right arm was no longer pointing towards the sky.

Half-way back to the cliff-edge, Smith said abruptly:

'Something struck Harrod on the back of the neck. I thought it might have been a rock. But there was no rock where he lay, only turf.'

'There was a rocky outcrop near by.'

'You don't break your neck on a rocky outcrop, then stand up and jump out into a snow-drift. Even had he rolled over into the drift, he could never have finished with his head seven feet out from the rock. He was struck by some hard metallic object, either the butt of a gun or the haft of a knife. The skin is broken but there is no bruising for the neck was broken immediately afterwards. When he was unconscious. To make us think it was an accident. It must have happened on the rock – there was no disturbance in the snow round Harrod – and it must have happened while he was upright. A tap on the neck, a quick neck-twist, then he fell or was pushed over the edge of the outcrop. Wonderful stuff, stone,' Smith finished bitterly. 'It leaves no footprints.'

Mary stopped and stared at him.

'Do you realize what you're saying?' She caught his speculative and very old-fashioned look, took his arm and went on quickly: 'No, I mean the implications. I'm sorry, I'm sorry, of course you do. John, I – I'm scared. Even all those months with you in Italy – well you know, nothing like this—' She broke off, then continued: 'Couldn't there – couldn't there be some other explanation?'

'Like he hit himself on the back of the head or the abominable snowman got him?'

She looked at him steadily, her dark eyes far too large in what could be seen of her hooded face. 'I don't deserve that, John. I *am* frightened.'

'Me, too.'

'I don't believe you.'

'Well, if I'm not, it's damn well time I started to be.'

Smith checked his descent when he estimated he was about forty feet from the base of the cliff. He took two turns of the nylon round his left leg, clamped it with his right, took a turn round his left arm, pulled off his right gauntlet with his teeth, stuffed it inside his tunic, eased out his Luger, slid the safety catch and went on his way again, checking his speed of descent with his gauntleted left hand. It was a reasonable enough expectation that whoever had tried to pull down the rope would be waiting there to finish off the job.

But there was no reception committee waiting, not, at least, at the spot where he touched down. He traversed a quick circle with his torch. There was nobody there and nothing there and the footprints that must have been there were long obscured by the drifting snow. Gun in one hand, torch in the other, he moved along the cliff face for thirty yards then moved out in a semi-circle until he arrived back at the cliff face. The rope-puller had evidently opted for discretion. Smith returned to the rope and jerked it. In two minutes he had Mary's kit-bag down and, a few minutes later, Mary herself. As soon as she had stepped out of the double bowline, Smith undid the knot, pulled the rope down from the top of the cliff and coiled it. So numbed and frozen were his hands by this time that the operation took him nearly fifteen minutes.

Rope over one shoulder, her kit-bag on the other, Smith led Mary to the fissure in the cliff side.

'Don't pitch the tent,' Smith said. 'Unroll it, put your sleeping bag on one half, get into it and pull the other half of the tent over you. Half an hour and you'll be covered with drifting snow. The snow will not only keep you warm, it'll hide you from any somnambulists. I'll be along in the morning before we leave.'

He walked away, stopped, looked back. Mary was still standing where he had left her, looking after him. There was no sag to her shoulders, no particular expression to her face, but for all that she looked oddly defenceless, lonely and forlorn, a quality as undefinable as it was unmistakable. Smith hesitated, then went back to her, unrolled her tent and sleeping bag, waited till she had climbed in, zipped up the bag and pulled the other half of the tent up to her chin. She smiled at him. He fixed the sleeping bag hood, pulled a corner of the tent over it and left, all without saying a word.

Locating his own tent was simple enough, a steady light burnt inside it. Smith beat the snow from his clothes, stooped and entered. Christiansen, Thomas and Carraciola were in their sleeping bags and were asleep or appeared to be. Torrance-Smythe was checking over their store of plastic explosives, fuses, detonators and grenades, while Schaffer was reading a paperback – in German – smoking a cigarette – also German – and faithfully guarding the radio. He put down the book and looked at Smith.

'OK?'

'OK.' Smith produced the code-book from his tunic. 'Sorry I was so long, but I thought I'd never find him. Drifting pretty badly up there.'

'We've arranged to take turns on watch,' Schaffer said. 'Half an hour each. It'll be dawn in three hours.'

Smith smiled. 'What are you guarding against in these parts?'

'The abominable snowman.'

The smile left Smith's face as quickly as it had come. He turned his attention to Harrod's code-book and spent about ten minutes in memorizing call-up signals and wave-frequencies and writing a message out in code. Before he had finished Schaffer had turned into his sleeping bag, leaving Torrance-Smythe on watch. Smith folded the message, tucked it in a pocket, rose, took the radio and a rubber ground-sheet to protect it from the snow.

'I'm going to move out a bit,' he said to Torrance-Smythe. 'Reception is lousy among trees. Besides, I don't want to wake everybody up. Won't be long.'

Two hundred yards from the tent, after having stopped twice and changed direction twice, Smith knelt with his back – and the rubber ground-sheet – to the drifting snow. He extended a fourteen feet telescopic aerial, adjusted a pre-selected call-up and cranked a handle. Four times he cranked the handle and on the fifth he got results. Someone was keeping a very close radio watch indeed.

'This is Danny Boy,' the set speaker crackled. The signal was faint and intermittent, but just comprehensible. 'Danny Boy replying to you. Over.'

Smith spoke into the mouth microphone. 'This is Broadsword. Can I speak to Father Machree or Mother Machree? Over.'

'Sorry. Unavailable. Over.'

'Code,' Smith said. 'Over.'

'Ready.'

Smith extracted the paper from his pocket and shone his torch on it. There were two lines containing meaningless jumbles of letters and, below that, the plain language translation, which read: 'SAFE LANDING HARROD DEAD WEATHER FINE PLEASE AWAIT MESSAGE 0800 GMT'. Smith read off the corresponding code figures and finished off: 'Have that delivered to Father Machree by 0700. Without fail.'

Torrance-Smythe looked up at Smith's return.

'Back already?' Surprise in his voice. 'You got through?'

'Not a chance,' Smith said disgustedly. 'Too many bloody mountains around.'

'Didn't try for very long, did you?'

'Two and a half minutes.' It was Smith's turn to look surprised. 'Surely you know that's the safe maximum?'

'You think there may be radio monitoring stations hereabouts?'

'Oh, no, not at all.' Smith's voice was heavy with sarcasm. 'You wouldn't expect to find radio monitors in the Schloss Adler, would you now?'

'Well, now.' Torrance-Smythe smiled tiredly. 'I believe someone did mention it was the southern HQ of the German Secret Service. Sorry, Major. It's not that I'm growing old, though there's that, too. It's just that what passes for my mind is so gummed up by cold and lack of sleep that I think it's stopped altogether.'

Smith pulled off his boots and snow-suit, climbed into his sleeping bag and pulled the radio close to him.

'Then it's time you had some sleep. My explosives expert is going to be no good to me if he can't tell a detonator from a door-knob. Go on. Turn in. I'll keep watch.'

'But we had arranged—'

'Arguments, arguments,' Smith sighed. 'Insubordination on every hand.' He smiled. 'Straight up, Smithy, I'm wide awake. I know I won't sleep tonight.'

One downright lie, Smith thought, and one statement of incontrovertible truth. He wasn't wide awake, he was physically and mentally exhausted and on the slightest relaxation of willpower oblivion would have overtaken him in seconds. But that he wouldn't sleep that night was beyond doubt: no power on earth would have let him sleep that night but, in the circumstances, it was perhaps wiser not to say so to Torrance-Smythe.

Chapter Three

The pre-dawn greyness was in the sky. Smith and his men had broken camp. Tent and sleeping bags were stored away and the cooking utensils – after a very sketchy breakfast scarcely deserving of the name – were being thrust into haversacks. There was no conversation, none at all: it wasn't a morning for speaking. All of them, Smith thought, looked more drawn, more exhausted, than they had done three hours ago: he wondered how he himself, who had had no sleep at all, must look. It was as well, he reflected, that mirrors were not part of their commando equipment. He looked at his watch.

'We'll leave in ten minutes,' he announced. 'Should give us plenty of time to be down in the tree line before sun-up. Assuming there are no more cliffs. Back in a moment. Visibility is improving and I think I'll go recce along the cliff edge. With any luck, maybe I can see the best way down.'

'And if you haven't any luck?' Carraciola asked sourly.

'We've still that thousand feet of nylon rope,' Smith said shortly.

He pulled on his snow-suit and left, angling off in the direction of the cliff. As soon as he was beyond the belt of the scrub pines and out of sight of the camp he changed direction uphill and broke into a run.

A single eye appeared under a lifted corner of snow-covered canvas as Mary Ellison heard the soft crunch of running footsteps in the snow. She heard the first two bars of a tuneless whistling of 'Lorelei', unzipped her sleeping bag and sat up. Smith was standing above her.

'Not already!' she said protestingly.

'Yes already. Come on. Up!'

'I haven't slept a wink.'

'Neither have I. I've been watching that damned radio all night – and watching to check that no somnambulists took a stroll in this direction.'

'You kept awake. You did that for me?'

'I kept awake. We're off. Start in five minutes. Leave your tent and kit-bag here, you won't be requiring them again. Take some food, something to drink, that's all. And for God's sake, don't get too close to us.' He glanced at his watch. 'We'll stop at 7 a.m. Check your watch. Exactly 7 a.m. And *don't* bump into us.'

'What do you think I am?' But Smith didn't tell her what he thought she was. He had already gone.

A thousand feet farther down the side of the Weissspitze the trees were something worth calling trees, towering conifers that soared sixty and seventy feet up into the sky. Into the clear sky, for the snow had stopped falling now. It was dawn.

The slope of the Weissspitze was still very steep, perhaps one in four or five. Smith, with his five men strung out behind him in single file, slipped and stumbled almost constantly: but the deep snow, Smith reflected, at least cushioned their frequent falls and as a mode of progress it was a damn sight preferable to shinning down vertical cliff-faces, on an impossible thin clothes-line. The curses of his bruised companions were almost continuous but serious complaints were marked by their total absence: there was no danger, they were making excellent time and they were now completely hidden in the deep belt of pines.

Two hundred yards behind them Mary Ellison carefully picked her way down the tracks made by the men below her. She slipped and fell only very occasionally for, unlike the men, she was carrying no over-balancing gear on her back. Nor had she any fear of being observed, of coming too close to Smith and the others: in still, frosty air on a mountain sound carries with a preternatural clarity and from the sound of the voices farther down the slope she could judge her distance from them to a nicety. For the twentieth time she looked at her watch: it was twenty minutes to seven.

Some time later, for much more than the twentieth time, Smith checked his watch again. It was exactly 7 o'clock. The dawn had gone and the light of full day-time filtered down through the snow-bent boughs of the conifers. Smith stopped and held up his hand, waiting until the other five had caught up with him.

'We must be half-way down now.' He shrugged off the heavy pack on his back and lowered it gratefully into the snow. 'I think it's time we had a look at the scenery.'

They piled their gear and moved off to the right. Within a minute the pines started to thin out and at a signal from Smith they all dropped to hands and knees and crawled forward the last few yards towards the edge of the belt of pines. Smith carried a telescope in his hand: Christiansen and Thomas both wore binoculars. Zeiss binoculars. Admiral Rolland had left nothing to chance. Beyond the last of the pines a mound of snow obstructed their view of the valley below. Shrouded from top to toe, in the all enveloping white of their snow-smocks, they completed the last few feet on their elbows and knees.

What lay below them was something out of a fairy tale, an impossibly beautiful scene from an impossibly beautiful fairy tale, a fairy tale set aeons back in the never-never land of the age of dreams, a kindlier land, a nobler land than man had ever known since first he had set his hand against his brother. A land that never was, Smith thought, a land that never was: but there it lay before them, the golden land that never was, the home of that most dreaded organization in the entire world, the German Gestapo. The impeccable incongruity of it all, Smith reflected, passed all belief.

The valley was bowl-shaped, open to the north, hemmed in by steeply rising hills to the east and west, closed off by the towering bulk of the Weissspitze to the south.

A scene of fantastic beauty. Nine thousand, seven hundred and ten feet in height, the second highest mountain in Germany, the Weissspitze soared up menacingly like another north wall of the Eiger, its dazzling whiteness caught in the morning sun, its starkly lovely outline sharply etched against the now cloudless blue of the sky. High up near the cone-shaped summit could be seen the line of black rock marking the cliff Smith and his men had descended during the night with, just below it, a much greater cliff-face on the plateau above which they had spent the night.

Directly opposite where they lay, and almost exactly on the same level, was the Schloss Adler itself. The castle of the eagle had been aptly named, an impregnable fortress, an inaccessible eyrie set between mountain and sky.

Just below the spot where the steep-sided slopes of the Weissspitze began to flatten out northwards into the head of the valley, a geological freak, known as a volcanic plug, jutted two hundred vertical feet up into the sparkling, ice-cold air. It was on this that the Schloss Adler had been built. The northern, western and eastern sides of this volcanic plug were sheer, perpendicular walls of rock, walls that swept up smoothly, without intermission or break into the structure of the castle itself: from where they lay, it was impossible to say where the one ended and the other began. To the south, a steeply-sloping ridgeback connected the plug to the equally sloping ramparts of the Weissspitze.

The castle itself was another dream, the dream of the apotheosis of medievalism. This dream, Smith was aware, was as illusory as the golden age of its setting. It wasn't medieval at all, it had been built as late as the mid-nineteenth century to the express order of one of the madder of the Bavarian monarchs who had suffered from a comprehensive list of delusions, of which grandeur had not been the least. But, delusions or not, he had had, as the deluded so often have – to the dismay and consternation of their allegedly saner brethren – impeccable taste. The castle was perfect for the valley, the valley for the castle. Any other combination would have been inconceivable.

The Schloss Adler was built in the form of a hollow square. It was towered, battlemented and crenellated, its most imposing aspects, two perfectly circular towers, the one to the east higher than that to the west, facing down the valley towards the north. Two smaller, but still magnificent towers, lay at the southern corners, facing the looming bulk of the Weissspitze. From where Smith lay, at some slight level above that of the castle, he could just see into the open square in its middle, outside access to which was obtained by a pair of huge iron gates at the rear. The sun had not yet climbed sufficiently high above the eastern hills for its rays to strike the castle directly, but, for all that, its incredibly white walls gleamed and glittered as if made of the most iridescent marble.

Below the soaring northern ramparts of the castle the valley fell away steeply to the Blau See, beautiful pine-fringed jewel of a lake of the deepest and most sparkling blue, a colour which with the green of the pines, the white dazzle of the snow and the brilliant, lighter blue of the sky above formed a combination of breath-taking loveliness. Impossibly lovely, Smith thought, a completely faithful colour reproduction of the scene would have had everybody shouting 'fake'.

From where they lay they could see that the belt of pines in which they lay hidden extended almost all the way down to the lake. Getting down there unobserved would be no problem at all. An almost exactly matching line of pines swept down the opposite – the eastern – side of the valley.

From the lake those two long sweeps of pines, climbing steadily upwards as they marched to the south, must have appeared like a pair of great curving horns almost meeting at the top of the lower of the two cliff-faces on the Weissspitze.

A small village lay at the head of the lake. Basically it consisted of a single wide street, perhaps two hundred yards in length, a railway station, two inevitable churches perched on two inevitable knolls and a thin scattering of houses climbing up the steep slopes on either side of the village. From the southern end of the village a road curved up the far side of the valley till it reached the ridge-back to the south of the castle: this ridge-back it ascended by a series of hairpin bends, the last of which led to the great doors guarding the forecourt at the back of the castle. The road, just then, was completely blocked by snow and sole access to the castle was obviously by means of the *Luftseilbahn*, an aerial cableway. Two cables stretched from the village straight up to the castle, crossing three supporting pylons en route. Even as they watched, a cable-car was completing the last section of its journey up to the castle. At a distance of not much more than a hundred feet from the glittering walls of the Schloss Adler it appeared to be climbing almost vertically.

On the Blau See, about a mile beyond the village, lay a very large group of regularly spaced huts, arranged in rectangular patterns. It bore an uncommonly close resemblance to a military encampment.

'Well, I'll be damned!' With an almost physical effort of will, Schaffer forced himself to look away and Smith could see the wonder reflected in his eyes. 'Is this for real, boss?'

It wasn't a question that called for an answer. Schaffer had summed up their collective feeling pretty well and there was nothing that anyone could add that wouldn't seem and sound superfluous. Prone in the snow, they watched in silence as the cable-car climbed agonizingly slowly up the last fifty feet towards the castle. It seemed as if it would never make it and Smith could almost palpably sense the empathy of his companions and himself as they willed that little car on the last few feet of its journey. But make it it did and it disappeared from sight under the roof of the cable header station that has been built into the western foot of the castle. The tension relaxed and Schaffer cleared his throat.

'Boss,' he said diffidently, 'there are a couple of minor points that occur to me. Requiring elucidation, one might say. First of all, if I didn't know better I'd say that was a military barracks down by that little old lake there.'

'You don't know better. That *is* a military barracks down by that little old lake there. And no ordinary military barracks either, I might say. That's the training HQ of the Jäger battalions of the Wehrmacht's Alpenkorps.'

'Oh, my gosh! The Alpine Corps! If I'd known this I'd never have come along. The Alpine Corps! Why didn't someone tell Ma Schaffer's nearest and dearest?'

'I thought you knew,' Smith said mildly. 'Why do you think we're not dressed as German sailors or Red Cross nurses?'

Schaffer unzipped his snow-smock, minutely examined his Alpenkorps uniform as if seeing it for the first time, then zipped it up again. He said carefully: 'You mean to say we're going to mingle, careless like, with the German Army.' He paused, looked wide-eyed at Smith's smiling nod, then went on incredulously: 'But – but we'll be recognized as strangers!'

'Training troops come and go all the time,' Smith said off-handedly. 'What's six new faces among six hundred new faces?'

'This is terrible,' Schaffer said gloomily.

'Worse than horses?' Smith smiled. 'After all, the Alpenkorps don't buck and trample all over you.'

'Horses don't carry machine-guns,' Schaffer said morosely.

'And your second point?'

'Ah, yes. The second point. There's the little matter of the old Schloss itself. Kinda forgotten our helicopter, haven't we? How do we get in?'

'A good point,' Smith conceded. 'We'll have to think about it. But I'll tell you this. If Colonel Wyatt-Turner can penetrate the German High Command and, more important, get away again, this should be a piece of cake for us.'

'He did what?' Schaffer demanded.

'Didn't you know?'

'How should I know?' Schaffer was irritated. 'Never met the guy till yesterday.'

'He spent the years '40 to '43 inside Germany. Served in the Wehrmacht for part of the time. Ended up in the GHQ in Berlin. Says he knows Hitler quite well.'

'Well, I'll be damned.' Schaffer paused for a long moment, finally arrived at a conclusion. 'The guy,' he said moodily, 'must be nuts.'

'Maybe. But if he can do it, we can. We'll figure a way. Let's get back among the trees.'

They inched their way back into cover, leaving Christiansen behind with Smith's telescope to keep watch. After they'd made a temporary camp, heated and drunk some coffee, Smith announced his intention of trying to contact London again.

He unpacked the radio and sat down on a kit-bag a few feet distant from the others. The switch that cut in the transmitter circuit was on the left hand side of the radio, the side remote from where the other four men were sitting. Smith switched on with a loud positive click, cranked the call-up handle with his left hand. With the very first crank his left hand moved the transmitting switch from 'On' to 'Off', the whirring of the call-up blanketing the sound. Smith cranked away diligently at intervals, stopping from time to time to make minute adjustments to the controls, then finally gave up and sat back, shaking his head in disgust.

'You'll never make it with all those trees around,' Torrance-Smythe observed.

'That must be it,' Smith agreed. 'I'll try the other side of the wood. Might have better luck there.'

He slung the transmitter over his shoulder and trudged off through the deep snow, cutting straight across to the other side of the belt of pines. When he thought he was safely out of eyeshot of the men at the camp, he checked with a quick look over his shoulder. They were out of sight. He turned more than ninety degrees left and hurried up the hill until he cut the tracks that he and his men had made on the way down. He followed the tracks uphill, whistling 'Lorelei', but whistling softly: in that frosty air, sound travelled dangerously far. He stopped whistling when Mary appeared from where she had been hiding behind a fallen pine.

'Hallo, darling,' she said brightly.

'We'll have less of the "darlings",' Smith said briskly. 'It's 8 a.m. Father Machree awaits. And keep your voice down.'

He sat on the fallen tree, cranked the handle and established contact almost immediately. The transmission from London was still very faint but clearer than it had been in the earlier hours of the morning.

'Father Machree is waiting,' the radio crackled. 'Hold. Hold.'

Smith held and the unmistakable voice of Admiral Rolland took over from the London operator.

'Position please, Broadsword.'

Smith consulted the piece of paper in his hand, again in code and plain language. The message read: WOODS DUE WEST CASTLE DESCENDING W.H. THIS EVENING. Smith read out the corresponding code letters.

There was a pause, presumably while Rolland was having the message decoded, then his voice came again.

'Understood. Proceed. Harrod killed accidentally?'

'No. Over.'

'By the enemy? Over.'

'No. What is the weather report? Over.'

'Deteriorating. Freshening winds, strong later. Snow. Over.'

Smith looked up at the still and cloudless sky above. He assumed that Rolland hadn't got his forecasts mixed up. He said: 'Time of next broadcast uncertain. Can you stand by? Over.'

'Am remaining HQ until operation complete,' Rolland said. 'Good luck. Goodbye.'

Smith closed up the radio and said thoughtfully to Mary: 'I didn't much care for the way he said goodbye there.'

In the naval Operations room in Whitehall, Admiral Rolland and Colonel Wyatt-Turner, one on either side of the radio operator manning a huge transceiver, looked at each other with heavy faces.

'So the poor devil was murdered,' Wyatt-Turner said flatly.

'A high price to pay for confirmation that we were right,' Rolland said sombrely. 'Poor devil, as you say. The moment we gave him that radio to carry we signed a death-warrant. I wonder who's next. Smith himself?'

'Not Smith.' Wyatt-Turner shook his head positively. 'Some people have a sixth sense. Smith has a seventh, eighth and ninth and a built-in radar set for danger. Smith can survive under any circumstances I can conceive of. I didn't pick him with a pin, sir. He's the best agent in Europe.'

'Except possibly yourself. And don't forget, Colonel, there may possibly be circumstances that even you can't conceive of.'

'Yes, that's so.' He looked directly at Rolland. 'What do you reckon his chances are, sir?'

'Chances?' Rolland's eyes were remote, unseeing. 'What do you mean, chances? He doesn't have any.'

Almost precisely the same thought was in Smith's mind as he lit a cigarette and looked at the girl beside him, careful not to let his thoughts show in his face. Not until that first sight he'd just had of the castle had the full realization of the apparent impossibility of their task struck him. Had he known what the precise physical situation had been, he doubted very much whether he would have come. Deep in the furthest recesses of his mind, he knew, although he would not admit it to himself, that there really was no room for the element of doubt. He wouldn't have come. But he had come. He was here and he had better do something about it.

He said to Mary: 'Have you had a squint at the old Schloss yet?'

'It's a fantastic place. How on earth do we ever get General Carnaby out of there?'

'Easy. We'll take a walk up there tonight, get inside and take him away.'

Mary stared at him in disbelief and waited for him to amplify his statement. He didn't. Finally, she said: 'That's all?'

'That's all.'

'The simplicity of true genius. You must have spent a lot of time working that one out.' When he still didn't reply, she went on, elaborately sarcastic: 'In the first place, of course, there'll be no trouble about getting in. You just go up to the main door and knock.'

'More or less. Then the door – or window – opens, I smile at you, say thank you and pass inside.'

'You what.'

'I smile and say thank you. Even in wartime, there's no reason why the little courtesies—'

'Please!' She was thoroughly exasperated now. 'If you can't talk sense—'

'*You* are going to open the door for *me*,' Smith explained patiently.

'Are you feeling all right?'

'The staff shortage in Germany is acute. The Schloss Adler is no exception. You're just the type they're looking for. Young, intelligent, good-looking, you can cook, polish, sew on Colonel Kramer's buttons—'

'Who's Colonel Kramer?' Her tone as much as her face showed the bewilderment in her mind.

'Deputy Chief of the German Secret Service.'

Mary said with conviction: 'You must be mad.'

'If I wasn't I wouldn't be doing this job.' He glanced at his watch. 'I've been gone too long and I fear that I'm surrounded by the odd suspicious mind. We move off at five. Exactly five. Down in the village there's a *Gasthaus* on the east side of the main street called "Zum Wilden Hirsch." "The Wild Deer." Remember it, "Zum Wilden Hirsch." We don't want you wandering into the wrong pub. Behind it there's a shed used as a beer cellar. It's always kept locked but there will be a key in the door tonight. I'll meet you there at exactly eight o'clock.'

He turned to go, but she caught him by the arm.

'How do you know all this?' she asked tensely. 'About the *Gasthaus* and the bottle store and the key being there and about Colonel Kramer and—'

'Ah, ah!' Smith shook his head admonishingly and touched her lips with his forefinger.

'Hand-book for spies, golden rule number one.' She drew away from him and stared down at the snow-covered ground, her voice low and bitter. 'Never ever tell anyone anything unless you have to.' She paused and looked up. 'Not even me?'

'Especially not you, poppet.' He patted her lightly on the cheek. 'Don't be late.'

He walked away down the slope leaving her looking after him with an expressionless face.

Lieutenant Schaffer lay stretched out and almost buried in the deep snow, half-hidden behind the bole of a pine, with a telescope to his eye. He twisted as he heard the soft crunch of snow behind him and saw Smith approaching on his hands and knees.

'Couldn't you knock or something?' Schaffer asked irritably.

'Sorry. Something you wanted to show me, so the boys say.'

'Yeah.' Schaffer handed Smith the telescope. 'Take a gander at this lot. Thought it might interest you.'

Smith took the telescope and fingered the very precise adjustment until he achieved maximum definition.

'Lower down,' Schaffer said. 'At the foot of the rock.'

Smith traversed the telescope down the sides of the Schloss Adler and the sheer walls of the volcanic plug until the fine cross-hairs came to rest on the snow-covered slopes at the foot. Moving across the slope he could see two soldiers with slung machine-carbines and, not on leashes, four dogs.

'My, my,' Smith murmured thoughtfully. 'I see what you mean.'

'Those are Dobermann pinschers, boss.'

'Well, they aren't toy poodles and that's a fact,' Smith agreed. He moved the telescope a little way up the walls of the volcanic plug, held it there.

'*And* floodlights.' he added softly.

He lowered the telescope again, past the patrolling soldiers and dogs, till it came to rest on a high wire fence that appeared to go all the way around the base of the volcanic plug.

'*And* a dinky little fence.'

'Fences,' Schaffer said pontifically, 'are made to be cut or climbed.'

'You try cutting or climbing this one, laddie, and you'll be cooked to a turn in nothing flat. A standard design, using a standard current of 2300 volt, single-phase, 60 cycle AC. All the best electric chairs have it.'

Schaffer shook his head. 'Amazing the lengths some folks will go to protect their privacy.'

'Fences, floods and Dobermanns,' Smith said. 'I don't think that combination will stop us, do you, Lieutenant?'

'Of course not. Stop us? Of course not!' He paused for some moments, then burst out: 'How in God's name do you propose—'

'We'll decide when the time comes,' Smith said easily.

'You mean you'll decide,' Schaffer said complainingly. 'Play it pretty close to the cuff, don't you?'

'That's because I'm too young to die.'

'Why me, for God's sake?' Schaffer demanded after a long pause. 'Why pick me for this job? This isn't my line of country, Major.'

'God knows,' Smith said frankly. 'Come to that, why me?'

Schaffer was in the middle of giving him a long and pointedly disbelieving look when he suddenly stiffened and cocked his head up to the sky in the direction of the unmistakably rackety whirr of a helicopter engine. Both men picked it up at once. It was coming from the north, over the Blau See, and heading directly towards them. It was a big military version and, even at that distance, the swastika markings were clearly distinguishable. Schaffer started to move backwards towards the line of pines.

'Exit Schaffer,' he announced hurriedly. 'The bloodhounds are out for us.'

'I don't think so,' Smith said. 'Stay where you are and pull your smock over your head.'

Quickly they pulled their white smocks over their heads until only their eyes, and Smith's telescope, partly buried in the snow, could be seen. From thirty yards in any direction, including straight up, they must have been quite invisible.

The helicopter swept up the valley still maintaining a course directly towards the spot where the two men lay hidden. When it was only a few hundred yards away even Smith began to feel uneasy and wondered if by some evil mischance the enemy knew or suspected their presence. They were bound to have heard the engines of the Lancaster, muted though they had been, during the night. Had some suspicious and intelligent character – and there would be no lack of those in the Schloss Adler – come up with the right answer to the question of the presence of this errant bomber in one of the most unlikely places in all Germany? Could picked members of the Alpenkorps be combing the pine woods even at that moment – and he, Smith, had been so confident that he hadn't even bothered to post a guard. Then, abruptly, when the helicopter was almost directly overhead, it side-slipped sharply to its left, sank down over the castle courtyard, hovered for a few moments and slowly descended. Smith surreptitiously mopped his forehead and applied his eye to the telescope.

The helicopter had landed. The rotor stopped, steps descended and a man climbed down to the courtyard floor. From his uniform, Smith decided, a very senior officer. Then he suddenly realized that it was a very very senior officer indeed. His face tightened as he pushed the telescope across to Schaffer. 'Take a good look,' he advised.

Schaffer took a good look, lowered the telescope as the man passed through a doorway. 'Pal of yours, boss?'

'I know him. Reichsmarschall Julius Rosemeyer. The Wehrmacht Chief of Staff.'

'My very first Reichsmarschall and me without my telescopic rifle,' Schaffer said regretfully. 'I wonder what his highness wants.'

'Same as us,' Smith said briefly.

'General Carnaby?'

'When you're going to ask the Allies' overall co-ordinator of planning a few questions about the Second Front you don't send just the corporal of the guard to interview him.'

'You don't think they might have come to take old Carnaby away?' Schaffer asked anxiously.

'Not a chance. The Gestapo never gives up its prisoners. In this country the Wehrmacht does what the Gestapo says.'

'Or else?'

'Or else. Off you go – they've more coffee on the brew back there. Send someone to relieve me in an hour.'

Admiral Rolland's weather forecast for the Sea turned out to be perfectly correct. As the endless shivering hours dragged slowly by the weather steadily deteriorated. By noon the sun was gone and a keen wind sprung up from the east. By early afternoon snow had begun to fall from the darkened sky, slowly at first then with increasing severity as the east wind steadily increased in strength and became bitingly cold. It looked like being a bad night, Smith thought. But a bad night that reduced visibility to near-zero and kept people indoors was what they wanted: it would have been difficult for them to saunter up to the Schloss Adler bathed in the warm light of a harvest moon. Smith checked his watch.

'Time to go.' He climbed stiffly to his feet and beat his arms to restore circulation. 'Call Thomas, will you.'

Rucksacks and kit-bags were slung and shouldered. Thomas, who had been keeping watch, appeared carrying Smith's telescope. Thomas was very far from being his usual cheerful self, and it wasn't just the fact that he'd spent the last hour exposed to the full force of wind and snow that had left him in such ill-humour.

'Is that damned radio working yet?' he asked Smith.

'Not a hope. Six tries, six failures. Why?'

'I'll tell you why,' Thomas said bitterly. 'Pity we couldn't get the Admiral to change his mind about the paratroops. A full troop train just got in, that's all.'

'Well, that's fine,' Smith said equably. 'The old hands will think we're new boys and the new boys will think we're old hands. Very convenient.'

Thomas looked thoughtfully at Smith.

'Very, *very* convenient.' He hesitated, then went on: 'How about loosening up a bit, Major?'

'What do you mean?'

'Come off it,' Carraciola said roughly. 'You know damn well what he means. It's our lives. Why do we have to go down into that damned village? And how do you intend to get Carnaby out? If we're to commit suicide, tell us why. You owe us that.'

'I owe you nothing,' Smith said flatly. 'I'll tell you nothing. And if you know nothing you can't talk. You'll be told when the time comes.'

'You, Smith,' Torrance-Smythe said precisely, 'are a cold-blooded devil.'

'It's been said before,' Smith said indifferently.

The village railway station was a small, two-track, end-of-the-line depot. Like all end-of-the-line depots it was characterized by rust, dilapidation, the barest functionalism of design and an odd pessimistically-expectant air of waiting for someone to come along and finish it off properly. At any time, its air of desolation was total. That night, completely deserted, with a high, gusting wind driving snow through pools of light cast by dim and swaying electric lamps, the ghostly impression of a place abandoned by man and by the world was almost overwhelming. It suited Smith's purpose perfectly.

He led his five snow-smock clad men quickly across the tracks and into the comparative shelter of the station buildings. They filed silently past the closed bookstall, the freight office, the booking office, flitted quickly into the shadows beyond and stopped.

Smith lowered the radio, shrugged off his rucksack, removed snow-smock and trousers and sauntered casually alongside the tracks – the thrifty Bavarians regarded platforms as a wasteful luxury. He stopped outside a door next to a bolted hatch which bore above it the legend GEPACK ANNAHME. He tried the door. It was locked. He made a quick survey to check that he was unobserved, stooped, examined the keyhole with a pencil flash, took a bunch of oddly shaped keys from his pockets and had the door opened in seconds. He whistled softly and was almost at once joined by the others, who filed quickly inside, already slipping off their packs as they went. Schaffer, bringing up the rear, paused and glanced up at the sign above the hatch.

'My God!' He shook his head. 'The left luggage office!'

'Where else?' Smith asked reasonably. He ushered Schaffer in, closed and locked the door behind him. Hooding his pencil torch until only a finger-width beam emerged, he passed by the luggage racks till he came to the far end of the room where a bay window was set in the wall. It was a perfectly ordinary sash window and he examined it very minutely, careful that at no time the pinpoint of light touched the glass to shine through to the street beyond. He turned his attention to the vertical wooden planking at the side of the window, took out his sheath knife and levered a plank away to expose a length of twin-cored flex stapled vertically to the wall. He split the cores, sliced through each in turn, replaced the plank and tested the lower sash of the window. It moved easily up and down.

'An interesting performance,' Schaffer observed. 'What was all that in aid of?'

'It's not always convenient to enter by the front door. Or, come to that, leave by it either.'

'A youth mis-spent in philandering or burgling,' Schaffer said sadly. 'How did you know it was wired for sound?'

'Even a small country station will have valuables stored in its left luggage office from time to time,' Smith said patiently. 'But it will *not* have a full-time baggage attendant. The attendant, booking clerk, ticket-collector, porter and station-master are probably all one man. So it's kept locked. But there's no point in barring the front door if your bag-snatcher can climb in through the back window. So your back window is grilled or wired. No grille – and a badly-fitting plank. Obvious.'

'Obvious to you, maybe,' Carraciola said sourly. 'All this – ah – expertise with skeleton keys and burglar alarms. The Black Watch you said you were in?'

'That's right.'

'Very odd training they give you in those Scottish regiments. Very odd indeed.'

' "Thorough" is the word you're searching for,' Smith said kindly. 'Let's go and have a drink.'

'Let's do that,' Carraciola said heavily. 'Remind me to get mine down in one go or ten gets you one that I'll never live to finish it.'

'It would be a shame to waste good beer,' Smith agreed. He waited until the last man was out, locked the door behind him and rejoined them as they walked out of the main station entrance under the 'Bahnhof' sign. They were now no longer carrying rucksacks or wearing snow-smocks. All were dressed in the uniforms of soldiers of a Jäger battalion, Smith as a major, Schaffer as a lieutenant and the other four as sergeants. Their uniforms were no longer as immaculately crease-free as they might have been nor for that matter, as Sergeant Harrod had observed, did they fit as well as they might have done. But in a village street or crowded bar, at night-time, they should pass muster. Or so Smith devoutly hoped.

It was a typical main street in a typical high alpine village. The buildings lining either side of the street, solid, rugged, four-square buildings, looked as if they had been defying the bitter Bavarian winters for a long long time and intended going on doing so for as long again. Nearly all the houses were of the wooden chalet type, with great sweeping eaves and balconies running the full width of the front of the houses. A few were of comparatively modern construction, with shingled walls, large double-glazed windows and fancy wrought-iron grille-work, but most were very old and low, planked with rough adze-cut wood, and having the interlocking wall-beams projecting at the corners.

There were no street lamps but neither was there any attempt at a blackout. Elongated rectangles of light from uncurtained windows patterned the snow-packed streets. Beyond the far or southern end of the street, intermittently seen through the sweeping curtains of snow, a cluster of bright lights seemed to hang suspended in the sky. Instinctively, almost, Smith stopped to gaze at this distant constellation and his men stopped with him. The lights of the Schloss Adler, the castle of the eagle, seemed impossibly remote, as unattainable as the mountains of the moon. Wordlessly, the men looked at them in long silence, then at one another, then, by mutual and still silent consent, moved on their way again, their boots crunching crisply in the beaten snow, their frozen breaths wisping away in the chill night wind.

The main street – the only street – was deserted, quite empty of life. Inevitably so, on so bitter a night. But if the street was deserted, the village was anything but: the sounds of laughter and singing and the babel of voices filled the night air and the nose-to-tail row of parked German trucks along one side of the street showed clearly enough just who was responsible for the singing and the laughter. For the training troops in the military barracks on the Blau See there was only one centre of entertainment for twenty miles around and this village was it: the *Gasthaüser* and *Weinstuben* were jammed to the doors with soldiers of the Alpenkorps, probably the most highly trained combat troops in Europe.

Schaffer said plaintively: 'I don't really feel like a drink, boss.'

'Nonsense,' Smith said encouragingly. 'You're just shy at the thought of meeting strangers.' He stopped in front of a *Gasthaus* with the legend 'Drei Könige' above the door. 'Here's a likely looking place, now. Hang on a minute.'

He climbed the steps, opened the door and looked inside. Down in the street the other five looked at one another, the same mingled apprehension and expectancy mirrored in every eye. Austrian *Schrammel* music, hauntingly and nostalgically evocative of a kindlier and happier age, flooded through the open doorway. The expressions on the faces of the men below didn't change. There was a time and a place for *Schrammel* music and this wasn't it.

Smith shook his head, closed the door and rejoined his men.

'Packed,' he said. 'Not even standing room.' He nodded across the street to another hostelry, the 'Eichhof,' a small, squat, beetle-browed building with adze-cut corner beams and an air of advanced dilapidation. 'Let's see what this has to offer.'

But the 'Eichhof' had nothing to offer. Regretfully but firmly Smith closed its front door and turned away.

'Jammed,' he announced. 'Besides, a low-class dump unsuitable for officers and NCOs of the Wehrmacht. But this next place looks more promising, don't you think?'

From the pointed silence it was apparent that the other five didn't think anything of the kind, and, in fact, apart from the factor of size, the third

Weinstube looked remarkably like the ones Smith had just passed up. 'Zum Wilden Hirsch', it was called, and above the sign was a snow-shrouded wooden carving of a wild deer.

Smith walked up the half-dozen steps to the front door and opened it. He winced as the blast of sound reached him, an almost physical assault upon the eardrums. Heaven knew the last two *Weinstuben* had been clamorous enough but compared to this place they now seemed, in retrospect, to have been invested in a cathedral silence. To the blaring accompaniment of a battery of discordant accordions what appeared, from the sheer volume of sound, to be an entire regiment were giving 'Lili Marlene' all they had. Smith glanced at his men, nodded and passed inside.

As the others followed, Schaffer paused in the doorway as Christiansen took his arm and said wonderingly: 'You think he thinks this *isn't* packed?'

'They must,' Schaffer conceded, 'have had them packed six deep in the other joints.'

Chapter Four

They weren't exactly stacked six deep inside 'Zum Wilden Hirsch' but they might well have been if the music-swaying crowd of elbow-jostling customers had assumed the horizontal instead of the perpendicular. He had never, Smith thought, seen so many people in one bar before. There must have been at least four hundred of them. To accommodate a number of that order called for a room of no ordinary dimensions, and this one wasn't. It was a very big room indeed. It was also a very very old room.

The floor of knotted pine sagged, the walls sagged and the massive smoke-blackened beams on the roof seemed to be about ready to fall down at any moment. In the middle of the room stood a huge black wood-burning stove, a stove stoked with such ferocious purpose that the cast-iron top cover glowed dull red. From just below the cover two six-inch twenty-foot long black-enamelled stove pipes led off to points high up on opposite sides of the room – a primitive but extremely efficient form of central heating. The three-sided settees – half booths – lining three walls of the room were of oak darkened by age and smoke and unknown centuries of customers, each booth having recessed holes for stowing newspapers rolled round slats of wood. The twenty or so tables scattered across the floor had hand-cut wooden tops of not less than three inches in thickness with chairs to match. Most of the back of the room was taken up by a solid oaken bar with a coffee-machine at one end, and, behind the bar, swing doors that presumably led to the kitchen. What little illumination there was in the room came from ceiling-suspended and very sooty oil lamps, each one with its generations-old patch of coal-black charred wood in the roof above.

Smith transferred his attention from the room to the customers in the room, a clientele of a composition such as one might expect to find in a high Alpine village with a military encampment at its back door. In one corner were a group of obvious locals, men with still, lean, aquiline, weather-beaten faces, unmistakably men of the mountains, many of them in intricately embroidered leather jackets and Tyrolean hats. They spoke little and drank quietly, as did another small group at the back of the room, perhaps a dozen or so nondescript civilians, clearly not locals, who drank sparingly from small Schnapps glasses. But ninety per cent of the customers were soldiers of the German Alpenkorps, some seated, many more standing, but all giving of their very best with 'Lili Marlene', and nearly all of them enthusiastically waving their pewter-capped litre Steinbechers in the air, happily oblivious, in that moment of tearfully nostalgic romanticism, of the fact that the amount of beer finding its way to comrades' uniforms and the floor was about the equivalent of a moderately heavy rainstorm.

Behind the bar was the obvious proprietor, a gargantuan three-hundred pounder with an impressive moon-like face and several girls busy filling trays with Steinbechers. Several others moved about the room, collecting or serving beer-mugs. One of them approaching in his direction caught Smith's eye.

It would have been surprising if she hadn't. It would have been surprising if she hadn't caught the attention of every man there. But there was no surprise. She did. She would have won any Miss Europe contest hands down if she had had a face other than her own which, though pleasant and plump, was rather plain. But any possible lack of attraction in that cheerfully smiling face was more than over-compensated for elsewhere. She was dressed in a gaily-patterned dirndl and Tyrolean blouse, had a hand-span waist, an hour-and-a-half-glass figure and an obvious predilection for low-cut blouses, that in terms of attracting local custom, must have been worth a fortune to the gigantic proprietor behind the bar. She drew a great deal of attention from the assembled soldiery, not all of it just consisting of admiring glances: if she weren't wearing armour-plating, Smith reflected, she must be permanently black and blue. She approached Smith, brushed back her blonde hair and smiled, the gesture as provocative as the smile.

'Can I help you, sir?'

'Dark beer, please,' Smith said politely. 'Six.'

'With pleasure, sir.' Again the provocative smile, this time accompanied by a half-appraising, half-lingering look from cornflower blue eyes, then she turned and walked away, if her method of locomotion could strictly be described as walking. Schaffer, a slightly dazed expression on his face, stared after her, then caught Smith by the arm.

'*Now* I know why I left Montana, boss.' His voice held something of the dazed quality on his face. 'It wasn't because of the horses after all.'

'Your mind on the job if you don't mind, Lieutenant.' Smith looked thoughtfully after the girl, rubbed his chin and said slowly: 'Barmaids know more about what's going on in their own manor than any chief of police – and that one looks as if she might know more than most. Yes, I'll do that.'

'Do what?' Schaffer asked suspiciously.

'Try to get next to her.'

'I saw her first,' Schaffer said plaintively.

'You can have the next dance,' Smith promised. The levity of the words were belied by the cool watchful expression on his face as his eyes constantly travelled the room. 'When you get your drinks, circulate. See if you can hear any mention of Carnaby or Reichsmarschall Rosemeyer.'

He caught sight of an empty chair by a corner table, moved across and sat in it, nodding politely to a rather bleary-eyed Alpenkorps captain deep in what appeared to be rather patronizing conversation with two lieutenants. The captain showed no more than a brief recognition of his presence and, as far as Smith could tell, no other person present was showing the slightest interest in either himself or his companions. The accordion band finished its stint more or less on the same note and at the same time and the singing of 'Lili Marlene' died away. For long seconds there was a profound and nostalgic silence, four hundred men alone with Lili Marlene under the barrack gate lantern, then, as if on cue, a babel of voices broke out all over the room: four hundred men with unfinished litre mugs do not remain sentimental for overly long.

He caught sight of the girl returning with six Steinbechers on a tray, pushing her way through the crowd and fending off admirers with a practised hand. She gave drinks to Smith's men who immediately but unostentatiously broke up and began to wander away into different parts of the room. The girl looked around, located Smith, smiled brightly, crossed to his table, and put the Steinbecher on it. Before she could straighten, Smith put his arm around her waist and pulled her on to his knee. The Jäger captain across the table broke off his conversation, stared across in startled disapproval, opened his mouth as if to speak, caught Smith's discouraging glance, decided to mind his own business and resumed his conversation. Smith, in his turn, looked away, squeezed the girl's waist, patted her knee and smiled what he hoped was a winning smile.

'And what might your name be, my Alpine rose?' His voice had a slightly slurred edge to it.

'Heidi.' She struggled to rise, but didn't really put her heart into it. 'Please, Major. I have work to do.'

'There is no more important work than entertaining soldiers of the Fatherland,' Smith said loudly. Holding Heidi firmly to forestall any attempt at escape, he took a long pull at his beer, then continued, quietly now, the mug still in front of his face: 'Shall I sing you a song?'

'What song?' Heidi asked warily. 'I hear too much singing.'

'I whistle better than I sing. Listen.' He whistled, very softly the first two bars of 'Lorelei'. 'Do you like that?'

Heidi stiffened and stared but immediately relaxed and smiled at him coquettishly.

'It's very nice, Major. And I'm sure you have a beautiful singing voice, too.'

Smith put his Steinbecher down with an unsteady bang that brought more disapproval from the other side of the table then lifted his hand to wipe the froth from his lips. Heidi smiled down at him, but the wary eyes weren't smiling.

Smith said from behind his hand: 'The men at the bar? The civilians? *Don't* turn round.'

'Gestapo.' She made another apparently futile attempt to free herself. 'From the castle.'

'One's a lip-reader.' Smith had the Steinbecher in front of his face again.

'I can tell. They're watching. Your room in five minutes. Hit me good and hard.'

Heidi stared at him in bewilderment, then yelped in pain as he pinched her, far from gently. She drew back, her right hand came over in a roundhouse swing and the sound of the slap could be heard clear across the crowded room, cutting sharply through the deep buzz of conversation. The voices died away, Steinbechers remained poised half-way towards lips, and every eye in the room turned until it was focused on the scene of the disturbance. Smith now had the exclusive and undivided attention of close on four hundred German soldiers which was exactly how he wanted it: no man anxious to avoid attention at all costs would ever do anything to incur the slightest risk of drawing that unwanted attention.

Heidi pushed herself to her feet, rubbed herself tenderly, snatched up the note which Smith had earlier placed on the table and stalked haughtily away. Smith, his already reddening face discomfited and tight in anger, rose, made to leave the table then halted when confronted by the Jäger captain who had already risen from his side of the table. He was a spruce, erect youngster, very much of the Hitler Jügend type, punctilious and correct but at that moment rather suffering from the effect of too many Steinbechers. Beneath the redly-dulled eyes lay a gleam which bespoke the not uncommon combination of self-importance and officious self-righteousness.

'Your conduct does not become an officer of the Wehrmacht,' he said loudly.

Smith did not reply at once. The embarrassed anger faded from his face to be replaced by an expressionlessly penetrating stare. He gazed unwinkingly into the captain's eyes for so long that the other finally looked away. When Smith's voice came it was too quiet to be heard even at the next table.

'*Herr* Major, when you talk to me, little man.' The tone was glacial: so now were also the eyes. 'Major Bernd Himmler. You may have heard of me?'

He paused significantly and the young captain seemed to shrink perceptibly before his eyes. Himmler, head of the Gestapo, was the most feared man in Germany. Smith could have been any relative of Himmler, possibly even his son.

'Report to me at 8 a.m. tomorrow morning,' Smith said curtly. He swung away without waiting for an answer. The Alpenkorps captain, suddenly very sober indeed, nodded wordlessly and sank wearily into his chair. As Smith strode towards the door the hubbub of conversation resumed. For the soldiers stationed in that remote military outpost, drinking beer, very large quantities of beer, was the only pastime: such incidents were no sooner seen than forgotten.

On his way to the door Smith stopped briefly by Schaffer and said: 'Well, I fouled that one up.'

'You could have handled it differently,' Schaffer conceded, then went on curiously: 'What did you say to him? The young Alpine Corps captain, I mean.'

'I gave him to understand that I was Himmler's son.'

'The Gestapo boss?' Schaffer asked incredulously. 'God above, you took a chance.'

'I couldn't afford to take a chance,' Smith said cryptically. 'I'll go try the "Eichhof". Better luck there, maybe. Back in ten minutes. Less.'

He left Schaffer looking uncertainly after him, made an urgent negative move of his hand towards Carraciola, who was approaching him, and passed outside. He moved a few paces along the wooden boardwalk, stopped and glanced briefly up and down the snow-filled street. It was deserted in both directions. He turned and walked quickly up a narrow alleyway which paralleled the side of 'Zum Wilden Hirsch'. At the rear stood a small wooden hut. Smith checked again that he was unobserved, opened the door quietly.

'Eight o'clock,' he said into the darkness. 'Come on.'

There was a rustle of clothes and Mary appeared in the doorway. She was shivering violently, her face blue-tinged with the extreme cold. She looked questioningly at Smith but he took her arm without a word and led her quickly to the back door of the *Gasthaus*. They entered a small hallway, dimly lit by an oil lamp, crossed it, climbed a flight of stairs, moved along a corridor and stopped at the second door on the right. They passed swiftly inside, Smith closing the door behind him.

It was a small room, plainly furnished, but from the chintz soft furnishings and toilet articles on a dressing-table, very obviously a feminine room. Mary sat down on the bed, hugging herself tightly to try to restore some warmth and looked up at Smith without any admiration in her face.

'I hope you're enjoying your little game,' she said bitterly. 'Seem to know your way around, don't you?'

'Instinct,' Smith explained. He stooped over the low-burning oil lamp by the bed, turned up the flame, glanced briefly about the room, located a battered leather case in one corner, swung it to the bed and snapped open the lid. The case contained women's clothing. He pulled Mary to her feet and said: 'Don't waste time. Take off your clothes. And when I say that, I mean your clothes. Every last stitch. Then get into that top outfit there. You'll find everything you need.'

Mary stared at him.

'Those clothes? Why on earth must I—'

'Don't *argue*. Now!'

'Now it is,' she said resignedly. 'You might at least turn your back.'

'Relax,' Smith said wearily. 'I have other things on my mind.' He crossed to the window, stood peering out through a crack in the chintz curtains and went on: 'Now, hurry. You're supposed to be coming off the bus from Steingaden that arrives in twenty minutes' time. You'll be carrying that case, which contains the rest of your clothes. Your name is Maria Schenk, you're from Düsseldorf, a cousin of a barmaid that works here, and you've had TB and been forced to give up your factory job and go to the mountains for your health. So you've got this new job, through this barmaid, in the Schloss Adler. And you have identity papers, travel permit, references and letters in appropriately post-marked envelopes to prove all of it. They're in that handbag in the case. Think you got all that?'

'I – I think so,' she said uncertainly. 'But if you'd only tell me—'

'For God's sake!' Smith said impatiently. 'Time, girl, time! Got it or not?'

'Maria Schenk, Düsseldorf, factory, TB, cousin here, Steingaden – yes, I have it.' She broke off to pull a ribbed blue wool dress over her head, smoothed it down and said wonderingly: 'It's a perfect fit! You'd think this dress was made for me!'

'It *was* made for you.' Smith turned round to inspect her. '36–26–36 or whatever. We – um – broke into your flat and borrowed a dress to use as a model. Thorough, that's us.'

'You broke into my flat?' she asked slowly.

'Well, now, you wouldn't want to go around like a refugee from a jumble sale,' Smith said reasonably. He looked at the dress with an approving eye. 'Does something for you.'

'I'd like to do something for you,' she said feelingly. Her eyes mirrored her bafflement, her total lack of understanding. 'But – but it must have taken *weeks* to prepare those clothes – and those papers!'

'Like enough,' Smith agreed. 'Our Forgery Section did a very special job on those papers. Had to, to get you into the lion's den.'

'Weeks,' Mary said incredulously. 'Weeks! But General Carnaby's plane crashed only yesterday morning.' She stared at him, registering successive expressions of confusion, accusation and, finally, downright anger. 'You *knew* it was going to crash!'

'Right first time, my poppet,' Smith said cheerfully. He gave her an affectionate pat. 'We rigged it.'

'*Don't* do that,' she snapped, then went on carefully, her face still tight with anger: 'There really *was* a plane crash?'

'Guaranteed. The plane crash-landed on the airfield HQ of the Bavarian Mountain Rescue pilots. Place called Oberhausen, about five miles from here. The place we'll be leaving from incidentally.'

'The place we'll be leaving—' She broke off, gazed at him a long moment then shook her head almost in despair. 'But – but in the plane I overheard you telling the men that if the mission failed or you had to split up that you were all to make a rendezvous at Frauenfeld, over the Swiss border.'

'Did you now?' There was mild interest in Smith's voice. 'I must be getting confused. Anyway, this Mosquito put down on the Oberhausen airfield riddled with machine-gun bullet holes. British machine-gun bullet holes, but what the hell, holes are holes.'

'And you'd risk the life of an American general – and all the plans for the Second Front—'

'Well, now, that's why I'm in such a hurry to get inside the Schloss Adler.' Smith cleared his throat. 'Not before they get his secrets out of him but before they find out that he's *not* an American general and knows no more about the Second Front than I do about the back of the moon.'

'What! He's a plant?'

'Name of Jones,' Smith nodded. 'Cartwright Jones. American actor. As a Thespian he's pretty second rate but he's a dead ringer for Carnaby.'

She looked at him with something like horror in her eyes.

'You'd risk an innocent—'

'He's getting plenty,' Smith interrupted. 'Twenty-five thousand dollars for a one-night stand. The peak of his professional career.'

There came a soft double knock on the door. A swift sliding movement of Smith's hand and a gun was suddenly there, a Mauser automatic, cocked and ready to go. Another swift movement and he was silently by the door, jerking it open. Smith put his gun away. Heidi came in, Smith shutting the door behind her.

'Well, cousins, here we are,' he announced. 'Mary – now Maria – and Heidi. I'm off.'

'You're off!' Mary said dazedly. 'But – but what am I supposed to *do*?'

'Heidi will tell you.'

Mary looked uncertainly at the other girl. 'Heidi?'

'Heidi. Our top secret agent in Bavaria since 1941.'

'Our – top—' Mary shook her head. 'I don't believe it!'

'Nobody would.' Smith surveyed Heidi's opulent charms with an admiring eye. 'Brother, what a disguise!'

Smith opened the back door of the *Gasthaus* with a cautious hand, moved swiftly outside and remained stock-still in the almost total darkness, waiting for his eyes to become accustomed to the change of light. The snow, he thought, was heavier than when they had first entered 'Zum Wilden Hirsch' and the wind had certainly freshened. It was bitingly cold.

Satisfied that he was unobserved, Smith turned to the left, took two steps and bit off an exclamation as he tripped over some unseen object and fell his length in the snow. He rolled over three times in the snow just in case any bystander might have a knife or gun and homicidal ideas about using them, then got to his feet with cat-like speed, his Mauser in one hand, his pencil-flash in the other. He snapped on the torch and swung round in a 360° turn. He was alone.

Alone, that was, but for the crumpled form over which he had tripped, an Alpenkorps sergeant lying face-down in the snow, a form lying still and curiously relaxed in that huddled shapelessness of death.

Smith stooped and rolled the figure over to expose the great red stain in the snow where the body had been lying. The pencil-flash rested briefly on the front of the tunic, a tunic gashed and soaked in blood. The beam of the torch moved up to the face. No more cloisters for this don, Smith thought in irrational emptiness, no more honey still for tea, and the fault is all mine and I can see it in his face. The already dulled and faded eyes of Torrance-Smythe stared up at him in the sightless reproach of death.

Smith straightened to his feet, his face remote and withdrawn, and quartered the immediate ground area with his light. There were no signs of a struggle but struggle there must have been, for some tunic buttons had been ripped off and the high collar torn open. Smithy had not died easily. Flash still in hand, Smith walked slowly along to the mouth of the narrow alleyway, then stopped. A confusion of footprints, dark smears of blood in the trodden snow, dark bare patches on the wooden walls of the *Gasthaus* where struggling men had staggered heavily against it – here was where the struggle had been. Smith switched off the light, returned both torch and gun to their hiding-places and stepped out into the street. On the one side was 'Zum Wilden Hirsch' with the sound of singing once again emanating from it, on the other side a brightly-lit telephone kiosk outside a Post Office. In the kiosk, talking animatedly on the telephone, was a uniformed figure, a soldier Smith had never seen before. The street itself was deserted.

Schaffer leaned negligently against the bar, the picture of complete and careless relaxation. His face belied him. It was grim and shocked and he was savagely shedding a cigarette between his fingers.

'Smithy!' Schaffer's voice was a low and vicious whisper. 'Not Smithy! You *sure*, boss?'

'I'm sure.' Smith's face still held the same remote and withdrawn expression, almost as if all feeling had been drained from him. 'You say he left in a hurry three minutes after I'd gone. So he wasn't after me. Who else left?'

'No idea.' Schaffer snapped the cigarette in half, dropped it to the floor. 'The place is packed. And there's another door. I *can't* believe it. Why old Smithy? *Why* Torrance-Smythe. He was the cleverest of us all.'

'That's why he's dead,' Smith said somberly. 'Now listen carefully. It's time you knew the score.'

Schaffer looked at him steadily and said: 'It's more than time.'

Smith began to speak in a very low voice, in fluent completely idiomatic German, careful that his back was turned to the Gestapo officers at the far end of the bar. After a minute or two he saw Heidi returning to the room through the doorway behind the bar but ignored her as she ignored him. Almost immediately afterwards a gradual diminution in the babel of talk, followed by an almost complete silence, made him fall quiet himself and follow the direction of the gaze of hundreds of soldiers all of whom were looking towards the door.

There was a reason for the silence, especially good reason, Smith thought, for soldiers almost totally cut off from womankind. Mary Ellison, clad in a belted rain-coat, with a scarf over her head and a battered suitcase in her hand, was standing in the doorway. The silence seemed to deepen. Women are rare at any time in a high Alpine *Gasthaus*, unaccompanied young women even rarer and beautiful young women on their own virtually unknown. For some moments Mary stood there uncertainly, as if unsure of her welcome or not knowing what to do. Then she dropped her bag, and her face lit up as she caught sight of Heidi, a face transformed with joy. Marlene Dietrich in *The Blue Angel*, Smith thought inconsequentially. With a face and a figure and an acting talent like that, she could have had Hollywood tramping a path of beaten gold to her doorstep . . . Through the silent room she and Heidi ran toward one another and embraced.

'My dear Maria! My dear Maria!' There was a break in Heidi's voice that made Smith reflect that Hollywood might have been well advised to tramp out two paths of beaten gold. 'So you came after all!'

'After all these years!' Mary hugged the other girl and kissed her again. 'It's wonderful to see you again, Cousin Heidi! Wonderful, wonderful, wonderful! Of *course* I came. Why ever not?'

'Well!' Heidi made no effort to lower her voice as she looked around significantly. 'They're a pretty rough lot, hereabouts. You should carry a gun, always. Hunter battalion, they call themselves. They're well named!'

The soldiers broke out into a roar of laughter and the normal hubbub of sound resumed almost at once. Arm in arm, Heidi led Mary across to the small group of civilians standing at the far end of the bar. She stopped in front of the man in the centre of the group, a dark, wiry, intelligent-faced man who looked very very tough indeed, and performed the introductions.

'Maria, this is Captain von Brauchitsch. He – um – works in the Schloss Adler. Captain, my cousin, Maria Schenk.'

Von Brauchitsch bowed slightly.

'You are fortunate in your cousins, Heidi. We were expecting you, Miss Schenk.' He smiled. 'But not someone as beautiful as this.'

Mary smiled in turn, her face puzzled. 'You were expecting—'

'He was expecting,' Heidi said dryly. 'It is the captain's business to know what is going on.'

'Don't make me sound so sinister, Heidi. You'll frighten Miss Schenk.' He glanced at his watch. 'The next cable-car leaves in ten minutes. If I might escort the young lady—'

'The young lady is going to my room first,' Heidi said firmly. 'For a wash-up and a Kaffee-Schnapps. Can't you see that she's half-dead with cold?'

'I do believe her teeth are chattering,' von Brauchitsch said with a smile. 'I thought it might have been me. Well, the cable-car after the next one, then.'

'And I'm going with her,' Heidi announced.

'Both of you?' Von Brauchitsch shook his head and smiled again. Von Brauchitsch was always smiling. 'My lucky night.'

'Permits, travel documents, identity cards and letters you have,' Heidi said. She fished up some papers from the recesses of her Tyrolean blouse and handed them to Mary who was sitting across from her on the bed in her room. 'Plan of the castle and instructions. Do your homework well then give them back to me. I'll take them up. You might be searched – they're a suspicious bunch up there. And drink up that Schnapps – first thing von Brauchitsch will do is to smell your breath. Just to check. He checks everything. He's the most suspicious of the lot.'

'He seemed a very pleasant man to me,' Mary said mildly.

'He's a very unpleasant Gestapo officer,' Heidi said dryly.

When Heidi returned to the bar, Smith and Schaffer had been rejoined by Carraciola, Thomas and Christiansen. All five appeared to be carefree in their drinking and chatting inconsequentially, but their low and urgent voices were evidence enough of the desperate worry in their minds. Or in the minds of some of them.

'You haven't seen old Smithy, then?' Smith asked quietly. 'None of you saw him go? Then where in hell has he got to?'

There was no reply, but the shrugs and worried frowns were reply enough. Christiansen said: 'Shall I go and have a look?'

'I don't think so,' Smith said. 'I'm afraid it's too late to go anywhere now.'

Both doors of 'Zum Wilden Hirsch' had suddenly burst open and half a dozen soldiers were coming quickly in through either door. All had slung machine-carbines, Schmeissers, at the ready. They fanned out along the walls and waited, machine-carbines horizontal, fingers on triggers, their eyes very calm, very watchful.

'Well, well,' Christiansen murmured. 'It was a nice war.'

The sudden and total silence was emphasized rather than broken by the crisp footfalls on the wooden floor as a full colonel of the Wehrmacht came striding into the room and looked coldly around him. The gargantuan proprietor of the *Gasthaus* came hurrying round from the back of the bar, tripping over chairs in the anxiety and fear limned so unmistakably clearly in his pumpkin of a face.

'Colonel Weissner!' It required no acute ear to catch the shake in the proprietor's voice. 'What in God's name—'

'No fault of yours, mein Herr.' The colonel's words were reassuring which was more than the tone of his voice was. 'But you harbour enemies of the state.'

'Enemies of the state.' In a matter of seconds the proprietor's complexion had changed from a most unbecoming puce to an even more unbecoming washed-out grey while his voice now quavered like a high-C tuning fork. 'What? I?. I. Josef Wartmann—'

'Please.' The colonel held up his hand for silence. 'We are looking for four or five Alpenkorps deserters from the Stuttgart military prison. To escape, they killed two officers and a guardroom sergeant. They were known to be heading this way.'

Smith nodded and said in Schaffer's ear: 'Very clever. Very clever indeed.'

'Now then,' Weissner continued briskly. 'If they're here, we'll soon have them. I want the senior officers present of drafts thirteen, fourteen and fifteen to come forward.' He waited until two majors and a captain came forward and stood at attention before him. 'You know all your officers and men by sight?'

The three officers nodded.

'Good. I wish you—'

'No need, Colonel.' Heidi had come round from behind the bar and now stood before Weissner, hands clasped respectfully behind her back. 'I know the man you're after. The ringleader.'

'Ah!' Colonel Weissner smiled. 'The charming—'

'Heidi, Herr Colonel. I have waited table on you up in the Schloss Adler.'

Weissner bowed gallantly. 'As if one could ever forget.'

'That one.' Her face full of a combination of righteous indignation and devotion to duty, Heidi pointed a dramatically accusing finger at Smith. 'That's the one, Herr Colonel. He – he pinched me!'

'My dear Heidi!' Colonel Weissner smiled indulgently. 'If we were to convict every man who ever harboured thoughts of—'

'Not that, Herr Colonel. He asked me what I knew or had heard about a man called General Cannabee – I think.'

'General Carnaby!' Colonel Weissner was no longer smiling. He glanced at Smith, motioned guards to close in on him, then glanced back at Heidi. 'What did you tell him?'

'Herr Colonel!' Heidi was stiff with outraged dignity. 'I hope I am a good German. *And* I value my engagements at the Schloss Adler.' She half-turned and pointed across the room. 'Captain von Brauchitsch of the Gestapo will vouch for me.'

'No need. We will not forget this, my dear child.' He patted her affectionately on the cheek, then turned to Smith, the temperature of his voice dropping from warm to sub-zero. 'Your accomplices, sir, and at once.'

'At once, my dear Colonel?' The look he gave Heidi was as glacial as the Colonel's voice. 'Surely not. Let's get our priorities straight. First, her thirty pieces of silver. Then us.'

'You talk like a fool,' Colonel Weissner said contemptuously. 'Heidi is a true patriot.'

'I'm sure she is,' Smith said bitterly.

Mary, her face still and shocked, stared down from the uncurtained crack in Heidi's dark room as Smith and the four others were led out of the front door of 'Zum Wilden Hirsch' and marched off down the road under heavy escort to where several command cars were parked on the far side of the street. Brusquely, efficiently, the prisoners were bundled into two of the cars, engines started up and within a minute both cars were lost to sight round a bend in the road. For almost a minute afterwards Mary stood there, staring out unseeingly on the swirling snow, then pulled the curtains together and turned back towards the darkened room.

She said in a whisper: 'How did it happen?'

A match scratched as Heidi lit and turned up the flame of the oil lamp.

'I can't guess.' Heidi shrugged. 'Someone, I don't know who, must have tipped Colonel Weissner off. But I put the finger on him.'

'Mary stared at her. 'You – you—'

'He'd have been found out in another minute anyway. They were strangers. But it strengthens our hand. I – and you – are now above suspicion.'

'Above suspicion!' Mary looked at her in disbelief then went on, almost wildly: 'But there's no point in going ahead now!'

'Is there not?' Heidi said thoughtfully. 'Somehow, I feel sorrier for Colonel Weissner than I do for Major Smith. Is not our Major Smith a man of resource? Or do our employers in Whitehall lie to us? When they told me he was coming here, they told me not to worry, to trust him implicitly. A man of infinite resource – those were their exact words – who can extricate himself from positions of utmost difficulty. They have a funny way of talking in Whitehall. But already I trust him. Don't you?'

There was no reply. Mary stared at the floor, her eyes bright with unshed tears. Heidi touched her arm and said softly. 'You love him as much as that?'

Mary nodded in silence.

'And does he love you?'

'I don't know. I just don't know. He's been too long in this business – even if he did know,' she said bitterly, 'he probably wouldn't tell himself.'

Heidi looked at her for a moment, shook her head and said: 'They should never have sent you. How can you hope to—' She broke off, shook her head again, and went on: 'It's too late now. Come on. We mustn't keep von Brauchitsch waiting.'

'But – but if he doesn't come? If he can't escape – and how *can* he escape?' She gestured despairingly at the papers lying on the bed. 'They're bound to check with Düsseldorf first thing in the morning about those forged references.'

Heidi said without any particular expression in her voice: 'I don't think he'd let *you* down, Mary.'

'No,' Mary said dolefully. 'I don't suppose he would.'

The big black Mercedes command car swept along the snow-packed road that paralleled the Blau See, the windscreen wipers just coping with the thickly-swirling snow that rushed greyly back at the windscreen through powerful headlight beams. It was an expensive car and a very comfortable one, but neither Schaffer up front nor Smith in the rear seat experienced any degree of comfort whatsoever, either mental or physical. On the mental side there was the bitter prospect of the inevitable firing squad and the knowledge that their mission was over even before it had properly begun: on the physical side they were cramped in the middle of their seats, Schaffer flanked by driver and guard, Smith by Colonel Weissner and guard, and both Smith and Schaffer were suffering from pain in the lower ribs: the owners of the Schmeisser machine-pistols, the muzzles of which were grinding into the captives' sides, had no compunction about letting their presence be known.

They were now, Smith estimated, half-way between village and barracks. Another thirty seconds and they would be through the barrack gates. Thirty seconds. No more.

'Stop this car!' Smith's voice was cold, authoritative with an odd undertone of menace. 'Immediately, do you hear? I must think.'

Colonel Weissner, startled, turned and stared at him. Smith ignored him completely. His face reflected an intensely frowning concentration, a thin-lipped anger barely under control, the face of a man to whom the thought of disobedience of his curt instruction was unthinkable: most certainly not the face of a man going to captivity and death. Weissner hesitated, but only fractionally. He gave an order and the big car began to slow.

'You oaf! You utter idiot!' Smith's tone, shaking with anger, was low and vicious, so low that only Weissner could hear it. 'You've almost certainly ruined everything and, by God, if you have, Weissner, you'll be without a regiment tomorrow!'

The car pulled into the roadside and stopped. Ahead, the red tail lights of the command car in front vanished into a snow-filled darkness. Weissner said brusquely, but with a barely perceptible tremor of agitation in his voice: 'What the devil are you talking about?'

'You knew about this American general, Carnaby?' Smith's face, eyes narrowed and teeth bared in anger, was within six inches of Weissner's. 'How?' He almost spat the word out.

'I dined in the Schloss Adler last night. I—'

Smith looked at him in total incredulity.

'Colonel Paul Kramer told you? He actually talked to you about him?' Weissner nodded wordlessly. 'Admiral Canaris' Chief of Staff! And now everybody knows. God in heaven, heads will roll for this.' He screwed the heels of his palms into his eyes, lowered his hands wearily to his thighs, gazed ahead unseeingly and shook his head, very slowly. 'This is too big, even for me.' He fished out his pass and handed it to Weissner, who examined it in the beam of a none too steady torch. 'Back to the barracks at once! I must get through to Berlin immediately. My uncle will know what to do.'

'Your uncle?' By what seemed a great effort of will Weissner looked up from the pass he held in his hand: his voice was no steadier than the torch. '*Heinrich* Himmler?'

'Who do you think?' Smith snarled. 'Mickey Mouse?' He dropped his voice to a low murmur. 'I trust you never have the privilege of meeting him, Colonel Weissner.' He gave Weissner the benefit of a long and speculative look singularly lacking in any encouragement, then turned away and prodded the driver, none too lightly, in the back. 'The barracks – and make it quick!'

The car moved off. Anything that the nephew of the dreaded Heinrich Himmler, Chief of the Gestapo, said was good enough for the driver.

Smith turned to the guard by his side. 'Take that damned thing out of my ribs!'

Angrily, he snatched the gun away. The guard, who had also heard of Himmler, meekly yielded up the machine-pistol. One second later he was doubled up in helpless retching agony as the butt of the Schmeisser smashed into his stomach and another second later Colonel Weissner was pinned against the window of his Mercedes as the muzzle of the Schmeisser ground into his right ear.

Smith said: 'If your men move, you die.'

'Okay.' Schaffer's calm voice from the front seat. 'I have their guns.'

'Stop the car,' Smith ordered.

The car came to a halt. Through the windscreen Smith could see the lights of the barracks guard-room, now less than two hundred yards away. He gave Weissner a prod with the Schmeisser muzzle.

'Out!'

Weissner's face was a mask of chagrined rage but he was too experienced a soldier even to hesitate. He got out.

'Three paces from the car,' Smith said. 'Face down on the snow. Hands clasped behind your head. Schaffer, your gun on your guard. Out beside the General, you.' This with his gun muzzle in the driver's neck.

Twenty seconds later, Schaffer at the wheel, they were on their way, leaving three men face downwards in the snow and the fourth, Smith's erstwhile guard, still doubled up in agony by the roadside.

'A creditable effort, young Himmler,' Schaffer said approvingly.

'I'll never be that lucky again,' Smith said soberly. 'Take your time passing the barracks. We don't want any of the sentries getting the wrong idea.'

At a steady twenty miles an hour they passed the main gates and then the secondary gates, apparently, as far as Smith could see, without exciting any comment. Just behind the three-pointed star on the car's radiator flew a small triangular pennant, the Camp Commandant's personal standard, and no one, it was safe to assume, would question the comings and goings of Colonel Weissner.

For half a mile or so beyond the secondary gates the road ran northwards in a straight line with, on the left, a sheer hundred-foot cliff dropping down into the waters of the Blau See, and, to the right, a line of pines, not more than fifty yards wide, backing up against another vertical cliff-face which soared up until lost in the snow and the darkness.

At the end of the half-mile straight, the road ahead swept sharply to the right to follow an indentation in the Blau See's shore-line, a dangerous corner marked by white fencing which would normally have been conspicuous enough by night-time but which was at the moment all but invisible against the all-enveloping background of snow. Schaffer braked for the corner. A thoughtful expression crossed his face and he applied still heavier pressure to the brake pedal and glanced at Smith.

'An excellent idea.' It was Smith's turn to be approving. 'We'll make an agent out of you yet.'

The Mercedes stopped. Smith gathered up the Schmeissers and pistols they had taken from Weissner and his men and got out. Schaffer wound down the driver's window, released the hand-brake, engaged gear and jumped out as the car began to move. With his right arm through the window Schaffer walked and then, as the car began to gather speed, ran along beside the Mercedes, his hand on the steering wheel. Twenty feet from the cliff edge he gave a last steering correction, jerked the quadrant hand throttle wide open and leapt aside as the car accelerated. The wooden fence never had a chance. With a splintering crash barely audible above the roaring of the engine at maximum revs in first gear, the Mercedes went through the barrier as if it had been made of cardboard, shot out over the edge of the cliff and disappeared from sight.

Smith and Schaffer reached the safety of an unbroken stretch of fencing and peered down just in time to see the car, upside down now and its headlamps still blazing, strike the surface of the lake with an oddly flat explosive sound, like distant gun fire. A column of water and weirdly phosphorescent spray reached half-way up the cliff side. When it subsided, they could at once locate from an underwater luminescence the position of the sinking car: the headlamps were still burning. Smith and Schaffer looked at each other then Smith thoughtfully removed his peaked cap and sent it sailing over the edge. The strong gusting wind blew the cap in against the cliff face, but it tumbled on down and landed, inside up, on still surfacing bubbles iridescently glittering from the light now far below. Then the light went out.

'So who cares?' Schaffer straightened up from the fencing and shrugged his shoulders. 'Wasn't our car. Back to the village, hey?'

'Not on your life,' Smith said emphatically. 'And I mean that – literally. Come on. Other way.'

Clutching their recently acquired weapons, they ran round the corner in the direction in which the car had been travelling. They had covered less than seventy yards when they heard the sound of car engines and saw wavering beams lighting up the splintered fence. Seconds later Smith and Schaffer were off the road, hidden in the pines and moving slowly back in the direction of a command car and two armoured cars that had now pulled up at the broken barrier.

'That's it, then, Herr Colonel.' An Alpenkorps sergeant with shoulder-slung gun peered gingerly over the edge of the cliff. 'Going too fast, saw it too late – or never saw it at all. The Blau See is over a hundred metres deep here, Herr Colonel. They're gone.'

'Maybe they're gone and maybe they're not. I wouldn't trust that lot as far as my front door.' Colonel Weissner's voice carried clearly and sounded bitter. 'They may have faked it and doubled back. Send one party of men straight into the pines there as far as the cliff wall. Five metre spacing. Let them use their torches. Then another party of men five hundred metres in the car back towards the camp. You go with them, Sergeant. Again spread out to the cliff-face. Let them come together. And be quick.'

Schaffer, from his hiding-place behind the bole of a pine, looked thoughtfully at Smith.

'I have to concede a point, boss, it's perhaps as well we didn't go straight back to the village. Cunning old devil, isn't he?'

'And what does that make me?' Smith murmured.

'Okay, okay. I'll concede that point, too.'

Five minutes passed. Comparatively little of the falling snow penetrated the thickly-matted branches of the pines and the two men could clearly see the occasional flicker of torches as the line of men nearest them moved away to the south, their lights probing behind tree-trunks and under windfalls as they searched for the two escaped prisoners. Colonel Wiessner paced up and down, slowly, beside his command car, his head bowed as if immersed in thought. From time to time he consulted his watch. As Smith watched, he moved out to the unbroken fencing and remained there, peering down towards the surface of the Blau See.

By and by Smith and Schaffer could hear the distant sound of muffled voices and within a minute the sergeant moved into the beam of the command car headlamps, approached Colonel Weissner and saluted.

'Not even a footprint, Herr Colonel.'

Weissner straightened and turned.

'There wouldn't be,' he said sombrely. 'I've just seen a hat floating in the water. A squalid end for such brave men, Sergeant. A squalid end.'

Chapter Five

The cable-car moved slowly out of the lower station at the beginning of its long climb up to the castle. An impossible climb, Mary thought, a dangerous and impossible climb. Peering through the front windows she could just distinguish the outline of the first pylon through the thinly-driving snow. The second and third pylons were invisible, but the intermittently shining cluster of lights suspended impossibly high in the sky showed clearly enough where they had to go. People have made it before, she thought dully, we'll probably make it, too. The way she felt then, with the bottom gone from her world, she didn't particularly care whether she made it or not.

The cable-car was a twelve-passenger vehicle, painted bright red outside, well-lit inside. There were no seats, only grab-rails along the two sides. That the grab-rails were very necessary became immediately and alarmingly obvious. The wind was now very strong and the car began to sway alarmingly only seconds after clearing the shelter of the lower station.

Apart from two soldiers and an apparent civilian, the only other passengers consisted of von Brauchitsch, Mary and Heidi, the last now with a heavy woollen coat and cossack fur hat over her ordinary clothes. Von Brauchitsch, holding on to the grab-rail with one hand, had his free arm round Mary's shoulders. He gave them a reassuring squeeze and smiled down at her.

'Scared?' he asked.

'No.' And she wasn't, she hadn't enough emotion left to be scared, but even with no hope left she was supposed to be a professional. 'No, I'm not scared. I'm terrified. I feel sea-sick already. Does – does this cable ever break?'

'Never.' Von Brauchitsch was reassurance itself. 'Just hang on to me and you'll be all right.'

'That's what he used to say to me,' Heidi said coldly.

'Fräulein,' von Brauchitsch explained patiently, 'I am gifted beyond the average, but I haven't yet managed to grow a third arm. Guests first.'

With a cupped cigarette in his hand, Schaffer leaned against the base of an unmistakable telephone pole and gazed thoughtfully into the middle distance.

There was reason both for the hooded cigarette and the thoughtful expression. Less than a hundred yards away from where he stood at the edge of the pines bordering the road running alongside the shore of the Blau See he could see guards, clearly illuminated by over-head lights, moving briskly to and fro in the vicinity of the barrack gates. Dimly seen behind them were the outline of the barracks themselves.

Schaffer shifted his stance and gazed upwards. The snow was almost gone now, the moon was threatening to break through, and he had no difficulty at all in distinguishing the form of Smith, his legs straddled across the lowest cross-bar.

Smith was busily employed with a knife, a specially designed commando knife which, among other advanced features, had a built-in wire cutter. Carefully, methodically, he brought the wire-cutter to bear. With eight consecutive snips eight consecutive telephone wires fell to the ground. Smith closed and pocketed his knife, disentangled his legs from the cross-bar, wrapped his arms round the pole and slid down to the ground. He grinned at Schaffer.

'Every little helps,' he said.

'Should hold them for a while,' Schaffer agreed. Once more they gathered up their guns and moved off to the east, vanishing into the pine woods which bordered the rear of the barracks.

The cable-car swayed more alarmingly than ever. It had now entered upon the last near-vertical lap of its journey. With von Brauchitsch's arm still around her shoulders, with her face still pressed against the front windows of the car, Mary stared up at the towering battlements, white as the driving snow, and thought that they reached up almost to the clouds themselves. As she watched, a break came in the wisping clouds and the whole fairy-tale castle was bathed in bright moonlight. Fear touched her eyes, she moistened her lips and gave an involuntary shiver. Nothing escaped von Brauchitsch's acute perception. He gave her shoulders another reassuring squeeze, perhaps the twentieth in that brief journey.

'Not to worry, Fräulein. It will be all right.'

'I hope so.' Her voice was the ghost of a whisper.

The same unexpected moonlight almost caught Smith and Schaffer. They had just crossed the station tracks and were moving stealthily along towards the left luggage office when the moon broke through. But they were still in the shadows of the over-hanging station roof. They pressed back into those shadows and peered along the tracks, past the hydraulic bumpers which marked the end of the line. Clearly now, sharply-limned as if in full daylight, red etched against the white, they could see one cable-car approaching the lower station, the other climbing the last few vertical feet towards the header station and, above that, the dazzling outline of the Schloss Adler glittering under the bright moon.

'That helps,' Schaffer said bitterly. 'That helps a lot.'

'Sky's still full of clouds,' Smith said mildly. He bent to the keyhole of the left luggage office, used his skeleton keys and moved inside. Schaffer followed, closing the door.

Smith located their rucksacks, cut a length of rope from the nylon, wrapped it round his waist and began stuffing some hand grenades and plastic explosives into a canvas bag. He raised his head as Schaffer diffidently cleared his throat.

'Boss?' This with an apprehensive glance through the window.

'Uh-huh?'

'Boss, has it occurred to you that Colonel Weissner probably knows all about this cache by this time? What I mean is, we may have company soon.'

'We may indeed,' Smith admitted. 'Surprised if we don't have. That's why I've cut this itsy-bitsy piece of rope off the big coil and why I'm taking the explosives and grenades only from my rucksack and yours. It's a very big coil – and no one knows what's inside our rucksacks. So it's unlikely that anything will be missed.'

'But the radio—'

'If we broadcast from here we might be caught in the act. If we take it away and they find it gone they'll know that that car at the bottom of the Blau See is empty. Is that it?'

'More or less.'

'So we compromise. We remove it, but we return it here after we've broadcast from a safe place.'

'What do you mean "safe place",' Schaffer demanded plaintively. The darkly saturnine face was unhappy. 'There isn't a safe place in Bavaria.'

'There's one not twenty yards away. Last place they'd look.' He tossed Schaffer a bunch of skeleton keys. 'Ever been inside a Bavarian ladies' cloakroom?'

Schaffer fielded the keys, stared at Smith, shook his head and left. Quickly he moved down the tracks, his torch flashing briefly on and off. Finally his torch settled on a doorway with, above it, the legend DAMEN.

Schaffer looked at it, pursed his lips, shrugged his shoulders and got to work on the lock.

Slowly, with apparently infinite labour, the cable-car completed the last few feet of its ascent and passed in under the roof of the Schloss Adler header station. It juddered to a halt, the front door opened and the passengers disembarked. They moved from the header station – built into the north-west base of the castle – up through a steeply-climbing twenty-five foot tunnel which had heavy iron doors and guards at either end. Passing the top gateway, they emerged into the courtyard, the entrance of which was sealed off by a massively-barred iron gate guarded by heavily armed soldiers and Dobermann pinschers. The courtyard itself was brightly illuminated by the light of dozens of uncurtained interior windows. In the very centre of the courtyard stood the helicopter which had that morning brought Reichsmarschall Rosemeyer to the Schloss Adler. Under the cover of a heavy tarpaulin – momentarily unnecessary because of the cessation of the snow – a dungareed figure, possibly the pilot, worked on the helicopter engine with the aid of a small but powerful arc-lamp.

Mary turned to von Brauchitsch, still holding a proprietary grip on her arm, and smiled ruefully.

'So many soldiers. So many men – and, I'm sure, so few women. What happens if I want to escape from the licentious soldiery?'

'Easy.' Von Brauchitsch really did have, Mary thought dully, a most charming smile. 'Just jump from your bedroom window. One hundred metres straight down and there you are. Free!'

The ladies' cloakroom in the station was a superlatively nondescript place, bleakly furnished with hard-backed benches, chairs, deal tables and a sagging wooden floor. The Spartans would have turned up their noses at it, in its sheer lack of decorative inspiration it could have been surpassed only by its counterpart in England. The expiring remains of a fire burnt dully in a black enamel stove.

Smith was seated by the central table, radio beside him, consulting a small book by the light of a hooded pencil-flash and writing on a slip of paper. He checked what he had written, straightened and handed the book to Schaffer.

'Burn it. Page by page.'

'Page by page? All?' Surprise in the saturnine face. 'You won't be requiring this any more?'

Smith shook his head and began to crank the radio handle.

There was a very much better fire in the Operations Room in Whitehall, a pine-log fire with a healthy crackle and flames of a respectable size. But the two men sitting on either side of the fire were a great deal less alert than the two men sitting by the dying embers of the fire in the Bavarian Alps. Admiral Rolland and Colonel Wyatt-Turner were frankly dozing, eyes shut, more asleep than awake. But they came to full wakefulness, jerking upright, almost instantly, when the long-awaited call-sign came through on the big transceiver manned by the civilian operator at the far end of the room. They glanced at each other, heaved themselves out of their deep arm-chairs.

'Broadsword calling Danny Boy.' The voice on the radio was faint but clear. 'Broadsword calling Danny Boy. You hear me? Over.'

The civilian operator spoke into his microphone, 'We hear you. Over.'

'Code. Ready? Over.'

'Ready. Over.'

Rolland and Wyatt-Turner were by the operator's shoulder now, his eyes fixed on his pencil as he began to make an instantaneous transcription of the meaningless jumble of letters beginning to come over the radio. Swiftly the message was spelt out: TORRANCE-SMYTHE MURDERED. THOMAS CHRISTIANSEN AND CARRACIOLA CAPTURED.

As if triggered by an unheard signal, the eyes of Rolland and Wyatt-Turner lifted and met. Their faces were strained and grim. Their eyes returned to the flickering pencil.

ENEMY BELIEVE SCHAFFER AND SELF DEAD, the message continued. EFFECTING ENTRY INSIDE THE HOUR. PLEASE HAVE TRANSPORT STANDING BY NINETY MINUTES. OVER.

Admiral Rolland seized the microphone from the operator.

'Broadsword! Broadsword! Do you know who I am, Broadsword?'

'I know who you are, sir. Over.'

'Pull out, Broadsword. Pull out now. Save yourselves. Over.'

'You – must – be – joking.' The words were spoken in slow motion, a perceptible pause between each pair. 'Over.'

'You heard me.' Rolland's voice was almost as slow and distinct. 'You *heard* me. That was an order, Broadsword.'

'Mary is already inside. Over and out.'

The transceiver went dead.

'He's gone, sir,' the operator said quietly.

'He's gone,' Rolland repeated mechanically. 'Dear God, he's gone.'

Colonel Wyatt-Turner moved away and sat down heavily in his chair by the fire. For such a big, burly man he appeared curiously huddled and shrunken. He looked up dully as Admiral Rolland sank into the opposite chair.

'It's all my fault.' The Colonel's voice was barely distinguishable. 'All my fault.'

'We did what we had to do. All *our* fault, Colonel. It was my idea.' He gazed into the fire. 'Now this – this on top of everything else.'

'Our worst day,' Wyatt-Turner agreed heavily. 'Our worst day ever. Maybe I'm too old.'

'Maybe we're all too old.' With his right forefinger Rolland began to tick off the fingers of his left hand. 'HQ Commander-in-Chief, Portsmouth. Secret alarm triggered. Nothing missing.'

'Nothing taken,' Wyatt-Turner agreed wearily. 'But the vigil emulsion plates show photostatic copies taken.'

'Two. Southampton. Barge-movement duplicates missing. Three, Plymouth. Time-lock in the naval HQ inoperative. We don't know what this means.'

'We can guess.'

'We can guess. Dover. Copy of a section of the Mulberry Harbour plans missing. An error? Carelessness? We'll never know. Five, Bradley's HQ guard sergeant missing. Could mean anything.'

'Could mean everything. All the troop movements for Overlord's Omaha beach are there.'

'Lastly, seven OS reports today. France, Belgium, Netherlands. Four demonstrably false. Other three unverifiable.'

For long moments there was a heavy, a defeated silence, finally broken by Wyatt-Turner.

'If there was ever any doubt, there's none now.' He spoke without looking up, his eyes gazing emptily into the fire. 'The Germans have almost total penetration here – and we have almost none on the continent. And now this – Smith and his men, I mean.'

'Smith and his men,' Rolland echoed. 'Smith and his men. We can write them off.'

Wyatt-Turner dropped his voice, speaking so softly that the radio operator couldn't overhear.

'And Operation Overlord, sir?'

'Operation Overlord,' Rolland murmured. 'Yes, we can write that off, too.'

'Intelligence is the first arm of modern warfare,' Wyatt-Turner said bitterly. 'Or has someone said that before?'

'No intelligence, no war.' Admiral Rolland pressed an intercom button. 'Have my car brought round. Coming, Colonel? To the airfield?'

'And a lot farther than that. If I have your permission, sir.'

'We've discussed it.' Admiral Rolland shrugged. 'I understand how you feel. Kill yourself if you must.'

'I've no intention.' Wyatt-Turner crossed to a cupboard and took out a Sten gun, turned to Rolland and smiled: 'We may encounter hostiles, sir.'

'You may indeed.' There was no answering smile on the Admiral's face.

'You heard what the man said?' Smith switched off the transmitter, telescoped the aerial and glanced across at Schaffer. 'We can pull out now.'

'Pull out now? Pull out now?' Schaffer was outraged. 'Don't you realize that if we do they'll get to Mary inside twelve hours.' He paused significantly, making sure he had all Smith's attention. 'And if they get to her they're bound to get to Heidi ten minutes later.'

'Come off it, Lieutenant,' Smith said protestingly. 'You've only seen her once, for five minutes.'

'So?' Schaffer was looking positively belligerent. 'How often did Paris see Helen of Troy? How often did Antony see Cleopatra. How often did Romeo—' He broke off then went on defiantly: 'And I don't care if she is a traitor spying on her own people.'

'She was born and brought up in Birmingham,' Smith said wearily.

'So who cares? I draw the line at nothing. Even if she is a Limey—' He paused. 'English?'

'Come on,' Smith said. 'Let's return this radio. We may have callers soon.'

'We mustn't be raising too many eyebrows,' Schaffer agreed.

They returned the radio, locked the left luggage office and were just moving towards the station exit when they were halted by the sound of truck engines and a siren's ululation. They pressed back against a wall as headlights lit up the station entrance. The leading truck came to a skidding halt not ten yards away.

Schaffer looked at Smith. 'Discretion, I think?'

'Discretion, indeed. Behind the booking office.'

The two men moved swiftly alongside the tracks and hid in the deep shadows behind the booking office. A sergeant, the one who had organized the search along the Blau See, came running through the entrance, followed by four soldiers, located the left luggage office, tried the door handle, reversed his machine-pistol and hammered the lock without effect, reversed his gun again, shot away the lock and passed inside, torch in hand. He appeared at the doorway almost at once.

'Tell the captain. They didn't lie. The Engländers' gear is here!' One of the soldiers left and the sergeant said to the three remaining men: 'Right. Get their stuff out and load it up.'

'There goes my last pair of cotton socks,' Schaffer murmured mournfully as their rucksacks were taken away. 'Not to mention my toothbrush and—'

He broke off as Smith caught his arm. The sergeant had stopped the man carrying the radio, taken it from him, placed his hand on it and stood quite still. He was directly under one of the small swinging electric lights and the expression on his face could clearly be seen to change from puzzlement to disbelief to complete and shocked understanding.

'Kapitan!' the sergeant shouted. 'Kapitan.'

An officer came hurrying through the station entrance.

'The radio, Kapitan! It's warm, very warm! It's been in use inside the last five minutes.'

'In the last five minutes? Impossible!' He stared at the sergeant. 'Unless—'

'Yes, Herr Kapitan. Unless.'

'Surround the station,' the officer shouted. 'Search every room.'

'Oh God!' Schaffer moaned. 'Why can't they leave us alone?'

'Quickly,' Smith said softly. He took Schaffer's arm and they moved through the dark shadows till they reached the ladies' cloakroom. Careful not to rattle his skeleton keys, Smith had the door open in seconds. They passed inside and locked the door behind them.

'This won't look so good in my obituary,' Schaffer said dolefully. There was a perceptible edge of strain under the lightly-spoken words.

'What won't?'

'Gave his life for his country in a ladies' lavatory in Upper Bavaria. How can a man RIP with that on his mind? . . . What's our friend outside saying?'

'If you shut up we might hear.'

'And when I say everywhere, I mean everywhere.' The German captain was barking out his commands in the best parade-ground fashion. 'If a door is locked, break it open. If you can't break it open, shoot the lock away. And if you don't want to die in the next five minutes, never forget that these are violent and extremely dangerous men almost certainly armed with stolen Schmeisser machine-pistols, apart from their own weapons. Make no attempt to capture them. Shoot on sight and shoot to kill.'

'You heard?' Smith said.

'I'm afraid I did.' There was a perceptible click as Schaffer cocked his machine-pistol.

They stood side-by-side in the darkness listening to the sounds of the search, the calling of voices, the hammering of rifle butts on wood, the splintering of yielding doors, the occasional short burst of machine-gun fire where a door, presumably, had failed to yield to more conventional methods of persuasion. The sounds of the approaching search grew very close.

'They're getting warm,' Schaffer murmured.

Schaffer had underestimated the temperature. Just as he finished speaking an unseen hand closed on the outer door handle and rattled the door furiously. Smith and Schaffer moved silently and took up position pressed close against the wall, one on either side of the door.

The rattling ceased. A heavy crashing impact from the outside shook the door on its hinges. A second such impact and the woodwork in the jamb by the lock began to splinter. Two more would do it, Smith thought, two more.

But there were no more.

'*Gott in Himmel*, Hans!' The voice beyond the door held – or appeared to hold – a mixture of consternation and outrage. 'What are you thinking of? Can't you read?'

'Can't I—' The second voice broke off abruptly and when it came again it was in tones of defensive apology. 'DAMEN! *Mein Gott*! DAMEN!' A pause. 'If you had spent as many years on the Russian Front as I have—' His voice faded as the two men moved away.

'God bless our common Anglo-Saxon heritage,' Schaffer murmured fervently.

'What are you talking about?' Smith demanded. He had released his tense grip on the Schmeisser and realized that the palms of his hands were damp.

'This misplaced sense of decency,' Schaffer explained.

'A far from misplaced and highly developed sense of self-preservation,' Smith said dryly. 'Would *you* like to come searching for a couple of reputed killers, like us, knowing that the first man to find us would probably be cut in half by a burst of machine-gun fire? Put yourself in their position. How do you think those men feel. How would you feel?'

'I'd feel very unhappy,' Schaffer said candidly.

'And so do they. And so they seize on any reasonable excuse not to investigate. Our two friends who have just left have no idea whatsoever whether we're in here or not and, what's more, the last thing they want to do is to find out.'

'Stop making with the old psychology. All that matters is that Schaffer is saved. Saved!'

'If you believe that,' Smith said curtly, 'you deserve to end up with a blindfold round your eyes.'

'How's that again?' Schaffer asked apprehensively.

'You and I,' Smith explained patiently, 'are not the only people who can put ourselves in the places of the searchers. You can bet your life that the captain can and more than likely the sergeant, too – you saw how quickly he caught on to the damn' radio. By and by one or other is going to come by, see this closed and undamaged door, blow his top and insist on a few of his men being offered the chance to earn a posthumous Iron Cross. What I mean is, Schaffer is not yet saved.'

'What do we do, boss?' Schaffer said quietly. 'I don't feel so funny any more.'

'We create a diversion. Here are the keys – this one. Put it in the lock and hold it ready to turn. We'll be leaving in a hurry – troops of this calibre can't be fooled for long.'

He dug into his knapsack, fished out a hand-grenade, crossed the cloakroom into the washroom and, in almost total darkness, felt his way across it to where the window at the back should have been, finally located it from the source of a faint wash of light. He pressed his nose against the glass but could see nothing, cursed softly as he realized a washroom window would always certainly be frosted, located the latch and slowly swung the window wide. With infinite caution, a fraction of an inch at a time, he thrust his head slowly through the window.

Nobody blew his head off. There were soldiers immediately to be seen, it was true, soldiers armed and at the ready, but they weren't looking in his direction: there were five of them, spread out in an arc of a circle, perhaps fifteen yards from the station entrance, and every machine-pistol was trained on that entrance. Waiting for the rabbits to bolt, Smith thought.

What was of much more interest was the empty truck parked only feet away from the window where he was: it was the reflected light from its side-lights that had enabled him to locate the window. Hoping that the truck was built along conventional lines, Smith armed the grenade, counted three, lobbed it under the back wheels of the truck and ducked behind the shelter of the washroom wall.

The two explosions – grenade and petrol tank – went off so almost simultaneously as to be indistinguishable in time. Shattered glass from the window above showered down on his head and his ear-drums hurt fiercely both from the roar of sound and the proximity to the explosive shock-wave. Smith made no attempt to inspect the damage he had done, less from the urgent need for haste to leave there than from the very obvious fact that the remains of the truck outside had burst into flames and to have lifted his head above that window-sill would have been a swift form of illuminated suicide: not that he could have done so in any event for the wind-driven flames from the truck were already beginning to lick through the shattered washroom window. On hands and knees Smith scuttled across the washroom floor, not rising till he had reached the cloakroom. Schaffer, who had his hand on the key and the door already open a fraction of an inch turned at Smith's approach.

'To the hills, boss?' he enquired.

'To the hills.'

The track-side of the station was, predictably, deserted: those who had not automatically run to investigate the source of the explosion would have as automatically assumed that the explosion was in some way connected with an escape attempt or resistance on the part of the hunted men. However it was, the result was the satisfactory same.

They ran along the tracks till they came to the bumpers at the end of the line, skirted these and continued running until they were safely among the scatter of houses that rose steeply up the hill-side on the eastern side of the village. They stopped to take breath and looked back the way they had come.

The station was on fire, not yet heavily on fire, but, with flames rising six to eight feet and black smoke billowing into the night sky, obviously already beyond any hope of extinction.

Schaffer said: 'They're not going to be very pleased.'

'I shouldn't think so.'

'What I mean is, they're really going to go after us now. With everything they have. They've Dobermann pinschers up at the castle and I've no doubt they have them at the camp too. They've only to bring them to the station, sniff our gear, have them circle the station, pick up our scent and that's it. Smith and Schaffer torn to shreds. I'll take on the Alpenkorps by numbers, but I draw the line at Dobermann pinschers, boss.'

'I thought it was horses you were scared of?' Smith said mildly.

'Horses, Dobermann pinschers, you name it, I'm scared of it. All it's got to have is four feet.' He looked gloomily at the burning station. 'I'd make a rotten vet.'

'No worry,' Smith assured him. 'We won't be here long enough for any of your four-footed pals to come bothering you.'

'No?' Schaffer looked at him suspiciously.

'The castle,' Smith said patiently. 'That's what we're here for. Remember?'

'I hadn't forgotten.' The flames from the blazing station were now licking thirty, forty feet up in the air. 'You gone and ruined a perfectly good station, you know that?'

'As you would say yourself,' Smith reminded him, 'it wasn't our station to start with. Come on. We've a call to make then we'll go see what kind of reception awaits us at the Schloss Adler.'

Mary Ellison was just at that moment discovering what the reception in the Schloss Adler was like. In her case it was none too pleasant. Von Brauchitsch and Heidi beside her, she was gazing around the great hall of the castle, stone walls, stone flags, a dark oaken roof, when a door at the end of the hall opened and a girl came towards them. There was an arrogance, a crisp authority about her: she marched, rather than walked.

But a very beautiful girl, Mary had to admit to herself, big, blonde, blue-eyed and beautiful. She could have been a pin-up girl for the Third Reich. At the moment, the blue eyes were very cold.

'Good-evening, Anne-Marie,' von Brauchitsch said. There was a marked lack of cordiality in his voice. 'This is the new girl, Fräulein Maria Schenk. Maria, this is the Colonel's secretary, in charge of all female staff.'

'Took your time about getting here, didn't you, Schenk?' If Anne-Marie had a soft, lilting, mellifluous voice she wasn't bothering to use it just then. She turned to Heidi and gave her an icy up-and-down. 'And why you? Just because we let you wait table when the Colonel has company—'

'Heidi is this girl's cousin,' von Brauchitsch interrupted brusquely. '*And* she has my permission.' The cold implication that she should confine herself to her duties was unmistakable.

Anne-Marie glared at him but made no attempt to press the point. Very few people would have done. Von Brauchitsch was just that sort of person.

'In here, Schenk.' Anne-Marie nodded to a side door. 'I have a few questions to ask.'

Mary looked at Heidi, then at von Brauchitsch, who shrugged and said: 'Routine investigation, Fräulein. I'm afraid you must.'

Mary preceded Anne-Marie through the doorway. The door was firmly closed behind them. Heidi and von Brauchitsch looked at each other. Heidi compressed her lips and the expression that momentarily flitted over her face about matched the one Anne-Marie had been wearing: von Brauchitsch made the age-old helpless gesture of lifting his shoulders high, palms of the hands turned up.

Within half a minute the reason for von Brauchitsch's helpless gesture became obvious. Through the door there came first the sound of a raised voice, a brief scuffle then a sharp cry of pain. Von Brauchitsch exchanged another resigned glance with Heidi, then turned as he heard heavy footsteps behind him. The man approaching was burly, weather-beaten, middle-aged and in civilian clothes: but although not in uniform he could never have been mistaken for anything other than an army officer. The heavy blue-shaven jowls, bull-neck, close-cropped hair and piercing blue eyes made him almost a caricature of the World War I Prussian Uhlan cavalry officer. That he was by no means as fossilized as he appeared was quite evident from the distinctly respectful manner in which von Brauchitsch addressed him.

'Good evening, Colonel Kramer.'

'Evening, Captain. Evening, Fräulein.' He had an unexpectedly gentle and courteous voice. 'You wear an air of expectancy?'

Before either could answer, the door opened and Anne-Marie and Mary entered: Mary gave the impression of having been pushed into the room. Anne-Marie was slightly flushed and breathing rather heavily, but otherwise her beautiful Aryan self. Mary's clothes were disordered, her hair dishevelled and it was obvious that she had been crying. Her cheeks were still tear-stained.

'We'll have no more trouble with *her*,' Anne-Marie announced with satisfaction. She caught sight of Kramer and the change in her tone was perceptible. 'Interviewing new staff, Colonel.'

'In your usual competent fashion, I see,' Colonel Kramer said dryly. He shook his head. 'When will you learn that respectable young girls do not like being forcibly searched and having their underclothes examined to see if they were made in Piccadilly or Gorki Street?'

'Security regulations,' Anne-Marie said defensively.

'Yes, yes.' Kramer's voice was brusque. 'But there are other ways.' He turned away impatiently. The engaging of female staff was not the problem of the deputy chief of the German Secret Service. While Heidi was helping

Mary to straighten her clothes, he went on, to von Brauchitsch: 'A little excitement in the village tonight?'

'Nothing for us.' Von Brauchitsch shrugged. 'Deserters.'

Kramer smiled.

'That's what I told Colonel Weissner to say. I think our friends are British agents.'

'What!'

'After General Carnaby, I shouldn't wonder,' Kramer said carelessly. 'Relax, Captain. It's over. Three of them are coming up for interrogation within the hour. I'd like you to be present later on. I think you'll find it most entertaining and – ah – instructive.'

'There were five of them, sir. I saw them myself when they were rounded up in "Zum Wilden Hirsch".'

'There *were* five,' Colonel Kramer corrected. 'Not now. Two of them – the leader and one other – are in the Blau See. They commandeered a car and went over a cliff.'

Mary, her back to the men and Anne-Marie, smoothed down her dress and slowly straightened. Her face was stricken. Anne-Marie turned, saw Mary's curiously immobile position and was moving curiously towards her when Heidi took Mary's arm and said quickly: 'My cousin looks ill. May I take her to her room?'

'All right.' Anne-Marie waved her hand in curt dismissal. 'The one you use when you are here.'

The room was bleak, monastic, linoleum-covered, with a made-up iron bed, chair, tiny dressing-table, a hanging cupboard and nothing else. Heidi locked the door behind them.

'You heard?' Mary said emptily. Her face was as drained of life as her voice.

'I heard – and I don't believe it.'

'Why should they lie?'

They believe it.' Heidi's tone was impatient, almost rough. 'It's time you stopped loving and started thinking. The Major Smiths of this world don't drive over cliff edges.'

'Talk is easy, Heidi.'

'So is giving up. *I* believe he is alive. And if he is, and if he comes here and you're gone or not there to help him, you know what he'll be then?' Mary made no reply, just gazed emptily into Heidi's face. 'He'll be dead. He'll be dead because you let him down. Would *he* let *you* down?'

Mary shook her head dumbly.

'Now then,' Heidi went on briskly. She reached first under her skirt then down the front of her blouse and laid seven objects on the table. 'Here we are. Lilliput .21 automatic, two spare magazines, ball of string, lead weight, plan of the castle and the instructions.' She crossed to a corner of the room, raised a loose floor-board, placed the articles beneath it and replaced the board. 'They'll be safe enough there.'

Mary looked at her for a long moment and showed her first spark of interest in an hour.

'You *knew* that board was loose,' she said slowly.

'Of course. I loosened it myself, a fortnight ago.'

'You – you knew about this as far back as then?'

'Whatever else?' Heidi smiled. 'Good luck, cousin.'

Mary sank on to the bed and sat there motionless for ten minutes after Heidi had gone, then rose wearily to her feet and crossed to her window. Her window faced to the north and she could see the line of pylons, the lights of the village and, beyond that, the darkened waters of the Blau See. But what dominated the entire scene were the redly-towering flames and billowing clouds of black smoke reaching up from some burning building at the far end of the village. For a hundred yards around it night had been turned into day and even if there had been a local fire brigade to hand it would have been clearly impossible for them to approach anywhere near the flames. When that first fire went out all that would be left would be smoking ashes. Mary wondered vaguely what it might mean.

She opened her window and leaned out, but cautiously. Even for a person as depressed as she was, there was no temptation to lean too far: castle walls and volcanic plug stretched vertically downwards for almost three hundred feet. She felt slightly dizzy.

To the left and below a cable-car left the castle header station and started to move down to the valley below. Heidi was in that car, leaning out a partially opened window and hopefully waving but Mary's eyes had again blurred with tears and she did not see her. She closed the window, turned away, lay down heavily on the bed and wondered again about John Smith, whether he were alive or dead. And she wondered again about the significance of that fire in the valley below.

Smith and Schaffer skirted the backs of the houses, shops and *Weinstuben* on the east side of the street, keeping to the dark shadows as far as it was possible. Their precautions, Smith realized, were largely superfluous: the undoubted centre of attraction that night was the blazing station and the street leading to it was jammed with hundreds of soldiers and villagers. It must, Smith thought, be a conflagration of quite some note, for although they could no longer see the fire itself, only the red glow in the sky above it, they could clearly hear the roaring crackle of the flames, flames three hundred yards away and with the wind blowing in the wrong direction. As a diversion, it was a roaring success.

They came to one of the few stone buildings in the village, a large barn-like affair with double doors at the back. The yard abutting the rear doors looked like an automobile scrap-yard. There were half-a-dozen old cars lying around, most of them without tyres, some rusted engines, dozens of small useless engine and body parts and a small mountain of empty oil drums. They picked their way carefully through the debris and came to the doors.

Schaffer used skeleton keys to effect and they were inside, doors closed and both torches on, inside fifteen seconds.

One side of the garage was given over to lathes or machine tools of one kind or another, but the rest of the floor space was occupied by a variety of vehicles, mostly elderly. What caught and held Smith's immediate attention, however, was a big yellow bus parked just inside the double front doors. It was a typically Alpine post-bus, with a very long overhang at the back to help negotiate mountain hairpin bends: the rear wheels were so far forward as to be almost in the middle of the bus. As was also common with Alpine post-buses in winter, it had a huge angled snow-plough bolted on to the front of the chasis. Smith looked at Schaffer.

'Promising, you think?'

'If I were optimistic enough to think we'd ever get back to this place,' Schaffer said sourly, 'I'd say it was very promising. You knew about this?'

'What do you think I am? A bus-diviner? Of course I knew about it.'

Smith climbed into the driver's seat. The keys were in the ignition. Smith switched on and watched the fuel gauge climb up to the half-full mark. He located the headlamps switch and turned it on. They worked. He pressed the starter button and the engine caught at once. Smith killed it immediately. Schaffer watched the performance with interest.

'I suppose you know you need a PSV licence to drive one of those, boss?'

'I have one around somewhere. Leave half the explosives in the back of the bus. And hurry. Heidi might be down with the next car.'

Smith climbed down from the driver's seat, went to the front doors, unbolted both, top and bottom, and pushed gently. The doors gave an inch, then stopped.

'Padlocked,' Smith said briefly.

Schaffer surveyed the massive steel plough on the front of the bus and shook his head sorrowfully.

'Poor old padlock,' he said.

The snow had stopped but the wind from the west was now very strong. The cold was intense. Masses of ragged dark cloud hurried across the sky and the entire valley was alternately cast into the deepest shadow or bathed in contrastingly dazzling light as the moon was alternately obscured by the clouds or shone through the shifting gaps between them. But there was no alternating light and shade at the far end of the village: the station still burnt furiously enough to render the moon's best efforts pretty ineffectual.

A cable-car was coming slowly down the valley, less than a hundred yards now from the lower station. Impelled by the powerfully gusting wind, it swung wildly, terrifyingly, across the night sky. But as it approached the end of its journey the motion quickly dampened down and disappeared altogether as it approached the station.

The cable-car jerked to a stop. Heidi, the only passenger, climbed out: understandably enough, she was looking rather pale. She walked down the steps at the back of the station, reached ground level then stopped dead as she heard the softly-whistled first few notes of 'Lorelei', She whirled round, then slowly approached two shapes, clad all in white, huddled by the side of the station.

'The Major Smiths of this world *don't* drive off cliff-tops,' she said calmly. She paused, then stepped forward suddenly and gave each man a quick hug and kiss on the cheek. 'But you had me a little worried there.'

'You just keep on worrying like that,' Schaffer said. 'No need to worry about him, though.'

Heidi waved a hand in the direction of the other end of the village. From the cable-car station on the lower slopes they had an excellent if distant view of the fire. 'Are you responsible for this?' she asked.

'It was a mistake,' Smith explained.

'Yeah. His hand slipped,' Schaffer added.

'You two should audition for a turn on vaudeville,' Heidi said dryly. Suddenly serious she said: 'Mary thinks you're both gone.'

'Weissner doesn't,' Smith said. 'The car that went over the cliff went without us. They're on to us.'

'Hardly surprising,' she murmured. 'Or hadn't you noticed the size of the fire.' She paused, then went on bleakly: 'They're not the only ones who are on to you. Kramer knows you're British agents after General Carnaby.'

'Well, well, well,' Smith said thoughtfully. 'I wonder what little bird has been whispering in Kramer's shell-like ear. One with a very long-range voice, methinks.'

'What *are* you talking about?'

'Nothing. It's not important.'

'It's not important! But don't you *see*?' Her voice was imploring, almost despairing. 'They *know* – or will any minute – that you're alive. They *know* who you are. They'll be expecting you up there.'

'Ah, but you overlook the subtleties, my dear Heidi,' Schaffer put in. 'What they *don't* know is that *we* are expecting *them* to be expecting *us*. At least, that's what I think I mean.'

'You're whistling in the dark, Lieutenant. And one last thing: your friends are being brought up to the castle any time now.'

'For interrogation?' Smith asked.

'I don't expect they've been asked up for tea,' she said acidly.

'Fair enough,' Smith nodded. 'We'll go up with them.'

'In the same car?' The words didn't question Smith's sanity, but the tone and expression did.

'Not "in". With.' Smith peered at his watch. 'The post-bus in Sulz's garage. Be there in eighty minutes. And oh! – bring a couple of crates of empty beer bottles.'

'Bring a couple of – oh, all right.' She shook her head in conviction. 'You're both mad.'

'Shines through in our every word and gesture,' Schaffer agreed, then, suddenly serious, added: 'Say a prayer for us, honey. And if you don't know any prayers, keep your fingers crossed till they ache.'

'Please come back,' she said. There was a catch in her voice. She hesitated, made to say more, turned and walked quickly away. Schaffer looked after her admiringly as she walked down the street.

'There goes the future Mrs Schaffer,' he announced. 'Bit tetchy and snappy, perhaps.' He pondered. 'But funny, I thought she was near crying at the end there.'

'Maybe you'd be tetchy and snappy and tearful if you'd been through what she's been in the past two and a half years,' Smith said sourly.

'Maybe she'd be less tetchy and tearful if she knew a bit more about what's going on.'

'I haven't the time to explain everything to everybody.'

'You can say that again. Devious, boss. That's the word for you.'

'Like enough.' Smith glanced at his watch. 'I wish to God they'd hurry up.'

'Speak for yourself.' Schaffer paused. 'When we – well, if we – get away, is she coming with us?'

'Is who coming with us?'

'Heidi, of course!'

'Heidi, of course. If we make it – and we can only do it through Mary, and Mary was introduced by—'

'Say no more.' He stared after the retreating figure and shook his head. 'She'll be a sensation in the Savoy Grill,' he said dreamily.

Chapter Six

The seconds crawled by and became minutes, and the minutes in turn piled up with agonizing slowness until almost quarter of an hour had passed. Brilliant moonshine and a contrastingly almost total darkness had alternated a score of times as the low, tattered, black clouds scudded across the valley, and the cold deepened until it reached down into the bones of the two watchers in the shadows. And still they waited. They waited because they had to: they couldn't reach the Schloss Adler without company and company was a long time in coming.

And they waited in silence, each man alone with his own thoughts. What was in Schaffer's mind Smith couldn't guess. Probably he was blissfully envisaging himself as the instigator of a series of uncontrollable stampedes in a selection of the better known hostelries in the West End of London. Smith's own thoughts were much more pragmatic and concerned solely with the immediate future. He was becoming concerned, and seriously concerned, about the intense cold and how it would affect their chances of making the trip up to the castle intact. Stamp their feet and flail their arms as they might, that numbing cold tightened its grip on them with every minute that passed. What they were about to do needed both physical strength and quick reactions in full measure, and that glacial cold was swiftly draining them of both. Briefly and bleakly he wondered what odds any reasonable bookmaker would have given against their chances of reaching the castle but dismissed the thought still-born. When no other option offered there was no point in figuring the percentages, and, besides, they were due to find out immediately: the long-awaited company was at hand.

Two Alpenkorps command cars, the leading one with wailing siren and flashing headlamps, swept up the village street just as the moon broke through the cloud-wrack once again, flooding the valley with light. Smith and Schaffer looked up at the moon, then at each other and then, wordlessly, moved back and pressed more deeply into the shadows on the west side of the lower station. The two metallic clicks seemed unnaturally loud as they eased forward the safety catches of their Schmeisser machine-pistols.

Engines stopped and headlamps faded and died almost on the same instant as the two cars pulled up beneath the steps. Men hurried out and lined up briefly before advancing single file up the station steps. A dozen altogether, Smith counted, an officer, eight guards and Carraciola, Thomas and Christiansen. All eight guards had their guns at the ready, which seemed a rather superfluous precaution as the three prisoners had their hands manacled behind their backs. Ergo, the guns weren't there to guard the prisoners but against any rescue attempt by Smith and Schaffer. He and Schaffer, Smith thought wryly, must be acquiring quite a reputation for themselves. But, nonetheless, a reassuring spectacle: if the Germans had known the true reason for his, Smith's, presence in Bavaria, they would also have known that they could have taken the three prisoners up with only a pea-shooter for protection and still have remained free from molestation.

The last of the twelve men passed inside the lower station. Smith touched Schaffer's arm. They slung their Schmeissers, scrambled quickly but quietly on to the ice-covered and steeply-sloping roof of the station and silently and with no little difficulty crawled forwards and upwards to the front edge of the roof under which the cable-car would appear as it moved out at the beginning of its long haul towards the castle. They were, Smith knew, terribly exposed: snow-suits or not, a casual passer-by in the street below had only to glance upwards and their detection was certain. Fortunately, there appeared to be no casual passers-by: the free entertainment provided by the burning station was drawing a full house. And then, as the cable began to move, the moon disappeared behind clouds.

They waited, tensely, till the leading edge of the cable-car appeared, swung their legs over the lip of the roof, waited till the suspension bracket passed beneath them, reached down for the cable, allowed themselves to be pulled off the roof, fell across the cable and lowered themselves gently until their feet touched the roof of the cable-car.

Mary walked softly along the dimly-lit, stone-flagged passage, counting off doors as she went. Outside the fifth she stopped, put her ear to it, stooped, glanced through the key-hole, knocked quietly and waited for a response. There was none. She knocked again, more loudly, with the same result. She turned the handle and found the door locked. From her small handbag she produced a set of skeleton keys. When the door yielded, she slipped quickly inside, closed the door and switched on the light.

The room was a considerable improvement on the one she had been given, although furnished with the same regulation iron bedstead. It was close-carpeted, boasted a couple of arm-chairs, and had a small chair with an Oberleutnant's uniform on it, a large wardrobe and a chest of drawers with a holstered belt, gun and binoculars resting on its glass top.

Mary locked the door, withdrew the key, crossed the room, lifted the lower sash window and looked down. She was, she saw, directly above the roof of the cable-car header station, a very steeply downward sloping roof the upper edge of which was built into the castle wall itself. She withdrew her head, removed from her handbag a ball of string with a heavy bolt attached to one end, laid it on the bed, picked up the binoculars and took up station by the window. Shivering in the bitter night wind, she adjusted the focus of the field-glasses, then traversed down the line of the aerial cables. And then she had it, dimly seen but unmistakable, the squat black outline of the cable-car, now half-way between the bottom and middle pylons, swaying madly, frighteningly, across the sky in the high and gusting wind.

Smith and Schaffer lay stretched out on the roof, clutching desperately to the suspension bracket, the only anchorage available. The roof was solidly coated with white-sheeted ice, they could find no purchase anywhere for their feet, and their bodies slid uncontrollably in all directions with the violent buffeting of the car beneath them. The sheer physical strain on hands and arms and shoulders was even worse than Smith had feared: and the worst was yet to come.

Schaffer twisted his head and peered downwards. It was a dizzy, vertiginous and frankly terrifying spectacle. The entire valley below seemed to be swinging through a forty-five degree arc. One second he was looking at the line of pines that bordered the western slope of the valley, then the floor of the valley rushed by beneath them and seconds later he was staring at the line of pines that swept up the eastern side of the valley. He twisted his head upwards, but that was no improvement; the lights of the Schloss Adler careened wildly through the same dizzy arc: it was like being on a combination of a roller-coaster, big dipper and runaway Ferris wheel with the notable exception, Schaffer thought bleakly, that the coaster, dipper and Ferris wheel were provided with safety belts and other securing devices designed to prevent the occupant from parting company with his machine. The wind howled its high and lonely threnody through the cables and the suspension bracket. Schaffer looked away, screwed his eyes shut, lowered his head between his outstretched arms and moaned.

'Still think the horse the world's worst form of transport?' Smith asked. His lips were close to Schaffer's ear.

'Give me my boots and saddle,' Schaffer said, then, even more despairingly, 'Oh, no! Not again!'

Once more, without any warning, the moon had broken through, flooding the two men in its pale cold light. Gauging the time when the strain on their arms was least, they pulled the snow hoods far over their heads and tried to flatten themselves even more closely on to the roof.

In the Schloss Adler two people were watching the wild upward progress of the cable-car, now brilliantly illuminated by the moon. Through Mary's field-glasses two clearly distinguishable shapes of men could be seen stretched out on the cable-car roof. For half a minute she kept the glasses trained on them, then slowly turned away, her eyes wide, almost staring, her face empty of expression. Fifty feet above her head a sentry with slung gun patrolling the battlements stopped and gazed down at the cable-car crawling up the valley. But he didn't gaze for long. Although booted, gauntleted and muffled to the ears, he shook with the cold. It was no night for idle spectating. He looked away indifferently and resumed his brisk sentry-go.

Indifference was a quality that was conspicuously lacking on top of the cable-car. The cable-car was on the last lap now, the section between the last pylon and the castle header station. Soon the moment of truth. A minute from then, Smith thought, and they could both well be lying broken and lifeless on the rocks two hundred feet below.

He twisted his head upwards. The cold moon still sailed across a clear gap in the sky but was closing rapidly towards another bank of cloud. The castle battlements, with the header station at the base, seemed almost vertically above his head. So steeply was the car rising on this last section that the volcanic plug itself was now less than fourteen yards away. His gaze followed the volcanic plug downwards till it reached its base: down there, on the slopes below, patrolling guards and their Dobermann pinschers were barely the size of beetles.

'Suits her, doesn't it?' Schaffer said suddenly. Harsh edges of strain burried in his voice and his face was tight and desperate. 'A lovely name.'

'What are you talking about?' Smith demanded.

'Heidi.'

'Oh, my God!' Smith stared up at the rapidly closing header station. 'Her name is Ethel.'

'You didn't have to tell me.' Schaffer tried to sound aggrieved but it didn't quite come off. He followed Smith's upward gaze and, after a long pause, said very slowly: 'Jesus! Look at the slope of that goddamned roof!'

'I've been looking.' Smith eased his knife from its sheath and made a quick grab at the suspension bracket as a particularly violent swing almost broke his grip with his other hand. 'Get your knife ready. And for God's sake don't lose it.'

The moon slid behind a black patch of cloud and the valley was flooded with darkness. Slowly, carefully, as the cable-car approached the header station and the swaying motion dampened down, Smith and Schaffer eased their way to the after end of the car, rose gingerly but swiftly to their feet and grabbed the cable with their free hands while their feet tried to find what precarious hold they could on the treacherously ice-sheathed roof.

The front of the car passed under the lip of the header station roof. A moment later the suspension bracket followed and Smith lunged forward and upwards, flinging himself bodily on to the roof. His right arm struck downwards and the knife blade pierced the coating of ice and imbedded itself firmly in the wood beneath. Less than a second later Schaffer had landed beside him, the downward arcing knife making contact at exactly the same instant as himself.

The blade broke off at the hilt. Schaffer opened his hand, dropped the haft and clawed desperately at the ice. The dragging nails ripped through the encrusting ice, quite failing to hold him. He reached his left hand to his mouth, tore off the gauntlet and dug both hands in with all the strength that was in him. He slowed, but not enough. His scrabbling toes failed to find any more purchase and he knew he was sliding out over the edge – and that when he went the first thing to halt his fall would be the rock-pile two hundred and fifty feet beneath at the base of the volcanic plug.

Smith had been badly winded by his fall. Several seconds elapsed before he realized that Schaffer wasn't where he should have been – lying on the roof beside him. He twisted round, saw the white blur of Schaffer's strained and desperate face, had a vague impression of Schaffer's eight finger-nails scoring their way through the ice as his body, already up to mid-thigh, slid inexorably over the edge and brought his left hand flashing down with a speed and power that, even in those circumstances, made Schaffer grunt in pain as the vice-like grip clamped over his right wrist.

For some seconds they lay like that, spreadeagled and motionless on the sloping roof, the lives of both dependent on the slim imbedded blade of Smith's knife; then Schaffer, urged by Smith's quivering left arm, began to inch his way slowly upwards. Thirty seconds later and he was level with Smith.

'This is a knife I have, not an ice-axe,' Smith said hoarsely. 'Won't take much more of this. Have you another knife?'

Schaffer shook his head. Momentarily, speech was beyond him.

'Piton?'

The same shake of the head.

'Your torch?'

Schaffer nodded, reached under the cumbersome snow-smock with his left hand and eventually managed to wriggle his torch free.

'Unscrew the bottom,' Smith said. 'Throw it away – and the battery.' Schaffer brought his left hand across to where his right was pinioned by Smith, removed base and battery, flattened the now empty cylinder base a little, reversed his grip and gouged the torch into the ice, downwards and towards himself. He moved his right hand and Smith released his grip. Schaffer remained where he was. Smith smiled and said: 'Try holding me.'

Schaffer caught Smith's left wrist. Tentatively, his hand still hooked in readiness, Smith removed his hand from the haft of the knife. Schaffer's imbedded torch held firm. Cautiously at first, then with increasing confidence as the sharp blade cut through the protective sheathing of ice, Smith carved out a secure handhold in the wooden roof of the station, passed his knife to Schaffer, wriggled out of his snow-smock, undid a few turns of the knotted rope round his waist and secured the free end to Schaffer's belt. He said: 'With the knife and torch, think you can make it?'

'Can I make it?' Schaffer tested both knife and and torch and smiled, a pretty strained effort, but his first for some time. 'After what I've been through – well, ever seen a monkey go up a coconut palm tree?'

Fifty feet above their heads, Mary withdrew from the window and laid the binoculars on the chest of drawers. Her hands shook and the metal of the binoculars rattled like castanets against the glass top. She returned to the window and began to pay out the weighted string.

Smith came up the last few feet of the sloping roof at the end of the rope, caught Schaffer's hand, stood upright on the flat inner section of the roof and at once began to unwind the rest of the knotted rope from his waist. Schaffer, although the temperature was far below freezing, wiped his brow like a man in a heat-wave.

'Brother!' He mopped his brow some more. 'If I can ever do you a favour, like lending you a car-fare—'

Smith grinned, clapped his shoulder, reached up into the gloom, caught the weighted end of the suspended string and quickly bent the nylon on to it. He gave two gentle tugs and the rope began to move upwards as Mary hauled it in through the window. Smith waited until two more gentle return tugs indicated that the rope was securely fastened and began to climb.

He was half-way up to the window when the moon broke through. In his Alpenkorps uniform he was perfectly silhouetted against the gleaming white of the castle walls. He hung there motionless, not daring to move, not so much as even daring to glance upwards or downwards lest the movement attract some hostile attention.

Twenty-five feet below him Schaffer peered cautiously over the edge of the header station roof. The guards and dogs were still patrolling the area round the roof of the volcanic plug. They had only to give one casual upwards glance and Smith's discovery was inevitable. Then some hair-prickling sixth sense made Schaffer look sharply upwards and he became very still indeed. The sentry, another circuit of the battlements completed, was standing with hands splayed out on the parapet, gazing out over the valley, perhaps watching the now dying flames from the burnt-out station: he had to lower his eyes only a fraction and that was that. Slowly, with his right hand, Schaffer brought up the Luger with the long perforated silencer screwed to its muzzle and laid it, in the best police fashion, across his left wrist. He had no doubt he could kill his man with one shot, the only question was when best to do it, how to weigh the balance of possibilities. If he waited until the man sighted them, he might give a warning shout or thrust himself back into cover before Schaffer could kill him. If he shot the sentry before he sighted them, then there would be no question of either escape or warning. But there was the possibility that the man might pitch forward over the battlements, crash off the roof of the header station and fall into the valley below, close by the patrolling men and dogs. A possibility only, Schaffer decided, not a probability: the slamming effect of the Luger shell would almost certainly knock him backwards off his feet. Schaffer had never before gunned down an unsuspecting man, but he coldly prepared to do so now. He lined up the luminous sight on the man's breast-bone and began to squeeze the trigger.

The moon went behind a cloud.

Slowly, stiffly, Schaffer lowered his gun. Schaffer, once again, wiped sweat from his forehead. He had the feeling that he wasn't through with brow-mopping for the night.

Smith reached the window, clambered over the sill, gave the rope two tugs as a signal for Schaffer to start climbing and passed into the room. It was almost totally dark inside, he'd just time to make out the iron bedstead which had been dragged to the window as anchorage for the rope when a pair of arms wound tightly round his neck and someone started murmuring incoherently in his ear.

'Easy on, easy on,' Smith protested. He was still breathing heavily and needed all the air he could get, but summoned enough energy to bend and kiss her. 'Unprofessional conduct, what's more. But I won't report it this time.'

She was still clinging to him, silent now, when Lieutenant Schaffer made his appearance, dragging himself wearily over the sill and collapsing on the iron bedstead. He was breathing very heavily indeed and had about him the air of one who has suffered much.

'Have they no elevators in this dump?' he demanded. It took him two breaths to get the words out.

'Out of training,' Smith said unsympathetically. He crossed to the door and switched on the light, hurriedly switched it off again. 'Damn. Get the rope in then pull the curtains.'

'This is the way they treated them in the Roman galleys,' Schaffer said bitterly. But he had the rope inside and the curtains closed in ten seconds. As Smith was manoeuvring the bed back into its original position, Schaffer was stuffing the nylon into their canvas bag, a bag, which, in addition to snowsuits and Schmeissers, contained some hand grenades and a stock of plastic explosives. He had just finished tying the neck of the bag when a key scraped in the lock.

Smith motioned Mary to stay where she was as he moved quickly to take up position behind the door: Schaffer, for all his alleged exhaustion, had dropped flat to the floor behind the bed with all the speed and silence of a cat. The door opened and a young Oberleutnant strode into the room, stopping short as he saw Mary, her hand to her mouth. His face registered astonishment, an astonishment almost immediately replaced by an anticipatory half-smile as he stepped forward beyond the opened door. Smith's arm came down and the young officer's eyes turned up in his head.

Smith studied the plans of the castle given him by Mary while Schaffer trussed up the Oberleutnant with the nylon, gagged him with tape and shoved him, jack-knifed, into the bottom of the cupboard. For good measure he pulled the top of the bed against the door.

'Ready when you are, boss.'

'That's now. I have my bearings. First left, down the stairs, third left. The gold drawing-room. Where Colonel Kramer holds court. Complete with minstrels' gallery.'

'What's a minstrel's gallery?' Schaffer enquired.

'A gallery for minstrels. Then the next right-hander takes us to the east wing. Down again, second left. Telephone exchange.'

'Why there?' Schaffer asked. 'We've already cut the lines.'

'Not the ones between here and the barracks, we haven't. Want them to whistle up a regiment of Alpenkorps?' He turned to Mary. 'Helicopter still here?'

'It was when I arrived.'

'The helicopter?' Schaffer showed his puzzlement. 'What gives with the whirlybird, then?'

'This gives with the whirlybird. They could use it either to whip Carnaby out of here – they *might* just be nervous if they think we're on the loose – or they might use it to block our getaway.'

'*If* we get away.'

'There's that. How are you on immobilizing helicopters, Lieutenant Schaffer? Your report states that you were an up-and-coming racing driver and a very competent mechanic before they scraped the bottom of the barrel and dragged you in.'

'I volunteered,' Schaffer said with dignity. 'About the competence, I dunno. But give me a four-pound hammer and I'll sure as little fishes immobilize anything from a bull-dozer to a bicycle.'

'And without the four-pounder? This is not a boiler-makers' convention.'

'I have been known to use finesse.'

Smith said to Mary: 'How can we get a sight of this machine?'

'Just five paces that way.' She pointed to the door. 'Every passage window in the Schloss Adler opens on to the courtyard.'

Smith opened the door, glanced up and down the passage and crossed to an opposite window. Schaffer was by his side.

The comings and goings of the moon made no difference to the state of illumination in the Schloss Adler courtyard. Two big overhead arc lamps burned by the heavily-barred entrance gates. A third burned at the opposite end of the courtyard, over the main doorway leading into the castle itself. At a height of about ten feet, four waterproof storm lamps were fastened to the east and west walls of the courtyard. Lights burned from a dozen windows on the east and northern sides. And the brightest light of all came from an arc-lamp that had been rigged above the helicopter and under the temporary protection of a stretched tarpaulin. A figure in green overalls and a high-peaked cap was working on the helicopter's engine. Smith touched

Schaffer's arm and they moved back into the room where Mary was waiting, closing the door behind them.

'Seems a straightforward operation,' Schaffer said. 'Fixing it so that the chopper doesn't fly again, I mean. I cross to the main gates, overpower the four men on guard, strangle the four Dobermann pinschers, knock off two or three other characters – armed characters – who appear to be patrolling the place all the time, overpower about twenty soldiers who appear to be drinking beer in some sort of canteen across the way, dispose of the guy who's working on the engine and *then* immobilize the chopper. I mean, just immobilizing the chopper itself wouldn't be anything, really, would it?'

'We'll think of something,' Smith said soothingly.

'I'll bet you think of something,' Schaffer said moodily. 'That's what I'm afraid of.'

'Time's a-wasting. We won't need those any more.'

Smith folded the plan, handed it to Mary, then frowned as she put it in her bag. 'You know better than that. The Lilliput: it should be on your person, not in the bag. Here.' He handed her the Mauser he'd taken from Colonel Weissner. 'This in your bag. Hide the Lilliput on you.'

'When I get to my room I will,' she said primly.

'All those leering Yankee lieutenants around,' Schaffer said sadly. 'Thank heavens I'm a changed man.'

'His mind is set on higher things,' Smith explained. He glanced at his watch. 'Give us thirty minutes.'

They slipped cautiously through the doorway then strode briskly and confidently along the passage, making no attempt to conceal their presence. The bag with the Schmeissers, rope, grenades and explosives Smith swung carelessly from one hand. They passed a bespectacled soldier carrying a sheaf of papers and a girl carrying a laden tray, neither of whom paid any attention to them. They turned right at the end of the passage, reached a circular flight of stairs and went down three floors until they came to the level of the courtyard. A short broad passage, with two doors on either side, took them to the main door leading out to the courtyard.

Smith opened the door and looked out. The scene was very much as Schaffer had feelingly described it, with far too many armed guards and police dogs around for anyone's peace of mind. The overalled mechanic was still at work on the helicopter's engine. Smith quietly closed the door and turned his attention to the nearest right-hand door in the passage. It was locked. He said to Schaffer: 'Keep an eye open at the end of the passage there.'

Schaffer went. As soon as he was in position, Smith brought out skeleton keys. The third key fitted and the door gave under his hand. He signalled Schaffer to return.

With the door closed and locked behind them, they looked around the room, a room faintly but for their purposes adequately lit by the backwash of light shining through the unshuttered window from the courtyard. It was, quite apparently, the fire-fighting HQ of the castle. The walls were hung with drums of rolled hoses, asbestos suits, helmets and fire-axes: wheeled handpumps, CO_2 cylinders and a variety of smaller cylinders for fighting oil and electrical fires took up much of the floor space.

'Ideal,' Smith murmured.

'Couldn't be better,' Schaffer agreed. 'What are you talking about?'

'If we leave anyone in here,' Smith explained, 'he's unlikely to be discovered unless there's an actual outbreak of fire. Agreed? So.' He took Schaffer by the arm and led him to the window. 'The lad working on the chopper there. About your size, wouldn't you say?'

'I wouldn't know,' Schaffer said. 'And if you've got in mind what I think you have in mind, then I don't want to know, either.'

Smith drew the shutters, crossed to the door and switched on the overhead light.

'You got any better ideas?'

'Give me time,' he complained.

'I can't give you what we haven't got. Take your jacket off and keep your Luger lined up on that door. I'll be back in a minute.'

Smith left, closing but not locking the door behind him. He passed through the outer doorway, walked a few paces across the courtyard, halted at the base of a set of steps leading up to the helicopter and looked up at the man working above him, a tall rangy man with a thin intelligent face and a lugubrious expression on it. If he'd been working bare-handed with metal tools in that freezing temperature, Smith thought, he'd have had a lugubrious expression on his face, too.

'You the pilot?' Smith asked.

'You wouldn't think so, would you?' the overalled man said bitterly. He laid down a spanner and blew on his hands. 'Back in Tempelhof I have two mechanics for this machine, one a farm-hand from Swabia, the other a blacksmith's assistant from the Harz. If I want to keep alive I do my own mechanics. What do you want?'

'Not me. Reichsmarschall Rosemeyer. The phone.'

'The Reichsmarschall?' The pilot was puzzled. 'I was speaking to him less than fifteen minutes ago.'

'A call just came through from the Chancellory in Berlin. It seems urgent.' Smith let a slight note of impatience creep into his voice. 'You better hurry. Through the main door there, then the first on the right.'

Smith stood aside as the pilot clambered down, looked casually around him. A guard with a leashed Dobermann was no more than twenty feet away, but paying no attention to them: with his pinched bluish face sunk deep in his upturned collar, his hands thrust down into his great-coat pockets and his frozen breath hanging heavily in the air, he was too busy concentrating on his own miseries to have time to spare for ridiculous suspicions. Smith turned to follow the pilot through the main door, unobtrusively unholstering his Luger and gripping it by the barrel.

Smith hadn't intended chopping down the pilot with his gun butt but was left with no option. As soon as the pilot had passed through the side door and seen Schaffer's Luger pointing at his chest from a distance of four feet his shoulders lifted – the preliminary, Smith knew, not to violence or resistance but to a shout for help. Schaffer caught him as he pitched forward and lowered him to the floor.

Quickly they unzipped the overall from the unconscious man, bound and gagged him and left him lying in a corner. The overall was hardly a perfect fit for Schaffer, but, then, overalls are rarely a perfect fit for anybody. Schaffer switched the pilot's hat for his own, pulled the peak low over his eyes and left.

Smith switched off the light, unshuttered the window, raised the lower sash and stood, Luger in hand, just far enough back from the window so as not to be seen from outside. Schaffer was already climbing the steps up to the helicopter. The guard was now only feet from the base of the ladder. He'd his hands out of his pockets now and was flailing his arms across his shoulders in an attempt to keep warm.

Thirty seconds later Schaffer climbed down the ladder again, carrying some pieces of equipment in his left hand. He reached the ground, lifted the piece of equipment for a closer inspection, shook his head in disgust, lifted his right hand in a vague half-greeting to the uncaring German guard and headed for the main door again. By the time he reached the fire-fighting room, Smith had the window shuttered again and the light on.

'That was quick,' Smith said approvingly.

'Fear lent him wings, as the saying goes,' Schaffer said sourly. 'I'm always quick when I'm nervous. Did you see the size of the teeth in that great slavering monster out there?' He held up the piece of equipment for inspection, dropped it to the floor and brought his heel down on it. 'Distributor cap. I'll bet they haven't another in Bavaria. Not for that engine. And now, I suppose, you want me to go and impersonate the telephone operator.'

'No. We don't want to exhaust all your Thespian stamina.'

'My what?' Schaffer asked suspiciously. 'That sounds kinda like a nasty crack to me.'

'Your acting resources. The only other impersonation you'll be called to make tonight is that of Lieutenant Schaffer, OSS, the innocent American abroad.'

'That shouldn't be too difficult,' Schaffer said bitterly. He draped the overalls he'd just removed over the unconscious pilot. 'A cold night. Anyway, the telephone exchange.'

'Soon. But I'd like to check first how far they've got with old Carnaby-Jones. Let's take a look.

Two floors higher up and midway along the central passage Smith stopped outside a doorway. At a nod from him, Schaffer reached for a light switch. Except for a faint glow of light at either end, the passage was now completely dark. Smith laid a gentle hand on the door-knob and quietly eased the door open. Fifteen inches, no more. Both men swiftly slid through the narrow gap, Smith quickly and softly closing the door to again.

The room, if so enormous a chamber could be called a room, must have been at least seventy feet long by thirty wide. The farther end of the room was brightly and warmly lit by three large chandeliers: comparatively, the end of the room where Smith and Schaffer stood was shrouded in near darkness.

They stood, not on the floor, but on a platform some dozen feet above the floor. It was a massive and grotesquely carved oaken minstrels' gallery which completely spanned the thirty-foot width of that end and ran perhaps a quarter of the way down both the longer sides of the room. There were rows of wooden benches, an organ on one side of the door through which they had just passed, a battery of organ pipes on the other. Whoever had built that place had obviously liked the organ and choir-singing: or maybe he just thought he did. From the centre of the front of the gallery, opposite the rear door, a flight of steps with intricately scrolled wooden banisters led down to what was very obviously the gold drawing-room.

It was aptly named, Smith thought. Everything in it was gold or golden or gilt. The enormous wall-to-wall carpet was deep gold in colour, the thickness of the pile would have turned a polar bear green with envy. The heavy baroque furniture, all twisted snakes and gargoyles' heads, was gilt, the huge couches and chairs covered in a dusty gold lamé. The chandeliers were gilded and, above the enormous white and gilt-plated fireplace, in which a crackling pine log fire burned, hung an almost equally enormous white and gilt-plated mirror. The great heavy curtains could have been made from beaten gold. The ceiling-high oak panelling, was a mistake, it continued to look obstinately like oak panelling, maybe the original covering gold paint had worn off. All in all, Smith reflected, it was a room only a mad Bavarian monarch could have conceived of, far less lived in.

Three men were seated comfortably round the great fire, to all appearances having an amicable discussion over after-dinner coffee and brandy, which was being served to them from – almost inevitably – a golden trolley by Anne-Marie. Anne-Marie, like the panelling was a disappointment: instead of a gold lamé dress she wore a long white silk sheath gown which, admittedly, went very well with her blonde colouring and snowtan. She looked as if she were about to leave for the opera.

The man with his back to him Smith had never seen before but, because he immediately recognized who the other men were, knew who this man must be: Colonel Paul Kramer, Deputy Chief of the German Secret Service, regarded by MI6 as having the most brilliant and formidable brain in German Intelligence. The man to watch, Smith knew, the man to fear. It was said of Kramer that he never made the same mistake twice – and that no one could remember when he'd last made a mistake for the first time.

As Smith watched, Colonel Kramer stirred, poured some more brandy from a Napoleon bottle by his side and looked first at the man on his left, a tall, ageing, but still good-looking man in the uniform of a Reichsmarschall of the Wehrmacht – at that moment, wearing a very glum expression on his face – then at the man seated opposite, an iron-grey-haired and very distinguished looking character in the uniform of a lieutenant general of the US Army. Without a comptometer to hand, it was difficult to say which of the two generals was wearing the more decorations.

Kramer sipped his brandy and said wearily: 'You make things very difficult for me, General Carnaby. Very, very difficult indeed.'

'The difficulties are of your own making, my dear Kramer,' Cartwright Jones said easily. 'Yours and General Rosemeyer's here . . . There *is* no difficulty.' He turned to Anne-Marie and smiled. 'If I might have some more of that excellent brandy, my dear. My word, we've nothing like this in SHAEF. Marooned in your Alpine redoubt or not, you people know how to look after yourselves.

In the gloom at the back of the minstrels' gallery, Schaffer nudged Smith with his elbow.

'What gives with old Carnaby-Jones knocking back the Napoleon, then?' he asked in a low indignant murmur. 'Why isn't he being turned on a spit or having the French fits coming out of scopolamine?'

'Ssh!' Smith's nudge carried a great deal more weight and authority than Schaffer's had done.

Jones smiled his thanks as Anne-Marie poured him some more brandy, sipped from the glass, sighed in satisfaction and continued: 'Or have you forgotten, General Rosemeyer, that Germany is also a signatory to The Hague conventions?'

'I haven't forgotten,' Rosemeyer said uncomfortably. 'And if I had my way . . . General, my hands are tied. I have my orders from Berlin.'

'And you can tell Berlin all they're entitled to know,' Jones said easily. 'I am General - Lieutenant General - George Carnaby, United States Army.'

'And Chief Co-ordinator of Planning for the Second Front,' Rosemeyer added morosely.

'The Second Front?' Jones asked with interest. 'What's that?'

Rosemeyer said heavily and with earnest gravity: 'General, I've done all I can. You must believe me. For thirty-six hours now, I've held off Berlin. I've persuaded - I've *tried* to persuade the High Command that the mere *fact* of your capture will compel the Allies to alter all their invasion plans. But this, it seems, is not enough. For the last time, may I request—'

'General George Carnaby,' Jones said calmly. 'United States Army.'

'I expected nothing else,' Rosemeyer admitted tiredly. 'How could I expect anything else from a senior army officer? I'm afraid the matter is now in Colonel Kramer's hands.'

Jones sipped some more brandy and eyed Kramer thoughtfully. 'The Colonel doesn't seem very happy about it either.'

'I'm not,' Kramer said. 'But the matter is out of my hands, too. I also have my orders. Anne-Marie will attend to the rest of it.'

'*This* charming young lady?' Jones was politely incredulous. 'A maestro of the thumb-screw?'

'Of the hypodermic syringe,' Kramer said shortly. 'She used to be a trained nurse.' A bell rang and Kramer picked up a phone by his side. 'Yes? Ah! They have, of course, been searched? Very good. Now.' He looked across at Jones. 'Well, well, well. Some interesting company coming up, General. Very interesting indeed. Parachutists. A rescue team - for you. I'm sure you'll be delighted to meet one another.'

'I really can't imagine what you're talking about,' Jones said idly.

'The rescue team we've seen before,' Smith murmured to Schaffer. 'And no doubt we'll be renewing old acquaintances before long. Come on.'

'What? Now?' Schaffer jerked an urgent thumb in the direction of Jones. 'Just when they're going to get to work on him?'

'Out of your social depth, Lieutenant,' Smith whispered. 'They're civilized. First, they finish the brandy. *Then* the works.'

'It's like I said,' Schaffer said mournfully. 'I'm from Montana.'

The two men left as quietly as they had come and as quietly closed the door behind them. Against the loom of light at either end of the corridor, they could see that the passage-way was clear. Smith switched on the light. They walked briskly along the passage, dropped down a flight of stairs, turned left and halted outside a doorway which bore above it the legend TELEFON ZENTRALE.

'Telephone exchange,' Schaffer said.

Smith shook his head in admiration, put his ear to the door, dropped to one knee, peered through the keyhole and, while still in that position, softly tried the handle. Whatever slight sound he made was masked by the muffled sound of a voice speaking over a telephone. The door was locked. Smith slowly released the handle, straightened and shook his head.

'Suspicious bunch of devils,' Schaffer said sourly. 'The skeletons.'

'The operator would hear us. Next door.'

Next door wasn't locked. The door gave before Smith's pressure on the handle. The room beyond was in total darkness and appeared to be empty.

'Moment, bitte!' a cold voice said behind them.

Quickly, but not too quickly, Smith and Schaffer turned round. A few feet away stood a soldier, levelled carbine in his hand, his eyes moving in active suspicion from the two men to the kit-bag in Smith's hands. Smith glared at the man, raised an imperative forefinger to his lips.

'Dummkopf!' Smith's voice was a low furious whisper through clenched teeth. *'Silenz! Engländer!'*

He turned away impatiently and peered tensely through the partly-opened doorway. Again he held up an imperious hand that commanded silence. After a few more seconds he straightened, lips compressed, looked significantly at Schaffer and moved slightly to one side. Schaffer took his position and started peering in turn. Curiosity, Smith could see, was replacing suspicion in the soldier's face. Schaffer straightened and said softly: 'What in God's name do we do?'

'I don't know,' Smith said in a worried whisper. 'Colonel Kramer told me he wanted them alive. But—'

'What is it?' the soldier demanded in a voice as low as their own. With the mention of Colonel Kramer the last of his suspicions had gone. 'Who is it?'

'You still here,' Smith said irritably. 'All right, go on. Have a look. But be quick!'

The soldier, his face and eyes now alight with intense curiosity and what might have been dreams of rapid promotion, moved forward on tiptoe as Schaffer courteously stepped to one side to let him see. A pair of Lugers grinding simultaneously into both temples effectively put an end to any idea of rapid military advancement that he might briefly have entertained. He was propelled, stumbling, into the room and, by the time he'd picked himself up and turned round, the door was closed, the light on and both pistols lined at his head.

'Those are silencers you see on our guns,' Smith said quietly. 'No heroics, no shooting. Dying for the Fatherland is one thing, dying uselessly for no reason at all is another and very stupid thing. Don't you agree?'

The soldier looked at them, calculated his chances, accepted the fact that he had none and nodded. Schaffer produced a length of rope and said: 'You may be over-eager, son, but you're no fool. Lie down with your hands behind your back.'

The room, Smith saw, was small and lined with metal shelves and filing cabinets. Some sort of storage room for office records. The chances of anyone coming along weren't high and it was, anyway, a chance they had to take. He waited till Schaffer had bound and gagged the prisoner, put his Luger away, helped Schaffer to bind the man to two of the metal poles supporting the shelves, turned to the window, slid up the lower sash and peered out.

The valley to the north stretched out before him, the lights of the village and the smouldering embers of the railway station visible through very gently falling snow. Smith looked to his right. The lighted window of the telephone exchange was only a few feet away. From the window a heavy lead-sheathed cable attached to a wire almost equally as heavy stretched down the castle wall into the darkness.

'That the one?' Schaffer was by his side now.

'That's the one. Let's have the rope.'

Smith eased his legs into a double bowline, wriggled over the window-sill and cautiously lowered himself to the full extent of his arms while Schaffer, standing by the window with the rope belayed round one of the stanchions of the shelving, took the strain. Smith released his grip on the sill and was lowered jerkily by Schaffer till he was about ten or twelve feet down. Then, using a free hand and both feet to fend himself off from the wall he began to swing himself in a pendulum arc across the face of the castle, an assist from Schaffer up above adding momentum to his swing. On the fifth swing the fingers of his left hand hooked round the lead cable and wire. As Schaffer eased off tension on the rope Smith got both hands round the cable and quickly climbed up the few feet to the window above. He was almost certain that the lead cable he had in his hands *was* the telephone outlet, but only almost: he had no desire to slice the blade of his knife through high-powered electricity supply lines.

He hitched a wary eye over the window-sill, saw that the telephone operator, his back almost directly to him, was talking animatedly on the phone, lifted himself another six inches, observed a cable of what appeared to be exactly similar dimensions to the one he was holding running along the skirting-board to some point behind the exchange and then not reappearing again. He lowered himself a couple of feet, grasped cable and wire firmly with his left hand, inserted the point of his knife between cable and wire a few inches below that and started sawing. A dozen powerful saw-cuts and he was through.

He replaced the knife in its sheath, hoisted himself up again and had another look through the window. The operator was still animated, but this time not with his voice but with a hand which he was using furiously to crank a handle at the side of the exchange. After a few seconds of this profitless exercise he gave up and just sat there staring at the switchboard and shaking his head in bafflement. Smith made a signal to Schaffer, released his grip on the cable and swung back across the castle wall.

Mary glanced at her watch for the tenth time in less than as many minutes, stubbed out the half-cigarette she'd been nervously smoking, rose from her chair, opened her hand-bag, checked that the safety catch of the Mauser inside was in the off position, closed the bag and crossed the room. She had just turned the handle and begun to open the door when knuckles rapped on the outside. She hesitated, glanced at the bag in her hand and looked round almost wildly to see where she could dispose of it. But it was too late to dispose of anything. The door opened and a cheerfully smiling von Brauchitsch stood framed in the doorway.

'Ah, Fräulein!' He glanced at the bag and smiled again. 'Lucky me! Just in time to escort you wherever you're going.'

'To escort me—' She broke off and smiled. 'My business is of no consequence. It can wait. You wanted to see me, Captain?'

'Naturally.'

'What about?'

'What about, she says! About nothing, that's what. Unless you call yourself nothing. Just to see you. Is that a crime? The prettiest girl we've seen—' He smiled again, this man who was always smiling, and took her arm. 'Come, a little Bavarian hospitality. Coffee. We have an armoury that's been converted into the finest *Kaffeestube*—'

'But - but my duties?' Mary said uncertainly. 'I must see the Colonel's secretary—'

'That one! Let her wait!' There was a marked lack of cordiality in von Brauchitsch's voice. 'You and I have a lot to talk about.'

'We have?' It was impossible to resist the infectious smile, not to reply in kind. 'Such as?'

'Düsseldorf.'

'Düsseldorf?'

'Of course! That's my home town, too.'

'Your home town, too!' She smiled again and gave his arm the briefest of squeezes. 'How small a world. That *will* be nice.'

She wondered vaguely, as she walked along, how one could smile and smile and, inside, feel as chilled as the tomb.

Chapter Seven

For the second time in fifteen minutes Smith and Schaffer stopped at the doorway outside the gold room's minstrels' gallery, switched out the passage light, paused, listened, then passed silently inside. This time, however, Smith reached through the crack of the almost closed door and switched the light back on again. He did not expect to be using that door again, that night or any night, and he had no wish to raise any eyebrows, however millimetric the raising: survival was a matter of the infinitely careful consideration of all possible dangers, no matter how remote that possibility might at times appear.

This time, Smith and Schaffer did not remain at the back of the minstrels' gallery. They moved slowly to the front, till they had come to the head of the broad flight of stairs leading down to the floor of the gold room and then sat down on the front oaken benches, one on each side of the gallery's passageway. They were still shrouded in deep gloom, completely invisible from below.

Colonel Kramer's stock of VSOP Napoleon brandy was certainly taking a beating that night, Smith reflected. The Colonel, Reichsmarschall Rosemeyer, Jones and Anne-Marie had been joined by three others - Carraciola, Thomas and Christiansen. Those last three were no longer manacled and under heavy guard. On the contrary there was no sign of any guard, and the three men were sitting deeply relaxed and side by side on one of the massive gold lamé-covered couches, glasses of brandy, and no small ones at that, in their hands. Even Anne-Marie now held a glass in her hand. It appeared to be an occasion for a celebration of some note.

Kramer lifted his glass towards the three men seated in the couch.

'Your health, gentlemen. Your very good health.' He turned to the Reichsmarschall. 'Three of the best in Europe, sir.'

'I suppose they are necessary,' Rosemeyer said in resigned distaste. 'At least, their courage is beyond dispute. Your health, gentlemen.'

'Your health, gentlemen,' Jones said bitterly. He sat forward in his chair and hurled his glass into the fire. The glass shattered and there was a momentary tongue of flame as the brandy ignited. '*That's* how I drink the health of double agents.'

Schaffer leaned across the passage-way and whispered: 'I thought you said he couldn't act?'

'Nobody's ever paid him twenty-five thousand bucks a night before,' Smith said sardonically.

'Tut, Tut, General. Best Venetian glass.' Kramer shook his head deprecatingly then smiled. 'But an understandable fit of pique. When your heroic rescuers turn out to be, well, birds of a different feather—'

'Double agents!' In his contempt, Jones almost spat out the words.

Kramer smiled again, tolerantly, and turned to the three men on the couch.

'And the return trip, gentlemen? As well organized as your outward journey?'

'That's about the one thing the close-mouthed so-and-so told us,' Carraciola said with some bitterness. 'A Mosquito bomber is to come to pick us up. Salen, a little village north of Frauenfeld in Switzerland. There's a little civilian airfield just to the north of Salen.'

Schaffer bent across the passage again and said in an admiring whisper: 'You really are a fearful liar.'

'So Salen it is,' Kramer was saying. 'We know all about it. The Swiss are very good at looking the wrong way when it suits them: but for reasons of our own we find it convenient not to protest too much. Odd things happen at Salen . . . However, a little message to London. Arrange pick-up times and so forth. Then a helicopter to the border – so much easier than walking, gentlemen – a rubber dinghy for the Rhine and then a short walk. You'll be back in Whitehall, reporting General Carnaby's transfer to Berlin, before you know it.'

'Back in London?' Thomas shook his head in slow emphasis. 'Not on your nelly, Colonel. With Smith and that Yank still at large? What happens if they find out what's really happening? What happens if they remain at large? What happens if they get a message through to London—'

'What do you take us for?' Kramer said tiredly. 'You will also, of course, be reporting the unfortunate demise of your leader. As soon as we located that still-warm radio set in the left luggage office we put on bloodhounds from the barracks. Your precious Major Smith was the last man to handle that set and he left a pretty clear trail. The hounds traced him along the east side of the village as far as a garage and then up to the lower station of the *Luftseilbahn*.'

'The cable-car?' Thomas was frankly disbelieving.

'The cable-car. Our Major Smith is either a very foolhardy or a very dangerous man – I must confess I know nothing of him. And there, at the lower station, the hounds completely lost the scent. The handlers circled the station with the hounds and then brought them into the cable-car itself. But the trail was cold. Our quarry appeared to have vanished into thin air.

'It was then that one of the searchers had the original idea of examining the thin air, so to speak. He climbed up and examined the roof of the lower station. Surprise, surprise, unmistakable signs in the snow and ice that two men had been up there before him. From that it was only a logical step to examine the roof of the cable-car itself, and sure enough—'

'They're inside!' Christiansen exclaimed.

'And won't get out again.' Colonel Kramer leaned back comfortably in his chair. 'Have no fear, gentlemen. Every exit is blocked – including the header station. We've doubled the guards outside and the rest have just begun to carry out a floor to floor search.'

In the gloom of the minstrels' gallery Smith and Schaffer exchanged thoughtful glances.

'I don't know,' Thomas said uneasily. 'He's a resourceful devil—'

Kramer held up a hand.

'Fifteen minutes. I guarantee it.' He shifted his glance to Jones. 'I don't pretend to look forward to this, General, but shall we get on with your – ah – medication?'

Jones glared at Carraciola, Christiansen and Thomas and said, very slowly and distinctly: 'You – bloody – swine!'

'Against all my principles, General Carnaby,' Rosemeyer said uncomfortably. 'But if we could only dispense with force—'

'Principles? You make me sick!' Jones stood up and made a strangled noise in his throat. 'The hell with you all! The Hague Conventions! Principles! Officers and gentlemen of the Third bloody Reich!' He stripped off his uniform jacket, rolled up a sleeve and sat down again.

There was a brief and uncomfortable silence, then Kramer nodded to Anne-Marie who put down her glass and moved off to a side door leading off the gold drawing-room. It was obvious to everyone that Anne-Marie wasn't feeling in the least uncomfortable: the half-smile on her face was as near to that of pleasurable anticipation as she could permit herself in the presence of Rosemeyer and Kramer.

Again Smith and Schaffer exchanged glances, no longer thoughtful glances, but the glances of men who know what they have to do and are committed to doing it. Carefully, silently, they eased themselves up from the choir-stalls, adjusted the straps of their shoulder-slung Schmeissers until the machine-pistols were in the horizontal position then started slowly down the stairs, well apart and as close as possible to their respective banisters, to minimize the danger of creaking treads.

They were half-way down, just beginning to emerge from the dark gloom of the gallery, when Anne-Marie re-entered the room. She was carrying a small stainless steel tray: on the tray were a glass beaker, a phial containing some colourless liquid and a hypodermic syringe. She set the tray down on an occasional table close to Jones and broke the phial into the narrow beaker.

Smith and Schaffer had reached the foot of the stairs and were now advancing towards the group round the fire-place. They had now completely emerged from the shadows, and were in full view of anyone who cared to turn his head. But no one cared to turn his head. Every seated person in the drawing-room was engrossed in the scene before him, watching in varying degrees of willing or unwilling fascination as Anne-Marie carefully filled the hypodermic syringe and held it up to the light to examine it. Smith and Schaffer continued to advance, their footfalls soundless on the luxuriously deep pile of the gold carpet.

Carefully, professionally, but with the trace of the smile still on her lips, Anne-Marie swabbed an area of Jones's forearm with cotton wool soaked in alcohol and then, as the watchers unconsciously bent forward in their seats, picked up Jones's wrist in one hand and the hypodermic in the other. The hypodermic hovered over the swabbed area as she located the vein she wanted.

'Just a waste of good scopolamine, my dear,' Smith said. 'You won't get anything out of him.'

There was a moment's frozen and incredulous stillness, the hypodermic syringe fell soundlessly to the floor, then everyone whirled round to stare at the two advancing figures, carbines moving gently from side to side. Predictably, Colonel Kramer was the first to recover and react. Almost imperceptibly, his hand began to drift to a button on a panel beside his chair.

'That button, Colonel,' Smith said conversationally.

Slowly, reluctantly, Kramer's hand retreated from the button.

'On the other hand,' Smith went on cordially, 'why not? By all means, if you wish.'

Kramer glanced at him in narrow-eyed and puzzled suspicion.

'You will notice, Colonel,' Smith continued by way of explanation, 'that my gun is not pointing at you. It is pointed at him' – he swung his gun to cover Carraciola – 'at him,' – the gun moved to Thomas – 'at him,' – it covered Christiansen – 'and at him!' Smith swung round abruptly and ground the muzzle of the Schmeisser into Schaffer's ribs. 'Drop that gun! Now!'

'Drop the gun?' Schaffer stared at him in shock and baffled consternation. 'What in the name of God—'

Smith stepped swiftly forward and, without altering his grip on his gun, ifted the barrel sharply upwards and drove the butt of the Schmeisser into Schaffer's stomach. Schaffer grunted in agony, doubled forward with both hands clutched over his midriff, then, seconds later, obviously in great pain, began to straighten slowly. Glaring at Smith, the dark eyes mad in his face, he slipped the shoulder strap and the Schmeisser fell to the carpet.

'Sit there.' With the muzzle of his gun Smith gestured to a chair half-way between Rosemeyer's and the couch where the three men were sitting.

Schaffer said slowly, painfully: 'You goddamned lousy, dirty, double-crossing—'

'That's what they all say. You're not even original.' The contempt in Smith's voice gave way to menace. 'That chair, Schaffer.'

Schaffer lowered himself with difficulty into his chair, rubbed his solar plexus and said, 'You —. If I live to be a hundred—'

'If you live to be a hundred you'll do nothing,' Smith said contemptuously. 'In your own idiom, Schaffer, you're a punk and a pretty second-rate one at that.' He settled himself comfortably in a chair beside Colonel Kramer. 'A simple-minded American,' he explained carelessly. 'Had him along for local colour.'

'I see,' Kramer said. It was obvious that he did not see. He went on uncertainly: 'If we might have an explanation—'

Smith waved him negligently to silence.

'All in good time, my dear Kramer, all in good time. As I was saying, my dear Anne-Marie—'

'How did you know her name was Anne-Marie?' Kramer asked sharply.

Smith smiled enigmatically, ignored him completely, and continued: 'As I was saying, scopolamine is a waste of time. All scopolamine will do, as you're all aware, is to reveal the truth about our friend here, which is that he is not Lieutenant General George Carnaby, Chief Co-ordinator of Planning for the Second Front, but a certain Cartwright-Jones, an American actor being paid precisely twenty-five thousand dollars to impersonate General Carnaby.' He looked over to Jones and bowed. 'My congratulations, Mr Jones. A very creditable performance. Pity you'll have to spend the rest of the war in a concentration camp.'

Kramer and Rosemeyer were on their feet, the others leaning far forward on the couch, an almost exactly identical expression of disbelief showing in every face. If Cartwright Jones had been earth's first visitor from outer space he couldn't possibly have been the object of more incredulous consternation.

'Well, well, well,' Smith said with interest. 'Surprise, surprise, surprise.' He tapped Kramer on the arm and gestured in the direction of Carraciola, Thomas and Christiansen. 'Odd, wouldn't you say, Kramer? They seem just as astonished as you are?'

'Is this true?' Rosemeyer demanded hoarsely of Jones. 'What he says? Do you deny—'

In a voice that was no more than a whisper, Jones said: 'How - how in God's name - who *are* you, sir?'

'A stranger in the night.' Smith waved a hand. 'Dropped in in the passing, you might say. Maybe the Allies will let you have that twenty-five thousand after the war. I wouldn't bank on it though. If international law allows you to shoot a captured enemy soldier dressed as a civilian, maybe the opposite holds good too.' Smith stretched and politely patted a yawn to extinction. 'And now, Anne-Marie, if I could - with your permission, my dear Kramer - have a glass of that excellent Napoleon. Clinging to the roofs of cable-cars works the devil with my circulation.'

The girl hesitated, looked at Kramer and Rosemeyer, found neither encouragement nor discouragement, shrugged, poured a glass and handed it to Smith, who sniffed the bouquet approvingly, drank a little and bowed again to Jones.

'My congratulations, sir. You are a connoisseur.' He sipped again, turned to Kramer and said sadly: 'To think you have been wasting such excellent liquor on enemies of the Third Reich.'

'Don't listen to him, Colonel Kramer, don't listen to him!' Carraciola shouted wildly. 'It's a bluff! He's just trying—'

Smith lined up his gun on Carraciola's chest and said softly: 'Keep quiet or I'll make you quiet, you damned traitor. You'll have your chance - *and* we'll see who's bluffing.' He lowered his gun to his knees and went on tiredly: 'Colonel Kramer, I don't fancy talking and having to keep a gun on this unlovely trio all the time. Have you a guard you can trust? A man who won't talk afterwards, I mean?'

He sat back in his chair, sipped his brandy and ignored the malevolent stares from his four erstwhile colleagues. Kramer looked at him for a very long moment, then nodded thoughtfully and reached for a phone.

The armoury – now converted into a *Kaffeestube* – of the Schloss Adler was very much in keeping with the remainder of the castle, something out of a medieval dream or nightmare, according to how individual tastes and inclinations lay. It was a large, darkly-panelled, stone-flagged room with enormous adzecut smoke-blackened beams and walls behung with ancient and rusty suits of armour, ancient and rusty weapons of all kinds and scores of armorial bearings, some of which could have been genuine. Three-sided half-booths lined the walls and half-a-dozen slab-topped monastery refectory tables, flanked by massive oak benches, paralleled the shorter axis of the room. The oil lamps, suspended by iron chains from the ceiling, were turned low, lending the atmosphere in the armoury an air of intimacy or brooding menace, according to one's original mood on entering. There was no doubt in Mary's mind as to its effect upon her. Her gaze followed half-a-dozen heavily armed and jack-booted men who were just leaving the armoury, then came back reluctantly to the man sitting close beside her in the corner booth.

'Well, what did I tell you?' von Brauchitsch said expansively. 'Coffee to match the surroundings!'

Coffee to match the surroundings, Mary thought, would have tasted of hemlock. She said: 'What did those men want? They seemed to be looking for someone.'

'Forget them. Concentrate on von Brauchitsch.'

'But you spoke to them. What did they *want*?'

'They say there are spies in the castle!' Von Brauchitsch threw his head back, laughed, and spread his hands palms up. 'Imagine! Spies in the Schloss Adler! The Gestapo HQ! They must have flown in on their broom-sticks. The military commandant is an old woman. He has spies in about once a week. Now what was I saying about Düsseldorf?' He broke off, glancing at her empty coffee cup. 'My apologies, my dear Fräulein. Come, more coffee.'

'No, really. I must go.'

Von Brauchitsch laughed again and put his hand on hers.

'Go where? There *is* nowhere to go inside the Schloss Adler. Nonsense, nonsense.' He turned in his seat and called: 'Fräulein! Two more coffees. And with Schnapps, this time.'

While he was ordering, Mary glanced quickly at her watch and a momentary expression of desperation crossed her face, but by the time von Brauchitsch turned back she was smiling sweetly at him. She said: 'You were saying about Düsseldorf—'

The company in the gold drawing-room had now been increased by one, a tall, cold-faced and hard-eyed sergeant who held a carbine cradled in a pair of strong and very capable looking hands. He was standing behind the couch on which Carraciola, Thomas and Christiansen were seated, and he was giving them his entire attention, apart from a frequent sideways glance at Schaffer. He had about him a reassuring air of competence.

'A very much more civilized arrangement,' Smith said approvingly. He rose, leaving his Schmeisser lying on the floor, crossed to the brandy decanter on the sideboard, poured himself another drink and made his way back to the fireplace where he placed his glass on the mantelpiece.

'This will take but minutes, only,' Smith said in a soft and ominous voice.

'Anne-Marie, bring in three more capsules of scopolamine.' He smiled at her. 'And I needn't remind *you* to bring the hypodermics.'

'Colonel Kramer!' Carraciola said desperately. 'This is madness! Are you going to allow—'

'Guard!' Smith's voice was harsh. 'If that man talks again, silence him!'

The guard jabbed his carbine muzzle none too lightly into Carraciola's back. Carraciola subsided, fuming, his fists clenched till the ivory showed.

'What do you take Reichsmarschall Rosemeyer and Colonel Kramer for?' Smith demanded cuttingly. 'Credulous fools? Little children? Imbeciles of your own calibre, who imagine you can get away with a cretinous masquerade of this nature? The scopolamine will be used *after* I have established my own bona-fides and *after* I have disproved yours. Anne-Marie?'

Anne-Marie smiled and marched away. It was not every night that she got the chance to administer three injections of scopolamine. Then she stopped and turned, eyebrows raised in interrogation, as Smith called her name again.

'One moment, Fräulein.' Smith, brandy glass in hand, was staring unseeingly into the middle distance and the watchers could see a slow smile coming to his face, a smile obviously heralding the birth of a new idea and one that pleased him very much. 'Of course, of course,' Smith said softly. 'And bring three note-books will you, my dear?'

'*Three* note-books?' Colonel Kramer's tone was neutral, his eyes watchful. '*Three* capsules? You give the impression that we have *four* enemies of the Reich here.'

'Only three enemies that matter,' Smith said in weary patience. 'The American?' The fact that he neither bothered to glance at Schaffer nor even permit a trace of contempt to creep into his voice showed unmistakably his opinion of the American. 'He doesn't even know what day of the week it is. Now then.' He picked up a cigar from an inlaid marquetry box, lit it and sipped some more brandy. 'Let's be fair and establish my bona-fides first. Pointers first, then proof. In the best judicial fashion.

'First, why did I invite another guard in and lay down my own gun?' He paused and went on sarcastically: 'Of course! Because I wanted to increase the odds against myself. Secondly, why didn't I kill Colonel Weissner and his men when I had them at my mercy – if, that is, I'm an enemy of the Third Reich – earlier this evening? I had some difficulty, I might tell you, in restraining our fire-eating American here from turning himself into a one-man firing squad. Very aggressive, he was.'

'I'll damned well tell you why,' Carraciola said viciously. 'Because you knew the shots would be heard!'

Smith sighed, lifted the flap of his jacket, produced an automatic and fired. The sound of the impact of the bullet thudding into the couch inches from Carraciola's shoulder completely blanketed the soft plop made by the automatic itself. Smith carelessly threw the silenced Luger into a nearby empty chair and smiled quizzically at Carraciola.

'Didn't know I had that, did you? I didn't kill Colonel Weissner because German does not kill German.'

'You are German?' Kramer's eyes were still watchful but the tone perhaps a shade less neutral.

'Johann Schmidt, at your service.' This with a little bow and click of the heels. 'Captain John Smith of the Black Watch.'

'From the Rhineland, by your accent?'

'Heidelberg.'

'But that is *my* home town.'

'Indeed?' Smith smiled his interest. 'Then I think we have a mutual friend.'

Momentarily, a faraway look came to Kramer's eyes and he said softly, apparently apropos of nothing: 'The columns of Charlemagne.'

'Ah, and the fountain in the courtyard of the dear old Friedrichsbau,' Smith said nostalgically. He glanced at Kramer, and the nostalgia gave way to a pseudo-mournful reproof. 'How could you, my dear Colonel? To proceed. Why – third point, I think – why did I stage this elaborate car accident – because I *knew* those three impostors wouldn't dare come into the open until they thought I was dead. Anyway, if I *were* the impostor, would I have come back when I knew the game was up? Anyway, to come back for what?' He smiled wearily and nodded at Jones. 'To rescue *another* impostor?'

Kramer said thoughtfully: 'I must say I'm rather beginning to look forward to hearing what our three friends here have to say.'

'I'll tell you *now* what I've bloody well got to say.' Christiansen was on his feet, ignoring the guard's gun, his voice shaking with fury. 'He's fooling you, he's fooling all of us. He's a damned liar and you're too damned stupid to see the wool over your eyes. A tissue of — lies, from beginning to end—'

'That will do!' Kramer's hand was up, his eyes bleak, his tone icy. 'You condemn yourselves from your own mouths. Every statement made so far by this officer is demonstrably true. Sergeant Hartmann' – this to the guard with the carbine – 'if any of those men speak again, do you think you could silence him without silencing him permanently?'

Hartmann produced a small woven-leather truncheon from his tunic and slipped the looped thong over his wrist.

'You know I can, Herr Colonel.'

'Good. Pray continue, Captain Schmidt.'

'Thank you. I hadn't finished.' Smith felt like pouring himself another brandy, a celebration brandy or, alternatively, pinning a medal on Christiansen for having so unerringly if unwittingly exposed the chink in Kramer's armour, a wounded intellectual vanity, the lacerated professional pride of a brilliant man being reminded of his capacity for being duped by one of those who had already duped him. 'For the same excellent reason I came here by the roof of the cable-car – they'd *never* have come into the open if they'd known I was here – and alive. Incidentally, Kramer, hasn't it occurred to you that it's impossible to enter the Schloss Adler from the roof of the header station without the assistance of a rope and someone inside?'

'Damnation!' Coming so soon after Christiansen's reminder of his fallibility, Smith's question left Kramer's self-confidence badly shaken. 'I never thought—'

'Von Brauchitsch,' Smith said carelessly. 'He had his orders direct from Berlin.' He placed his glass on the mantelpiece, walked across and stood before the three spies. 'Tell me, how did I know Jones was an impostor? Why did you *not* know he was one? And if I'm not what I claim to be then what in God's name am I doing here at all? Perhaps you would like to explain that?'

The three men glanced up at him in baleful silence.

'Perhaps they would indeed,' Kramer said heavily. He came and stood by Smith, staring down at the three men with an oddly expressionless gaze that was more disturbing than any show of anger could ever have been. After another and longer silence he said: 'Captain Schmidt, this has gone far enough.'

'Not yet.'

'I require no more,' Kramer persisted.

'I promised you proof – those were but the pointers. A proof to satisfy the Deputy Chief of the German Secret Service – and that proof is in three parts. A yes or no, Colonel Kramer, if you please. Do you or do you not know the name of our top man in Britain?' Kramer nodded. 'Then suppose we ask them?'

The three men on the couch looked at each other, then at Smith. They looked in silence. Thomas licked dry lips, a movement that did not go unnoticed by Kramer. Smith produced a small red note-book from his tunic pocket, removed a rubber band, tore out the central page, then carefully replaced the band on the book and the book in his pocket. He wrote something on the page and handed it to Kramer, who glanced at it and nodded. Smith took the paper from him, walked across to the fire and burned it.

'Now then,' Smith said. 'You have here, in the Schloss Adler, the most powerful radio transmitter in Central Europe—'

'You are singularly well-informed, Captain Schmidt,' Kramer said wryly.

'Smith. I live Smith. I breathe Smith. I *am* Smith. Put a radio-telephone call through to Field-Marshal Kesselring's HQ in Northern Italy. Ask for his Chief of Military Intelligence.'

Kramer said softly: 'The mutual friend you mentioned?'

'An old alumnus of Heidelberg University,' Smith nodded. 'Colonel Wilhelm Wilner.' He smiled. 'Willi-Willi.'

'You know that? Then it will not be necessary to call him.'

'Admiral Canaris would like you to.'

'And you know my chief, too?' Kramer's voice was even softer.

'My self-esteem urges me to say that I do – but modesty and the truth compels me to admit I don't,' Smith said disarmingly. 'I just work for him.'

'I'm convinced already, convinced beyond all doubt,' Rosemeyer said. 'But do as he says, Colonel.'

Kramer did as he was told. He put a call through to the radio room, hung up and waited patiently. Smith lay back in his armchair, brandy in one hand, cigar in the other, the picture of relaxed confidence. If Schaffer and the three men on the couch beside him were either relaxed or confident they entirely failed to show it. Behind them their guard watched his four charges hopefully, as if eager to show his expertise with a blackjack. If either Rosemeyer or Jones were thinking any thoughts at all, those thoughts didn't break through to the surface. Anne-Marie, not quite knowing what was going on, hovered around indecisively, a tentative smile of anticipation still on her face. She was the only person who moved during the period of waiting and that only because Smith crooked a finger at her and indicated his empty brandy glass: so complete was the ascendancy he had achieved that she obeyed the unspoken command without hesitation and brought back a very generous measure of brandy which she set down on his side-table to the accompaniment of a winning smile. Smith gave her a winning smile in return. But no one spoke, not once, during that seemingly interminable wait.

The phone bell rang.

Kramer lifted it and, after a few preliminary exchanges, presumably with operators, said: 'Colonel Wilhelm Wilner. My dear friend, Willi-Willi. How are you.' After the introductory courtesies were over, Kramer said: 'We have an agent here who claims to know you. A Captain John Smith. Have you ever – ah, so you know him? Good, good!' A pause, then he continued: 'Could you describe him?'

He listened intently, looking at Smith as a voice crackled over the receiver. Suddenly he beckoned to Smith, who rose and crossed over to where Kramer was sitting.

'Your left hand,' Kramer said to Smith, took it in his own, then spoke into the phone. 'Yes, the tip of the little finger is missing ... and the right forearm has what?' Smith bared his right forearm without being told. 'Yes, yes, two parallel scars, three centimetres apart ... What's that? ... Tell him he's a traitor?'

'And tell him he's a renegade.' Smith smiled.

'And you're a renegade,' Kramer said on the phone. 'Chambertin, you say. Ah! Thank you, thank you. Goodbye, my old friend.' He replaced the receiver.

'We both prefer French wine,' Smith said apologetically and by way of explanation.

'Our top double agent in the Mediterranean,' Kramer said wonderingly. 'And I'd never even heard of you.'

'Maybe that's why he is what he is,' Rosemeyer said dryly.

'I've been lucky.' Smith shrugged then said briskly: 'Well, then. My credentials?'

'Impeccable,' Kramer said. 'My God, they're impeccable.'

'So,' Smith said grimly. 'Now for our friends' credentials. As you know, Christiansen, Thomas and Carraciola – the real Christiansen, Thomas and Carraciola – while working for—'

'What in God's name are you talking about?' Christiansen shouted. He was on his feet, his face suffused with uncontrollable anger. 'The real Christiansen—' His eyes turned up as Hartmann's blackjack caught him behind the ear and he sagged to the floor.

'He was warned,' Kramer said grimly. 'You didn't hit him too hard, Sergeant?'

'A two-minute tap,' Hartmann said reassuringly.

'Good. I think you may now proceed without interruption, my dear Schmidt.'

'Smith,' Smith corrected him. 'As I was saying, our real agents while working for the British counter-espionage have not only been responsible for the deep infiltration of the German Secret Service into the British espionage network in France and the Low Countries but have also set up an excellent chain of spies in England – a most successful ring, as Admiral Canaris well knows.'

'It's not my territory,' Kramer said. 'But that, of course, I know.'

Smith said coldly: 'To your feet, you impostors, and sit at the table there. Sergeant, lend a hand to that man on the floor there. He appears to be coming round.'

Their faces baffled and uncomprehending, Carraciola and Thomas made their way towards the table and sat down, where they were shortly joined by a very shaky and sick-looking Christiansen. The sergeant remained by him just long enough to ensure that he didn't fall off his chair, then took three paces back and covered them all with his carbine again.

From the other side of the table Smith flung down in front of the three men the little note-books that Anne-Marie had brought. Then he produced his own elastic-banded note-book from his pocket and laid it on the small table beside Kramer.

'If they are who they claim to be,' Smith said quietly, 'it would be reasonable, would it not, my dear Kramer, to expect them to be able to write the names and the addresses or contacts of our agents in England and of the British agents who have been supplanted on the Continent by our men.' He paused significantly. 'And then compare their lists with the genuine one in my book there.'

'It would indeed,' Kramer said slowly. 'Proof at one stroke. Masterly, my dear Captain Schmidt – Smith, I mean.' He smiled, almost wanly. 'I'm afraid I'm not myself tonight. But tell me, Captain.' He touched the banded note-book by his side. 'This list of agents – I mean, carrying it around on your person. Does this not contravene every rule we have?'

'Of course it does. Rules can only be broken by the man who made them. You think that even I would dare without his authority? Admiral Walter Canaris will be in his Berlin office now.' Smith nodded towards the telephone.

'What do you take me for.' Kramer smiled and turned to the three men at the table. 'Well, you heard.'

'There's something terribly far wrong—' Carraciola began despairingly.

'There is indeed,' Kramer interrupted bleakly.

'I don't *doubt* Smith's bona-fides.' Carraciola was almost in anguish now. 'Not any more. But there's been some ghastly mistake—'

'You are the ones who have made it,' Smith said curtly.

'Write,' Kramer commanded. 'Sergeant Hartmann.'

Sergeant Hartmann stepped forward, his leather-thonged blackjack at the ready. The three men bent their heads and wrote.

Chapter Eight

The armoury was almost deserted now. Some time previously, a couple of sergeants had entered, moved around among the coffee tables and taken at least a score of grumbling men away for unspecified duties. Mary did not have to guess at what those unspecified duties might be. She glanced secretly at her watch for what must have been the twentieth time, rubbed her forehead wearily, rose to her feet and smiled palely at von Brauchitsch.

'I'm so sorry, Captain. I must go. I really must go. A most dreadful headache.'

'I *am* sorry, my dear Maria.' A troubled contrition had replaced his habitual smile. 'You should have told me earlier. You don't look at all well. A long journey from the Rhineland, then all this Schnapps—'

'I'm afraid I'm not used to it,' Mary said ruefully. 'I'll be all right when I've lain down.'

'Of course, of course. Come, my dear, let me escort you to your room.'

'No, no!' Then, realizing she had spoken with uncalled-for vehemence, she smiled again and touched his hand. 'I'll be all right. Really I will.'

'Captain von Brauchitsch knows what's best.' The face was serious but friendly, the voice authoritative but with an underlying tone of humour, and Mary knew there was no answer to it. 'I positively insist. Come along.'

He tucked her arm protectively under his and led her from the armoury.

Arm in arm they walked along the passage-way leading from the armoury-cum-*Kaffeestube* towards the central block of the castle. The passage-way, in contrast to the last time they had walked along there, was completely deserted and Mary commented on the fact.

'It's the witches on their broomsticks,' von Brauchitsch laughed. 'The commandant hasn't caught them yet, but give him another few years and you never know. All those poor souls you saw being hauled out of the armoury are now probably poking about the eaves or climbing up the flagpoles. You never know where spies get to nowadays.'

'You seem to treat the possibility lightly enough,' Mary said.

'I'm a Gestapo officer. I'm paid and trained to use my head, not an overheated imagination,' he said curtly, then squeezed her arm and apologized. 'Sorry, that tone of voice was aimed at someone else, not you.' He halted abruptly, peered out a window into the courtyard and said: 'Now that is strange.'

'What's strange?'

'The helicopter there,' von Brauchitsch said thoughtfully. 'Army regulations state that High Command helicopters must be kept in instant readiness at all times. But that one has part of its engine cover dismantled and a tarpaulin stretched in position over it. Wouldn't call that instant readiness, would you?'

'I suppose helicopters need repairing from time to time the same as any other machine.' Her throat was suddenly dry and she wished von Brauchitsch wouldn't hold her so closely: he was bound to notice her accelerating heart-beat. 'What's so unusual about that?'

'What's so unusual is that there was no one working on that machine almost half an hour ago when we first passed by here,' von Brauchitsch said. 'Unheard of for a Reichsmarschall's personal pilot to walk away and leave a job half done.'

'Would it be unheard of for him to take a piece of mechanism inside and repair it under cover?' Mary asked sweetly. 'Or perhaps you haven't seen a thermometer tonight?'

'I'm getting as bad as the old commandant and his witch-hunts,' von Brauchitsch said sadly. He moved on, shaking his head. 'You see before you a horrible example of the dangers of being too long in my business: the obvious answer is far too obvious for shrewd and cunning intellects like ours. I must remember that later on tonight.'

'You're going to exercise this great mind again tonight?' Mary asked lightly.

'In there, as a matter of fact.' Von Brauchitsch nodded as they passed by an ornate door. 'The gold drawing-room.' He glanced at his watch. 'In twenty minutes! So soon! Your charming company, Fräulein.'

'Thank you, kind sir. You – you have an appointment?' Her heart was back at its old tricks again.

'An evening of musical appreciation. Even the Gestapo has its finer side. We are going to listen to a nightingale sing.' He quickened his pace. 'Sorry, Fräulein, but I've just remembered I've one or two reports to prepare.'

'I'm sorry if I've kept you from your work, Captain,' she said demurely. How much does he know, she thought wildly, how much does he suspect, what action has he suddenly decided to take? The von Brauchitschs of this world didn't just suddenly remember anything for the excellent reason that they never forgot it in the first place. 'It's been most kind of you.'

'The pleasure was one-sided,' von Brauchitsch protested gallantly. 'Mine and mine alone.' He stopped outside her bedroom door, took her hand in his and smiled. 'Goodnight, my dear Maria. You really are the most charming girl.'

'Goodnight.' She returned smile for smile. 'And thank you.'

'We really must get to know each other better,' von Brauchitsch said in farewell. He opened her door, bowed, kissed her hand, gently closed the door behind her and rubbed his chin thoughtfully. 'Very much better, my dear Maria,' he said softly to himself. 'Very much better indeed.'

Carraciola, Thomas and Christiansen bent over their notebooks and scribbled furiously. At least the first two did: Christiansen had not yet recovered from the blow on the head and was making heavy weather of his writing. Kramer, who was standing apart with Smith and talking to him in low tones, looked at them in curiosity and with just a trace of uneasiness.

'They seem to be finding plenty of inspiration from somewhere,' he said carefully.

'The spectacle of an open grave is often thought-provoking,' Smith said cynically.

'I am afraid I don't quite follow.'

'Do you know what those men will be fifteen minutes from now?'

'I'm tired,' Kramer said. He sounded it. 'Please don't play with words, Captain Schmidt.'

'Smith. In fifteen minutes they'll be dead. And they know it. They're fighting desperately for extra minutes to live: when you have as little time as they have, even a minute is a prize snatched from eternity. Or the last despairing fling of the ruined gambler. Call it what you like.'

'You wax lyrical, Captain,' Kramer grumbled. He paced up and down for almost a minute, no longer troubling to watch the men at the table, then stopped and planted himself squarely in front of Smith. 'All right,' he said wearily. 'I've been on the spit long enough. I confess I'm baffled. Out with it. What in God's name is behind all this?'

'The simplicity of true genius, my dear Kramer. Admiral Rolland, the head of MI6. And he *is* a genius, make no mistake.'

'So he's a genius,' Kramer said impatiently. 'Well?'

'Carraciola, Thomas and Christiansen were caught three weeks ago. Now, as you are aware, they were concerned only with north-west Europe and were not known here.'

'By reputation, they were.'

'Yes, yes. But only that. Admiral Rolland reckoned that if three fully-briefed men impersonated our three captured men and were despatched here for a perfectly plausible reason, they would be *persona grata* of some note, honoured guests and completely accepted by you. And, of course, once they were accepted by you, they could operate inside the Schloss Adler with complete security and safety.'

'And?'

'Well, don't you see?' It was Smith's turn to be impatient. 'Rolland knew that if General Carnaby—' he broke off and scowled across the room at Carnaby-Jones – 'or that impostor masquerading as General Carnaby were taken here, his opposite number in the German Army would be sent to interrogate him.' Smith smiled. 'Even in Britain they are aware that the prophet must go to the mountain, not the mountain to the prophet: the Army calls upon the Gestapo, not vice versa.'

'Go on, go on!'

'The Wehrmacht Chief of Staff, Reichsmarschall Julius Rosemeyer, would have been just as priceless to the Allies as General Carnaby to us.'

'The Reichsmarschall!' Kramer spoke in a shocked whisper, his eyes straying across the room to Rosemeyer. 'Kidnap!'

'Your precious trusted agents there,' Smith said savagely. 'And they would have got away with it.'

'My God! God in heaven! It's – it's diabolical!'

'Isn't it?' Smith said. 'Isn't it just?'

Kramer left him abruptly, crossed the room to Rosemeyer and sat down in the chair beside him. For perhaps two minutes they talked together in low tones, occasionally glancing in Smith's direction. Kramer it was, Smith could see, who did most of the talking. Rosemeyer who did all of the reacting. Kramer, Smith reflected, must be putting it across rather well: a printed diagram could have been no clearer than the successive expressions of curiosity, puzzlement, astonishment and, finally, shocked realization that reflected on Rosemeyer's face. After some seconds' silence, both men rose to their feet and walked across to where Smith stood. The Reichsmarschall, Smith saw, was a little paler than normal, and when he spoke it required neither a sensitive ear nor imagination to detect a slight tremor in his voice.

He said: 'This is an incredible story, Captain Smith, incredible. But inevitable. It must be. The only explanation that can cover all the facts, put all the pieces of the jig-saw together.' He attempted a smile. 'To change the metaphor, I must say that it comes as a considerable shock to find that one is the missing key in a baffling code. I am eternally in your debt, Captain Smith.'

'Germany is eternally in your debt,' Kramer said. 'You have done her a great service. We shall not forget this. I am sure the Führer will personally wish to honour you with some mark of his esteem.'

'You are too kind, gentlemen,' Smith murmured. 'To do my duty is reward enough.' He smiled faintly. 'Perhaps our Führer will give me two or three weeks' leave – the way I feel tonight my nerves aren't what they were. But if you gentlemen will excuse me – my present task is not yet completed.'

He moved away and walked slowly up and down, brandy glass in hand, behind the three men bent over the table. From time to time he glanced at one of the note-books and smiled in weary cynicism, neither the smile nor the significance of the smile going unremarked by anyone in the room except the three writing men. He stopped behind Thomas, shook his head in disbelief and said, 'My God!'

'Let's finish it now!' Rosemeyer demanded impatiently.

'If you please, Reichsmarschall, let us play this charade out to the bitter end.'

'You have your reasons?'

'I most certainly have.'

Briskly, but not hurriedly, von Brauchitsch walked away from Mary's room, his footfalls echoing crisply on the stone-flagged corridor. Once round the corner of the corridor he broke into a run.

He reached the courtyard and ran across to the helicopter. There was no one there. Quickly he ran up a few steps and peered through the Perspex cupola of the cockpit. He reached ground again and hailed the nearest guard, who came stumbling across, a leashed Dobermann trailing behind him.

'Quickly,' von Brauchitsch snapped. 'Have you seen the pilot?'

'No, Herr Major,' the guard answered nervously. He was an elderly man, long past front-line service and held the Gestapo in great fear. 'Not for a long time.'

'What do you mean by a long time?' von Brauchitsch demanded.

'I don't know. That's to say,' the guard added hastily, 'half an hour. More. Three-quarters, I would say, Herr Major.'

'Damnation,' von Brauchitsch swore. 'So long. Tell me, when the pilot is carrying out repairs is there a place near here he uses as a work-shop?'

'Yes, sir.' The guard was eager to oblige with some positive information. 'That door there, sir. The old grain store.'

'Is he in there now?'

'I don't know, Herr Major.'

'You should know,' von Brauchitsch said coldly. 'It's your job to keep your eyes open. Well, just don't stand there, oaf! Go and find out!'

The elderly guard trotted away while von Brauchitsch, shaking his head angrily over his impatience with the old soldier, crossed the courtyard and questioned the guards at the gate, three tough, competent, young storm-troopers who, unlike the patrol guard, could be guaranteed not to miss anything. He received the same negative answer there.

He strode back towards the helicopter and intercepted the elderly guard running from the old grain store.

'There's nobody there, Herr Major.' He was slightly out of breath and highly apprehensive at being the bearer of what might be ill news. 'It's empty.'

'It would be,' von Brauchitsch nodded. He patted the old shoulder and smiled. 'No fault of yours, my friend. You keep a good watch.'

Unhurriedly, almost, now, he made for the main entrance door, pulling out a set of master keys as he went. He struck oil with the first door he opened. The pilot lay there, still unconscious, the smashed distributor cap lay beside him, the pair of overalls lying on top of him a mute but entirely sufficient explanation of the way in which the distributor cap had been removed without detection. Von Brauchitsch took a torch from a long rack on the wall, cut the pilot's bonds, freed his gag and left him lying there with the door wide open. The passage outside was a heavily travelled one, and someone was bound to be along soon.

Von Brauchitsch ran up the stairs to the passage leading to the bedrooms, slowed down, walked easily, casually past Mary's bedroom and stopped at the fifth door beyond that. He used his master keys and passed inside, switching on the light as he went in. He crossed the room, lifted the lower sash window and nodded when he saw that nearly all the snow on the sill had been brushed or rubbed away. He leaned farther out, switched on his torch and flashed the beam downwards. The roof of the header station was fifty feet directly below and the markings and footprints in the snow told their own unmistakable story.

Von Brauchitsch straightened, looked at the odd position of the iron bedstead against the wardrobe door and tugged the bed away. He watched the wardrobe door burst open and the bound and gagged figure inside roll to the floor without as much as hoisting an eyebrow. This had been entirely predictable. From the depths of the bound man's groans it was obvious that he was coming round. Von Brauchitsch cut him free, removed his gag and left. There were more urgent matters demanding his attention than holding the hands of young Oberleutnants as they held their heads and groaned their way back to consciousness.

He stopped outside Mary's room, put his ear to the door and listened. No sound. He put his eye to the keyhole and peered. No light. He knocked. No reply. He used his master keys and passed inside. No Mary.

'Well, well, well,' von Brauchitsch murmured. 'Very interesting indeed.'

'Finished?' Smith asked.

Thomas nodded. Christiansen and Carraciola glowered. But all three were sitting back and it was obvious that all three were, in fact, finished. Smith walked along behind them, reaching over their shoulders for the note-books. He took them across the room and laid them on the little table by Kramer's chair.

'The moment of truth,' Smith said quietly. 'One book should be enough.'

Kramer, reluctantly almost, picked up the top book and began to read. Slowly he began to leaf his way through the pages. Smith drained his glass and sauntered unconcernedly across the room to the decanter on the sideboard. He poured some brandy, carefully recapped the bottle, walked a few aimless steps and halted. He was within two feet of the guard with the carbine.

He sipped his brandy and said to Kramer: 'Enough?'

Kramer nodded.

'Then compare it with my original.'

Kramer nodded. 'As you say, the moment of truth.'

He picked up the note-book, slid off the rubber band and opened the cover. The first page was blank. So was the next. And the next . . . Frowning, baffled, Kramer lifted his eyes to look across the room to Smith.

Smith's brandy glass was falling to the ground as Smith himself, with a whiplash violent movement of his body brought the side of his right hand chopping down on the guard's neck. The guard toppled as if a bridge had fallen on him. Glasses on the sideboard tinkled in the vibration of his fall.

Kramer's moment of utter incomprehension vanished. The bitter chagrin of total understanding flooded his face. His hand stretched out towards the alarm button.

'Uh-uh! Not the buzzer, Mac!' The blow that had struck down the guard had held no more whiplash than the biting urgency in Schaffer's voice. He was stretched his length on the floor where he'd dived to retrieve the Schmeisser now trained, rock steady, on Kramer's heart. For the second time that night, Kramer's hand withdrew from the alarm button.

Smith picked up the guard's carbine, walked across the room and changed it for his silenced Luger. Schaffer, his gun still trained on Kramer, picked himself up from the floor and glared at Smith.

'A second-rate punk,' he said indignantly. 'A simple-minded American. That's what you said. Don't know what goddamned day of the week it is, do I?'

'All I could think of on the spur of the moment,' Smith said apologetically.

'That makes it even worse,' Schaffer complained. 'And did you have to clobber me so goddamned realistically?'

'Local colour. What are you complaining about? It worked.' He walked across to Kramer's table, picked up the three notebooks and buttoned them securely inside his tunic. He said to Schaffer: 'Between them, they shouldn't have missed anything . . . Well, time to be gone. Ready, Mr Jones?'

'And hurry about it,' Schaffer added. 'We have a street-car to catch. Well, anyhow, a cable-car.'

'It's a chicken farm in the boondocks for me.' Jones looked completely dazed and he sounded exactly the same way. 'Acting? My God, I don't know anything about it.'

'This is all you want?' Kramer was completely under control again, calm, quiet, the total professional. 'Those books? Just those books?'

'Well, just about. Lots of nice names and addresses. A bedtime story for MI6.'

'I see.' Kramer nodded his understanding. 'Then those men are, of course, what they claim to be?'

'They've been under suspicion for weeks. Classified information of an invaluable nature was going out and false – and totally valueless – information was coming in. It took two months' work to pin-point the leakages and channels of false information to one or more of the departments controlled by those men. But we knew we could never prove it on them – we weren't even sure if there was more than one traitor and had no idea who that one might be – and, in any event, proving it without finding out their contacts at home and abroad would have been useless. So we – um – thought this one up.'

'You mean, *you* thought it up, Captain Smith,' Rosemeyer said.

'What does it matter?' Smith said indifferently.

'True. It doesn't. But something else does.' Rosemeyer smiled faintly. 'When Colonel Kramer asked you if the books were all you wanted, you said "just about". Indicating that there was possibly something else. It is your hope to kill two birds with one stone, to invite me to accompany you?'

'If you can believe that, Reichsmarschall Rosemeyer,' Smith said unkindly, 'it's time you handed your baton over to someone else. I have no intention of binding you hand and foot and carrying you over the Alps on my shoulder. The only way I could take you is at the point of a gun and I very much fear that you are a man of honour, a man to whom the safety of his skin comes a very long way behind his loyalty to his country. If I pointed this gun at you and said to get up and come with us or be gunned down, nobody in this room doubts that you'd just keep on sitting. So we must part.'

'You are as complimentary as you are logical.' Rosemeyer smiled, a little, bitter smile. 'I wish the logic had struck me as forcibly when we were discussing this very subject a few minutes ago.'

'It is perhaps as well it didn't,' Smith admitted.

'But – but Colonel Wilner?' Kramer said. 'Field-Marshal Kesselring's Chief of Intelligence. Surely he's not—'

'Rest easy. Willi-Willi is not on our pay-roll. What he said he believed to be perfectly true. He believes me to be the top double-agent in Italy. I've been feeding him useless, false and out-of-date information for almost two years. Tell him so, will you?'

'Kind of treble agent, see?' Schaffer said in a patient explaining tone. 'That's one better than double.'

'Heidelberg?' Kramer asked.

'Two years at the University. Courtesy of the – um – Foreign Office.'

Kramer shook his head. 'I still don't understand—'

'Sorry. We're going.'

'In fact, we're off,' Schaffer said. 'Read all about it in the post-war memoirs of Pimpernel Schaffer—'

He broke off as the door opened wide. Mary stood framed in the doorway and the Mauser was very steady in her hand. She let it fall to her side with a sigh of relief.

'Took your time about getting here, didn't you?' Smith said severely. 'We were beginning to get a little worried about you.'

'I'm sorry. I just couldn't get away. Von Brauchitsch—'

'No odds, young lady.' Schaffer made a grandiose gesture with his right arm. 'Schaffer was here.'

'The new girl who arrived tonight!' Kramer whispered. He looked slightly dazed. 'The cousin of that girl from the—'

'None else,' Smith said. 'She's the one who has been helping me to keep Willi-Willi happy for a long time past. *And* she's the one who opened the door for us tonight.'

'Boss,' Schaffer said unhappily. 'Far be it for me to rush you—'

'Coming now.' Smith smiled at Rosemeyer. 'You were right, the books weren't all I wanted. You were right, I did want company. But unlike you, Reichsmarschall, those I want have a high regard for their own skins and are entirely without honour. And so they will come.' His gun waved in the direction of Carraciola, Thomas and Christiansen. 'On your feet, you three. You're coming with us.'

'Coming with us?' Schaffer said incredulously. 'To England?'

'To stand trial for treason. It's no part of my duties to act as public executioner . . . God alone knows how many hundreds and thousands of lives they've cost already. Not to mention Torrance-Smythe and Sergeant Harrod.' He looked at Carraciola, and his eyes were very cold. 'I'll never know, but I think you were the brains. It was you who killed Harrod back up there on the mountain. If you could have got that radio code-book you could have cracked our network in South Germany. That would have been something, our network here has never been penetrated. The radio code-book was a trap that didn't spring . . . And you got old Smithy. You left the pub a couple of minutes after I did tonight and he followed you. But he couldn't cope with a man—'

'Drop those guns.' Von Brauchitsch's voice was quiet and cold and compelling. No one had heard or seen the stealthy opening of the door. He stood just inside, about four feet from Mary and he had a small-calibre automatic in his right hand. Smith whirled round, his Luger lining up on the doorway, hesitated a fatal fraction of a second because Mary was almost directly in line with von Brauchitsch. Von Brauchitsch, his earlier gallantry of the evening yielding to a coldly professional assessment of the situation, had no such inhibitions. There was a sharp flat crack, the bullet passed through Mary's sleeve just above the elbow and Smith exclaimed in pain as he clutched his bleeding hand and heard his flying Luger strike against some unidentified furniture. Mary tried to turn round but von Brauchitsch was too quick and too strong. He jumped forward, hooked his arm round her and caught her wrist with the gun and thrust his own over her shoulder. She tried to struggle free. Von Brauchitsch squeezed her wrist, she cried out in pain, her hand opened and her gun fell to the floor. Von Brauchitsch seemed to notice none of this, his unwinking right eye, the only vulnerable part of him that could be seen behind Mary's gun, was levelled along the barrel of his automatic.

Schaffer dropped his gun.

'You shouldn't have tried it,' von Brauchitsch said to Smith. 'An extremely silly thing to do . . . In your circumstances, I'd have done exactly the same silly thing.' He looked at Kramer. 'Sorry for the delay, Herr Colonel. But I *thought* the young lady was very anxious and restive. *And* she knows precious little about her native Düsseldorf. *And* she doesn't know enough not to let people hold her hand when she's telling lies – as she does most of the time.' He released the girl and half turned her round, smiling down at her. 'A delightful hand, my dear – but what a fascinating variation of pulse rates.'

'I don't know what you're talking about and I don't care.' Kramer gave vent to a long luxurious sigh and drooped with relief. 'Well *done*, my boy, well done. My God! Another minute—' He heaved himself to his feet, crossed over to Schaffer, prudently keeping clear of von Brauchitsch's line of fire, searched him for hidden weapons, found none, did the same to Smith with the same results, looked at Mary and hesitated. 'Well, I don't see how she very well can be, but . . . I wonder. Anne-Marie?'

'Certainly, Herr Colonel. It will be a pleasure. We've met before and she knows my methods. Don't you my dear?' With a smile as nearly wolf-like as any beautiful Aryan could give, Anne-Marie walked across to Mary and struck her viciously across the face. Mary cried in pain, staggered back against the wall and crouched there, eyes too wide in a pale face, palms pressed behind her for support from the wall, a trickle of blood coming from the corner of her mouth. 'Well?' Anne-Marie demanded. 'Have you a gun.'

'Anne-Marie!' There was protest and aversion in Kramer's face. 'Must you—'

'I know how to deal with cheap little spies like her!' She turned to Mary and said: 'I'm afraid they don't like watching how I get results. In there!'

She caught Mary by the hair, pulled her to the side door, opened it and pushed her violently inside. The sound of her body crashing to the floor and another gasp of pain came together. Anne-Marie closed the door behind them.

For the next ten seconds or so there could be clearly heard the sound of blows and muffled cries of pain. Von Brauchitsch waved Smith and Schaffer back with his gun, advanced, hitched a seat on the edge of one of the big arm-chairs, winced as he listened to the sound of the struggle and said to Kramer dryly: 'I somehow think the young lady would have preferred me to search her. There's a limit to the value of false modesty.'

'I'm afraid Anne-Marie sometimes lets her enthusiasm carry her away,' Kramer conceded. His mouth was wrinkled in distaste.

'Sometimes?' Von Brauchitsch winced again as more sounds filtered through the door, the crash of a body against a wall, a shriek of pain, low sobbing moans, then silence. 'Always. When the other girl is as young and beautiful as herself.'

'It's over now,' Kramer sighed. 'It's all over now.' He looked at Smith and Schaffer. 'We'll fix that hand first, then – well, one thing about the Schloss Adler, there is no shortage of dungeons.' He broke off, the fractional widening of his eyes matching a similar slumping of his shoulders, and he said carefully to von Brauchitsch: 'You are far too good a man to lose, Captain. It would seem that we were wasting our sympathy on the wrong person. There's a gun four feet from you pointing at the middle of your back.'

Von Brauchitsch, his gun-hand resting helplessly on his thigh, turned slowly round and looked over his shoulder. There was indeed a gun pointing at the middle of his back, a Lilliput .21 automatic, and the hand that held it was disconcertingly steady, the dark eyes cool and very watchful. Apart from the small trickle of blood from her cut lip and rather dishevelled hair, Mary looked singularly little the worse for wear.

'It's every parent's duty,' Schaffer said pontifically, 'to encourage his daughter to take up Judo.' He took the gun from von Brauchitsch's unresisting hand, retrieved his own Schmeisser, walked across to the main door and locked it. 'Far too many folk coming in here without knocking.' On his way back he looked through the open door of the room, whistled, grinned and said to Mary: 'It's a good job I have my thoughts set on someone else. I wouldn't like to be married to you if you lost your temper. That's a regular sickbay dispensary in there. Fix the major's hand as best you can. I'll watch them.' He hoisted his Schmeisser and smiled almost blissfully: 'Oh, brother, how I'll watch them.'

And he watched them. While Mary attended to Smith's injured hand in the small room where Anne-Marie had so lately met her Waterloo, Schaffer herded his six charges into one of the massive couches, took up position by the mantelpiece, poured himself some brandy, sipped it delicately and gave the prisoners an encouraging smile from time to time. There were no answering smiles. For all Schaffer's nonchalance and light-hearted banter there was about him not only a coldly discouraging competence with the weapon in his hand but also the unmistakable air of one who would, when the need arose and without a second's hesitation, squeeze the trigger and keep on squeezing it. Being at the wrong end of a Schmeisser machine-pistol does not make for an easy cordiality in relationships.

Smith and Mary emerged from the side room, the latter carrying a cloth-covered tray. Smith was pale and had his right hand heavily bandaged. Schaffer looked at the hand then lifted an enquiring eyebrow to Mary.

'Not so good.' She looked a little pale herself. 'Forefinger and thumb are both smashed. I've patched it as best I can but I'm afraid it's a job for a surgeon.'

'If I can survive Mary's first aid,' Smith said philosophically, 'I can survive anything. We have a more immediate little problem here.' He tapped his tunic. 'Those names and addresses here. Might be an hour or two before we get them through to England and then another hour or two before those men can be rounded up.' He looked at the men seated on the couch. '*You* could get through to them in a lot less than that and warn them. So we have to ensure your silence for a few hours.'

'We could ensure it for ever, boss,' Schaffer said carelessly.

'That won't be necessary. As you said yourself, it's a regular little dispensary in there.' He removed the tray cloth to show bottles and hypodermic syringes. He held up a bottle in his left hand. 'Nembutal. You'll hardly feel the prick.'

Kramer stared at him. 'Nembutal? I'll be damned if I do.'

Smith said in a tone of utter conviction: 'You'll be dead if you don't.'

Chapter Nine

Smith halted outside the door marked RADIO RAUM, held up his hand for silence, looked at the three scowling captives and said: 'Don't even *think* of tipping anyone off or raising the alarm. I'm not all that keen on taking you back to England. Lieutenant Schaffer, I think we might immobilize those men a bit more.'

'We might at that,' Schaffer agreed. He went behind each of the three men in turn, ripped open the top buttons on their tunics and pulled the tunics down their backs until their sleeves reached their elbows and said in the same soft voice: 'That'll keep their hands out of trouble for a little.'

'But not their feet. Don't let them come anywhere near you,' Smith said to Mary. 'They've nothing to lose. Right, Lieutenant, when you're ready.'

'Ready now.' Carefully, silently, Schaffer eased open the door of the radio room. It was a large, well-lit, but very bleak room, the two main items of furniture being a massive table by the window on the far wall and, on the table, an almost equally massive transceiver in gleaming metal: apart from two chairs and a filing cabinet the room held nothing else, not even as much as a carpet to cover the floorboards.

Perhaps it was the lack of a carpet that betrayed them. For the first half of Schaffer's stealthy advance across the room the operator, his back to them, sat smoking a cigarette in idle unconcern, listening to soft Austrian *Schrammel* music coming in over his big machine: suddenly, alerted by the faintest whisper of sound from a creaking floorboard or just by some sixth sense, he whirled round and jumped to his feet. And he thought as quickly as he moved. Even as he raised his arms high in apparently eager surrender, he appeared to move slightly to his right, shifting the position of his right foot. There came the sudden strident clamour of an alarm bell ringing in the passage outside, Schaffer leapt forward, his Schmeisser swinging, and the operator staggered back against his transceiver then slid unconscious to the floor. But Schaffer was too late. The bell rang and kept on ringing.

'That's all I need!' Smith swore bitterly. 'That's all I bloody well need.' He ran through the radio room door out into the passage, located the glass-cased alarm bell some feet away and struck it viciously with the butt of his Schmeisser. The shattered glass tinkled to the floor and the clangour abruptly ceased.

'Inside!' Smith gestured to the open doorway of the radio room. 'All of you. Quickly.' He ushered them all inside, looked around, saw a side door leading off to the right and said to Mary: 'Quickly. What's in there? Schaffer!'

'Horatio hold the bridge,' Schaffer murmured. He moved across and took up position at the radio room door. 'We could have done without this, boss.'

'We could do without a lot of things in this world,' Smith said wearily. He glanced at Mary. 'Well?'

'Storage rooms for radio spares, looks like.'

'You and Jones take those three in there. If they breathe, kill them.'

Jones looked down at the gun held gingerly in his hand and said: 'I am not a serviceman, sir.'

'I have news for you,' Smith said. 'Neither am I.'

He crossed hurriedly to the transceiver, sat down and studied the confusing array of dials, knobs and switches. For fully twenty seconds he sat there, just looking.

Schaffer said from the doorway: 'Know how to work it, boss?'

'A fine time to ask me,' Smith said. 'We'll soon find out, won't we?' He switched the machine to 'Send', selected the ultra short wave band and lined up his transmitting frequency. He opened another switch and picked up a microphone.

'Broadsword calling Danny Boy,' he said. 'Broadsword calling Danny Boy. Can you hear me? Can you hear me?'

Nobody heard him or gave indication of hearing him. Smith altered the transmitting frequency fractionally and tried again. And again. And again. After the sixth or seventh repetition, Smith started as a crash of machine-pistol fire came from the doorway. He twisted round. Schaffer was stretched full length on the floor, smoke wisping from the barrel of his Schmeisser.

'We got callers, boss,' Schaffer said apologetically. 'Don't think I got any but I sure as hell started their adrenalin moving around.'

'Broadsword calling Danny Boy,' Smith said urgently, insistingly. 'Broadsword calling Danny Boy. For God's sake, why don't they answer?'

'They can't come round the corner of the passage without being sawn in half.' Schaffer spoke comfortably from his uncomfortable horizontal position on the floor. 'I can hold them off to Christmas. So what's the hurry?'

'Broadsword calling Danny Boy. Broadsword calling Danny Boy. How long do you think it's going to be before someone cuts the electricity?'

'For God's sake, Danny Boy,' Schaffer implored. 'Why don't you answer? Why don't you answer?'

'Danny Boy calling Broadsword.' The voice on the radio was calm and loud and clear, so free from interference that it might have come from next door. 'Danny Boy—'

'One hour, Danny Boy,' Smith interrupted. 'One hour. Understood? Over.'

'Understood. You have it, Broadsword?' The voice was unmistakably that of Admiral Rolland's. 'Over.'

'I have it,' Smith said. 'I have it all.'

'All sins are forgiven. Mother Machree coming to meet you. Leaving now.'

There came another staccato crash of sound as Schaffer loosed off another burst from his Schmeisser. Admiral Rolland's voice on the radio said: 'What was that?'

'Static,' Smith said. He didn't bother to switch off. He rose, took three paces back and fired a two-second burst from his machine-pistol, his face twisting in pain as the recoil slammed into his shattered hand. No one would ever use that particular radio again. He glanced briefly at Schaffer, but only briefly: the American's face, though thoughtful, was calm and unworried: there were those who might require helpful words, encouragement and reassurance, but Schaffer was not one of them. Smith moved swiftly across to the window and lifted the lower sash with his left hand.

The moon was almost obscured behind some darkly drifting cloud. A thin weak light filtered down into the half-seen obscurity of the valley below. Once again the snow was beginning to fall, gently. The air was taut, brittle, in the intensity of its coldness, an arctic chill that bit to the bone. The icy wind that gusted through the room could have come off the polar ice-cap.

They were on the east side of the castle, Smith realized, the side remote from the cable-car header station. The base of the volcanic plug was shrouded in a gloom so deep that it was impossible to be sure whether or not the guards and Dobermanns were patrolling down there: and, for the purposes of present survival, it didn't really matter. Smith withdrew from the window, pulled the nylon from the kit-bag, tied one end securely to the metal leg of the radio table, threw the remainder of the rope out into the night then, with his left hand, thoroughly scuffed and rubbed away the frozen encrusted snow on both the window-sill and for two or three feet beneath it: it would, he thought, have to be a hypercritical eye that didn't immediately register the impression that there had been fairly heavy and recent traffic over the sill. He wondered, vaguely, whether the rope reached as far as the ground and dismissed the thought as soon as it had occurred to him: again, it didn't really matter.

He crossed the room to where Schaffer lay spread-eagled in the doorway. The key was in the lock on the inside of the door and the lock, he observed with satisfaction, was on the same massive scale as everything else in the Schloss Adler. He said to Schaffer: 'Time to close the door.'

'Let's wait till they show face again then discourage them some more,' Schaffer suggested. 'It's been a couple of minutes since the last lad peeked his head round the corner there. Another peek, another salvo from Schaffer and it might give us another couple of minutes' grace – enough time to make it feasible for us to have shinned down that little rope there and make our getaway.'

'I should have thought of that.' An icy snow-laden gust of wind blew across the room, from open window through open door, and Smith shivered. 'My God, it's bitter!'

'Loss of blood,' Schaffer said briefly, then added, unsympathetically: 'And all that brandy you guzzled back there. When it comes to opening pores—'

He broke off and lay very still, lowering his head a fraction to sight along the barrel of his Schmeisser. He said softly: 'Give me your torch, boss.'

'What is it?' Smith whispered. He handed Schaffer the torch.

'Discretion,' Schaffer murmured. He switched on the torch and placed it on the floor, pushing it as far away from himself as he could. 'I reckon if I were in their place I'd be discreet, too. There's a stick poking round the corner of the passage and the stick has a mirror tied to it. Only, they haven't got it angled right.'

Smith peered cautiously round the door jamb, just in time to see stick and suspended mirror being withdrawn from sight, presumably to make adjustments. A few seconds later and the stick appeared again, this time with the mirror angled at more or less forty-five degrees. Mirror and stick disintegrated under the flatly staccato hammering of Schaffer's machine-pistol. Schaffer stood up, took careful aim at the single overhead light illuminating the passage and fired one shot. Now the sole light in the passage came from the torch on the floor, the light from which would not only effectively conceal from the Germans at the far end of the passage what was going on at the radio room door but, indeed, make it very difficult to decide whether or not the door itself was open or shut.

Smith and Schaffer moved back into the radio room, soundlessly closed the door behind them and as soundlessly turned the key in the lock. Schaffer used the leverage of his Schmeisser to bend the key so that it remained firmly jammed in the wards of the lock.

They waited. At least two minutes passed, then they heard the sound of excited voices at the far end of the passage followed almost at once by the sound of heavy boots pounding down the passage. They moved away from the door, passed inside the radio spares room, leaving just a sufficient crack in the doorway to allow a faint backwash of light to filter through. Smith said softly: 'Mary, you and Mr Jones for Thomas there. A gun in each temple.' He took Christiansen for himself, forced him to kneel and ground his gun into the back of his neck. Schaffer backed Carraciola against a wall, the muzzle of his Schmeisser pressed hard against his teeth. At the other end of the machine-pistol Schaffer smiled pleasantly, his teeth a pale gleam in the near darkness. The stillness inside the little room was complete.

The half-dozen Germans outside the radio room door bore no resemblance to the elderly guard von Brauchitsch had interrogated in the courtyard. They were elite soldiers of the Alpenkorps, ruthless men who had been ruthlessly trained. No one made any move to approach the door handle or lock: the machine-like efficiency with which they broached that door without risk to themselves was clearly the result of a well-drilled procedure for handling situations of precisely this nature.

At a gesture from the Oberleutnant in charge, a soldier stepped forward and with two diagonal sweeps emptied the magazine of his machine-pistol through the door. A second used his machine-pistol to stitch a neat circle in the wood, reversed his gun and knocked in the wooden circle with the butt. A third armed two grenades and lobbed them accurately through the hole provided while a fourth shot away the lock. The soldiers pressed back on each side of the door. The two flat cracks of the exploding grenades came almost simultaneously and smoke came pouring through the circular hole in the door.

The door was kicked open and the men rushed inside. There was no longer any need to take precautions – any men who had been in the same confined space as those two exploding grenades would be dead men now. For a moment there was confusion and hesitation until the blue acrid smoke was partially cleared away by the powerful cross-draught then the Oberleutnant, locating the source of this draught with the aid of a small hand-torch, ran across to the open window, checked at the sight of the rope disappearing over the sill, leaned out the window, rubbed his now-streaming eyes and peered downwards along the beam of his torch. The beam reached perhaps half-way down the side of the volcanic plug. There was nothing to be seen. He caught the rope in his free hand and jerked it savagely: it was as nearly weightless as made no difference. For a moment he focused his torch on the disturbed snow on the window-ledge then swung back into the room.

'*Gott in Himmel!*' he shouted. 'They've got away. They're down already! Quickly, the nearest phone!'

'Well, now.' Schaffer listened to the fading sound of running footsteps, removed the muzzle of his Schmeisser from Carraciola's teeth and smiled approvingly. 'That was a good boy.' Gun in Carraciola's back, he followed Smith out into the wrecked radio room and said thoughtfully: 'It isn't going to take them too long to find out there are no footprints in the snow down there.'

'It's going to take them even less time to discover that this rope is gone.' Swiftly, ignoring the stabbing pain in his right hand, Smith hauled the nylon in through the window. 'We're going to need it. *And* we're going to need some distractions.'

'I'm distracted enough as it is,' Schaffer said.

'Take four or five plastic explosives, each with different fuse length settings. Chuck them into rooms along the corridor there.'

'Distractions coming up.' Schaffer extracted some plastic explosives from the kit-bag, cut the slow-burning RDX fuses off to varying lengths, crimped on the chemical igniters, said, 'Consider it already done,' and left.

The first three rooms he came to were locked and he wasted neither time nor the precious ammunition of his silenced Luger in trying to open them. But each of the next five rooms was unlocked. In the first three, all bedrooms, he placed charges in a Dresden fruit bowl, under an officer's cap and under a pillow: in the fourth room, a bathroom, he placed it behind a WC and in the fifth, a store-room, high up on a shelf beside some highly inflammable-looking cardboard cartons.

Smith, meanwhile, had ushered the others from the still smoke-filled, eye-watering, throat-irritating atmosphere of the radio room into the comparatively purer air of the passageway beyond, and was waiting the return of Schaffer when his face became suddenly thoughtful at the sight of some fire-fighting gear – a big CO_2 extinguisher, buckets of sand and a fireman's axe – on a low platform by the passage wall.

'You *are* slipping, Major Smith.' Mary's eyes were red-rimmed and her tear-streaked face white as paper, but she could still smile at him. 'Distractions, you said. I've had the same thought myself, and I'm only me.'

Smith gave her a half-smile, the way his hand hurt he felt he couldn't afford the other half, and tried the handle of a door beside the low platform, a door lettered AKTEN RAUM – Records Office. Such a door, inevitably, was locked. He took the Luger in his left hand, placed it against the lock, squeezed the trigger and went inside.

It certainly looked like a Records Office. The room was heavily shelved and piled ceiling-high with files and papers. Smith crossed to the window, opened it wide to increase the draught then scattered large piles of paper on the floor and put a match to them. The paper flared up at once, the flames feet high within seconds.

'Kinda forgot this, didn't you?' Schaffer had returned and was bearing with him the large CO_2 cylinder. He crossed to the window. 'Gardyloo or mind your heads or whatever the saying is.'

The cylinder disappeared through the open window. The room was already so furiously ablaze that Schaffer had difficulty in finding his way back to the door again. As he stumbled out, his clothes and hair singed and face smoke-blackened, a deep-toned bell far down in the depths of the Schloss Adler began to ring with a strident urgency. 'For God's sake, what next,' Schaffer said in despair. 'The fire brigade?'

'Just about,' Smith said bitterly. 'Damn it, why couldn't I have checked first? Now they know where we are.'

'A heat-sensing device linked to an indicator?'

'What else? Come on.'

They ran along the central passage-way, driving the prisoners in front of them, dropped down a central flight of stairs and were making for the next when they heard the shouting of voices and the clattering of feet on treads as soldiers came running up from the castle courtyard.

'Quickly! In behind there!' Smith pointed to a curtained alcove. 'Hurry up! Oh, God – I've forgotten something!' He turned and ran back the way he had come.

'Where the hell has he—' Schaffer broke off as he realized the approaching men were almost upon them, whirled and jabbed the nearest prisoner painfully with the muzzle of his Schmeisser. 'In that alcove. Fast,' In the dim light behind the curtains he changed his machine-pistol for the silenced Luger. 'Don't even think of touching those curtains. With the racket that bell's making, they won't even hear you die.'

Nobody touched the curtains. Jack-booted men, gasping heavily for breath, passed by within feet of them. They clattered furiously up the next flight of stairs, the one Smith and the others had just descended, and then the footsteps stopped abruptly. From the next shouted words it was obvious that they had just caught sight of the fire and had abruptly and for the first time realized the magnitude of the task they had to cope with.

'Emergency! Sergeant, get on that phone!' It was the voice of the Oberleutnant who had led the break-in to the radio room. 'Fire detail at the double! Hoses, more CO_2 cylinders. Where in God's name is Colonel Kramer. Corporal! Find Colonel Kramer at once.'

The corporal didn't answer, the sound of jutting heels striking the treads as he raced down the stairs was answer enough. He ran by the alcove and ran down the next flight of stairs until the sound of his footfalls was lost in the metallic clamour of the alarm bell. Schaffer risked a peep through a crack in the curtains just as Smith came running up on tiptoe.

'Where the hell have you been?' Schaffer's voice was low and fierce.

'Come on, come on! Out of it!' Smith said urgently. 'No, Jones, *not* down that flight of stairs, you want to meet a whole regiment of Alpenkorps coming up it? Along the passage to the west wing. We'll use the side stairs. For God's sake, hurry. This place will be like Piccadilly Circus in a matter of seconds.'

Schaffer pounded along the passage beside Smith and when he spoke again the anxiety-born fierceness of tone had a certain plaintive equality to it. 'Well, where the bloody hell have you been?'

'The man we left tied up in the room beside the telephone exchange. The Records Office is directly above. I just remembered. I cut him free and dragged him out to the passage. He'd have burnt to death.'

'You did that, did you?' Schaffer said wonderingly. 'You do think of the most goddamned unimportant things, don't you?'

'It's a point of view. Our friend lying in the passage back there wouldn't share your sentiments. Right, down those stairs and straight ahead. Mary, you know the door.'

Mary knew the door. Fifteen paces from the foot of the stairs she stopped. Smith spared a glance through the passage window on his left. Already smoke and flame were showing through the windows and embrasures in the north-east tower of the castle. In the courtyard below, dozens of soldiers were running around, most of them without what appeared to be any great sense of purpose or direction. One man there wasn't running. He was the overalled helicopter pilot and he was standing very still indeed, bent low over the engine. As Smith watched he slowly straightened, lifted his right arm and shook his fist in the direction of the burning tower.

Smith turned away and said to Mary: 'Sure this is the room? Two stories below the window we came in?'

Mary nodded. 'No question. This is it.'

Smith tried the door handle: the room was locked. The time for skeleton keys and such-like finesse was gone: he placed the barrel of his Luger against the lock.

The corporal despatched by his Oberleutnant to locate Colonel Kramer was faced by the same problem when he turned the handle of the gold drawing-room, for when Smith and the others had left there for the last time Schaffer had locked the door and thoughtfully thrown the key out a convenient passage window. The corporal first of all knocked respectfully. No reply. He knocked loudly, with the same lack of result. He depressed the handle and used his shoulder and all he did was to hurt his shoulder. He battered at the lock area with the butt of his Schmeisser but the carpenters who had built the Schloss Adler doors had known what they were about. He hesitated, then brought his machine-pistol right way round and fired a burst through the lock, praying to heaven that Colonel Kramer wasn't sleeping in a chair in direct line with the keyhole.

Colonel Kramer was sleeping all right, but nowhere near the direct line of the keyhole. He was stretched out on the gold carpet with a considerately-placed pillow under his head. The corporal advanced slowly into the drawing-room, his eyebrows reaching for his hair and his face almost falling apart in shocked disbelief. Reichsmarschall Rosemeyer was stretched out beside the Colonel. Von Brauchitsch and a sergeant were sprawled in arm-chairs, heads lolling on their shoulders, while Anne-Marie – a very dishevelled and somewhat bruised-looking Anne-Marie – was stretched out on one of the big gold-lamé couches.

Like a man in a daze, still totally uncomprehending, the corporal approached Kramer, knelt by his side and then shook him by the shoulder, with gentle respect at first and then with increasing vigour. After some time it was borne in upon him that he could shake the Colonel's shoulder all night and that would be all he would have for it.

And then, illogically and for the first time, he noticed that all the men were without jackets, and that everyone, including Anne-Marie, had their left sleeves rolled up to the elbow. He looked slowly around the drawing-room and went very still as his gaze rested on a tray with bottles, beakers and hypodermic syringes. Slowly, on the corporal's face, shocked incomprehension was replaced by an equally shocked understanding. He took off through the doorway like the favourite in the Olympics 100 metres final.

Schaffer tied the nylon rope round the head of the iron bedstead, tested the security of the knot, lifted the lower sash window, pushed the rope through and peered unhappily down the valley. At the far end of the village a pulsating red glow marked the smouldering embers of what had once been the railway station. The lights of the village itself twinkled clearly. Immediately below and to the right of where he stood could be seen four patrolling guards with as many dogs – Kramer hadn't spoken idly when he'd said the outside guards had been doubled – and the ease with which he could spot them Schaffer found all too readily understandable when he twisted his head and stared skywards through the thinly driving snow. The moon had just emerged from behind a black bar of cloud and was sailing across a discouragingly large stretch of empty sky. Even the stars could be seen.

'I'm going to feel a mite conspicuous out there, boss,' Schaffer said complainingly. 'And there's a wolf-pack loose down below there.'

'Wouldn't matter if they had a battery of searchlights trained on this window,' Smith said curtly. 'Not now. We've no option. Quickly!'

Schaffer nodded dolefully, eased himself through the window, grasped the rope and halted momentarily as a muffled explosion came from the eastern wing of the castle.

'Number one,' Schaffer said with satisfaction. 'Bang goes a bowl of Dresden fruit – or a Dresden bowl of fruit. I do hope,' he added anxiously, 'that there's nobody using the toilet next door to where that bang just went off.'

Smith opened his mouth to make impatient comment but Schaffer was already gone. Fifteen feet only and he was standing on the roof of the header station. Smith eased himself awkwardly over the sill, wrapped the rope round his right forearm, took the strain with his left hand and looked at Mary. She gave him an encouraging smile, but there was nothing encouraging about her expression when she transferred her gaze back to the three men who were lined up facing a wall, their hands clasped behind their necks.

Carnaby-Jones was also covering them but, in his case, he held the gun as if it might turn and bite him at any moment.

Smith joined Schaffer on the roof of the header station. Both men crouched low to minimize the chances of being spotted from below. For the first ten feet out from the wall the roof was quite flat then dropped away sharply at an angle of thirty degrees. Smith thoughtfully regarded this steep slope and said: 'We don't want a repeat performance of what happened to us last time we were out there. We could do with a good piton to hammer into the castle wall here. Or the roof. Some sort of belay for our rope.'

'Pitons we don't need. Look at this.' With his bare hands Schaffer scraped at the snow-encrusted roof of the header station to reveal a fine wire netting and, below that, iron bars covering a pane of plate glass perhaps two feet by one. 'Skylights, I believe they're called. Those bars look pretty firm to me.'

He laid both hands on one of the bars and tugged firmly. It remained secure. Smith laid his left hand on the same bar and they pulled together. It still remained secure. Schaffer grinned in satisfaction, passed the rope round the bar and made no mistake about the knot he tied. Smith sat down on the roof and put his hand to the rope. Schaffer caught his wrist and firmly broke Smith's grip.

'No, you don't.' Schaffer lifted Smith's right hand: the thick wrapping of bandages were already sodden, saturated with blood. 'You can win your VC next time out. This time, you'd never make it. This one is on me.' He paused and shook his head in wonder. 'My God, Schaffer, you don't know what you're saying.'

He removed the kit-bag he'd been carrying round his neck, crawled to the break in the roof, gripped the rope and slid smoothly down the sloping surface. As he approached the roof edge he turned round with infinite care until he was pointing head downwards. Slowly, inch by almost imperceptible inch, the rope above him caught securely between his feet, he lowered himself still farther until his head was projecting over the edge of the roof. He peered downwards.

He was, he discovered, directly above one of the cables. Two hundred feet below, but to his left, this time, guards and Dobermanns were floundering uphill through the deep snow at the best speed they could make, heading for the main entrance, to the castle courtyard. The word had gone out, Schaffer realized, and every available man was being pulled in either to fight the fire or to help in the search for the men who had started the fire. Which meant, Schaffer concluded, that some of the garrison must have checked the state of the ground beneath the radio room window and found there nothing but virgin and undisturbed snow. . .

He twisted his head and looked upwards. There was no sign of any guard patrolling the battlements, which was what he would have expected: there was no point in keeping a posted lookout for an enemy without when every indication pointed to the fact that the enemy was still within.

Schaffer eased himself downwards another perilous six inches till head and shoulders were over the edge of the roof. Only two things mattered now: was there a winch attendant or guard inside the header station and, if there were, could he, Schaffer, hold on to the rope with one hand while with the other he wriggled his Luger free and shoot the guard? Schaffer doubted it. His OSS training had been wide-ranging and intensive but no one had ever thought it necessary that they should master the techniques of a high-wire circus acrobat. His mouth very dry and his heart pounding so heavily as to threaten to dislodge his precarious hand- and toe-holds, Schaffer craned his head and looked inside.

There was neither guard nor winch attendant inside: or, if there were any such, he was so well concealed that Schaffer couldn't see him. But logic said that no one would be hiding there for there was no conceivable reason why anyone should be hiding: logic also said that any person who might have been there would, like the patrolling guards below and the sentry on the battlements, have been called inside the castle to help fight fire and enemy. All Schaffer could see was a cable-car, heavy winching machinery and heavy banks of lead-acid batteries: he was soon convinced that that was all that there was to see. No cause for concern.

But what he did see, something that did dismay him considerably, was that there was only one way for him to get into the station. There was no possibility of his sliding down the rope on to the floor of the station for the excellent reason that the roof of the station, in typically Alpine eaves fashion, overhung the floor by at least six feet. The only way in was by dropping down on to the *Luftseilbahn's* heavy steel cable then overhanding himself up inside the station. Schaffer wasted no time in considering whether this was physically possible. It *had* to be possible. There was no other way in.

Carefully and with no little difficulty Schaffer inched himself back up the rope and the slope of the roof until he was about three feet clear of the edge. He eased his foot-grip on the rope and swung round through 180° until he was once more facing up the slope with his legs now dangling over the edge. He looked up. The crouched figure of Smith showed tension in every line although the face was as expressionless as ever. Schaffer lifted one hand, made a circle with thumb and forefinger, then eased himself over the edge until his searching feet found the cable.

He eased himself farther until he was sitting astride the cable, transferred his grip to the cable and swung down until he was suspended by hands and feet and looked up towards the moon. As a view, Schaffer reflected, it was vastly preferable to contemplating that two hundred foot drop down into the valley below. He started to climb.

He almost failed to make it. For every six inches he made up the cable, he slid back five. The cable was covered by a diabolically slippery coating of oil and sheath ice and only by clenching his fists till his forearms ached could he make any kind of progress at all and the fact that the cable stretched up at forty-five degrees made the difficult the well-nigh impossible. Such a means of locomotion would have been suicidal for the virtually one-handed Smith and quite impossible for either Mary or Carnaby-Jones. Once, after he had made about twelve feet, Schaffer looked down to gauge his chances if he let go and dropped down to the floor beneath, and rapidly concluded that the chances were either that he would break both legs or, if he landed at all awkwardly, would pitch out two hundred feet down to the valley below. As Schaffer later recounted it, this last possibility combined with the vertiginous view of the long long way to the floor of the valley, did him more good than an extra pair of arms. Ten seconds later, sweating and gasping like a long distance runner and very close to the last stages of exhaustion, he hauled himself on to the roof of the cable-car.

He lay there for a full minute until the trembling in his arms eased and pulse and breathing rates returned to not more than a man in a high fever might expect to have, lowered himself quietly and wearily to the floor, took out his Luger, slid the safety catch and began to make a quick check that the header station really was empty of the enemy, a superfluous precaution, reason told him, any concealed person would have been bound both to see and hear his entry, but instinct and training went deeper than reason. There was no one there. He looked behind winches, electric motors and batteries. He had the place to himself.

The next thing was to ensure that he continued to have the place to himself. At the lower end of the sloping archway leading up to the castle courtyard, the heavy iron door stood wide. He passed through this doorway and padded softly up the cobbled pathway until he came to the courtyard exit. Here, too, was another iron gate, as wide open as the other. Schaffer moved as far forward as the shadowing safety of the tunnel's overhang permitted and looked cautiously around the scene before him.

There was certainly, he had to admit, plenty to be seen and under more auspicious circumstances it would have done his heart good. The courtyard scene was as frenzied as the earlier glimpse they had had from the passage, but this time the action was much more purposive and controlled. Shouting, gesticulating figures were supervising the unrolling of hoses, the coupling-up of hydrants, the relays of men carrying extinguishers and buckets of sand. The main gates stood open and unguarded, even the sentries must have been pressed into action: not that the unguarded doors offered any warmly beckoning escape route. Only a suicide would have tried making his escape through a courtyard crowded with sixty or seventy scurrying Alpenkorps troops.

Over to his left the helicopter still stood forlorn and useless. There was no sign of the pilot. Suddenly a loud flat explosion echoed inside the confining walls of the square. Schaffer lifted his head to locate its source, saw fresh clouds of smoke billowing from an upper window in the east wing and briefly wondered which of his diversionary explosives that might be. But only for a brief moment. Some instinct made him glance to his right and his face went very still. The men he'd seen floundering up the slope outside, guards with the Dobermann pinschers, were coming through the main gate, the clouds of frozen breath trailing in the air behind them evidence enough of their exhausting run uphill through that knee-high snow. Schaffer backed away slowly and silently: German soldiers he could cope with or avoid but Dobermanns were out of his class. He swung the heavy iron door to, careful not to make the least whisper of sound, slid home two heavy bolts, ran quickly down the arched passage-way, closed and padlocked the lower door and put the key in his pocket.

He looked up, startled, at a loud crashing of glass and the subsequent tinkle as the shattered fragments tinkled to the floor. Automatically, the barrel of his Luger followed his glance.

'Put that cannon away,' Smith said irritably. Schaffer could clearly see his face now, pressed close to the iron bars. 'Who do you think is up here – Kramer and company?'

'It's my nerves,' Schaffer explained coldly. 'You haven't been through what Lieutenant Schaffer's just been through. How are things up there?'

'Carraciola and friends are face down on the roof, freezing to death in the snow and Mary has the Schmeisser on them. Jones is still up there. Won't even put his head outside. Says he's no head for heights. I've given up arguing with him. How are things your end?'

'Quiet. If anyone is having any passing thoughts about the cable-car, there are no signs of it. Both doors to the courtyard are locked. They're iron and even if someone does start having suspicious thoughts, they should hold them for a while. And, boss, the way I came in is strictly for the birds. And I mean strictly. What you need is wings. Your hand the way it is you could never make it. Mary and the old boy couldn't try it. Carraciola and the rest – well, who cares about Carraciola and the rest.'

'What winch controls are there?' Smith asked.

'Well, now.' Schaffer approached the winch. 'A small lever marked "*Normal*" and "*Notfall*"—'

'Are there batteries down there?' Smith interrupted.

'Yeah. Any amount.'

'Put the lever to "*Notfall*" – "Emergency." They could cut off the main power from inside the castle.'

'OK, it's done. Then there are Start and Stop buttons, a big mechanical handbrake and a gear lever affair marked "Forwards" and "Backwards". With a neutral position.'

'Start the motor,' Smith ordered. Schaffer pressed the 'Start' button and a generator whined into life, building up to its maximum revolutions after perhaps ten seconds. 'Now release the brake and select forward gear. If it works, stop the car and try the other gear.'

Schaffer released the brake and engaged gear, sliding the gear handle progressively over successive stops. The car moved forward, gently at first, but gathering speed until it was clear of the header station roof. After a few more feet Schaffer stopped the car, engaged reverse gear and brought the car back up into its original position. He looked up at Smith. 'Smooth, huh?'

'Lower it down till it's half-way past the edge of the roof. We'll slide down the rope on to the top of the cable-car then you can bring us up inside.'

'Must be all the fish you eat,' Schaffer said admiringly. He set the car in motion.

'I'm sending Carraciola, Thomas and Christiansen down first,' Smith said. 'I wouldn't care for any of us to be on the top of the same cable-car as that lot. Think you can hold them till we get down?'

'You don't improve morale by being insulting to subordinate officers,' Schaffer said coldly.

'I didn't know you'd any left. While you're doing that I'll have another go at persuading Juliet up there to come and join us.' He prodded Carraciola with a far from gentle toe. 'You first. Down that rope and on to the top of the cable-car.'

Carraciola straightened until he was kneeling, glanced down the slope of the roof to the depths of the valley beyond.

'You're not getting me on that lot. Not ever.' He shook his head in finality, then stared up at Smith, his black eyes implacable in their hate. 'Go on, shoot me. Kill me now.'

'I'll kill you if you ever try to escape,' Smith said. 'Don't you know that, Carraciola?'

'Sure I know it. But you won't kill me in cold blood, just standing here. You're a man of principle, aren't you, Major? Ethics, that's the word. The kind of noble sucker who risks his life to free an enemy soldier who might burn to death. Why don't you shoot, Major?'

'Because I don't have to.' With his left hand Smith grabbed Carraciola's hair and jerked his head back till Carraciola, gasping with the pain of it, was staring skywards, while he reversed the grip on his Luger and raised it high. Nausea and pain flooded through him as the ends of the broken finger-bone grated together, but none of this showed in his face. 'I just knock you out, tie a rope round your waist and lower you down over the edge, maybe eight or ten feet. Schaffer eases out the car till it touches you, then he climbs in the back door, goes to the front door and hauls you inside. You can see my right hand's not too good, maybe I won't be able to tie a secure enough knot round you, maybe I won't be able to hold you, maybe Schaffer might let you go when he's hauling you inside. I don't much care, Carraciola.'

'You double-dealing bastard!' Tears of pain filled Carraciola's eyes and his voice was low and venomous. 'I swear to God I'll live to make you wish you'd never met me.'

'Too late.' Smith thrust him away contemptuously and Carraciola had to grab wildly at the rope to prevent himself from sliding over the break of the roof. 'I've been wishing that ever since I found out who and what you really are. Vermin soil my hands. Move now or I damn well will shoot you. Why the hell should I bother taking you back to England?'

Carraciola believed him. He slid down the rope until first his feet then his hands found the security of the supporting bracket of the cable-car. Smith gestured with his gun towards Thomas. Thomas went without a word. Ten seconds later Christiansen followed him. Smith watched the cable-car begin to move up inside the station, then looked upwards to the window from which the rope dangled.

'Mr Jones?'

'I'm still here.' Carnaby-Jones's voice had a quaver to it and he didn't as much as venture to risk a glance over the windowsill.

'Not for much longer, I hope,' Smith said seriously. 'They'll be coming for you, Mr Jones. They'll be coming any moment now. I hate to say this, but I must. It is my duty to warn you what will happen to you, an enemy spy. You'll be tortured, Mr Jones – not simply everyday tortures like pulling out your teeth and toe-nails, but unspeakable tortures I can't mention with Miss Ellison here – and then you'll finish in the gas chambers. *If* you're still alive.'

Mary clutched his arm. 'Would they – would they really do that?'

'Good God, no!' Smith stared at her in genuine surprise. 'What on earth would they want to do that for?' He raised his voice again: 'You'll die in a screaming agony, Mr Jones, an agony beyond your wildest dreams. And you'll take a long time dying. Hours. Maybe days. And screaming. Screaming all the time.'

'What in God's name am I to do?' The desperate voice from above was no longer quavering, it vibrated like a broken bed-spring. 'What *can* I do?'

'You can slide down that rope,' Smith said brutally. 'Fifteen feet. Fifteen little feet, Mr Jones. My God, you could do that in a pole vault.'

'I can't.' The voice was a wail. 'I simply can't.'

'Yes, you can,' Smith urged. 'Grab the rope now, close your eyes, out over the sill and down. Keep your eyes closed. We can catch you.'

'I can't! I can't!'

'Oh God!' Smith said despairingly. 'Oh, my God! It's too late now.'

'It's too – what in heaven's name do you mean?'

'The lights are going on along the passage,' Smith said, his voice low and tense. 'And that window. And the next. They're coming for you, Mr Jones, they're coming now. Oh God, when they strip you off and strap you down on the torture table—'

Two seconds later Carnaby-Jones was over the sill and sliding down the nylon rope. His eyes were screwed tightly shut. Mary said, admiringly: 'You really are the most fearful liar ever.'

'Schaffer keeps telling me the same thing,' Smith admitted. 'You can't all be wrong.'

The cable-car, with the three men clinging grimly to the suspension bracket, climbed slowly up into the header station and jerked to a halt. One by one the three men, under the persuasion of Schaffer's gently waving Luger, lowered themselves the full length of their arms and dropped the last two or three feet to the floor. The last of them, Thomas, seemed to land awkwardly, exclaimed in muffled pain and fell heavily sideways. As he fell, his hands shot out and grabbed Schaffer by the ankles. Schaffer, immediately off-balance, flung up his arms in an attempt to maintain equilibrium and, before he could even begin to bring his arms down again, was winded by a diving rugby tackle by Christiansen. He toppled backwards, his back smashing into a generator with an impact that drove from his lungs what little breath had been left in them. A second later and Christiansen had his gun, driving the muzzle cruelly into a throat gasping for air.

Carraciola was already at the lower iron door, shaking it fiercely. His eye caught sight of the big padlock in its hasp. He swung round, ran back towards Schaffer, knocked aside the gun in Christiansen's hand and grabbed Schaffer by the throat.

'That padlock. Where's the key to that bloody padlock?' The human voice can't exactly emulate the hiss of a snake, but Carraciola's came pretty close to it then. 'That door has been locked from the inside. You're the only person who could have done it. *Where is that key?*'

Schaffer struggled to a sitting position, feebly pushing aside Carraciola's hand. 'I can't breathe!' The moaning, gasping breathing lent credence to the words. 'I can't breathe. I – I'm going to be sick.'

'Where *is* that damned key?' Carraciola demanded.

'Oh God, I feel ill!' Schaffer hoisted himself slowly to a kneeling position, his head bent, retching sounds coming from his throat. He shook his head from side to side, as if to clear away the muzziness, then slowly raised it, his eyes unfocused. He mumbled: 'What do you want? What did you say?'

'The key!' If the need for silence hadn't been paramount, Carraciola's voice would have been a frustrated scream of rage. Half-a-dozen times, in brutal and rapid succession, he struck Schaffer across the face with the palm and back of his hand. 'Where is that key?'

'Easy on, easy on!' Thomas caught Carraciola's hand. 'Don't be such a damned fool. You want him to talk, don't you?'

'The key. Yes, the key.' Schaffer hoisted himself wearily to his feet and stood there swaying, eyes half-closed, face ashen, blood trickling from both corners of his mouth. 'The batteries there, I think I hid them behind the batteries. I don't know, I can't think. No, wait.' The words came in short, anguished gasps. 'I didn't. I meant to, but I didn't.' He fumbled in his pocket, eventually located the key and brought it out, offering it vaguely in Carraciola's direction. Carraciola, the beginnings of a smile on his face, reached out for the key but, before he could reach it Schaffer abruptly straightened and with a convulsive jerk of his arm sent the key spinning through the open end of the station to land in the valley hundreds of feet below. Carraciola stared after the vanished key in total incredulity then, his suffused and enraged face mute evidence of his complete loss of self-control, stooped, picked up Schaffer's fallen Schmeisser and swung it viciously across the American's head and face. Schaffer fell like a tree.

'Well,' Thomas said acidly. 'Now that we've got that out of our system, we can shoot the lock away.'

'You can commit suicide with ricochets – that door's iron, man.' Carraciola had indeed got it out of his system for he was back on balance again. He paused, then smiled slowly. 'What the hell are we all thinking of? Let's play it clever. If we did get through that door the first thing we'd probably collect would be a chestful of machine-gun bullets. Remember, the only people who know who we really are have bloody great doses of Nembutal inside them and are liable to remain unconscious for a long time. To the rest of the garrison we're unknowns – and to the few who saw us arrive, we're prisoners. In both cases we're automatically enemies.'

'So?' Thomas was impatient.

'So, as I say, we play it clever. We go down in this cable-car and play it clever again. We phone old Weissner. We ask him to phone the Schloss Adler, tell him where Smith is and, in case Smith does manage to get down to the village on the other cable-car after us, we ask him to have a reception committee waiting for him at the lower station. Then we go to the barracks – they're bound to have a radio there – and get in touch with you know who. Flaws?'

'Nary a flaw.' Christiansen grinned. 'And then we all live happily ever afterwards. Come on, what are we waiting for?'

'Into the cable-car, you two.' Carraciola waited until they had boarded, walked across the floor until he was directly under the smashed skylight and called: 'Boss!' Schaffer's silenced Luger was in his hand.

On the roof above Smith stiffened, handed the trembling Carnaby-Jones – his eyes were still screwed shut – over to the care of Mary, took two steps towards the skylight and stopped. It was Wyatt-Turner who had said of Smith that he had a built-in radar set against danger and Carraciola's voice had just started it up into instantaneous operation and had it working with a clarity and precision that would have turned Decca green with envy.

'Schaffer?' Smith called softly. 'Lieutenant Schaffer? Are you there?'

'Right here, boss.' Mid-west accent, Schaffer to the life. Smith's radarscope went into high and had it been geared to warning bells he'd have been deafened for life. He dropped to hands and knees and crawled soundlessly forward. He could see the floor of the station now. The first thing that came into his vision was a bank of batteries, then an outflung hand, then, gradually the rest of the spread-eagled form of Schaffer. Another few inches forward and he sensed as much as saw a long finger pointing in his direction and flung himself to one side. The wind from the Luger's shell rifled his hair. Down below someone cursed in anger and frustration.

'That's the last chance you'll ever have, Carraciola,' Smith said. From where he lay he could just see Schaffer's face – or the bloody mask that covered his face. It was impossible to tell whether he was alive or dead. He looked dead.

'Wrong again. Merely the postponement of a pleasure. We're leaving now, Smith. I'm going to start the motor. Want Schaffer to get his – Christiansen has the Schmeisser on him. Don't try anything.'

'You make for that control panel,' Smith said, 'and your first step into my line of vision will be your last. I'll cut you down, Carraciola. Schaffer's dead. I can see he's dead.'

'He's damn all of the kind dead. He's just been clobbered by a gun butt.'

'I'll cut you down,' Smith said monotonously.

'Goddam it, I tell you he's not dead!' Carraciola was exasperated now.

'I'm going to kill you,' Smith said quietly. 'If I don't, the first guards through that door surely will. You can see what we've done to their precious Schloss Adler – it's well alight. Can't you guess the orders that have gone out – shoot on sight. Any stranger, shoot on sight – and shoot to kill. You're a stranger, Carraciola.'

'For God's sake, will you listen to me?' There was desperation in the voice now. 'I can prove it. He *is* alive. What can you see from up there?'

The signal strengths of Smith's danger radar set began to fade. He said: 'I can see Schaffer's head.'

'Watch it, then.' There was a thud and a silenced Luger bounced to a stop a few inches from Schaffer's head. A moment later Carraciola himself came into Smith's field of vision. He looked up at Smith and at the Schmeisser muzzle staring down at him and said: 'You won't be needing that.' He stooped over Schaffer, pinched his nose with one hand and clamped his other hand over the mouth. Within seconds the unconscious man, fighting for the air that would not come, began to move his head and to raise feeble hands in the direction of his face. Carraciola took his hands away, looked up at Smith and said: 'Don't forget, Christiansen has still that Schmeisser on him.'

Carraciola walked confidently across to the control panel, made the generator switch, released the mechanical handbrake and engaged gear, pushing the lever all the way across. The cable-car leapt forward with a violent jerk. Carraciola ran for it, jumped inside, turned and slammed the door of the cable-car.

On the roof above, Smith laid down his useless Schmeisser and pushed himself wearily to his feet. His face was bleak and bitter.

'Well, that's it, then,' Mary said. Her voice was unnaturally calm. 'Finish. All finish. Operation Overlord – and us. If that matters.'

'It matters to me.' Smith took out his silenced automatic and held it in his good left hand. 'Keep an eye on Junior here.'

Chapter Ten

'No!' For perhaps two dazed, incredulous seconds that were the longest seconds she had ever known, Mary had quite failed to gather Smith's intention: when shocked understanding did come, her voice rose to a scream. 'No! No! For God's sake, no!'

Smith ignored the heart-broken voice, the desperate clutching hand and walked to the end of the flat section of the roof. At the lower edge of the steeply sloping roof section the leading edge of the cable-car had just come into view: a cable-car with, inside it, three men who were exchanging delighted grins and thumping one another joyously on the back.

Smith ran down the ice-coated pitch of the roof, reached the edge and jumped. The cable-car was already seven or eight feet beyond him and almost as far below. Had the cable-car not been going away from him he must surely have broken both legs. As it was, he landed with a jarring teeth-rattling crash, a crash that caused the cable-car to shudder and sway and his legs to buckle and slide from beneath him on the ice-coated roof. His injured right hand failed to find a purchase on the suspension bracket and in his blindly despairing grab with his left hand he was forced to drop his Luger. It slid to the edge of the roof and fell away into the darkness of the valley below. Smith wrapped both arms round the suspension bracket and fought to draw some whooping gasps of air into his starving lungs: he had been completely winded by the fall.

In their own way, the three men inside the cable-car were as nearly stunned as Smith himself. The smiles had frozen on their faces and Christiansen's arm was still poised in mid-air where it had been arrested by the sound and the shock of Smith's landing on the cable-car roof. Carraciola, predictably, was the first to recover and react. He snatched the Schmeisser from Christiansen and pointed it upwards.

The cable-car was now forty to fifty feet clear of the castle and the high wind was beginning to swing it, pendulum-like, across the sky. Smith, weakened by the impact of the fall, the pain in his hand and the loss of blood, hung on grimly and dizzily to the suspension bracket, his body athwart the roof of the car. He felt sick and exhausted and there seemed to be a mist in front of his eyes.

From shoulder to knee and only inches from his body a venomous burst of machine-pistol fire stitched a pattern of holes in the cable-car roof: the mists cleared away from Smith's eyes more quickly than he would have believed possible. A Schmeisser magazine held far more shells than that. They would wait a second or two to see if a falling body passed any of the side windows – with that violently swinging transverse movement it was virtually impossible for anyone to fall off over the leading or trailing ends of the car – and if none came, then they would fire again. But where? What would be the next area of roof chosen for treatment? Would the gunman fire at random or to a systematic pattern? It was impossible to guess. Perhaps at that very moment the muzzle of the Schmeisser was only two inches from the middle of his spine. The very thought was enough to galvanize Smith into a quick roll that stretched him out over the line of holes that had just been made. It was unlikely that the gunman would fire in exactly the same place again, but even that was a gamble, the gunman might figure just as Smith was doing and traverse the same area again. But he wasn't figuring the same as Smith, the next burst was three feet away towards the trailing end of the car.

Using the suspension bracket as support, Smith pulled himself to his feet until he was quite vertical, hanging on to the cable itself. This way, the possible target area was lessened by eighty per cent. Quickly, soundlessly, sliding his hands along the cable, he moved forward until he was standing at the very front of the car.

The cable-car's angle of arc through the sky was increasing with every swing of the pendulum. The purchase for his feet was minimal, all the strain came on his arms, and by far the greater part of that on his sound left arm. There was nothing smoothly progressive about the cable-car's sideways motion through the sky, it jumped and jerked and jarred and jolted like a Dervish dancer in the last seconds before total collapse. The strain on the left arm was intolerable, it felt as if the shoulder sinews were being torn apart: but shoulder sinews are reparable whereas the effects of a Schmeisser blast at point blank range were not. And it seemed, to Smith, highly unlikely that anybody would waste a burst on the particular spot where he was standing, the obvious position for any roof passenger who didn't want to be shaken off into the valley below was flat out on the roof with his arms wrapped for dear life round one of the suspension arm's support brackets.

His reasoning was correct. There were three more bursts, none of which came within feet of him, and then no more. Smith knew that he would have to return to the comparative security of the suspension arm and return there soon. He was nearly gone. The grip of his left hand on the cable was weakening, this forced him to strengthen the grip of his right hand and the resulting agony that travelled like an electric shock from his hand up his arm clear to the right hand side of his head served only to compound the weakness. He would have to get back, and he would have to get back now. He prayed that the Schmeisser's magazine was empty.

And then, and for another reason, he knew that he had no option but to go now: and he knew his prayer hadn't been answered. The leading door of the cable-car opened and a head and a hand appeared. The head was Carraciola's: the hand held the Schmeisser. Carraciola was looking upwards even as he leaned out and he saw Smith immediately: he leaned farther out still, swung the Schmeisser one-handedly until the stock rested on his shoulder and squeezed the trigger.

Under the circumstances accurate aiming was impossible but at a distance of four feet accurate aiming was the last thing that mattered. Smith had already let go of the cable and wàs flinging himself convulsively backward when the first of the bullets ripped off his left hand epaulette. The second grazed his left shoulder, a brief burning sensation, but the rest of the burst passed harmlessly over his head. He landed heavily, stretched out blindly, located and grasped one of the suspension arms and scuttled crab-like round the base of the suspension arm until he had it and what little pathetic cover it offered between him and Carraciola.

For Carraciola was coming after him and Carraciola was coming to mak' siccar. He had the gun still in his hand and that gun could have very few shells indeed left in the magazine: it would be no part of Carraciola's plan to waste any of those shells. Even as Smith watched, Carraciola seemed to rise effortlessly three feet into the air – a feat of levitation directly attributable to the powerful boost given him by Thomas and Christiansen – jack-knifed forward at hip level and flattened his body on top of the cable-car roof: his legs still dangled over the leading edge. A suicidal move, Smith thought in brief elation, Carraciola had made a fatal mistake: with neither hand hold nor purchase on that ice-coated roof, he must slide helplessly over the edge at the first jerk or jolt of the cable-car. But the elation was brief indeed for Carraciola had made no mistake. He had known what Smith hadn't: where to find a secure lodgment for his hand on the smooth expanse of that roof. Within seconds his scrabbling fingers had found safety – a gash in the cable-car roof that had been torn open by one of the bursts from the Schmeisser. Carraciola's fingers hooked securely and he pulled himself forward until he was in a kneeling position, his toes hooked over the leading edge.

Smith reached up with his wounded hand and clawed desperately for a grenade in the canvas bag slung over his left shoulder, at the same time pushing himself as far back as his anchoring left hand, clutched round a suspension bracket, would permit: at that range a grenade could do almost as much damage to himself as to Carraciola. His legs slid back until his feet projected over the trailing edge and he cried out in pain as a tremendous pressure, a bone-breaking, skin tearing pressure, was applied to his shins, half-way between knees and feet: someone had him by the ankles and that someone seemed determined to separate his feet from the rest of his body. Smith twisted his head round but all he could see was a pair of hands round his ankles, knuckles bone-white in the faint wash of moonlight. And no one man's weight, Smith realized, could have caused that agonizing pain in his shins. His companion must have had him by the waist, whether to increase the pressure or to ensure his safety if Smith did slide over the end. The reasons were immaterial: the effect was the same. He tried to draw up his legs but with a pinning weight of well over 200 lbs., any movement was quite impossible.

Smith risked a quick glance forward, but Carraciola hadn't moved, the cable-car was now half-way between the header station and the top pylon, the pendulum swing was at its maximum and Carraciola, still in his kneeling position, was hanging on for his life. Smith abandoned his attempt to reach for a grenade which could now serve no purpose whatsoever, unsheathed his knife, clasped the haft in the three good fingers of his right hand, twisted round and tried to strike at those hands that were causing him such excruciating agony. He couldn't get within fifteen inches of them.

His legs were breaking: his left arm was breaking: and his clenched grip on the support was slowly beginning to open. He had only seconds to go, Smith knew, and so he had nothing in the world to lose. He changed his grip on his knife, caught the tip of the blade between his broken thumb and the rest of his fingers, turned and threw the knife as powerfully and as accurately as his smashed hand and pain-dimmed eyes would permit. The stinging pain in his left ankle and the scream of pain from the trailing door were simultaneous: immediately, all the pressure on his ankles vanished: a second later, Christiansen, whom Thomas had managed to drag back inside the cable-car, was staring stupidly at the knife that transfixed his right wrist.

In that one instant Smith had won and he had lost. Or so it most surely seemed, for he was defenceless now: Carraciola had bided his time, calculated his chances and flung himself forward until he had reached the safety of the suspension bracket. Now he pulled himself slowly to his feet, his left arm round the suspension arm itself, his left leg twined securely round one of the brackets. The Schmeisser pointed into Smith's face.

'Only one bullet left.' Carraciola's smile was almost pleasant. 'I had to make sure, you see.'

Perhaps he hadn't lost, Smith thought, perhaps he hadn't lost after all. Because of the pinioning effect of Christiansen's hands on his ankles he'd been unaware, until now, how much less difficult it had become to maintain position on that ice-sheathed roof, unaware how much the pendulum swaying of the cable-car had been reduced. And it seemed that, even now, Carraciola was still unaware of it, or, if the change of motion had registered with him, the reason for it had not. With a conscious effort of will Smith shifted his by now half-hypnotized gaze from the staring muzzle of the Schmeisser to a point just over Carraciola's shoulder. The suspension arm of the first pylon was less than twenty feet away.

'Too bad, Smith.' Carraciola steadied the barrel of his machine pistol. 'Comes to us all. Be seeing you.'

'Look behind you,' Smith said.

Carraciola half-smiled in weary disbelief that anyone should try that ancient one on him. Smith glanced briefly, a second time, over Carraciola's shoulder, winced and looked away. The disbelief vanished from Carraciola's face as if a light had been switched off. Some sixth sense or instantaneous flash of comprehension or just some sudden certainty of knowledge made him twist round and glance over his shoulder. He cried out in terror, the last sound he ever made. The steel suspension arm of the pylon smashed into his back. Both his back and inter-twined leg broke with a simultaneous crack that could have been heard a hundred yards away. One second later he was swept from the roof of the cable-car but by that time Carraciola was already dead. From the open rearward door of the car, Thomas and Christiansen, their shocked faces mirroring their stunned disbelief, watched the broken body tumbling down into the darkness of the valley below.

Shaking like a man with the ague and moving like an old man in a dream, Smith slowly and painfully hauled himself forward until he was in a sitting position with an arm and leg wound round one of the after arms of the supporting bracket. Still in the same dream-like slow motion he lifted his head and gazed down the valley. The other cable-car, moving up-valley on its reciprocal course, had just passed the lower-most of the three pylons. With luck, his own cable-car might be the first to arrive at the central pylon. With luck. Not, of course, that the question of luck entered into it any more: he had no options or alternatives left, he had to do what he had to do and luck was the last factor to be taken into consideration.

From his kit-bag Smith extracted two packets of plastic explosives and wedged them firmly between the roof of the car and the two after arms of the suspension bracket, making sure that the tear strip igniters were exposed and ready to hand. Then he braced himself, sitting upright, against the suspension bracket, using both arms and legs to anchor himself and prepared to sit it out once more as the cable-car, approaching mid-section of its second lap between the first and central pylons, steadily increased its swaying angle of arc across the night sky.

It was foolish of him, he knew, to sit like that. The snow had momentarily stopped, and the full moon, riding palely in an empty sky, was flooding the valley with a wash of ghostly light. Sitting as he was he must, he realized, be clearly visible from either the castle or the lower station: but apart from the fact that he doubted whether concealment mattered any longer he knew there was nothing he could do about it, there wasn't the strength left in his one good arm to allow him to assume the prone spread-eagled position that he and Schaffer had used on the way up.

He wondered about Schaffer, wondered about him in a vaguely woolly detached way for which exhaustion, loss of blood and the bitter cold were almost equally responsible. He wondered about the others, too, about the elderly man and the girl perched on top of the header station roof, about the two men inside the cable-car: but Mary and Carnaby-Jones were helpless to do anything to help and the chances of the unarmed Thomas and Christiansen carrying out another roof-top sortie were remote indeed: Carraciola had carried a Schmeisser, and they had seen what had happened to Carraciola. Schaffer, it was Schaffer who mattered.

Schaffer was feeling even more vague and woolly than Smith, if for different reasons. He was waking, slowly and painfully, from a very bad dream and in this dream he could taste salt in his mouth and hear a soft urgent feminine voice calling his name, calling it over and over again. In normal times Schaffer would have been all for soft feminine voices, urgent or not, but he wished that this one would stop for it was all part of the bad dream and in this bad dream someone had split his head in half and he knew the pain wouldn't go until he woke up. He moaned, put the palms of his hands on the floor and tried to prop himself up. It took a long time, it took an eternity, for someone had laid one of the girders from the Forth bridge across his back, but at last he managed to straighten both his arms, his head hanging down between them. His head didn't feel right, it didn't even feel like his head, for, apart from the fact that there seemed to be a butcher's cleaver stuck in it, it seemed to be stuffed with cotton wool, grey and fuzzy round the edges. He shook his head to clear it and this was a mistake for the top of his head fell off. Or so it felt to Schaffer as the blinding coruscation of multi-coloured lights before his eyes arranged themselves into oddly kaleidoscopic patterns. He opened his eyes and the patterns dimmed and the lights began to fade: gradually, beneath his eyes the pattern of floorboards began to resolve themselves, and, on the board, the outlines of hands. His own hands.

He was awake, but this was one of those bad dreams which stayed with you even when you were awake. He could still taste salt – the salt of blood – his head still felt as if one incautious shake would have it rolling across the floor and that soft and urgent voice was still calling.

'Lieutenant Schaffer! Lieutenant Schaffer! Wake up, Lieutenant, wake up! Can you hear me?'

He'd heard that voice before, Schaffer decided, but he couldn't place it. It must have been a long time ago. He twisted his head to locate the source of the voice – it seemed to come from above – and the kaleidoscopic whirligig of colours were back in position again, revolving more quickly than ever. Head-shaking and head-twisting, Schaffer decided, were contra-indicated. He returned his head slowly to its original position, managed to get his knees under him, crawled forward in the direction of some dimly-seen piece of machinery and hauled himself shakily to his feet.

'Lieutenant! Lieutenant Schaffer! I'm up here.'

Schaffer turned and lifted his head in an almost grotesque slow motion and this time the whole universe of brightly dancing stars was reduced to the odd constellation or two. He recognized the voice from the distant past now, it was that of Mary Ellison, he even thought he recognized the pale strained face looking down from above, but he couldn't be sure, his eyes weren't focusing as they should. He wondered dizzily what the hell she was doing up there staring down at him through what appeared to be the bars of a shattered sky-light: his mind, he dimly realized, was operating with all the speed and subtle fluency of a man swimming upstream against a river of black molasses.

'Are you – are you all right?' Mary asked.

Schaffer considered this ridiculous question carefully. 'I expect I shall be,' he said with great restraint. 'What happened?'

'They hit you with your own gun.'

'That's right.' Schaffer nodded and immediately wished he hadn't. He gingerly fingered a bruise on the back of his head. 'In the face. I must have struck my head as—' He broke off and turned slowly to face the door. 'What was that?'

'A dog. It sounded like a dog barking.'

'That's what I thought.' His voice slurred and indistinct, he staggered drunkenly across to the lower iron door and put his ear to it. 'Dogs,' he said. 'Lots of dogs. And lots and lots of hammering. Sledge-hammers, like enough.' He left the door and walked back to the centre of the floor, still staggering slightly. 'They're on to us and they're coming for us. Where's the Major?'

'He went after them.' The voice was empty of all feeling. 'He jumped on to the top of the cable-car.'

'He did, eh?' Schaffer received the news as if Smith's action had been the most natural and inevitable thing in the world. 'How did he make out?'

'How did he make—' There was life back in her voice now, a shocked anger at Schaffer's apparent callousness. She checked herself and said: 'There was a fight and I think someone fell off the roof. I don't know who it was.'

'It was one of them,' Schaffer said positively.

'One of – how can you say that?'

'The Major Smiths of this world don't drive over the edge of a cliff. Quotation from the future Mrs Schaffer. The Major Smiths of this world don't fall off the roofs of cable-cars. Quotation from the future Mrs Schaffer's future husband.'

'You're recovering,' Mary said coldly. 'But I think you're right. There's still someone sitting on top of the cable-car and it wouldn't be one of them, would it?'

'How do you know there's someone sitting—'

'Because I can see him,' she said impatiently. 'It's bright moonlight. Look for yourself.'

Schaffer looked for himself, then rubbed a weary forearm across aching eyes. 'I have news for you, love,' he said. 'I can't even see the damn' cable-car.'

The cable-car was ten yards away from the central pylon. Smith, upright now, stooped, tore off the two friction fuses, straightened and, holding the cable in his left hand, took up position just on the inner side of the car roof. At the last moment he released his grip on the cable and stretched both arms out before him to break the impact of his body against the suspension arm. The ascending car on the other cable was now almost as close to the central pylon as his own. It didn't seem possible that he could make it in time.

The impact of the horizontal suspension arm drove the thought from his mind and all the breath from his body; had it not been for the buffering effect of his outstretched arms, Smith was sure, some of his ribs must have gone. As it was, he was almost completely winded but he forced himself to ignore the pain and his heaving lungs' demand for oxygen, swung his feet up till they rested on the lower cross-girder, hooked his hands round the upper girder and made his way quickly across to the other side. At least, his hands and his feet moved quickly, but the steel was so thickly coated in clear smooth ice that his scrabbling feet could find almost no purchase whatsoever on the lower girder. He had reached no farther than the middle when the ascending car began to pass under its suspension arm. For the first time that night Smith blessed the brightness of the moon. He took two more slipping, sliding steps and launched himself towards the ice-coated cable that glittered so brightly in the pale moonlight.

His left hand caught the cable, his right arm hooked over it and the cable itself caught him high up on the chest. He had made no mistake about the location of his hand and arm, but his sliding take-off had caused his body to fall short and the cable slid up under his chin with a jerk that threatened to decapitate him. His legs swung out far beneath him, swung back and touched the roof as he lowered himself to the full extent of his left arm. He released his grip on the cable, dropped on all fours and reached out blindly but successfully for one of the arms of the suspension bracket. For long seconds he knelt there, retching uncontrollably as he was flooded by the nausea and pain from his throat and still winded lungs: then, by and by, the worst of it passed and he lay face down on the floor as the cable-car began to increase its pendulum swing with the increasing distance from the central pylon. He would not have believed that a man could be so totally exhausted and yet still have sufficient residual strength and sufficient self-preservation instinct to hang on to that treacherous and precarious hand-hold on that ice-coated roof.

Long seconds passed and some little measure of strength began to return to his limbs and body. Wearily, he hauled himself up into a sitting position, twisted round and gazed back down the valley.

The cable-car he had so recently abandoned was now hardly more than fifty yards from the lowermost pylon. Thomas and Christiansen sat huddled in the middle, the latter wrapping a makeshift bandage round his injured hand. Both fore and aft doors were still open as they were when the abortive attack on Smith had been made. That neither of the two men had ventured near the extremities of the car to try to close either of the doors was proof enough of the respect, if not fear, in which Smith was now held.

From the roof of the cable-car came a brilliant flash of light, magnesium-blinding in its white intensity: simultaneously there came the sound of two sharp explosions, so close together as to be indistinguishable in time. The two rear supports of the suspension bracket broke and the car, suspended now by only the two front supports, tilted violently, the front going up, the rear down.

Inside, the angle of the floor of the car changed in an instant from the horizontal to at least thirty degrees. Christiansen was flung back towards the still open rear door. He grabbed despairingly at the side – but he grabbed with his wounded hand. Soundlessly, he vanished through the open doorway and as soundlessly fell to the depths of the valley below.

Thomas, with two sound hands and faster reactions, had succeeded in saving himself – for the moment. He glanced up and saw where the roof was beginning to buckle and break as the forward two suspension arm support brackets, now subjected to a wrenching lateral pressure they had never been designed to withstand, began to tear their retaining bolts free. Thomas struggled up the steeply inclined floor till he stood in the front doorway: because of the tilt of the car, now almost 45° as the front supports worked loose, the leading edge of the roof was almost touching the car. Thomas reached up, grabbed the cable with both hands, and had just cleared his legs from the doorway when the two front supports tore free from the roof in a rending screech of metal. The cable-car fell away, slowly turning end over end.

Despite the cable's violent buffeting caused by the sudden release of the weight of the car, Thomas had managed to hang on. He twisted round and saw the suspension arm of the lowest pylon only feet away. The sudden numbing of all physical and mental faculties was accurately and shockingly reflected in the frozen fear of his face, the lips drawn back in a snarling rictus of terror. The knuckles of the hands gleamed like burnished ivory. And then, suddenly, there were no hands there, just the suspension arm and the empty wire and a long fading scream in the night.

As his cable-car approached the header station, Smith edged well forward to clear the lip of the roof. From where he crouched it was impossible to see the east wing of the Schloss Adler but if the columns of dense smoke now drifting across the valley were anything to go by, the fire seemed to have an unshakable hold. Clouds were again moving across the moon and this could be both a good thing and a bad thing: a good thing in that it would afford them cover and help obscure those dense clouds of smoke, a bad thing in that it was bound to highlight the flames from the burning castle. It could only be a matter of time, Smith reflected, before the attention of someone in the village or the barracks beyond was caught by the fire or the smoke. Or, he thought grimly, by the increasing number of muffled explosions coming from the castle itself. He wondered what might be the cause of them: Schaffer hadn't had the time to lay all those distractions.

The roof of the cable-car cleared the level of the floor of the header station and Smith sagged in relief as he saw the figure standing by the controls of the winch. Schaffer. A rather battered and bent Schaffer, it was true, an unsteady Schaffer, a Schaffer with one side of his face masked in blood, a Schaffer who from his peering and screwed-up expression had obviously some difficulty in focusing his gaze. But undoubtedly Schaffer and as nearly a going concern as made no odds. Smith felt energy flow back into him, he hadn't realized just how heavily he had come to depend on the American: with Schaffer by his side it was going to take a great deal to stop them now.

Smith glanced up as the roof of the header station came into view. Mary and Carnaby-Jones were still there, pressed back against the castle wall. He lifted a hand in greeting, but they gave no sign in return. Ghosts returning from the dead, Smith thought wryly, weren't usually greeted by a wave of the hand.

Schaffer, for all the trouble he was having with his eyes and his still obviously dazed condition, seemed to handle the winch controls immaculately. It may have been – and probably was – the veriest fluke, but he put the gear level in neutral and applied the brake to bring the cable-car to rest exactly half-way in under the lip of the roof. First Mary and then Jones came sliding down the nylon rope on to the roof of the car, Jones with his eyes screwed tightly shut. Neither of them spoke a word, not even when Schaffer had brought them up inside and they had slid down on to the floor of the station.

'Hurry! Hurry!' Smith flung open the rear door of the cable-car. 'Inside, all of you!' He retrieved Schaffer's Luger from the floor, then whirled round as he heard the furious barking of dogs followed bv the sound of heavy sledges battering against the iron door leading from the station. The first of the two defences must have been carried away: now the second was under siege.

Mary and a stumbling Schaffer were already inside the cable-car. Jones, however, had made no move to go. He stood there, Smith's Schmeisser in his hand, listening to the furious hammering on the door. His face seemed unconcerned. He said, apologetically: 'I'm not very good at heights, I'm afraid. But this is different.'

'Get inside!' Smith almost hissed the words.

'No.' Jones shook his head. 'You hear. They'll be through any minute. I'll stay.'

'For God's sake!' Smith shouted in exasperation.

'I'm twenty years older than any of you.'

'Well, there's that.' Smith nodded consideringly, held out his right hand, said, 'Mr Jones. Good luck,' brought across his left hand and half-dragged, half-carried the dazed Jones into the cable-car. Smith moved quickly across to the controls, engaged gear all the way, released the handbrake and ran after the moving car.

As they moved out from below the roof of the station, the sound of the assault on the inner door seemed to double in its intensity. In the Schloss Adler, Smith reflected, there would be neither pneumatic chisels nor oxy-acetylene equipment for there could be no conceivable call for either, but, even so, it didn't seem to matter: with all the best will in the world a couple of iron hasps couldn't for long withstand an attack of that nature. Thoughtfully, Smith closed the rear door. Schaffer was seated, his elbows on his knees, his head in his hands. Mary was kneeling on the floor, Jones's head in her lap, looking down at the handsome silvery-haired head. He couldn't see her expression but was dolefully certain that she was even then preparing a homily about the shortcomings of bullies who went around clobbering elderly and defenceless American actors. Almost two minutes passed in complete silence before Carnaby-Jones stirred, and, when he did, Mary herself stirred and looked up at Smith. To his astonishment, she had a half-smile on her face.

'It's all right,' she said. 'I've counted ten. In the circumstances, it was the only argument to use.' She paused and the smile faded. 'I thought you were gone then.'

'You weren't the only one. After this I retire. I've used up a lifetime's luck in the past fifteen minutes. You're not looking so bright yourself.'

'I'm not feeling so bright.' Her face was pale and strained as she braced herself against the wild lurching of the cable-car. 'If you want to know, I'm sea-sick. I don't go much on this form of travel.'

Smith tapped the roof. 'You want to try travelling steerage on one of those,' he said feelingly. 'You'd never complain about first-class travel again. Ah! Pylon number two coming up. Almost half-way.'

'*Only* half-way.' A pause. 'What happens if they break through that door up there?'

'Reverse the gear lever and up we go.'

'Like it or not?'

'Like it or not.'

Carnaby-Jones struggled slowly to a sitting position, gazed uncomprehendingly around him until he realized where he was, rubbed his jaw tenderly and said to Smith: 'That was a dirty trick.'

'It was all of that,' Smith acknowledged. 'I'm sorry.'

'I'm not.' Jones smiled shakily. 'Somehow, I don't really think I'm cut out to be a hero.'

'Neither am I, brother, neither am I,' Schaffer said mournfully. He lifted his head from his hands and looked slowly around. His eyes were still glassy and only partially focusing but a little colour was returning to his right cheek, the one that wasn't masked in blood. 'Our three friends. What became of our three friends?'

'Dead.'

'Dead?' Schaffer groaned and shook his head. 'Tell me about it sometime. But not now.'

'He doesn't know what he's missing,' Smith said unsympathetically. 'The drama of it all escapes him, which is perhaps just as well. Is the door up above there still standing or are the hinges or padlocks going? Is someone rushing towards the winch controls – Is there—'

'Stop it!' Mary's voice was sharp, high-pitched and carried overtones of hysteria. 'Stop talking like that!'

'Sorry,' Smith said contritely. He reached out and touched her shoulder. 'Just whistling in the dark, that's all. Here comes the last pylon. Another minute or so and we're home and dry.'

'Home and dry,' Schaffer said bitterly. 'Wait till I have that Savoy Grill menu in my hand. *Then* I'll be home and dry.'

'Some people are always thinking of their stomachs,' Smith observed. At that moment he was thinking of his own and it didn't feel any too good. No stomach does when it feels as if it has a solid lead ball, a chilled lead ball lodged in it with an icy hand squeezing from the outside. His heart was thumping slowly, heavily, painfully in his chest and he was having difficulty in speaking for all the saliva seemed to have evaporated from his mouth. He became suddenly aware that he was unconsciously leaning backward, bracing himself for the moment when the cable-car jerked to a stand-still then started climbing back up to the Schloss Adler again. I'll count to ten, he said to himself, then if we get that far without being checked, I'll count to nine, and then – And then he caught sight of Mary's face, a dead-white, scared and almost haggard face that made her look fifteen years older than she was, and felt suddenly ashamed of himself. He sat on the bench, and squeezed her shoulder. 'We'll be all right,' he said confidently. All of a sudden he found it easy to speak again. 'Uncle John has just said so, hasn't he? You wait and see.'

She looked up at him, trying to smile. 'Is Uncle John always right?'

'Always,' Smith said firmly.

Twenty seconds passed. Smith rose to his feet, walked to the front of the cable-car and peered down. Though the moon was obscured he could just dimly discern the shape of the lower section. He turned to look at the others. They were all looking at him.

'Not much more than a hundred feet to go,' Smith said. 'I'm going to open that door in a minute. Well, a few seconds. By that time we won't be much more than fifteen feet above the ground. Twenty, at the most. If the car stops, we jump. There's two or three feet of snow down there. Should cushion our fall enough to give an even chance of not breaking anything.'

Schaffer parted his lips to make some suitable remark, thought better of it and returned head to hands in weary silence. Smith opened the leading door, did his best to ignore the icy blast of wind that gusted in through the opening, and looked vertically downwards, realizing that he had been over-optimistic in his assessment of the distance between cable-car and ground. The distance was at least fifty feet, a distance sufficient to arouse in even the most optimistic mind dismaying thoughts of fractured femurs and tibias. And then he dismissed the thought, for an even more dismaying factor had now to be taken into consideration: in the far distance could be heard the sound of sirens, in the far distance could be seen the wavering beams of approaching headlamps. Schaffer lifted his head. The muzziness had now left him, even if his sore head had not.

'Enter, left, reinforcements,' he announced. 'This wasn't on the schedule, boss. Radio gone, telephone gone, helicopter gone—'

'Just old-fashioned.' Smith pointed towards the rear window. 'They're using smoke signals.'

'Jeez!' Schaffer stared out the rear windows, his voice awe-struck. 'For stone, it sure burns good!'

Schaffer was in no way exaggerating. For stone, it burnt magnificently. The Schloss Adler was well and truly alight, a conflagration in which smoke had suddenly become an inconsiderable and, indeed, a very minor element. It was wreathed in flames, almost lost to sight in flames, towering flames that now reached up almost to the top of the great round tower to the north-east. Perched on its volcanic plug half-way up the mountain-side against the dimly seen back-drop of the unseen heights of the Weissspitze, the blazing castle, its effulgence now beginning to light up the entire valley and quite drowning out the pale light of a moon again showing through, was an incredibly fantastic sight from some equally incredible and fantastic fairy tale.

'One trusts that they are well insured,' Schaffer said. He was on his feet now, peering down towards the lower station. 'How far, boss? And how far down?'

'Thirty feet. Maybe twenty-five. And fifteen feet down.' The lights of the leading cars were passing the still smouldering embers of the station. 'We have it made, Lieutenant Schaffer.'

'We have it made.' Schaffer cursed and staggered as the car jerked to a violent and abrupt stop. 'Almost, that is.'

'All out!' Smith shouted. 'All out!'

'There speaks the eternal shop steward,' Schaffer said. 'Stand back, I've got two good hands.' He brushed by Smith, clutched the door jamb with his left hand, pulled Mary towards him, transferred his grip from waist to wrist and dropped her out through the leading door, lowering her as far as the stretch of his left arm would permit. When he let her go, she had less than three feet to fall. Within three seconds he had done the same with Carnaby-Jones. The cable-car jerked and started to move back up the valley. Schaffer practically bundled Smith out of the car, wincing in pain as he momentarily took all of Smith's two hundred pound weight, then slid out of the doorway himself, hung momentarily from the doorway at the full stretch of his arms, then dropped six feet into the soft yielding snow. He staggered, but maintained balance.

Smith was beside him. He had fished out a plastic explosive from the bag on his back and torn off the friction fuse. He handed the package to Schaffer and said: 'You have a good right arm.'

'I have a good right arm. Horses, no. Baseball, yes.' Schaffer took aim and lobbed the explosive neatly through the doorway of the disappearing cable-car. 'Like that?'

'Like that. Come on.' Smith turned and, catching Mary by the arm while Schaffer hustled Carnaby-Jones along, ran down the side of the lower station and into the shelter of the nearest house bare seconds before a command car, followed by several trucks crammed with soldiers, slid to a skidding halt below the lower station. Soldiers piled out of the trucks, following an officer, clearly identifiable as Colonel Weissner, up the steps into the lower station.

The castle burned more fiercely than ever, a fire obviously totally out of control. Suddenly, there was the sharp crack of an explosion and the ascending cable-car burst into flames. The car, half-way up to the first pylon, swung in great arcs across the valley, its flames fanned by the wind, and climbed steadily upwards into the sky until its flame was lost in the greater flame of the Schloss Adler.

Crouched in the shelter of the house, Schaffer touched Smith's arm. 'Sure you wouldn't like to go and burn down the station as well?'

'Come on,' Smith said. 'The garage.'

Chapter Eleven

Colonel Wyatt-Turner leaned over in the co-pilot's seat, pressed his face against the side-screen and stared down unhappily at the ground. The Mosquito bomber, all engines and plywood, was, he was well aware, the fastest warplane in the world: even so, he hadn't been prepared for anything quite so fast as this.

Normal flying, of course, imparts no sensation of speed, but then, Wing Commander Carpenter wasn't engaged in normal flying; he was engaged in what Wyatt-Turner regarded as highly abnormal flying and flying, moreover, that was liable to bring them to disaster at any second. Carpenter was giving a ground-level performance of some spectacular note, skimming across fields, brushing tree-tops, skirting small hills that stood in his way, and Wyatt-Turner didn't like any of it one little bit. What he liked even less was the appalling speed of their own moon-shadow flitting over the ground beneath them; and what he liked least of all was the increasing number of occasions on which plane and shadow came within almost touching distance of each other. In an effort to keep his mind off what must inevitably happen when and if the gap were finally closed he withdrew his almost mesmerised stare and glanced at his watch.

'Twenty-five minutes.' He looked at the relaxed figure in the pilot's seat, at the world-weary face that contrasted so oddly with the magnificent panache of the red handlebar moustache. 'Can you make it in time?'

'I can make it,' Carpenter said comfortably. 'Point is, will they?'

'God only knows. I don't see how they can. Both the Admiral and I are convinced that they're trapped in the Schloss Adler. Besides, the whole countryside must be up in arms by this time. What chance *can* they have?'

'And that is why you came?'

'I sent them,' Wyatt-Turner said emptily. He glanced through the side-screen and recoiled as plane and shadow seemed to touch as they skimmed over the top of a pine forest. He said plaintively: 'Must you fly so close to the damned ground?'

'Enemy radar, old chap,' Carpenter said soothingly. 'We're safer down here among the bushes.'

Smith, with Mary and Jones behind him and Schaffer bringing up the rear, skirted the backs of the houses on the east side of the village street and cautiously made their way through the automobile junkyard to the rear double doors of Sulz's garage. Smith had his skeleton keys in his hand and was just reaching for the padlock when one of the doors opened quietly inwards. Heidi stood there. She stared at them as if they were creatures from another world, then up at the burning castle, then wordlessly, questioningly, at Smith.

'All here in black and white.' Smith patted his tunic. 'Into the bus.'

Smith waited till they had filed through the door, closed it, crossed to a small barred window at the front of the garage and peered out cautiously.

The street was packed with a milling crowd of people, most of them soldiers, nearly all unarmed men who had come hurrying out from the various *Weinstuben* to watch the burning Schloss Adler. But there were plenty of armed soldiers nearby – two truck-loads not thirty yards from the garage, not to mention three more truck-loads even farther up the street at the foot of the lower station. Farther down the street a motor-cycle patrol was parked outside 'Zum Wilden Hirsch'. The one real physical obstacle in the way of their escape was a small command car, manned, parked directly outside the doors of Sulz's garage. Smith looked at the car thoughtfully, decided that this was an obstacle that could be overcome. He withdrew from the window and crossed over to the doors to check that the four bolts were still withdrawn.

Mary and Carnaby-Jones had already made their way into the bus. As Heidi went to follow, Schaffer caught her by the shoulders, kissed her briefly and smiled at her. She looked at him in surprise.

'Well, aren't you glad to see me?' Schaffer demanded. 'I've had a *terrible* time up there. Good God, girl, I might have been killed.'

'Not as handsome as you were two hours ago.' She smiled, gently touched his face where Carraciola's handiwork with the Schmeisser had left its bloody mark, and added over her shoulder as she climbed into the bus: 'And that's as long as you've known me.'

'Two hours! I've aged twenty years tonight. And that, lady, is one helluva long courtship. Oh, God!' He watched in wearily resigned despair as Smith climbed into the driver's seat and switched on the ignition. 'Here we go for another twenty. On the floor, everyone.'

'How about you?' Heidi asked.

'Me?' Schaffer's surprise seemed genuine. He smashed the front window with the butt of the Schmeisser, reversed the gun, released the trigger and knelt on the floor. 'I'm the conductor. It's against regulations.'

The middle finger of Smith's blood-stained, bandaged hand reached for the starter button and the big diesel caught at once. Smith started to back towards the rear of the garage. Two perfectly good cars, a Mercedes and an Opel, lay in his way and by the time that Smith – whose expression betrayed no awareness of their presence – reached the back of the garage neither were fit for anything other than the scrap-heap that lay beyond the rear doors. Smith stopped, engaged first gear, revved up the engine and let in the clutch with a bang. The bus jerked forward, gathering speed as it went.

Smith aimed the angled point of the massive snow-plough at the junction of the double doors and for all the resistance the doors offered they might have been made of brown paper. With a splintering crash that sent shattered door-planks flying through the air like so much confetti, the bus roared out into the street, Smith spinning the wheel violently to the right as they careened into the crowded thoroughfare.

Crowded the thoroughfare might have been, but the pedestrians, the rubber-neckers gazing at the funeral pyre of the Schloss Adler, had had at least sufficient warning given them by the accelerating clamour of the post-bus's diesel to fling themselves clear as the bus came crashing through the doors. But the command car had no such opportunity for escape. Before either of the two occupants of the front seat – a sergeant with his hands resting lightly on the wheel, a major with a radio telephone in one hand, a thin cigar with a long ash in the other – were properly aware of what was happening, their car was swept up and carried away on the post-bus's snow-plough. For fifteen, perhaps even twenty yards, the command car was carried along, precariously balanced, on the broad blade of the snow-plough, before dropping off to one side. Miraculously enough, it landed on even keel, all four wheels still on the ground. The dazed major still had the telephone in one hand, the cigar in the other: he hadn't even lost the ash from his cigar.

Farther down the street, outside 'Zum Wilden Hirsch', a group of Alpenkorps motor-cyclists standing just outside the door stared incredulously up the street. Their first reaction, their immediate conclusion was either that Zep Salzmann, the highly popular driver of the post-bus, had gone mad or that the accelerator had jammed on the floor-boards. Disillusionment was rapid. They heard the unmistakable sound of an engine changing up quickly through the gears and caught a brief glimpse of Smith hunched over the steering wheel and of Schaffer crouched behind, the Schmeisser sticking out through the right-hand shattered windscreen: then the post-bus's headlamps switched on and they could see no more. But they had seen enough. One quick command from their sergeant and the motor-cycle patrol leapt for their machines, began to kick them into life.

But Smith also had seen enough. He blew a warning blast on his town horn, twisted the wheel and slewed the bus into the side of the street. His intentions were unmistakable and the motor-cycle patrol's decision to elect for discretion in lieu of suicidal valour was as immediate as it was automatic. They frantically abandoned their machines and flung themselves for their lives up the steps of 'Zum Wilden Hirsch'.

There was a thunderous series of metallic bangs interspersed with the eldritch screeches of torn and tortured metal as the snow-plough smashed into the motor-cycles and swept them along in its giant maw. As Smith straightened out into the middle of the road again several of them slid off the angled blade and crashed with a great splintering of wood and buckling of metal into the boarded sidewalk: the machines were no longer recognisable as motor-cycles. Two of them, however, still remained perched on the blade.

The post-bus was still accelerating with Smith's accelerator foot flat on the floor-boards. The headlamps were flashing rapidly, alternately main beam and dipped, and the streets ahead were clearing with corresponding rapidity: but the moment when the last few straggling pedestrians were galvanized into jumping for safety came when Smith switched on the Alpine horn.

In the mountains, the Alpine post-bus has absolute priority over every other vehicle in the road and its penetrating and stentorian three-toned post-horn is the symbol of its total authority, of its unquestioned right to complete priority at all times. The sound of that horn – whether the post-bus is in sight or not – is the signal for all vehicles or pedestrians to stop or move well into the side of the road, a signal that is immediately and automatically obeyed, for the absolute entitlement to the right of way of the official post-bus is deeply ingrained into the minds of all Alpine dwellers, and has been from earliest childhood. A magic wand might have made a better job of clearing that village street, but not all that much better; vehicles and pedestrians alike pressed into the sides of the street as if some powerful magnetic affinity had just been developed between them and the walls of the houses. The expression on faces ranged from astonishment to blank incomprehension. Hostility there was none: there had been no time for any to develop for events were moving far too swiftly and comprehension hadn't even begun to overtake the events. The bus had now reached the end of the village street and still not one shot had been fired.

At the sharp left-hand corner at the foot of the street the two remaining motor-cycles slid off the snow-plough and smashed into a low stone wall: two more absolute certainties, Smith thought inconsequentially, for the automobile cemetery behind Sulz's garage. Ahead of him now he could see the road stretch almost arrow-straight alongside the dark waters of the Blau See. He switched off the Alpine horn button, changed his mind and switched it on again: that horn was worth a pair of machine-guns any day.

'Don't you know any other tunes?' Schaffer asked irritably. He shivered in the icy blast from the smashed front window, and sat on the floor to get what little shelter he could. 'Give me a call when you require my services. A mile from now, I'd say.'

'What do you mean, a mile from now?'

'The barrack gates. That guy in the command car had a radio phone.'

'He had, had he?' Smith spared him a brief glance. 'Why didn't you shoot him?'

'I'm a changed man, boss.' Schaffer sighed. 'Something splendid has just come into my life.'

'Besides, you didn't have a chance.'

'Besides, as you say, I didn't have a chance.' Schaffer twisted round and looked through the rear windows of the bus for signs of pursuit, but the road behind them was empty. For all that, Schaffer reflected, the rearward view was one not lacking in interest: the Schloss Adler, now completely enveloped in flames, a reddish-white inferno by this time lighting up for half a mile around the startling incongruity of its snow and ice covered setting, was clearly beyond saving: arsonist's dream or fireman's nightmare, the castle was finished: before dawn it would be an empty and desolate shell, a gaunt and blackened ruin to haunt and desecrate for generations to come the loveliest fairy-tale valley he had ever seen.

Schaffer shortened his gaze and tried to locate the three others, but all were on the floor, under seats and completely concealed. He cursed as the shaking and shuddering bus lurched violently, throwing him against the right-hand front door, then straightened and peered at the illuminated dashboard.

'God save us all,' he said piously. 'Ninety!'

'Kilometres,' Smith said patiently.

'Ah!' Schaffer said as he watched Smith's foot move quickly from accelerator to brake, hoisted a wary eye over the lower edge of the shattered windscreen and whistled softly. The barrack gates were barely two hundred yards away: both the area around the guard-house and the parade ground beyond were brilliantly illuminated by overhead flood-lamps: scores of armed soldiers seemed to be running around in purposeless confusion, a totally erroneous impression as Schaffer almost immediately realized. They were running towards and scrambling aboard trucks and command cars and they weren't wasting any time about it either.

'A hive of activity and no mistake,' Schaffer observed. 'I wonder—' He broke off, his eyes widening. A giant tank came rumbling into view past the guard-house, turned right on to the road, stopped, swivelled 180° on its tracks, completely blocking the road: the gun turret moved fractionally until it was lined up on the headlights of the approaching bus. 'Oh, my gosh!' Schaffer's shocked whisper was just audible over the fading sound of the post-bus's diesel. 'A Tiger tank. And that's an 88-millimetre cannon, boss.'

'It's not a pop-gun, and that's a fact,' Smith agreed. 'Flat on the floor.' He reached forward, pulled a switch, and the eighteen-inch long semaphore indicator began to wave gently up and down. Smith first dipped his main headlights, then switched them off altogether, covering the last thirty yards on side-lamps alone and praying that all those signs of peaceful normality might help to keep nervous fingers away from the firing button of the most lethal tank cannon ever devised.

The fingers, for whatever reason, left the button alone. Smith slowed to a walking pace, turned right through the guard-house gates and stopped. Taking care to keep his injured right hand well out of sight, he wound down his window and leaned out, left elbow over the sill as three guards, led by a sergeant and all with machine-pistols at the ready, closed in on the driver's cab.

'Quickly!' Smith shouted. 'Telephone. Surgeon to the sick-bay.' He jerked his thumb over his shoulder. 'Colonel Weissner. They got him twice. Through the lungs. For God's sake, don't just *stand* there!'

'But – but the post-bus!' the sergeant protested. 'We had a call from—'

'Drunk, by God!' Smith swore savagely. 'He'll be court-martialled in the morning.' His voice dropped menacingly. 'And you, if the Colonel dies. Move!'

Smith engaged gear and drove off, still at walking pace. The sergeant, reassured by the sight of a major's uniform, the fact that the bus was moving into the barracks, the slow speed with which it was moving and, above all, by the authoritative clamour of the Alpine horn which Smith still had not switched off, ran for the nearest phone.

Still crawling along in first gear, Smith carefully edged the post-bus through the press of men and machines, past a column of booted and gauntleted soldiers mounted on motor-cycles, past armoured vehicles and trucks, all with engines already running, some already moving towards the gates – but not moving as quickly towards the gates as Smith would have wished. Ahead of the post-bus was a group of officers, most of them obviously senior, talking animatedly. Smith slowed down the bus even more and leaned from the window.

'They're trapped!' he called excitedly. 'Upstairs in "Zum Wilden Hirsch". They've got Colonel Weissner as hostage. Hurry, for God's sake!'

He broke off as he suddenly recognised one of the officers as the Alpenkorps captain to whom in his temporary capacity of Major Bernd Himmler, he'd spoken in 'Zum Wilden Hirsch' earlier that evening. A second later the recognition was mutual, the captain's mouth fell open in total incredulity and before he had time to close it Smith's foot was flat on the accelerator and the bus heading for the southern gates, soldiers flinging themselves to both sides to avoid the scything sweep of the giant snow-plough. Such was the element of surprise that fully thirty yards had been covered before most of the back windows of the bus were holed and broken, the shattering of glass mingling with the sound of the ragged fusillade of shots from behind. And then Smith, wrenching desperately on the wheel, came careering through the southern gates back on to the main road, giving them at least temporary protection from the sharp-shooters on the parade ground.

But they had, it seemed, only changed from the frying pan to the fire. Temporary protection they might have obtained from one enemy – but from another and far deadlier enemy they had no protection at all. Smith all but lost control of the bus as something struck a glancing blow low down on his cab door, ricocheted off into the night with a viciously screaming whine and exploded in a white flash of snow-flurried light less than fifty yards ahead.

'The Tiger tank,' Schaffer shouted. 'That goddamned 88-millimetre—'

'Get down!' Smith jack-knifed down and to one side of the wheel until his eyes were only an inch above the foot of the windscreen. 'That one was low. The next one—'

The next one came through the top of the back door, traversed the length of the bus and exited through the front of the roof, just above the windscreen. This time there was no explosion.

'A dud?' Schaffer said hopefully. 'Or maybe a dummy practice—'

'Dummy nothing!' Upright again, Smith was swinging the bus madly, dangerously, from side to side of the road in an attempt to confuse the tank gunner's aim. 'Armour-piercing shells, laddie, designed to go through two inches of steel plate in a tank before they explode.' He winced and ducked low as a third shell took out most of the left-hand windows of the bus, showering himself and Schaffer with a flying cloud of shattered glass fragments. 'Just let one of those shells strike a chassis member, instead of thin sheet metal, or the engine block, or the snow-plough—'

'Don't!' Schaffer begged. 'Just let it creep up on me all unbeknownst, like.' He paused, then continued: 'Taking his time, isn't he? Lining up for the Sunday one.'

'No,' Smith glanced in the rear-view mirror and steadied the wildly swaying bus up on a steadier course. 'Never thought I'd be glad to see a few car-loads or truck loads of Alpenkorps coming after me.' He changed into top gear and pushed the accelerator to the floor. 'I'm happy to make an exception this time.'

Schaffer turned and looked through the shattered rear windows. He could count at least three pairs of headlights on the road behind them, with two others swinging out through the southern gates: between them, they effectively blotted the post-bus from the view of the tank gunner.

'Happy isn't the word for it. Me, I'm ecstatic. Tiger tanks are one thing but little itsy-bitsy trucks are another.' Schaffer strode rapidly down the central aisle, passing by Mary, Heidi and Carnaby-Jones, all of whom were struggling rather shakily to their feet, and looked at the crates stacked in the rear seats.

'Six crates!' he said to Heidi. 'And we asked for only two. Honey, you're going to make me the happiest man alive.' He opened the rear door and began to empty the contents of the crate on to the road. A few of the bottles just bounced harmlessly on ridges of hard-packed snow, but the speed of the bus was now such that most of them shattered on impact.

The first of the two leading pursuit cars was within three hundred yards of the bus when it ran into the area of broken glass. From Schaffer's point of view it was impossible to tell what exactly happened, but such indications as could be gathered by long-range sight and sound were satisfying enough.

The headlights of the leading car suddenly began to slew violently from side to side, the screeching of brakes was clearly audible above the sound of the post-bus's diesel, but not nearly as loud as the rending crash of metal as the second car smashed into the rear of the first. For a few seconds both cars seemed locked together, then they skidded wildly out of control, coming to rest with the nose of the first car in the right hand ditch, the tail of the second in the left hand ditch. The headlamps of both cars had failed just after the moment of impact but there was more than sufficient illumination from the lamps of the first of the trucks coming up behind them to show that the road was completely blocked.

'Neat,' Schaffer said admiringly. 'Very neat, Schaffer.' He called to Smith: 'That'll hold them, boss.'

'Sure, it'll hold them,' Smith said grimly. 'It'll hold them for all of a minute. You can't burst heavy truck tyres that way and it won't take them long to bull-doze those cars out of the way. Heidi?'

Heidi walked forward, shivering in the icy gale blowing through both the shattered front and side windows. 'Yes, Major?'

'How far to the turn off?'

'A mile.'

'And to the wooden bridge – what do you call it, Zur Alten Brücke?'

'Another mile.'

'Three minutes. At the most, that.' He raised his voice. 'Three minutes, Lieutenant. Can you do it?'

'I can do it.' Schaffer was already lashing together packages of plastic explosives. He used transparent adhesive tape, leaving long streamers dangling from the bound packages. He had just secured the last package in position when he lurched heavily as the post-bus, now clear of the Blau See and running through a pine forest, swung abruptly to the left on to a side road.

'Sorry,' Smith called. 'Almost missed that one. Less than a mile, Lieutenant.'

'No panic,' Schaffer said cheerfully. He fished out a knife to start cutting the fuses to their shortest possible length, then went very still indeed as he glanced through where the rear windows had once been. In the middle distance were the vertically wavering beams of powerful headlights, closing rapidly. The cheerfulness left Schaffer's voice. 'Well, maybe there is a little bit panic, at that. I've got bad news, boss.'

'And I have a rear mirror. How far, Heidi?'

'Next corner.'

While Schaffer worked quickly on the fuses, Smith concentrated on getting the post-bus round the next corner as quickly as possible without leaving the road. And then they were on and round the corner and the bridge was no more than a hundred yards away.

It was not, Smith thought, a bridge he would have chosen to have crossed with a bicycle, much less a six ton bus. Had it been a bridge crossing some gently meandering stream, then, yes, possibly: but not a bridge such as this one was, a fifty-foot bridge surfaced with untied railway sleepers, spanning a ravine two hundred feet in depth and supported by trestles, very ancient wooden trestles which, from what little he could see of them from his acute angle of approach, he wouldn't have trusted to support the tables at the vicar's garden party.

Smith hit this elderly and decrepit edifice at forty miles per hour. A more cautious and understandable approach might have been to crawl over it at less than walking pace but Smith's conviction that the less time he spent on each ancient sleeper the better was as instantaneous as it was complete. The heavy snow chains on each tyre bit into and dislodged each successive sleeper with a terrifying rumble, the post-bus bounced up and down as if on a giant cake-walk while the entire structure of the bridge swayed from side to side like the bridge of a destroyer at speed in a heavy cross-sea. It had been Smith's original intention to stop in the middle of the bridge but once embarked upon the crossing he would no more have done so than dallied to pick up an edelweiss in the path of an Alpine avalanche. Ten feet from the edge of the bridge he stamped on the brakes and skidded to a sliding halt, on solid ground again, in less than twenty yards.

Schaffer had already the back door open and the two packages of plastic explosives in his hands before the bus stopped. Five seconds after hitting the road he was back on the bridge again, skipping nimbly over a dozen dislodged sleepers until he had arrived at the main supports of the central trestle. It took him less than twenty seconds to tape one package to the right hand support, cross the bridge and tape the second package to the left hand support. He heard the deepening roar of a rapidly approaching engine, glanced up, saw the swathe of unseen headlamp beams shining round the corner they had just passed, tore off the ignition fuse, crossed the bridge, tore off the other and raced for the bus. Smith had already the bus in gear and was moving away when Schaffer flung himself through the back doorway and was hauled inside by helping hands.

Schaffer twisted round till he was sitting on the passage-way, his legs dangling through the open doorway, just in time to see the headlamps of the pursuing car sweep into sight round the corner. It was now less than a hundred yards from the bridge, and accelerating. For a brief, almost panic-stricken, moment, Schaffer wondered wildly if he had cut the fuses short enough, he hadn't realized the following car had been quite as close as it was: and from the tense and strained expressions on the faces of the two girls and the man beside him, expressions sensed rather than seen, he knew that exactly the same thought was in their minds.

The two loud, flat detonations, each fractionally preceded by the brilliant white flash characteristic of the plastic explosive, came within one second of each other. Baulks of timber and railway sleepers were hurled forty feet into the air, spinning lazily around in a curious kind of slow motion, many of them falling back again on to the now tottering support structure with an impact sufficient to carry away the central trestle. One moment, a bridge: the next, an empty ravine with, on the far side of it, the wildly swinging headlamp beams as the driver flung his car from side to side in a nothing-to-be-lost attempt to prevent the car from sliding over the edge of the ravine. It seemed certain that he must fail until the moment when the car, sliding broadside on along the road, struck a large rock, rolled over twice and came to a halt less than six feet from the edge of the ravine.

Schaffer shook his head in wonder, rose, closed the rear door, sat in the back seat, lit a cigarette, tossed the spent match through the smashed rear window and observed: 'You're a lucky lot to have me around.'

'All this and modesty too,' Heidi said admiringly.

'A rare combination,' Schaffer acknowledged. 'You'll find lots of other pleasant surprises in store for you as we grow old together. How far to this airfield now?'

'Five miles. Perhaps eight minutes. But this is the only road in. With the bridge gone, there's no hurry now.'

'That's as maybe. Schaffer is anxious to be gone. Tell me, honey, were *all* those beer bottles empty?'

'The ones we threw away were.'

'I just simply don't deserve you,' Schaffer said reverently.

'We're thinking along the same lines at last,' Heidi said acidly.

Schaffer grinned, took two beer bottles and went forward to relieve Smith, who moved out only too willingly with the bus still in motion. Smith's right hand, Schaffer saw, hadn't a scrap of bandage left that wasn't wholly saturated in blood and the face was very pale. But he made no comment.

Three minutes later they were out of the forest, running along through open farm-land, and five minutes after that, acting on Heidi's directions, Schaffer swung the bus through a narrow gateway on the left hand side of the road. The headlamps successively illuminated two small hangars, a narrow, cleared runway stretching into the distance and, finally, a bullet-riddled Mosquito bomber with a crumpled under-carriage.

'Ain't that a beautiful sight, now?' Schaffer nodded at the damaged plane. 'Carnaby-Jones's transport?'

Smith nodded. 'It began with a Mosquito and it will end – we hope – in a Mosquito. This is Oberhausen airfield HQ of the Bavarian Mountain Rescue pilots.'

'Three cheers for the Bavarian Mountain Rescue pilots.' Schaffer stopped the bus facing up the length of the runway, switched off the lights and turned off the engine. They sat silently in the darkness, waiting.

Colonel Wyatt-Turner glanced through the side-screen and breathed with relief as, for the first time that night, the ground fell away sharply beneath the Mosquito. He said sarcastically: 'Losing your nerve, Wing Commander?'

'I lost that September 3rd, 1939,' Carpenter said cheerfully. 'Got to climb. Can't expect to see any recognition signals down among the bushes there.'

'You're sure we're on the right course?'

'No question. That's the Weissspitze there. Three minutes' flying time.' Carpenter paused and went on thoughtfully. 'Looks uncommon like Guy Fawkes night up there, don't you think.'

The Wing Commander was hardly exaggerating. In the far distance the silhouette of the Weissspitze was but dimly seen, but there was no mistaking the intensity of the great fire blazing half-way up the mountain-side. Occasionally, great gouts of red flame and what looked like gigantic fireworks could be seen soaring high above the main body of the fire.

'Explosives or boxes of ammunition going up, I'd say,' Carpenter said pensively. 'That's the Schloss Adler, of course. Were any of your boys carrying matches?'

'They must have been.' Wyatt-Turner stared impassively at the distant blaze. 'It's quite a sight.'

'It's all of that,' Carpenter agreed. He touched Wyatt-Turner's arm and pointed forwards and down. 'But there's a sight that's far finer, the most beautiful sight I've ever seen.'

Wyatt-Turner followed the pointing finger. Less than two miles away, about five hundred feet below, a pair of headlamps were flashing regularly on and off, once every two seconds. With a conscious effort of will he looked away and glanced briefly at Carpenter, but almost at once was back on the flashing headlamps. He stared at them hypnotically and shook his head in slow and total disbelief.

Schaffer had the headlights switched on main beam, illuminating the runway, and the post-bus engine running as the black squat shape of the Mosquito, air-brakes fully extended, lined up for its approach to the runway, and had the bus itself moving, accelerating quickly through the gears, as the Mosquito sank down over the top of the bus and settled down beautifully without the slightest suspicion of a bounce.

Within a minute Schaffer brought the bus to a skidding halt only yards from the now stationary plane. Half a minute later, with all five of them safely inside the plane, Carpenter had the Mosquito turned through 180° and was standing hard on the brakes as he brought the engines up to maximum revolutions. And then they were on their way, gathering speed so rapidly that they were air-borne two hundred yards before the end of the runway. For the first mile of their climb Carpenter kept the plane heading almost directly towards the blazing castle that now redly illuminated the entire valley, then the funeral pyre of the Schloss Adler vanished for the last time as the Mosquito banked and headed for the north-west and home.

Chapter Twelve

Wing Commander Carpenter took the Mosquito up to five thousand feet and kept it there. The time for dodging around among the bushes was past for, on the outward journey, Carpenter had been concerned only that no German station pick him up long enough to form even a rough guess as to where he was going. But now he didn't care if every radar station in the country knew where he was going: he was going home to England, mission accomplished, and there wasn't a warplane in Europe that could catch him. Wing Commander Carpenter pulled luxuriously at his evil-smelling briar. He was well content.

His five newly-acquired passengers were, perhaps, a fraction less content. They lacked Carpenter's well-upholstered pilot's seat. The interior of the Mosquito made no concessions whatsoever to passenger comfort. It was bleak, icy, cramped – it didn't require much space to carry a 4000 lb. bomb load, the Mosquito's maximum – and totally devoid of seating in any form. The three men and the two girls squatted uncomfortably on thin palliasses, the expressions on their faces pretty accurately reflecting their acute discomfort. Colonel Wyatt-Turner, still holding across his knees the Sten gun he'd had at the ready in case any trouble had developed on the ground or the flashing lights of the truck had been a German ruse, was sitting sideways in the co-pilot's seat so that he could see and talk to the pilot and the passengers at the same time. He had accepted without question or apparent interest Smith's brief explanation of the two girls' presence as being necessary to escape Gestapo vengeance. Colonel Wyatt-Turner had other and weightier matters on his mind.

Smith looked up from the bleeding mangled hand that Mary was re-bandaging with the plane's first aid kit and said to the Colonel: 'It was good of you to come in person to meet us, sir.'

'It wasn't good of me at all,' Wyatt-Turner said frankly. 'I'd have gone mad if I'd stayed another minute in London – I *had* to know. It was I who sent you all out here.' He sat without speaking for some time, then went on heavily: 'Torrance-Smythe gone, Sergeant Harrod, and now, you say, Carraciola, Christiansen and Thomas. All dead. A heavy price, Smith, a terrible price. My best men.'

'All of them, sir?' Smith asked softly.

'I'm getting old.' Wyatt-Turner shook his head wearily and drew a hand across his eyes. 'Did you find out who—'

'Carraciola.'

'Carraciola! Ted Carraciola? Never! I can't believe it.'

'*And* Christiansen.' Smith's voice was still quiet, still even. '*And* Thomas.'

'And Christiansen? And Thomas?' He looked consideringly at Smith. 'You've been through a lot, Major Smith. You're not well.'

'I'm not as well as I was,' Smith admitted. 'But I was well enough when I killed them?'

'You – *you* killed them?'

'I've killed a traitor before now. You know that.'

'But – but traitors! All three of them. Impossible. I can't believe it! I *won't* believe it!'

'Then maybe you'll believe this, sir.' Smith produced one of the note-books from his tunic and handed it to Wyatt-Turner. 'The names and addresses or contacts of every German agent in southern England *and* the names of all British agents in north-west Europe who have been supplanted by German agents. You will recognise Carraciola's writing. He wrote this under duress.'

Slowly, like a man in a dream, Wyatt-Turner reached out and took the note-book. For three minutes he examined the contents, leafing slowly, almost reluctantly through the pages, then finally laid the book down with a sigh.

'This is the most important document in Europe, the most important document I have even seen.' Wyatt-Turner sighed. 'The nation is deeply in your debt, Major Smith.'

'Thank you, sir.'

'Or would have been. It's a great pity it will never have the chance to express its gratitude.' He lifted the Sten from his knees and pointed it at Smith's heart. 'You will do nothing foolish, will you, Major Smith?'

'What in God's name—' Carpenter twisted in his seat and stared at Wyatt-Turner in startled and total disbelief.

'Concentrate on your flying, my dear Wing Commander.' Wyatt-Turner waved the Sten gently in Carpenter's direction. 'Your course will do for the present. We'll be landing at Lille airport within the hour.'

'The guy's gone nuts!' Schaffer's voice was a shocked whisper.

'If he has,' Smith said drily, 'he went nuts some years ago. Ladies and gentlemen, I give you the most dangerous spy in Europe, the most successful double agent of all time.' He paused for reaction, but the silence remained unbroken: the enormity of the revelation of Wyatt-Turner's duplicity was too great for immediate comprehension. Smith continued: 'Colonel Wyatt-Turner, you will be court-martialled this afternoon, sentenced, removed to the Tower then taken out, blind-folded and shot at eight o'clock tomorrow morning.'

'You knew?' Wyatt-Turner's affable self-confidence had completely deserted him and his voice, low and strained, was barely distinguishable above the clamour of the engines. 'You knew about me?'

'I knew about you,' Smith nodded. 'But we all knew about you, didn't we, Colonel? Three years, you claimed, behind the German lines, served with the Wehrmacht and finally penetrated the Berlin High Command. Sure you did. With the help of the Wehrmacht and the High Command. But when the tide of war turned and you could no longer feed the Allies with false and misleading reports about proposed German advances, then you were allowed to escape back to England to feed the Germans true and accurate reports about Allied planes – *and* give them all the information they required to round up British agents in north-west Europe. How many million francs do you have in your numbered account in Zurich, Colonel?'

Wing Commander Carpenter stared straight ahead through the windscreen, and said very slowly: 'Frankly, old chap, this is preposterous.'

'Try batting an eyelid and see just how preposterous that Sten gun is,' Smith suggested. He looked at Wyatt-Turner again. 'You underestimated Admiral Rolland, I'm afraid. He's had his suspicions about you and the four section leaders of Department C for months. But he was wrong about Torrance-Smythe.'

'Guess away.' Wyatt-Turner had recovered his composure and most of his self-confidence. 'It'll pass the time till we get to Lille.'

'Unfortunately for you, there is no guess-work. Admiral Rolland recalled me – and Mary – from Italy: he could no longer be sure of anyone in London. You know how corruption spreads? Played it very clever, did the Admiral. He told you he had his suspicions about one of his section leaders, but didn't know which. So, when General Carnaby crashed, he put up to you the idea of sending the section officers to the rescue – and made damn sure that you never once had the opportunity of talking to any of them in private before they took off.'

'That – that was why I was called in?' Schaffer looked as if he had been sand-bagged. 'Because you couldn't trust—'

'For all we knew, MI6 was riddled . . . Well, Colonel, you weren't too happy until Rolland asked *you* to pick the leader. So you picked me. Rolland knew you would. You'd only just met me for the first time, but you knew from Kesselring's military intelligence chief, through your pal Admiral Canaris, that I was their top double agent. Or thought you did. Rolland was the only man on either side who knew I wasn't. For you, I was the ideal choice. Rolland made certain that you didn't have the chance of talking to *me* either, but you weren't worried. You knew that I would know what to do.' Smith smiled bleakly. 'I'm happy to say I did. It must have been quite a shock to your system this afternoon when he told you what I really was.'

'You knew that? You knew all that?' Wyatt-Turner's newfound composure had vanished, his voice was quiet and vicious. He lifted the Sten slightly. 'What goes on, Smith?'

'All pre-arranged to force your hand. We had everything – except proof – about you. I got that proof this evening. Colonel Kramer *knew* that we were coming, *knew* we were after General Carnaby.' He nodded towards Jones. 'Incidentally meet Cartwright Jones, an American actor.'

'What?' Wyatt-Turner forced out the word as if a pair of powerful hands were squeezing on his wind-pipe.

'General Carnaby is spending a quiet weekend at the Admiral's country house in Wiltshire. As a stand-in, Mr Jones was quite admirable. He had them all as deceived as that faked plane crash – you will have realized by now that it was a deliberate crash-landing.' Wyatt-Turner tried to speak, but the words failed to come: his mouth was working and the colour had drained from his ruddy face. 'And why did Kramer know? He knew because you had informed Berlin as soon as Rolland had put the plan to you. *Nobody else had the chance to. And* he knew that we would be in "Zum Wilden Hirsch" this evening. He knew because I told you on the radio broadcast this morning and you lost no time in passing the good word on.'

'Are you sure?' Heidi asked. 'Couldn't the informant have been whichever of the men – Carraciola or Christiansen or Thomas – who killed Torrance-Smythe. There's a phone box just outside the inn.'

'I know. No, he didn't have time. I left the inn for exactly seven minutes. Three minutes after I'd left, Torrance-Smythe did the same – to follow one of the three others he'd just seen leaving. Smithy was clever and he knew something was far wrong. He—'

'*How* did he know?' Schaffer demanded.

'We'll never be sure. I think we'll find that he was a highly-skilled lip-reader. Anyway, he caught the man he'd seen leaving in the phone booth outside the Post Office – before he'd had time to get through to either Weissner or Kramer. There was a fight to the death. By the time the killer had dragged Smithy around to the back and returned to the booth, someone else was occupying it. I saw him. So the killer had to go back into the inn. Kramer it was who told Weissner – and the Colonel here who told Kramer.'

'Very interesting.' There was a sneer in Wyatt-Turner's voice, but a sneer belied by the deep unease in his face. 'Fascinating, in fact. Quite finished, Major Smith?'

'Finished.' Smith sighed. 'You just had to come to meet us, hadn't you, Colonel? This was the last door to life left open to you. In my final broadcast I told the Admiral "I have it all". He told you what that meant – all the names, all the addresses. We could never have got at you through Carraciola, Christiansen or Thomas – they were too close to you in MI6, you were too cagey and they never knew who they were working for. You used intermediaries – and all their names are in that book. You *knew* they'd put the finger on you – when it's a choice between taking a walk to the gallows and talking – well, it's not much of a choice, is it?'

Wyatt-Turner didn't answer. He turned to Carpenter and said: 'Lay off a course for Lille airport.'

'Don't bother,' Smith said.

Wyatt-Turner lined his Sten on Smith. 'Give me one good reason why I shouldn't shoot you now.'

'I can do that,' Smith nodded. 'Why do you think that Admiral Rolland accompanied you to the airport. He never has before.'

'Go on.' Wyatt's voice was hard, abrupt, but his eyes were sick, sick with the sudden certainty of defeat and death.

'To make quite certain that you took that Sten and only that Sten with you. Tell me, can you see two parallel scores where the stock meets the barrel?'

Wyatt-Turner stared at him for a long moment than glanced down quickly at the Sten. There were two unmistakable parallel scratches exactly where Smith had said they would be. Wyatt-Turner looked up again, his face contorted, desperation replacing the sickness in his eyes.

'That's right,' Smith said. 'I personally filed off the firing pin exactly thirty-six hours ago.' With his left hand Smith reached awkwardly under his tunic flap and brought out his silenced Luger. Wyatt-Turner, with his Sten lined up on Smith's head and the muzzle less than three feet from Smith's face, squeezed the trigger time and again, and each convulsive contraction of his forefinger was rewarded by a dry and empty click. With a stunned almost uncomprehending expresson on his face, Wyatt-Turner slowly lowered the Sten to the floor, then quickly whirled in his seat, jerked open the door and threw the note-book out into the night. He turned and smiled bleakly at Smith.

'The most important document in Europe, I believe I called it.'

'So you did.' Smith handed his gun to Schaffer, reached under his tunic and brought out two more books. 'Duplicates.'

'Duplicates!' The smile slowly faded from the heavily-jowled face, leaving it frozen in defeat. 'Duplicates,' he whispered. He looked slowly around them all and then finally back at Smith, who had retrieved his gun from Schaffer. He said: 'Are you going to shoot me?'

'No.'

Wyatt-Turner nodded, slid back the door to its widest extent and said: 'Can you really see me in the Tower?' He stepped forward into the doorway.

'No.' Smith shook his head. 'No, I can't see that.'

'Mind the step,' said Schaffer. His voice was cold and empty, his face was carved from stone.

'Well, now, time to make a call.' Smith slid shut the door, scrambled painfully into the co-pilot's seat and looked at Mary. 'The Admiral must be getting worried by this time.'

'Time to make a call,' Mary repeated mechanically. She stared at him as if seeing a ghost. 'How can you sit there – just after – how can you be so *calm*?'

'Because it's no shock to me, silly. I *knew* he was going to die.'

'You knew – of course, of course,' she murmured.

'Now then,' Smith went on, deliberately brisk-voiced as he took her hand. 'You realize what this means, don't you?'

'Do I realize what what means?' She was still ashen-faced.

'You and I are all washed up,' Smith explained patiently. 'Finished. In Italy, in north-west Europe. I won't even be allowed to fight as a soldier because if I were captured I'd still be shot as a spy.'

'So?'

'So, for us, the war is over. For the first time we can think of ourselves.

OK?' He squeezed her hand and she smiled shakily in reply. 'OK. Wing Commander, may I use your radio?'

'So that's the way he went.' Admiral Rolland, telephone in hand and standing by the big transceiver in his London Operations HQ, looked old and very very tired. 'Maybe it's all for the best, Smith. And you have all the information you want?'

Smith's voice crackled over the earphone. 'Everything, sir.'

'Magnificent, magnificent! I have all the police forces in the country alerted. As soon as we get that book . . . There's a car waiting for you at the airport. See you in an hour.'

'Yes, sir. There's one thing, sir, a small thing. I want to get married this morning.'

'You what?' Grey bushy eyebrows lifted towards the mane of white hair.

'I want to get married,' Smith explained slowly and patiently. 'To Miss Mary Ellison.'

'But you can't,' Rolland protested. 'This morning! Impossible! There are such things as banns, permits, the registrar's office will be shut today—'

'After all I've done for you,' Smith interrupted reproachfully.

'Blackmail, sir! You play on an old man's gratitude. Downright blackmail!' Rolland banged down the phone, smiled tiredly and picked up another phone. 'Operator? Put me through to the Forgery Section.'

Wing Commander Carpenter, his pipe well alight and by his elbow a cup of coffee newly poured from a vacuum flask, was his old imperturbable self again. Smith talked quietly to Mary while Jones had his eyes closed and appeared to be asleep.

Farther aft in the fuselage, Schaffer had his arm around Heidi, who was making no attempt to fight him off.

'Right,' Schaffer said. 'So we go to this pub tonight, see—'

'You said the Savoy Grill,' Heidi reminded him.

'A rose by any other name . . . So we go to this pub, and we'll have paté, smoked trout, sirloin of Aberdeen-Angus—'

'Aberdeen-Angus!' Heidi looked at him in amusement. 'Forgotten the war, haven't you? Forgotten rationing? More like a sirloin of horse meat.'

'Honey.' Schaffer took her hands and spoke severely and earnestly. 'Honey, don't ever again mention that word to me. I'm allergic to horses.'

'You eat them?' Heidi gazed at him in astonishment. 'In Montana?'

'I fall off them,' Schaffer said moodily. 'Everywhere.'

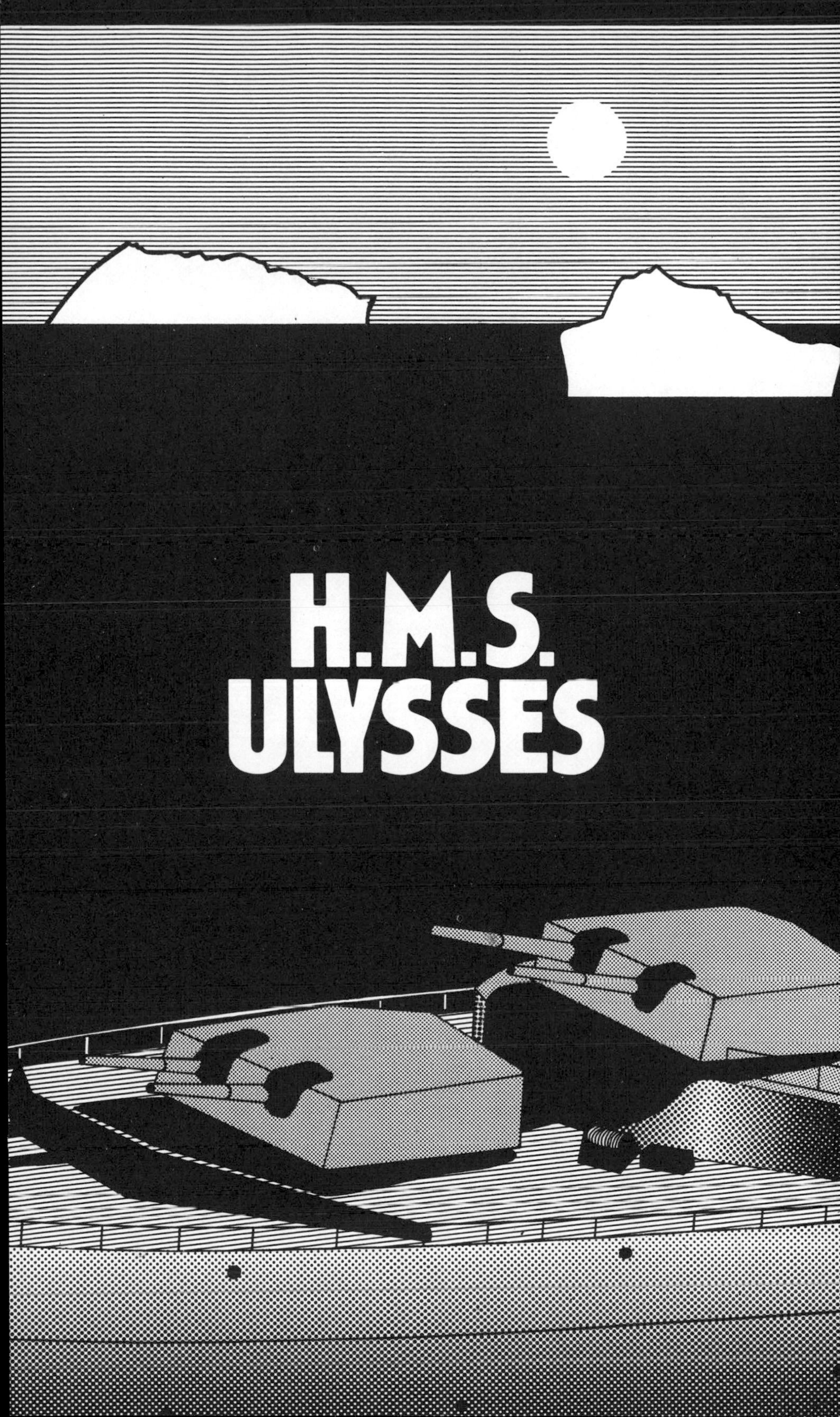
H.M.S.
ULYSSES

H.M.S.Ulysses

To Gisela

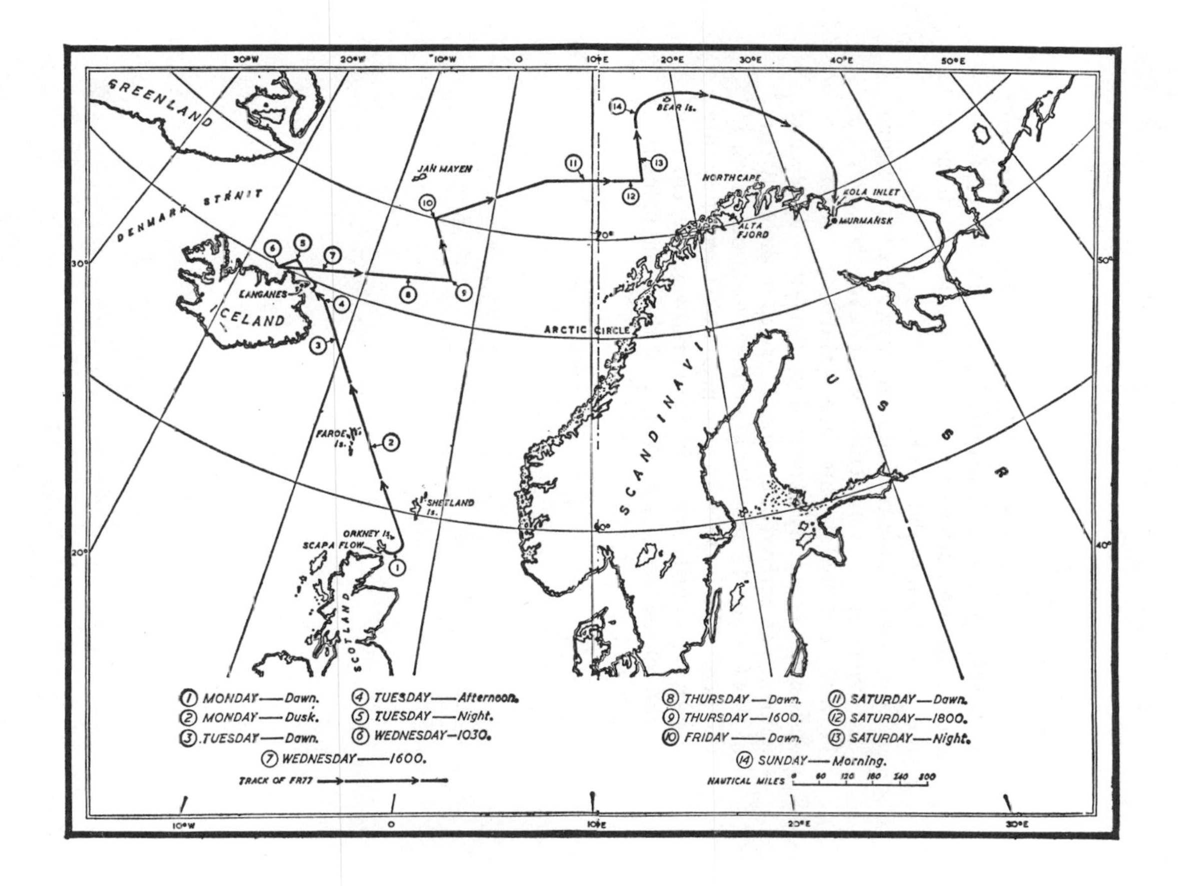
GREENLAND
DENMARK STRAIT
ICELAND
LANGANES
JAN MAYEN
FAROE Is.
SHETLAND Is.
ORKNEY Is.
SCAPA FLOW
SCOTLAND
BEAR Is.
NORTHCAPE
ALTA FJORD
KOLA INLET
MURMANSK
ARCTIC CIRCLE
SCANDINAVI
U S S R
① MONDAY—Dawn.
② MONDAY—Dusk.
③ TUESDAY—Dawn.
④ TUESDAY—Afternoon.
⑤ TUESDAY—Night.
⑥ WEDNESDAY—1030.
⑦ WEDNESDAY—1600.
⑧ THURSDAY—Dawn.
⑨ THURSDAY—1600.
⑩ FRIDAY—Dawn.
⑪ SATURDAY—Dawn.
⑫ SATURDAY—1800.
⑬ SATURDAY—Night.
⑭ SUNDAY—Morning.
TRACK OF FR77
NAUTICAL MILES 0 60 120 180 240 300

H.M.S. Ulysses

I wish to acknowledge my debt to my elder brother, Ian L. MacLean, Master Mariner, for the considerable technical help and advice on matters maritime given me in the preparation of this book.

To avoid possible confusion it must be clearly stated that there is no connection whatsoever between the H.M.S. *Ulysses* of this book and the Ulster-class destroyer – now fully converted to a frigate – of the same name which entered operational service in the early part of 1944, some 12 months after the events described in this book. Nor is there any connection between any ship herein mentioned as being in Scapa Flow or participating in the convoy and any naval ship of the same name that has served, or is serving, in the Royal Navy.

A.M.

Come, my friends,
'Tis not too late to seek a newer world.
Push off, and sitting well in order smite
The sounding furrows; for my purpose holds
To sail beyond the sunset, and the baths
Of all the western stars, until I die.
It may be that the gulfs will wash us down:
It may be we shall touch the Happy Isles,
And see the great Achilles whom we knew.
Though much is taken, much abides; and though
We are not now that strength which in old days
Moved earth and heaven: that which we are, we are;
One equal temper of heroic hearts,
Made weak by time and fate but strong in will
To strive, to seek, to find, and not to yield.

ALFRED LORD TENNYSON

Chapter One

Prelude: Sunday Afternoon

Slowly, deliberately, Starr crushed out the butt of his cigarette. The gesture, Captain Vallery thought, held a curious air of decision and finality. He knew what was coming next, and, just for a moment, the sharp bitterness of defeat cut through that dull ache that never left his forehead nowadays. But it was only for a moment – he was too tired really, far too tired to care.

'I'm sorry, gentlemen, genuinely sorry.' Starr smiled thinly. 'Not for the orders, I assure you – the Admiralty decision, I am personally convinced, is the only correct and justifiable one in the circumstances. But I do regret your – ah – inability to see our point of view.'

He paused, proffered his platinum cigarette case to the four men sitting with him round the table in the Rear-Admiral's day cabin. At the four mute headshakes the smile flickered again. He selected a cigarette, slid the case back into the breast pocket of his double-breasted grey suit. Then he sat back in his chair, the smile quite gone. It was not difficult to visualize, beneath that pin-stripe sleeve, the more accustomed broad hand and golden stripes of Vice-Admiral Vincent Starr, Assistant Director of Naval Operations.

'When I flew north from London this morning,' he continued evenly, 'I was annoyed. I was very annoyed. I am – well, I am a fairly busy man. The First Sea Lord, I thought, was wasting my time as well as his own. When I return, I must apologize. Sir Humphrey was right. He usually is . . . '

His voice trailed off to a murmur, and the flint-wheel of his lighter rasped through the strained silence. He leaned forward on the table and went on softly.

'Let us be perfectly frank, gentlemen. I expected – I surely had a right to expect – every support and full co-operation from you in settling this unpleasant business with all speed. Unpleasant business?' He smiled wryly. 'Mincing words won't help. Mutiny, gentlemen, is the generally accepted term for it – a capital offence, I need hardly remind you. And yet what do I find?' His glance travelled slowly round the table. 'Commissioned officers in His Majesty's Navy, including a Flag-Officer, sympathizing with – if not actually condoning – a lower-deck mutiny!'

He's overstating it, Vallery thought dully. He's provoking us. The words, the tone, were a question, a challenge inviting reply.

There was no reply. The four men seemed apathetic, indifferent. Four men, each an individual, each secure in his own personality – yet, at that moment, so strangely alike, their faces heavy and still and deeply lined, their eyes so quiet, so tired, so very old.

'You are not convinced, gentlemen?' he went on softly. 'You find my choice of words a trifle – ah – disagreeable?' He leaned back. 'Hm . . .

"mutiny." ' He savoured the word slowly, compressed his lips, looked round the table again. 'No, it doesn't sound too good, does it, gentlemen? You would call it something else again, perhaps?' He shook his head, bent forward, smoothed out a signal sheet below his fingers.

' "Returned from strike on Lofotens," ' he read out: ' "1545 – boom passed: 1610 – finished with engines: 1630 – provisions, stores lighters alongside, mixed seaman-stoker party detailed unload lubricating drums: 1650 – reported to Captain stokers refused to obey CPO Hartley, then successively Chief Stoker Hendry, Lieutenant (E.) Grierson and Commander (E.): ringleaders apparently Stokers Riley and Petersen: 1705 – refused to obey Captain: 1715 – Master at Arms and Regulating PO assaulted in performance of duties." ' He looked up. 'What duties? Trying to arrest the ringleaders?'

Vallery nodded silently.

' "1715 – seaman branch stopped work, apparently in sympathy: no violence offered: 1725 – broadcast by Captain, warned of consequences: ordered to return to work: order disobeyed: 1730 – signal to C-in-C *Duke of Cumberland*, for assistance." '

Starr lifted his head again, looked coldly across at Vallery.

'Why, incidentally, the signal to the Admiral? Surely your own marines—'

'My orders,' Tyndall interrupted bluntly. 'Turn our own marines against men they've sailed with for two and half years? Out of the question! There's no matelot – boot-neck antipathy on *this* ship, Admiral Starr: they've been through far too much together. . . . Anyway,' he added dryly, 'it's wholly possible that the marines would have refused. And don't forget that if we had used our own men, and they had quelled this – ah – mutiny, the *Ulysses* would have been finished as a fighting ship.'

Starr looked at him steadily, dropped his eyes to the signal again.

' "1830 – Marine boarding party from *Cumberland*: no resistance offered to boarding: attempted to arrest, six, eight suspected ringleaders: strong resistance by stokers and seamen, heavy fighting poop-deck, stokers' mess-deck and engineers' flat till 1900; no firearms used, but 2 dead, 6 seriously injured, 35-40 minor casualties." ' Starr finished reading, crumpled the paper in an almost savage gesture. 'You know, gentlemen, I believe you have a point after all.' The voice was heavy with irony. ' "Mutiny" is hardly the term. Fifty dead and injured: "Pitched battle" would be much nearer the mark.'

The words, the tone, the lashing bite of the voice provoked no reaction whatsoever. The four men still sat motionless, expressionless, unheeding in a vast indifference.

Admiral Starr's face hardened.

'I'm afraid you have things just a little out of focus, gentlemen. You've been up here a long time and isolation distorts perspective. Must I remind senior officers that, in wartime, individual feelings, trials and sufferings are of no moment at all? The Navy, the country – they come first, last and all the time.' He pounded the table softly, the gesture insistent in its restrained urgency. 'Good God, gentlemen,' he ground out, 'the future of the world is at stake – and you, with your selfish, your inexcusable absorption in your own petty affairs, have the colossal effrontery to endanger it!'

Commander Turner smiled sardonically to himself. A pretty speech, Vincent boy, very pretty indeed – although perhaps a thought reminiscent of Victorian melodrama: the clenched teeth act was definitely overdone. Pity he didn't stand for Parliament – he'd be a terrific asset to any Government Front Bench. Suppose the old boy's really too honest for that, he thought in vague surprise.

'The ringleaders will be caught and punished – heavily punished.' The voice was harsh now, with a bitter edge to it. 'Meantime the 14th Aircraft Carrier Squadron will rendezvous at Denmark Strait as arranged, at 1030 Wednesday instead of Tuesday – we radioed Halifax and held up the sailing. You will proceed to sea at 0600 tomorrow.' He looked across at Rear-Admiral Tyndall. 'You will please advise all ships under your command at once, Admiral.'

Tyndall – universally known throughout the Fleet as Farmer Giles – said nothing. His ruddy features, usually so cheerful and crinkling, were set and grim: his gaze, heavy-lidded and troubled, rested on Captain Vallery and he wondered just what kind of private hell that kindly and sensitive man was suffering right then. But Vallery's face, haggard with fatigue, told him nothing: that lean and withdrawn asceticism was the complete foil. Tyndall swore bitterly to himself.

'I don't really think there's more to say, gentlemen,' Starr went on smoothly. 'I won't pretend you're in for an easy trip – you know yourselves what happened to the last three major convoys – PQ 17, FR 71 and 74. I'm afraid we haven't yet found the answer to acoustic torpedoes and glider bombs. Further, our intelligence in Bremen and Kiel – and this is substantiated by recent experience in the Atlantic – report that the latest U-boat policy is to get the escorts first. . . . Maybe the weather will save you.'

You vindictive old devil, Tyndall thought dispassionately. Go on, damn you – enjoy yourself.

'At the risk of seeming rather Victorian and melodramatic' – impatiently Starr waited for Turner to stifle his sudden fit of coughing – 'we may say that the *Ulysses* is being given the opportunity of – ah – redeeming herself.' He pushed back his chair. 'After that, gentlemen, the Med. But first – FR 77 to Murmansk, come hell or high water!' His voice broke on the last word and lifted into stridency, the anger burring through the thin veneer of suavity. 'The *Ulysses* must be made to realize that the Navy will never tolerate disobedience of orders, dereliction of duty, organized revolt and sedition!'

'Rubbish!'

Starr jerked back in his chair, knuckles whitening on the armrest. His glance whipped round and settled on Surgeon-Commander Brooks, on the unusually vivid blue eyes so strangely hostile now under that magnificent silver mane.

Tyndall, too, saw the angry eyes. He saw, also, the deepening colour in Brooks's face, and moaned softly to himself. He knew the signs too well – old Socrates was about to blow his Irish top. Tyndall made to speak, then slumped back at a sharp gesture from Starr.

'What did you say, Commander?' The Admiral's voice was very soft and quite toneless.

'Rubbish,' repeated Brooks distinctly. 'Rubbish. That's what I said. "Let's be perfectly frank," you say. Well, sir, I'm being frank. "Dereliction of duty, organized revolt and sedition" my foot! But I suppose you have to call it something, preferably something well within your own field of experience. But God only knows by what strange association and sleight-of-hand mental transfer, you equate yesterday's trouble aboard the *Ulysses* with the only clearly-cut code of behaviour thoroughly familiar to yourself.' Brooks paused for a second: in the silence they heard the thin, high wail of a bosun's pipe – a passing ship, perhaps. 'Tell me, Admiral Starr,' he went on quietly, 'are we to drive out the devils of madness by whipping – a quaint old medieval custom – or maybe, sir, by drowning – remember the Gadarene swine? Or perhaps a month or two in cells, you think, is the best cure for tuberculosis?'

'What in heaven's name are you talking about, Brooks?' Starr demanded angrily. 'Gadarene swine, tuberculosis – what *are* you getting at, man? Go on – explain.' He drummed his fingers impatiently on the table, eyebrows arched high into his furrowed brow. 'I hope, Brooks,' he went on silkily, 'that you can justify this – ah – insolence of yours.'

'I'm quite sure that Commander Brooks intended no insolence, sir.' It was Captain Vallery speaking for the first time. 'He's only expressing—'

'Please, Captain Vallery,' Starr interrupted, 'I am quite capable of judging these things for myself, I think.' His smile was very tight. 'Well, go on, Brooks.'

Commander Brooks looked at him soberly, speculatively.

'Justify myself?' He smiled wearily. 'No, sir, I don't think I can.' The slight inflection of tone, the implications, were not lost on Starr, and he flushed slightly. 'But I'll try to explain,' continued Brooks. 'It may do some good.'

He sat in silence for a few seconds, elbow on the table, his hand running through the heavy silver hair – a favourite mannerism of his. Then he looked up abruptly.

'When were you last at sea, Admiral Starr?' he inquired.

'Last at sea?' Starr frowned heavily. 'What the devil has that got to do with you, Brooks – or with the subject under discussion?' he asked harshly.

'A very great deal.' Brooks retorted. 'Would you please answer my question, Admiral?'

'I think you know quite well, Brooks,' Starr replied evenly, 'that I've been at Naval Operations HQ in London since the outbreak of war. What are you implying, sir?'

'Nothing. Your personal integrity and courage are not open to question. We all know that. I was merely establishing a fact.' Brooks hitched himself forward in his chair.

'I'm a naval doctor, Admiral Starr – I've been a doctor for over thirty years now.' He smiled faintly. 'Maybe I'm not a very good doctor, perhaps I don't keep quite so abreast of the latest medical developments as I might, but I believe I can claim to know a great deal about human nature – this is no time for modesty – about how the mind works, about the wonderfully intricate interaction of mind and body.

' "Isolation distorts perspective" – these were your words, Admiral Starr. "Isolation" implies a cutting off, a detachment from the world, and your implication was partly true. But – and this, sir, is the point – there are more worlds than one. The Northern Seas, the Arctic, the black-out route to Russia – these are another world, a world utterly distinct from yours. It is a world, sir, of which you cannot possibly have any conception. In effect, you are completely isolated from *our* world.'

Starr grunted, whether in anger or derision it was difficult to say, and cleared his throat to speak, but Brooks went on swiftly.

'Conditions obtain there without either precedent or parallel in the history of war. The Russian Convoys, sir, are something entirely new and quite unique in the experience of mankind.'

He broke off suddenly, and gazed out through the thick glass of the scuttle at the sleet slanting heavily across the grey waters and dun hills of the Scapa anchorage. No one spoke. The Surgeon-Commander was not finished yet: a tired man takes time to marshal his thoughts.

'Mankind, of course, can and does adapt itself to new conditions.' Brooks spoke quietly, almost to himself. 'Biologically and physically, they have had to do so down the ages, in order to survive. But it takes time, gentlemen, a great deal of time. You can't compress the natural changes of twenty centuries into a couple of years: neither mind nor body can stand it. You can try, of course, and such is the fantastic resilience and toughness of man that he can tolerate it – for extremely short periods. But the limit, the saturation capacity for adaption is soon reached. Push men beyond that limit and anything can happen. I say "anything" advisedly, because we don't yet know the precise form the crack-up will take – but crack-up there always is. It may be physical, mental, spiritual – I don't know. But this I do know, Admiral Starr – the crew of the *Ulysses* has been pushed to the limit – and clear beyond.'

'Very interesting, Commander.' Starr's voice was dry, sceptical. 'Very interesting indeed – and most instructive. Unfortunately your theory – and it's only that, of course – is quite untenable.'

Brooks eyed him steadily.

'That sir, is not even a matter of opinion.'

'Nonsense, man, nonsense!' Starr's face was hard in anger. 'It's a matter of fact. Your premises are completely false.' Starr leaned forward, his forefinger punctuating every word. 'This vast gulf you claim to lie between the convoys to Russia and normal operational work at sea – it just doesn't exist. Can you point out any one factor or condition present in these Northern waters which is not to be found somewhere else in the world? Can you, Commander Brooks?'

'No, sir.' Brooks was quite unruffled. 'But I can point out a frequently overlooked fact – that differences of degree and association can be much greater and have far more far-reaching effects than differences in kind. Let me explain what I mean.

'Fear can destroy a man. Let's admit it – fear is a natural thing. You get it in every theatre of war – but nowhere, I suggest, so intense, so continual as in the Arctic convoys.

'Suspense, tension can break a man – any man. I've seen it happen too often, far, far too often. And when you're keyed up to snapping point, sometimes for seventeen days on end, when you have constant daily reminders of what may happen to you in the shape of broken, sinking ships and broken, drowning bodies – well, we're men, not machines. Something has to go – and does. The Admiral will not be unaware that after the last two trips we shipped nineteen officers and men to sanatoria – mental sanatoria?'

Brooks was on his feet now, his broad, strong fingers splayed over the polished table surfaces, his eyes boring into Starr's.

'Hunger burns out a man's vitality, Admiral Starr. It saps his strength, slows his reactions, destroys the will to fight, even the will to survive. You are surprised, Admiral Starr? Hunger, you think – surely that's impossible in the well-provided ships of today? But it's not impossible, Admiral Starr. It's inevitable. You keep on sending us out when the Russian season's over, when the nights are barely longer than the days, when twenty hours out of the twenty-four are spent on watch or at action stations, and you expect us to feed well!' He smashed the flat of his hand on the table. 'How the hell can we, when the cooks spend nearly all their time in the magazines, serving the turrets, or in damage control parties? Only the baker and butcher are excused – and so we live on corned beef sandwiches. For weeks on end! Corned beef sandwiches!' Surgeon-Commander Brooks almost spat in disgust.

Good old Socrates, thought Turner happily, give him hell. Tyndall, too, was nodding his ponderous approval. Only Vallery was uncomfortable – not because of what Brooks was saying, but because Brooks was saying it. He, Vallery, was the captain: the coals of fire were being heaped on the wrong head.

'Fear, suspense, hunger.' Brooks's voice was very low now. 'These are the things that break a man, that destroy him as surely as fire or steel or pestilence could. These are the killers.

'But they are nothing, Admiral Starr, just nothing at all. They are only the henchmen, the outriders, you might call them, of the Three Horsemen of the Apocalypse – cold, lack of sleep, exhaustion.

'Do you know what it's like up there, between Jan Mayen and Bear Island on a February night, Admiral Starr? Of course you don't. Do you know what it's like when there's sixty degrees of frost in the Arctic – and it still doesn't freeze? Do you know what it's like when the wind, twenty degrees below zero, comes screaming off the Polar and Greenland ice-caps and slices through the thickest clothing like a scalpel? When there's five hundred tons of ice on the deck, where five minutes' direct exposure means frostbite, where the bows crash down into a trough and the spray hits you as solid ice, where even a torch battery dies out in the intense cold? Do you, Admiral Starr, do you?' Brooks flung the words at him, hammered them at him.

'And do you know what it's like to go for days on end without sleep, for weeks with only two or three hours out of the twenty-four? Do you know the sensation, Admiral Starr? That fine-drawn feeling with every nerve in your body and cell in your brain stretched taut to breaking point, pushing you over the screaming edge of madness. Do you know it, Admiral Starr? It's the most exquisite agony in the world, and you'd sell your friends, your family, your hopes of immortality for the blessed privilege of closing your eyes and just letting go.

'And then there's the tiredness, Admiral Starr, the desperate weariness that never leaves you. Partly it's the debilitating effect of the cold, partly lack of sleep, partly the result of incessantly bad weather. You know yourself how exhausting it can be to brace yourself even for a few hours on a rolling, pitching deck: our boys have been doing it for months – gales are routine on the Arctic run. I can show you a dozen, two dozen old men, not one of them a day over twenty.'

Brooks pushed back his chair and paced restlessly across the cabin. Tyndall and Turner glanced at each other, then over at Vallery, who sat with head and shoulders bowed, eyes resting vacantly on his clasped hands on the table. For the moment, Starr might not have existed.

'It's a vicious, murderous circle.' Brooks went on quickly. He was leaning against the bulkhead now, hands deep in his pockets, gazing out sightlessly through the misted scuttle. 'The less sleep you have, the tireder you are: the more tired you become, the more you feel the cold. And so it goes on. And then, all the time, there's the hunger and the terrific tension. Everything interacts with everything else: each single factor conspires with the others to crush a man, break him physically and mentally, and lay him wide open to disease. Yes, Admiral – disease.' He smiled into Starr's face, and there was no laughter in his smile. 'Pack men together like herring in a barrel, deprive 'em of every last ounce of resistance, batten 'em below decks for days at a time, and what do you get? TB. It's inevitable.' He shrugged. 'Sure, I've only isolated a few cases so far – but I *know* that active pulmonary TB is rife in the lower deck.

'I saw the break-up coming months ago.' He lifted his shoulders wearily. 'I wanted the Fleet Surgeon several times. I wrote the Admiralty twice. They were sympathetic – and that's all. Shortage of ships, shortage of men . . .

'The last hundred days did it, sir – on top of the previous months. A hundred days of pure bloody hell and not a single hour's shore leave. In port only twice – for ammunitioning: all oil and provisions from the carriers at sea. And every day an eternity of cold and hunger and danger and suffering. In the name of God,' Brooks cried, 'we're not machines!'

He levered himself off the wall and walked over to Starr, hands still thrust deep in his pockets.

'I hate to say this in front of the Captain, but every officer in the ship – except Captain Vallery – knows that the men would have mutinied, as you call it, long ago, but for one thing – Captain Vallery. The intense personal loyalty of the crew to the Captain, the devotion almost to the other side of idolatry is something quite unique in my experience, Admiral Starr.'

Tyndall and Turner both murmured approval. Vallery still sat motionless.

'But there was a limit even to that. It had to come. And now you talk of punishing, imprisoning these men. Good God above, you might as well hang a man for having leprosy, or send him to penal servitude for developing ulcers!' Brooks shook his head in despair. 'Our crew are equally guiltless. They just couldn't help it. They can't see right from wrong any more. They can't think straight. They just want a rest, they just want peace, a few days' blessed quiet. They'll give anything in the world for these things and they *can't* see beyond them. Can't you see that, Admiral Starr? Can't you? Can't you?'

For perhaps thirty seconds there was silence, complete, utter silence, in the Admiral's cabin. The high, thin whine of the wind, the swish of the hail seemed unnaturally loud. Then Starr was on his feet, his hands stretching out for his gloves: Vallery looked up, for the first time, and he knew that Brooks had failed.

'Have my barge alongside, Captain Vallery. At once, please.' Starr was detached, quite emotionless. 'Complete oiling, provisioning and ammunitioning as soon as possible. Admiral Tyndall, I wish you and your squadron a successful voyage. As for you, Commander Brooks, I quite see the point of your argument – at least, as far as you are concerned.' His lips parted in a bleak, wintry smile. 'You are quite obviously overwrought, badly in need of some leave. Your relief will be aboard before midnight. If you will come with me, Captain . . . '

He turned to the door and had taken only two steps when Vallery's voice stopped him dead, poised on one foot.

'One moment, sir, if you please.'

Starr swung round. Captain Vallery had made no move to rise. He sat still, smiling. It was a smile compounded of deference, of understanding – and of a curious inflexibility. It made Starr feel vaguely uncomfortable.

'Surgeon-Commander Brooks,' Vallery said precisely, 'is a quite exceptional officer. He is invaluable, virtually irreplaceable and the *Ulysses* needs him badly. I wish to retain his services.'

'I've made my decision, Captain,' Starr snapped. 'And it's final. You know, I think, the powers invested in me by the Admiralty for this investigation.'

'Quite, sir.' Vallery was quiet, unmoved, 'I repeat, however, that we cannot afford to lose an officer of Brooks's calibre.'

The words, the tone, were polite, respectful; but their significance was unmistakable. Brooks stepped forward, distress in his face, but before he could speak, Turner cut in smoothly, urbanely.

'I assume I wasn't invited to this conference for purely decorative purposes.' He tilted back in his chair, his eyes fixed dreamily on the deckhead. 'I feel it's time I said something. I unreservedly endorse old Brooks's remarks – every word of them.'

Starr, white-mouthed and motionless, looked at Tyndall. 'And you, Admiral?'

Tyndall looked up quizzically, all the tenseness and worry gone from his face. He looked more like a West Country Farmer Giles than ever. He supposed wryly, that his career was at stake; funny, he thought how suddenly unimportant a career could become.

'As Officer Commanding, maximum squadron efficiency is my sole concern. Some people *are* irreplaceable. Captain Vallery suggests Brooks is one of these. I agree.'

'I see, gentlemen, I see,' Starr said heavily. Two spots of colour burned high up on his cheekbones. 'The convoy has sailed from Halifax, and my hands are tied. But you make a great mistake, gentlemen, a great mistake, in pointing pistols at the head of the Admiralty. We have long memories in Whitehall. We shall – ah – discuss the matter at length on your return. Good-day, gentlemen, good-day.'

Shivering in the sudden chill, Brooks clumped down the ladder to the upper deck and turned for'ard past the galley into the Sick Bay. Johnson, the Leading Sick Bay Attendant, looked out from the dispensary.

'How are our sick and suffering, Johnson?' Brooks inquired. 'Bearing up manfully?'

Johnson surveyed the eight beds and their occupants morosely.

'Just a lot of bloody chancers, sir. Half of them are a damned sight fitter than I am. Look at Stoker Riley there – him with the broken finger and whacking great pile of *Reader's Digests*. Going through all the medical articles, he is, and roaring out for sulph., penicillin and all the latest antibiotics. Can't pronounce half of them. Thinks he's dying.'

'A grievous loss,' the Surgeon-Commander murmured. He shook his head. 'What Commander Dodson sees in him I don't know. . . . What's the latest from hospital?'

The expression drained out of Johnson's face.

'They're just off the blower, sir,' he said woodenly. 'Five minutes ago. Ordinary Seaman Ralston died at three o'clock.'

Brooks nodded heavily. Sending that broken boy to hospital had only been a gesture anyway. Just for a moment he felt tired, beaten. 'Old Socrates,' they called him, and he was beginning to feel his age these days – and a bit more besides. Maybe a good night's sleep would help, but he doubted it. He sighed.

'Don't feel too good about all this, Johnson, do you?'

'Eighteen, sir. Exactly eighteen.' Johnson's voice was low, bitter. 'I've just been talking to Burgess – that's him in the next bed. Says Ralston steps out across the bathroom coaming, a towel over his arm. A mob rushes past, then this bloody great ape of a boot-neck comes tearing up and bashes him over the skull with his rifle. Never knew what him him, sir – and he never knew why.'

Brooks smiled faintly.

'That's what they call – ah – seditious talk, Johnson,' he said mildly.

'Sorry, sir. Suppose I shouldn't – it's just that I—'

'Never mind, Johnson. I asked for it. Can't stop anyone from thinking. Only, don't think out loud. It's – it's prejudicial to naval discipline. . . . I think your friend Riley wants you. Better get him a dictionary.'

He turned and pushed his way through the surgery curtains. A dark head – all that could be seen behind the dentist's chair – twisted round. Johnny Nicholls, Acting Surgeon Lieutenant, rose quickly to his feet, a pile of report cards dangling from his left hand.

'Hallo, sir. Have a pew.'

Brooks grinned.

'An excellent thing, Lieutenant Nicholls, truly gratifying, to meet these days a junior officer who knows his place. Thank you, thank you.'

He climbed into the chair and sank back with a groan, fiddling with the neck-rest.

'If you'll just adjust the foot-rest, my boy . . . so. Ah – thank you.' He leaned back luxuriously, eyes closed, head far back on the rest, and groaned again. 'I'm an old man, Johnny, my boy, just an ancient has-been.'

'Nonsense, sir,' Nicholls said briskly. 'Just a slight malaise. Now, if you'll let me prescribe a suitable tonic . . . '

He turned to a cupboard, fished out two tooth-glasses and a dark-green, ribbed bottle marked 'Poison.' He filled the glasses and handed one to Brooks. 'My personal recommendation. Good health, sir!'

Brooks looked at the amber liquid, then at Nicholls.

'Heathenish practices they taught you at these Scottish Universities, my boy . . . Admirable fellers, some of these old heathens. What is it this time, Johnny?'

'First-class stuff,' Nicholls grinned. 'Produce of the Island of Coll.'

The old surgeon looked at him suspiciously.

'Didn't know they had any distilleries up there.'

'They haven't. I only said it was made in Coll. . . . How did things go up top, sir?'

'Bloody awful. His nibs threatened to string us all from the yardarm. Took a special dislike to me – said I was to be booted off the ship instanter. Meant it, too.'

'You!' Nicholls's brown eyes, deep-sunk just now and red-rimmed from sleeplessness, opened wide. 'You're joking, sir, of course.'

'I'm not. But it's all right – I'm not going. Old Giles, the skipper and Turner – the crazy idiots – virtually told Starr that if I went he'd better start looking around for another Admiral, Captain and Commander as well. They shouldn't have done it, of course – but it shook old Vincent to the core. Departed in high dudgeon, muttering veiled threats . . . not so veiled, either, come to think of it.'

'Damned old fool!' said Nicholls feelingly.

'He's not really, Johnny. Actually, he's a brilliant bloke. You don't become a DNO for nothing. Master strategist and tactician, Giles tells me, and he's not really as bad as we're apt to paint him; to a certain extent we can't blame old Vincent for sending us out again. Bloke's up against an insoluble problem. Limited resources at his disposal, terrific demands for ships and men in half a dozen other theatres. Impossible to meet half the claims made on him; half the time he's operating on little better than a shoe-string. But he's still an inhuman, impersonal sort of cuss – doesn't understand men.'

'And the upshot of it all?'

'Murmansk again. Sailing at 0600 tomorrow.'

'What! Again? This bunch of walking zombies?' Nicholls was openly incredulous. 'Why, they can't do that, sir! They – they just can't!'

'They're doing it anyway, my boy. The *Ulysses* must – ah – redeem itself.' Brooks opened his eyes. 'Gad the very thought appals me. If there's any of that poison left, my boy . . . '

Nicholls shoved the depleted bottle back into the cupboard, and jerked a resentful thumb in the direction of the massive battleship clearly visible through the porthole, swinging round her anchor three or four cable-lengths away.

'Why always us, sir? It's always us. Why don't they send that useless floating barracks out once in a while? Swinging round that bloody great anchor, month in, month out—'

'Just the point,' Brooks interrrupted solemnly. 'According to the Kapok Kid, the tremendous weight of empty condensed milk cans and herring-in-tomato sauce tins accumulated on the ocean bed over the past twelve months completely defeats all attempts to weigh anchor.'

Nicholls didn't seem to hear him.

'Week in, week out, months and months on end, they send the *Ulysses* out. They change the carriers, they rest the screen destroyers – but never the *Ulysses*. There's no let-up. Never, not once. But the *Duke of Cumberland* – all it's fit for is sending hulking great brutes of marines on board here to massacre sick men, crippled men, men who've done more in a week than—'

'Easy, boy, easy,' the Commander chided. 'You can't call three dead men and the bunch of wounded heroes lying outside there a massacre. The marines were only doing their job. As for the *Cumberland* – well, you've got to face it. We're the only ship in the Home Fleet equipped for carrier command.'

Nicholls drained his glass and regarded his superior officer moodily.

'There are times, sir, when I positively love the Germans.'

'You and Johnson should get together sometime,' Brooks advised. 'Old Starr would have you both clapped in irons for spreading alarm and . . . Hallo, hallo!' He straightened up in his chair and leaned forward. 'Observe the old *Duke* there, Johnny! Yards of washing going up from the flag-deck and matelots running – actually running – up to the fo'c'sle head. Unmistakable signs of activity. By Gad, this *is* uncommon surprising! What d'ye make of it, boy?'

'Probably learned that they're going on leave.' Nicholls growled. 'Nothing else could possibly make that bunch move so fast. And who are we to grudge them the just rewards for their labours? After so long, so arduous, so dangerous a spell of duty in Northern waters . . . '

The first shrill blast of a bugle killed the rest of the sentence. Instinctively, their eyes swung round on the crackling, humming loudspeaker, then on each other in sheer, shocked disbelief. And then they were on their feet, tense, expectant: the heart-stopping urgency of the bugle-call to action stations never grows dim.

'Oh, my God, no!' Brooks moaned. 'Oh, no, no! Not again! Not in Scapa Flow!'

'Oh, God, no! Not again – *not in Scapa Flow*!'

These were the words in the mouths, the minds, the hearts of 727 exhausted, sleep-haunted, bitter men that bleak winter evening in Scapa Flow. That they thought of, and that only could they think of as the scream of the bugle stopped dead all work on decks and below decks, in engine-rooms and boiler-rooms, on ammunition lighters and fuel tenders, in the galleys and in the offices. And that only could the watch below think of – and that with an even more poignant despair – as the strident blare seared through the bliss of oblivion and brought them back, sick at heart, dazed in mind and stumbling on their feet, to the iron harshness of reality.

It was, in a strangely indefinite way, a moment of decision. It was the moment that could have broken the *Ulysses*, as a fighting ship, for ever. It was the moment that bitter, exhausted men, relaxed in the comparative safety of a land-locked anchorage, could have chosen to make the inevitable stand against authority, against that wordless, mindless compulsion and merciless insistence which was surely destroying them. If ever there was such a moment, this was it.

The moment came – and passed. It was no more than a fleeting shadow, a shadow that flitted lightly across men's minds and was gone, lost in the rush of feet pounding to action stations. Perhaps self-preservation was the reason. But that was unlikely – the *Ulysses* had long since ceased to care. Perhaps it was just naval discipline, or loyalty to the captain, or what the psychologists call conditioned reflex – you hear the scream of brakes and you immediately jump for your life. Or perhaps it was something else again.

Whatever it was, the ship – all except the port watch anchor party – was closed up in two minutes. Unanimous in their disbelief that this could be happening to them in Scapa Flow, men went to their stations silently or vociferously, according to their nature. They went reluctantly, sullenly, resentfully, despairingly. But they went.

Rear-Admiral Tyndall went also. He was not one of those who went silently. He climbed blasphemously up to the bridge, pushed his way through the port gate and clambered into his high-legged arm-chair in the for'ard port corner of the compass platform. He looked at Vallery.

'What's the flap, in heaven's name, Captain?' he demanded testily. 'Everything seems singularly peaceful to me.'

'Don't know yet, sir.' Vallery swept worried eyes over the anchorage. 'Alarm signal from C-in-C, with orders to get under way immediately.'

'Get under way! But why, man, why?'

Vallery shook his head.

Tyndall groaned. 'It's all a conspiracy, designed to rob old men like ourselves of their afternoon sleep,' he declared.

'More likely a brainwave of Starr's to shake us up a bit,' Turner grunted.

'No.' Tyndall was decisive. 'He wouldn't try that – wouldn't dare. Besides, by his lights, he's not a vindictive man.'

Silence fell, a silence broken only by the patter of sleet and hail, and the weird haunting pinging of the Asdic. Vallery suddenly lifted his binoculars.

'Good lord, sir, look at that! The *Duke*'s slipped her anchor!'

There was no doubt about it. The shackle-pin had been knocked out and the bows of the great ship were swinging slowly round as it got under way.

'What in the world—?' Tyndall broke off and scanned the sky. 'Not a plane, not a paratrooper in sight, no radar reports, no Asdic contacts, no sign of the German Grand Fleet steaming through the boom—'

'She's signalling us, sir!' It was Bentley speaking, Bentley, the Chief Yeoman of Signals. He paused and went on slowly: 'Proceed to our anchorage at once. Make fast to north buoy.'

'Ask them to confirm,' Vallery snapped. He took the fo'c'sle phone from the communication rating.

'Captain here, Number One. How is she? Up and down? Good.' He turned to the officer of the watch. 'Slow ahead both: Starboard 10.' He looked over at Tyndall's corner, brows wrinkled in question.

'Search me,' Tyndall growled. 'Could be the latest in parlour games – a sort of nautical musical chairs, you know. . . . Wait a minute, though! Look! The *Cumberland* – all her 5.25's are at maximum depression!'

Vallery's eyes met his.

'No, it can't be! Good God, do you think—?'

The blare of the Asdic loudspeaker, from the cabinet immediately abaft of the bridge, gave him his answer. The voice of Leading Asdic Operator Chrysler was clear, unhurried.

'Asdic – bridge. Asdic – bridge. Echo, Red 30. Repeat, Red 30. Strengthening. Closing.'

The captain's incredulity leapt and died in the same second.

'Alert Director Control! Red 30. All AA guns maximum depression. Underwater target. Torps' – this to Lieutenant Marshall, the Canadian Torpedo Officer – 'depth charge stations.'

He turned back to Tyndall.

'It can't be, sir – it just can't! A U-boat I presume it is – in Scapa Flow. Impossible!'

'Prien didn't think so,' Tyndall grunted.

'Prien?'

'Kapitan-Leutnant Prien – gent who scuppered the *Royal Oak*.'

'It couldn't happen again. The new boom defences—'

'Would keep out any normal submarines,' Tyndall finished. His voice dropped to a murmur. 'Remember what we were told last month about our midget two-man subs – the chariots? The ones to be taken over to Norway by Norwegian fishing-boats operating from the Shetlands. Could be that the Germans have hit on the same idea.'

'Could be,' Vallery agreed. He nodded sardonically. 'Just look at the *Cumberland* go – straight for the boom.' He paused for a few seconds, his eyes speculative, then looked back at Tyndall. 'How do you like it, sir?'

'Like what, Captain?'

'Playing Aunt Sally at the fair.' Vallery grinned crookedly. 'Can't afford to lose umpteen million pounds worth of capital ship. So the old *Duke* hares out to sea and safety, while we moor near her anchor berth. You can bet German Naval Intelligence has the bearing of her anchorage down to a couple of inches. These midget subs carry detachable warheads and if there's going to be any fitted, they're going to be fitted to us.'

Tyndall looked at him. His face was expressionless. Asdic reports were continuous, reporting steady bearing to port and closing distances.

'Of course, of course,' the Admiral murmured. 'We're the whipping boy. Gad, it makes me feel bad!' His mouth twisted and he laughed mirthlessly. 'Me? This is the final straw for the crew. That hellish last trip, the mutiny, the marine boarding party from the *Cumberland*, action stations in harbour – and now this! Risking our necks for that – that . . . ' He broke off, spluttering, swore in anger, then resumed quietly:

'What are you going to tell the men, Captain? Good God, it's fantastic! I feel like mutiny myself . . . ' He stopped short, looked inquiringly past Vallery's shoulder.

The Captain turned round.

'Yes, Marshall?'

'Excuse me, sir. This – er – echo.' He jerked a thumb over his shoulder. 'A sub, sir – possibly a pretty small one?' The transatlantic accent was very heavy.

'Likely enough, Marshall. Why?'

'Just how Ralston and I figured it, sir.' He grinned. 'We have an idea for dealing with it.'

Vallery looked out through the driving sleet, gave helm and engine orders, then turned back to the Torpedo Officer. He was coughing heavily, painfully, as he pointed to the glassed-in anchorage chart.

'If you're thinking of depth-charging our stern off in these shallow waters—'

'No, sir. Doubt whether we could get a shallow enough setting anyway. My idea – Ralston's to be correct – is that we take out the motor-boat and a few 25-lb. scuttling charges, 18-second fuses and chemical igniters. Not much of a kick from these, I know, but a miniature sub ain't likely to have helluva – er – very thick hulls. And if the crews are sitting on top of the ruddy things instead of inside – well, it's curtains for sure. It'll kipper 'em.'

Vallery smiled.

'Not bad at all, Marshall. I think you've got the answer there. What do you think, sir?'

'Worth trying, anyway,' Tyndall agreed. 'Better than waiting around like a sitting duck.'

'Go ahead then, Torps.' Vallery looked at him quizzically. 'Who are your explosives experts?'

'I figured on taking Ralston—'

'Just what I thought. You're taking nobody, laddie,' said Vallery firmly. 'Can't afford to lose my torpedo officer.'

Marshall looked pained, then shrugged resignedly.

'The Chief TGM and Ralston – he's the senior LTO. Good men both.'

'Right. Bentley – detail a man to accompany them in the boat. We'll signal Asdic bearings from here. Have him take a portable Aldis with him.' He dropped his voice. 'Marshall?'

'Sir?'

'Ralston's young brother died in hospital this afternoon.' He looked across at the Leading Torpedo Operator, a tall, blond, unsmiling figure dressed in faded blue overalls beneath his duffel. 'Does he know yet?'

The Torpedo Officer stared at Vallery, then looked round slowly at the LTO. He swore, softly, bitterly, fluently.

'Marshall!' Vallery's voice was sharp, imperative, but Marshall ignored him, his face a mask, oblivious alike to the reprimand in the Captain's voice and the lashing bite of the sleet.

'No, sir,' he stated at length, 'he doesn't know. But he did receive some news this morning. Croydon was pasted last week. His mother and three sisters live there – lived there. It was a land-mine, sir – there was nothing left.' He turned abruptly and left the bridge.

Fifteen minutes later it was all over. The starboard whaler and the motor-boat on the port side hit the water with the *Ulysses* still moving up to the mooring. The whaler, buoy-jumper aboard, made for the buoy, while the motor-boat slid off at a tangent.

Four hundred yards away from the ship, in obedience to the flickering instructions from the bridge, Ralston fished out a pair of pliers from his overalls and crimped the chemical fuse. The Gunner's Mate stared fixedly at his stop-watch. On the count of twelve the scuttling charge went over the side.

Three more, at different settings, followed it in close succession, while the motor-boat cruised in a tight circle. The first three explosions lifted the stern and jarred the entire length of the boat, viciously – and that was all. But with the fourth, a great gout of air came gushing to the surface, followed by a long stream of viscous bubbles. As the turbulence subsided, a thin slick of oil spread over a hundred square yards of sea. . . .

Men, fallen out from Action Stations, watched with expressionless faces as the motor-boat made it back to the *Ulysses* and hooked on to the falls just in time: the Hotchkiss steering-gear was badly twisted and she was taking in water fast under the counter.

The *Duke of Cumberland* was a smudge of smoke over a far headland.

Cap in hand, Ralston sat down opposite the Captain. Vallery looked at him for a long time in silence. He wondered what to say, how best to say it. He hated to have to do this.

Richard Vallery also hated war. He always had hated it and he cursed the day it had dragged him out of his comfortable retirement. At least, 'dragged' was how he put it; only Tyndall knew that he had volunteered his services to the Admiralty on 1st September, 1939, and had had them gladly accepted.

But he hated war. Not because it interfered with his life-long passion for music and literature, on both of which he was a considerable authority, not even because it was a perpetual affront to his aestheticism, to his sense of rightness and fitness. He hated it because he was a deeply religious man, because it grieved him to see in mankind the wild beasts of the primeval jungle, because he thought the cross of life was already burden enough without the gratuitous infliction of the mental and physical agony of war, and, above all, because he saw war all too clearly as the wild and insensate folly it was, as a madness of the mind that settled nothing, proved nothing – except the old, old truth that God was on the side of the big battalions.

But some things he had to do, and Vallery had clearly seen that this war had to be his also. And so he had come back to the service, and had grown older as the bitter years passed, older and frailer, and more kindly and tolerant and understanding. Among Naval Captains, indeed among men, he was unique. In his charity, in his humility, Captain Richard Vallery walked alone. It was a measure of the man's greatness that this thought never occurred to him.

He sighed. All that troubled him just now was what he ought to say to Ralston. But it was Ralston who spoke first.

'It's all right, sir.' The voice was a level monotone, the face very still. 'I know. The Torpedo Officer told me.'

Vallery cleared his throat.

'Words are useless, Ralston, quite useless. Your young brother – and your family at home. All gone. I'm sorry, my boy, terribly sorry about it all.' He looked up into the expressionless face and smiled wryly. 'Or maybe you think that these are all words – you know, something formal, just a meaningless formula.'

Suddenly, surprisingly, Ralston smiled briefly.

'No, sir, I don't. I can appreciate how you feel, sir. You see, my father – well, he's a captain too. He tells me he feels the same way.'

Vallery looked at him in astonishment.

'Your father, Ralston? Did you say—'

'Yes, sir.' Vallery could have sworn to a flicker of amusement in the blue eyes, so quiet, so self-possessed, across the table. 'In the Merchant Navy, sir – a tanker captain – 16,000 tons.'

Vallery said nothing, Ralston went on quietly:

'And about Billy, sir – my young brother. It's – it's just one of these things. It's nobody's fault but mine – I asked to have him aboard here. I'm to blame, sir – only me.' His lean brown hands were round the brim of his hat, twisting it, crushing it. How much worse will it be when the shattering impact of the double blow wears off, Vallery wondered, when the poor kid begins to think straight again?

'Look, my boy, I think you need a few days' rest, time to think things over.' God, Vallery thought, what an inadequate, what a futile thing to say. 'PRO is making out your travelling warrant just now. You will start fourteen days' leave as from tonight.'

'Where is the warrant made out for, sir?' The hat was crushed now, crumpled between the hands. 'Croydon?'

'Of course. Where else—' Vallery stopped dead; the enormity of the blunder had just hit him.

'Forgive me, my boy. What a damnably stupid thing to say!'

'Don't send me away, sir,' Ralston pleaded quietly. 'I know it sounds – well, it sounds corny, self-pitying, but the truth is I've nowhere to go. I belong here – on the *Ulysses*. I can do things all the time – I'm busy – working, sleeping – I don't have to talk about things – I can do things . . .'

The self-possession was only the thinnest veneer, taut and frangible, with the quiet desperation immediately below.

'I can get a chance to help pay 'em back,' Ralston hurried on. 'Like crimping these fuses today – it – well, it was a privilege. It was more than that – it was – oh, I don't know. I can't find the words, sir.'

Vallery knew. He felt sad, tired, defenceless. What could he offer this boy in place of this hate, this very human, consuming flame of revenge? Nothing, he knew, nothing that Ralston wouldn't despise, wouldn't laugh at. This was not the time for pious platitudes. He sighed again, more heavily this time.

'Of course you shall remain, Ralston. Go down to the Police Office and tell them to tear up your warrant. If I can be of any help to you at any time—'

'I understand, sir. Thank you very much. Good night, sir.'

'Good night, my boy.'

The door closed softly behind him.

Chapter Two

Monday Morning

'Close all water-tight doors and scuttles. Hands to stations for leaving harbour.' Impersonally, inexorably, the metallic voice of the broadcast system reached into every farthest corner of the ship.

And from every corner of the ship men came in answer to the call. They were cold men, shivering involuntarily in the icy north wind, sweating pungently as the heavy falling snow drifted under collars and cuffs, as numbed hands stuck to frozen ropes and metal. They were tired men, for fuelling, provisioning and ammunitioning had gone on far into the middle watch: few had had more than three hours' sleep.

And they were still angry, hostile men. Orders were obeyed, to be sure, with the mechanical efficiency of a highly-trained ship's company; but obedience was surly, acquiescence resentful, and insolence lay ever close beneath the surface. But Divisional Officers and NCOs handled the men with velvet gloves. Vallery had been emphatic about that.

Illogically enough, the highest pitch of resentment had not been caused by the *Cumberland*'s prudent withdrawal. It had been produced the previous evening by the routine broadcast. 'Mail will close at 2000 tonight.' Mail! Those who weren't working non-stop round the clock were sleeping like the dead with neither the heart nor the will even to think of writing. Leading Seaman Doyle, the doyen of 'B' mess-deck and a venerable three-badger (thirteen years' undiscovered crime, as he modestly explained his good-conduct stripes) had summed up the matter succinctly: 'If my old Missus was Helen of Troy and Jane Russell rolled into one – and all you blokes wot have seen the old dear's photo know that the very idea's a shocking libel on either of them ladies – I still wouldn't send her even a bleedin' postcard. You gotta draw a line somewhere. Me, for my scratcher.' Whereupon he had dragged his hammock from the rack, slung it with millimetric accuracy beneath a hot-air louvre – seniority carries its privileges – and was asleep in two minutes. To a man, the port watch did likewise: the mail bag had gone ashore almost empty. . . .

At 0600, exactly to the minute, the *Ulysses* slipped her moorings and steamed slowly towards the boom. In the grey half-light, under leaden, lowering clouds, she slid across the anchorage like an insubstantial ghost, more often than not half-hidden from view under sudden, heavy flurries of snow.

Even in the relatively clear spells, she was difficult to locate. She lacked solidity, substance, definition of outline. She had a curious air of impermanence, of volatility. An illusion, of course, but an illusion that accorded well with a legend – for a legend the *Ulysses* had become in her own brief lifetime. She was known and cherished by merchant seamen, by the men who sailed the bitter seas of the North, from St John's to Archangel, from the Shetlands to Jan Mayen, from Greenland to far reaches of Spitzbergen, remote on the edge of the world. Where there was danger, where there was death, there you might look to find the *Ulysses*, materializing wraith-like from a fog-bank, or just miraculously, being there when the bleak twilight of an Arctic dawn brought with it only the threat, at times almost the certainty, of never seeing the next.

A ghost-ship, almost, a legend. The *Ulysses* was also a young ship, but she had grown old in the Russian Convoys and on the Arctic patrols. She had been there from the beginning, and had known no other life. At first she had operated alone, escorting single ships or groups of two or three: later, she had operated with corvettes and frigates, and now she never moved without her squadron, the 14th Escort Carrier group.

But the *Ulysses* had never really sailed alone. Death had been, still was, her constant companion. He laid his finger on a tanker, and there was the erupting hell of a high-octane detonation; on a cargo liner, and she went to the bottom with her load of war supplies, her back broken by a German torpedo; on a destroyer, and she knifed her way into the grey-black depths of the Barents Sea, her still-racing engines her own executioners; on a U-boat, and she surfaced violently to be destroyed by gunfire, or slid down gently to the bottom of the sea, the dazed, shocked crew hoping for a cracked pressure hull and merciful instant extinction, dreading the endless gasping agony of suffocation in their iron tomb on the ocean floor. Where the *Ulysses* went, there also went death. But death never touched her. She was a lucky ship. A lucky ship and a ghost-ship and the Arctic was her home.

Illusion, of course, this ghostliness, but a calculated illusion. The *Ulysses* was designed specifically for one task, for one ocean, and the camouflage experts had done a marvellous job. The special Arctic camouflage, the broken, slanting diagonals of grey and white and washed-out blues merged beautifully, imperceptibly into the infinite shades of grey and white, the cold, bleak grimness of the barren northern seas.

And the camouflage was only the outward, the superficial indication of her fitness for the North.

Technically, the *Ulysses* was a light cruiser. She was the only one of her kind, a 5500-ton modification of the famous *Dido* type, a forerunner of the

Black Prince class. Five hundred and ten feet long, narrow in her fifty-foot beam with a raked stem, square cruiser stern and long fo'c'sle deck extending well abaft the bridge – a distance of over two hundred feet, she looked and was a lean, fast and compact warship, dangerous and durable.

'Locate: engage: destroy.' These are the classic requirements of a naval ship in wartime, and to do each, and to do it with maximum speed and efficiency, the *Ulysses* was superbly equipped.

'Location, for instance. The human element, of course, was indispensable, and Vallery was far too experienced and battle-wise a captain to underestimate the value of the unceasing vigil of look-outs and signalmen. The human eye was not subject to blackout, technical hitches or mechanical breakdowns. Radio reports, too, had their place and Asdic, of course, was the only defence against submarines.

But the *Ulysses*'s greatest strength in location lay elsewhere. She was the first completely equipped radar ship in the world. Night and day, the radar scanners atop the fore and main tripod masts swept ceaselessly in a 360° arc, combing the far horizons, searching, searching. Below, in the radar rooms – eight in all – and in the Fighter Direction rooms, trained eyes, alive to the slightest abnormality, never left the glowing screens. The radar's efficiency and range were alike fantastic. The makers, optimistically, as they had thought, had claimed a 40–45 mile operating range for their equipment. On the *Ulysses*'s first trials after her refit for its installation, the radar had located a Condor, subsequently destroyed by a Blenheim, at a range of eighty-five miles.

Engage – that was the next step. Sometimes the enemy came to you, more often you had to go after him. And then, one thing alone mattered – speed.

The *Ulysses* was tremendously fast. Quadruple screws powered by four great Parsons single-reduction geared turbines – two in the for'ard, two in the after engine-room – developed an unbelievable horse-power that many a battleship, by no means obsolete, could not match. Officially, she was rated at 33.5 knots. Off Arran, in her full-power trials, bows lifting out of the water, stern dug in like a hydroplane, vibrating in every Clyde-built rivet, and with the tortured, seething water boiling whitely ten feet above the level of the poop-deck, she had covered the measured mile at an incredible 39.2 knots – the nautical equivalent of 45 mph. And the 'Dude' – Engineer-Commander Dobson – had smiled knowingly, said he wasn't half trying and just wait till the *Abdiel* or the *Manxman* came along, and he'd show them something. But as these famous mine-laying cruisers were widely believed to be capable of 44 knots, the wardroom had merely sniffed 'Professional jealousy' and ignored him. Secretly, they were as proud of the great engines as Dobson himself.

Locate, engage – and destroy. Destruction. That was the be-all, the end-all. Lay the enemy along the sights and destroy him. The *Ulysses* was well equipped for that also.

She had four twin gun-turrets, two for'ard, two aft, 5.25 quick-firing and dual-purpose – equally effective against surface targets and aircraft. These were controlled from the Director Towers, the main one for'ard, just above and abaft of the bridge, the auxiliary aft. From these towers, all essential data about bearing, wind-speed, drift, range, own speed, enemy speed, respective angles of course were fed to the giant electronic computing tables in the Transmitting Station, the fighting heart of the ship, situated, curiously enough, in the very bowels of the *Ulysses*, deep below the water-line, and thence automatically to the turrets as two simple factors – elevation and training. The turrets, of course, could also fight independently.

These were the main armament. The remaining guns were purely AA – the batteries of multiple pom-poms, firing two-pounders in rapid succession, not particularly accurate but producing a blanket curtain sufficient to daunt any enemy pilot, and isolated clusters of twin Oerlikons, high-precision, high-velocity weapons, vicious and deadly in trained hands.

Finally, the *Ulysses* carried her depth-charges and torpedoes – 36 charges only, a negligible number compared to that carried by many corvettes and destroyers, and the maximum number that could be dropped in one pattern was six. But one depth-charge carries 450 lethal pounds of Amatol, and the *Ulysses* had destroyed two U-boats during the preceding winter. The 21-inch torpedoes, each with its 750-pound warhead of TNT, lay sleek and menacing, in the triple tubes on the main deck, one set on either side of the after funnel. These had not yet been blooded.

This, then was the *Ulysses*. The complete, the perfect fighting machine, man's ultimate, so far, in his attempt to weld science and savagery into an instrument of destruction. The perfect fighting machine – but only so long as it was manned and serviced by a perfectly-integrating smoothly-functioning team. A ship – any ship – can never be better than its crew. And the crew of the *Ulysses* was disintegrating, breaking up: the lid was clamped on the volcano, but the rumblings never ceased.

The first signs of further trouble came within three hours of clearing harbour. As always, minesweepers swept the channel ahead of them, but, as always, Vallery left nothing to chance. It was one of the reasons why he – and the *Ulysses* – had survived thus far. At 0620 he streamed paravanes – the slender, torpedo-shaped bodies which angled out from the bows, one on either side, on special paravane wire. In theory, the wires connecting mines to their moorings on the floor of the sea were deflected away from the ship, guided out to the paravanes themselves and severed by cutters: the mines would then float to the top to be exploded or sunk by small arms.

At 0900, Vallery ordered the paravanes to be recovered. The *Ulysses* slowed down. The First Lieutenant, Lieutenant-Commander Carrington, went to the fo'c'sle to supervise operations: seamen, winch drivers, and the Subs. in charge of either side closed up to their respective stations.

Quickly the recovery booms were freed from their angled crutches, just abaft the port and starboard lights, swung out and rigged with recovery wires. Immediately, the three-ton winches on 'B' gun-deck took the strain, smoothly, powerfully; the paravanes cleared the water.

Then it happened. It was AB Ferry's fault that it happened. And it was just ill-luck that the port winch was suspect, operating on a power circuit with a defective breaker, just ill-luck that Ralston was the winch-driver, a taciturn, bitter-mouthed Ralston to whom, just then, nothing mattered a damn, least of all what he said and did. But it was Carslake's responsibility that the affair developed into what it did.

Sub-Lieutenant Carslake's presence there, on top of the Carley floats, directing the handling of the port wire, represented the culmination of a series of mistakes. A mistake on the part of his father, Rear-Admiral, Rtd., who had seen in his son a man of his own calibre, had dragged him out of

Cambridge in 1939 at the advanced age of twenty-six and practically forced him into the Navy: a weakness on the part of his first CO, a corvette captain who had known his father and recommended him as a candidate for a commission: a rare error of judgment on the part of the selection board of the *King Alfred*, who had granted him his commission; and a temporary lapse on the part of the Commander, who had assigned him to his duty, in spite of Carslake's known incompetence and inability to handle men.

He had the face of an overbred racehorse, long, lean and narrow, with prominent pale-blue eyes and protruding upper teeth. Below his scanty fair hair, his eyebrows were arched in a perpetual question mark: beneath the long, pointed nose, the supercilious curl of the upper lip formed the perfect complement to the eyebrows. His speech was a shocking caricature of the King's English: his short vowels were long, his long ones interminable: his grammar was frequently execrable. He resented the Navy, he resented his long overdue promotion to Lieutenant, he resented the way the men resented him. In brief, Sub-Lieutenant Carslake was the quintessence of the worst by-product of the English public-school system. Vain, superior, uncouth and ill-educated, he was a complete ass.

He was making an ass of himself now. Striving to maintain balance on the rafts, feet dramatically braced at a wide angle, he shouted unceasing commands at his men. CPO Hartley groaned aloud, but kept otherwise silent in the interests of discipline. And AB Ferry felt himself under no such restraints.

' 'Ark at his Lordship,' he murmured to Ralston. 'All for the Skipper's benefit.' He nodded at where Vallery was leaning over the bridge, twenty feet above Carslake's head. 'Impresses him no end, so his nibs reckons.'

'Just you forget about Carslake and keep your eyes on that wire,' Ralston advised. 'And take these damned great gloves off. One of these days—'

'Yes, yes, I know,' Ferry jeered. 'The wire's going to snag 'em and wrap me round the drum.' He fed in the hawser expertly. 'Don't you worry, chum, it's never going to happen to me.'

But it did. It happened just then. Ralston, watching the swinging paravane closely, flicked a glance inboard. He saw the broken strand inches from Ferry, saw it hook viciously into the gloved hand and drag him towards the spinning drum before Ferry had a chance to cry out.

Ralston's reaction was immediate. The foot-brake was only six inches away – but that was too far. Savagely he spun the control wheel, full ahead to full reverse in a split second. Simultaneously with Ferry's cry of pain as his forearm crushed against the lip of the drum came a muffled explosion and clouds of acrid smoke from the winch as £500 worth of electric motor burnt out in a searing flash.

Immediately the wire began to run out again, accelerating momentarily under the dead weight of the plunging paravane. Ferry went with it. Twenty feet from the winch the wire passed through a snatch-block on the deck: if Ferry was lucky, he might lose only his hand.

He was less than four feet away when Ralston's foot stamped viciously on the brake. The racing drum screamed to a shuddering stop, the paravanes crashed down into the sea and the wire, weightless now, swung idly to the rolling of the ship.

Carslake scrambled down off the Carley, his sallow face suffused with anger. He strode up to Ralston.

'You bloody fool!' he mouthed furiously. 'You've lost us that paravane. By God, LTO, you'd better explain yourself! Who the hell gave you orders to do anything?'

Ralston's mouth tightened, but he spoke civilly enough.

'Sorry, sir. Couldn't help it – it had to be done. Ferry's arm—'

'To hell with Ferry's arm!' Carslake was almost screaming with rage. 'I'm in charge here – and I give the orders. Look! Look!' He pointed to the swinging wire. 'Your work Ralston, you – you blundering idiot! It's gone, gone, do you understand, *gone*?'

'Well, now, so it is.' The eyes were bleak, the tone provocative, as he looked back at Carslake and patted the winch. 'And don't forget this – it's gone too, and it costs a ruddy sight more than any paravane.'

'I don't want any of your damned impertinence!' Carslake shouted. His mouth was working, his voice shaking with passion. 'What you need is to have some discipline knocked into you and, by God, I'm going to see you get it, you insolent young bastard!'

Ralston flushed darkly. He took one quick step forward, his fist balled, then relaxed heavily as the powerful hands of CPO Hartley caught his swinging arm. But the damage was done now. There was nothing for it but the bridge.

Vallery listened calmly, patiently, as Carslake made his outraged report. He felt far from patient. God only knew, he thought wearily, he had more than enough to cope with already. But the unruffled professional mask of detachment gave no hint of his feelings.

'Is this true, Ralston?' he asked quietly, as Carslake finished his tirade. 'You disobeyed orders, swore at the Lieutenant and insulted him?'

'No, sir.' Ralston sounded as weary as the Captain felt. 'It's not true.' He looked at Carslake, his face expressionless, then turned back to the Captain. 'I didn't disobey orders – there were none. Chief Petty Officer Hartley knows that.' He nodded at the burly impassive figure who had accompanied them to the bridge. 'I didn't swear at him. I hate to sound like a sea-lawyer, sir, but there are plenty of witnesses that Sub-Lieutenant Carslake swore at me – several times. And if I insulted him' – he smiled faintly – 'it was pure self-defence.'

'This is no place for levity, Ralston.' Vallery's voice was cold. He was puzzled – the boy baffled him. The bitterness, the brittle composure – he could understand these; but not the flickering humour. 'As it happens, I saw the entire incident. Your promptness, your resource, saved that rating's arm, possibly even his life – and against that a lost paravane and wrecked winch are nothing.' Carslake whitened at the implied rebuke. 'I'm grateful for that – thank you. As for the rest, Commander's Defaulters tomorrow morning. Carry on, Ralston.'

Ralston compressed his lips, looked at Vallery for a long moment, then saluted abruptly and left the bridge.

Carslake turned round appealingly.

'Captain, sir . . . ' He stopped at the sight of Vallery's upraised hand.

'Not now, Carslake. We'll discuss it later.' He made no attempt to conceal the dislike in his voice. 'You may carry on, Lieutenant. Hartley – a word with you.'

Hartley stepped forward. Forty-four years old, CPO Hartley was the Royal Navy at its best. Very tough, very kindly and very competent, he enjoyed the admiration of all, ranging from the vast awe of the youngest Ordinary Seaman to the warm respect of the Captain himself. They had been together from the beginning.

'Well, Chief, let's have it. Between ourselves.'

'Nothing to it really, sir.' Hartley shrugged. 'Ralston did a fine job. Sub-Lieutenant Carslake lost his head. Maybe Ralston *was* a bit sassy, but he was provoked. He's only a kid, but he's a professional – and he doesn't like being pushed around by amateurs.' Hartley paused and looked up at the sky. 'Especially bungling amateurs.'

Vallery smothered a smile.

'Could that be interpreted as – er – a criticism, Chief?'

'I suppose so, sir.' He nodded forward. 'A few ruffled feathers down there, sir. Men are pretty sore about this. Shall I—?'

'Thanks, Chief. Play it down as much as possible.'

When Hartley had gone, Vallery turned to Tyndall.

'Well, you heard it, sir? Another straw in the wind.'

'A straw?' Tyndall was acid. 'Hundreds of straws. More like a bloody great cornstack. . . . Find out who was outside my door last night?'

During the middle watch, Tyndall had heard an unusual scraping noise outside the wardroom entry to his day cabin, had gone to investigate himself: in his hurry to reach the door, he'd knocked a chair over, and seconds later he had heard a clatter and the patter of running feet in the passage outside; but, when he had thrown the door open, the passage had been empty. Nothing there, nothing at all – except a file on the deck, below the case of Navy Colt .445s; the chain on the trigger guards was almost through.

Vallery shook his head.

'No idea at all, sir.' His face was heavy with worry. 'Bad, really bad.'

Tyndall shivered in an icy flurry. He grinned crookedly.

'Real Captain Teach Stuff, eh? Pistols and cutlasses and black eye-patches, storming the bridge . . . '

Vallery shook his head impatiently.

'No, not that. You know it, sir. Defiance, maybe, but – well, no more. The point is, a marine is on guard at the keyboard – just round the corner of that passage. Night and day. Bound to have seen him. He denies—'

'The rot has gone that far?' Tyndall whistled softly. 'A black day, Captain. What does our fire-eating young Captain of Marines say to that?'

'Foster? Pooh-poohs the very idea – and just about twists the ends of his moustache off. Worried to hell. So's Evans, his Colour-Sergeant.'

'So am I!' said Tyndall feelingly. He glared into space. The Officer of the Watch, who happened to be in his direct line of vision, shifted uncomfortably. 'Wonder what old Socrates thinks of it all, now? Maybe only a pill-roller, but the wisest head we've got. . . . Well, speak of the devil!'

The gate had just swung open, and a burly, unhappy-looking figure, duffel-coated, oilskinned and wearing a Russian beaverskin helmet – the total effect was of an elderly grizzly bear caught in a thunderstorm – shuffled across the duckboards of the bridge. He brought up facing the Kent screen – an inset, circular sheet of glass which revolved at high speed and offered a clear view in all weather conditions – rain, hail, snow. For half a minute he peered miserably through this and obviously didn't like what he saw.

He sniffed loudly and turned away, beating his arms against the cold.

'Ha! A deck officer on the bridge of HM Cruisers. The romance, the glamour! Ha!' He hunched his oilskinned shoulders, and looked more miserable than ever. 'No place this for a civilized man like myself. But you know how it is, gentlemen – the clarion call of duty. . . . '

Tyndall chuckled.

'Give him plenty of time, Captain. Slow starters, these medics, you know, but—'

Brooks cut in, voice and face suddenly serious.

'Some more trouble, Captain. Couldn't tell it over the phone. Don't know how much it's worth.'

'Trouble?' Vallery broke off, coughed harshly into his handkerchief. 'Sorry,' he apologized. 'Trouble? There's nothing else, old chap. Just had some ourselves.'

'That bumptious young fool, Carslake? Oh, I know all right. My spies are everywhere. Bloke's a bloody menace. . . . However, my story.

'Young Nicholls was doing some path. work late last night in the dispensary – on TB specimens. Two, three hours in there. Lights out in the bay, and the patients either didn't know or had forgotten he was there. Heard Stoker Riley – a real trouble-maker, that Riley – and the others planning a locked-door, sit-down strike in the boiler-room when they return to duty. A sit-down strike in a boiler-room. Good lord, it's fantastic! Anyway, Nicholls let it slide – pretended he hadn't heard.'

'What!' Vallery's voice was sharp, edged with anger. 'And Nicholls ignored it, didn't report it to me! Happened last night, you say. Why wasn't I told – immediately? Get Nicholls up here – now. No, never mind.' He reached out to pick up the bridge phone. 'I'll get him myself.'

Brooks laid a gauntleted hand on Vallery's arm.

'I wouldn't do that, sir. Nicholls is a smart boy – very smart indeed. He knew that if he let the men know they had been overheard, they would know that he must report it to you. And then you'd have been bound to take action – and open provocation of trouble is the last thing you want. You said so yourself in the wardroom last night.'

Vallery hesitated. 'Yes, yes, of course I said that, but – well, Doc, this is different. It could be a focal point for spreading the idea to—'

'I told you, sir,' Brooks interrupted softly. 'Johnny Nicholls is a very smart boy. He's got a big notice, in huge red letters, outside the Sick Bay door: "Keep clear: Suspected scarlet fever infection." Kills me to watch 'em. Everybody avoids the place like the plague. Not a hope of communicating with their pals in the Stokers' Mess.'

Tyndall guffawed at him, and even Vallery smiled slightly.

'Sounds fine, Doc. Still, I should have been told last night.'

'Why should you be woken up and told every little thing in the middle of the night?' Brooks's voice was brusque. 'Sheer selfishness on my part, but what of it? When things get bad, you damn' well carry this ship on your back – and when we've all got to depend on you, we can't afford to have you anything less than as fit as possible. Agreed, Admiral?'

Tyndall nodded solemnly. 'Agreed, O Socrates. A very complicated way of saying that you wish the Captain to have a good night's sleep. But agreed.'

Brooks grinned amiably. 'Well, that's all, gentlemen. See you all at the court-martial – I hope.' He cocked a jaundiced eye over a shoulder, into the thickening snow. 'Won't the Med. be wonderful, gentlemen?' He sighed and slid effortlessly into his native Galway brogue. 'Malta in the spring. The beach at Sliema – with the white houses behind – where we picnicked, a hundred years ago. The soft winds, me darlin' boys, the *warm* winds, the blue skies and Chianti under a striped umbrella—'

'Off!' Tyndall roared. 'Get off this bridge, Brooks, or I'll—'

'I'm gone already,' said Brooks. 'A sit-down strike in the boiler-room! Ha! First thing you know, there'll be a rash of male suffragettes chaining themselves to the guard-rails!' The gate clanged shut behind him.

Vallery turned to the Admiral, his face grave.

'Looks as if you were right about the cornstack, sir.'

Tyndall grunted, non-committally.

'Maybe. Trouble is, the men have nothing to do right now except brood and curse and feel bitter about everything. Later on it'll be all right – perhaps.'

'When we get – ah – busier, you mean?'

'Mmm. When you're fighting for your life, to keep the ship afloat – well, you haven't much time for plots and pondering over the injustices of fate. Self-preservation is still the first law of nature. . . . Speaking to the men tonight, Captain?'

'Usual routine broadcast, yes. In the first dog, when we're all closed up to dusk action stations.' Vallery smiled briefly. 'Make sure that they're all awake.'

'Good. Lay it on, thick and heavy. Give 'em plenty to think about – and, if I'm any judge of Vincent Starr's hints, we're going to *have* plenty to think about this trip. It'll keep 'em occupied.'

Vallery laughed. The laugh transformed his thin sensitive face. He seemed genuinely amused.

Tyndall lifted an interrogatory eyebrow. Vallery smiled back at him.

'Just passing thoughts, sir. As Spencer Faggot would have said, things have come to a pretty pass. . . . Things are bad indeed, when only the enemy can save us.'

Chapter Three

Monday Afternoon

All day long the wind blew steadily out of the nor'-nor'-west. A strong wind, and blowing stronger. A cold wind, a sharp wind full of little knives, it carried with it snow and ice and the strange dead smell born of the forgotten ice-caps that lie beyond the Barrier. It wasn't a gusty, blowy wind. It was a settled, steady kind of wind, and it stayed fine on the starboard bow from dawn to dusk. Slowly, stealthily, it was lifting a swell. Men like Carrington, who knew every sea and port in the world, like Vallery and Hartley, looked at it and were troubled and said nothing.

The mercury crept down and the snow lay where it fell. The tripods and yardarms were great, glistening Xmas trees, festooned with woolly stays and halliards. On the mainmast, a brown smear appeared now and then, daubed on by a wisp of smoke from the after funnel, felt rather than seen: in a moment, it would vanish. The snow lay on the deck and drifted. It softened the anchor-cables on the fo'c'sle deck into great, fluffy ropes of cotton-wool, and drifted high against the breakwater before 'A' turret. It piled up against the turrets and superstructure, swished silently into the bridge and lay there slushily underfoot. It blocked the great eyes of the Director's range-finder, it crept unseen along passages, it sifted soundlessly down hatches. It sought out the tiniest unprotected chink in metal and wood, and made the mess-decks dank and clammy and uncomfortable: it defied gravity and slid effortlessly up trouser legs, up under the skirts of coats and oilskins, up under duffel hoods, and made men thoroughly miserable. A miserable world, a wet world, but always and predominantly a white world of softness and beauty and strangely muffled sound. All day long it fell, this snow, fell steadily and persistently, and the *Ulysses* slid on silently through the swell, a ghost ship in a ghost world.

But not alone in her world. She never was, these days. She had companionship, a welcome, reassuring companionship, the company of the 14th Aircraft Squadron, a tough, experienced and battle-hardened escort group, almost as legendary now as that fabulous Force 8, which had lately moved South to take over that other suicide run, the Malta convoys.

Like the *Ulysses*, the squadron steamed NNW all day long. There were no dog-legs, no standard course alterations. Tyndall abhorred the zig-zag, and, except on actual convoy and then only in known U-boat waters, rarely used it. He believed – as many captains did – that the zig-zag was a greater potential source of danger than the enemy. He had seen the *Curaçoa*, 4200 tons of cockle-shell cruiser, swinging on a routine zig-zag, being trampled into the grey depths of the Atlantic under the mighty forefoot of the *Queen Mary*. He never spoke of it, but the memory stayed with him.

The *Ulysses* was in her usual position – the position dictated by her role of Squadron flagship – as nearly as possible in the centre of the thirteen warships.

Dead ahead steamed the cruiser *Stirling*. An old Cardiff class cruiser, she was a solid reliable ship, many years older and many knots slower than the *Ulysses*, adequately armed with five single six-inch guns, but hardly built to hammer her way through the Arctic gales: in heavy seas, her wetness was proverbial. Her primary role was squadron defence: her secondary, to take over the squadron if the flagship were crippled or sunk.

The carriers – *Defender, Invader, Wrestler* and *Blue Ranger* – were in position to port and starboard, the *Defender* and *Wrestler* slightly ahead of the *Ulysses*, the others slightly astern. It seemed *de rigeur* for these escort carriers to have names ending in -er and the fact that the Navy already had a *Wrestler* – a Force 8 destroyer (and a *Defender*, which had been sunk some time previously off Tobruk) – was blithely ignored. These were not the 35,000-ton giants of the regular fleet – ships like the *Indefatigable* and the *Illustrious* – but 15-20,000-ton auxiliary carriers, irreverently known as banana boats. They were converted merchantmen, American-built: these had been fitted out at Pascagoula, Mississippi, and sailed across the Atlantic by mixed British-American crews.

They were capable of eighteen knots, a relatively high speed for a single-screw ship – the *Wrestler* had two screws – but some of them had as many as four Busch-Sulzer Diesels geared to the one shaft. Their painfully rectangular flight-decks, 450 feet in length, were built up above the open fo'c'sle – one could see right under the flight-deck for'ard of the bridge – and flew off about thirty fighters – Grummans, Sea-fires or, most often, Corsairs – or twenty light bombers. They were odd craft, awkward, ungainly and singularly unwarlike; but over the months they had done a magnificent job of providing umbrella cover against air attack, of locating and destroying enemy ships and submarines: their record of kills, above, on and below the water was impressive and frequently disbelieved by the Admiralty.

Nor was the destroyer screen calculated to inspire confidence among the naval strategists at Whitehall. It was a weird hodge-podge, and the term 'destroyer' was a purely courtesy one.

One, the *Nairn*, was a River class frigate of 1500 tons: another, the *Eager*, was a Fleet Minesweeper, and a third, the *Gannet*, better known as *Huntley and Palmer*, was a rather elderly and very tired Kingfisher corvette, supposedly restricted to coastal duties only. There was no esoteric mystery as to the origin of her nickname – a glance at her silhouette against the sunset was enough. Doubtless her designer had worked within Admiralty specifications: even so, he must have had an off day.

The *Vectra* and the *Viking* were twin-screwed, modified 'V' and 'W' destroyers, in the superannuated class now, lacking in speed and fire-power, but tough and durable. The *Baliol* was a diminutive Hunt class destroyer which had no business in the great waters of the North. The *Portpatrick*, a skeleton-lean four stacker, was one of the fifty lend-lease World War I destroyers from the United States. No one even dared guess at her age. An intriguing ship at any time, she became the focus of all eyes in the fleet and a source of intense interest whenever the weather broke down. Rumour had it that two of her sister ships had overturned in the Atlantic during a gale; human nature being what it is, everyone wanted a grandstand view whenever weather conditions deteriorated to an extent likely to afford early confirmation of these rumours. What the crew of the *Portpatrick* thought about it all was difficult to say.

These seven escorts, blurred and softened by the snow, kept their screening stations all day – the frigate and mine-sweeper ahead, the destroyers at the sides, and the corvette astern. The eighth escort, a fast, modern 'S' class destroyer, under the command of the Captain (Destroyers), Commander Orr, prowled restlessly around the fleet. Every ship commander in the squadron envied Orr his roving commission, a duty which Tyndall had assigned him in self-defence against Orr's continual pestering. But no one objected, no one grudged him his privilege: the *Sirrus* had an uncanny nose for trouble, an almost magnetic affinity for U-boats lying in ambush.

From the warmth of the *Ulysses's* wardroom – long, incongruously comfortable, running fifty feet along the starboard side of the fo'c'sle deck – Johnny Nicholls gazed out through the troubled grey and white of the sky. Even the kindly snow, he reflected, blanketing a thousand sins, could do little for these queer craft, so angular, so graceless, so obviously out-dated.

He supposed he ought to feel bitter at My Lords of the Admiralty, with their limousines and arm-chairs and elevenses, with their big wall-maps and pretty little flags, sending out this raggle-taggle of a squadron to cope with the pick of the U-boat packs, while they sat comfortably, luxuriously at home. But the thought died at birth: it was, he knew, grotesquely unjust. The Admiralty would have given them a dozen brand-new destroyers – if they had them. Things, he knew, were pretty bad, and the demands of the Atlantic and the Mediterranean had first priority.

He supposed, too, he ought to feel cynical, ironic, at the sight of these old and worn-out ships. Strangely, he couldn't. He knew what they could do, what they had done. If he felt anything at all towards them, it was something uncommonly close to admiration – perhaps even pride. Nicholls stirred uncomfortably and turned away from the porthole. His gaze fell on the somnolent form of the Kapok Kid, flat on his back in an arm-chair, an enormous pair of fur-lined flying-boots perched above the electric fire.

The Kapok Kid, Lieutenant the Honourable Andrew Carpenter, RN, Navigator of the *Ulysses* and his best friend – he was the one to feel proud, Nicholls thought wryly. The most glorious extrovert Nicholls had ever known, the Kapok Kid was equally at home anywhere – on a dance floor or in the cockpit of a racing yacht at Cowes, at a garden party, on a tennis court or at the wheel of his big crimson Bugatti, windscreen down and the loose ends of a seven-foot scarf streaming out behind him. But appearances were never more deceptive. For the Kapok Kid, the Royal Navy was his whole life, and he lived for that alone. Behind that slightly inane façade lay, besides a first-class brain, a deeply romantic streak, an almost Elizabethan love for sea and ships which he sought, successfully, he imagined, to conceal from all his fellow-officers. It was patently obvious that no one ever thought it worth the mentioning.

Theirs was a curious friendship, Nicholls mused. An attraction of opposites, if ever there was one. For Carpenter's hail-fellow ebullience, his natural reserve and reticence were the perfect foil: over against his friend's near-idolatry of all things naval stood his own thorough-going detestation of all that the Kapok Kid so warmly admired. Perhaps because of that over-developed sense of individuality and independence, that bane of so many highland Scots, Nicholls objected strongly to the thousand and one pin-pricks of discipline, authority and bureaucratic naval stupidity which were a constant affront to his intelligence and self-respect. Even three years ago, when the war had snatched him from the wards of a great Glasgow hospital, his first year's internship barely completed, he had his dark suspicions that the degree of compatibility between himself and the Senior Service would prove to be singularly low. And so it had proved. But, in spite of this antipathy – or perhaps because of it and the curse of a Calvinistic conscience – Nicholls had become a first-class officer. But it still disturbed him vaguely to discover in himself something akin to pride in the ships of his squadron.

He sighed. The loudspeaker in the corner of the wardroom had just crackled into life. From bitter experience, he knew that broadcast announcements seldom presaged anything good.

'Do you hear there? Do you hear there?' The voice was metallic, impersonal: the Kapok Kid slept on in magnificent oblivion. 'The Captain will broadcast to the ship's company at 1730 tonight. Repeat. The Captain will broadcast to the ship's company at 1730 tonight. That is all.'

Nicholls prodded the Kapok Kid with a heavy toe. 'On your feet, Vasco. Now's the time if you want a cuppa char before getting up there and navigating.' Carpenter stirred, opened a red-rimmed eye: Nicholls smiled down encouragingly. 'Besides, it's lovely up top now – sea rising, temperature falling and a young blizzard blowing. Just what you were born for, Andy, boy!'

The Kapok Kid groaned his way back to consciousness, struggled to a sitting position and remained hunched forward, his straight flaxen hair falling over his hands.

'What's the matter now?' His voice was querulous, still slurred with sleep. Then he grinned faintly. 'Know where I was, Johnny?' he asked reminiscently. 'Back on the Thames, at the Grey Goose, just up from Henley. It was summer, Johnny, late in summer, warm and very still. Dressed all in green, she was—'

'Indigestion,' Nicholls cut in briskly. 'Too much easy living. . . . It's four-thirty, and the old man's speaking in an hour's time. Dusk stations at any time – we'd better eat.'

Carpenter shook his head mournfully. 'The man has no soul, no finer feelings.' He stood up and stretched himself. As always, he was dressed from head to foot in a one-piece overall of heavy, quilted kapok – the silk fibres encasing the seeds of the Japanese and Malayan silk-cotton tree: there was a great, golden 'J' embroidered on the right breast pocket: what it stood for was anyone's guess. He glanced out through the porthole and shuddered.

'Wonder what's the topic for tonight, Johnny?'

'No idea. I'm curious to see what his attitude, his tone is going to be, how he's going to handle it. The situation, to say the least, is somewhat – ah – delicate.' Nicholls grinned, but the smile didn't touch his eyes. 'Not to mention the fact that the crew don't know that they're off to Murmansk again – although they must have a pretty good idea.'

'Mmm.' The Kapok Kid nodded absently. 'Don't suppose the old man'll try to play it down – the hazards of the trip, I mean, or to excuse himself – you know, put the blame where it belongs.'

'Never.' Nicholls shook his head decisively. 'Not the skipper. Just not in his nature. Never excuses himself – and never spares himself.' He stared into the fire for a long time, then looked up quietly at the Kapok Kid. 'The skipper's a very sick man, Andy – very sick indeed.'

'What!' The Kapok Kid was genuinely startled. 'A very sick . . . Good lord, you're joking! You must be, Why—'

'I'm not,' Nicholls interrupted flatly, his voice very low. Winthrop, the padre, an intense, enthusiastic, very young man with an immense zest for life and granitic convictions on every subject under the sun, was in the far corner of the wardroom. The zest was temporarily in abeyance – he was sunk in exhausted slumber. Nicholls liked him, but preferred that he should not hear – the padre would talk. Winthrop, Nicholls had often thought, would never have made a successful priest – confessional reticence would have been impossible for him.

'Old Socrates says he's pretty far through – and he knows,' Nicholls continued. 'Old man phoned him to come to his cabin last night. Place was covered in blood and he was coughing his lungs up. Acute attack of haemoptysis. Brooks has suspected it for a long time, but the Captain would never let him examine him. Brooks says a few more days of this will kill him.' He broke off, glanced briefly at Winthrop. 'I talk too much,' he said abruptly. 'Getting as bad as the old padre there. Shouldn't have told you,

I suppose – violation of professional confidence and all that. All this under your hat, Andy.'

'Of course, of course.' There was a long pause. 'What you mean is, Johnny – he's dying?'

'Just that. Come on, Andy – char.'

Twenty minutes later, Nicholls made his way down to the Sick Bay. The light was beginning to fail and the *Ulysses* was pitching heavily. Brooks was in the surgery.

'Evening, sir. Dusk stations any minute now. Mind if I stay in the bay tonight?'

Brooks eyed him speculatively.

'Regulations,' he intoned, 'say that the Action Stations position of the Junior Medical Officer is aft in the Engineer's Flat. Far be it from me—'

'Please.'

'Why? Lonely, lazy or just plain tired?' The quirk of the eyebrows robbed the words of all offence.

'No. Curious. I want to observe the reactions of Stoker Riley and his – ah – confederates to the skipper's speech. Might be most instructive.'

'Sherlock Nicholls, eh? Right-o, Johnny. Phone the Damage Control Officer aft. Tell him you're tied up. Major operation, anything you like. Our gullible public and how easily fooled. Shame.'

Nicholls grinned and reached for the phone.

When the bugle blared for dusk Action Stations, Nicholls was sitting in the dispensary. The lights were out, the curtains almost drawn. He could see into every corner of the brightly lit Sick Bay. Five of the men were asleep. Two of the others – Petersen, the giant, slow-spoken stoker, half Norwegian, half-Scots, and Burgess, the dark little cockney – were sitting up in bed, talking softly, their eyes turned towards the swarthy, heavily-built patient lying between them. Stoker Riley was holding court.

Alfred O'Hara Riley had, at a very early age indeed, decided upon a career of crime, and beset, though he subsequently was, by innumerable vicissitudes, he had clung to this resolve with an unswerving determination: directed towards almost any other sphere of activity, his resolution would have been praiseworthy, possibly even profitable. But praise and profit had passed Riley by.

Every man is what environment and heredity makes him. Riley was no exception, and Nicholls, who knew something of his upbringing, appreciated that life had never really given the big stoker a chance. Born of a drunken, illiterate mother in a filthy, overcrowded and fever-ridden Liverpool slum, he was an outcast from the beginning: allied to that, his hairy, ape-like figure, the heavy prognathous jaw, the twisted mouth, the wide flaring nose, the cunning black eyes, squinting out beneath the negligible clearance between hairline and eyebrows that so accurately reflected the mental capacity within, were all admirably adapted to what was to become his chosen vocation. Nicholls looked at him and disapproved without condemning; for a moment, he had an inkling of the tragedy of the inevitable.

Riley was never at any time a very successful criminal – his intelligence barely cleared the moron level. He dimly appreciated his limitations, and had left the higher, more subtle forms of crime severely alone. Robbery –

preferably robbery with violence – what his *mêtier*. He had been in prison six times, the last time for two years.

His induction into the Navy was a mystery which baffled both Riley and the authorities responsible for his being there. But Riley had accepted this latest misfortune with equanimity, and gone through the bomb-shattered 'G' and 'H' blocks in the Royal Naval Barracks, Portsmouth, like a high wind through a field of corn, leaving behind him a trail of slashed suitcases and empty wallets. He had been apprehended without much difficulty, done sixty days' cells, then been drafted to the *Ulysses* as a stoker.

His career of crime aboard the *Ulysses* had been brief and painful. His first attempted robbery had been his last – a clumsy and incredibly foolish rifling of a locker in the marine sergeants' mess. He had been caught red-handed by Colour-Sergeant Evans and Sergeant MacIntosh. They had preferred no charges against him and Riley had spent the next three days in the Sick Bay. He claimed to have tripped on the rung of a ladder and fallen twenty feet to the boiler-room floor. But the actual facts of the case were common knowledge, and Turner had recommended his discharge. To everyone's astonishment, not least that of Stoker Riley, Dodson, the Engineer Commander had insisted he be given a last chance, and Riley had been reprieved.

Since that date, four months previously, he had confined his activities to stirring up trouble. Illogically but understandably, his brief encounter with the marines had swept away his apathetic tolerance of the Navy: a smouldering hatred took its place. As an agitator, he had achieved a degree of success denied him as a criminal. Admittedly, he had a fertile field for operations; but credit – if that is the word – was due also to his shrewdness, his animal craft and cunning, his hold over his crewmates. The husky, intense voice, his earnestness, his deep-set eyes, lent Riley a strangely elemental power – a power he had used to its maximum effect a few days previously when he had precipitated the mutiny which had led to the death of Ralston, the stoker, and the marine – mysteriously dead from a broken neck. Beyond any possible doubt, their deaths lay at Riley's door; equally beyond doubt, that could never be proved. Nicholls wondered what new devilment was hatching behind these lowering, corrugated brows, wondered how on earth it was that that same Riley was continually in trouble for bringing aboard the *Ulysses* and devotedly tending every stray kitten, every broken-winged bird he found.

The loudspeaker crackled, cutting through his thoughts, stilling the low voices in the Sick Bay. And not only there, but throughout the ship, in turrets and magazines, in engine-rooms and boiler-rooms, above and below deck everywhere, all conversation ceased. Then there was only the wind, the regular smash of the bows into the deepening troughs, the muffled roar of the great boiler-room intake fans and the hum of a hundred electric motors. Tension lay heavy over the ship, over 730 officers and men, tangible, almost, in its oppression.

'This is the Captain speaking. Good evening.' The voice was calm, well modulated, without a sign of strain or exhaustion. 'As you all know, it is my custom at the beginning of every voyage to inform you as soon as possible of what lies in store for you. I feel that you have a right to know, and that it is my duty. It's not always a pleasant duty – it never has been during recent months. This time, however, I'm almost glad.' He paused, and the words came, slow and measured. 'This is our last operation as a unit of the Home Fleet. In a month's time, God willing, we will be in the Med.'

Good for you, thought Nicholls. Sweeten the pill, lay it on, thick and heavy. But the Captain had other ideas.

'But first, gentlemen, the job on hand. It's the mixture as before – Murmansk again. We rendezvous at 1030 Wednesday, north of Iceland, with a convoy from Halifax. There are eighteen ships in this convoy – big and fast – all fifteen knots and above. Our third Fast Russian convoy, gentlemen – FR77, in case you want to tell your grandchildren about it,' he added dryly. 'These ships are carrying tanks, planes, aviation spirit and oil – nothing else.

'I will not attempt to minimize the dangers. You know how desperate is the state of Russia today, how terribly badly she needs these weapons and fuel. You can also be sure that the Germans know too – and that her Intelligence agents will already have reported the nature of this convoy and the date of sailing.' He broke off short, and the sound of his harsh, muffled coughing into a handkerchief echoed weirdly through the silent ship. He went on slowly. 'There are enough fighter planes and petrol in this convoy to alter the whole character of the Russian war. The Nazis will stop at nothing – I repeat, nothing – to stop this convoy from going through to Russia.

'I have never tried to mislead or deceive you. I will not now. The signs are not good. In our favour we have, firstly, our speed, and secondly – I hope – the element of surprise. We shall try to break through direct for the North Cape.

'There are four major factors against us. You will all have noticed the steady worsening of the weather. We are, I'm afraid, running into abnormal weather conditions – abnormal even for the Arctic. It may – I repeat "may" – prevent U-boat attacks: on the other hand it may mean losing some of the smaller units of our screen – we have no time to heave to or run before bad weather. FR77 is going straight through. . . . And it almost certainly means that the carriers will be unable to fly off fighter cover.'

Good God, has the skipper lost his senses, Nicholls wondered. He'll wreck any morale that's left. Not that there is any left. What in the world—

'Secondly,' the voice went on, calm, inexorable, 'we are taking no rescue ships on this convoy. There will be no time to stop. Besides, you all know what happened to the *Stockport* and the *Zafaaran*. You're safer where you are.[1]

'Thirdly, two – possibly three – U-boat packs are known to be strung out along latitude seventy degrees and our Northern Norway agents report a heavy mustering of German bombers of all types in their area.

'Finally, we have reason to believe that the *Tirpitz* is preparing to move out.' Again he paused, for an interminable time, it seemed. It was as if he knew the tremendous shock carried in these few words, and wanted to give

[1] Rescue ships, whose duties were solely what their name implies, were a feature of many of the earlier convoys. The *Zafaaran* was lost in one of the war's worst convoys. The *Stockport* was torpedoed. She was lost with all hands, including all those survivors rescued from other sunken ships.

it time to register. 'I need not tell you what that means. The Germans may risk her to stop the convoy. The Admiralty hope they will. During the latter part of the voyage, capital units of the Home Fleet, including possibly the aircraft-carriers *Victorious* and *Furious*, and three cruisers, will parallel our course at twelve hours' steaming distance. They have been waiting a long time, and we are the bait to spring the trap. . . .

'It is possible that things may go wrong. The best-laid plans . . . or the trap may be late in springing shut. This convoy must still get through. If the carriers cannot fly off cover, the *Ulysses* must cover the withdrawal of FR77. You will know what that means. I hope this is all perfectly clear.'

There was another long bout of coughing, another long pause, and when he spoke again the tone had completely changed. He was very quiet.

'I know what I am asking of you. I know how tired, how hopeless, how sick at heart you all feel. I know – no one knows better – what you have been through, how much you need, how much you deserve a rest. Rest you shall have. The entire ship's company goes on ten days' leave from Portsmouth on the eighteenth, then for refit in Alexandria.' The words were casual, as if they carried no significance for him. 'But before that – well, I know it seems cruel, inhuman – it must seem so to you – to ask you to go through it all again, perhaps worse than you've ever gone through before. But I can't help it – no one can help it.' Every sentence, now, was punctuated by long silences: it was difficult to catch his words, so low and far away.

'No one has any right to ask you to do it, I least of all . . . least of all. I know you *will* do it. I know you will not let me down. I know you will take the *Ulysses* through. Good luck. Good luck and God bless you. Good night.'

The loudspeakers clicked off, but the silence lingered on. Nobody spoke and nobody moved. Not even the eyes moved. Those who had been looking at the 'speakers still gazed on, unseeingly; or stared down at their hands; or down into the glowing butts of forbidden cigarettes, oblivious to the acrid smoke that laced exhausted eyes. It was strangely as if each man wanted to be alone, to look into his own mind, follow his thoughts out for himself, and knew that if his eyes caught another's he would no longer be alone. A strange hush, a supernatural silence, the wordless understanding that so rarely touches mankind: the veil lifts and drops again and a man can never remember what he has seen but knows that he has seen something and that nothing will ever be quite the same again. Seldom, all too seldom it comes: a sunset of surpassing loveliness, a fragment from some great symphony, the terrible stillness which falls over the huge rings of Madrid and Barcelona as the sword of the greatest of the matadors sinks inevitably home. And the Spaniards have the word for it – 'the moment of truth.'

The Sick Bay clock, unnaturally loud, ticked away one minute, maybe two. With a heavy sigh – it seemed ages since he had breathed last – Nicholls softly pulled to the sliding door behind the curtains and switched on the light. He looked round at Brooks, looked away again.

'Well, Johnny?' The voice was soft, almost bantering.

'I just don't know, sir, I don't know at all.' Nicholls shook his head. 'At first I thought he was going – well, make a hash of it. You know, scare the lights out of 'em. And good God!' he went on wonderingly, 'that's exactly what he did do. Piled it on – gales, *Tirpitz*, hordes of subs. – and yet . . .' His voice trailed off.

'And yet?' Brooks echoed mockingly. 'That's just it. Too much intelligence – that's the trouble with the young doctors today. I saw you – sitting there like a bogus psychiatrist, analysing away for all you were worth at the probable effect of the speech on the minds of the wounded warriors without, and never giving it a chance to let it register on yourself.' He paused and went on quietly.

'It was beautifully done, Johnny. No, that's the wrong word – there was nothing premeditated about it. But don't you see? As black a picture as man could paint: points out that this is just a complicated way of committing suicide: no silver lining, no promises, even Alex. thrown in as a casual afterthought. Builds 'em up, then lets 'em down. No inducements, no hope, no appeal – and yet the appeal was tremendous. . . . What was it, Johnny?'

'I don't know.' Nicholls was troubled. He lifted his head abruptly, then smiled faintly. 'Maybe there *was* no appeal. Listen.' Noiselessly, he slid the door back, flicked off the lights. The rumble of Riley's harsh voice, low and intense, was unmistakable.

'— just a lot of bloody clap-trap. Alex.? The Med.? Not on your – life, mate. You'll never see it. You'll never even see Scapa again. Captain Richard Vallery, DSO! Know what that old bastard wants, boys? Another bar to his DSO. Maybe even a VC. Well, by Christ's, he's not going to have it! Not at my expense. Not if I can – well help it. "I know you won't let me down," ' he mimicked, his voice high-pitched. 'Whining old bastard!' He paused a moment, then rushed on.

'The *Tirpitz*! Christ Almighty! The *Tirpitz*! We're going to stop it – us! This bloody toy ship! Bait, he says, bait!' His voice rose. 'I tell you, mates, nobody gives a damn about us. Direct for the North Cape! They're throwing us to the bloody wolves! And that old bastard up top —'

'Shaddap!' It was Petersen who spoke, his voice a whisper, low and fierce. His hand stretched out, and Brooks and Nicholls in the surgery winced as they heard Riley's wrist-bones crack under the tremendous pressure of the giant's hand. Often I wonder about you, Riley,' Petersen went on slowly. 'But not now, not any more. You make me sick!' He flung Riley's hand down and turned away.

Riley rubbed his wrist in agony, and turned to Burgess.

'For God's sake, what's the matter with him? What the hell . . .' He broke off abruptly. Burgess was looking at him steadily, kept looking for a long time. Slowly, deliberately, he eased himself down in bed, pulled the blankets up to his neck and turned his back on Riley.

Brooks rose quickly to his feet, closed the door and pressed the light switch.

'Act I, Scene I. Cut! Lights!' he murmured. 'See what I mean, Johnny?'

'Yes, sir.' Nicholls nodded slowly. 'At least, I think so.'

'Mind you, my boy, it won't last. At least, not at that intensity.' He grinned. 'But maybe it'll take us the length of Murmansk. You never know.'

'I hope so, sir. Thanks for the show.' Nicholls reached up for his duffel-coat. 'Well, I suppose I'd better make my way aft.'

'Off you go, then. And, oh – Johnny —'

'Sir?'

'That scarlet-fever notice-board of yours. On your way aft you might consign it to the deep. I don't think we'll be needing it any more.'

Nicholls grinned and closed the door softly behind him.

Chapter Four

Monday Night

Dusk action stations dragged out its interminable hour and was gone. That night, as on a hundred other nights, it was just another nagging irritation, a pointless precaution that did not even justify its existence, far less its meticulous thoroughness. Or so it seemed. For although at dawn enemy attacks were routine, at sunset they were all but unknown. It was not always so with other ships, indeed it was rarely so, but then, the *Ulysses* was a lucky ship. Everyone knew that. Even Vallery knew it, but he also knew why. Vigilance was the first article of his sailor's creed.

Soon after the Captain's broadcast, radar had reported a contact, closing. That it was an enemy plane was certain: Commander Westcliffe, Senior Air Arm Officer, had before him in the Fighter Direction Room a wall map showing the operational routes of all Coastal and Ferry Command planes, and this was a clear area. But no one paid the slightest attention to the report, other than Tyndall's order for a 45° course alteration. This was as routine as dusk Action Stations themselves. It was their old friend Charlie coming to pay his respects again.

'Charlie' – usually a four-engine Focke-Wulf Condor – was an institution on the Russian Convoys. He had become to the seamen on the Murmansk run very much what the albatros had been the previous century to sailing men, far south in the Roaring Forties: a bird of ill-omen, half feared but almost amicably accepted, and immune from destruction – though with Charlie, for a different reason. In the early days, before the advent of cam-ships and escort carriers, Charlie frequently spent the entire day, from first light to last, circling a convoy and radioing to base pin-point reports of its position.[1]

Exchanges of signals between British ships and German reconnaissance planes were not unknown, and apocryphal stories were legion. An exchange of pleasantries about the weather was almost commonplace. On several occasions Charlie had plaintively asked for his position and been given highly-detailed latitude and longitude bearings which usually placed him somewhere in the South Pacific; and, of course, a dozen ships claimed the authorship of the story wherein the convoy Commodore sent the signal, 'Please fly the other way round. You are making us dizzy,' and Charlie had courteously acknowledged and turned in his tracks.

Latterly, however, amiability had been markedly absent, and Charlie,

[1] Cam-ships were merchant ships with specially strengthened fo'c'sles. On these were fitted fore-and-aft angled ramps from which fighter planes, such as modified Hurricanes, were catapulted for convoy defence. After breaking off action, the pilot had either to bale out or land in the sea. 'Hazardous' is rather an inadequate word to describe the duties of this handful of very gallant pilots: the chances of survival were not high.

grown circumspect with the passing of the months and the appearance of ship-borne fighters, rarely appeared except at dusk. His usual practice was to make a single circle of the convoy at a prudent distance and then disappear into the darkness.

That night was no exception. Men caught only fleeting glimpses of the Condor in the driving snow, then quickly lost it in the gathering gloom. Charlie would report the strength, nature and course of the Squadron, although Tyndall had little hope that the German Intelligence would be deceived as to their course. A naval squadron, near the sixty-second degree of latitude, just east of the Faroes, and heading NNE, wouldn't make sense to them – especially as they almost certainly knew of the departure of the convoy from Halifax. Two and two, far too obviously totted up to four.

No attempt was made to fly off Seafires – the only plane with a chance to overhaul the Condor before it disappeared into the night. To locate the carrier again in almost total darkness, even on a radio beam, was difficult: to land at night, extremely dangerous; and to land, by guess and by God, in the snow and blackness on a pitching, heaving deck, a suicidal impossibility. The least miscalculation, the slightest error of judgment and you had not only lost a plane but a drowned pilot. A ditched Seafire, with its slender, torpedo-shaped fuselage and the tremendous weight of the great Rolls-Royce Merlin in its nose, was a literal death-trap. When it went down into the sea, it just kept on going.

Back on to course again, the *Ulysses* pushed blindly into the gathering storm. Hands fell out from Action Stations, and resumed normal Defence Stations – watch and watch, four on, four off. Not a killing routine, one would think: twelve hours on, twelve hours off a day – a man could stand that. And so he could, were that all. But the crew also spent three hours a day at routine Action Stations, every second morning – the forenoon watch – at work (this when they were off-watch) and God only knew how many hours at Action Stations. Beyond all this, all meals – when there were meals – were eaten in their off-duty time. A total of three to four hours' sleep a day was reckoned unusual: forty-eight hours without sleep hardly called for comment.

Step by step, fraction by menacing fraction, mercury and barograph crept down in a deadly dualism. The waves were higher now, their troughs deeper, their shoulders steeper, and the bone chilling wind lashed the snow into a blinding curtain. A bad night, a sleepless night, both above deck and below, on watch and off.

On the bridge, the First Lieutenant, the Kapok Kid, signalmen, the Searchlight LTO, look-outs and messengers peered out miserably into the white night and wondered what it would be like to be warm again. Jerseys, coats, overcoats, duffels, oilskins, scarves, balaclavas, helmets – they wore them all, completely muffled except for a narrow eye-slit in the woollen cocoon, and still they shivered. They wrapped arms and forearms round, and rested their feet on the steam pipes which circled the bridge, and froze. Pom-pom crews huddled miserably in the shelter of their multiple guns, stamped their feet, swung their arms and swore incessantly. And the lonely Oerlikon gunners, each jammed in his lonely cockpit, leaned against the built-in 'black' heaters and fought off the Oerlikon gunner's most insidious enemy – sleep.

The Starboard watch, in the mess-decks below, were little happier. There were no bunks for the crew of the *Ulysses*, only hammocks, and these were never slung except in harbour. There were good and sufficient reasons for this. Standards of hygiene on a naval warship are high, compared even to the average civilian home: the average matelot would never consider climbing into his hammock fully dressed – and no one in his senses would have dreamed of undressing on the Russian Convoys. Again, to an exhausted man, the prospect and the actual labour of slinging and then lashing a hammock were alike appalling. And the extra seconds it took to climb out of a hammock in an emergency could represent the margin between life and death, while the very existence of a slung hammock was a danger to all, in that it impeded quick movement. And finally, as on that night of a heavy head sea, there could be no more uncomfortable place than a hammock slung fore and aft.

And so the crew slept where it could, fully clothed even to duffel coats and gloves. On tables and under tables, on narrow nine-inch stools, on the floor, in hammock racks – anywhere. The most popular place on the ship was on the warm steel deck-plates in the alleyway outside the galley, at night-time a weird and spectral tunnel, lit only by a garish red light. A popular sleeping billet, made doubly so by the fact that only a screen separated it from the upper-deck, a scant ten feet away. The fear of being trapped below decks in a sinking ship was always there, always in the back of men's minds.

Even below decks, it was bitterly cold. The hot-air systems operated efficiently only on 'B' and 'C' mess-decks, and even there the temperature barely cleared freezing point. Deckheads dripped constantly and the condensation on the bulkheads sent a thousand little rivulets to pool on the corticene floor. The atmosphere was dank and airless and terribly chill – the ideal breeding ground for the TB, so feared by Surgeon-Commander Brooks. Such conditions, allied with the constant pitching of the ship and the sudden jarring vibrations which were beginning to develop every time the bows crashed down, made sleep almost impossible, at best a fitful, restless unease.

Almost to a man, the crew slept – or tried to sleep – with heads pillowed on inflated lifebelts. Blown up, bent double then tied with tape, these lifebelts made very tolerable pillows. For this purpose, and for this alone, were these lifebelts employed, although standing orders stated explicitly that lifebelts were to be worn at all times during action and in known enemy waters. These orders were completely ignored, not least of all by those Divisional Officers whose duty it was to enforce them. There was enough air trapped in the voluminous and bulky garments worn in these latitudes to keep a man afloat for at least three minutes. If he wasn't picked up in that time, he was dead anyway. It was shock that killed, the tremendous shock of a body at 96° F being suddenly plunged into a liquid temperature some 70° lower – for in the Arctic waters, the sea temperature often falls below normal freezing point. Worse still, the sub-zero wind lanced like a thousand stilettos through the saturated clothing of a man who had been submerged in the sea, and the heart, faced with an almost instantaneous 100° change in body temperature, just stopped beating. But it was a quick death, men said, quick and kind and merciful.

At ten minutes to midnight the Commander and Marshall made their way to the bridge. Even at this late hour and in the wicked weather, the Commander was his usual self, imperturbable and cheerful, lean and piratical, a throw-back to the Elizabethan buccaneers, if ever there was one. He had an unflagging zest for life. The duffel hood, as always, lay over his shoulders, the braided peak of his cap was tilted at a magnificent angle. He groped for the handle of the bridge gate, passed through, stood for a minute, accustoming his eyes to the dark, located the First Lieutenant and thumped him resoundingly on the back.

'Well, watchman, and what of the night?' he boomed cheerfully. 'Bracing, yes, decidedly so. Situation completely out of control as usual, I suppose? Where are all our chickens this lovely evening?' He peered out into the snow, scanned the horizon briefly, then gave up. 'All gone to hell and beyond, I suppose.'

'Not too bad,' Carrington grinned. An RNR officer and an ex-Merchant Navy captain in whom Vallery reposed complete confidence, Lieutenant-Commander Carrington was normally a taciturn man, grave and unsmiling. But a particular bond lay between him and Turner, the professional bond of respect which two exceptional seamen have for each other. 'We can see the carriers now and then. Anyway, Bowden and his backroom boys have 'em all pinned to an inch. At least, that's what they say.'

'Better not let old Bowden hear you say that,' Marshall advised. 'Thinks radar is the only step forward the human race has taken since the first man came down from the trees.' He shivered uncontrollably and turned his back on the driving wind. 'Anyway, I wish to God I had his job,' he added feelingly. 'This is worse than winter in Alberta!'

'Nonsense, my boy, stuff and nonsense!' the Commander roared. 'Decadent, that's the trouble with you youngsters nowadays. This is the only life for a self-respecting human being.' He sniffed the icy air appreciatively and turned to Carrington. 'Who's on with you tonight, Number One?'

A dark figure detached itself from the binnacle and approached him.

'Ah, there you are. Well, well, 'pon my soul, if it isn't our navigating officer, the Honourable Carpenter, lost as usual and dressed to kill in his natty gent's suiting. Do you know, Pilot, in that outfit you look like a cross between a deep-sea diver and that advert for Michelin tyres?'

'Ha!' said the Kapok Kid aggrievedly. 'Sniff and scoff while you may, sir.' He patted his quilted chest affectionately. 'Just wait till ye're all down there in the drink together, everybody else dragged down or frozen to death, me drifting by warm and dry and comfortable, maybe smoking the odd cigarette—'

'Enough. Be off. Course, Number One?'

'Three-twenty, sir. Fifteen knots.'

'And the Captain?'

'In the shelter.' Carrington jerked his head towards the reinforced steel circular casing at the after end of the bridge. This supported the Director Tower, the control circuits to which ran through a central shaft in the casing. A sea-bunk – a spartan, bare settee – was kept there for the Captain's use. 'Sleeping, I hope,' he added, 'but I very much doubt it. Gave orders to be called at midnight.'

'Why?' Turner demanded.

'Oh, I don't know. Routine, I suppose. Wants to see how things are.'

'Cancel the order,' Turner said briefly. 'Captain's got to learn to obey orders like anybody else – especially doctor's orders. I'll take full responsibility. Good night, Number One.'

The gate clanged shut and Marshall turned uncertainly towards the Commander.

'The Captain, sir. Oh, I know it's none of my business, but' – he hesitated – 'well, is he all right?'

Turner looked quickly around him. His voice was unusually quiet.

'If Brooks had his way, the old man would be in hospital.' He was silent for a moment, then added soberly. 'Even then, it might be too late.'

Marshall said nothing. He moved restlessly around, then went aft to the port searchlight control position. For five minutes, an intermittent rumble of voices drifted up to the Commander. He glanced up curiously on Marshall's return.

'That's Ralston, sir,' the Torpedo Officer explained. 'If he'd talk to anybody, I think he'd talk to me.'

'And does he?'

'Sure – but only what *he* wants to talk about. As for the rest, no dice. You can almost see the big notice round his neck – "Private – Keep Off." Very civil, very courteous and completely unapproachable. I don't know what the hell to do about him.'

'Leave him be,' Turner advised. 'There's nothing anyone can do.' He shook his head. 'My God, what a lousy break life's given that boy!'

Silence fell again. The snow was lifting now, but the wind still strengthening. It howled eerily through masts and rigging, blending with a wild and eldritch harmony into the haunting pinging of the Asdic. Weird sounds both, weird and elemental and foreboding, that rasped across the nerves and stirred up nameless, atavistic dreads of a thousand ages past, long buried under the press of civilization. An unholy orchestra, and, over years, men grew to hate it with a deadly hatred.

Half-past twelve came, one o'clock, then half-past one. Turner's thought turned fondly towards coffee and cocoa. Coffee or cocoa? Cocoa, he decided, a steaming potent brew, thick with melted chocolate and sugar. He turned to Chrysler, the bridge messenger, younger brother of the Leading Asdic Operator.

'WT – Bridge. WT – Bridge.' The loudspeaker above the Asdic cabinet crackled urgently, the voice hurried, insistent. Turner jumped for the hand transmitter, barked an acknowledgment.

'Signal from *Sirrus*. Echoes, port bow, 300, strong, closing. Repeat, echoes, port bow, strong, closing.'

'Echoes, WT? Did you say "echoes"?'

'Echoes, sir. I repeat, echoes.'

Even as he spoke, Turner's hand cut down on the gleaming phosphorescence of the Emergency Action Stations switch.

Of all sounds in this earth, there is none so likely to stay with a man to the end of his days as the EAS. There is no other sound even remotely like it. There is nothing noble or martial or blood-stirring about it. It is simply a whistle, pitched near the upper limit of audio-frequency, alternating, piercing, atonic, alive with a desperate urgency and sense of danger: knife-like, it sears through the most sleep-drugged brain and has a man – no matter how exhausted, how weak, how deeply sunk in oblivion – on his feet in seconds, the pulse-rate already accelerating to meet the latest unknown, the adrenalin already pumping into his blood-stream.

Inside two minutes, the *Ulysses* was closed up to Action Stations. The

Commander had moved aft to the After Director Tower, Vallery and Tyndall were on the bridge.

The *Sirrus*, two miles away to port, remained in contact for half an hour. The *Viking* was detached to help her, and, below-deck in the *Ulysses*, the peculiar, tinny clanging of depth-charging was clearly heard at irregular intervals. Finally, the *Sirrus* reported. 'No success: contact lost: trust you have not been disturbed.' Tyndall ordered the recall of the two destroyers, and the bugle blew the stand-down.

Back on the bridge, again, the Commander sent for his long overdue cocoa. Chrysler departed to the seaman's for'ard galley – the Commander would have no truck with the wishy-washy liquid concocted for the officers' mess – and returned with a steaming jug and a string of heavy mugs, their handles threaded on a bent wire. Turner watched with approval the reluctance with which the heavy, viscous liquid poured glutinously over the lip of the jug, and nodded in satisfaction after a preliminary taste. He smacked his lips and sighed contentedly.

'Excellent, young Chrysler, excellent! You have the gift. Torps., an eye on the ship, if you please. Must see where we are.'

He retired to the chart-room on the port side, just aft of the compass platform, and closed the black-out door. Relaxed in his chair, he put his mug on the chart-table and his feet beside it, drew the first deep inhalation of cigarette smoke into his lungs. Then he was on his feet, cursing: the crackle of the WT loudspeaker was unmistakable.

This time it was the *Portpatrick*. For one reason and another, her reports were generally treated with a good deal of reserve, but this time she was particularly emphatic. Commander Turner had no option; again he reached for the EAS switch.

Twenty minutes later the stand-down sounded again, but the Commander was to have no cocoa that night. Three times more during the hours of darkness all hands closed up to Action Stations, and only minutes, it seemed, after the last stand-down, the bugle went for dawn stations.

There was no dawn as we know it. There was a vague, imperceptible lightening in the sky, a bleak, chill greyness, as the men dragged themselves wearily back to their action stations. This, then, was war in the northern seas. No death and glory heroics, no roaring guns and spitting Oerlikons, no exaltation of the spirit, no glorious defiance of the enemy: just worn-out sleepless men, numbed with cold and sodden duffels, grey and drawn and stumbling on their feet with weakness and hunger and lack of rest, carrying with them the memories, the tensions, the cumulative physical exhaustion of a hundred such endless nights.

Vallery, as always, was on the bridge. Courteous, kind and considerate as ever, he looked ghastly. His face was haggard, the colour of putty, his bloodshot eyes deep-sunk in hollowed sockets, his lips bloodless. The severe haemorrhage of the previous night and the sleepless night just gone had taken terrible toll of his slender strength.

In the half-light, the squadron came gradually into view. Miraculously, most of them were still in position. The frigate and minesweeper were together and far ahead of the fleet – during the night they had been understandably reluctant to have their tails tramped on by a heavy cruiser or a carrier. Tyndall appreciated this and said nothing. The *Invader* had lost position during the night, and lay outside the screen on the port quarter. She received a very testy signal indeed, and came steaming up to resume station, corkscrewing violently in the heavy cross seas.

Stand-down came at 0800. At 0810 the port watch was below, making tea, washing, queueing up at the galley for breakfast trays, when a muffled explosion shook the *Ulysses*. Towels, soap, cups, plates and trays went flying or were left where they were: blasphemous and bitter, the men were on their way before Vallery's hand closed on the Emergency switch.

Less than half a mile away the *Invader* was slewing round in a violent half-circle, her flight-deck tilted over at a crazy angle. It was snowing heavily again now, but not heavily enough to obscure the great gouts of black oily smoke belching up for-ard of the *Invader*'s bridge. Even as the crew of the *Ulysses* watched, she came to rest, wallowing dangerously in the troughs between the great waves.

'The fools, the crazy fools!' Tyndall was terribly bitter, unreasonably so; even to Vallery, he would not admit how much he was now feeling the burden, the strain of command that sparked off his now almost chronic irritability. 'This is what happens, Captain, when a ship loses station! And it's as much my fault as theirs – should have sent a destroyer to escort her back.' He peered through his binoculars, turned to Vallery. 'Make a signal please: "Estimate of damage – please inform." . . . That damned U-boat must have trailed her from first light, waiting for a line-up.'

Vallery said nothing. He knew how Tyndall must feel to see one of his ships heavily damaged, maybe sinking. The *Invader* was still lying over at the same unnatural angle, the smoke rising in a steady column now. There was no sign of flames.

'Going to investigate, sir?' Vallery inquired.

Tyndall bit his lip thoughtfully and hesitated.

'Yes, I think we'd better do it ourselves. Order squadron to proceed, same speed, same course. Signal the *Baliol* and the *Nairn* to stand by the *Invader*.'

Vallery, watching the flags fluttering to the yardarm, was aware of someone at his elbow. He half-turned.

'That was no U-boat, sir.' The Kapok Kid was very sure of himself. 'She can't have been torpedoed.'

Tyndall overheard him. He swung round in his chair, glared at the unfortunate navigator.

'What the devil do you know about it, sir?' he growled. When the Admiral addressed his subordinates as 'sir,' it was time to take to the boats. The Kapok Kid flushed to the roots of his blond hair, but he stood his ground.

'Well, sir, in the first place the *Sirrus* is covering the *Invader*'s port side, though well ahead, ever since your recall signal. She's been quartering that area for some time. I'm sure Commander Orr would have picked her up. Also, it's far too rough for any sub to maintain periscope depth, far less line up a firing track. And if the U-boat did fire, it wouldn't only fire one – six more likely, and, from that firing angle, the rest of the squadron must have been almost a solid wall behind the *Invader*. But no one else has been hit. . . . I did three years in the trade, sir.'

'I did ten,' Tyndall growled. 'Guesswork, Pilot, just guesswork.'

'No, sir,' Carpenter persisted. 'It's not. I can't swear to it' – he had his binoculars to his eyes – but I'm almost sure the *Invader* is going astern.

Could only be because her bows – below the waterline that is – have been damaged or blown off. Must have been a mine, sir, probably acoustic.'

'Ah, of course, of course!' Tyndall was very acid. 'Moored in 6000 feet of water, no doubt?'

'A *drifting* mine, sir,' the Kapok Kid said patiently. 'Or an old acoustic torpedo – spent German torpedoes don't always sink. Probably a mine, though.'

'Suppose you'll be telling me next what mark it is and when it was laid,' Tyndall growled. But he was impressed in spite of himself. And the *Invader* was going astern, although slowly, without enough speed to give her steerage way. She still wallowed helplessly in the great troughs.

An Aldis clacked acknowledgment to the winking light on the *Invader*. Bently tore a sheet off a signal pad, handed it to Vallery.

' "*Invader* to Admiral," ' the Captain read. ' "Am badly holed, starboard side for'ard, very deep. Suspect drifting mine. Am investigating extent of damage. Will report soon." '

Tyndall took the signal from him and read it slowly. Then he looked over his shoulder and smiled faintly.

'You were dead right, my boy, it seems. Please accept an old curmudgeon's apologies.'

Carpenter murmured something and turned away, brick-red again with embarrassment. Tyndall grinned faintly at the Captain, then became thoughtful.

'I think we'd better talk to him personally, Captain. Barlow, isn't it? Make a signal.'

They climbed down two decks to the Fighter Direction room. Westcliffe vacated his chair for the Admiral.

'Captain Barlow?' Tyndall spoke into the hand-piece.

'Speaking.' The sound came from the loudspeaker above his head.

'Admiral here, Captain. How are things?'

'We'll manage, sir. Lost most of our bows, I'm afraid. Several casualties. Oil fires, but under control. WT doors all holding, and engineers and damage control parties are shoring up the cross-bulkheads.'

'Can you go ahead at all, Captain?'

'Could do, sir, but risky – in this, anyway.'

'Think you could make it back to base?'

'With this wind and sea behind us, yes. Still take three-four days.'

'Right-o, then.' Tyndall's voice was gruff. 'Off you go. You're no good to us without bows! Damned hard luck, Captain Barlow. My commiserations. And oh! I'm giving you the *Baliol* and *Nairn* as escorts and radioing for an ocean-going tug to come out to meet you – just in case.'

'Thank you, sir. We appreciate that. One last thing – permission to empty starboard squadron fuel tanks. We've taken a lot of water, can't get rid of it all – only way to recover our trim.'

Tyndall sighed. 'Yes, I was expecting that. Can't be helped and we can't take it off you in this weather. Good luck, Captain. Goodbye.'

'Thank you very much, sir. Goodbye.'

Twenty minutes later, the *Ulysses* was back on station in the squadron. Shortly afterwards, they saw the *Invader*, not listing quite so heavily now, head slowly round to the south-east, the little Hunt class destroyer and the frigate, one on either side, rolling wickedly as they came round with her. In another ten minutes, watchers on the *Ulysses* had lost sight of them, buried in a flurrying snow squall. Three gone and eleven left behind; but it was the eleven who now felt so strangely alone.

Chapter Five

Tuesday

The *Invader* and her troubles were soon forgotten. All too soon, the 14th Aircraft Carrier Squadron had enough, and more than enough, to worry about on their own account. They had their own troubles to overcome, their own enemy to face – an enemy far more elemental and far more deadly than any mine or U-boat.

Tyndall braced himself more firmly against the pitching, rolling deck and looked over at Vallery. Vallery, he thought for the tenth time that morning, looked desperately ill.

'What do you make of it, Captain? Prospects aren't altogether healthy, are they?'

'We're for it, sir. It's really piling up against us. Carrington has spent six years in the West Indies, has gone through a dozen hurricanes. Admits he's seen a barometer lower, but never one so low with the pressure still falling so fast – not in these latitudes. This is only a curtain-raiser.'

'This will do me nicely, meantime, thank you,' Tyndall said dryly. 'For a curtain-raiser, it's doing not so badly.'

It was a masterly understatement. For a curtain-raiser, it was a magnificent performance. The wind was fairly steady, about Force 9 on the Beaufort scale, and the snow had stopped. A temporary cessation only, they all knew – far ahead to the north-west the sky was a peculiarly livid colour. It was a dull glaring purple, neither increasing nor fading, faintly luminous and vaguely menacing in its uniformity and permanence. Even to men who had seen everything the Arctic skies had to offer, from pitchy darkness on a summer's noon, right through the magnificent displays of Northern Lights to that wonderfully washed-out blue that so often smiles down on the stupendous calms of the milk-white seas that lap edge of the Barrier, this was something quite unknown.

But the Admiral's reference had been to the sea. It had been building up, steadily, inexorably, all during the morning. Now, at noon, it looked uncommonly like an eighteenth-century print of a barque in a storm – serried waves of greenish-grey, straight, regular and marching uniformly along, each decoratively topped with frothing caps of white. Only here, there were 500 feet between crest and crest, and the squadron, heading almost directly into it, was taking hearty punishment.

For the little ships, already burying their bows every fifteen seconds in a creaming smother of cascading white, this was bad enough, but another, a more dangerous and insidious enemy was at work – the cold. The temperature had long sunk below freezing point, and the mercury was still shrinking down, close towards the zero mark.

The cold was now intense: ice formed in cabins and mess-decks: fresh-water systems froze solid: metal contracted, hatch-covers jammed, door hinges locked in frozen immobility, the oil in the searchlight controls gummed up and made them useless. To keep a watch, especially a watch on the bridge, was torture: the first shock of that bitter wind seared the lungs, left a man fighting for breath: if he had forgotten to don gloves – first the silk gloves, then the woollen mittens, then the sheepskin gauntlets – and touched a handrail, the palms of the hands seared off, the skin burnt as by white-hot metal: on the bridge, if he forgot to duck when the bows smashed down into a trough, the flying spray, solidified in a second into hurtling slivers of ice, lanced cheek and forehead open to the bone: hands froze, the very marrow of the bones numbed, the deadly chill crept upwards from feet to calves to thighs, nose and chin turned white with frostbite and demanded immediate attention: and then, by far the worst of all, the end of the watch, the return below deck, the writhing, excruciating agony of returning circulation. But, for all this, words are useless things, pale shadows of reality. Some things lie beyond the knowledge and the experience of the majority of mankind, and here imagination finds itself in a world unknown.

But all these things were relatively trifles, personal inconveniences to be shrugged aside. The real danger lay elsewhere. It lay in the fact of ice.

There were over three hundred tons of it already on the decks of the *Ulysses*, and more forming every minute. It lay in a thick, even coat over the main deck, the fo'c'sle, the gun-decks and the bridges: it hung in long, jagged icicles from coamings and turrets and rails: it trebled the diameter of every wire, stay and halliard, and turned slender masts into monstrous trees, ungainly and improbable. It lay everywhere, a deadly menace, and much of the danger lay in the slippery surface it presented – a problem much more easily overcome on a coal-fired merchant ship with clinker and ashes from its boilers, than in the modern, oil-fired warships. On the *Ulysses*, they spread salt and sand and hoped for the best.

But the real danger of the ice lay in its weight. A ship, to use technical terms, can be either stiff or tender. If she's stiff, she has a low centre of gravity, rolls easily, but whips back quickly and is extremely stable and safe. If she's tender, with a high centre of gravity, she rolls reluctantly but comes back even more reluctantly, is unstable and unsafe. And if a ship were tender, and hundreds of tons of ice piled high on its decks, the centre of gravity rose to a dangerous height. It could rise to a fatal height. . . .

The escort carriers and the destroyers, especially the *Portpatrick,* were vulnerable, terribly so. The carriers, already unstable with the great height and weight of their reinforced flight-decks, provided a huge, smooth, flat surface to the falling snow, ideal conditions for the formation of ice. Earlier on, it had been possible to keep the flight-decks relatively clear – working parties had toiled incessantly with brooms and sledges, salt and steam hoses. But the weather had deteriorated so badly now that to send out a man on that wildly pitching, staggering flight-deck, glassy and infinitely treacherous, would be to send him to his death. The *Wrestler* and *Blue Ranger* had modified heating systems under the flight-decks – modified, because, unlike the British ships, these Mississippi carriers had planked flight-decks: in such extreme conditions, they were hopelessly inefficient.

Conditions aboard the destroyers were even worse. They had to contend not only with the ice from the packed snow, but with ice from the sea itself. As regularly as clockwork, huge clouds of spray broke over the destroyers' fo'c'sles as the bows crashed solidly, shockingly into the trough and rising shoulder of the next wave: the spray froze even as it touched the deck, even before it touched the deck, piling up the solid ice, in places over a foot thick, from the stem aft beyond the breakwater. The tremendous weight of the ice was pushing the little ships down by their heads; deeper, with each successive plunge ever deeper, they buried their noses in the sea, and each time, more and more sluggishly, more and more reluctantly, they staggered laboriously up from the depths. Like the carrier captains, the destroyer skippers could only look down from their bridges, helpless, hoping.

Two hours passed, two hours in which the temperature fell to zero, hesitated, then shrank steadily beyond it, two hours in which the barometer tumbled crazily after it. Curiously, strangely, the snow still held off, the livid sky to the north-west was as far away as ever, and the sky to the south and east had cleared completely. The squadron presented a fantastic picture now, little toy-boats of sugar-icing, dazzling white, gleaming and sparkling in the pale, winter sunshine, pitching crazily through the ever-lengthening, ever-deepening valleys of grey and green of the cold Norwegian Sea, pushing on towards that far horizon, far and weird and purply glowing, the horizon of another world. It was an incredibly lovely spectacle.

Rear-Admiral Tyndall saw nothing beautiful about it. A man who was wont to claim that he never worried, he was seriously troubled now. He was gruff, to those on the bridge, gruff to the point of discourtesy and the old geniality of the Farmer Giles of even two months ago was all but gone. Ceaselessly his gaze circled the fleet; constantly, uncomfortably, he twisted in his chair. Finally he climbed down, passed through the gate and went into the Captain's shelter.

Vallery had no light on and the shelter was in semi-darkness. He lay there on his settee, a couple of blankets thrown over him. In the half-light, his face looked ghastly, corpse-like. His right hand clutched a balled handkerchief, spotted and stained: he made no attempt to hide it. With a painful effort, and before Tyndall could stop him, he had swung his legs over the edge of the settee and pulled forward a chair. Tyndall choked off his protest, sank gracefully into the seat.

'I think your curtain's just about to go up, Dick. . . . What on earth ever induced me to become a squadron commander?'

Vallery grinned sympathetically. 'I don't particularly envy you, sir. What are you going to do now?'

'What would *you* do?' Tyndall countered dolefully.

Vallery laughed. For a moment his face was transformed, boyish almost, then the laugh broke down into a bout of harsh, dry coughing. The stain spread over his handkerchief. Then he looked up and smiled.

'The penalty for laughing at a superior officer. What would I do? Heave to, sir. Better still, tuck my tail between my legs and run for it.'

Tyndall shook his head.

'You never were a very convincing liar, Dick.'

Both men sat in silence for a moment, then Vallery looked up.

'How far to go, exactly, sir?'

'Young Carpenter makes it 170 miles, more or less.'

'One hundred and seventy.' Vallery looked at his watch. 'Twenty hours to go – in this weather. We *must* make it!'

Tyndall nodded heavily. 'Eighteen ships sitting out there – nineteen, counting the sweeper from Hvalfjord – not to mention old Starr's blood pressure . . .'

He broke off as a hand rapped on the door and a head looked in.

'Two signals, Captain, sir.'

'Just read them out, Bentley, will you?'

'First is from the *Portpatrick*: "Sprung bow-plates: making water fast: pumps coming: fear further damage: please advise." '

Tyndall swore. Vallery said calmly: 'And the other?'

'From the *Gannet*, sir. "Breaking up." '

'Yes, yes. And the rest of the message?'

'Just that, sir. "Breaking up." '

'Ha! One of these taciturn characters,' Tyndall growled. 'Wait a minute, Chief, will you?' He sank back in his chair, hand rasping his chin, gazing at his feet, forcing his tired mind to think.

Vallery murmured something in a low voice, and Tyndall looked up, his eyebrows arched.

'Troubled waters, sir. Perhaps the carriers—'

Tyndall slapped his knee. 'Two minds with but a single thought. Bentley, make two signals. One to all screen vessels – tell 'em to take position – astern – close astern – of the carriers. Other to the carriers. Oil hose, one each through port and starboard loading ports, about – ah – how much would you say, Captain?'

'Twenty gallons a minute, sir?'

'Twenty gallons it is. Understand, Chief? Right-o, get 'em off at once. And Chief – tell the Navigator to bring his chart here.' Bentley left, and he turned to Vallery. 'We've got to fuel later on, and we can't do it here. Looks as if this might be the last chance of shelter this side of Murmansk. . . . And if the next twenty-four hours are going to be as bad as Carrington forecasts, I doubt whether some of the little ships could live through it anyway. . . . Ah! Here you are, Pilot. Let's see where we are. How's the wind, by the way?'

'Force 10, sir.' Bracing himself against the wild lurching of the *Ulysses*, the Kapok Kid smoothed out the chart on the captain's bunk. 'Backing slightly.'

'North-west, would you say, Pilot?' Tyndall rubbed his hands. 'Excellent. Now, my boy, our position?'

'12.40 west. 66.15 north,' said the Kapok Kid precisely. He didn't even trouble to consult the chart. Tyndall lifted his eyebrows but made no comment.

'Course?'

'310, sir.'

'Now, if it were necessary for us to seek shelter for fuelling—'

'Course exactly 290, sir. I've pencilled it in – there. Four and a half hours' steaming, approximately.'

'How the devil—' Tyndall exploded. 'Who told you to – to—' He spluttered into a wrathful silence.

'I worked it out five minutes ago, sir. It – er – seemed inevitable. 290

would take us a few miles inside the Langanes peninsula. There should be plenty shelter there. Carpenter was grave, unsmiling.

'Seemed inevitable!' Tyndall roared. 'Would you listen to him, Captain Vallery? Inevitable! And it's only just occurred to me! Of all the . . . Get out! Take yourself and that damned comic-opera fancy dress elsewhere!'

The Kapok Kid said nothing. With an air of injured innocence he gathered up his charts and left. Tyndall's voice halted him at the door.

'Pilot!'

'Sir?' The Kapok Kid's eyes were fixed on a point above Tyndall's head.

'As soon as the screen vessels have taken up position, tell Bentley to send them the new course.'

'Yes, sir. Certainly.' He hesitated, and Tyndall chuckled. 'All right, all right,' hc said resignedly. 'I'll say it again – I'm just a crusty old curmudgeon . . . and shut that damned door! We're freezing in here.'

The wind was rising more quickly now and long ribbons of white were beginning to streak the water. Wave troughs were deepening rapidly, their sides steepening, their tops blown off and flattened by the wind. Gradually, but perceptibly to the ear now, the thin, lonely whining in the rigging was climbing steadily up the register. From time to time, large chunks of ice, shaken loose by the increasing vibration, broke off from the masts and stays and spattered on the deck below.

The effect of the long oil-slicks trailing behind the carriers was almost miraculous. The destroyers, curiously mottled with oil now, were still plunging astern, but the surface tension of the fuel held the water and spray from breaking aboard. Tyndall, justifiably, was feeling more than pleased with himself.

Towards half-past four in the afternoon, with shelter still a good fifteen miles away, the elation had completely worn off. There was a whole gale blowing now and Tyndall had been compelled to signal for a reduction in speed.

From deck level, the seas now were more than impressive. They were gigantic, frightening. Nicholls stood with the Kapok Kid, off watch now, on the main deck, under the port whaler, sheltering in the lee of the fo'c'sle deck. Nicholls, clinging to a davit to steady himself, and leaping back now and then to avoid a deluge of spray, looked over to where the *Defender*, the *Vultra* and *Viking* tailing behind, were pitching madly, grotesquely, under that serene blue sky. The blue sky above, the tremendous seas below. There was something almost evil, something literally spine-chilling, in that macabre contrast.

'They never told me anything about this in the Medical School,' Nicholls observed at last. 'My God, Andy,' he added in awe, 'have you ever seen anything like this?'

'Once, just once. We were caught in a typhoon off the Nicobars. I don't think it was as bad as this. And Number One says this is damn' all compared to what's coming tonight – and he knows. God, I wish I was back in Henley!'

Nicholls looked at him curiously.

'Can't say I know the First Lieutenant well. Not a very – ah – approachable customer, is he? But everyone – old Giles, the skipper, the Commander, yourself – they all talk about him with bated breath. What's so extra special about him? I respect him, mind you – everyone seems to – but dammit to hell, he's no superman.'

'Sea's beginning to break up,' the Kapok Kid murmured absently. 'Notice how every now and again we're beginning to get a wave half as big again as the others? Every seventh wave, the old sailors say. No, Johnny, he's not a superman. Just the greatest seaman you'll ever see. Holds two master's-tickets – square-rigged and steam. He was going round the Horn in Finnish barques when we were still in our prams. Commander could tell you enough stories about him to fill a book.' He paused then went on quietly:

'He really is one of the few great seamen of today. Old Blackbeard Turner is no slouch himself, but he'll tell anyone that he can't hold a candle to Jimmy. . . . I'm no hero-worshipper, Johnny. You know that. But you can say about Carrington what they used to say about Shackleton – when there's nothing left and all hope is gone, get down on your knees and pray for him. Believe me, Johnny, I'm damned glad he's here.'

Nicholls said nothing. Surprise held him silent. For the Kapok Kid, flippancy was a creed, derogation second nature: seriousness was a crime and anything that smacked of adulation bordered on blasphemy. Nicholls wondered what manner of man Carrington must be.

The cold was vicious. The wind was tearing great gouts of water off the wave-tops, driving the atomized spray at bullet speed against fo'c'sle and sides. It was impossible to breathe without turning one's back, without wrapping layers of wool round mouth and nose. Faces blue and white, shaking violently with the cold, neither suggested, neither even thought of going below. Men hypnotized, men fascinated by the tremendous seas, the towering waves, 1000, 2000 feet in length, long, sloping on the lee side, steep-walled and terrifying on the other, pushed up by a sixty knot wind and by some mighty force lying far to the north-west. In these gigantic troughs, a church steeple would be lost for ever.

Both men turned round as they heard the screen door crashing behind them. A duffel-coated figure, cursing fluently, fought to shut the heavy door against the pitching of the *Ulysses*, finally succeeded in heaving the clips home. It was Leading Seaman Doyle, and even though his beard hid three-quarters of what could be seen of his face, he still looked thoroughly disgusted with life.

Carpenter grinned at him. He and Doyle had served a commission together on the China Station. Doyle was a very privileged person.

'Well, well, the Ancient Mariner himself! How are things down below, Doyle?'

'Bloody desperate, sir!' His voice was as lugubrious as his face. 'Cold as charity, sir, and everything all over the bloody place. Cups, saucers, plates in smithereens. Half the crew—'

He broke off suddenly, eyes slowly widening in blank disbelief. He was staring out to sea between Nicholls and Carpenter.

'Well, what about half the crew? . . . What's the matter, Doyle?'

'Christ Almighty!' Doyle's voice was slow, stunned: it was almost a prayer. 'Oh, Christ Almighty!' The voices rose sharply on the last two syllables.

The two officers twisted quickly round. The *Defender* was climbing – all 500 feet of her was literally climbing – up the lee side of a wave that staggered the imagination, whose immensity completely defied immediate comprehension. Even as they watched, before shocked minds could grasp the significance of it all, the *Defender* reached the crest, hesitated, crazily tilted up her stern till screw and rudder were entirely clear of the water, then crashed down, down, down. . . .

Even at two cable-lengths' distance in that high wind, the explosive smash of the plummeting bows came like a thunder-clap. An aeon ticked by, and still the *Defender* seemed to keep on going under, completely buried now, right back to the bridge island, in a sea of foaming white. How long she remained like that, arrowed down into the depths of the Arctic, no one could afterwards say: then slowly, agonizingly, incredibly, great rivers of water cascaded off her bows, she broke surface again. Broke surface, to present to frankly disbelieving eyes a spectacle entirely without precedent, anywhere, at any time. The tremendous, instantaneous, upthrusting pressure of unknown thousands of tons of water had torn the open flight-deck completely off its mountings and bent it backwards, in a great, sweeping 'U,' almost as far as the bridge. It was a sight to make men doubt their sanity, to leave them stupefied, to leave them speechless – all that is, except the Kapok Kid. He rose magnificently to the occasion.

'My word!' he murmured thoughtfully. 'That *is* unusual.'

Another such wave, another such shattering impact and it would have been the end for the *Defender*. The finest ships, the stoutest, most powerful vessels, are made only of thin, incredibly thin, sheets of metal, and metal, twisted and tortured as was the *Defender*'s, could never have withstood another such impact.

But there were no more such waves, no more such impacts. It had been a freak wave, one of these massive, inexplicable contortions of the sea which have occurred, with blessed infrequency, from time immemorial, in all the great seas of the world whenever Nature wanted to show mankind, an irreverent, over-venturesome mankind, just how puny and pitifully helpless a thing mankind really is. . . . There were no more such waves and, by five o'clock, although land was still some eight to ten miles away, the squadron had moved into comparative shelter behind the tip of the Langanes peninsula.

From time to time, the captain of the *Defender*, who seemed to be enjoying himself hugely, sent reassuring messages to the Admiral. He was making a good deal of water, but he was managing nicely, thank you. He thought the latest shape in flight-decks very fashionable, and a vast improvement on the old type; straight flight-decks lacked imagination, he thought, and didn't the Admiral think so too. The vertical type, he stated, provided excellent protection against wind and weather, and would make a splendid sail with the wind in the right quarter. With his last message, to the effect that he thought that it would be rather difficult to fly off planes, a badly-worried Tyndall lost his temper and sent back such a blistering signal that all communications abruptly ceased.

Shortly before six o'clock, the squadron hove-to under the shelter of Langanes, less than two miles offshore. Langanes is low-lying, and the wind, still climbing the scale, swept over it and into the bay beyond without a break; but the sea, compared to an hour ago, was mercifully calm, although the ships still rolled heavily. At once the cruisers and the screen vessels – except the *Portpatrick* and the *Gannet* – moved alongside the carriers, took oil hoses aboard. Tyndall, reluctantly and after much heart-searching, had decided that the *Portpatrick* and *Gannet* were suspect, a potential liability: they were to escort the crippled carrier back to Scapa.

Exhaustion, an exhaustion almost physical, almost tangible, lay heavily over the mess-decks and the wardroom of the *Ulysses*. Behind lay another sleepless night, another twenty-four hours with peace unknown and rest impossible. With dull tired minds, men heard the broadcast that the *Defender*, the *Portpatrick* and the *Gannet* were to return to Scapa when the weather moderated. Six gone now, only eight left – half the carrier force gone. Little wonder that men felt sick at heart, felt as if they were being deserted, as if, in Riley's phrase, they were being thrown to the wolves.

But there was remarkably little bitterness, a puzzling lack of resentment which, perhaps, sprung only from sheer passive acceptance. Brooks was aware of it, this inaction of feeling, this unnatural extinction of response, and was lost for a reason to account for it. Perhaps, he thought, this was the nadir, the last extremity when sick men and sick minds cease altogether to function, the last slow-down of all vital processes, both human and animal. Perhaps this was just the final apathy. His intellect told him that was reasonable, more, it was inevitable. . . . And all the time some fugitive intuition, some evanescent insight, was thrusting upon him an awareness, a dim shadowy awareness of something altogether different; but his mind was too tired to grasp it.

Whatever it was, it wasn't apathy. For a brief moment that evening, a white-hot anger ran through the ship like a flame, then resentment of the injustice which had provoked it. That there had been cause for anger even Vallery admitted; but his hand had been forced.

It had all happened simply enough. During routine evening tests, it had been discovered that the fighting lights on the lower yardarm were not working. Ice was at once suspected as being the cause.

The lower yardarm, on this evening dazzling white and heavily coated with snow and ice, paralleled the deck, sixty feet above it, eighty feet above the waterline. The fighting lights were suspended below the outer tip: to work on these, a man had either to sit on the yardarm – a most uncomfortable position as the heavy steel WT transmission aerial was bolted to its upper length – or in a bosun's chair suspended from the yardarm. It was a difficult enough task at any time: tonight, it had to be done with the maximum speed, because the repairs would interrupt radio transmission – the 3000-volt steel 'Safe-to-Transmit' boards (which broke the electrical circuits) had to be withdrawn and left in the keeping of the Officer of the Watch during the repair: it had to be done – very precise, finicky work had to be done – in that sub-zero temperature: it had to be done on that slippery, glass-smooth yardarm, with the *Ulysses* rolling regularly through a thirty-degree arc: the job was more than ordinarily difficult – it was highly dangerous.

Marshall did not feel justified in detailing the duty LTO for the job, especially as that rating was a middle-aged and very much overweight reservist, long past his climbing prime. He asked for volunteers. It was inevitable that he should have picked Ralston, for that was the kind of man Ralston was.

The task took half an hour – twenty minutes to climb the mast, edge out to the yardarm tip, fit the bosun's chair and lifeline, and ten minutes for the actual repair. Long before he was finished, a hundred, two hundred tired men, robbing themselves of sleep and supper, had come on deck and huddled there in the bitter wind, watching in fascination.

Ralston swung in a great arc across the darkening sky, the gale plucking viciously at his duffel and hood. Twice, wind and wave flung him out, still in his chair, parallel to the yardarm, forcing him to wrap both arms around the yardarm and hang on for his life. On the second occasion he seemed to strike his face against the aerial for he held his head for a few seconds afterwards, as if he were dazed. It was then that he lost his gauntlets – he must have had them in his lap, while making some delicate adjustment: they dropped down together, disappeared over the side.

A few minutes later, while Vallery and Turner were standing amidships examining the damage the motor-boat had suffered in Scapa Flow, a short, stocky figure came hurriedly out of the after screen door, made for the fo'c'sle at an awkward stumbling run. He pulled up abruptly at the sight of the Captain and the Commander: they saw it was Hastings, the Master-at-Arms.

'What's the matter, Hastings?' Vallery asked curtly. He always found it difficult to conceal his dislike for the Master-at-Arms, his dislike for his harshness, his uncalled-for severity.

'Trouble on the bridge, sir,' Hastings jerked out breathlessly. Vallery could have sworn to a gleam of satisfaction in his eye. 'Don't know exactly what – could hardly hear a thing but the wind on the phone. . . . I think you'd better come, sir.'

They found only three people on the bridge: Etherton, the gunnery officer, one hand still clutching a phone, worried, unhappy: Ralston, his hands hanging loosely by his sides, the palms raw and torn, the face ghastly, the chin with the dead pallor of frostbite, the forehead masked in furrowed, frozen blood: and, lying in a corner, Sub-Lieutenant Carslake, moaning in agony, only the whites of his eyes showing, stupidly fingering his smashed mouth, the torn, bleeding gaps in his prominent upper teeth.

'Good God!' Vallery ejaculated. 'Good God above!' He stood there, his hand on the gate, trying to grasp the significance of the scene before him. Then his mouth clamped shut and he swung round on the Gunnery Officer.

'What the devil's happened here, Etherton?' he demanded harshly. 'What *is* all this? Has Carslake—'

'Ralston hit him, sir,' Etherton broke in.

'Don't be so bloody silly, Guns!' Turner grunted.

'Exactly!' Vallery's voice was impatient. 'We can see that. Why?'

'A WT messenger came up for the "Safe-to-Transmit" boards. Carslake gave them to him – about ten minutes ago, I – I think.'

'You think! Where were you, Etherton, and why did you permit it? You know very well . . .' Vallery broke off short, remembering the presence of Ralston and the MAA.

Etherton muttered something. His words were inaudible in the gale.

Vallery bent forward. 'What did you say, Etherton—'

'I was down below, sir.' Etherton was looking at the deck. 'Just – just for a moment, sir.'

'I see. You were down below.' Vallery's voice was controlled now, quiet and even; his eyes held an expression that promised ill for Etherton. He looked round at Turner. 'Is he badly hurt, Commander?'

'He'll survive,' said Turner briefly. He had Carslake on his feet now, still moaning, his hand covering his smashed mouth.

For the first time, the Captain seemed to notice Ralston. He looked at him for a few seconds – an eternity on that bitter, storm-lashed bridge –

then spoke, monosyllabic, ominous, thirty years of command behind the word.

'Well?'

Ralston's face was frozen, expressionless. His eyes never left Carslake.

'Yes, sir. I did it. I hit him – the treacherous, murdering bastard!'

'Ralston!' The MAA's voice was a whiplash.

Suddenly Ralston's shoulders sagged. With an effort, he looked away from Carslake, looked wearily at Vallery.

'I'm sorry. I forgot. He's got a stripe on his arm – only ratings are bastards.' Vallery winced at the bitterness. 'But he—'

'You've got frostbite.'

'Rub your chin, man!' Turner interrupted sharply.

Slowly, mechanically, Ralston did as he was told. He used the back of his hand. Vallery winced again as he saw the palm of the hand, raw and mutilated, skin and flesh hanging in strips. The agony of that bare-handed descent from the yardarm. . . .

'He tried to murder me, sir. It was deliberate.' Ralston sounded tired.

'Do you realize what you are saying?' Vallery's voice was as icy as the wind that swept over Langanes. But he felt the first, faint chill of fear.

'He tried to murder me, sir,' Ralston repeated tonelessly. 'He returned the boards five minutes before I left the yardarm. WT must have started transmitting just as soon as I reached the mast, coming down.'

'Nonsense, Ralston. How dare you—'

'He's right, sir.' It was Etherton speaking. He was replacing the receiver carefully, his voice unhappy. 'I've just checked.'

The chill of fear settled deeper on Vallery's mind. Almost desperately he said:

'Anyone can make a mistake. Ignorance may be culpable, but—'

'Ignorance!' The weariness had vanished from Ralston as if it had never been. He took two quick steps forward. 'Ignorance! I gave him these boards, sir, when I came to the bridge. I asked for the Officer of the Watch and he said *he* was – I didn't know the Gunnery Officer was on duty, sir. When I told him that the boards were to be returned only to me, he said: "I don't want any of your damned insolence, Ralston. I know my job – you stick to yours. Just you get up there and perform your heroics." He *knew*, sir.'

Carslake burst from the Commander's supporting arm, turned and appealed wildly to the Captain. The eyes were white and staring, the whole face working.

'That's a lie, sir! It's a damned, filthy lie!' He mouthed the words, slurred them through smashed lips. 'I never said . . .'

The words crescendoed into a coughing, choking scream as Ralston's fist smashed viciously, terribly into the torn, bubbling mouth. He staggered drunkenly through the port gate, crashed into the chart house, slid down to lie on the deck, huddled and white and still. Both Turner and the MAA had at once leapt forward to pinion the LTO's arms, but he made no attempt to move.

Above and beyond the howl of the wind, the bridge seemed strangely silent. When Vallery spoke, his voice was quite expressionless.

'Commander, you might phone for a couple of our marines. Have Carslake taken down to his cabin and ask Brooks to have a look at him. Master-at-Arms?'

'Sir?'

'Take this rating to the Sick Bay, let him have any necessary treatment. Then put him in cells. With an armed guard. Understand?'

'I understand, sir.' There was no mistaking the satisfaction in Hastings's voice.

Vallery, Turner and the Gunnery Officer stood in silence as Ralston and the MAA left, in silence as two burly marines carried Carslake, still senseless, off the bridge and below. Vallery moved after them, broke step at Etherton's voice behind him.

'Sir?'

Vallery did not even turn round. 'I'll see you later, Etherton.'

'No, sir. Please. This is important.'

Something in the Gunnery Officer's voice held Vallery. He turned back, impatiently.

'I'm not concerned with excusing myself, sir. There's no excuse.' The eyes were fixed steadily on Vallery. 'I was standing at the Asdic door when Ralston handed the boards to Carslake. I overheard them – every word they said.'

Vallery's face became very still. He glanced at Turner, saw that he, too, was waiting intently.

'And Ralston's version of the conversation?' In spite of himself, Vallery's voice was rough, edged with suspense.

'Completely accurate, sir.' The words were hardly audible. 'In every detail. Ralston told the exact truth.'

Vallery closed his eyes for a moment, turned slowly, heavily away. He made no protest as he felt Turner's hand under his arm, helping him down the steep ladder. Old Socrates had told him a hundred times that he carried the ship on his back. He could feel the weight of it now, the crushing burden of every last ounce of it.

Vallery was at dinner with Tyndall, in the Admiral's day cabin, when the message arrived. Sunk in private thought, he gazed down at his untouched food as Tyndall smoothed out the signal.

The Admiral cleared his throat.

'On course. On time. Sea moderate, wind freshening. Expect rendezvous as planned. Commodore 77.'

He laid the signal down. 'Good God! Seas moderate, fresh wind! Do you reckon he's in the same damned ocean as us?'

Vallery smiled faintly.

'This is it, sir.'

'This is it,' Tyndall echoed. He turned to the messenger.

'Make a signal. "You are running into severe storm. Rendezvous unchanged. You may be delayed. Will remain at rendezvous until your arrival." That clear enough, Captain?'

'Should be, sir. Radio silence?'

'Oh, yes. Add "Radio silence. Admiral, 14th ACS." Get it off at once, will you? Then tell WT to shut down themselves.'

The door shut softly. Tyndall poured himself some coffee, looked across at Vallery.

'That boy still on your mind, Dick?'

Vallery smiled non-committally, lit a cigarette. At once he began to cough harshly.

'Sorry, sir,' he apologized. There was silence for some time, then he looked up quizzically.

'What mad ambition drove me to become a cruiser captain?' he asked sadly.

Tyndall grinned. 'I don't envy you. . . . I seem to have heard this conversation before. What are you going to do about Ralston, Dick?'

'What would *you* do, sir?' Vallery countered.

'Keep him locked up till we return from Russia. On a bread-and-water diet, in irons if you like.'

Vallery smiled.

'You never were a very good liar, John.'

Tyndall laughed. '*Touché*!' He was warmed, secretly pleased. Rarely did Richard Vallery break through his self-imposed code of formality. 'A heinous offence, we all know, to clout one of HM commissioned officers, but if Etherton's story is true, my only regret is that Ralston didn't give Brooks a really large-scale job of replanning that young swine's face.'

'It's true, all right, I'm afraid,' said Vallery soberly. 'What it amounts to is that naval discipline – oh, how old Starr would love this – compels me to punish a would-be murderer's victim!' He broke off in a fresh paroxysm of coughing, and Tyndall looked away: he hoped the distress wasn't showing in his face, the pity and anger he felt that Vallery – that very perfect, gentle knight, the finest gentleman and friend he had ever known – should be coughing his heart out, visibly dying on his feet, because of the blind inhumanity of an SNO in London, two thousand miles away. 'A victim,' Vallery went on at last, 'who has already lost his mother, brother and three sisters. . . . I believe he has a father at sea somewhere.'

'And Carslake?'

'I shall see him tomorrow. I should like you to be there, sir. I will tell him that he will remain an officer of this ship till we return to Scapa, then resign his commission. . . . I don't think he'd care to appear at a court-martial, even as a witness,' he finished dryly.

'Not if he's sane, which I doubt,' Tyndall agreed. A sudden thought struck him. 'Do you think he *is* sane?' he frowned.

'Carslake,' Vallery hesitated. 'Yes, I think so, sir. At least, he was. Brooks isn't so sure. Says he didn't like the look of him tonight – something queer about him, he thinks, and in these abnormal conditions small provocations are magnified out of all proportion.' Vallery smiled briefly. 'Not that Carslake is liable to regard the twin assaults on pride and person as a small provocation.'

Tyndall nodded agreement. 'He'll bear watching. . . . Oh, damn! I wish the ship would stay still. Half my coffee on the tablecloth. Young Spicer' – he looked towards the pantry – 'will be as mad as hell. Nineteen years old and a regular tyrant. . . . I thought these would be sheltered waters, Dick?'

'So they are, compared to what's waiting for us. Listen!' He cocked his head to the howling of the wind outside. 'Let's see what the weather man has to say about it.'

He reached for the desk phone, asked for the transmitting station. After a brief conversation he replaced the receiver.

'TS says the anemometer is going crazy. Gusting up to eighty knots. Still north-west. Temperature steady at ten below.' He shivered. 'Ten below!' Then looked consideringly at Tyndall. 'Barometer almost steady at 27.8.'

'What!'

'27.8. That's what they say. It's impossible, but that's what they say.' He glanced at his wrist-watch. 'Forty-five minutes, sir. . . . This is a very complicated way of committing suicide.'

They were silent for a minute, then Tyndall spoke for both of them, answering the question in both their minds.

'We must go, Dick. We must. And by the way, our fire-eating young Captain (D), the doughty Orr, wants to accompany us in the *Sirrus*. . . . We'll let him tag along a while. He has things to learn, that young man.'

At 2020 all ships had completed oiling. Hove to, they had had the utmost difficulty in keeping position in that great wind; but they were infinitely safer than in the open sea. They were given orders to proceed when the weather moderated, the *Defender* and escorts to Scapa, the squadron to a position 100 miles ENE of rendezvous. Radio silence was to be strictly observed.

At 2030 the *Ulysses* and *Sirrus* got under way to the East. Lights winked after them, messages of good luck. Fluently, Tyndall cursed the squadron for the breach of darken-ship regulations, realized that, barring themselves there was no one on God's earth to see the signals anyway, and ordered a courteous acknowledgment.

At 2045, still two miles short of Langanes point, the *Sirrus* was plunging desperately in mountainous seas, shipping great masses of water over her entire fo'c'sle and main deck, and, in the darkness, looking far less like a destroyer than a porpoising submarine.

At 2050, at reduced speed, she was observed to be moving in close to such slight shelter as the land afforded there. At the same time, her six-inch Aldis flashed her signal: 'Screen doors stove in: "A" turret not tracking: flooding port boiler-room intake fans.' And on the *Sirrus*'s bridge Commander Orr swore in chagrin as he received the *Ulysses*'s final message: 'Lesson without words, No. 1. Rejoin squadron at once. You can't come out to play with the big boys.' But he swallowed his disappointment, signalled: 'Wilco. Just you wait till I grow up,' pulled the *Sirrus* round in a madly swinging half-circle and headed thankfully back for shelter. Aboard the flagship, it was lost to sight almost immediately.

At 2100, the *Ulysses* moved out into the Denmark Strait.

Chapter Six

Tuesday Night

It was the worst storm of the war. Beyond all doubt, had the records been preserved for Admiralty inspection, that would have proved to be incomparably the greatest storm, the most tremendous convulsion of nature since these recordings began. Living memory aboard the *Ulysses* that night, a vast accumulation of experience in every corner of the globe, could certainly recall nothing even remotely like it, nothing that would even begin to bear comparison as a parallel or precedent.

At ten o'clock, with all doors and hatches battened shut, with all traffic prohibited on the upper deck, with all crews withdrawn from gun-turrets and magazines and all normal deck watchkeeping stopped for the first time since her commissioning, even the taciturn Carrington admitted that the Caribbean hurricanes of the autumns of '34 and '37 – when he'd run out of searoom, been forced to heave-to in the dangerous right-hand quadrant of both these murderous cyclones – had been no worse than this. But the two ships he had taken through these – a 3000-ton tramp and a superannuated tanker on the New York asphalt run – had not been in the same class for seaworthiness as the *Ulysses*. He had little doubt as to her ability to survive. But what the First Lieutenant did not know, what nobody had any means of guessing, was that this howling gale was still only the deadly overture. Like some mindless and dreadful beast from an ancient and other world, the Polar monster crouched on its own doorstep, waiting. At 2230, the *Ulysses* crossed the Arctic Circle. The monster struck.

It struck with a feral ferocity, with an appalling savagery that smashed minds and bodies into a stunned unknowingness. Its claws were hurtling rapiers of ice that slashed across a man's face and left it welling red: it's teeth were that sub-zero wind, gusting over 120 knots, that ripped and tore through the tissue paper of Arctic clothing and sunk home to the bone: its voice was the devil's orchestra, the roar of a great wind mingled with the banshee shrieking of tortured rigging, a requiem for fiends: its weight was the crushing power of the hurricane wind that pinned a man helplessly to a bulkhead, fighting for breath, or flung him off his feet to crash in some distant corner, broken-limbed and senseless. Baulked of prey in its 500-mile sweep across the frozen wastes of the Greenland ice-cap, it goaded the cruel sea into homicidal alliance and flung itself, titanic in its energy, ravenous in its howling, upon the cockleshell that was the *Ulysses*.

The *Ulysses* should have died then. Nothing built by man could ever have hoped to survive. She should just have been pressed under to destruction, or turned turtle, or had her back broken, or disintegrated under these mighty hammer-blows of wind and sea. But she did none of these things.

How she ever survived the insensate fury of that first attack, God only knew. The great wind caught her on the bow and flung her round in a 45° arc and pressed her far over on her side as she fell – literally fell – forty heart-stopping feet over and down the precipitous walls of a giant trough. She crashed into the valley with a tremendous concussion that jarred every plate, every Clyde-built rivet in her hull. The vibration lasted an eternity as overstressed metal fought to re-adjust itself, as steel compressed and stretched far beyond specified breaking loads. Miraculously she held, but the sands were running out. She lay far over on her starboard side, the gunwales dipping: half a mile away, towering high above the mast-top, a great wall of water was roaring down on the helpless ship.

The 'Dude' saved the day. The 'Dude,' alternatively known as 'Persil,' but officially as Engineer-Commander Dodson, immaculately clad as usual in overalls of the most dazzling white, had been at his control position in the engine-room when that tremendous gust had struck. He had no means of knowing what had happened. He had no means of knowing that the ship was not under command, that no one on the bridge had as yet recovered from that first shattering impact: he had no means of knowing that the quarter-master had been thrown unconscious into a corner of the wheel-house, that his mate, almost a child in years, was too panic-stricken to dive for the madly-spinning wheel. But he did know that the *Ulysses* was listing crazily, almost broadside on, and he suspected the cause.

His shouts on the bridge tube brought no reply. He pointed to the port controls, roared 'Slow' in the ear of the Engineer WO – then leapt quickly for the starboard wheel.

Fifteen seconds later and it would have been too late. As it was, the accelerating starboard screw brought her round just far enough to take that roaring mountain of water under her bows, to dig her stern in to the level of the depth-charge rails, till forty feet of her airborne keel lay poised above the abyss below. When she plunged down, again that same shuddering vibration enveloped the entire hull. The fo'c'sle disappeared far below the surface, the sea flowing over and past the armoured side of 'A' turret. But she was bows on again. At once the 'Dude' signalled his WO for more revolutions, cut back the starboard engine.

Below decks, everything was an unspeakable shambles. On the mess-decks, steel lockers in their scores had broken adrift, been thrown in a dozen different directions, bursting hasps, and locks, spilling their contents everywhere. Hammocks had been catapulted from their racks, smashed crockery littered the decks: tables were twisted and smashed, broken stools stuck up at crazy angles, books, papers, teapots, kettles and crockery were scattered in insane profusion. And amidst this jumbled, sliding wreckage, hundreds of shouting, cursing, frightened and exhausted men struggled to their feet, or knelt, or sat, or just lay still.

Surgeon-Commander Brooks and Lieutenant Nicholls, with an inspired, untiring padre as good as a third doctor, were worked off their feet. The veteran Leading SBA Johnson, oddly enough, was almost useless – he was violently sick much of the time, seemed to have lost all heart: no one knew why – it was just one of these things and he had taken all he could.

Men were brought into the Sick Bay in their dozens, in their scores, a constant trek that continued all night long as the *Ulysses* fought for her life, a trek that soon overcrowded the meagre space available and turned the wardroom into an emergency hospital. Bruises, cuts, dislocations, concussions, fractures – the exhausted doctors experienced everything that night. Serious injuries were fortunately rare, and inside three hours there were only nine bed-patients in the Sick Bay, including AB Ferry, his already mangled arm smashed in two places – a bitterly protesting Riley and his fellow-mutineers had been unceremoniously turfed out to make room for the more seriously injured.

About 2330, Nicholls was called to treat the Kapok Kid. Lurching, falling and staggering in the wildly gyrating ship, he finally found the Navigator in his cabin. He looked very unhappy. Nicholls eyed him speculatively, saw the deep, ugly gash on his forehead, the swollen ankle peeping out below the Kapok Kid's Martian survival suit. Bad enough, but hardly a borderline case, although one wouldn't have thought so from the miserable, worried expression. Nicholls grinned inwardly.

'Well, Horatio,' he said unkindly, 'what's supposed to be the matter with you? Been drinking again?'

'It's my back, Johnny,' he muttered. He turned face-down on the bunk. 'Have a look at it, will you?'

Nicholls's expression changed. He moved forward, then stopped short.

'How the hell can I,' he demanded irritably, 'when you're wearing that damned ugly suit of yours?'

'That's what I mean,' said the Kapok Kid anxiously. 'I was thrown against the searchlight controls – all knobs and nasty, sharp projections. Is it torn? Is it ripped, cut in any way? Are the seams—'

'Well, for God's sake! Do you mean to tell me—?' Nicholls sank back incredulously on a locker.

The Kapok Kid looked at him hopefully.

'Does that mean it's all right?'

'Of course it's all right! If it's a blasted tailor you want, why the hell—'

'Enough!' The Kapok Kid swung briskly on to the side of his bunk, lifting an admonitory hand. 'There is work for you, sawbones.' He touched his bleeding forehead. 'Stitch this up and waste no time about it. A man of my calibre is urgently needed on the bridge. . . . I'm the only man on this ship who has the faintest idea where we are.'

Busy with a swab. Nicholls grinned. 'And where are we?'

'I don't know,' said the Kapok Kid frankly. 'That's what's so urgent about it. . . . But I do know where I was! Back in Henley. Did I ever tell you . . .?'

The *Ulysses* did not die. Time and again that night, hove to with the wind fine of her starboard bow, as her bows crashed into and under the far shoulder of a trough, it seemed that she could never shake free from the great press of water. But time and again she did just that, shuddering, quivering under the fantastic strain. A thousand times before dawn officers and men blessed the genius of the Clyde ship-yard that had made her: a thousand times they cursed the blind malevolence of that great storm that put the *Ulysses* on the rack.

Perhaps 'blind' was not the right word. The storm wielded its wild hate with an almost human cunning. Shortly after the first onslaught, the wind had veered quickly, incredibly so and in defiance of all the laws, back almost to the north again. The *Ulysses* was on a lee shore, forced to keep pounding into gigantic seas.

Gigantic – and cunning also. Roaring by the *Ulysses*, a huge comber would suddenly whip round and crash on deck, smashing a boat to smithereens. Inside an hour, the barge, motor-boat and two whalers were gone, their shattered timbers swept away in the boiling cauldron. Carley rafts were broken off by the sudden hammer-blows of the same cunning waves, swept over the side and gone for ever: four of the Balsa floats went the same way.

But the most cunning attack of all was made right aft on the poop-deck. At the height of the storm a series of heavy explosions, half a dozen in as many seconds, almost lifted the stern out of the water. Panic spread like wildfire in the after mess-decks: practically every light abaft the after engine-room smashed or failed. In the darkness of the mess-decks, above the clamour, high-pitched cries of 'Torpedoed!' 'Mined!' 'She's breaking up!' galvanized exhausted, injured men, even those – more than half – in various degrees of prostration from seasickness, into frantic stampeding towards doors and hatches, only to find doors and hatches jammed solidly by the intense cold. Here and there, the automatic battery lamps had clicked on when the lighting circuits failed: glowing little pin-points, they played on isolated groups of white, contorted faces, sunken-eyed and straining, as they struggled through the yellow pools of light. Conditions were ripe for disaster when a voice, harsh, mocking, cut cleanly through the bedlam. The voice was Ralston's: he had been released before nine o'clock, on the Captain's orders: the cells were in the very forepeak of the ship, and conditions there were impossible in a head sea: even so, Hastings had freed him only with the worst possible grace.

'It's our own depth charges! Do you hear me, you bloody fools – it's our own depth charges!' It was not so much the words as the biting mockery, that stopped short the panic, halted dazed, unthinking men in their tracks. 'They're *our* depth charges, I tell you! They must have been washed over the side!'

He was right. The entire contents of a rack had broken adrift, lifted from their cradles by some freak wave, and tumbled over the side. Through some oversight, they had been left set at their shallow setting – those put on for the midget submarine in Scapa – and had gone off almost directly under the ship. The damage, it seemed, was only minor.

Up in 'A' mess-deck, right for'ard, conditions were even worse. There was more wreckage on the decks and far more seasickness – not the green-faced, slightly ludicrous malaise of the cross-channel steamer, but tearing rendering conversions, dark and heavy with blood – for the bows had been rearing and plunging, rearing and plunging, thirty, forty, fifty feet at a time for endless, hopeless hours; but there was an even more sinister agent at work, rapidly making the mess-deck untenable.

At the for'ard end of the capstan flat, which adjoined the mess-deck, was the battery-room. In here were stored, or on charge a hundred and one different batteries, ranging from the heavy lead-acid batteries weighing over a hundred pounds to the tiny nickel-cadmium cells for the emergency lighting. Here, too, were stored earthenware jars of prepared acid and big, glass carboys of undiluted sulphuric. These last were permanently stored: in heavy weather, the big batteries were lashed down.

No one knew what had happened. It seemed likely – certain, indeed – that acid spilt from the batteries by the tremendous pitching had eaten through the lashings. Then a battery must have broken loose and smashed another, and another, and another, and then the jars and carboys until the entire floor – fortunately of acid-resisting material – was awash to a depth of five or six inches in sulphuric acid.

A young torpedoman, on a routine check, had opened the door and seen the splashing sea of acid inside. Panicking, and recalling vaguely that caustic soda, stored in quantities just outside, was a neutralizer for sulphuric, he had emptied a forty-pound carton of it into the battery-room: he was in the Sick Bay now, blinded. The acid fumes saturated the capstan flat, making entry impossible without breathing equipment, and was seeping back, slowly, insidiously, into the mess-deck: more deadly still hundreds of gallons of salt water from sprung deckplates and broken capstan speaking tubes were surging crazily around the flat: already the air was tainted with the first traces of chlorine gas. On the deck immediately above, Hartley and two seamen, belayed with ropes, had made a brief, hopelessly gallant attempt to plug the gaping holes: all three, battered into near senselessness by the great waves pounding the fo'c'sle, were dragged off within a minute.

For the men below, it was discomfort, danger and desperate physical illness: for the bare handful of men above, the officers and ratings on the bridge, it was pure undiluted hell. But a hell not of our latter-day imagining, a strictly Eastern and Biblical conception, but the hell of our ancient North-European ancestors, of the Vikings, the Danes, the Jutes, of Beowulf and the monster-haunted meres – the hell of eternal cold.

True, the temperature registered a mere 10° below zero – 42° of frost. Men have been known to live, even to work in the open, at far lower temperatures. What is not so well known, what is barely realized at all, is that when freezing point has been passed, every extra mile per hour of wind is *equivalent*, in terms of pure cold as it reacts on a human being, to a 1° drop in temperature. Not once, but several times that night, before it had finally raced itself to destruction, the anemometer had recorded gusts of over 125 mph, wave-flattening gusts that sundered stays and all but tore the funnels off. For minutes on end, the shrieking, screaming wind held steady at 100 mph and above – the total equivalent, for these numbed, paralysed creatures on the bridge, of something well below a 100° below zero.

Five minutes at a time was enough for any man on the bridge, then he had to retire to the Captain's shelter. Not that manning the bridge was more than a gesture anyway – it was impossible to look into that terrible wind: the cold would have seared the eyeballs blind, the ice would have gouged them out. And it was impossible even to see through the Kent Clear-view windscreens. They still spun at high speed, but uselessly: the ice-laden storm, a gigantic sandblaster, had starred and abraded the plate glass until it was completely opaque.

It was not a dark night. It was possible to see above, abeam and astern. Above, patches of night-blue sky and handfuls of stars could be seen at fleeting intervals, obscured as soon as seen by the scudding, shredded cloud-wrack. Abeam and astern, the sea was an inky black, laced with boiling white. Gone now were the serried ranks of yesterday, gone, too, the decorative whitecaps: here now were only massive mountains of water, broken and confused, breaking this way and that, but always tending south. Some of these moving ranges of water – by no stretch of the imagination, only by proxy, could they be called waves – were small, insignificant – in size of a suburban house: others held a million tons of water, towered seventy to eighty feet, looming terrifyingly against the horizon, big enough to drown a cathedral. . . . As the Kapok Kid remarked, the best thing to do with these waves was to look the other way. More often than not, they passed harmlessly by, plunging the *Ulysses* into the depths: rarely, they curled over and broke their tops into the bridge, soaking the unfortunate Officer of the Watch. He had then to be removed at once or he would literally have frozen solid within a minute.

So far they had survived, far beyond the expectation of any man. But, as they were blind ahead, there was always the worry of what would come next. Would the next sea be normal – for that storm, that was – or some nameless juggernaut that would push them under for ever? The suspense never lifted, a suspense doubled by the fact that when the *Ulysses* reared and crashed down, it did so soundlessly, sightlessly. They could judge its intensity only by movement and vibration: the sound of the sea, everything, was drowned in the Satanic cacophony of that howling wind in the upper works and rigging.

About two in the morning – it was just after the depth-charge explosions – some of the senior officers had staged their own private mutiny. The Captain, who had been persuaded to go below less than an hour previously, exhausted and shaking uncontrollably with cold, had been wakened by the depth-charging and had returned to the bridge. He found his way barred by the Commander and Commander Westcliffe, who bundled him quietly but firmly into the shelter. Turner heaved the door to, switched on the light. Vallery was more puzzled than angry.

'What – what in the world does this mean?' he demanded.

'Mutiny!' boomed Turner happily. His face was covered in blood from flying splinters of ice. 'On the High Seas, is the technical term, I believe. Isn't that so, Admiral?'

'Exactly,' the Admiral agreed. Vallery swung round, startled: Tyndall was lying in state on the bunk. 'Mind you, I've no jurisdiction over a Captain in his own ship; but I can't see a thing.' He lay back on the bunk, eyes elaborately closed in seeming exhaustion. Only Tyndall knew that he wasn't pretending.

Vallery said nothing. He stood there clutching a handrail, his face grey and haggard, his eyes blood-red and drugged with sleep. Turner felt a knife twist inside him as he looked at him. When he spoke, his voice was low and earnest, so unusual for him that he caught and held Vallery's attention.

'Sir, this is no night for a naval captain. Danger from any quarter except the sea itself just doesn't exist. Agreed?'

Vallery nodded silently.

'It's a night for a seaman, sir. With all respect, I suggest that neither of us is in the class of Carrington – he's just a different breed of man.'

'Nice of you to include yourself, Commander,' Vallery murmured. 'And quite unnecessary.'

'The first Lieutenant will remain on the bridge all night. So will Westcliffe here. So will I.'

'Me, too,' grunted Tyndall. 'But I'm going to sleep.' He looked almost as tired, as haggard as Vallery.

Turner grinned. 'Thank you, sir. Well, Captain, I'm afraid it's going to be a bit overcrowded here tonight. . . . We'll see you after breakfast.'

'But—'

'But me no buts,' Westcliffe murmured.

'Please,' Turner insisted. 'You will do us a favour.'

Vallery looked at him. 'As Captain of the *Ulysses* . . .' His voice tailed off. 'I don't know what to say.'

'I do,' said Turner briskly, his hand on Vallery's elbow. 'Let's go below.'

'Don't think I can manage by myself, eh?' Vallery smiled faintly.

'I do. But I'm taking no chances. Come along, sir.'

'All right, all right.' He sighed tiredly. 'Anything for a quiet life . . . and a night's sleep!'

Reluctantly, with a great effort, Lieutenant Nicholls dragged himself up from the mist-fogged depths of exhausted sleep. Slowly, reluctantly, he opened his eyes. The *Ulysses*, he realized, was still rolling as heavily, plunging as sickeningly as ever. The Kapok Kid, forehead swathed in bandages, the rest of his face pocked with blood, was bending over him. He looked disgustingly cheerful.

'Hark, hark, the lark, etcetera,' the Kapok Kid grinned. 'And how are we this morning?' he mimicked unctuously. The Hon. Carpenter held the medical profession in low esteem.

Nicholls focused blurred eyes on him.

'What's the matter, Andy? Anything wrong?'

'With Messrs. Carrington and Carpenter in charge,' said the Kapok Kid loftily, 'nothing could be wrong. Want to come up top, see Carrington do his stuff? He's going to turn the ship round. In this little lot, it should be worth seeing!'

'What! Dammit to hell! Have you woken me just—'

'Brother, when this ship turns, you would wake up anyway – probably on the deck with a broken neck. But as it so happens, Jimmy requires your assistance. At least, he requires one of these heavy plate-glass squares which I happen to know you have in great numbers in the dispensary. But the dispensary's locked – I tried it,' he added shamelessly.

'But what – I mean – plate glass—'

'Come and see for yourself,' the Kapok Kid invited.

It was dawn now, a wild and terrible dawn, fit epilogue for a nightmare. Strange, trailing bands of misty-white vapour swept by barely at mast-top level, but high above the sky was clear. The seas, still gigantic, were shorter now, much shorter, and even steeper: the *Ulysses* was slowed right down, with barely enough steerage way to keep her head up – and even then, taking severe punishment in the precipitous head seas. The wind had dropped to a steady fifty knots – gale force: even at that, it seared like fire in Nicholls's lungs as he stepped out on the flap-deck, blinded him with ice and cold. Hastily he wrapped scarves over his entire face, clambered up to the bridge by touch and instinct. The Kapok Kid followed with the glass. As they climbed, they heard the loudspeakers crackling some unintelligible message.

Turner and Carrington were alone on the twilit bridge, swathed like mummies. Not even their eyes were visible – they wore goggles.

' 'Morning, Nicholls,' boomed the Commander. 'It *is* Nicholls, isn't it?' He pulled off his goggles, his back turned to the bitter wind, threw them away in disgust. 'Can't see damn' all through these bloody things . . . Ah, Number One, he's got the glass.'

Nicholls crouched in the for'ard lee of the compass platform. In a corner, the duckboards were littered with goggles, eye shields and gas-masks. He jerked his head towards them.

'What's this – a clearance sale?'

'We're turning, Doc.' It was Carrington who answered, his voice calm and precise as ever, without a trace of exhaustion. 'But we've got to see where we're going, and as the Commander says, all these damn' things there are useless – mist up immediately they're put on – it's too cold. If you'll just hold it – so – and if you would wipe it, Andy?'

Nicholls looked at the great seas. He shuddered.

'Excuse my ignorance, but why turn round at all?'

'Because it will be impossible very shortly,' Carrington answered briefly. Then he chuckled. 'This is going to make me the most unpopular man in the ship. We've just broadcast a warning. Ready, sir?'

'Stand by, engine-room: stand by, wheelhouse. Ready, Number One.'

For thirty seconds, forty-five, a whole minute, Carrington stared steadily, unblinkingly through the glass. Nicholls's hands froze. The Kapok Kid rubbed industriously. Then:

'Half-ahead, port!'

'Half-ahead, port!' Turner echoed.

'Starboard 20!'

'Starboard 20!'

Nicholls risked a glance over his shoulder. In the split second before his eyes blinded, filled with tears, he saw a huge wave bearing down on them, the bows already swinging diagonally away from it. Good God! Why hadn't Carrington waited until that was past?

The great wave flung the bows up, pushed the *Ulysses* far over to starboard, then passed under. The *Ulysses* staggered over the top, corkscrewed wickedly down the other side, her masts, great gleaming tree trunks thick and heavy with ice, swinging in a great arc as she rolled over, burying her port rails in the rising shoulder of the next sea.

'Full ahead port!'

'Full ahead port!'

'Starboard 30!'

'Starboard 30!'

The next sea, passing beneath, merely straightened the *Ulysses* up. And then, at last, Nicholls understood. Incredibly, because it had been impossible to see so far ahead, Carrington had known that two opposing wave systems were due to interlock in an area of comparative calm: how he had sensed it, no one knew, would ever know, not even Carrington himself: but he was a great seaman, and he had known. For fifteen, twenty seconds, the sea was a seething white mass of violently disturbed, conflicting waves – of the type usually found, on a small scale, in tidal races and overfalls – and the *Ulysses* curved gratefully through. And then another great sea, towering almost to bridge height, caught her on the far turn of the quarter circle. It struck the entire length of the *Ulysses* – for the first time that night – with tremendous weight. It threw her far over on her side, the lee rails vanishing. Nicholls was flung off his feet, crashed heavily into the side of the bridge, the glass shattering. He could have sworn he heard Carrington laughing. He clawed his way back to the middle of the compass platform.

And still the great wave had not passed. It towered high above the trough into which the *Ulysses*, now heeled far over to 40°, had been so contemptuously flung, bore down remorselessly from above and sought, in a lethal silence and with an almost animistic savagery, to press her under. The inclinometer swung relentlessly over – 45°, 50°, 53°, and hung there an eternity, while men stood on the side of the ship, braced with their hands on the deck, numbed minds barely grasping the inevitable. This was the end. The *Ulysses* could never come back.

A lifetime ticked agonizingly by. Nicholls and Carpenter looked at each other, blank-faced, expressionless. Tilted at that crazy angle, the bridge was sheltered from the wind. Carrington's voice, calm, conversational, carried with amazing clarity.

'She'd go to 65° and still come back,' he said matter-of-factly. 'Hang on to your hats, gentlemen. This is going to be interesting.'

Just as he finished, the *Ulysses* shuddered, then imperceptibly, then slowly, then with vicious speed lurched back and whipped through an arc of 90°, then back again. Once more Nicholls found himself in the corner of the bridge. But the *Ulysses* was almost round.

The Kapok Kid, grinning with relief, picked himself up and tapped Carrington on the shoulder.

'Don't look now, sir, but we have lost our mainmast.'

It was a slight exaggeration, but the top fifteen feet, which had carried the after radar scanner, were undoubtedly gone. That wicked, double whiplash, with the weight of the ice, had been too much.

'Slow ahead both! Midships!'

'Slow ahead both! Midships!'

'Steady as she goes!'

The *Ulysses* was round.

The Kapok Kid caught Nicholls's eye, nodded at the First Lieutenant.

'See what I mean, Johnny?'

'Yes.' Nicholls was very quiet. 'Yes, I see what you mean.' Then he grinned suddenly. 'Next time you make a statement, I'll just take your word for it, if you don't mind. These demonstrations of proof take too damn' much out of a person!'

Running straight before the heavy stern sea, the *Ulysses* was amazingly steady. The wind, too, was dead astern now, the bridge in magical shelter. The scudding mist overhead had thinned out, was almost gone. Far away to the south-east a dazzling white sun climbed up above a cloudless horizon. The long night was over.

An hour later, with the wind down to thirty knots, radar reported contacts to the west. After another hour, with the wind almost gone and only a heavy swell running, smoke plumes tufted above the horizon. At 1030, in position, on time, the *Ulysses* rendezvoused with the convoy from Halifax.

Chapter Seven

Wednesday Night

The convoy came steadily up from the west, rolling heavily in cross seas, a rich argosy, a magnificent prize for any German wolf-pack. Eighteen ships in this argosy, fifteen big, modern cargo ships, three 16,000-ton tankers, carrying a freight far more valuable, infinitely more vital, than any fleet of quinqueremes or galleons had ever known. Tanks, planes and petrol – what were gold and jewels, silks and the rarest of spices compared to these? £10,000,000, £20,000,000 – the total worth of that convoy was difficult to estimate: in any event, its real value was not to be measured in terms of money.

Aboard the merchant ships, crews lined the decks as the *Ulysses* steamed up between the port and centre lines. Lined the decks and looked and wondered – and thanked their Maker they had been wide of the path of that great storm. The *Ulysses*, seen from another deck, was a strange sight: broken-masted, stripped of her rafts, with her boat falls hauled taut over empty cradles, she glistened like crystal in the morning light: the great wind had blown away all snow, had abraded and rubbed and polished the ice to a satin-smooth, transparent gloss: but on either side of the bows and before the bridge were huge patches of crimson, where the hurricane sand-blaster of that long night had stripped off camouflage and base coats, exposing the red lead below.

The American escort was small – a heavy cruiser with a sea plane for spotting, two destroyers and two near-frigates of the coastguard type. Small, but sufficient: there was no need of escort carriers (although these frequently sailed with the Atlantic convoys) because the Luftwaffe could not operate so far west, and the wolf-packs, in recent months, had moved north and east of Iceland: there, they were not only nearer base – they could more easily lie astride the converging convoy routes to Murmansk.

ENE they sailed in company, freighters, American warships and the *Ulysses* until, late in the afternoon, the box like silhouette of an escort carrier bulked high against the horizon. Half an hour later, at 1600, the American escorts slowed, dropped astern and turned, winking farewell messages of good luck. Aboard the *Ulysses*, men watched them depart with mixed feelings. They knew these ships had to go, that another convoy would already be mustering off the St Lawrence. There was none of the envy, the bitterness one might expect – and had indeed been common enough only a few weeks ago – among these exhausted men who carried the brunt of the war. There was instead a careless acceptance of things as they were, a quasi-cynical bravado, often a queer, high nameless pride that hid itself beneath twisted jests and endless grumbling.

The 14th Aircraft Carrier Squadron – or what was left of it – was only two miles away now. Tyndall, coming to the bridge, swore fluently as he saw that a carrier and mine-sweeper were missing. An angry signal went out to Captain Jeffries of the *Stirling*, asking why orders had been disobeyed, where the missing ships were.

An Aldis flickered back its reply. Tyndall sat grim-faced and silent as Bentley read out the signal to him. The *Wrestler*'s steering gear had broken down during the night. Even behind Langanes the weather position had been severe, had worsened about midnight when the wind had veered to the north. The *Wrestler*, even with two screws, had lost almost all steering command, and, in zero visibility and an effort to maintain position, had gone too far ahead and grounded on the Vejle bank. She had grounded on the top of the tide. She had still been there, with the mine-sweeper *Eager* in attendance, when the squadron had sailed shortly after dawn.

Tyndall sat in silence for some minutes. He dictated a WT signal to the *Wrestler*, hesitated about breaking radio silence, countermanded the signal, and decided to go to see for himself. After all, it was only three hours' steaming distance. He signalled the *Stirling*: 'Take over squadron command: will rejoin in the morning,' and ordered Vallery to take the *Ulysses* back to Langanes.

Vallery nodded unhappily, gave the necessary orders. He was worried, badly so, was trying hard not to show it. The least of his worries was himself, although he knew, but never admitted to anyone, that he was a very sick man. He thought wryly that he didn't have to admit it anyway – he was amused and touched by the elaborate casualness with which his officers sought to lighten his load, to show their concern for him.

He was worried, too, about his crew – they were in no fit state to do the lightest work, to survive that killing cold, far less sail the ship and fight her through to Russia. He was depressed, also, over the series of misfortunes that had befallen the squadron since leaving Scapa: it augured ill for the future, and he had no illusions as to what lay ahead for the crippled squadron. And always, a gnawing torment at the back of his mind, he worried about Ralston.

Ralston – that tall throwback to his Scandinavian ancestors, with his flaxen hair and still blue eyes. Ralston, whom nobody understood, with whom nobody on the ship had an intimate friendship, who went his own unsmiling, self-possessed way. Ralston, who had nothing left to fight for, except memories, who was one of the most reliable men in the *Ulysses*, extraordinarily decisive, competent and resourceful in any emergency – and who again found himself under lock and key. And for nothing that any reasonable and just man could call fault of his own.

Under lock and key – that was what hurt. Last night, Vallery had gladly seized the excuse of bad weather to release him, had intended to forget the matter, to let sleeping dogs lie. But Hastings, the Master-At-Arms, had exceeded his duty and returned him to cells during the forenoon watch. Masters-At-Arms – disciplinary Warrant Officers, in effect – had never been particularly noted for a humane, tolerant and ultra-kindly attitude to life in general or the lower deck in particular – they couldn't afford to be. But even amongst such men, Hastings was an exception – a machine-like seemingly emotionless creature, expressionless, unbending, strict, fair according to his lights, but utterly devoid of heart and sympathy. If Hastings were not careful, Vallery mused, he might very well go the same way as Lister, until recently the highly unpopular Master-At-Arms of the *Blue Ranger*. Not, when he came to think of it, that anyone knew what had happened to Lister, except that he had been so misguided as to take a walk on the flight-deck on a dark and starless night . . .

Vallery sighed. As he had explained to Foster, his hands were tied. Foster, the Captain of Marines, with an aggrieved and incensed Colour-Sergeant Evans standing behind him, had complained bitterly at having his marines withdrawn for guard duty, men who needed every minute of sleep they could snatch. Privately, Vallery had sympathized with Foster, but he couldn't afford to countermand his original order – not, at least, until he had held a Captain's Defaulters and placed Ralston under open arrest . . . He sighed again, sent for Turner and asked him to break out grass lines, a manila and a five-inch wire on the poop. He suspected that they would be needed shortly, and, as it turned out, his preparations were justified.

Darkness had fallen when they moved up to the Vejle bank, but locating the *Wrestler* was easy – her identification challenge ten minutes ago had given her approximate position, and now her squat bulk loomed high before them, a knife-edged silhouette against the pale afterglow of sunset. Ominously, her flight-deck raked perceptibly towards the stern, where the *Eager* lay, apparently at anchor. The sea was almost calm here – there was only a gentle swell running.

Aboard the *Ulysses*, a hooded, pin-hole Aldis started to chatter.

'Congratulations! How are you fast?'

From the *Wrestler*, a tiny light flickered in answer. Bentley read aloud as the message came.

'Bows aft 100 feet.'

'Wonderful,' said Tyndall bitterly. 'Just wonderful! Ask him, "How is steering-gear?" '

Back came the answer: 'Diver down: transverse fracture of post: dockyard job.'

'My God!' Tyndall groaned. 'A dockyard job! That's handy. Ask him, "What steps have you taken?" '

'All fuel and water pumped aft. Kedge anchor. *Eager* towing. Full astern, 1200–1230.'

The turn of the high tide, Tyndall knew. 'Very successful, very successful indeed,' he growled. 'No, you bloody fool, don't send that. Tell him to prepare to receive towing wire, bring own towing chain aft.'

'Message understood,' Bentley read.

'Ask him, "How much excess squadron fuel have you?" '

'800 tons.'

'Get rid of it.'

Bentley read, 'Please confirm.'

'Tell him to empty the bloody stuff over the side!' Tyndall roared.

The light on the *Wrestler* flickered and died in hurt silence.

At midnight the *Eager* steamed slowly ahead of the *Ulysses*, taking up the wire that led back to the cruiser's fo'c'sle capstan: two minutes later, the *Ulysses* began to shudder as the four great engines boiled up the shallow water into a seething mud-stained cauldron. The chain from the poop-deck to the *Wrestler*'s stern was a bare fifteen fathoms in length, angling up at 30°. This would force the carrier's stern down – only a fraction, but in this situation every ounce counted – and give more positive buoyancy to the grounded bows. And much more important – for the racing screws were now aerating the water, developing only a fraction of their potential thrust – the proximity of the two ships helped the *Ulysses*'s screws reinforce the action of the *Wrestler*'s in scouring out a channel in the sand and mud beneath the carrier's keel.

Twenty minutes before high tide, easily, steadily, the *Wrestler* slid off. At once the blacksmith on the *Ulysses*'s bows knocked off the shackle securing the *Eager*'s towing wire, and the *Ulysses* pulled the carrier, her engines shut down, in a big half-circle to the east.

By one o'clock the *Wrestler* was gone, the *Eager* in attendance and ready to pass a head rope for bad weather steering. On the bridge of the *Ulysses*, Tyndall watched the carrier vanish into the night, zig-zagging as the captain tried to balance the steering on the two screws.

'No doubt they'll get the hang of it before they get to Scapa,' he growled. He felt cold, exhausted and only the way an Admiral can feel when he has lost three-quarters of his carrier force. He sighed wearily and turned to Vallery.

'When do you reckon we'll overtake the convoy?'

Vallery hesitated: not so the Kapok Kid.

'0805,' he answered readily and precisely. 'At twenty-seven knots, on the intersection course I've just pencilled out.'

'Oh, my God!' Tyndall groaned. 'That stripling again. What did I ever do to deserve him. As it happens, young man, it's imperative that we overtake before dawn.'

'Yes, sir.' The Kapok Kid was imperturbable. 'I thought so myself. On my alternative course, 33 knots, thirty minutes before dawn.'

'I thought so myself! Take him away!' Tyndall raved. 'Take him away or I'll wrap his damned dividers round . . .' He broke off, climbed stiffly out of his chair, took Vallery by the arm. 'Come on, Captain. Let's go below. What the hell's the use of a couple of ancient has-beens like us getting in the way of youth?' He passed out the gate behind the Captain, grinning tiredly to himself.

The *Ulysses* was at dawn Action Stations as the shadowy shapes of the convoy, a bare mile ahead, lifted out of the greying gloom. The great bulk of the *Blue Ranger*, on the starboard quarter of the convoy, was unmistakable. There was a moderate swell running, but not enough to be uncomfortable: the breeze was light, from the west, the temperature just below zero, the sky chill and cloudless. The time was exactly 0700.

At 0702, the *Blue Ranger* was torpedoed. The *Ulysses* was two cable-lengths away, on her starboard quarter: those on the bridge felt the physical shock of the twin explosions, heard them shattering the stillness of the dawn as they saw two searing columns of flame fingering skywards, high above the *Blue Ranger*'s bridge and well aft of it. A second later they heard a signalman shouting something unintelligible, saw him pointing forwards and downwards. It was another torpedo, running astern of the carrier, trailing its evil phosphorescent wake across the heels of the convoy, before spending itself in the darkness of the Arctic.

Vallery was shouting down the voice-pipe, pulling round the *Ulysses*, still doing upwards of twenty knots, in a madly heeling, skidding turn, to avoid collision with the slewing carrier. Three sets of Aldis lamps and the fighting lights were already stuttering out the 'Maintain Position' code signal to ships in the convoy. Marshall, on the phone, was giving the stand-by order to the depth-charge LTO: gun barrels were already depressing, peering hungrily into the treacherous sea. The signal to the *Sirrus* stopped short, unneeded: the destroyer, a half-seen blue in the darkness, was already knifing its way through the convoy, white water piled high at its bows, headed for the estimated position of the U-boat.

The *Ulysses* sheered by parallel to the burning carrier, less than 150 feet away; travelling so fast, heeling so heavily and at such close range, it was impossible to gather more than a blurred impression, a tangled, confused memory of heavy black smoke laced with roaring columns of flame, appalling in that near-darkness, of a drunkenly listing flight-deck, of Grummans and Corsairs cartwheeling grotesquely over the edge to splash icy clouds of spray in shocked faces, as the cruiser slewed away; and then the *Ulysses* was round, heading back south for the kill.

Within a minute, the signal-lamp of the *Vectra*, up front with the convoy, started winking. 'Contact, Green 70, closing: Contact, Green 70, closing.'

'Acknowledge,' Tyndall ordered briefly.

The Aldis had barely begun to clack when the *Vectra* cut through the signal.

'Contacts, repeat contacts. Green 90, Green 90. Closing. Very close. Repeat contacts, contacts.'

Tyndall cursed softly.

'Acknowledge. Investigate.' He turned to Vallery. 'Let's join him, Captain. This is it. Wolf-pack Number One – and in force. No bloody right to be here,' he added bitterly. 'So much for Admiralty Intelligence!'

The *Ulysses* was round again, heading for the *Vectra*. It should have been growing lighter now, but the *Blue Ranger*, her squadron fuel tanks on fire, a gigantic torch against the eastern horizon, had the curious effect of throwing the surrounding sea into heavy darkness. She lay almost athwart of the flagship's course for the *Vectra*, looming larger every minute. Tyndall had his night glasses to his eyes, kept on muttering: 'The poor bastards, the poor bastards!'

The *Blue Ranger* was almost gone. She lay dead in the water, heeled far over to starboard, ammunition and petrol tanks going up in a constant series of crackling reports. Suddenly, a succession of dull, heavy explosions rumbled over the sea: the entire bridge island structure lurched crazily sideways, held, then slowly, ponderously, deliberately, the whole massive body of it toppled majestically into the glacial darkness of the sea. God only knew how many men perished with it, deep down in the Arctic, trapped in its iron walls. They were the lucky ones.

The *Vectra*, barely two miles ahead now, was pulling round south in a tight circle. Vallery saw her, altered course to intercept. He heard Bentley shouting something unintelligible from the fore corner of the compass platform. Vallery shook his head, heard him shouting again, his voice desperate with some nameless urgency, his arm pointing frantically over the windscreen, and leapt up beside him.

The sea was on fire. Flat, calm, burdened with hundreds of tons of fuel oil, it was a vast carpet of licking, twisting flames. That much, for a second, and that only, Vallery saw: then with heart-stopping shock, with physically sickening abruptness, he saw something else again: the burning sea was alive with swimming, struggling men. Not a handful, not even dozens, but literally hundreds, soundlessly screaming, agonizingly dying in the barbarous contrariety of drowning and cremation.

'Signal from *Vectra*, sir.' It was Bentley speaking, his voice abnormally matter-of-fact. ' "Depth-charging. 3, repeat 3 contacts. Request immediate assistance." '

Tyndall was at Vallery's side now. He heard Bentley, looked a long second at Vallery, following his sick, fascinated gaze into the sea ahead.

For a man in the sea, oil is an evil thing. It clogs his movements, burns his eyes, sears his lungs and tears away his stomach in uncontrollable paroxysms of retching; but oil on fire is a hellish thing, death by torture, a slow, shrieking death by drowning, by burning, by asphyxiation – for the flames devour all the life-giving oxygen on the surface of the sea. And not even in the bitter Arctic is there the merciful extinction by cold, for the insulation of an oil-soaked body stretches a dying man on the rack for eternity, carefully preserves him for the last excruciating refinement of agony. All this Vallery knew.

He knew, too, that for the *Ulysses* to stop, starkly outlined against the burning carrier, would have been suicide. And to come sharply round to starboard, even had there been time and room to clear the struggling, dying men in the sea ahead, would have wasted invaluable minutes, time and to spare for the U-boats ahead to line up firing-tracks on the convoy; and the *Ulysses*'s first responsibility was to the convoy. Again all this Vallery knew. But, at that moment, what weighed most heavily with him was common humanity. Fine off the port bow, close in to the *Blue Ranger*, the oil was heaviest, the flames fiercest, the swimmers thickest: Vallery looked back over his shoulder at the Officer of the Watch.

'Port 10!'

'Port 10, sir.'

'Midships!'

'Midships, sir.'

'Steady as she goes!'

For ten, fifteen seconds the *Ulysses* held her course, arrowing through the burning sea to the spot where some gregariously atavistic instinct for self-preservation held two hundred men knotted together in a writhing, seething mass, gasping out their lives in hideous agony. For a second a great gout of flame leapt up in the centre of the group, like a giant, incandescent magnesium flare, a flame that burnt the picture into the hearts and minds of the men on the bridge with a permanence and searing clarity that no photographic plate could ever have reproduced: men on fire, human torches beating insanely at the flames that licked, scorched and then incinerated clothes, hair and skin: men flinging themselves almost out of the water, backs arched like tautened bows, grotesque in convulsive crucifixion: men lying dead in the water, insignificant, featureless little oil-stained mounds in an oil-soaked plain: and a handful of fear-maddened men, faces inhumanly contorted, who saw the *Ulysses* and knew what was coming, as they frantically thrashed their way to a safety that offered only a few more brief seconds of unspeakable agony before they gladly died.

'Starboard 30!' Vallery's voice was low, barely a murmur, but it carried clearly through the shocked silence on the bridge.

'Starboard 30, sir.'

For the third time in ten minutes, the *Ulysses* slewed crazily round in a racing turn. Turning thus, a ship does not follow through the line of the bows cutting the water; there is a pronounced sideways or lateral motion, and the faster and sharper the turn, the more violent the broadside skidding motion, like a car on ice. The side of the *Ulysses*, still at an acute angle, caught the edge of the group on the port bow: almost on the instant, the entire length of the swinging hull smashed into the heart of the fire, into the thickest press of dying men.

For most of them, it was just extinction, swift and glad and merciful. The tremendous concussion and pressure waves crushed the life out of them, thrust them deep down into the blessed oblivion of drowning, thrust them down and sucked them back into the thrashing vortex of the four great screws . . .

On board the *Ulysses*, men for whom death and destruction had become the stuff of existence, to be accepted with the callousness and jesting indifference that alone kept them sane – these men clenched impotent fists, mouthed meaningless, useless curses over and over again and wept heedlessly like little children. They wept as pitiful, charred faces, turned up towards the *Ulysses* and alight with joy and hope, petrified into incredulous staring horror, as realization dawned and the water closed over them; as hate-filled men screamed insane invective, both arms raised aloft, shaking fists white-knuckled through the dripping oil as the *Ulysses* trampled them under: as a couple of young boys were sucked into the maelstrom of the propellors, still giving the thumbs-up sign: as a particularly shocking case, who looked as if he had been barbecued on a spit and had no right to be alive, lifted a scorified hand to the blackened hole that had been his mouth, flung to the bridge a kiss in token of endless gratitude; and wept, oddly, most of all, at the inevitable humorist who lifted his fur cap high above his head and bowed gravely and deeply, his face into the water as he died.

Suddenly, mercifully, the sea was empty. The air was strangely still and quiet, heavy with the sickening stench of charred flesh and burning Diesel, and the *Ulysses*'s stern was swinging wildly almost under the black pall overhanging the *Blue Ranger* amidships, when the shells struck her.

The shells – three 3.7s – came from the *Blue Ranger*. Certainly, no living gun-crews manned these 3.7s – the heat must have ignited the bridge fuses in the cartridge cases. The first shell exploded harmlessly against the armour-plating: the second wrecked the bosun's store, fortunately empty: the third penetrated No. 3 Low Power Room via the deck. There were nine men in there – an officer, seven ratings and Chief-Torpedo Gunner's Mate Noyes. In that confined space, death was instantaneous.

Only seconds later a heavy rumbling explosion blew out a great hole along the waterline of the *Blue Ranger* and she fell slowly, wearily right over on her starboard side, her flight-deck vertical to the water, as if content to die now that, dying, she had lashed out at the ship that had destroyed her crew.

On the bridge, Vallery still stood on the yeoman's platform, leaning over the starred, opaque windscreen. His head hung down, his eyes were shut and he was retching desperately, the gushing blood – arterial blood – ominously bright and scarlet in the erubescent glare of the sinking carrier. Tyndall stood there helplessly beside him, not knowing what to do, his mind numbed and sick. Suddenly, he was brushed unceremoniously aside by the Surgeon-Commander, who pushed a white towel to Vallery's mouth and led him gently below. Old Brooks, everyone knew, should have been at his Action Stations position in the Sick Bay: no one dared say anything.

Carrington straightened the *Ulysses* out on course, while he waited for Turner to move up from the after Director tower to take over the bridge. In three minutes the cruiser was up with the *Vectra,* methodically quartering for a lost contact. Twice the ships regained contact, twice they dropped heavy patterns. A heavy oil slick rose to the surface: possibly a kill, probably a ruse, but in any event, neither ship could remain to investigate further. The convoy was two miles ahead now, and only the *Stirling* and *Viking* were there for its protection – a wholly inadequate cover and powerless to save the convoy from any determined attack.

It was the *Blue Ranger* that saved FR77. In these high latitudes, dawn comes slowly, interminably: even so, it was more than half-light, and the merchant ships, line ahead through that very gentle swell, lifted clear and sharp against a cloudless horizon, a U-boat Commander's dream – or would have been, had he been able to see them. But, by this time, the convoy was completely obscured from the wolf-pack lying to the south: the light westerly wind carried the heavy black smoke from the blazing carrier along the southern flank of the convoy, at sea level, the perfect smoke-screen, dense, impenetrable. Why the U-boats had departed from their almost invariable practice of launching dawn attacks from the north, so as to have their targets between themselves and the sunrise, could only be guessed. Tactical surprise, probably, but whatever the reason it was the saving of the convoy. Within an hour, the thrashing screws of the convoy had left the wolf-pack far behind – and FR77, having slipped the pack, was far too fast to be overtaken again.

Aboard the flagship, the WT transmitter was chattering out a coded signal to London. There was little point, Tyndall had decided, in maintaining radio silence now; the enemy knew their position to a mile. Tyndall smiled grimly as he thought of the rejoicing in the German Naval High Command at the news that FR77 was without any air cover whatsoever; as a starter, they could expect Charlie within the hour.

The signal read: 'Admiral, 14 ACS: To DNC, London. Rendezvoused FR77 1030 yesterday. Weather conditions extreme. Severe damage to Carriers: *Defender, Wrestler* unserviceable, returning base under escort: *Blue Ranger* torpedoed 0702, sunk 0730 today: Convoy Escorts now *Ulysses, Stirling, Sirrus, Vectra, Viking*: no mine-sweepers – *Eager* to base, mine-sweeper from Hvalfjord failed rendezvous: Urgently require air support: Can you detach carrier battle squadron: Alternatively, permission return base. Please advise immediately.'

The wording of the message, Tyndall pondered, could have been improved. Especially the bit at the end – probably sounded sufficiently like a threat to infuriate old Starr, who would only see in it pusillanimous confirmation of his confirmation of his conviction of the *Ulysses*'s – and Tyndall's – unfitness for the job . . . Besides, for almost two years now – since long before the sinking of the *Hood* by the *Bismarck* – it had been Admiralty policy not to break up the Home Fleet squadrons by detaching capital ships or carriers. Old battleships, too slow for modern inter-naval surface action – vessels such as the *Ramillies* and the *Malaya* – were used for selected Arctic convoys: with that exception, the official strategy was based on keeping the Home Fleet intact, containing the German Grand Fleet – and risking the convoys . . . Tyndall took a last look round the convoy, sighed wearily and eased himself down to the duckboards. What the hell, he thought, let it go. If it wasted his time sending it, it would also waste old Starr's time reading it.

He clumped his way heavily down the bridge ladders, eased his bulk through the door of the Captain's cabin, hard by the FDR. Vallery, partly undressed, was lying in his bunk, between very clean, very white sheets: their knife-edged ironing crease-marks contrasted oddly with the spreading crimson stain. Vallery himself, gaunt-cheeked and cadaverous beneath dark stubble of beard, red eyes sunk deep in great hollow sockets, looked corpse-like, already dead. From one corner of his mouth blood trickled down a parchment cheek. As Tyndall shut the door, Vallery lifted a wasted hand, all ivory knuckles and blue veins, in feeble greeting.

Tyndall closed the door carefully, quietly. He took his time, time and to spare to allow the shock to drain out of his face. When he turned round, his face was composed, but he made no attempt to disguise his concern.

'Thank God for old Socrates!' he said feelingly. 'Only man in the ship who can make you see even a modicum of sense.' He parked himself on the edge of the bed. 'How do you feel, Dick?'

Vallery grinned crookedly. There was no humour in his smile.

'All depends what you mean, sir. Physically or mentally? I feel a bit worn out – not really ill, you know. Doc says he can fix me up – temporarily anyway. He's going to give me a plasma transfusion – says I've lost too much blood.'

'Plasma?'

'Plasma. Whole blood would be a better coagulant. But he thinks it may prevent – or minimize – future attacks . . .' He paused, wiped some froth off his lips, and smiled again, as mirthlessly as before. 'It's not really a doctor and medicine I need, John – it's a padre – and forgiveness.' His voice trailed off into silence. The cabin was very quiet.

Tyndall shifted uncomfortably and cleared his throat noisily. Rarely had he been so conscious that he was, first and last, a man of action.

'Forgiveness? What on earth do you mean, Dick?' He hadn't meant to speak so loudly, so harshly.

'You know damn' well what I mean,' Vallery said mildly. He was a man who was rarely heard to swear, to use the most innocuous oath. 'You were with me on the bridge this morning.'

For perhaps two minutes neither man said a word. Then Vallery broke into a fresh paroxysm of coughing. The towel in his hand grew dark, sodden, and when he leaned back on his pillow Tyndall felt a quick stab of fear. He bent quickly over the sick man, sighed in soundless relief as he heard the quick, shallow breathing.

Vallery spoke again, his eyes still closed.

'It's not so much the men who were killed in the Low Power Room.' He seemed to be talking to himself, his voice a drifting murmur. 'My fault, I suppose – I took the *Ulysses* too near the *Ranger*. Foolish to go near a sinking ship, especially if she's burning . . . But just one of these things, just one of the risks . . . they happen . . .' The rest was a blurred, dying whisper. Tyndall couldn't catch it.

He rose abruptly to his feet, pulling his gloves on.

'Sorry, Dick,' he apologized. 'Shouldn't have come – shouldn't have stayed so long. Old Socrates will give me hell.'

'It's the others – the boys in the water.' Vallery might never have heard him. 'I hadn't the right – I mean, perhaps some of them would . . .' Again his voice was lost for a moment, then he went on strongly: 'Captain Richard Vallery, DSO – judge, jury and executioner. Tell me, John, what am I going to say when *my* turn comes?'

Tyndall hesitated, heard the authoritative rap on the door and jerked round, his breath escaping in a long, inaudible sigh of thankfulness.

'Come in,' he called.

The door opened and Brooks walked in. He stopped short at the sight of the Admiral, turned to the white-coated assistant behind him, a figure weighed down with stands, bottles, tubing and various paraphernalia.

'Remain outside, Johnson, will you?' he asked. 'I'll call you when I want you.'

He closed the door, crossed the cabin and pulled a chair up to the Captain's bunk. Vallery's wrist between his fingers, he looked coldly across at Tyndall. Nicholls, Brooks remembered, was insistent that the Admiral was far from well. He looked tired, certainly, but more unhappy than tired . . . The pulse was very fast, irregular.

'You've been upsetting him,' Brooks accused.

'Me? Good God, no!' Tyndall was injured. 'So help me, Doc, I never said—'

'Not guilty, Doc.' It was Vallery who spoke, his voice stronger now. 'He never said a word. *I'm* the guilty man – guilty as hell.'

Brooks looked at him for a long moment. Then he smiled, smiled in understanding and compassion.

'Forgiveness, sir. That's it, isn't it?' Tyndall stared in surprise, looked at him in wonder.

Vallery opened his eyes. 'Socrates!' he murmured. 'You would know.'

'Forgiveness,' Brooks mused. 'Forgiveness. From whom – the living, the dead – or the Judge?'

Again Tyndall started. 'Have you – have you been listening outside? How can you—?'

'From all three, Doc. A tall order, I'm afraid.'

'From the dead, sir, you are quite right. There would be no forgiveness: only their blessing, for there is nothing to forgive. I'm a doctor, don't forget – I saw those boys in the water . . . you sent them home the easy way. As for the Judge – you know, "The Lord giveth, the Lord taketh away. Blessed be the name of the Lord" – the Old Testament conception of the Lord who takes away in His own time and His own way, and to hell with mercy and charity.' He smiled at Tyndall. 'Don't look so shocked, sir. I'm not being blasphemous. If that were the Judge, Captain, neither you nor I – nor the Admiral – would ever want any part of him. But you know it isn't so . . .'

Vallery smiled faintly, propped himself up on his pillow. 'You make good medicine, Doctor. It's a pity you can't speak for the living also.'

'Oh, can't I?' Brooks smacked his hand on his thigh, guffawed in sudden recollection. 'Oh, my word, it was magnificent!' He laughed again in genuine amusement. Tyndall looked at Vallery in mock despair.

'Sorry,' Brooks apologized. 'Just fifteen minutes ago a bunch of sympathetic stokers deposited on the deck of the Sick Bay the prone and extremely unconscious form of one of their shipmates. Guess who? None other than our resident nihilist, our old friend Riley. Slight concussion and assorted facial injuries, but he should be restored to the bosom of his mess-deck by nightfall. Anyway, he insists on it – claims his kittens need him.'

Vallery looked up, amused, curious.

'Fallen down the stokehold again, I presume?'

'Exactly the question I put, sir – although it looked more as if he had fallen into a concrete mixer. "No, sir," says one of the stretcher-bearers. "He tripped over the ship's cat." "Ship's cat?" I says. "What ship's cat?" So he turns to his oppo and says: "Ain't we got a ship's cat, Nobby?" Whereupon the stoker yclept Nobby looks at him pityingly and says: " 'E's got it all wrong, sir. Poor old Riley just came all over queer – took a weak turn, 'e did. I 'ope 'e ain't 'urt 'isself?" He sounded quite anxious.'

'What had happened?' Tyndall queried.

'I let it go at that. Young Nicholls took two of them aside, promised no action and had it out of them in a minute flat. Seems that Riley saw in this morning's affair a magnificent opportunity for provoking trouble. Cursed you for an inhuman, cold-blooded murderer and, I regret to say, cast serious aspersions on your immediate ancestors – and all of this, mind you, where he thought he was safe – among his own friends. His friends half-killed him . . . You know, sir, I envy you . . .'

He broke off, rose abruptly to his feet.

'Now, sir, if you'll just lie down and roll up your sleeve . . . Oh, damn!'

'Come in.' It was Tyndall who answered the knock. 'Ah, for me, young Chrysler. Thank you.'

He looked up at Vallery. 'From London – in reply to my signal.' He turned it over in his hand two or three times. 'I suppose I have to open it some time,' he said reluctantly.

The Surgeon-Commander half-rose to his feet.

'Shall I—'

'No, no, Brooks. Why should you? Besides, it's from our mutual friend, Admiral Starr. I'm sure you'd like to hear what he's got to say, wouldn't you?'

'No, I wouldn't.' Brooks was very blunt. 'I can't imagine it'll be anything good.'

Tyndall opened the signal, smoothed it out.

'DNO to Admiral Commanding 14 ACS,' he read slowly. '*Tirpitz* reported preparing to move out. Impossible detach Fleet carrier: FR77 vital: proceed Murmansk all speed: good luck: Starr.' Tyndall paused, his mouth twisted. 'Good luck! He might have spared us that!'

For a long time the three men looked at each other, silently, without expression. Characteristically, it was Brooks who broke the silence.

'Speaking of forgiveness,' he murmured quietly, 'what I want to know is – who on God's earth, above or below it, is ever going to forgive that vindictive old bastard?'

Chapter Eight

Thursday Night

It was still only afternoon, but the grey Arctic twilight was already thickening over the sea as the *Ulysses* dropped slowly astern. The wind had died away completely; again the snow was falling, steadily, heavily, and visibility was down to a bare cable-length. It was bitterly cold.

In little groups of three and four, officers and men made their way aft to the starboard side of the poop-deck. Exhausted, bone-chilled men, mostly sunk in private and bitter thought, they shuffled wordlessly aft, dragging feet kicking up little puffs of powdery snow. On the poop, they ranged themselves soundlessly behind the Captain or in a line inboard and aft of the long, symmetrical row of snow-covered hummocks that heaved up roundly from the unbroken whiteness of the poop.

The Captain was flanked by three of his officers – Carslake, Etherton and the Surgeon-Commander. Carslake was by the guard-rail, the lower half of his face swathed in bandages to the eyes. For the second time in twenty-four hours he had waylaid Vallery, begged him to reconsider the decision to deprive him of his commission. On the first occasion Vallery had been adamant, almost contemptuous: ten minutes ago he had been icy and abrupt, had threatened Carslake with close arrest if he annoyed him again. And now Carslake just stared unseeingly into the snow and gloom, pale-blue eyes darkened and heavy with hate.

Etherton stood just behind Vallery's left shoulder, shivering uncontrollably. Above the white, jerking line of compressed mouth, cheek and jaw muscles were working incessantly: only his eyes were steady, dulled in sick fascination at the curious mound at his feet. Brooks, too, was tight-lipped, but there the resemblance ended: red of face and wrathful blue of eye, he fumed and seethed as can only a doctor whose orders have been openly flouted by the critically ill. Vallery, as Brooks had told him, forcibly and insubordinately, had no bloody right to be there, was all sorts of a damned fool for leaving his bunk. But, as Vallery had mildly pointed out, somebody had to conduct a funeral service, and that was the Captain's duty if the padre couldn't do it. And this day the padre couldn't do it, for it was the padre who lay dead at his feet . . . At his feet, and at the feet of Etherton – the man who had surely killed him.

The padre had died four hours ago, just after Charlie had gone. Tyndall had been far out in his estimate. Charlie had not appeared within the hour. Charlie had not appeared until mid-morning, but when he did come he had the company of three of his kind. A long haul indeed from the Norwegian coast to this, the 10th degree west of longitude, but nothing for these giant Condors – Focke-Wulf 200s – who regularly flew the great dawn to dusk half-circle from Trondheim to Occupied France, round the West Coast of the British Isles.

Condors in company always meant trouble, and these were no exception. They flew directly over the convoy, approaching from astern: the barrage from merchant ships and escorts was intense, and the bombing attack was pressed home with a marked lack of enthusiasm: the Condors bombed from a height of 7000 feet. In that clear, cold morning air the bombs were in view almost from the moment they cleared the bomb-bays: there was time to spare to take avoiding action. Almost at once the Condors had broken off the attack and disappeared to the east impressed, but apparently unharmed, by the warmth of their reception.

In the circumstances, the attack was highly suspicious. Circumspect Charlie might normally be on reconnaissance, but on the rare occasions that he chose to attack he generally did so with courage and determination. The recent sally was just too timorous, the tactics too obviously hopeless. Possibly, of course, recent entrants to the Luftwaffe were given to a discretion so signally lacking in their predecessors, or perhaps they were under strict orders not to risk their valuable craft. But probably, almost certainly, it was thought, that futile attack was only diversionary and the main danger lay elsewhere. The watch over and under the sea was intensified.

Five, ten, fifteen minutes passed and nothing had happened. Radar and Asdic screens remained obstinately clear. Tyndall finally decided that there was no justification for keeping the entire ship's company, so desperately in need of rest, at Action Stations for a moment longer and ordered the stand-down to be sounded.

Normal Defence Stations were resumed. All forenoon work had been cancelled, and officers and ratings off watch, almost to a man, went to snatch what brief sleep they could. But not all. Brooks and Nicholls had their patients to attend to: the Navigator returned to the chart-house: Marshall and his Commissioned Gunner, Mr Peters, resumed their interrupted routine rounds: and Etherton, nervous, anxious, over-sensitive and desperately eager to redeem himself for his share in the Carslake-Ralston episode, remained huddled and watchful in the cold, lonely eyrie of the Director Tower.

The sharp, urgent call from the deck outside came to Marshall and Peters as they were talking to the Leading Wireman in charge of No. 2 Electrical Shop. The shop was on the port side of the fo'c'sle deck cross-passage which ran athwartships for'ard of the wardroom, curving aft round the trunking of 'B' turret. Four quick steps had them out of the shop, through the screen door and peering over the side through the freshly falling snow, following the gesticulating finger of an excited marine. Marshall glanced at the man, recognized him immediately: it was Charteris, the only ranker known personally to every officer in the ship – in port, he doubled as wardroom barman.

'What is it, Charteris?' he demanded. 'What are you seeing? Quickly, man!'

'There, sir! Look! Out there – no, a bit more to your right! It's – it's a sub, sir, a U-boat!'

'What? What's that? A U-boat?' Marshall half-turned as the Rev. Winthrop, the padre, squeezed to the rail between himself and Charteris. 'Where? Where is it? Show me, show me!'

'Straight ahead, padre. I can see it now – but it's a damned funny shape for a U-boat – if you'll excuse the language,' Marshall added hastily. He caught the war-like, un-Christian gleam in Winthrop's eyes, smothered a laugh and peered through the snow at the strange squat shape which had now drifted almost abreast of them.

High up in the Tower, Etherton's restless, hunting eyes had already seen it, even before Charteris. Like Charteris, he immediately thought it was a U-boat caught surfacing in a snowstorm – the pay-off of the attack by the Condors: the thought that Asdic or radar would certainly have picked it up never occurred to him. Time, speed – that was the essence, before it vanished. Unthinkingly, he grabbed the phone to the for'ard multiple pom-pom.

'Director – pom-pom!' he barked urgently. 'U-boat, port 60. Range 100 yards, moving aft. Repeat, port 60. Can you see it? . . . No, no, port 60 – 70 now!' he shouted desperately. 'Oh, good, good! Commence tracking.'

'On target, sir,' the receiver crackled in his ear.

'Open fire – continuous!'

'Sir – but, sir – Kingston's not here. He went—'

'Never mind Kingston!' Etherton shouted furiously. Kingston, he knew, was Captain of the Gun. 'Open fire, you fools – now! I'll take responsibility.' He thrust the phone back on the rest, moved across to the observation panel . . . The realization, sickening, shocking, fear seared through his mind and he lunged desperately for the phone.

'Belay the last order!' he shouted wildly. 'Cease fire! Cease fire! Oh, my God, my God, my God!' Through the receiver came the staccato, angry bark of the two-pounder. The receiver dropped from his hand, crashed against the bulkhead. It was too late.

It was too late because he had committed the cardinal sin – he had forgotten to order the removal of the muzzle-covers – the metal plates that sealed off the flash-covers of the guns when not in use. And the shells were fused to explode on contact . . .

The first shell exploded inside its barrel, killing the trainer and seriously wounding the communication number: the other three smashed through their flimsy covers and exploded within a second of each other, a few feet from the faces of the four watchers on the fo'c'sle deck.

All four were untouched, miraculously untouched by the flying, screaming metal. It flew outwards and downwards, a red-hot iron hail sizzling into the sea. But the blast of the explosion was backwards, and the power of even a few pounds of high explosive detonating at arm's length is lethal.

The padre died instantly, Peters and Charteris within seconds, and all from the same cause – telescoped occiputs. The blast hurled them backwards off their feet, as if flung by a giant hand, the backs of their heads smashing to an eggshell pulp against the bulkhead. The blood seeped darkly into the snow, was obliterated in a moment.

Marshall was lucky, fantastically so. The explosion – he said afterwards that it was like getting in the way of the driving piston of the Coronation Scot – flung him through the open door behind him, ripped off the heels of both shoes as they caught on the storm-sill: he braked violently in mid-air, described a complete somersault, slithered along the passage and smashed squarely into the trunking of 'B' turret, his back framed by the four big spikes of the butterfly nuts securing an inspection hatch. Had he been standing a foot to the right or the left, had his heels been two inches higher as he catapulted through the doorway, had he hit the turret a hair's-breath to the left or right – Lieutenant Marshall had no right to be alive. The laws of chance said so, overwhelmingly. As it was, Marshall was now sitting up in the Sick Bay, strapped, broken ribs making breathing painful, but otherwise unharmed.

The upturned lifeboat, mute token of some earlier tragedy on the Russian Convoys, had long since vanished into the white twilight.

Captain Vallery's voice, low and husky, died softly away. He stepped back, closing the Prayer Book, and the forlorn notes of the bugle echoed briefly over the poop and died in the blanketing snow. Men stood silently, unmovingly, as, one by one, the thirteen figures shrouded in weighted canvas slid down the tipped plank, down from under the Union Flag, splashed heavily into the Arctic and were gone. For long seconds, no one moved. The unreal, hypnotic effect of that ghostly ritual of burial held tired, sluggish minds in unwilling thrall, held men oblivious to cold and discomfort. Even when Etherton half-stepped forward, sighed, crumpled down quietly, unspectacularly in the snow, the trance-like hiatus continued. Some ignored him, others glanced his way, incuriously. It seemed absurd, but it struck Nicholls, standing in the background, that they might have stayed there indefinitely, the minds and the blood of men slowing up, coagulating, freezing, while they turned to pillars of ice. Then suddenly, with exacerbating abruptness, the spell was shattered: the strident scream of the Emergency Stations whistle seared through the gathering gloom.

It took Vallery about three minutes to reach the bridge. He rested often, pausing on every second or third step of the four ladders that reached up to the bridge: even so, the climb drained the last reserves of his frail strength. Brooks had to half-carry him through the gate. Vallery clung to the binnacle, fighting for breath through foam-flecked lips; but his eyes were alive, alert as always, probing through the swirling snow.

'Contact closing, closing: steady on course, interception course: speed unchanged.' The radar loudspeaker was muffled, impersonal; but the calm precise tones of Lieutenant Bowden were unmistakable.

'Good, good! We'll fox him yet!' Tyndall, his tired, sagging face lit up in almost beaming anticipation, turned to the Captain. The prospect of action always delighted Tyndall.

'Something coming up from the SSW, Captain. Good God above, man, what are you doing here?' He was shocked at Vallery's appearance. 'Brooks! Why in heaven's name—?'

'Suppose *you* try talking to him?' Brooks growled wrathfully. He slammed the gate shut behind him, stalked stiffly off the bridge.

'What's the matter with him?' Tyndall asked of no one in particular. 'What the hell am I supposed to have done?'

'Nothing, sir,' Vallery pacified him. 'It's all my fault – disobeying doctor's orders and what have you. You were saying—?'

'Ah, yes. Trouble, I'm afraid, Captain.' Vallery smiled secretly as he saw the satisfaction, the pleased anticipation creep back into the Admiral's face. 'Radar reports a surface vessel approaching, big, fast, more or less on interception course for us.'

'And not ours, of course?' Vallery murmured. He looked up suddenly. 'By jove, sir, it couldn't be—?'

'The *Tirpitz*?' Tyndall finished for him. He shook his head in decision. 'My first thought, too, but no. Admiralty and Air Force are watching her like a broody hen over her eggs. If she moves a foot, we'll know . . . Probably some heavy cruiser.'

'Closing. Closing. Course unaltered.' Bowden's voice, clipped, easy, was vaguely reminiscent of a cricket commentator's. 'Estimated speed 24, repeat 24 knots.'

His voice crackled into silence as the WT speaker came to life.

'WT – bridge. WT – bridge. Signal from convoy: *Stirling* – Admiral. Understood. Wilco. Out.'

'Excellent, excellent! From Jeffries,' Tyndall explained. 'I sent him a signal ordering the convoy to alter course to NNW. That should take 'em well clear of our approaching friend.'

Vallery nodded. 'How far ahead is the convoy, sir?'

'Pilot!' Tyndall called and leaned back expectantly.

'Six – six and a half miles.' The Kapok Kid's face was expressionless.

'He's slipping,' Tyndall said mournfully. 'The strain's telling. A couple of days ago he'd have given us the distance to the nearest yard. Six miles – far enough, Captain. He'll never pick 'em up. Bowden says he hasn't even picked us up yet, that the intersection of courses must be pure coincidence . . . I gather Lieutenant Bowden has a poor opinion of German radar.'

'I know. I hope he's right. For the first time the question is of rather more than academic interest.' Vallery gazed to the South, his binoculars to his eyes: there was only the sea, the thinning snow. 'Anyway, this came at a good time.'

Tyndall arched a bushy eyebrow.

'It was strange, down there on the poop.' Vallery was hesitant. 'There was something weird, uncanny in the air. I didn't like it, sir. It was desperately – well, almost frightening. The snow, the silence, the dead men – thirteen dead men – I can only guess how the men felt, about Etherton, about anything. But it wasn't good – don't know how it would have ended—'

'Five miles,' the loudspeaker cut in. 'Repeat, five miles. Course, speed, constant.'

'Five miles,' Tyndall repeated in relief. Intangibles bothered him. 'Time to trail our coats a little, Captain. We'll soon be in what Bowden reckons is his radar range. Due east, I think – it'll look as if we're covering the tail of the convoy and heading for the North Cape.'

'Starboard 10,' Vallery ordered. The cruiser came gradually round, met, settled on her new course: engine revolutions were cut down till the *Ulysses* was cruising along at 26 knots.

One minute, five passed, then the loudspeaker blared again.

'Radar – bridge. Constant distance, altering on interception course.'

'Excellent! Really excellent!' The Admiral was almost purring. 'We have him, gentlemen. He's missed the convoy . . . Commence firing by radar!'

Vallery reached for the Director handset.

'Director? Ah, it's you, Courtney . . . good, good . . . you just do that.'

Vallery replaced the set, looked across at Tyndall.

'Smart as a whip, that boy. He's had "X" and "Y" lined up, tracking for the past ten minutes. Just a matter of pressing a button, he says.'

'Sounds uncommon like our friends here.' Tyndall jerked his head in the direction of the Kapok Kid, then looked up in surprise. 'Courtney? Did you say "Courtney"? Where's Guns?'

'In his cabin, as far as I know. Collapsed on the poop. Anyway, he's in no fit state to do his job . . . Thank God I'm not in that boy's shoes. I can imagine . . .'

The *Ulysses* shuddered, and the whip-like crash of 'X' turret drowned Vallery's voice as the 5.25 shells screamed away into the twilight. Seconds later, the ship shook again as the guns of 'Y' turret joined in. Thereafter the guns fired alternately, one shell at a time, every half-minute: there was no point in wasting ammunition when the fall of shot could not be observed; but it was probably the bare minimum necessary to infuriate the enemy and distract his attention from everything except the ship ahead.

The snow had thinned away now to a filmy curtain of gauze that blurred, rather than obscured the horizon. To the west, the clouds were lifting, the sky lightening in sunset. Vallery ordered 'X' turret to cease fire, to load with starshell.

Abruptly, the snow was gone and the enemy was there, big and menacing, a black featureless silhouette with the sudden flush of sunset striking incongruous golden gleams from the water creaming high at her bows.

'Starboard 30!' Vallery snapped. 'Full ahead. Smoke-screen!' Tyndall nodded compliance. It was no part of his plan to become embroiled with a German heavy cruiser or pocket battleship . . . especially at an almost point-blank range of four miles.

On the bridge, half a dozen pairs of binoculars peered aft, trying to identify the enemy. But the fore-and-aft silhouette against the reddening sky was difficult to analyse, exasperatingly vague and ambiguous. Suddenly, as they watched, white gouts of flame lanced out from the heart of the silhouette:

simultaneously, the starshell burst high up in the air, directly above the enemy, bathing him in an intense, merciless white glare, so that he appeared strangely naked and defenceless.

An illusory appearance. Everyone ducked low, in reflex instinct, as the shells whistled just over their heads and plunged into the sea ahead. Everyone, that is, except the Kapok Kid. He bent an impassive eye on the Admiral as the latter slowly straightened up.

'Hipper Class, sir,' he announced. '10,000 tons, 8-inch guns, carries aircraft.'

Tyndall looked at his unsmiling face in long suspicion. He cast around in his mind for a suitably crushing reply, caught sight of the German cruiser's turrets belching smoke in the sinking glare of the starshell.

'My oath!' he exclaimed. 'Not wasting much time, are they? And damned good shooting!' he added in professional admiration as the shells hissed into the sea through the *Ulysses*'s boiling wake, about 150 feet astern. 'Bracketed in the first two salvoes. They'll straddle us next time.'

The *Ulysses* was still heeling round, the black smoke beginning to pour from the after funnel, when Vallery straightened, clapped his binoculars to his eyes. Heavy clouds of smoke were mushrooming from the enemy's starboard deck, just for'ard of the bridge.

'Oh, well done, young Courtney!' he burst out. 'Well done indeed!'

'Well done indeed!' Tyndall echoed. 'A beauty! Still, I don't think we'll stop to argue the point with them . . . Ah! Just in time, gentlemen! Gad, that was close!' The stern of the *Ulysses*, swinging round now almost to the north, disappeared from sight as a salvo crashed into the sea, dead astern, one of the shells exploding in a great eruption of water.

The next salvo – obviously the hit on the enemy cruiser hadn't affected her fire-power – fell a cable length's astern. The German was now firing blind. Engineer Commander Dodson was making smoke with a vengeance, the oily, black smoke flattening down on the surface of the sea, rolling, thick, impenetrable. Vallery doubled back on course, then headed east at high speed.

For the next two hours, in the dusk and darkness, they played cat and mouse with the 'Hipper' class cruiser, firing occasionally, appearing briefly, tantalizingly, then disappearing behind a smoke-screen, hardly needed now in the coming night. All the time, radar was their eyes and their ears and never played them false. Finally, satisfied that all danger to the convoy was gone, Tyndall laid a double screen in a great curving 'U,' and vanished to the south-west, firing a few final shells, not so much in token of farewell as to indicate direction of departure.

Ninety minutes later, at the end of a giant half-circle to port, the *Ulysses* was sitting far to the north, while Bowden and his men tracked the progress of the enemy. He was reported as moving steadily east, then, just before contact was lost, as altering course to the south-east.

Tyndall climbed down from his chair, numbed and stiff. He stretched himself luxuriantly.

'Not a bad night's work, Captain, not bad at all. What do you bet our friend spends the night circling to the south and east at high speed, hoping to come up ahead of the convoy in the morning?' Tyndall felt almost jubilant, in spite of his exhaustion. 'And by that time FR77 should be 200 miles to the north of him . . . I suppose, Pilot, you have worked out intersection courses for rejoining the convoy at all speeds up to a hundred knots?'

'I think we should be able to regain contact without much difficulty,' said the Kapok Kid politely.

'It's when he is at his most modest,' Tyndall announced, 'that he sickens me most . . . Heavens above, I'm frozen to death. . . . Oh, damn! Not more trouble, I hope?'

The communication rating behind the compass platform picked up the jangling phone, listened briefly.

'For you, sir,' he said to Vallery. 'The Surgeon Lieutenant.'

'Just take the message, Chrysler.'

'Sorry, sir. Insists on speaking to you himself.' Chrysler handed the receiver into the bridge. Vallery smothered an exclamation of annoyance, lifted the receiver to his ear.

'Captain, here. Yes, what is it? . . . What? . . . *What*! Oh, God, no! . . . Why wasn't I told? . . . Oh, I see. Thank you, thank you.'

Vallery handed the receiver back, turned heavily to Tyndall. In the darkness, the Admiral felt, rather than saw the sudden weariness, the hunched defeat of the shoulders.

'That was Nicholls.' Vallery's voice was flat, colourless. 'Lieutenant Etherton shot himself in his cabin, five minutes ago.'

At four o'clock in the morning, in heavy snow, but in a calm sea, the *Ulysses* rejoined the convoy.

By mid-morning of that next day, a bare six hours later Admiral Tyndall had become an old weary man, haggard, haunted by remorse and bitter self-criticism, close, very close, to despair. Miraculously, in a matter of hours, the chubby cheeks had collapsed in shrunken flaccidity, draining blood had left the florid cheeks a parchment grey, the sunken eyes had dulled in blood and exhaustion. The extent and speed of the change wrought in that tough and jovial sailor, a sailor seemingly impervious to the most deadly vicissitudes of war, was incredible: incredible and disturbing in itself, but infinitely more so in its wholly demoralizing effect on the men. To every arch there is but one keystone . . . or so any man must inevitably think.

Any impartial court of judgment would have cleared Tyndall of all guilt, would have acquitted him without a trial. He had done what he thought right, what any commander would have done in his place. But Tyndall sat before the merciless court of his own conscience. He could not forget that it was he who had re-routed the convoy so far to the north, that it was he who had ignored official orders to break straight for the North Cape, that it was exactly on latitude 70 N – where their Lordships had told him they would be – that FR77 had, on that cold, clear windless dawn, blundered straight into the heart of the heaviest concentration of U-boats encountered in the Arctic during the entire course of the war.

The wolf-pack had struck at its favourite hour – the dawn – and from its favourite position – the north-east, with the dawn in its eyes. It struck cruelly, skilfully and with a calculated ferocity. Admittedly, the era of Kapitan Leutnant Prien – his U-boat long ago sent to the bottom with all hands by the destroyer *Wolverine* – and his illustrious contemporaries, the heyday of the great U-boat Commanders, the high noon of individual brilliance and great personal gallantry, was gone. But in its place – and generally acknowledged to be even more dangerous, more deadly – were the concerted, highly integrated mass attacks of the wolf-packs, methodical, machine-like, almost reduced to a formula, under a single directing command.

The *Cochella*, third vessel in the port line, was the first to go. Sister ship to the *Vytura* and the *Varella*, also accompanying her in FR77, the *Cochella* carried over 3,000,000 gallons of 100-octane petrol. She was hit by at least three torpedoes: the first two broke her almost in half, the third triggered off a stupendous detonation that literally blew her out of existence. One moment she was there, sailing serenely through the limpid twilight of sunrise: the next moment she was gone. Gone, completely, utterly gone, with only a seething ocean, convulsed in boiling white, to show where she had been: gone, while stunned eardrums and stupefied minds struggled vainly to grasp the significance of what had happened: gone, while blind reflex instinct hurled men into whatever shelter offered as a storm of lethal metal swept over the fleet.

Two ships took the full force of the explosion. A huge mass of metal – it might have been a winch – passed clear through the superstructure of the *Sirrus*, a cable-length away on the starboard: it completely wrecked the radar office. What happened to the other ship immediately astern, the impossibly-named *Tennessee Adventurer*, was not clear, but almost certainly her wheelhouse and bridge had been severely damaged: she had lost steering control, was not under command.

Tragically, this was not at first understood, simply because it was not apparent. Tyndall, recovering fast from the sheer physical shock of the explosion, broke out the signal for an emergency turn to port. The wolf-pack, obviously, lay on the port hand, and the only action to take to minimize further losses, to counter the enemy strategy, was to head straight towards them. He was reasonably sure that the U-boats would be bunched – generally, they strung out only for the slow convoys. Besides, he had adopted this tactic several times in the past with a high degree of success. Finally, it cut the U-boats' target to an impossible tenth, forcing on them the alternative of diving or the risk of being trampled under.

With the immaculate precision and co-ordination of Olympic equestrians, the convoy heeled steadily over to starboard, slewed majestically round, trailing curved, white wakes phosphorescently alive in the near-darkness that still clung to the surface of the sea. Too late, it was seen that the *Tennessee Adventurer* was not under command. Slowly, then with dismaying speed, she came round to the east, angling directly for another merchantman, the *Tobacco Planter*. There was barely time to think, to appreciate the inevitable: frantically, the *Planter*'s helm went hard over in an attempt to clear the other astern, but the wildly swinging *Adventurer*, obviously completely out of control, matched the *Planter*'s tightening circle, foot by inexorable foot, blind malice at the helm.

She struck the *Planter* with sickening violence just for'ard of the bridge. The *Adventurer*'s bows, crumpling as they went, bit deeply into her side, fifteen, twenty feet in a chaos of tearing, rending metal: the stopping power of 10,000 tons deadweight travelling at 15 knots is fantastic. The wound was mortal, and the *Planter*'s own momentum, carrying her past, wrenched her free from the lethal bows, opening the wound to the hungry sea and hastened her own end. Almost at once she began to fill, to list heavily to starboard. Aboard the *Adventurer*, someone must have taken over command:

her engine stopped, she lay motionless alongside the sinking ship, slightly down by the head.

The rest of the convoy cleared the drifting vessels, steadied west by north. Far out on the starboard hand, Commander Orr, in the *Sirrus*, clawed his damaged destroyer round in a violent turn, headed back towards the crippled freighters. He had gone less than half a mile when he was recalled by a vicious signal from the flagship. Tyndall was under no illusions. The *Adventurer*, he knew, might remain there all day, unharmed – it was obvious that the *Planter* would be gone in a matter of minutes – but that would be a guarantee neither of the absence of U-boats nor of the sudden access of misguided enemy chivalry: the enemy would be there, would wait to the last possible second before dark in the hope that some rescue destroyer would heave to alongside the *Adventurer*.

In that respect, Tyndall was right. The *Adventurer* was torpedoed just before sunset. Three-quarters of the ship's company escaped in lifeboats, along with twenty survivors picked up from the *Planter*. A month later the frigate *Esher* found them, in three lifeboats tied line ahead, off the bitter, iron coast of Bear Island, heading steadily north. The Captain, alert and upright, was still sitting in the stern-sheets, empty eye-sockets searching for some lost horizon, a withered claw locked to the tiller. The rest were sitting or lying about the boats, one actually standing, his arm cradled around the mast, and all with shrunken sun-blackened lips drawn back in hideous mirth. The log-book lay beside the Captain, empty: all had frozen to death on that first night. The young frigate commander had cast them adrift, watched them disappear over the northern rim of the world, steering for the Barrier. And the Barrier is the region of the great silence, the seas of incredible peace, so peaceful, so calm, so cold that they may be there yet, the dead who cannot rest. A mean and shabby end for the temple of the spirit . . . It is not known whether the Admiralty approved the action of the captain of the frigate.

But in the major respect, that of anticipating enemy disposition, the Admiral was utterly wrong. The wolf-pack commander had outguessed him and it was arguable that Tyndall should have foreseen this. His tactic of swinging an entire convoy into the face of a torpedo attack was well known to the enemy: it was also well known that his ship was the *Ulysses*, and the *Ulysses*, the only one of her kind, was familiar, by sight or picture silhouette, to every U-boat commander in the German Navy: and it had been reported, of course, that it was the *Ulysses* that was leading FR77 through to Murmansk. Tyndall should have expected, expected and forestalled the long overdue counter.

For the submarine that had torpedoed the *Cochella* had been the last, not the first, of the pack. The others had lain to the south of the U-boat that had sprung the trap, and well to the west of the track of FR77 – clear beyond the reach of Asdic. And when the convoy wheeled to the west, the U-boats lined up leisurely firing tracks as the ships steamed up to cross their bows at right angles. The sea was calm, calm as a millpond, an extraordinary deep, Mediterranean blue. The snow-squalls of the night had passed away. Far to the north-east a brilliant sun was shouldering itself clear of the horizon, its level rays striking a great band of silver across the Arctic, highlighting the ships, shrouded white in snow, against the darker sea and sky beyond. The conditions were ideal, if one may use the word 'ideal' to describe the prologue to a massacre.

Massacre, an almost total destruction there must inevitably have been but for the warning that came almost too late. A warning given neither by radar nor Asdic, nor by any of the magically efficient instruments of modern detection, but simply by the keen eyes of an eighteen-year-old Ordinary Seaman – and the God-sent rays of the rising sun.

'Captain, sir! Captain, sir!' It was young Chrysler who shouted. His voice broke in wild excitement, his eyes were glued to the powerful binoculars clamped on the port searchlight control position. 'There's something flashing to the south, sir! It flashed twice – there it goes again!'

'Where, boy?' Tyndall shouted. 'Come on, where, where?' In his agitation, Chrysler had forgotten the golden rule of the reporting look-out – bearing must come first.

'Port 50, sir – no, port 60 . . . I've lost sight of it now, sir.'

Every pair of glasses on the bridge swung round on the given bearing. There was nothing to be seen, just nothing at all. Tyndall shut his telescope slowly, shrugged his shoulders eloquent in disbelief.

'Maybe there *is* something,' said the Kapok Kid doubtfully. 'How about the sea catching a periscope making a quick circle sweep?'

Tyndall looked at him, silent, expressionless, looked away, stared straight ahead. To the Kapok Kid he seemed strange, different. His face was set, stonily impassive, the face of a man with twenty ships and 5000 lives in his keeping, the face of a man who has already made one wrong decision too many.

'There they go again!' Chrysler screamed. 'Two flashes – no, *three* flashes!' He was almost beside himself with excitement, literally dancing in an agony of frustration. 'I did see them, sir, I *did*. I *did*. Oh, please, sir, please!'

Tyndall had swung round again. Ten long seconds he gazed at Chrysler, who had left his binoculars, and was gripping the gate in gauntleted hands, shaking it in anguished appeal. Abruptly, Tyndall made up his mind.

'Hard aport, Captain. Bentley – the signal!'

Slowly, on the unsupported word of an eighteen-year-old, FR77 came round to the south, slowly, just too slowly. Suddenly, the sea was alive with running torpedoes – three, five, ten – Vallery counted thirty in as many seconds. They were running shallow and their bubbling trails, evil, ever-lengthening, rose swiftly to the surface and lay there milkily on the glassy sea, delicately evanescent shafts for arrowheads so lethal. Parallel in the centre, they fanned out to the east and west to embrace the entire convoy. It was a fantastic sight: no man in that convoy had ever seen anything remotely like it.

In a moment the confusion was complete. There was no time for signals. It was every ship for itself in an attempt to avoid wholesale destruction: and confusion was worse confounded by the ships in the centre and outer lines, that had not yet seen the wakes of the streaking torpedoes.

Escape for all was impossible: the torpedoes were far too closely bunched. The cruiser *Stirling* was the first casualty. Just when she seemed to have cleared all danger – she was far ahead where the torpedoes were thickest – she lurched under some unseen hammer-blow, slewed round crazily and steamed away back to the east, smoke hanging heavily over her poop. The *Ulysses*, brilliantly handled, heeled over on maximum rudder and under the counter-thrusting of her great screws, slid down an impossibly narrow lane between four torpedoes, two of them racing by a bare boat's length from either side: she was still a lucky ship. The destroyers, fast, highly manoeuvrable, impeccably handled, bobbed and weaved their way to safety with almost contemptuous ease, straightened up and headed south under maximum power.

The merchant ships, big, clumsy, relatively slow, were less fortunate. Two ships in the port line, a tanker and a freighter, were struck: miraculously, both just staggered under the numbing shock, then kept on coming. Not so the big freighter immediately behind them, her holds crammed with tanks, her decks lined with them. She was torpedoed three times in three seconds: there was no smoke, no fire no spectacular after-explosion: sieved and ripped from stern to stem, she sank quickly, quietly, still on even keel, dragged down by the sheer weight of metal. No one below decks had even the slightest chance of escaping.

A merchantman in the centre line, the *Belle Isle*, was torpedoed amidships. There were two separate explosions – probably she had been struck twice – and she was instantly on fire. Within seconds, the list to port was pronounced, increasing momentarily: gradually her rails dipped under, the outslung lifeboats almost touching the surface of the sea. A dozen, fifteen men were seen to be slipping, sliding down the sheering decks and hatch-covers, already half-submerged, towards the nearest lifeboat. Desperately they hacked at belly-band securing ropes, piled into the lifeboat in grotesquely comical haste, pushed it clear of the dipping davits, seized the oars and pulled frantically away. From beginning to end, hardly a minute had elapsed.

Half a dozen powerful strokes had them clear beyond their ship's counter: two more took them straight under the swinging bows of the *Walter A. Baddeley*, her companion tank-carrier in the starboard line. The consummate seamanship that had saved the *Baddeley* could do nothing to save the lifeboat: the little boat crumpled and splintered like a matchwood toy, catapulting screaming men into the icy sea.

As the big, grey hull of the *Baddeley* slid swiftly by them, they struck out with insane strength that made nothing of their heavy Arctic clothing. At such times, reason vanishes: the thought that if, by some God-given miracle, they were to escape the guillotine of the *Baddeley*'s single great screw, they would do so only to die minutes later in the glacial cold of the Arctic, never occurred to them. But, as it happened, death came by neither metal nor cold. They were still struggling, almost abreast the poop, vainly trying to clear the rushing, sucking vortex of water, when the torpedoes struck the *Baddeley*, close together and simultaneously, just for'ard of the rudder.

For swimming men who have been in the close vicinity of an underwater high explosion there can be no shadow of hope: the effect is inhuman, revolting, shocking beyond conception: in such cases, experienced doctors, pathologists even, can with difficulty bring themselves to look upon what were once human beings . . . But for these men, as so often in the Arctic, death was kind, for they died unknowing.

The *Walter A. Baddeley*'s stern had been almost completely blown off. Hundreds of tons of water were already rushing in the great, gaping hole below the counter, racing through cross-bulkheads fractured by the explosion, smashing open engine-boiler room watertight doors buckled by the blast, pulling her down by the stern, steadily, relentlessly, till her taffrail dipped salute to the waiting Arctic. For a moment, she hung there. Then, in quick succession from deep inside the hull, came a muffled explosion, the ear-shattering, frightening roar of escaping high-pressure steam and the thunderous crash of massive boilers rending away from their stools as the ship upended. Almost immediately the shattered stern lurched heavily, sunk lower and lower till the poop was completely gone, till the dripping forefoot was tilted high above the sea. Foot by foot the angle of tilt increased, the stern plunged a hundred, two hundred feet under the surface of the sea, the bows rearing almost as high against the blue of the sky, buoyed up by half a million cubic feet of trapped air.

The ship was exactly four degrees off the vertical when the end came. It was possible to establish this angle precisely, for it was just at that second, half a mile away aboard the *Ulysses*, that the shutter clicked, the shutter of the camera in Lieutenant Nicholls's gauntleted hands.

A camera that captured an unforgettable picture – a stark, simple picture of a sinking ship almost vertically upright against a pale-blue sky. A picture with a strange lack of detail, with the exception only of two squat shapes, improbably suspended in mid-air: these were 30-ton tanks, broken loose from their foredeck lashings, caught in midflight as they smashed down on the bridge structure, awash in the sea. In the background was the stern of the *Belle Isle,* the screw out of the water, the Red Duster trailing idly in the peaceful sea.

Bare seconds after the camera had clicked, the camera was blown from Nicholls's hands, the case crumpling against a bulkhead, the lens shattering but the film still intact. Panic-stricken the seamen in the lifeboat may have been, but it wasn't unreasoning panic: in No. 2 hold, just for'ard of the fire, the *Belle Isle* had been carrying over 1000 tons of tank ammunition . . . Broken cleanly in two, she was gone inside a minute: the *Baddeley*'s bows, riddled by the explosion, slid gently down behind her.

The echoes of the explosion were still rolling out over the sea in ululating diminuendo when they were caught up and flung back by a series of muffled reports from the South. Less than two miles away, the *Sirrus, Vectra* and *Viking*, dazzling white in the morning sun, were weaving a crazily intricate pattern over the sea, depth-charges cascading from either side of their poop-decks. From time to time, one or other almost disappeared behind towering mushrooms of erupting water and spray, reappearing magically as the white columns fell back into the sea.

To join in the hunt, to satisfy the flaming, primitive lust for revenge – that was Tyndall's first impulse. The Kapok Kid looked at him furtively and wondered, wondered at the hunched rigidity, the compressed lipless mouth, the face contorted in white and bitter rage – a bitterness directed not least against himself. Tyndall twisted suddenly in his seat.

'Bentley! Signal the *Stirling* – ascertain damage.' The *Stirling* was more than a mile astern now, but coming round fast, her speed at least twenty knots.

'Making water after engine-room,' Bentley read eventually. 'Store-rooms flooded, but hull damage slight. Under control. Steering gear jammed. On emergency steering. Am all right.'

'Thank God for that! Signal, "Take over: proceed east." Come on, Captain, let's give Orr a hand to deal with these murdering hounds!'

The Kapok Kid looked at him in sudden dismay.

'Sir!'

'Yes, yes, Pilot! What is it?' Tyndall was curt, impatient.

'How about that first U-boat?' Carpenter ventured. 'Can't be much more than a mile to the south, sir. Shouldn't we—?'

'God Almighty!' Tyndall swore. His face was suffused with anger. 'Are you trying to tell me . . .?' He broke off abruptly, stared at Carpenter for a long moment. 'What did you say, Pilot?'

'The boat that sunk the tanker, sir,' the Kapok Kid said carefully. 'She could have reloaded by now and she's in a perfect position—'

'Of course, of course,' Tyndall muttered. He passed a hand across his eyes, flickered a glance at Vallery. The Captain had his head averted. Again the hand passed across the tired eyes. 'You're quite right, Pilot, quite right.' He paused, then smiled. 'As usual, damn you!'

The *Ulysses* found nothing to the north. The U-boat that had sunk the *Cochella* and sprung the trap had wisely decamped. While they were quartering the area, they heard the sound of gunfire, saw the smoke erupting from the *Sirrus*'s 4.7s.

'Ask him what all the bloody fuss is about,' Tyndall demanded irritably. The Kapok Kid smiled secretly: the old man had life in him yet.

'*Vectra* and *Viking* damaged, probably destroyed U-boat,' the message read. '*Vectra* and self sunk surfaced boat. How about you?'

'How about you!' Tyndall exploded. 'Damn his confounded insolence! How about you? He'll have the oldest, bloody mine-sweeper in Scapa for his next command . . . This is all your fault, Pilot!'

'Yes, sir. Sorry, sir. Maybe he's only asking in a spirit of – ah – anxious concern.'

'How would you like to be his Navigator in his next command?' said Tyndall dangerously. The Kapok Kid retired to his charthouse.

'Carrington!'

'Sir?' The First Lieutenant was his invariable self, clear-eyed, freshly shaven, competent, alert. The sallow skin – hall-mark of all men who have spent too many years under tropical suns – was unshadowed by fatigue. He hadn't slept for three days.

'What do you make of that?' He pointed to the north-west. Curiously woolly grey clouds were blotting out the horizon; before them the sea dusked to indigo under wandering catspaws from the north.

'Hard to say, sir,' Carrington said slowly. 'Not heavy weather, that's certain . . . I've seen this before, sir – low, twisting cloud blowing up on a fine morning with a temperature rise. Very common in the Aleutians and the Bering Sea, sir – and there it means fog, heavy mist.'

'And you, Captain?'

'No idea, sir.' Vallery shook his head decisively. The plasma transfusion seemed to have helped him. 'New to me – never seen it before.'

'Thought not,' Tyndall grunted. 'Neither have I – that's why I asked Number One first . . . If you think it's fog that's coming up, Number One, let me know, will you? Can't afford to have convoy and escorts scattered over half the Arctic if the weather closes down. Although, mind you,' he added bitterly, 'I think they'd be a damned sight safer without us!'

'I can tell you now, sir.' Carrington had that rare gift – the ability to make a confident, quietly unarguable assertion without giving the slightest offence. 'It's fog.'

'Fair enough.' Tyndall never doubted him. 'Let's get the hell out of it. Bentley – signal the destroyers: "Break off engagement. Rejoin convoy." And Bentley – add the word "Immediate." ' He turned to Vallery. 'For Commander Orr's benefit.'

Within the hour, merchant ships and escorts were on station again, on a north-east course at first to clear any further packs on latitude 70. To the south-east, the sun was still bright: but the first thick, writhing tendrils of the mist, chill and dank, were already swirling round the convoy. Speed had been reduced to six knots: all ships were streaming fog-buoys.

Tyndall shivered, climbed stiffly from his chair as the stand-down sounded. He passed through the gate, stopped in the passage outside. He laid a glove on Chrysler's shoulder, kept it there as the boy turned round in surprise.

'Just wanted a squint at these eyes of yours, laddie,' he smiled. 'We owe them a lot. Thank you very much – we will not forget.' He looked a long time into the young face, forgot his own exhaustion and swore softly in sudden compassion as he saw the red-rimmed eyes, the white, maculated cheeks stained with embarrassed pleasure.

'How old are you, Chrysler?' he asked abruptly.

'Eighteen, sir ... in two days' time.' The soft West Country voice was almost defiant.

'He'll be eighteen – in two days' time!' Tyndall repeated slowly to himself. 'Good God! Good God above!' He dropped his hand, walked wearily aft to the shelter, entered, closed the door behind him.

'He'll be eighteen – in two days' time,' he repeated, like a man in a daze.

Vallery propped himself up on the settee. 'Who? Young Chrysler?'

Tyndall nodded unhappily.

'I know.' Vallery was very quiet. 'I know how it is ... He did a fine job today.'

Tyndall sagged down in a chair. His mouth twisted in bitterness.

'The only one ... Dear God, what a mess!' He drew heavily on a cigarette, stared down at the floor. 'Ten green bottles, hanging on a wall,' he murmured absently.

'I beg your pardon, sir?'

'Fourteen ships left Scapa, eighteen St John – the two components of FR77,' Tyndall said softly. 'Thirty-two ships in all. And now' – he paused – 'now there are seventeen – and three of these damaged. I'm counting the *Tennessee Adventurer* as a dead duck.' He swore savagely. 'Hell's teeth, how I hate leaving ships like that, sitting targets for any murdering ...' He stopped short, drew on his cigarette again, deeply. 'Doing wonderfully, amn't I?'

'Ah, nonsense, sir!' Vallery interrupted, impatient, almost angry. 'It wasn't any fault of yours that the carriers had to return.'

'Meaning that the rest was my fault?' Tyndall smiled faintly, lifted a hand to silence the automatic protest. 'Sorry, Dick, I know you didn't mean that – but it's true, it's true. Six merchant boys gone in ten minutes – six! And we shouldn't have lost one of them.' Head bent, elbows on knees, he screwed the heels of his palms into exhausted eyes. 'Rear-Admiral Tyndall, master strategist,' he went on softly. 'Alters convoy course to run smack into a heavy cruiser, alter it again to run straight into the biggest wolf-pack I've ever known – and just where the Admiralty said they would be ... No matter what old Starr does to me when I get back, I've no kick coming. Not now, not after this.'

He rose heavily to his feet. The light of the single lamp caught his face. Vallery was shocked at the change.

'Where to, now, sir?' he asked.

'The bridge. No, no, stay where you are, Dick.' He tried to smile, but the smile was a grimace that flickered only to die. 'Leave me in peace while I ponder my next miscalculation.'

He opened the door, stopped dead as he heard the unmistakable whistling of shells close above, heard the EAS signal screaming urgently through the fog. Tyndall turned his head slowly, looked back into the shelter.

'It looks,' he said bitterly, 'as if I've already made it.'

Chapter Nine

Friday Morning

The fog, Tyndall saw, was all around them now. Since that last heavy snowfall during the night, the temperature had risen steadily, quickly. But it had beguiled only to deceive: the clammy, icy feathers of the swirling mist now struck doubly chill.

He hurried through the gate, Vallery close behind him. Turner, steel helmet trailing, was just leaving for the After Tower. Tyndall stretched out his hand, stopped him.

'What is it, Commander?' he demanded. 'Who fired? Where? Where did it come from?'

'I don't know, sir. Shells came from astern, more or less. But I've a damned good idea who it is.' His eyes rested on the Admiral a long, speculative moment. 'Our friend of last night is back again.' He turned abruptly, hurried off the bridge.

Tyndall looked after him, perplexed, uncomprehending. Then he swore, softly, savagely, and jumped for the radar handset.

'Bridge. Admiral speaking. Lieutenant Bowden at once!' The loudspeaker crackled into immediate life.

'Bowden speaking, sir.'

'What the devil are you doing down there?' Tyndall's voice was low, vicious. 'Asleep, or what? We are being attacked Lieutenant Bowden. By a surface craft. This may be news to you.' He broke off, ducked low as another salvo screamed overhead and crashed into the water less than half a mile ahead: the spray cascaded over the decks of a merchantman, glimpsed momentarily in a clear lane between two rolling fog-banks. Tyndall straightened up quickly, snarled into the mouth-piece. 'He's got our range, and got it accurately. In God's name, Bowden, where is he?'

'Sorry, sir.' Bowden was cool, unruffled. 'We can't seem to pick him up. We still have the *Adventurer* on our screens, and there appears to be a very slight distortion on his bearing, sir - approximately 300 . . . I suggest the enemy ship is still screened by the *Adventurer* or, if she's closer, is on the *Adventurer*'s direct bearing.'

'How near?' Tyndall barked.

'Not near, sir. Very close to the *Adventurer*. We can't distinguish either by size or distance.'

Tyndall dangled the transmitter from his hand. He turned to Vallery.

'Does Bowden really expect me to believe that yarn?' he asked angrily. 'A million to one coincidence like that - an enemy ship accidentally chose and holds the only possible course to screen her from our radar. Fantastic!'

Vallery looked at him, his face without expression.

'Well?' Tyndall was impatient. 'Isn't it?'

'No, sir,' Vallery answered quietly. 'It's not. Not really. And it wasn't accidental. The U-pack would have radioed her, given our bearing and course. The rest was easy.'

Tyndall gazed at him through a long moment of comprehension, screwed his eyes shut and shook his head in short fierce jerks. It was a gesture compounded of self-criticism, the death of disbelief, the attempt to clear a woolly, exhausted mind. Hell, a six-year-old could have seen that . . . A shell whistled into the sea a bare fifty yards to port. Tyndall didn't flinch, might never have seen or heard it.

'Bowden?' He had the transmitter to his mouth again.

'Sir?'

'Any change in the screen?'

'No, sir. None.'

'And are you still of the same opinion?'

'Yes, sir! Can't be anything else.'

'And close to the *Adventurer*, you say?'

'Very close, I would say.'

'But, good God, man, the *Adventurer* must be ten miles astern by now!'

'Yes, sir. I know. So is the bandit.'

'What! Ten miles! But, but—'

'He's firing by radar, sir,' Bowden interrupted. Suddenly the metallic voice sounded tired. 'He must be. He's also tracking by radar, which is why he's keeping himself in line with our bearings on the *Adventurer*. And he's extremely accurate . . . I'm afraid, Admiral, that his radar is at least as good as ours.'

The speaker clicked off. In the sudden strained silence on the bridge, the crash of breaking ebonite sounded unnaturally loud as the transmitter slipped from Tyndall's hand, fractured in a hundred pieces. The hand groped forward, he clutched at a steam pipe as if to steady himself. Vallery stepped towards him, arms outstretched in concern, but Tyndall brushed by unseeingly. Like an old spent man, like a man from whose ancient bones and muscles all the pith has long since drained, he shuffled slowly across the bridge, oblivious of a dozen mystified eyes, dragged himself up on to his high stool.

You fool, he told himself bitterly, savagely, oh, you bloody old fool! He would never forgive himself, never, never, never! All along the line he had been out-thought, out-guessed and out-manoeuvred by the enemy. They had taken him for a ride, made an even bigger bloody fool out of him than his good Maker had ever intended. Radar! Of course, that was it! The blind assumption that German radar had remained the limited, elementary thing that Admiralty and Air Force Intelligence had reported it to be last year! Radar – and as good as the British. As good as the *Ulysses*'s – and everybody had believed that the *Ulysses* was incomparably the most efficient – indeed the only efficient – radar ship in the world. As good as our own – probably a damned sight better. But had the thought ever occurred to him? Tyndall writhed in sheer chagrin, in agony of spirit, and knew the bitter taste of self-loathing. And so, this morning, the pay-off: six ships, three hundred men gone to the bottom. May God forgive you, Tyndall, he thought dully, may God forgive you. You sent them there . . . Radar!

Last night, for instance. When the *Ulysses* had been laying a false trail to the east, the German cruiser had obligingly tagged behind, the perfect foil to his, Tyndall's genius. Tyndall groaned in mortification. Had tagged behind, firing wildly, erratically each time the *Ulysses* had disappeared behind a smoke-screen. Had done so to conceal the efficiency of her radar, to conceal the fact that, during the first half-hour at least, she must have been tracking the escaping convoy as it disappeared to the NNW – a process made all the easier by the fact that he, Tyndall, had expressly forbidden the use of the zig-zag!

And then, when the *Ulysses* had so brilliantly circled, first to the south and then to the north again, the enemy must have had her on his screen – constantly. And later, the biter bit with a vengeance, the faked enemy withdrawal to the south-east. Almost certainly, he, too, had circled to the north again, picked up the disappearing British cruiser on the edge of his screen, worked out her intersection course as a cross check on the convoy's, and radioed ahead to the wolf-pack, positioning them almost to the foot.

And now, finally, the last galling blow to whatever shattered remnants of his pride were left him. The enemy had opened fire at extreme range, but with extreme accuracy – a dead give-away to the fact that the firing was radar-controlled. And the only reason for it must be the enemy's conviction that the *Ulysses*, by this time, must have come to the inevitable conclusion that the enemy was equipped with a highly sensitive radar transmitter. The inevitable conclusion! Tyndall had never even begun to suspect it. Slowly, oblivious to the pain, he pounded his fist on the edge of the windscreen. God, what a blind, crazy stupid fool he'd been! Six ships, three hundred men. Hundreds of tanks and planes, millions of gallons of fuel lost to Russia; how many more thousands of dead Russians, soldiers and civilians, did that represent? And the broken, sorrowing families, he thought incoherently, families throughout the breadth of Britain: the telegram boys cycling to the little houses in the Welsh valleys, along the wooded lanes of Surrey, to the lonely reek of the peat-fire, remote in the Western Isles, to the lime-washed cottages of Donegal and Antrim: the empty homes across the great reaches of the New World, from Newfoundland and Maine to the far slopes of the Pacific. These families would never know that it was he, Tyndall, who had so criminally squandered the lives of husbands, brothers, sons – and that was worse than no consolation at all.

'Captain Vallery?' Tyndall's voice was only a husky whisper. Vallery crossed over, stood beside him, coughing painfully as the swirling fog caught nose and throat, lancinated inflamed lungs. It was a measure of Tyndall's distressed preoccupation that Vallery's obvious suffering quite failed to register.

'Ah, there you are. Captain, this enemy cruiser must be destroyed.'

Vallery nodded heavily. 'Yes, sir. How?'

'How?' Tyndall's face, framed in the moisture-beaded hood of his duffel, was haggard and grey: but he managed to raise a ghost of a smile. 'As well hung for a sheep . . . I propose to detach the escorts – including ourselves – and nail him.' He stared out blindly into the fog, his mouth bitter. 'A simple tactical exercise – maybe within even my limited compass.' He broke off suddenly, stared over the side then ducked hurriedly: a shell had exploded in the water – a rare thing – only yards away, erupting spray showering down on the bridge.

'We – the *Stirling* and ourselves – will take him from the south,' he continued, 'soak up his fire and radar. Orr and his death-or-glory boys will approach from the north. In this fog, they'll get very close before releasing their torpedoes. Conditions are all against a single ship – he shouldn't have much chance.'

'All the escorts,' Vallery said blankly. 'You propose to detach *all* the escorts?'

'That's exactly what I propose to do, Captain.'

'But – but – perhaps that's exactly what he wants,' Vallery protested.

'Suicide? A glorious death for the Fatherland? Don't you believe it!' Tyndall scoffed. 'That sort of thing went out with Langesdorff and Middelmann.'

'No, sir!' Vallery was impatient. 'He wants to pull us off, to leave the convoy uncovered.'

'Well, what of it?' Tyndall demanded. 'Who's going to find them in this lot?' He waved an arm at the rolling, twisting fog-banks. 'Dammit, man, if it weren't for their fog-buoys, even our ships couldn't see each other. So I'm damned sure no one else could either.'

'No?' Vallery countered swiftly. 'How about another German cruiser fitted with radar? Or even another wolf-pack? Either could be in radio contact with our friend astern – and he's got our course to the nearest minute!'

'In radio contact? Surely to God our WT is monitoring all the time?'

'Yes, sir. They are. But I'm told it's not easy on the VHF ranges.'

Tyndall grunted non-committally, said nothing. He felt desperately tired and confused; he had neither the will nor the ability to pursue the argument further. But Vallery broke in on the silence, the vertical lines between his eyebrows etched deep with worry.

'And why's our friend sitting steadily on our tails, pumping the odd shell among us, unless he's concentrating on driving us along a particular course? It reduces his chance of a hit by 90 per cent – and cuts out half his guns.'

'Maybe he's expecting us to reason like that, to see the obvious.' Tyndall was forcing himself to think, to fight his way through a mental fog no less nebulous and confusing than the dank mist that swirled around him. 'Perhaps he's hoping to panic us into altering course – to the north, of course – where a U-pack *may* very well be.'

'Possible, possible,' Vallery conceded. 'On the other hand, he may have gone a step further. Maybe he wants us to be too clever for our own good. Perhaps he expects us to see the obvious, to avoid it, to continue on our present course – and so do exactly what he wants us to do . . . He's no fool, sir – we know that now.'

What was it that Brooks had said to Starr back in Scapa, a lifetime ago? 'That fine-drawn feeling . . . that exquisite agony . . . every cell in the brain stretched taut to breaking point, pushing you over the screaming edge of madness.' Tyndall wondered dully how Brooks could have known, could have been so damnably accurate in his description. Anyway, he knew now, knew what it was to stand on the screaming edge . . . Tyndall appreciated dimly that he was at the limit. That aching, muzzy forehead where to think was to be a blind man wading through a sea of molasses. Vaguely he realized that this must be the first – or was it the last? – symptom of a nervous breakdown . . . God only knew there had been plenty of them aboard the *Ulysses* during the past months . . . But he was still the Admiral . . . He must *do* something, *say* something.

'It's no good guessing, Dick,' he said heavily. Vallery looked at him sharply – never before had old Giles called him anything but 'Captain' on the bridge. 'And we've got to do something. We'll leave the *Vectra* as a sop to our consciences. No more.' He smiled wanly. 'We must have at least two destroyers for the dirty work. Bentley – take this signal for WT. "To all escort vessels and Commander Fletcher on the *Cape Hatteras* . . ." '

Within ten minutes, the four warships, boring south-east through the impenetrable wall of fog, had halved the distance that lay between them and the enemy. The *Stirling, Viking* and *Sirrus* were in constant radio communication with the *Ulysses* – they had to be, for they travelled as blind men in an invious world of grey and she was their eyes and their ears.

'Radar – bridge. Radar – bridge.' Automatically, every eye swung round, riveted on the loudspeaker. 'Enemy altering course to south: increasing speed.'

'Too late!' Tyndall shouted hoarsely. His fists were clenched, his eyes alight with triumph. 'He's left it too late!'

Vallery said nothing. The seconds ticked by, the *Ulysses* knifed her way through cold fog and icy sea. Suddenly, the loudspeaker called again.

'Enemy 180° turn. Heading south-east. Speed 28 knots.'

'28 knots? He's on the run!' Tyndall seemed to have gained a fresh lease of life. 'Captain, I propose that the *Sirrus* and *Ulysses* proceed south-east at maximum speed, engage and slow the enemy. Ask WT to signal Orr. Ask Radar enemy's course.'

He broke off, waited impatiently for the answer.

'Radar – bridge. Course 312. Steady on course. Repeat, steady on course.'

'Steady on course,' Tyndall echoed. 'Captain, commence firing by radar. We have him, we have him!' he cried exultantly. 'He's waited too long! We have him, Captain!'

Again Vallery said nothing. Tyndall looked at him, half in perplexity, half in anger. 'Well, don't you agree?'

'I don't know, sir.' Vallery shook his head doubtfully. 'I don't know at all. Why did he wait so long? Why didn't he turn and run the minute we left the convoy?'

'Too damn' sure of himself!' Tyndall growled.

'Or too sure of something else,' Vallery said slowly. 'Maybe he wanted to make good and sure that we *would* follow him.'

Tyndall growled again in exasperation, made to speak then lapsed into silence as the *Ulysses* shuddered from the recoil of 'A' turret. For a moment, the billowing fog on the fo'c'sle cleared, atomized by the intense heat and flash generated by the exploding cordite. In seconds, the grey shroud had fallen once more.

Then, magically it was clear again. A heavy fog-bank had rolled over them, and through a gap in the next they caught a glimpse of the *Sirrus* dead on the beam, a monstrous bone in her teeth, scything to the south-east at something better than 34 knots. The *Stirling* and the *Viking* were already lost in the fog astern.

'He's too close,' Tyndall snapped. 'Why didn't Bowden tell us? We can't bracket the enemy this way. Signal the *Sirrus*: "Steam 317 five minutes." Captain, same for us. 5 south, then back on course.'

He had hardly sunk back in his chair, and the *Ulysses*, mist-shrouded again, was only beginning to answer her helm when the WT loudspeaker switched on.

'WT - bridge. WT - bridge—'

The twin 5.25s of 'B' turret roared in deafening unison, flame and smoke lancing out through the fog. Simultaneously, a tremendous crash and explosion heaved up the duckboards beneath the feet of the men in the bridge catapulting them all ways, into each other, into flesh-bruising, bone-breaking metal, into the dazed confusion of numbed minds and bodies fighting to reorientate themselves under the crippling handicap of stunning shock, of eardrums rended by the blast, of throat and nostrils stung by acrid fumes, of eyes blinded by dense black smoke. Throughout it all, the calm impersonal voice of the WT transmitter repeated its unintelligible message.

Gradually the smoke cleared away. Tyndall pulled himself drunkenly to his feet by the rectifying arm of the binnacle: the explosion had blown him clean out of his chair into the centre of the compass platform. He shook his head, dazed, uncomprehending. Must be tougher than he'd imagined: all that way - and he couldn't remember bouncing. And that wrist, now - that lay over at a damned funny angle. His own wrist, he realized with mild surprise. Funny, it didn't hurt a bit. And Carpenter's face there, rising up before him: the bandages were blown off, the gash received on the night of the great storm gaping wide again, the face masked with blood . . . That girl at Henley, the one he was always talking about - Tyndall wondered, inconsequently, what she would say if she saw him now . . . Why doesn't the WT transmitter stop that insane yammering? . . . Suddenly his mind was clear.

'My God! Oh, God!' He stared in disbelief at the twisted duckboards, the fractured asphalt beneath his feet. He released his grip on the binnacle, lurched forward into the windscreen: his sense of balance had confirmed what his eyes had rejected: the whole compass platform tilted forward at an angle of 15 degrees.

'What is it, Pilot?' His voice was hoarse, strained, foreign even to himself. 'In God's name, what's happened? A breech explosion in "B" turret?'

'No, sir.' Carpenter drew his forearm across his eyes: the kapok sleeve came away covered in blood. 'A direct hit, sir - smack in the superstructure.'

'He's right, sir.' Carrington had hoisted himself far over the windscreen, was peering down intently. Even at that moment, Tyndall marvelled at the man's calmness, his almost inhuman control. 'And a heavy one. It's wrecked the for'ard pom-pom and there's a hole the size of a door just below us . . . It must be pretty bad inside, sir.'

Tyndall scarcely heard the last words. He was kneeling over Vallery, cradling his head in his one good arm. The Captain lay crumpled against the gate, barely conscious, his stertorous breathing interrupted by rasping convulsions as he choked on his own blood. His face was deathly white.

'Get Brooks up here, Chrysler – the Surgeon-Commander, I mean!' Tyndall shouted. 'At once!'

'WT – bridge. WT – bridge. Please acknowledge. Please acknowledge.' The voice was hurried, less impersonal, anxiety evident even in its metallic anonymity.

Chrysler replaced the receiver, looked worriedly at the Admiral.

'Well?' Tyndall demanded. 'Is he on his way?'

'No reply, sir.' The boy hesitated. 'I think the line's gone.'

'Hell's teeth!' Tyndall roared. 'What are you doing standing there, then? Go and get him. Take over, Number One, will you? Bentley – have the Commander come to the bridge.'

'WT – bridge. WT – bridge.' Tyndall glared up at the speaker in exasperation, then froze into immobility as the voice went on. 'We have been hit aft. Damage Control reports coding-room destroyed. Number 6 and 7 Radar Offices destroyed. Canteen wrecked. After control tower severely damaged.'

'The After control tower!' Tyndall swore, pulled off his gloves, wincing at the agony of his broken hand. Carefully, he pillowed Vallery's head on the gloves, rose slowly to his feet. 'The After Tower! And Turner's there! I hope to God . . .'

He broke off, made for the after end of the bridge at a stumbling run. Once there he steadied himself, his hand on the ladder rail, and peered apprehensively aft.

At first he could see nothing, not even the after funnel and mainmast. The grey, writhing fog was too dense, too maddeningly opaque. Then suddenly, for a mere breath of time, an icy catspaw cleared away the mist, cleared away the dark, convoluted smoke-pall above the after superstructure. Tyndall's hand tightened convulsively on the rail, the knuckles whitening to ivory.

The after superstructure had disappeared. In its place was a crazy mass of jumbled twisted steel, with 'X' turret, normally invisible from the bridge, showing up clearly beyond, apparently unharmed. But the rest was gone – radar offices, coding-room, police office, canteen, probably most of the after galley. Nothing, nobody could have survived there. Miraculously, the truncated mainmast still stood, but immediately aft of it, perched crazily on top of this devil's scrapheap, the After Tower, fractured and grotesquely askew, lay over at an impossible angle of 60°, its range-finder gone. And Commander Turner had been in there . . . Tyndall swayed dangerously on top of the steel ladder, shook his head again to fight off the fog clamping down on his mind. There was a heavy, peculiarly dull ache just behind his forehead, and the fog seemed to be spreading from there . . . A lucky ship, they called the *Ulysses*. Twenty months on the worst run and in the worst waters in the world and never a scratch . . . But Tyndall had always known that some time, some place, her luck would run out.

He heard hurried steps clattering up the steel ladder, forced his blurred eyes to focus themselves. He recognized the dark, lean face at once: it was Leading Signalman Davies, from the flag deck. His face was white, his breathing short and quick. He opened his mouth to speak, then checked himself, his eyes staring at the handrail.

'Your hand, sir!' He switched his startled gaze from the rail to Tyndall's eyes. 'Your hand! You've no gloves on, sir!'

'No?' Tyndall looked down as if faintly astonished he had a hand. 'No, I haven't, have I? Thank you, Davies.' He pulled his hand off the smooth frozen steel, glanced incuriously at the raw, bleeding flesh. 'It doesn't matter. What is it, boy?'

'The Fighter Direction Room, sir!' Davies's eyes were dark with remembered horror. 'The shell exploded in there. It's – it's just gone, sir. And the Plot above . . .' He stopped short, his jerky voice lost in the crash of the guns of 'A' turret. Somehow it seemed strangely unnatural that the main armament still remained effective. 'I've just come from the FDR and the Plot, sir,' Davies continued, more calmly now. 'They – well, they never had a chance.'

'Including Commander Westcliffe?' Dimly, Tyndall realized the futility of clutching at straws.

'I don't know, sir. It's – it's just bits and pieces in the FDR, if you follow me. But if he was there—'

'He would be,' Tyndall interrupted heavily. 'He never left it during Action Stations . . .'

He stopped abruptly, broken hands clenched involuntarily as the high-pitched scream and impact explosion of HE shells blurred into shattering cacophony, appalling in its closeness.

'My God!' Tyndall whispered. 'That was close! Davies! What the hell! . . .'

His voice choked off in an agonized grunt, arms flailing wildly at the empty air, as his back crashed against the deck of the bridge, driving every last ounce of breath from his body. Wordlessly, convulsively, propelled by desperately thrusting feet and launched by the powerful back-thrust of arms pivoting on the handrails, Davies had just catapulted himself up the last three steps of the ladder, head and shoulders socketing into the Admiral's body with irresistible force. And now Davies, too, was down, stretched his length on the deck, spreadeagled across Tyndall's legs. He lay very still.

Slowly, the cruel breath rasping his tortured lungs, Tyndall surfaced from the black depths of unconsciousness. Blindly, instinctively he struggled to sit up, but his broken hand collapsed under the weight of his body. His legs didn't seem to be much help either: they were quite powerless, as if he were paralysed from the waist down. The fog was gone now, and blinding flashes of colour, red, green and white were coruscating brilliantly across the darkening sky. Starshells? Was the enemy using a new type of starshell? Dimly, with a great effort of will, he realized that there must be some connection between these dazzling flashes and the now excruciating pain behind his forehead. He reached up the back of his right hand: his eyes were still screwed tightly shut . . . Then the realization faded and was gone.

'Are you all right, sir? Don't move. We'll soon have you out of this!' The voice, deep, authoritative, boomed directly above the Admiral's head. Tyndall shrank back, shook his head in imperceptible despair. It was Turner who was speaking, and Turner, he knew, was gone. Was this, then, what it was like to be dead, he wondered dully. This frightening, confused world of blackness and blinding light at the same time, a dark-bright world of pain and powerlessness and voices from the past?

Then suddenly, of their own volition almost, his eyelids flickered and were open. Barely a foot above him were the lean, piratical features of the Commander, who was kneeling anxiously at his side.

'Turner! Turner?' A questioning hand reached out in tentative hope, clutched gratefully, oblivious to the pain, at the reassuring solidity of the Commander's arm. 'Turner! It *is* you! I thought—'

'The After Tower, eh?' Turner smiled briefly. 'No, sir – I wasn't within a mile of it. I was coming here, just climbing up to the fo'c'sle deck, when that first hit threw me back down to the main deck . . . How are you, sir?'

'Thank God! Thank God! I don't know how I am. My legs . . . What in the name of heaven is that?'

His eyes focusing normally again, widened in baffled disbelief. Just above Turner's head, angling for'ard and upward to port, a great white tree-trunk stretched as far as he could see in either direction. Reaching up, he could just touch the massive bole with his hand.

'The foremast, sir,' Turner explained. 'It was sheared clean off by that last shell, just above the lower yardarm. The back blast flung it on to the bridge. Took most of the AA tower with it, I'm afraid – and caved in the Main Tower. I don't think young Courtney could have had much chance . . . Davies saw it coming – I was just below him at the time. He was very quick—'

'Davies!' Tyndall's dazed mind had forgotten all about him. 'Of course! Davies!' It must be Davies who was pinioning his legs. He craned his neck forward, saw the huddled figure at his feet, the great weight of the mast lying across his back. 'For God's sake, Commander, get him out of that!'

'Just lie down, sir, till Brooks gets here. Davies is all right.'

'All right? All right!' Tyndall was almost screaming, oblivious to the silent figures who were gathering around him. 'Are you mad, Turner? The poor bastard must be in agony!' He struggled frantically to rise, but several pairs of hands held him down, firmly, carefully.

'He's all right, sir.' Turner's voice was surprisingly gentle. 'Really he is, sir. He's all right. Davies doesn't feel a thing. Not any more.' And all at once the Admiral knew and he fell back limply to the deck, his eyes closed in shocked understanding.

His eyes were still shut when Brooks appeared, doubly welcome in his confidence and competence. Within seconds, almost, the Admiral was on his feet, shocked, badly bruised, but otherwise unharmed. Doggedly, and in open defiance of Brooks, Tyndall demanded that he be assisted to the bridge. His eyes lit up momentarily as he saw Vallery standing shakily on his feet, a white towel to his mouth. But he said nothing. His head bowed, he hoisted himself painfully into his chair.

'WT – bridge. WT – bridge. Please acknowledge signal.'

'Is that bloody idiot still there?' Tyndall demanded querulously. 'Why doesn't someone—?'

'You've only been gone a couple of minutes, sir,' the Kapok Kid ventured.

'Two minutes!' Tyndall stared at him, lapsed into silence. He glanced down at Brooks, busy bandaging his right hand. 'Have you nothing better to do, Brooks?' he asked harshly.

'No, I haven't,' Brooks replied truculently. 'When shells explode inside four walls, there isn't much work left for a doctor . . . except signing death certificates,' he added brutally. Vallery and Turner exchanged glances. Vallery wondered if Brooks had any idea how far through Tyndall was.

'WT – bridge. WT – bridge. *Vectra* repeats request for instruction. Urgent. Urgent.'

'The *Vectra*!' Vallery glanced at the Admiral, silent now and motionless, and turned to the bridge messenger. 'Chrysler! Get through to WT. Any way you can. Ask them to repeat the first message.'

He looked again at Turner, following the Admiral's sick gaze over the side. He looked down, recoiled in horror, fighting down the instant nausea. The gunner in the sponson below – just another boy like Chrysler – must have seen the falling mast, must have made a panic-stricken attempt to escape. He had barely cleared his cockpit when the radar screen, a hundred square feet of meshed steel carrying the crushing weight of the mast as it had snapped over the edge of the bridge, had caught him fairly and squarely. He lay still now, mangled, broken, something less than human, spreadeagled in outflung crucifixion across the twin barrels of his Oerlikon.

Vallery turned away, sick in body and mind. God, the craziness, the futile insanity of war. Damn that German cruiser, damn those German gunners, damn them, damn them! . . . But why should he? They, too, were only doing a job – and doing it terribly well. He gazed sightlessly at the wrecked shambles of his bridge. What damnably accurate gunnery! He wondered, vaguely, if the *Ulysses* had registered any hits. Probably not, and now, of course, it was impossible. It was impossible now because the *Ulysses*, still racing south-east through the fog, was completely blind, both radar eyes gone, victims to the weather and the German guns. Worse still, all the Fire Control towers were damaged beyond repair. If this goes on, he thought wryly, all we'll need is a set of grappling irons and a supply of cutlasses. In terms of modern naval gunnery, even although her main armament was intact, the *Ulysses* was hopelessly crippled. She just didn't have a chance. What was it that Stoker Riley was supposed to have said – 'being thrown to the wolves'? Yes, that was it – 'thrown to the wolves.' But only a Nero, he reflected wearily, would have blinded a gladiator before throwing him into the arena.

All firing had ceased. The bridge was deadly quiet. Silence, complete silence, except for the sound of rushing water, the muffled roar of the great engine-room intake fans, the monotonous, nerve-drilling pinging of the Asdic – and these, oddly enough, only served to deepen the great silence.

Every eye, Vallery saw, was on Admiral Tyndall. Old Giles was mumbling something to himself, too faint to catch. His face, shockingly grey, haggard and blotched, still peered over the side. He seemed fascinated by the sight of the dead boy. Or was it the smashed Radar screen? Had the full significance of the broken scanner and wrecked Director Towers dawned on him yet? Vallery looked at him for a long moment, then turned away: he knew that it had.

'WT – bridge. WT – bridge.' Everyone on the bridge jumped, swung round in nerve-jangled startlement. Everyone except Tyndall. He had frozen into a graven immobility.

'Signal from *Vectra*. First Signal. Received 0952.' Vallery glanced at his watch. Only six minutes ago! Impossible!

'Signal reads: "Contacts, contacts, 3, repeat 3. Amend to 5. Heavy concentration of U-boats, ahead and abeam. Am engaging." '

Every eye on the bridge swung back to Tyndall. His, they knew, the responsibility, his the decision – taken alone, against the advice of his senior officer – to leave the convoy almost unguarded. Impersonally, Vallery admired the baiting, the timing, the springing of the trap. How would old Giles react to this, the culmination of a series of disastrous miscalculations – miscalculations for which, in all fairness, he could not justly be blamed . . . But he would be held accountable. The iron voice of the loudspeaker broke in on his thoughts.

'Second signal reads: "In close contact. Depth-charging. Depth-charging. One vessel torpedoed, sinking. Tanker torpedoed, damaged, still afloat, under command. Please advise. Please assist. Urgent. Urgent!" '

The speaker clicked off. Again that hushed silence, strained, unnatural. Five seconds it lasted, ten, twenty – then everyone stiffened, looked carefully away.

Tyndall was climbing down from his chair. His movements were stiff, slow with the careful faltering shuffle of the very old. He limped heavily. His right hand, startling white in its snowy sheath of bandage, cradled his broken wrist. There was about him a queer, twisted sort of dignity, and if his face held any expression at all, it was the far-off echo of a smile. When he spoke, he spoke as a man might talk to himself, aloud.

'I am not well,' he said. 'I am going below.' Chrysler, not too young to have an inkling of the tragedy, held open the gate, caught Tyndall as he stumbled on the step. He glanced back over his shoulder, a quick, pleading look, caught and understood Vallery's compassionate nod. Side by side, the old and the young, they moved slowly aft. Gradually, the shuffling died away and they were gone.

The shattered bridge was curiously empty now, the men felt strangely alone. Giles, the cheerful, buoyant, indestructible Giles was gone. The speed, the extent of the collapse was not for immediate comprehension: the only sensation at the moment was that of being unprotected and defenceless and alone.

'Out of the mouths of babes and sucklings . . .' Inevitably, the first to break the silence was Brooks. 'Nicholls always maintained that . . .' He stopped short, his head shaking in slow incredulity. 'I must see what I can do,' he finished abruptly, and hurried off the bridge.

Vallery watched him go, then turned to Bentley. The Captain's face, haggard, shadowed with grizzled beard, the colour of death in the weird half-light of the fog, was quite expressionless.

'Three signals, Chief. First to *Vectra*. "Steer 360°. Do not disperse. Repeat, do not disperse. Am coming to your assistance." ' He paused, then went on: 'Sign it, "Admiral, 14 ACS." Got it? . . . Right. No time to code it. Plain language. Send one of your men to the WT at once.'

'Second: To *Stirling, Sirrus* and *Viking*. "Abandon pursuit immediate. Course north-east. Maximum speed." Plain language also.' He turned to the Kapok Kid. 'How's your forehead, Pilot? Can you carry on?'

'Of course, sir.'

'Thank you, boy. You heard me? Convoy re-routed north – say in a few minutes' time, at 1015. 6 knots. Give me an intersection course as soon as possible.'

'Third signal, Bentley: To *Stirling, Sirrus* and *Viking*: "Radar out of action. Cannot pick you up on screen. Stream fog-buoys. Siren at two-minute intervals." Have that message coded. All acknowledgments to the bridge at once. Commander!'

'Sir?' Turner was at his elbow.

'Hands to defence stations. It's my guess the pack will have gone before we get there. Who'll be off watch?'

'Lord only knows,' said Turner frankly. 'Let's call it port.'

Vallery smiled faintly. 'Port it is. Organize two parties. First of port to clear away all loose wreckage: over the side with the lot – keep nothing. You'll need the blacksmith and his mate, and I'm sure Dodson will provide you with an oxy-acetylene crew. Take charge yourself. Second of port as burial party. Nicholls in charge. All bodies recovered to be laid out in the canteen when it's clear . . . Perhaps you could give me a full report of casualties and damage inside the hour?'

'Long before that, sir. . . . Could I have a word with you in private?'

They walked aft. As the shelter door shut behind them, Vallery looked at the Commander curiously, half-humorously. 'Another mutiny, perhaps, Commander?'

'No, sir.' Turner unbuttoned his coat, his hand struggling into the depths of a hip-pocket. He dragged out a flat half-bottle, held it up to the light. 'Thank the Lord for that!' he said piously. 'I was afraid it got smashed when I fell. . . . Rum, sir. Neat. I know you hate the stuff, but never mind. Come on, you need this!'

Vallery's brows came down in a straight line.

'Rum. Look here, Commander, do you—?'

'To hell with KRs and AFOs!' Turner interrupted rudely. 'Take it – you need it badly! You've been hurt, you've lost a lot more blood and you're almost frozen to death.' He uncorked it, thrust the bottle into Vallery's reluctant hands. 'Face facts. We need you – more than ever now – and you're almost dead on your feet – and I mean dead on your feet,' he added brutally. 'This might keep you going a few more hours.'

'You put things so nicely,' Vallery murmured. 'Very well. Against my better judgment . . .'

He paused, the bottle to his mouth.

'And you give me an idea, Commander. Have the bosun break out the rum. Pipe "Up spirits." Double ration to each man. They, too, are going to need it.' He swallowed, pulled the bottle away, and the grimace was not for the rum.

'Especially,' he added soberly, 'the burial party.'

Chapter Ten

Friday Afternoon

The switch clicked on and the harsh fluorescent light flooded the darkening surgery. Nicholls woke with a start, one hand coming up automatically to shield exhausted eyes. The light hurt. He screwed his eyes to slits, peered painfully at the hands of his wrist-watch. Four o'clock! Had he been asleep that long? God, it was bitterly cold!

He hoisted himself stiffly forward in the dentist's chair, twisted his head round. Brooks was standing with his back to the door, snow-covered hood framing his silver hair, numbed fingers fumbling with a packet of cigarettes. Finally he managed to pull one out. He looked up quizzically over a flaring match-head.

'Hallo, there, Johnny! Sorry to waken you, but the skipper wants you. Plenty of time, though.' He dipped the cigarette into the dying flame, looked up again. Nicholls, he thought with sudden compassion, looked ill, desperately tired and over-strained; but no point in telling him so. 'How are you? On second thoughts, don't tell me! I'm a damned sight worse myself. Have you any of that poison left?'

'Poison, sir?' The levity was almost automatic, part of their relationship with each other. 'Just because you make one wrong diagnosis? The Admiral will be all right—'

'Gad! The intolerance of the very young – especially on the providentially few occasions that they happen to be right. . . . I was referring to that bottle of bootleg hooch from the Isle of Mull.'

'Coll,' Nicholls corrected. 'Not that it matters – you've drunk it all, anyway,' he added unkindly. He grinned tiredly at the Commander's crestfallen face, then relented. 'But we do have a bottle of Talisker left.' He crossed over to the poison cupboard, unscrewed the top of a bottle marked 'Lysol.' He heard, rather than saw, the clatter of glass against glass, wondered vaguely, with a kind of clinical detachment, why his hands were shaking so badly.

Brooks drained his glass, sighed in bliss as he felt the grateful warmth sinking down inside him.

'Thank you, my boy. Thank you. You have the makings of a first-class doctor.'

'You think so, sir? I don't. Not any longer. Not after today.' He winced, remembering. 'Forty-four of them, sir, over the side in ten minutes, one after the other, like – like so many sacks of rubbish.'

'Forty-four?' Brooks looked up. 'So many, Johnny?'

'Not really, sir. That was the number of missing. About thirty, rather, and God only knows how many bits and pieces. . . . It was a brush and shovel job in the FDR.' He smiled, mirthlessly. 'I had no dinner, today. I don't think anybody else in the burial party had either. . . . I'd better screen that port-hole.'

He turned away quickly, walked across the surgery. Low on the horizon, through the thinly-falling snow, he caught intermittent sight of an evening star. That meant that the fog was gone – the fog that had saved the convoy, had hidden them from the U-boats when it had turned so sharply to the north. He could see the *Vectra*, her depth-charge racks empty and nothing to show for it. He could see the *Vytura*, the damaged tanker, close by, almost awash in the water, hanging grimly on to the convoy. He could see four of the Victory ships, big, powerful, reassuring, so pitifully deceptive in their indestructible permanence. . . . He slammed the scuttle, screwed home the last butterfly nut, then swung round abruptly.

'Why the hell don't we turn back?' he burst out. 'Who does the old man think he's kidding – us or the Germans? No air cover, no radar, not the faintest chance of help! The Germans have us pinned down to an inch now – and it'll be easier still for them as we go on. And there's a thousand miles to go!' His voice rose. 'And every bloody enemy ship, U-boat and plane in the Arctic smacking their lips and waiting to pick us off at their leisure.' He shook his head in despair. 'I'll take my chance with anybody else, sir. You know that. But this is just murder – or suicide. Take your pick, sir. It's all the same when you're dead.'

'Now, Johnny, you're not—'

'*Why* doesn't he turn back?' Nicholls hadn't even heard the interruption. 'He's only got to give the order. What does he want? Death or glory? What's he after? Immortality at my expense, at *our* expense?' He swore, bitterly. 'Maybe Riley was right. Wonderful headlines. "Captain Richard Vallery, DSO, has been posthumously awarded—" '

'Shut up!' Brooks's eye was as chill as the Arctic ice itself, his voice a biting lash.

'You dare to talk of Captain Vallery like that!' he said softly. 'You dare to besmirch the name of the most honourable . . .' He broke off, shook his head in wrathful wonder. He paused to pick his words carefully, his eyes never leaving the other's white, strained face.

'He is a good officer, Lieutenant Nicholls, maybe even a great officer: and that just doesn't matter a damn. What does matter is that he is the finest gentleman – I say "gentleman" – I've ever known, that ever walked the face of this graceless, God-forsaken earth. He is not like you or me. He is not like anybody at all. He walks alone, but he is never lonely, for he has company all the way . . . men like Peter, like Bede, like St Francis of Assisi.' He laughed shortly. 'Funny, isn't it – to hear an old reprobate like myself talk like this? Blasphemy, even, you might call it – except that the truth can never be blasphemy. And I *know*.'

Nicholls said nothing. His face was like a stone.

'Death, glory, immortality,' Brooks went on relentlessly. 'These were your words, weren't they? Death?' He smiled and shook his head again. 'For Richard Vallery, death doesn't exist. Glory? Sure, he wants glory, we all want glory, but all the *London Gazettes* and Buckingham Palaces in the world can't give *him* the kind of glory he wants: Captain Vallery is no longer a child, and only children play with toys. . . . As for immortality.' He laughed, without a trace of rancour now, laid a hand on Nicholls's shoulder.

'I ask you, Johnny – wouldn't it be damned stupid to ask for what he has already?'

Nicholls said nothing. The silence lengthened and deepened, the rush of air from the ventilation louvre became oppressively loud. Finally, Brooks coughed, looked meaningfully at the 'Lysol' bottle.

Nicholls filled the glasses, brought them back. Brooks caught his eyes, held them, and was filled with sudden pity. What was that classical understatement of Cunningham's during the German invasion of Crete – 'It is inadvisable to drive men beyond a certain point.' Trite but true. True even for men like Nicholls. Brooks wondered what particular private kind of hell that boy had gone through that morning, digging out the shattered, torn bodies of what had once been men. And, as the doctor in charge, he would have had to examine them all – or all the pieces he could find. . . .

'Next step up and I'll be in the gutter.' Nicholls's voice was very low. 'I don't know what to say, sir. I don't know what made me say it. . . . I'm sorry.'

'Me too,' Brooks said sincerely. 'Shooting off my mouth like that! And I mean it.' He lifted his glass, inspected the contents lovingly. 'To our enemies, Johnny: their downfall and confusion, and don't forget Admiral Starr.' He drained the glass at a gulp, set it down, looked at Nicholls for a long moment.

'I think you should hear the rest, too, Johnny. You know, why Vallery doesn't turn back.' He smiled wryly. 'It's not because there are as many of these damned U-boats behind us as there are in front – which there undoubtedly are.' He lit a fresh cigarette, went on quietly:

'The Captain radioed London this morning. Gave it as his considered opinion that FR77 would be a goner – "annihilated" was the word he used and, as a word, they don't come any stronger – long before it reached the North Cape. He asked at least to be allowed to go north about, instead of east for the Cape. . . . Pity there was no sunset to-night, Johnny,' he added half-humorously. 'I would have liked to see it.'

'Yes, yes,' Nicholls was impatient. 'And the answer?'

'Eh! Oh, the answer. Vallery expected it immediately.' Brooks shrugged. 'It took four hours to come through.' He smiled, but there was no laughter in his eyes. 'There's something big, something on a huge scale brewing up somewhere. It can only be some major invasion – this under your hat, Johnny?'

'Of course, sir!'

'What it is I haven't a clue. Maybe even the long-awaited Second Front. Anyway, the support of the Home Fleet seems to be regarded as vital to success. But the Home Fleet is tied up – by the *Tirpitz*. And so the orders have gone out – get the *Tirpitz*. Get it at all costs.' Brooks smiled, and his face was very cold. 'We're big fish, Johnny, we're important people. We're the biggest, juiciest bait ever offered up the biggest, juiciest prize in the world today – although I'm afraid the trap's a trifle rusty at the hinges. . . . The signal came from the First Sea Lord – and Starr. The decision was taken at Cabinet level. We go on. We go east.'

'We are the "all costs," ' said Nicholls flatly. 'We are expendable.'

'We are expendable,' Brooks agreed. The speaker above his head clicked on, and he groaned. 'Hell's bells, here we go again!'

He waited until the clamour of the Dusk Action Stations' bugle had died away, stretched out a hand as Nicholls hurried for the door.

'Not you, Johnny. Not yet. I told you, the skipper wants you. On the bridge, ten minutes after Stations begin.'

'What? On the bridge? What the hell for?'

'Your language is unbecoming to a junior officer,' said Brooks solemnly. 'How did the men strike you today?' he went on inconsequently. 'You were working with them all morning. Their usual selves?'

Nicholls blinked, then recovered.

'I suppose so.' He hesitated. 'Funny, they seemed a lot better a couple of days ago, but – well, now they're back to the Scapa stage. Walking zombies. Only more so – they can hardly walk now.' He shook his head. 'Five, six men to a stretcher. Kept tripping and falling over things. Asleep on their feet – eyes not focusing, too damned tired to look where they're going.'

Brooks nodded. 'I know, Johnny, I know. I've seen it myself.'

'Nothing mutinous, nothing sullen about them any more.' Nicholls was puzzled, seeking tiredly to reduce nebulous, scattered impressions to a homogeneous coherence. 'They've neither the energy nor the initiative left for a mutiny now, anyway, I suppose, but it's not that. Kept muttering to themselves in the FDR: "Lucky bastard." "He died easy" – things like that. Or "Old Giles – off his bleedin' rocker." And you can imagine the shake of the head. But no humour, none, not even the grisly variety you usually . . .' He shook his own head. 'I just don't know, sir. Apathetic, indifferent, hopeless – call 'em what you like. I'd call 'em lost.'

Brooks looked at him a long moment, then added gently:

'Would you now?' He mused. 'And do you know, Johnny, I think you'd be right. . . . Anyway,' he continued briskly, 'get up there. Captain's going to make a tour of the ship.'

'What!' Nicholls was astounded. 'During action stations? Leave the bridge?'

'Just that.'

'But – but he can't, sir. It's – it's unprecedented!'

'So's Captain Vallery. That's what I've been trying to tell you all evening.'

'But he'll kill himself!' Nicholls protested wildly.

'That's what I said,' Brooks agreed wryly. 'Clinically, he's dying. He should be dead. What keeps him going God only knows – literally. It certainly isn't plasma or drugs. . . . Once in a while, Johnny, it's salutary for us to appreciate the limits of medicine. Anyway, I talked him into taking you with him. . . . Better not keep him waiting.'

For Lieutenant Nicholls, the next two hours were borrowed from purgatory. Two hours, the Captain took to his inspection, two hours of constant walking, of climbing over storm-sills and tangled wreckage of steel, of squeezing and twisting through impossibly narrow apertures, of climbing and descending a hundred ladders, two hours of exhausting torture in the bitter, heart-sapping cold of a sub-zero temperature. But it was a memory that was to stay with him always, that was never to return without filling him with warmth, with a strange and wonderful gratitude.

They started on the poop – Vallery, Nicholls and Chief Petty Officer Hartley – Vallery would have none of Hastings, the Master-at-Arms, who usually accompanied the Captain on his rounds. There was something oddly reassuring about the big, competent Chief. He worked like a Trojan that night, opening and shutting dozens of watertight doors, lifting and lowering countless heavy hatches, knocking off and securing the thousand clips that held these doors and hatches in place, and before ten minutes had passed, lending a protesting Vallery the support of his powerful arm.

They climbed down the long, vertical ladder to 'Y' magazine, a dim and gloomy dungeon thinly lit with pinpoints of garish light. Here were the butchers, bakers and candlestick makers – the non-specialists in the purely offensive branches. 'Hostilities only' ratings, almost to a man, in charge of a trained gunner, they had a cold, dirty and unglamorous job, strangely neglected and forgotten – strangely, because so terribly dangerous. The four-inch armour encasing them offered about as much protection as a sheet of newspaper to an eight-inch armour-piercing shell or a torpedo. . . .

The magazine walls – walls of shells and cartridge cases – were soaking wet, dripping constantly visibly, with icy condensation. Half the crew were leaning or lying against the racks, blue, pinched, shivering with cold, their breath hanging heavily in the chill air: the others were trudging heavily round and round the hoist, feet splashing in pools of water, lurching, stumbling with sheer exhaustion, gloved hands buried in their pockets, drawn, exhausted faces sunk on their chests. Zombies, Nicholls thought wonderingly, just living zombies. Why don't they lie down?

Gradually, everyone became aware of Vallery's presence, stopped walking or struggling painfully erect, eyes too tired, minds too spent for either wonder or surprise.

'As you were, as you were,' Vallery said quickly. 'Who's in charge here?'

'I am sir.' A stocky overalled figure walked slowly forward, halted in front of Vallery.

'Ah, yes. Gardiner, isn't it?' He gestured to the men circling the hoist. 'What in the world is all this for, Gardiner?'

'Ice,' said Gardiner succinctly. 'We have to keep the water moving or it'll freeze in a couple of minutes. We can't have ice on the magazine floor, sir.'

'No, no, of course not! But – but the pumps, the draincocks?'

'Solid!'

'But surely – this doesn't go on all the time?'

'In flat weather – all the time, sir.'

'Good God!' Vallery shook his head incredulously, splashed his way to the centre of the group, where a slight, boyish figure was coughing cruelly into a corner of an enormous green and white muffler. Vallery placed a concerned arm across the shaking shoulders.

'Are you all right, boy?'

'Yes, sir. 'Course Ah am!' He lifted a thin white face racked with pain. 'Ah'm fine,' he said indignantly.

'What's your name?'

'McQuater, sir.'

'And what's your job, McQuater?'

'Assistant cook, sir.'

'How old are you?'

'Eighteen, sir.' Merciful heavens, Vallery thought, this isn't a cruiser I'm running – it's a nursery!

'From Glasgow, eh?' He smiled.

'Yes, sir.' Defensively.

'I see.' He looked down at the deck, at McQuater's boots half-covered in water. 'Why aren't you wearing your seaboots?' he asked abruptly.

'We don't get issued with them, sir.'

'But your feet, man! They must be soaking!'

'Ah don't know, sir. Ah think so. Anyway,' McQuater said simply, 'it doesna matter. Ah canna feel them.'

Vallery winced. Nicholls, looking at the Captain, wondered if he realized the distressing, pathetic picture he himself presented with his sunken, bloodless face, red, inflamed eyes, his mouth and nose daubed with crimson, the inevitable dark and sodden hand-towel clutched in his left glove. Suddenly unaccountably, Nicholls felt ashamed of himself: that thought, he knew, could never occur to this man.

Vallery smiled down at McQuater.

'Tell me son, honestly – are you tired?'

'Ah am that   Ah mean, aye, aye, sir.'

'Me too,' Vallery confessed. 'But – you can carry on a bit longer?'

He felt the frail shoulders straighten under his arm.

' 'Course Ah can, sir!' The tone was injured, almost truculent. '*'Course* Ah can!'

Vallery's gaze travelled slowly over the group, his dark eyes glowing as he heard a murmured chorus of assent. He made to speak, broke off in a harsh coughing and bent his head. He looked up again, his eyes wandering once more over the circle of now-anxious faces, then turned abruptly away.

'We won't forget you,' he murmured indistinctly. 'I promise you, we won't forget you.' He splashed quickly away, out of the pool of water, out of the pool of light, into the darkness at the foot of the ladder.

Ten minutes later, they emerged from 'Y' turret. The night sky was cloudless now, brilliant with diamantine stars, little chips of frozen fire in the dark velvet of that fathomless floor. The cold was intense. Captain Vallery shivered involuntarily as the turret door slammed behind them.

'Hartley?'

'Sir?'

'I smelt rum in there!'

'Yes, sir. So did I.' The Chief was cheerful, unperturbed. 'Proper stinking with it. Don't worry about it though, sir. Half the men in the ship bottle their rum ration, keep it for action stations.'

'Completely forbidden in regulations, Chief. You know that as well as I do!'

'I know. But there's no harm, sir. Warms 'em up – and if it gives them Dutch courage, all the better. Remember that night the for'ard pom-pom got two Stukas?'

'Of course.'

'Canned to the wide. Never have done it otherwise. . . . And now, sir, they *need* it.'

'Suppose you're right, Chief. They do and I don't blame them.' He chuckled. 'And don't worry about my knowing – I've always known. But it smelled like a saloon bar in there. . . .'

They climbed up to 'X' turret – the marine turret – then down to the magazine. Wherever he went, as in 'Y' magazine, Vallery left the men the better for his coming. In personal contact, he had some strange indefinable power that lifted men above themselves, that brought out in them something they had never known to exist. To see dull apathy and hopelessness slowly give way to resolution, albeit a kind of numbed and desperate resolve, was to see something that baffled the understanding. Physically and mentally, Nicholls knew, these men had long since passed the point of no return.

Vaguely, he tried to figure it out, to study the approach and technique. But the approach varied every time, he saw, was no more than a natural reaction to different sets of circumstances as they presented themselves, a reaction utterly lacking in calculation or finesse. There *was* no technique. Was pity, then, the activating force, pity for the heart-breaking gallantry of a man so clearly dying? Or was it shame – if *he* can do it, if *he* can still drive that wasted mockery of a body, if he can kill himself just to come to see if *we're* all right – if he can do that and smile – then, by God, we can stick it out, too? That's it, Nicholls said to himself, that's what it is, pity and shame, and he hated himself for thinking it, and not because of the thought, but because he knew he lied. . . . He was too tired to think anyway. His mind was woolly, fuzzy round the edges, his thoughts disjointed, uncontrolled. Like everyone else's. Even Andy Carpenter, the last man you would suspect of it – he felt that way, too, and admitted it. . . . He wondered what the Kapok Kid would have to say to this. . . . The Kid was probably wandering too, but wandering in his own way, back as always on the banks of the Thames. He wondered what the girl in Henley was like. Her name started with 'J' – Joan, Jean – he didn't know: the Kapok Kid had a big golden 'J' on the right breast of his kapok suit – *she* had put it there. But what was she like? Blonde and gay, like the Kid himself? Or dark and kind and gentle, like St Francis of Assisi? St Francis of Assisi? Why in the world did he – ah, yes, old Socrates had been talking about him. Wasn't he the man of whom Axel Munthe . . .

'Nicholls! Are you all right?' Vallery's voice was sharp with anxiety.

'Yes, of course, sir.' Nicholls shook his head, as if to clear it. 'Just gathering wool. Where to now, sir?'

'Engineers' Flat, Damage Control parties, Switchboard, Number 3 Low Power room – no, of course, that's gone – Noyes was killed there, wasn't he? . . . Hartley, I'd appreciate it if you'd let my feet touch the deck occasionally. . . .'

All these places they visited in turn and a dozen others besides – not even the remotest corner, the most impossible of access, did Vallery pass by, if he knew a man was there, closed up to his action station.

They came at last to the engine and boiler-room, to the gulping pressure changes on unaccustomed eardrums as they went through the airlocks, to the antithetically breath-taking blast of heat as they passed inside. In 'A' boiler-room, Nicholls insisted on Vallery's resting for some minutes. He was grey with pain and weakness, his breathing very distressed. Nicholls noticed Hartley talking in a corner, was dimly aware of someone leaving the boiler-room.

Then his eyes caught sight of a burly, swarthy stoker, with bruised cheeks and the remnants of a gorgeous black eye, stalking across the floor. He carried a canvas chair, set it down with a thump behind Vallery.

'A seat, sir,' he growled.

'Thank you, thank you.' Vallery lowered himself gratefully, then looked up in surprise. 'Riley?' he murmured, then switched his glance to Hendry, the Chief Stoker. 'Doing his duty with a minimum of grace, eh?'

Hendry stirred uncomfortably.

'He did it off his own bat, sir.'

'I'm sorry,' Vallery said sincerely. 'Forgive me, Riley. Thank you very much.' He stared after him in puzzled wonder, looked again at Hendry, eyebrows lifted in interrogation.

Hendry shook his head.

'Search me, sir. I've no idea. He's a queer fish. Does things like that. He'd bend a lead pipe over your skull without batting an eyelid – and he's got a mania for looking after kittens and lame dogs. Or if you get a bird with a broken wing – Riley's your man. But he's got a low opinion of his fellowmen, sir.'

Vallery nodded slowly, without speaking, leaned against the canvas back and closed his eyes in exhaustion. Nicholls bent over him.

'Look, sir,' he urged quietly, 'why not give it up? Frankly, sir, you're killing yourself. Can't we finish this some other time?'

'I'm afraid not, my boy.' Vallery was very patient. 'You don't understand. "Some other time" will be too late.' He turned to Hendry. 'So you think you'll manage all right, Chief?'

'Don't you worry about us, sir.' The soft Devon voice was grim and gentle at the same time. 'Just you look after yourself. The stokers won't let you down, sir.'

Vallery rose painfully to his feet, touched him lightly on the arm. 'Do you know, Chief, I never thought you would. . . . Ready, Hartley?' He stopped short, seeing a giant duffel-coated figure waiting at the foot of the ladder, the face below the hood dark and sombre. 'Who's that? Oh, I know. Never thought stokers got so cold,' he smiled.

'Yes, sir, it's Petersen,' Hartley said softly, 'He's coming with us.'

'Who said so? And – and Petersen? Wasn't that—?'

'Yes, sir. Riley's – er — lieutenant in the Scapa business . . . Surgeon Commander's orders, sir. Petersen's going to give us a hand.'

'Us? Me, you mean.' There was no resentment, no bitterness in Vallery's voice. 'Hartley, take my advice – never let yourself get into the hands of the doctors. . . . You think he's safe?' he added half-humorously.

'He'd probably kill the man who looked sideways at you,' Hartley stated matter-of-factly. 'He's a good man, sir. Simple, easily led – but good.'

At the foot of the ladder, Petersen stepped aside to let them pass, but Vallery stopped, looked up at the giant towering six inches above him, into the grave, blue eyes below the flaxen hair.

'Hallo, Petersen. Hartley tells me you're coming with us. Do you really want to? You don't have to, you know.'

'Please, Captain.' The speech was slow and precise, the face curiously dignified in unhappiness. 'I am very sorry for what has happened—'

'No, no!' Vallery was instantly contrite. 'You misunderstand. It's a bitter night up top. But I would like it very much if you would come. Will you?'

Petersen stared at him, then began slowly to smile, his face darkening with pleasure. As the Captain set foot on the first step, the giant arm came round him. The sensation, as Vallery described it later, was very much like going up in a lift.

From there they visited Engineer Commander Dodson in his engine-room, a cheerful, encouraging, immensely competent Dodson, an engineer to his finger-tips in his single-minded devotion to the great engines under his care. Then aft to the Engineer's Flat, up the companionway between the wrecked Canteen and the Police Office, out on to the upper deck. After the heat of the boiler-room, the 100° drop in temperature, a drop that strangled breath with the involuntary constriction of the throat and made a skin-crawling mockery of 'Arctic clothing,' was almost literally paralysing.

The starboard torpedo tubes – the only ones at the standby – were only four paces away. The crew, huddled in the lee of the wrecked bosun's store – the one destroyed by the *Blue Ranger*'s shells – were easily located by the stamping of frozen feet, the uncontrollable chattering of teeth.

Vallery peered into the gloom. 'LTO there?'

'Captain, sir?' Surprise, doubt in the voice.

'Yes. How are things going?'

'All right, sir.' He was still off-balance, hesitant. 'I think young Smith's left foot is gone, sir – frostbite.'

'Take him below – at once. And organize your crew into ten minute watches: one to keep a telephone watch here, the other four in the Engineer's Flat. From now on. You understand?' He hurried away, as if to avoid the embarrassment of thanks, the murmurs of smiling gladness.

They passed the torpedo shop, where the spare torpedoes and compressed air cylinders were stored, climbed the ladder to the boat-deck. Vallery paused a moment, one hand on the boat-winch, the other holding the bloody scarf, already frozen almost solid, to mouth and nose. He could just distinguish the shadowy bulkiness of merchantmen on either side: their masts, though, were oddly visible, swinging lazily, gently against the stars as the ships rolled to a slight swell, just beginning. He shuddered, pulled his scarf higher round his neck. God, it was cold! He moved for'ard, leaning heavily on Petersen's arm. The snow, three to four inches deep, cushioned his footsteps as he came up behind an Oerlikon gun. Quietly, he laid a hand on the shoulder of the hooded gunner hunched forward in his cockpit.

'Things all right, gunner?'

No reply. The man appeared to stir, moved forward, then fell still again.

'I said, "Are you all right?" ' Vallery's voice had hardened. He shook the gunner by the shoulder, turned impatiently to Hartley.

'Asleep, Chief! At Action Stations! We're all dead from lack of sleep, I know – but his mates below are depending on him. There's no excuse. Take his name!'

'Take his name!' Nicholls echoed softly, bent over the cockpit. He shouldn't speak like this, he knew, but he couldn't help it. 'Take his name,' he repeated. 'What for? His next of kin? This man is dead.'

The snow was beginning to fall again, cold and wet and feathery, the wind lifting a perceptible fraction. Vallery felt the first icy flakes, unseen in the darkness, brushing his cheeks, heard the distant moan of the wind in the rigging, lonely and forlorn. He shivered.

'His heater's gone.' Hartley withdrew an exploratory hand, straightened up. He seemed tired. 'These Oerlikons have black heaters bolted to the side of the cockpit. The gunners lean against them, sir, for hours at a time. . . . I'm afraid the fuse must have blown. They've been warned against this, sir, a thousand times.'

'Good God! Good God!' Vallery shook his head slowly. He felt old, terribly tired. 'What a useless, futile way to die. . . . Have him taken to the Canteen, Hartley.'

'No good, sir.' Nicholls straightened up also. 'It'll have to wait. What with the cold and the quick onset of rigor mortis – well, it'll have to wait.'

Vallery nodded assent, turned heavily away. All at once, the deck 'speaker aft of the winch blared into raucous life, a rude desecration that shattered the chilled hush of the evening.

'Do you hear there? Do you hear there? Captain, or notify Captain, to contact bridge immediately, please.' Three times the message was repeated, then the 'speaker clicked off.

Quickly Vallery turned to Hartley.

'Where's the nearest phone, Chief?'

'Right here, sir.' Hartley turned back to the Oerlikon, stripped earphones and chest mouthpiece from the dead man. 'That is, if the AA tower is still manned?'

'What's left of it is.'

'Tower? Captain to speak to bridge. Put me through.' He handed the receiver to Vallery. 'Here you are, sir.'

'Thank you. Bridge? Yes, speaking. . . . Yes, yes. . . . Very good. Detail the *Sirrus*. . . . No, Commander, nothing I can do anyway – just maintain position, that's all.' He took the handset off, handed it back to Hartley.

'Asdic contact from *Viking*,' he said briefly. 'Red 90.' He turned, looked out over the dark sea, realized the futility of his instinctive action, and shrugged. 'We've sent the *Sirrus* after him. Come on.'

Their tour of the boat-deck gun-sites completed with a visit to the midships' pom-pom crew, bone-chilled and shaking with cold, under the command of the bearded Doyle, respectfully sulphurous in his outspoken comments on the weather, they dropped down to the main deck again. By this time Vallery was making no protest at all, not even of the most token kind, against Petersen's help and support. He was too glad of them. He blessed Brooks for his foresight and thoughtfulness, and was touched by the rare delicacy and consideration that prompted the big Norwegian to withdraw his supporting arm whenever they spoke to or passed an isolated group of men.

Inside the port screen door and just for'ard of the galley, Vallery and Nicholls, waiting as the others knocked the clamps off the hatch leading down to the stokers' mess, heard the muffled roar of distant depth-charges – there were four in all – felt the pressure waves strike the hull of the *Ulysses*. At the first report Vallery had stiffened, head cocked in attention, eyes fixed on infinity, in the immemorial manner of a man whose ears are doing the work for all the senses. Hesitated a moment, shrugged, bent his arm to hook a leg over the hatch coaming. There was nothing he could do.

In the centre of the stokers' mess was another, heavier hatch. This, too, was opened. The ladder led down to the steering position, which, as in most modern warships, was far removed from the bridge, deep in the heart of the ship below the armour-plating. Here, for a couple of minutes, Vallery talked quietly to the quartermaster, while Petersen, working in the confined space just outside, opened the massive hatch – 450 lbs. of steel, actuated by a counter-balancing pulley weight – which gave access to the hold, to the very bottom of the *Ulysses*, to the Transmitting Station and No. 2 Low Power Room.

A mazing, confusing mystery of a place, this Low Power Room, confusing to the eye and ear. Round every bulkhead, interspersed with scores of switches, breakers and rheostats, were ranged tiered banks of literally hundred of fuses, baffling to the untrained eye in their myriad complexity. Baffling, too, was the function of a score or more of low-power generators, nerve-drilling in the frenetic dissonance of their high-pitched hums. Nicholls straightened up at the foot of the ladder and shuddered involuntarily. A bad place, this. How easily could mind and nerves slide over the edge of insanity under the pounding, insistent clamour of the desynchronized cacophony!

Just then there were only two men there – an Electric Artificer and his assistant, bent over the big Sperry master gyro, making some latitude adjustment to the highly complex machinery of the compass. They looked up quickly, tired surprise melting into tired pleasure. Vallery had a few words with them – speech was difficult in that bedlam of sound – then moved over to the door of the TS.

He had his glove on the door handle when he froze to complete stillness. Another pattern had exploded, much closer this time, two cable lengths distant, at most. Depth-charges, they knew, but only because reason and experience told them: deep down in the heart of an armour-plated ship there is no sense of explosion, no roar of erruption from a detonating depth-charge. Instead, there is a tremendous, metallic clang, peculiarly tinny in calibre, as if some giant with a giant sledge had struck the ship's side and found the armour loose.

The pattern was followed almost immediately by another two explosions, and the *Ulysses* was still shuddering under the impact of the second when Vallery turned the handle and walked in. The others filed in after the Captain, Petersen closing the door softly behind him. At once the clamour of the electric motors died gratefully away in the hushed silence of the TS.

The TS, fighting heart of the ship, lined like the Low Power Room though it was by banks of fuses, was completely dominated by the two huge electronic computing tables occupying almost half the floor space. These, the vital links between the Fire Control Towers and the turrets, were generally the scene of intense, controlled activity: but the almost total destruction of the towers that morning had made them all but useless, and the undermanned TS was strangely quiet. Altogether, there were only eight ratings and an officer manning the tables.

The air in the TS, a TS prominently behung with 'No Smoking' notices, was blue with tobacco smoke hanging in a flat, lazily drifting cloud near the deckhead – a cloud which spiralled thinly down to smouldering cigarette ends. For Nicholls there was something oddly reassuring in these burning cigarettes: in the unnatural bow-taut stillness, in the inhuman immobility of the men, it was the only guarantee of life.

He looked, in a kind of detached curiosity, at the rating nearest him. A thin, dark-haired man, he was sitting hunched forward, his elbow on the table, the cigarette clipped between his fingers a bare inch from his half-open mouth. The smoke was curling up, lacing its smarting path across vacant, sightless eyes oblivious to the irritation, the ash on the cigarette, itself almost two inches in length, drooping slightly. Vaguely, Nicholls wondered how long he had been sitting there motionless, utterly motionless . . . and why?

Expectancy, of course. That was it – expectancy. It was too obvious. Waiting, just waiting. Waiting for what? For the first time it struck Nicholls, struck him with blinding clarity, what it was to wait, to wait with the bowstring of the nerves strung down at inhuman tension, strung down far beyond quivering to the tautened immobility of snapping point, to wait for the torpedo that would send them crashing into oblivion. For the first time he realized why it was that men who could, invariably it seemed, find something complainingly humorous in any place and every place never joked about the TS. A death trap is not funny. The TS was twenty feet below water level: for'ard of it was 'B' magazine, aft of it 'A' boiler-room, on either side of it were fuel tanks, and below it was the unprotected bottom, prime target for acoustic mines and torpedoes. They were ringed, surrounded, by the elements, the threat of death, and it needed only a flash, a wandering spark, to trigger off the annihilating reality. . . . And above them, in the one in a thousand chance of survival, was a series of hatches which could all too easily warp and lock solid under the metal-twisting shock of an explosion. Besides, the primary idea was that the hatches, deliberately heavy in construction, should *stay* shut in the event of damage, to seal off the flooded compartments below. The men in the TS knew this.

'Good-evening. Everything all right down here?' Vallery's voice, quiet and calm as ever, sounded unnaturally loud. Startled faces, white and strained, twisted round, eyes opening in astonishment; the depth-charging, Nicholls realized, had masked their approach.

'Wouldn't worry too much about the racket outside,' Vallery went on reassuringly. 'A wandering U-boat, and the *Sirrus* is after him. You can thank your stars you're here and not in that sub.'

No one else had spoken. Nicholls, watching them, saw their eyes flickering back from Vallery's face to the forbidden cigarettes, understood their discomfort, their embarrassment at being caught red-handed by the Captain.

'Any reports from the main tower, Brierley?' he asked the officer in charge. He seemed unaware of the strain.

'No, sir. Nothing at all. All quiet above.'

'Fine!' Vallery sounded positively cheerful. 'No news is good news.' He brought his hand out from his pocket, proffered his cigarette case to Brierley. 'Smoke? And you Nicholls?' He took one himself replaced the case, absently picked up a box of matches lying in front of the nearest gunner and if he noticed the gunner's startled disbelief, the slow beginnings of a smile, the tired shoulders slumping fractionally in a long, soundless sigh of relief, he gave no sign.

The thunderous clanging of more depth-charges drowned the rasping of the match, drowned Vallery's harsh, convulsive coughing as the smoke reached his lungs. Only the reddening of the sodden hand-towel betrayed him. As the last vibration died away, he looked up, concern in his eyes.

'Good God! Does it always sound like that down here?'

Brierley smiled faintly. 'More or less, sir. Usually more.'

Vallery looked slowly round the men in the TS, nodded for'ard.

' "B" magazine there, isn't it?'

'Yes, sir.'

'And nice big fuel tanks all around you?'

Brierley nodded. Every eye was on the Captain.

'I see. Frankly, I'd rather have my own job – wouldn't have yours for a pension. . . . Nicholls, I think we'll spend a few minutes down here, have our smoke in peace. Besides,' – he grinned – 'think of the increased fervour with which we'll count our blessings when we get out of here!'

He stayed five minutes, talking quietly to Brierley and his men. Finally, he stubbed out his cigarette, took his leave and started for the door.

'Sir.' The voice stopped him on the threshold, the voice of the thin dark gunner whose matches he had borrowed.

'Yes, what is it?'

'I thought you might like this.' He held out a clean, white towel. 'That one you've got is - well, sir, I mean it's—'

'Thank you.' Vallery took the towel without any hesitation. 'Thank you very much.'

Despite Petersen's assistance, the long climb up to the upper deck left Vallery very weak. His feet were dragging heavily.

'Look, sir, this is madness!' Nicholls was desperately anxious. 'Sorry, sir, I didn't mean that, but - well, come and see Commander Brooks, please!'

'Certainly.' The reply was a husky whisper. 'Our next port of call anyway.'

Half a dozen paces took them to the door of the Sick Bay. Vallery insisted on seeing Brooks alone. When he came out of the surgery after some time, he seemed curiously refreshed, his step lighter. He was smiling, and so was Brooks. Nicholls lagged behind as the Captain left.

'Give him anything, sir?' he asked. 'Honest to God, he's killing himself!'

'He took something, not much.' Brooks smiled softly. 'I know he's killing himself, so does he. But he knows why, and I know why, and he knows I know why. Anyway, he feels better. Not to worry, Johnny!'

Nicholls waited at the top of the ladder outside the Sick Bay, waited for the Captain and others to come up from the telephone exchange and No. 1 Low Power Room. He stood aside as they climbed the coaming, but Vallery took his arm, walked him slowly for'ard past the Torpedo Office, nodding curtly to Carslake, in nominal charge of a Damage Control party, Carslake, face still swathed in white, looked back with eyes wild and staring and strange, his gaze almost devoid of recognition. Vallery hesitated, shook his head, then turned to Nicholls, smiling.

'BMA in secret session, eh?' he queried. 'Never mind, Nicholls, and don't worry. *I'm* the one who should be worrying.'

'Indeed, sir? Why?'

Vallery shook his head again. 'Rum in the gun turrets, cigarettes in the TS, and now a fine old whisky in a "Lysol" bottle. Thought Commander Brooks was going to poison me - and what a glorious death! Excellent stuff, and the Surgeon Commander's apologies to you for broaching your private supplies.'

Nicholls flushed darkly, began to stammer an apology but Vallery but him off.

'Forget it, boy, forget it. What does it matter? But it makes me wonder what we're going to find next. An opium den in the Capstan Flat, perhaps, or dancing girls in "B" turret?'

But they found nothing in these or any other places, except cold, misery and hunger-haunted exhaustion. As ever, Nicholls saw, they - or rather, Vallery - left the men the better of their coming. But they themselves were now in a pretty bad state, Nicholls realized. His own legs were made of rubber, he was exhausted by continuous shivering: where Vallery found the strength to carry on, he couldn't even begin to imagine. Even Petersen's great strength was flagging, not so much from half-carrying Vallery as from the ceaseless hammering of clips frozen solid on doors and hatches.

Leaning against a bulkhead, breathing heavily after the ascent from 'A' magazine, Nicholls looked hopefully at the Captain. Vallery saw the look, interpreted it correctly, and shook his head, smiling.

'Might as well finish it, boy. Only the Capstan Flat. Nobody there anyway, I expect, but we might as well have a look.'

They walked slowly round the heavy machinery in the middle of the Capstan Flat, for'ard past the Battery Room and Sail-maker's Shop, past the Electrical Workshop and cells to the locked door of the Painter's Shop, the most for'ard compartment in the ship.

Vallery reached his hand forward, touched the door symbolically, smiled tiredly and turned away. Passing the cell door, he casually flicked open the inspection port, glanced in perfunctorily and moved on. Then he stopped dead, wheeled round and flung open the inspection port again.

'What in the name of – Ralston! What on earth are you doing here?' he shouted.

Ralston smiled. Even through the thick plate glass it wasn't a pleasant smile and it never touched the blue eyes. He gestured to the barred grille, indicating that he could not hear.

Impatiently, Vallery twisted the grille handle.

'What are you doing here, Ralston?' he demanded. The brows were drawn down heavily over blazing eyes. 'In the cells – and at this time! Speak up, man! Tell me!' Nicholls looked at Vallery in slow surprise. The old man – angry! It was unheard of? Shrewdly, Nicholls decided that he'd rather not be the object of Vallery's fury.

'I was locked up here, sir.' The words were innocuous enough, but their tone said, 'What a damned silly question.' Vallery flushed faintly.

'When?'

'At 1030 this morning, sir.'

'And by whom, may I inquire?'

'By the Master-At-Arms, sir.'

'On what authority?' Vallery demanded furiously.

Ralston looked at him a long moment without speaking. His face was expressionless. 'On yours, sir.'

'Mine!' Vallery was incredulous. 'I didn't tell him to lock you up!'

'You never told him not to,' said Ralston evenly. Vallery winced: the oversight, the lack of consideration was his, and that hurt badly.

'Where's your night Action Station?' he asked sharply.

'Port tubes, sir.' That, Vallery realized, explained why only the starboard crew had been closed up.

'And why – why have you been left here during Action Stations? Don't you know it's forbidden, against all regulations?'

'Yes, sir.' Again the hint of the wintry smile. 'I know. But does the Master-At-Arms know?' He paused a second, smiled again. 'Or maybe he just forgot,' he suggested.

'Hartley!' Vallery was on balance again, his tone level and grim. 'The Master-At-Arms here, immediately: see that he brings his keys!' He broke into a harsh bout of coughing, spat some blood into the towel, looked at Ralston again.

'I'm sorry about this, my boy,' he said slowly. 'Genuinely sorry.'

'How's the tanker?' Ralston asked softly.

'What? What did you say?' Vallery was unprepared for the sudden switch. 'What tanker?'

'The one that was damaged this morning, sir.'

'Still with us.' Vallery was puzzled. 'Still with us, but low in the water. Any special reason for asking?'

'Just interested, sir.' The smile was wary, but this time it was a smile. 'You see—'

He stopped abruptly as a deep, muffled roar crashed through the silent night, the pressure blast listing the *Ulysses* sharply to starboard. Vallery lurched, staggered and would have fallen but for Petersen's sudden arm. He braced himself against the righting roll, looked at Nicholls in sudden dismay. The sound was all too familiar.

Nicholls gazed back at him, sorry to his heart for this fresh burden for a dying man, and nodded slowly, in reluctant agreement with the unspoken thought in Vallery's eyes.

'Afraid you're right, sir. Torpedo. Somebody's stopped a packet.'

'Do you hear there!' The capstan flat speaker was hurried, intense, unnaturally loud in the aftermath of silence. 'Do you hear there! Captain on the bridge: urgent. Captain on the bridge: urgent. Captain on the bridge: urgent. . . .'

Chapter Eleven

Friday Evening

Bent almost double, Captain Vallery clutched the handrail of the port ladder leading up to the fo'c'sle. Desperately, he tried to look out over the darkened water, but he could see nothing. A mist, a dark and swirling and roaring mist flecked with blood, a mist shot through with dazzling light swam before his eyes and he was blind. His breath came in great whooping gasps that racked his tortured lungs: his lower ribs were clamped in giant pincers, pincers that were surely crushing him. That stumbling, lurching run from the forepeak, he dimly realized, had all but killed him. Close, too damn' close, he thought. I must be more careful in future. . . .

Slowly his vision cleared, but the brilliant light remained. Heavens above, Vallery thought, a blind man could have seen all there was to see here. For there was nothing to be seen but the tenebrous silhouette, so faint as to be almost imagined, of a tanker deep, deep in the water – and a great column of flame, hundreds of feet in height, streaking upwards from the heart of the dense mushroom of smoke that obscured the bows of the torpedoed ship. Even at the distance of half a mile, the roaring of the flames was almost intolerable. Vallery watched appalled. Behind him he could hear Nicholls swearing, softly, bitterly, continuously.

Vallery felt Petersen's hand on his arm. 'Does the Captain wish to go up to the bridge?'

'In a moment, Petersen, in a moment. Just hang on.' His mind was functioning again, his eyes, conditioned by forty years' training, automatically sweeping the horizon. Funny, he thought, you can hardly see the tanker – the *Vytura*, it must be – she's shielded by that thick pall of smoke, probably; but the other ships in the convoy, white, ghost-like, sharply etched against the indigo blue of the sky, were bathed in that deadly glare. Even the stars had died.

He became aware that Nicholls was no longer swearing in repetitious monotony, that he was talking to him.

'A tanker, isn't it, sir? Hadn't we better take shelter? Remember what happened to that other one!'

'What one?' Vallery was hardly listening.

'The *Cochella*. A few days ago, I think it was. Good God, no! It was only this morning!'

'When tankers go up, they go up, Nicholls.' Vallery seemed curiously far away. 'If they just burn, they may last long enough. Tankers die hard, terribly hard, my boy: they live where any other ship would sink.'

'But – but she must have a hole the size of a house in her side!' Nicholls protested.

'No odds,' Vallery replied. He seemed to be waiting, watching for something. 'Tremendous reserve buoyancy in these ships. Maybe 27 sealed tanks, not to mention coffer-dams, pump-rooms, engine-rooms. . . . Never heard of the Nelson device for pumping compressed air into a tanker's oil tanks to give it buoyancy, to keep it afloat? Never heard of Captain Dudley Mason and the *Ohio*? Never heard of . . .' He broke off suddenly, and when he spoke again, the dreaming lethargy of the voice was gone.

'I thought so!' he exclaimed, his voice sharp with excitement. 'I thought so! The *Vytura*'s still under way, still under command! Good God, she must still be doing almost 15 knots! The bridge, quick!'

Vallery's feet left the deck, barely touched it again till Petersen set him down carefully on the duckboards in front of the startled Commander. Vallery grinned faintly at Turner's astonishment, at the bushy eyebrows lifting over the dark, lean buccaneer's face, leaner, more recklessly chiselled than ever in the glare of the blazing tanker. If ever a man was born 400 years too late, Vallery thought inconsequentially; but what a man to have around!

'It's all right, Commander.' He laughed shortly. 'Brooks thought I needed a Man Friday. That's Stoker Petersen. Over-enthusiastic, maybe a trifle apt to take orders too literally. . . . But he was a Godsend to me tonight. . . . But never mind me.' He jerked his thumb towards the tanker, blazing even more whitely now, difficult to look at, almost, as the noonday sun. 'How about him?'

'Makes a bloody fine lighthouse for any German ship or plane that happens to be looking for us,' Turner growled. 'Might as well send a signal to Trondheim giving our lat. and long.'

'Exactly,' Vallery nodded. 'Besides setting up some beautiful targets for the sub that got the *Vytura* just now. A dangerous fellow, Commander. That was a brilliant piece of work – in almost total darkness, too.'

'Probably a scuttle somebody forgot to shut. We haven't the ships to keep checking them all the time. And it wasn't so damned brilliant, at least not for him. The *Viking*'s in contact right now, sitting over the top of him. . . . I sent her right away.'

'Good man!' Vallery said warmly. He turned to look at the burning tanker, looked back at Turner, his face set. 'She'll have to go, Commander.'

Turner nodded slowly. 'She'll have to go,' he echoed.

'It *is* the *Vytura*, isn't it?'

'That's her. Same one that caught it this morning.'

'Who's the master?'

'Haven't the foggiest,' Turner confessed. 'Number One, Pilot? Any idea where the sailing list is?'

'No, sir.' The Kapok Kid was hesitant, oddly unsure of himself. 'Admiral had them, I know. Probably gone, now.'

'What makes you think that?' Vallery asked sharply.

'Spicer, his pantry steward, was almost choked with smoke this afternoon, found him making a whacking great fire in his bath,' the Kapok Kid said miserably. 'Said he was burning vital documents that must not fall into enemy hands. Old newspapers, mostly, but I think the list must have been among them. It's nowhere else.'

'Poor old . . .' Turner remembered just in time that he was speaking to the Admiral, broke off, shook his head in compassionate wonder. 'Shall I send a signal to Fletcher on the *Cape Hatteras*?'

'Never mind.' Vallery was impatient. 'There's no time. Bentley – to the master, *Vytura*: "Please abandon ship immediately: we are going to sink you." '

Suddenly Vallery stumbled, caught hold of Turner's arm.

'Sorry,' he apologized. 'I'm afraid my legs are going. Gone, rather.' He smiled up wryly at the anxious faces. 'No good pretending any longer, is there? Not when your legs start a mutiny on their own. Oh, dear God, I'm done!'

'And no bloody wonder!' Turner swore. 'I wouldn't treat a mad dog the way you treat yourself! Come on, sir. Admiral's chair for you – now. If you don't, I'll get Petersen to you,' he threatened, as Vallery made to protest. The protest died in a smile, and Vallery meekly allowed himself to be helped into a chair. He signed deeply, relaxed into the God-sent support of the back and arms of the chair. He felt ghastly, powerless, his wasted body a wide sea of pain, and deadly cold; all these things, but also proud and grateful – Turner had never even suggested that he go below.

He heard the gate crash behind him, the murmur of voices, then Turner was at his side.

'The Master-At-Arms, sir. Did you send for him?'

'I certainly did.' Vallery twisted in his chair, his face grim. 'Come here, Hastings!'

The Master-At-Arms stood at attention before him. As always, his face was a mask, inscrutable, expressionless, almost inhuman in that fierce light.

'Listen carefully.' Vallery had to raise his voice above the roar of the flames: the effort even to speak was exhausting. 'I have no time to talk to you now. I will see you in the morning. Meantime, you will release Leading Seaman Ralston immediately. You will then hand over your duties, your papers and your keys to Regulating Petty Officer Perrat. Twice, now, you have overstepped the limits of your authority: that is insolence, but it can be overlooked. But you have also kept a man locked in cells during Action Stations. The prisoner would have died like a rat in a trap. You are no longer Master-At-Arms of the *Ulysses*. That is all.'

For a couple of seconds Hastings stood rigidly in shocked unbelieving silence, then the iron discipline snapped. He stepped forward, arms raised in appeal, the mask collapsed in contorted bewilderment.

'Relieved of my duties? Relieved of my duties! But, sir, you can't do that! you can't . . .'

His voice broke off in a gasp of pain as Turner's iron grip closed over his elbow.

'Don't say "can't" to the Captain,' he whispered silkily in his ear. 'You heard him? Get off the bridge!'

The gate clicked behind him. Carrington said, conversationally: 'Somebody's using his head aboard the *Vytura* – fitted a red filter to his Aldis. Couldn't see it otherwise.'

Immediately the tension eased. All eyes were on the winking red light, a hundred feet aft of the flames, and even then barely distinguishable. Suddenly it stopped.

'What does he say, Bentley?' Vallery asked quickly.

Bentley coughed apologetically. 'Message reads: "Are you hell. Try it and I will ram you. Engine intact. We can make it." '

Vallery closed his eyes for a moment. He was beginning to appreciate how old Giles must have felt. When he looked up again, he had made his decision.

'Signal: "You are endangering entire convoy. Abandon ship at once. Repeat, at once."' He turned to the Commander, his mouth bitter. 'I take off my hat to him. How would *you* like to sit on top of enough fuel to blow you to Kingdom Come. . . . Must be oil in some of his tanks. . . . God, how I hate to have to threaten a man like that!'

'I know, sir,' Turner murmured. 'I know how it is. . . . Wonder what the *Viking*'s doing out there? Should be hearing from her now?'

'Send a signal,' Vallery ordered. 'Ask for information.' He peered aft, searched briefly for the Torpedo Lieutenant. 'Where's Marshall?'

'Marshall?' Turner was surprised. 'In the Sick Bay, of course. Still on the injured list, remember – four ribs gone?'

'Of course, or course!' Vallery shook his head tiredly, angry with himself. 'And the Chief Torpedo Gunner's Mate – Noyes, isn't it? – he was killed yesterday in Number 3. How about Vickers?'

'He was in the FDR.'

'In the FDR,' Vallery repeated slowly. He wondered why his heart didn't stop beating. He was long past the stage of chilled bone and coagulating blood. His whole body was a great block of ice. . . . He had never known that such cold could exist. It was very strange, he thought, that he was no longer shivering. . . .

'I'll do it myself, sir,' Turner interrupted his wandering. 'I'll take over the bridge Torpedo Control – used to be the worst Torps. officer on the China Station.' He smiled faintly. 'Perhaps the hand has not lost what little cunning it ever possessed!'

'Thank you.' Vallery was grateful. 'You just do that.'

'We'll have to take him from starboard,' Turner reminded him. 'Port control was smashed this morning – foremast didn't do it any good. . . . I'll go check the Dumaresq.[1] . . . Good God!' His hand gripped Vallery's shoulder with a strength that made him wince. 'It's the Admiral, sir! He's coming on the bridge!'

Incredulously, Vallery twisted round in his chair. Turner was right. Tyndall was coming through the gate, heading purposefully towards him. In the deep shadow cast by the side of the bridge, he seemed disembodied. The bare head, sparsely covered with thin, straggling wisps of white, the grey, pitifully-shrunken face, the suddenly stooped shoulders, unaccountably thin under black oilskins, all these were thrown into harsh relief by the flames. Below, nothing was visible. Silently, Tyndall padded his way across the bridge, stood waiting at Vallery's side.

Slowly, leaning on Turner's ready arm, Vallery climbed down. Unsmiling, Tyndall looked at him, nodded gravely, hoisted himself into his seat. He picked up the binoculars from the ledge before him, slowly quartered the horizon.

It was Turner who noticed it first.

'Sir! You've no gloves on, sir!'

'What? What did you say?' Tyndall replaced the glasses, looked incredulously at his blood-stained, bandaged hands. 'Ah! Do you know, I *knew* I had forgotten something. That's the second time. Thank you, Commander.' He smiled courteously, picked up the binoculars again, resumed his quartering of the horizon. All at once Vallery felt another, deadlier chill pass through him, and it had nothing to do with the bitter chill of the Arctic night.

Turner hesitated helplessly for a second, then turned quickly to the Kapok Kid.

'Pilot! Haven't I seen gauntlets hanging in your chart-house?'

'Yes, sir. Right away!' The Kapok Kid hurried off the bridge.

Turner looked up at the Admiral again.

'Your head, sir – you've nothing on. Wouldn't you like a duffel coat, a hood, sir?'

'A hood?' Tyndall was amused. 'What in the world for? I'm not cold. . . . If you'll excuse me, Commander?' He turned the binoculars full into the glare of the blazing *Vytura*. Turner looked at him again, looked at Vallery, hesitated, then walked aft.

Carpenter was on his way back with the gloves when the WT loudspeaker clicked on.

'WT – bridge. WT – bridge. Signal from *Viking*: "Lost contact. Am continuing search." '

'Lost contact!' Vallery exclaimed. Lost contact – the worst possible thing that could have happened! A U-boat out there, loose, unmarked, and the whole of FR77 lit up like a fairground. A fairground, he thought bitterly, clay pipes in a shooting gallery and with about as much chance of hitting back once contact had been lost. Any second now. . . .

He wheeled round, clutched at the binnacle for support. He had forgotten how weak he was, how the tilting of the shattered bridge affected balance.

'Bentley! No reply from the *Vytura* yet?'

[1] The Dumaresq was a miniature plotting table on which such relevant factors as corresponding speeds and courses were worked out to provide firing tracks for the torpedoes.

'No, sir,' Bentley was as concerned as the Captain, as aware of the desperate need for speed. 'Maybe his power's gone – no, no, no, there he is now, sir!'

'Captain, sir.'

Vallery looked round. 'Yes, Commander, what is it? Not more bad news, I hope?'

' 'Fraid so, sir. Starboard tubes won't train – jammed solid.'

'Won't train,' Vallery snapped irritably. 'That's nothing new, surely. Ice, frozen snow. Chip it off, use boiling water, blow-lamps, any old—'

'Sorry, sir.' Turner shook his head regretfully. 'Not that. Rack and turntable buckled. Must have been either the shell that got the bosun's store or Number 3 Low Power Room – immediately below. Anyway – kaput!'

'Very well, then!' Vallery was impatient. 'It'll have to be the port tubes.'

'No bridge control left, sir,' Turner objected. 'Unless we fire by local control?'

'No reason why not, is there?' Vallery demanded. 'After all, that's what torpedo crews are trained for. Get on to the port tubes – I assume the communication line there is still intact – tell them to stand by.'

'Yes, sir.'

'And Turner?'

'Sir?'

'I'm sorry.' He smiled crookedly. 'As old Giles used to say of himself, I'm just a crusty old curmudgeon. Bear with me, will you?'

Turner grinned sympathetically, then sobered quickly. He jerked his head forward.

'How is he, sir?'

Vallery looked at the Commander for a long second, shook his head, almost imperceptibly. Turner nodded heavily and was gone.

'Well, Bentley? What does he say?'

'Bit confused, sir,' Bentley apologized. 'Couldn't get it all. Says he's going to leave the convoy, proceed on his own. Something like that, sir.'

Proceed on his own! That was no solution, Vallery knew. He might still burn for hours, a dead give-away, even on a different course. But to proceed on his own! An unprotected crippled, blazing tanker – and a thousand miles to Murmansk, the worst thousand miles in all the world! Vallery closed his eyes. He felt sick to his heart. A man like that, and a ship like that – and he had to destroy them both!

Suddenly Tyndall spoke.

'Port 30!' he ordered. His voice was loud, authoritative. Vallery stiffened in dismay. Port 30! They'd turn into the *Vytura*.

There was a couple of seconds' silence, then Carrington, Officer of the Watch, bent over the speaking-tube, repeated: 'Port 30.' Vallery started forward, stopped short as he saw Carrington gesturing at the speaking-tube. He'd stuffed a gauntlet down the mouthpiece.

'Midships!'

'Midships, sir!'

'Steady! Captain?'

'Sir?'

'That light hurts my eyes,' Tyndall complained. 'Can't we put that fire out?'

'We'll try, sir.' Vallery walked across, spoke softly. 'You look tired, sir. Wouldn't you like to go below?'

'What? Go below! Me!'

'Yes, sir. We'll send for you if we need you,' he added persuasively.

Tyndall considered this for a moment, shook his head grimly.

'Won't do, Dick. Not fair to you. . . .' His voice trailed away and he muttered something that sounded like 'Admiral Tyndall,' but Vallery couldn't be sure.

'Sir? I didn't catch—'

'Nothing!' Tyndall was very abrupt. He looked away towards the *Vytura*, exclaimed in sudden pain, flung up an arm to protect his eyes. Vallery, too, started back, eyes screwed up to shut out the sudden blinding flash of flame from the *Vytura*.

The explosion crashed in their ears almost simultaneously, the blast of the pressure wave sent them reeling. The *Vytura* had been torpedoed again, right aft, close to her engine-room, and was heavily on fire there. Only the bridge island, amidships, was miraculously free from smoke and flames. Even in the moment of shock, Vallery thought, 'She must go now. She can't last much longer.' But he knew he was deluding himself, trying to avoid the inevitable, the decision he must take. Tankers, as he'd told Nicholls, died hard, terribly hard. Poor old Giles, he thought unaccountably, poor old Giles.

He moved aft to the port gate. Turner was shouting angrily into the telephone.

'You'll damn' well do what you're told, do you hear? Get them out immediately! Yes, I said "immediately"!'

Vallery touched his arm in surprise. 'What's the matter, Commander?'

'Of all the bloody insolence!' Turner snorted. 'Telling *me* what to do!'

'Who?'

'The LTO on the tubes. Your friend Ralston!' said Turner wrathfully.

'Ralston! Of course!' Vallery remembered now. 'He told me that was his night Action Stations. What's wrong?'

'What's wrong: Says he doesn't think he can do it. Doesn't like to, doesn't wish to do it, if you please. Blasted insubordination!' Turner fumed.

Vallery blinked at him. 'Ralston – are you sure? But of course you are. . . . I wonder. . . . That boy's been through a very private hell, Turner. Do you think—'

'I don't know what to think!' Turner lifted the phone again. 'Tubes nine-oh? At last! . . . What? What did you say? . . . Why don't we . . . Gunfire! Gunfire!' He hung up the receiver with a crash, swung round on Vallery.

'Asks me, pleads with me, for gunfire instead of torpedoes! He's mad, he must be! But mad or not, I'm going down there to knock some sense into that mutinous young devil!' Turner was angrier than Vallery had ever seen him. 'Can you get Carrington to man this phone, sir?'

'Yes, yes, of course!' Vallery himself had caught up some of Turner's anger. 'Whatever his sentiments, this is no time to express them!' he snapped. 'Straighten him up. . . . Maybe I've been too lenient, too easy, perhaps he thinks we're in his debt, at some psychological disadvantage, for the shabby treatment he's received. . . . All right, all right, Commander!' Turner's mounting impatience was all too evident. 'Off you go. Going into attack in three or four minutes.' He turned abruptly, passed into the compass platform.

'Bentley!'

'Sir?'

'Last signal—'

'Better have a look, sir,' Carrington interrupted. 'He's slowing up.'

Vallery stepped forward, peered over the windscreen. The *Vytura*, a roaring mass of flames was falling rapidly astern.

'Clearing the davits, sir!' the Kapok Kid reported excitedly. 'I think – yes, yes, I can see the boat coming down!'

'Thank God for that!' Vallery whispered. He felt as though he had been granted a new lease of life. Head bowed, he clutched the screen with both hands – reaction had left him desperately weak. After a few seconds he looked up.

'WT code signal to *Sirrus*,' he ordered quietly. ' "Circle well astern. Pick up survivors from the *Vytura*'s lifeboat." '

He caught Carrington's quick look and shrugged. 'It's a better than even risk, Number One, so to hell with Admiralty orders. God,' he added with sudden bitterness, 'wouldn't I love to see a boatload of the "no-survivors-will-be-picked-up" Whitehall warriors drifting about in the Barents Sea!' He turned away, caught sight of Nicholls and Petersen.

'Still here, are you, Nicholls? Hadn't you better get below?'

'If you wish, sir.' Nicholls hesitated, nodded forward towards Tyndall. 'I thought, perhaps—'

'Perhaps you're right, perhaps you're right.' Vallery shook his head in weary perplexity. 'We'll see. Just wait a bit, will you?' He raised his voice. 'Pilot!'

'Sir?'

'Slow ahead both!'

'Slow ahead both, sir!'

Gradually, then more quickly, way fell off the *Ulysses* and she dropped slowly astern of the convoy. Soon, even the last ships in the lines were ahead of her, thrashing their way to the north-east. The snow was falling more thickly now, but still the ships were bathed in that savage glare, frighteningly vulnerable in their naked helplessness.

Seething with anger, Turner brought up short at the port torpedoes. The tubes were out, their evil, gaping mouths, highlighted by the great flames, pointing out over the intermittent refulgence of the rolling swell. Ralston, perched high on the unprotected control position above the central tube, caught his eye at once.

'Ralston!' Turner's voice was harsh, imperious. 'I want to speak to you!'

Ralston turned round quickly, rose, jumped on to the deck. He stood facing the Commander. They were of a height, their eyes on a level, Ralston's still, blue, troubled, Turner's dark and stormy with anger.

'What the hell's the matter with you, Ralston?' Turner ground out. 'Refusing to obey orders, is that it?'

'No, sir.' Ralston's voice was quiet, curiously strained. 'That's not true.'

'Not true!' Turner's eyes were narrowed, his fury barely in check. 'Then what's all this bloody claptrap about not wanting to man the tubes? Are you thinking of emulating Stoker Riley? Or have you just taken leave of your senses – if any?'

Ralston said nothing.

The silence, a silence all too easily interpreted as dumb insolence, infuriated Turner. His powerful hands reached out, grasped Ralston's duffel coat. He pulled the rating towards him, thrust his face close to the other's.

'I asked a question, Ralston,' he said softly. 'I haven't had an answer. I'm waiting. What *is* all this?'

'Nothing, sir.' Distress in his eyes, perhaps, but no fear. 'I – I just don't want to, sir. I hate to do it – to send one of our own ships to the bottom!' The voice was pleading now, blurred with overtones of desperation: Turner was deaf to them. 'Why does she have to go, sir!' he cried. 'Why? Why? Why?'

'None of your bloody business – but as it so happens she's endangering the entire convoy!' Turner's face was still within inches of Ralston's. 'You've got a job to do, orders to obey. Just get up there and obey them! Go on!' he roared, as Ralston hesitated. 'Get up there!' He fairly spat the words out.

Ralston didn't move.

'There are other LTOs, sir!' His arms lifted high in appeal, something in the voice cut through Turner's blind anger: he realized, almost with shock, that this boy was desperate. 'Couldn't *they*—?'

'Let someone else do the dirty work, eh? That's what you mean, isn't it? Turner was bitingly contemptuous. 'Get them to do what you won't do yourself, you – you contemptible young bastard! Communications Number? Give me your set. I'll take over from the bridge.' He took the phone, watched Ralston climb slowly back up and sit hunched forward, head bent over the Dumaresq.

'Number One? Commander speaking. All set here. Captain there?'

'Yes, sir. I'll call him.' Carrington put down the phone, walked through the gate.

'Captain, sir. Commander's on the—'

'Just a moment!' The upraised hand, the tenseness of the voice stopped him. 'Have a look. No. 1. What do you think?' Vallery pointed towards the *Vytura*, past the oil-skinned figure of the Admiral. Tyndall's head was sunk on his chest, and he was muttering incoherently to himself.

Carrington followed the pointing finger. The lifeboat, dimly visible through the thickening snow, had slipped her falls while the *Vytura* was still under way. Crammed with men, she was dropping quickly astern under the great twisting column of flame – dropping far too quickly astern as the First Lieutenant suddenly realized. He turned round, found Vallery's eyes, bleak and tired and old, on his own. Carrington nodded slowly.

'She's picking up, sir. Under way, under command. . . . What are you going to do, sir?'

'God help me, I've no choice. Nothing from the *Viking*, nothing from the *Sirrus*, nothing from our Asdic – and that U-boat's still out there. . . . Tell Turner what's happened. Bentley!'

'Sir?'

'Signal the *Vytura*.' The mouth, whitely compressed, belied the eyes – eyes dark and filled with pain. ' "Abandon ship. Torpedoing you in three minutes. Last signal." Port 20, Pilot!'

'Port 20 it is, sir.'

The *Vytura* was breaking off tangentially, heading north. Slowly, the *Ulysses* came round, almost paralleling her course, now a little astern of her.

'Half-ahead, Pilot!'

'Half-ahead it is, sir.'

'Pilot!'

'Sir?'

'What's Admiral Tyndall saying? Can you make it out?'

Carpenter bent forward, listened, shook his head. Little flurries of snow fell off his fur helmet.

'Sorry, sir. Can't make him out – too much noise from the *Vytura*. . . . I think he's humming, sir.'

'Oh, God!' Vallery bent his head, looked up again, slowly, painfully. Even so slight an effort was labour intolerable.

He looked across to the *Vytura*, stiffened to attention. The red Aldis was winking again. He tried to read it, but it was too fast: or perhaps his eyes were just too old, or tired: or perhaps he just couldn't think any more. . . . There was something weirdly hypnotic about that tiny crimson light flickering between these fantastic curtains of flame, curtains sweeping slowly, ominously together, majestic in their inevitability. And then the little red light had died, so unexpectedly, so abruptly, that Bentley's voice reached him before the realization.

'Signal from the *Vytura*, sir.'

Vallery tightened his grip on the binnacle. Bentley guessed the nod, rather than saw it.

'Message reads: "Why don't you — off. Nuts to the Senior Service. Tell him I send all my love." ' The voice died softly away, and there was only the roaring of the flames, the lost pinging of the Asdic.

'All my love.' Vallery shook his head in silent wonderment. 'All my love! He's crazy! He must be. "All my love," and I'm going to destroy him. . . . Number One!'

'Sir?'

'Tell the Commander to stand by!'

Turner repeated the message from the bridge, turned to Ralston.

'Stand by, LTO!' He looked out over the side, saw that the *Vytura* was slightly ahead now, that the *Ulysses* was still angling in on an interception course. 'About two minutes now, I should say.' He felt the vibration beneath his feet dying away, knew the *Ulysses* was slowing down. Any second now, and she'd start slewing away to starboard. The receiver crackled again in his ear, the sound barely audible above the roaring of the flames. He listened, looked up. ' "X" and "Y" only. Medium settings. Target 11 knots.' He spoke into the phone. 'How long?'

'How long, sir?' Carrington repeated.

'Ninety seconds,' Vallery said huskily. 'Pilot – starboard 10.' He jumped, startled, as he heard the crash of falling binoculars, saw the Admiral slump forward, face and neck striking cruelly on the edge of the windscreen, the arms dangling loosely from the shoulders.

'Pilot!'

But the Kapok Kid was already there. He slipped an arm under Tyndall, took most of the dead weight off the biting edge of the screen.

'What's the matter, sir?' His voice was urgent, blurred with anxiety. 'What's wrong?'

Tyndall stirred slightly, his cheek lying along the edge of the screen.

'Cold, cold, cold,' he intoned. The quavering tones were those of an old, a very old man.

'What? What did you say, sir?' the Kapok Kid begged.

'Cold. I'm cold. I'm terribly cold! My feet, my feet!' The old voice wandered away, and the body slipped into a corner of the bridge, the grey face upturned to the falling snow.

Intuition, an intuition amounting to a sudden sick certainty, sent the Kapok Kid plunging to his knees. Vallery heard the muffled exclamation, saw him straighten up and swing round, his face blank with horror.

'He's – he's got nothing on, sir,' he said unsteadily. 'He's barefoot! They're frozen – frozen solid!'

'Barefoot?' Vallery repeated unbelievingly. 'Barefoot! It's not possible!'

'And pyjamas, sir! That's all he's wearing!'

Vallery lurched forward, peeling off his gloves. He reached down, felt his stomach turn over in shocked nausea as his fingers closed on ice-chilled skin. Bare feet! And pyjamas! Bare feet – no wonder he'd padded so silently across the duckboards! Numbly, he remembered that the last temperature reading had shown 35° of frost. And Tyndall, feet caked in frozen snow and slush, had been sitting there for almost five minutes! . . . He felt great hands under his armpits, felt himself rising effortlessly to his feet. Petersen. It *could* only be Petersen, of course. And Nicholls behind him.

'Leave this to me, sir. Right, Petersen, take him below.' Nicholls's brisk, assured voice, the voice of a man competent in his own element, steadied Vallery, brought him back to the present, and the demands of the present, more surely than anything else could have done. He became aware of Carrington's clipped, measured voice, reeling off course, speed, directions, saw the *Vytura* 50° off the port bow, dropping slowly, steadily aft. Even at that distance, the blast of heat was barely tolerable – what in the name of heaven was it like on the bridge of the *Vytura*?

'Set course, Number One,' he called. 'Local control.'

'Set course, local control.' Carrington might have been on a peace-time exercise in the Solent.

'Local control,' Turner repeated. He hung up the set, looked round. 'You're on your own, Ralston,' he said softly.

There was no reply. The crouched figure on the control position, immobile as graved stone, gave no sign that he had heard.

'Thirty seconds!' Turner said sharply. 'All lined up?'

'Yes, sir.' The figure stirred. 'All lined up.' Suddenly, he swung round, in desperate, final appeal. 'For God's sake, sir! Is there no other—'

'Twenty seconds!' Turner said viciously. 'Do you want a thousand lives on your lily-livered conscience? And if you miss . . .'

Ralston swung slowly back. For a mere breath of time, his face was caught full in the harsh glare of the *Vytura*: with sudden shock, Turner saw that the eyes were masked with tears. Then he saw the lips move. 'Don't worry, sir. I won't miss.' The voice was quite toneless, heavy with nameless defeat.

Perplexed, now, rather than angry, and quite uncomprehending, Turner saw the left sleeve come up to brush the eyes, saw the right hand stretch forward, close round the grip of 'X' firing lever. Incongruously, there sprang to Turner's mind the famous line of Chaucer, 'In goon the spears full sadly in arrest.' In the closing of that hand there was the same heart-stopping decision, the same irrevocable finality.

Suddenly, so suddenly that Turner started in spite of himself, the hand jerked convulsively back. He heard the click of the tripping lever, muffled roar in the explosion chamber, the hiss of compressed air, and the torpedo was gone, its evil sleekness gleaming fractionally in the light of the flames before it crashed below the surface of the sea. It was hardly gone before the tubes shuddered again and the second torpedo was on its way.

For five, ten seconds Turner stared out, fascinated, watching the arrowing wakes of bubbles vanish in the distance. A total of 1500 lbs. of Amatol in these warheads – God help the poor bastards aboard the *Vytura*. . . . The deck 'speaker clicked on.

'Do you hear there? Do you hear there? Take cover immediately! Take cover immediately!' Turner stirred, tore his eyes away from the sea, looked up, saw that Ralston was still crouched in his seat.

'Come down out of there, you young fool!' he shouted. 'Want to be riddled when the *Vytura* goes up? Do you hear me?'

Silence. No word, no movement, only the roaring of the flames.

'Ralston!'

'I'm all right, sir.' Ralston's voice was muffled: he did not even trouble to turn his head.

Turner swore, leapt up on the tubes, dragged Ralston from his seat, pulled him down to the deck and into shelter. Ralston offered no resistance: he seemed sunk in a vast apathy, an uncaring indifference.

Both torpedoes struck home. The end was swift, curiously unspectacular. Listeners – there were no watchers – on the *Ulysses* tensed themselves for the shattering detonation, but the detonation never came. Broken-backed and tired of fighting, the *Vytura* simply collapsed in on her stricken mid-ships, lay gradually, wearily over on her side and was gone.

Three minutes later, Turner opened the door of the Captain's shelter, pushed Ralston in before him.

'Here you are, sir,' he said grimly. 'Thought you might like to see what a conscientious objecter looks like!'

'I certainly do!' Vallery laid down the log-book, turned a cold eye on the torpedoman, looked him slowly up and down. 'A fine job, Ralston, but it doesn't excuse your conduct. Just a minute, Commander.'

He turned back to the Kapok Kid. 'Yes, that seems all right, Pilot. It'll make good reading for their lordships,' he added bitterly. 'The ones the Germans don't get, we finish off for them. . . . Remember to signal the *Hatteras* in the morning, ask for the name of the master of the *Vytura*.'

'He's dead. . . . You needn't trouble yourself!' said Ralston bitterly, then staggered as the Commander's open hand smashed across his face. Turner was breathing heavily, his eyes dark with anger.

'You insolent young devil!' he said softly. 'That was just a little too much from you.'

Ralston's hand came up slowly, fingering the reddening weal on his cheek.

'You misunderstand me, sir.' There was no anger, the voice was a fading murmur, they had to strain to catch his words. 'The master of the *Vytura* – I can tell you his name. It's Ralston. Captain Michael Ralston. He was my father.'

Chapter Twelve

Saturday

To all things an end, to every night its dawn; even to the longest night when dawn never comes, there comes at last the dawn. And so it came for FR77, as grey, as bitter, as hopeless as the night had been long. But it came.

It came to find the convoy some 350 miles north of the Arctic Circle, steaming due east along the 72nd parallel of latitude, half-way between Jan Mayen and the North Cape. 8° 45′ east, the Kapok Kid reckoned, but he couldn't be sure. In heavy snow and with ten-tenth cloud, he was relying on dead reckoning: he had to, for the shell that had destroyed the FDR had wrecked the Automatic Pilot. But roughly 600 nautical miles to go. 600 miles, 40 hours, and the convoy – or what would be left of it by that time – would be in the Kola Inlet, steaming up-river to Polyarnoe and Murmansk . . . 40 hours.

It came to find the convoy – 14 ships left in all – scattered over three square miles of sea and rolling heavily in the deepening swell from the NNE: 14 ships, for another had gone in the deepest part of the night. Mine, torpedo? Nobody knew, nobody ever would know. The *Sirrus* had stopped, searched the area for an hour with hooded ten-inch signalling lamps. There had been no survivors. Not that Commander Orr had expected to find any – not with the air temperature 6° below zero.

It came after a sleepless night of never-ending alarms, of continual Asdic contacts, of constant depth-charging that achieved nothing. Nothing, that is, from the escorts' point of view: but for the enemy, it achieved a double-edged victory. It kept exhausted men at Action Stations all night long, blunting, irreparably perhaps, the last vestiges of the knife-edged vigilance on which the only hope – it was never more – of survival in the Arctic depended. More deadly still, it had emptied the last depth-charge rack in the convoy. . . . It was a measure of the intensity of the attack, of the relentlessness of the persecution, that this had never happened before. But it had happened now. There was not a single depth-charge left – not one. The fangs were drawn, the defences were down. It was only a matter of time before the wolf-packs discovered that they could strike at will. . . .

And with the dawn, of course, came dawn Action Stations, or what would have been dawn stations had the men not already been closed up for fifteen hours, fifteen endless hours of intense cold and suffering, fifteen hours during which the crew of the *Ulysses* had been sustained by cocoa and one bully-beef sandwich, thin, sliced and stale, for there had been no time to bake the previous day. But dawn stations were profoundly significant in themselves: they prolonged the waiting another interminable two hours – and to a man rocking on his feet from unimaginable fatigue, literally holding convulsively jerking eyelids apart with finger and thumb while a starving brain, which is less a brain than a well fine-drawn agony, begs him to let go, let go just for a second, just this once and never again, even a minute is brutal eternity: and they were still more important in that they were recognized as the Ithuriel hour of the Russian Convoys, the testing time when every man stood out clearly for what he was. And for the crew of a mutiny ship, for men already tried and condemned, for physically broken and mentally scourged men who neither could nor would ever be the same again in body or mind, the men of the *Ulysses* had no need to stand in shame. Not all, of course, they were only human; but many had found, or were finding, that the point of no return was not necessarily the edge of the precipice: it could be the bottom of the valley, the beginning of the long climb up the far slope, and when a man had once begun that climb he never looked back to that other side.

For some men, neither precipice nor valley ever existed. Men like Carrington, for instance. Eighteen consecutive hours on the bridge now, he was still his own indestructible self, alert with that relaxed watchfulness that never flagged, a man of infinite endurance, a man who could never crack, who you knew could never crack, for the imagination baulked at the very idea. Why he was what he was, no man could tell. Such, too, were men like Chief Petty Officer Hartley, like Chief Stoker Hendry, like Colour-Sergeant Evans and Sergeant MacIntosh; four men strangely alike, big, tough, kindly, no longer young, steeped in the traditions of the Service. Taciturn, never heard to speak of themselves, they were under no illusions as to their importance: they knew – as any Naval officer would be the first to admit – that, as the senior NCOs, they, and not any officer, were the backbone of the Royal Navy; and it was from their heavy sense of responsibility that sprung their rock-like stability. And then of course, there were men – a handful only – like Turner and the Kapok Kid and Dodson, whom dawn found as men above themselves, men revelling in danger and exhaustion, for only thus could they realize themselves, for only this had they been born. And finally, men like Vallery, who had collapsed just after midnight, and was still asleep in the shelter, and Surgeon Commander Brooks: wisdom was their sheet anchor, a clear appreciation of the relative insignificance both of themselves and the fate of FR77, a coldly intellectual appraisal of, married to an infinite compassion for, the follies and suffering of mankind.

At the other end of the scale, dawn found men – a few dozen, perhaps – gone beyond recovery. Gone in selfishness, in self-pity and in fear, like Carslake, gone because their armour, the trappings of authority, had been stripped off them, like Hastings, or gone, like Leading SBA Johnson and a score of others, because they had been pushed too far and had no sheet anchor to hold them.

And between the two extremes were those – the bulk of the men – who had touched zero and found that endurance can be infinite – and found in this realization the springboard for recovery. The other side of the valley *could* be climbed, but not without a staff. For Nicholls, tired beyond words from a long night standing braced against the operating table in the surgery, the staff was pride and shame. For Leading Seaman Doyle, crouched miserably into the shelter of the for'ard funnel, watching the pinched agony, the perpetual shivering of his young midships pom-pom crew, it was pity; he would, of course, have denied this, blasphemously. For young Spicer, Tyndall's devoted pantry-boy, it was pity, too – pity and a savage grief for the dying man in the Admiral's cabin. Even with both legs amputated below the knee, Tyndall should not have been dying. But the fight, the resistance was gone, and Brooks knew old Giles would be glad to go. And for scores, perhaps for hundreds, for men like the tubercular-ridden McQuater, chilled to death in sodden clothes, but no longer staggering drunkenly round the hoist in 'Y' Turret, for the heavy rolling kept the water on the move: like Petersen, recklessly squandering his giant strength in helping his exhausted mates: like Chrysler, whose keen young eyes, invaluable now that Radar was gone, never ceased to scan the horizons: for men like these, the staff was Vallery, the tremendous respect and affection in which he was held, the sure knowledge that they could never let him down.

These, then, were the staffs, the intangible sheet anchors that held the *Ulysses* together that bleak and bitter dawn – pride, pity, shame, affection, grief – and the basic instinct for self-preservation although the last, by now, was an almost negligible factor. Two things were never taken into the slightest account as the springs of endurance: never mentioned, never even considered, they did not exist for the crew of the *Ulysses*: two things the sentimentalists at home, the gallant leader writers of the popular press, the propagandizing purveyors of nationalistic claptrap would have had the world believe to be the source of inspiration and endurance – hatred of the enemy, love of kinsfolk and country.

There was no hatred of the enemy. Knowledge is the prelude to hate, and they did not know the enemy. Men cursed the enemy, respected him, feared him and killed him if they could: if they didn't, the enemy would kill them. Nor did men see themselves as fighting for King and country: they saw the necessity for war, but objected to camouflaging this necessity under a spurious cloak of perfervid patriotism: they were just doing what they were told, and if they didn't, they would be stuck against a wall and shot. Love of kinsfolk – that had some validity, but not much. It was natural to want to protect your kin, but this was an equation where the validity varied according to the factor of distance. It was a trifle difficult for a man crouched in his ice-coated Oerlikon cockpit off the shores of Bear Island to visualize himself as protecting that rose-covered cottage in the Cotswolds. . . . But for the rest, the synthetic national hatreds and the carefully cherished myth of King and country, these are nothing and less than nothing when mankind stands at the last frontier of hope and endurance: for only the basic, simple human emotions, the positive ones of love and grief and pity and distress, can carry a man across that last frontier.

Noon, and still the convoy, closed up in tight formation now, rolled eastwards in the blinding snow. The alarm halfway through dawn stations had been the last that morning. Thirty-six hours to go, now, only thirty-six hours. And if this weather continued, the strong wind and blinding snow that made flying impossible, the near-zero visibility and heavy seas that would blind any periscope . . . there was always that chance. Only thirty-six hours.

Admiral John Tyndall died a few minutes after noon. Brooks, who had sat with him all morning, officially entered the cause of death as 'post-operative shock and exposure.' The truth was that Giles had died because he no longer wished to live. His professional reputation was gone: his faith, his confidence in himself were gone, and there was only remorse for the hundreds of men who had died: and with both legs gone, the only life he had ever known, the life he had so loved and cherished and to which he had devoted forty-five glad and unsparing years, that life, too, was gone for ever. Giles died gladly, willingly. Just on noon he recovered consciousness, looked at Brooks and Vallery with a smile from which every trace of madness had vanished. Brooks winced at the grey smile, mocking shadow of the famous guffaw of the Giles of another day. Then he closed his eyes and muttered something about his family – Brooks knew he had no family. His eyes opened again, he saw Vallery as if for the first time, rolled his eyes till he saw Spicer. 'A chair for the Captain, my boy.' Then he died.

He was buried at two o'clock, in the heart of a blizzard. The Captain's voice, reading the burial service, was shredded away by snow and wind: the Union flag was flapping emptily on the tilted board before the men knew he was gone: the bugle notes were broken and distant and lost, far away and fading like the horns of Elfland: and then the men, two hundred of them at least, turned silently away and trudged back to their frozen mess-decks.

Barely half an hour later, the blizzard had died, vanished as suddenly as it had come. The wind, too, had eased, and though the sky was still dark and heavy with snow, though the seas were still heavy enough to roll 15,000-ton ships through a 30° arc, it was clear that the deterioration in the weather had stopped. On the bridge, in the turrets, in the mess-decks, men avoided each other's eyes and said nothing.

Just before 1500, the *Vectra* picked up an Asdic contact. Vallery received the report, hesitated over his decision. If he sent the *Vectra* to investigate, and if the *Vectra* located the U-boat accurately and confined herself, as she would have to do, to describing tight circles above the submarine, the reason for this freedom from depth-charging would occur to the U-boat captain within minutes. And then it would only be a matter of time – until he decided it was safe to surface and use his radio – that every U-boat north of the Circle would know that FR77 could be attacked with impunity. Further, it was unlikely that any torpedo attack would be made under such weather conditions. Not only was periscope observation almost impossible in the heavy seas, but the U-boat itself would be a most unstable firing platform: wave motion is not confined to the surface of the water – the effects can be highly uncomfortable and unstabilizing thirty, forty, fifty feet down – and are appreciable, under extreme conditions, at a depth of almost a hundred feet. On the other hand, the U-boat captain might take a 1000–1 chance, might strike home with a lucky hit. Vallery ordered the *Vectra* to investigate.

He was too late. The order would have been too late anyway. The *Vectra* was still winking acknowledgment of the signal, had not begun to turn, when the rumble of a heavy explosion reached the bridge of the *Ulysses*. All eyes swept round a full circle of the horizon, searching for smoke and flame, for the canted deck and slewing ship that would show where the torpedo had gone home. They found no sign, none whatsoever, until almost half a minute had passed. Then they noticed, almost casually, that the *Electra*, leading ship in the starboard line, was slowing up, coming to a powerless stop, already settling in the water on an even keel, with no trace of tilt either for'ard or aft. Almost certainly, she had been holed in the engine-room.

The Aldis on the *Sirrus* had begun to flash. Bentley read the message, turned to Vallery.

'Commander Orr requests permission to go alongside, port side, take off survivors.'

'Port, is it?' Turner nodded. 'The sub's blind side. It's a fair chance, sir – in a calm sea. As it is . . .' He looked over at the *Sirrus*, rolling heavily in the beam sea, and shrugged. 'Won't do her paintwork any good.'

'Her cargo?' Vallery asked. 'Any idea? Explosives?' He looked round, saw the mute headshakes, turned to Bentley.

'Ask *Electra* if she's carrying any explosives as cargo.'

Bentley's Aldis chattered, fell silent. After half a minute, it was clear that there was going to be no reply.

'Power gone, perhaps, or his Aldis smashed,' the Kapok Kid ventured. 'How about one flag for explosives, two for none?'

Vallery nodded in satisfaction. 'You heard, Bentley?'

He looked over the starboard quarter as the message went out. The *Vectra* was almost a mile distant rolling, one minute, pitching the next as she came round in a tight circle. She had found the killer, and her depth-charge racks were empty.

Vallery swung back, looked across to the *Electra*. Still no reply, nothing. . . . Then he saw two flags fluttering up to the yardarm.

'Signal the *Sirrus*,' he ordered. ' "Go ahead: exercise extreme care." '

Suddenly, he felt Turner's hand on his arm.

'Can you hear 'em?' Turner asked.

'Hear what?' Vallery demanded.

'Lord only knows. It's the *Vectra*. Look!'

Vallery followed the pointing finger. At first, he could see nothing, then all at once he saw little geysers of water leaping up in the *Vectra*'s wake, geysers swiftly extinguished by the heavy seas. Then, faintly, his straining ear caught the faraway murmur of underwater explosions, all but inaudible against the wind.

'What the devil's the *Vectra* doing?' Vallery demanded. 'And what's she using?'

'Looks like fireworks to me,' Turner grunted. 'What do you think, Number One?'

'Scuttling charges – 25-pounders,' Carrington said briefly.

'He's right, sir' Turner admitted. 'Of course that's what they are. Mind you, he might as well be using fireworks,' he added disparagingly.

But the Commander was wrong. A scuttling charge has less than a tenth part of the disruptive power of a depth-charge – but one lodged snugly in the conning-tower or exploding alongside a steering plane could be almost as lethal. Turner had hardly finished speaking when a U-boat – the first the *Ulysses* had seen above water for almost six months – porpoised high above the surface of the sea, hung there for two or three seconds, then crashed down on even keel, wallowing wickedly in the troughs between the waves. The dramatic abruptness of her appearance – one moment the empty sea, the next a U-boat rolling in full view of the entire convoy – took every ship by surprise – including the *Vectra*. She was caught on the wrong foot, moving away on the outer leg of a figure-of-eight turn. Her pom-pom opened up immediately, but the pom-pom, a notoriously inaccurate gun in the best of circumstances, is a hopeless proposition on the rolling, heeling deck of a destroyer making a fast turn in heavy weather: the Oerlikons registered a couple of hits on the conning-tower, twin Lewises peppered the hull with as much effect as a horde of angry hornets; but by the time the *Vectra* was round, her main armament coming to bear, the U-boat had disappeared slowly under the surface.

In spite of this, the *Vectra*'s 4·7s opened up, firing into the sea where the U-boat had submerged, but stopping almost immediately when two shells in succession had ricocheted off the water and whistled dangerously through the convoy. She steadied on course, raced over the position of the submerged U-boat: watchers on the *Ulysses*, binoculars to their eyes, could just distinguish duffel-coated figures on the *Vectra*'s poop-deck hurling more scuttling charges over the side. Almost at once, the *Vectra*'s helm went hard over and she clawed her way back south again, guns at maximum depression pointing down over her starboard side.

The U-boat must have been damaged, more severely this time, by either the shells or the last charges. Again she surfaced, even more violently than before, in a seething welter of foam, and again the *Vectra* was caught on the wrong foot, for the submarine had surfaced off her port bow, three cable-lengths away.

And this time, the U-boat was up to stay. Whatever Captain and crew lacked, it wasn't courage. The hatch was open, and men were swarming over the side of the conning-tower to man the gun, in a token gesture of defiance against crushing odds.

The first two men over the side never reached the gun – breaking, sweeping waves, waves that towered high above the submarine's deck, washed them over the side and they were gone. But others flung themselves forward to take their places, frantically training their gun through a 90° arc to bear on the onrushing bows of the *Vectra*. Incredibly – for the seas were washing over the decks, seas which kept tearing the men from their posts, and the submarine was rolling with impossible speed and violence – their first shell, fired over open sights, smashed squarely into the bridge of the *Vectra*. The first shell and the last shell, for the crew suddenly crumpled and died, sinking down by the gun or pitching convulsively over the side.

It was a massacre. The *Vectra* had two Bolton-Paul Defiant night-fighter turrets, quadruple hydraulic turrets complete with astrodome, bolted to her fo'c'sle, and these had opened up simultaneously, firing, between them, something like a fantastic total of 300 shells every ten seconds. That often misused cliché 'hail of lead' was completely accurate here. It was impossible for a man to live two seconds on the exposed deck of that U-boat, to hope to escape that lethal storm. Man after man kept flinging himself over the coaming in suicidal gallantry, but none reached the gun.

Afterwards, no one aboard the *Ulysses* could say when they first realized that the *Vectra*, pitching steeply through the heavy seas, was going to ram the U-boat. Perhaps her Captain had never intended to do so. Perhaps he had expected the U-boat to submerge, had intended to carry away conning-tower and periscope standard, to make sure that she could not escape again. Perhaps he had been killed when that shell had struck the bridge. Or perhaps he had changed his mind at the last second, for the *Vectra*, which had been arrowing in on the conning-tower, suddenly slewed sharply to starboard.

For an instant, it seemed that she might just clear the U-boat's bows, but the hope died the second it was born. Plunging heavily down the sheering side of a gaping trough, the *Vectra*'s forefoot smashed down and through the hull of the submarine, some thirty feet aft of the bows, slicing through the toughened steel of the pressure hull as if it were cardboard. She was still plunging, still driving down, when two shattering explosions, so close together as to be blurred into one giant blast, completely buried both vessels under a sky-rocketing mushroom of boiling water and twisted steel. The why of the explosion was pure conjecture; but what had happened was plain enough. Some freak of chance must have triggered off the TNT – normally an extremely stable and inert disruptive – in a warhead in one of the U-boat's tubes: and then the torpedoes in the storage racks behind and possibly, probably even, the for'ard magazine of the *Vectra* had gone up in sympathetic detonation.

Slowly, deliberately almost, the great clouds of water fell back into the sea, and the *Vectra* and the U-boat – or what little was left of them – came abruptly into view. To the watchers on the *Ulysses*, it was inconceivable that either of them should still be afloat. The U-boat was very deep in the water, seemed to end abruptly just for'ards of the gun platform: the *Vectra* looked as if some great knife had sheared her athwartships, just for'ard of the bridge. The rest was gone, utterly gone. And throughout the convoy unbelieving minds were still wildly rejecting the evidence of their eyes when the shattered hull of the *Vectra* lurched into the same trough as the U-boat, rolled heavily, wearily, over on top of her, bridge and mast cradling the conning-tower of the submarine. And then the water closed over them and they were gone, locked together to the bottom of the sea.

The last ships in the convoy were two miles away now, and in the broken seas, at that distance, it was impossible to see whether there were any survivors. It did not seem likely. And if there were, if there were men over there, struggling, swimming, shouting for help in the murderous cold of that glacial sea, they would be dying already. And they would have been dead long before any rescue ship could even have turned round. The convoy steamed on, beating steadily east. All but two, that is – the *Electra* and the *Sirrus*.

The *Electra* lay beam on to the seas, rolling slowly, sluggishly, dead in the water. She had now a list of almost 15° to port. Her decks, fore and aft of the bridge, were lined with waiting men. They had given up their attempt to abandon ship by lifeboat when they had seen the *Sirrus* rolling up behind them, fine on the port quarter. A boat had been swung out on its davits, and with the listing of the *Electra* and the rolling of the sea it had proved impossible to recover it. It hung now far out from the ship's side, swinging wildly at the end of its davits about twenty feet above the sea. On his approach, Orr had twice sent angry signals, asking the falls to be cut. But the lifeboat remained there, a menacing pendulum in the track of the *Sirrus*: panic, possibly, but more likely winch brakes jammed solid with ice. In either event, there was no time to be lost: another ten minutes and the *Electra* would be gone.

The *Sirrus* made two runs past in all – Orr had no intention of stopping alongside, of being trampled under the the 15,000-ton deadweight of a toppling freighter. On his first run he steamed slowly by at five knots, at a distance of twenty feet – the nearest he dared go with the set of the sea rolling both ships towards each other at the same instant.

As the *Sirrus*'s swinging bows slid up past the bridge of the *Electra*, the waiting men began to jump. They jumped as the *Sirrus*'s fo'c'sle reared up level with their deck, they jumped as it plunged down fifteen, twenty feet below. One man carrying a suitcase and Burberry stepped nonchalantly across both sets of guard-rails during the split second that they were relatively motionless to each other: others crashed sickeningly on to the ice-coated steel deck far below, twisting ankles, fracturing legs and thighs, dislocating hip-joints. And two men jumped and missed; above the bedlam of noise, men heard the blood-chilling, bubbling scream of one as the swinging hulls crushed the life out of him, the desperate, terror-stricken cries of the other as the great, iron wall of the *Electra* guided him into the screws of the *Sirrus*.

It was just then that it happened and there could be no possible reflection on Commander Orr's seamanship: he had handled the *Sirrus* brilliantly. But even his skill was helpless against these two successive freak waves, twice the size of the others. The first flung the *Sirrus* close in to the *Electra*, then passing under the *Electra*, lurched her steeply to port as the second wave heeled the *Sirrus* far over to starboard. There was a grinding, screeching crash. The *Sirrus*'s guard-rails and upper side plates buckled and tore along a 150-foot length: simultaneously, the lifeboat smashed endwise into the front of the bridge, shattering into a thousand pieces. Immediately, the telegraphs jangled, the water boiled whitely at the *Sirrus*'s stern – shocked realization of its imminence and death itself must have been only a merciful hair's-breadth apart for the unfortunate man in the water – and then the destroyer was clear, sheering sharply away from the *Electra*.

In five minutes the *Sirrus* was round again. It was typical of Orr's ice-cold, calculating nerve and of the luck that never deserted him that he should this time choose to rub the *Sirrus*'s shattered starboard side along the length of the *Electra* – she was too low in the water now to fall on him – and that he should do so in a momentary spell of slack water. Willing hands caught men as they jumped, cushioned their fall. Thirty seconds and the destroyer was gone again and the decks of the *Electra* were deserted. Two minutes later and a muffled roar shook the sinking ship – her boilers going. And then she toppled slowly over on her side: masts and smokestack lay along the surface of the sea, dipped and vanished: the straight-back of bottom and keel gleamed fractionally, blackly, against the grey of sea and sky, and was gone. For a minute, great gouts of air rushed turbulently to the surface. By and by the bubbles grew smaller and smaller and then there were no more.

The *Sirrus* steadied on course, crowded decks throbbing as she began to pick up speed, to overtake the convoy. Convoy No. FR77. The convoy the Royal Navy would always want to forget. Thirty-six ships had left Scapa and St John's. Now there were twelve, only twelve. And still almost thirty-two hours to the Kola Inlet. . . .

Moodily, even his tremendous vitality and zest temporarily subdued, Turner watched the *Sirrus* rolling up astern. Abruptly he turned away, looked furtively, pityingly at Captain Vallery, no more now than a living skeleton driven by God only knew what mysterious force to wrest hour after impossible hour from death. And for Vallery now, death, even the hope of it, Turner suddenly realized, must be infinitely sweet. He looked, and saw the shock and sorrow in that grey mask, and he cursed, bitterly, silently. And then these tired, dull eyes were on him and Turner hurriedly cleared his throat.

'How many survivors does that make in the *Sirrus* now?' he asked.

Vallery lifted weary shoulders in the ghost of a shrug.

'No idea, Commander. A hundred, possibly more. Why?'

'A hundred,' Turner mused. 'And no-survivors-will-be-picked-up. I'm just wondering what old Orr's going to say when he dumps that little lot in Admiral Starr's lap when we get back to Scapa Flow!'

Chapter Thirteen

Saturday Afternoon

The *Sirrus* was still a mile astern when her Aldis started flickering. Bentley took the message, turned to Vallery.

'Signal, sir. "Have 25–30 injured men aboard. Three very serious cases, perhaps dying. Urgently require doctor." '

'Acknowledge,' Vallery said. He hesitated a moment, then: 'My compliments to Surgeon-Lieutenant Nicholls. Ask him to come to the bridge.' He turned to the Commander, grinned faintly. 'I somehow don't see Brooks at his athletic best in a breeches buoy on a day like this. It's going to be quite a crossing.'

Turner looked again at the *Sirrus*, occasionally swinging through a 40° arc as she rolled and crashed her way up from the west.

'It'll be no picnic,' he agreed. 'Besides, breeches buoys aren't made to accommodate the likes of our venerable chief surgeon.' Funny, Turner thought, how matter-of-fact and offhand everyone was: nobody had as much as mentioned the *Vectra* since she'd rammed the U-boat.

The gate creaked. Vallery turned round slowly, acknowledged Nicholls's sketchy salute.

'The *Sirrus* needs a doctor,' he said without preamble. 'How do you fancy it?'

Nicholls steadied himself against the canted bridge and the rolling of the cruiser. Leave the *Ulysses* – suddenly, he hated the thought, was amazed at himself for his reaction. He, Johnny Nicholls, unique, among the officers anyway, in his thorough-going detestation and intolerance of all things naval – to feel like that! Must be going soft in the head. And just as suddenly he knew that his mind wasn't slipping, knew why he wanted to stay. It was not a matter of pride or principle or sentiment: it was just that – well, just that he belonged. The feeling of belonging – even to himself he couldn't put it more accurately, more clearly than that, but it affected him strangely, powerfully. Suddenly he became aware that curious eyes were on him, looked out in confusion over the rolling sea.

'Well?' Vallery's voice was edged with impatience.

'I don't fancy it at all,' Nicholls said frankly. 'But of course I'll go, sir. Right now?'

'As soon as you can get your stuff together,' Vallery nodded.

'That's now. We have an emergency kit packed all the time.' He cast a jaundiced eye over the heavy sea again. 'What am I supposed to do sir – jump?'

'Perish the thought!' Turner clapped him on the back with a large and jovial hand. 'You haven't a thing to worry about,' he boomed cheerfully. 'you positively won't feel a thing – these, if I recall rightly, were your exact words to me when you extracted that old molar of mine two-three weeks back.' He winced in painful recollection. 'Breeches buoy, laddie, breeches buoy!'

'Breeches buoy!' Nicholls protested. 'Haven't noticed the weather, have you? I'll be going up and down like a blasted yo-yo!'

'The ignorance of youth,' Turner shook his head sadly. 'We'll be turning into the sea, of course. It'll be like a ride in a Rolls, my boy! We're going to rig it now.' He turned away. 'Chrysler – get on to Chief Petty Officer Hartley. Ask him to come up to the bridge.'

Chrysler gave no sign of having heard. He was in his usual favourite position these days – gloved hands on the steam pipes, the top half of his face crushed into the rubber eyepiece of the powerful binoculars on the starboard searchlight control. Every few seconds a hand would drop, revolve the milled training rack a fraction. Then again the complete immobility.

'Chrysler!' Turner roared. 'Are you deaf?'

Three, four, five more seconds passed in silence. Every eye was on Chrysler when he suddenly jerked back, glanced down at the bearing indicator, then swung round. His face was alive with excitement.

'Green one-double-oh!' he shouted. 'Green one-double-oh! Aircraft. Just on the horizon!' He fairly flung himself back at his binoculars. 'Four, seven – no, *ten*! Ten aircraft!' he yelled.

'Green one-double-oh?' Turner had his glasses to his eyes. 'Can't see a thing! Are you sure, boy?' he called anxiously.

'Still the same, sir.' There was no mistaking the agitated conviction in the young voice.

Turner was through the gate and beside him in four swift steps. 'Let me have a look,' he ordered. He gazed through the glasses, twisted the training rack once or twice, then stepped back slowly, heavy eyebrows lowering in anger.

'There's something bloody funny here, young man!' he growled. 'Either your eyesight or your imagination? And if you ask me—'

'He's right,' Carrington interrupted calmly. 'I've got 'em, too.'

'So have I, sir!' Bentley shouted.

Turner wheeled back to the mounted glasses, looked through them briefly, looked round at Chrysler.

'Remind me to apologize some day!' he smiled, and was back on the compass platform before he had finished speaking.

'Signal to convoy,' Vallery was saying rapidly. 'Code H. Full ahead, Number One. Bosun's mate? Broadcaster: stand by all guns. Commander?'

'Sir?'

'Independent targets, independent fire all AA guns? Agreed? And the turrets?'

'Couldn't say yet. . . . Chrysler, can you make out—'

'Condors, sir,' Chrysler anticipated him.

'Condors!' Turner stared in disbeleief. 'A dozen Condors! Are you sure that . . . Oh, all right, all right!' he broke off hastily. 'Condors they are.' He shook his head in wonderment, turned to Vallery. 'Where's my bloody tin hat? Condors, he says!'

'So Condors they are,' Vallery repeated, smiling. Turner marvelled at the repose, the unruffled calm.

'Bridge targets, independent fire control for all turrets?' Vallery went on.

'I think so, sir.' Turner looked at the two communication ratings just aft of the compass platform – one each on the group phones to the for'ard and after turrets. 'Ears pinned back, you two. And hop to it when you get the word.'

Vallery beckoned to Nicholls.

'Better get below, young man,' he advised. 'Sorry your little trip's been postponed.'

'I'm not,' Nicholls said bluntly.

'No?' Vallery was smiling. 'Scared?'

'No, sir,' Nicholls smiled back. 'Not scared. And you know I wasn't.'

'I know you weren't,' Vallery agreed quietly. 'I know – and thank you.'

He watched Nicholls walk off the bridge, beckoned to the WT messenger, then turned to the Kapok Kid.

'When was our last signal to the Admiralty, Pilot? Have a squint at the log.'

'Noon yesterday,' said the Kapok Kid readily.

'Don't know what I'll do without you,' Vallery murmured. 'Present position?'

'72.20 north, 13.40 east.'

'Thank you.' He looked at Turner. 'No point in radio silence now, Commander?'

Turner shook his head.

'Take this message,' Vallery said quickly. 'To DNO, London. . . . How are our friends doing, Commander?'

'Circling well to the west, sir. Usual high altitude, gambit from the stern, I suppose,' he added morosely. 'Still,' he brightened, 'cloud level's barely a thousand feet.'

Vallery nodded. 'FR77, 1600. 72.20, 13.40. Steady on 090. Force 9, north, heavy swell: "Situation desperate. Deeply regret Admiral Tyndall died 1200 today. Tanker *Vytura* torpedoed last night, sunk by self. *Washington State* sunk 0145 today. *Vectra* sunk 1515, collision U-boat. *Electra* sunk 1530. Am being heavily attacked by twelve, minimum twelve, Focke-Wulf 200s." A reasonable assumption, I think, Commander,' he said wryly, 'and it'll shake their Lordships. They're of the opinion there aren't so many Condors in the whole of Norway. "Imperative send help. Air cover essential. Advise immediately." Get that off at once, will you?'

'Your nose, sir!' Turner said sharply.

'Thank you.' Vallery rubbed the frostbite, dead white in the haggard grey and blue of his face, gave up after a few seconds: the effort was more trouble than it was worth, drained away too much of his tiny reserves of strength. 'My God, it's bitter, Commander!' he murmured quietly.

Shivering, he pulled himself to his feet, swept his glasses over FR77. Code H was being obeyed. The ships were scattered over the sea apparently at random, broken out from the two lines ahead which would have made things far too simple for bomb-aimers in aircraft attacking from astern. They would have to aim now for individual targets. Scattered, but not too scattered – close enough together to derive mutual benefit from the convoy's concerted barrage. Vallery nodded to himself in satisfaction and twisted round, his glasses swivelling to the west.

There was no mistaking them now, he thought – they were Condors, all right. Almost dead astern now, massive wingtips dipping, the big four-engined planes banked slowly, ponderously to starboard, then straightened on a 180° overtaking course. And they were climbing, steadily climbing.

Two things were suddenly clear to Vallery, two things the *enemy* obviously knew. They had known where to find FR77 – the Luftwaffe was not given to sending heavy bombers out over the Arctic on random hazard: they hadn't even bothered to send Charlie on reconnaissance. For a certainty, some submarine had located them earlier on, given their position and course: at any distance at all, their chance of seeing a periscope in that heavy sea had been remote. Further, the Germans *knew* that the *Ulysses*'s radar was gone. The Focke-Wulfs were climbing to gain the low cloud, would break cover only seconds before it was time to bomb. Against radar-controlled fire, at such close range, it would have been near suicide. But they *knew* it was safe.

Even as he watched, the last of the labouring Condors climbed through the low, heavy ceiling, was completely lost to sight. Vallery shrugged wearily, lowered his binoculars.

'Bentley?'

'Sir?'

'Code R. Immediate.'

The flags fluttered up. For fifteen, twenty seconds – it seemed ten times as long as that to the impatient Captain – nothing happened. And then, like rolling toy marionettes under the hand of a master puppeteer, the bows of every ship in the convoy began to swing round – those to the port of the *Ulysses* to the north, those to the starboard to the south. When the Condors broke through – two minutes, at the most, Vallery reckoned, they would find beneath them only the empty sea. Empty, that is, except for the *Ulysses* and the *Stirling*, ships admirably equipppped to take care of themselves. And then the Condors would find themselves under heavy cross-fire from the merchant ships and destroyers, and too late – at that low altitude, much too late – to alter course for fore-and-aft bombing runs on the freighters. Vallery smiled wryly to himself. As a defensive tactic, it was little enough, but the best he could do in the circumstances. . . . He could hear Turner barking orders through the loudspeaker, was more than content to leave the defence of the ship in the Commander's competent hands. If only he himself didn't feel so tired. . . .

Ninety seconds passed, a hundred, two minutes – and still no sign of the Condors. A hundred eyes stared out into the cloud-wrack astern: it remained obstinately, tantalizingly grey and featureless.

Two and a half minutes passed. Still there was nothing.

'Anybody seen anything?' Vallery asked anxiously. His eyes never left that patch of cloud astern. 'Nothing? Nothing at all?' The silence remained, oppressive, unbroken.

Three minutes. Three and a half. Four. Vallery looked away to rest his straining eyes, caught Turner looking at him, caught the growing apprehension, the slow dawn and strengthening of surmise in the lean face. Wordlessly, at the same instant, they swung round, staring out into the sky ahead.

'That's it!' Vallery said quickly. 'You're right, Commander you must be!' He was aware that everyone had turned now, was peering ahead as intently as himself. 'They've by-passed us, they're going to take us from ahead. Warn the guns! Dear God, they almost had us!' he whispered softly.

'Eyes skinned, everyone!' Turner boomed. The apprehension was gone, the irrepressible joviality, the gratifying anticipation of action was back again. 'And I mean everyone! We're all in the same boat together. No joke intended. Fourteen days' leave to the first man to sight a Condor!'

'Effective as from when?' the Kapok Kid asked dryly.

Turner grinned at him. Then the smile died, the head lifted sharply in sudden attention.

'Can you hear 'em?' he asked. His voice was soft, almost as if he feared the enemy might be listening. 'They're up there, somewhere – damned if I can tell where, though. If only that wind—'

The vicious, urgent thudding of the boat-deck Oerlikons stopped him dead in mid-sentence, had him whirling round and plunging for the broadcast transmitter in one galvanic, concerted movement. But even then he was too late – he would have been too late anyway. The Condors – the first three in line ahead, were already visible – were already through the cloud, 500 feet up and barely half a mile away – dead astern. *Astern.* The bombers must have circled back to the west as soon as they had reached the clouds, completely fooled them as to their intentions. . . . Six seconds – six seconds is time and to spare for even a heavy bomber to come less than half a mile in a shallow dive. There was barely time for realization, for the first bitter welling of mortification and chagrin when the Condors were on them.

It was almost dusk, now, the weird half-light of the Arctic twilight. Tracers, glowing hot pinpoints of light streaking out through the darkening sky, were clearly seen, at first swinging erratically, fading away to extinction in the far distance, then steadying, miraculously dying in the instant of birth as they sank home into the fuselages of the swooping Condors. But time was too short – the guns were on target for a maximum of two seconds – and these giant Focke-Wulfs had a tremendous capacity for absorbing punishment. The leading Condor levelled out about three hundred feet, its medium 250-kilo bombs momentarily paralleling its line of flight, then arching down lazily towards the *Ulysses*. At once the Condor pulled its nose up in maximum climb, the four great engines labouring in desynchronized clamour, as it sought the protection of the clouds.

The bombs missed. They missed by about thirty feet, exploding on contact with the water just abaft the bridge. For the men in the TS, engine-and boiler-rooms, the crash and concussion must have been frightful – literally earshattering. Waterspouts, twenty feet in diameter at their turbulent bases, streaked up whitely into the twilight, high above the truncated masts, hung there momentarily, then collapsed in drenching cascades on the bridge and boat-deck aft, soaking, saturating, every gunner on the pom-pom and in the open Oerlikon cockpits. The temperature stood at 2° above zero – 30° of frost.

More dangerously, the blinding sheets of water completely unsighted the gunners. Apart from a lone Oerlikon on a sponson below the starboard side of the bridge, the next Condor pressed home its attack against a minimum of resistance. The approach was perfect, dead fore-and-aft on the centre line; but the pilot overshot, probably in his anxiety to hold course. Three bombs this time: for a second, it seemed that they must miss, but the first smashed into the fo'c'sle between the breakwater and the capstan, exploding in the flat below, heaving up the deck in a tangled wreckage of broken steel. Even as the explosion died, the men on the bridge could hear a curious clanking rattle: the explosion must have shattered the fo'c'sle capstan and Blake stopper simultaneously, and sheared the retaining shackle on the anchor cable, and the starboard anchor, completely out of control, was plummeting down to the depths of the Arctic.

The other bombs fell into the sea directly ahead, and from the *Stirling*, a mile ahead, it seemed that the *Ulysses* disappeared under the great column of water. But the water subsided, and the *Ulysses* steamed on, apparently unharmed. From dead ahead, the sweeping lift of the bows hid all damage, and there was neither flames nor smoke – hundreds of gallons of water, falling from the sky and pouring in through the great jagged holes in the deck, had killed any fire there was. The *Ulysses* was still a lucky ship. . . . And then, at last, after twenty months of the fantastic escapes, the fabulous good fortune that had made her a legend, a byword for immunity throughout all the north, the luck of the *Ulysses* ran out.

Ironically, the *Ulysses* brought disaster on herself. The main armament, the 5.25s aft, had opened up now, was pumping its 100-lb. shells at the diving bombers, at point-blank range and over equivalent of open sights. The very first shell from 'X' turret sheared away the starboard wing of the third Condor between the engines, tore it completely away to spin slowly like a fluttering leaf into the darkly-rolling sea. For a fraction of a second the Focke-Wulf held on course, then abruptly the nose tipped over and the giant plane screamed down in an almost vertical dive, her remaining engines inexplicably accelerating to a deafening crescendo as she hurtled arrow-straight for the deck of the *Ulysses*.

There was no time to take any avoiding action, no time to think, no time even to hope. A cluster of jettisoned bombs crashed into the boiling wake – the *Ulysses was* already doing upwards of thirty knots – and two more crashed through the poop-deck, the first exploding in the after seamen's mess-deck, the other in the marines' mess-deck. One second later, with a tremendous roar and in a blinding sheet of gasoline flame, the Condor itself, at a speed of upwards of three hundred m.p.h., crashed squarely into the front of 'Y' turret.

Incredibly, that was the last attack on the *Ulysses* – incredibly, because the *Ulysses* was defenceless now, wide open to any air attack from astern. 'Y' turret was gone, 'X' turret, still magically undamaged, was half-buried under the splintered wreckage of the Condor, blinded by the smoke and leaping flame. The boat-deck Oerlikons, too, had fallen silent. The gunners, half-drowned under the deluge of less than a minute ago, were being frantically dragged from their cockpits: a difficult enough task at any time, it was almost impossible with their clothes already frozen solid, their duffels cracking and crackling like splintering matchwood as the men were dragged over the side of their cockpits. With all speed, they were rushed below, thrust into the galley passage to thaw, literally to thaw: agony, excruciating agony, but the only alternative to the quick and certain death which would have come to them in their ice-bound cockpits.

The remaining Condors had pulled away in a slow climbing turn to starboard. They were surrounded, bracketed fore and aft and on either side, by scores of woolly, expanding puffs of exploding AA shells, but they flew straight through these, charmed, unhurt. Already, they were beginning to disappear into the clouds, to settle down on a south-east course for home. Strange, Vallery thought vaguely, one would have expected them to hammer home their initial advantage of surprise, to concentrate on the crippled *Ulysses*: certainly, thus far the Condor crews had shown no lack of courage. . . . He gave it up, turned his attention to more immediate worries. And there was plenty to worry about.

The *Ulysses* was heavily on fire aft – a deck and mess-deck fire, admittedly, but potentially fatal for all that – 'X' and 'Y' magazines were directly below. Already, dozens of men from the damage control parties were running aft, stumbling and falling on the rolling ice-covered deck, unwinding the hose drums behind them, occasionally falling flat on their faces as two ice-bound coils locked together, the abruptly tightening hose jerking them off their feet. Others stumbled past them, carrying the big, red foam-extinguishers on their shoulders or under their arms. One unfortunate seaman – AB Ferry, who had left the Sick Bay in defiance of strict orders – running down the port alley past the shattered Canteen, slipped and fell abreast 'X' turret: the port wing of the Condor, even as it had sheared off and plunged into the sea, had torn away the guard-rails here, and Ferry, hands and feet scrabbling frantically at the smooth ice of the deck, his broken arm clawing uselessly at one of the remaining stanchions, slid slowly, inevitably over the side and was gone. For a second, the high-pitched, fear-stricken shriek rose thin and clear above the roaring of the flames, died abruptly as the water closed over him. The propellers were almost immediately below.

The men with the extinguishers were the first into action, as, indeed, they had to be when fighting a petrol fire – water would only have made matters worse, have increased the area of the fire by washing the petrol in all directions, and the petrol, being lighter than water, immiscible and so floating to the top, would have burned as furiously as ever. But the foam-extinguishers were of only limited efficiency, not so much because several release valves had jammed solid in the intense cold as because of the intense white heat which made close approach almost impossible, while the smaller carbontet. extinguishers, directed against electrical fires below, were shockingly ineffective: these extinguishers had never been in action before and the crew of the *Ulysses* had known for a long time of the almost magical properties of the extinguisher liquid for removing the most obstinate stains and marks in clothes. You may convince a WT rating of the lethal nature of 2000 volts: you may convince a gunner of the madness of matches in a magazine: you may convince a torpedoman of the insanity of juggling with fulminate of mercury: but you will never convince any of them of the criminal folly of draining off just a few drops of carbontetrachloride. . . . Despite stringent periodical checks, most of the extinguishers were only half-full. Some were completely empty.

The hoses were little more effective. Two were coupled up to the starboard mains and the valves turned: the hoses remained lifeless, empty. The starboard salt-water line had frozen solid – common enough with fresh-water systems, this, but not with salt. A third hose on the port side was coupled up, but the release valve refused to turn: attacked with hammers and crowbars, it sheered off at the base – at extremely low temperatures, molecular changes occur in metals, cut tensile strength to a fraction – the high-pressure water drenching everyone in the vicinity. Spicer, the dead Admiral's pantry-boy, a stricken-eyed shadow of his former cheerful self, flung away his hammer and wept in anger and frustration. The other port valve worked, but it took an eternity for the water to force its way through the flattened frozen hose.

Gradually, the deck fire was brought under control – less through the efforts of the firefighters than the fact that there was little inflammable material left after the petrol had burnt off. Hoses and extinguishers were then directed through the great jagged rents on the poop to the fires roaring in the mess-deck below, while two asbestos-suited fighters clambered over and struggled through the red-hot, jangled mass of smoking wreckage on the poop. Nicholls had one of the suits, Leading Telegraphist Brown, a specialist in rescue work, the other.

Brown was the first on the scene. Picking his way gingerly, he climbed up to the entrance of 'Y' turret. Watchers in the port and starboard alleyways saw him pause there, fighting to tie back the heavy steel door – it had been crashing monotonously backwards and forwards with the rolling of the cruiser. Then they saw him step inside. Less than ten seconds later they saw him appear at the door again, on his knees and clutching desperately at the side for support. His entire body was arching convulsively and he was being violently sick into his oxygen mask.

Nicholls saw this, wasted time neither on 'Y' turret nor on the charred skeletons still trapped in the incinerated fuselage of the Condor. He climbed quickly up the vertical steel ladders to 'X' gun-deck, moved round to the back and tried to open the door. The clips were jammed, immovable – whether from cold or metal distortion he did not know. He looked round for some lever, stepped aside as he saw Doyle, duffel coat smouldering, haggard face set and purposeful under the beard, approaching with a sledge in his hand. A dozen heavy, well-directed blows – the clanging, Nicholls thought, must be almost intolerable inside the hollow amplifier of the turret – and the door was open. Doyle secured it, stepped aside to let Nicholls enter.

Nicholls climbed inside. There had been no need to worry about that racket outside, he thought wryly. Every man in the turret was stone dead. Colour-Sergeant Evans was sitting bolt upright in his seat, rigid and alert in death as he had been in life: beside him lay Foster, the dashing, fiery Captain of Marines, whom death became so ill. The rest were all sitting or lying quietly at their stations, apparently unharmed and quite unmarked except for an occasional tiny trickle of blood from ear and mouth, trickles already coagulated in the intense cold – the speed of the *Ulysses* had carried the flames aft, away from the turret. The concussion must have been tremendous, death instantaneous. Heavily, Nicholls bent over the communications number, gently detached his headset, and called the bridge.

Vallery himself took the message, turned back to Turner. He looked old, defeated.

'That was Nicholls,' he said. Despite all he could do, the shock and sorrow showed clearly in every deeply-etched line in that pitiably wasted face. ' "Y" turret is gone – no survivors. "X" turret seems intact – but everyone inside is dead. Concussion, he says. Fires in the after mess-deck still not under control. . . . Yes, boy, what is it?'

' "Y" magazine, sir,' the seaman said uncertainly. 'They want to speak to the gunnery officer.'

'Tell them he's not available,' Vallery said shortly. 'We haven't time . . .' He broke off, looked up sharply. 'Did you say "*Y*" magazine? Here, let me have that phone.'

He took the receiver, pushed back the hood of his duffel coat.

'Captain speaking, "Y" magazine. What is it? . . . What? Speak up man, I can't hear you. . . . Oh, damn!' He swung round on the bridge LTO. 'Can you switch this receiver on to the relay amplifier? I can't hear a . . . Ah, that's better.'

The amplifier above the chart-house crackled into life – a peculiarly throaty, husky life, doubly difficult to understand under the heavy overlay of a slurred Glasgow accent.

'Can ye hear me now?' the speaker boomed.

'I can hear you.' Vallery's own voice echoed loudly over the amplifier. 'McQuater, isn't it?'

'Aye, it's me, sir. How did ye ken?' Even through the 'speaker the surprise was unmistakable. Shocked and exhausted though he was, Vallery found himself smiling.

'Never mind that now, McQuater. Who's in charge down there – Gardiner, isn't it?'

'Yes, sir. Gardiner.'

'Put him on, will you?' There was a pause.

'Ah canna, sir. Gardiner's deid.'

'Dead!' Vallery was incredulous. 'Did you say "dead," McQuater?'

'Aye, and he's no' the only one.' The voice was almost truculent, but Vallery's ear caught the faint tremor below. 'Ah was knocked oot masel', but Ah'm fine now.'

Vallery paused, waited for the boy's bout of hoarse, harsh coughing to pass.

'But – but – what happened?'

'How should Ah know – Ah mean, Ah dinna ken – Ah don't know, sir. A helluva bang and then – ach, Ah'm no' sure whit happened. . . . Gardiner's mooth's all blood.'

'How – how many of you are left?'

'Just Barker, Williamson and masel', sir. Naebody else – just us.'

'And – and they're all right, McQuater?'

'Ach, they're fine. But Barker thinks he's deein'. He's in a gey bad wey. Ah think he's gone clean aff his trolley, sir.'

'He's *what*?'

'Loony, sir,' McQuater explained patiently. 'Daft. Some bluidy nonsense aboot goin' to meet his Maker, and him wi' naething behind him but a lifetime o' swindlin' his fellow-man.' Vallery heard Turner's sudden chuckle, remembered that Barker was the canteen manager. 'Williamson's busy shovin' cartridges back into the racks – floor's littered with the bluidy things.'

'McQuater!' Vallery's voice was sharp, automatic in reproof.

'Aye, Ah'm sorry, sir. Ah clean forgot. . . . Whit's to be done, sir?'

'Done about what?' Vallery demanded impatiently.

'This place, sir. "Y" magazine. Is the boat on fire ootside? It's bilin' in here – hotter than the hinges o' hell!'

'What! What did you say?' Vallery shouted. This time he forgot to reprimand McQuater. 'Hot, did you say? How hot? Quickly, boy!'

'Ah canna touch the after bulkheid, sir,' McQuater answered simply. 'It 'ud tak 'the fingers aff me.'

'But the sprinklers – what's the matter with them?' Vallery shouted. 'Aren't they working? Good God, boy, the magazine will go up any minute!'

'Aye.' McQuater's voice was noncommittal. 'Aye, Ah kinna thought that might be the wey o' it. No, sir, the sprinklers are na working' – and it's already 20 degrees above the operatin' temperature, sir.'

'Don't just stand there,' Vallery said desperately. 'Turn them on by hand! The water in the sprinklers can't possibly be frozen if it's as hot as you say it is. Hurry, man, hurry. If the mag. goes up, the *Ulysses* is finished. For God's sake, hurry!'

'Ah've tried them, sir,' McQuater said softly. 'It's nae bluidy use. They're solid!'

'Then break them open! There must be a tommy bar lying about somewhere. Smash them open, man! Hurry!'

'Aye, richt ye are, sir. But – but if Ah do that, sir, how am Ah to shut the valves aff again?' There was a note almost of quiet desperation in the boy's voice – some trick of reproduction in the amplifier, Vallery guessed.

'You can't! It's impossible! But never mind that!' Vallery said impatiently, his voice ragged with anxiety. 'We'll pump it all out later. Hurry, McQuater, hurry!'

There was a brief silence followed by a muffled shout and a soft thud, then they heard a thin metallic clanging echoing through the amplifier, a rapid, staccato succession of strokes. McQuater must have been raining a veritable hail of blows on the valve handles. Abruptly, the noise ceased.

Vallery waited until he heard the phone being picked up, called anxiously: 'Well, how is it? Sprinklers all right?'

'Goin' like the clappers, sir.' There was a new note in his voice, a note of pride and satisfaction. 'Ah've just crowned Barker wi' the tommy bar,' he added cheerfully.

'You've *what*?'

'Laid oot old Barker,' said McQuater distinctly. 'He tried to stop me. Windy auld bastard. . . . Ach, he's no' worth mentionin'. . . . My they sprinklers are grand things, sir. Ah've never seen them workin' before. Place is ankle deep a'ready. And the steam's fair sizzlin' aff the bulkheid!'

'That's enough!' Vallery's voice was sharp. 'Get out at once – and make sure that you take Barker with you.'

'Ah saw a picture once. In the Paramount in Glasgow, Ah think. Ah must've been flush.' The tone was almost conversational, pleasurably reminiscent. Vallery exchanged glances with Turner, saw that he too, was fighting off the feeling of unreality. '*Rain*, it was cried. But it wasnae hauf as bad as this. There certainly wisnae hauf as much bluidy steam! Talk aboot the hothouse in the Botanic Gardens!'

'McQuater!' Vallery roared. 'Did you hear me? Leave at once, I say! At once, do you hear?'

'Up to ma knees a'ready!' McQuater said admiringly. 'It's gey cauld. . . . Did you say somethin' sir?'

'I said, "Leave at once!" ' Vallery ground out. 'Get out!'

'Aye, Ah see. "Get oot." Aye. Ah thought that was what ye said. Get oot. Well, it's no that easy. As a matter o' fact, we canna. Hatchway's buckled and the hatch-cover, too – jammed deid solid, sir.'

The echo from the speaker boomed softly over the shattered bridge, died away in frozen silence. Unconsciously, Vallery lowered the telephone, his eyes wandering dazedly over the bridge. Turner, Carrington, the Kapok Kid, Bentley, Chrysler and the others – they were all looking at him, all with the same curiously blank intensity blurring imperceptibly into the horror of understanding – and he knew that their eyes and faces only mirrored his own. Just for a second, as if to clear his mind, he screwed his eyes tightly shut, then lifted the phone again.

'McQuater! McQuater! Are you still there?'

'Of course Ah'm here!' Even through the speaker, the voice was peevish, the asperity unmistakable. 'Where the hell—?'

'Are you sure it's jammed, boy?' Vallery cut in desperately. 'Maybe if you took a tommy-bar to the clips—'

'Ah could take a stick o' dynamite to the bluidy thing and it 'ud make no difference,' McQuater said matter-of-factly. 'Onywey, it's just aboot red-hot a'ready – the hatch, Ah mean. There must be a bluidy great fire directly ootside it.'

'Hold on a minute,' Vallery called. He turned round. 'Commander, have Dodson send a stoker to the main magazine flooding valve aft: stand by to shut off.'

He crossed over to the nearest communication number.

'Are you on the poop phone just now? Good! Give it to me. . . . Hallo, Captain here. Is – ah, it's you, Hartley. Look, give me a report on the state of the mess-deck fires. It's desperately urgent. There are ratings trapped in "Y" magazine, the sprinklers are on and the hatch-cover's jammed. . . . Yes, yes, I'll hold on.'

He waited impatiently for the reply, gloved hand tapping mechanically on top of the phone box. His eyes swept slowly over the convoy, saw the freighters, steaming in to take up position again. Suddenly he stiffened, eyes unseeing.

'Yes, Captain speaking. . . . Yes. . . . Yes. Half an hour, maybe an hour. . . . Oh, God, no! You're quite certain? . . . No, that's all.'

He handed the receiver back, looked up slowly, his face drained of expression.

'Fire in the seamen's mess is under control,' he said dully. 'The marines' mess is an inferno – directly on top of "Y" magazine. Hartley says there isn't a chance of putting it out for an hour at least. . . . I think you'd better get down there, Number One.'

A whole minute passed, a minute during which there was only the pinging of the Asdic, the regular crash of the sea as the *Ulysses* rolled in the heavy troughs.

'Maybe the magazine's cool enough now,' the Kapok Kid suggested at length. 'Perhaps we could shut off the water long enough . . .' His voice trailed away uncertainly.

'Cool enough?' Turner cleared his throat noisily. 'How do we know? Only McQuater could tell us . . .' He stopped abruptly, as he realized the implications of what he was saying.

'We'll ask him,' Vallery said heavily. He picked up the phone again. 'McQuater?'

'Hallo!'

'Perhaps we could shut off the sprinklers outside, if it's safe. Do you think the temperature . . .?'

He broke off, unable to complete the sentence. The silence stretched out, taut and tangible, heavy with decision. Vallery wondered numbly what McQuater was thinking, what he himself would have thought in McQuater's place.

'Hing on a minute,' the speaker boomed abruptly. 'Ah'll have a look up top.'

Again that silence, again that tense unnatural silence lay heavily over the bridge. Vallery started as the speaker boomed again.

'Jings, Ah'm b——d. Ah couldna climb that ladder again for twenty-four points in the Treble Chance. . . . Ah'm on the ladder now, but Ah'm thinkin' Ah'll no' be on it much longer.'

'Never mind . . .' Vallery checked himself, aghast at what he had been about to say. If McQuater fell off, he'd drown like a rat in that flooded magazine.

'Oh, aye. The magazine.' In the intervals between the racked bouts of coughing, the voice was strangely composed. 'The shells up top are just aboot meltin'. Worse than ever, sir.'

'I see.' Vallery could think of nothing else to say. His eyes were closed and he knew he was swaying on his feet. With an effort, he spoke again. 'How's Williamson?' It was all he could think of.

'Near gone. Up to his neck and hangin' on to the racks.' McQuater coughed again. 'Says he's a message for the Commander and Carslake.'

'A – a message?'

'Uh-huh! Tell old Blackbeard to take a turn to himself and lay off the bottle,' he said with relish. The message for Carslake was unprintable.

Vallery didn't even feel shocked.

'And yourself, McQuater?' he said. 'No message, nothing you would like . . .' He stopped, conscious of the grotesque inadequacy, the futility of what he was saying.

'Me? Ach, there's naething Ah'd like . . . Well, maybe a transfer to the *Spartiate*, but Ah'm thinking maybe it's a wee bit ower later for that.[1] Williamson!' The voice had risen to a sudden urgent shout. 'Williamson! Hing on, boy, Ah'm coming!' They heard the booming clatter in the speaker as McQuater's phone crashed against metal, and then there was only the silence.

'McQuater!' Vallery shouted into the phone. 'McQuater! Answer me, man. Can you hear me? McQuater!' But the speaker above him remained

[1] H.M.S. *Spartiate* was a shore establishment. Naval HQ for the West of Scotland. It was at St Enoch's Hotel, Glasgow.

dead, finally, irrevocably dead. Vallery shivered in the icy wind. That magazine, that flooded magazine . . . less than twenty-four hours since he had been there. He could see it now, see it clearly as he had seen it last night. Only now he saw it dark, cavernous with only the pinpoints of emergency lighting, the water welling darkly, slowly up the sides, saw that little, pitifully wasted Scots boy with the thin shoulders and pain-filled eyes, struggling desperately to keep his mate's head above that icy water, exhausting his tiny reserves of strength with the passing of every second. Even now, the time must be running out and Vallery knew hope was gone. With a sudden clear certainty he knew that when those two went down, they would go down together. McQuater would never let go. Eighteen years old, just eighteen years old. Vallery turned away, stumbling blindly through the gate on to the shattered compass platform. It was beginning to snow again and darkness was falling all around them.

Chapter Fourteen

Saturday Evening I

The *Ulysses* rolled on through the Arctic twilight. She rolled heavily, awkwardly, in seas of the wrong critical length, a strange and stricken sight with both masts gone, with all boats and rafts gone, with shattered fore-and-aft superstructure, with a crazily tilted bridge and broken, mangled after turret, half-buried in the skeleton of the Condor's fuselage. But despite all that, despite, too, the great garish patches of red lead and gaping black holes in fo'c'sle and poop – the latter welling with dark smoke laced with flickering lances of flame – she still remained uncannily ghost-like and graceful, a creature of her own element, inevitably at home in the Arctic. Ghost-like, graceful, and infinitely enduring . . . and still deadly. She still had her guns – and her engines. Above all, she had these great engines, engines strangely blessed with endless immunity. So, at least, it seemed . . .

Five minutes dragged themselves interminably by, five minutes during which the sky grew steadily darker, during which reports from the poop showed that the firefighters were barely holding their own, five minutes during which Vallery recovered something of his normal composure. But he was now terribly weak.

A bell shrilled, cutting sharply through the silence and the gloom. Chrysler answered it, turned to the bridge.

'Captain, sir. After engine-room would like to speak to you.'

Turner looked at the Captain, said quickly: 'Shall I take it, sir?'

'Thank you.' Vallery nodded his head gratefully. Turner nodded in turn, crossed to the phone.

'Commander speaking. Who is it? . . . Lieutenant Grierson. What is it, Grierson? Couldn't be good news for a change?'

For almost a minute Turner remained silent. The others on the bridge could hear the faint crackling of the earpiece, sensed rather than saw the taut attention, the tightening of the mouth.

'Will it hold?' Turner asked abruptly. 'Yes, yes, of course. . . . Tell him we'll do our best up here. . . . Do that. Half-hourly, if you please.'

'It never rains, et cetera,' Turner growled, replacing the phone. 'Engine running rough, temperature hotting up. Distortion in inner starboard shaft. Dodson himself is in the shaft tunnel right now. Bent like a banana, he says.'

Vallery smiled faintly. 'Knowing Dodson, I suppose that means a couple of thou out of alignment.'

'Maybe.' Turner was serious. 'What does matter is that the main shaft bearing's damaged and the lubricating line fractured.'

'As bad as that?' Vallery asked softly.

'Dodson is pretty unhappy. Says the damage isn't recent – thinks it began the night we lost our depth-charges.' Turner shook his head. 'Lord knows what stresses that shaft's undergone since. . . . I suppose to-night's performance brought it to a head. . . . The bearing will have to be lubricated by hand. Wants engine revs. at a minimum or engine shut off altogether. They'll keep us posted.'

'And no possibility of repair?' Vallery asked wryly.

'No, sir. None.'

'Very well, then. Convoy speed. And Commander?'

'Sir?'

'Hands to stations all night. You needn't tell 'em so – but, well, I think it would be wise. I have a feeling—'

'What's that!' Turner shouted. 'Look! What the hell's she doing?' His finger was stabbing towards the last freighter in the starboard line: her guns were blazing away at some unseen target, the tracers lancing whitely through the twilight sky. Even as he dived for the broadcaster, he caught sight of the *Viking*'s main armament belching smoke and jagged flame.

'All guns! Green 110! Aircraft! Independent fire, independent targets! Independent fire, independent targets!' He heard Vallery ordering starboard helm, knew he was going to bring the for'ard turrets to bear.

They were too late. Even as the *Ulysses* began to answer her helm, the enemy planes were pulling out of their approach dives. Great, clumsy shapes, these planes, forlorn and insubstantial in the murky gloom, but identifiable in a sickening flash by the clamour of suddenly racing engines. Condors, without a shadow of doubt. Condors that had outguessed them again, that gliding approach, throttles cut right back, muted roar of the engines drifting downwind, away from the convoy. Their timing, their judgment of distance, had been superb.

The freighter was bracketed twice, directly hit by at least seven bombs: in the near-darkness, it was impossible to see the bombs going home, but the explosions were unmistakable. And as each plane passed over, the decks were raked by savage bursts of machine-gun fire. Every gun position on the freighter was wide open, lacking all but the most elementary frontal protection: the Dems, Naval Ratings on the LA guns, Royal Marine Artillerymen on the HA weapons, were under no illusions as to their life expectancy when they joined the merchant ships on the Russian run. . . . For such few gunners as survived the bombing, the vicious stuttering of these machine-guns was almost certainly their last sound on earth.

As the bombs plummeted down on the next ship in line, the first freighter was already a broken-backed mass of licking, twisting flames. Almost certainly, too, her bottom had been torn out: she had listed heavily, and now slowly and smoothly broke apart just aft of the bridge as if both parts were hinged below the water-line, and was gone before the clamour of the last aero engine had died away in the distance.

Tactical surprise had been complete. One ship gone, a second slewing wildly to an uncontrolled stop, deep in the water by the head, and strangely disquieting and ominous in the entire absence of smoke, flame or any movement at all, a third heavily damaged but still under command. Not one Condor had been lost.

Turner ordered the cease-fire – some of the gunners were still firing blindly into the darkness: trigger-happy, perhaps, or just that the imagination plays weird tricks on woolly minds and sunken blood-red eyes that had known no rest for more hours and days than Turner could remember. And then, as the last Oerlikon fell silent, he heard it again – the drone of the heavy aero engines, the sound welling then ebbing again like breakers on a distant shore, as the wind gusted and died.

There was nothing anyone could do about it. The Focke-Wulf, although lost in the low cloud, was making no attempt to conceal its presence: the ominous drone was never lost for long. Clearly, it was circling almost directly above.

'What do you make of it, sir?' Turner asked.

'I don't know,' Vallery said slowly. 'I just don't know at all. No more visits from the Condors, I'm sure of that. It's just that little bit too dark – and they know they won't catch us again. Tailing us, like as not.'

'Tailing us! It'll be black as tar in half an hour!' Turner disagreed. 'Psychological warfare, if you ask me.'

'God knows,' Vallery sighed wearily. 'All I know is that I'd give all my chances, here and to come, for a couple of Corsairs, or radar, or fog, or another such night as we had in the Denmark Straits.' He laughed shortly, broke down in a fit of coughing. 'Did you hear me?' he whispered. 'I never though I'd ask for that again. . . . How long since we left Scapa, Commander?'

Turner thought briefly. 'Five – six days, sir.'

'Six days!' He shook his head unbelievingly. 'Six days. And – and thirteen ships – we have thirteen ships now.'

'Twelve,' Turner corrected quietly. 'Another's almost gone. Seven freighters, the tanker and ourselves. Twelve . . . I wish they'd have a go at the old *Stirling* once in a while,' he added morosely.

Vallery shivered in a sudden flurry of snow. He bent forward, head bent against the bitter wind and slanting snow, sunk in unmoving thought. Presently he stirred.

'We will be off the North Cape at dawn,' he said absently. 'Things may be a little difficult, Commander. They'll throw in everything they've got.'

'We've been round there before,' Turner conceded.

'Fifty-fifty on our chances.' Vallery did not seem to have heard him, seemed to be talking to himself. '*Ulysses* and the Sirens – "it may be that the gulfs will wash us down." . . . I wish you luck, Commander.'

Turner stared at him. 'What do you mean—?'

'Oh, myself too.' Vallery smiled, his head lifting up. 'I'll need all the luck, too.' His voice was very soft.

Turner did what he had never done before, never dreamed he would do. In the near-darkness he bent over the Captain, pulled his face round gently and searched it with troubled eyes. Vallery made no protest, and after a few seconds Turner straightened up.

'Do me a favour, sir,' he said quietly. 'Go below. I can take care of things – and Carrington will be up before long. They're gaining control aft.'

'No, not to-night.' Vallery was smiling, but there was a curious finality about the voice. 'And it's no good dispatching one of your minions to summon old Socrates to the bridge. Please, Commander, I want to stay here – I want to see things to-night.'

'Yes, yes, of course.' Suddenly, strangely, Turner no longer wished to argue. He turned away. 'Chrysler! I'll give you just ten minutes to have a gallon of boiling coffee in the Captain's shelter. . . . And you're going to go in there for half an hour,' he said firmly, turning to Vallery, 'and drink the damned stuff, or – or—'

'Delighted!' Vallery muttered. 'Laced with your incomparable rum, of course?'

'Of course! Eh – oh, yes, damn that Williamson!' Turner growled irritably. He paused, went on slowly: 'Shouldn't have said that. . . . Poor bastards, they'll have had it by this time. . . .' He fell silent, then cocked his head listening. 'I wonder how long old Charlie means to keep stooging around up there,' he murmured.

Vallery cleared this throat, coughed, and before he could speak the WT broadcaster clicked on.

'WT – bridge. WT – bridge. Two messages.'

'One from the dashing Orr, for a fiver,' Turner grunted.

'First from the *Sirrus*. "Request permission to go alongside, take off survivors. As well hung for a sheep as a lamb." '

Vallery stared through the thinly falling snow, through the darkness of the night and over the rolling sea.

'In *this* sea?' he murmured. 'And as near dark as makes no difference. He'll kill himself!'

'That's nothing to what old Starr's going to do to him when he lays hands on him!' Turner said cheerfully.

'He hasn't a chance. I – I could never ask a man to do that. There's no justification for such a risk. Besides, the merchant-man's been badly hit. There can't be many left alive aboard.'

Turner said nothing.

'Make a signal,' Vallery said clearly. ' "Thank you. Permission granted. Good luck." And tell WT to go ahead.'

'Second signal from London for Captain. Decoding. Messenger leaving for bridge immediately.'

'To Officer Commanding, 14 ACS, FR77,' the speaker boomed after a few seconds. ' "Deeply distressed at news. Imperative maintain 090. Battle squadron steaming SSE at full speed on interception course. Rendezvous approx. 1400 tomorrow. Their Lordships expressly command best wishes Rear-Admiral Vallery. DNO, London." '

The speaker clicked off and there was only the lost pinging of the Asdic, the throbbing monotony of the prowling Condor's engines, the lingering memory of the gladness in the broadcaster's voice.

'Uncommon civil of their Lordships,' murmured the Kapok Kid, rising to the occasion as usual. 'Downright decent, one might almost say.'

'Bloody long overdue,' Turner growled. 'Congratulations, sir,' he added warmly. 'Signs of grace at last along the banks of the Thames.' A murmur of pleasure ran round the bridge: discipline or not, no one made any attempt to hide his satisfaction.

'Thank you, thank you.' Vallery was touched, deeply touched. Promise of help at long, long last, a promise which might hold – almost certainly held – for each and every member of his crew the difference between life and death – and they could only think to rejoice in his promotion! Dead men's shoes, he thought, and thought of saying it, but dismissed the idea immediately: a rebuff, a graceless affront to such genuine pleasure.

'Thank you very much,' he repeated. 'But gentlemen, you appear to have missed the only item of news of any real significance—'

'Oh, no, we haven't,' Turner growled. 'Battle squadron – ha! Too—late as usual. Oh, to be sure, they'll be in at the death – or shortly afterwards, anyway. Perhaps in time for a few survivors. I suppose the *Illustrious* and the *Furious* will be with them?'

'Perhaps. I don't know.' Vallery shook his head, smiling. 'Despite my recent – ah – elevation, I am not yet in their Lordship's confidence. But there'll be some carriers, and they could fly off a few hours away, give us air cover from dawn.'

'Oh, no, they won't,' said Turner prophetically. 'The weather will break down, make flying off impossible. See if I'm not right.'

'Perhaps, Cassandra, perhaps,' Vallery smiled. 'We'll see. . . . What was that, Pilot? I didn't quite . . .'

The Kapok Kid grinned.

'It's just occurred to me that tomorrow's going to be a big day for our junior doctor – he's convinced that no battleship ever puts out to sea except for a Spithead review in peacetime.'

'That reminds me,' Vallery said thoughtfully. 'Didn't we promise the *Sirrus*—?'

'Young Nicholls is up to his neck in work,' Turner cut in. 'Doesn't love us – the Navy rather – overmuch, but he sure loves his job. Borrowed a fire-fighting suit, and Carrington says he's already . . .' He broke off, looked up sharply into the thin, driving snow. 'Hallo! Charlie's getting damned nosy, don't you think?'

The roar of the Condor's engines was increasing every second: the sound rose to a clamouring crescendo as the bomber roared directly overhead, barely a couple of hundred feet above the broken masts, died away to a steady drone as the plane circled round the convoy.

'WT to escorts!' Vallery called quickly. 'Let him go – don't touch him! No starshells – nothing. He's trying to draw us out, to have us give away our position. . . . It's not likely that the merchant ships . . . Oh, God! The fools, the fools! Too late, too late!'

A merchantman in the port line had opened up – Oerlikons or Bofors, it was difficult to say. They were firing blind, completely blind: and in a high wind, snow and darkness, the chance of locating a plane by sound alone was impossibly remote.

The firing did not last long – ten, fifteen seconds at the outside. But long enough – and the damage was done. Charlie had pulled off, and straining apprehensive ears caught the sudden deepening of the note of the engines as the boosters were cut in for maximum climb.

'What do you make of it, sir?' Turner asked abruptly.

'Trouble.' Vallery was quiet but certain. 'This has never happened before – and it's not psychological warfare, as you call it, Commander: he doesn't even rob us of our sleep – not when we're this close to the North Cape. And he can't hope to trail us long: a couple of quick course alterations and – ah!' He breathed softly. 'What did I tell you, Commander?'

With a suddenness that blocked thought, with a dazzling glare that struck whitely, cruelly at singeing eyeballs, night was transformed into day. High above the *Ulysses* a flare had burst into intense life, a flare which tore apart the falling snow like filmy, transparent gauze. Swinging wildly under its parachute with the gusting of the wind, the flare was drifting slowly seawards, towards a sea no longer invisible but suddenly black as night, towards a sea where every ship, in its glistening sheath of ice and snow, was silhouetted in dazzling whiteness against the inky backdrop of sea and sky.

'Get that flare!' Turner was barking into the transmitter. 'All Oerlikons, all pom-poms, get that flare!' He replaced the transmitter. 'Might as well throw empty beer bootles at it with the old girl rolling like this,' he muttered. 'Lord, gives you a funny feeling, this!'

'I know,' the Kapok Kid supplied. 'Like one of these dreams where you're walking down a busy street and you suddenly realize that all you're wearing is a wrist-watch. "Naked and defenceless," is the accepted term, I believe. For the non-literary, "caught with the pants down." ' Absently he brushed the snow off the quilted kapok, exposing the embroidered 'J' on the breast pocket, while his apprehensive eyes probed into the circle of darkness outside the pool of light. 'I don't like this at all,' he complained.

'Neither do I.' Vallery was unhappy. 'And I don't like Charlie's sudden disappearance either.'

'He hasn't disappeared,' Turner said grimly. 'Listen!' They listened, ears straining intently, caught the intermittent, distant thunder of the heavy engines. 'He's 'way astern of us, closing.'

Less than a minute later the Condor roared overhead again, higher this time, lost in the clouds. Again he released a flare, higher, much higher than the last, and this time squarely over the heart of the convoy.

Again the roar of the engines died to a distant murmur, again the desynchronized clamour strengthened as the Condor overtook the convoy a second time. Glimpsed only momentarily in the inverted valleys between the scudding clouds, it flew wide, this time, far out on the port hand, riding clear above the pitiless glare of the sinking flares. And, as it thundered by, flares exploded into blazing life – four of them, just below cloud level, at four-second intervals. The northern horizon was alive with light, glowing and pulsating with a fierce flame that threw every tiny detail into the starkest relief. And to the south there was only the blackness: the rim of the pool of light stopped abruptly just beyond the starboard line of ships.

It was Turner who first appreciated the significance, the implications of this. Realization struck at him with the galvanic effect of sheer physical shock. He gave a hoarse cry, fairly flung himself at the broadcast transmitter: there was no time to await permission.

' "B" turret!' he roared. 'Starshells to the south. Green 90, green 90. Urgent! Urgent! Starshells, green 90. Maximum elevation 10. Close settings. Fire when you are ready!' He looked quickly over his shoulder. 'Pilot! Can you see—?'

' "B" turret training, sir.'

'Good, good!' He lifted the transmitter again. 'All guns! All guns! Stand by to repel air attack from starboard. Probable bearing green 90. Hostiles probably torpedo-bombers.' Even as he spoke, he caught sight of the intermittent flashing of the fighting lights on the lower yardarm: Vallery was sending out an emergency signal to the convoy.

'You're right, Commander,' Vallery whispered. In the gaunt pallor, in the skin taut stretched across the sharp and fleshless bones, his face, in that blinding glare, was a ghastly travesty of humanity; it was a death's-head, redeemed only by the glow of the deep-sunken eyes, the sudden flicker of bloodless lids as the whip-lash crash of 'B' turret shattered the silence. 'You must be,' he went on slowly. 'Every ship silhouetted from the north – and a maximum run-in from the south under cover of darkness.' He broke off suddenly as the shells exploded in great overlapping globules of light, two miles to the south. 'You *are* right,' he said gently. 'Here they come.'

They came from the south, wing-tip to wing-tip, flying in three waves with four or five planes in each wave. They were coming in at about 500 feet, and even as the shells burst their noses were already dipping into the plane of the shallow attack dive of the torpedo-bomber. And as they dived, the bombers fanned out, as if in search of individual targets – or what seemed, at first sight, to be individual targets. But within seconds it became obvious that they were concentrating on two ships and two ships alone – the *Stirling* and the *Ulysses*. Even the ideal double target of the crippled merchantman and the destroyer *Sirrus*, almost stopped alongside her, was strictly ignored. They were flying under orders.

'B' turret pumped out two more starshells at minimum settings, reloaded with HE. By this time, every gun in the convoy had opened up, the barrage was intense: the torpedo-bombers – curiously difficult to identify, but looking like Heinkels – had to fly through a concentrated lethal curtain of steel and high explosive. The element of surprise was gone: the starshells of the *Ulysses* had gained a priceless twenty seconds.

Five bombers were coming at the *Ulysses* now, fanned out to disperse fire, but arrowing in on a central point. They were levelling off, running in on firing tracks almost at wave-top height, when one of them straightened up a fraction too late, brushed lightly against a cresting wave-top, glanced harmlessly off, then catapulted crazily from wave-top to wave-top – they were flying at right angles to the set of the sea – before disappearing in a trough. Misjudgment of distance or the pilot's windscreen suddenly obscured by a flurry of snow – it was impossible to say.

A second later the leading plane in the middle disintegrated in a searing burst of flame – a direct hit on its torpedo warhead. A third plane, behind and to the west, sheered off violently to the left to avoid the hurtling debris, and the subsequent dropping of its torpedo was no more than an empty gesture. It ran half a cable length behind the *Ulysses*, spent itself in the empty sea beyond.

Two bombers left now, pressing home their attack with suicidal courage, weaving violently from side to side to avoid destruction. Two seconds passed, three, four – and still they came on, through the falling snow and intensely heavy fire, miraculous in their immunity. Theoretically, there is no target so easy to hit as a plane approaching directly head on: in practice, it never worked out that way. In the Arctic, the Mediterranean, the Pacific, the relative immunity of the torpedo-bombers, the high percentage of successful attacks carried out in the face of almost saturation fire, never failed to confound the experts. Tension, over-anxiety, fear – these were part of the trouble, at least: there are no half measures about a torpedo-bomber – you get him or he gets you. And there is nothing more nerve-racking – always, of course, with the outstanding exception of the screaming, near-vertical power-dive of the gull-winged Stuka dive-bomber – than to see a torpedo-bomber looming hugely, terrifyingly over the open sights of your gun and know that you have just five inexorable seconds to live. . . . And with the *Ulysses*, of course, the continuous rolling of the cruiser in the heavy cross-sea made accuracy impossible.

These last two bombers came in together, wing-tip to wing-tip. The plane nearer the bows dropped its torpedo less than two hundred yards away, pulled up in a maximum climbing turn to starboard, a fusillade of light cannon and machine-gun shells smashing into the upper works of the bridge: the torpedo hit the water obliquely, porpoised high into the air, then crashed back again nose first into a heavy wave, diving steeply into the sea: it passed under the *Ulysses*.

But seconds before that the last torpedo-bomber had made its attack – made its attack and failed and died. It had come roaring in less than ten feet above the waves, had come straight on without releasing its torpedo, without gaining an inch in height, until the crosses on the upper sides of the wings could be clearly seen, until it was less than a hundred yards away. Suddenly, desperately, the pilot had begun to climb: it was immediately obvious that the torpedo release mechansim had jammed, either through mechanical failure or icing in the intense cold: obviously, too, the pilot had intended to release the torpedo at the last minute, had banked on the sudden decrease of weight to lift him over the *Ulysses*.

The nose of the bomber smashed squarely into the for'ard funnel, the starboard wing shearing off like cardboard as it scythed across the after leg of the tripod mast. There was an instantaneous, blinding sheet of gasoline flame, but neither smoke nor explosion. A moment later the crumpled, shattered bomber, no longer a machine but a torn and flaming crucifix, plunged into the hissing sea a dozen yards away. The water had barely closed over it when a gigantic underwater explosion heeled the *Ulysses* far over to starboard, a vicious hammer-blow that flung men off their feet and shattered the lighting system on the port side of the cruiser.

Commander Turner hoisted himself painfully to his feet, shook his head to clear it of the cordite fumes and the dazed confusion left by cannon shells exploding almost at arm's length. The shock of the detonating torpedo hadn't thrown him to the duckboards – he'd hurled himself there five seconds previously as the flaming guns of the other bomber had raked the bridge from point-blank range.

His first thought was for Vallery. The Captain was lying on his side, crumpled strangely against the binnacle. Dry-mouthed, cold with a sudden chill that was not of that Polar wind, Turner bent quickly, turned him gently over.

Vallery lay still, motionless, lifeless. No sign of blood, no gaping wound – thank God for that! Turner peeled off a glove, thrust a hand below duffel coat and jacket, thought he detected a faint, a very faint beating of the heart. Gently he lifted the head off the frozen slush, then looked up quickly. The Kapok Kid was standing above him.

'Get Brooks up here, Pilot,' he said swiftly. 'It's urgent!'

Unsteadily, the Kapok Kid crossed over the bridge. The communication rating was leaning over the gate, telephone in his hand.

'The Sick Bay, quickly!' the Kapok Kid ordered. 'Tell the Surgeon Commander . . . ' He stopped suddenly, guessed that the man was still too dazed to understand. 'Here, give me that phone!' Impatiently, he stretched out his hand and grabbed the telephone, then stiffened in horror as the man slipped gradually backwards, extended arms trailing stiffly over the top of the gate until they disappeared. Carpenter opened the gate, stared down at the dead man at his feet: there was a hole the size of his gloved fist between his shoulder blades.

He lay alongside the Asdic Cabinet, a cabinet, the Kapok Kid now saw for the first time, riddled and shattered with machine-gun bullets and shells. His first thought was the numbing appreciation that the set must be smashed beyond recovery, that their last defence against the U-boats was gone. Hard on the heels of that came the sickening realization that there had been an Asdic operator inside there. . . . His eyes wandered away, caught sight of Chrysler rising to his feet by the torpedo control. He, too, was staring at the Asdic cabinet, his face drained of expression. Before the Kapok Kid could speak, Chrysler lurched forward, battering frantically, blindly at the jammed door of the cabinet. Like a man in a dream, the Kapok Kid heard him sobbing. . . . And then he remembered. The Asdic operator – his name was Chrysler too. Sick to his heart, the Kapok Kid lifted the phone again. . . .

Turner pillowed the Captain's head, moved across to the starboard corner of the compass platform. Bentley, quiet, unobtrusive as always, was sitting on the deck, his back wedged between two pipes, his head pillowed peacefully on his chest. His hand under Bentley's chin, Turner gazed down into the sightless eyes, the only recognizable feature of what had once been a human face. Turner swore in savage quiet, tried to prise the dead fingers locked round the hand-grip of the Aldis, then gave up. The barred beam shone eerily across the darkening bridge.

Methodically, Turner searched the bridge-deck for further casualties. He found three others and it was no consolation at all that they must have died unknowing. Five dead men for a three-second burst – a very fair return, he thought bitterly. Standing on the after ladder, his face stilled in unbelief as he realized that he was staring down into the heart of the shattered for'ard funnel. More he could not see: the boat deck was already blurred into featureless anonymity in the dying glare of the last of the flares. He swung on his heel, returned to the compass platform.

At least, he thought grimly, there was no difficulty in seeing the *Stirling*. What was it that he had said – said less than ten minutes ago? 'I wish they'd have a go at the *Stirling* once in a while.' Something like that. His mouth twisted. They'd had a go, all right. The *Stirling*, a mile ahead, was slewing away to starboard, to the south-east, her for'ard superstructure enveloped in a writhing cocoon of white flame. He stared through his night glasses, tried to assess the damage; but a solid wall of flame masked the superstructure, from the fo'c'sle deck clear abaft the bridge. He could see nothing there, just nothing – but he could see, even in that heavy swell, that the *Stirling* was listing to starboard. It was learned later that the *Stirling* had been struck twice: she had been torpedoed in the for'ard boiler-room, and seconds later a bomber had crashed into the side of her bridge, her torpedo still slung beneath the belly of her fuselage: almost certainly, in the light of the similar occurrence on the *Ulysses*, severe icing had jammed the release mechanism. Death must have been instantaneous for every man on the bridge and the decks below; among the dead were Captain Jeffries, the First Lieutenant and the Navigator.

The last bomber was hardly lost in the darkness when Carrington replaced the poop phone, turned to Hartley.

'Think you can manage now, Chief? I'm wanted on the bridge.'

'I think so, sir.' Hartley, blackened and stained with smoke and extinguisher foam, passed his sleeve wearily across his face. 'The worst is over. . . . Where's Lieutenant Carslake? Shouldn't he—?'

'Forget him,' Carrington interrupted brusquely. 'I don't know where he is, nor do I care. There's no need for us to beat about the bush, Chief – we're better without him. If he returns, *you're* still in charge. Look after things.'

He turned away, walked quickly for'ard along the port alley. On the packed snow and ice, the pad of his rubber seaboots was completely soundless.

He was passing the shattered canteen when he saw a tall, shadowy figure standing in the gap between the snow-covered lip of the outer torpedo tube and the end stanchion of the guard-rails, trying to open a jammed extinguisher valve by striking it against the stanchion. A second later, he saw another blurred form detach itself stealthily from the shadows, creep up stealthily behind the man with the extinguisher, a heavy bludgeon of wood or metal held high above his head.

'Look out!' Carrington shouted. 'Behind you!'

It was all over in two seconds – the sudden, flailing rush of the attacker, the crash as the victim, lightning fast in his reactions, dropped his extinguisher and fell crouched to his knees, the thin piercing scream of anger and terror as the attacker catapulted over the stooping body and through the gap between tubes and rails, the splash – and then the silence.

Carrington ran up to the man on the deck, helped him to his feet. The last flare had not yet died, and it was still light enough for him to see who it was – Ralston, the LTO. Carrington gripped his arms, looked at him anxiously.

'Are you all right? Did he get you? Good God, who on earth—?'

'Thank you, sir.' Ralston was breathing quickly, but his face was almost expressionless again. 'That was too close! Thank you very much, sir.'

'But who on earth—?' Carrington repeated in wonder.

'Never saw him, sir.' Ralston was grim. 'But I know who it was – Sub-Lieutenant Carslake. He's been following me around all night, never let me out of his sight, not once. Now I know why.'

It took much to disturb the First Lieutenant's iron equanimity, but now he shook his head in slow disbelief.

'I knew there was bad blood!' he murmured. 'But that it should come to this! What the Captain will say to this I just—'

'Why tell him?' Ralston said indifferently. 'Why tell anyone? Perhaps Carslake had relations. What good will it do to hurt them, to hurt anyone. Let anyone think what they like.' He laughed shortly. 'Let them think he died a hero's death fire-fighting, fell over the side, anything.' He looked down into the dark, rushing water, then shivered suddenly. 'Let him go, sir, please. He's paid.'

For a long second Carrington, too, stared down over the side, looked back at the tall boy before him. Then he clapped his arm, nodded slowly and turned away.

Turner heard the clanging of the gate, lowered the binoculars to find Carrington standing by his side, gazing wordlessly at the burning cruiser. Just then Vallery moaned softly, and Carrington looked down quickly at the prone figure at his feet.

'My God! The Old Man! Is he hurt badly, sir?'

'I don't know, Number One. If not, it's a bloody miracle,' he added bitterly. He stooped down, raised the dazed Captain to a sitting position.

'Are you all right, sir?' he asked anxiously. 'Do you – have you been hit?'

Vallery shuddered in a long, exhausting paroxysm of coughing, then shook his head feebly.

'I'm all right,' he whispered weakly. He tried to grin, a pitiful, ghastly travesty of a smile in the reflected light from the burning Aldis. 'I dived for the deck, but I think the binnacle got in my way.' He rubbed his forehead, already bruised and discoloured. 'How's the ship, Commander?'

'To hell with the ship!' Turner said roughly. He passed an arm round Vallery, raised him carefully to his feet. 'How are things aft, Number One?'

'Under control. Still burning, but under control. I left Hartley in charge.' He made no mention of Carslake.

'Good! Take over. Radio *Stirling, Sirrus*, see how they are. Come on, sir. Shelter for you!'

Vallery protested feebly, a token protest only, for he was too weak to stand. He checked involuntarily as he saw the snow falling whitely through the barred beam of the Aldis, slowly followed the beam back to its source.

'Bentley?' he whispered. 'Don't tell me . . .' He barely caught the Commander's wordless nod, turned heavily away. They passed by the dead man stretched outside the gate, then stopped at the Asdic cabinet. A sobbing figure was crouched into the angle between the shelter and the jammed and shattered door of the hut, head pillowed on the forearm resting high against the door. Vallery laid a hand on the shaking shoulder, peered into the averted face.

'What is it? Oh, it's you, boy.' The white face had been lifted towards him. 'What's the matter, Chrysler?'

'The door, sir!' Chrysler's voice was muffled, quivering. 'The door – I can't open it.'

For the first time, Vallery looked at the cabinet, at the gashed and torn metal. His mind was still dazed, exhausted, and it was almost by a process of association that he suddenly, horrifyingly thought of the gashed and mangled operator that must lie behind that locked door.

'Yes,' he said quietly. 'The door's buckled. . . . There's nothing anyone can do. Chrysler.' He looked more closely at the grief-dulled eyes. 'Come on, my boy, there's no need—'

'My brother's in there, sir.' The words, the hopeless despair, struck Vallery like a blow. Dear God! He had forgotten. . . . Of course – Leading Asdic Operator Chrysler. . . . He stared down at the dead man at his feet, already covered with a thin layer of snow.

'Have that Aldis unplugged, Commander, will you?' he asked absently. 'And Chrysler?'

'Yes, sir.' A flat monotone.

'Go below and bring up some coffee, please.'

'Coffee, sir!' He was bewildered, uncomprehending. 'Coffee! But – but – my brother—'

'I know,' Vallery said gently. 'I know. Bring some coffee, will you?'

Chrysler stumbled off. When the shelter door closed behind them, clicking on the light, Vallery turned to the Commander.

'Cue for moralizing on the glories of war,' he murmured quietly. '*Dulce et decorum*, and the proud privilege of being the sons of Nelson and Drake. It's not twenty-four hours since Ralston watched his father die. . . . And now this boy. Perhaps—'

'I'll take care of things,' Turner nodded. He hadn't yet forgiven himself for what he had said and done to Ralston last night, in spite of Ralston's quick friendliness, the ready acceptance of his apologies. 'I'll keep him busy out of the way till we open up the cabinet. . . . Sit down, sir. Have a swig of this.' He smiled faintly. 'Friend Williams having betrayed my guilty secret. . . . Hallow! Company.'

The light clicked off and a burly figure bulked momentarily against the grey oblong of the doorway. The door shut, and Brooks stood blinking in the sudden light, red of face and gasping for breath. His eyes focused on the bottle in Turner's hand.

'Ha!' he said at length. 'Having a bottle party, are we? All contributions gratefully received, I have no doubt.' He opened his case on a convenient table, was rummaging inside when someone rapped sharply on the door.

'Come in,' Vallery called.

A signalman entered, handed a note to Vallery. 'From London, sir, Chief says there may be some reply.'

'Thank you. I'll phone down.'

The door opened and closed again. Vallery looked up at an empty-handed Turner.

'Thanks for removing the guilty evidence so quickly,' he smiled. Then he shook his head. 'My eyes – they don't seem so good. Perhaps you would read the signal, Commander?'

'And perhaps *you* would like some decent medicine,' Brooks boomed, 'instead of that filthy muck of Turner's.' He fished in his bag, produced a bottle of amber liquid. 'With all the resources of modern medicine – well, practically all, anyway – at my disposal, I can find nothing to equal this.'

'Have you told Nicholls?' Vallery was stretched out on the settee now, eyes closed, the shadow of a smile on his bloodless lips.

'Well, no,' Brooks confessed. 'But plenty of time. Have some?'

'Thanks. Let's have the good news, Turner.'

'Good news!' The sudden deadly quiet of the Commander's voice fell chilly over the waiting men. 'No, sir, it's not good news.

' "Rear-Admiral Vallery, Commanding 14 ACS, FR77." ' The voice was drained of all tone and expression. ' "*Tirpitz*, escorting cruisers, destroyers, reported moving out Alta Fjord sunset. Intense activity Alta Fjord airfield. Fear sortie under air cover. All measures avoid useless sacrifice Merchant, Naval ships. DNO, London." ' With deliberate care Turner folded the paper, laid it on the table. 'Isn't that just wonderful,' he murmured. 'Whatever next?'

Vallery was sitting bolt upright on the settee, blind to the blood trickling down crookedly from one corner of his mouth. His face was calm, unworried.

'I think I'll have that glass, now, Brooks, if you don't mind,' he said quietly. The *Tirpitz*. The *Tirpitz*. He shook his head tiredly, like a man in a dream. The *Tirpitz* – the name that no man mentioned without a far-off echo of awe and fear, the name that had completely dominated North Atlantic naval strategy during the past two years. Moving out at last, an armoured Colossus, sister-ship to that other Titan that had destroyed the *Hood* with one single, savage blow – the *Hood*, the darling of the Royal Navy, the most powerful ship in the world – or so men had thought. What chance had *their* tiny cockle-shell cruiser. . . . Again he shook his head, angrily this time, forced himself to think of the present.

'Well, gentlemen, I suppose time bringeth all things – even the *Tirpitz*. It had to come some day. Just our ill luck – the bait was too close, too tempting.'

'My young colleague is going to be just delighted,' Brooks said grimly. 'A *real* battleship at long, long last.'

'Sunset,' Turner mused. 'Sunset. My God! he said sharply, 'even allowing for negotiating the fjord they'll be on us in four hours on this course!'

'Exactly,' Vallery nodded. 'And it's no good running north. They'll overtake us before we're within a hundred miles of them.'

'Them? Our big boys up north?' Turner scoffed. 'I hate to sound like a gramophone record, but you'll recall my earlier statement about them – too—late as usual!' He paused, swore again. 'I hope that old bastard Starr's satisfied at last!' he finished bitterly.

'Why all the gloom?' Vallery looked up quizzically, went on softly. 'We can still be back, safe and sound in Scapa in forty-eight hours. "Avoid useless sacrifice Merchant, Naval ships," he said. The *Ulysses* is probably the fastest ship in the world today. It's simple, gentlemen.'

'No, no!' Brooks moaned. 'Too much of an anti-climax. I couldn't stand it!'

'Do another PQ17?'[1] Turner smiled, but the smile never touched his eyes. 'The Royal Navy could never stand it: Captain – Rear-Admiral Vallery would never permit it; and speaking for myself and, I'm fairly certain, this bunch of cut-throat mutineers of ours – well, I don't think we'd ever sleep so sound o'nights again.'

'Gad!' Brooks murmured. 'The man's a poet!'

'You're right, Turner.' Vallery drained his glass, lay back exhausted. 'We don't seem to have much option. . . . What if we receive orders for a – ah – high-speed withdrawal?'

'You can't read,' Turner said bluntly. 'Remember, you just said your eyes are going back on you.'

[1] PQ17, a large mixed convoy – it included over 30 British, American and Panamanian ships – left Iceland for Russia under the escort of half a dozen destroyers and perhaps a dozen smaller craft, with a mixed Anglo-American cruiser and destroyer squadron in immediate support. A shadow covering force – again Anglo-American – comprising one aircraft carrier, two battleships, three cruisers and a flotilla of destroyers, lay to the north. As with FR77, they formed the spring of the trap that closed too late.

The time was midsummer, 1942, a suicidal season for the attempt, for in June and July, in these high latitudes, there is no night. About longitude 20° east, the convoy was heavily attacked by U-boats and aircraft.

On the same day as the attack began – 4th July – the covering cruiser squadron was radioed that the *Tirpitz* had just sailed from Alta Fjord. (This was not the case: the *Tirptiz* did make a brief, abortive sortie on the afternoon of the 5th, but turned back the same evening: rumour had it that she had been damaged by torpedoes from a Russian submarine.) The support squadron and convoy escorts immediately withdrew to the west at high speed, leaving PQ17 to their fate, leaving them to scatter and make their unescorted way to Russia as best they could. The feelings of the crews of the merchant ships at this save-their-own-skins desertion and betrayal by the Royal Navy can be readily imagined. Their fears, too, can be readily imagined, but even their darkest forebodings never conceived the dreadful reality: 23 merchant ships were sent to the bottom – by U-boats and aircraft. The *Tirpitz* was not seen, never came anywhere near the convoy; but even the threat had driven the naval squadrons to flight.

The author does not know all the facts concerning PQ17, nor does he seek to interpret those he does know: still less does he seek to assign blame. Curiously enough, the only definite conclusion is that no blame can be attached to the commander of the squadron, Admiral Hamilton. He had no part of the decision to withdraw – the order came from the Admiralty, and was imperative. But one does not envy him.

It was a melancholy and bitter incident, all the more unpalatable in that it ran so directly counter to the traditions of a great Service; one wonders what Sir Philip Sydney would have thought, or, in more modern times, Kennedy of the *Rawalpindi* or Fegen of the *Jervis Bay*. But there was no doubt what the Merchant Navy thought. What they still think. From most of the few survivors, there can be no hope of forgiveness. They will, probably, always remember: the Royal Navy would desperately like to forget. It is difficult to blame either.

' "Souls that have toiled and wrought and fought with me," ' Vallery quoted softly. 'Thank you, gentlemen. You make things very easy for me.' He propped himself on an elbow, his mind made up. He smiled at Turner, and his face was almost boyish again.

'Inform all merchant ships, all escorts. Tell them to break north.'

Turner stared at him.

'North? Did you say "north"?' But the Admiralty—'

'North, I said,' Vallery repeated quietly. 'The Admiralty can do what they like about it. We've played along long enough. We've sprung the trap. What more can they want? This way there's a chance – an almost hopeless chance, perhaps, but a fighting chance. To go east is suicide.' He smiled again, almost dreamily. 'The end is not all-important,' he said softly. 'I don't think I'll have to answer for this. Not now – not ever.'

Turner grinned at him, his face lit up. 'North, you said.'

'Inform C-in-C.' Vallery went on. 'Ask Pilot for an interception course. Tell the convoy we'll tag along behind, give 'em as much cover as we can, as long as we can. . . . As long as we can. Let us not delude ourselves. 1000 to 1 at the outside. . . . Nothing else we can do, Commander?'

'Pray,' Turner said succinctly.

'And sleep,' Brooks added. 'Why don't you have half an hour, sir?'

'Sleep!' Vallery seemed genuinely amused. 'We'll have all the time in the world to sleep, just by and by.'

'You have a point,' Brooks conceded. 'You are very possibly right.'

Chapter Fifteen

Saturday Evening II

Messages were pouring in to the bridge now, messages from the merchant ships, messages of dismayed unbelief asking for confirmation of the *Tirpitz* breakout: from the *Stirling*, replying that the superstructure fire was now under control and that the engine-room watertight bulkheads were holding; and one from Orr of the *Sirrus*, saying that his ship was making water to the capacity of the pumps - he had been in heavy collision with the sinking merchantman - that they had taken off forty-four survivors, that the *Sirrus* had already done her share and couldn't she go home? The signal had arrived after the *Sirrus*'s receipt of the bad news. Turner grinned to himself: no inducement on earth, he knew, could have persuaded Orr to leave now.

The messages kept pouring in, by visual signal or WT. There was no point in maintaining radio silence to outwit enemy monitor positions; the enemy knew where they were to a mile. Nor was there any need to prohibit light signalling - not with the *Stirling* still burning furiously enough to illuminate the sea for a mile around. And so the messages kept on coming - messages of fear and dismay and anxiety. But, for Turner, the most disquieting message came neither by lamp nor by radio.

Fully quarter of an hour had elapsed since the end of the attack and the *Ulysses* was rearing and pitching through the head seas on her new course of 350°, when the gate of the bridge crashed open and a panting, exhausted man stumbled on to the compass platform. Turner, back on the bridge again, peered closely at him in the red glare from the *Stirling*, recognized him as a stoker. His face was masked in sweat, the sweat already caking to ice in the intense cold. And in spite of that cold, he was hatless, coatless, clad only in a pair of thin dungarees. He was shivering violently, shivering from excitement and not because of the icy wind - he was oblivious to such things.

Turner seized him by the shoulder.

'What is it, man?' he demanded anxiously. The stoker was still too breathless to speak. 'What's wrong? Quickly!'

'The TS, sir!' The breathing was so quick, so agonized, that the words blurred into a gasping exhalation. 'It's full of water!'

'The TS!' Turner was incredulous. 'Flooded! When did this happen?'

'I'm not sure, sir.' He was still gasping for breath. 'But there was a bloody awful explosion, sir, just about amid—'

'I know! I know!' Turner interrupted impatiently. 'Bomber carried away the for'ard funnel, exploded in the water, port side. But that was fifteen minutes ago, man! Fifteen minutes! Good God, they would have—'

'TS switchboard's gone, sir.' The stoker was beginning to recover, to huddle against the wind, but frantic at the Commander's deliberation and delay, he straightened up and grasped Turner's duffel without realizing what he was doing. The note of urgency deepened still further. 'All the power's gone, sir. And the hatch is jammed! The men can't get out!'

'The hatch-cover jammed!' Turner's eyes narrowed in concern. 'What happened?' he rapped out. 'Buckled?'

'The counter-weight's broken off, sir. It's on top of the hatch. We can only get it open an inch. You see, sir—'

'Number One!' Turner shouted.

'Here, sir.' Carrington was standing just behind him. 'I heard. . . . Why can't you open it?'

'It's the *TS* hatch!' the stoker cried desperately. 'A quarter of a bloody ton if it's an ounce, sir. You know – the one below the ladder outside the wheelhouse. Only two men can get at it at the same time. We've tried. . . . Hurry, sir. *Please.*'

'Just a minute.' Carrington was calm, unruffled, infuriatingly so. 'Hartley? No, still fire-fighting. Evans, MacIntosh – dead.' He was obviously thinking aloud. 'Bellamy, perhaps?'

'What is it, Number One?' Turner burst out. He himself had caught up the anxiety, the impatience of the stoker. 'What are you trying—?'

'Hatch-cover plus pulley – 1000 lbs,' Carrington murmured. 'A special man for a special job.'

'Petersen, sir!' The stoker had understood immediately. 'Petersen!'

'Of course!' Carrington clapped gloved hands together. 'We're on our way, sir. Acetylene? No time! Stoker – crow-bars, sledges. . . . Perhaps if you would ring the engine-room, sir?'

But Turner already had the phone in his hand.

Aft on the poop-deck, the fire was under control, all but in a few odd corners where the flames were fed by a fierce through draught. In the mess-decks, bulkheads, ladders, mess partitions, lockers had been twisted and buckled into strange shapes by the intense heat: on deck, the gasoline-fed flames, incinerating the two and three-quarter inch deck plating and melting the caulking as by some gigantic blow-torch, had cleanly stripped all covering and exposed the steel deck-plates, plates dull and red glowing evilly, plates that hissed and spat as heavy snowflakes drifted down to sibilant extinction.

On and below decks, Hartley and his crews, freezing one moment, reeling in the blast of heat the next, toiled like men insane. Where their wasted, exhausted bodies found the strength God only knew. From the turrets, from the Master-At-Arms's office, from mess-decks and emergency steering position, they pulled out man after man who had been there when the Condor had crashed: pulled them out, looked at them, swore, wept and plunged back into the aftermath of that holocaust, oblivious of pain and danger, tearing aside wreckage, wreckage still burning, still red-hot, with charred and broken gloves: and when the gloves fell off, they used their naked hands.

As the dead were ranged in the starboard alleyway, Leading Seaman Doyle was waiting for them. Less than half an hour previously, Doyle had been in the for'ard galley passage, rolling in silent agony as frozen body and clothes thawed out after the drenching of his pom-pom. Five minutes later, he had been back on his gun, rock-like, unflinching, as he pumped shell after shell over open sights into the torpedo bombers. And now, steady and enduring as ever, he was on the poop. A man of iron, and a face of iron, too, that night, the bearded leonine head still and impassive as he picked up one dead man after the other, walked to the guard-rail and dropped his burden gently over the side. How many times he repeated that brief journey that night, Doyle never knew: he had lost count after the first twenty or so. He had no right to do this, of course: the navy was very strong on decent burial, and this was not decent burial. But the sailmakers were dead and no man would or could have sewn up these ghastly charred heaps in the weighted and sheeted canvas. The dead don't care, Doyle thought dispassionately – let them look after themselves. So, too, thought Carrington and Hartley, and they made no move to stop him.

Beneath their feet, the smouldering mess-decks rang with hollow reverberating clangs as Nicholls and Leading Telegraphist Brown, still weirdly garbed in their white asbestos suits, swung heavy sledges against the securing clips of 'Y' magazine hatch. In the smoke and gloom and their desperate haste, they could hardly see each other, much less the clips: as often as not they missed their strokes and the hammers went spinning out of numbed hands into the waiting darkness.

Time yet, Nicholls thought desperately, perhaps there is time. The main flooding valve had been turned off five minutes ago: it was possible, barely possible, that the two trapped men inside were clinging to the ladder, above water level.

One clip, one clip only was holding the hatch-cover now. With alternate strokes of their sledges, they struck it with vicious strength. Suddenly, unexpectedly, it sheared off at its base and the hatch-cover crashed open under the explosive up-surge of the compressed air beneath. Brown screamed in agony, a single coughing shout of pain, as the bone-crashing momentum of the swinging hatch crashed into his right hip, then fell to the deck where he lay moaning quietly.

Nicholls did not even spare him a glance. He leant far through the hatch, the powerful beam of his torch stabbing downwards into the gloom. And he could see nothing, nothing at all – not what he wanted to see. All he saw was the water, dark and viscous and evil, water rising and falling, water flooding and ebbing in the eerie oilbound silence as the *Ulysses* plunged and lifted in the heavy seas.

'Below!' Nicholls called loudly. The voice, a voice, he noted impersonally, cracked and shaken with strain, boomed and echoed terrifyingly down the iron tunnel. 'Below!' he shouted again. 'Is there anybody there?' He strained his ears for the least sound, for the faintest whisper of an answer, but none came.

'McQuater!' He shouted a third time. 'Williamson! Can you hear me?' Again he looked, again he listened, but there was only the darkness and the muffled whisper of the oil-slicked water swishing smoothly from side to side. He stared again down the light from the torch, marvelled that any surface could so quickly dissipate and engulf the brilliance of that beam. And beneath that surface. . . . He shivered. The water – even the water seemed to be dead, old and evil and infinitely horrible. In sudden anger, he shook his head to clear it of these stupid, primitive fears: his imagination – he'd have to watch it. He stepped back, straightened up. Gently, carefully, he closed the swinging hatch. The mess-deck echoed as his sledge swung down on the clips, again and again and again.

Engineer-Commander Dodson stirred and moaned. He struggled to open his eyes but his eyelids refused to function. At least, he thought that they did for the blackness around remained as it was, absolute, impenetrable, almost palpable.

He wondered dully what had happened, how long he had been there, what had happened. And the side of his head – just below the ear – that hurt abominably. Slowly, with clumsy deliberation, he peeled off his glove, reached up an exploratory hand. It came away wet and sticky: his hair, he realized with mild surprise, was thickly matted with blood. It must be blood – he could feel it trickling slowly, heavily down the side of his cheek.

And that deep, powerful vibration, a vibration overlain with an indefinable note of strain that set his engineer's teeth on edge – he could hear it, almost feel it, immediately in front of him. His bare hand reached out, recoiled in instant reflex as it touched something smooth and revolving – and burning hot.

The shaft tunnel! Of course. That's where he was – the shaft tunnel. They'd discovered fractured lubricating pipes on the port shafts too, and he'd decided to keep this engine turning. He knew they'd been attacked. Down here in the hidden bowels of the ship, sound did not penetrate: he had heard nothing of the aircraft engines: he hadn't even heard their own guns firing – but there had been no mistaking the jarring shock of the 5.25s surging back on their hydraulic recoils. And then – a torpedo perhaps, or a near miss by a bomb. Thank God he'd been sitting facing inboard when the *Ulysses* had lurched. The other way round and it would have been curtains for sure when he'd been flung across the shaft coupling and wrapped round . . .

The shaft! Dear God, the shaft! It was running almost red-hot on dry bearings! Frantically, he pawed around, picked up his emergency lamp and twisted its base. There was no light. He twisted it again with all his strength, reached up, felt the jagged edges of broken screen and bulb, and flung the useless lamp to the deck. He dragged out his pocket torch: that, too, was smashed. Desperate now, he searched blindly around for his oil can: it was lying on its side, the patent spring top beside it. The can was empty.

No oil, none. Heaven only knew how near that overstressed metal was to the critical limit. He didn't. He admitted that: even to the best engineers, metal fatigue was an incalculable unknown. But, like all men who had spent a lifetime with machines, he had developed a sixth sense for these things – and, right now, that sixth sense was jabbing at him, mercilessly, insistently. Oil – he would have to get oil. But he knew he was in bad shape, dizzy, weak from shock and loss of blood, and the tunnel was long and slippery and dangerous – and unlighted. One slip, one stumble against or over that merciless shaft. . . . Gingerly, the Engineer-Commander stretched out his hand again, rested his hand for an instant on the shaft, drew back sharply in sudden pain. He lifted his hand to his cheek, knew that it was not friction that had flayed and burnt the skin off the tips of his fingers. There was no choice. Resolutely, he gathered his legs under him, swayed dizzily to his feet, his back bent against the arching convexity of the tunnel.

It was then that he noticed it for the first time – a light, a swinging tiny pinpoint of light, imponderably distant in the converging sides of that dark tunnel, although he knew it could be only yards away. He blinked, closed his eyes and looked again. The light was still there, advancing steadily, and he could hear the shuffling of feet now. All at once he felt weak, light-headed: gratefully he sank down again, his feet safely braced once more against the bearing block.

The man with the light stopped a couple of feet away, hooked the lamp on to an inspection bracket, lowered himself carefully and sat beside Dodson. The rays of the lamp fell full on the dark heavy face, the jagged brows and prognathous jaw: Dodson stiffened in sudden surprise.

'Riley! Stoker Riley!' His eyes narrowed in suspicion and conjecture. 'What the devil are you doing here?'

'I've brought a two-gallon drum of lubricating oil,' Riley growled. He thrust a Thermos flask into the Engineer-Commander's hands. 'And here's some coffee. I'll 'tend to this – you drink that. . . . Suffering Christ! This bloody bearing's red-hot!'

Dodson set down the Thermos with a thump.

'Are you deaf?' he asked harshly. 'Why are *you* here? Who sent you? Your station's in "B" boiler-room!'

'Grierson sent me,' Riley said roughly. His dark face was impassive. 'Said he couldn't spare his engine-room men – too bloody valuable. . . . Too much?' The oil, thick, viscous, was pouring slowly on to the overheated bearing.

'*Lieutenant* Grierson!' Dodson was almost vicious, his voice a whip-lash of icy correction. 'And that's a damned lie, Riley! Lieutenant Grierson never sent you: I suppose you told *him* that somebody else had sent you?'

'Drink your coffee,' Riley advised sourly. 'You're wanted in the engine-room.'

The Engineer-Commander clenched his fist, restrained himself with difficulty.

'You damned insolent bastard!' he burst out. Abruptly, control came back and he said evenly: 'Commander's Defaulters in the morning. You'll pay for this, Riley!'

'No, I won't.' Confound him, Dodson thought furiously, he's actually grinning, the insolent . . .

He checked his thought.

'Why not?' he demanded dangerously.

'Because you won't report me.' Riley seemed to be enjoying himself hugely.

'Oh so that's it!' Dodson glanced swiftly round the darkened tunnel, and his lips tightened as he realized for the first time how completely alone they were: in sudden certainty he looked back at Riley, big and hunched and menacing. Smiling yet, but no smile, Dodson thought, could ever transform that ugly brutal face. The smile on the face of the tiger. . . . Fear, exhaustion, never-ending strain – they did terrible things to a man and you couldn't blame him for what he had become, or for what he was born. . . . But his, Dodson's, first responsibility was to himself. Grimly, he remembered how Turner had berated him, called him all sorts of a fool for refusing to have Riley sent to prison.

'So that's it, eh?' he repeated softly. He turned himself, feet thrusting solidly against the block. 'Don't be so sure, Riley. I can give you twenty-five years, but—'

'Oh, for Christ's sake!' Riley burst out impatiently. 'What are you talking about, sir? Drink your coffee – please. You're wanted in the engine-room, I tell you!' he repeated impatiently.

Uncertainly, Dodson relaxed, unscrewed the cap of the Thermos. He had a sudden, peculiar feeling of unreality, as if he were a spectator, some bystander in no way involved in this scene, this fantastic scene. His head, he realized, still hurt like hell.

'Tell me, Riley,' he asked softly, 'what makes you so sure I won't report you?'

'Oh, you can report me all right.' Riley was suddenly cheerful again. 'But I won't be at the Commander's table tomorrow morning.'

'No?' It was half-challenge, half-question.

'No,' Riley grinned. ''Cos there'll *be* no Commander *and* no table tomorrow morning.' He clasped his hands luxuriously behind his head. 'In fact, there'll be no nothin'.'

Something in the voice, rather than in the words, caught and held Dodson's attention. He knew, with instant conviction, that though Riley might be smiling, he wasn't joking. Dodson looked at him curiously, but said nothing.

'Commander's just finished broadcastin',' Riley continued. 'The *Tirpitz* is out – we have four hours left.'

The bald, flat statement, the complete lack of histrionics, of playing for effect, left no possible room for doubt. The *Tirpitz* – out. The *Tirpitz* – out. Dodson repeated the phrase to himself, over and over again. Four hours, just four hours to go. . . . He was surprised at his own reaction, his apparent lack of concern.

'Well?' Riley was anxious now, restive. 'Are you goin' or aren't you? I'm not kiddin', sir – you're wanted – urgent!'

'You're a liar,' Dodson said pleasantly. 'Why did you bring the coffee?'

'For myself.' The smile was gone, the face set and sullen. 'But I thought you needed it – you don't look so good to me. . . . They'll fix you up back in the engine-room.'

'And that's just where you're going, right now!' Dodson said evenly.

Riley gave no sign that he had heard.

'On your way, Riley,' Dodson said curtly. 'That's an order!'

'—off!' Riley growled. 'I'm stayin'. You don't require to have three—great gold stripes on your sleeve to handle a bloody oil can,' he finished derisively.

'Possibly not.' Dodson braced against a sudden, violent pitch, but too late to prevent himself lurching into Riley. 'Sorry, Riley. Weather's worsening, I'm afraid. Well, we – ah – appear to have reached an impasse.'

'What's that?' Riley asked suspiciously.

'A dead-end. A no-decision fight. . . . Tell me, Riley,' he asked quietly. 'What brought you here?'

'I told you!' Riley was aggrieved. 'Grierson – *Lieutenant* Grierson sent me.'

'What brought you here?' Dodson persisted. It was as if Riley had not spoken.

'That's my—business!' Riley answered savagely.

'What brought you here?'

'Oh, for Christ's sake leave me alone!' Riley shouted. His voice echoed loudly along the dark tunnel. Suddenly he turned round full-face, his mouth twisted bitterly. 'You know bloody well why I came.'

'To do me in, perhaps?'

Riley looked at him a long second, then turned away. His shoulders were hunched, his head held low.

'You're the only bastard in this ship that ever gave me a break,' he muttered. 'The only bastard I've ever *known* who ever gave me a chance,' he amended slowly. 'Bastard,' Dodson supposed, was Riley's accolade of friendship, and he felt suddenly ashamed of his last remark. 'If it wasn't for you,' Riley went on softly, 'I'd 'a' been in cells the first time, in a civvy jail the second. Remember, sir?'

Dodson nodded. 'You were rather foolish, Riley,' he admitted.

'Why did you do it?' The big stoker was intense, worried. 'God, everyone knows what I'm like—'

'Do they? I wonder. . . . I thought you had the makings of a better man than you—'

'Don't give me that bull!' Riley scoffed. '*I* know what I'm like. I know what I am. I'm no—good! Everybody says I'm no—good! And they're right. . . .' He leaned forward. 'Do you know somethin'? I'm a Catholic. Four hours from now . . .' He broke off. 'I should be on my knees, shouldn't I?' he sneered. 'Repentance, lookin' for – what do they call it?'

'Absolution?'

'Aye. That's it. Absolution. And do you know what?' He spoke slowly, emphatically. 'I don't give a single, solitary damn!'

'Maybe you don't have to,' Dodson murmured. 'For the last time, get back to that engine-room!'

'No!'

The Engineer-Commander sighed, picked up the Thermos.

'In that case, perhaps you would care to join me in a cup of coffee?'

Riley looked up, grinned, and when he spoke it was in a very creditable imitation of Colonel Chinstrap of the famous ITMA radio programme.

'Ectually, I don't mind if I do!'

Vallery rolled over on his side, his legs doubled up, his hand automatically reaching for the towel. His emaciated body shook violently, and the sound of the harsh, retching cough beat back at him from the iron walls of his shelter. God, he thought, oh, God, it's never been as bad as this before. Funny, he thought, it doesn't hurt any more, not even a little bit. The attack eased. He looked at the crimson, sodden towel, flung it in sudden disgust and with what little feeble strength was left into the darkest corner of the shelter.

'You carry this damned ship on your back!' Unbidden, old Socrates's phrase came into his mind and he smiled faintly. Well, if ever they needed him, it was now. And if he waited any longer, he knew he could never be able to go.

He sat up, sweating with the effort, swung his legs carefully over the side. As his feet touched the deck, the *Ulysses* pitched suddenly, steeply, and he fell forward against a chair, sliding helplessly to the floor. It took an eternity of time, an infinite effort to drag himself to his feet again: another effort like that, he knew, would surely kill him.

And then there was the door – that heavy, steel door. Somehow he had to open it, and he knew he couldn't. But he laid hold of the handle and the door opened, and suddenly, miraculously, he was outside, gasping as the cruel, sub-zero wind seared down through his throat and wasted lungs.

He looked fore and aft. The fires were dying, he saw, the fires on the *Stirling* and on his own poop-deck. Thank God for that at least. Beside him, two men had just finished levering the door off the Asdic cabinet, were flashing a torch inside. But he couldn't bear to look: he averted his head, staggered with outstretched hands for the gate of the compass platform.

Turner say him coming, hurried to meet him, helped him slowly to his chair.

'You've no right to be here,' he said quietly. He looked at Vallery for a long moment. 'How are you feeling, sir?'

'I'm a good deal better, now, thanks,' Vallery replied. He smiled and went on: 'We Rear-Admirals have our responsibilities, you know, Commander: it's time I began to earn my princely salary.'

'Stand back, there!' Carrington ordered curtly. 'Into the wheelhouse or up on the ladder – all of you. Let's have a look at this.'

He looked down at the great, steel hatch-cover. Looking at it, he realized he'd never before appreciated just how solid, how massive that cover was. The hatch-cover, open no more than an inch, was resting on a tommy-bar. He noticed the broken, stranded pulley, the heavy counterweight lying against the sill of the wheelhouse. So that's off, he thought: thank the Lord for that, anyway.

'Have you tried a block and tackle?' he asked abruptly.

'Yes, sir,' the man nearest him replied. He pointed to a tangled heap in a corner. 'No use, sir. The ladder takes the strain all right, but we can't get the hook under the hatch, except sideways – and then it slips off all the time.' He gestured to the hatch. 'And every clip's either bent – they were opened by sledges – or at the wrong angle. . . . I think I know how to use a block and tackle, sir.'

'I'm sure you do,' Carrington said absently. 'Here, give me a hand, will you?'

He hooked his fingers under the hatch, took a deep breath. The seaman at one side of the cover – the other side was hard against the after bulkhead – did the same. Together they strained, thighs and backs quivering under the strain. Carrington felt his face turning crimson with effort, heard the blood pounding in his ears, and relaxed. They were only killing themselves and that damned cover hadn't shifted a fraction – someone had done remarkably well to open it even that far. But even though they were tired and anything but fit, Carrington thought, two men should have been able to raise an edge of that hatch. He suspected that the hinges were jammed – or the deck buckled. If that were so, he mused, even if they could hook on a tackle, it would be of little help. A tackle was of no use when a sudden, immediate application of force was required; it always yielded that fraction before tightening up.

He sank to his knees, put his mouth to the edge of the hatch.

'Below there!' he called. 'Can you hear me?'

'We can hear you.' The voice was weak, muffled. 'For God's sake get us out of here. We're trapped like rats!'

'Is that you, Brierley? Don't worry – we'll get you out. How's the water down there?'

'Water? More bloody oil than water! There must be a fracture right through the port oil tank. I think the ring main passage must be flooded, too.'

'How deep is it?'

'Three-quarters way up already! We're standing on generators, hanging on to switchboards. One of our boys is gone already – we couldn't hold him.' Even muffled by the hatch, the strain, the near-desperation in the voice was all too obvious. 'For pity's sake, hurry up!'

'I said we'd get you out!' Carrington's voice was sharp, authoritative. The confidence was in his voice only, but he knew how quickly panic could spread down there. 'Can you push from below at all?'

'There's room for only one on the ladder,' Brierley shouted. 'It's impossible to get any pressure, any leverage upwards.' There was a sudden silence, then a series of muffled oaths.

'What's up?' Carrington called sharply.

'It's difficult to hang on,' Brierley shouted. 'There are waves two feet high down there. One of the men was washed off there. . . . I think he's back again. It's pitch dark down here.'

Carrington heard the clatter of heavy footsteps above him, and straightened up. It was Petersen. In that narrow space, the blond Norwegian stoker looked gigantic. Carrington looked at him, looked at the immense span of shoulder, the great depth of chest, one enormous hand hanging loosely by his side, the other negligently holding three heavy crowbars and a sledge as if they were so many lengths of cane. Carrington looked at him, looked at the still, grave eyes so startlingly blue under the flaxen hair, and all at once he felt oddly confident, reassured.

'We can't open this, Petersen,' Carrington said baldly. 'Can you?'

'I will try, sir.' He laid down his tools, stooped, caught the end of the tommy-bar projecting beneath the corner of the cover. He straightened quickly, easily: the hatch lifted a fraction, then the bar, putty-like in its apparent malleability, bent over almost to a right angle.

'I think the hatch is jammed.' Petersen wasn't even breathing heavily. 'It will be the hinges, sir.'

He walked round the hatch, peered closely at the hinges, then grunted in satisfaction. Three times the heavy sledge, swung with accuracy and all the power of these great shoulders behind them, smashed squarely into the face of the outer hinge. On the third stroke the sledge snapped. Petersen threw away the broken shaft in disgust, picked up another, much heavier crowbar.

Again the bar bent, but again the hatch-cover lifted – an inch this time. Petersen picked up the two smaller sledges that had been used to open clips, hammered at the hinges till these sledges, too, were broken and useless.

This time he used the last two crowbars together, thrust under the same corner of the hatch. For five, ten seconds he remained bent over them, motionless. He was breathing deeply, quickly, now, then suddenly the breathing stopped. The sweat began to pour off his face, his whole body to quiver under that titanic strain: then slowly, incredibly, both crowbars began to bend.

Carrington watched, fascinated. He had never seen anything remotely like this before: he was sure no one else had either. Neither of these bars, he would have sworn, would have bent under less than half a ton of pressure. It was fantastic, but it was happening: and as the giant straightened, they were bending more and more. Then suddenly, so unexpectedly that everyone jumped, the hatch sprang open five or six inches and Petersen crashed backwards against the bulkhead, the bars falling from his hand and splashing into the water below.

Petersen flung himself back at the hatch, tigerish in his ferocity. His fingers hooked under the edge, the great muscles of his arms and shoulders lifted and locked as he tugged and pulled at that massive hatch-cover. Three times he heaved, four times, then on the fifth the hatch almost literally leapt up with a screech of tortured metal and smashed shudderingly home into the retaining latch of the vertical stand behind. The hatch was open. Petersen just stood there smiling – no one had seen Petersen smile for a long time – his face bathed in sweat, his great chest rising and falling rapidly as his starved lungs sucked in great draughts of air.

The water level in the Low Power Room was within two feet of the hatch: sometimes, when the *Ulysses* plunged into a heavy sea, the dark, oily liquid splashed over the hatch coaming into the flat above. Quickly, the trapped men were hauled to safety. Soaked in oil from head to foot, their eyes gummed and blinded, they were men overcome by reaction, utterly spent and on the verge of collapse, so far gone that even in their fear could do no more than cling helplessly to the ladder, would almost certainly have slipped back into the surging blackness below; but Petersen bent over and plucked them clean out of the Low Power Room as if they had been little children.

'Take these men to the Sick Bay at once!' Carrington ordered. He watched the dripping, shivering men being helped up the ladder, then turned to the giant stoker with a smile. 'We'll all thank you later, Petersen. We're not finished yet. This hatch must be closed and battened down.'

'It will be difficult, sir,' Petersen said gravely.

'Difficult or not, it *must* be done.' Carrington was emphatic. Regularly, now, the water was spilling over the coaming, was lapping the sill of the wheelhouse. 'The emergency steering position is gone: if the wheelhouse is flooded, we're finished.'

Petersen said nothing. He lifted the retaining latch, pulled the protesting hatch-cover down a foot. Then he braced his shoulder against the latter, planted his feet on the cover and straightened his back convulsively: the cover screeched down to 45°. He paused, bent his back like a bow, his hands taking his weight on the ladder, then pounded his feet again and again on the edge of the cover. Fifteen inches to go.

'We need heavy hammers, sir.' Petersen said urgently.

'No time!' Carrington shook his head quickly. 'Two more minutes and it'll be impossible to shut the hatch-cover against the water pressure. Hell!' he said bitterly. 'If it were only the other way round – closing from below. Even I could lever it shut!'

Again Petersen said nothing. He squatted down by the side of the hatch, gazed into the darkness beneath his feet.

'I have an idea, sir,' he said quickly. 'If two of you would stand on the hatch, push against the ladder. Yes, sir, that way – but you could push harder if you turned your back to me.'

Carrington laid the heels of his hands against the iron steps of the ladder, heaved with all his strength. Suddenly he heard a splash, then a metallic clatter, whirled round just in time to see a crowbar clutched in an enormous hand disappear below the edge of the hatch. There was no sign of Petersen. Like many big, powerful men, he was lithe and cat-like in his movements: he'd gone down over the edge of that hatch without a sound.

'Petersen!' Carrington was on his knees by the hatch. 'What the devil do you think you're doing? Come out of there, you bloody fool! Do you want to drown?'

There was no reply. Complete silence below, a silence deepened by the gentle susurration of the water. Suddenly the quiet was broken by the sound of metal striking against metal, then by a jarring screech as the hatch dropped six inches. Before Carrington had time to think, the hatch-cover dropped farther still. Desperately, the First Lieutenant seized a crowbar, thrust it under the hatch-cover: a split second later the great steel cover thudded down on top of it. Carrington had his mouth to the gap now.

'In the name of God, Petersen,' he shouted, 'Are you sane? Open up, open up at once, do you hear?'

'I can't.' The voice came and went as the water surged over the stoker's head. 'I won't. You said yourself . . . there is no time . . . this was the only way.'

'But I never meant—'

'I know. It does not matter . . . it is better this way.' It was almost impossible to make out what he was saying. 'Tell Captain Vallery that Petersen says he is very sorry. . . . I tried to tell the Captain yesterday.'

'Sorry! Sorry for what?' Madly Carrington flung all his strength against the iron bar: the hatch-cover did not even quiver.

'The dead marine in Scapa Flow. . . . I did not mean to kill him, I could never kill any man. . . . But he angered me,' the big Norwegian said simply. 'He killed my friend.'

For a second, Carrington stopped straining at the bar. Petersen! Of course – who but Petersen could have snapped a man's neck like that. Petersen, the big, laughing Scandinavian, who had so suddenly changed overnight into a grave unsmiling giant, who stalked the deck, the mess-decks and alleyways by day and by night, who was never seen to smile or sleep. With a sudden flash of insight, Carrington saw clear through the tortured mind of that kind and simple man.

'Listen, Petersen,' he begged. 'I don't give a damn about that. Nobody shall ever know, I promise you. Please, Petersen, just—'

'It is better this way.' The muffled voice was strangely content. 'It is not good to kill a man . . . it is not good to go on living. . . . I know. . . . Please, it is important – you will tell my Captain – Petersen is sorry and filled with shame. . . . I do this for my Captain.' Without warning, the crowbar was plucked from Carrington's hand. The cover clanged down in position. For a minute the wheelhouse flat rang to a succession of muffled, metallic blows. Suddenly the clamour ceased and there was only the rippling surge of the water outside the wheelhouse and the creak of the wheel inside as the *Ulysses* steadied on course.

The clear sweet voice soared high and true above the subdued roar of the engine-room fans, above the whine of a hundred electric motors and the sound of the rushing of the waters. Not even the metallic impersonality of the loudspeakers could detract from the beauty of that singing voice. . . . It was a favourite device of Vallery's when the need for silence was not paramount, to pass the long, dark hours by coupling up the record-player to the broadcast system.

Almost invariably, the musical repertoire was strictly classical – or what is more often referred to, foolishly and disparagingly, as the popular classics. Bach, Beethoven, Tchaikovski, Lehar, Verdi, Delius – these were the favourites. 'No. I in B flat minor,' 'Air on a G string,' 'Moonlight on the Alster,' 'Claire de Lune,' 'The Skater's Waltz' – the crew of the *Ulysses* could never have enough of these. 'Ridiculous,' 'impossible' – it is all too easy to imagine the comments of those who equate the matelot's taste in music with the popular conception of his ethics and morals; but those same people have never heard the hushed, cathedral silence in the crowded hangar of a great aircraft carrier in Scapa Flow as Yehudi Menuhin's magic bow sang across the strings of the violin, swept a thousand men away from the harsh urgencies of reality, from the bitter memories of the last patrol or convoy, into the golden land of music.

But now a girl was singing. It was Deanna Durbin, and she was singing 'Beneath the Lights of Home,' that most heartbreakingly nostalgic of all songs. Below decks and above, bent over the great engines or huddled by their guns, men listened to the lovely voice as it drifted through the darkened ship and the falling snow, and turned their minds inwards and thought of home, thought of the bitter contrast and the morning that would not come. Suddenly, half-way through, the song stopped.

'Do you hear there?' the speakers boomed. 'Do you hear there? This – this is the Commander speaking.' The voice was deep and grave and hesitant: it caught and held the attention of every man in the ship.

'I have bad news for you.' Turner spoke slowly, quietly. 'I am sorry – I . . .' He broke off, then went on more slowly still. 'Captain Vallery died five minutes ago.' For a moment the 'speaker was silent, then crackled again. 'He died on the bridge, in his chair. He knew he was dying and I don't think he suffered at all. . . . He insisted – he insisted that I thank you for the way you all stood by him. "Tell them" – these were his words, as I remember – "tell them," he said, "that I couldn't have carried on without them, that they are the best crew that God ever gave a Captain.' Then he said – it was the last thing he said: "Give them my apologies. After all they've done for me – well, well, tell them I'm terribly sorry to let them down like this." That was all he said – just "Tell them I'm sorry." And then he died.'

Chapter Sixteen

Saturday Night

Richard Vallery was dead. He died grieving, stricken at the thought that he was abandoning the crew of the *Ulysses*, leaving them behind, leaderless. But it was only for a short time, and he did not have to wait long. Before the dawn, hundreds more, men in the cruisers, the destroyers and the merchantmen, had died also. And they did not die as he had feared under the guns of the *Tirpitz* – another grim parallel with PQ17, for the *Tirpitz* had not left Alta Fjord. They died, primarily, because the weather had changed.

Richard Vallery was dead, and with his death a great change had come over the men of the *Ulysses*. When Vallery died, other things died also, for he took these things with him. He took with him the courage, the kindliness, the gentleness, the unshakable faith, the infinitely patient and understanding endurance, all these things which had been so peculiarly his own. And now these things were gone and the *Ulysses* was left without them and it did not matter. The men of the *Ulysses* no longer needed courage and all the adjuncts of courage, for they were no longer afraid. Vallery was dead and they did not know how much they respected and loved that gentle man until he was gone. But then they knew. They knew that something wonderful, something that had become an enduring part of their minds and memories, something infinitely fine and good, was gone and they would never know it again, and they were mad with grief. And, in war, a grief-stricken man is the most terrible enemy there is. Prudence, caution, fear, pain – for the grief-stricken man these no longer exist. He lives only to lash out blindly at the enemy, to destroy, if he can, the author of his grief. Rightly or wrongly, the *Ulysses* never thought to blame the Captain's death on any but the enemy. There was only, for them, the sorrow and the blind hate. Zombies, Nicholls had called them once, and the *Ulysses* was more than ever a ship manned by living zombies, zombies who prowled restlessly, incessantly, across the snow and ice of the heaving decks, automatons living only for revenge.

The weather changed just before the end of the middle watch. The seas did not change – FR77 was still butting into the heavy, rolling swell from the north, still piling up fresh sheets of glistening ice on their labouring fo'c'sles. But the wind dropped, and almost at once the snowstorm blew itself out, the last banks of dark, heavy cloud drifting away to the south. By four o'clock the sky was completely clear.

There was no moon that night, but the stars were out, keen and sharp and frosty as the icy breeze that blew steadily out of the north.

Then, gradually, the sky began to change. At first there was only a barely perceptible lightening on the northern rim then, slowly, a pulsating flickering band of light began to broaden and deepen and climb steadily above the horizon, climbing higher to the south with the passing of every minute. Soon that pulsating ribbon of light was paralleled by others, streamers in the most delicate pastel shades of blue and green and violet, but always and predominantly white. And always, too, these lanes of multi-coloured light grew higher and stronger and brighter: at the climax, a great band of white stretched high above the convoy, extending from horizon to horizon. . . . These were the Northern Lights, at any time a spectacle of beauty and wonder, and this night surpassing lovely: down below, in ships clearly illumined against the dark and rolling seas, the men of FR77 looked up and hated them.

On the bridge of the *Ulysses*, Chrysler of the uncanny eyesight and super-sensitive hearing, was the first to hear it. Soon everyone else heard it too, the distant roar, throbbing and intermittent, of a Condor approaching from the south. After a time they became aware that the Condor was no longer approaching, but sudden hope died almost as it was born. There was no mistaking it now – the deeper, heavier note of a Focke-Wulf in maximum climb. The Commander turned wearily to Carrington.

'It's Charlie, all right,' he said grimly. 'The bastard's spotted us. He'll already have radioed Alta Fjord and a hundred to one in anything you like that he's going to drop a marker flare at 10,000 feet or so. It'll be seen fifty miles away.'

'Your money's sake.' The First Lieutenant was withering. 'I never bet against dead certs. . . . And then, by and by, maybe a few flares at a couple of thousand?'

'Exactly!' Turner nodded. 'Pilot, how far do you reckon we're from Alta Fjord – in flying time, I mean?'

'For a 200-knot plane, just over an hour,' the Kapok Kid said quietly. His ebullience was gone: he had been silent and dejected since Vallery had died two hours previously.

'An hour!' Carrington exclaimed. 'And they'll *be* here. My God, sir,' he went on wonderingly, 'they're really out to get us. We've never been bombed nor torpedoed at night before. We've never had the *Tirpitz* after us before. We never—'

'The *Tirpitz*,' Turner interrupted. 'Just where the hell *is* that ship? She's had time to come up with us. Oh, I know it's dark and we've changed course,' he added, as Carrington made to object, 'but a fast destroyer screen would have picked us – Preston!' He broke off, spoke sharply to the Signal Petty Officer. 'Look alive, man! That ship's flashing us.'

'Sorry, sir.' The signalman, swaying on his feet with exhaustion, raised his Aldis, clacked out an acknowledgment. Again the light on the merchant-man began to wink furiously.

' "Transverse fracture engine bedplate." ' Preston read out. ' "Damage serious: shall have to moderate speed." '

'Acknowledge,' said Turner curtly. 'What ship is that, Preston?'

'The *Ohio Freighter*, sir.'

'The one that stopped a tin fish a couple of days back?'

'That's her, sir.'

'Make a signal. "Essential maintain speed and position." ' Turner swore. 'What a time to choose for an engine breakdown. . . . Pilot, when do we rendezvous with the Fleet?'

'Six hours' time, sir: exactly.'

'Six hours.' Turner compressed his lips. 'Just six hours – perhaps!' he added bitterly.

'Perhaps?' Carrington murmured.

'Perhaps,' Turner affirmed. 'Depends entirely on the weather. C-in-C won't risk capital ships so near the coast unless he can fly off fighter cover against air attack. And, if you ask me, that's why the *Tirpitz* hasn't turned up yet – some wandering U-boat's tipped him off that our Fleet Carriers are steaming south. He'll be waiting on the weather. . . . What's he saying now, Preston?' The *Ohio*'s signal lamp had flashed briefly, then died.

' "Imperative slow down," ' Preston repeated. '"Damage severe. Am slowing down." '

'He is, too,' Carrington said quietly. He looked up at Turner, at the set face and dark eyes, and knew the same thought was in the Commander's mind as was in his own. 'He's a goner, sir, a dead duck. He hasn't a chance. Not unless—'

'Unless what?' Turner asked harshly. 'Unless we leave him an escort? Leave what escort, Number One? The *Viking* – the only effective unit we've left?' He shook his head in slow decision. 'The greatest good of the greatest number: that's how it has to be. They'll know that. Preston, send "Regret cannot leave you standby. How long to effect repairs?" '

The flare burst even before Preston's hand could close on the trigger. It burst directly over FR77. It was difficult to estimate the height – probably six to eight thousand feet – but at that altitude it was no more than an incandescent pin-point against the great band of the Northern Lights arching majestically above. But it was falling quickly, glowing more brightly by the second: the parachute, if any, could have been only a steadying drogue.

The cracking of the WT 'speaker broke through the stuttering chatter of the Aldis.

'WT – bridge. WT – bridge. Message from *Sirrus*: "Three survivors dead. Many dying or seriously wounded. Medical assistance urgent, repeat urgent." ' The 'speaker died, just as the *Ohio* started flickering her reply.

'Send for Lieutenant Nicholls,' Turner ordered briefly. 'Ask him to come up to the bridge at once.'

Carrington stared down at the dark broad seas, seas flecked with milky foam: the bows of the *Ulysses* were crashing down heavily, continuously.

'You're going to risk it, sir?'

'I must. You'd do the same, Number One. . . . What does the *Ohio* say, Preston?'

' "I understand. Too busy to look after the Royal Navy anyway. We will make up on you. Au revoir!" '

'We will make up on you. Au revoir.' Turner repeated softly. 'He lies in his teeth, and he knows it. By God!' he burst out. 'If anyone ever tells me the Yankee sailors have no guts – I'll push his perishing face in. Preston, send: "Au revoir. Good luck." . . . Number One, I feel like a murderer.' He rubbed his hand across his forehead, nodded towards the shelter where Vallery lay stretched out, and strapped to his settee. 'Month in, month out, he's been taking these decisions. It's no wonder . . .' He broke off as the gate creaked open.

'Is that you, Nicholls? There is work for you, my boy. Can't have you medical types idling around uselessly all day long.' He raised his hand. 'All right, all right,' he chuckled. 'I know. . . . How are things on the surgical front?' he went on seriously.

'We've done all we can, sir. There was very little left for us to do,' Nicholls said quietly. His face was deeply lined, haggard to the point of emaciation. 'But we're in a bad way for supplies. Hardly a single dressing left. And no anaesthetics at all – except what's left in the emergency kit. The Surgeon-Commander refuses to touch those.'

'Good, good,' Turner murmured. 'How do you feel, laddie?'

'Awful.'

'You look it,' Turner said candidly. 'Nicholls – I'm terribly sorry, boy – I want you to go over to the *Sirrus*.'

'Yes, sir.' There was no surprise in the voice: it hadn't been difficult to guess why the Commander had sent for him. 'Now?'

Turner nodded without speaking. His face, the lean strong features, the heavy brows and sunken eyes were quite visible now in the strengthening light of the plunging flare. A face to remember, Nicholls thought.

'How much kit can I take with me, sir?'

'Just your medical gear. No more. You're not travelling by Pullman, laddie!'

'Can I take my camera, my films?'

'All right.' Turner smiled briefly. 'Looking forward keenly to photographing the last seconds of the *Ulysses*, I suppose. . . . Don't forget that the *Sirrus* is leaking like a sieve. Pilot – get through to the WT. Tell the *Sirrus* to come alongside, prepare to receive medical officer by breeches buoy.'

The gate creaked again. Turner looked at the bulky figure stumbling wearily on to the compass platform. Brooks, like every man in the crew was dead on his feet; but the blue eyes burned as brightly as ever.

'My spies are everywhere,' he announced. 'What's this about the *Sirrus* shanghaiing young Johnny here?'

'Sorry, old man,' Turner apologized. 'It seems things are pretty bad on the *Sirrus*.'

'I see.' Brooks shivered. It might have been the thin threnody of the wind in the shattered rigging, or just the iceladen wind itself. He shivered again, looked upwards at the sinking flare. 'Pretty, very pretty,' he murmured. 'What are the illuminations in aid of?'

'We are expecting company,' Turner smiled crookedly. 'An old world custom, O Socrates – the light in the window and what have you.' He stiffened abruptly, then relaxed, his face graven in granitic immobility. 'My mistake,' he murmured. 'The company has already arrived.'

The last words were caught up and drowned in the rumbling of a heavy explosion. Turner had known it was coming – he'd seen the thin stiletto of flame stabbing skywards just for'ard of the *Ohio Freighter*'s bridge. The sound had taken five or six seconds to reach them – the *Ohio* was already a mile distant on the starboard quarter, but clearly visible still under the luminance of the Northern Lights – the Northern Lights that had betrayed her, almost stopped in the water, to a wandering U-boat.

The *Ohio Freighter* did not remain visible for long. Except for the moment of impact, there was neither smoke, nor flame, nor sound. But her back must have been broken, her bottom torn out – and she was carrying a full cargo of nothing but tanks and ammunition. There was a curious dignity about her end – she sank quickly, quietly, without any fuss. She was gone in three minutes.

It was Turner who finally broke the heavy silence on the bridge. He turned away and in the light of the flare his face was not pleasant to see.

'Au revoir,' he muttered to no one in particular. 'Au revoir. That's what he said, the lying . . .' He shook his head angrily, touched the Kapok Kid on the arm. 'Get through to WT,' he said sharply. 'Tell the *Viking* to sit over the top of that sub till we get clear.'

'Where's it all going to end?' Brooks's face was still and heavy in the twilight.

'God knows! How I hate those murdering bastards!' Turner ground out. 'Oh, I know, I know, we do the same – but give me something I can see, something I can fight, something—'

'You'll be able to see the *Tirpitz* all right,' Carrington interrupted dryly. 'By all accounts, she's big enough.'

Turner looked at him, suddenly smiled. He clapped his arm, then craned his head back, staring up at the shimmering loveliness of the sky. He wondered when the next flare would drop.

'Have you a minute to spare, Johnny?' The Kapok Kid's voice was low. 'I'd like to speak to you.'

'Sure.' Nicholls looked at him in surprise. 'Sure, I've a minute, ten minutes – until the *Sirrus* comes up. What's wrong, Andy?'

'Just a second.' The Kapok Kid crossed to the Commander. 'Permission to go to the charthouse, sir?'

'Sure you've got your matches?' Turner smiled. 'OK. Off you go.'

The Kapok Kid smiled faintly, said nothing. He took Nicholls by the arm, led him into the charthouse, flicked on the lights and produced his cigarettes. He looked steadily at Nicholls as he dipped his cigarette into the flickering pool of flame.

'Know something, Johnny?' he said abruptly. 'I reckon I must have Scotch blood in me.'

'Scots,' Nicholls corrected. 'And perish the very thought.'

'I'm feeling – what's the word? – fey, isn't it? I'm feeling fey tonight, Johnny.' The Kapok Kid hadn't even heard the interruption. He shivered. 'I don't know why – I've never felt this way before.'

'Ah, nonsense! Indigestion, my boy,' Nicholls said briskly. But he felt strangely uncomfortable.

'Won't wash this time,' Carpenter shook his head, half-smiling. 'Besides, I haven't eaten a thing for two days. I'm on the level, Johnny.' In spite of himself, Nicholls was impressed. Emotion, gravity, earnestness – these were utterly alien to the Kapok Kid.

'I won't be seeing you again,' the Kapok Kid continued softly. 'Will you do me a favour, Johnny?'

'Don't be so bloody silly,' Nicholls said angrily. 'How the hell do you—?'

'Take this with you.' The Kapok Kid pulled out a slip of paper, thrust it into Nicholls's hands. 'Can you read it?'

'I can read it.' Nicholls had stilled his anger. 'Yes, I can read it.' There was a name and address on the sheet of paper, a girl's name and a Surrey address. 'So that's her name,' he said softly. 'Juanita . . . Juanita.' He pronounced it carefully, accurately, in the Spanish fashion. 'My favourite song and my favourite name,' he murmured.

'Is it?' the Kapok Kid asked eagerly. 'Is it indeed? And mine, Johnny.' He paused. 'If, perhaps – well, if I don't – well, you'll go to see her, Johnny?'

'What are you talking about, man?' Nicholls felt embarrassed. Half-impatiently, half-playfully, he tapped him on the chest. 'Why, with that suit on, you could *swim* from here to Murmansk. You've said so yourself, a hundred times.'

The Kapok Kid grinned up at him. The grin was a little crooked.

'Sure, sure, I know, I know – will you go, Johnny?'

'Dammit to hell, yes!' Nicholls snapped. 'I'll go – and it's high time I was going somewhere else. Come on!' He snapped off the lights, pulled back the door, stopped with his foot halfway over the sill. Slowly, he stepped back inside the charthouse, closed the door and flicked on the light. The Kapok Kid hadn't moved, was gazing quietly at him.

'I'm sorry, Andy,' Nicholls said sincerely. 'I don't know what made me—'

'Bad temper,' said the Kapok Kid cheerfully. 'You always did hate to think that I was right and you were wrong!'

Nicholls caught his breath, closed his eyes for a second. Then he stretched out his hand.

'All the best, Vasco.' It was an effort to smile. 'And don't worry. I'll see her if – well, I'll see her, I promise you. Juanita. . . . But if I find *you* there,' he went on threateningly, 'I'll—'

'Thanks, Johnny. Thanks a lot.' The Kapok Kid was almost happy. 'Good luck, boy. . . . Vaya con Dios. That's what she always said to me, what she said before I came away. "Vaya con Dios." '

Thirty minutes later, Nicholls was operating aboard the *Sirrus*.

The time was 0445. It was bitterly cold, with a light wind blowing steadily from the north. The seas were heavier than ever, longer between the crests, deeper in their gloomy troughs, and the damaged *Sirrus*, labouring under a mountain of ice, was making heavy weather of it. The sky was still clear, a sky of breath-taking purity, and the stars were out again, for the Northern Lights were fading. The fifth successive flare was drifting steadily seawards.

It was at 0445 that they heard it – the distant rumble of gunfire far to the south – perhaps a minute after they had seen the incandescent brilliance of a burning flare on the rim of the far horizon. There could be no doubt as to what was happening. The *Viking*, still in contact with the U-boat, although powerless to do anything about it, was being heavily attacked. And the attack must have been short, sharp and deadly, for the firing ceased soon after it had begun. Ominously, nothing came through on the WT. No one ever knew what had happened to the *Viking*, for there were no survivors.

The last echo of the *Viking*'s guns had barely died away before they heard the roar of the engines of the Condor, at maximum throttle in a shallow dive. For five, perhaps ten seconds – it seemed longer than that, but not long enough for any gun in the convoy to begin tracking him accurately – the great Focke-Wulf actually flew beneath his own flare, and then was gone. Behind him, the sky opened up in a blinding coruscation of flame, more dazzling, more hurtful, than the light of the noonday sun. So intense, so extraordinary the power of those flares, so much did pupils contract and eyelids narrow in instinctive self-protection, that the enemy bombers were through the circle of light and upon them before anyone fully realized what was happening. The timing, the split-second co-operation between marker planes and bombers were magnificent.

There were twelve planes in the first wave. There was no concentration on one target, as before: not more than two attacked any ship. Turner, watching from the bridge, watching them swoop down steeply and level out before even the first gun in the *Ulysses* had opened up, caught his breath in sudden dismay. There was something terribly familiar about the speed, the approach, the silhouette of these planes. Suddenly he had it – Heinkels, by God! Heinkel 111s. And the Heinkel 111, Turner knew, carried that weapon he dreaded above all others – the glider bomb.

And then, as if he had touched a master switch, every gun on the *Ulysses* opened up. The air filled with smoke, the pungent smell of burning cordite: the din was indescribable. And all at once, Turner felt fiercely, strangely happy. . . . To hell with them and their glider bombs, he thought. This was war as he liked to fight it: not the cat-and-mouse, hide-and-seek frustration of trying to outguess the hidden wolf-packs, but war out in the open, where he could see the enemy and hate him and love him for fighting as honest men should and do his damnedest to destroy him. And, Turner knew, if they could at all, the crew of the *Ulysses* would destroy him. It needed no great sensitivity to direct the sea-change that had overtaken his men – yes, *his* men now: they no longer cared for themselves: they had crossed the frontier of fear and found that nothing lay beyond it and they would keep on feeding their guts and squeezing their triggers until the enemy overwhelmed them.

The leading Heinkel was blown out of the sky, and fitting enough it was 'X' turret that destroyed it – 'X' turret, the turret of dead marines, the turret that had destroyed the Condor, and was now manned by a scratch marine crew. The Heinkel behind lifted sharply to avoid the hurtling fragments of fuselage and engines, dipped, flashed past the cruiser's bows less than a boat-length away, banked steeply to port under maximum power, and swung back in on the *Ulysses*. Every gun on the ship was caught on the wrong foot, and seconds passed before the first one was brought to bear – time and to spare for the Heinkel to angle in at 60°, drop his bomb and slew frantically away as the concentrated fire of the Oerlikons and pom-poms closed in on him. Miraculously, he escaped.

The winged bomb was high, but not high enough. It wavered, steadied, dipped, then glided forwards and downwards through the drifting smoke of the guns to strike home with a tremendous, deafening explosion that shook the *Ulysses* to her keel and almost shattered the eardrums of those on deck.

To Turner, looking aft from the bridge, it seemed that the *Ulysses* could never survive this last assault. An ex-torpedo officer and explosives expert himself, he was skilled in assessing the disruptive power of high explosive: never before had he been so close to so powerful, so devastating an explosion. He had dreaded these glider bombs, but even so he had underestimated their power: the concussion had been double, treble what he had been expecting.

What Turner did not know was that what he had heard had been not one explosion but two, but so nearly simultaneous as to be indistinguishable. The glider bomb, by a freakish chance had crashed directly into the port torpedo tubes. There had been only one torpedo left there – the other two had sent the *Vytura* to the bottom – and normally Amatol, the warhead explosive, is extremely stable and inert, even when subjected to violent shock: but the bursting bomb had been too close too powerful: sympathetic detonation had been inevitable.

Damage was extensive and spectacular: it was severe, but not fatal. The side of the *Ulysses* had been ripped open, as by a giant can-opener, almost to the water's edge: the tubes had vanished: the decks were holed and splintered: the funnel casing was a shambles, the funnel itself tilting over to port almost to fifteen degrees; but the greatest energy of the explosion had been directed aft, most of the blast expending itself over the open sea, while the galley and canteen, severely damaged already, were no more than a devil's scrapyard.

Almost before the dust and debris of the explosion had settled, the last of the Heinkels was disappearing, skimming the waves, weaving and twisting madly in evasive action, pursued and hurried by a hundred glowing streams of tracer. Then, magically, they were gone, and there was only the sudden deafening silence and the flares, drooping slowly to extinction, lighting up the pall above the *Ulysses*, the dark clouds of smoke rolling up from the shattered *Stirling* and a tanker with its after superstructure almost gone. But not one of the ships in FR77 had faltered or stopped; and they had destroyed five Heinkels. A costly victory, Turner mused, if it could be called a victory; but he knew the Heinkels would be back. It was not difficult to imagine the fury, the hurt pride of the High Command in Norway: as far as Turner knew, no Russian Convoy had ever sailed so far south before.

Riley eased a cramped leg, stretched it gently so as to avoid the great spinning shaft. Carefully he poured some oil on to the bearing, carefully, so as not to disturb the Engineer Commander, propped in sleep between the tunnel wall and Riley's shoulder. Even as Riley drew back, Dodson stirred, opened heavy, gummed lids.

'Good God above!' he said wearily. 'You still here, Riley?' It was the first time either of them had spoken for hours.

'It's a — good job I *am* here,' Riley growled. He nodded towards the bearing. 'Bloody difficult to get a fire-hose down to this place, I should think!' That was unfair Riley knew: he and Dodson had been taking it in half-hour turns to doze and feed the bearing. But he felt he had to say something: he was finding it increasingly difficult to keep on being truculent to the Engineer Commander.

Dodson grinned to himself, said nothing. Finally, he cleared his throat, murmured casually: 'The *Tirpitz* is taking its time about making its appearance, don't you think?'

'Yes, sir.' Riley was uncomfortable. 'Should 'a' been here long ago, damn her!'

'Him,' Dodson corrected absently. '*Admiral von Tirpitz*, you know. . . . Why don't you give up this foolishness, Riley?'

Riley grunted, said nothing. Dodson sighed, then brightened.

'Go and get some more coffee, Riley, I'm parched!'

'No.' Riley was blunt. '*You* get it.'

'As a favour, Riley.' Dodson was very gentle. 'I'm damned thirsty!'

'Oh, all right.' The big stoker swore, climbed painfully to his feet. 'Where'll I get it?'

'Plenty in the engine-room. If it's not iced water they're swigging, it's coffee. But no iced water for me.' Dodson shivered.

Riley gathered up the Thermos, stumbled along the passage. He had only gone a few feet when they felt the *Ulysses* shudder under the recoil of the heavy armament. Although they did not know it, it was the beginning of the air attack.

Dodson braced himself against the wall, saw Riley do the same, paused a second then hurry away in an awkward, stumbling run. There was something grotesquely familiar in that awkward run, Dodson thought. The guns surged back again and the figure scuttled even faster, like a giant crab in a panic. . . . *Panic*, Dodson thought: that's it, panic-stricken. Don't blame the poor bastard – I'm beginning to imagine things myself down here. Again the whole tunnel vibrated, more heavily this time – that must be 'X' turret, almost directly above. No, I don't blame him. Thank God he's gone. He smiled quietly to himself. I won't be seeing friend Riley again – he isn't all that of a reformed character. Tiredly, Dodson settled back against the wall. On my own at last, he murmured to himself, and waited for the feeling of relief. But it never came. Instead, there was only a vexation and loneliness, a sense of desertion and a strangely empty disappointment.

Riley was back inside a minute. He came back with that same awkward crab-like run, carrying a three-pint Thermos jug and two cups, cursing fluently and often as he slipped against the wall. Panting, wordlessly, he sat down beside Dodson, poured out a cup of steaming coffee.

'Why the hell did you have to come back?' Dodson demanded harshly. 'I don't want you and—'

'You wanted coffee,' Riley interrupted rudely. 'You've got the bloody stuff. Drink it.'

At that instant the explosion and the vibration from the explosion in the port tubes echoed weirdly down the dark tunnel, the shock flinging the two men heavily against each other. His whole cup of coffee splashed over Dodson's leg: his mind was so tired, his reactions so slow, that his first realization was of how damnably cold he was, how chill that dripping tunnel. The scalding coffee had gone right through his clothes, but he could feel neither warmth nor wetness: his legs were numbed, dead below the knees. Then he shook his head, looked up at Riley.

'What in God's name was that? What's happening? Did you—?'

'Haven't a clue. Didn't stop to ask.' Riley stretched himself luxuriously, blew on his steaming coffee. Then a happy thought struck him, and a broad cheerful grin came as near to transforming that face as would ever be possible.

'It's probably the *Tirpitz*,' he said hopefully.

Three times more during that terrible night, the German squadrons took off from the airfield at Alta Fjord, throbbed their way nor'-nor'-west through the bitter Arctic night, over the heaving Arctic sea, in search of the shattered remnants of FR77. Not that the search was difficult – the Focke-Wulf Condor stayed with them all night, defied their best attempts to shake him off. He seemed to have an endless supply of these deadly flares, and might very well have been – in fact, almost certainly was – carrying nothing else. And the bombers had only to steer for the flares.

The first assault – about 0545 – was an orthodox bombing attack, made from about 3000 feet. The planes seemed to be Dorniers, but it was difficult to be sure, because they flew high above a trio of flares sinking close to the water level. As an attack, it was almost but not quite abortive, and was pressed home with no great enthusiasm. This was understandable: the barrage was intense. But there were two direct hits, one on a merchantman, blowing away most of the fo'c'sle, the other on the *Ulysses*. It sheered through the flag deck and the Admiral's day cabin, and exploded in the heart of the Sick Bay. The Sick Bay was crowded with the sick and dying, and, for many, that bomb must have come as a God-sent release, for the *Ulysses* had long since run out of anaesthetics. There were no survivors. Among the dead was Marshall, the Torpedo Officer, Johnson, the Leading SBA, the Master-At-Arms who had been lightly wounded an hour before by a splinter from the torpedo tubes, Burgess, strapped helplessly in a strait-jacket – he had suffered concussion on the night of the great storm and gone insane. Brown, whose hip had been smashed by the hatch-cover of 'Y' magazine, and Brierley, who was dying anyway, his lungs saturated and rotted away with fuel oil. Brooks had not been there.

The same explosion had also shattered the telephone exchange: barring only the bridge-gun phones, and the bridge-engine phones and speaking-tubes, all communication lines in the *Ulysses* were gone.

The second attack at 7 a.m., was made by only six bombers – Heinkels again, carrying glider-bombs. Obviously flying strictly under orders, they ignored the merchantmen and concentrated their attack solely on the cruisers. It was an expensive attack: the enemy lost all but two of their force in exchange for a single hit aft on the *Stirling*, a hit which, tragically, put both after guns out of action.

Turner, red-eyed and silent, bareheaded in that sub-zero wind, and pacing the shattered bridge of the *Ulysses*, marvelled that the *Stirling* still floated, still fought back with everything she had. And then he looked at his own ship, less a ship, he thought wearily, than a floating shambles of twisted steel still scything impossibly through those heavy seas, and marvelled all the more. Broken, burning cruisers, cruisers ravaged and devastated to the point of destruction, were nothing new for Turner: he had seen the *Trinidad* and the *Edinburgh* being literally battered to death on these same Russian convoys. But he had never seen any ship, at any time, such inhuman, murderous punishment as the *Ulysses* and the obsolete *Stirling* and still live. He would not have believed it possible.

The third attack came just before dawn. It came with the grey half-light, an attack carried out with great courage and the utmost determination by fifteen Heinkel 111 glider-bombers. Again the cruisers were the sole targets, the heavier attack by far being directed against the *Ulysses*. Far from shirking the challenge and bemoaning their ill-luck the crew of the *Ulysses*, that strange and selfless crew of walking zombies whom Nicholls had left behind, welcomed the enemy gladly, even joyfully, for how can one kill an enemy if he does not come to you? Fear, anxiety, the near-certainty of death – these did not exist. Home and country, families, wives and sweethearts, were names, only names: they touched a man's mind, these thoughts, touched it and lifted and were gone as if they had never been. 'Tell them,' Vallery had said, 'tell them they are the best crew God ever gave a captain.' Vallery. *That* was what mattered, that and what Vallery stood for, that something that had been so inseparably a part of that good and kindly man that you never saw it because it *was* Vallery. And the crew hoisted the shells, slammed the breeches and squeezed their triggers, men uncaring, men oblivious of anything and everything, except the memory of the man who had died apologizing because he had let them down, except the sure knowledge that they could not let Vallery down. Zombies, but inspired zombies, men above themselves, as men commonly are when they know the next step, the inevitable step has them clear to the top of the far side of the valley. . . .

The first part of the attack was launched against the *Stirling*. Turner saw two Heinkels roaring in in a shallow dive, improbably surviving against heavy, concentrated fire at point-blank range. The bombs, delayed action and armour-piercing, struck the *Stirling* amidships, just below deck level, and exploded deep inside, in the boiler-room and engine-room. The next three bombers were met with only pom-pom and Lewis fire: the main armament for'ard had fallen silent. With sick apprehension. Turner realized what had happened: the explosion had cut the power to the turrets.[1] Ruthlessly, contemptuously almost, the bombers brushed aside the puny opposition: every bomb went home. The *Stirling*, Turner saw, was desperately wounded. She was on fire again, and listing heavily to starboard.

The suddenly lifting crescendo of aero engines spun Turner round to look to his own ship. There were five Heinkels in the first wave, at different heights and approach angles so as to break up the pattern of AA fire, but all converging on the after end of the *Ulysses*. There was so much smoke and noise that Turner could only gather confused, broken impressions. Suddenly, it seemed, the air was filled with glider-bombs and the tearing, staccato crash of the German cannon and guns. One bomb exploded in mid-air, just for'ard of the after funnel and feet away from it: a maiming, murderous storm of jagged steel scythed across the boat-deck, and all Oerlikons and the pom-poms fell immediately silent, their crews victim to shrapnel or concussion. Another plunged through the deck and Engineers' Flat and turned the WT office into a charnel house. The remaining two that struck were higher, smashing squarely into 'X' gun-deck and 'X' turret. The turret was split open around the top and down both sides as by a giant cleaver, and blasted off its mounting, to lie grotesquely across the shattered poop.

Apart from the boat-deck and turret gunners, only one other man lost his life in that attack, but that man was virtually irreplaceable. Shrapnel from the first bomb had burst a compressed air cylinder in the torpedo workshop, and Hartley, the man who, above all, had become the back-bone of the *Ulysses* had taken shelter there, only seconds before. . . .

[1] It is almost impossible for one single explosion, or even several in the same locality, to destroy or incapacitate all the dynamos in a large naval vessel, or to sever all the various sections of the Ring Main, which carries the power around the ship. When a dynamo or its appropriate section of the Ring Main suffered damage, the interlinking fuses automatically blew, isolating the damaged section. Theoretically, that is. In practice, it does not always happen that way – the fuses may not rupture and the entire system breaks down. Rumour – very strong rumour – had it that at least one of HM capital ships was lost simply because the Dynamo Fuse Release Switches – fuses of the order of 800 amps – failed to blow, leaving the capital ship powerless to defend itself.

The *Ulysses* was running into dense black smoke, now – the *Stirling* was heavily on fire, her fuel tanks gone. What happened in the next ten minutes, no one ever knew. In the smoke and flame and agony, they were moments borrowed from hell and men could only endure. Suddenly, the *Ulysses* was out in the clear, and the Heinkels, all bombs gone, were harrying her, attacking her incessantly with cannon and machine-gun, ravening wolves with their victim on its knees, desperate to finish it off. But still, here and there, a gun fired on the *Ulysses.*

Just below the bridge, for instance – there was a gun firing there. Turner risked a quick glance over the side, saw the gunner pumping his tracers into the path of a swooping Heinkel. And then the Heinkel opened up, and Turner flung himself back, knocking the Kapok Kid to the deck. Then the bomber was gone and the guns were silent. Slowly, Turner hoisted himself to his feet, peered over the side: the gunner was dead, his harness cut to ribbons.

He heard a scuffle behind him, saw a slight figure fling off a restraining hand, and climb to the edge of the bridge. For an instant, Turner saw the pale, staring face of Chrysler, Chrysler who had neither smiled nor even spoken since they had opened up the Asdic cabinet; at the same time he saw three Heinkels forming up to starboard for a fresh attack.

'Get down, you young fool!' Turner shouted. 'Do you want to commit suicide?'

Chrysler looked at him, eyes wide and devoid of recognition, looked away and dropped down to the sponson below. Turner lifted himself to the edge of the bridge and looked down.

Chrysler was struggling with all his slender strength, struggling in a strange and frightening silence, to drag the dead man from his Oerlikon cockpit. Somehow, with a series of convulsive, despairing jerks, he had him over the side, had laid him gently to the ground, and was climbing into the cockpit. His hand, Turner saw, was bare and bleeding, stripped to the raw flesh – then out of the corner of his eyes he saw the flame of the Heinkel's guns and flung himself backward.

One second passed, two, three – three seconds during which cannon shells and bullets smashed against the reinforced armour of the bridge – then, as a man in a daze, he heard the twin Oerlikons opening up. The boy must have held his fire to the very last moment. Six shots the Oerlikon fired – only six, and a great, grey shape, stricken and smoking, hurtled over the bridge barely at head height, sheared off its port wing on the Director Tower and crashed into the sea on the other side.

Chrysler was still sitting in the cockpit. His right hand was clutching his left shoulder, a shoulder smashed and shattered by a cannon shell, trying hopelessly to stem the welling arterial blood. Even as the next bomber straightened out on its strafing run, even as he flung himself backwards, Turner saw the mangled, bloody hand reach out for the trigger grip again.

Flat on the duckboards beside Carrington and the Kapok Kid, Turner pounded his fist on the deck in terrible frustration of anger. He thought of Starr, the man who had brought all this upon them, and hated him as he would never have believed he could hate anybody. He could have killed him then. He thought of Chrysler, of the excruciating hell of that gun-rest pounding into that shattered shoulder, of brown eyes glazed and shocked with pain and grief. If he himself lived, Turner swore, he would recommend that boy for the Victoria Cross. Abruptly the firing ceased and a Heinkel swung off sharply to starboard, smoke pouring from both its engines.

Quickly, together with the Kapok Kid, Turner scrambled to his feet, hoisted himself over the side of the bridge. He did it without looking, and he almost died then. A burst of fire from the third and last Heinkel – the bridge was always the favourite target – whistled past his head and shoulders: he felt the wind of their passing fan his cheek and hair. Then, winded from the convulsive back-thrust that had sent him there, he was stretched full length on the duckboards again. They were only inches from his eyes, these duckboards, but he could not see them. All he could see was the image of Chrysler, a gaping wound the size of a man's hand in his back, slumped forward across the Oerlikons, the weight of his body tilting the barrels grotesquely skywards. Both barrels had still been firing, were still firing, would keep on firing until the drums were empty, for the dead boy's hand was locked across the trigger.

Gradually, one by one, the guns of the convoy fell silent, the clamour of the aero engines began to fade in the distance. The attack was over.

Turner rose to his feet, slowly and heavily this time. He looked over the side of the bridge, stared down into the Oerlikon gunpit, then looked away, his face expressionless.

Behind him, he heard someone coughing. It was a strange, bubbling kind of cough. Turner whirled round, then stood stock-still, his hands clenched tightly at his sides.

The Kapok Kid, with Carrington kneeling helplessly at his side, was sitting quietly on the boards, his back propped against the legs of the Admiral's chair. From left groin to right shoulder through the middle of the embroidered 'J' on the chest, stretched a neat, straight, evenly-spaced pattern of round holes, stitched in by the machine-gun of the Heinkel. The blast of the shells must have hurtled him right across the bridge.

Turner stood absolutely still. The Kid, he knew with sudden sick certainty, had only seconds to live: he felt that any sudden move on his part would snap the spun-silk thread that held him on to life.

Gradually, the Kapok Kid became aware of his presence, of his steady gaze, and looked up tiredly. The vivid blue of his eyes were dulled already, the face white and drained of blood. Idly, his hand strayed up and down the punctured kapok, fingering the gashes. Suddenly he smiled, looked down at the quilted suit.

'Ruined,' he whispered. 'Bloody well ruined!' Then the wandering hand slipped down to his side, palm upward, and his head slumped forward on his chest. The flaxen hair stirred idly in the wind.

Chapter Seventeen

Sunday Morning

The *Stirling* died at dawn. She died while still under way, still plunging through the heavy seas, her mangled, twisted bridge and superstructure glowing red, glowing white-hot as the wind and sundered oil tanks lashed the flames into an incandescent holocaust. A strange and terrible sight, but not unique: thus the *Bismarck* had looked, whitely incandescent, just before the *Shropshire*'s torpedoes had sent her to the bottom.

The *Stirling* would have died anyway – but the Stukas made siccar. The Northern Lights had long since gone: now, too, the clear skies were going, and dark cloud was banking heavily to the north. Men hoped and prayed that the cloud would spread over FR77, and cover it with blanketing snow. But the Stukas got there first.

The Stukas – the dreaded gull-winged Junkers 87 dive-bombers – came from the south, flew high over the convoy, turned, flew south again. Level with, and due west of the *Ulysses*, rear ship in the convoy, they started to turn once more: then, abruptly, in the classic Stuka attack pattern, they peeled off in sequence, port wings dipping sharply as they half-rolled, turned and fell out of the sky, plummetting arrow-true for their targets.

Any plane that hurtles down in undeviating dive on waiting gun emplacements has never a chance. Thus spoke the pundits, the instructors in the gunnery school of Whale Island, and proceeded to prove to their own satisfaction the evident truth of their statement, using AA guns and duplicating the situation which would arise insofar as it lay within their power. Unfortunately, they couldn't duplicate the Stuka.

'Unfortunately,' because in actual battle, the Stuka was the only factor in the situation that really mattered. One had only to crouch behind a gun, to listen to the ear-piercing, screaming whistle of the Stuka in its near-vertical dive, to flinch from its hail of bullets as it loomed larger and larger in the sights, to know that nothing could now arrest the flight of that underslung bomb, to appreciate the truth of that. Hundreds of men alive today – the lucky ones who endured and survived a Stuka attack – will readily confirm that the war produced nothing quite so nerve-rending, quite so demoralizing as the sight and sound of those Junkers with the strange dihedral of the wings in the last seconds before they pulled out of their dive.

But one time in a hundred, maybe one time in a thousand, when the human factor of the man behind the gun ceased to operate, the pundits could be right. This was the thousandth time, for fear was a phantom that had vanished in the night: ranged against the dive-bombers were only one multiple pom-pom and half a dozen Oerlikons – the for'ard turrets could not be brought to bear – but these were enough, and more, in the hands of men inhumanly calm, ice-cool as the Polar wind itself, and filled with an almost dreadful singleness of purpose. Three Stukas in almost as many seconds were clawed out of the sky, two to crash harmlessly in the sea, a third to bury itself with tremendous impact in the already shattered day cabin of the Admiral.

The chances against the petrol tanks not erupting in searing flame or of the bomb not exploding were so remote as not to exist: but neither happened. It hardly seemed to call for comment – in extremity, courage becomes routine – when the bearded Doyle abandoned his pom-pom, scrambled up to the fo'c'sle deck, and flung himself on top of the armed bomb rolling heavily in scuppers awash with 100 per cent octane petrol. One tiny spark from Doyle's boot or from the twisted, broken steel of the Stuka rubbing and grinding against the superstructure would have been trigger enough: the contact fuse in the bomb was still undamaged, and as it slipped and skidded over the ice-bound deck, with Doyle hanging desperately on, it seemed animistically determined to smash its delicate percussion nose against a bulkhead or stanchion.

If Doyle thought of these things, he did not care. Coolly, almost carelessly, he kicked off the only retaining clip left on a broken section of the guard-rail, slid the bomb, fins first, over the edge, tipped the nose sharply to clear the detonator. The bomb fell harmlessly into the sea.

It fell into the sea just as the first bomb sliced contemptuously through the useless one-inch deck armour of the *Stirling* and crashed into the engine-room. Three, four, five, six other bombs buried themselves in the dying heart of the cruiser, the lightened Stukas lifting away sharply to port and starboard. From the bridge of the *Ulysses*, there seemed to be a weird, unearthly absence of noise as the bombs went home. They just vanished into the smoke and flame, engulfed by the inferno.

No one blow finished the *Stirling*, but a mounting accumulation of blows. She had taken too much and she could take no more. She was like a reeling boxer, a boxer over-matched against an unskilled but murderous opponent, sinking under an avalance of blows.

Stony-faced, bitter beyond words at his powerlessness, Turner watched her die. Funny, he thought tiredly, she's like all the rest. Cruisers, he mused in a queerly detached abstraction, must be the toughest ships in the world. He'd seen many go, but none easily, cleanly, spectacularly. No sudden knock-out, no *coup de grâce* for them – always, always, they had to be battered to death.... Like the *Stirling*. Turner's grip on the shattered windscreen tightened till his forearms ached. To him, to all good sailors, a well-loved ship was a well-loved friend: for fifteen months, now, the old and valiant *Stirling* had been their faithful shadow, had shared the burden of the *Ulysses* in the worst convoys of the war: she was the last of the old guard, for only the *Ulysses* had been longer on the blackout run. It was not good to watch a friend die: Turner looked away, stared down at the ice-covered duckboards between his feet, his head sunk between hunched shoulders.

He could close his eyes, but he could not close his ears. He winced, hearing the monstrous, roaring hiss of boiling water and steam as the white-hot superstructure of the *Stirling* plunged deeply into the ice-chilled Arctic. For fifteen, twenty seconds that dreadful, agonized sibilation continued, then stopped in an instant, the sound sheared off as by a guillotine. When Turner looked up, slowly, there was only the rolling, empty sea ahead, the big oil-slicked bubbles rising to the top, bubbles rising only to be punctured as they broke the surface by the fine rain falling back into the sea from the great clouds of steam already condensing in that bitter cold.

The *Stirling* was gone, and the battered remnants of FR77 pitched and plunged steadily onwards to the north. There were seven ships left now – the four merchantmen, including the Commodore's ship, the tanker, the *Sirrus* and the *Ulysses*. None of them was whole: all were damaged, heavily damaged, but none so desperately hurt as the *Ulysses*. Seven ships, only seven: thirty-six had set out for Russia.

At 0800 Turner signalled the *Sirrus*: 'WT gone. Signal C-in-C course, speed, position. Confirm 0930 as rendezvous. Code.'

The reply came exactly an hour later. 'Delayed heavy seas. Rendezvous approx 1030. Impossible fly off air cover. Keep coming. C-in-C.'

'Keep coming!' Turner repeated savagely. 'Would you listen to him! "Keep coming," he says! What the hell does he expect us to do – scuttle ourselves?' He shook his head in angry despair. 'I hate to repeat myself,' he said bitterly. 'But I must. Too bloody late as usual!'[1]

Dawn and daylight had long since come, but it was growing darker again. Heavy grey clouds, formless and menacing, blotted out the sky from horizon to horizon. They were snow clouds, and, please God, the snow would soon fall: that could save them now, that and that alone.

But the snow did not come – not then. Once more, there came instead the Stukas, the roar of their engines rising and falling as they methodically quartered the empty sea in search of the convoy – Charlie had left at dawn. But it was only a matter of time before the dive-bomber squadron found the tiny convoy; ten minutes from the time of the first warning of their approach, the leading Junkers 87 tipped over its wing and dropped out of the sky.

Ten minutes – but time for a council and plan of desperation. When the Stukas came, they found the convoy stretched out in line abreast, the tanker *Varella* in the middle, two merchantmen in close line ahead on either side of it, the *Sirrus* and the *Ulysses* guarding the flanks. A suicidal formation in submarine waters – a torpedo from port or starboard could hardly miss them all. But weather conditions were heavily against submarines, and the formation offered at least a fighting chance against the Stukas. If they approached from astern – their favourite attack technique – they would run into the simultaneous massed fire of seven ships; if they approached from the sides, they must first attack the escorts, for no Stuka would present its unprotected underbelly to the guns of a warship. . . . They elected to attack from either side, five from the east, four from the west. This time, Turner noted, they were carrying long-range fuel tanks.

Turner had no time to see how the *Sirrus* was faring. Indeed, he could hardly see how his own ship was faring, for thick acrid smoke was blowing back across the bridge from the barrels of 'A' and 'B' turrets. In the gaps

[1] It is regrettable but true – the Home Fleet squadron was almost always too late. The Admiralty could not be blamed – the capital ships were essential for the blockade of the *Tirpitz*, and they did not dare risk them close inshore against land-based bombers. The long awaited trap *did* eventually snap shut: but it caught only the heavy cruiser *Scharnhorst* and not the *Tirpitz*. It never caught the great ship. She was destroyed at her anchorage in Alta Fjord by Lancaster bombers of the Royal Air Force.

of sound between the crash of the 5.25s, he could hear the quick-fire of Doyle's midship pom-pom, the vicious thudding of the Oerlikons.

Suddenly, startling in its breath-taking unexpectedness, two great beams of dazzling white stabbed out through the mirk and gloom. Turner stared, then bared his teeth in fierce delight. The 44-inch searchlights! Of course! The great searchlights, still on the official secret list, capable of lighting up an enemy six miles away! What a fool he had been to forget them – Vallery had used them often, in daylight and in dark, against attacking aircraft. No man could look into those terrible eyes, those flaming arcs across the electrodes and not be blinded.

Blinking against the eye-watering smoke. Turner peered aft to see who was manning the control position. But he knew who it was before he saw him. It could only be Ralston – searchlight control, Turner remembered, was his day action station: besides, he could think of no one other than the big, blond torpedoman with the gumption, the quick intelligence to burn the lamps on his own initiative.

Jammed in the corner of the bridge by the gate, Turner watched him. He forgot his ship, forgot even the bombers – he personally could do nothing about them anyway – as he stared in fascination at the man behind the controls.

His eyes were glued to the sights, his face expressionless, absolutely; but for the gradual stiffening of back and neck as the sight dipped in docile response to the delicate caress of his fingers on the wheel, he might have been carved from marble: the immobility of the face, the utter concentration was almost frightening.

There was not a flicker of feeling or emotion: never a flicker as the first Stuka weaved and twisted in maddened torment, seeking to escape that eye-staring flame, not even a flicker as it swerved violently in its dive, pulled out too late and crashed into the sea a hundred yards short of the *Ulysses*.

What was the boy thinking of? Turner wondered. His mother, his sisters, entombed under the ruins of a Croydon bungalow: of his brother, innocent victim of that mutiny – how impossible that mutiny seemed now! – in Scapa Flow: of his father, dead by his son's own hand? Turner did not know, could not even begin to guess: clairvoyantly, almost, he knew that it was too late, that no one would ever know now.

The face was inhumanly still. There wasn't a shadow of feeling as the second Stuka overshot the *Ulysses*, dropped its bomb into the open sea: not a shadow as a third blew up in mid-air: not a trace of emotion when the guns of the next Stuka smashed one of the lights . . . not even when the cannon shells of the last smashed the searchlight control, tore half his chest away. He died instantaneously, stood there a moment as if unwilling to abandon his post, then slumped back quietly on to the deck. Turner bent over the dead boy, looked at the face, the eyes upturned to the first feathery flakes of falling snow. The eyes, the face, were still the same, mask-like, expressionless. Turner shivered and looked away.

One bomb, and one only, had struck the *Ulysses*. It had struck the fo'c'sle deck just for'ard of 'A' turret. There had been no casualties, but some freak of vibration and shock had fractured the turret's hydraulic lines. Temporarily, at least, 'B' was the only effective remaining turret in the ship.

The *Sirrus* hadn't been quite so lucky. She had destroyed one Stuka – the merchantmen had claimed another – and had been hit twice, both bombs exploding in the after mess-deck. The *Sirrus*, overloaded with survivors, was carrying double her normal complement of men, and usually that mess-deck would have been crowded: during action stations it was empty. Not a man had lost his life – not a man was to lose his life on the destroyer *Sirrus*: she was never damaged again on the Russian convoys.

Hope was rising, rising fast. Less than an hour to go, now, and the battle squadron would be there. It was dark, dark with the gloom of an Arctic storm, and heavy snow was falling, hissing gently into the dark and rolling sea. No plane could find them in this – and they were almost beyond the reach of shore-based aircraft, except, of course, for the Condors. And it was almost impossible weather for submarines.

'It may be we shall touch the Happy Isles.' Carrington quoted softly.

'What?' Turner looked up, baffled. 'What did you say, Number One?'

'Tennyson.' Carrington was apologetic. 'The Captain was always quoting him. . . . Maybe we'll make it yet.'

'Maybe, maybe.' Turner was non-committal. 'Preston!'

'Yes, sir, I see it.' Preston was staring to the north where the signal lamp of the *Sirrus* was flickering rapidly.

'A ship, sir!' he reported excitedly. '*Sirrus* says naval vessel approaching from the north!'

'From the north! Thank God! Thank God!' Turner shouted exultantly. 'From the north! It must be them! They're ahead of time. . . . I take it all back. Can you see anything, Number One?'

'Not a thing, sir. Too thick – but it's clearing a bit, I think. . . . There's the *Sirrus* again.'

'What does she say, Preston?' Turner asked anxiously.

'Contact. Sub. contact. Green 30. Closing.'

'Contact! At this late hour!' Turner groaned, then smashed his fist down on the binnacle. He swore fiercely.

'By God, she's not going to stop us now! Preston, signal the *Sirrus* to stay . . .'

He broke off, looked incredulously to the north. Up there in the snow and gloom, stilettos of white flame had lanced out briefly, vanished again. Carrington by his side now, he stared unwinkingly north, saw shells splashing whitely in the water under the bows of the Commodore's ship, the *Cape Hatteras*: then he saw the flashes again, stronger, brighter this time, flashes that lit up for a fleeting second the bows and superstructure of the ship that was firing.

He turned slowly, to find that Carrington, too, had turned, was gazing at him with set face and bitter eyes. Turner, grey and haggard with exhaustion and the sour foretaste of ultimate defeat, looked in turn at his First Lieutenant in a long moment of silence.

'The answer to many questions,' he said softly. 'That's why they've been softening up the *Stirling* and ourselves for the past couple of days. The fox is in among the chickens. It's our old pal the *Hipper* cruiser come to pay us a social call.'

'It is.'

'So near and yet . . .' Turner shrugged. 'We deserved better than this. . . .' He grinned crookedly. 'How would you like to die a hero's death?'

'The very idea appals me!' boomed a voice behind him. Brooks had just arrived on the bridge.

'Me, too,' Turner admitted. He smiled: he was almost happy again. 'Have we any option, gentlemen?'

'Alas, no,' Brooks said sadly.

'Full ahead both!' Carrington called down the speaking-tube: it was by way of his answer.

'No, no,' Turner chided gently. 'Full *power*, Number One. Tell them we're in a hurry: remind them of the boasts they used to make about the *Abdiel* and the *Manxman* . . . Preston! General emergency signal: "Scatter: proceed independently to Russian ports." '

The upper deck was thick with freshly fallen snow, and the snow was still falling. The wind was rising again and, after the warmth of the canteen where he had been operating, it struck at Johnny Nicholls's lungs with sudden, searing pain: the temperature, he guessed, must be about zero. He buried his face in his duffel coat, climbed laboriously, haltingly up the ladders to the bridge. He was tired, deadly weary, and he winced in agony every time his foot touched the deck: his splinted left leg was shattered just above the ankle – shrapnel from the bomb in the after mess-deck.

Peter Orr, commander of the *Sirrus*, was waiting for him at the gate of the tiny bridge.

'I thought you might like to see this, Doc.' The voice was strangely high-pitched for so big a man. 'Rather I thought you would want to see this,' he corrected himself. 'Look at her go!' he breathed. 'Just look at her go!'

Nicholls looked out over the port side. Half a mile away on the beam, the *Cape Hatteras* was blazing furiously, slowing to a stop. Some miles to the north, through the falling snow, he could barely distinguish the vague shape of the German cruiser, a shape pinpointed by the aming guns still mercilessly pumping shells into the sinking ship. Every shot went home: the accuracy of their gunnery was fantastic.

Half a mile astern on the port quarter, the *Ulysses* was coming up. She was sheeted in foam and spray, the bows leaping almost clear of the water, then crashing down with a pistol-shot impact easily heard, even against the wind, on the bridge of the *Sirrus*, as the great engines thrust her through the water, faster, faster, with the passing of every second.

Nicholls gazed, fascinated. This was the first time he'd seen the *Ulysses* since he'd left her and he was appalled. The entire upperworks, fore and aft, were a twisted, unbelievable shambles of broken steel: both masts were gone, the smoke-stacks broken and bent, the Director Tower shattered and grotesquely askew: smoke was still pluming up from the great holes in fo'c'sle and poop, the after turrets, wrenched from their mountings, pitched crazily on the deck. The skeleton of the Condor still lay athwart 'Y' turret, a Stuka was buried to the wings in the fo'c'sle deck, and she was, he knew, split right down to the water level abreast the torpedo tubes. The *Ulysses* was something out of a nightmare.

Steadying himself against the violent pitching of the destroyer, Nicholls stared and stared, numbed with horror and disbelief. Orr looked at him, looked away as a messenger came to the bridge.

'Rendezvous 1015,' he read. '1015! Good lord, 25 minutes' time! Do you hear that, Doc? 25 minutes' time!'

'Yes, sir,' Nicholls said absently: he hadn't heard him.

Orr looked at him, touched his arm, pointed to the *Ulysses*.

'Bloody well incredible, isn't it?' he murmured.

'I wish to God I was aboard her,' Nicholls muttered miserably. 'Why did they send me—? Look! What's that?'

A huge flag, a flag twenty feet in length, was streaming out below the yardarm of the *Ulysses*, stretched taut in the wind of its passing. Nicholls had never seen anything remotely like it: the flag was enormous, red and blue and whiter than the driving snow.

'The battle ensign,' Orr murmured. 'Bill Turner's broken out the battle ensign.' He shook his head in wonder. 'To take time off to do that *now* – well, Doc, only Turner would do that. You know him well?'

Nicholls nodded silently.

'Me, too,' Orr said simply. 'We are both lucky men.'

The *Sirrus* was still doing fifteen knots, still headed for the enemy, when the *Ulysses* passed them by a cable-length away as if they were stopped in the water.

Long afterwards, Nicholls could never describe it all accurately. He had a hazy memory of the *Ulysses* no longer plunging and lifting, but battering through waves and troughs on a steady even keel, the deck angling back sharply from a rearing forefoot to the counter buried deep in the water, fifteen feet below the great boiling tortured sea of white that arched up in seething magnificence above the shattered poop-deck. He could recall, too, that 'B' turret was firing continuously, shell after shell screaming away through the blinding snow, to burst in brilliant splendour over and on the German cruiser: for 'B' turret had only starshells left. He carried, too, a vague mental picture of Turner waving ironically from the bridge, of the great ensign streaming stiffly astern, already torn and tattered at the edges. But what he could never forget, what he would hear in his heart and mind as long as he lived, was the tremendous, frightening roar of the great boiler-room intake fans as they sucked in mighty draughts of air for the starving engines. For the *Ulysses* was driving through the heavy seas under maximum power, at a speed that should have broken her shuddering back, should have burnt out the great engines. There was no doubt as to Turner's intentions: he was going to ram the enemy, to destroy him and take him with him, at a speed of just on or over forty incredible knots.

Nicholls gazed and gazed and did not know what to think: he felt sick at heart, for that ship was part of him now, his good friends, especially the Kapok Kid – for he did not know that the Kid was already dead – they, too, were part of him, and it is always terrible to see the end of a legend, to see it die, to see it going into the gulfs. But he felt, too, a strange exultation; she was dying but what a way to die! And if ships had hearts, had souls, as the old sailing men declared, surely the *Ulysses* would want it this way too.

She was still doing forty knots when, as if by magic, a great gaping hole appeared in her bows just above the water-line. Shell-fire, possibly, but unlikely at that angle. It must have been a torpedo from the U-boat, not yet located: a sudden dip of the bows could have coincided with the upthrust of a heavy sea forcing a torpedo to the surface. Such things had happened before: rarely, but they happened. . . . The *Ulysses* brushed aside the torpedo, ignored the grievous wound, ignored the heavy shells crashing into her and kept on going.

She was still doing forty knots, driving in under the guns of the enemy, guns at maximum depression, when 'A' magazine blew up, blasted off the entire bows in one shattering detonation. For a second, the lightened fo'c'sle reared high into the air: then it plunged down, deep down, into the shoulder of a rolling sea. She plunged down and kept on going down, driving down to the black floor of the Arctic, driven down by the madly spinning screws, the still thundering engines her own executioner.

Chapter Eighteen

Epilogue

The air was warm and kind and still. The sky was blue, a deep and wonderful blue, with little puffs of cotton-wool cloud drifting lazily to the far horizon. The street-gardens, the hanging birdcage flower-baskets, spilled over with blue and yellow and red and gold, all the delicate pastel shades and tints he had almost forgotten had ever existed: every now and then an old man or a hurrying housewife or a young man with a laughing girl on his arm would stop to admire them, then walk on again, the better for having seen them. The nesting birds were singing, clear and sweet above the distant roar of the traffic, and Big Ben was booming the hour as Johnny Nicholls climbed awkwardly out of the taxi, paid off the driver and hobbled slowly up the marble steps.

His face carefully expressionless, the sentry saluted, opened the heavy swing door. Nicholls passed inside, looked around the huge hall, saw that both sides were lined with heavy, imposing doors: at the far end, beneath the great curve of the stairs and overhanging the widely convex counter of the type usually found in banks, hung a sign: 'Typist Pool: Inquiries.'

The tip-tap of the crutches sounded unnaturally loud on the marble floor as he limped over to the counter. Very touching and melodramatic, Nicholls, he thought dispassionately: trust the audience are having their money's worth. Half a dozen typists had stopped work as if by command, were staring at him in open curiosity, hands resting limply on their machines. A trim young wren, red-haired and shirt-sleeved, came to the counter.

'Can I help you, sir?' The quiet voice, the blue eyes were soft with concern. Nicholls, catching a glimpse of himself in a mirror behind her, a glimpse of a scuffed uniform jacket over a grey fisherman's jersey, of blurred, sunken eyes and gaunt, pale cheeks, admitted wryly to himself that he couldn't blame her. He didn't have to be a doctor to know that he was in pretty poor shape.

'My name is Nicholls, Surgeon-Lieutenant Nicholls. I have an appointment—'

'Lieutenant Nicholls. . . . H.M.S. *Ulysses*!' The girl drew in her breath sharply. 'Of course, sir. They're expecting you.' Nicholls looked at her, looked at the Wrens sitting motionless in the chairs, caught the intense, wondering expression in their eyes, the awed gaze with which one would regard beings from another planet. It made him feel vaguely uncomfortable.

'Upstairs, I suppose?' He hadn't meant to sound so brusque.

'No, sir.' The Wren came quietly round the counter. 'They – well, they heard you'd been wounded, sir,' she murmured apologetically. 'Just across the hall here, please.' She smiled at him, slowed her step to match his halting walk.

She knocked, held open the door, announced him to someone he couldn't see, and closed the door softly behind him when he had passed through.

There were three men in the room. The one man he recognized, Vice-Admiral Starr, came forward to meet him. He looked older, far older, far more tired than when Nicholls had last seen him – hardly a fortnight previously.

'How are you, Nicholls?' he asked. 'Not walking so well, I see.' Under the assurance, the thin joviality so flat and misplaced, the harsh edge of strain burred unmistakably. 'Come and sit down.'

He led Nicholls across to the table, long, big and covered with leather. Behind the table, framed against huge wall-maps, sat two men. Starr introduced them. One, big, beefy, red of face, was in full uniform, the sleeves ablaze with the broad band and four stripes of an Admiral of the Fleet: the other was a civilian, a small, stocky man with iron-grey hair, eyes still and wise and old. Nicholls recognized him immediately, would have known anyway from the deference of both the Admirals. He reflected wryly that the Navy was indeed doing him proud: such receptions were not for all. . . . But they seemed reluctant to begin the reception, Nicholls thought – he had forgotten the shock his appearance must give. Finally, the grey-haired man cleared his throat.

'How's the leg, boy?' he asked. 'Looks pretty bad to me.' His voice was low, but alive with controlled authority.

'Not too bad, thank you, sir,' Nicholls answered. 'Two, three weeks should see me back on the job.'

'You're taking two months, laddie,' said the grey-haired man quietly. 'More if you want it.' He smiled faintly. 'If anyone asks, just tell 'em I said so. Cigarette?'

He flicked the big table-lighter, sat back in his chair. Temporarily, he seemed at a loss as to what to say next. Then he looked up abruptly.

'Had a good trip home?'

'Very fair, sir. VIP treatment all the way. Moscow, Teheran, Cairo, Gib.' Nicholls's mouth twisted. 'Much more comfortable than the trip out.' He paused, inhaled deeply on his cigarette, looked levelly across the table. 'I would have preferred to come home in the *Sirrus*.'

'No doubt,' Starr broke in acidly. 'But we cannot afford to cater for the personal prejudices of all and sundry. We were anxious to have a first-hand account of FR77 – and particularly the *Ulysses* – as soon as possible.'

Nicholls's hands clenched on the edge of his chair. The anger had leapt in him like a flame, and he knew that the man opposite was watching closely. Slowly he relaxed, looked at the grey-haired man, interrogative eyebrows mutely asking confirmation.

The grey-haired man nodded.

'Just tell us all you know,' he said kindly. 'Everything – about everything. Take your time.'

'From the beginning?' Nicholls asked in a low voice.

'From the beginning.'

Nicholls told them. He would have liked to tell the story, right as it fell out, from the convoy before FR77 straight through to the end. He did his best, but it was a halting story, strangely lacking in conviction. The atmosphere, the surroundings were wrong – the contrast between the peaceful warmth of these rooms and the inhuman cold and cruelty of the Arctic was an immense gulf that could be bridged only by experience and understanding. Down here, in the heart of London, the wild, incredible tale he had to tell fell falsely, incredibly even on his own ears. Half-way through, he looked at his listeners, almost gave up. Incredulity? No, it wasn't that – at least, not with the grey-haired man and the Admiral of the Fleet. Just a baffled incomprehension, an honest failure to understand.

It wasn't so bad when he stuck to the ascertainable facts, the facts of carriers crippled by seas, of carriers mined, stranded and torpedoed: the facts of the great storm, of the desperate struggle to survive: the facts of the gradual attrition of the convoy, of the terrible dying of the two gasoline tankers, of the U-boats and bombers sent to the bottom, of the *Ulysses*, battering through the snowstorm at 40 knots, blown up by the German cruiser, of the arrival of the battle squadron, of the flight of the cruiser before it could inflict further damage, of the rounding-up of the scattered convoy, of the curtain of Russian fighters in the Barents Sea, of the ultimate arrival in the Kola Inlet of the battered remnants of FR77 – five ships in all.

It was when he came to less readily ascertainable facts, to statements that could never be verified at all, that he sensed the doubt, the something more than wonder. He told the story as calmly, as unemotionally as he could: the story of Ralston, Ralston of the fighting lights and the searchlights, of his father and family: of Riley, the ringleader of the mutiny and his refusal to leave the shaft tunnel: of Petersen, who had killed a marine and gladly given his own life: of McQuater and Chrysler and Doyle and a dozen others.

For a second, his own voice broke uncertainly as he told the story of the half-dozen survivors from the *Ulysses*, picked up by the *Sirrus* soon afterwards. He told how Brooks had given his lifejacket to an ordinary seaman, who amazingly survived fifteen minutes in that water: how Turner, wounded in head and arm, had supported a dazed Spicer till the *Sirrus* came plunging alongside, had passed a bowline round him, and was gone before anything could be done: how Carrington, that enduring man of iron, a baulk of splintered timber under his arms, had held two men above water till rescue came. Both men – Preston was one – had died later: Carrington had climbed the rope unaided, clambered over the guard-rails dangling a left-leg with the foot blown off above the ankle. Carrington would survive: Carrington was indestructible. Finally, Doyle, too, was gone: they had thrown him a rope, but he had not seen it, for he was blind.

But what the three men really wanted to know, Nicholls realized, was how the *Ulysses* had been, how a crew of mutineers had borne themselves. He had told them, he knew, things of wonder and of splendour, and they could not reconcile these with men who would take up arms against their own ship, in effect, against their own King.

So Nicholls tried to tell them, then knew, as he tried, that he could never tell them. For what was there to tell? That Vallery had spoken to the men over the broadcast system: how he had gone among them and made them almost as himself, on that grim, exhausting tour of inspection: how he had spoken of them as he died: and how, most of all, his death had made them men again? For that was all that there was to tell, and these things were just nothing at all. With sudden insight, Nicholls saw that the meaning of that strange transformation of the men of the *Ulysses*, a transformation of bitter, broken men to men above themselves, could neither be explained nor understood, for all the meaning was in Vallery, and Vallery was dead.

Nicholls felt tired, now, desperately so. He knew he was far from well. His mind was cloudy, hazy in retrospect, and he was mixing things up: his sense of chronological time was gone, he was full of hesitations and uncertainties. Suddenly he was overwhelmed by the futility of it all, and he broke off slowly, his voice trailing into silence.

Vaguely, he heard the grey-haired man ask something in a quiet voice, and he muttered aloud, unthinking.

'What was that? What did you say?' The grey-haired man was looking at him strangely. The face of the Admiral behind the table was impassive. Starr's, he saw, was open in disbelief.

'I only said, "They were the best crew God ever gave a Captain," ' Nicholls murmured.

'I see.' The old, tired eyes looked at him steadily, but there was no other comment. Fingers drumming on the table, he looked slowly at the two Admirals, then back to Nicholls again.

'Take things easy for a minute, boy. . . . If you'll just excuse us . . .'

He rose to his feet, walked slowly over to the big, bay windows at the other end of the long room, the others following. Nicholls made no move, did not even look after them: he sat slumped in the chair, looking dejectedly, unseeingly, at the crutches on the floor between his feet.

From time to time, he could hear a murmur of voices. Starr's high-pitched voice carried most clearly. 'Mutiny ship, sir . . . never the same again . . . better this way.' There was a murmured reply, too low to catch, then he heard Starr saying, '. . . finished as a fighting unit.' The grey-haired man said something rapidly, his tone sharp with disagreement, but the words were blurred. Then the deep, heavy voice of the Fleet Admiral said something about 'expiation,' and the grey-haired man nodded slowly. Then Starr looked at him over his shoulder, and Nicholls knew they were talking about him. He thought he heard the words 'not well' and 'frightful strain,' but perhaps he was imagining it.

Anyway, he no longer cared. He was anxious for one thing only, and that was to be gone. He felt an alien in an alien land, and whether they believed him or not no longer mattered. He did not belong here, where everything was so sane and commonplace and real – and withal a world of shadows.

He wondered what the Kapok Kid would have said had he been here, and smiled in fond reminiscence: the language would have been terrible, the comments rich and barbed and pungent. Then he wondered what Vallery would have said, and he smiled again at the simplicity of it all, for Vallery would have said: 'Do not judge them, for they do not understand.'

Gradually, he became aware that the murmuring had ceased, that the three men were standing above him. His smile faded, and he looked up slowly to see them looking down strangely at him, their eyes full of concern.

'I'm damnably sorry, boy,' the grey-haired man said sincerely. 'You're a sick man and we've asked far too much of you. A drink, Nicholls? It was most remiss—'

'No, thank you, sir.' Nicholls straightened himself in his chair. 'I'll be perfectly all right.' He hesitated. 'Is – is there anything else?'

'No, nothing at all.' The smile was genuine, friendly. 'You've been a great help to us, Lieutenant, a great help. And a fine report. Thank you very much indeed.'

A liar and a gentleman, Nicholls thought gratefully. He struggled to his feet, reached out for his crutches. He shook hands with Starr and the Admiral of the Fleet, and said goodbye. The grey-haired man accompanied him to the door, his hand beneath Nicholls's arm.

At the door Nicholls paused.

'Sorry to bother you but – when do I begin my leave, sir?'

'As from now,' the other said emphatically. 'And have a good time. God knows you've earned it, my boy. . . . Where are you going?'

'Henley, sir.'

'Henley! I could have sworn you were Scots.'

'I am, sir – I have no family.'

'Oh. . . . A girl, Lieutenant?'

Nicholls nodded silently.

The grey-haired man clapped him on the shoulder, and smiled gently. 'Pretty, I'll be bound?'

Nicholls looked at him, looked away to where the sentry was already holding open the street doors, and gathered up his crutches.

'I don't know, sir,' he said quietly. 'I don't know at all. I've never seen her.'

He tip-tapped his way across the marble flags, passed through the heavy doors and limped out into the sunshine.

ICE STATION
ZEBRA

Ice Station Zebra

To Lachlan, Michael and Alistair

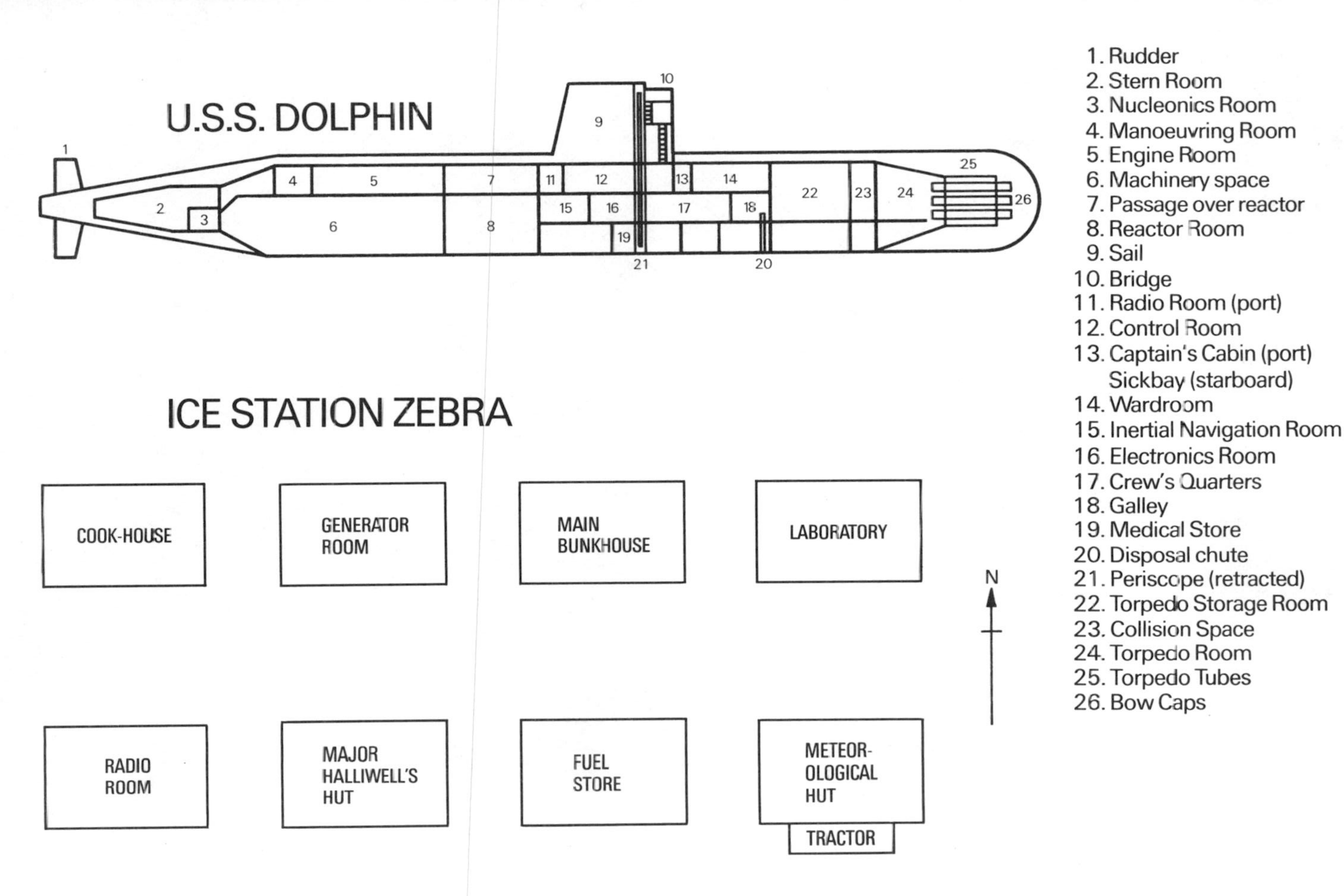
U.S.S. DOLPHIN
1. Rudder
2. Stern Room
3. Nucleonics Room
4. Manoeuvring Room
5. Engine Room
6. Machinery space
7. Passage over reactor
8. Reactor Room
9. Sail
10. Bridge
11. Radio Room (port)
12. Control Room
13. Captain's Cabin (port)
Sickbay (starboard)
14. Wardroom
15. Inertial Navigation Room
16. Electronics Room
17. Crew's Quarters
18. Galley
19. Medical Store
20. Disposal chute
21. Periscope (retracted)
22. Torpedo Storage Room
23. Collision Space
24. Torpedo Room
25. Torpedo Tubes
26. Bow Caps
ICE STATION ZEBRA
COOK-HOUSE
GENERATOR ROOM
MAIN BUNKHOUSE
LABORATORY
RADIO ROOM
MAJOR HALLIWELL'S HUT
FUEL STORE
METEOR-OLOGICAL HUT
TRACTOR
N

Chapter One

Commander James D. Swanson of the United States Navy was short, plump and crowding forty. He had jet black hair topping a pink cherubic face, and with the deep permanent creases of laughter lines radiating from his eyes and curving round his mouth he was a dead ringer for the cheerful, happy-go-lucky extrovert who is the life and soul of the party where the guests park their brains along with their hats and coats. That, anyway, was how he struck me at first glance but on the reasonable assumption that I might very likely find some other qualities in the man picked to command the latest and most powerful nuclear submarine afloat I took a second and closer look at him and this time I saw what I should have seen the first time if the dank grey fog and winter dusk settling down over the Firth of Clyde hadn't made seeing so difficult. His eyes. Whatever his eyes were they weren't those of the gladhanding wisecracking *bon vivant*. They were the coolest, clearest grey eyes I'd ever seen, eyes that he used as a dentist might his probe, a surgeon his lancet or a scientist his electronic microscope. Measuring eyes. They measured first me and then the paper he held in his hand but gave no clue at all as to the conclusions arrived at on the basis of measurements made.

'I'm sorry, Dr Carpenter.' The south-of-the-Mason–Dixon-line voice was quiet and courteous, but without any genuine regret that I could detect, as he folded the telegram back into its envelope and handed it to me. 'I can accept neither this telegram as sufficient authorization nor yourself as a passenger. Nothing personal, you know that; but I have my orders.'

'Not sufficient authorization?' I pulled the telegram from its cover and pointed to the signature. 'Who do you think this is – the resident window-cleaner at the Admiralty?'

It wasn't funny, and as I looked at him in the failing light I thought maybe I'd overestimated the depth of the laughter lines in the face. He said precisely: 'Admiral Hewson is commander of the Nato Eastern Division. On Nato exercises I come under his command. At all other times I am responsible only to Washington. This is one of those other times. I'm sorry. And I must point out, Dr Carpenter, that you could have arranged for anyone in London to send this telegram. It's not even on a naval message form.'

He didn't miss much, that was a fact, but he was being suspicious about nothing. I said: 'You could call him up by radio-telephone, Commander.'

'So I could,' he agreed. 'And it would make no difference. Only accredited American nationals are allowed aboard this vessel – and the authority must come from Washington.'

'From the Director of Underseas Warfare or Commander Atlantic submarines?' He nodded, slowly, speculatively, and I went on: 'Please radio them and ask them to contact Admiral Hewson. Time is very short, Commander.' I might have added that it was beginning to snow and that I was getting colder by the minute, but I refrained.

He thought for a moment, nodded, turned and walked a few feet to a portable dockside telephone that was connected by a looping wire to the long dark shape lying at our feet. He spoke briefly, keeping his voice low, and hung up. He barely had time to rejoin me when three duffel-coated figures came hurrying up an adjacent gangway, turned in our direction and stopped when they reached us. The tallest of the three tall men, a lean rangy character with wheat-coloured hair and the definite look of a man who ought to have had a horse between his legs, stood slightly in advance of the other two. Commander Swanson gestured towards him.

'Lieutenant Hansen, my executive officer. He'll look after you till I get back.' The commander certainly knew how to choose his words.

'I don't need looking after,' I said mildly. 'I'm all grown up now and I hardly ever feel lonely.'

'I shall be as quick as I can, Dr Carpenter,' Swanson said. He hurried off down the gangway and I gazed thoughtfully after him. I put out of my mind any idea I might have had about the Commander US Atlantic Submarines picking his captains from the benches in Central Park. I had tried to effect an entrance aboard Swanson's ship and if such an entrance was unauthorized he didn't want me taking off till he'd found out why. Hansen and his two men, I guessed, would be the three biggest sailors on the ship.

The ship. I stared down at the great black shape lying almost at my feet. This was my first sight of a nuclear-engined submarine, and the *Dolphin* was like no submarine that I had ever seen. She was about the same length as a World War II long-range ocean-going submarine but there all resemblance ceased. Her diameter was at least twice that of any conventional submarine. Instead of having the vaguely boat-shaped lines of her predecessors, the *Dolphin* was almost perfectly cylindrical in design: instead of the usual V-shaped bows, her fore end was completely semi-spherical. There was no deck, as such: the rounded sheer of sides and bows rose smoothly to the top of the hull then fell as smoothly away again, leaving only a very narrow fore-and-aft working space so dangerously treacherous in its slippery convexity that it was permanently railed off in harbour. About a hundred feet back from the bows the slender yet massive conning-tower reared over twenty feet above the deck, for all the world like the great dorsal fin of some monstrous shark: half-way up the sides of the conning-tower and thrust out stubbily at right angles were the sweptback auxiliary diving planes of the submarine. I tried to see what lay farther aft but the fog and the thickening snow swirling down from the north of Loch Long defeated me. Anyway, I was losing interest. I'd only a thin raincoat over my clothes and I could feel my skin start to gooseflesh under the chill fingers of that winter wind.

'Nobody said anything about us having to freeze to death,' I said to Hansen. 'That naval canteen there. Would your principles prevent you from accepting a cup of coffee from Dr Carpenter, that well-known espionage agent?'

He grinned and said: 'In the matter of coffee, friend, I have no principles. Especially to-night. Someone should have warned us about those Scottish winters.' He not only looked like a cowboy, he talked like one: I was an expert on cowboys as I was sometimes too tired to rise to switch off the TV set. 'Rawlings, go tell the captain that we are sheltering from the elements.'

While Rawlings went to the dockside phone Hansen led the way to the nearby neon-lit canteen. He let me precede him through the door then made for the counter while the other sailor, a red-complexioned character about the size and shape of a polar bear, nudged me gently into an angled bench seat in one corner of the room. They weren't taking too many chances with me. Hansen came and sat on the other side of me, and when Rawlings returned he sat squarely in front of me across the table.

'As neat a job of corralling as I've seen for a long time,' I said approvingly. 'You've got nasty suspicious minds, haven't you?'

'You wrong us,' Hansen said sadly. 'We're just three friendly sociable guys carrying out our orders. It's Commander Swanson who has the nasty suspicious mind, isn't that so, Rawlings?'

'Yes, indeed, Lieutenant,' Rawlings said gravely. 'Very security-minded, the captain is.'

I tried again. 'Isn't this very inconvenient for you?' I asked. 'I mean, I should have thought that every man would have been urgently required aboard if you're due to sail in less than two hours' time.'

'You just keep on talking, Doc,' Hansen said encouragingly. There was nothing encouraging about his cold blue Arctic eyes. 'I'm a right good listener.'

'Looking forward to your trip up to the ice-pack?' I inquired pleasantly.

They operated on the same wavelength, all right. They didn't even look at one another. In perfect unison they all hitched themselves a couple of inches closer to me, and there was nothing imperceptible about the way they did it either. Hansen waited, smiling in a pleasantly relaxed fashion until the waitress had deposited four steaming mugs of coffee on the table, then said in the same encouraging tone: 'Come again, friend. Nothing we like to hear better than top classified information being bandied about in canteens. How the hell do *you* know where we're going?'

I reached up my hand beneath my coat lapel and it stayed there, my right wrist locked in Hansen's right hand.

'We're not suspicious or anything,' he said apologetically. 'It's just that we submariners are very nervous on account of the dangerous life we lead. Also, we've a very fine library of films aboard the *Dolphin* and every time a character in one of those films reaches up under his coat it's always for the same reason and that's not just because he's checking to see if his wallet's still there.'

I took his wrist with my free hand, pulled his arm away and pushed it down on the table. I'm not saying it was easy, the US Navy clearly fed its submariners on a high protein diet, but I managed it without bursting a blood-vessel. I pulled a folded newspaper out from under my coat and laid it down. 'You wanted to know how the hell I knew where you were going,' I said. 'I can read, that's why. That's a Glasgow evening paper I picked up in Renfrew Airport half an hour ago.'

Hansen rubbed his wrist thoughtfully, then grinned. 'What did you get your doctorate in, Doc? Weight-lifting? About that paper – how could you have got it in Renfrew half an hour ago?'

'I flew down here. Helicopter.'

'A whirlybird, eh? I heard one arriving a few minutes ago. But that was one of ours.'

'It had US Navy written all over it in four-foot letters,' I conceded, 'and the pilot spent all his time chewing gum and praying out loud for a quick return to California.'

'Did you tell the skipper this?' Hansen demanded.

'He didn't give me the chance to tell him anything.'

'He's got a lot on his mind and far too much to see to,' Hansen said. He unfolded the paper and looked at the front page. He didn't have far to look to find what he wanted: the two-inch banner headlines were spread over seven columns.

'Well, would you look at this.' Lieutenant Hansen made no attempt to conceal his irritation and chagrin. 'Here we are, pussy-footing around in this God-forsaken dump, sticking-plaster all over our mouths, sworn to eternal secrecy about mission and destination and then what? I pick up this blasted Limey newspaper and here are all the top-secret details plastered right across the front page.'

'You are kidding, Lieutenant,' said the man with the red face and the general aspect of a polar bear. His voice seemed to come from his boots.

'I am not kidding, Zabrinski,' Hansen said coldly, 'as you would appreciate if you had ever learned to read. "Nuclear submarine to the rescue," it says. "Dramatic dash to the North Pole." God help us, the North Pole. And a picture of the *Dolphin*. And of the skipper. Good lord, there's even a picture of me.'

Rawlings reached out a hairy paw and twisted the paper to have a better look at the blurred and smudged representation of the man before him. 'So there is. Not very flattering, is it, Lieutenant? But a speaking likeness, mind you, a speaking likeness. The photographer has caught the essentials perfectly.'

'You are utterly ignorant of the first principles of photography,' Hansen said witheringly. 'Listen to this lot. "The following joint statement was issued simultaneously a few minutes before noon (GMT) to-day in both London and Washington: 'In view of the critical condition of the survivors of Drift Ice Station Zebra and the failure either to rescue or contact them by conventional means, the United States Navy has willingly agreed that the United States nuclear submarine *Dolphin* be dispatched with all speed to try to effect contact with the survivors.

' "The *Dolphin* returned to its base in the Holy Loch, Scotland, at dawn this morning after carrying out extensive exercises with the Nato naval forces in the Eastern Atlantic. It is hoped that the *Dolphin* (Commander James D. Swanson, USN, commanding) will sail at approximately 7 p.m. (GMT) this evening.

' "The laconic understatement of this communique heralds the beginning of a desperate and dangerous rescue attempt which must be without parallel in the history of the sea or the Arctic. It is now sixty hours—" '

' "Desperate," you said, Lieutenant?' Rawlings frowned heavily. ' "Dangerous," you said? The captain will be asking for volunteers?'

'No need. I told the captain that I'd already checked with all eighty-eight enlisted men and that they'd volunteered to a man.'

'You never checked with me.'

'I must have missed you out. Now kindly clam up, your executive officer is talking. "It is now sixty hours since the world was electrified to learn of the disaster which had struck Drift Ice Station Zebra, the only British meteorological station in the Arctic, when an English-speaking ham radio operator in Bodo, Norway picked up the faint SOS from the top of the world.

' "A further message, picked up less than twenty-four hours ago by the British trawler *Morning Star* in the Barents Sea makes it clear that the position of the survivors of the fuel oil fire that destroyed most of Drift Ice Station Zebra in the early hours of Tuesday morning is desperate in the extreme. With their oil fuel reserves completely destroyed and their food stores all but wiped out, it is feared that those still living cannot long be expected to survive in the twenty-below temperatures – fifty degrees of frost – at present being experienced in that area.

' "It is not known whether all the prefabricated huts, in which the expedition members lived, have been destroyed.

' "Drift Ice Station Zebra, which was established only in the late summer of this year, is at present in an estimated position of 85° 40′ N 21° 30′ E, which is only about three hundred miles from the North Pole. Its position cannot be known with certainty because of the clockwise drift of the polar ice-pack.

' "For the past thirty hours long-range supersonic bombers of the American, British and Russian air forces have been scouring the polar ice-pack searching for Station Zebra. Because of the uncertainty about the Drift Station's actual position, the complete absence of daylight in the Arctic at this time of year and the extremely bad weather conditions they were unable to locate the station and forced to return." '

'They didn't have to locate it,' Rawlings objected. 'Not visually. With the instruments those bombers have nowadays they could home in on a humming-bird a hundred miles away. The radio operator at the Drift Station had only to keep on sending and they could have used that as a beacon.'

'Maybe the radio operator is dead,' Hansen said heavily. 'Maybe his radio has packed up on him. Maybe the fuel that was destroyed was essential for running the radio. All depends what source of power he used.'

'Diesel-electric generator,' I said. 'He had a standby battery of Nife cells. Maybe he's conserving the batteries, using them only for emergencies. There's also a hand-cranked generator, but its range is pretty limited.'

'How do you know that?' Hansen asked quietly. 'About the type of power used?'

'I must have read it somewhere.'

'You must have read it somewhere.' He looked at me without expression, then turned back to his paper. ' "A report from Moscow," ' he read on, ' "states that the atomic-engined *Dvina*, the world's most powerful ice-breaker, sailed from Murmansk some twenty hours ago and is proceeding at high speed towards the Arctic pack. Experts are not hopeful about the outcome for at this late period of the year the ice-pack had already thickened and compacted into a solid mass which will almost certainly defy the efforts of any vessel, even those of the *Dvina*, to smash its way through.

' "The use of the submarine *Dolphin* appears to offer the only slender hope of life for the apparently doomed survivors of Station Zebra. The odds against success must be regarded as heavy in the extreme. Not only will the *Dolphin* have to travel several hundred miles continuously submerged under the polar ice-cap, but the possibilities of its being able to break through the ice-cap at any given place or to locate the survivors are very remote. But undoubtedly if any ship in the world can do it it is the *Dolphin*, the pride of the United States Navy's nuclear submarine fleet." '

Hansen broke off and read on silently for a minute. Then he said: 'That's about all. A story giving all the known details of the *Dolphin*. That, and a lot of ridiculous rubbish about the enlisted men in the *Dolphin's* crew being the *èlite* of the cream of the US Navy.'

Rawlings looked wounded. Zabrinski, the polar bear with the red face, grinned, fished out a pack of cigarettes and passed them around. Then he became serious again and said: 'What are those crazy guys doing up there at the top of the world anyway?'

'Meteorological, lunkhead,' Rawlings informed him. 'Didn't you hear the lieutenant say so? A big word, mind you,' he conceded generously, 'but he made a pretty fair stab at it. Weather station to you, Zabrinski.'

'I still say they're crazy guys,' Zabrinski rumbled. 'Why do they do it, Lieutenant?'

'I suggest you ask Dr Carpenter about it,' Hansen said dryly. He stared through the plate-glass windows at the snow whirling greyly through the gathering darkness, his eyes bleak and remote, as if he were already visualizing the doomed men drifting to their death in the frozen immensity of the polar ice-cap. 'I think he knows a great deal more about it than I do.'

'I know a little,' I admitted. 'There's nothing mysterious or sinister about what I know. Meteorologists now regard the Arctic and the Antarctic as the two great weather factories of the world, the areas primarily responsible for the weather that affects the rest of the hemisphere. We already know a fair amount about Antarctic conditions, but practically nothing about the Arctic. So we pick a suitable ice-floe, fill it with huts crammed with technicians and all sorts of instruments and let them drift around the top of the world for six months or so. Your own people have already set up two or three of those stations. The Russians have set up at least ten, to the best of my knowledge, most of them in the East Siberian Sea.'

'How do they establish those camps, Doc?' Rawlings asked.

'Different ways. Your people prefer to establish them in winter-time, when the pack freezes up enough for plane landings to be made. Someone flies out from, usually, Point Barrow in Alaska and searches around the polar pack till they find a suitable ice-floe – even when the ice is compacted and frozen together into one solid mass an expert can tell which pieces are going to remain as good-sized floes when the thaw comes and the break-in begins. Then they fly out all huts, equipment, stores and men by ski-plane and gradually build the place up.

'The Russians prefer to use a ship in summer-time. They generally use the *Lenin*, a nuclear-engined ice-breaker. It just batters its way into the summer pack, dumps everything and everybody on the ice and takes off before the big freeze-up starts. We used the same technique for Drift Ice Station Zebra – our one and only ice station. The Russians lent us the *Lenin* – all countries are only too willing to co-operate on meteorological research as everyone benefits by it – and took us pretty deep into the ice-pack north of Franz Josef Land. Zebra has already moved a good bit from its original position – the polar ice-cap, just sitting on top of the Arctic Ocean, can't quite manage to keep up with the west-east spin of the earth so that it has a slow westward movement in relation to the earth's crust. At the present moment it's about four hundred miles due north of Spitzbergen.'

'They're still crazy,' Zabrinski said. He was silent for a moment then looked speculatively at me. 'You in the Limey navy, Doc?'

'You must forgive Zabrinski's manners, Dr Carpenter,' Rawlings said coldly. 'But he's denied the advantages that the rest of us take for granted. I understand he was born in the Bronx.'

'No offence,' Zabrinski said equably. 'Royal Navy, I meant. Are you, Doc?'

'Attached to it, you might say.'

'Loosely, no doubt,' Rawlings nodded. 'Why so keen on an Arctic holiday, Doc? Mighty cool up there, I can tell you.'

'Because the men on Drift Station Zebra are going to be badly in need of medical aid. If there are any survivors, that is.'

'We got our own medico on board and he's no slouch with a stethoscope, or so I've heard from several who have survived his treatment. A well-spoken-of quack.'

'Doctor, you ill-mannered lout,' Zabrinski said severely.

'That's what I meant,' Rawlings apologized. 'It's not often that I get the chance to talk to an educated man like myself, and it just kinda slipped out. The point is, the *Dolphin*'s already all buttoned up on the medical side.'

'I'm sure it is.' I smiled. 'But any survivors we might find are going to be suffering from advanced exposure, frostbite and probably gangrene. The treatment of those is rather a speciality of mine.'

'Is it now?' Rawlings surveyed the depths of his coffee cup. 'I wonder how a man gets to be a specialist in those things?'

Hansen stirred and withdrew his gaze from the darkly-white world beyond the canteen windows.

'Dr Carpenter is not on trial for his life,' he said mildly. 'The counsel for the prosecution will kindly pack it in.'

They packed it in. This air of easy familiarity between officer and men, the easy camaraderie, the mutually tolerant disparagement with the deceptively misleading overtones of knock-about comedy, was something very rare in my experience but not unique. I'd seen it before, in first-line RAF bomber crews, a relationship found only among a close-knit, close-living group of superbly trained experts each of whom is keenly aware of their complete interdependence. The casually informal and familiar attitude was a token not of the lack of discipline but of the complete reverse: it was the token of a very high degree of self-discipline, of the regard one man held for another not only as a highly-skilled technician in his own field but also as a human being. It was clear, too, that a list of unwritten rules governed their conduct. Off-hand and frequently completely lacking in outward respect though Rawlings and Zabrinski were in their attitude towards Lieutenant Hansen, there was an invisible line of propriety over which it was inconceivable that they would ever step: for Hansen's part, he scrupulously avoided any use of his authority when making disparaging remarks at the expense of the two enlisted men. It was also clear, as now, who was boss.

Rawlings and Zabrinski stopped questioning me and had just embarked upon an enthusiastic discussion of the demerits of the Holy Loch in particular and Scotland in general as a submarine base when a jeep swept past the canteen windows, the snow whirling whitely, thickly, through the swathe of the headlights. Rawlings jumped to his feet in mid-sentence, then subsided slowly and thoughtfully into his chair.

'The plot,' he announced, 'thickens.'

'You saw who it was?' Hansen asked.

'I did indeed. Andy Bandy, no less.'

'I didn't hear that, Rawlings,' Hansen said coldly.

'Vice-Admiral John Garvie, United States Navy, sir.'

'Andy Bandy, eh?' Hansen said pensively. He grinned at me. 'Admiral Garvie, Officer Commanding US Naval Forces in Nato. Now this is very interesting, I submit. I wonder what he's doing here.'

'World War III has just broken out,' Rawlings announced. 'It's just about time for the Admiral's first martini of the day and no lesser crisis—'

'He didn't by any chance fly down with you in that chopper from Renfrew this afternoon?' Hansen interrupted shrewdly.

'No.'

'Know him, by any chance?'

'Never even heard of him until now.'

'Curiouser and curiouser,' Hansen murmured.

A few minutes passed in desultory talk – the minds of Hansen and his two men were obviously very much on the reason for the arrival of Admiral Garvie – and then a snow-filled gust of chilled air swept into the canteen as the door opened and a blue-coated sailor came in and crossed to our table.

'The captain's compliments, Lieutenant. Would you bring Dr Carpenter to his cabin, please?'

Hansen nodded, rose to his feet and led the way outside. The snow was beginning to lie now, the darkness was coming down fast and the wind from the north was bitingly chill. Hansen made for the nearest gangway, halted at its head as he saw seamen and dockyard workers, insubstantial and spectral figures in the swirling flood-lit snow, carefully easing a slung torpedo down the for'ard hatch, turned and headed towards the after gangway. We clambered down and at the foot Hansen said: 'Watch your step, Doc. It's a mite slippery hereabouts.'

It was all that, but with the thought of the ice-cold waters of the Holy Loch waiting for me if I put a foot wrong I made no mistake. We passed through the hooped canvas shelter covering the after hatch and dropped down a steep metal ladder into a warm, scrupulously clean and gleaming engine-room packed with a baffling complexity of grey-painted machinery and instrument panels, its every corner brightly illuminated with shadowless fluorescent lighting.

'Not going to blindfold me, Lieutenant?' I asked.

'No need.' He grinned. 'If you're on the up and up, it's not necessary. If you're not on the up and up it's still not necessary, for you can't talk about what you've seen – not to anyone that matters – if you're going to spend the next few years staring out from behind a set of prison bars.'

I saw his point. I followed him for'ard, our feet soundless on the black rubber decking past the tops of a couple of huge machines readily identifiable as turbo-generator sets for producing electricity. More heavy banks of instruments, a door, then a thirty-foot-long very narrow passageway. As we passed along its length I was conscious of a heavy vibrating hum from beneath my feet. The *Dolphin*'s nuclear reactor had to be somewhere. This would be it, here. Directly beneath us. There were circular hatches on the passageway deck and those could only be covers for the heavily-leaded glass windows, inspection ports which would provide the nearest and only approach to the nuclear furnace far below.

The end of the passage, another heavily-clipped door, and then we were into what was obviously the control centre of the *Dolphin*. To the left was a partitioned-off radio room, to the right a battery of machines and dialled panels of incomprehensible purpose, straight ahead a big chart table. Beyond that again, in the centre were massive mast housings and, still farther on, the periscope stand with its twin periscopes. The whole control room was twice the size of any I'd ever seen in a conventional submarine but, even so, every square inch of bulkhead space seemed to be taken up by one type or another of highly-complicated looking machines or instrument banks: even the deckhead was almost invisible, lost to sight above thickly twisted festoons of wires, cables and pipes of a score of different kinds.

The for'ard port side of the control room was for all the world like a replica of the flight-deck of a modern multi-engined jet airliner. There were two separate yoke aircraft-type control columns, facing on to banks of hooded calibrated dials. Behind the yokes were two padded leather chairs, each chair, I could see, fitted with safety-belts to hold the helmsman in place. I wondered vaguely what type of violent manoeuvres the *Dolphin* might be capable of when such safety-belts were obviously considered essential to strap the helmsman down.

Opposite the control platform, on the other side of the passageway leading forward from the control room, was a second partitioned-off room. There was no indication what this might be and I wasn't given time to wonder. Hansen hurried down the passage, stopped at the first door on his left, and knocked. The door opened and Commander Swanson appeared.

'Ah, there you are. Sorry you've been kept waiting, Dr Carpenter. We're sailing at six-thirty, John' – this to Hansen. 'You can have everything buttoned up by then?'

'Depends how quickly the loading of the torpedoes goes, Captain.'

'We're taking only six aboard.'

Hansen lifted an eyebrow, made no comment. He said: 'Loading them into the tubes?'

'In the racks. They have to be worked on.'

'No spares?'

'No spares.'

Hansen nodded and left. Swanson led me into his cabin and closed the door behind him.

Commander Swanson's cabin was bigger than a telephone booth, I'll say that for it, but not all that much bigger to shout about. A built-in bunk, a folding washbasin, a small writing-bureau and chair, a folding camp-stool, a locker, some calibrated repeater instrument dials above the bunk and that was it. If you'd tried to perform the twist in there you'd have fractured yourself in a dozen places without ever moving your feet from the centre of the floor.

'Dr Carpenter,' Swanson said, 'I'd like you to meet Admiral Garvie, Commander US Nato Naval Forces.'

Admiral Garvie put down the glass he was holding in his hand, rose from the only chair and stretched out his hand. As he stood with his feet together, the far from negligible clearance between his knees made it easy to understand the latter part of his 'Andy Bandy' nickname: like Hansen, he'd have been at home on the range. He was a tall florid-faced man with white hair, white eyebrows and a twinkle in the blue eyes below: he had that certain indefinable something about him common to all senior naval officers the world over, irrespective of race or nationality.

'Glad to meet you, Dr Carpenter. Sorry for the – um – lukewarm reception you received, but Commander Swanson was perfectly within his rights in acting as he did. His men have looked after you?'

'They permitted me to buy them a cup of coffee in the canteen.'

He smiled. 'Opportunists all, those nuclear men. I feel that the good name of American hospitality is in danger. Whisky, Dr Carpenter?'

'I thought American naval ships were dry, sir.'

'So they are, my boy, so they are. Except for a little medicinal alcohol, of course. My personal supply.' He produced a hip-flask about the size of a canteen, reached for a convenient tooth-glass. 'Before venturing into the remoter fastnesses of the Highlands of Scotland the prudent man takes the necessary precautions. I have to make an apology to you, Dr Carpenter. I saw your Admiral Hewson in London last night and had intended to be here this morning to persuade Commander Swanson here to take you aboard. But I was delayed.'

'Persuade, sir?'

'Persuade.' He sighed. 'Our nuclear submarine captains, Dr Carpenter, are a touchy and difficult bunch. From the proprietary attitude they adopt towards their submarines you'd think that each one of them was a majority shareholder in the Electric Boat Company of Groton, where most of those boats are built.' He raised his glass. 'Success to the commander and yourself. I hope you manage to find those poor devils. But I don't give you one chance in a thousand.'

'I think we'll find them, sir. Or Commander Swanson will.'

'What makes you so sure?' He added slowly, 'Hunch?'

'You could call it that.'

He laid down his glass and his eyes were no longer twinkling. 'Admiral Hewson was most evasive about you, I must say. Who are you, Carpenter? *What* are you?'

'Surely he told you, Admiral? Just a doctor attached to the navy to carry out—'

'A naval doctor?'

'Well, not exactly. I—'

'A civilian, is it?'

I nodded, and the admiral and Swanson exchanged looks which they were at no pains at all to conceal from me. If they were happy at the prospect of having aboard America's latest and most secret submarine a man who was not only a foreigner but a civilian to boot, they were hiding it well. Admiral Garvie said: 'Well, go on.'

'That's all. I carry out environmental health studies for the services. How men react to extremes of environmental conditions, such as in the Arctic or the tropics, how they react to conditions of weightlessness in simulated space flights or to extremes of pressure when having to escape from submarines. Mainly—'

'Submarines.' Admiral Garvie pounced on the word. 'You have been to sea in submarines, Dr Carpenter. Really sailed in them, I mean?'

'I had to. We found that simulated tank escapes were no substitute for the real thing.'

The admiral and Swanson looked unhappier than ever. A foreigner – bad. A foreign civilian – worse. But a foreign civilian with at least a working knowledge of submarines – terrible. I didn't have to be beaten over the head to see their point of view. I would have felt just as unhappy in their shoes.

'What's your interest in Drift Ice Station Zebra, Dr Carpenter?' Admiral Garvie asked bluntly.

'The Admiralty asked me to go there, sir.'

'So I gather, so I gather,' Garvie said wearily. 'Admiral Hewson made that quite plain to me already. Why *you*, Carpenter?'

'I have some knowledge of the Arctic, sir. I'm supposed to be an expert on the medical treatment of men subjected to prolonged exposure, frostbite and gangrene. I might be able to save lives or limbs that your own doctor aboard might not.'

'I could have half a dozen such experts here in a few hours,' Garvie said evenly. 'Regular serving officers of the United States Navy, at that. That's not enough, Carpenter.'

This was becoming difficult. I tried again. I said: 'I know Drift Station Zebra. I helped select the site. I helped establish the camp. The commandant, a Major Halliwell, has been my closest friend for many years.' The last was only half the truth but I felt that this was neither the time nor the place for over-elaboration.

'Well, well,' Garvie said thoughtfully. 'And you still claim you're just an ordinary doctor?'

'My duties are flexible, sir.'

'I'll say they are. Well, then, Carpenter, if you're just a common-or-garden sawbones, how do you explain this?' He picked a signal form from the table and handed it to me. 'This has just arrived in reply to Commander Swanson's radioed query to Washington about you.'

I looked at the signal. It read: 'Dr Neil Carpenter's bonafides beyond question. He may be taken into your fullest, repeat fullest confidence. He is to be extended every facility and all aid short of actually endangering the safety of your submarine and the lives of your crew.' It was signed by the Director of Naval Operations.

'Very civil of the Director of Naval Operations, I must say.' I handed back the signal. 'With a character reference like this, what are you worrying about. That ought to satisfy anyone.'

'It doesn't satisfy me,' Garvie said heavily. 'The ultimate responsibility for the safety of the *Dolphin* is mine. This signal more or less gives you *carte blanche* to behave as you like, to ask Commander Swanson to act in ways that might be contrary to his better judgment. I can't have that.'

'Does it matter what you can or can't have? You have your orders. Why don't you obey them?'

He didn't hit me. He didn't even bat an eyelid. He wasn't activated by pique about the fact that he wasn't privy to the reason for the seeming mystery of my presence there, he was genuinely concerned about the safety of the submarine. He said: 'If I think it more important that the *Dolphin* should remain on an active war footing rather than to go haring off on a wild-goose chase to the Arctic, or if I think you constitute a danger to the submarine, I can countermand the DNO's orders. I'm the C-in-C on the spot. And I'm not satisfied.'

This was damnably awkward. He meant every word he said and he didn't look the type who would give a hoot for the consequences if he believed himself to be in the right. I looked at both men, looked at them slowly and speculatively, the unmistakable gaze, I hoped, of a man who was weighing others in the balance: what I was really doing was thinking up a suitable story that would satisfy both. After I had given enough time to my weighing-up – and my thinking – I dropped my voice a few decibels and said: 'Is that door soundproof?'

'More or less,' Swanson said. He'd lowered his own voice to match mine.

'I won't insult either of you by swearing you to secrecy or any such rubbish,' I said quietly. 'I want to put on record the fact that what I am about to tell you I am telling you under duress, under Admiral Garvie's threat to refuse me transport if I don't comply with his wishes.'

'There will be no repercussions,' Garvie said.

'How do you know? Not that it matters now. Well, gentlemen, the facts are these. Drift Ice Station Zebra is officially classed as an Air Ministry meteorological station. Well, it belongs to the Air Ministry all right, but there's not more than a couple of qualified meteorologists among its entire personnel.'

Admiral Garvie refilled the toothglass and passed it to me without a word, without a flicker of change in his expression. The old boy certainly knew how to play it cool.

'What you will find there,' I went on, 'are some of the most highly skilled men in the world in the fields of radar, radio, infra-red and electronic computers, operating the most advanced instruments ever used in those fields. We know now, never mind how, the count-down succession of signals the Russians use in the last minute before launching a missile. There's a huge dish aerial in Zebra that can pick up and amplify any such signals within seconds of it beginning. Then long-range radar and infra-red home in on that bearing and within three minutes of the rocket's lift-off they have its height, speed and course pin-pointed to an infinitesimal degree of error. The computers do this, of course. One minute later the information is in the hands of all the anti-missile stations between Alaska and Greenland. One minute more and solid fuel infra-red homing anti-missile rockets are on their way; then the enemy missiles will be intercepted and harmlessly destroyed while still high over the Arctic regions. If you look at a map you will see that in its present position Drift Ice Station Zebra is sitting practically on Russia's missile doorstep. It's hundreds of miles in advance of the present DEW line – the distant early warning system. Anyway, it renders the DEW line obsolete.'

'I'm only the office boy around those parts,' Garvie said quietly. 'I've never heard of any of this before.'

I wasn't surprised. I'd never heard any of it myself either, not until I'd just thought it up a moment ago. Commander Swanson's reactions, if and when we ever got to Drift Station Zebra, were going to be very interesting. But I'd cross that bridge when I came to it. At present, my only concern was to get there.

'Outside the Drift Station itself,' I said, 'I doubt if a dozen people in the world know what goes on there. But now you know. And you can appreciate how vitally important it is to the free world that this base be maintained in being. If anything has happened to it we want to find out just as quick as possible *what* has happened so that we can get it operating again.'

'I still maintain that you're not an ordinary doctor,' Garvie smiled. 'Commander Swanson, how soon can you get under way?'

'Finish loading the torpedoes, move alongside the *Hunley*, load some final food stores, pick up extra Arctic clothing and that's it, sir.'

'Just like that? You said you wanted to make a slow-time dive out in the loch to check the planes and adjust the underwater trim – those missing torpedoes up front are going to make a difference you know.'

'That's before I heard Dr Carpenter. Now I want to get up there just as fast as he does, sir. I'll see if immediate trim checks are necessary: if not, we can carry them out at sea.'

'It's your boat,' Garvie acknowledged. 'Where are you going to accommodate Dr Carpenter, by the way?'

'There's space for a cot in the Exec's and Engineer's cabin.' He smiled at me. 'I've already had your suitcase put in there.'

'Did you have much trouble with the lock?' I inquired.

He had the grace to colour slightly. 'It's the first time I've ever seen a combination lock on a suitcase,' he admitted. 'It was that, more than anything else – and the fact that we couldn't open it – that made the admiral and myself so suspicious. I've still one or two things to discuss with the admiral, so I'll take you to your quarters now. Dinner will be at eight to-night.'

'I'd rather skip dinner, thanks.'

'No one ever gets seasick on the *Dolphin*, I can assure you,' Swanson smiled.

'I'd appreciate the chance to sleep instead. I've had no sleep for almost three days and I've been travelling non-stop for the past fifty hours. I'm just tired, that's all.'

'That's a fair amount of travelling.' Swanson smiled. He seemed almost always to be smiling, and I supposed vaguely that there would be some people foolish enough to take that smile always at its face value. 'Where were you fifty hours ago, Doctor?'

'In the Antarctic.'

Admiral Garvie gave me a very old-fashioned look indeed, but he let it go at that.

Chapter Two

When I awoke I was still heavy with sleep, the heaviness of a man who has slept for a long time. My watch said nine-thirty, and I knew it must be the next morning, not the same evening: I had been asleep for fifteen hours.

The cabin was quite dark. I rose, fumbled for the light switch, found it and looked around. Neither Hansen nor the engineer officer was there: they must have come in after I had gone to sleep and left before I woke. I looked around some more, and then I listened. I was suddenly conscious of the almost complete quiet, the stillness, the entire lack of any perceptible motion. I might have been in the bedroom of my own house. What had gone wrong? What hold-up had occurred? Why in God's name weren't we under way? I'd have sworn the previous night that Commander Swanson had been just as conscious of the urgency as I had been.

I had a quick wash in the folding Pullman-type basin, passed up the need for a shave, pulled on shirt, trousers and shoes and went outside. A few feet away a door opened to starboard off the passage. I went along and walked in. The officers' wardroom, without a doubt, with one of them still at breakfast, slowly munching his way through a huge plateful of steak, eggs and French fries, glancing at a magazine in a leisurely fashion and giving every impression of a man enjoying life to the luxurious full. He was about my own age, big, inclined to fat – a common condition, I was to find, among the entire crew who ate so well and exercised so little – with close-cropped black hair already greying at the temples and a cheerful intelligent face. He caught sight of me, rose and stretched out a hand.

'Dr Carpenter, it must be. Welcome to the wardroom. I'm Benson. Take a seat, take a seat.'

I said something, appropriate but quick, then asked: 'What's wrong? What's been the hold-up? Why aren't we under way?'

'That's the trouble with the world to-day,' Benson said mournfully. 'Rush, rush, rush. And where does all the hurry get them? I'll tell you—'

'Excuse me. I must see the captain.' I turned to leave but he laid a hand on my arm.

'Relax, Dr Carpenter. We *are* at sea. Take a seat.'

'At sea? On the level? I don't feel a thing.'

'You never do when you're three hundred feet down. Maybe four hundred. I don't,' he said expansively, 'concern myself with those trifles. I leave them to the mechanics.'

'Mechanics?'

'The captain, engineer officer, people like those.' He waved a hand in a generously vague gesture to indicate the largeness of the concept he understood by the term 'mechanics'. 'Hungry?'

'We've cleared the Clyde?'

'Unless the Clyde extends to well beyond the north of Scotland, the answer to that is, yes, we have.'

'Come again?'

He grinned. 'At the last check we were well into the Norwegian Sea, about the latitude of Bergen.'

'This is still only Tuesday morning?' I don't know if I looked stupid: I certainly felt it.

'It's still only Tuesday morning.' He laughed. 'And if you can work out from that what kind of speed we have been making in the last fifteen hours we'd all be obliged if you'd keep it to yourself.' He leaned back in his seat and lifted his voice. 'Henry!'

A steward, white-jacketed, appeared from what I took to be the pantry. He was a tall thin character with a dark complexion and the long lugubrious face of a dyspeptic spaniel. He looked at Benson and said in a meaningful voice: '*Another* plate of French fries, Doc?'

'You know very well that I never have more than one helping of that carbohydrated rubbish,' Benson said with dignity. 'Not, at least, for breakfast. Henry, this is Dr Carpenter.'

'Howdy,' Henry said agreeably.

'Breakfast, Henry,' Benson said. 'And, remember, Dr Carpenter is a Britisher. We don't want him leaving with a low opinion of the chow served up in the United States Navy.'

'If anyone aboard this ship has a low opinion of the food,' Henry said darkly, 'they hide it pretty well. Breakfast. The works. Right away.'

'Not the works, for heaven's sake,' I said. 'There are some things we decadent Britishers can't face up to first thing in the morning. One of them is French fries.'

He nodded approvingly and left. I said: 'Dr Benson, I gather.'

'Resident medical officer aboard the *Dolphin*, no less,' he admitted. 'The one who's had his professional competence called into question by having a competing practitioner called in.'

'I'm along for the ride. I assure you I'm not competing with anyone.'

'I know you're not,' he said quickly. Too quickly. Quickly enough so that I could see Swanson's hand in this, could see him telling his officers to lay of quizzing Carpenter too much. I wondered again what Swanson was going to say when and if we ever arrived at the Drift Station and he found out just how fluent a liar I was. Benson went on, smiling, 'There's no call for even one medico aboard this boat, far less two.'

'You're not overworked?' From the leisurely way he was going about his breakfast it seemed unlikely.

'Overworked! I've sickbay call once a day and no one ever turns up – except the morning after we arrive in port with a long cruise behind us and then there are liable to be a few sore heads around. My main job, and what is supposed to be my speciality, is checking on radiation and atmosphere pollution of one kind or another – in the olden submarine days the atmosphere used to get pretty foul after only a few hours submerged but we have to stay down for months, if necessary.' He grinned. 'Neither job is very exacting. We issue each member of the crew with a dosimeter and periodically check a film badge for radiation dosage – which is invariably less than you'd get sitting on the beach on a moderately warm day.

'The atmospheric problem is even easier. Carbon dioxide and carbon monoxide are the only things we have to worry about. We have a scrubbing machine that absorbs the breathed-out carbon dioxide from the atmosphere and pumps it out into the sea. Carbon monoxide – which we could more or less eliminate if we forbade cigarette smoking, only we don't want a mutiny on our hands when we're three hundred feet down – is burned to dioxide by a special heater and then scrubbed as usual. And even that hardly worries me, I've a very competent engineman who keeps those machines in tip-top condition.' He sighed. 'I've a surgery here that will delight your heart, Dr Carpenter. Operating table, dentist's chair, the lot, and the biggest crisis I've had yet is a cigarette burn between the fingers sustained by a cook who fell asleep during one of the lectures.'

'Lectures?'

'I've got to do something if I'm not to go round the bend. I spend a couple of hours a day keeping up with all the latest medical literature but what good is that if you don't get a chance to practise it? So I lecture. I read up about places we're going to visit and everyone listens to those talks. I give lectures on general health and hygiene and some of them listen to those. I give lectures on the perils of overeating and under-exercise and no one listens to those. I don't listen to them myself. It was during one of those that the cook got burned. That's why our friend Henry, the steward, adopts his superior and critical attitude towards the eating habits of those who should obviously be watching their habits. He eats as much as any two men aboard but owing to some metabolic defect he remains as thin as a rake. Claims it's all due to dieting.'

'It all sounds a bit less rigorous than the life of the average G.P.'

'It is, it is.' He brightened. 'But I've got one job – a hobby to me – that the average G.P. can't have. The ice-machine. I've made myself an expert on that.'

'What does Henry think about it?'

'What? Henry?' He laughed. 'Not that kind of ice-machine. I'll show you later.'

Henry brought food and I'd have liked the *maîtres d'hôtel* of some allegedly five-star hotels in London to be there to see what a breakfast should be like. When I'd finished and told Benson that I didn't see that his lectures on the dangers of overweight were going to get him very far, he said: 'Commander Swanson said you might like to see over the ship. I'm at your complete disposal.'

'Very kind of you both. But first I'd like to shave, dress and have a word with the captain.'

'Shave if you like. No one insists on it. As for dress, shirt and pants are the rig of the day here. And the captain told me to tell you that he'd let you know immediately anything came through that could possibly be of any interest to you.'

So I shaved and then had Benson take me on a conducted tour of this city under the sea: the *Dolphin*, I had to admit made any British submarine I'd ever seen look like a relic from the Ice Age.

To begin with, the sheer size of the vessel was staggering. So big had the hull to be to accommodate the huge nuclear reactor that it had internal accommodation equivalent to that of a 3,000-ton surface ship, with three decks instead of the usual one and lower hold found in the conventional submarine. The size, combined with the clever use of pastel paints for all accommodation spaces, working spaces and passageways, gave an overwhelming impression of lightness, airiness and above all, spaciousness.

He took me first, inevitably, to his sickbay. It was at once the smallest and most comprehensively equipped surgery I'd ever seen, whether a man wanted a major operation or just a tooth filled, he could have himself accommodated there. Neither clinical nor utilitarian, however, was the motif Benson had adopted for the decoration of the one bulkhead in his surgery completely free from surgical or medical equipment of any kind – a series of film stills in colour featuring every cartoon character I'd ever seen, from Popeye to Pinnochio, with, as a two-foot square centrepiece, an immaculately cravatted Yogi Bear industriously sawing off from the top of a wooden signpost the first word of a legend which read 'Don't feed the bears.' From deck to deckhead, the bulkhead was covered with them.

'Makes a change from the usual pin-ups,' I observed.

'I get inundated with those, too,' Benson said regretfully. 'Film librarian, you know. Can't use them, supposed to be bad for discipline. However. Lightens the morgue-like atmosphere, what? Cheers up the sick and suffering, I like to think – and distracts their attention while I turn up page 217 in the old textbook to find out what's the matter with them.'

From the surgery we passed through the wardroom and officers' quarters and dropped down a deck to the crew's living quarters. Benson took me through the gleaming tiled washrooms, the immaculate bunk-room, then into the crew's mess hall.

'The heart of the ship,' he announced. 'Not the nuclear reactor, as the uninformed maintain, but here. Just look at it. Hifi, juke box, record player, coffee machine, ice-cream machine, movie theatre, library and the home of all the card-sharps on the ship. What chance has a nuclear reactor against this lot? The old-time submariners would turn in their graves if they could see this: compared to the prehistoric conditions they lived in we must seem completely spoiled and ruined. Maybe we are, then again maybe we're not: the old boys never had to stay submerged for months at a time. This is also where I send them to sleep with my lectures on the evils of overeating.' He raised his voice for the benefit of seven or eight men who were sitting about the tables, drinking coffee, smoking and reading. 'You can observe for yourself, Dr Carpenter, the effects of my lectures in dieting and keeping fit. Did you ever see a bunch of more out-of-condition fat-bellied slobs in your life?'

The men grinned cheerfully. They were obviously well used to this sort of thing: Benson was exaggerating and they knew it. Each of them looked as if he knew what to do with a knife and fork when he got them in his hands, but that was about as far as it went. All had a curious similarity, big men and small men, the same characteristic as I'd seen in Zabrinski and Rawlings – an air of calmly relaxed competence, a cheerful imperturbability, that marked them out as being the men apart that they undoubtedly were.

Benson conscientiously introduced me to everyone, telling me exactly what their function aboard ship was and in turn informing them that I was a Royal Navy doctor along for an acclimatization trip. Swanson would have told him to say this, it was near enough the truth and would stop speculation on the reason for my presence there.

Benson turned into a small compartment leading off the mess hall. 'The air purification room. This is Engineman Harrison. How's our box of tricks, Harrison?'

'Just fine, Doc, just fine. CO reading steady on thirty parts a million.' He entered some figures up in a log book, Benson signed it with a flourish, exchanged a few more remarks and left.

'Half my day's toil done with one stroke of the pen,' he observed. 'I take it you're not interested in inspecting sacks of wheat, sides of beef, bags of potatoes and about a hundred different varieties of canned goods.'

'Not particularly. Why?'

'The entire for'ard half of the deck beneath our feet – a storage hold, really – is given up mainly to that. Seems an awful lot, I know, but then a hundred men can get through an awful lot of food in three months, which is the minimum time we must be prepared to stay at sea if the need arises. We'll pass up the inspection of the stores, the sight of all that food just makes me feel I'm fighting a losing battle all the time, and have a look where the food's cooked.'

He led the way for'ard into the galley, a small square room all tiles and glittering stainless steel. A tall, burly, white-coated cook turned at our entrance and grinned at Benson. 'Come to sample to-day's lunch, Doc?'

'I have not,' Benson said coldly. 'Dr Carpenter, the chief cook and my arch-enemy, Sam MacGuire. What form does the excess of calories take that you are proposing to thrust down the throats of the crew to-day?'

'No thrusting required,' said MacGuire happily. 'Cream soup, sirloin of beef, no less, roast potatoes and as much apple pie as a man can cope with. All good nourishing food.'

Benson shuddered. He made to leave the galley, stopped and pointed at a heavy bronze ten-inch tube that stood about four feet above the deck of the galley. It had a heavy hinged lid and screwed clamps to keep the lid in position. 'This might interest you, Dr Carpenter. Guess what?'

'A pressure cooker?'

'Looks like it, doesn't it? This is our garbage disposal unit. In the old days when a submarine had to surface every few hours garbage disposal was no problem, you just tipped the stuff over the side. But when you spend weeks on end cruising at three hundred feet you can't just walk up to the upper deck and tip the waste over the side: garbage disposal becomes quite a problem. This tube goes right down to the bottom of the *Dolphin*. There's a heavy watertight door at the lower end corresponding to this one, with interlocking controls which made it impossible for both doors to be open at the same time – it would be curtains for the *Dolphin* if they were. Sam here, or one of his henchmen, sticks the garbage into nylon mesh or polythene bags, weighs them with bricks—'

'Bricks, you said?'

'Bricks. Sam, how many bricks aboard this ship?'

'Just over a thousand at the latest count, Doc.'

'Regular builder's yard, aren't we?' Benson grinned. 'Those bricks are to ensure that the garbage bags sink to the bottom of the sea and not float to the surface – even in peacetime we don't want to give our position away to anyone. In go three or four bags, the top door is clamped shut and the bags pumped out under pressure. Then the outer door is closed again. Simple.'

'Yes.' For some reason or other this odd contraption had a curious fascination for me. Days later I was to remember my inexplicable interest in it and wonder whether, after all, I wasn't becoming psychic with advancing years.

'It's not worth all that attention,' Benson said good-humouredly. 'Just an up-to-date version of the old rubbish chute. Come on, a long way to go yet.'

He led the way from the galley to a heavy steel door set in a transverse bulkhead. Eight massive clips to release, then replace after we had passed through the doorway.

'The for'ard torpedo storage room.' Benson's voice was lowered, for at least half of the sixteen or so bunks that lined the bulkheads or were jammed up close to the torpedoes and racks were occupied and every man occupying them was sound asleep. 'Only six torpedoes as you can see. Normally there's stowage for twelve plus another six constantly kept loaded in the torpedo tubes. But those six are all we have just now. We had a malfunction in two of our torpedoes of the newest and more or less untested radio-controlled type – during the Nato exercises just ended – and Admiral Garvie ordered the lot removed for inspection when we got back to the Holy Loch. The *Hunley*, that's our depot ship, carries experts for working on those things. However, they were no sooner taken off yesterday morning than this Drift Station operation came our way and Commander Swanson insisted on having at least six of them put back on straight away.' Benson grinned. 'If there's one thing a submarine skipper hates it's putting to sea without his torpedoes. He feels he might just as well stay at home.'

'Those torpedoes are still not operational?'

'I don't know whether they are or not. Our sleeping warriors here will do their best to find out when they come to.'

'Why aren't they working on them now?'

'Because before our return to the Clyde they were working on them for nearly sixty hours non-stop trying to find out the cause of the malfunction – and if it existed in the other torpedoes. I told the skipper that if he wanted to blow up the *Dolphin* as good a way as any was to let those torpedo-men keep on working – they were starting to stagger around like zombies and a zombie is the last person you want to have working on the highly-complicated innards of a torpedo. So he pulled them off.'

He walked the length of the gleaming torpedoes and halted before another steel door in a cross bulkhead. He opened this, and beyond, four feet away, was another such heavy door set in another such bulkhead. The sills were about eighteen inches above deck level.

'You don't take many chances in building these boats, do you?' I asked. 'It's like breaking into the Bank of England.'

'Being a nuclear sub doesn't mean that we're not as vulnerable to underwater hazards as the older ships,' Benson said. 'We are. Ships have been lost before because the collision bulkhead gave way. The hull of the *Dolphin* can withstand terrific pressures, but a relatively minor tap from a sharp-edged object can rip us wide like an electric can-opener. The biggest danger is surface collision which nearly always happens at the bows. So, to make doubly sure in the event of a bows collision, we have those double collision bulkheads – the first submarine ever to have them. Makes fore and aft movement here a bit difficult but you've no idea how much more soundly we all sleep at night.'

He closed the after door behind him and opened the for'ard one: we found ourselves in the for'ard torpedo room, a narrow cramped compartment barely long enough to permit torpedoes to be loaded or withdrawn from their tubes. Those tubes,with their heavy-hinged rear doors, were arranged close together in two vertical banks of three. Overhead were the loading rails with heavy chain tackles attached. And that was all. No bunks in here and I didn't wonder: I wouldn't have liked to be the one to sleep for'ard of those collision bulkheads.

We began to work our way aft and had reached the mess hall when a sailor came up and said that the captain wanted to see me. I followed him up the wide central stairway into the control room, Dr Benson a few paces behind to show that he wasn't being too inquisitive. Commmander Swanson was waiting for me by the door of the radio room.

'Morning Doctor. Slept well?'

'Fifteen hours. What do you think? And breakfasted even better. What's up, Commander.' Something was up, that was for sure: for once, Commander Swanson wasn't smiling.

'Message coming through about Drift Station Zebra. Has to be decoded first but that should take minutes only.' Decoding or not, it seemed to me that Swanson already had a fair idea of the content of that message.

'When did we surface?' I asked. A submarine loses radio contact as soon as it submerges.

'Not since we left the Clyde. We are close on three hundred feet down right now.'

'This is a *radio* message that's coming through?'

'What else? Times have changed. We still have to surface to transmit but we can receive down to our maximum depth. Somewhere in Connecticut is the world's largest radio transmitter using an extremely low frequency which can contact us at this depth far more easily than any other radio station can contact a surface ship. While we're waiting, come and meet the drivers.'

He introduced me to some of his control centre crew – as with Benson it seemed to be a matter of complete indifference to him whether it was officer or enlisted man – finally stopped by an officer sitting just aft of the periscope stand, a youngster who looked as if he should still be in high school. 'Will Raeburn,' Swanson said. 'Normally we pay no attention to him but after we move under the ice he becomes the most important man on the ship. Our navigation officer. Are we lost, Will?'

'We're just there, Captain.' He pointed to a tiny pin-point of light on the Norwegian Sea chart spread out below the glass on the plotting-table. 'Gyro and sins are checking to a hair.'

'Sins?' I said.

'You may well look surprised, Dr Carpenter,' Swanson said. 'Lieutenant Raeburn here is far too young to have any sins. He is referring to S.I.N.S. – Ship's Inertial Navigational System – a device once used for guiding intercontinental missiles and now adapted for submarine use, specifically nuclear submarines. No point in my elaborating, Will's ready to talk your head off about it if he manages to corner you.' He glanced at the chart position. 'Are we getting along quickly enough to suit you, Doctor?'

'I still don't believe it,' I said.

'We cleared the Holy Loch a bit earlier than I expected, before seven,' Swanson admitted. 'I had intended to carry out some slow-time dives to adjust trim – but it wasn't necessary. Even the lack of twelve torpedoes up in the nose didn't make her as stern-heavy as I'd expected. She's so damned big that a few tons more or less here or there doesn't seem to make any difference to her. So we just came haring on up—'

He broke off to accept a signal sheet from a sailor, and read through it slowly, taking his time about it. Then he jerked his head, walked to a quiet corner of the control centre and faced me as I came up to him. He still wasn't smiling.

'I'm sorry,' he said. 'Major Halliwell, the commandant of the Drift Station – you said last night he was a very close friend of yours?'

I felt my mouth begin to go dry. I nodded, took the message from him. It read: 'A further radio message, very broken and difficult to decipher, was received 0945 Greenwich Mean Time from Drift Ice Station Zebra by the British trawler *Morning Star*, the vessel that picked up the previous broadcast. Message stated that Major Halliwell, Officer Commanding, and three others unnamed critically injured or dead, no indication who or how many of the four are dead. Others, number again unknown, suffering severely from burns and exposure. Some message about food and fuel, atmospheric conditions and weakness in transmission made it quite indecipherable. Understood from very garbled signal that survivors in one hut, unable to move because of weather. Word 'icestorm' clearly picked up. Apparently details of wind speed and temperature but unable to make out.

'*Morning Star* several times attempted contact Drift Station Zebra immediately afterwards. No acknowledgment.

'*Morning Star*, at request of British Admiralty, has abandoned fishing grounds and is moving closer in to Barrier to act as listening post. Message ends.'

I folded the paper and handed it back to Swanson. He said again: 'Sorry about this, Carpenter.'

'Critically injured or dead,' I said. 'In a burnt-out station on the ice-cap in winter, what's the difference?' My voice fell upon my ears as the voice of another man, a voice flat and lifeless, a voice empty of all emotion. 'Johnny Halliwell and three of his men. Johnny Halliwell. Not the kind of man you would meet often, Commander. A remarkable man. Left school at fifteen when his parents died to devote himself to the support of a brother eight years younger than himself. He slaved, he scraped, he sacrificed, he devoted many of the best years of his life to doing everything for his young brother, including putting him through a six-year University course. Not till then did he think of himself, not till then did he get married. He leaves a lovely wife and three marvellous kids. Two nieces and a nephew not yet six months old.'

'Two nieces—' He broke off and stared at me. 'Good God, your brother? *Your* brother?' He didn't, for the moment seem to find anything peculiar in the difference of surname.

I nodded silently. Young Lieutenant Raeburn approached us, an odd expression of anxiety on his face, but Swanson abruptly waved him away without seeming even to glance in his direction. He shook his head slowly and was still shaking it when I said abruptly: 'He's tough. He may be one of the survivors. He may live. We must get Drift Station Zebra's position. We *must* get it.'

'Maybe they haven't got it themselves,' Swanson said. You could see he was grateful for something to talk about. 'It *is* a drifting station, remember. The weather being what it is, it may have been days since they got their last fixes – and for all we know their sextants, chronometers and radio direction finders have been lost in the fire.'

'They must know what their latest fix was, even although it was a week ago. They must have a fairly accurate idea of the speed and direction of their drift. They'll be able to provide approximate data. The *Morning Star* must be told to keep transmitting non-stop with a continuous request for their position. If you surface now, can you contact the *Morning Star*?'

'I doubt it. The trawler must be the best part of a thousand miles north of us. His receiver wouldn't be big enough to pull us in – which is another way of saying that our transmitter is too small.'

'The BBC have plenty of transmitters that are big enough. So have the Admiralty. Please ask one or other to contact the *Morning Star* and ask it to make a continuous send for Zebra's position.'

'They could do that themselves direct.'

'Sure they could. But they couldn't hear the reply. The *Morning Star* can – if there's any reply. And she's getting closer to them all the time.'

'We'll surface now,' Swanson nodded. He turned away from the chart table we'd been standing beside and headed for the diving stand. As he passed the plotting table he said to the navigator: 'What was it you wanted, Will?'

Lieutenant Raeburn turned his back on me and lowered his voice, but my hearing has always been a little abnormal. He whispered: 'Did you see his face, Captain? I thought he was going to haul off and clobber you one.'

'I thought the same thing myself,' Swanson murmured. 'For a moment. But I think I just happened to be in his line of vision, that's all.'

I went forward to my cabin and lay down in the cot.

Chapter Three

'There it is, then,' said Swanson. 'That's the Barrier.'

The *Dolphin*, heading due north, her great cylindrical bulk at one moment completely submerged, the next showing clear as she rolled heavily through the steep quartering seas, was making less than three knots through the water, the great nuclear-powered engines providing just enough thrust to the big twin eight-foot propellers to provide steerage way and no more: thirty feet below where we stood on the bridge the finest sonar equipment in the world was ceaselessly probing the waters all around us but even so Swanson was taking no chances on the effects of collision with a drifting ice-block. The noonday Arctic sky was so overcast that the light was no better than that of late dusk. The bridge thermometer showed the sea temperature as 28° F, the air temperature as −16° F. The gale-force wind from the north-east was snatching the tops off the rolling steel-grey waves and subjecting the steep-walled sides of the great conning-tower – sail, the crew called it – to the ceaseless battering of a bullet-driven spray that turned to solid ice even as it struck. The cold was intense.

Shivering uncontrollably, wrapped in heavy duffel-coat and oilskins and huddled against the illusory shelter of the canvas wind-dodger, I followed the line of Swanson's pointing arm: even above the high thin shrill whine of the wind and the drum-fire of the flying spray against the sail, I could hear the violent chattering of his teeth. Less than two miles away a long, thin, greyish-white line, at that distance apparently smooth and regular, seemed to stretch the entire width of the northern horizon. I'd seen it before and it wasn't much to look at but it was a sight a man never got used to, not because of itself but because of what it represented, the beginning of the polar ice-cap that covered the top of the world, at this time of year a solid compacted mass of ice that stretched clear from where we lay right across to Alaska on the other side of the world. And we had to go under that mass. We had to go under it to find men hundreds of miles away, men who might be already dying, men who might be already dead. Who probably were dead. Men, dying or dead, whom we had to seek out by guess and by God in that great wasteland of ice stretching out endlessly before us, for we did not know where they were.

The relayed radio message we had received just forty-nine hours previously had been the last. Since then, there had been only silence. The trawler *Morning Star* had been sending almost continuously in the intervening two days, trying to raise Drift Station Zebra, but out of that bleak desert of ice to the north had come nothing but silence. No word, no signal, no faintest whisper of sound had come out of that desolation.

Eighteen hours previously the Russian atomic-engined *Dvina* had reached the Barrier and had started on an all-out and desperate attempt to smash its way into the heart of the ice-cap. In this early stage of winter the ice was neither so thick nor so compacted as it would be at the time of its maximum density, in March, and the very heavily armoured and powerfully engined *Dvina* was reputed to be able to break through ice up to a thickness of eighteen feet: given fair conditions, the *Dvina* was widely believed to be capable of battering its way to the North Pole. But the conditions of the rafted ice had proved abnormal to a degree and the attempt a hopeless one. The *Dvina* had managed to crash its way over forty miles into the ice-cap before being permanently stopped by a thick wall of rafter ice over twenty feet in height and probably more than a hundred deep. The *Dvina*, according to reports, had sustained heavy damage to its bows and was still in the process of extricating itself, with the greatest difficulty, from the pack. A very gallant effort that had achieved nothing except an improvement in East-West relations to an extent undreamed of for many years.

Nor had the Russian efforts stopped there. Both they and the Americans had made several flights over the area with front-line long-range bombers. Through the deep overcast and driving ice- and snow-filled winds those planes had criss-crossed the suspected area a hundred times, searching with their fantastically accurate radar. But not one single radar sighting had been reported. Various reasons had been put forward to explain the failure, especially the failure of the Strategic Air Command's B52 bomber whose radar was known to be easily capable of picking out a hut against contrasting background from ten thousand feet and in pitch darkness. It had been suggested that the huts were no longer there: that the radar's eye was unable to distinguish between an ice-sheathed hut and the thousands of ice-hummocks which dot the polar cap in winter; and that they had been searching in the wrong area in the first place. The most probable explanation was that the radar waves had been blurred and deflated by the dense clouds of ice-spicules blowing over the area. Whatever the reason, Drift Ice Station Zebra remained as silent as if no life had ever been there, as lost as if it had never existed.

'There's no percentage in staying up here and getting frozen to death.' Commander Swanson's voice was a half-shout, it had to be to make him heard. 'If we're going under that ice, we might as well go now.' He turned his back to the wind and stared out to the west where a big broad-beamed trawler was rolling heavily and sluggishly in the seas less than a quarter of a mile away. The *Morning Star*, which had closed right up to the edge of the ice-pack over the last two days, listening, waiting, and all in vain, was about to return to Hull: her fuel reserves were running low.

'Make a signal,' Swanson said to the seaman by his side. ' "We are about to dive and proceed under the ice. We do not expect to emerge for minimum four days, are prepared to remain maximum fourteen." ' He turned to me and said: 'If we can't find them in that time . . .' and left the sentence unfinished.

I nodded, and he went on: ' "Many thanks for your splendid co-operation. Good luck and a safe trip home." ' As the signalman's lamp started chattering out its message, he said wonderingly: 'Do those fishermen trawl up in the Arctic the entire winter?'

'They do.'

'The whole winter. Fifteen minutes and I'm about dead. Just a bunch of decadent Limeys, that's what they are.' A lamp aboard the *Morning Star* flickered for some seconds and Swanson said: 'What reply?'

' "Mind your heads under that ice. Good luck and goodbye." '

'Everybody below,' Swanson said. As the signalman began to strip the canvas dodger I dropped down a ladder into a small compartment beneath, wriggled through a hatch and down a second ladder to the pressure hull of the submarine, another hatch, a third ladder and then I was on the control deck of the *Dolphin*. Swanson and the signalman followed, then last of all Hansen, who had to close the two heavy watertight doors above.

Commander Swanson's diving technique would have proved a vast disappointment to those brought up on a diet of movie submarines. No frenzied activity, no tense steely-eyed men hovering over controls, no Tannoy calls of "Dive, dive, dive," no blaring of klaxons. Swanson reached down a steel-spring microphone, said quietly: 'This is the captain. We are about to move under the ice. Diving now,' hung up and said: 'Three hundred feet.'

The chief electronics technician leisurely checked the rows of lights indicating all hatches, surface openings and valves closed to the sea. The disc lights were out: the slot lights burned brightly. Just as leisurely he re-checked them, glanced at Swanson and said: 'Straight line shut, sir.' Swanson nodded. Air hissed loudly out of the ballast tanks, and that was it. We were on our way. It was about as wildly exciting as watching a man push a wheelbarrow. And there was something oddly reassuring about it all.

Ten minutes later Swanson came up to me. In the past two days I'd come to know Commander Swanson fairly well, like him a lot and respect him tremendously. The crew had complete and implicit faith in him. I was beginning to have the same thing. He was a kindly genial man with a vast knowledge of every aspect of submarining, a remarkable eye for detail, an even more remarkably acute mind and an imperturbability that remained absolute under all conditions. Hansen, his executive officer and clearly no respecter of persons, had said flatly that Swanson was the best submarine officer in the Navy. I hoped he was right, that was the kind of man I wanted around in conditions like those.

'We're about to move under the ice now, Dr Carpenter,' he said. 'How do you feel about it?'

'I'd feel better if I could see where we were going.'

'We can see,' he said. 'We've the best eyes in the world aboard the *Dolphin*. We've got eyes that look down, around, ahead and straight up. Our downward eye is the fathometer or echo-sounder that tells us just how deep the water below our keel is – and as we have about five thousand feet of water below our keel at this particular spot we're hardly likely to bump into underwater projections and its use right now is purely a formality. But no responsible navigation officer would ever think of switching it off. We have two sonar eyes for looking around and ahead, one sweeping the ship, another searching out a fifteen-degree path on either side of the bow. Sees everything, hears everything. You drop a spanner on a warship twenty miles away and we know all about it. Fact. Again it seems purely a formality. The sonar is searching for underwater ice stalactites forced down by the pressure of rafted ice above, but in five trips under the ice and two to the Pole I've never seen underwater stalactites or ridges deeper than 200 feet, and we're at 300 feet now. But we still keep them on.'

'You might bump into a whale?' I suggested.

'We might bump into another submarine.' He wasn't smiling. 'And that would be the end of both of us. What with the Russian and our own nuclear submarines busy criss-crossing to and fro across the top of the world the underside of the polar ice-cap is getting more like Times Square every day.'

'But surely the chances—'

'What are the chances of mid-air collision to the only two aircraft occupying ten thousand square miles of sky? On paper, they don't exist. There have been three such collisions this year already. So we keep the sonar pinging. But the really important eye, when you're under the ice, is the one that looks up. Come and have a squint at it.'

He led the way to the after starboard end of the control room where Dr Benson and another man were busy studying a glassed-in eye-level machine which outwardly consisted of a seven-inch-wide moving ribbon of paper and an inked stylus that was tracing a narrow straight black line along it. Benson was engrossed in adjusting some of the calibrated controls.

'The surface fathometer,' Swanson said. 'Better known as the ice-machine. It's not really Dr Benson's machine at all, we have two trained operators aboard, but as we see no way of separating him from it without actually court-martialling him, we take the easy way out and let him be.' Benson grinned, but his eye didn't leave the line traced by the stylus. 'Same principle as the echo-sounding machine, it just bounces an echo back from the ice – when there is any. That thin black line you see means open water above. When we move under the ice the stylus has an added vertical motion which not only indicates the presence of ice but also gives us its thickness.'

'Ingenious,' I said.

'It's more than that. Under the ice it can be life or death for the *Dolphin*. It certainly means life or death for Drift Station Zebra. If we ever get its position we can't get at it until we break through the ice and this is the only machine that can tell us where the ice is thinnest.'

'No open water at this time of year? No leads?'

'Polynyas, we call them. None. Mind you, the ice-pack is never static, not even in winter, and surface pressure changes can very occasionally tear the ice apart and expose open water. With air temperatures such as you get in winter you can guess how long the open water stays in a liquid condition. There's a skin of ice on it in five minutes, an inch in an hour and a foot inside two days. If we get to one of those frozen over polynyas inside, say, three days, we've a fair chance of breaking through.'

'With the conning-tower?'

'That's it. The sail. All new nuclear subs have specially strengthened sails designed for one purpose only – breaking through Arctic ice. Even so we have to go pretty gently as the shock, of course, is transmitted to the pressure hull.'

I thought about this a bit then said: 'What happens to the pressure hull if you come up too fast – as I understand may happen with a sudden change in salinity and sea temperature – and you find out at the last minute that you've drifted away from the indicated area of thin ice and have ten solid feet of the stuff above you?'

'That's it,' he said. 'Like you say, it's the last minute. Don't even think about such things, far less talk about them: I can't afford to have nightmares on this job.' I looked at him closely, but he wasn't smiling any more. He lowered his voice. 'I don't honestly think that there is one member of the crew of the *Dolphin* who doesn't get a little bit scared when we move in under the ice. I know I do. I think this is the finest ship in the world, Dr Carpenter, but there are still a hundred things that can go wrong with it and if anything happens to the reactor or the steam turbines or the electrical generators – then we're already in our coffin and the lid screwed down. The ice-pack above is the coffin lid. In the open sea most of those things don't matter a damn – we just surface or go to snorkel depth and proceed on our diesels. But for diesels you need air – and there's no air under the ice-pack. So if anything happens we either find a polynya to surface in, one chance in ten thousand at this time of year, before our standby battery packs up or – well, that's it.'

'This is all very encouraging,' I said.

'Isn't it?' He smiled, none too soon for me. 'It'll never happen. What's the worthy Benson making all the racket about?'

'Here it is,' Benson called. 'The first drift-block. And another. And another! Come and have a look, Doctor.'

I had a look. The stylus, making a faint soft hissing sound, was no longer tracing out a continuously horizontal line but was moving rapidly up and down across the paper, tracing out the outline of the block of ice passing astern above us. Another thin straight line, more agitated vertical movements of the stylus, and again another block of ice had gone. Even as I watched the number of thin horizontal lines became fewer and fewer and shorter and shorter until eventually they disappeared altogether.

'That's it, then,' Swanson nodded. 'We'll take her deep now, real deep, and open up all the stops.'

When Commander Swanson had said he was going to hurry, he'd meant every word of it. In the early hours of the following morning I was awakened from a deep sleep by a heavy hand on my shoulder. I opened my eyes, blinked against the glare of the overhead light then saw Lieutenant Hansen.

'Sorry about the beauty sleep, Doc,' he said cheerfully. 'But this is it.'

'This is what?' I said irritably.

'85° 35′ north, 21° 20′ east – the last estimated position of Drift Station Zebra. At least, the last estimated position with estimated correction for polar drift.'

'Already?' I glanced at my watch, not believing it. 'We're there already?'

'We have not,' Hansen said modestly, 'been idling. The skipper suggests you come along and watch us at work.'

'I'll be right with you.' When and if the *Dolphin* managed to break through the ice and began to try her one in a million chance of contacting Drift Station Zebra, I wanted to be there.

We left Hansen's cabin and had almost reached the control room when I lurched, staggered and would have fallen but for a quick grab at a handrail that ran along one side of the passageway. I hung on grimly as the *Dolphin* banked violently sideways and round like a fighter plane in a tight turn. No submarine in my experience had ever been able to begin to behave even remotely in that fashion. I understood now the reasons for the safety belts on the diving control seats.

'What the hell's up?' I said to Hansen. 'Avoiding some underwater obstruction ahead?'

'Must be a possible polynya. Some place where the ice is thin, anyway. As soon as we spot a possible like that we come around like a chicken chasing its own tail just so we don't miss it. It makes us very popular with the crew, especially when they're drinking coffee or soup.'

We passed into the control room. Commander Swanson, flanked by the navigator and another man, was bent over the plotting table, examining something intently. Farther aft a man at the surface fathometer was reading out ice thickness figures in a quiet unemotional voice. Commander Swanson looked up from the chart.

'Morning, Doctor. John, I think we may have something here.'

Hansen crossed to the plot and peered at it. There didn't seem to be much to peer at – a tiny pin-point of light shining through the glass top of the plot and a squared sheet of chart paper marked by a most unseamanlike series of wavering black lines traced out by a man with a pencil following the track of the tiny moving light. There were three red crosses superimposed on the paper, two very close together, and just as Hansen was examining the paper the crewman manning the ice-machine – Dr Benson's enthusiasm for his toy did not, it appeared, extend to the middle of the night – called out 'Mark!' Immediately the black pencil was exchanged for a red and a fourth cross made.

' "Think" and "may" are just about right, Captain,' Hansen said. 'It looks awfully narrow to me.'

'It looks the same way to me, too,' Swanson admitted. 'But it's the first break in the heavy ice that we've had in an hour, almost. And the farther north we go, the poorer our chances. Let's give it a go. Speed?'

'One knot,' Raeburn said.

'All back one-third,' Swanson said. No sharp imperatives, not ever, in the way Swanson gave his orders, more a quiet and conversational suggestion, but there was no mistaking the speed with which one of the crewmen strapped into the diving-stand bucket seat leaned forward to telegraph the order to the engine-room. 'Left full rudder.'

Swanson bent over to check the plot, closely watching the tiny pin-point of light and tracing pencil move back towards the approximate centre of the elongated quadrangle formed by the four red crosses. 'All stop,' he went on. 'Rudder amidships.' A pause then: 'All ahead one-third. So. All stop.'

'Speed zero,' Raeburn said.

'120 feet,' Swanson said to the diving officer. 'But gently, gently.'

A strong steady hum echoed in the control centre. I asked Hansen: 'Blowing ballast?'

He shook his head. 'Just pumping the stuff out. Gives a far more precise control of rising speed and makes it easier to keep the sub on an even keel. Bringing a stopped sub up on a dead even keel is no trick for beginners. Conventional subs never try this sort of thing.'

The pumps stopped. There came the sound of water flooding back into the tanks as the diving officer slowed up the rate of ascent. The sound faded.

'Secure flooding,' the diving officer said. 'Steady on 120 feet.'

'Up periscope,' Swanson said to the crewman by his side. An overhead lever was engaged and we could hear the hiss of high-pressure oil as the hydraulic piston began to lift the starboard periscope off its seating. The gleaming cylinder rose slowly against the pressure of the water outside until finally the foot of the periscope cleared its well. Swanson opened the hinged handgrips and peered through the eyepiece.

'What does he expect to see in the middle of the night at this depth?' I asked Hansen.

'Never can tell. It's rarely completely dark, as you know. Maybe a moon, maybe only stars – but even starlight will show as a faint glow through the ice – if the ice is thin enough.'

'What's the thickness of the ice above, in this rectangle?'

'The sixty-four thousand dollar question,' Hansen admitted, 'and the answer is that we don't know. To keep that ice-machine to a reasonable size the graph scale has to be very small. Anything between four and forty inches. Four inches we go through like the icing on a wedding cake: forty inches and we get a very sore head indeed.' He nodded across to Swanson. 'Doesn't look so good. That grip he's twisting is to tilt the periscope lens upwards and that button is for focusing. Means he's having trouble in finding anything.'

Swanson straightened. 'Black as the earl of hell's waistcoat,' he said conversationally. 'Switch on hull and sail floodlights.'

He stooped and looked again. For a few seconds only. 'Pea-soup. Thick and yellow and strong. Can't see a thing. Let's have the camera, shall we?'

I looked at Hansen, who nodded to a white screen that had just been unshuttered on the opposite bulkhead. 'All mod cons, Doc. Closed circuit TV. Camera is deck mounted under toughened glass and can be remotely controlled to look up or round.'

'You could do with a new camera, couldn't you?' The TV screen was grey, fuzzy, featureless.

'Best that money can buy,' Hansen said. 'It's the water. Under certain conditions of temperature and salinity it becomes almost completely opaque when floodlit. Like driving into a heavy fog with your headlights full on.'

'Floodlights off,' Swanson said. The screen became quite blank. 'Floodlights on.' The same drifting misty grey as before. Swanson sighed and turned to Hansen. 'Well, John?'

'If I were paid for imagining things,' Hansen said carefully, 'I could imagine I see the top of the sail in that left corner. Pretty murky out there, Captain. Heigh-ho for the old blind man's buff, is that it?'

'Russian roulette, I prefer to call it.' Swanson had the clear unworried face of a man contemplating a Sunday afternoon in a deck-chair. 'Are we holding position?'

'I don't know.' Raeburn looked up from the plot. 'It's difficult to be sure.'

'Sanders?' This to the man at the ice-machine.

'Thin ice, sir. Still thin ice.'

'Keep calling. Down periscope.' He folded the handles up and turned to the diving officer. 'Take her up like we were carrying a crate of eggs atop the sail and didn't want to crack even one of them.'

The pumps started again. I looked around the control room. Swanson excepted, everyone was quiet and still and keyed-up. Raeburn's face was beaded with sweat and Sanders's voice was too calm and impersonal by half as he kept repeating: 'Thin ice, thin ice,' in a low monotone. You could reach out and touch the tension in the air.. I said quietly to Hansen: 'Nobody seems very happy. There's still a hundred feet to go.'

'There's forty feet,' Hansen said shortly. 'Readings are taken from keel level and there's sixty feet between the keel and the top of the sail. Forty feet minus the thickness of the ice – and maybe a razor-sharp or needle-pointed stalactite sticking down ready to skewer the *Dolphin* through the middle. You know what that means?'

'That it's time I started getting worried too?'

Hansen smiled, but he wasn't feeling like smiling. Neither was I, not any more.

'Ninety feet,' the diving officer said.

'Thin ice, thin ice,' Sanders intoned.

'Switch off the deck flood, leave the sail flood on,' Swanson said. 'And keep that camera moving. Sonar?'

'All clear,' the sonar operator reported. 'All clear all round.' A pause, then: 'No, hold it, hold it! Contact dead astern!'

'How close?' Swanson asked quickly.

'Too close to say. Very close.'

'She's jumping!' the diving officer called out sharply. '80, 75.' The *Dolphin* had hit a layer of colder water or extra salinity.

'Heavy ice, heavy ice!' Sanders called out urgently.

'Flood emergency!' Swanson ordered – and this time it was an order.

I felt the sudden build-up of air pressure as the diving officer vented the negative tank and tons of sea-water poured into the emergency diving tank, but it was too late. With a shuddering jarring smash that sent us staggering the *Dolphin* crashed violently into the ice above, glass tinkled, lights went out and the submarine started falling like a stone.

'Blow negative to the mark!' the diving officer called. High pressure air came boiling into the negative tank – at our rate of falling we would have been flattened by the sea-pressure before the pumps could even have begun to cope with the huge extra ballast load we had taken aboard in seconds. Two hundred feet, two hundred and fifty and we were still falling. Nobody spoke, everybody just stood or sat in a frozen position staring at the diving stand. It required no gift for telepathy to know the thought in every mind. It was obvious that the *Dolphin* had been struck aft by some underwater pressure ridge at the same instant as the sail had hit the heavy ice above: if the *Dolphin* had been holed aft this descent wasn't going to stop until the pressure of a million tons of water had crushed and flattened the hull and in a flicker of time snuffed out the life of every man inside it.

'Three hundred feet,' the diving officer called out. 'Three fifty – and she's slowing! She's slowing.'

The *Dolphin* was still falling, sluggishly passing the four-hundred-foot mark, when Rawlings appeared in the control room, tool-kit in one hand, a crate of assorted lamps in the other.

'It's unnatural,' he said. He appeared to be addressing the shattered lamp above the plot which he had immediately begun to repair. 'Contrary to the laws of nature, I've always maintained. Mankind was never meant to probe beneath the depths of the ocean. Mark my words, those new-fangled inventions will come to a bad end.'

'So will you, if you don't keep quiet,' Commander Swanson said acidly. But there was no reprimand in his face, he appreciated as well as any of us the therapeutic breath of fresh air that Rawlings had brought into that tension-laden atmosphere. 'Holding?' he went on to the diving officer.

The diving officer raised a finger and grinned. Swanson nodded, swung the coiled-spring microphone in front of him. 'Captain here,' he said calmly. 'Sorry about that bump. Report damage at once.'

A green light flashed in the panel of a box beside him. Swanson touched a switch and a loudspeaker in the deckhead crackled.

'Manoeuvring room here.' The manoeuvring room was in the after end of the upper level engine-room, towards the stern. 'Hit was directly above us here. We could do with a box of candles and some of the dials and gauges are out of kilter. But we still got a roof over our heads.'

'Thank you, Lieutenant. You can cope?'

'Sure we can.'

Swanson pressed another switch. 'Stern room?'

'We still attached to the ship?' a cautious voice inquired.

'You're still attached to the ship,' Swanson assured him. 'Anything to report?'

'Only that there's going to be an awful lot of dirty laundry by the time we get back to Scotland. The washing-machine's had a kind of fit.'

Swanson smiled and switched off. His face was untroubled, he must have had a special sweat-absorbing mechanism on his face, I felt I could have done with a bath towel. He said to Hansen: 'That was bad luck. A combination of a current where a current had no right to be, a temperature inversion where a temperature inversion had no right to be, and a pressure ridge where we least expected it. Not to mention the damned opacity of the water. What's required is a few circuits until we know this polynya like the backs of our hands, a small offset to allow for drift and a little precautionary flooding as we approach the ninety-foot mark.'

'Yes, sir. That's what's required. Point is, what are we going to do?'

'Just that. Take her up and try again.'

I had my pride so I refrained from mopping my brow. They took her up and tried again. At 200 feet and for fifteen minutes Swanson juggled propellers and rudder till he had the outline of the frozen polynya above as accurately limned on the plot as he could ever expect to have it. Then he positioned the *Dolphin* just outside one of the boundary lines and gave an order for a slow ascent.

'One twenty-feet,' the diving officer said. 'One hundred ten.'

'Heavy ice,' Sanders intoned. 'Still heavy ice.'

Sluggishly the *Dolphin* continued to rise. Next time in the control room, I promised myself, I wouldn't forget that bath towel. Swanson said: 'If we've overestimated the speed of the drift, there's going to be another bump I'm afraid.' He turned to Rawlings who was still busily repairing lights. 'If I were you, I'd suspend operations for the present. You may have to start all over again in a moment and we don't carry all that number of spares aboard.'

'One hundred feet,' the diving officer said. He didn't sound as unhappy as his face looked.

'The water's clearing,' Hansen said suddenly. 'Look.'

The water had cleared, not dramatically so, but enough. We could see the top corner of the sail clearly outlined on the TV screen. And then suddenly, we could see something else again, heavy ugly ridged ice not a dozen feet above the sail.

Water flooding into the tanks. The diving officer didn't have to be told what to do, we'd gone up like an express lift the first time we'd hit a different water layer and once like that was enough in the life of any submarine.

'Ninety feet,' he reported. 'Still rising.' More water flooded in, then the sound died away. 'She's holding. Just under ninety feet.'

'Keep her there.' Swanson stared at the TV screen. 'We're drifting clear and into the polynya – I hope.'

'Me too,' Hansen said. 'There can't be more than a couple of feet between the top of the sail and that damned ugly stuff.'

'There isn't much room,' Swanson acknowledged. 'Sanders?'

'Just a moment, sir. The graph looks kinda funny – no we're clear.' He couldn't keep the excitement out of his voice. 'Thin ice!'

I looked at the screen. He was right. I could see the vertical edge of a wall of ice move slowly across the screen, exposing clear water above.

'Gently, now, gently,' Swanson said. 'And keep the camera on the ice wall at the side, then straight up, turn about.'

The pumps began to throb again. The ice wall, less than ten yards away, began to drift slowly down past us.

'Eighty-five feet,' the diving officer reported. 'Eighty.'

'No hurry,' Swanson said. 'We're sheltered from that drift by now.'

'Seventy-five feet.' The pumps stopped, and water began to flood into the tanks. 'Seventy.' The *Dolphin* was almost stopped now, drifting upwards as gently as thistledown. The camera switched upwards, and we could see the top corner of the sail clearly outlined with a smooth ceiling of ice floating down to meet it. More water gurgled into the tanks, the top of the sail met the ice with a barely perceptible bump and the *Dolphin* came to rest.

'Beautifully done,' Swanson said warmly to the diving officer. 'Let's give that ice a nudge. Are we slewing?'

'Bearing constant.'

Swanson nodded. The pumps hummed, pouring out water, lightening ship, steadily increasing positive buoyancy. The ice stayed where it was. More time passed, more water pumped out, and still nothing happened. I said softly to Hansen: 'Why doesn't he blow the main ballast? You'd get a few hundred tons of positive buoyancy in next to no time and even if that ice is forty inches thick it couldn't survive all that pressure at a concentrated point.'

'Neither could the *Dolphin*,' Hansen said grimly. 'With a suddenly induced big positive buoyancy like that, once she broke through she'd go up like a cork from a champagne bottle. The pressure hull might take it, I don't know, but sure as little apples the rudder would be squashed flat as a piece of tin. Do you want to spend what little's left of your life travelling in steadily decreasing circles under the polar ice-cap?'

I didn't want to spend what little was left of my life in travelling in steadily decreasing circles under the ice-cap so I kept quiet. I watched Swanson as he walked across to the diving stand and studied the banked dials in silence for some seconds. I was beginning to become a little apprehensive about what Swanson would do next: I was beginning to realize, and not slowly either, that he was a lad who didn't give up very easily.

'That's enough of that lot,' he said to the diving officer. 'If we go through now with all this pressure behind us we'll be airborne. This ice is even thicker than we thought. We've tried the long steady shove and it hasn't worked. A sharp tap is obviously what is needed. Flood her down, but gently, to eighty feet or so, a good sharp whiff of air into the ballast tanks and we'll give our well-known imitation of a bull at a gate.'

Whoever had installed the 240-ton air-conditioning unit in the *Dolphin* should have been prosecuted, it just wasn't working any more. The air was very hot and stuffy – what little there was of it, that was. I looked around cautiously and saw that everyone else appeared to be suffering from this same shortage of air, all except Swanson, who seemed to carry his own built-in oxygen cylinder around with him. I hoped Swanson was keeping in mind the fact that the *Dolphin* had cost 120 million dollars to build. Hansen's narrowed eyes held a definite core of worry and even the usually imperturbable Rawlings was rubbing a bristly blue chin with a hand the size and shape of a shovel. In the deep silence after Swanson had finished speaking the scraping noise sounded unusually loud, then was lost in the noise of water flooding into the tanks.

We stared at the screen. Water continued to pour into the tanks until we could see a gap appear between the top of the sail and the ice. The pumps started up, slowly, to control the speed of descent. On the screen, the cone of light thrown on to the underside of the ice by the flood-lamp grew fainter and larger as we dropped, then remained stationary, neither moving nor growing in size. We had stopped.

'Now,' said Swanson. 'Before that current gets us again.'

There came the hissing roar of compressed air under high pressure entering the ballast tanks. The *Dolphin* started to move sluggishly upwards while we watched the cone of light on the ice slowly narrow and brighten.

'More air,' Swanson said.

We were rising faster now, closing the gap to the ice all too quickly for my liking. Fifteen feet, twelve feet, ten feet.

'More air,' Swanson said.

I braced myself, one hand on the plot, the other on an overhead grab bar. On the screen, the ice was rushing down to meet us. Suddenly the picture quivered and danced, the *Dolphin* shuddered, jarred and echoed hollowly along its length, more lights went out, the picture came back on the screen, the sail was still lodged below the ice, then the *Dolphin* trembled and lurched and the deck pressed against our feet like an ascending elevator. The sail on the TV vanished, nothing but opaque white taking its place. The diving officer, his voice high with strain that had not yet found relief, called out. 'Forty feet, forty feet.' We had broken through.

'There you are now,' Swanson said mildly. 'All it needed was a little perseverance.' I looked at the short plump figure, the round good-humoured face, and wondered for the hundredth time why the nerveless iron men of this world so very seldom look the part.

I let my pride have a holiday. I took my handkerchief from my pocket, wiped my face and said to Swanson: 'Does this sort of thing go on all the time?'

'Fortunately, perhaps, no.' He smiled. He turned to the diving officer. 'We've got our foothold on this rock. Let's make sure we have a good belay.'

For a few second more compressed air was bled into the tanks, then the diving officer said: 'No chance of her dropping down now, Captain.'

'Up periscope.'

Again the long gleaming silver tube hissed up from its well. Swanson didn't even bother folding down the hinged handles. He peered briefly into the eyepiece, then straightened.

'Down periscope.'

'Pretty cold up top?' Hansen asked.

Swanson nodded. 'Water on the lens must have frozen solid as soon as it hit that air. Can't see a thing.' He turned to the diving officer. 'Steady at forty?'

'Guaranteed. And all the buoyancy we'll ever want.'

'Fair enough.' Swanson looked at the quartermaster who was shrugging his way into a heavy sheepskin coat. 'A little fresh air, Ellis, don't you think?'

'Right away, sir.' Ellis buttoned his coat and added: 'Might take some time.'

'I don't think so,' Swanson said. 'You may find the bridge and hatchways jammed with broken ice but I doubt it. My guess is that that ice is so thick that it will have fractured into very large sections and fallen outside clear of the bridge.'

I felt my ears pop with the sudden pressure change as the hatch swung up and open and snapped back against its standing latch. Another more distant sound as the second hatch-cover locked open and then we heard Ellis on the voice-tube.

'All clear up top.'

'Raise the antennae,' Swanson said. 'John, have them start transmitting and keep transmitting until their fingers fall off. Here we are and here we stay – until we raise Drift Ice Station Zebra.'

'If there's anyone left alive there,' I said.

'There's that, of course,' Swanson said. He couldn't look at me. 'There's always that.'

Chapter Four

This, I thought, death's dreadful conception of a dreadful world, must have been what had chilled the hearts and souls of our far-off Nordic ancestors when life's last tide slowly ebbed and they had tortured their failing minds with fearful imaginings of a bleak and bitter hell of eternal cold. But it had been all right for the old boys, all they had to do was to imagine it, we had to experience the reality of it and I had no doubt at all in my mind as to which was the easier. The latter-day Eastern conception of hell was more comfortable altogether, at least a man could keep reasonably warm there.

One thing sure, nobody could keep reasonably warm where Rawlings and I were, standing a half-hour watch on the bridge of the *Dolphin* and slowly freezing solid. It had been my own fault entirely that our teeth were chattering like frenzied castanets. Half an hour after the radio room had started transmitting on Drift Ice Station Zebra's wavelength and all without the slightest whisper by way of reply or acknowledgment, I had suggested to Commander Swanson that Zebra might possibly be able to hear us without having sufficient power to send a reply but that they might just conceivably let us have an acknowledgment some other way. I'd pointed out that Drift Stations habitually carried rockets – the only way to guide home any lost members of the party if radio communication broke down – and radio-sondes and rockoons. The sondes were radio-carrying balloons which could rise to a height of twenty miles to gather weather information: the rockoons, radio rockets fired from balloons, could rise even higher. On a moonlit night such as this, those balloons, if released, would be visible at least twenty miles away: if flares were attached to them, at twice that distance. Swanson had seen my point, called for volunteers for the first watch and in the circumstances I hadn't had much option. Rawlings had offered to accompany me.

It was a landscape – if such a bleak, barren and featureless desolation could be called a landscape – from another and ancient world, weird and strange and oddly frightening. There were no clouds in the sky, but there were no stars either: this I could not understand. Low on the southern horizon a milky misty moon shed its mysterious light over the dark lifelessness of the polar ice-cap. Dark, not white. One would have expected moonlit ice to shine and sparkle and glitter with the light of a million crystal chandeliers – but it was dark. The moon was so low in the sky that the dominating colour on the ice-cap came from the blackness of the long shadows cast by the fantastically ridged and hummocked ice: and where the moon did strike directly the ice had been so scoured and abraded by the assaults of a thousand ice-storms that it had lost almost all its ability to reflect light of any kind.

This ridged and hummocked ice-cap had a strange quality of elusiveness, of impermanence, of evanescence: one moment there, definitively hard and harsh and repellent in its coldly contrasting blacks and whites, the next, ghost-like blurring coalescing and finally vanishing like a shimmering mirage fading and dying in some ice-bound desert. But this was no trick of the eye or imagination, it was the result of a ground-level ice-storm that rose and swirled and subsided at the dictates of an icy wind that was never less than strong and sometimes gusted up to gale force, a wind that drove before it a swirling rushing fog of billions of needle-pointed ice-spicules. For the most part, standing as we were on the bridge twenty feet above the level of the ice – the rest of the *Dolphin* might never have existed as far as the eye could tell – we were above this billowing ground-swell of ice particles; but occasionally the wind gusted strongly, the spicules lifted, drummed demoniacally against the already ice-sheathed starboard side of the sail, drove against the few exposed inches of our skin with all the painfully stinging impact of a sand-blaster held at arm's length; but unlike a sand-blaster, the pain-filled shock of those spear-tipped spicules was only momentary, each wasp-like sting carried with it its own ice-cold anaesthetic and all surface sensation was quickly lost. Then the wind would drop, the furious rattling on the sail would fade and in the momentary contrast of near-silence we could hear the stealthy rustling as of a million rats advancing as the ice-spicules brushed their blind way across the iron-hard surface of the polar cap. The bridge thermometer stood at −21° F. −53° of frost. If I were a promoter interested in developing a summer holiday resort, I thought, I wouldn't pay very much attention to this place.

Rawlings and I stamped our feet, flailed our arms across our chests, shivered non-stop, took what little shelter we could from the canvas wind-break, rubbed our goggles constantly to keep them clear, and never once, except when the ice-spicules drove into our faces, stopped examining every quarter of the horizon. Somewhere out there on those frozen wastes was a lost and dying group of men whose lives might depend upon so little a thing as the momentary misting up of one of our goggles. We stared out over those shifting ice-sands until our eyes ached. But that was all we had for it, just aching eyes. We saw nothing, nothing at all. The ice-cap remained empty of all signs of life. Dead.

When our relief came Rawlings and I got below with all the speed our frozen and stiffened limbs would allow. I found Commander Swanson sitting on a canvas stool outside the radio room. I stripped off outer clothes, face coverings and goggles, took a steaming mug of coffee that had appeared from nowhere and tried not to hop around too much as the blood came pounding back into arms and legs.

'How did you cut yourself like that?' Swanson asked, concern in his voice. 'You've a half-inch streak of blood right across your forehead.'

'Flying ice, it just looks bad.' I felt tired and pretty low. 'We're wasting our time transmitting. If the men on Drift Station Zebra were without any shelter it's no wonder all signals ceased long ago. Without food and shelter no one could last more than a few hours in that lot. Neither Rawlings nor I is a wilting hothouse flower but after half an hour up there we've both just about had it.'

'I don't know,' Swanson said thoughtfully. 'Look at Amundsen. Look at Scott, at Peary. They *walked* all the way to the Poles.'

'A different breed of men, Captain. Either that or the sun shone for them. All I know is that half an hour is too long to be up there. Fifteen minutes is enough for anyone.'

'Fifteen minutes it shall be.' He looked at me, face carefully empty of all expression. 'You haven't much hope?'

'If they're without shelter. I've none.'

'You told me they had an emergency power pack of Nife cells for powering their transmitter,' he murmured. 'You also said those batteries will retain their charge indefinitely, years if necessary, irrespective of the weather conditions under which they are stored. They must have been using that battery a few days ago when they sent out their first SOS. It wouldn't be finished already.'

His point was so obvious that I didn't answer. The battery wasn't finished: the men were.

'I agree with you,' he went on quietly. 'We're wasting our time. Maybe we should just pack up and go home. If we can't raise them, we'll never find them.'

'Maybe not. But you're forgetting your directive from Washington, Commander.'

'How do you mean?'

'Remember? I'm to be extended every facility and all aid short of actually endangering the safety of the submarine and the lives of the crew. At the present moment we're doing neither. If we fail to raise them I'm prepared for a twenty-mile sweep on foot round this spot in the hope of locating them. If that fails we could move to another polynya and repeat the search. The search area isn't all that big, there's a fair chance, but a chance, that we might locate the station eventually. I'm prepared to stay up here all winter till we do find them.'

'You don't call that endangering the lives of my men? Making extended searches of the ice-cap, on foot, in mid-winter?'

'Nobody said anything about endangering the lives of your men.'

'You mean – you mean you'd go it alone.' Swanson stared down at the deck and shook his head. 'I don't know what to think. I don't know whether to say you're crazy or whether to say I'm beginning to understand why they – whoever "they" may be – picked you for the job, Dr Carpenter.' He sighed, then regarded me thoughtfully. 'One moment you say there's no hope, the next that you're prepared to spend the winter here, searching. If you don't mind my saying so, Doctor, it just doesn't make sense.'

'Stiff-necked pride,' I said. 'I don't like throwing my hand in on a job before I've even started it. I don't know what the attitude of the United States Navy is on that sort of thing.'

He gave me another speculative glance, I could see he believed me the way a fly believes the spider on the web who has just offered him safe accommodation for the night. He smiled. He said: 'The United States Navy doesn't take offence all that easily, Dr Carpenter. I suggest you catch a couple of hours' sleep while you can. You'll need it all if you're going to start walking towards the North Pole.'

'How about yourself? You haven't been to bed at all to-night.'

'I think I'll wait a bit.' He nodded towards the door of the radio room. 'Just in case anything comes through.'

'What are they sending? Just the call sign?'

'Plus request for position and a rocket, if they have either. I'll let you know immediately anything comes through. Good night, Dr Carpenter. Or rather, good morning.'

I rose heavily and made my way to Hansen's cabin.

The atmosphere round the 8 a.m. breakfast table in the wardroom was less than festive. Apart from the officer on deck and the engineer lieutenant on watch, all the *Dolphin*'s officers were there, some just risen from their bunks, some just heading for them, none of them talking in anything more than monosyllables. Even the ebullient Dr Benson was remote and withdrawn. It seemed pointless to ask whether any contact had been established with Drift Station Zebra, it was painfully obvious that it hadn't. And that after almost five hours' continuous sending. The sense of despondency and defeat, the unspoken knowledge that time had run out for the survivors of Drift Station Zebra hung heavy over the wardroom.

No one hurried over his meal – there was nothing to hurry for – but by and by they rose one by one and drifted off, Dr Benson to his sick-bay call, the young torpedo officer, Lieutenant Mills, to supervise the efforts of his men who had been working twelve hours a day for the past two days to iron out the faults in the suspect torpedoes, a third to relieve Hansen, who had the watch, and three others to their bunks. That left only Swanson, Raeburn and myself. Swanson, I knew, hadn't been to bed at all the previous night, but for all that he had the rested clear-eyed look of a man with eight solid hours behind him.

The steward, Henry, had just brought in a fresh pot of coffee when we heard the sound of running footsteps in the passageway outside and the quartermaster burst into the wardroom. He didn't quite manage to take the door off its hinges, but that was only because the Electric Boat Company put good solid hinges on the doors of their submarines.

'We got it made!' he shouted, and then perhaps recollecting that enlisted men were expected to conduct themselves with rather more decorum in the wardroom, went on: 'We've raised them, Captain, we've raised them!'

'What!' Swanson could move twice as fast as his comfortable figure suggested and he was already half-out of his chair.

'We are in radio contact with Drift Ice Station Zebra, sir,' Ellis said formally.

Commander Swanson got to the radio room first, but only because he had a head start on Raeburn and myself. Two operators were on watch, both leaning forward towards their transmitters, one with his head bent low, the other with his cocked to one side, as if those attitudes of concentrated listening helped them to isolate and amplify the slightest sounds coming through the earphones clamped to their heads. One of them was scribbling away mechanically on a signal pad. DSY, he was writing down, DSY repeated over and over again. DSY. The answering call-sign of Drift Station Zebra. He stopped writing as he caught sight of Swanson out of the corner of one eye.

'We've got 'em, Captain, no question. Signal very weak and intermittent but—'

'Never mind the signal!' It was Raeburn who made this interruption without any by-your-leave from Swanson. He tried, and failed, to keep the rising note of excitement out of his voice and he looked more than ever like a youngster playing hookey from high school. 'The bearing? Have you got their bearing? That's all that matters.'

The other operator swivelled in his seat and I recognized my erstwhile guard, Zabrinski. He fixed Raeburn with a sad and reproachful eye.

'Course we got their bearing, Lieutenant. First thing we did. O-forty-five, give or take a whisker. North-east, that is.'

'Thank you, Zabrinski,' Swanson said dryly. 'O-forty-five is north-east. The navigating officer and I wouldn't have known. Position?'

Zabrinski shrugged and turned to his watchmate, a man with a red face, leather neck and a shining polished dome where his hair ought to have been. 'What's the word, Curly?'

'Nothing. Just nothing.' Curly looked at Swanson. 'Twenty times I've asked for his position. No good. All he does is send out his call-sign. I don't think he's hearing us at all, he doesn't even know we're listening, he just keeps sending his call-sign over and over again. Maybe he hasn't switched his aerial in to "receive".'

'It isn't possible,' Swanson said.

'It is with this guy,' Zabrinski said. 'At first Curly and I thought that it was the signal that was weak, then we thought it was the operator who was weak or sick, but we were wrong, he's just a ham-handed amateur.'

'You can tell?' Swanson asked.

'You can always tell. You can—' He broke off, stiffened and touched his watchmate's arm.

Curly nodded. 'I got it,' he said matter-of-factly. 'Position unknown, the man says.'

Nobody said anything, not just then. It didn't seem important that he couldn't give us his position, all that mattered was that we were in direct contact. Raeburn turned and ran forward across the control room. I could hear him speak rapidly on the bridge telephone. Swanson turned to me.

'Those balloons you spoke of earlier. The ones on Zebra. Are they free or captive?'

'Both.'

'How do the captive ones work?'

'A free-running winch, nylon cord marked off in hundreds and thousands of feet.'

'We'll ask them to send a captive balloon up to 5,000 feet,' Swanson decided. 'With flares. If they're within thirty or forty miles we ought to see it, and if we get its elevation and make an allowance for the effect of wind on it, we should get a fair estimate of distance . . . What is it, Brown?' This to the man Zabrinski called 'Curly.'

'They're sending again,' Curly said. 'Very broken, fades a lot. "God's sake, hurry." Just like that, twice over. "God's sake hurry." '

'Send this,' Swanson said. He dictated a brief message about the balloons. 'And send it real slow.'

Curly nodded and began to transmit. Raeburn came running back into the radio room.

'The moon's not down yet,' he said quickly to Swanson. 'Still a degree or two above the horizon. I'm taking a sextant up top and taking a moon-sight. Ask them to do the same. That'll give us the latitude difference and if we know they're o-forty-five of us we can pin them down to a mile.'

'It's worth trying,' Swanson said. He dictated another message to Brown. Brown transmitted the second message immediately after the first. We waited for the answer. For all of ten minutes we waited. I looked at the men in the radio room, they all had the same remote withdrawn look of men who are there only physically, men whose minds are many miles away. They were all at the same place and I was too, wherever Drift Ice Station Zebra was.

Brown started writing again, not for long. His voice this time was still matter-of-fact, but with overtones of emptiness. He said: ' "All balloons burnt. No moon." '

'No moon.' Raeburn couldn't hide the bitterness, the sharpness of his disappointment. 'Damn! Must be pretty heavy overcast up there. Or a bad storm.'

'No,' I said. 'You don't get local weather variations like that on the ice-cap. The conditions will be the same over 50,000 square miles. The moon is down. For them, the moon is down. Their latest estimated position must have been pure guesswork, and bad guesswork at that. They must be at least a hundred miles farther north and east than we had thought.'

'Ask them if they have any rockets,' Swanson said to Brown.

'You can try,' I said. 'It'll be a waste of time. If they are as far off as I think, their rockets would never get above our horizon. Even if they did, we wouldn't see them.'

'It's always a chance, isn't it?' Swanson asked.

'Beginning to lose contact, sir,' Brown reported. 'Something there about food but it faded right out.'

'Tell them if they have any rockets to fire them at once,' Swanson said. 'Quickly now, before you lose contact.'

Four times in all Brown sent the message before he managed to pick up a reply. Then he said: 'Message reads: "Two minutes." Either this guy is pretty far through or his transmitter batteries are. That's all. "Two minutes," he said.'

Swanson nodded wordlessly and left the room. I followed. We picked up coats and binoculars and clambered up to the bridge. After the warmth and comfort of the control room, the cold seemed glacial, the flying ice-spicules more lancet-like than ever. Swanson uncapped the gyro-repeater compass, gave us the line of o-forty-five, told the two men who had been keeping watch what to look for and where.

A minute passed, two minutes, five. My eyes began to ache from staring into the ice-filled dark, the exposed part of my face had gone completely numb and I knew that when I removed those binoculars I was going to take a fair bit of skin with them.

A phone bell rang. Swanson lowered his glasses, leaving two peeled and bloody rings round his eyes – he seemed unaware of it, the pain wouldn't come until later – and picked up the receiver. He listened briefly, hung up.

'Radio room,' he said. 'Let's get below. All of us. The rockets were fired three minutes ago.'

We went below. Swanson caught sight of his face reflected in a glass gauge and shook his head. 'They must have shelter,' he said quietly. 'They must. Some hut left. Or they would have been gone long ago.' He went into the radio room. 'Still in contact?'

'Yeah.' Zabrinski spoke. 'Off and on. It's a funny thing. When a dicey contact like this starts to fade it usually gets lost and stays lost. But this guy keeps coming back. Funny.'

'Maybe he hasn't even got batteries left,' I said. 'Maybe all they have is a hand-cranked generator. Maybe there's no one left with the strength to crank it for more than a few moments at a time.'

'Maybe,' Zabrinski agreed. 'Tell the captain that last message, Curly.'

' "Can't late many tours," ' Brown said. 'That's how the message came through. "Can't late many tours." I think it should have read "Can't last many hours." Don't see what else it can have been.'

Swanson looked at me briefly, glanced away again. I hadn't told anyone else that the commandant of the base was my brother and I knew he hadn't told anyone either. He said to Brown: 'Give them a time-check. Ask them to send their call-signs five minutes every hour on the hour. Tell them we'll contact them again within six hours at most, maybe only four. Zabrinski, how accurate was that bearing?'

'Dead accurate, Captain. I've had plenty of re-checks. O-forty-five exactly.'

Swanson moved out into the control centre. 'Drift Station Zebra can't see the moon. If we take Dr Carpenter's word for it that weather conditions are pretty much the same all over, that's because the moon is below their horizon. With the elevation we have of the moon, and knowing their bearing, what's Zebra's minimum distance from us?'

'A hundred miles, as Dr Carpenter said,' Raeburn confirmed after a short calculation. 'At least that.'

'So. We leave here and take a course o-forty. Not enough to take us very far from their general direction but it will give us enough offset to take a good cross-bearing eventually. We will go exactly a hundred miles and try for another polynya. Call the executive officer, secure for diving.' He smiled at me. 'With two cross-bearings and an accurately measured base-line, we can pin them down to a hundred yards.'

'How do you intend to measure a hundred miles under the ice? Accurately, I mean?'

'Our inertia navigation computer does it for me. It's very accurate, you wouldn't believe just how accurate. I can dive the *Dolphin* off the eastern coast of the United States and surface again in the Eastern Mediterranean within five hundred yards of where I expect to be. Over a hundred miles I don't expect to be twenty yards out.'

Radio aerials were lowered, hatches screwed down and within five minutes the *Dolphin* had dropped down from her hole in the ice and was on her way. The two helmsmen at the diving stand sat idly smoking, doing nothing: the steering controls were in automatic interlock with the inertial navigation system which steered the ship with a degree of accuracy and sensitivity impossible to human hands. For the first time I could feel a heavy jarring vibration rumbling throughout the length of the ship: 'can't last many hours' the message had said: the *Dolphin* was under full power.

I didn't leave the control room that morning. I spent most of the time peering over the shoulder of Dr Benson who had passed his usual five minutes in the sick-bay waiting for the patients who never turned up and then had hurried to his seat by the ice-machine. The readings on that machine meant living or dying to the Zebra survivors. We had to find another polynya to surface in to get a cross-bearing: no cross-bearing, no hope. I wondered for the hundredth time how many of the survivors of the fire were still alive. From the quiet desperation of the few garbled messages that Brown and Zabrinski had managed to pick up I couldn't see that there would be many.

The pattern traced out by the hissing stylus on the chart was hardly an encouraging sight. Most of the time it showed the ice overhead to be of a thickness of ten feet or more. Several times the stylus dipped to show thicknesses of thirty to forty feet, and once it dipped down almost clear of the paper, showing a tremendous inverted ridge of at least 150 feet in depth. I tried to imagine what kind of fantastic pressures created by piled-up log-jams of rafted ice on the surface must have been necessary to force ice down to such a depth: but I just didn't have the imagination to cope with that sort of thing.

Only twice in the first eighty miles did the stylus trace out the thin black line that meant thin ice overhead. The first of those polynyas might have accommodated a small rowing boat, but it would certainly never have looked at the *Dolphin*: the other had hardly been any bigger.

Shortly before noon the hull vibration died away as Swanson gave the order for a cutback to a slow cruising speed. He said to Benson: 'How does it look?'

'Terrible. Heavy ice all the way.'

'Well, we can't expect a polynya to fall into our laps straight away,' Swanson said reasonably, 'We're almost there. We'll make a grid search. Five miles east, five miles west, a quarter-mile farther to the north each time.'

The search began. An hour passed, two, then three. Raeburn and his assistant hardly ever raised their heads from the plotting table where they were meticulously tracing every movement the *Dolphin* was making in its criss-cross search under the sea. Four o'clock in the afternoon. The normal background buzz of conversation, the occasional small talk from various groups in the control centre, died away completely. Benson's occasional 'Heavy ice, still heavy ice,' growing steadily quieter and more dispirited, served only to emphasize and deepen the heavy brooding silence that had fallen. Only a case-hardened undertaker could have felt perfectly at home in that atmosphere. At the moment, undertakers were the last people I wanted to think about.

Five o'clock in the afternoon. People weren't looking at each other any more, far less talking. Heavy ice, still heavy ice. Defeat, despair, hung heavy in the air. Heavy ice, still heavy ice. Even Swanson had stopped smiling, I wondered if he had in his mind's eye what I now constantly had in mine, the picture of a haggard, emaciated, bearded man with his face all but destroyed with frostbite, a frozen, starving, dying man draining away the last few ounces of his exhausted strength as he cranked the handle of his generator and tapped out his call-sign with lifeless fingers, his head bowed as he strained to listen above the howl of the ice-storm for the promise of aid that never came. Or maybe there was no one tapping out a call-sign any more. They were no ordinary men who had been sent to man Drift Ice Station Zebra but there comes a time when even the toughest, the bravest, the most enduring will abandon all hope and lie down to die. Perhaps he had already lain down to die. Heavy ice, still heavy ice.

At half past five Commander Swanson walked across to the ice-machine and peered over Benson's shoulder. He said: 'What's the average thickness of that stuff above?'

'Twelve to fifteen feet,' Benson said. His voice was low and tired. 'Nearer fifteen, I would say.'

Swanson picked up a phone. 'Lieutenant Mills? Captain here. What is the state of readiness of those torpedoes you're working on? . . . Four? . . . Ready to go? . . . Good. Stand by to load. I'm giving this search another thirty minutes, then it's up to you. Yes that is correct. We shall attempt to blow a hole through the ice.' He replaced the phone.

Hansen said thoughtfully: 'Fifteen feet of ice is a helluva lot of ice. And that ice will have a tamping effect and will direct 90 per cent of the explosive force down the way. You think we *can* blow a hole through fifteen feet of ice, Captain?'

'I've no idea,' Swanson admitted. 'How can anyone know until we try it?'

'Nobody ever tried to do this before?' I asked.

'No. Not in the US Navy, anyway. The Russians may have tried it, I wouldn't know. They don't,' he added dryly, 'keep us very well informed on those matters.'

'Aren't the underwater shock waves liable to damage the *Dolphin*?' I asked. I didn't care for the idea at all, and that was a fact.

'If they do, the Electric Boat Company can expect a pretty strong letter of complaint. We shall explode the warhead electronically about 1,000 yards after it leaves the ship – it has to travel eight hundred yards anyway before a safety device unlocks and permits the warhead to be armed. We shall be bows-on to the detonation and with a hull designed to withstand the pressures this one is, the shock effects should be negligible.'

'Very heavy ice,' Benson intoned. 'Thirty feet, forty feet, fifty feet. Very, very heavy ice.'

'Just too bad if your torpedo ended up under a pile like the stuff above us just now,' I said. 'I doubt if it would even chip off the bottom layer.'

'We'll take care that doesn't happen. We'll just find a suitably large layer of ice of normal thickness, kind of back off a thousand yards and then let go.'

'Thin ice!' Benson's voice wasn't a shout, it was a bellow. 'Thin ice. No, by God, clear water! Clear water! Lovely clear, clear water!'

My immediate reaction was that either the ice-machine or Benson's brain had blown a fuse. But the officer at the diving panel had no such doubts for I had to grab and hang on hard as the *Dolphin* heeled over violently to port and came curving round, engines slowing, in a tight circle to bring her back to the spot where Benson had called out. Swanson watched the plot, spoke quietly and the big bronze propellers reversed and bit into the water to bring the *Dolphin* to a stop.

'How's it looking now, Doc?' Swanson called out.

'Clear, clear water,' Benson said reverently. 'I got a good picture of it. It's pretty narrow, but wide enough to hold us. It's long, with a sharp left-hand dog-leg, for it followed us round through the first forty-five degrees of our curve.'

'One fifty feet,' Swanson said.

The pumps hummed. The *Dolphin* drifted gently upwards like an airship rising from the ground. Briefly, water flooded back into the tanks. The *Dolphin* hung motionless.

'Up periscope,' Swanson said.

The periscope hissed up slowly into the raised position. Swanson glanced briefly through the eyepiece, then beckoned me. 'Take a look,' he beamed. 'As lovely a sight as you'll ever see.'

I took a look. If you'd made a picture of what could be seen above and framed it you couldn't have sold the result even if you added Picasso's name to it: but I could see what he meant. Solid black masses on either side with a scarcely lighter strip of dark jungle green running between them on a line with the fore-and-aft direction of the ship. An open lead in the polar pack.

Three minutes later we were lying on the surface of the Arctic Ocean, just under two hundred and fifty miles from the Pole.

The rafted, twisted ice-pack reared up into contorted ridges almost fifty feet in height, towering twenty feet above the top of the sail, so close you could almost reach out and touch the nearest ridge. Three or four of those broken and fantastically hummocked icehills we could see stretching off to the west and then the light of the floodlamp failed and we could see no more. Beyond that there was only blackness.

To the east we could see nothing at all. To have stared out to the east with opened eyes would have been to be blinded for life in a very few seconds: even goggles became clouded and scarred after the briefest exposure. Close in to the *Dolphin*'s side you could, with bent head and hooded eyes, catch, for a fleeting part of a second, a glimpse of black water, already freezing over: but it was more imagined than seen.

The wind, shrieking and wailing across the bridge and through raised antennae, showed at consistently over 60 m.p.h. on the bridge anemometer. The ice-storm was no longer the gusting, swirling fog of that morning but a driving wall of stiletto-tipped spears, near-lethal in its ferocity, high speed ice-spicule lances that would have skewered their way through the thickest cardboard or shattered in a second a glass held in your hand. Over and above the ululating threnody of the wind we could hear an almost constant grinding, crashing and deep-throated booming as millions of tons of racked and tortured ice, under the influence of the gale and some mighty pressure centre, heaven knew how many hundreds of miles away, reared and twisted and tore and cracked, one moment forming another rafted ridge as a layer of ice, perhaps ten feet thick, screeched and roared and clambered on to the shoulders of another and then another, the next rending apart in indescribably violent cacophony to open up a new lead, black wind-torn water that started to skim over with ice almost as soon as it was formed.

'Are we both mad? Let's get below.' Swanson cupped his hands to my ear and had to shout, but even so I could hardly hear him above that hellish bedlam of sound.

We clambered down into the comparatively sudden stillness of the control room. Swanson untied his parka hood and pulled off scarf and goggles that had completely masked his face. He looked at me and shook his head wonderingly.

'And some people talk about the white silence of the Arctic. My God, a boilermaker's shop is like a library reading-room compared to that lot.' He shook his head again. 'We stuck our noses out a few times above the ice-pack last year, but we never saw anything like this. Or heard it. Winter-time, too. Cold, sure, damned cold, and windy, but never so bad that we couldn't take a brief stroll on the ice, and I used to wonder about those stories of explorers being stuck in their tents for days on end, unable to move. But I know now why Captain Scott died.'

'It is pretty nasty,' I admitted. 'How safe are we here, Commander?'

'That's anybody's guess,' Swanson shrugged. 'The wind's got us jammed hard against the west wall of this polynya and there's maybe fifty yards of open water to starboard. For the moment we're safe. But you can hear and see that pack is on the move, and not slowly either. The lead we're in was torn open less than an hour ago. How long? Depends on the configuration of the ice, but those polynyas can close up damned quickly at times, and while the hull of the *Dolphin* can take a fair old pressure, it can't take a million tons of ice leaning against it. Maybe we can stay here for hours, maybe only for minutes. Whichever it is, as soon as that east wall comes within ten feet of the starboard side we're dropping down out of it. You know what happens when a ship gets caught in the ice.'

'I know. They get squeezed flat, are carried round the top of the world for a few years then one day are released and drop to the bottom, two miles straight down. The United States Government wouldn't like it, Commander.'

'The prospects of further promotion for Commander Swanson would be poor,' Swanson admitted. 'I think—'

'Hey!' The shout came from the radio room. 'Hey, c'm here.'

'I rather think Zabrinski must be wanting me,' Swanson murmured. He moved off with his usual deceptive speed and I followed him into the radio room. Zabrinski was sitting half-turned in his chair, an ear-to-ear beam on his face, the earphones extended in his left hand. Swanson took them, listened briefly, then nodded.

'DSY,' he said softly. 'DSY, Dr Carpenter. We have them. Got the bearing? Good.' He turned to the doorway, saw the quartermaster. 'Ellis, ask the navigating officer to come along as soon as possible.'

'We'll pick 'em all up yet, Captain,' Zabrinski said jovially. The smile on the big man's face, I could see now, didn't extend as far as his eyes. 'They must be a pretty tough bunch of boys out there.'

'Very tough, Zabrinski,' Swanson said absently. His eyes were remote and I knew he was listening to the metallic cannonading of the ice-spicules, a billion tiny pneumatic chisels drumming away continuously against the outer hull of the submarine, a sound loud enough to make low speech impossible. 'Very tough. Are you in two-way contact?'

Zabrinski shook his head and turned away. He'd stopped smiling. Raeburn came in, was handed a sheet of paper and left for his plotting table. We went with him. After a minute or two he looked up, and said: 'If anyone fancies a Sunday afternoon's walk, this is it.'

'So close?' Swanson asked.

'So very close. Five miles due east, give or take half a mile. Pretty fair old bloodhounds, aren't we?'

'We're just lucky,' Swanson said shortly. He walked back to the radio room. 'Talking to them yet?'

'We've lost them altogether.'

'Completely?'

'We only had 'em a minute, Captain. Just that. Then they faded. Got weaker and weaker. I think Doc Carpenter here is right, they're using a hand-cranked generator.' He paused, then said idly: 'I've a six-year-old-daughter who could crank one of those machines for five minutes without turning a hair.'

Swanson looked at me, then turned away without a word. I followed him to the unoccupied diving stand. From the bridge access hatch we could hear the howl of the storm, the grinding ice with its boom and scream that spanned the entire register of hearing. Swanson said: 'Zabrinski put it very well . . . I wonder how long this damnable storm is going to last?'

'Too long. I have a medical kit in my cabin, a fifty-ounce flask of medicinal alcohol and cold-weather clothes. Could you supply me with a thirty-pound pack of emergency rations, high protein high-calorie concentrates, Benson will know what I mean.'

'Do you mean what I think you mean?' Swanson said slowly. 'Or am I just going round the bend?'

'What's this about going round the bend?' Hansen had just come through the doorway leading to the for'ard passageway, and the grin on his face was clear enough indication that though he'd caught Swanson's last words he'd caught neither the intonation nor the expression on Swanson's face. 'Very serious state of affairs, going round the bend. I'll have to assume command

and put you in irons, Captain. Something about it in regulations, I dare say.'

'Dr Carpenter is proposing to sling a bag of provisions on his back and proceed to Drift Station Zebra on foot.'

'You've picked them up again?' Just for the moment Hansen had forgotten me. 'You really got them? And a cross-bearing?'

'Just this minute. We've hit it almost on the nose. Five miles, young Raeburn says.'

'My God! Five miles. Only five miles!' Then the elation vanished from voice and face as if an internal switch had been touched. 'In weather like this it might as well be five hundred. Even old Amundsen couldn't have moved ten yards through this stuff.'

'Dr Carpenter evidently thinks he can improve on Amundsen's standard's,' Swanson said dryly. 'He's talking about walking there.'

Hansen looked at me for a long and considering moment, then turned back to Swanson. 'I think maybe it's Doc Carpenter we should be clapping in the old irons.'

'I think maybe it is,' Swanson said.

'Look,' I said. 'There are men out there on Drift Station Zebra. Maybe not many, not now, but there are some. One, anyway. Men a long way past being sick. Dying men. To a dying man it takes only the very smallest thing to spell out the difference between life and death. I'm a doctor, I know. The smallest thing. An ounce of alcohol, a few ounces of food, a hot drink, some medicine. Then they'll live. Without those little things they will surely die. They're entitled to what smallest aid they can get, and I'm entitled to take whatever risks I care to see they get it. I'm not asking anyone else to go, all I'm asking is that you implement the terms of your orders from Washington to give me all possible assistance without endangering the *Dolphin* or its crew. Threatening to stop me is not my idea of giving assistance. And I'm not asking you to endanger your submarine or the lives of your men.'

Swanson gazed at the floor. I wondered what he was thinking of: the best way to stop me, his orders from Washington, or the fact that he was the only man who knew that the commandant on Zebra was my brother. He said nothing.

'You must stop him, Captain,' Hansen said urgently. 'Any other man you saw putting a pistol to his head or a razor to his throat, you'd stop that man. This is the same. He's out of his mind, he's wanting to commit suicide.' He tapped the bulkhead beside him. 'Good God, Doc, why do you think we have the sonar operators in here on duty even when we're stopped. So that they can tell us when the ice wall on the far side of the polynya starts to close in on us, that's why. And *that's* because it's impossible for any man to last thirty seconds on the bridge or see an inch against the ice-storm up there. Just take a quick twenty-second trip up there, up on the bridge, and you'll change your mind fast enough, I guarantee.'

'We've just come down from the bridge,' Swanson said matter-of-factly.

'And he still wants to go? It's like I say, he's crazy.'

'We could drop down now,' Swanson said. 'We have the position. Perhaps we can find a polynya within a mile, half a mile of Zebra. That would be a different proposition altogether.'

'Perhaps you could find a needle in a haystack,' I said. 'It took you six hours to find this one, and even at that we were lucky. And don't talk about torpedoes, the ice in this area is rafted anything up to a hundred feet in depth. Pretty much all over. You'd be as well trying to blast your way through with a .22. Might be twelve hours, might be days before we could break through again. I can get there in two-three hours.'

'*If* you don't freeze to death in the first hundred yards,' Hansen said. '*If* you don't fall down a ridge and break your leg. *If* you don't get blinded in a few minutes. *If* you don't fall into a newly-opened polynya that you can't see, where you'll either drown or, if you manage to get out, freeze solid in thirty seconds. And even if you do survive all those things, I'd be grateful if you'd explain to me exactly how you propose to find your way blind to a place five miles away. You can't carry a damn' great gyro weighing about half a ton on your back, and a magnetic compass is useless in those latitudes. The magnetic north pole is a good bit *south* of where we are now and a long way to the west. Even if you *did* get some sort of bearing from it, in the darkness and the ice-storm you could still miss the camp – or what's left of it – by only a hundred yards and never know it. And even if by one chance in a million you do manage to find your way there, how on earth do you ever expect to find your way back again. Leave a paper-trail? A five-mile ball of twine. Crazy is hardly the word for it.'

'I may break a leg, drown or freeze,' I conceded. 'I'll take my chance on that. Finding my way there and back is no great trick. You have a radio bearing on Zebra and know exactly where it lies. You can take a radio bearing on any transmitter. All I have to do is to tote a receiver-transmitter radio along with me, keep in touch with you and you can keep me on the same bearing as Zebra. It's easy.'

'It would be,' Hansen said, 'except for one little thing. We don't have any such radio.'

'I have a twenty-mile walkie-talkie in my case,' I said.

'Coincidence, coincidence,' Hansen murmured. 'Just happened to bring it along, no doubt. I'll bet you have all sorts of funny things in that case of yours, haven't you, Doc?'

'What Dr Carpenter has in his case is really no business of ours,' Swanson said in mild reproof. He hadn't thought so earlier. 'What does concern us is his intention to do away with himself. You really can't expect us to consent to this ridiculous proposal, Dr Carpenter.'

'No one's asking you to consent to anything,' I said. 'Your consent is not required. All I'm asking you to do is to stand to one side. And to arrange for that food provision pack for me. If you won't, I'll have to manage without.'

I left and went to my cabin. Hansen's cabin, rather. But even although it wasn't my cabin that didn't stop me from turning the key in the lock as soon as I had passed through the door.

Working on the likely supposition that if Hansen did come along soon he wasn't going to be very pleased to find the door of his own cabin locked against him, I wasted no time. I spun the combination lock on the case and opened the lid. At least three-quarters of the available space was taken up by Arctic survival clothing, the very best that money could buy. It hadn't been my money that had bought it.

I stripped off the outer clothes I was wearing, pulled on long open-mesh underwear, woollen shirt and cord breeches, then a triple-knit wool parka lined with pure silk. The parka wasn't quite standard, it had a curiously shaped suède-lined pocket below and slightly to the front of the left armpit, and a differently shaped suède-lined pocket on the right-hand side. I dug swiftly to the bottom of my case and brought up three separate items. The first of these, a nine-millimetre Mannlicher-Schoenauer automatic, fitted into the left-hand pocket as securely and snugly as if the pocket had been specially designed for it, which indeed it had: the other items, spare magazine clips, fitted as neatly into the right-hand pocket.

The rest of the dressing didn't take long. Two pairs of heavy-knit woollen socks, felt undershoes and then the furs – caribou for the outer parka and trousers, wolverine for the hood, sealskin for the boots and reindeer for the gloves, which were pulled on over other layers of silk gloves and woollen mittens. Maybe a polar bear would have had a slight edge over me when it came to being equipped to survive an Arctic blizzard, but there wouldn't have been much in it.

I hung snow-mask and goggles round my neck, stuck a rubberized waterproofed torch into the inside pocket of the fur parka, unearthed my walkie-talkie and closed the case. I set the combination again. There was no need to set the combination any more, not now that I had the Mannlicher-Schoenauer under my arm, but it would give Swanson something to do while I was away. I shoved my medicine case and a steel flask of alcohol in a rucksack and unlocked the door.

Swanson was exactly where I'd left him in the control room. So was Hansen. So were two others who had not been there when I had left, Rawlings and Zabrinski. Hansen, Rawlings, and Zabrinski, the three biggest men in the ship. The last time I'd seen them together was when Swanson had whistled them up from the *Dolphin* in the Holy Loch to see to it that I didn't do anything he didn't want me to do. Maybe Commander Swanson had a one-track mind. Hansen, Rawlings, and Zabrinski. They looked bigger than ever.

I said to Swanson: 'Do I get those iron rations or not?'

'One last formal statement,' Swanson said. His first thoughts, as I came waddling into the control centre, must have been that a grizzly bear was loose inside his submarine, but he hadn't batted an eyelid. 'For the record. Your intentions are suicidal, your chances are non-existent. I cannot give my consent.'

'All right, your statement is on record, witnesses and all. The iron rations.'

'I cannot give my consent because of a fresh and dangerous development. One of our electronic technicians was carrying out a routine calibration test on the ice-machine just now and an overload coil didn't function. Electric motor burnt out. No spares, it will have to be rewired. You realize what that means. If we're forced to drop down I can't find my way to the top again. Then it's curtains for everybody – everybody left above the ice, that is.'

I didn't blame him for trying, but I was vaguely disappointed in him: he'd had time to think up a better one than that. I said: 'The iron rations, Commander. Do I get them?'

'You mean to go through with this? After what I've said?'

'Oh, for God's sake. I'll do without the food.'

'My executive officer, Torpedoman Rawlings and Radioman Zabrinski,' Swanson said formally, 'don't like this.'

'I can't help what they like or don't like.'

'They feel they can't let you go through with it,' he persisted.

They were more than big. They were huge. I could get past them the way a lamb gets past a starving lion. I had a gun all right but with that one-piece parka I was wearing I'd practically have to undress myself to get at it and Hansen, in that Holy Loch canteen, had shown just how quickly he could react when he saw anyone making a suspicious move. And even if I did get my gun out, what then? Men like Hansen, like Rawlings and Zabrinski, didn't scare. I couldn't bluff them with a gun. And I couldn't use the gun. Not against men who were just doing their duty.

'They *won't* let you go through with it,' Swanson went on, 'unless, that is, you will permit them to accompany you, which they have volunteered to do.'

'Volunteered,' Rawlings sniffed. 'You, you, and you.'

'I don't want them,' I said.

'Gracious, ain't he?' Rawlings asked of no one in particular. 'You might at least have said thanks, Doc.'

'You are putting the lives of your men in danger, Commander Swanson. You know what your orders said.'

'Yes. I also know that in Arctic travels, as in mountaineering and exploring, a party has always double the chances of the individual. I also know that if it became known that we had permitted a civilian doctor to set off on his own for Drift Station Zebra while we were all too scared to stir from our nice warm sub, the name of the United States Navy would become pretty muddy.'

'What do your men think of your making them risk their lives to save the good name of the submarine service?'

'You heard the captain,' Rawlings said. 'We're volunteers. Look at Zabrinski there, anyone can see that he is a man cast in a heroic mould.'

'Have you thought of what happens' I said, 'if the ice closes in when we're away and the captain has to take the ship down?'

'Don't even talk of it,' Zabrinski urged. 'I'm not all that heroic.'

I gave up. I'd no option but to give up. Besides, like Zabrinski, I wasn't all that heroic and I suddenly realized that I would be very glad indeed to have those three men along with me.

Chapter Five

Lieutenant Hansen was the first man to give up. Or perhaps 'give up' is wrong, the meaning of the words was quite unknown and the thought totally alien to Hansen, it would be more accurate to say that he was the first of us to show any glimmerings of common sense. He caught my arm, brought his head close to mine, pulled down his snow mask and shouted: 'No farther, Doc. We must stop.'

'The next ridge,' I yelled back. I didn't know whether he'd heard me or not, as soon as he'd spoken he'd pulled his mask back up into position again to protect the momentarily exposed skin against the horizontally driving ice-storm, but he seemed to understand for he eased his grip on the rope round my waist and let me move ahead again. For the past two and a half hours Hansen, Rawlings and I had each taken his turn at being the lead man on the end of the rope, while the other three held on to it some ten yards behind, the idea being not that the lead man should guide the others but that the others should save the life of the lead man, should the need arise. And the need already had arisen, just once, Hansen, slipped and scrambling on all-fours across a fractured and upward sloping raft of ice, had reached gropingly forward with his arms into the blindness of the night and the storm and found nothing there. He had fallen eight vertical feet before the rope had brought him up with a vicious jerk that had been almost as painful for Rawlings and myself, who had taken the brunt of the shock, as it had been for Hansen. For nearly two minutes he'd dangled above the wind-torn black water of a freshly opened lead before we'd managed to drag him back to safety. It had been a close thing, far too close a thing, for in far sub-zero temperatures with a gale-force wind blowing, even a few seconds' submersion in water makes the certainty of death absolute, the process of dissolution as swift as it is irreversible. In those conditions the clothes of a man pulled from the water become a frozen and impenetrable suit of armour inside seconds, an armour that can neither be removed nor chipped away. Petrified inside this ice-shroud, a man just simply and quickly freezes to death – in the unlikely event, that is, of his heart having withstood the thermal shock of the body surface being exposed to an almost instantaneous hundred degree drop in temperature.

So now I stepped forward very cautiously, very warily indeed, feeling the ice ahead of me with a probe we'd devised after Hansen's near accident – a chopped-off five foot length of rope which we'd dipped into the water of the lead then exposed to the air until it had become as rigid as a bar of steel. At times I walked, at times I stumbled, at times, when a brief lull in the gale-force wind, as sudden as it was unexpected, would catch me off balance I'd just fall forward and continue on hands and knees, for it was quite as easy that way. It was during one of those periods when I was shuffling blindly forward on all-fours that I realized that the wind had, for the time being, lost nearly all of its violence and that I was no longer being bombarded by that horizontally driving hail of flying ice-spicules. Moments later my probe made contact with some solid obstacle in my path: the vertical wall of a rafted ice ridge. I crawled thankfully into its shelter, raised my goggles and pulled out and switched on my torch as the others came blindly up to where I lay.

Blindly. With arms outstretched they pawed at the air before them like sightless men, which for the past two and a half hours was exactly what they had been. For all the service our goggles had given us we might as well have stuck our heads in gunny sacks before leaving the *Dolphin*. I looked at Hansen, the first of the three to come up. Goggles, snow-mask, hood, clothing – the entire front part of his body from top to toe was deeply and solidly encrusted in a thick and glittering layer of compacted ice, except for some narrow cracks caused by joint movements of legs and arms. As he drew close to me I could hear him splintering and crackling a good five feet away.

Long ice-feathers streamed back from his head, shoulders and elbows; as an extra-terrestrial monster from one of the chillier planets, such as Pluto, he'd have been a sensation in any horror movie. I suppose I looked much the same.

We huddled close together in the shelter of the wall. Only four feet above our heads the ice-storm swept by in a glittering grey-white river. Rawlings, sitting on my left, pushed up his goggles, looked down at his ice-sheathed furs and started to beat himself with his fist across the chest to break up the covering. I reached out a hand and caught his arm.

'Leave it alone,' I said.

'Leave it alone?' Rawling's voice was muffled by his snow-mask, but not so muffled that I couldn't hear the chattering of his teeth. 'This damn' suit of armour weighs a ton. I'm out of training for this kind of weight-lifting, Doc.'

'Leave it alone. If it weren't for that ice, you'd have frozen to death by this time: it's insulating you from that wind and the ice-storm. Let's see the rest of your face. And your hands.'

I checked him and the two others for frost-bite, while Hansen checked me. We were still lucky. Blue and mottled and shaking with cold, but no frost-bite. The furs of the other three might not have been quite as fancy as mine, but they were very adequate indeed. Nuclear subs always got the best of everything, and Arctic clothing was no exception. But although they weren't freezing to death I could see from their faces and hear from their breathing that they were pretty far gone in exhaustion. Thrusting into the power of that ice-storm was like wading upstream against the current of a river of molasses: that was energy-sapping enough, but the fact that we had to spend most of our time clambering over, slipping on, sliding and falling across fractured ice or making detours round impassable ridges while being weighed down with forty pound packs on our back and heaven only knew how many additional pounds of ice coating our furs in front had turned our trudge across that contorted treacherous ice into a dark and frozen nightmare.

'The point of no return, I think,' Hansen said. His breathing, like Rawlings's, was very quick, very shallow, almost gasping. 'We can't take much more of this, Doc.'

'You ought to listen to Dr Benson's lectures a bit more.' I said reprovingly. 'All this ice-cream and apple pie and lolling around in your bunks is no training for this sort of thing.'

'Yeah?' He peered at me. 'How do *you* feel?'

'A mite tired,' I admitted. 'Nothing much to speak of.' Nothing much to speak of, my legs felt as if they were falling off, that was all, but the goad of pride was always a useful one to have to hand. I slipped off my rucksack and brought out the medicinal alcohol. 'I suggest fifteen minutes' break. Any more and we'll just start stiffening up completely. Meantime, a little drop of what we fancy will help keep the old blood corpuscles trudging around.'

'I thought medical opinion was against alcohol in low temperatures,' Hansen said doubtfully. 'Something about opening the pores.'

'Name me any form of human activity,' I said, 'and I'll find you a group of doctors against it. Spoilsports. Besides, this isn't alcohol, it's very fine Scotch whisky.'

'You should have said so in the first place. Pass it over. Not too much for Rawlings and Zabrinski, they're not used to the stuff. Any word, Zabrinski?'

Zabrinski, with the walkie-talkie's aerial up and one earphone tucked in below the hood of his parka, was talking into the microphone through cupped hands. As the radio expert, Zabrinski had been the obvious man to handle the walkie-talkie and I'd given it to him before leaving the submarine. This was also the reason why Zabrinski wasn't at any time given the position of lead man in our trudge across the pack ice. A heavy fall or immersion in water would have finished the radio he was carrying slung on his back: and if the radio were finished then so would we be, for without the radio not only had we no hope of finding Drift Station Zebra, we wouldn't have a chance in a thousand of ever finding our way back to the *Dolphin* again. Zabrinski was built on the size and scale of a medium-sized gorilla and was about as durable; but we couldn't have treated him more tenderly had he been made of Dresden china.

'It's difficult,' Zabrinski said. 'Radio's O.K., but this ice-storm causes such damn' distortion and squeaking – no, wait a minute, though, wait a minute.'

He bent his head over the microphone, shielding it from the sound of the storm, and spoke again through cupped hands. 'Zabrinski here . . . Zabrinski. Yeah, we're all kinda tuckered out, but Doc here seems to think we'll make it. . . . Hang on, I'll ask him.'

He turned to me. 'How far do you reckon we've come, they want to know.'

'Four miles.' I shrugged. 'Three and a half, four and a half. You guess it.'

Zabrinski spoke again, looked interrogatively at Hansen and myself, saw our headshakes and signed off. He said: 'Navigating officer says we're four-five degrees north of where we should be and that we'll have to cut south if we don't want to miss Zebra by a few hundred yards.'

It could have been worse. Over an hour had passed since we'd received the last bearing position from the *Dolphin* and, between radio calls, our only means of navigating had been by judging the strength and direction of the wind in our faces. When a man's face is completely covered and largely numb it's not a very sensitive instrument for gauging wind direction – and for all we knew the wind might be either backing or veering. It could have been a lot worse and I said so to Hansen.

'It could be worse,' he agreed heavily. 'We could be travelling in circles or we could be dead. Barring that, I don't see how it could be worse.' He gulped down the whisky, coughed, handed the flask top back to me. 'Things look brighter now. You honestly think we can make it?'

'A little luck, that's all. You think maybe our packs are too heavy? That we should abandon some of it here?' The last thing I wanted to do was to abandon any of the supplies we had along with us: eighty pounds of food, a stove, thirty pounds of compressed fuel tablets, 100 ounces of alcohol, a tent, and a very comprehensive medical kit; but if it was to be abandoned I wanted the suggestion to be left to them, and I was sure they wouldn't make it.

'We're abandoning nothing,' Hansen said. Either the rest or the whisky had done him good, his voice was stronger, his teeth hardly chattering at all.

'Let the thought die stillborn,' Zabrinski said. When first I'd seen him in Scotland he had reminded me of a polar bear and now out here on the ice-cap, huge and crouched in his ice-whitened furs, the resemblance was redoubled. He had the physique of a bear, too, and seemed completely tireless; he was in far better shape than any of us. 'This weight on my bowed shoulders is like a bad leg: an old friend that gives me pain, but I wouldn't be without it.'

'You?' I asked Rawlings.

'I am conserving my energy,' Rawlings announced. 'I expect to have to carry Zabrinski later on.'

We pulled the starred, abraded and now thoroughly useless snow-goggles over our eyes again, hoisted ourselves stiffly to our feet and moved off to the south to find the end of and round the high ridge that here blocked our path. It was by far the longest and most continuous ridge we'd encountered yet, but we didn't mind, we required to make a good offing to get us back on course and not only were we doing just that but we were doing it in comparative shelter and saving our strength by so doing. After perhaps four hundred yards the ice wall ended so abruptly, leading to so sudden and unexpected an exposure to the whistling fury of the ice-storm that I was bowled completely off my feet. An express train couldn't have done it any better. I hung on to the rope with one hand, clawed and scrambled my way back on to my feet with the help of the other, shouted a warning to the others, and then we were fairly into the wind again, holding it directly in our faces and leaning far forward to keep our balance.

We covered the next mile in less than half an hour. The going was easier now, much easier than it had been, although we still had to make small detours round rafted, compacted and broken ice: on the debit side, we were all of us, Zabrinski excepted, pretty far gone in exhaustion, stumbling and falling far more often than was warranted by the terrain and the strength of the ice-gale: for myself, my leaden dragging legs felt as if they were on fire, each step now sent a shooting pain stabbing from ankle clear to the top of the thigh. For all that, I think I could have kept going longer than any of them, even Zabrinski, for I had the motivation, the driving force that would have kept me going hours after my legs would have told me that it was impossible to carry on a step farther. Major John Halliwell. My elder, my only brother. Alive or dead. Was he alive or was he dead, this one man in the world to whom I owed everything I had or had become? Was he dying, at that very moment when I was thinking of him, was he dying? His wife, Mary, and his three children who spoilt and ruined their bachelor uncle as I spoilt and ruined them: whatever way it lay they would have to know and only I could tell them. Alive or dead? My legs weren't mine, the stabbing fire that tortured them belonged to some other man, not to me. I had to know, I had to know, and if I had to find out by covering whatever miles lay between me and Drift Ice Station Zebra on my hands and knees, then I would do just that. I would find out. And over and above the tearing anxiety as to what had happened to my brother there was yet another powerful motivation, a motivation that the world would regard as of infinitely more importance than the life or death of the commandant of the station. As infinitely more important than the living or dying of the score of men who manned that desolate polar outpost. Or so the world would say.

The demented drumming of the spicules on my mask and ice-sheathed furs suddenly eased, the gale wind fell away and I found myself standing in the grateful shelter of an ice-ridge even higher than the last one we'd used for shelter. I waited for the others to come up, asked Zabrinski to make a position check with the *Dolphin* and doled out some more of the medicinal alcohol. More of it than on the last occasion. We were in more need of it.

Both Hansen and Rawlings were in a very distressed condition, their breath whistling in and out of their lungs in the rapid, rasping, shallow panting of a long-distance runner in the last tortured moments of his final exhaustion. I became gradually aware that the speed of my own breathing matched theirs almost exactly, it required a concentrated effort of will-power to hold my breath even for the few seconds necessary to gulp down my drink. I wondered vaguely if perhaps Hansen hadn't had the right of it, maybe the alcohol wasn't good for us. But it certainly tasted as if it were.

Zabrinski was already talking through cupped hands into the microphone. After a minute or so he pulled the earphones out from under his parka and buttoned up the walkie-talkie set. He said: 'We're either good or lucky or both. The *Dolphin* says we're exactly on the course we ought to be on.' He drained the glass I handed him and sighed in satisfaction. 'Well, that's the good part of the news. Here comes the bad part. The sides of the polynya the *Dolphin* is lying in are beginning to close together. They're closing pretty fast. The captain estimates he'll have to get out of it in two hours. Two at the most.' He paused, then finished slowly: 'And the ice-machine is still on the blink.'

'The ice-machine,' I said stupidly. Well, anyway, I felt stupid, I don't know how I sounded. 'Is the ice—?'

'It sure is, brother,' Zabrinski said. He sounded tired. 'But you didn't believe the skipper, did you, Dr Carpenter? You were too clever for that.'

'Well, that's a help,' Hansen said heavily. 'That makes everything just perfectly splendid. The *Dolphin* drops down, the ice closes up, and there we are, the *Dolphin* below, us on top and the whole of the polar ice-cap between us. They'll almost certainly never manage to find us again, even if they do fix the ice-machine. Shall we just lie down and die now or shall we first stagger around in circles for a couple of hours and then lie down and die?'

'It's tragic,' Rawlings said gloomily. 'Not the personal aspect of it, I mean the loss to the United States Navy. I think I may fairly say, Lieutenant, that we are – or were – three promising young men. Well, you and me, anyway. I think Zabrinski there had reached the limit of his potentialities. He reached them a long time ago.'

Rawlings got all this out between chattering teeth and still painful gasps of air. Rawlings, I reflected, was very much the sort of person I would like to have by my side when things began to get awkward, and it looked as if things were going to become very awkward indeed. He and Zabrinski had, as I'd found out, established themselves as the home-spun if slightly heavy-handed humorists on the *Dolphin*; for reasons known only to themselves both men habitually concealed intelligence of a high order and advanced education under a cloak of genial buffoonery.

'Two hours yet,' I said. 'With this wind at our back we can be back in the sub in well under an hour. We'd be practically blown back there.'

'And the men on Drift Station Zebra?' Zabrinski asked.

'We'd have done our best. Just one of those things.'

'We are profoundly shocked, Dr Carpenter,' Rawlings said. The tone of genial buffoonery was less noticeable than usual.

'Deeply dismayed,' Zabrinski added, 'by the very idea.' The words were light, but the lack of warmth in the voice had nothing to do with the bitter wind.

'The only dismaying thing around here is the level of intelligence of certain simple-minded sailors,' Hansen said with some asperity. He went on, and I wondered at the conviction in his voice: 'Sure, Dr Carpenter thinks we should go back. That doesn't include him. Dr Carpenter wouldn't turn back now for all the gold in Fort Knox.' He pushed himself wearily to his feet. 'Can't be much more than half a mile to go now. Let's get it over with.'

In the backwash of light from my torch I saw Rawlings and Zabrinski glance at each other, saw them shrug their shoulders at the same moment. Then they, too, were on their feet and we were on our way again.

Three minutes later Zabrinski broke his ankle.

It happened in an absurdly simple fashion, but for all its simplicity it was a wonder that nothing of the same sort had happened to any of us in the previous three hours. After starting off again, instead of losing our bearing by working to the south and north until we had rounded the end of the ice ridge blocking our path, we elected to go over it. The ridge was all of ten feet high but by boosting and pulling each other we reached the top without much difficulty. I felt my way forward cautiously, using the ice-probe – the torch was useless in that ice-storm and my goggles completely opaque. After twenty feet crawling across the gently downward sloping surface I reached the far side of the ridge and stretched down with the probe.

'Five feet,' I called to the others as they came up. 'It's only five feet.' I swung over the edge, dropped down and waited for the others to follow. Hansen came first, then Rawlings, both sliding down easily beside me. What happened to Zabrinski was impossible to see, he either misjudged his distance from the edge or a sudden easing of the wind made him lose his footing. Whatever the cause, I heard him call out, the words whipped away and lost by the wind, as he jumped down beside us. He seemed to land squarely and lightly enough on his feet, then cried out sharply and fell heavily to the ground.

I turned my back to the ice-storm, raised the useless snow-goggles and pulled out my torch. Zabrinski was half-sitting, half-lying on the ice, propped up on his right elbow and cursing steadily and fluently and, as far as I could tell because of the muffling effect of his snow-mask, without once repeating himself. His right heel was jammed in a four-inch crack in the ice, one of the thousands of such fractures and fissures that criss-crossed the pressure areas of the pack: his right leg was bent over at an angle to the outside, an angle normally impossible for any leg to assume. I didn't need to have a medical diploma hung around my neck to tell that the ankle was gone: either that or the lowermost part of the tibia, for the ankle was so heavily encased in a stout boot with lace binding that most of the strain must have fallen on the shin bone. I hoped it wasn't a compound fracture, but it was an unreasonable hope: at that acute angle the snapped bone could hardly have failed to pierce the skin. Compound or not, it made no immediate difference, I'd no intention of examining it: a few minutes' exposure of the lower part of his leg in those temperatures was as good a way as any of ensuring that Zabrinski went through the rest of his life with one foot missing.

We lifted his massive bulk, eased the useless foot out of the crack in the ice and lowered him gently to a sitting position. I unslung the medical kit from my back, knelt beside him and asked: 'Does it hurt badly?'

'No, it's numb, I hardly feel a thing.' He swore disgustedly. 'What a crazy thing to do. A little crack like that. How stupid can a man get?'

'You wouldn't believe me if I told you,' Rawlings said acidly. He shook his head. 'I prophesied this, I prophesied this. I said it would end up with me carrying this gorilla here.'

I had splints to the injured leg and taped them as tightly as possible over the boot and the furs, trying not to think of the depth of trouble we were in now. Two major blows in one. Not only had we lost the indispensable services of the strongest man in our party, we now had an extra 220 lbs. – at least – of weight, of dead-weight, to carry along with us. Not to mention his 40-lb. pack. Zabrinski might almost have read my thoughts.

'You'll have to leave me here, Lieutenant,' he said to Hansen. His teeth were rattling, with shock and cold. 'We must be almost there now. You can pick me up on the way back.'

'Don't talk rubbish,' Hansen said shortly. 'You know damn' well we'd never find you again.'

'Exactly,' Rawlings said. His teeth were like Zabrinski's, stuttering away irregularly like an asthmatic machine-gun. He knelt on the ice to support the injured man's bulk. 'No medals for morons. It says so in the ship's articles.'

'But you'll never get to Zebra,' Zabrinski protested. 'If you have to carry me—'

'You heard what I said,' Hansen interrupted. 'We're not leaving you.'

'The lieutenant is perfectly correct,' Rawlings agreed. 'You aren't the hero type, Zabrinski. You haven't the face for it, for one thing. Now clam up while I get some of this gear off your back.'

I finished tightening the splints and pulled mittens and fur gloves back on my silk-clad but already frozen hands. We shared out Zabrinski's load among the three of us, pulled goggles and snow-masks back into position, hoisted Zabrinski to his one sound leg, turned into the wind and went on our way again. It would be truer to say that we staggered on our way again.

But now, at last and when we most needed it, luck was with us. The ice-cap stretched away beneath our feet level and smooth as the surface of a frozen river. No ridges, no hummocks, no crevasses, not even the tiny cracks one of which had crippled Zabrinski. Just billiard flat unbroken ice and not even slippery, for its surface had been scoured and abraded by the flying ice-storm.

Each of us took turns at being lead man, the other two supporting a Zabrinski who hopped along in uncomplaining silence on one foot. After maybe three hundred yards of this smooth ice, Hansen, who was in the lead at the moment, stopped so suddenly and unexpectedly that we bumped into him.

'We're there!' he yelled above the wind. 'We've made it. We're there! Can't you smell it?'

'Smell what?'

'Burnt fuel oil. Burnt rubber. Don't you get it?'

I pulled down my snow-mask, cupped my hands to my face and sniffed cautiously. One sniff was enough. I hitched up my mask again, pulled Zabrinski's arm more tightly across my shoulder and followed on after Hansen.

The smooth ice ended in another few feet. The ice sloped up sharply to a level plateau and it took the three of us all of what pitifully little strength remained to drag Zabrinski up after us. The acrid smell of burning seemed to grow more powerful with every step we took. I moved forward, away from the others, my back to the storm, goggles down and sweeping the ice with semicircular movements of my torch. The smell was strong enough now to make my nostrils wrinkle under the mask. It seemed to be coming from directly ahead. I turned round into the wind, protectively cupped hand over my eyes, and as I did my torch struck something hard and solid and metallic. I lifted my torch and vaguely through the driving ice I could just make out the ghostly hooped steel skeleton, ice-coated on the windward side, fire-charred on the leeward side, of what had once been a nissen-shaped hut.

We had found Drift Ice Station Zebra.

I waited for the others to come up, guided them past the gaunt and burnt-out structure, then told them to turn backs to wind and lift their goggles. For maybe ten seconds we surveyed the ruin in the light of my torch. No one said anything. Then we turned round into the wind again.

Drift Station Zebra had consisted of eight separate huts, four in each of two parallel rows, thirty feet between the two rows, twenty feet between each two huts in the rows – this to minimize the hazard of fire spreading from hut to hut. But the hazard hadn't been minimized enough. No one could be blamed for that. No one, except in the wildest flights of nightmarish imagination, could have envisaged what must indeed have happened – exploding tanks and thousands of gallons of blazing oil being driven through the night by a gale-force wind. And, by a double inescapable irony, fire, without which human life on the polar ice-cap cannot survive, is there the most dreaded enemy of all: for although the entire ice-cap consists of water, frozen water, there is nothing that can melt that water and so put out the fire. Except fire itself. I wondered vaguely what had happened to the giant chemical fire-extinguishers housed in every hut.

Eight huts, four in each row. The first two on either side were completely gutted. No trace remained of the walls, which had been of two layers of weather-proofed bonded ply that had enclosed the insulation of shredded glass-fibre and kapok: on all of them even the aluminium-sheeted roofs had disappeared. In one of the huts we could see charred and blackened generator machinery, ice-coated on the windward side, bent and twisted and melted almost out of recognition: one could only wonder at the furnace ferocity of the heat responsible.

The fifth hut – the third on the right-hand side – was a gutted replica of the other four, the framing even more savagely twisted by the heat. We were just turning away from this, supporting Zabrinski and too sick at heart even to speak to each other, when Rawlings called out something unintelligible. I leaned closer to him and pulled back my parka hood.

'A light!' he shouted. 'A light. Look, Doc – across there!'

And a light there was, a long narrow strangely white vertical strip of light from the hut opposite the charred wreck by which we stood. Leaning sideways into the storm we dragged Zabrinski across the intervening gap. For the first time my torch showed something that was more than a bare framework of steel. This was a hut. A blackened, scorched and twisted hut with a roughly nailed-on sheet of plywood where its solitary window had been, but nevertheless a hut. The light was coming from a door standing just ajar at the sheltered end. I laid my hand on the door, the one unscorched thing I'd seen so far in Drift Station Zebra. The hinges creaked like a rusty gate in a cemetery at midnight and the door gave beneath my hand. We passed inside.

Suspended from a hook in the centre of the ceiling a hissing Coleman lamp threw its garish light, amplified by the glittering aluminium ceiling, over every corner and detail of that eighteen by ten hut. A thick but transparent layer of ice sheathed the aluminium roof except for a three-foot circle directly above the lamp, and the ice spread from the ceiling down the plywood walls all the way to the door. The wooden floor, too, was covered with ice, except where the bodies of the men lay. There may have been ice under them as well. I couldn't tell.

My first thought, conviction rather, and one that struck at me with a heart-sapping sense of defeat, with a chill that even the polar storm outside had been unable to achieve, was that we had arrived too late. I had seen many dead men in my life, I knew what dead men looked like, and now I was looking at just that many more. Shapeless, huddled, lifeless forms lying under a shapeless mass of blankets, mackinaws, duffels and furs, I wouldn't have bet a cent on my chances of finding one heart-beat among the lot of them. Lying packed closely together in a rough semicircle at the end of the room remote from the door, they were utterly still, as unmoving as men would be if they had been lying that way for a frozen eternity. Apart from the hissing of the pressure-lamp there was no sound inside the hut other than the metallic drumfire of the ice-spicules against the ice-sheathed eastern wall of the hut.

Zabrinski was eased down into a sitting position against a wall. Rawlings unslung the heavy load he was carrying on his back, unwrapped the stove, pulled off his mittens and started fumbling around for the fuel tablets. Hansen pulled the door to behind him, slipped the buckles of his rucksack and wearily let his load of tinned food drop to the floor of the shack.

For some reason, the voice of the storm outside and the hissing of the Coleman inside served only to heighten the deathly stillness in the hut, and the unexpected metallic clatter of the falling cans made me jump. It made one of the dead men jump, too. The man nearest to me by the left-hand wall suddenly moved, rolled over and sat up, bloodshot faded eyes staring out unbelievingly from a frostbitten, haggard and cruelly burnt face, the burns patchily covered by a long dark stubble of beard. For long seconds he looked at us unblinkingly, then, some obscure feeling of pride making him ignore the offer of my outstretched arm, he pushed himself shakily and with obvious pain to his feet. Then the cracked and peeling lips broke into a grin.

'You've been a bleedin' long time getting here.' The voice was hoarse and weak and cockney as the Bow Bells themselves. 'My name's Kinnaird. Radio operator.'

'Whisky?' I asked.

He grinned again, tried to lick his cracked lips, and nodded. The stiff tot of whisky went down his throat like a man in a barrel going over the Niagara Falls, one moment there, the next gone for ever. He bent over, coughing harshly until the tears came to his eyes, but when he straightened life was coming back into those same lack-lustre eyes and colour touching the pale emaciated cheeks.

'If you go through life saying "Hallo" in this fashion, mate,' he observed, 'then you'll never lack for friends.' He bent and shook the shoulder of the man beside whom he had been lying. 'C'mon, Jolly, old boy, where's your bleedin' manners. We got company.'

It took quite a few shakes to get Jolly, old boy, awake, but when he did come to he was completely conscious and on his feet with remarkable speed in the one case and with remarkable nimbleness in the other. He was a short, chubby character with china-blue eyes, and although he was as much in need of a shave as Kinnaird, there was still colour in his face and the round good-humoured face was far from emaciated: but frost-bite had made a bad mess of both mouth and nose. The china-blue eyes, flecked with red and momentarily wide in surprise, crinkled into a grin of welcome. Jolly, old boy, I guess, would always adjust fast to circumstances.

'Visitors, eh?' His deep voice held a rich Irish brogue. 'And damned glad we are to see you, too. Do the honours, Jeff.'

'We haven't introduced ourselves,' I said. 'I'm Dr Carpenter and this—'

'Regular meeting of the BMA, old boy,' Jolly said. I was to find out later that he used the phrase 'old boy' in every second or third sentence, a mannerism which went strangely with his Irish accent.

'Dr Jolly?'

'The same. Resident medical officer, old boy.'

'I see. This is Lieutenant Hansen of the United States Navy submarine *Dolphin*—'

'Submarine?' Jolly and Kinnaird stared at each other, then at us. 'You said "submarine," old top?'

'Explanations can wait. Torpedoman Rawlings. Radioman Zabrinski.' I glanced down at the huddled men on the floor, some of them already stirring at the sound of voices, one or two propping themselves up on their elbows. 'How are they?'

'Two or three pretty bad burn cases,' Jolly said. 'Two or three far gone with cold and exhaustion, but not so far gone that food and warmth wouldn't have them right as rain in a few days. I made them all huddle together like this for mutual warmth.'

I counted them. Including Jolly and Kinnaird, there were twelve all told. I said: 'Where are the others?'

'The others?' Kinnaird looked at me in momentary surprise, then his face went bleak and cold. He pointed a thumb over his shoulder. 'In the next hut, mate.'

'Why?'

'Why?' He rubbed a weary forearm across bloodshot eyes. 'Because we don't fancy sleeping with a roomful of corpses, that's why.'

'Because you don't—' I broke off and stared down at the men at my feet. Seven of them were awake now, three of them propped on elbows, four still lying down, all seven registering various degrees of dazed bewilderment: the three who were still asleep – or unconscious – had their faces covered by blankets. I said slowly. 'There were nineteen of you.'

'Nineteen of us,' Kinnaird echoed emptily. 'The others – well, they never had a chance.'

I said nothing. I looked carefully at the faces of the conscious men, hoping to find among them the one face I wanted to see, hoping perhaps that I had not immediately recognized it because frost-bite or hunger or burns had made it temporarily unrecognizable. I looked very carefully indeed and I knew that I had never seen any of those faces before.

I moved over to the first of the three still sleeping figures and lifted the blanket covering the face. The face of a stranger. I let the blanket drop. Jolly said in puzzlement: 'What's wrong? What do you want?'

I didn't answer him. I picked my way round recumbent men, all staring uncomprehendingly at me, and lifted the blanket from the face of the second sleeping man. Again I let the blanket drop and I could feel my mouth go dry, the slow heavy pounding of my heart. I crossed to the third man, then stood there hesitating, knowing I must find out, dreading what I must find. Then I stooped quickly and lifted the blanket. A man with a heavily bandaged face. A man with a broken nose and a thick blond beard. A man I had never seen in my life before. Gently I spread the blanket over his face and straightened up. Rawlings, I saw, already had the solid-fuel stove going.

'That should bring the temperature up to close to freezing,' I said to Dr Jolly. 'We've plenty of fuel. We've also brought food, alcohol, a complete medical kit. If you and Kinnaird want to start in on those things now I'll give you a hand in a minute. Lieutenant, that was a polynya, that smooth stretch we crossed just before we got here? A frozen lead?'

'Couldn't be anything else.' Hansen was looking at me peculiarly, a wondering expression on his face. 'These people are obviously in no fit state to travel a couple of hundred yards, far less four or five miles. Besides, the skipper said he was going to be squeezed down pretty soon. So we whistle up the Dolphin and have them surface at the back door?'

'Can he find that polynya – without the ice-machine, I mean?'

'Nothing simpler. I'll take Zabrinski's radio, move a measured two hundred yards to the north, send a bearing signal, move two hundred yards to the south and do the same. They'll have our range to a yard. Take a couple of hundred yards off that and the *Dolphin* will find itself smack in the middle of the polynya.'

'But still under it. I wonder how thick that ice is. You had an open lead to the west of the camp some time ago, Dr Jolly. How long ago?'

'A month. Maybe five weeks. I can't be sure.'

'How thick?' I asked Hansen.

'Five feet, maybe six. Couldn't possibly break through it. But the captain's always had a hankering to have a go with his torpedoes.' He turned to Zabrinski. 'Still fit to operate that radio of yours?'

I left them to it. I'd hardly been aware of what I'd been saying, anyway. I felt sick and old and empty and sad, and deathly tired. I had my answer now. I'd come 12,000 miles to find it, I'd have gone a million to avoid it. But the inescapable fact was there and now nothing could ever change it. Mary, my sister-in-law and her three wonderful children – she would never see her husband again, they would never see their father again. My brother was dead and no one was ever going to see him again. Except me. I was going to see him now.

I went out, closing the door behind me, moved round the corner of the hut and lowered my head against the storm. Ten seconds later I reached the door of the last hut in the line. I used the torch to locate the handle, twisted it, pushed and passed inside.

Once it had been a laboratory: Now it was a charnel house, a house of the dead. The laboratory equipment had all been pushed roughly to one side and the cleared floor space covered with the bodies of dead men. I knew they were dead men, but only because Kinnaird had told me so: hideously charred and blackened and grotesquely misshapen as they were, those carbonized and contorted lumps of matter could have been any form of life or indeed no form of life at all. The stench of incinerated flesh and burnt diesel fuel was dreadful. I wondered which of the men in the other hut had had the courage, the iron resolution, to bring those grisly burdens, the shockingly disfigured remains of their former comrades into this hut. They must have had strong stomachs.

Death must have been swift, swift for all of them. Theirs had not been the death of men trapped by fire, it had been the death of men who had themselves been on fire. Caught, drenched, saturated by a gale-borne sea of burning oil, they must have spent the last few seconds of life as incandescently blazing human torches before dying in insane screaming agony. They must have died as terribly as men can ever die.

Something about one of the bodies close to me caught my attention. I stooped and focused the torch beam on what had once been a right hand, now no more than a blackened claw with the bone showing through. So powerful had been the heat that it had warped, but not melted, the curiously shaped gold ring on the third finger. I recognized that ring, I had been with my sister-in-law when she had bought it.

I was conscious of no grief, no pain, no revulsion. Perhaps, I thought dully, those would come later when the initial shock had worn off. But I didn't think so. This wasn't the man I remembered so well, the brother to whom I owed everything, a debt that could never now be repaid. This charred mass of matter before me was a stranger, so utterly different from the man who lived on in my memory, so changed beyond all possibility of recognition that my numbed mind in my exhausted body just could not begin to bridge the gap.

As I stood there, staring down, something ever so slightly off-beat about the way the body lay caught my professional attention. I stooped low, very low, and remained bent over for what seemed a long time. I straightened, slowly, and as I did I heard the door behind me open. I whirled round and saw that it was Lieutenant Hansen. He pulled down his snow-mask, lifted up his goggles, looked at me and then at the man at my feet. I could see shock draining expression and colour from his face. Then he looked up at me.

'So you lost out, Doc?' I could hardly hear the husky whisper above the voice of the storm. 'God, I'm sorry.'

'What do you mean?'

'Your brother?' He nodded at the man at my feet.

'Commander Swanson told you?'

'Yeah. Just before we left. That's why we came.' His gaze moved in horrified fascination over the floor of the hut, and his face was grey, like old parchment. 'A minute, Doc, just a minute.' He turned and hurried through the doorway.

When he came back he looked better, but not much. He said: 'Commander Swanson said that that was why he had to let you go.'

'Who else knows?'

'Skipper and myself. No one else.'

'Keep it that way, will you? As a favour to me.'

'If you say so, Doc.' There was curiosity in his face now, and puzzlement, but horror was still the dominant expression. 'My God, have you ever seen anything like it?'

'Let's get back to the others,' I said. 'We're doing nobody any good by staying here.'

He nodded without speaking. Together we made our way back to the other hut. Apart from Dr Jolly and Kinnaird, three other men were on their feet now, Captain Folsom, an extraordinarily tall thin man with savagely burnt face and hands who was second in command of the base, Hewson, a dark-eyed taciturn character, a tractor driver and engineer who had been responsible for the diesel generators, and a cheerful Yorkshireman, Naseby, the camp cook. Jolly, who had opened my medical kit and was applying fresh bandages to the arms of the men still lying down, introduced them, then turned back to his job. He didn't seem to need my help, not for the moment anyway. I heard Hansen say to Zabrinski: 'In contact with the *Dolphin*?'

'Well, no.' Zabrinski stopped sending his call-sign and shifted slightly to ease his broken ankle. 'I don't quite know how to put this, Lieutenant, but the fact is that this little ol' set here seems to have blown a fuse.'

'Well, now,' Hansen said heavily. 'That *is* clever of you, Zabrinski. You mean you can't raise them?'

'I can hear them, they can't hear me.' He shrugged, apologetically. 'Me and my clumsy feet, I guess. It wasn't just only my ankle that went when I took that tumble out there.'

'Well, can't you repair the damn' thing?'

'I don't think so, Lieutenant.'

'Damn it, you're supposed to be a radioman.'

'That's so,' Zabrinski acknowledged reasonably. 'But I'm not a magician. And with a couple of numbed and frozen hands, no tools, an old-type set without a printed circuit and the code signs in Japanese – well, even Marconi would have called it a day.'

'*Can* it be repaired?' Hansen insisted.

'It's a transistor set. No valves to smash. I expect it could be repaired. But it might take hours, Lieutenant – I'd even have to fake up a set of tools first.'

'Well, fake them. Anything you like. Only get that thing working.'

Zabrinski said nothing. He held out the headphones to Hansen. Hansen looked at Zabrinski, then at the phones, took them without a word and listened briefly. Then he shrugged, handed back the phones and said: 'Well, I guess there *is* no hurry to repair that radio.'

'Yeah,' Zabrinski said. 'Awkward, you might say, Lieutenant.'

'What's awkward,' I asked.

'Looks as if *we're* going to be next on the list for a rescue party,' Hansen said heavily. 'They're sending a more or less continuous signal: "Ice closing rapidly, return at once." '

'I was against this madness from the very beginning,' Rawlings intoned from the floor. He stared down at the already melting lumps of frozen tinned soup and stirred it moodily with a fork. 'A gallant attempt, men, but foredoomed to failure.'

'Keep your filthy fingers out of that soup and kindly clam up,' Hansen said coldly. He turned suddenly to Kinnaird. 'How about *your* radio set. Of course, that's it. We have fit men here to crank your generator and—'

'I'm sorry.' Kinnaird smiled the way a ghost might smile. 'It's not a hand-powered generator, that was destroyed, it's a battery set. The batteries are finished. Completely finished.'

'A battery set, you said?' Zabrinski looked at him in mild surprise. 'Then what caused all the power fluctuations when you were transmitting?'

'We kept changing over the nickel cadmium cells to try to make the most of what little power was left in them: we'd only fifteen left altogether, most of them were lost in the fire. That caused the power fluctuations. But even Nife cells don't last for ever. They're finished, mate. The combined power left in those cells would light a pencil torch.'

Zabrinski didn't say anything. No one said anything. The ice-spicules drummed incessantly against the east wall, the Coleman hissed, the solid-fuel stove purred softly: but the sole effect of those three sounds was to make the silence inside seem that little bit more absolute. No one looked at his neighbours, everyone stared down at the floor with the fixed and steadfast gaze of an entomologist hunting for traces of woodworm. Any newspaper printing a picture taken at that instant wouldn't have found it any too easy to convince its readers that the men on Drift Ice Station Zebra had been rescued just ten minutes previously, and rescued from certain death at that. The readers would have pointed out that one might have expected a little more jubilation in the atmosphere, a touch, perhaps, of lighthearted relief, and they wouldn't have been far wrong at that, there wasn't very much gaiety around.

After the silence had gone on just that little too long I said to Hansen: 'Well, that's it, then. We don't have to hire any electronic computer to work this one out. Someone's got to get back to the *Dolphin* and get back there now. I'm nominating myself.'

'No!' Hansen said violently, then more quietly: 'Sorry, friend, but the skipper's orders didn't include giving permission to anyone to commit suicide. You're staying here.'

'So I stay here,' I nodded. This wasn't the time to tell him I didn't need his permission for anything, far less was it the time to start flourishing the Mannlicher-Schoenauer. 'So we all stay here. And then we all die here. Quietly, without any fighting, without any fuss, we just lie down and die here. I suppose you reckon that comes under the heading of inspiring leadership. Amundsen would have loved that.' It wasn't fair, but then I wasn't feeling fairminded at the moment.

Nobody's going any place,' Hansen said. 'I'm not my brother's keeper, Doc, but for all that I'll be damned if I let you kill yourself. You're not fit, none of us is fit to make the return trip to the *Dolphin* – not after what we've just been through. That's one thing. The next thing is that without a transmitter from which the *Dolphin* can pick up our directional bearings, we could never hope to find the *Dolphin* again. The third thing is that the closing ice will probably have forced the *Dolphin* to drop down before anyone could get half-way there. And the last thing is that if we failed to find the *Dolphin* either because we missed her or because she was gone, we could never make our way back to Zebra again: we wouldn't have the strength and we would have nothing to guide us back anyway.'

'The odds offered aren't all that attractive,' I admitted.

'What odds are you offering on the ice-machine being repaired?'

Hansen shook his head, said nothing. Rawlings started stirring his soup again, carefully not looking up, he didn't want to meet the anxious eyes, the desperate eyes, in that circle of haggard and frost-bitten faces any more than I did. But he looked up as Captain Folsom pushed himself away from the support of a wall and took a couple of unsteady steps towards us. It didn't require any stethoscope to see that Folsom was in a pretty bad way.

'I am afraid that we don't understand,' he said. His voice was slurred and indistinct, the puffed and twisted lips had been immobilized by the savage charring of his face: I wondered bleakly how many months of pain would elapse, how many visits to the surgeon's table, before Folsom could show that face to the world again. In the very remote event, that was, of our ever getting him to hospital. 'Would you please explain? What is the difficulty?'

'Simply this,' I said. 'The *Dolphin* has an ice fathometer, a device for measuring the thickness of the overhead ice. Normally, even if Commander Swanson – the captain of the *Dolphin* – didn't hear from us, we could expect him on our doorstep in a matter of hours. He has the position of this Drift Station pinned down pretty closely. All he would have to do is to drop down, come under us here, start a grid search with his ice fathometer and it would be only minutes before he would locate the relatively thin ice out in that lead there. But things aren't normal. The ice-machine has broken down and if it stays that way he'll never find that lead. That's why I want to go back there. Now. Before Swanson's forced to dive by the closing ice.'

'Don't see it, old boy,' Jolly said. 'How's that going to help? Can *you* fix this ice what-you-may-call-it.'

'I don't have to. Commander Swanson knows his distance from this camp give or take a hundred yards. All I have to do is to tell him to cover the distance less quarter of a mile and loose off a torpedo. That ought—'

'Torpedo?' Jolly asked. 'Torpedo? To break through the ice from beneath?'

'That's it. It's never been tried before. I suppose there's no reason why it shouldn't work if the ice is thin enough and it won't be all that thick in the lead out there. I don't really know.'

'They'll be sending planes, you know, Doc,' Zabrinski said quietly. 'We started transmitting the news as soon as we broke through and everybody will know by now that Zebra has been found – at least, they'll know exactly where it is. They'll have the big bombers up here in a few hours.'

'Doing what?' I asked. 'Sculling around uselessly in the darkness up above? Even if they do have the exact position, they still won't be able to see what's left of this station because of the darkness and the ice-storm. Perhaps they can with radar, it's unlikely, but even if they do, what then? Drop supplies? Maybe. But they won't dare drop supplies directly on us for fear of killing us. They'd have to drop them some distance off – and even a quarter-mile would be too far away for any chance we'd ever have of finding stuff in those conditions. As for landing – even if weather conditions were perfect, no plane big enough to have the range to fly here could ever hope to land on the ice-cap. You know that.'

'What's your middle name, Doc?' Rawlings asked dolefully. 'Jeremiah?'

'The greatest good of the greatest number,' I said. 'The old yardstick, but there's never been a better one. If we just hole up here without making any attempt to help ourselves and the ice-machine remains useless, then we're all dead. All sixteen of us. If I make it there safely, then we're all alive. Even if I don't, the ice-machine may be fixed and there would only be one lost then.' I started pulling on my mittens. 'One is less than sixteen.'

'We might as well make it two,' Hansen sighed and began to pull on his own gloves. I was hardly surprised, when he'd last spoken he'd talked at first of 'you' having no chance and finished by saying that 'we' had none and it hadn't required any psychiatrist to follow his quick shift in mental orientation: whatever men like Hansen were hand-picked for, it wasn't for any predilection for shifting the load to others' shoulders when the going became sticky.

I didn't waste time arguing with him.

Rawlings got to his feet.

'One skilled volunteer for the soup-stirring,' he requested. 'Those two wouldn't get as far as the door there without my holding their hands. I shall probably get a medal for this. What's the highest decoration awarded in peace-time, Lieutenant?'

'There are no medals given for soup-stirring, Rawlings,' Hansen said, 'which is what you are going to keep on doing. You're staying right here.'

'Uh-uh.' Rawlings shook his head. 'Prepare yourself to deal with your first mutiny, Lieutenant. I'm coming with you. I can't lose. If we get to the *Dolphin* you'll be too damned glad and happy to have made it to dream of reporting me, apart from being a fair-minded man who will have to admit that our safe arrival back at the ship will be entirely due to Torpedoman Rawlings.' He grinned. 'And if we don't make it – well, you can't very well report it, can you, Lieutenant?'

Hansen walked across to him. He said quietly: 'You know that there's more than an even chance that we won't reach the *Dolphin*. That would leave twelve pretty sick men here, not to mention Zabrinski with a broken ankle, and with no one to look after them. They must have one fit man to look after them. You couldn't be that selfish, now, could you, Rawlings? Look after them, will you? As a favour to me?'

Rawlings looked at him for long seconds, then squatted down and started stirring the soup again.

'As a favour to me, you mean,' he said bitterly. 'OK, I'll stay. As a favour to me. Also to prevent Zabrinski tripping over his legs again and breaking another ankle.' He stirred the soup viciously. Well, what are you waiting for? The skipper may be making up his mind to dive any minute.'

He had a point. We brushed off protests and attempts to stop us made by Captain Folsom and Dr Jolly and were ready to leave in thirty seconds. Hansen was through the door first. I turned and looked at the sick and emaciated and injured survivors of Drift Station Zebra. Folsom, Jolly, Kinnaird, Hewson, Naseby and seven others. Twelve men altogether. They couldn't all be in cahoots together, so it had to be a single man, maybe two, acting in concert. I wondered who those men might be, those men I would have to kill, that person or persons who had murdered my brother and six other men on Drift Ice Station Zebra.

I pulled the door to behind me and followed Hansen out into the dreadful night.

Chapter Six

We had been tired, more than tired, even before we had set out. We had been leaden-legged, bone-weary, no more than a short hand-span from total exhaustion. But for all that we flitted through the howling darkness of that night like two great white ghosts across the dimly seen whiteness of a nightmare lunar landscape. We were no longer bowed under the weight of heavy packs. Our backs were to that gale-force wind so that for every laborious plodding step we had made on our way to Zebra, we now covered five, with so little a fraction of our earlier toil that at first it seemed all but effortless. We had no trouble in seeing where we were going, no fear of falling into an open lead or of crippling ourselves against some unexpected obstacle, for with our useless goggles removed and powerful torch beams dancing erratically ahead of us as we jog-trotted along, visibility was seldom less than five yards, more often near to ten. Those were the physical aids that helped us on our way but even more sharply powerful as spur to our aching legs was that keen and ever-growing fear that dominated our minds to the exclusion of all else, the fear that Commander Swanson had already been compelled to drop down and that we would be left to die in that shrieking wasteland: with our lacking both shelter and food, the old man with the scythe would not be keeping us waiting too long.

We ran, but we did not run too fast, for to have done that would have been to have the old man tapping us on the shoulder in very short order indeed. In far sub-zero temperatures, there is one thing that the Eskimo avoids as he would the plague – over-exertion, in those latitudes more deadly, even than the plague itself. Too much physical effort while wearing heavy furs inevitably results in sweat, and when the effort ceases, as eventually cease it must, the sweat freezes on the skin: the only way to destroy that film of ice is by further exertion, producing even more sweat, the beginnings of a vicious and steadily narrowing circle that can have only one end. So though we ran it was only at a gentle jog-trot, hardly more than a fast walk: we took every possible precaution against overheating.

After half an hour, perhaps a little more, I called for a brief halt in the shelter of a steep ice-wall. Twice in the past two minutes Hansen had stumbled and fallen where there hadn't appeared to be any reason to stumble and fall: and I had noticed that my own legs were more unsteady than the terrain warranted.

'How are you making out?' I asked.

'Pretty bushed, Doc.' He sounded it, too, his breathing quick and rasping and shallow. 'But don't write me off yet. How far do you reckon we've come?'

'Three miles, near enough.' I patted the ice-wall behind us. 'When we've had a couple of minutes I think we should try climbing this. Looks like a pretty tallish hummock to me.'

'To try to get into the clear above the ice-storm?' I nodded my head and he shook his. 'Won't do you any good, Doc. This ice-storm must be at least twenty feet thick, and even if you do get above it the *Dolphin* will still be below it. She's only got the top of her sail clear above the ice.'

'I've been thinking,' I said. 'We've been so lost in our own woes and sorrows that we have forgotten about Commander Swanson. I think we have been guilty of underestimating him pretty badly.'

'It's likely enough. Right now I'm having a full-time job worrying about Lieutenant Hansen. What's on your mind?'

'Just this. The chances are better than fifty-fifty that Swanson believes we are on the way back to the *Dolphin*. After all, he's been ordering us to return for quite some time; and if he thinks we didn't get the order because something has happened to us or to the radio, he'll still figure that we will be returning.'

'Not necessarily. Radio or not, we might still be pushing on for Drift Station Zebra.'

'No. Definitely not. He'll be expecting us to be smart enough to figure it the way he would; and smart enough to see that that is the way he *would* figure it. He would know that if our radio broke down before we got to Zebra that it would be suicidal for us to try to find it without radio bearing – but that it *wouldn't* be suicidal for us to try to make it back to the *Dolphin*, for he would be hoping that we would have sufficient savvy to guess that he would put a lamp in the window to guide the lost sheep home.'

'My God, Doc, I believe you've got it! Of course he would, of course he would. Lordy, lordy, what am I using for brains?' He straightened and turned to face the ice-wall.

Pushing and pulling, we made it together to the top. The summit of the rafted ice hummock was less than twenty feet above the level of the ice-pack and not quite high enough. We were still below the surface of that gale-driven river of ice-spicules. Occasionally, for a brief moment of time, the wind force would ease fractionally and let us have a brief glimpse of the clear sky above but only occasionally and for a fraction of a second. And if there was anything to be seen in that time, we couldn't see it.

'There'll be other hummocks,' I shouted in Hansen's ear. 'Higher hummocks.' He nodded without answering. I couldn't see the expression on his face but I didn't have to see it. The same thought was in both our minds: we could see nothing because there was nothing to see. Commander Swanson hadn't put a lamp in the window, for the window was gone, the *Dolphin* forced to dive to avoid being crushed by the ice.

Five times in the next twenty mintues we climbed hummocks, and five times we climbed down, each time more dejected, more defeated. By now I was pretty far gone, moving in a pain-filled nightmare: Hansen was in even worse case, lurching and staggering around like a drunken man. As a doctor, I knew well of the hidden and unsuspected resources that an exhausted man can call on in times of desperate emergency; but I knew too, that those resources are not limitless and that we were pretty close to the end. And when that end came we would just lie down in the lee of an ice-wall and wait for the old man to come along: he wouldn't keep us waiting long.

Our sixth hummock all but defeated us. It wasn't that it was hard to climb, it was well ridged with foot and hand holds in plenty, but the sheer physical effort of climbing came very close to defeating us. And then I dimly began to realize that part of the effort was due to the fact that this was by far the highest hummock we had found yet. Some colossal pressures had concentrated on this one spot, rafting and log-jamming the ice-pack until it had risen a clear thirty feet above the general level: the giant underwater ridge beneath must have stretched down close on two hundred feet towards the black floor of the Arctic.

Eight feet below the summit our heads were in the clear: on the summit itself, holding on to each other for mutual support against the gale, we could look down on the ice-storm whirling by just beneath our feet: a fantastic sight, a great grey-white sea of undulating turbulence, a giant rushing river that stretched from horizon to horizon. Like so much else in the high Arctic the scene had an eerie and terrifying strangeness about it, a mindless desolation that belonged not to earth but to some alien and long-dead planet.

We scanned the horizon to the west until our eyes ached. Nothing. Nothing at all. Just that endless desolation. From due north to due south, through 180°, we searched the surface of that great river; and still we saw nothing. Three minutes passed. Still nothing. I began to feel the ice running in my blood.

On the remote off-chance that we might already have by-passed the *Dolphin* to the north or south, I turned and peered towards the east. It wasn't easy, for that far sub-zero gale of wind brought tears to the eyes in an instant of time; but at least it wasn't impossible, we no longer had to contend with the needle-pointed lances of the ice-spicules. I made another slow 180° sweep of the eastern horizon, and again, and again. Then I caught Hansen's arm.

'Look there,' I said. 'To the north-east. Maybe quarter of a mile away, maybe half a mile. Can you see anything?'

For several seconds Hansen squinted along the direction of my outstretched hand, then shook his head. 'I see nothing. What do you think you see?'

'I don't know. I'm not sure. I can imagine I see a very faint touch of luminescence on the surface of the ice-storm there, maybe just a fraction of a shade whiter than the rest.'

For a full half-minute Hansen stared out through cupped hands. Finally he said: 'It's no good. I don't see it. But then my eyes have been acting up on me for the past half-hour. But I can't even *imagine* I see anything.'

I turned away to give my streaming eyes a rest from that icy wind and then looked again. 'Damn it,' I said, 'I can't be sure that there is anything there; but I can't be sure that there isn't, either.'

'What do you fancy it would be?' Hansen's voice was dispirited, with overtones of hopelessness. 'A light?'

'A searchlight shining vertically upwards. A searchlight that's not able to penetrate that ice-storm.'

'You're kidding yourself, Doc,' Hansen said wearily. 'The wish father to the thought. Besides, that would mean that we had already passed the *Dolphin*. It's not possible.'

'It's not impossible. Ever since we started climbing those damned ice-hummocks I've lost track of time and space. It *could* be.'

'Do you still see it?' The voice was empty, uninterested, he didn't believe me and he was just making words.

'Maybe my eyes are acting up, too,' I admitted. 'But, damn it, I'm still not sure that I'm not right.'

'Come on, Doc, let's go.'

'Go where?'

'I don't know.' His teeth chattered so uncontrollably in that intense cold that I could scarcely follow his words. 'I guess it doesn't matter very much where—'

With breath-taking abruptness, almost in the centre of my imagined patch of luminescence and not more than four hundred yards away, a swiftly climbing rocket burst through the rushing river of ice-spicules and climbed high into the clear sky trailing behind it a fiery tale of glowing red sparks. Five hundred feet it climbed, perhaps six hundred, then burst into a brilliantly incandescent shower of crimson stars, stars that fell lazily back to earth again, streaming away to the west on the wings of the gale and dying as they went, till the sky was colder and emptier than ever before.

'You still say it doesn't matter very much where we go?' I asked Hansen. 'Or maybe you didn't see that little lot?'

'What I just saw,' he said reverently, 'was the prettiest ol' sight that Ma Hansen's little boy ever did see – or ever will see.' He thumped me on the back, so hard that I had to grab him to keep my balance. 'We got it made, Doc!' he shouted. 'We got it made. Suddenly I have the strength of ten. Home sweet home, here we come.'

Ten minutes later we were home.

'God this is wonderful,' Hansen sighed. He stared in happy bemusement from the captain to me to the glass in his hand to the water dripping from the melting ice on his furs on to the corticene decking of the captain's tiny cabin. 'The warmth, the light, the comfort and home sweet home. I never thought I'd see any of it again. When that rocket went up, Skipper, I was just looking around to pick a place to lay me down and die. And don't think I'm joking, for I'm not.'

'And Dr Carpenter?' Swanson smiled.

'Defective mental equipment somewhere,' Hansen said. 'He doesn't seem to know how to set about giving up. I think he's just mule-headed. You get them like that.'

Hansen's slightly off-beat, slightly irrational talk had nothing to do with the overwhelming relief and relaxation that comes after moments of great stress and tension. Hansen was too tough for that. I knew that and I knew that Swanson knew it also. We'd been back for almost twenty minutes now, we'd told our story, the pressure was off, a happy ending for all seemed in sight and normalcy was again almost the order of the day. But when the strain is off and conditions are back to normal a man has time to start thinking about things again. I knew only too well what was in Hansen's mind's eye, that charred and huddled shapelessness that had once been my brother. He didn't want me to talk about him, and for that I didn't blame him; he didn't want me even to think about him, although he must have known that that was impossible. The kindest men nearly always are like that, hard and tough and cynical on the outside, men who have been too kind and showed it.

'However it was,' Swanson smiled, 'you can consider yourselves two of the luckiest men alive. That rocket you saw was the third last we had, it's been a regular fourth of July for the past hour or so. And you reckon Rawlings, Zabrinski and the survivors on Zebra are safe for the present?'

'Nothing to worry about for the next couple of days,' Hansen nodded. 'They'll be OK. Cold, mind you, and a good half of them desperately in need of hospital treatment, but they'll survive.'

'Fine. Well, this is how it is. This lead here stopped closing in about half an hour ago, but it doesn't matter now, we can drop down any time and still hold our position. What does matter is that we have located the fault in the ice-machine. It's a damnably tricky and complicated job and I expect it will take several hours to fix. But I think we'll wait until it is fixed before we try anything. I'm not too keen on this idea of making a dead reckoning approach to this lead near Zebra then loosing off a shot in the dark. Since there's no desperate hurry, I'd rather wait till we got the ice fathometer operating again, make an accurate survey of this lead then fire a torpedo up through the middle. If the ice is only four or five feet thick there, we shouldn't have much trouble blowing a hole through.'

'That would be best,' Hansen agreed. He finished off his medicinal alcohol – an excellent bourbon – rose stiffly to his feet and stretched. 'Well, back to the old treadmill again. How many torpedoes in working order?'

'Four, at the last count.'

'I may as well go help young Mills load them up now. If that's OK by you, Skipper.'

'It is not OK by me,' Swanson said mildly, 'and if you'll take a quick gander at that mirror there you'll understand why. You're not fit to load a slug into an airgun far less a torpedo into its tube. You haven't just been on a Sunday afternoon stroll, you know. A few hours' sleep, John, then we'll see.'

Hansen didn't argue. I couldn't imagine anyone arguing with Commander Swanson. He made for the door. 'Coming, Doc?'

'In a moment. Sleep well.'

'Yeah. Thanks.' He touched me lightly on the shoulder and smiled through bloodshot and exhausted eyes. 'Thanks for everything. Good-night, all.'

When he was gone Swanson said: 'It was pretty wicked out there to-night?'

'I wouldn't recommend it for an old ladies' home Sunday afternoon outing.'

'Lieutenant Hansen seems to imagine he's under some kind of debt to you,' he went on inconsequentially.

'Imagination, as you say. They don't come any better than Hansen. You're damned lucky to have him as an exec.'

'I know that.' He hesitated, then said quietly: 'I promise you, I won't mention this again – but, well, I'm most damnably sorry, Doctor.'

I looked at him and nodded slowly. I knew he meant it, I knew he had to say it, but there's not much you can say in turn to anything like that. I said: 'Six others died with him, Commander.'

He hesitated again. 'Do we – do we take the dead back to Britain with us?'

'Could I have another drop of that excellent bourbon, Commander. Been a very heavy run on your medicinal alcohol in the past few hours, I'm afraid.' I waited till he had filled my glass then went on: 'We don't take them back with us. They're not dead men, they're just unrecognizable and unidentifiable lumps of charred matter. Let them stay here.'

His relief was unmistakable and he was aware of it for he went on hurriedly, for something to say: 'All this equipment for locating and tracking the Russian missiles. Destroyed?'

'I didn't check.' He'd find out for himself soon enough that there had been no such equipment. How he'd react to that discovery in light of the cock-and-bull story I'd spun to himself and Admiral Garvie in the Holy Loch I couldn't even begin to guess. At the moment I didn't even care. It didn't seem important, nothing seemed important, not any more. All at once I felt tired, not sleepy, just deathly tired, so I pushed myself stiffly to my feet, said good-night and left.

Hansen was in his bunk when I got back to his cabin, his furs lying where he had dropped them. I checked that he was no longer awake, slipped off my own furs, hung them up and replaced the Mannlicher-Schoenauer in my case. I lay down in my cot to sleep, but sleep wouldn't come. Exhausted though I was, I had never felt less like sleep in my life.

I was too restless and unsettled for sleep, too many problems coming all at once were causing a first-class log-jam in my mind. I got up, pulled on shirt and denim pants, and made my way to the control room. I spent the better part of what remained of the night there, pacing up and down, watching two technicians repairing the vastly complicated innards of the ice-machine, reading the messages of congratulation which were still coming in, talking desultorily to the officer on deck and drinking endless cups of coffee. It passed the night for me and although I hadn't closed an eye I felt fresh and almost relaxed by the time morning came.

At the wardroom breakfast table that morning everyone seemed quietly cheerful. They knew they had done a good job, the whole world was telling them they had done a magnificent job, and you could see that they all regarded that job as being as good as over. No one appeared to doubt Swanson's ability to blow a hole through the ice. If it hadn't been for the presence of the ghost at the feast, myself, they would have been positively jovial.

'We'll pass up the extra cups of coffee this morning, gentlemen,' Swanson said. 'Drift Station Zebra is still waiting for us and even although I'm assured everyone there will survive, they must be feeling damned cold and miserable for all that. The ice-machine has been in operation for almost an hour now, at least we hope it has. We'll drop down right away and test it and after we've loaded the torpedoes – two should do it, I fancy – we'll blow our way up into this lead at Zebra.'

Twenty minutes later the *Dolphin* was back where she belonged, 150 feet below the surface of the sea – or the ice-cap. After ten minutes' manoeuvring, with a close check being kept on the plotting table to maintain our position relative to Drift Station Zebra, it was clear that the ice-machine was behaving perfectly normally again, tracing out the inverted ridges and valleys in the ice with its usual magical accuracy. Commander Swanson nodded his satisfaction.

'That's it, then.' He nodded to Hansen and Mills, the torpedo officer. 'You can go ahead now. Maybe you'd like to accompany them, Dr Carpenter. Or is loading torpedoes old hat to you?'

'Never seen it,' I said truthfully. 'Thanks, I'd like to go along.' Swanson was as considerate towards men as he was towards his beloved *Dolphin* which was why every man in the ship swore by him. He knew, or suspected that, apart from the shock I felt at my brother's death, I was worried stiff about other things: he would have heard, although he hadn't mentioned it to me and hadn't even asked me how I had slept, that I'd spent the night prowling aimlessly and restlessly above the control room: he knew I would be grateful for any distraction, for anything that would relieve my mind, however temporarily, of whatever it was that was troubling it. I wondered just how much that extraordinarily keen brain knew or guessed. But that was an unprofitable line of thought so I put it out of my mind and went along with Hansen and Mills. Mills was another like Raeburn, the navigation officer, he looked to me more like a college undergraduate than the highly competent officer he was, but I supposed it was just another sign that I was growing old.

Hansen crossed to a panel by the diving console and studied a group of lights. The night's sleep had done Hansen a great deal of good and, apart from the abraded skin on his forehead and round the cheekbones where the ice-spicules of last night had done their work, ihe was again his normal cheerfully-cynical relaxed self, fresh and rested and fit. He waved his hand at the panel.

'The torpedo safety light, Dr Carpenter. Each green light represents a closed torpedo tube door. Six doors that open to the sea – bow caps, we call them – six rear doors for loading the torpedoes. Only twelve lights but we study them very, very carefully – just to make sure that all the lights are green. For if any of them were red – any of the top six, that is, which represent the sea doors – well, that wouldn't be so good, would it?' He looked at Mills. 'All green?'

'All green,' Mills echoed.

We moved for'ard along the wardroom passage, and dropped down the wide companionway into the crew's mess. From there we moved into the for'ard torpedo storage room. Last time I'd been there, on the morning after our departure from the Clyde, nine or ten men had been sleeping in their bunks; now all the bunks were empty. Five men were waiting for us: four ratings and a Petty Officer Bowen whom Hansen, no stickler for protocol, addressed as Charlie.

'You will see now,' Hansen observed to me, 'why officers are more highly paid than enlisted men, and deservedly so. While Charlie and his gallant men skulk here behind two sets of collision bulkheads, we must go and test the safety of the tubes. Regulations. Still, a cool head, and an iron nerve: we do it gladly for our men.'

Bowen grinned and unclipped the first collision bulkhead door. We stepped over the eighteen-inch sill, leaving the five men behind, and waited until the door had been clipped up again before opening the for'ard collision bulkhead door and stepping over the second sill into the cramped torpedo room. This time the door was swung wide open and hooked back on a heavy standing catch.

'All laid down in the book of rules,' Hansen said. 'the only time the two doors can be opened at the same time is when we're actually loading the torpedoes.' He checked the position of metal handles at the rear of the tubes, reached up, swung down a steel-spring microphone and flicked a switch. 'Ready to test tubes. All manual levers shut. All lights showing green?'

'All lights still green.' The answering voice from the overhead squawk box was hollow, metallic, queerly impersonal.

'You already checked,' I said mildly.

'So we check again. Same old book of rules.' He grinned. 'Besides, my grandpa died at ninety-seven and I aim to beat his record. Take no chances and you run no risk. What are they to be, George?'

'Three and four.' I could see the brass plaques on the circular rear doors of the tubes, 2, 4 and 6 on the port side, 1, 3 and 5 on the starboard. Lieutenant Mills was proposing to use the central tubes on each side.

Mills unhooked a rubber torch from the bulkhead and approached number 3 first. Hansen said: 'Still no chances. First of all George opens the test cock in the rear door which will show if there is any water at all in the tubes. Shouldn't be, but sometimes a little gets past the bow caps. If the test cock shows nothing, then he opens the door and shines his torch up to examine the bow cap and see that there is no obstruction in the tube. How's it, George?'

'OK, number three.' Three times Mills lifted the test cock handle and no trace of water appeared. 'Opening the door now.'

He hauled on the big lever at the rear, pulled it clear and swung back the heavy circular door. He shone his torch up the gleaming inside length of the tube, then straightened. 'Clean as a whistle and dry as a bone.'

'That's not the way he was taught to report it,' Hansen said sorrowfully. 'I don't know what the young officers are coming to these days. Right, George, number four.'

Mills grinned, secured the rear door on number 3 and crossed to number 4. He lifted the test cock handle and said: 'Oh-oh.'

'What is it?' Hansen asked.

'Water,' Mills said tersely.

'Is there much? Let's see?'

'Just a trickle.'

'Is that bad?' I asked.

'It happens,' Hansen said briefly. He joggled the handle up and down and another spoonful of water appeared. 'You can get a slightly imperfect bow-cap and if you go deep enough to build up sufficient outside pressure you can get a trickle of water coming in. Probably what has happened in this case. If the bow-cap was open, friend, at this depth the water would come out of that spout like a bullet. But no chances, no chances.' He reached for the microphone again. 'Number four bow-cap still green? We have a little water here.'

'Still green.'

Hansen looked down at Mills. 'How's it coming?'

'Not so much now.'

'Control centre,' Hansen said into the microphone. 'Check the trim chit, just to make sure.'

There was a pause, then the box crackled again.

'Captain here. All tubes showing "Empty." Signed by Lieutenant Hansen and the foreman engineer.'

'Thank you, sir.' Hansen switched off and grinned. 'Lieutenant Hansen's word is good enough for me any day. How's it now?'

'Stopped.'

'Open her up.'

Mills tugged the heavy lever. It moved an inch or two, then stuck. 'Uncommon stiff,' he commented.

'You torpedomen never heard of anything called lubricating oil?' Hansen demanded. 'Weight, George, weight.'

Mills applied more weight. The lever moved another couple of inches. Mills scowled, shifted his feet to get maximum purchase and heaved just as Hansen shouted: 'No! Stop! For God's sake, stop!'

He was too late. He was a lifetime too late. The lever snapped clear, the heavy circular rear door smashed open as violently as if it had been struck by some gigantic battering ram and a roaring torrent of water burst into the for'ard torpedo room. The sheer size, the enormous column of water was staggering. It was like a giant hosepipe, like one of the outlet pipes of the Boulder Dam. It caught up Lieutenant Mills, already badly injured by the flailing sweep of that heavy door and swept him back across the torpedo room to smash heavily against the after bulkhead; for a moment he half-stood there, pinned by the power of that huge jet, then slid down limply to the deck.

'Blow all main ballast!' Hansen shouted into the microphone. He was hanging on to a rear torpedo door to keep from being carried away and even above the thunderous roar of the waters his voice carried clearly. 'Emergency. Blow all main ballast. Number four tube open to the sea. Blow all main ballast!' He released his grip, staggered across the deck trying to keep his balance in the madly swirling already foot-deep waters. 'Get out of here, for God's sake.'

He should have saved his energy and breath. I was already on my way out of there. I had Mills under the arms and was trying to drag him over the high sill of the for'ard collision bulkhead and I was making just no headway at all. The proper trim of a submarine is a delicate thing at the best of times and even after these few seconds the nose of the *Dolphin*, heavy with the tons of water that had already poured in, was beginning to cant sharply downwards: trying to drag Mills and at the same time keep my balance on that sloping deck with knee-high water boiling around me was more than I could do; but suddenly Hansen had Mills by the feet and I stumbled off-balance, tripped over the high sill and fell backwards into the confined space between the two collision bulkheads, dragging Mills after me.

Hansen was still on the other side of the bulkhead. I could hear him cursing steadily, monotonously and as if he meant it as he struggled to unhook the heavy door from its standing catch. Because of the steep downward pitch of the *Dolphin*'s deck he had to lean all his weight against the massive steel door to free the catch, and with his insecure footing among the swirling waters on that sloping slippery deck he was obviously having the devil's own time trying to release it. I let Mills lie, jumped over the sill, flung my shoulder against the door and with the suddenly added pressure the latch clicked free. The heavy door at once swung half-shut, carrying us along with it and knocking us both off our feet into the battering-ram path of that torrent still gushing from number 4 tube. Coughing and spluttering we scrambled upright again, crossed the sill and, hanging on to a clip handle apiece, tried to drag the door shut.

Twice we tried and twice we failed. The water boiled in through the tube and its level was now almost lipping the top of the sill. With every second that passed the downward angle of the *Dolphin* increased and with every extra degree of steepness the task of pulling that door uphill against the steadily increasing gravity became more and more difficult.

The water began to spill over the sill on to our feet.

Hansen grinned at me. At least, I thought for a moment he was grinning, but the white teeth were clamped tightly together and there was no amusement at all in his eyes. He shouted above the roar of the water: 'It's now or never.'

A well-taken point. It was indeed now or never. At a signal from Hansen we flung our combined weights on to those clip-handles each with one hand to a clip while the other braced against the bulkhead to give maximum purchase. We got the door to within four inches. It swung open. We tried again. Still four inches and I knew that all our strength had gone into that one.

'Can you hold it for a moment?' I shouted.

He nodded. I shifted both hands to the lower corner clip, dropped to the deck, braced my feet against the sill and straightened both legs in one convulsive jerk. The door crashed shut, Hansen jammed his clip home, I did the same with mine and we were safe. For the moment we were safe.

I left Hansen to secure the remaining clips and started knocking the clips off the after collision bulkhead door. I'd only got as far as the first one when the others started falling off by themselves. Petty Officer Bowen and his men, on the other side of that door, needed no telling that we wanted out of there just as fast as possible. The door was pulled open and my ear drums popped with the abrupt fall in air pressure. I could hear the steady echoing roar of air blasting into the ballast tanks under high pressure. I hoisted Mills by the shoulders, strong competent hands lifted him out and over the sill and a couple of seconds later Hansen and I were beside him.

'In God's name!' Petty Officer Bowen said to Hansen. 'What's gone wrong?'

'Number four tube open to the sea.'

'Jesus!'

'Clip up that door,' Hansen ordered. 'But good.' He left at a dead run, clawing his way up the sharply sloping deck of the torpedo storage room. I took a look at Lieutenant Mills – one short look was all I needed – and followed after Hansen. Only I didn't run. Running wasn't going to help anybody now.

The roar of compressed air filled the ship, the ballast tanks were rapidly emptying, but still the *Dolphin* continued on its deadly dive, arrowing down for the dark depths of the Arctic: not even the massive compressed-air banks of the submarine could hope to cope so soon with the effects of the scores of tons of sea-water that had already flooded into the for'ard torpedo room: I wondered bleakly if they would ever be able to cope at all. As I walked along the wardroom passage, using the hand-rail to haul myself up that crazily canted deck, I could feel the entire submarine shudder beneath my feet. No doubt about what that was, Swanson had the great turbines turning over at maximum revolutions, the big bronze propellers threshing madly in reverse, trying to bite deep into the water to slow up the diving submarine.

You can smell fear. You can smell it and you can see it and I could do both as I hauled my way into the control centre of the *Dolphin* that morning. Not one man as much as flickered an eye in my direction as I passed by the sonar room. They had no eyes for me. They had no eyes for anybody: tense, strained, immobile, with hunted faces, they had eyes for one thing only – the plummetting needle on the depth gauge.

The needle was passing the six-hundred-feet mark. Six hundred feet. No conventional submarine I'd ever been on could have operated at this depth. Could have survived at this depth. Six hundred and fifty. I thought of the fantastic outside pressure that represented and I felt far from happy. Someone else was feeling far from happy also, the young seaman manning the inboard diving seat. His fists were clenched till the knuckles showed, a muscle was jumping in his cheek, a nerve twitching in his neck and he had the look on his face of a man who sees the bony finger of death beckoning.

Seven hundred feet. Seven hundred and fifty. Eight hundred. I'd never heard of a submarine that had reached that depth and lived. Neither, apparently, had Commander Swanson.

'We have just set up a new mark, men,' he said. His voice was calm and relaxed and although he was far too intelligent a man not to be afraid, no trace of it showed in tone or manner. 'Lowest recorded dive ever, as far as I am aware. Speed of descent?'

'No change.'

'It will change soon. The torpedo room must be about full now – apart from the pocket of air compressed under high pressure.' He gazed at the dial and tapped his teeth thoughtfully with a thumb-nail – this, for Swanson, was probably the equivalent of going into hysterics. 'Blow the diesel tanks: blow the fresh-water tanks.' Imperturbable though he sounded, Swanson was close to desperation for this was the counsel of despair: thousands of miles from home and supplies, yet jettisoning all the diesel and drinking water, the lack of either of which could make all the difference between life and death. But, at that moment, it didn't matter: all that mattered was lightening ship.

'Main ballast tanks empty,' the diving officer reported. His voice was hoarse and strained.

Swanson nodded, said nothing. The volume of the sound of the compressed air had dropped at least seventy-five per cent and the suddenly comparative silence was sinister, terrifying, as if it meant that the *Dolphin* was giving up the fight. Now we had only the slender reserves of the fresh water and diesel to save us: at the rate at which the *Dolphin* was still diving I didn't see how it could.

Hansen was standing beside me. I noticed blood dripping from his left hand to the deck and when I looked more closely I could see that two of his fingers were broken. It must have happened in the torpedo room. At the moment, it didn't seem important. It certainly didn't seem important to Hansen. He was entirely oblivious of it.

The pressure gauge fell farther and still farther. I knew now that nothing could save the *Dolphin*. A bell rang. Swanson swung down a microphone and pressed a button.

'Engine-room here,' a metallic voice came through. 'We must slow down. Main bearings beginning to smoke, she'll seize up any moment.'

'Maintain revolutions.' Swanson swung back the microphone. The youngster at the diving console, the one with the jumping cheek muscles and the nervous twitch, started to mumble, 'Oh, dear God, oh, dear God,' over and over again, softly at first, then the voice climbing up the scale to hysteria. Swanson moved two paces, touched him on the shoulder. 'Do you mind, laddie? I can hardly hear myself think.' The mumblings stopped and the boy sat quite still, his face carved from grey granite, the nerve in his neck going like a trip-hammer.

'How much more of this will she take?' I asked casually. At least, I meant it to sound casual but it came out like the croak of an asthmatic bullfrog.

'I'm afraid we're moving into the realms of the unknown,' Swanson admitted calmly. 'One thousand feet plus. If that dial is right, we passed the theoretical implosion point – where the hull should have collapsed – fifty feet ago. At the present moment she's being subjected to well over a million tons of pressure.' Swanson's repose, his glacial calm, was staggering, they must have scoured the whole of America to find a man like that. If ever there was the right man in the right place at the right time it was Commander Swanson in the control room of a runaway submarine diving to depths hundreds of feet below what any submarine had ever experienced before.

'She's slowing,' Hansen whispered.

'She's slowing,' Swanson nodded.

She wasn't slowing half fast enough for me. It was impossible that the pressure hull could hold out any longer. I wondered vaguely what the end would be like, then put the thought from my mind, I would never know anything about it, anyway. At that depth the pressure must have been about twenty tons to the square foot, we'd have been squashed as flat as flounders before our senses could even begin to record what was happening to us.

The engine-room call-up bell rang again. The voice this time was imploring, desperate. 'We must ease up, Captain. Switch gear is turning red hot. We can see it glowing.'

'Wait till it's white hot, then you can complain about it,' Swanson said curtly. If the engines were going to break down they were going to break down; but until they did he'd tear the life out of them in an attempt to save the *Dolphin*. Another bell rang.

'Control room?' The voice was harsh, high-pitched. 'Crew's mess deck here. Water is beginning to come in.' For the first time, every eye in the control room turned away from the depth gauge and fixed itself on that loudspeaker. The hull was giving at last under the fantastic pressure, the crushing weight. One little hole, one tiny threadlike crack as a starting point and the pressure hull would rip and tear and flatten like a toy under a steam-hammer. A quick glance at the strained, shocked faces showed this same thought in every mind.

'Where?' Swanson demanded.

'Starboard bulkhead.'

'How much?'

'A pint or two, just trickling down the bulkhead. And it's getting worse. It's getting worse all the time. For God's sake, Captain, what are we going to do?'

'What are you going to do?' Swanson echoed. 'Mop the damn' stuff up, of course. You don't want to live in a dirty ship, do you?' He hung up.

'She's stopped. She's stopped.' Four words and a prayer. I'd been wrong about every eye being on the loudspeaker, one pair of eyes had never left the depth gauge, the pair belonging to the youngster at the console.

'She's stopped,' the diving officer confirmed. His voice had a shake in it.

No one spoke. The blood continued to drip unheeded from Hansen's crushed fingers. I thought that I detected, for the first time, a faint sheen of sweat on Swanson's brow, but I couldn't be sure. The deck still shuddered beneath our feet as the giant engines strove to lift the *Dolphin* out of those deadly depths, the compressed air still hissed into the diesel and fresh-water tanks. I could no longer see the depth gauge, the diving officer had drawn himself up so close to it that he obscured most of it from me.

Ninety seconds passed, ninety seconds that didn't seem any longer than a leap year, ninety interminable seconds while we waited for the sea to burst into our hull and take us for its own, then the diving officer said: 'Ten feet. *Up*'

'Are you sure?' Swanson asked.

'A year's pay.'

'We're not out of the wood yet,' Swanson said mildly. 'The hull can still go – it should have gone a damn' long time ago. Another hundred feet – that means a couple of tons less pressure to the square foot – and I think we'll have a chance. At least a fifty-fifty chance. And after that the chances will improve with every foot we ascend; and as we ascend the highly compressed air in the torpedo room will expand, driving out water and so lightening ship.'

'Still rising,' the diving officer said. 'Still rising. Speed of ascent changed.'

Swanson walked across to the diving stand and studied the slow movement of the depth gauge dial. 'How much fresh water left?'

'Thirty per cent.'

'Secure blowing fresh-water ballast. Engines all back two-thirds.'

The roar of compressed air fell away and the deck vibration eased almost to nothing as the engine revolutions fell from emergency power to two-third full speed.

'Speed of ascent unchanged,' the diving officer reported. 'One hundred feet up.'

'Secure blowing diesel.' The roar of compressed air stopped completely. 'All back one-third.'

'Still rising. Still rising.'

Swanson took a silk handkerchief from his pocket and wiped his face and neck. 'I was a little worried there,' he said to no one in particular, 'and I don't much care who knows it.' He reached for a microphone and I could hear his voice booming faintly throughout the ship.

'Captain here. All right, you can all start breathing again. Everything is under control, we're on our way up. As a point of interest we're still over three hundred feet deeper than the lowest previous submarine dive ever recorded.'

I felt as if I had just been through the rollers of a giant mangle. We all looked as if we'd just been through the rollers of a giant mangle. A voice said: 'I've never smoked in my life, but I'm starting now. Someone give me a cigarette.' Hansen said: 'When we get back to the States do you know what I'm going to do?'

'Yes,' Swanson said. 'You're going to scrape together your last cent, go up to Groton and throw the biggest, the most expensive party ever for the men who built this boat. You're too late, Lieutenant, I thought of it first.' He checked abruptly and said sharply: 'What's happened to your hand?'

Hansen lifted his left hand and stared at it in surprise. 'I never even knew I'd been scratched. Must have happened with that damn' door in the torpedo room. There's a medical supply box there, Doc. Would you fix this.'

'You did a damn' fine job there, John,' Swanson said warmly. 'Getting that door closed, I mean. Couldn't have been easy.'

'It wasn't. All pats on the back to our friend here,' Hansen said. 'He got it closed, not me. And if we hadn't got it closed—'

'Or if I'd let you load the torpedoes when you came back last night,' Swanson said grimly. 'When we were sitting on the surface and the hatches wide open. We'd have been eight thousand feet down now and very, very dead.'

Hansen suddenly snatched his hand away. 'My God!' he said remorsefully. 'I'd forgotten. Never mind this damned hand of mine. George Mills, the torpedo officer. He caught a pretty bad smack. You'd better see him first. Or Doc Benson.'

I took his hand back. 'No hurry for either of us. Your fingers first. Mills isn't feeling a thing.'

'Good lord!' Astonishment showed in Hansen's face, maybe shock at my callousness. 'When he recovers consciousness—'

'He'll never recover consciousness again,' I said. 'Lieutenant Mills is dead.'

'What!' Swanson's fingers bit deeply, painfully into my arm. ' "Dead," did you say?'

'That column of water from number four tube came in like an express train,' I said tiredly. 'Flung him right back against the after bulkhead and smashed in the occiput – the back of his head – like an eggshell. Death must have been instantaneous.'

'Young George Mills,' Swanson whispered. His face had gone very pale. 'Poor young beggar. His first trip on the *Dolphin*. And now – just like that. Killed.'

'Murdered,' I said.

'What!' If Commander Swanson didn't watch out with his fingers he'd have my upper arm all black and blue. 'What was that you said?'

' "Murdered," I said. "Murdered," I meant.'

Swanson stared at me for a long moment, his face empty of expression, but the eyes strained and tired and suddenly somehow old. He wheeled, walked across to the diving officer, spoke a few words to him and returned. 'Come on,' he said abruptly. 'You can fix up the lieutenant's hand in my cabin.'

Chapter Seven

'You realize the seriousness of what you are saying?' Swanson asked. 'You are making a grave accusation—'

'Come off it,' I said rudely. 'This is not a court of law and I'm not accusing anyone. All I say is that murder has been done. Whoever left that bow-cap door open is directly responsible for the death of Lieutenant Mills.'

'What do you mean "left the door open"? Who says anyone left the door open? It could have been due to natural causes. And even if – I can't see it – that door had been left open, you can't accuse a man of murder because of carelessness or forgetfulness or because—'

'Commander Swanson,' I said. 'I'll go on record as saying that you are probably the best naval officer I have ever met. But being best at that doesn't mean that you're best at everything. There are noticeable gaps in your education, Commander, especially in the appreciation of the finer points of skulduggery. You require an especially low and devious type of mind for that and I'm afraid that you just haven't got it. Doors left open by natural causes, you say. What natural causes?'

'We've hit the ice a few hefty smacks,' Swanson said slowly. 'That could have jarred it open. Or when we poked through the ice last night a piece of ice, a stalactite, say, could have—'

'Your tubes are recessed, aren't they. Mighty oddly-shaped stalactite that would go down then bend in at a right angle to reach the door – and even then it would only shut it more tightly.'

'The doors are tested every time we're in harbour,' Commander Swanson persisted quietly. 'They're also opened when we open tubes to carry out surface trimming tests in dock. Any dockyard has pieces of waste, rope and other rubbish floating around that could easily have jammed a door open.'

'The safety lights showed the doors shut.'

'They could have been opened just a crack, not enough to disengage the safety contact.'

'Open a crack! Why do you think Mills is dead? If you've ever seen the jet of water that hits the turbine blades in a hydro-electric plant, then you'll know how that water came in. A crack? My God! How are those doors operated?'

'Two ways. Remote control, hydraulic, just press a button: then there are manually-operated levers in the torpedo room itself.'

I turned to Hansen. He was sitting on the bunk beside me, his face pale as I splinted his broken fingers. I said: 'Those hand-operated levers. Were they in the shut position?'

'You heard me say so in there. Of course they were. First thing we always check.'

'Somebody doesn't like you,' I said to Swanson. 'Or somebody doesn't like the *Dolphin*. Or somebody knew that the *Dolphin* was going searching for the Zebra survivors and they didn't like that either. So they sabotaged the ship. You will remember you were rather surprised you didn't have to correct the *Dolphin*'s trim? It had been your intention to carry out a slow-time dive to check the underwater trim because you thought that would have been affected by the fact that you had no torpedoes in the for'ard tubes. But surprise, surprise. She didn't need any correction.'

'I'm listening,' Swanson said quietly. He was with me now. He was with me all the way. He cocked an eyebrow as we heard water flooding back into the tanks. The repeater gauge showed 200 feet, Swanson must have ordered his diving officer to level off at that depth. The *Dolphin* was still canted nose downwards at an angle of about 25°.

'She didn't need any correcting because some of her tubes were already full of water. For all I know maybe number three tube, the one we tested and found OK is the only one that is *not* full of water. Our clever little pal left the doors open, disconnected the hand-operated levers so that they appeared to be in the shut position when they were actually open and crossed over a few wires in a junction box so that the open position showed green while the closed showed red. A man who knew what he was about could have done it in a few minutes. Two men who knew what they were about could have done it in no time at all. I'll lay anything you like that when you're eventually in a position to check you'll find the levers disconnected, the wires crossed and the inlets of the test-cocks blocked with sealing-wax, quick-drying paint or even chewing-gum so that when the test-cocks were opened nothing would show and you would assume the tubes to be empty.'

'There was a trickle from the test-cock in number four tube,' Hansen objected.

'Low-grade chewing-gum.'

'The murderous swine,' Swanson said calmly. His restraint was far more effective than the most thunderous denunciations could ever have been. 'He could have murdered us all. But for the grace of God and the Groton boatyard shipwrights he would have murdered us all.'

'He didn't mean to,' I said. 'He didn't mean to kill anyone. You had intended to carry out a slow-time dive to check trim in the Holy Loch before you left that evening. You told me so yourself. Did you announce it to the crew, post it up in daily orders or something like that?'

'Both.'

'So. Our pal knew. He also knew that you carried out those checks when the boat is still awash or just under the surface. When you checked the tubes to see if they were OK, water would come in, too much water to permit the rear doors to be shut again, but not under such high pressure that you wouldn't have time and to spare to close the for'ard collision bulkhead door and make a leisurely retreat in good order. What would have happened? Not much. At the worst you would have settled down slowly to the bottom and stayed there. Not deep enough to worry the *Dolphin*. In a submarine of even ten years ago it might have been fatal for all, because of the limited air supply. Not to-day when your air purifying machines can let you stay down for months at a time. You just float up your emergency indicator buoy and telephone, tell your story, sit around and drink coffee till a naval diver comes down and replaces the bow cap, pump out the torpedo room and surface again. Our unknown pal – or pals – didn't mean to kill anyone. But they did mean to delay you. And they would have delayed you. We know now that you could have got to the surface under your own steam, but even so your top brass would have insisted that you go into dock for a day or two to check that everything was OK.'

'Why should anyone want to delay us?' Swanson asked. I though he had an unnecessarily speculative look in his eyes, but it was hard to be sure, Commander Swanson's face showed exactly what Commander Swanson wanted it to show and no more.

'My God, do you think I know the answer to that one?' I said irritably.

'No. No, I don't think so.' He could have been more emphatic about it. 'Tell me, Dr Carpenter, do you suspect some member of the *Dolphin*'s crew to be responsible?'

'Do you really need an answer to that one?'

'I supppose not,' he sighed. 'Going to the bottom of the Arctic Ocean is not a very attractive way of committing suicide, and if any member of the crew had jinxed things he'd damn' soon have unjinxed them as soon as he realized that we weren't going to carry out trim checks in shallow water. Which leaves only the civilian dockyard workers in Scotland – and every one of them has been checked and rechecked and given a top-grade security clearance.'

'Which means nothing. There are plushy Moscow hotels and British and American prisons full of people who had top-grade security clearances . . . What are you going to do now, Commander. About the *Dolphin*, I mean?'

'I've been thinking about it. In the normal course of events the thing to do would be to close the bow-cap of number four and pump out the torpedo room, then go in and close the rear door of number four. But the bow-cap door won't close. Within a second of John's telling us that number four was open to the sea the diving officer hit the hydraulic button – the one that closes it by remote control. You saw for yourself that nothing happened. It must be jammed.'

'You bet your life it's jammed,' I said grimly. 'A sledgehammer might do some good but pressing buttons won't.'

'I could go back to that lead we've just left, surface again and send a diver under the ice to investigate and see what he can do, but I'm not going to ask any man to risk his life doing that. I could retreat to the open sea, surface and fix it there, but not only would it be a damned slow and uncomfortable trip with the *Dolphin* canted at this angle, it might take us days before we got back here again. And some of the Drift Station Zebra men are pretty far through. It might be too late.'

'Well, then,' I said. 'You have the man to hand, Commander. I told you when I first met you that environmental health studies were my speciality, especially in the field of pressure extremes when escaping from submarines. I've done an awful lot of simulated sub escapes, Commander. I do know a fair amount about pressures, how to cope with them and how I react to them myself.'

'How do you react to them, Dr Carpenter?'

'A high tolerance. They don't worry me much.'

'What do you have in mind?'

'You know damn' well what I have in mind,' I said impatiently. 'Drill a hole in the door of the after collision bulkhead, screw in a high-pressure hose, open the door, shove someone in the narrow space between the two collision bulkheads and turn up the hose until the pressure between the collision bulkheads equals that in the torpedo room. You have the clips eased off the for'ard collision door. When the pressures are equalized it opens at a touch, you walk inside, close number four rear door and walk away again. That's what you had in mind wasn't it?'

'More or less,' he admitted. 'Except that *you* are no part of it. Every man on this ship has made simulated escapes. They all know the effects of pressure. And most of them are a great deal younger than you.'

'Suit yourself,' I said. 'But age has little to do with the ability to stand stresses. You didn't pick a teen-ager as the first American to orbit the earth, did you? As for simulated escapes, making a free ascent up a hundred-foot tank is a different matter altogether from going inside an iron box, waiting for the slow build-up of pressure, working under that pressure, then waiting for the slow process of decompression. I've seen young men, big, tough, very, very fit young men break up completely under those circumstances and almost go crazy trying to get out. The combination of physiological and psychological factors involved is pretty fierce.'

'I think,' Swanson said slowly, 'that I'd sooner have you – what do the English say, batting on a sticky wicket – than almost any man I know. But there's a point you've overlooked. What would the Admiral Commanding Atlantic Submarines say to me if he knew I'd let a civilian go instead of one of my own men?'

'If you *don't* let me go, I know what he'll say. He'll say: "We must reduce Commander Swanson to lieutenant, j-g., because he had on board the *Dolphin* an acknowledged expert in this speciality and refused, out of stiff-necked pride, to use him, thereby endangering the lives of his crew and the safety of his ship."'

Swanson smiled a pretty bleak smile, but with the desperately narrow escape we had just had, the predicament we were still in and the fact that his torpedo officer was lying dead not so many feet away, I hardly expected him to break into gales of laughter. He looked at Hansen: 'What do you say, John?'

'I've seen more incompetent characters than Dr Carpenter,' Hansen said. 'Also, he gets about as nervous and panic-stricken as a bag of Portland cement.'

'He has qualifications you do not look to find in the average medical man,' Swanson agreed. 'I shall be glad to accept your offer. One of my men will go with you. That way the dictates of common sense and honour are both satisfied.'

It wasn't all that pleasant, not by quite a way, but it wasn't all that terribly bad either. It went off exactly as it could have been predicted it would go off. Swanson cautiously eased the *Dolphin* up until her stern was just a few feet beneath the ice: this reduced the pressure in the torpedo room to a minimum, but even at that the bows were still about a hundred feet down.

A hole was drilled in the after collision bulkhead door and an armoured high-pressure hose screwed into position. Dressed in porous rubber suits and equipped with an aqualung apiece, a young torpedoman by the name of Murphy and I went inside and stood in the gap between the two collision bulkheads. High-powered air hissed into the confined space. Slowly the pressure rose: twenty, thirty, forty, fifty pounds to the square inch. I could feel the pressure on lungs and ears, the pain behind the eyes, the slight wooziness that comes from the poisonous effect of breathing pure oxygen under such pressure. But I was used to it, I knew it wasn't going to kill me: I wondered if young Murphy knew that. This was the stage where the combined physical and mental effects became too much for most people, but if Murphy was scared or panicky or suffering from bodily distress he hid it well. Swanson would have picked his best man and to be the best man in a company like that Murphy had to be something very special.

We eased off the clips on the for'ard bulkhead door, knocked them off cautiously as the pressures equalized. The water in the torpedo room was about two feet above the level of the sill and as the door came ajar the water boiled whitely through into the collision space while compressed air hissed out from behind us to equalize the lowering pressure of the air in the torpedo room. For about ten seconds we had to hang on grimly to hold the door and maintain our balance while water and air fought and jostled in a seething maelstrom to find their own natural levels. The door opened wide. The water level now extended from about thirty inches up on the collision bulkhead to the for'ard deckhead of the torpedo room. We crossed the sill, switched on our waterproof torches and ducked under.

The temperature of that water was about 28° F. – four below freezing. Those porous rubber suits were specially designed to cope with icy waters but even so I gasped with the shock of it – as well as one can gasp when breathing pure oxygen under heavy pressure. But we didn't linger, for the longer we remained there the longer we would have to spend decompressing afterwards. We half-walked, half-swum towards the fore end of the compartment, located the rear door on number 4 tube and closed it, but not before I had a quick look at the inside of the pressure cock. The door itself seemed undamaged: the body of the unfortunate Lieutenant Mills had absorbed its swinging impact and prevented it from being wrenched off its hinges. It didn't seem distorted in any way, and fitted snugly into place. We forced its retaining lever back into place and left.

Back in the collision compartment we gave the prearranged taps on the door. Almost at once we heard the subdued hum of a motor as the high-speed extraction pumps in the torpedo room got to work, forcing the water out through the hull. Slowly the water level dropped and as it dropped the air pressure as slowly decreased. Degree by degree the *Dolphin* began to come back on even keel. When the water was finally below the level of the for'ard sill we gave another signal and the remaining over-pressure air was slowly bled out through the hose.

A few minutes later, as I was stripping off the rubber suit, Swanson asked: 'Any trouble?'

'None. You picked a good man in Murphy.'

'The best. Many thanks, Doctor.' He lowered his voice. 'You wouldn't by any chance—'

'You know damned well I would,' I said. 'I did. Not sealing-wax, not chewing-gum, not paint. Glue, Commander Swanson. That's how they blocked the test-cock inlet. The old-fashioned animal hide stuff that comes out of a tube. Ideal for the job.'

'I see,' he said, and walked away.

The *Dolphin* shuddered along its entire length as the torpedo hissed out of its tube – number 3 tube, the only one in the submarine Swanson could safely rely upon.

'Count it down,' Swanson said to Hansen. 'Tell me when we should hit, tell me when we should hear it hit.'

Hansen looked at the stop-watch in his bandaged hand and nodded. The seconds passed slowly. I could see Hansen's lips move silently. Then he said: 'We should be hitting – now,' and two or three seconds later: 'We should be hearing – now.'

Whoever had been responsible for the settings and time calculations on that torpedo had known what he was about. Just on Hansen's second 'now' we felt as much as heard the clanging vibration along the *Dolphin*'s hull as the shock-waves from the exploding war-head reached us. The deck shook briefly beneath our feet but the impact was nowhere nearly as powerful as I had expected. I was relieved. I didn't have to be a clairvoyant to know that everyone was relieved. No submarine had ever before been in the vicinity of a torpedo detonating under the ice-pack: no one had known to what extent the tamping effect of overhead ice might have increased the pressure and destructive effect of the lateral shock-waves.

'Nicely,' Swanson murmured. 'Very nicely done indeed. Both ahead one-third. I hope that bang had considerably more effect on the ice than it had on our ship.' He said to Benson at the ice-machine: 'Let us know as soon as we reach the lead, will you?'

He moved to the plotting table. Raeburn looked up and said: 'Five hundred yards gone, five hundred to go.'

'All stop,' Swanson said. The slight vibration of the engine died away. 'We'll just mosey along very carefully indeed. That explosion may have sent blocks of ice weighing a few tons apiece pretty far down into the sea. I don't want to be doing any speed at all if we meet any of them on the way up.'

'Three hundred yards to go,' Raeburn said.

'All clear. All clear all round,' the sonar room reported.

'Still thick ice,' Benson intoned. 'Ah! That's it. We're under the lead. Thin ice. Well, five or six feet.'

'Two hundred yards,' Raeburn said. 'It checks.'

We drifted slowly onwards. At Swanson's orders the propellers kicked over once or twice then stopped again.

'Fifty yards,' Raeburn said. 'Near enough.'

'Ice reading?'

'No change? Five feet, about.'

'Speed?'

'One knot.'

'Position?'

'One thousand yards exactly. Passing directly under target area.'

'And nothing on the ice-machine. Nothing at all?'

'Not a thing.' Benson shrugged and looked at Swanson. The captain walked across and watched the inked stylus draw its swiftly etched vertical lines on the paper.

'Peculiar, to say the least of it,' Swanson murmured. 'Seven hundred pounds of very high-grade amatol in that lot. Must be uncommonly tough ice in those parts. Again to say the least of it. We'll go up to ninety feet and make a few passes under the area. Floodlights on, TV on.'

So we went up to ninety feet and made a few passes and nothing came of it. The water was completely opaque, the floods and camera useless. The ice-machine stubbornly registered four to six feet – it was impossible to be more accurate – all the time.

'Well, that seems to be it,' Hansen said. 'We back off and have another go?'

'Well, I don't know,' Swanson said pensively. 'What say we just try to shoulder our way up?'

'Shoulder our way up?' Hansen wasn't with him: neither was I. 'What kind of shoulder is going to heave five feet of ice to one side?'

'I'm not sure. The thing is, we've been working from unproved assumptions and that's always a dangerous basis. We've been assuming that if the torpedo didn't blow the ice to smithereens it would at least blow a hole in it. Maybe it doesn't happen that way at all. Maybe there's just a big upward pressure of water distributed over a fair area that heaves the ice up and breaks it into pretty big chunks that just settle back into the water again in their original position in the pattern of a dried-up mud hole with tiny cracks all round the isolated sections. But with cracks all round. Narrow cracks, but there. Cracks so narrow that the ice-machine couldn't begin to register them even at the slow speed we were doing.' He turned to Raeburn. 'What's our position?'

'Still in the centre of the target area, sir.'

'Take her up till we touch the ice,' Swanson said.

He didn't have to add any cautions about gentleness. The diving officer took her up like floating thistledown until we felt a gentle bump.

'Hold her there,' Swanson said. He peered at the TV screen but the water was so opaque that all definition vanished half-way up the sail. He nodded to the diving officer. 'Kick her up – hard.'

Compressed air roared into the ballast tanks. Seconds passed without anything happening then all at once the *Dolphin* shuddered as something very heavy and very solid seemed to strike the hull. A moment's pause, another solid shock then we could see the edge of a giant segment of ice sliding down the face of the TV screen.

'Well, now, I believe I might have had a point there,' Swanson remarked. 'We seem to have hit a crack between two chunks of ice almost exactly in the middle. Depth?'

'Forty-five.'

'Fifteen feet showing. And I don't think we can expect to lift the hundreds of tons of ice lying over the rest of the hull. Plenty of positive buoyancy?'

'All we'll ever want.'

'Then we'll call it a day at that. Right, Quartermaster, away you go up top and tell us what the weather is like.'

I didn't wait to hear what the weather was like. I was interested enough it in, but I was even more interested in ensuring that Hansen didn't come along to his cabin in time to find me putting on the Mannlicher-Schoenauer along with my furs. But this time I stuck it not in its special holster but in the outside pocket of my caribou trousers. I thought it might come in handier there.

It was exactly noon when I clambered over the edge of the bridge and used a dangling rope to slide down a great rafted chunk of ice that slanted up almost to the top of the sail. The sky had about as much light in it as a late twilight in winter when the sky is heavy with grey cloud. The air was as bitter as ever, but the weather had improved for all that. The wind was down now, backed round to the north-east, seldom gusting at more than twenty m.p.h., the ice-spicules rising no more than two or three feet above the ice-cap. Nothing to tear your eyes out. To be able to see where you were going on that damned ice-cap made a very pleasant change.

There were eleven of us altogether – Commander Swanson himself, Dr Benson, eight enlisted men and myself. Four of the men were carrying stretchers with them.

Even seven hundred pounds of the highest grade conventional explosive on the market hadn't managed to do very much damage to the ice in that lead. Over an area of seventy yards square or thereabouts the ice had fractured into large fragments curiously uniform in size and roughly hexagonal in shape but fallen back so neatly into position that you couldn't have put a hand down most of the cracks between the adjacent fragments of ice: many of the cracks, indeed, were already beginning to bind together. A poor enough performance for a torpedo war-head – until you remembered that though most of its disruptive power must have been directed downwards it had still managed to lift and fracture a chunk of ice-cap weighing maybe 5,000 tons. Looked at in that way, it didn't seem such a puny effort after all. Maybe we'd been pretty lucky to achieve what we had.

We walked across to the eastern edge of the lead, scrambled up on to the ice-pack proper and turned round to get our bearings, to line up on the unwavering white finger of the searchlight that reached straight up into the gloom of the sky. No chance of getting lost this time. While the wind stayed quiet and the spicules stayed down you could see that lamp in the window ten miles away.

We didn't even need to take any bearings. A few steps away and up from the edge of the lead and we could see it at once. Drift Station Zebra. Three huts, one of them badly charred, five blackened skeletons of what had once been huts. Desolation.

'So that's it,' Swanson said in my ear. 'Or what's left of it. I've come a long way to see this.'

'You nearly went a damned sight longer and never saw it,' I said. 'To the floor of the Arctic, I mean. Pretty, isn't it?'

Swanson shook his head slowly, moved on. There were only a hundred yards to go. I led the way to the nearest intact hut, opened the door and passed inside.

The hut was about thirty degrees warmer than the last time I had been there, but still bitterly cold. Only Zabrinski and Rawlings were awake. The hut smelt of burnt fuel, disinfectant, iodine, morphine and a peculiar aroma arising from a particularly repulsive looking hash that Rawlings was industriously churning around in a dixie over the low stove.

'Ah, there you are,' Rawlings said conversationally. He might have been hailing a neighbour who'd phoned a minute previously to see if he could come across to borrow the lawnmower rather than greeting men he'd been fairly certain he'd never see again. 'The time is perfect – just about to ring the dinner bell, Captain. Care for some Maryland chicken – I think.'

'Not just at the moment, thank you,' Swanson said politely. 'Sorry about the ankle, Zabrinski. How is it?'

'Just fine, Captain, just fine. In a plaster cast.' He thrust out a foot, stiffly.

'The Doc here – Dr Jolly – fixed me up real nice. Had much trouble last night?' This was for me.

'Dr Carpenter had a great deal of trouble last night,' Swanson said. 'And we've had a considerable amount since. But later. Bring that stretcher in here. You first, Zabrinski. As for you, Rawlings, you can stop making like Escoffier. The *Dolphin*'s less than a couple of hundred yards from here. We'll have you all aboard in half an hour.'

I heard a shuffling noise behind me. Dr Jolly was on his feet, helping Captain Folsom to his. Folsom looked even weaker than he had done yesterday: his face, bandaged though it was, certainly looked worse.

'Captain Folsom,' I introduced him. 'Dr Jolly. This is Commander Swanson, captain of the *Dolphin*. Dr Benson.'

'*Doctor* Benson, you said, old boy?' Jolly lifted an eyebrow. 'My word, the pill-rolling competition's getting a little fierce in these parts. And Commander. By jove, but we're glad to see you fellows.' The combination of the rich Irish brogue and the English slang of the twenties fell more oddly than ever on my ear, he reminded me of educated Singhalese I'd met with their precise, lilting, standard southern English interlarded with the catch-phrases of forty years ago. Topping, old bean, simply too ripping for words.

'I can understand that,' Swanson smiled. He looked around the huddled unmoving men on the floor, men who might have been living or dead but for the immediate and smoky condensation from their shallow breathing, and his smile faded. He said to Captain Folsom: 'I cannot tell you how sorry I am. This has been a dreadful thing.'

Folsom stirred and said something but we couldn't make out what it was. Although his shockingly burnt face had been bandaged since I'd seen him last it didn't seem to have done him any good: he was talking inside his mouth all right but the ravaged cheek and mouth had become so paralysed that his speech didn't emerge as any recognizable language. The good side of his face, the left, was twisted and furrowed and the eye above almost completely shut. This had nothing to do with any sympathetic neuro-muscular reaction caused by the wickedly charred right cheek. The man was in agony. I said to Jolly: 'No morphine left?' I'd left him, I'd thought, with more than enough of it.

'Nothing left,' he said tiredly. 'I used the lot. The lot.'

'Dr Jolly worked all through the night,' Zabrinski said quietly. 'Eight hours. Rawlings and himself and Kinnaird. They never stopped once.'

Benson had his medical kit open. Jolly saw it and smiled, a smile of relief, a smile of exhaustion. He was in far worse case than he'd been the previous evening. He hadn't had all that much in him when he'd started. But he'd worked. He'd worked a solid eight hours. He'd even fixed up Zabrinski's ankle. A good doctor. Conscientious, Hippocratic, anyway. He was entitled to relax. Now that there were other doctors here, he'd relax. But not before.

He began to ease Folsom into a sitting position and I helped him. He slid down himself, his back to the wall. 'Sorry, and all that, you know,' he said. His bearded frost-bitten face twisted into the semblance of a grin. 'A poor host.'

'You can leave everything to us now, Dr Jolly,' Swanson said quietly. 'You've got all the help that's going. One thing. All those men fit to be moved?'

'I don't know.' Jolly rubbed an arm across bloodshot, smudged eyes. 'I don't know. One or two of them slipped pretty far back last night. It's the cold. Those two. Pneumonia, I think. Something an injured man could fight off in a few days back home can be fatal here. It's the cold,' he repeated. 'Uses up ninety per cent of his energy not in fighting illness and infection but just generating enough heat to stay alive.'

'Take it easy,' Swanson said. 'Maybe we'd better change our minds about that half-hour to get you all aboard. Who's first for the ambulance, Dr Benson?' Not Dr Carpenter. Dr Benson. Well, Benson was his own ship's doctor. But pointed, all the same. A regrettable coolness, as sudden in its onset as it was marked in degree, had appeared in his attitude towards me, and I didn't have to be beaten over the head with a heavy club to guess at the reason for the abrupt change.

'Zabrinski, Dr Jolly, Captain Folsom and this man here,' Benson said promptly.

'Kinnaird, radio operator,' Kinnaird identified himself. 'We never thought you'd make it, mate.' This to me. He dragged himself somehow to his feet and stood there swaying. 'I can walk.'

'Don't argue,' Swanson said curtly. 'Rawlings stop stirring that filthy mush and get to your feet. Go with them. How long would it take you to run a cable from the boat, fix up a couple of big electric heaters in here, some lights?'

'Alone?'

'All the help you want, man.'

'Fifteen minutes. I could rig a phone, sir.'

'That would be useful. When the stretcher bearers come back bring blankets, sheets, hot water. Wrap the water containers in the blankets. Anything else, Dr Benson?'

'Not now, sir.'

'That's it then. Away you go.'

Rawlings lifted the spoon from the pot, tasted it, smacked his lips in appreciation and shook his head sadly. 'It's a crying shame,' he said mournfully. 'It really is.' He went out in the wake of the stretcher bearers.

Of the eight men left lying on the floor, four were conscious. Hewson the tractor-driver, Naseby the cook, and two others who introduced themselves as Harrington. Twins. They'd even been burnt and frost-bitten in the same places. The other four were either sleeping or in coma. Benson and I started looking them over, Benson much more carefully than myself, very busy with thermometer and stethoscope. Looking for signs of pneumonia. I didn't think he'd have to look very far. Commander Swanson looked speculatively around the cabin, occasionally throwing a very odd look in my direction, occasionally flailing his arms across his chest to keep the circulation going. He had to. He didn't have the fancy furs I had and in spite of the solid-fuel stove the place was like an ice-box.

The first man I looked at was lying on his side in the far right-hand corner of the room. He had half-open eyes, just showing the lower arcs of his pupils, sunken temples, marble-white forehead and the only part of his face that wasn't bandaged was as cold as the marble in a winter graveyard. I said: 'Who is this?'

'Grant. John Grant.' Hewson, the dark quiet tractor-driver answered me. 'Radio operator. Kinnaird's side-kick. How's it with him?'

'He's dead. He's been dead quite some time.'

'Dead?' Swanson said sharply. 'You sure?' I gave him my aloof professional look and said nothing. He went on to Benson: 'Anybody too ill to be moved?'

'Those two here, I think,' Benson said. He wasn't noticing the series of peculiar looks Swanson was letting me have, so he handed me his stethoscope. After a minute I straightened and nodded.

'Third-degree burns,' Benson said to Swanson. 'What we can see of them, that is. Both high temperatures, both very fast, very weak and erratic pulses, both with lung fluids.'

'They'd have a better chance inside the *Dolphin*,' Swanson said.

'You'll kill them getting there,' I said. 'Even if you could wrap them up warmly enough to take them back to the ship, hauling them up to the top of the sail and then lowering them vertically through those hatchways would finish them off.'

'We can't stay out in that lead indefinitely,' Swanson said. 'I'll take the responsibility for moving them.'

'Sorry, Captain.' Benson shook his head gravely. 'I agree with Dr Carpenter.'

Swanson shrugged and said nothing. Moments later the stretcher bearers were back, followed soon after by Rawlings and three other enlisted men carrying cables, heaters, lamps and a telephone. It took only a few minutes to button the heaters and lamps on to the cable. Rawlings cranked the call-up generator of his field-phone and spoke briefly into the mouthpiece. Bright lights came on and the heaters started to crackle and after a few seconds glow.

Hewson, Naseby and the Harrington twins left by stretcher. When they'd gone I unhooked the Coleman lamp. 'You won't be needing this now,' I said. 'I won't be long.'

'Where are you going?' Swanson's voice was quiet.

'I won't be long,' I repeated. 'Just looking around.'

He hesitated, then stood to one side. I went out, moved round a corner of the hut and stopped. I heard the whirr of the call-up bell, a voice on the telephone. It was only a murmur to me, I couldn't make out what was being said. But I'd expected this.

The Coleman storm lantern flickered and faded in the wind, but didn't go out. Stray ice-spicules struck against the glass, but it didn't crack or break, it must have been one of those specially toughened glasses immune to a couple of hundred degrees' temperature range between the inside and the outside.

I made my way diagonally across to the only hut left on the south side. No trace of burning, charring or even smoke-blackening on the outside walls. The fuel store must have been the one next to it, on the same side and to the west, straight downwind: that almost certainly must have been its position to account for the destruction of all the other huts, and the grotesquely buckled shape of its remaining girders made this strong probability a certainty. Here had been the heart of the fire.

Hard against the side of the undamaged hut was a lean-to shed, solidly built. Six feet high, six wide, eight long. The door opened easily. Wooden floor, gleaming aluminium for the sides and ceiling, big black heaters bolted to the inside and outside walls. Wires led from those and it was no job for an Einstein to guess that they led – or had led – to the now destroyed generator house. This lean-to shed would have been warm night and day. The squat low-slung tractor that took up nearly all the floor space inside would have started any time at the touch of a switch. It wouldn't start at the turn of a switch now, it would take three or four blow-torches and the same number of strong men even to turn the engine over once. I closed the door and went into the main hut.

It was packed with metal tables, benches, machinery and every modern device for the automatic recording and interpretation of every conceivable observed detail of the Arctic weather. I didn't know what the functions of most of the instruments were and I didn't care. This was the meteorological office and that was enough for me. I examined the hut carefully but quickly and there didn't seem to be anything odd or out of place that I could see. In one corner, perched on an empty wooden packing case, was a portable radio transmitter with listening phones – transceivers, they called them nowadays. Near it, in a box of heavy oiled wood, were fifteen Nife cells connected up in series. Hanging from a hook on the wall was a two-volt test lamp. I touched its bare leads to the outside terminals of the battery formed by the cells. Had those cells left in them even a fraction of their original power that test lamp should have burnt out in a white flash. It didn't even begin to glow. I tore a piece of flex from a nearby lamp and touched its ends to the terminals. Not even the minutest spark. Kinnaird hadn't been lying when he had said that his battery had been completely dead. But, then, I hadn't for a moment thought he'd been lying.

I made my way to the last hut – the hut that held the charred remnants of the seven men who had died in the fire. The stench of charred flesh and burnt diesel seemed stronger, more nauseating than ever. I stood in the doorway and the last thing I wanted to do was to approach even an inch closer. I peeled off fur and woollen mittens, set the lamp on a table, pulled out my torch and knelt by the first dead man.

Ten minutes passed and all I wanted was out of there. There are some things that doctors, even hardened pathologists, will go a long way to avoid. Bodies that have been too long in the sea is one; bodies that have been in the immediate vicinity of under-water explosion is another; and men who have literally been burned alive is another. I was beginning to feel more than slightly sick; but I wasn't going to leave there until I was finished.

The door creaked open. I turned and watched Commander Swanson come in. He'd been a long time, I'd expected him before then. Lieutenant Hansen, his damaged left hand wrapped in some thick woollen material, came in after him. That was what the phone call had been about, the Commander calling up reinforcements. Swanson switched off his torch, pushed up his snow-goggles and pulled down his mask. His eyes narrowed at the scene before him, his nostrils wrinkled in involuntary disgust, and the colour drained swiftly from his ruddy cheeks. Both Hansen and I had told him what to expect, but he hadn't been prepared for this: not often can the imagination encompass the reality. For a moment I thought he was going to be sick, but then I saw a slight tinge of colour touch the cheekbones and I knew he wasn't.

'Dr Carpenter,' he said in a voice in which the unsteady huskiness seemed only to emphasize the stilted formality, 'I wish you to return at once to the ship where you will remain confined to your quarters. I would prefer you went voluntarily, accompanied by Lieutenant Hansen here. I wish no trouble. I trust you don't either. If you do, we can accommodate you. Rawlings and Murphy are waiting outside that door.'

'Those are fighting words, Commander,' I said, 'and very unfriendly. Rawlings and Murphy are going to get uncommon cold out there.' I put my right hand in my caribou pants pocket – the one with the gun in it – and surveyed him unhurriedly. 'Have you had a brainstorm?'

Swanson looked at Hansen and nodded in the direction of the door. Hansen half-turned, then stopped as I said: 'Very high-handed, aren't we? I'm not worth an explanation, is that it?'

Hansen looked uncomfortable. He didn't like any part of this. I suspected Swanson didn't either, but he was going to do what he had to do and let his feelings look elsewhere.

'Unless you're a great deal less intelligent than I believe – and I credit you with a high intelligence – you know exactly what the explanation is. When you came aboard the *Dolphin* in the Holy Loch both Admiral Garvie and myself were highly suspicious of you. You spun us a story about being an expert in Arctic conditions and of having helped set up this station here. When we wouldn't accept that as sufficient authority or reason to take you along with us you told a highly convincing tale about this being an advanced missile-warning outpost and even although it was peculiar that Admiral Garvie had never heard of it, we accepted it. The huge dish aerial you spoke of, the radar masts, the electronic computers – what's happened to them, Dr Carpenter? A bit insubstantial, weren't they? Like all figments of the imagination.'

I looked at him, considering, and let him go on.

'There never were any of those things, were there? You're up to the neck in something very murky indeed, my friend. What it is I don't know nor, for the moment, do I care. All I care for is the safety of the ship, the welfare of the crew and bringing the Zebra survivors safely back home and I'm taking no chances at all.'

'The wishes of the British Admiralty, the orders from your own Director of Underseas Warfare – those mean nothing to you?'

'I'm beginning to have very strong reservations about the way those orders were obtained,' Swanson said grimly. 'You're altogether too mysterious for my liking, Dr Carpenter – as well as being a fluent liar.'

'Those are harsh, harsh words, Commander.'

'The truth not infrequently sounds that way. Will you please come?'

'Sorry. I'm not through here yet.'

'I see. John, will you—'

'I can give you an explanation. I see I have to. Won't you listen?'

'A third fairy-story?' A headshake. 'No.'

'And I'm not ready to leave. Impasse.'

Swanson looked at Hansen, who turned to go. I said: 'Well, if you're too stiff-necked to listen to me, call up the bloodhounds. Isn't it just luck, now, that we have three fully-qualified doctors here?'

'What do you mean?'

'I mean this.' Guns have different characteristics in appearance. Some look relatively harmless, some ugly, some business-like, some wicked-looking. The Mannlicher-Schoenauer in my hand just looked plain downright wicked. Very wicked indeed. The white light from the Coleman glittered off the blued metal, menacing and sinister. It was a great gun to terrify people with.

'You wouldn't use it,' Swanson said flatly.

'I'm through talking. I'm through asking for a hearing. Bring on the bailiffs, friend.'

'You're bluffing, mister,' Hansen said savagely. 'You don't dare.'

'There's too much at stake for me not to dare. Find out now. Don't be a coward. Don't hide behind your enlisted men's backs. Don't order them to get themselves shot.' I snapped off the safety-catch. 'Come and take it from me yourself.'

'Stay right where you are, John,' Swanson said sharply. 'He means it. I suppose you have a whole armoury in that combination-lock suitcase of yours,' he said bitterly.

'That's it. Automatic carbines, six-inch naval guns, the lot. But for a small-size situation a small-size gun. Do I get my hearing?'

'You get your hearing.'

'Send Rawlings and Murphy away. I don't want anyone else to know anything about this. Anyway, they're probably freezing to death.'

Swanson nodded. Hansen went to the door, opened it, spoke briefly and returned. I laid the gun on the table, picked up my torch and moved some paces away. I said: 'Come and have a look at this.'

They came. Both of them passed by the table with the gun lying there and didn't even look at it. I stopped before one of the grotesquely misshapen charred lumps lying on the floor. Swanson came close and stared down. His face had lost whatever little colour it had regained. He made a queer noise in his throat.

'That ring, that gold ring—' he began, then stopped short.

'I wasn't lying about that.'

'No. No you weren't. I – I don't know what to say. I'm most damnably—'

'It doesn't matter,' I said roughly. 'Look here. At the back. I'm afraid I had to remove some of the carbon.'

'The neck,' Swanson whispered. 'It's broken.'

'Is that what you think?'

'Something heavy, I don't know, a beam from one of the huts, must have fallen—'

'You've just seen one of those huts. They have no beams. There's an inch and half of the vertebrae missing. If anything sufficiently heavy to smash off an inch and a half of the backbone had struck him, the broken piece would be imbedded in his neck. It's not. It was blown out. He was shot from the front, through the base of the throat. The bullet went out the back of the neck. A soft-nosed bullet – you can tell by the size of the exit hole – from a powerful gun, something like a .38 Colt or Luger or Mauser.'

'Good God above!' For the first time, Swanson was badly shaken. He stared at the thing on the floor, then at me. 'Murdered. You mean he was murdered.'

'Who would have done this?' Hansen said hoarsely. 'Who, man, who? And in God's name, why?'

'I don't know who did it.'

Swanson looked at me, his eyes strange. 'You just found this out?'

'I found out last night.'

'You found out last night.' The words were slow, far-spaced, a distinct hiatus between each two. 'And all the time since, aboard the ship, you never said – you never showed – my God, Carpenter, you're inhuman.'

'Sure,' I said. 'See that gun there. It makes a loud bang and when I use it to kill the man who did this I won't even blink. I'm inhuman, all right.'

'I was speaking out of turn. Sorry.' Swanson was making a visible effort to bring himself under normal control. He looked at the Mannlicher-Schoenauer, then at me, then back at the gun. 'Private revenge is out, Carpenter. No one is going to take the law into his own hands.'

'Don't make me laugh out loud. A morgue isn't a fit place for it. Besides, I'm not through showing you things yet. There's more. Something that I've just found out now. Not last night.' I pointed to another huddled black shape on the ground. 'Care to have a look at this man here?'

'I'd rather not,' Swanson said steadily. 'Suppose you tell us?'

'You can see from where you are. The head. I've cleaned it up. Small hole in the front, in the middle of the face and slightly to the right; larger exit hole at the back of the top of the head. Same gun. Same man behind the gun.'

Neither man said anything. They were too sick, too shocked to say anything.

'Queer path the bullet took,' I went on. 'Ranged sharply upwards. As if the man who fired the shot had been lying or sitting down while his victim stood above him.'

'Yes.' Swanson didn't seem to have heard me. 'Murder. Two murders. This is a job for the authorities, for the police.'

'Sure,' I said. 'For the police. Let's just ring the sergeant at the local station and ask him if he would mind stepping this way for a few minutes.'

'It's not a job for us,' Swanson persisted. 'As captain of an American naval vessel with a duty to discharge I am primarily interested in bringing my ship and the Zebra survivors back to Scotland again.'

'Without endangering the ship?' I asked. 'With a murderer aboard the possibility of endangering the ship does not arise?'

'We don't know he is – or will be – aboard.'

'You don't even begin to believe that yourself. You know he will be. You know as well as I do why this fire broke out and you know damn' well that it was no accident. If there was any accidental element about it it was just the size and extent of the fire. The killer may have miscalculated that. But both time and weather conditions were against him: I don't think he had very much option. The only possible way in which he could obliterate all traces of his crime was to have a fire of sufficient proportions to obliterate those traces. He would have got off with it too, if I hadn't been here, if I hadn't been convinced before we left port that something was very far wrong indeed. But he would take very good care that he wouldn't obliterate himself in the process. Like it or not, Commander, you're going to have a killer aboard your ship.'

'But all of those men have been burned, some very severely—'

'What the hell did you expect? That the unknown X would go about without a mark on him, without as much as a cigarette burn, proclaiming to the world that he had been the one who had been throwing matches about and had then thoughtfully stood to one side? Local colour. He *had* to get himself burnt.'

'It doesn't follow,' Hansen said. 'He wasn't to know that anyone was going to get suspicious and start investigating.'

'You'll be well advised to join your captain in keeping out of the detecting racket,' I said shortly. 'The men behind this are top-flight experts with far-reaching contacts – part of a criminal octopus with tentacles so long that it can even reach out and sabotage your ship in the Holy Loch. Why they did that, I don't know. What matters is that top-flight operators like those *never* take chances. They always operate on the assumption that they *may* be found out. They take every possible precaution against every possible eventuality. Besides, when the fire was at its height – we don't know the story of that, yet – the killer would have had to pitch in and rescue those trapped. It would have seemed damned odd if he hadn't. And so he got burnt.'

'My God.' Swanson's teeth were beginning to chatter with the cold but he didn't seem to notice it. 'What a hellish set-up.'

'Isn't it? I dare say there's nothing in your navy regulations to cover this lot.'

'But what – what are we going to do?'

'We call the cops. That's me.'

'What do you mean?'

'What I say. I have more authority, more official backing, more scope, more power and more freedom of action than any cop you ever saw. You must believe me. What I say is true.'

'I'm beginning to believe it *is* true,' Swanson said in slow thoughtfulness. 'I've been wondering more and more about you in the past twenty-four hours. I've kept telling myself I was wrong, even ten minutes before I kept telling myself. You're a policeman? Or detective?'

'Naval officer. Intelligence. I have credentials in my suitcase which I am empowered to show in an emergency.' It didn't seem the time to tell him just how wide a selection of credentials I did have. 'This is the emergency.'

'But – but you are a doctor.'

'Sure I am. A navy doctor – on the side. My speciality is investigating sabotage in the UK armed forces. The cover-up of research doctor is the ideal one. My duties are deliberately vague and I have the power to poke and pry into all sorts of corners and situations and talk to all sorts of people on the grounds of being an investigating psychologist that would be impossible for the average serving officer.'

There was a long silence, then Swanson said bitterly: 'You might have told us before this.'

'I might have broadcast it all over your Tannoy system. Why the hell should I? I don't want to trip over blundering amateurs every step I take. Ask any cop. The biggest menace of his life is the self-appointed Sherlock. Besides, I couldn't trust you, and before you start getting all hot and bothered about that I might add that I don't mean you'd deliberately give me away or anything like that but that you may inadvertently give me away. Now I've no option but to tell you what I can and chance the consequences. Why couldn't you just have accepted that directive from your Director of Naval Operations and acted accordingly?'

'Directive?' Hansen looked at Swanson. 'What directive?'

'Orders from Washington to give Dr Carpenter here *carte blanche* for practically everything. Be reasonable, Carpenter. I don't like operating in the dark and I'm naturally suspicious. You came aboard in highly questionable circumstances. You knew too damn' much about submarines. You were as evasive as hell. You had this sabotage theory all cut and dried. Damn it, man, of course I had reservations. Wouldn't you have had, in my place?'

'I suppose so. I don't know. Me, I obey orders.'

'Uh-huh. And your orders in this case?'

'Meaning what exactly is all this about,' I sighed. 'It would have to come to this. You must be told now – and you'll understand why your Director of Naval Operations was so anxious that you give me every help possible.'

'We can believe this one?' Swanson asked.

'You can believe this one. The story I spun back in the Holy Loch wasn't all malarkey – I just dressed it up a bit to make sure you'd take me along. They did indeed have a very special item of equipment here – an electronic marvel that was used for monitoring the count-down of Soviet missiles and pin-pointing their locations. This machine was kept in one of the huts now destroyed – the second from the west in the south now. Night and day a giant captive radio-sonde balloon reached thirty thousand feet up into the sky – but it had no radio attached. It was just a huge aerial. Incidentally, I should think that is the reason why the oil fuel appears to have been flung over so large an area – an explosion caused by the bursting of the hydrogen cylinders used to inflate the balloons. They were stored in the fuel hut.'

'Did everybody in Zebra know about this monitoring machine?'

'No. Most of them thought it a device for investigating cosmic rays. Only four people knew what it really was – my brother and the three others who all slept in the hut that housed this machine. Now the hut is destroyed. The free world's most advanced listening-post. You wonder why your DNO was so anxious?'

'Four men?' Swanson looked at me, a faint speculation still in his eye. 'Which four men, Dr Carpenter?'

'Do you have to ask? Four of the seven men you see lying here, Commander.'

He stared down at the floor then looked quickly away. He said: 'You mentioned that you were convinced even before we left port that something was far wrong. Why?'

'My brother had a top-secret code. We had messages sent by himself – he was an expert radio operator. One said that there had been two separate attempts to wreck the monitor. He didn't go into details. Another said that he had been attacked and left unconscious when making a midnight check and found someone bleeding off the gas from the hydrogen cylinders – without the radio-sonde aerial the monitor would have been useless. He was lucky, he was out only for a few minutes, as long again and he would have frozen to death. In the circumstances did you expect me to believe that the fire was unconnected with the attempts to sabotage the monitor?'

'But how would anyone *know* what it was?' Hansen objected. 'Apart from your brother and the other three men, that is?' Like Swanson, he glanced at the floor and, like Swanson looked as hurriedly away. 'For my money this is the work of a psycho. A madman. A coldly calculating criminal would – well, he wouldn't go in for wholesale murder like this. But a psycho would.'

'Three hours ago,' I said, 'before you loaded the torpedo into number three tube you checked the manually controlled levers and the warning lights for the tube bow-caps. In the one case you found that the levers had been disconnected in the open position: in the other you found that the wires had been crossed in a junction-box. Do you think that was the work of a psycho? Another psycho?'

He said nothing. Swanson said: 'What can I do to help, Dr Carpenter?'

'What are you willing to do, Commander?'

'I will not hand over command of the *Dolphin*.' He smiled, but he wasn't feeling like smiling. 'Short of that, I – and the crew of the *Dolphin* – are at your complete disposal. You name, it, Doctor, that's all.'

'This time you believe my story?'

'This time I believe your story.'

I was pleased about that, I almost believed it myself.

Chapter Eight

The hut where we'd found all the Zebra survivors huddled together was almost deserted when we got back to it – only Dr Benson and the two very sick men remained. The hut seemed bigger now, somehow, bigger and colder, and very shabby and untidy like the remnants of a church rummage sale where the housewives have trained for a couple of months before moving up to battle stations. Pieces of clothing, bedding, frayed and shredded blankets, gloves, plates, cutlery and dozens of odds and ends of personal possessions lay scattered all over the floor. The sick men had been too sick – and too glad to be on their way – to worry overmuch about taking too many of their various knick-knacks out of there. All they had wanted out of there was themselves. I didn't blame them.

The two unconscious men had their scarred and frost-bitten faces towards us. They were either sleeping or in a coma. But I took no chances. I beckoned Benson and he came and stood with us in the shelter of the west wall.

I told Benson what I'd told the commander and Hansen. He had to know. As the man who would be in the most constant and closest contact with the sick men, he had to know. I suppose he must have been pretty astonished and shaken, but he didn't show it. Doctors' faces behave as doctors tell them to, when they come across a patient in a pretty critical state of health they don't beat their breasts and break into loud lamentations, as this tends to discourage the patient. This now made three men from the *Dolphin*'s crew who knew what the score was – well, half the score, anyway. Three was enough. I only hoped it wasn't too much.

Thereafter Swanson did the talking: Benson would take it better from him than he would from me. Swanson said: 'Where were you thinking of putting the sick men we've sent back aboard?'

'In the most comfortable places I can find. Officers' quarters, crew's quarters, scattered all over so that no one is upset too much. Spread the load, so to speak.' He paused. 'I didn't know of the latest – um – development at the time. Things are rather different now.'

'They are. Half of them in the wardroom, the other half in the crew's mess – no, the crew's quarters. No reason why they shouldn't be fixed up comfortably. If they wonder at this, you can say it's for ease of medical treatment and that they can all be under constant medical watch, like heart patients in a ward. Get Dr Jolly behind you in this, he seems a co-operative type. And I've no doubt he'll support you in your next move – that all patients are to be stripped, bathed and provided with clean pyjamas. If they're too ill to move, bed-bath. Dr Carpenter here tells me that prevention of infection is of paramount importance in cases of severe burn injuries.'

'And their clothes?'

'You catch on more quickly than I did,' Swanson grunted. 'All their clothes to be taken away and labelled. All contents to be removed and labelled. The clothes, for anyone's information, are to be disinfected and laundered.'

'It might help if I am permitted to know just what we are looking for,' Benson suggested.

Swanson looked at me.

'God knows,' I said. 'Anything and everything. One thing certain – you won't find a gun. Be especially careful in labelling gloves – when we get back to Britain we'll have the experts test them for nitrates from the gun used.'

'If anyone has brought aboard anything bigger than a postage stamp I'll find it,' Benson promised.

'Are you sure?' I asked. 'Even if you brought it aboard yourself?'

'Eh? Me? What the devil are you suggesting?'

'I'm suggesting that something may have been shoved inside your medical kit, even your pockets, when you weren't looking.'

'Good lord.' He dug feverishly into his pockets. 'The idea never occurred to me.'

'You haven't the right type of nasty suspicious mind,' Swanson said dryly. 'Off you go. You too, John.'

They left, and Swanson and I went inside. Once I'd checked that the two men really were unconscious, we went to work. It must have been many years since Swanson had policed a deck or parade-ground, far less doubled as scavenger, but he took to it in the manner born. He was assiduous, painstaking, and missed nothing. Neither did I. We cleared a corner of the hut and brought across there every single article that was either lying on the floor or attached to the still ice-covered walls. Nothing was missed. It was either shaken, turned over, opened or emptied according to what it was. Fifteen minutes and we were all through. If there was anything bigger than a matchstick to be found in that room then we would have found it. But we found nothing. Then we scattered everything back over the floor again until the hut looked more or less as it had been before our search. If either of the two unconscious men came to I didn't want him knowing that we had been looking for anything.

'We're no great shakes in the detecting business,' Swanson said. He looked slightly discouraged.

'We can't find what isn't there to be found. And it doesn't help that we don't know what we're looking for. Let's try for the gun now. May be anywhere, he may even have thrown it away on the ice-cap, though I think that unlikely. A killer never likes to lose his means of killing – and he couldn't have been sure that he wouldn't require it again. There aren't so very many places to search. He wouldn't have left it here, for this is the main bunkhouse and in constant use. That leaves only the met. office and the lab. where the dead are lying.'

'He could have hidden it among the ruins of one of the burnt-out huts,' Swanson objected.

'Not a chance. Our friend has been here for some months now, and he must know exactly the effect those ice-storms have. The spicules silt up against any object that lies in their path. The metal frameworks at the bases of the destroyed buildings are still in position, and the floors of the huts – or where the wooden floors used to be – are covered with solid ice to a depth of from four to six inches. He would have been as well to bury his gun in quick-setting concrete.'

We started on the meteorological hut. We looked in every shelf, every box, every cupboard and had just started ripping the backs off the metal cabinets that housed the meteorological equipment when Swanson said abruptly: 'I have an idea. Back in a couple of minutes.'

He was better than his word. He was back in a minute flat, carrying in his hands four objects that glittered wetly in the lamplight and smelled strongly of petrol. A gun – a Luger automatic – the haft and broken-off blade of a knife and two rubber-wrapped packages which turned out to be spare magazines for the Luger. He said: 'I guess this was what you were looking for.'

'Where did you find them?'

'The tractor. In the petrol tank.'

'What made you think of looking there?'

'Just luck. I got to thinking about your remark that the guy who had used this gun might want to use it again. But if he was to hide it anywhere where it was exposed to the weather it might have become jammed up with ice. Even if it didn't, he might have figured that the metal would contract so that the shells wouldn't fit or that the firing mechanism and lubricating oil would freeze solid. Only two things don't freeze solid in these sub-zero temperatures – alcohol and petrol. You can't hide a gun in a bottle of gin.'

'It wouldn't have worked,' I said. 'Metal would still contract – the petrol is as cold as the surrounding air.'

'Maybe he didn't know that. Or if he did, maybe he just thought it was a good place to hide it, quick and handy.' He looked consideringly at me as I broke the butt and looked at the empty magazine, then said sharply: 'You're smearing that gun a little, aren't you?'

'Fingerprints? Not after being in petrol. He was probably wearing gloves anyway.'

'So why did you want it?'

'Serial number. May be able to trace it. It's even possible that the killer had a police permit for it. It's happened before, believe it or not. And you must remember that the killer believed there would be no suspicion of foul play, far less that a search would be carried out for the gun.

'Anyway, this knife explains the gun. Firing guns is a noisy business and I'm surprised – I was surprised – that the killer risked it. He might have waked the whole camp. But he had to take the risk because he'd gone and snapped off the business end of this little sticker here. This is a very slender blade, the kind of blade it's very easy to snap unless you know exactly what you're doing, especially when extreme cold makes the metal brittle. He probably struck a rib or broke the blade trying to haul it out – a knife slides in easily enough but it can jam against cartilage or bone when you try to remove it.'

'You mean – you mean the killer murdered a *third* man?' Swanson asked carefully. 'With this knife?'

'The third man but the first victim,' I nodded. 'The missing half of the blade will be stuck inside someone's chest. But I'm not going to look for it – it would be pointless and take far too long.'

'I'm not sure that I don't agree with Hansen,' Swanson said slowly. 'I know it's impossible to explain away the sabotage on the boat – but, my God, this looks like the work of a maniac. All this – all this senseless killing.'

'All this killing,' I agreed. 'But not senseless – not from the point of view of the killer. No, don't ask me, I don't know what his point of view was – or is. I know – you know – why he started the fire: what we don't know is why he killed those men in the first place.'

Swanson shook his head, then said: 'Let's get back to the other hut. I'll phone for someone to keep a watch over those sick men. I don't know about you, but I'm frozen stiff. And you had no sleep last night.'

'I'll watch them meantime,' I said. 'For an hour or so. And I've some thinking to do, some very hard thinking.'

'You haven't much to go on, have you?'

'That's what makes it so hard.'

I'd said to Swanson that I didn't have much to go on, a less than accurate statement, for I didn't have anything to go on at all. So I didn't waste any time thinking. Instead I took a lantern and went once again to the lab. where the dead men lay. I was cold and tired and alone, and the darkness was falling and I didn't very much fancy going there. Nobody would have fancied going there, a place of dreadful death which any sane person would have avoided like the plague. And that was why I was going there, not because I wasn't sane, but because it was a place that no man would ever voluntarily visit – unless he had an extremely powerful motivation, such as the intention of picking up some essential thing he had hidden there in the near certainty that no one else would ever go near the place. It sounded complicated, even to me. I was very tired. I made a fuzzy mental note to ask around, when I got back to the *Dolphin*, to find out who had suggested shifting the dead men in there.

The walls of the lab. were lined with shelves and cupboards containing jars and bottles and retorts and test-tubes and such-like chemical junk, but I didn't give them more than a glance. I went to the corner of the hut where the dead men lay most closely together, shone my torch along the side of the room and found what I was looking for in a matter of seconds – a floorboard standing slightly proud of its neighbours. Two of the blackened contorted lumps that had once been men lay across that board. I moved them just far enough, not liking the job at all, then lifted one end of the loose floorboard.

It looked as if someone had had it in mind to start up a supermarket. In the six-inch space between the floor and the base of the hut were stacked dozens of neatly arranged cans – soup, beef, fruit, vegetables, a fine varied diet with all the proteins and vitamins a man could want. Someone had had no intention of going hungry. There was even a small pressure-stove and a couple of gallons of kerosene to thaw out the cans. And to one side, lying flat, two rows of gleaming Nife cells – there must have been about forty in all.

I replaced the board, left the lab. and went across to the meteorological hut again. I spent over an hour there, unbuttoning the backs of metal cabinets and peering into their innards, but I found nothing. Not what I had hoped to find, that was. But I did come across one very peculiar item, a small green metal box six inches by four by two, with a circular control that was both switch and tuner, and two glassed-in dials with neither figures nor marking on them. At the side of the box was a brass-rimmed hole.

I turned the switch and one of the dials glowed green, a magic-eye tuning device with the fans spread well apart. The other dial stayed dead. I twiddled the tuner control but nothing happened. Both the magic eye and the second dial required something to activate them – something like a pre-set radio signal. The hole in the side would accommodate the plug of any standard telephone receiver. Not many people would have known what this was, but I'd seen one before – a transistorized homing device for locating the direction of a radio signal, such as emitted by the 'Sarah' device on American space capsules which enables searchers to locate it once it has landed in the sea.

What legitimate purpose could be served by such a device in Drift Ice Station Zebra? When I'd told Swanson and Hansen of the existence of a console for monitoring rocket-firing signals from Siberia, that much of my story, anyway, had been true. But that had called for a giant aerial stretching far up into the sky: this comparative toy couldn't have ranged a twentieth of the distance to Siberia.

I had another look at the portable radio transmitter and the now exhausted Nife batteries that served them. The dialling counter was still tuned into the waveband which the *Dolphin* had picked up the distress signals. There was nothing for me there. I looked more closely at the nickel-cadmium cells and saw that they were joined to one another and to the radio set by wire-cored rubber leads with very powerfully spring-loaded saw-tooth clips on the terminals: those last ensured perfect electrical contact as well as being very convenient to use. I undid two of the clips, brought a torch-beam to bear and peered closely at the terminals. The indentations made by the sharpened steel saw-teeth were faint but unmistakable.

I made my way back to the laboratory hut, lifted the loose floorboard again and shone the torch on the Nife cells lying there. At least half of the cells had the same characteristic markings. Cells that looked fresh and unused, yet they had those same markings and if anything was certain it was that those cells had been brand-new and unmarked when Drift Ice Station Zebra had been first set up. A few of the cells were tucked so far away under adjacent floorboards that I had to stretch my hand far in to reach them. I pulled out two and in the space behind I seemed to see something dark and dull and metallic.

It was too dark to distinguish clearly what the object was but after I'd levered up another two floorboards I could see without any trouble at all. It was a cylinder about thirty inches long and six in diameter with brass stopcock and mounted pressure gauge registering 'full': close beside it was a package about eighteen inches square and four thick, stencilled with the words 'RADIO-SONDE BALLOONS". Hydrogen, batteries, balloons, corned beef and mulligatawny soup. A catholic enough assortment of stores by any standards; but there wouldn't have been anything haphazard about the choice of that assortment.

When I made it back to the bunkhouse, the two patients were still breathing. That was about all I could say for myself, too, I was shaking with the cold and even clamping my teeth together couldn't keep them from chattering. I thawed out under the big electric heaters until I was only half-frozen, picked up my torch and moved out again into the wind and the cold and the dark. I was a sucker for punishment, that was for sure.

In the next twenty minutes I made a dozen complete circuits of the camp, moving a few yards farther out with each circuit. I must have walked over a mile altogether and that was all I had for it, just the walk and a slight touch of frost-bite high up on the cheekbones, the only part of my face, other than the eyes, exposed to that bitter cold. I knew I had frost-bite for the skin had suddenly ceased to feel cold any more and was quite dead to the touch. Enough was enough and I had a hunch that I was wasting my time anyway. I headed back to the camp.

I passed between the meteorological hut and the lab. and was just level with the eastern end of the bunkhouse when I sensed as much as saw something odd out of the corner of my eye. I steadied the torch-beam on the east wall and peered closely at the sheath of ice that had been deposited there over the days by the ice-storm. Most of the encrustation was of a homogeneous greyish-white, very smooth and polished, but it wasn't all grey-white: it was speckled here and there with dozens of black flecks of odd shapes and sizes, none of them more than an inch square. I tried to touch them but they were deeply imbedded in and showing through the gleaming ice. I went to examine the east wall of the meteorological hut, but it was quite innocent of any such black flecking. So was the east wall of the lab.

A short search inside the meteorological hut turned up a hammer and screw-driver. I chipped away a section of the black-flecked ice, brought it into the bunkhouse and laid it on the floor in front of one of the big electrical heaters. Ten minutes later I had a small pool of water and, lying in it, the sodden remains of what had once been fragments of burnt paper. This was very curious indeed. It meant that there were scores of pieces of burnt paper imbedded in the east wall of the bunkhouse. Just there: nowhere else. The explanation, of course, could be completely innocuous: or not, as the case might be.

I had another look at the two unconscious men. They were warm enough and comfortable enough but that was about all you could say for them. I couldn't see them as fit enough to be moved inside the next twenty-four hours. I lifted the phone and asked for someone to relieve me and when two seamen arrived, I made my way back to the *Dolphin*.

There was an unusual atmosphere aboard ship that afternoon, quiet and dull and almost funereal. It was hardly to be wondered at. As far as the crew of the *Dolphin* had been concerned, the men manning Drift Ice Station Zebra had been just so many ciphers, not even names, just unknowns. But now the burnt, frost-bitten, emaciated survivors had come aboard ship, sick and suffering men each with a life and individuality of his own, and the sight of those wasted men still mourning the deaths of their eight comrades had suddenly brought home to every man on the submarine the full horror of what had happened on Zebra. And, of course less than seven hours had elapsed since their own torpedo officer, Lieutenant Mills, had been killed. Now, even although the mission had been successful, there seemed little enough reason for celebration. Down in the crew's mess the hi-fi and the juke-box were stilled. The ship was like a tomb.

I found Hansen in his cabin. He was sitting on the edge of his pullman bunk, still wearing his fur trousers, his face bleak and hard and cold. He watched me in silence as I stripped off my parka, undid the empty holster tied round my chest, hung it up and stuck inside it the automatic I'd pulled from my caribou pants. Then he said suddenly: 'I wouldn't take them off, Doc. Not if you want to come with us, that is.' He looked at his own furs and his mouth was bitter. 'Hardly the rig of the day for a funeral, is it?'

'You mean—'

'Skipper's in his cabin. Boning up on the burial service. George Mills and that assistant radio operator – Grant, wasn't it – who died out there to-day. A double funeral. Out on the ice. There's some men there already, chipping a place with crowbars and sledges at the base of a hummock.'

'I saw no one.'

'Port side. To the west.'

'I thought Swanson would have taken young Mills back to the States. Or Scotland.'

'Too far. And there's the psychological angle. You could hardly dent the morale of this bunch we have aboard here far less shoot it to pieces, but carrying a dead man as a shipmate is an unhappy thing. He's had permission from Washington . . .' He broke off uncertainly, looked quietly up at me and then away again. I didn't have any need of telepathy to know what was in his mind.

'The seven men on Zebra?' I shook my head. 'No, no funeral service for them. How could you? I'll pay my respects some other way.'

His eyes flickered up at the Mannlicher-Schoenauer hanging in its holster, then away again. He said in a quiet savage voice: 'Goddam his black murderous soul. That devil's aboard here, Carpenter. Here. On our ship.' He smacked a bunched fist hard against the palm of his other hand. 'Have you no idea what's behind this, Doc? No idea who's responsible?'

'If I had, I wouldn't be standing here. Any idea how Benson is getting along with the sick and injured?'

'He's all through. I've just left him.'

I nodded, reached up for the automatic and stuck it in the pocket of my caribou pants. Hansen said quietly: 'Even aboard here?'

'Especially aboard here.' I left him and went along to the surgery. Benson was sitting at his table, his back to his art gallery of technicolour cartoons, making entries in a book. He looked up as I closed the door behind me.

'Find anything?' I asked.

'Nothing that I would regard as interesting. Hansen did most of the sorting. You may find something.' He pointed to neatly folded piles of clothing on the deck, several small attache-cases and a few polythene bags, each labelled. 'Look for yourself. How about the two men left out on Zebra?'

'Holding their own. I think they'll be OK, but it's too early to say yet.' I squatted on the floor, went carefully through all the pockets in the clothes and found, as I had expected, nothing. Hansen wasn't the man to miss anything. I felt every square inch of the lining areas and came up with the same results. I went through the small cases and the polythene bags, small items of clothing and personal gear, shaving kits, letters, photographs, two or three cameras. I broke open the cameras and they were all empty. I said to Benson: 'Dr Jolly brought his medical case aboard with him?'

'Wouldn't even trust one of your own colleagues, would you?'

'No.'

'Neither would I.' He smiled with his mouth only. 'You're an evil influence. I went through every item in it. Not a thing. I even measured the thickness of the bottom of the case. Nothing there.'

'Good enough for me. How are the patients?'

'Nine of them,' Benson said. 'The psychological effect of knowing that they're safe has done them more good than any medication ever could.' He consulted cards on his desk. 'Captain Folsom is the worst. No danger, of course, but his facial burns are pretty savage. We've arranged to have a plastic surgeon standing by in Glasgow when we return. The Harrington twins, both met. officers, are rather less badly burnt, but very weak, from both cold and hunger. Food, warmth and rest will have them on their feet in a couple of days again. Hassard, another met. officer, and Jeremy, a lab. technician, moderate burns, moderate frost-bite, fittest of the lot otherwise – it's queer how different people react so differently to hunger and cold. The other four – Kinnaird, the senior radio operator, Dr Jolly, Naseby, the cook, and Hewson, the tractor-driver and and man who was in charge of the generator – are much of a muchness: they're suffering most severely of all from frost-bite, especially Kinnaird, all with moderate burns, weak, of course, but recovering fast. Only Folsom and the Harrington twins have consented to become bed-patients. The rest we've provided with rigouts of one sort or another. They're all lying down, of course, but they won't be lying down long. All of them are young, tough, and basically very fit – they don't pick children or old men to man places like Drift Station Zebra.'

A knock came to the door and Swanson's head appeared. He said, 'Hallo, back again,' to me then turned to Benson. 'A small problem of medical discipline here, Doctor.' He stood aside to let us see Naseby, the Zebra cook, standing close behind him, dressed in a US Navy's petty officer's uniform. 'It seems that your patients have heard about the funeral service. They want to go along – those who are able, that is – to pay their last respects to their colleagues. I understand and sympathize, of course, but their state of health—'

'I would advise against it, sir,' Benson said. 'Strongly.'

'You can advise what you like, mate,' a voice came from behind Naseby. It was Kinnaird, the cockney radio operator, also clad in blue. 'No offence. Don't want to be rude or ungrateful. But I'm going. Jimmy Grant was my mate.'

'I know how you feel,' Benson said. 'I also know how *I* feel about it – your condition, I mean. You're in no fit state to do anything except lie down. You're making things very difficult for me.'

'I'm the captain of this ship,' Swanson put in mildly. 'I can forbid it, you know. I can say "No," and make it stick.'

'And you are making things difficult for us, sir,' Kinnaird said. 'I don't reckon it would advance the cause of Anglo-American unity very much if we started hauling off at our rescuers an hour or two after they'd saved us from certain death.' He smiled faintly. 'Besides, look at what it might do to our wounds and burns.'

Swanson cocked an eyebrow at me. 'Well, they're your countrymen.'

'Dr Benson is perfectly correct,' I said. 'But it's not worth a civil war. If they could survive five or six days on that damned ice-cap, I don't suppose a few minutes more is going to finish them off.'

'Well, if it does,' Swanson said heavily, 'we'll blame you.'

If I ever had any doubt about it I didn't have then, not after ten minutes out in the open. The Arctic ice-cap was no place for a funeral; but I couldn't have imagined a more promising set-up for a funeral director who wanted to drum up some trade. After the warmth of the *Dolphin* the cold seemed intense and within five minutes we were all shivering violently. The darkness was as nearly absolute as it ever becomes on the ice-cap, the wind was lifting again and thin flurries of snow came gusting through the night. The solitary floodlamp served only to emphasize the ghostly unreality of it all, the huddled circle of mourners with bent heads, the two shapeless canvas-wrapped forms lying huddled at the base of an ice-hummock, Commander Swanson bent over his book, the wind and the snow snatching the half-heard mumble from his lips as he hurried through the burial service. I caught barely one word in ten of the committal and then it was all over, no meaningless rifle salutes, no empty blowing of bugles, just the service and the silence and the dark shapes of stumbling men hurriedly placing fragments of broken ice over the canvas-sheeted forms. And within twenty-four hours the eternally drifting spicules and blowing snow would have sealed them for ever in their icy tomb, and there they might remain for ever, drifting in endless circles about the North Pole; or some day, perhaps a thousand years from then, an ice-lead might open up and drop them down to the uncaring floor of the Arctic, their bodies as perfectly preserved as if they had died only that day. It was a macabre thought.

Heads bent against the snow and ice, we hurried back to the shelter of the *Dolphin*. From the ice-cap to the top of the sail it was a climb of over twenty feet up the almost vertically inclined huge slabs of ice that the submarine had pushed upwards and sideways as she had forced her way through. Hand-lines had been rigged from the top of the sail but even then it was a fairly tricky climb. It was a set-up where with the icy slope, the frozen slippery ropes, the darkness and the blinding effect of the snow and ice, an accident could all too easily happen. And happen it did.

I was about six feet up, giving a hand to Jeremy, the lab. technician from Zebra whose burnt hands made it almost impossible for him to climb alone, when I heard a muffled cry above me. I glanced up and had a darkly-blurred impression of someone teetering on top of the sail, fighting for his balance, then jerked Jeremy violently towards me to save him from being swept away as that same someone lost his footing, toppled over backwards and hurtled down past us on to the ice below. I winced at the sound of the impact, two sounds, rather, a heavy muffled thud followed immediately by a sharper, crisper crack. First the body, then the head. I half imagined that I heard another sound afterwards, but couldn't be sure. I handed Jeremy over to the care of someone else and slithered down an ice-coated rope, not looking forward very much to what I must see. The fall had been the equivalent of a twenty-foot drop on to a concrete floor.

Hansen had got there before me and was shining his torch down not on to one prostrate figure as I had expected, but two. Benson and Jolly, both of them out cold.

I said to Hansen: 'Did you see what happened?'

'No. Happened too quickly. All I know is that it was Benson that did the falling and Jolly that did the cushioning. Jolly was beside me only a few seconds before the fall.'

'If that's the case then Jolly probably saved your doctor's life. We'll need to strap them in stretchers and haul them up and inside. We can't leave them out here.'

'Stretchers? Well, yes, if you say so. But they might come round any minute.'

'One of them might. But one of them is not going to come round for a long time. You heard that crack when a head hit the ice, it was like someone being clouted over the head with a fence-post. And I don't know which it is yet.'

Hansen left. I stooped over Benson and eased back the hood of the duffel-coat he was wearing. A fence-post was just about right. The side of his head, an inch above the right ear, was a blood-smeared mess, a three-inch long gash in the purpling flesh with the blood already coagulating in the bitter cold. Two inches farther forward and he'd have been a dead man, the thin bone behind the temple would have shattered under such an impact. For Benson's sake, I hoped the rest of his skull was pretty thick. No question but that this had been the sharp crack I'd heard.

Benson's breathing was very shallow, the movement of his chest barely discernible. Jolly's, on the other hand, was fairly deep and regular. I pulled back his anorak hood, probed carefully over his head and encountered a slight puffiness far back, near the top of the left-hand side. The inference seemed obvious. I hadn't been imagining things when I thought I had heard a second sound after the sharp crack caused by Benson's head striking against the ice. Jolly must have been in the way of the falling Benson, not directly enough beneath him to break his fall in any way but directly enough to be knocked backwards on to the ice and clout the back of his head as he fell.

It took ten minutes to have them strapped in stretchers, taken inside and placed in a couple of temporary cots in the sick-bay. With Swanson waiting anxiously I attended to Benson first, though there was little enough I could do, and had just started on Jolly when his eyes flickered and he slowly came back to consciousness, groaning a bit and trying to hold the back of his head. He made to sit up in his cot but I restrained him.

'Oh, lord, my head.' Several times he squeezed his eyes tightly shut, opened them wide, focused with difficulty on the bulkhead riotous with the colour of Benson's cartoon characters, then looked away as if he didn't believe it. 'Oh, my word, that must have been a dilly. Who did it, old boy?'

'Did what?' Swanson asked.

'Walloped me on the old bean. Who? Eh?'

'You mean to say you don't remember?'

'Remember?' Jolly said irritably. 'How the devil should I . . .' He broke off as his eye caught sight of Benson in the adjacent cot, a huddled figure under the blankets with only the back of his head and a big gauze pack covering his wound showing. 'Of course, of course. Yes, that's it. He fell on top of me, didn't he?'

'He certainly did,' I said. 'Did you try to catch him?'

'Catch him? No, I didn't try to catch him. I didn't try to get out of the way either. It was all over in half a second. I just don't remember a thing about it.' He groaned a bit more then looked across at Benson. 'Came a pretty nasty cropper, eh? Must have done.'

'Looks like it. He's very severely concussed. There's X-ray equipment here and I'll have a look at his head shortly. Damned hard luck on you too, Jolly.'

'I'll get over it,' he grunted. He pushed off my hand and sat up. 'Can I help you?'

'You may not,' Swanson said quietly. 'Early supper then twelve hours solid for you and the eight others, Doctor, and those are *my* doctor's orders. You'll find supper waiting in the wardroom now.'

'Aye, aye, sir.' Jolly gave a ghost of a smile and pushed himself groggily to his feet. 'That bit about the twelve hours sounds good to me.'

After a minute or two, when he was steady enough on his feet, he left. Swanson said: 'What now?'

'You might inquire around to see who was nearest or near to Benson when he slipped climbing over the edge of the bridge. But discreetly. It might do no harm if at the same time you hinted around that maybe Benson had just taken a turn.'

'What are *you* hinting at?' Swanson asked slowly.

'Did he fall or was he pushed? that's what I'm hinting at.'

'Did he fall or . . .' He broke off then went on warily: 'Why should anyone want to push Dr Benson?'

'Why should anyone want to kill seven – eight, now – men in Drift Ice Station Zebra?'

'You have a point,' Swanson acknowledged quietly. He left.

Making X-ray pictures wasn't very much in my line but apparently it hadn't been very much in Dr Benson's line either for he'd written down, for his own benefit and guidance, a detailed list of instructions for the taking and development of X-ray pictures. I wondered how he would have felt if he had known that the first beneficiary of his meticulous thoroughness was to be himself. The two finished negatives I came up with wouldn't have caused any furore in the Royal Photographic Society, but they were enough for my wants.

By and by Commander Swanson returned, closing the door behind him. I said: 'Ten gets one that you got nothing.'

'You won't die a poor man,' he nodded. 'Nothing is what it is. So Chief Torpedoman Patterson tells me, and you know what he's like.'

I knew what he was like. Patterson was the man responsible for all discipline and organization among the enlisted men and Swanson had said to me that he regarded Patterson, and not himself, as the most indispensable man on the ship.

'Patterson was the man who reached the bridge immediately before Benson,' Swanson said. 'He said he heard Benson cry out, swung round and saw him already beginning to topple backwards. He didn't recognize who it was at the time, it was too dark and snowy for that. He said he had the impression that Benson had already had one hand and one knee on the bridge coaming when he fell backwards.'

'A funny position in which to start falling backwards,' I said. 'Most of his body weight must already have been inboard. And even if he did topple outwards he would surely still have had plenty of time to grab the coaming with both hands.'

'Maybe he did take a turn,' Swanson suggested. 'And don't forget that the coaming is glass-slippery with its smooth coating of ice.'

'As soon as Benson disappeared Patterson ran to the side to see what had happened to him?'

'He did,' Swanson said wearily. 'And he said there wasn't a person within ten feet of the top of the bridge when Benson fell.'

'And who *was* ten feet below?'

'He couldn't tell. Don't forget how black it was out there on the ice-cap and that the moment Patterson had dropped into the brightly lit bridge he'd lost whatever night-sight he'd built up. Besides, he didn't wait for more than a glance. He was off for a stretcher even before you or Hansen got to Benson. Patterson is not the sort of man who has to be told what to do.'

'So it's a dead end there?'

'A dead end.'

I nodded, crossed to a cupboard and brought back the two X-rays, still wet, held in their metal clips. I held them up to the light for Swanson's inspection.

'Benson?' he asked, and when I nodded peered at them more closely and finally said: 'That line there – a fracture?'

'A fracture. And not a hair-line one either, as you can see. He really caught a wallop.'

'How bad is it? How long before he comes out of this coma – he *is* in a coma?'

'He's all that. How long? If I were a lad fresh out of medical school I'd let you have a pretty confident estimate. If I were a top-flight brain surgeon I'd say anything from half an hour to a year or two, because people who really know what they are talking about are only too aware that we know next to nothing about the brain. Being neither, I'd guess at two or three days – and my guess could be hopelessly wrong. There may be cerebral bleeding. I don't know. I don't think so. Blood-pressure, respiration and temperature shows no evidence of organic damage. And now you know as much about it as I do.'

'Your colleagues wouldn't like that.' Swanson smiled faintly. 'This cheerful confession of ignorance does nothing to enhance the mystique of your profession. How about your other patients – the two men still out in Zebra?'

'I'll see them after supper. Maybe they'll be fit enough to be brought here to-morrow. Meanwhile, I'd like to ask a favour of you. Could you lend me the services of your Torpedoman Rawlings? And would you have any objections to his being taken into our confidence?'

'Rawlings? I don't know why you want him, but why Rawlings? The officers and petty officers aboard this ship are the pick of the United States Navy. Why not one of them? Besides, I'm not sure that I like the idea of passing on to an enlisted man secrets denied to my officers.'

'They're strictly non-naval secrets. The question of hierarchy doesn't enter into it. Rawlings is the man I want. He's got a quick mind, quick reflexes, and a dead-pan give-away-nothing expression that is invaluable in a game like this. Besides, in the event – the unlikely event, I hope – of the killer suspecting that we're on to him, he wouldn't look for any danger from one of your enlisted men because he'd be certain that we wouldn't let them in on it.'

'What do you want him for?'

'To keep a night guard on Benson here.'

'On Benson?' A fractional narrowing of the eyes, that could have been as imagined as real, was the only change in Swanson's impassive face. 'So you don't think it was an accident, do you?'

'I don't honestly know. But I'm like yourself when you carry out a hundred and one different checks, most of which you know to be unnecessary, before you take your ship to sea – I'm taking no chances. If it wasn't an accident – then someone might have an interest in doing a really permanent job next time.'

'But how can Benson represent a danger to anyone?' Swanson argued. 'I'll wager anything you like, Carpenter, that Benson doesn't – or didn't – know a thing about them that could point a finger at anyone. If he did, he'd have told me straight away. He was like that.'

'Maybe he saw or heard something the significance of which he didn't then realize. Maybe the killer is frightened that if Benson has time enough to think about it the significance will dawn on him. Or maybe it's all a figment of my overheated imagination: maybe he just fell. But I'd still like to have Rawlings.'

'You shall have him.' Swanson rose to his feet and smiled. 'I don't want you quoting that Washington directive at me again.'

Two minutes later Rawlings arrived. He was dressed in a light brown shirt and overall pants, obviously his own conception of what constituted the well-dressed submariner's uniform, and for the first time in our acquaintance he didn't smile a greeting. He didn't even glance at Benson on his cot. His face was still and composed, without any expression.

'You sent for me, sir?' 'Sir,' not 'Doc.'

'Take a seat, Rawlings.' He sat, and as he did I noticed the heavy bulge in the twelve-inch thigh pocket on the side of his overall pants. I nodded and said: 'What have you got there? Doesn't do much for the cut of your natty suiting, does it?'

He didn't smile. He said. 'I always carry one or two tools around with me. That's what the pocket is for.'

'Let's see this particular tool,' I said.

He hesitated briefly, shrugged and, not without some difficulty, pulled a heavy gleaming drop-forged steel pipe-wrench from the pocket. I hefted it in my hand.

'I'm surprised at you, Rawlings,' I said. 'What do you think the average human skull is made of – concrete? One little tap with this thing and you're up on a murder or manslaughter charge.' I picked up a roll of bandage. 'Ten yards of this wrapped round the business end will automatically reduce the charge to one of assault and battery.'

'I don't know what you're talking about,' he said mechanically.

'I'm talking about the fact that when Commander Swanson, Lieutenant Hansen and I were inside the laboratory this afternoon and you and Murphy were outside, you must have kind of leaned your ear against the door and heard more than was good for you. You know there's something far wrong and though you don't know what your motto is "be prepared". Hence the cosh. Correct?'

'Correct.'

'Does Murphy know?'

'No.'

'I'm a naval intelligence officer. Washington know all about me. Want the captain to vouch for me?'

'Well, no.' The first faint signs of a grin. 'I heard you pull a gun on the skipper, but you're still walking about loose. You must be in the clear.'

'You heard me threaten the captain and Lieutenant Hansen with a gun. But then you were sent away. You heard nothing after that?'

'Nothing.'

'Three men have been murdered in Zebra. Two shot, one knifed. Their bodies were burned to conceal traces of the crime. Four others died in the fire. The killer is aboard this ship.'

Rawlings said nothing. His eyes were wide, his face pale and shocked. I told him everything I'd told Swanson and Hansen and emphasized that he was to keep it all to himself. Then I finished: 'Dr Benson here has been seriously hurt. A deliberate attempt for God knows what reason, may have been made on his life. We don't know. But if it was a deliberate attempt, then it's failed – so far.'

Rawlings had brought himself under control. He said, his voice as empty of expression as his face: 'Our little pal might come calling again?'

'He may. No member of the crew except the captain, the executive officer or I will come here. Anyone else – well, you can start asking him questions when he recovers consciousness.'

'You recommended ten yards of this bandage, Doc?'

'It should be enough. And only a gentle tap, for God's sake. Above and behind the ear. You might sit behind that curtain there where no one can see you.'

'I'm feeling lonesome to-night,' Rawlings murmured. He broke open the bandage, started winding it around the head of the wrench and glanced at the cartoon-decorated bulkhead beside him. 'Even old Yogi Bear ain't no fit companion for me to-night. I hope I have some other company calling.'

I left him there. I felt vaguely sorry for anyone who should come calling, killer or not. I felt, too, that I had taken every possible precaution. But when I left Rawlings there guarding Benson I did make one little mistake. Just one. I left him guarding the wrong man.

The second accident of the day happened so quickly, so easily, so inevitably that it might almost have been just that – an accident.

At supper that evening I suggested that, with Commander Swanson's permission, I'd have a surgery at nine next morning; because of enforced neglect most of the burn wounds were suppurating fairly badly, requiring constant cleaning and changing of coverings: I also thought it about time that an X-ray inspection be made of Zabrinski's broken ankle. Medical supplies in the sick-bay were running short. Where did Benson keep his main supplies? Swanson told me and detailed Henry, the steward, to show me where it was.

About ten that night, after I'd returned from seeing the two men out on Zebra, Henry led me through the now deserted control room and down the ladder which led to the inertial navigation room and the electronics space, which abutted on it. He undid the strong-back clamp on the square heavy steel hatch in a corner of the electronics room and with an assist from me – the hatch must have weighed about 150 pounds – swung it up and back until the hatch clicked home on its standing latch.

Three rungs on the inside of the hatch-cover led on to the vertical steel ladder that reached down to the deck below. Henry went down first, snapping on the light as he went, and I followed.

The medical storage room, though tiny, was equipped on the same superbly lavish scale as was everything else on the *Dolphin*. Benson, as thoroughly meticulous in this as he had been in his outlining of X-ray procedure, had everything neatly and logically labelled so that it took me less than three minutes to find everything I wanted. I went up the ladder first, stopped near the top, stretched down and took the bag of supplies from Henry, swung it up on the deck above, then reached up quickly with my free hand to grab the middle of the three rungs welded on the lower side of the hatch cover to haul myself up on to the deck of the electronics space. But I didn't haul myself up. What happened was that I hauled the hatch cover down. The retaining latch had become disengaged, and the 150-pound dead weight of that massive cover was swinging down on top of me before I could even begin to realize what was happening.

I fell half-sideways, half-backwards, pulling the hatch cover with me. My head struck against the hatch coaming. Desperately I ducked my head forward – if it had been crushed between the coaming and the falling cover the two sides of my skull would just about have met in the middle – and tried to snatch my left arm back inside. I was more or less successful with my head – I had it clear of the coaming and was ducking so quickly that the impact of the cover was no more than enough to give me a slight headache afterwards; but my left arm was a different matter altogether. I almost got it clear – but only almost. If my left hand and wrist had been strapped to a steel block and a gorilla had had a go at it with a sledge-hammer, the effect couldn't have been more agonizing. For a moment or two I hung there, trapped, dangling by my left wrist, then the weight of my body tore the mangled wrist and hand through the gap and I crashed down to the deck beneath. Then the gorilla seemed to have another go with the sledge-hammer and consciousness went.

'I won't beat about the bush, old lad,' Jolly said. 'No point in it with a fellow pill-roller. Your wrist is a mess – I had to dig half your watch out of it. The middle and little fingers are broken, the middle in two places. But the permanent damage, I'm afraid, is to the back of your hand – the little and ring finger tendons have been sliced.'

'What does that mean?' Swanson asked.

'It means that in his left hand he'll have to get by with two fingers and a thumb for the rest of his life,' Jolly said bluntly.

Swanson swore softly and turned to Henry. 'How in God's name could you have been so damnably careless? An experienced submariner like you? You know perfectly well that you are required to make a visual check every time a hatch cover engages in a standing latch. Why didn't you?'

'I didn't need to, sir,' Henry was looking more dyspeptic and forlorn than ever. 'I heard it click and I gave a tug. It was fixed, all right. I can swear to it, sir.'

'How could it have been fixed? Look at Dr Carpenter's hand. Just a hair-line engagement and the slightest extra pressure – my God, why can't you people obey regulations?'

Henry stared at the deck in silence. Jolly, who was understandably looking about as washed-out as I felt, packed away the tools of his trade, advised me to take a couple of days off, gave me a handful of pills to take, said a weary good-night and climbed up the ladder leading from the electronics space, where he had been fixing my hand. Swanson said to Henry: 'You can go now, Baker.' It was the first time I'd ever heard anyone address Henry by his surname, a sufficient enough token of what Swanson regarded as the enormity of his crime. 'I'll decide what to do about this in the morning.'

'I don't know about the morning,' I said after Henry was gone. 'Maybe the next morning. Or the one after that. Then you can apologize to him. You and me both. That cover was locked on its standing latch. *I* checked it visually, Commander Swanson.'

Swanson gave me his cool impassive look. After a moment he said quietly: 'Are you suggesting what I think you are suggesting?'

'Someone took a risk,' I said. 'Not all that much of a risk, though – most people are asleep now and the control room was deserted at the moment that mattered. Someone in the wardroom to-night heard me ask your permission to go down to the medical store and heard you giving your okay. Shortly after that nearly everyone turned in. One man didn't – he kept awake and hung around patiently until I came back from the Drift Station. He followed us down below – he was lucky, Lieutenant Sims, your officer on deck, was taking star-sights up on the bridge and the control room was empty – and he unhooked the latch but left the hatch cover in a standing position. There was a slight element of gambling as to whether I would come up first, but not all that much, it would have been a matter of elementary courtesy, he would have thought, for Henry to see me up first. Anyway, he won his gamble, slight though it was. After that our unknown friend wasn't quite so lucky – I think he expected the damage to be a bit more permanent.'

'I'll get inquiries under way immediately,' Swanson said. 'Whoever was responsible, someone must have seen him. Someone must have heard him leaving his cot—'

'Don't waste your time, Commander. We're up against a highly intelligent character who doesn't overlook the obvious. Not only that but word of your inquiries is bound to get around and you'd scare him under cover where I'd never get at him.'

'Then I'll just keep the whole damned lot under lock and key until we get back to Scotland,' Swanson said grimly. '*That* way there'll be no more trouble.'

'That way we'll *never* find out who the murderer of my brother and the six – seven now – others are. Whoever it is has to be given sufficient rope to trip himself up.'

'Good lord, man, we can't just sit back and let things be done to us.' A hint of testiness in the commander's voice and I couldn't blame him. 'What do we – what do *you* propose to do now?'

'Start at the beginning. To-morrow morning we'll hold a court of inquiry among the survivors. Let's find out all we can about that fire. Just an innocent above-board fact-finding inquiry – for the Ministry of Supply, let us say. I've an idea we might turn up something very interesting indeed.'

'You think so?' Swanson shook his head. 'I don't believe it. I don't believe it for a moment. Look what's happened to you. It's obvious, man, that someone knows or suspects that you're on to them. They'll take damned good care to give nothing away.'

'You think that's why I was clouted to-night?'

'What other reason could there be?'

'Was that why Benson was hurt?'

'We don't know that he was. Deliberately, I mean. May have been pure coincidence.'

'Maybe it was,' I agreed. 'And again maybe it wasn't. My guess, for what it's worth, is that the accident or accidents have nothing at all to do with any suspicions the killer may have that we're on to him. Anyway, let's see what to-morrow brings.'

It was midnight when I got back to my cabin. The engineer officer was on watch and Hansen was asleep so I didn't put on any light lest I disturb him. I didn't undress, just removed my shoes, lay down on the cot and pulled a cover over me.

I didn't sleep. I couldn't sleep. My left arm from the elbow downwards still felt as if it were caught in a bear-trap. Twice I pulled from my pocket the pain-killers and sleeping-tablets that Jolly had given me and twice I put them away.

Instead I just lay there and thought and the first and most obvious conclusion I came up with was that there was someone aboard the *Dolphin* who didn't care any too much for the members of the medical profession. Then I got to wondering why the profession was so unpopular and after half an hour of beating my weary brain-cells around I got silently to my feet and made my way on stockinged soles to the sick-bay.

I passed inside and closed the door softly behind me. A red night-light burnt dully in one corner of the bay, just enough to let me see the huddled form of Benson lying on a cot. I switched on the overhead light, blinked in the sudden fierce wash of light and looked at the curtain at the other end of the bay. Nothing stirred behind it. I said: 'Just kind of take your itching fingers away from that pipewrench, Rawlings. It's me, Carpenter.'

The curtain was pulled to one side and Rawlings appeared, the pipe-wrench, with its bandage-wrapped head, dangling from one hand. He had a disappointed look on his face.

'I was expecting someone else,' he said reproachfully. 'I was kinda hoping – my God, Doc, what's happened to your arm?'

'Well may you ask, Rawlings. Our little pal had a go at me to-night. I think he wanted me out of the way. Whether he wanted me out of the way permanently or not I don't know, but he near as a toucher succeeded.' I told him what had happened, then asked him: 'Is there any man aboard you can trust absolutely?' I knew the answer before I had asked the question.

'Zabrinski,' he said unhesitatingly.

'Do you think you could pussy-foot along to wherever it is that he's sleeping and bring him here without waking up anyone?'

He didn't answer my questions. He said: 'He can't walk, Doc, you know that.'

'Carry him. You're big enough.'

He grinned and left. He was back with Zabrinski inside three minutes. Three-quarters of an hour later, after telling Rawlings he could call off his watch, I was back in my cabin.

Hansen was still asleep. He didn't wake even when I switched on a side light. Slowly, clumsily, painfully, I dressed myself in my furs, unlocked my case and drew out the Luger, the two rubber-covered magazines and the broken knife which Commander Swanson had found in the tractor's petrol tank. I put those in my pocket and left. As I passed through the control room I told the officer on deck that I was going out to check on the two patients still left out in the camp. As I had pulled a fur mitten over my injured hand he didn't raise any eyebrows, doctors were a law to themselves and I was just the good healer *en route* to give aid and comfort to the sick.

I did have a good look at the two sick men, both of whom seemed to me to be picking up steadily, then said 'good-night' to the two *Dolphin* crewmen who were watching over them. But I didn't go straight back to the ship. First I went to the tractor shed and replaced the gun, magazines and broken knife in the tractor tank. Then I went back to the ship.

Chapter Nine

'I'm sorry to have to bother you with all these questions,' I said pleasantly. 'But that's the way it is with all government departments. A thousand questions in quadruplicate and each of them more pointlessly irritating than the rest. But I have this job to do and the report to be radioed off as soon as possible and I would appreciate all the information and co-operation you can give me. First off, has anyone any idea at all how this damnable fire started?'

I hoped I sounded like a Ministry of Supply official which was what I'd told them I was – making a Ministry of Supply report. I'd further told them, just to nip any eyebrow-raising in the bud, that it was the Ministry of Supply's policy to send a doctor to report on any accident where loss of life was involved. Maybe this was the case. I didn't know and I didn't care.

'Well, I was the first to discover the fire, I think,' Naseby, the Zebra cook, said hesitantly. His Yorkshire accent was very pronounced. He was still no picture of health and strength but for all that he was a hundred per cent improved on the man I had seen yesterday. Like the other eight survivors of Drift Ice Station Zebra who were present in the wardroom that morning, a long night's warm sleep and good food had brought about a remarkable change for the better. More accurately, like seven others. Captain Folsom's face had been so hideously burnt that it was difficult to say what progress he was making although he had certainly had a good enough breakfast, almost entirely liquid, less than half an hour previously.

'It must have been about two o'clock in the morning,' Naseby went on. 'Well, near enough two. The place was already on fire. Burning like a torch, it was. I—'

'What place?' I interrupted. 'Where were you sleeping?'

'In the cookhouse. That was also our dining-hall. Farthest west hut in the north row.'

'You slept there alone?'

'No. Hewson, here, and Flanders and Bryce slept there also. Flanders and Bryce, they're – they were – lab. technicians. Hewson and I slept at the very back of the hut, then there were two big cupboards, one each side, that held all the food stores, then Flanders and Bryce slept in the dining-hall itself, by a corner of the galley.'

'They were nearest the door?'

'That's right. I got up, coughing and choking with smoke, very groggy, and I could see flames already starting to eat through the east wall of the hut. I shook Hewson then ran for the fire extinguisher – it was kept by the door. It wouldn't work. Jammed solid with the cold, I suppose. I don't know. I ran back in again. I was blind by this time, you never saw smoke like it in your life. I shook Flanders and Bryce and shouted at them to get out then I bumped into Hewson and told him to run and wake Captain Folsom here.'

I looked at Hewson. 'You woke Captain Folsom?'

'I went to wake him. But not straight away. The whole camp was blazing like the biggest Fifth of November bonfire you ever saw and flames twenty feet high were sweeping down the lane between the two rows of huts. The air was full of flying oil, a lot of it burning. I had to make a long swing to the north to get clear of the oil and the flames.'

'The wind was from the east?'

'Not quite. Not that night. South-east, I would say. East-south-east would be more like it, rather. Anyway, I gave a very wide berth to the generator house – that was the one next the dining-hall in the north row – and reached the main bunkhouse. That was the one you found us in.'

'Then you woke Captain Folsom?'

'He was already gone. Shortly after I'd left the dining-hall the fuel drums in the fuel storage hut – that was the one directly south of the main bunkhouse – started exploding. Like bloody great bombs going off they were, the noise they made. They would have waked the dead. Anyway, they woke Captain Folsom. He and Jeremy here' – he nodded at a man sitting across the table from him – 'had taken the fire extinguisher from the bunkhouse and tried to get close to Major Halliwell's hut.'

'That was the one directly west of the fuel store?'

'That's right. It was an inferno. Captain Folsom's extinguisher worked well enough but he couldn't get close enough to do any good. There was so much flying oil in the air that even the extinguisher foam seemed to burn.'

'Hold on a minute,' I said. 'To get back to my original question. How did the fire start?'

'We've discussed that a hundred times among ourselves,' Dr Jolly said wearily. 'The truth is, old boy, we haven't a clue. We know *where* it started all right: match the huts destroyed against the wind direction that night and it could only have been in the fuel store. But how? It's anybody's guess. I don't see that it matters a great deal now.'

'I disagree. It matters very much. If we could find out how it started we might prevent another such tragedy later on. That's why I'm here. Hewson, you were in charge of the fuel store and generator hut. Have you no opinion on this?'

'None. It *must* have been electrical, but how I can't guess. It's possible that there was a leakage from one of the fuel drums and that oil vapour was present in the air. There were two black heaters in the fuel store, designed to keep the temperature up to zero Fahrenheit, so that the oil would always flow freely. Arcing across the make and break of the thermostats might have ignited the gas. But it's only a wild guess, of course.'

'No possibility of any smouldering rags or cigarette ends being the cause?'

Hewson's face turned a dusky red.

'Look, mister, I know my job. Burning rags, cigarette ends – I know how to keep a bloody fuel store—'

'Keep your shirt on,' I interrupted. 'No offence. I'm only doing *my* job.' I turned back to Naseby. 'After you'd sent Hewson here to rouse up Captain Folsom, what then?'

'I ran across to the radio room – that's the hut due south of the cookhouse and west of Major Halliwell's—'

'But those two lab. technicians – Flanders and Bryce, wasn't it – surely you checked they were awake and out of it before you left the dining-hall?'

'God help me, I didn't.' Naseby stared down at the deck, his shoulders hunched, his face bleak. 'They're dead. It's my fault they're dead. But you don't know what it was like inside that dining-hall. Flames were breaking through the east wall, the place was full of choking smoke and oil, I couldn't see, I could hardly breathe. I shook them both and shouted at them to get out. I shook them hard and I certainly shouted loud enough.'

'I can bear him out on that,' Hewson said quietly. 'I was right beside him at the time.'

'I didn't wait,' Naseby went on. 'I wasn't thinking of saving my own skin. I thought Flanders and Bryce were all right and that they would be out the door on my heels. I wanted to warn the others. It wasn't – it wasn't until minutes later that I realized that there was no sign of them. And then – well, then it was too late.'

'You ran across to the radio room. That's where you slept, Kinnaird, wasn't it?'

'That's where I slept, yes.' His mouth twisted. 'Me and my mate Grant, the boy that died yesterday. And Dr Jolly slept in the partitioned-off east end of the hut. That's where he had his surgery and the little cubby-hole where he carried out his tests on ice samples.'

'So your end would have started to go on fire first?' I said to Jolly.

'Must have done,' he agreed. 'Quite frankly, old chap, my recollection of the whole thing is just like a dream – a nightmare, rather. I was almost asphyxiated in my sleep, I think. First thing I remember was young Grant bending over me, shaking me and shouting. Can't recall what he was shouting but it must have been that the hut was on fire. I don't know what I said or did, probably nothing, for the next thing I clearly remember was being hit on both sides of the face, and not too gently either. But, by jove, it worked! I got to my feet and he dragged me out of my office into the radio room. I owe my life to young Grant. I'd just enough sense left to grab the emergency medical kit that I always kept packed.'

'What woke Grant?'

'Naseby, here, woke him.' Kinnaird said. 'He woke us both, shouting and hammering on the door. If it hadn't been for him Dr Jolly and I would both have been goners, the air inside that place was like poison gas and I'm sure if Naseby hadn't shouted on us we would never have woken up. I told Grant to waken the doctor while I tried to get the outside door open.'

'It was locked?'

'The damned thing was jammed. That was nothing unusual at night. During the day when the heaters were going full blast to keep the huts at a decent working temperature the ice around the doors tended to melt: at night, when we got into our sleeping-bags, we turned our heaters down and the melted ice froze hard round the door openings, sealing it solid. That happened most nights in most of the huts – usually had to break our way out in the morning. But I can tell you that I didn't take too long to burst it open that night.'

'And then?'

'I ran out,' Kinnaird said. 'I couldn't see a thing for black smoke and flying oil. I ran maybe twenty yards to the south to get some idea of what was happening. The whole camp seemed to be on fire. When you're woken up like that at two in the morning, half-blinded, half-asleep and groggy with fumes your mind isn't at its best, but thank God I'd enough left of my mind to realize that an S O S radio message was the one thing that was going to save our lives. So I went back inside the radio hut.'

'We all owe our lives to Kinnaird.' Speaking for the first time was Jeremy, a burly red-haired Canadian who had been chief technician on the base. 'And if I'd been a bit quicker with my hands we'd have all been dead.'

'Oh, for Christ's sake, mate, shut up,' Kinnaird growled.

'I won't shut up,' Jeremy said soberly. 'Besides, Dr Carpenter wants a full report. I was first out of the main bunkhouse after Captain Folsom here. As Hewson said, we tried the extinguisher on Major Halliwell's hut. It was hopeless from the beginning but we had to do it – after all, we knew there were four men trapped in there. But, like I say, it was a waste of time. Captain Folsom shouted that he was going to get another extinguisher and told me to see how things were in the radio room.

'The place was ablaze from end to end. As I came round as close as I could to the door at the west end I saw Naseby here bending over Dr Jolly, who'd keeled over as soon as he had come out into the fresh air. He shouted to me to give him a hand to drag Dr Jolly clear and I was just about to when Kinnaird, here, came running up. I saw he was heading straight for the door of the radio room.' He smiled without humour. 'I thought he had gone off his rocker. I jumped in front of him, to stop him. He shouted at me to get out of the way. I told him not to be crazy and he yelled at me – you had to yell to make yourself heard above the roar of the flames – that he had to get the portable radio out, that all the oil was gone and the generator and the cookhouse with all the food were burning up. He knocked me down and the next I saw was him disappearing through that door. Smoke and flames were pouring through the doorway. I don't know how he ever got out alive.'

'Was that how you got your face and hands so badly burnt?' Commander Swanson asked quietly. He was standing in a far corner of the wardroom, having taken no part in the discussion up till now, but missing nothing all the same. That was why I had asked him to be present: just because he was a man who missed nothing.

'I reckon so, sir.'

'I fancy that should earn a trip to Buckingham Palace,' Swanson murmured.

'The hell with Buckingham Palace,' Kinnaird said violently. 'How about my mate, eh? How about young Jimmy Grant? Can he make the trip to Buckingham Palace? Not now he can't, the poor bastard. Do you know what he was doing? He was still *inside* the radio room when I went back in, sitting at the main transmitter, sending out an S O S on our regular frequency. His clothes were on fire. I dragged him off his seat and shouted to him to grab some Nife cells and get out. I caught up the portable transmitter and a nearby box of Nife cells and ran through the door. I thought Grant was on my heels but I couldn't hear anything, what with the roar of flames and the bursting of fuel drums the racket was deafening. Unless you'd been there you just can't begin to imagine what it was like. I ran far enough clear to put the radio and cells in a safe place. Then I went back. I asked Naseby, who was still trying to bring Dr Jolly round, if Jimmy Grant had come out. He said he hadn't. I started to run for the door again – and, well, that's all I remember.'

'I clobbered him,' Jeremy said with gloomy satisfaction. 'From behind. I had to.'

'I could have killed you when I came round,' Kinnaird said morosely. 'But I guess you saved my life at that.'

'I certainly did, brother.' Jeremy grimaced. 'That was my big contribution that night. Hitting people. After Naseby, here, had brought Dr Jolly round he suddenly started shouting: 'Where's Flanders and Bryce, where's Flanders and Bryce?' Those were the two who had been sleeping with Hewson and himself in the cookhouse. A few others had come down from the main bunkhouse by that time and the best part of a minute had elapsed before we realized that Flanders and Bryce weren't among them. Naseby, here, started back for the cookhouse at a dead run. He was making for the doorway, only there was no doorway left, just a solid curtain of fire where the doorway used to be. I swung at him as he passed and he fell and hit his head on the ice.' He looked at Naseby. 'Sorry again, Johnny, but you were quite crazy at the moment.'

Naseby rubbed his jaw and grinned wearily. 'I can still feel it. And God knows you were right.'

'Then Captain Folsom arrived, along with Dick Foster, who also slept in the main bunkhouse,' Jeremy went on. 'Captain Folsom said he'd tried every other extinguisher on the base and that all of them were frozen solid. He'd heard about Grant being trapped inside the radio room and he and Foster were carrying a blanket apiece, soaked with water. I tried to stop them but Captain Folsom ordered me to stand aside.' Jeremy smiled faintly. 'When Captain Folsom orders people to stand aside – well, they do just that.'

'He and Foster threw the wet blankets over their heads and ran inside. Captain Folsom was out in a few seconds, carrying Grant. I've never seen anything like it, they were burning like human torches. I don't know what happened to Foster, but he never came out. By that time the roofs of both Major Halliwell's hut and the cookhouse had fallen in. Nobody could get anywhere near either of those buildings. Besides, it was far too late by then, Major Halliwell and the three others inside the major's hut and Flanders and Bryce inside the cookhouse must already have been dead. Dr Jolly, here, doesn't think they would have suffered very much – asphyxiation would have got them, like enough, before the flames did.'

'Well,' I said slowly, 'that's as clear a picture of what must have been a very confusing and terrifying experience as we're ever likely to get. It wasn't possible to get anywhere near Major Halliwell's hut?'

'You couldn't have gone within fifteen feet of it and hoped to live,' Naseby said simply.

'And what happened afterwards?'

'I took charge, old boy,' Jolly said. 'Wasn't much to take charge of, though, and what little there was to be done could be done only by myself – fixing up the injured, I mean. I made 'em all wait out there on the ice-cap until the flames had died down a bit and there didn't seem to be any more likelihood of further fuel drums bursting then we all made our way to the bunkhouse where I did the best I could for the injured men. Kinnaird here, despite pretty bad burns, proved himself a first-class assistant doctor. We bedded down the worst of them. Young Grant was in a shocking condition – 'fraid there never really was very much hope for him. And – well, that was about all there was to it.'

'You had no food for the next few days and nights?'

'Nothing at all, old boy. No heat either, except for the standby Coleman lamps that were in the three remaining huts. We managed to melt a little water from the ice, that was all. By my orders everyone remained lying down and wrapped up in what was available in order to conserve energy and warmth.'

'Bit rough on you,' I said to Kinnaird. 'Having to lose any hard-earned warmth you had every couple of hours in order to make those S O S broadcasts.'

'Not only me,' Kinnaird said. 'I'm no keener on frost-bite than anyone else. Dr Jolly insisted that everyone who could should take turn about at sending out the S O S's. Wasn't hard. There was a pre-set mechanical call-up and all anyone had to do was to send this and listen in on the earphones. If any message came through I was across to the met. office in a flash. It was actually Hewson, here, who contacted the ham operator in Bodo and Jeremy who got through to that trawler in the Barents Sea. I carried on from there, of course. Apart from them there were Dr Jolly and Naseby, here, to give a hand, so it wasn't so bad. Hassard, too, took a turn after the first day – he'd been more or less blinded on the night of the fire.'

'You remained in charge throughout, Dr Jolly?' I asked.

'Bless my soul, no. Captain Folsom, here, was in a pretty shocked condition for the first twenty-four hours, but when he'd recovered from that he took over. I'm only a pill-roller, old boy. As a leader of men and a dashing man of action – well, no, quite frankly, old top, I don't see myself in that light at all.'

'You did damned well, all the same.' I looked round the company. 'That most of you won't be scarred for life is due entirely to the quick and highly efficient treatment Dr Jolly gave you under almost impossible circumstances. Well, that's all. Must be a pretty painful experience for all of you, having to relive that night again. I can't see that we can ever hope to find out how the fire started, just one of those chance in a million accidents, what the insurance companies call an act of God. I'm certain, Hewson, that no shadow of negligence attaches to you and that your theory on the outbreak of fire is probably correct. Anyway, although we've paid a hellishly high cost, we've learnt a lesson – never again to site a main fuel store within a hundred yards of the camp.'

The meeting broke up. Jolly bustled off to the sick-bay, not quite managing to conceal his relish at being the only medical officer aboard who wasn't *hors de combat.* He had a busy couple of hours ahead of him – changing bandages on burns, checking Benson, X-raying Zabrinski's broken ankle and resetting the plaster.

I went to my cabin, unlocked my case, took out a small wallet, relocked my case and went to Swanson's cabin. I noticed that he wasn't smiling quite so often now as when I'd first met him in Scotland. He looked up as I came in answer to his call and said without preamble: 'If those two men still out in the camp are in any way fit to be moved I want them both aboard at once. The sooner we're back in Scotland and have some law in on this the happier I'll be. I warned you that this investigation of yours would turn up nothing. Lord knows how short a time it will be before someone else gets clobbered. God's sake, Carpenter, we have a murderer running loose.'

'Three things,' I said. 'Nobody's going to get clobbered any more, that's almost for certain. Secondly, the law, as you call it, wouldn't be allowed to touch it. And in the third place, the meeting this morning was of some use. It eliminated three potential suspects.'

'I must have missed something that you didn't.'

'Not that. I knew something that you didn't. I knew that under the floor of the laboratory were about forty Nife cells in excellent condition – but cells that had been used.'

'The hell you did,' he said softly. 'Sort of forgot to tell me, didn't you?'

'In this line of business I never tell anyone anything unless I think he can help me by having that knowledge.'

'You must win an awful lot of friends and influence an awful lot of people,' Swanson said dryly.

'It gets embarrassing. Now, who could have used cells? Only those who left the bunkhouse from time to time to send out the S O S's. That cuts out Captain Folsom and the Harrington twins – there's no question of any of the three of them having left the bunkhouse at any time. They weren't fit to. So that leaves Hewson, Naseby, Dr Jolly, Jeremy, Hassard and Kinnaird. Take your choice. One of them is a murderer.'

'Why did they want those extra cells?' Swanson asked. 'And if they had those extra cells why did they risk their lives by relying on those dying cells that they did use. Does it make sense to you?'

'There's sense in everything,' I said. If you want evasion, Carpenter has it. I brought out my wallet, spread cards before him. He picked them up, studied them and returned them to my wallet.

'So now we have it,' he said calmly. 'Took quite a while to get round to it, didn't you? The truth, I mean. Officer of M.I.6. Counter-espionage. Government agent, eh? Well, I won't make any song and dance about it, Carpenter, I've known since yesterday what you must be: you couldn't be anything else.' He looked at me in calm speculation. 'You fellows never disclose your identity unless you have to.' He left the logical question unspoken.

'Three reasons why I'm telling you. You're entitled to some measure of my confidence. I want you on my side. And because of what I'm about to tell you, you'd have known anyway. Have you ever heard of the Perkin-Elmer Roti satellite missile tracker camera?'

'Quite a mouthful,' he murmured. 'No.'

'Heard of Samos? Samos III?'

'Satellite and Missile Observation System?' He nodded. 'I have. And what conceivable connection could that have with a ruthless killer running amok on Drift Station Zebra?'

So I told him what connection it could have. A connection that was not only conceivable, not only possible, not only probable, but absolutely certain. Swanson listened very carefully, very attentively, not interrupting even once and at the end of it he leaned back in his chair and nodded. 'You have the right of it, no doubt about that. The question is, who? I just can't wait to see this fiend under close arrest and armed guard.'

'You'd clap him in irons straight away?'

'Good God!' He stared at me. 'Wouldn't you?'

'I don't know. Yes, I do. I'd leave him be. I think our friend is just a link in a very long chain and if we give him enough rope he'll not only hang himself, he'll lead us to the other members of the chain. Besides, I'm not all that sure that there *is* only one murderer: killers have been known to have accomplices before now, Commander.'

'Two of them? You think there may be two killers aboard my ship?' He pursed his lips and squeezed his chin with a thoughtful hand, Swanson's nearest permissible approach to a state of violent agitation. Then he shook his head definitely. 'There may only be one. If that is so, and I knew who he was, I'd arrest him at once. Don't forget, Carpenter, we've hundreds of miles to go under the ice before we're out in the open sea. We can't watch all six of them all the time and there are a hundred and one things that a man with even only a little knowledge of submarines could do that would put us all in mortal danger. Things that wouldn't matter were we clear of the ice, things that would be fatal under it.'

'Aren't you rather overlooking the fact that if the killer did us in he'd also be doing himself in?'

'I don't necessarily share your belief in his sanity. All killers are a little crazy. No matter how excellent their reasons for killing, the very fact that they do kill makes them a rogue human being, an abnormal. You can't judge them by normal standards.'

He was only half-right, but unfortunately that half might apply in this case. Most murderers kill in a state of extreme emotional once-in-a-lifetime stress and never kill again. But our friend in this case had every appearance of being a stranger to emotional stress of any kind – and, besides, he'd killed a great deal more than once.

'Well,' I said doubtfully. 'Perhaps. Yes, I think I do agree with you.' I refrained from specifying our common ground for agreement. 'Who's your candidate for the high jump, Commander?'

'I'm damned if I know. I listened to every word that was said this morning. I watched the face of each man who spoke – and the faces of the ones who weren't speaking. I've been thinking nonstop about it since and I'm still damned if I have a clue. How about Kinnaird?'

'He's the obvious suspect, isn't he? But only because he's a skilled radio operator. I could train a man in a couple of days to send and receive in morse. Slow, clumsy, he wouldn't know a thing about the instrument he was using, but he could still do it. Any of them may easily have been competent enough to operate a radio. The fact that Kinnaird is a skilled operator may even be a point in his favour.'

'Nife cells were removed from the radio cabin and taken to the laboratory,' Swanson pointed out. 'Kinnaird had the easiest access to them. Apart from Dr Jolly who had his office and sleeping quarters in the same hut.'

'So that would point a finger at Kinnaird or Jolly?'

'Well, wouldn't it?'

'Certainly. Especially if you will agree that the presence of those tinned foods under the lab. floor also points a finger at Hewson and Naseby, both of whom slept in the cookhouse where the food was stored, and that the presence of the radio-sonde balloon and the hydrogen in the lab. also points a finger at Jeremy and Hassard, one a met. officer and the other a technician who would have had the easiest access to those items.'

'That's right, confuse things,' Swanson said irritably. 'As if they weren't confused enough already.'

'I'm not confusing things. All I'm saying is that if you admit a certain possibility for a certain reason then you must admit similar possibilities for similar reasons. Besides, there are points in Kinnaird's favour. He risked his life to go back into the radio room to bring out the portable transmitter. He risked almost certain suicide when he tried to go in the second time to bring out his assistant, Grant, and probably would have died if Jeremy hadn't clobbered him. Look what happened to that man Foster who went in there immediately afterwards with a wet blanket over his head – *he* never came out.

'Again, would Kinnaird have mentioned the Nife cells if he had any guilt complex about them? But he did. That, incidentally, might have been why Grant, the assistant radio operator, collapsed in there and later died – Kinnaird had told him to bring out the other Nife cells and he was overcome because he stayed there too long looking for things that had already been removed from the hut. And there's one final point: we have Naseby's word for it that the door of the radio room was jammed, presumably by ice. Had Kinnaird been playing with matches a few moments previously, that door wouldn't have had time to freeze up.'

'If you let Kinnaird out,' Swanson said slowly, 'you more or less have to let Dr Jolly out too.' He smiled. 'I don't see a member of your profession running round filling people full of holes, Dr Carpenter. Repairing holes is their line of business, not making them. Hippocrates wouldn't have liked it.'

'I'm not letting Kinnaird out,' I said. 'But I'm not going off half-cocked and pinning a murder rap on him either. As for the ethics of my profession – would you like a list of the good healers who have decorated the dock in the Old Bailey? True, we have nothing on Jolly. His part in the proceedings that night seems to have consisted in staggering out from the radio room, falling flat on his face and staying there till pretty near the end of the fire. That, of course, has no bearing upon whatever part he might have taken in the proceedings prior to the fire. Though against that possibility there's the fact of the jammed door, the fact that Kinnaird or Grant would have been almost bound to notice if he had been up to something – Jolly's bunk was at the back of the radio room and he would have had to pass Kinnaird and Grant to get out, not forgetting that he would also have to stop to pick up the Nife cells. And there is one more point in his favour – an apparent point, that is. I still don't think that Benson's fall was an accident and if it was no accident it is difficult to see how Jolly could have arranged it while he was at the foot of the sail and Benson at the top and it's even more difficult to see why he should have stood at the foot of the sail and let Benson fall on top of him.'

'You're putting up a very good defence case for both Jolly and Kinnaird,' Swanson murmured.

'No. I'm only saying what a defence lawyer would say.'

'Hewson,' Swanson said slowly. 'Or Naseby, the cook. Or Hewson *and* Naseby. Don't you think it damned funny that those two, who were sleeping at the back or east side of the cookhouse, which was the first part of the hut to catch fire, should have managed to escape while the other two – Flanders and Bryce, wasn't it – who slept in the middle should have suffocated in there? Naseby said he shouted at them and shook them violently. Maybe he could have shouted and shaken all night without result. Maybe they were already unconscious – or dead. Maybe they had seen Naseby or Hewson or both removing food supplies and had been silenced. Or maybe they had been silenced *before* anything had been removed. And don't forget the gun. It was hidden in the petrol tank of the tractor, a pretty damn' funny place for a man to hide anything. But nothing funny about the idea occurring to Hewson, was there? He was the tractor-driver. And he seems to have taken his time about getting around to warn Captain Folsom. He said he had to make a wide circuit to avoid the flames but apparently Naseby didn't find it so bad when he went to the radio room. Another thing, a pretty telling point, I think, he said that when he was on the way to the bunkhouse the oil drums in the fuel store started exploding. If they only started exploding then how come all the huts – the five that were eventually destroyed, that is – were already uncontrollably on fire. They were uncontrollably on fire because they were saturated by flying oil so the first explosions, must have come a long time before then. And, apart from warning Folsom – who had already been warned – Hewson doesn't seem to have done very much after the fire started.'

'You'd make a pretty good prosecuting counsel yourself, Commander. But wouldn't you think there is just too *much* superficially against Hewson? That a clever man wouldn't have allowed so much superficial evidence to accumulate against him? You would have thought that, at least, he would have indulged in a little fire-fighting heroics to call attention to himself?'

'No. You're overlooking the fact that he would never have had reason to expect that there would be any investigation into the causes of the fire? That the situation would never arise where he – or anyone else, for that matter – would have to justify their actions and behaviour if accusations were to be levelled against them?'

'I've said it before and I say it again. People like that *never* take a chance. They always act on the assumption that they *may* be found out.'

'How could they be found out?' Swanson protested. 'How could they possibly expect to have suspicion aroused?'

'You don't think it possible that they suspect that we are on to them?'

'No, I don't.'

'That wasn't what you were saying last night after that hatch fell on me,' I pointed out. 'You said it was obvious that someone was on to me.'

'Thank the lord that all I have to do is the nice uncomplicated job of running a nuclear submarine,' Swanson said heavily. 'The truth is, I don't know what to think any more. How about this cook fellow – Naseby?'

'You think he was in cahoots with Hewson?'

'If we accept the premise that the men in the cookhouse who were not in on this business had to be silenced, and Naseby wasn't, then he must have been, mustn't he? But, dammit, how then about his attempt to rescue Flanders and Bryce?'

'May just have been a calculated risk. He saw how Jeremy flattened Kinnaird when he tried to go back into the radio-room a second time and perhaps calculated that Jeremy would oblige again if he tried a similar but fake rescue act.'

'Maybe Kinnaird's second attempt was also fake,' Swanson said. 'After all, Jeremy had already tried to stop him once.'

'Maybe it was,' I agreed. 'But Naseby. If he's your man, why should he have said that the radio room door was jammed with ice, and that he had to burst it open. That gives Kinnaird and Jolly an out – and a murderer wouldn't do anything to put any other potential suspect in the clear.'

'It's hopeless,' Swanson said calmly. 'I say let's put the whole damn' crowd of them under lock and key.'

'That would be clever,' I said. 'Yes, let's do just that. That way we'll never find out who the murderer is. Anyway, before you start giving up, remember it's even more complicated than that. Remember you're passing up the two most obvious suspects of all – Jeremy and Hassard, two tough, intelligent birds who, if they were the killers, were clever enough to see that *nothing* pointed the finger against them. Unless, of course, there might have been something about Flanders and Bryce that Jeremy didn't want anyone to see, so he stopped Naseby from going back into the cookhouse. Or not.'

Swanson almost glared at me. Watching his submarine plummeting out of control beyond the 1000-feet mark was something that rated maybe the lift of an eyebrow; but this was something else again. He said: 'Very well, then, we'll let the killer run loose and wreck the *Dolphin* at his leisure. I must have very considerable confidence in you, Dr Carpenter. I feel sure my confidence will not be misplaced. Tell me one last thing. I assume you are a highly skilled investigator. But I was puzzled by one omission in your questioning. A vital question, I should have thought.'

'Who suggested moving the corpses into the lab. knowing that by doing so he would be making his hiding-place for the cached material a hundred per cent foolproof?'

'I apologize.' He smiled faintly. 'You had your reasons, of course.'

'Of course. You're not sure whether or not the killer is on to the fact that we are on to him. I'm sure. I know he's not. But had I asked that question, he'd have known immediately that there could be only one reason for my asking it. Then he would have known I was on to him. Anyway, it's my guess that Captain Folsom gave the order, but the original suggestion, carefully camouflaged so that Folsom may no longer be able to pin it down, would have come from another quarter.'

Had it been a few months earlier with the summer Arctic sun riding in the sky, it would have been a brilliant day. As it was, there was no sun not in that latitude and so late in the year, but for all that the weather was about as perfect as it was possible for it to be. Thirty-six hours – the time that had elapsed since Hansen and I had made that savage trip back to the *Dolphin* – had brought about a change that seemed pretty close to miraculous. The knifing east wind had died, completely. That flying sea of ice-spicules was no more. The temperature had risen at least twenty degrees and the visibility was as perfect as visibility on the winter ice-pack ever is.

Swanson, sharing Benson's viewpoint on the crew's over-sedentary mode of existence and taking advantage of the fine weather, had advised everyone not engaged in actual watch-keeping to take advantage of the opportunity offered to stretch their legs in the fresh air. It said much for Swanson's powers of persuasion that by eleven that morning the *Dolphin* was practically deserted; and of course the crew, to whom Drift Ice Station Zebra was only so many words, were understandably curious to see the place, even the shell of the place, that had brought them to the top of the world.

I took my place at the end of the small queue being treated by Dr Jolly. It was close on noon before he got round to me. He was making light of his own burns and frost-bite and was in tremendous form, bustling happily about the sick-bay as if it had been his own private domain for years.

'Well,' I said, 'the pill-rolling competition wasn't so fierce after all, was it? I'm damned glad there was a third doctor around. How are things on the medical front?'

'Coming along not too badly, old boy,' he said cheerfully. 'Benson's picking up very nicely, pulse, respiration, blood-pressure close to normal, level of unconsciousness very slight now, I should say. Captain Folsom's still in considerable pain, but no actual danger, of course. The rest have improved a hundred per cent, little thanks to the medical fraternity: excellent food, warm beds and the knowledge that they're safe have done them more good than anything we could ever do. Anyway, it's done me a lot of good, by jove!'

'And them,' I agreed. 'All your friends except Folsom and the Harrington twins have followed most of the crew on to the ice and I'll wager that if you had suggested to them forty-eight hours ago that they'd willingly go out there again in so short a time, they'd have called for a strait-jacket.'

'The physical and mental recuperative power of homo sapiens,' Jolly said jovially. 'Beyond belief at times, old lad, beyond belief. Now, let's have a look at that broken wing of yours.'

So he had a look, and because I was a colleague and therefore inured to human suffering he didn't spend any too much time in molly-coddling me, but by hanging on to the arm of my chair and the shreds of my professional pride I kept the roof from falling in on me. When he was finished he said: 'Well, that's the lot, except for Brownell and Bolton, the two lads out on the ice.'

'I'll come with you,' I said. 'Commander Swanson is waiting pretty anxiously to hear what we have to say. He wants to get away from here as soon as possible.'

'Me, too,' Jolly said fervently. 'But what's the commander so anxious about?'

'Ice. You never know the hour or minute it starts to close in. Want to spend the next year or two up here?'

Jolly grinned, thought over it for a bit, then stopped grinning. He said apprehensively: 'How long are we going to be under this damned ice? Before we reach the open sea, I mean?'

'Twenty-four hours, Swanson says. Don't look so worried, Jolly. Believe me, it's far safer under this stuff than among it.'

With a very unconvinced look on his face Jolly picked up his medical kit and led the way from the sick-bay. Swanson was waiting for us in the control room. We climbed up the hatches, dropped down over the side and walked over to the Drift Station.

Most of the crew had already made their way out there. We passed numbers of them on the way back and most of them looked grim or sick or both and didn't even glance up as we passed. I didn't have to guess why they looked as they did, they'd been opening doors that they should have left closed.

With the sharp rise in outside temperature and the effect of the big electric heaters having been burning there for twenty-four hours the bunkhouse hut was now, if anything, overheated, with the last traces of ice long vanished from walls and ceiling. One of the men, Brownell, had recovered consciousness and was sitting up, supported, and drinking soup provided by one of the two men who had been keeping watch over him.

'Well,' I said to Swanson, 'here's one ready to go.'

'No doubt about that,' Jolly said briskly. He bent over the other, Bolton, for some seconds, then straightened and shook his head. 'A very sick man, Commander, very sick. I wouldn't care to take the responsibility of moving him.'

'I might be forced to take the responsibility myself,' Swanson said bluntly. 'Let's have another opinion on this.' His tone and words, I thought, could have been more diplomatic and conciliatory; but if there were a couple of murderers aboard the *Dolphin* there was a thirty-three and a third per cent chance that Jolly was one of them and Swanson wasn't forgetting it for a moment.

I gave Jolly an apologetic half-shrug, bent over Bolton and examined him as best I could with only one hand available for the task. I straightened and said: 'Jolly's right. He is pretty sick. But I think he might just stand the transfer to the ship.'

' "Might just" is not quite the normally accepted basis for deciding the treatment of a patient,' Jolly objected.

'I know it's not. But the circumstances are hardly normal either.'

'I'll take the responsibility,' Swanson said. 'Dr Jolly, I'd be most grateful if you would supervise the transport of those two men back to the ship. I'll let you have as many men as you want straight away.'

Jolly protested some more, then gave in with good grace. He supervised the transfer, and very competent he was about it too. I remained out there a little longer, watching Rawlings and some others dismantling heaters and lights and rolling up cables and, after the last of them was gone and I was alone, I made my way round to the tractor shed.

The broken haft of the knife was still in the tank of the tractor. But not the gun and not the two magazines. Those were gone. And whoever had taken them it hadn't been Dr Jolly, he hadn't been out of my sight for two consecutive seconds between the time he'd left the *Dolphin* and the time of his return to it.

At three o'clock that afternoon we dropped down below the ice and headed south for the open sea.

Chapter Ten

The afternoon and evening passed quickly and pleasantly enough. Closing our hatches and dropping down from our hardly won foothold in that lead had had a symbolic significance at least as important as the actual fact of leaving itself. The thick ceiling of ice closing over the hull of the *Dolphin* was a curtain being drawn across the eye of the mind. We had severed all physical connection with Drift Ice Station Zebra, a home of the dead that might continue to circle slowly about the Pole for mindless centuries to come; and with the severance had come an abrupt diminution of the horror and the shock which had hung pall-like over the ship and its crew for the past twenty-four hours. A dark door had swung to behind us and we had turned our backs on it. Mission accomplished, duty done, we were heading for home again and the sudden upsurge of relief and happiness among the crew to be on their way again, their high anticipation of port and leave, was an almost tangible thing. The mood of the ship was close to that of lighthearted gaiety. But there was no gaiety in my mind, and no peace: I was leaving too much behind. Nor could there be any peace in the minds of Swanson and Hansen, of Rawlings and Zabrinski: they knew we were carrying a killer aboard, a killer who had killed many times. Dr Benson knew also, but for the moment Dr Benson did not count: he still had not regained consciousness and I held the very unprofessional hope that he wouldn't for some time to come. In the twilight world of emergence from coma a man can start babbling and say all too much.

Some of the Zebra survivors had asked if they could see around the ship and Swanson agreed. In light of what I had told him in his cabin that morning, he must have agreed very reluctantly indeed, but no trace of this reluctance showed in his calmly smiling face. To have refused their request would have been rather a churlish gesture, for all the secrets of the *Dolphin* were completely hidden from the eye of the layman. But it wasn't good manners that made Swanson give his consent: refusing a reasonable request could have been responsible for making someone very suspicious indeed.

Hansen took them around the ship and I accompanied them, less for the exercise or interest involved than for the opportunity it gave me to keep a very close eye indeed on their reactions to their tour. We made a complete circuit of the ship, missing out only the reactor room, which no one could visit, anyway, and the inertial navigation-room which had been barred to me also. As we moved around I watched them all, and especially two of them, as closely as it is possible to watch anyone without making him aware of your observation, and I learned precisely what I had expected to learn – nothing. I'd been crazy even to hope I'd learn anything, our pal with the gun was wearing a mask that had been forged into shape and riveted into position. But I'd had to do it, anyway: playing in this senior league I couldn't pass up the one chance in a million.

Supper over, I helped Jolly as best I could with his evening surgery. Whatever else Jolly was, he was a damn' good doctor. Quickly and efficiently he checked and where necessary rebandaged the walking cases, examined and treated Benson and Folsom then asked me to come right aft with him to the nucleonics laboratory in the stern room which had been cleared of deck gear to accommodate the four other bed patients, the Harrington twins, Brownell and Bolton. The sick-bay itself had only two cots for invalids and Benson and Folsom had those.

Bolton, despite Jolly's dire predictions, hadn't suffered a relapse because of his transfer from the hut to the ship – which had been due largely to Jolly's extremely skilful and careful handling of the patient and the stretcher into which he had been lashed. Bolton, in fact, was conscious now and complaining of severe pain in his badly burned right forearm. Jolly removed the burn covering and Bolton's arm was a mess all right, no skin left worth speaking of, showing an angry violent red between areas of suppuration. Different doctors have different ideas as to the treatment of burns: Jolly favoured a salve-coated aluminium foil which he smoothed across the entire burn area then lightly bandaged in place. He then gave him a pain-killing injection and some sleeping tablets, and briskly informed the enlisted man who was keeping watch that he was to be informed immediately of any change or deterioration in Bolton's condition. A brief inspection of the three others, a changed bandage here and there and he was through for the night.

So was I. For two nights now I had had practically no sleep – what little had been left for me the previous night had been ruined by the pain in my left hand. I was exhausted. When I got to my cabin, Hansen was already asleep and the engineer officer gone.

I didn't need any of Jolly's sleeping pills that night.

I awoke at two o'clock. I was sleep-drugged, still exhausted and felt as if I had been in bed about five minutes. But I awoke in an instant and in that instant I was fully awake.

Only a dead man wouldn't have stirred. The racket issuing from the squawk box just above Hansen's bunk was appalling: a high-pitched, shrieking, atonic whistle, two-toned and altering pitch every half-second, it drilled stiletto-like against my cringing ear-drums. A banshee in its death agonies could never have hoped to compete with that lot.

Hansen already had his feet on the deck and was pulling on clothes and shoes in desperate haste. I had never thought to see that slow-speaking laconic Texan in such a tearing hurry, but I was seeing it now.

'What in hell's name is the matter?' I demanded. I had to shout to make myself heard above the shricking of the alarm whistle.

'Fire!' His face was shocked and grim. 'The ship's on fire. And under this goddamned ice!'

Still buttoning his shirt, he hurdled my cot, crashed the door back on its hinges and was gone.

The atonic screeching of the whistle stopped abruptly and the silence fell like a blow. Then I was conscious of something more than silence – I was conscious of a complete lack of vibration throughout the ship. The great engines had stopped. And then I was conscious of something else again: feathery fingers of ice brushing up and down my spine. Why had the engines stopped? What could make a nuclear engine stop so quickly and what happened once it did? My God, I thought, maybe the fire is coming from the reactor room itself. I'd looked into the heart of the uranium atomic pile through a heavily leaded glass inspection port and seen the indescribable unearthly radiance of it, a nightmarish coalescence of green and violet and blue, the new 'dreadful light' of mankind. What happened when this dreadful light ran amok? I didn't know, but I suspected I didn't want to be around when it happened.

I dressed slowly, not hurrying. My damaged hand didn't help me much but that wasn't why I took my time. Maybe the ship was on fire, maybe the nuclear power plant had gone out of kilter. But if Swanson's superbly trained crew couldn't cope with every emergency that could conceivably arise then matters weren't going to be improved any by Carpenter running around in circles shouting: 'Where's the fire?'

Three minutes after Hansen had gone I walked along to the control room and peered in: if I was going to be in the way then this was as far as I was going to go. Dark acrid smoke billowed past me and a voice – Swanson's – said sharply: 'Inside and close that door.'

I pulled the door to and looked around the control room. At least, I tried to. It wasn't easy. My eyes were already streaming as if someone had thrown a bag of pepper into them and what little sight was left them didn't help me much. The room was filled with black evil-smelling smoke, denser by far and more throat-catching than the worst London fog. Visibility was no more than a few feet, but what little I could see showed me men still at their stations. Some were gasping, some were half-choking, some were cursing softly, all had badly watering eyes, but there was no trace of panic.

'You'd have been better on the other side of that door.' Swanson said dryly. 'Sorry to have barked at you, Doctor, but we want to limit the spread of the smoke as much as possible.'

'Where's the fire?'

'In the engine-room.' Swanson could have been sitting on his front porch at home discussing the weather. 'Where in the engine-room we don't know. It's pretty bad. At least, the smoke is. The extent of the fire we don't know, because we can't locate it. Engineer officer says it's impossible to see your hand in front of your face.'

'The engines,' I said. 'They've stopped. Has anything gone wrong?'

He rubbed his eyes with a handkerchief, spoke to a man who was pulling on a heavy rubber suit and a smoke-mask, then turned back to me.

'We're not going to be vaporized, if that's what you mean.' I could have sworn he was smiling. 'The atomic pile can only fail safe no matter what happens. If anything goes wrong the uranium rods slam down in very quick time indeed – a fraction under a one-thousandth of a second – stopping the whole reaction. In this case, though, we shut it off ourselves. The men in the manoeuvring-room could no longer see either the reactor dials or the governor for the control rods. No option but to shut it down. The engine-room crew have been forced to abandon the engine and manoeuvring-rooms and take shelter in the stern room.'

Well, that was something at least. We weren't going to be blown to pieces, ignobly vaporized on the altar of nuclear advancement; good old-fashioned suffocation, that was to be our lot. 'So what do we do?' I asked.

'What we should do is surface immediately. With fourteen feet of ice overhead that's not easy. Excuse me, will you?'

He spoke to the now completely masked and suited man who was carrying a small dialled box in his hands. They walked together past the navigator's chart desk and ice-machine to the heavy door opening on the passage that led to the engine-room over the top of the reactor compartment. They unclipped the door, pushed it open. A dense blinding cloud of dark smoke rolled into the room as the masked man stepped quickly into the passageway and swung the door to behind him. Swanson clamped the door shut, walked, temporarily blinded, back to the control position and fumbled down a roof microphone.

'Captain speaking.' His voice echoed emptily through the control centre. 'The fire is located in the engine-room. We do not know yet whether it is electrical, chemical or fuel oil: the source of the fire has not been pin-pointed. Acting on the principle of being prepared for the worst, we are now testing for a radiation leak.' So that was what the masked man had been carrying, a Geiger counter. 'If that proves negative, we shall try for a steam leak; and if that is negative we shall carry out an intensive search to locate the fire. It will not be easy as I'm told visibility is almost zero. We have already shut down all electrical circuits in the engine-room, lighting included, to prevent an explosion in the event of atomized fuel being present in the atmosphere. We have closed the oxygen intake valves and isolated the engine-room from the air-cleaning system in the hope that the fire will consume all available oxygen and burn itself out.

'All smoking is prohibited until further notice. Heaters, fans, and all electrical circuits other than communication lines to be switched off – and that includes the juke-box and the ice-cream machine. All lamps to be switched off except those absolutely essential. All movement is to be restricted to a minimum. I shall keep you informed of any progress we may make.'

I became aware of someone standing by my side. It was Dr Jolly, his normally jovial face puckered and woebegone, the tears flowing down his face. Plaintively he said to me: 'This *is* a bit thick, old boy, what? I'm not sure that I'm so happy now about being rescued. And all those prohibitions – no smoking, no power to be used, no moving around – do those mean what I take them to mean?'

'I'm afraid they do indeed.' It was Swanson who answered Jolly's question for him. 'This, I'm afraid, is every nuclear submarine captain's nightmare come true – fire under the ice. At one stroke we're not only reduced to the level of a conventional submarine – we're two stages worse. In the first place, a conventional submarine wouldn't be under the ice, anyway. In the second place, it has huge banks of storage batteries, and even if it were beneath the ice it would have sufficient reserve power to steam far enough south to get clear of the ice. Our reserve battery is so small that it wouldn't take us a fraction of the way.'

'Yes, yes,' Jolly nodded. 'But this no smoking, no moving—'

'That same very small battery, I'm afraid, is the only source left to us for power for the air-purifying machines, for lighting, ventilation, heating – I'm afraid the *Dolphin* is going to get very cold in a short time – so we have to curtail its expenditure of energy on those things. So no smoking, minimum movement – the less carbon dioxide breathed into the atmosphere the better. But the real reason for conserving electric energy is that we need it to power the heaters, pumps and motors that have to be used to start up the reactor again. If that battery exhausts itself before we get the reactor going – well, I don't have to draw a diagram.'

'You're not very encouraging, are you, Commander?' Jolly complained.

'No, not very. I don't see any reason to be,' Swanson said dryly.

'I'll bet you'd trade in your pension for a nice open lead above us just now,' I said.

'I'd trade in the pension of every flag officer in the United States Navy,' he said matter-of-factly. 'If we could find a polynya I'd surface, open the engine-room hatch to let most of the contaminated air escape, start up our diesel – it takes its air direct from the engine-room – and have the rest of the smoke sucked out in nothing flat. As it is, that diesel is about as much use to me as a grand piano.'

'And the compasses?' I asked.

'That's another interesting thought,' Swanson agreed. 'If the power output from our reserve battery falls below a certain level, our three Sperry gyro-compass systems and the N6A – that's the inertial guidance machine – just pack up. After that we're lost, completely. Our magnetic compass is quite useless in these latitudes – it just walks in circles.'

'So we would go around and around in circles, too,' Jolly said thoughtfully. 'For ever and ever under the jolly old ice-cap, what? By jove, Commander, I'm really beginning to wish we'd stayed up at Zebra.'

'We're not dead yet, Doctor . . . Yes, John?' This to Hansen, who had just come up.

'Sanders, sir. On the ice-machine. Can he have a smoke mask. His eyes are watering pretty badly.'

'Give him anything you like in the ship.' Swanson said, 'just so long as he can keep his eyes clear to read that graph. And double the watch on the ice-machine. If there's a lead up there only the size of a hair, I'm going for it. Immediate report if the ice thickness falls below, say, eight or nine feet.'

'Torpedoes?' Hansen asked. 'There hasn't been ice thin enough for that in three hours. And at the speed we're drifting there won't be for three months. I'll go keep the watch myself. I'm not much good for anything else, this hand of mine being the way it is.'

'Thank you. First you might tell Engineman Harrison to turn off the CO_2 scrubber and monoxide burners. Must save every amp of power we have. Besides, it will do this pampered bunch of ours the world of good to sample a little of what the old-time submariners had to experience when they were forced to stay below maybe twenty hours at a time.'

'That's going to be pretty rough on our really sick men,' I said. 'Benson and Folsom in the sick-bay, the Harrington twins, Brownell and Bolton in the nucleonics lab, right aft. They've got enough to contend with without foul air as well.'

'I know,' Swanson admitted. 'I'm damnably sorry about it. Later on, when – and if – the air gets really bad, we'll start up the air-purifying systems again but blank off every place except the lab. and sick-bay.' He broke off and turned round as a fresh wave of dark smoke rolled in from the suddenly opened after door. The man with the smoke mask was back from the engine-room and even with my eyes streaming in that smoke-filled acrid atmosphere I could see he was in a pretty bad way. Swanson and two others rushed to meet him, two of them catching him as he staggered into the control room, the third quickly swinging the heavy door shut against the darkly-evil clouds of smoke.

Swanson pulled off the man's smoke mask. It was Murphy, the man who had accompanied me when we'd closed the torpedo tube door. People like Murphy and Rawlings, I thought, always got picked for jobs like this.

His face was white and he was gasping for air, his eyes upturned in his head. He was hardly more than half-conscious, but even that foul atmosphere in the control centre must have seemed to him like the purest mountain air compared to what he had just been breathing for within thirty seconds his head had begun to clear and he was able to grin up painfully from where he'd been lowered into a chair.

'Sorry, Captain,' he gasped. 'This smoke-mask was never meant to cope with the stuff that's in the engine-room. Pretty hellish in there, I tell you.' He grinned again. 'Good news, Captain. No radiation leak.'

'Where's the Geiger counter?' Swanson asked quietly.

'It's had it, I'm afraid, sir. I couldn't see where I was going in there, honest, sir, you can't see three inches in front of your face. I tripped and damn' near fell down into the machinery space. The counter did fall down. But I'd a clear check before then. Nothing at all.' He reached up to his shoulder and unclipped his film badge. 'This'll show, sir.'

'Have that developed immediately. That was very well done, Murphy,' he said warmly. 'Now nip for'ard to the mess room. You'll find some really clear air there.'

The film badge was developed and brought back in minutes. Swanson took it, glanced at it briefly, smiled and let out his breath in a long slow whistle of relief. 'Murphy was right. No radiation leak. Thank God for that, anyway. If there had been well, that was that, I'm afraid.'

'The for'ard door of the control room opened, a man passed through, and the door was as quickly closed. I guessed who it was before I could see him properly.'

'Permission from Chief Torpedoman Patterson to approach you, sir,' Rawlings said with brisk formality. 'We've just seen Murphy, pretty groggy he is, and both the Chief and I think that youngsters like that shouldn't be—'

'Am I to understand that you are volunteering to go next, Rawlings?' Swanson asked. The screws of responsibility and tension were turned hard down on him, but I could see that it cost him some effort to keep his face straight.

'Well, not exactly volunteering, sir. But – well, who else is there.'

'The torpedo department aboard this ship,' Swanson observed acidly, 'always did have a phenomenally high opinion of itself.'

'Let him try an underwater oxygen set,' I said. 'Those smoke-masks seem to have their limitations.'

'A steam leak, Captain?' Rawlings asked. 'That what you want me to check on?'

'Well, you seem to have been nominated, voted for and elected by yourself,' Swanson said. 'Yes, a steam leak.'

'That the suit Murphy was wearing?' Rawlings pointed to the clothes on the desk.

'Yes. Why?'

'You'd have thought there would be some signs of moisture or condensation if there had been a steam leak, sir.'

'Maybe. Maybe soot and smoke particles are holding the condensing steam in suspension. Maybe it was hot enough in there to dry off any moisture that did reach his suit. Maybe a lot of things. Don't stay too long in there.'

'Just as long as it takes me to get things fixed up,' Rawlings said confidently. He turned to Hansen and grinned. 'You baulked me once back out there on the ice-cap, Lieutenant, but sure as little apples I'm going to get that little old medal this time. Bring undying credit on the whole ship, I will.'

'If Torpedoman Rawlings will ease up with his ravings for a moment,' Hansen said, 'I have a suggestion to make, Captain. I know he won't be able to take off his mask inside there but if he would give a call-up signal on the engine telephone or ring through on the engine answering telegraph every four or five minutes we'd know he was O.K. If he doesn't, someone can go in after him.'

Swanson nodded. Rawlings pulled on suit and oxygen apparatus and left. That made it the third time the door leading to the engine compartment had been opened in a few minutes and each time fresh clouds of that black and biting smoke had come rolling in. Conditions were now very bad inside the control room, but someone had issued a supply of goggles all round and a few were wearing smoke-masks.

A phone rang. Hansen answered, spoke briefly and hung up.

'That was Jack Cartwright, Skipper.' Lieutenant Cartwright was the main propulsion officer, who'd been on watch in the manoeuvring-room and had been forced to retreat to the stern room. 'Seems he was overcome by the fumes and was carried back into the stern room. Says he's O.K. now and could we send smoke-masks or breathing apparatus for himself and one of his men – they can't get at the ones in the engine-room. I told him yes.'

'I'd certainly feel a lot happier if Jack Cartwright was in there investigating in person,' Swanson admitted. 'Send a man, will you?'

'I thought I'd take them myself. Someone else can double on the ice-machine.'

Swanson glanced at Hansen's injured hand, hesitated then nodded. 'Right. But straight through the engine-room and straight back.'

Hansen was on his way inside a minute. Five minutes later he was back again. He stripped off his breathing equipment. His face was pale and covered in sweat.

'There's fire in the engine-room, all right,' he said grimly. 'Hotter than the hinges of hell. No trace of sparks or flames but that doesn't mean a thing, the smoke in there is so thick that you couldn't see a blast furnace a couple of feet away.'

'See Rawlings?' Swanson asked.

'No. Has he not rung through?'

'Twice, but—' He broke off as the engine-room telegraph rang. 'So. He's still O.K. How about the stern room, John?'

'Damn' sight worse than it is here. The sick men aft there are in a pretty bad way, especially Bolton. Seems the smoke got in before they could get the door shut.'

'Tell Harrison to start up his air scrubbers. But for the lab. only. Blank off the rest of the ship.'

Fifteen minutes passed, fifteen minutes during which the engine-room telegraph rang three times, fifteen minutes during which the air became thicker and fouler and steadily less breathable, fifteen minutes during which a completely equipped fire-fighting team was assembled in the control centre, then another billowing cloud of black smoke announced the opening of the after door.

It was Rawlings. He was very weak and had to be helped out of his breathing equipment and his suit. His face was white and streaming sweat, his hair and clothes so saturated with sweat that he might easily have come straight from an immersion in the sea. But he was grinning triumphantly.

'No steam leak, Captain, that's for certain.' It took him three breaths to get that out. 'But fire down below in the machinery space. Sparks flying all over the shop. Some flame, not much. I located it, sir. Starboard high-pressure turbine. The lagging's on fire.'

'You'll get that medal, Rawlings,' Swanson said, 'even if I have to make the damn' thing myself.' He turned to the waiting firemen. 'You heard. Starboard turbine. Four at a time, fifteen minutes maximum. Lieutenant Raeburn, the first party. Knives, claw-hammers, pliers, crow-bars, CO_2. Saturate the lagging first then rip it off. Watch out for flash flames when you're pulling it off. I don't have to warn you about the steam pipes. Now on your way.'

They left. I said to Swanson: 'Doesn't sound so much. How long will it take. Ten minutes, quarter of an hour?'

He looked at me sombrely. 'A minimum of three or four hours – if we're lucky. It's hell's own maze down in the machinery space there. Valves, tubes, condensers and miles of that damned steam piping that would burn your hands off if you touched it. Working conditions even normally are so cramped as to be almost impossible. Then there's that huge turbine housing with this thick insulation lagging wrapped all round it – and the engineers who fitted it meant it to stay there for keeps. Before they start they have to douse the fire with the CO_2 extinguishers and even that won't help much. Every time they rip off a piece of charred insulation the oil-soaked stuff below will burst into flames again as soon as it comes into contact with the oxygen in the atmosphere.'

'Oil-soaked?'

'That's where the whole trouble must lie,' Swanson exclaimed. 'Wherever you have moving machinery you must have oil for lubrication. There's no shortage of machinery down in the machine space – and no shortage of oil either. And just as certain materials are strongly hygroscopic so that damned insulation has a remarkable affinity for oil. Where there's any around, whether in its normal fluid condition or in fine suspension in the atmosphere that lagging attracts it as a magnet does iron filings. And it's as absorbent as blotting-paper.'

'But what could have caused the fire?'

'Spontaneous combustion. There have been cases before. We've run over 50,000 miles in this ship now and in that time I suppose the lagging has become thoroughly saturated. We've been going at top speed ever since we left Zebra and the excess heat generated has set the damn thing off . . . John, no word from Cartwright yet?'

'Nothing.'

'He must have been in there for the best part of twenty minutes now.'

'Maybe. But he was just beginning to put his suit on – himself and Ringman – when I left. That's not to say they went into the engine-room straight away. I'll call the stern room.' He did, spoke then hung up, his face grave. 'Stern room says that they have been gone twenty-five minutes. Shall I investigate, sir?'

'You stay right here. I'm not—'

He broke off as the after door opened with a crash and two men came staggering out – rather, one staggering, the other supporting him. The door was heaved shut and the men's masks removed. One man I recognized as an enlisted man who had accompanied Raeburn: the other was Cartwright, the main propulsion officer.

'Lieutenant Raeburn sent me out with the lieutenant here,' the enlisted man said. 'He's not so good, I think, Captain.'

It was a pretty fair diagnosis. He wasn't so good and that was a fact. He was barely conscious but none the less fighting grimly to hang on to what few shreds of consciousness were left him.

'Ringman,' he jerked out. 'Five minutes – five minutes ago. We were going back—'

'Ringman,' Swanson prompted with a gentle insistence. 'What about Ringman?'

'He fell. Down into the machinery space. I – I went after him, tried to lift him up the ladder. He screamed. God, he screamed. I – he—'

He slumped in his chair, was caught before he fell to the floor. I said: 'Ringman. Either a major fracture or internal injuries.'

'Damn!' Swanson swore softly. 'Damn and blast it all. A fracture. Down there. John, have Cartwright carried through to the crew's mess. A fracture!'

'Please have a mask and suit ready for me,' Jolly said briskly. 'I'll fetch Dr Benson's emergency kit from the sick-bay.'

'You?' Swanson shook his head. 'Damned decent, Jolly. I appreciate it but I can't let you—'

'Just for once, old boy, the hell with your navy regulations,' Jolly said politely. 'The main thing to remember, Commander, is that I'm aboard this ship too. Let us remember that we all – um – sink or swim together. No joke intended.'

'But you don't know how to operate those sets—'

'I can learn, can't I?' Jolly said with some asperity. He turned and left.

Swanson looked at me. He was wearing goggles, but they couldn't hide the concern in his face. He said, curiously hesitant: 'Do you think—'

'Of course Jolly's right. You've no option. If Benson were fit you know very well you'd have him down there in jig-time. Besides, Jolly is a damned fine doctor.'

'You haven't been down there, Carpenter. It's a metal jungle. There isn't room to splint a broken finger far less—'

'I don't think Dr Jolly will try to fix or splint anything. He'll just give Ringman a jab that will lay him out so that he can be brought up here without screaming in agony all the way.'

Swanson nodded, pursed his lips and walked away to examine the ice fathometer. I said to Hansen: 'It's pretty bad, isn't it?'

'You can say that again, friend. It's worse than bad. Normally, there should be enough air in the submarine to last us maybe sixteen hours. But well over half the air in the ship, from here right aft is already practically unbreathable. What we have left can't possibly last us more than a few hours. Skipper's boxed in on three sides. If he doesn't start the air purifiers up the men working down in the machinery space are going to have the devil of a job doing anything. Working in near-zero visibility with breathing apparatus on you're practically as good as blind – the floods will make hardly any difference. If he does start up the purifiers in the engine-room, the fresh oxygen will cause the fire to spread. And, when he starts them up, of course, that means less and less power to get the reactor working again.'

'That's very comforting,' I said. 'How long will it take you to restart the reactor?'

'At least an hour. That's after the fire has been put out and everything checked for safety. At least an hour.'

'And Swanson reckoned three or four hours to put the fire out. Say five, all told. It's a long time. Why doesn't he use some of his reserve power cruising around to find a lead?'

'An even bigger gamble than staying put and trying to put out the fire. I'm with the skipper. Let's fight the devil we know rather than dice with the one we don't.'

Medical case in hand, Jolly came coughing and spluttering his way back into the control centre and started pulling on suit and breathing apparatus. Hansen gave him instructions on how to operate it and Jolly seemed to get the idea pretty quickly. Brown, the enlisted man who'd helped Cartwright into the control centre, was detailed to accompany him. Jolly had no idea of the location of the ladder leading down from the upper engine-room to the machinery space.

'Be as quick as you can,' Swanson said. 'Remember, Jolly, you're not trained for this sort of thing. I'll expect you back inside ten minutes.'

They were back in exactly four minutes. They didn't have an unconscious Ringman with them either. The only unconscious figure was that of Dr Jolly, whom Brown half-carried, half-dragged over the sill into the control room.

'Can't say for sure what happened,' Brown gasped. He was trembling from the effort he had just made, Jolly must have out-weighed him by at least thirty pounds. 'We'd just got into the engine-room and shut the door. I was leading and suddenly Dr Jolly fell against me – I reckon he must have tripped over something. He knocked me down. When I got to my feet he was lying there behind me. I put the torch on him. Out cold, he was. His mask had been torn loose. I put it on as best I could and pulled him out.'

'My word,' Hansen said reflectively. 'The medical profession on the *Dolphin is* having a rough time.' He gloomily surveyed the prone figure of Dr Jolly as it was carried away towards the after door and relatively fresh air. 'All three sawbones out of commission now. That's very handy, isn't it, Skipper?'

Swanson didn't answer. I said to him: 'The injection for Ringman. Would you know what to give, how to give it and where?'

'No.'

'Would any of your crew?'

'I'm in no position to argue, Dr Carpenter.'

I opened Jolly's medical kit, hunted among the bottles on the lid rack until I found what I wanted, dipped a hypodermic and injected it in my left forearm, just where the bandage ended. 'Pain-killer,' I said. 'I'm just a softy. But I want to be able to use the forefinger and thumb of that hand.' I glanced across at Rawlings, as recovered as anyone could get in that foul atmosphere, and said: 'How are you feeling now?'

'Just resting lightly.' He rose from his chair and picked up his breathing equipment. 'Have no fears, Doc. With Torpedoman First-class Rawlings by your side—'

'We have plenty of fresh men still available aft, Dr Carpenter,' Swanson said.

'No. Rawlings. It's for his own sake. Maybe he'll get two medals now for this night's work.'

Rawlings grinned and pulled the mask over his head. Two minutes later we were inside the engine-room.

It was stiflingly hot in there, and visibility, even with powerful torches shining, didn't exceed eighteen inches, but for the rest it wasn't too bad. The breathing apparatus functioned well enough and I was conscious of no discomfort. At first, that was.

Rawlings took my arm and guided me to the head of a ladder that reached down to the deck of the machinery space. I heard the penetrating hiss of a fire-extinguisher and peered around to locate its source.

A pity they had no submarines in the Middle Ages, I thought, the sight of that little lot down there would have given Dante an extra fillip when he'd started in on his *Inferno*. Over on the starboard side two very powerful floodlamps had been slung above the huge turbine: the visibility they gave varied from three to six feet, according to the changing amount of smoke given off by the charred and smouldering insulation. At the moment, one patch of the insulation was deeply covered in a layer of white foam – carbon dioxide released under pressure immediately freezes anything with which it comes in contact. As the man with the extinguisher stepped back, three others moved forward in the swirling gloom and started hacking and tearing away at the insulation. As soon as a sizeable strip was dragged loose the exposed lagging below immediately burst into flames reaching the height of a man's head, throwing into sharp relief weird masked figures leaping backwards to avoid being scorched by the flames. And then the man with the CO_2 would approach again, press his trigger, the blaze would shrink down, flicker and die, and a coat of creamy-white foam would bloom where the fire had been. Then the entire process would be repeated all over again. The whole scene with the repetitively stylized movements of the participants highlit against a smoky oil-veined background of flickering crimson was somehow weirdly suggestive of the priests of a long-dead and alien culture offering up some burnt sacrifice on their bloodstained pagan altar.

It also made me see Swanson's point: at the painfully but necessarily slow rate at which those men were making progress, four hours would be excellent par for the course. I tried not to think what the air inside the *Dolphin* would be like in four hours' time.

The man with the extinguisher – it was Raeburn – caught sight of us, came across and led me through a tangled maze of steam pipes and condensers to where Ringman was lying. He was on his back, very still, but conscious: I could see the movement of the whites of his eyes behind his goggles. I bent down till my mask was touching his.

'Your leg?' I shouted.

He nodded.

'Left?'

He nodded again, reached out gingerly and touched a spot halfway down the shin-bone. I opened the medical case, pulled out scissors, pinched the clothes on his upper arm between finger and thumb and cut a piece of the material away. The hypodermic came next and within two minutes he was asleep. With Rawlings's help I laid splints against his leg and bandaged them roughly in place. Two of the fire-fighters stopped work long enough to help us drag him up the ladder and then Rawlings and I took him through the passage above the reactor room. I became aware that my breathing was now distressed, my legs shaking and my whole body bathed in sweat.

Once in the control centre I took off my mask and immediately began to cough and sneeze uncontrollably, tears streaming down my cheeks. Even in the few minutes we had been gone the air in the control room had deteriorated to a frightening extent.

Swanson said: 'Thank you, Doctor. What's it like in there?'

'Quite bad. Not intolerable, but not nice. Ten minutes is long enough for your fire-fighters at one time.'

'Fire-fighters I have in plenty. Ten minutes it shall be.'

A couple of burly enlisted men carried Ringman through to the sick-bay. Rawlings had been ordered for'ard for rest and recuperation in the comparatively fresh air of the messroom, but elected to stop off at the sick-bay with me. He'd glanced at my bandaged left hand and said: 'Three hands are better than one, even although two of them do happen to belong to Rawlings.'

Benson was restless and occasionally murmuring, but still below the level of consciousness. Captain Folsom was asleep, deeply so, which I found surprising until Rawlings told me that there were no alarm boxes in the sick-bay and that the door was completely soundproofed.

We laid Ringman down on the examination table and Rawlings slit up his left trouser leg with a pair of heavy surgical scissors. It wasn't as bad as I had feared it would be, a clean fracture of the tibia, not compound: with Rawlings doing most of the work we soon had his leg fixed up. I didn't try to put his leg in traction; when Jolly, with his two good hands, had completely recovered he'd be able to make a better job of it than I could.

We'd just finished when a telephone rang. Rawlings lifted it quickly before Folsom could wake, spoke briefly and hung up.

'Control room,' he said. I knew from the wooden expression on his face that whatever news he had for me, it wasn't good. 'It was for you. Bolton, the sick man in the nucleonics lab., the one you brought back from Zebra yesterday afternoon. He's gone. About two minutes ago.' He shook his head despairingly. 'My God, another death.'

'No,' I said. 'Another murder.'

Chapter Eleven

The *Dolphin* was an ice-cold tomb. At half past six that morning, four and a half hours after the outbreak of the fire, there was still only one dead man inside the ship, Bolton. But as I looked with bloodshot and inflamed eyes at the men sitting or lying about the control room – no one was standing any more – I knew that within an hour, two at the most, Bolton would be having company. By ten o'clock, at the latest, under those conditions, the *Dolphin* would be no more than a steel coffin with no life left inside her.

As a ship, the *Dolphin* was already dead. All the sounds we associated with a living vessel, the murmurous pulsation of great engines, the high-pitched whine of generators, the deep hum of the air-conditioning unit, the unmistakable transmission from the sonar, the clickety-clack from the radio room, the soft hiss of air, the brassy jingle from the juke-box, the whirring fans, the rattle of pots from the galley, the movement of men, the talking of men – all those were gone. All those vital sounds, the heart-beats of a living vessel, were gone; but in their place was not silence but something worse than silence, something that bespoke not living but dying, the frighteningly rapid, hoarse, gasping breathing of lung-tortured men fighting for air and for life.

Fighting for air. That was the irony of it. Fighting for air while there were still many days' supply of oxygen in the giant tanks. There were some breathing sets aboard, similar to the British Built-in Breathing System which takes a direct oxy-nitrogen mixture from tanks, but only a few, and all members of the crew had had a turn at those, but only for two minutes at a time. For the rest, for the more than ninety per cent without those systems, there was only the panting straining agony that leads eventually to death. Some portable closed-circuit sets were still left, but those were reserved exclusively for the fire-fighters.

Oxygen was occasionally bled from the tanks directly into the living spaces and it just didn't do any good at all; the only effect it seemed to have was to make breathing even more cruelly difficult by heightening the atmospheric pressure. All the oxygen in the world was going to be of little avail as long as the level of carbon dioxide given off by our anguished breathing mounted steadily with the passing of each minute. Normally, the air in the *Dolphin* was cleaned and circulated throughout the ship every two minutes, but the giant 200-ton air-conditioner responsible for this was a glutton for the electric power that drove it; and the electricians' estimate was that the reserve of power in the stand-by battery, which alone could reactivate the nuclear power-plant, was already dangerously low. So the concentration of carbon dioxide increased steadily towards lethal levels and there was nothing we could do about it.

Increasing, too, in what passed now for air, were the Freon fumes from the refrigerating machinery and the hydrogen fumes from the batteries. Worse still, the smoke was now so thick that visibility, even in the for'ard parts of the ship, was down to a few feet, but that smoke had to remain also, there was no power to operate the electrostatic precipitators and even when those had been briefly tried they had proved totally inadequate to cope with the concentration of billions of carbon particles held in suspension in the air. Each time the door to the engine-room was opened – and that was progressively oftener as the strength of the fire-fighters ebbed – fresh clouds of that evil acrid smoke rolled through the submarine. The fire in the engine-room had stopped burning over two hours previously; but now what remained of the redly-smouldering insulation round the starboard high-pressure turbine gave off far more smoke and fumes than flames could ever have done.

But the greatest enemy of all lay in the mounting count of carbon monoxide, that deadly, insidious, colourless, tasteless, odourless gas with its murderous affinity for the red blood cells – five hundred times that of oxygen. On board the *Dolphin* the normal permissible tolerance of carbon monoxide in the air was thirty parts in a million. Now the reading was somewhere between four and five hundred parts in a million. When it reached a thousand parts, none of us would have more than minutes to live.

And then there was the cold. As Commander Swanson had grimly prophesied, the *Dolphin*, with the steam pipes cooled down and all heaters switched off, had chilled down to the sub-freezing temperature of the sea outside, and was ice-cold. In terms of absolute cold, it was nothing – a mere two degrees below zero on the centigrade scale. But in terms of cold as it reacted on the human body it was very cold indeed. Most of the crew were without warm clothing of any kind – in normal operating conditions the temperature inside the *Dolphin* was maintained at a steady 22° C. regardless of the temperature outside – they were both forbidden to move around and lacked the energy to move around to counteract the effects of the cold, and what little energy was left in their rapidly weakening bodies was so wholly occupied in forcing their labouring chest muscles to gulp in more and ever more of that foul and steadily worsening air that they had none at all left to generate sufficient animal heat to ward off that dank and bitter cold. You could actually *hear* men shivering, could listen to their violently shaking limbs knocking and rat-tat-tatting helplessly against bulkheads and deck, could hear the chattering of their teeth, the sound of some of them, far gone in weakness, whimpering softly with the cold: but always the dominant sound was that harsh strangled moaning, a rasping and frightening sound, as men sought to suck air down into starving lungs.

With the exception of Hansen and myself – both of whom were virtually one-handed – and the sick patients, every man in the *Dolphin* had taken his turn that night in descending into the machinery space and fighting that red demon that threatened to slap us all. The number in each fire-fighting group had been increased from four to eight and the time spent down there shortened to three or four minutes, so that efforts could be concentrated and more energy expended in a given length of time; but because of the increasingly Stygian darkness in the machinery space, the ever-thickening coils of oily black smoke, and the wickedly cramped and confined space in which the men had to work, progress had been frustratingly, maddeningly slow; and entered into it now, of course, was the factor of that dreadful weakness that now assailed us all, so that men with the strength only of little children were tugging and tearing at the smouldering insulation in desperate near-futility and seemingly making no progress at all.

I'd been down again in the machinery space, just once, at 5.30 a.m. to attend to Jolly who had himself slipped, fallen and laid himself out while helping an injured crewman up the ladder, and I knew I would never forget what I had seen there, dark and spectral figures in a dark and spectral and swirling world, lurching and staggering around like zombies in some half-forgotten nightmare, swaying and stumbling and falling to the deck or down into the bilges now deep-covered in great snowdrifts of carbon dioxide foam and huge smoking blackened chunks of torn-off lagging. Men on the rack, men in the last stages of exhaustion. One little spark of fire, one little spark of an element as old as time itself and all the brilliant technological progress of the twentieth century was set at nothing, the frontiers of man's striving translated in a moment from the nuclear age to the dark unknown of pre-history.

Every dark hour brings forth its man and there was no doubt in the minds of the crew of the *Dolphin* that that dark night had produced its own here. Dr Jolly. He had made a swift recovery from the effects of his first disastrous entry into the engine-room that night, appearing back in the control centre only seconds after I had finished setting Ringman's broken leg. He had taken the news of Bolton's death pretty badly, but never either by word or direct look did he indicate to either Swanson or myself that the fault lay with us for insisting against his better judgment on bringing on board the ship a man whose life had been hanging in the balance even under the best of conditions. I think Swanson was pretty grateful for that and might even have got around to apologizing to Jolly had not a fire-fighter come through from the engine-room and told us that one of his team had slipped and either twisted or broken an ankle – the second of many minor accidents and injuries that were to happen down in the machinery space that night. Jolly had reached for the nearest closed-circuit breathing apparatus before we could try to stop him and was gone in a minute.

We eventually lost count of the number of trips he made down there that night. Fifteen at least, perhaps many more, by the time six o'clock had come my mind was beginning to get pretty fuzzy round the edges. He'd certainly no lack of customers for his medical skill. Paradoxically enough, the two main types of injury that night were diametrically opposite in nature: burning and freezing, burning from the red-hot lagging – and, earlier, the steam pipes – and freezing from a carelessly directed jet of carbon dioxide against exposed areas of face or hands. Jolly never failed to answer a call, not even after the time he'd given his own head a pretty nasty crack. He would complain bitterly to the captain, old boy, for rescuing him from the relative safety and comfort of Drift Ice Station Zebra, crack some dry joke, pull on his mask and leave. A dozen speeches to Congress or Parliament couldn't have done what Jolly did that night in cementing Anglo-American friendship.

About 6.45 a.m. Chief Torpedoman Patterson came into the control centre. I suppose he walked through the doorway, but that was only assumption, from where I sat on the deck between Swanson and Hansen you couldn't see half-way to the door; but when he came up to Swanson he was crawling on his hands and knees, head swaying from side to side, whooping painfully, his respiration rate at least fifty to the minute. He was wearing no mask of any kind and was shivering constantly.

'We must do something, Captain,' he said hoarsely. He spoke as much when inhaling as when exhaling, when your breathing is sufficiently distressed one is as easy as the other. 'We've got seven men passed out now between the for'ard torpedo room and the crew's mess. They're pretty sick men, Captain.'

'Thank you, Chief.' Swanson, also without a mask, was in as bad a way as Patterson, his chest heaving, his breath hoarsely rasping, tears and sweat rolling down the greyness of his face. 'We will be as quick as possible.'

'More oxygen,' I said. 'Bleed more oxygen into the ship.'

'Oxygen? More oxygen?' He shook his head. 'The pressure is too high as it is.'

'Pressure won't kill them.' I was dimly aware through my cold and misery and burning chest and eyes that my voice sounded just as strange as did those of Swanson and Patterson. 'Carbon monoxide will kill them. Carbon monoxide is what is killing them now. It's the relative proportion of CO_2 to oxygen that matters. It's too high, it's far too high. That's what's going to finish us all off.'

'More oxygen,' Swanson ordered. 'Even the unnecessary acknowledgment of my words would have cost too much. More oxygen.'

Valves were turned and oxygen hissed into the control room and, I know, into the crew spaces. I could feel my ears pop as the pressure swiftly built up, but that was all I could feel. I certainly couldn't feel any improvement in my breathing, a feeling that was borne out when Patterson, noticeably weaker this time, crawled back and croaked out the bad news that he now had a dozen unconscious men on his hands.

I went for'ard with Patterson and a closed-circuit oxygen apparatus - one of the few unexhausted sets left - and clamped it for a minute or so on to the face of each unconscious man in turn, but I knew it was but a temporary palliative, the oxygen revived them but within a few minutes of the mask being removed most of them slipped back into unconsciousness again. I made my way back to the control room, a dark dungeon of huddled men nearly all lying down, most of them barely conscious. I was barely conscious myself. I wondered vaguely if they felt as I did, if the fire from the lungs had now spread to the remainder of the body, if they could see the first slight changes in colour in their hands and faces, the deadly blush of purple, the first unmistakable signs of a man beginning to die from carbon monoxide poisoning. Jolly, I noticed, still hadn't returned from the engine-room: he was keeping himself permanently on hand, it seemed, to help those men who were in ever increasingly greater danger of hurting themselves and their comrades, as their weakness increased, as their level of care and attention and concentration slid down towards zero.

Swanson was where I'd left him, propped on the deck against the plotting table. He smiled faintly as I sank down beside himself and Hansen.

'How are they, Doctor?' he whispered. A whisper, but a rock-steady whisper. The man's monolithic calm had never cracked and I realized dimly that here was a man who could never crack; you do find people like that, once in a million or once in a lifetime. Swanson was such a man.

'Far gone,' I said. As a medical report it maybe lacked a thought in detail but it contained the gist of what I wanted to say and it saved me energy.

'You will have your first deaths from carbon monoxide poisoning within the hour.'

'So soon?' The surprise was in his red, swollen streaming eyes as well as in his voice. 'Not so soon, Doctor. It's hardly – well, it's hardly started to take effect.'

'So soon,' I said. 'Carbon monoxide poisoning is very rapidly progressive. Five dead within the hour. Within two hours fifty. At least fifty.'

'You take the choice out of my hands,' he murmured. 'For which I am grateful. John, where is our main propulsion officer. His hour has come.'

'I'll get him.' Hansen hauled himself wearily to his feet, an old man making his last struggle to rise from his deathbed, and at that moment the engine-room door opened and blackened exhausted men staggered into the control room. Waiting men filed out to take their place. Swanson said to one of the men who had just entered: 'Is that you, Will?'

'Yes, sir.' Lieutenant Raeburn, the navigating officer, pulled off his mask and began to cough, rackingly, painfully. Swanson waited until he had quieted a little.

'How are things down there, Will?'

'We've stopped making smoke, Skipper.' Raeburn wiped his streaming face, swayed dizzily and lowered himself groggily to the floor. 'I think we've drowned out the lagging completely.'

'How long to get the rest of it off?'

'God knows. Normally, ten minutes. The way we are – an hour. Maybe longer.'

'Thank you. Ah!' He smiled faintly as Hansen and Cartwright appeared out of the smoke-filled gloom. 'Our main propulsion officer. Mr Cartwright, I would be glad if you would put the kettle on to boil. What's the record for activating the plant, getting steam up and spinning the turbo-generators?'

'I couldn't say, Skipper.' Red-eyed, coughing, smoke-blackened and obviously in considerable pain, Cartwright nevertheless straightened his shoulders and smiled slowly. 'But you may consider it broken.'

He left. Swanson heaved himself to his feet with obvious weakness – except for two brief inspection trips to the engine-room he had not once worn any breathing apparatus during those interminable and pain-filled hours. He called for power on the broadcast circuit, unhooked a microphone and spoke in a calm clear strong voice: it was an amazing exhibition in self-control, the triumph of a mind over agonized lungs still starving for air.

'This is your captain speaking,' he said. 'The fire in the engine-room is out. We are already reactivating our power plant. Open all watertight doors throughout the ship. They are to remain open until further orders. You may regard the worst of our troubles as lying behind us. Thank you for all you have done.' He hooked up the microphone, and turned to Hansen. 'The worst *is* behind, John – if we have enough power left to reactivate the plant.'

'Surely the worst is still to come,' I said. 'It'll take you how long, three-quarters of an hour, maybe an hour to get your turbine generators going and your air-purifying equipment working again. How long do you think it will take your air cleaners to make any noticeable effect on this poisonous air?'

'Half an hour. At least that. Perhaps more.'

'There you are then.' My mind was so woolly and doped now that I had difficulty in finding words to frame my thoughts, and I wasn't even sure that my thoughts were worth thinking. 'An hour and a half at least – and you said the worst was over. The worst hasn't even begun.' I shook my head, trying to remember what it was that I had been going to say next, then remembered. 'In an hour and a half one out of every four of your men will be gone.'

Swanson smiled. He actually, incredibly, smiled. He said: 'As Sherlock used to say to Moriarty, I think not, Doctor. Nobody's going to die of monoxide poisoning. In fifteen minutes' time we'll have fresh breathable air throughout the ship.'

Hansen glanced at me just as I glanced at him. The strain had been too much, the old man had gone off his rocker. Swanson caught our interchange of looks and laughed, the laugh changing abruptly to a bout of convulsive coughing as he inhaled too much of that poisoned smoke-laden atmosphere. He coughed for a long time then gradually quietened down.

'Serves me right,' he gasped. 'Your faces . . . Why do you think I ordered the watertight doors opened, Doctor?'

'No idea.'

'John?'

Hansen shook his head. Swanson looked at him quizzically and said: 'Speak to the engine-room. Tell them to light up the diesel.'

'Yes, sir,' Hansen said woodenly. He made no move.

'Lieutenant Hansen is wondering whether he should fetch a strait-jacket,' Swanson said. 'Lieutenant Hansen knows that a diesel engine is never *never* lit up when a submarine is submerged – unless with a snorkel which is useless under ice – for a diesel not only uses air straight from the engine-room atmosphere, it gulps it down in great draughts and would soon clear away all the air in the ship. Which is what I want. We bleed compressed air under fairly high pressure into the forepart of the ship. Nice clean fresh air. We light up the diesel in the after part – it will run rough at first because of the low concentration of oxygen in this poisonous muck – but it will run. It will suck up much of this filthy air, exhausting its gases over the side, and as it does it will lower the atmospheric pressure aft and the fresh air will make its way through from for'ard. To have done this before now would have been suicidal, the fresh air would only have fed the flames until the fire was out of control. But we can do it now. We can run it for a few minutes only, of course, but a few minutes will be ample. You are with me, Lieutenant Hansen?'

Hansen was with him all right, but he didn't answer. He had already left.

Three minutes passed, then we heard, through the now open passageway above the reactor room, the erratic sound of a diesel starting, fading, coughing, then catching again – we learned later that the engineers had had to bleed off several ether bottles in the vicinity of the air intake to get the engine to catch. For a minute or two it ran roughly and erratically and seemed to be making no impression at all on that poisonous air: then, imperceptibly, almost, at first, then with an increasing degree of definition, we could see the smoke in the control room, illuminated by the single lamp still left burning there, begin to drift and eddy towards the reactor passage. Smoke began to stir and eddy in the corners of the control room as the diesel sucked the fumes aft, and more smoke-laden air, a shade lighter in colour, began to move in from the wardroom passageway, pulled in by the decreasing pressure in the control room, pushed in by the gradual build-up of fresh air in the forepart of the submarine as compressed air was bled into the living spaces.

A few more minutes made the miracle. The diesel thudded away in the engine-room, running more sweetly and strongly as air with a higher concentration of oxygen reached its intake, and the smoke in the control room drained steadily away to be replaced by a thin greyish mist from the forepart of the ship that was hardly deserving of the name of smoke at all. And that mist carried with it air, an air with fresh life-giving oxygen, an air with a proportion of carbon dioxide and carbon monoxide that was now almost negligible. Or so it seemed to us.

The effect upon the crew was just within the limits of credibility. It was as if a wizard had passed through the length of the ship and touched them with the wand of life. Unconscious men, men for whom death had been less than half an hour away, began to stir, some to open their eyes: sick, exhausted, nauseated and pain-racked men who had been lying or sitting on the decks in attitudes of huddled despair sat up straight or stood, their faces breaking into expressions of almost comical wonderment and disbelief as they drew great draughts down into their aching lungs and found that it was not poisonous gases they were inhaling but fresh breathable air: men who had made up their minds for death began to wonder how they could ever have thought that way. As air went, I suppose, it was pretty sub-standard stuff and the Factory Acts would have had something to say about it; but, for us, no pine-clad mountain air ever tasted half so sweet.

Swanson kept a careful eye on the gauges recording the air pressure in the submarine. Gradually it sunk down to the fifteen pounds at which the atmosphere was normally kept, then below it; he ordered the compressed air to be released under higher pressure and then when the atmospheric pressure was back to normal ordered the diesel stopped and the compressed air shut off.

'Commander Swanson,' I said. 'If you ever want to make admiral you can apply to me for a reference any time.'

'Thank you.' He smiled. 'We have been very lucky.' Sure we had been lucky, the way men who sailed with Swanson would always be lucky.

We could hear now the sounds of pumps and motors as Cartwright started in on the slow process of bringing the nuclear power plant to life again. Everyone knew that it was touch and go whether there would be enough life left in the batteries for that, but, curiously, no one seemed to doubt that Cartwright would succeed; we had been through too much to entertain even the thought of failure now.

Nor did we fail. At exactly eight o'clock that morning Cartwright phoned to say that he had steam on the turbine blades and that the *Dolphin* was a going proposition again. I was glad to hear it.

For three hours we cruised along at slow speed while the air-conditioning plant worked under maximum pressure to bring the air inside the *Dolphin* back to normal. After that Swanson slowly stepped up our speed until we had reached about fifty per cent of normal cruising speed, which was as fast as the propulsion officer deemed it safe to go. For a variety of technical reasons it was impractical for the *Dolphin* to operate without all turbines in commission, so we were reduced to the speed of the slowest and, without lagging on it, Cartwright didn't want to push the starboard high-pressure turbine above a fraction of its power. This way, it would take us much longer to clear the ice-pack and reach the open sea but the captain, in a broadcast, said that if the limit of the ice-pack was where it had been when we'd first moved under it – and there was no reason to think it should have shifted more than a few miles – we should be moving out into the open sea about four o'clock the following morning.

By four o'clock of that afternoon, members of the crew, working in relays, had managed to clear away from the machinery space all the debris and foam that had accumulated during the long night. After that, Swanson reduced all watches to the barest skeletons required to run the ship so that as many men as possible might sleep as long as possible. Now that the exultation of victory was over, now that the almost intolerable relief of knowing that they were not after all to find their gasping end in a cold iron tomb under the ice-cap had begun to fade, the inevitable reaction, when it did come, was correspondingly severe. A long and sleepless night behind them; hours of cruelly back-breaking toil in the metal jungle of the machinery space; that lifetime of tearing tension when they had not known whether they were going to live or die but had believed they were going to die: the poisonous fumes that had laid them all on the rack: all of those combined had taken cruel toll of their reserves of physical and mental energy and the crew of the *Dolphin* were now sleep-ridden and exhausted as they had never been. When they lay down to sleep they slept at once, like dead men.

I didn't sleep. Not then, not at four o'clock. I couldn't sleep. I had too much to think about, like how it had been primarily my fault, through a mistake, miscalculation or sheer pig-headedness, that the *Dolphin* and her crew had been brought to such desperate straits: like what Commander Swanson was going to say when he found out how much I'd kept from him, how little I'd told him. Still, if I had kept him in the dark so long, I couldn't see that there would be much harm in it if I kept him in the dark just that little time longer. It would be time enough in the morning to tell him all I knew. His reactions would be interesting, to say the least. He might be striking some medals for Rawlings, but I had the feeling that he wouldn't be striking any for me. Not after I'd told him what I'd have to.

Rawlings. That was the man I wanted now. I went to see him, told him what I had in mind and asked him if he would mind sacrificing a few hours' sleep during the night. As always, Rawlings was co-operation itself.

Later that evening I had a look at one or two of the patients. Jolly, exhausted by his Herculean efforts of the previous night, was fathoms deep in slumber, so Swanson had asked if I would deputize for him. So I did, but I didn't try very hard. With only one exception they were sound asleep and none of them was in so urgent need of medical attention that there would have been any justification for waking him up. The sole exception was Dr Benson, who had recovered consciousness late that afternoon. He was obviously on the mend but complained that his head felt like a pumpkin with someone at work on it with a riveting gun so I fed him some pills and that was the extent of the treatment. I asked him if he had any idea as to what had been the cause of his fall from the top of the sail, but he was either too woozy to remember or just didn't know. Not that it mattered now. I already knew the answer.

I slept for nine hours after that, which was pretty selfish of me considering that I had asked Rawlings to keep awake half the night; but then I hadn't had much option about that, for Rawlings was in the position to perform for me an essential task that I couldn't perform for myself.

Some time during the night we passed out from under the ice-cap into the open Arctic Ocean again.

I awoke shortly after seven, washed, shaved and dressed as carefully as I could with one hand out of commission, for I believe a judge owes it to his public to be decently turned out when he goes to conduct a trial, then breakfasted well in the wardroom. Shortly before nine o'clock I walked into the control room. Hansen had the watch. I went up to him and said quietly; so that I couldn't be overheard: 'Where is Commander Swanson?'

'In his cabin.'

'I'd like to speak to him and yourself. Privately.'

Hansen looked at me speculatively, nodded, handed over the watch to the navigator and led the way to Swanson's cabin. We knocked, went in and closed the door behind us. I didn't waste any time in preamble.

'I know who the killer is,' I said. 'I've no proof but I'm going to get it now. I would like you to be on hand. If you can spare the time.'

They'd used up all their emotional responses and reactions during the previous thirty hours so they didn't throw up their hands or do startled double-takes or make any of the other standard signs of incredulousness. Instead Swanson just looked thoughtfully at Hansen, rose from his table, folded the chart he'd been studying and said dryly: 'I think we might spare the time, Dr Carpenter. I have never met a murderer.' His tone was impersonal, even light, but the clear grey eyes had gone very cold indeed. 'It will be quite an experience to meet a man with eight deaths on his conscience.'

'You can count yourself lucky that it is only eight,' I said. 'He almost brought it up to the hundred mark yesterday morning.'

This time I did get them. Swanson stared at me, then said softly: 'What do you mean?'

'Our pal with the gun also carries a box of matches around with him,' I said. 'He was busy with them in the engine-room in the early hours of yesterday morning.'

'Somebody *deliberately* tried to set the ship on fire?' Hansen looked at me in open disbelief. 'I don't buy that, Doc.'

'I buy it,' Swanson said. 'I buy anything Dr Carpenter says. We're dealing with a madman, Doctor. Only a madman would risk losing his life along with the lives of a hundred others.'

'He miscalculated,' I said mildly. 'Come along.'

They were waiting for us in the wardroom as I'd arranged, eleven of them in all – Rawlings, Zabrinski, Captain Folsom, Dr Jolly, the two Harrington twins, who were now just barely well enough to be out of bed, Naseby, Hewson, Hassard, Kinnaird and Jeremy. Most of them were seated round the wardroom table except for Rawlings, who opened the door for us, and Zabrinski, his foot still in the cast, who was sitting in a chair in one corner of the room, studying an issue of the *Dolphin Daze*, the submarine's own mimeographed newspaper. Some of them made to get to their feet as we came in but Swanson waved them down. They sat, silently, all except Dr Jolly who boomed out a cheerful: 'Good morning, Captain. Well, well, this is an intriguing summons. Most intriguing. What is it you want to see us about, Captain?'

I cleared my throat. 'You must forgive a small deception. It is I who wants to see you, not the captain.'

'You?' Jolly pursed his lips and looked at me speculatively. 'I don't get it, old boy. Why you?'

'I have been guilty of another small deception. I am not, as I gave you to understand, attached to the Ministry of Supply. I am an agent of the British Government. An officer of MI6 counter-espionage.'

Well, I got my reaction, all right. They just sat there, mouths wide open like newly-landed fish, staring at me. It was Jolly, always a fast adjuster, who recovered first.

'Counter-espionage, by jove! Counter-espionage! Spies and cloaks and daggers and beautiful blondes tucked away in the wardrobes – or wardroom, should I say. But why – but why are you *here*? What do you – well, what *can* you want to see us about, Dr Carpenter?'

'A small matter of murder,' I said.

'Murder!' Captain Folsom spoke for the first time since coming aboard ship, the voice issuing from that savagely burnt face no more than a strangled croak. 'Murder?'

'Two of the men lying up there now in the Drift Station lab. were dead *before* the fire. They had been shot through the head. A third had been knifed. I would call that murder, wouldn't you?'

Jolly groped for the table and lowered himself shakily into his seat. The rest of them looked as if they were very glad that they were already sitting down.

'It seems so superfluous to add,' I said, adding it all the same, 'that the murderer is in this room now.'

You wouldn't have thought it, not to look at them. You could see at a glance that none of those high-minded citizens could possibly be a killer. They were as innocent as life's young morning, the whole lot of them, pure and white as the driven snow.

Chapter Twelve

It would be an understatement to say that I had the attention of the company. Maybe had I been a two-headed visitor from outer space, or had been about to announce the result of a multi-million pound sweepstake in which they held the only tickets, or was holding straws for them to pick to decide who should go before the firing squad – maybe then they might have given me an even more exclusive degree of concentration. But I doubt it. It wouldn't have been possible.

'If you'll bear with me,' I began, 'first of all I'd like to give you a little lecture in camera optics – and don't ask me what the hell that has to do with murder, it's got everything to do with it, as you'll find out soon enough.

'Film emulsion and lens quality being equal, the clarity of detail in any photograph depends upon the focal length of the lens – that is, the distance between the lens and the film. As recently as fifteen years ago the maximum focal length of any camera outside an observatory was about fifty inches. Those were used in reconnaissance planes in the later stages of the Second World War. A small suitcase lying on the ground would show up on a photograph taken from a height of ten miles, which was pretty good for those days.

'But the American Army and Air Force wanted bigger and better aerial cameras, and the only way this could be done was by increasing the focal length of the lens. There was obviously a superficial limit to this length because the Americans wanted this camera to fit into a plane – or an orbiting satellite – and if you wanted a camera with a focal length of, say, 250 inches, it was obviously going to be quite impossible to install a twenty-foot camera pointing vertically downwards in a plane or small satellite. But scientists came up with a new type of camera using the folded lens principle, where the light, instead of coming down a long straight barrel, is bounced round a series of angled mirrored corners, which permits the focal length to be increased greatly without having to enlarge the camera itself. By 1950 they'd developed a hundred-inch focal length lens. It was quite an improvement on the World War II cameras which could barely pick up a suitcase at ten miles – this one could pick up a cigarette packet at ten miles. Then, ten years later, came what they called the Perkin-Elmer Roti satellite missile tracker, with a focal length of five hundred inches – equivalent to a barrel type camera forty feet long: this one could pick up a cube of sugar at ten miles.'

I looked inquiringly around the audience for signs of inattention. There were no signs of inattention. No lecturer ever had a keener audience than I had there.

'Three years later,' I went on, 'another American firm had developed this missile tracker into a fantastic camera that could be mounted in even a small-size satellite. Three years' non-stop work to create this camera – but they reckoned it worth it. We don't know the focal length, it's never been revealed: we do know that, given the right atmospheric conditions, a white saucer on a dark surface will show up clearly from 300 miles up in space. This on a relatively tiny negative capable of almost infinite enlargement – for the scientists have also come up with a completely new film emulsion, still super-secret and a hundred times as sensitive as the finest films available on the commercial market to-day.

'This was to be fitted to the two-ton satellite the Americans called Samos III – Samos for Satellite and Missile Observation System. It never was. This, the only camera of its kind in the world, vanished, hi-jacked in broad daylight and, as we later learned, dismantled, flown from New York to Havana by a Polish jet-liner which had cleared for Miami and so avoided customs inspection.

'Four months ago this camera was launched in a Soviet satellite on a polar orbit, crossing the American middle west seven times a day. Those satellites can stay up indefinitely, but in just three days, with perfect weather conditions, the Soviets had all the pictures they ever wanted – pictures of every American missile launching base west of the Mississippi. Every time this camera took a picture of a small section of the United States another smaller camera in the satellite, pointing vertically upwards, took a fix on the stars. Then it was only a matter of checking map co-ordinates and they could have a Soviet inter-continental ballistic missile ranged in on every launching-pad in America. But first they had to have the pictures.

'Radio transmission is no good, there's far too much quality and detail lost in the process – and you must remember this was a relatively tiny negative in the first place. So they had to have the actual films. There are two ways of doing this – bring the satellite back to earth or have it eject a capsule with the films. The Americans, with their Discoverer tests, have perfected the art of using planes to snatch falling capsules from the sky. The Russians haven't, although we do know they have a technique for ejecting capsules should a satellite run amok. So they had to bring the satellite down. They planned to bring it down some two hundred miles east of the Caspian. But something went wrong. Precisely what we don't know, but our experts say that it could only have been due to the fact that the retro-rockets on one side of the capsule failed to fire when given the radio signal to do so. You are beginning to understand, gentlemen?'

'We are beginning to understand indeed.' It was Jeremy who spoke, his voice very soft. 'The satellite took up a different orbit.'

'That's what happened. The rockets firing on one side didn't slow her up any that mattered, they just knocked her far off course. A new and wobbly orbit that passed through Alaska, south over the Pacific, across Grahamland in Antarctica and directly south of South America, up over Africa and Western Europe, then round the North Pole in a shallow curve, maybe two hundred miles distant from it at the nearest point.

'Now, the only way the Russians could get the films was by ejecting the capsule, for with retro-rockets firing on one side only they knew that even if they did manage to slow up the satellite sufficiently for it to leave orbit, they had no idea where it would go. But the damnably awkward part of it from the Russian's viewpoint was that nowhere in its orbit of the earth did the satellite pass over the Soviet Union or any sphere of Communist influence whatsoever. Worse, ninety per cent of its travel was over open sea and if they brought it down there they would never see their films again as the capsule is so heavily coated with aluminium and Pyroceram to withstand the heat of re-entry into the atmosphere that it was much heavier than water. And as I said, they had never developed the American know-how of snatching falling capsules out of the air – and you will appreciate that they couldn't very well ask the Americans to do the job for them.

'So they decided to bring it down in the only safe place open to them – either the polar ice-cap in the north or the Antarctic in the south. You will remember Captain, that I told you that I had just returned from the Antarctic. The Russians have a couple of geophysical stations there and, up until a few days ago, we thought that there was a fifty-fifty chance that the capsule might be brought down there. But we were wrong. Their nearest station in the Antarctic was 300 miles from the path of orbit – and no field parties were stirring from home.'

'So they decided to bring it down in the vicinity of Drift Ice Station Zebra?' Jolly asked quietly. It was a sign of his perturbation that he didn't even call me 'old boy.'

'Drift Ice Station Zebra wasn't even in existence at the time the satellite went haywire, although all preparations were complete. We had arranged for Canada to lend us a St Lawrence ice-breaker to set up the station but the Russians in a burst of friendly goodwill and international co-operation offered us the atomic-powered *Lenin*, the finest ice-breaker in the world. They wanted to make good and sure that Zebra was set up and set up in good time. It was. The east-west drift of the ice-cap was unusually slow this year and almost eight weeks elapsed after the setting up of the station until it was directly beneath the flight trajectory of the satellite.'

'You *knew* what the Russians had in mind?' Hansen asked.

'We knew. But the Russians had no idea whatsoever that we were on to them. They had no idea that one of the pieces of equipment which was landed at Zebra was a satellite monitor which would tell Major Halliwell when the satellite received the radio signal to eject the capsule.' I looked slowly round the Zebra survivors. 'I'll wager none of you knew that. But Major Halliwell did – and the three other men who slept in his hut where this machine was located.

'What we did not know was the identity of the member of Zebra's company that had been suborned by the Russians. We were certain someone *must* have been but had no idea who it was. Every one of you had first-class security clearances. But someone was suborned – and that someone, when he arrived back in Britain, would have been a wealthy man for the rest of his days. In addition to leaving what was in effect an enemy agent planted in Zebra, the Soviets also left a portable monitor – an electronic device for tuning in on a particular radio signal which would be activated inside the capsule at the moment of its ejection from the satellite. A capsule can be so accurately ejected 300 miles up that it will land within a mile of its target, but the ice-cap is pretty rough territory and dark most of the time, so this monitor would enable our friend to locate the capsule which would keep on emitting its signal for at least, I suppose, twenty-four hours after landing. Our friend took the monitor and went out looking for the capsule. He found it, released it from its drogue and brought it back to the station. You are still with me, gentlemen? Especially one particular gentleman?'

'I think we are all with you, Dr Carpenter,' Commander Swanson said softly. 'Every last one of us.'

'Fine. Well, unfortunately, Major Halliwell and his three companions also knew that the satellite had ejected its capsule – don't forget that they were monitoring this satellite twenty-four hours a day. They knew that someone was going to go looking for it pretty soon, but who that someone would be they had no idea. Anyway, Major Halliwell posted one of his men to keep watch. It was a wild night, bitterly cold, with a gale blowing an ice-storm before it, but he kept a pretty good watch all the same. He either bumped into our friend returning with the capsule or, more probably, saw a light in a cabin, investigated, found our friend stripping the film from the capsule and, instead of going quietly away and reporting to Major Halliwell, he went in and challenged this man. If that was the way of it, it was a bad mistake, the last he ever made. He got a knife between the ribs.' I gazed at all the Zebra survivors in turn. 'I wonder which one of you did it? Whoever it was, he wasn't very expert. He broke off the blade inside the chest. I found it there.' I was looking at Swanson and he didn't bat an eyelid. He knew I hadn't found the blade there: he had found the haft in the petrol tank. But there was time enough to tell them that.

'When the man he had posted didn't turn up, Major Halliwell got worried.

It must have been something like that. I don't know and it doesn't matter. Our friend with the broken knife was on the alert now, he knew someone was on to him – it must have come as a pretty severe shock, he'd thought himself completely unsuspected – and when the second man the Major sent turned up he was ready for him. He had to kill him – for the first man was lying dead in his cabin. Apart from his broken knife he'd also a gun. He used it.

'Both those men had come from Halliwell's cabin, the killer knew that Halliwell must have sent them and that he and the other man still in the major's cabin would be around in double quick time if the second watcher didn't report back immediately. He decided not to wait for that – he'd burnt his boats anyway. He took his gun, went into Major Halliwell's cabin and shot him and the other man as they lay on their beds. I know that because the bullets in their heads entered low from the front and emerged high at the back – the angle the bullets would naturally take if the killer was standing at the foot of their beds and fired at them as they were lying down. I suppose this is as good a time as any to say that my name is not really Carpenter. It's Halliwell. Major Halliwell was my elder brother.'

'Good God!' Dr Jolly whispered. 'Good God above!'

'One thing the killer knew it was essential to do right away – to conceal the traces of his crime. There was only one way – burn the bodies out of all recognition. So he dragged a couple of drums of oil out of the fuel store, poured them against the walls of Major Halliwell's hut – he'd already pulled in there the first two men he'd killed – and set fire to it. For good measure he also set fire to the fuel store. A thorough type, my friends, a man who never did anything by halves.'

The men seated around the wardroom table were dazed and shocked, uncomprehending and incredulous. But they were only incredulous because the enormity of the whole thing was beyond them. But not beyond them all.

'I'm a man with a curious turn of mind,' I went on. 'I wondered why sick, burnt, exhausted men had wasted their time and their little strength in shifting the dead men into the lab. Because someone had suggested that it might be a good thing to do, the decent thing to do. The real reason, of course, was to discourage anyone from going there. I looked under the floor-boards and what did I find? Forty Nife cells in first-class condition, stores of food, a radio-sonde balloon and a hydrogen cylinder for inflating the balloon. I had expected to find the Nife cells – Kinnaird, here, has told us that there were a good many reserves, but Nife cells won't be destroyed in a fire. Buckled and bent a bit, but not destroyed. I hadn't expected to find the other items of equipment, but they made everything clear.

'The killer had had bad luck on two counts – being found out and with the weather. The weather really put the crimp on all his plans. The idea was that when conditions were favourable he'd send the films up into the sky attached to a radio-sonde balloon which could be swept up by a Russian plane: snatching a falling capsule out of the sky is very tricky indeed; snaring a stationary balloon is dead easy. The relatively unused Nife cells our friend used for keeping in radio touch with his pals to let them know when the weather had cleared and when he was going to send the balloon up. There is no privacy on the air-waves, so he used a special code; when he no longer had any need for it he destroyed the code by the only safe method of destruction in the Arctic – fire. I found scores of pieces of charred paper embedded in the walls of one of the huts where the wind had carried them from the met. office after our friend had thrown the ashes away.

'The killer also made sure that only those few worn-out Nife cells were used to send the S O S's and to contact the *Dolphin*. By losing contact with us so frequently, and by sending such a blurred transmission, he tried to delay our arrival here so as to give the weather a chance to clear up and let him fly off his balloon. Incidentally you may have heard radio reports – it was in all the British newspapers – that Russian as well as American and British planes scoured this area immediately after the fire. The British and Americans were looking for Zebra: the Russians were looking for a radio-sonde balloon. So was the ice-breaker *Dvina* when it tried to smash its way through here a few days ago. But there have been no more Russian planes: our friend radioed *his* friends to say that there was no hope of the weather clearing, that the *Dolphin* had arrived and that they would have to take the films back with them on the submarine.'

'One moment, Dr Carpenter,' Swanson interrupted in a careful sort of voice. 'Are you saying that those films are aboard this ship now?'

'I'll be very much surprised if they aren't, Commander. The other attempt to delay us, of course, was by making a direct attack on the *Dolphin* itself. When it became known that the *Dolphin* was to make an attempt to reach Zebra, orders went through to Scotland to cripple the ship. Red Clydeside is no more red than any other maritime centre in Britain, but you'll find Communists in practically every shipyard in the country – and, more often than not, their mates don't know who they are. There was no intention, of course, of causing any fatal accident – and, as far as whoever was responsible for leaving the tube doors open was concerned, there was no reason why there should be. International espionage in peacetime shuns violence – which is why our friend here is going to be very unpopular with his masters. Like Britain or America, they'll adopt any legitimate or illegitimate tactic to gain their espionage end – but they stop short of murder, just as we do. Murder was no part of the Soviet plan.'

'Who is it, Dr Carpenter?' Jeremy said very quietly. 'For God's sake, who is it? There's nine of us here and – do you *know* who it is?'

'I know. And only six, not nine, can be under suspicion. The ones who kept radio watches after the disaster. Captain Folsom and the two Harringtons here were completely immobilized. We have the word of all of you for that. So that, Jeremy, just leaves yourself, Kinnaird, Dr Jolly, Hassard, Naseby and Hewson. Murder for gain, and high treason. There's only one answer for that. The trial will be over the day it begins: three weeks later it will all be over. You're a very clever man, my friend. You're more than that, you're brilliant. But I'm afraid it's the end of the road for you, Dr Jolly.'

They didn't get it. For long seconds they didn't get it. They were too shocked, too stunned. They'd heard my words all right, but the meaning hadn't registered immediately. But it was beginning to register now for like marionettes under the guidance of a master puppeteer they all slowly turned their heads and stared at Jolly. Jolly himself rose slowly to his feet and took two paces towards me, his eyes wide, his mouth working.

'Me?' His voice was low and hoarse and unbelieving. '*Me*? Are you – are you mad, Dr Carpenter? In the name of God, man—'

I hit him. I don't know why I hit him, a crimson haze seemed to blur my vision, and Jolly was staggering back to crash on the deck, holding both hands to smashed lips and nose, before I could realize what I had done. I think if I had had a knife or a gun in my hand then, I would have killed him. I would have killed him the way I would have killed a fer-de-lance, a black widow spider or any other such dark and evil and deadly thing, without thought or compunction or mercy. Gradually the haze cleared from my eyes. No one had stirred. No one had stirred an inch. Jolly pushed himself painfully to his knees and then his feet and collapsed heavily in his seat by the table. He was holding a blood-soaked handkerchief to his face. There was utter silence in the room.

'My brother, Jolly,' I said. 'My brother and all the dead men on Zebra. Do you know what I hope?' I said. 'I hope that something goes wrong with the hangman's rope and that you take a long, long time to die.'

He took the handkerchief from his mouth.

'You're crazy man,' he whispered between smashed and already puffing lips. 'You don't know what you are saying.'

'The jury at the Old Bailey will be the best judge of that. I've been on to you now, Jolly, for almost exactly sixty hours.'

'What did you say?' Swanson demanded. 'You've known for sixty hours!'

'I knew I'd have to face your wrath some time or other, Commander,' I said. Unaccountably, I was beginning to feel very tired, weary and heart-sick of the whole business. 'But if you had known who he was you'd have locked him up straightaway. You said so in so many words. I wanted to see where the trail led to in Britain, who his associates and contacts would be. I had splendid visions of smashing a whole spy ring. But I'm afraid the trail is cold. It ends right here. Please hear me out.

'Tell me, did no one think it strange that when Jolly came staggering out of his hut when it caught fire that he should have collapsed and remained that way? Jolly claimed that he had been asphyxiated. Well, he wasn't asphyxiated inside the hut because he managed to come out under his own steam. Then he collapsed. Curious. Fresh air invariably revives people. But not Jolly. He's a special breed. He wanted to make it clear to everyone that he had nothing to do with the fire. Just to drive home the point, he has repeatedly emphasized that he is not a man of action. If he isn't, then I've never met one.'

'You can hardly call that proof of guilt,' Swanson interrupted.

'I'm not adducing evidence,' I said wearily. 'I'm merely introducing pointers. Pointer number two. You, Naseby, felt pretty bad about your failure to wake up your two friends, Flanders and Bryce. You could have shaken them for an hour and not woken them up. Jolly, here, used either ether or chloroform to lay them out. This was after he had killed Major Halliwell and the three others; but before he started getting busy with matches. He realized that if he burnt the place down there might be a long, long wait before rescue came and he was going to make damned certain that he wasn't going to go hungry. If the rest of you had died from starvation – well, that was just your bad luck. But Flanders and Bryce lay between him and the food. Didn't it strike you as very strange, Naseby, that your shouting and shaking had no effect. The only reason could be that they had been drugged – and only one man had access to drugs. Also, you said that both Hewson and yourself felt pretty groggy. No wonder. It was a pretty small hut and the chloroform or ether fumes had reached and affected Hewson and yourself – normally you'd have smelt it on waking up, but the stink of burning diesel obliterates every other smell. Again, I know this is not proof of any kind.

'Third pointer. I asked Captain Folsom this morning who had given the orders for the dead men to be put in the lab. He said he had. But, he remembered, it was Jolly's suggestion to him. Something learnedly medical about helping the morale of the survivors by putting the charred corpses out of sight.

'Fourth pointer. Jolly said that *how* the fire started was unimportant. A crude attempt to side-track me. Jolly knew as well as I did that it was all-important. I suppose, by the way, Jolly, that you deliberately jammed all the fire-extinguishers you could before you started the fire. About that fire, Commander. Remember you were a bit suspicious of Hewson, here, because he said the fuel drums hadn't started exploding until he was on his way to the main bunkhouse. He was telling the truth. There were no fewer than four drums in the fuel stores that didn't explode – the ones Jolly, here, used to pour against the huts to start the fire. How am I doing, Dr Jolly?'

'It's all a nightmare,' he said very quietly. 'It's a nightmare. Before God. I know nothing of any of this.'

'Pointer number five. For some reason that is unclear to me Jolly wanted to delay the *Dolphin* on its return trip. He could best do this, he reckoned, if Bolton and Brownell, the two very sick men still left out on the station could he judged to be too sick to be transferred to the *Dolphin*. The snag was, there were two other doctors around who might say that they *were* fit to be transferred. So he tried, with a fair measure of success, to eliminate us.

'First Benson. Didn't it strike you as strange, Commander, that the request for the survivors to be allowed to attend the funeral of Grant and Lieutenant Mills should have come from Naseby in the first place, then Kinnaird? Jolly, as the senior man of the party with Captain Folsom, here, temporarily unfit, was the obvious man to make the approach – but he didn't want to go calling too much attention to himself. Doubtless by dropping hints, he engineered it so that someone else should do it for him. Now Jolly had noticed how glass-smooth and slippery the ice-banked sides of the sail were and he made a point of seeing that Benson went up the rope immediately ahead of him. You must remember it was almost pitch dark – just light enough for Jolly to make out the vague outline of Benson's head from the wash of light from the bridge as it cleared the top of the rail. A swift outward tug on the rope and Benson overbalanced. It seemed that he had fallen on top of Jolly. But only seemed. The loud sharp crack I heard a fraction of a second after Benson's body struck was not caused by his head hitting the ice – it was caused by Jolly, here, trying to kick his head off. Did you hurt your toes much, Jolly?'

'You're mad,' he said mechanically. 'This is utter nonsense. Even if it wasn't nonsense, you couldn't prove a word of it.'

'We'll see. Jolly claimed that Benson fell on top of him. He even flung himself on the ice and cracked his head to give some verisimilitude to his story – our pal never misses any of the angles. I felt the slight bump on his head. But he wasn't laid out. He was faking. He recovered just that little bit too quickly and easily when he got back to the sick-bay. And it was then that he made his first mistake, the mistake that put me on to him – and should have put me on guard for an attack against myself. You were there, Commander.'

'I've missed everything else,' Swanson said bitterly. 'Do you want me to spoil a hundred per cent record?'

'When Jolly came to he saw Benson lying there. All he could see of him was a blanket and a big gauze pack covering the back of his head. As far as Jolly was concerned, it could have been anybody – it had been pitch dark when the accident occurred. But what did he say? I remember his exact words. He said: "Of course, of course. Yes, that's it. He fell on top of me, didn't he?" *He never thought to ask who it was* – the natural, the inevitable question in the circumstances. But Jolly didn't have to ask. He knew.'

'He knew.' Swanson stared at Jolly with cold bleak eyes and there was no doubt in his mind now about Jolly. 'You have it to rights, Dr Carpenter. He knew.'

'And then he had a go at me. Can't prove a thing, of course. But he was there when I asked you where the medical store was, and he no doubt nipped down smartly behind Henry and myself and loosened the latch on the hatch-cover. But he didn't achieve quite the same high degree of success this time. Even so, when we went out to the station next morning he still tried to stop Brownell and Bolton from being transferred back to the ship by saying Bolton was too ill. But you overruled him.'

'I was right about Bolton,' Jolly said. He seemed strangely quiet now. 'Bolton died.'

'He died,' I agreed. 'He died because you murdered him and for Bolton alone I can make certain you hang. For a reason I still don't know, Jolly was still determined to stop this ship. Delay it, anyway. I think he wanted only an hour or two's delay. So he proposed to start a small fire, nothing much, just enough to cause a small scare and have the reactor shut down temporarily. As the site of his fire he chose the machinery space – the one place in the ship where he could casually let something drop and where it would lie hidden, for hours if need be, among the maze of pipes down there. In the sick-bay he concocted some type of delayed action chemical fuse which would give off plenty of smoke but very little flame – there are a dozen combinations of acids and chemicals that can bring this about and our friend will be a highly-trained expert well versed in all of them. Now all Jolly wanted was an excuse to pass through the engine-room when it would be nice and quiet and virtually deserted. In the middle of the night. He fixed this too. He can fix anything. He is a very, very clever man indeed is our pal here; he's also an utterly ruthless fiend.

'Late on the evening of the night before the fire the good healer here made a round of his patients. I went with him. One of the men he treated was Bolton in the nucleonics lab. – and, of course, to get to the nucleonics lab. you have to pass through the engine-room. There was an enlisted man watching over the patients and Jolly left special word that he was to be called at any hour if Bolton became any worse. He was called. I checked with the engine-room staff after the fire. The engineer officer was on watch and two others were in the manoeuvring-room but an engine-man carrying out a routine lubrication job saw him passing through the engine-room about 1.30 a.m. in answer to a call from the man watching over the patients. He took the opportunity to drop his little chemical fuse as he was passing by the machinery space. What he didn't know was that his little toy lodged on or near the oil-saturated lagging on the housing of the starboard turbo-generator and that when it went off it would generate sufficient heat to set the lagging on fire.'

Swanson looked at Jolly, bleakly and for a long time, then turned to me and shook his head. 'I can't wear that, Dr Carpenter. This phone call because a patient just happens to turn sick. Jolly is not the man to leave *anything* to chance.'

'He isn't,' I agreed. 'He didn't. Up in the refrigerator in the sick-bay I have an exhibit for the Old Bailey. A sheet of aluminium foil liberally covered with Jolly's fingerprints. Smeared on this foil is the remains of a salve. That foil was what Jolly had bandaged on to Bolton's burnt forearm that night, just after he had given him pain-killing shots – Bolton was suffering very badly. But before Jolly put the salve on the foil he spread on something else first – a layer of sodium chloride – common or garden household salt. Jolly knew that the drugs he had given Bolton would keep him under for three or four hours; he also knew that by the time Bolton had regained consciousness body heat would have thinned the salve and brought the salt into contact with the raw flesh on the forearm. Bolton, he knew, when he came out from the effects of the drugs, would come out screaming in agony. Can you imagine what it must have been like: the whole forearm a mass of raw flesh – and covered with salt? When he died soon after, he died from shock. Our good healer here – a lovable little lad, isn't he?

'Well, that's Jolly. Incidentally, you can discount most of the gallant doctor's heroism during the fire – although he was understandably as anxious as any of us that we survive. The first time he went into the engine-room it was too damned hot and uncomfortable for his liking so he just lay down on the floor and let someone carry him for'ard to where the fresh air was. Later—'

'He'd his mask off,' Hansen objected.

'He took it off. *You* can hold your breath for ten or fifteen seconds – don't you think Jolly can too? Later on, when he was performing his heroics in the engine-room it was because conditions there were better, conditions outside were worse – and because by going into the engine-room he was entitled to a closed-circuit breathing set. Jolly got more clean air last night than any of us. He doesn't mind if he causes someone to die screaming his head off in agony – but he himself isn't going to suffer the slightest degree of hardship. Not if he can help it. Isn't that so, Jolly?'

He didn't answer.

'Where are the films, Jolly?'

'I don't know what you are talking about,' he said in a quiet toneless voice. 'Before God, my hands are clean.'

'How about your fingerprints on that foil with the salt on it?'

'Any doctor can make a mistake.'

'My God! Mistake! Where are they, Jolly – the films?'

'For God's sake leave me alone,' he said tiredly.

'Have it your own way.' I looked at Swanson. 'Got some nice secure place where you can lock this character up?'

'I certainly have,' Swanson said grimly. 'I'll conduct him there in person.'

'No one's conducting anyone anywhere,' Kinnaird said. He was looking at me and I didn't care very much for the way he was looking at me. I didn't care very much either for what he held in his hand, a very nasty-looking

Luger. It was cradled in his fist as if it had grown there and it was pointing straight between my eyes.

Chapter Thirteen

'Clever, clever counter-espionage, Carpenter,' Dr Jolly murmured. 'How swiftly the fortunes of war change, old boy. But you shouldn't be surprised really. You haven't found out anything that actually matters, but surely you should have found out enough to realize that you are operating out of your class. Please don't try anything foolish. Kinnaird is one of the finest pistol shots I have ever known – and you will observe how strategically he's placed so that everyone in the room is covered.'

He delicately patted his still-bleeding mouth with a handkerchief, rose, went behind me and ran his hands quickly down my clothes.

'My word,' he said. 'Not even carrying a gun. You really are unprepared, Carpenter. Turn round, will you, so that your back is to Kinnaird's gun?'

I turned round. He smiled pleasantly then hit me twice across the face with all his strength, first with the back of his right hand and then with the back of the left. I staggered, but didn't fall down. I could taste the salt of blood.

'Can't even call it regrettable loss of temper,' Jolly said with satisfaction. 'Did it deliberately and with malice aforethought. Enjoyed it, too.'

'So Kinnaird was the killer,' I said slowly, thickly. 'He was the man with the gun?'

'Wouldn't want to take all the credit, mate,' Kinnaird said modestly. 'Let's say we sorted them out fifty-fifty.'

'*You* were the one who went out with the monitor to find the capsule,' I nodded. 'That's why you got your face so badly frost-bitten.'

'Got lost,' Kinnaird admitted. 'Thought I'd never find the damned station again.'

'Jolly and Kinnaird,' Jeremy said wonderingly. 'Jolly and Kinnaird. Your own mates. You two filthy murderous—'

'Be quiet,' Jolly ordered. 'Kinnaird, don't bother answering questions. Unlike Carpenter here, I take no pleasure in outlining my *modus operandi* and explaining at length how clever I've been. As you observed, Carpenter, I'm a man of action. Commander Swanson, get on that phone there, call up your control room, order your ship to surface and steam north.'

'You're becoming too ambitious, Jolly,' Swanson said calmly. 'You can't hi-jack a submarine.'

'Kinnaird,' Jolly said. 'Point your gun at Hansen's stomach. When I reach the count of five, pull the trigger. One, two, three—'

Swanson half-raised a hand in acknowledgment of defeat, crossed to the wall-phone, gave the necessary orders, hung up and came back to stand beside me. He looked at me without either respect or admiration. I looked round all the other people in the room. Jolly, Hansen and Rawlings standing, Zabrinski sitting on a chair by himself with the now disregarded copy of the *Dolphin Daze* on his knees, all the others sitting round the table, Kinnaird well clear of them, the gun very steady in his hand. So very steady. No one seemed to be contemplating any heroics. For the most part everyone was too shocked, too dazed, to think of anything.

'Hi-jacking a nuclear submarine is an intriguing prospect – and no doubt would be a highly profitable one, Commander Swanson,' Jolly said. 'But I know my limitations. No, old top, we shall simply be leaving you. Not very many miles from here is a naval vessel with a helicopter on its after deck. In a little while, Commander, you will send a wireless message on a certain frequency giving our position: the helicopter will pick us up. And even if your crippled engine would stand the strain I wouldn't advise you to come chasing after that ship with ideas about torpedoing it or anything of that dramatic ilk. Apart from the fact that you wouldn't like to be responsible for triggering off a nuclear war, you couldn't catch it, anyway. You won't even be able to see the ship, Commander – and if you did it wouldn't matter, anyway. It has no nationality markings.'

'Where are the films?' I asked.

'They're already aboard that naval vessel.'

'They're *what*?' Swanson demanded. 'How in hell's name can they be?'

'Sorry and all that, old boy. I repeat that unlike Carpenter, here, I don't go around shooting off my mouth. A professional, my dear captain, *never* gives information about his methods.'

'So you get off with it,' I said bitterly. My mouth felt thick and swollen.

'Don't see what's to stop us. Crimes don't always come home to roost, you know.'

'Eight men murdered,' I said wonderingly. 'Eight men. You can stand there and cheerfully admit that you are responsible for the deaths of eight men.'

'Cheerfully?' he said consideringly. 'No, not cheerfully. I'm a professional, and a professional never kills unnecessarily. But this time it was necessary. That's all.'

'That's the second time you've used the word "professional",' I said slowly. 'I was wrong on one theory. You weren't just suborned after the Zebra team had been picked. You've been at this game a long time – you're too good not to have been.'

'Fifteen years, old lad,' Jolly said calmly. 'Kinnaird and I – we were the best team in Britain. Our usefulness in that country, unfortunately, is over. I should imagine that our – um – exceptional talents can be employed elsewhere.'

'You admit to all those murders?' I asked.

He looked at me in sudden cold speculation. 'A damned funny question, Carpenter. Of course. I've told you. Why?'

'And do you, Kinnaird?'

He looked at me in bleak suspicion. 'Why ask?'

'You answer my question and I'll answer yours.' At the corner of my range of vision I could see Jolly looking at me with narrowed eyes. He was very sensitive to atmosphere, he knew there was something off-key.

'You know damn' well what I did, mate,' Kinnaird said coldly.

'So there we have it. In the presence of no less than twelve witnesses, you both confess to murder. You shouldn't have done that, you know. I'll answer your question, Kinnaird. I wanted to have an oral confession from you because, apart from the sheet of aluminium foil and something I'll mention in a minute, we have no actual proof at all against either of you. But now we have your confessions. Your great talents are not going to be used in any other sphere, I'm afraid. You'll never see that helicopter or that naval vessel. You'll both die jerking on the end of a rope.'

'What rubbish is this?' Jolly asked contemptuously. But there was worry under the contempt. 'What last-minute despairing bluff are you trying to pull, Carpenter?'

I ignored his question. I said: 'I've been on to Kinnaird, here, for some sixty hours also, Jolly. But I had to play it this way. Without letting you gain what appeared to be the upper hand you would never have admitted to the crimes. But now you have.'

'Don't fall for it, old boy,' Jolly said to Kinnaird. 'It's just some desperate bluff. He never had any idea that you were in on this.'

'When I knew you were one of the killers,' I said to Jolly, 'I was almost certain Kinnaird had to be another. You shared the same cabin and unless Kinnaird had been sapped or drugged he had to be in on it. He was neither. He was in on it. That door wasn't jammed when Naseby ran round to the radio room to warn you – the two of you were leaning all your weight against it to give the impression that it had been closed for hours and that ice had formed.

'By the same token, young Grant, the assistant radio operator, was in cahoots with you – or he wasn't. If he wasn't, he would have to be silenced. He wasn't. So you silenced him. After I'd caught on to the two of you I had a good look at Grant. I went out and dug him up from where we'd buried him. Rawlings and I. I found a great big bruise at the base of his neck. He surprised you in something, or he woke when you knifed or shot one of Major Halliwell's men, and you laid him out. You didn't bother killing him, you were about to set the hut on fire and incinerate him, so killing would have been pointless. But you didn't reckon on Captain Folsom, here, going in and bringing him out – alive.

'That was most damnably awkward for you, wasn't it, Jolly? He was unconscious but when and if he recovered consciousness he could blow the whole works on you. But you couldn't get at him to finish him off, could you? The bunkhouse was full of people, most of them suffering so severely that sleep was impossible for them. When we arrived on the scene you got desperate. Grant was showing signs of regaining consciousness. You took a chance, but not all that much of a chance. Remember how surprised I was to find that you had used up all my morphine? Well, I *was* surprised then. But not now. I know now where it went. You gave him an injection of morphine – and you made damn' sure the hypodermic had a lethal dose. Am I correct?'

'You're cleverer than I thought you were,' he said calmly. 'Maybe I have misjudged you a little. But it still makes no difference, old boy.'

'I wonder. If I'd known about Kinnaird so long why do you think I allowed a situation to develop where you could apparently turn the tables?'

'Apparently is not the word you want. And the answer to your question is easy. You didn't know Kinnaird *had* a gun.'

'No?' I looked at Kinnaird. 'Are you sure that thing works?'

'Don't come that old stuff with me, mate,' Kinnaird said in contempt.

'I just wondered,' I said mildly. 'I thought perhaps the petrol in the tractor's tank might have removed all the lubricating oil.'

Jolly came close to me, his face tight and cold. 'You *knew* about this? What goes on, Carpenter?'

'It was actually Commander Swanson, here, who found the gun in the tank,' I said. 'You had to leave it there because you knew you'd all be getting a good clean-up and medical examination when we got you on board and it would have been bound to be discovered. But a murderer – a professional, Jolly – will never part with his gun unless he is compelled to. I knew if you got the slightest chance you would go back for it. So I put it back in the tank.'

'The hell you did!' Swanson was as nearly angry as I'd ever seen him. 'Forgot to tell me, didn't you?'

'I must have done. That was after I'd cottoned on to you, Jolly. I wasn't *absolutely* sure you had a partner, but I knew if you had it must be Kinnaird. So I put the gun back there in the middle of the night and I made good and certain that you, Jolly, didn't get the chance to go anywhere near the tractor shed at any time. But the gun vanished that following morning when everyone was out sampling the fresh air. So then I knew you had an accomplice. But the real reason for planting that gun, of course, is that without it you'd never have talked. But now you have talked and it's all finished. Put up that gun, Kinnaird.'

'I'm afraid your bluff's run out mate.' The gun was pointing directly at my face.

'Your last chance, Kinnaird. Please pay attention to what I am saying. Put up that gun or you will be requiring the services of a doctor within twenty seconds.'

He said something, short and unprintable. I said: 'It's on your own head. Rawlings, you know what to do.'

Every head turned towards Rawlings who was standing leaning negligently against a bulkhead, his hands crossed lightly in front of him. Kinnaird looked too, the Luger following the direction of his eyes. A gun barked, the sharp flat crack of a Mannlicher-Schoenauer, Kinnaird screamed and his gun spun from his smashed hand. Zabrinski, holding my automatic in one hand and his copy of the *Dolphin Daze* – now with a neat charred hole through the middle – in the other, regarded his handiwork admiringly then turned to me. 'Was that how you wanted it done, Doc?'

'That was exactly how I wanted it done, Zabrinski. Thank you very much. A first-class job.'

'A first-class job,' Rawlings sniffed. He retrieved the fallen Luger and pointed it in Jolly's general direction. 'At four feet even Zabrinski couldn't miss.' He dug into a pocket, pulled out a roll of bandage and tossed it to Jolly. 'We kinda thought we might be having to use this so we came prepared. Dr Carpenter said your pal here would be requiring the services of a doctor. He is. You're a doctor. Get busy.'

'Do it yourself,' Jolly snarled. No 'old boy,' no 'old top.' The *bonhomie* was gone and gone for ever.

Rawlings looked at Swanson and said woodenly: 'Permission to hit Dr Jolly over the head with this little old gun, sir?'

'Permission granted,' Swanson said grimly. But no further persuasion was necessary. Jolly cursed and started ripping the cover off the bandage.

For almost a minute there was silence in the room while we watched Jolly carry out a rough, ready and far from gentle repair job on Kinnaird's hand. Then Swanson said slowly: 'I still don't understand how in the devil Jolly got rid of the film.'

'It was easy. Ten minutes thinking and you'd get it. They waited until we had cleared the ice-cap then they took the films, shoved them in a waterproof bag, attached a yellow dye marker to the bag then pumped it out through the garbage disposal unit in the galley. Remember, they'd been on a tour of the ship and seen it – although the suggestion was probably radioed them by a naval expert. I had Rawlings posted on watch in the early hours of this morning and he saw Kinnaird go into the galley about half past four. Maybe he just wanted a ham sandwich, I don't know. But Rawlings says he had the bag and marker with him when he sneaked in and empty hands when he came out. The bag would float to the surface and the marker stain thousands of square yards of water. The naval ship up top would have worked out our shortest route from Zebra to Scotland and would be within a few miles of our point of exit from the ice-pack. It could probably have located it without the helicopter: but the chopper made it dead certain.

'Incidentally, I was being rather less than accurate when I said I didn't know the reason for Jolly's attempts to delay us. I knew all along. He'd been told that the ship couldn't reach our exit point until such and such a time and that it was vital to delay us until then. Jolly, here, even had the effrontery to check with me what time we would be emerging from the ice-pack.'

Jolly looked up from Kinnaird's hand and his face was twisted in a mask of malevolence.

'You win, Carpenter. So you win. All along the line. But you lost out in the only thing that really mattered. They got the films – the films showing the location, as you said, of nearly every missile base in America. And that was all that mattered. Ten million pounds couldn't buy that information. But we got it.' He bared his teeth in a savage smile. 'We may have lost out, Carpenter, but we're professionals. We did our job.'

'They got the films, all right,' I acknowledged. 'And I'd give a year's salary to see the faces of the men who develop them. Listen carefully, Jolly. Your main reason in trying to cripple Benson and myself was not so much that you could have the say-so on Bolton's health and so delay us: your main reason, your over-riding reason, was that you wanted to be the only doctor on the ship so that it could only be you who would carry out the X-ray on Zabrinski's ankle here and remove the plaster cast. Literally everything hinged on that: basically, nothing else mattered. That was why you took such a desperate chance in crippling me when you heard me say I intended to X-ray Zabrinski's ankle the following morning. That was the one move you made that lacked the hall-mark of class – of a professional – but then I think you were close to panic. You were lucky.

'Anyway, you removed the plaster cast two mornings ago and also the films which you had hidden there in oilskin paper when you'd fixed the plaster on to Zabrinski's leg the first night we arrived in Zebra. A perfect hiding-place. You could always, of course, have wrapped them in bandages covering survivors' burns, but that would be too dicey. The cast was brilliant.

'Unfortunately for you and your friends I had removed the original plaster during the previous night, extracted the films from the oiled paper and replaced them with others. That, incidentally, is the second piece of evidence I have on you. There are two perfect sets of prints on the leaders of the satellite films – yours and Kinnaird's. Along with the salt-covered aluminium foil and the confession freely made in front of witnesses that guarantees you both the eight o'clock walk to the gallows. The gallows and failure, Jolly. You weren't even a professional. Your friends will never see those films.'

Mouthing soundless words through smashed lips, his face masked in madness and completely oblivious to the two guns, Jolly flung himself at me. He had taken two steps and two only when Rawling's gun caught him, not lightly, on the side of the head. He crashed to the floor as if the Brooklyn bridge had fallen in on top of him. Rawlings surveyed him dispassionately.

'Never did a day's work that gave me profounder satisfaction,' he said conversationally. 'Except, perhaps, those pictures I took with Dr Benson's camera to give Dr Carpenter, here, some negatives to shove inside that oiled paper.'

'Pictures of what?' Swanson asked curiously.

Rawlings grinned happily. 'All those pin-ups in Doc Benson's sick-bay. Yogi Bear, Donald Duck, Pluto, Popeye, Snow-white and the seven dwarfs – you name it, I got it. The lot. Each a guaranteed work of art – and in glorious Technicolor.' He smiled a beatific smile. 'Like Doc Carpenter, here, I'd give a year's pay to see their faces when they get around to developing those negatives.'

WHEN EIGHT BELLS TOLL

When Eight Bells Toll

To Paul and Xenia

Chapter One

Dusk Monday – 3 a.m. Tuesday

The Peacemaker Colt has now been in production, without change in design, for a century. Buy one to-day and it would be indistinguishable from the one Wyatt Earp wore when he was the Marshal of Dodge City. It is the oldest hand-gun in the world, without question the most famous and, if efficiency in its designated task of maiming and killing be taken as criterion of its worth, then it is also probably the best hand-gun ever made. It is no light thing, it is true, to be wounded by some of the Peacemaker's more highly esteemed competitors, such as the Luger or Mauser: but the high-velocity, narrow-calibre, steel-cased shell from either of those just goes straight through you, leaving a small neat hole in its wake and spending the bulk of its energy on the distant landscape whereas the large and unjacketed soft-nosed lead bullet from the Colt mushrooms on impact, tearing and smashing bone and muscle and tissue as it goes and expending all its energy on you.

In short when a Peacemaker's bullet hits you in, say, the leg, you don't curse, step into shelter, roll and light a cigarette one-handed then smartly shoot your assailant between the eyes. When a Peacemaker bullet hits your leg you fall to the ground unconscious, and if it hits the thigh-bone and you are lucky enough to survive the torn arteries and shock, then you will never walk again without crutches because a totally disintegrated femur leaves the surgeon with no option but to cut your leg off. And so I stood absolutely motionless, not breathing, for the Peacemaker Colt that had prompted this unpleasant train of thought was pointed directly at my right thigh.

Another thing about the Peacemaker: because of the very heavy and varying trigger pressure required to operate the semi-automatic mechanism, it can be wildly inaccurate unless held in a strong and steady hand. There was no such hope here. The hand that held the Colt, the hand that lay so lightly yet purposefully on the radio-operator's table, was the steadiest hand I've ever seen. It was literally motionless. I could see the hand very clearly. The light in the radio cabin was very dim, the rheostat of the angled table lamp had been turned down until only a faint pool of yellow fell on the scratched metal of the table, cutting the arm off at the cuff, but the hand was very clear. Rock-steady, the gun could have lain no quieter in the marbled hand of a statue. Beyond the pool of light I could half sense, half see the dark outline of a figure leaning back against the bulkhead, head slightly tilted to one side, the white gleam of unwinking eyes under the peak of a hat. My eyes went back to the hand. The angle of the Colt hadn't varied by a fraction of a degree. Unconsciously, almost, I braced my right leg to meet the impending shock. Defensively, this was a very good move, about as useful as holding up a sheet of newspaper in front of me. I wished to God that

Colonel Sam Colt had gone in for inventing something else, something useful, like safety-pins.

Very slowly, very steadily, I raised both hands, palms outward, until they were level with my shoulders. The careful deliberation was so that the nervously inclined wouldn't be deceived into thinking that I was contemplating anything ridiculous, like resistance. It was probably a pretty superfluous precaution as the man behind that immobile pistol didn't seem to have any nerves and the last thought I had in my head was that of resistance. The sun was long down but the faint red after-glow of sunset still loomed on the north-west horizon and I was perfectly silhouetted against it through the cabin doorway. The lad behind the desk probably had his left hand on the rheostat switch ready to turn it up and blind me at an instant's notice. And there was that gun. I was paid to take chances. I was paid even to step, on occasion, into danger. But I wasn't paid to act the part of a congenital and suicidal idiot. I hoisted my hands a couple of inches higher and tried to look as peaceful and harmless as possible. The way I felt, that was no feat.

The man with the gun said nothing and did nothing. He remained completely still. I could see the white blur of teeth now. The gleaming eyes stared unwinkingly at me. The smile, the head cocked slightly to one side, the negligent relaxation of the body – the aura in that tiny cabin of a brooding and sardonic menace was so heavy as to be almost palpable. There was something evil, something frighteningly unnatural and wrong and foreboding in the man's stillness and silence and cold-blooded cat-and-mouse indifference. Death was waiting to reach out and touch with his icy forefinger in that tiny cabin. In spite of two Scots grandparents I'm in no way psychic or fey or second-sighted, as far as extra-sensory perception goes I've about the same degree of receptive sensitivity as a lump of old lead. But I could smell death in the air.

'I think we're both making a mistake,' I said. 'Well, you are. Maybe we're both on the same side.' The words came with difficulty, a suddenly dry throat and tongue being no aid to clarity of elocution, but they sounded all right to me, just as I wanted them to sound, low and calm and soothing. Maybe he was a nut case. Humour him. Anything. Just stay alive. I nodded to the stool at the front corner of his desk. 'It's been a hard day. Okay if we sit and talk? I'll keep my hands high, I promise you.'

The total reaction I got was nil. The white teeth and eyes, the relaxed contempt, that iron gun in that iron hand. I felt my own hands begin to clench into fists and hastily unclenched them again, but I couldn't do anything about the slow burn of anger that touched me for the first time.

I smiled what I hoped was a friendly and encouraging smile and moved slowly towards the stool. I faced him all the time, the cordial smile making my face ache and the hands even higher than before. A Peacemaker Colt can kill a steer at sixty yards, God only knew what it would do to me. I tried to put it out of my mind, I've only got two legs and I'm attached to them both.

I made it with both still intact. I sat down, hands still high, and started breathing again. I'd stopped breathing but hadn't been aware of it, which was understandable enough as I'd had other things on my mind, such as crutches, bleeding to death and such-like matters that tend to grip the imagination.

The Colt was as motionless as ever. The barrel hadn't followed me as I'd moved across the cabin, it was still pointing rigidly at the spot where I'd been standing ten seconds earlier.

I moved fast going for that gun-hand, but it was no breakneck dive. I didn't, I was almost certain, even have to move fast, but I haven't reached the advanced age in which my chief thinks he honours me by giving me all the dirtiest jobs going by ever taking a chance: when I don't have to.

I eat all the right foods, take plenty of exercise and, even although no insurance company in the world will look at me, their medical men would pass me any time, but even so I couldn't tear that gun away. The hand that had looked like marble felt like marble, only colder. I'd smelled death all right, but the old man hadn't been hanging around with his scythe at the ready, he'd been and gone and left this lifeless shell behind him. I straightened, checked that the windows were curtained, closed the door noiselessly, locked it as quietly and switched on the overhead light.

There's seldom any doubt about the exact time of a murder in an old English country house murder story. After a cursory examination and a lot of pseudo-medical mumbo-jumbo, the good doctor drops the corpse's wrist and says, 'The decedent deceased at 11.57 last night' or words to that effect, then, with a thin deprecatory smile magnanimously conceding that he's a member of the fallible human race, adds, 'Give or take a minute or two.' The good doctor outside the pages of the detective novel finds it rather more difficult. Weight, build, ambient temperature and cause of death all bear so heavily and often unpredictably on the cooling of the body that the estimated time of death may well lie in a span of several hours.

I'm not a doctor, far less a good one, and all I could tell about the man behind the desk was that he had been dead long enough for rigor mortis to set in but not long enough for it to wear off. He was stiff as a man frozen to death in a Siberian winter. He'd been gone for hours. How many, I'd no idea.

He wore four gold bands on his sleeves, so that would seem to make him the captain. The captain in the radio cabin. Captains are seldom found in the radio cabin and never behind the desk. He was slumped back in his chair, his head to one side, the back of it resting against a jacket hanging from a hook on the bulkhead, the side of it against a wall cabinet. Rigor mortis kept him in that position but he should have slipped to the floor or at least slumped forward on to the table before rigor mortis had set in.

There were no outward signs of violence that I could see but on the assumption that it would be stretching the arm of coincidence a bit far to assume that he had succumbed from natural causes while preparing to defend his life with his Peacemaker I took a closer look. I tried to pull him upright but he wouldn't budge. I tried harder, I heard the sound of cloth ripping, then suddenly he was upright, then fallen over to the left of the table, the right arm pivoting stiffly around and upwards, the Colt an accusing finger pointing at heaven.

I knew now how he had died and why he hadn't fallen forward before. He'd been killed by a weapon that projected from his spinal column, between maybe the sixth and seventh vertebrae, I couldn't be sure, and the handle of this weapon had caught in the pocket of the jacket on the bulkhead and held him there.

My job was one that had brought me into contact with a fair number of people who had died from a fair assortment of unnatural causes, but this was the first time I'd ever seen a man who had been killed by a chisel. A half-inch wood chisel, apparently quite ordinary in every respect except that its wooden handle had been sheathed by a bicycle's rubber hand-grip, the kind that doesn't show fingerprints. The blade was imbedded to a depth of at least four inches and even allowing for an edge honed to a razor sharpness it had taken a man as powerful as he was violent to strike that blow. I tried to jerk the chisel free, but it wouldn't come. It often happens that way with a knife: bone or cartilage that has been pierced by a sharp instrument locks solid over the steel when an attempt is made to withdraw it. I didn't try again. The chances were that the killer himself had tried to move it and failed. He wouldn't have wanted to abandon a handy little sticker like that if he could help it. Maybe someone had interrupted him. On maybe he had a large supply of half-inch wood chisels and could afford to leave the odd one lying around carelessly in someone's back.

Anyway, I didn't really want it. I had my own. Not a chisel but a knife. I eased it out of the plastic sheath that had been sewn into the inner lining of my coat, just behind the neck. It didn't look so much, a four-inch handle and a little double-edged three-inch blade. But that little blade could slice through a two-inch manila with one gentle stroke and the point was the point of a lancet. I looked at it and looked at the inner door behind the radio table, the one that led to the radio-operator's sleeping cabin, then I slid a little fountain-pen torch from my breast pocket, crossed to the outer door, switched off the overhead lamp, did the same for the table lamp and stood there waiting.

How long I stood there I couldn't be sure. Maybe two minutes, maybe as long as five. Why I waited, I don't know. I told myself I was waiting until my eyes became adjusted to the almost total darkness inside the cabin, but I knew it wasn't that. Maybe I was waiting for some noise, the slightest imagined whisper of stealthy sound, maybe I was waiting for something, anything, to happen – or maybe I was just scared to go through that inner door. Scared for myself? Perhaps I was. I couldn't be sure. Or perhaps I was scared of what I would find behind that door. I transferred the knife to my left hand – I'm right-handed but ambidextrous in some things – and slowly closed my fingers round the handle of the inner door.

It took me all of twenty seconds to open that door the twelve inches that was necessary for me to squeeze through the opening. In the very last half-inch the damned hinges creaked. It was a tiny sound, a sound you wouldn't normally have heard two yards away. With my steel-taut nerves in the state they were in, a six-inch naval gun going off in my ear would have sounded muffled by contrast. I stood petrified as any graven image, the dead man by my side was no more immobile than I. I could hear the thump of my accelerating heartbeat and savagely wished the damned thing would keep quiet.

If there was anyone inside waiting to flash a torch in my face and shoot me, knife me or do a little fancy carving up with a chisel, he was taking his time about it. I treated my lungs to a little oxygen, stepped soundlessly and sideways through the opening. I held the flash at the full outstretch extent of my right arm. If the ungodly are going to shoot at a person who is shining a torch at them they generally aim in the very close vicinity of the torch as the unwary habitually hold a torch in front of them. This, as I had learnt many years previously from a colleague who'd just had a bullet extracted from the lobe of his left lung because of this very unwariness, was a very unwise thing to do. So I held the torch as far from my body as possible, drew my left arm back with the knife ready to go, hoping fervently that the reactions of any person who might be in that cabin were slower than mine, and slid forward the switch of the torch.

There was someone there all right, but I didn't have to worry about his reactions. Not any more. He'd none left. He was lying face down on the bunk with that huddled shapeless look that belongs only to the dead. I made a quick traverse of the cabin with the pencil beam. The dead man was alone. As in the radio cabin, there was no sign of a struggle.

I didn't even have to touch him to ascertain the cause of death. The amount of blood that had seeped from that half-inch incision in his spine wouldn't have filled a tea-spoon. I wouldn't have expected to find more; when the spinal column has been neatly severed the heart doesn't go on pumping long enough to matter a damn. There would have been a little more internal bleeding, but not much.

The curtains were drawn. I quartered every foot of the deck, bulkheads and furniture with my flash. I don't know what I expected to find: what I found was nothing. I went out, closed the door behind me and searched the radio cabin with the same results. There was nothing more for me here, I had found all I wanted to find, all I had never wanted to find. And I never once looked at the faces of the two dead men. I didn't have to, they were faces I knew as well as the face that looked back at me every morning out of my shaving mirror. Seven days previously they had dined with me and our chief in our favourite pub in London and they had been as cheerful and relaxed as men in their profession can ever be, their normal still watchfulness overlaid by the momentary savouring of the lighter side of life they knew could never really be for them. And I had no doubt they had gone on being as still and watchful as ever, but they hadn't been watchful enough and now they were only still. What had happened to them was what inevitably happened to people in our trade, which would inevitably happen to myself when the time came. No matter how clever and strong and ruthless you were, sooner or later you would meet up with someone who was cleverer and stronger and more ruthless than yourself. And that someone would have a half-inch wood chisel in his hand and all your hardly won years of experience and knowledge and cunning counted for nothing for you never saw him coming and you never saw him coming because you had met your match at last and then you were dead.

And I had sent them to their deaths. Not willingly, not knowingly, but the ultimate responsibility had been mine. This had all been my idea, my brain-child and mine alone, and I'd overriden all objections and fast-talked our very doubtful and highly sceptical chief into giving if not his enthusiastic approval at least his grudging consent. I'd told the two men, Baker and Delmont, that if they played it my way no harm would come to them so they'd trusted me blindly and played it my way and now they lay dead beside me. No hesitation, gentlemen, put your faith in me, only see to it that you make your wills first of all.

There was nothing more to be done here now. I'd sent two men to their deaths and that couldn't be undone. It was time to be gone.

I opened that outer door the way you'd open the door to a cellar you knew to be full of cobras and black widow spiders. The way *you* would open the door, that is: were cobras and black widow spiders all I had to contend with aboard that ship, I'd have gone through that door without a second thought, they were harmless and almost lovable little creatures compared to some specimens of homo sapiens that were loose on the decks of the freighter *Nantesville* that night.

With the door opened at its fullest extent I just stood there. I stood there for a long time without moving a muscle of body or limbs, breathing shallowly and evenly, and when you stand like that even a minute seems half a lifetime. All my being was in my ears. I just stood there and listened. I could hear the slap of waves against the hull, the occasional low metallic rumble as the *Nantesville* worked against wind and tide on its moorings, the low moan of the strengthening night wind in the rigging and, once, the far-off lonely call of a curlew. Lonesome sounds, safe sounds, sounds of the night and nature. Not the sounds I was listening for. Gradually, these sounds too became part of the silence. Foreign sounds, sounds of stealth and menace and danger, there were none. No sound of breathing, no slightest scrape of feet on steel decks, no rustle of clothing, nothing. If there was anyone waiting out there he was possessed of a patience and immobility that was superhuman and I wasn't worried about superhumans that night, just about humans, humans with knives and guns and chisels in their hands. Silently I stepped out over the storm sill.

I've never paddled along the night-time Orinoco in a dug-out canoe and had a thirty-foot anaconda drop from a tree, wrap a coil around my neck and start constricting me to death and what's more I don't have to go there now to describe the experience for I know exactly what it feels like. The sheer animal power, the feral ferocity of the pair of huge hands that closed round my neck from behind was terrifying, something I'd never known of, never dreamed of. After the first moment of blind panic and shocked paralysis, there was only one thought in my mind: it comes to us all and now it has come to me, someone who is cleverer and stronger and more ruthless than I am.

I lashed back with all the power of my right foot but the man behind me knew every rule in the book. His own right foot, travelling with even more speed and power than mine, smashed into the back of my swinging leg. It wasn't a man behind me, it was a centaur and he was shod with the biggest set of horseshoes I'd ever come across. My leg didn't just feel as if it had been broken, it felt as if it had been cut in half. I felt his left toe behind my left foot and stamped on it with every vicious ounce of power left me but when my foot came down his toe wasn't there any more. All I had on my feet was a pair of thin rubber swimming moccasins and the agonizing jar from the steel deck plates shot clear to the top of my head. I reached up my hands to break his little fingers but he knew all about that too for his hands were clenched into iron-hard balls with the second knuckle grinding into the carotid artery. I wasn't the first man he'd strangled and unless I did something pretty quickly I wasn't going to be the last either. In my ears I could hear the hiss of compressed air escaping under high pressure and behind my eyes the shooting lines and flashes of colour were deepening and brightening by the moment.

What saved me in those first few seconds were the folded hood and thick rubberized canvas neck ruff of the scuba suit I was wearing under my coat. But it wasn't going to save me many seconds longer, the life's ambition of the character behind me seemed to be to make his knuckles meet in the middle of my neck. With the progress he was making that wouldn't take him too long, he was half-way there already.

I bent forward in a convulsive jerk. Half of his weight came on my back, that throttling grip not easing a fraction, and at the same time he moved his feet as far backwards as possible – the instinctive reaction to my move, he would have thought that I was making a grab for one of his legs. When I had him momentarily off-balance I swung round in a short arc till both our backs were towards the sea. I thrust backwards with all my strength, one, two, three steps, accelerating all the way. The *Nantesville* didn't boast of any fancy teak guard-rails, just small-section chain, and the small of the strangler's back took our combined charging weights on the top chain.

If I'd taken that impact I'd have broken my back or slipped enough discs to keep an orthopaedic surgeon in steady employment for months. But no shouts of agony from this lad. No gasps, even. Not a whisper of sound. Maybe he was a deaf mute – I'd heard of several dead mutes possessed of this phenomenal strength, part of nature's compensatory process, I suppose.

But he'd been forced to break his grip, to grab swiftly at the upper chain to save us both from toppling over the side into the cold dark waters of Loch Houron. I thrust myself away and spun round to face him, my back against the radio office bulkhead. I needed that bulkhead, too – any support while my swimming head cleared and a semblance of life came back into my numbed right leg.

I could see him now as he straightened up from the guard-rail. Not clearly – it was too dark for that – but I could see the white blur of face and hands and the general outline of his body.

I'd expected some towering giant of a man, but he was no giant – unless my eyes weren't focusing properly, which was likely enough. From what I could see in the gloom he seemed a compact and well enough made figure, but that was all. He wasn't even as big as I was. Not that that meant a thing – George Hackenschmidt was a mere five foot nine and a paltry fourteen stone when he used to throw the Terrible Turk through the air like a football and prance around the training ring with eight hundred pounds of cement strapped to his back just to keep him in trim. I had no compunction or false pride about running from a smaller man and as far as this character was concerned the farther and faster the better. But not yet. My right leg wasn't up to it. I reached my hand behind my neck and brought the knife down, holding it in front of me, the blade in the palm of my hand so that he couldn't see the sheen of steel in the faint starlight.

He came at me calmly and purposefully, like a man who knew exactly what he intended to do and was in no doubt at all as to the outcome of his intended action. God knows I didn't doubt he had reason enough for his confidence. He came at me sideways so that my foot couldn't damage him, with his right hand extended at the full stretch of his arm. A one track mind. He was going for my throat again. I waited till his hand was inches from my face then jerked my own right hand violently upwards. Our hands smacked solidly together as the blade sliced cleanly through the centre of his palm.

He wasn't a deaf mute after all. Three short unprintable words, an unjustified slur on my ancestry, and he stepped quickly backwards, rubbed the back and front of his hand against his clothes then licked it in a queer animal-like gesture. He peered closely at the blood, black as ink in the starlight, welling from both sides of his hand.

'So the little man has a little knife has he?' he said softly. The voice was a shock. With this caveman-like strength I'd have expected a caveman-like intelligence and voice to match, but the words came in the calm, pleasant, cultured almost accentless speech of the well-educated southern Englishman. 'We shall have to take the little knife from him, shan't we?' He raised his voice. 'Captain Imrie?' At least, that's what the name sounded like.

'Be quiet, you fool!' The urgent irate voice came from the direction of the crew accommodation aft. 'Do you want to—'

'Don't worry, Captain.' The eyes didn't leave me. 'I have him. Here by the wireless office. He's armed. A knife. I'm just going to take it away from him.'

'You have him? You have him? Good, good, good!' It was the kind of a voice a man uses when he's smacking his lips and rubbing his hands together: it was also the kind of voice that a German or Austrian uses when he speaks English. The short guttural 'gut' was unmistakable. 'Be careful. This one I want alive. Jacques! Henry! Kramer! All of you. Quickly! The bridge. Wireless office.'

'Alive,' the man opposite me said pleasantly, 'can also mean not quite dead.' He sucked some more blood from the palm of his hand. 'Or will you hand over the knife quietly and peaceably? I would suggest—'

I didn't wait for more. This was an old technique. You talked to an opponent who courteously waited to hear you out, not appreciating that half-way through some well-turned phrase you were going to shoot him through the middle when, lulled into a sense of temporary false security, he least expected it. Not quite cricket, but effective, and I wasn't going to wait until it took effect on me. I didn't know how he was coming at me but I guessed it would be a dive, either head or feet first and that if he got me down on the deck I wouldn't be getting up again. Not without assistance. I took a quick step forward, flashed my torch a foot from his face, saw the dazzled eyes screw shut for the only fraction of time I'd ever have and kicked him.

It wasn't as hard as it might have been, owing to the fact that my right leg still felt as if it were broken, nor as accurate, because of the darkness, but it was a pretty creditable effort in the circumstances and it should have left him rolling and writhing about the deck, whooping in agony. Instead he just stood there, unable to move, bent forward and clutching himself with his hands. He was more than human, all right. I could see the sheen of his eyes, but I couldn't see the expression in them, which was just as well as I don't think I would have cared for it very much.

I left. I remembered a gorilla I'd once seen in Basle Zoo, a big black monster who used to twist heavy truck tyres into figures of eight for light exercise. I'd as soon have stepped inside that cage as stay around that deck when this lad became more like his old self again. I hobbled forward round the corner of the radio office, climbed up a life-raft and stretched myself flat on the deck.

The nearest running figures, some with torches, were already at the foot of the companionway leading up to the bridge. I had to get right aft to the rope with the rubber-covered hook I'd swung up to swarm aboard. But I couldn't do it until the midship decks were clear. And then, suddenly, I couldn't do it at all: now that the need for secrecy and stealth was over someone had switched on the cargo loading lights and the midships and foredecks were bathed in a brilliant dazzle of white. One of the foredeck arc lamps was on a jumbo mast, just for'ard of and well above where I was lying. I felt as exposed as a fly pinned to a white ceiling. I flattened myself on that deck as if I were trying to push myself through it.

They were up the companionway and by the radio office now. I heard the sudden exclamations and curses and knew they'd found the hurt man: I didn't hear his voice so I assumed he wasn't able to speak yet.

The curt, authoritative German-accented voice took command.

'You cackle like a flock of hens. Be silent. Jacques, you have your machine-pistol?'

'I have my pistol Captain.' Jacques had the quiet competent sort of voice that I would have found reassuring in certain circumstances but didn't very much care for in the present ones.

'Go aft. Stand at the entrance to the saloon and face for'ard. Cover the midships decks. We will go to the fo'c'sle and then come aft in line abreast and drive him to you. If he doesn't surrender to you, shoot him through the legs. I want him alive.'

God, this was worse that the Peacemaker Colt. At least that fired only one shot at a time. I'd no idea what kind of machine-pistol Jacques had, probably it fired bursts of a dozen or more. I could feel my right thigh muscle begin to stiffen again, it was becoming almost a reflex action now.

'And if he jumps over the side, sir?'

'Do I have to tell you, Jacques?'

'No, sir.'

I was just as clever as Jacques was. He didn't have to tell me either. That nasty dry taste was back in my throat and mouth again. I'd a minute left, no more, and then it would be too late. I slid silently to the side of the radio office roof, the starboard side, the side remote from the spot where Captain Imrie was issuing curt instructions to his men, lowered myself soundlessly to the deck and made my way to the wheelhouse.

I didn't need my torch in there, the backwash of light from the big arc-lamps gave me all the illumination I wanted. Crouching down, to keep below window level, I looked around and saw what I wanted right away – a metal box of distress flares.

Two quick flicks of the knife severed the lashings that secured the flare-box to the deck. One piece of rope, perhaps ten feet in all, I left secured to a handle of the box. I pulled a plastic bag from the pocket of my coat, tore off the coat and the yachtsman's rubber trousers that I was wearing over my scuba suit, stuffed them inside and secured the bag to my waist. The coat and trousers had been essential. A figure in a dripping rubber diving suit walking across the decks of the *Nantesville* would hardly have been likely to escape comment whereas in the dusk and with the outer clothing I had on I could have passed for a crewman and, indeed, had done so twice at a distance: equally important, when I'd left the port of Torbay in my rubber dinghy it had been broad daylight and the sight of a scuba-clad figure putting to sea towards evening wouldn't have escaped comment either, as the curiosity factor of the inhabitants of the smaller ports of the Western Highlands and Islands did not, I had discovered, lag noticeably behind that of their mainland brethren. Some would put it even more strongly than that.

Still crouching low, I moved out through the wheelhouse door on to the starboard wing of the bridge. I reached the outer end and stood up straight. I had to, I had to take the risk, it was now or never at all, I could hear the crew already beginning to move forward to start their search. I lifted the flare box over the side, eased it down the full length of the rope and started to swing it slowly, gently, from side to side, like a leadsman, preparing to cast his lead.

The box weighed at least forty pounds, but I barely noticed the weight. The pendulum arc increased with every swing I made. It had reached an angle of about forty-five degrees on each swing now, pretty close to the maximum I could get and both time and my luck must be running out, I felt about as conspicuous as a trapeze artist under a dozen spotlights and just about as vulnerable too. As the box swung aft on its last arc I gave the rope a final thrust to achieve all the distance and momentum I could, opened my hands at the extremity of the arc and dropped down behind the canvas wind-dodger. It was as I dropped that I remembered I hadn't holed the damned box, I had no idea whether it would float or sink but I did have a very clear idea of what would happen to me if it didn't sink. One thing for sure, it was too late to worry about it now.

I heard a shout come from the main deck, some twenty or thirty feet aft of the bridge. I was certain I had been seen but I hadn't. A second after the shout came a loud and very satisfactory splash and a voice I recognized as Jacques's shouting: 'He's gone over the side. Starboard abaft the bridge. A torch quick!' He must have been walking aft as ordered, seen this dark blur falling, heard the splash and come on the inevitable conclusion. A dangerous customer who thought fast, was Jacques. In three seconds he'd told his mates all they required to know: what had happened, where and what he wanted done as the necessary preliminary to shooting me full of holes.

The men who had been moving forward to start the sweep for me now came running aft, pounding along the deck directly beneath where I was crouching on the wing of the bridge.

'Can you see him, Jacques?' Captain Imrie's voice, very quick, very calm.

'Not yet, sir.'

'He'll be up soon.' I wished he wouldn't sound so damned confident. 'A dive like that must have knocked most of the breath out of him. Kramer, two men and into the boat. Take lamps and circle around. Henry, the box of grenades. Carlo, the bridge, quick. Starboard searchlight.'

I'd never thought of the boat, that was bad enough, but the grenades! I felt chilled. I knew what an underwater explosion, even a small explosion, can do to the human body, it was twenty times as deadly as the same explosion on land. And I had to, I just had to, be in that water in minutes. But at least I could do something about that searchlight, it was only two feet above my head. I had the power cable in my left hand, the knife in my right and had just brought the two into contact when my mind stopped thinking about those damned grenades and started working again. Cutting that cable would be about as clever as leaning over the wind-dodger and yelling 'Here I am, come and catch me' – a dead giveaway that I was still on board. Clobbering Carlo from behind as he came up the ladder would have the same effect. And I couldn't fool them twice. Not people like these. Hobbling as fast as I could I passed through the wheelhouse on to the port wing, slid down the ladder and ran towards the forepeak. The foredeck was deserted.

I heard a shout and the harsh chatter of some automatic weapon – Jacques and his machine-pistol, for a certainty. Had he imagined he'd seen something, had the box come to the surface, had he actually seen the box and mistaken it for me in the dark waters? It must have been the last of these – he wouldn't have wasted ammunition on anything he'd definitely recognized as a box. Whatever the reason, it had all my blessing. If they thought I was floundering about down there, riddled like a Gruyère cheese, then they wouldn't be looking for me up here.

They had the port anchor down. I swung over the side on a rope, got my feet in the hawse-pipe, reached down and grabbed the chain. The international athletics board should have had their stop-watches on me that night, I must have set a new world record for shinning down anchor chains.

The water was cold but my exposure suit took care of that. It was choppy, with a heavy tide running, both of which suited me well. I swam down the port side of the *Nantesville*, underwater for ninety per cent of the time and I saw no one and no one saw me: all the activity was on the starboard side of the vessel.

My aqualung unit and weights and flippers were where I had left them, tied to the top of the rudder post – the *Nantesville* was not much more than half-way down to her marks and the top of the post not far under water. Fitting on an aqualung in choppy seas with a heavy tide running isn't the easiest of tasks but the thought of Kramer and his grenades was a considerable help. Besides I was in a hurry to be gone for I had a long way to go and many things to do when I arrived at my destination.

I could hear the engine note of the lifeboat rising and falling as it circled off the ship's starboard side but at no time did it come within a hundred feet of me. No more shots were fired and Captain Imrie had obviously decided against using the grenades. I adjusted the weights round my waist, dropped down into the dark safety of the waters, checked my direction on my luminous wrist compass and started to swim. After five minutes I came to the surface and after another five felt my feet ground on the shore of the rocky islet where I'd cached my rubber dinghy.

I clambered up on the rocks and looked back. The *Nantesville* was ablaze with light. A searchlight was shining down into the sea and the lifeboat still circling around. I could hear the steady clanking of the anchor being weighed. I hauled the dinghy into the water, climbed in, unshipped the two stubby oars and paddled off to the south-west. I was still within effective range of the searchlight but its chances of picking up a black-clad figure in a low-silhouette black dinghy on those black waters were remote indeed.

After a mile I shipped the oars and started up the outboard. Or tried to start it up. Outboards always work perfectly for me, except when I'm cold, wet and exhausted. Whenever I really need them, they never work. So I took to the stubby oars again and rowed and rowed and rowed, but not for what seemed any longer than a month. I arrived back at the *Firecrest* at ten to three in the morning.

Chapter Two

Tuesday: 3 a.m. – dawn

'Calvert?' Hunslett's voice was a barely audible murmur in the darkness.

'Yes.' Standing there above me on the *Firecrest*'s deck, he was more imagined than seen against the blackness of the night sky. Heavy clouds had rolled in from the south-west and the last of the stars were gone. Big heavy drops of cold rain were beginning to spatter off the surface of the sea. 'Give me a hand to get the dinghy aboard.'

'How did it go?'

'Later. This first.' I climbed up the accommodation ladder, painter in hand. I had to lift my right leg over the gunwale. Stiff and numb and just beginning to ache again, it could barely take my weight. 'And hurry. We can expect company soon.'

'So that's the way of it,' Hunslett said thoughtfully, 'Uncle Arthur *will* be pleased about this.'

I said nothing to that. Our employer, Rear-Admiral Sir Arthur Arnford-Jason, KCB and most of the rest of the alphabet, wasn't going to be pleased at all. We heaved the dripping dinghy inboard, unclamped the outboard and took them both on to the foredeck.

'Get me a couple of waterproof bags,' I said. 'Then start getting the anchor chain in. Keep it quiet – leave the brake pawl off and use a tarpaulin.'

'We're leaving?'

'We would if we had any sense. We're staying. Just get the anchor up and down.'

By the time he'd returned with the bags I'd the dinghy deflated and in its canvas cover. I stripped off my aqualung and scuba suit and stuffed them into one of the bags along with the weights, my big-dialled waterproof watch and the combined wrist-compass and depth-gauge. I put the outboard in the other bag, restraining the impulse just to throw the damn' thing overboard: an outboard motor was a harmless enough object to have aboard any boat, but we already had one attached to the wooden dinghy hanging from the davits over the stern.

Hunslett had the electric windlass going and the chain coming in steadily. An electric windlass is in itself a pretty noiseless machine: when weighing anchor all the racket comes from four sources – the chain passing through the hawse-pipe, the clacking of the brake pawl over the successive stops, the links passing over the drum itself and the clattering of the chain as it falls into the chain locker. About the first of these we could do nothing: but with the brake pawl off and a heavy tarpaulin smothering the sound from the drum and chain locker, the noise level was surprisingly low. Sound travels far over the surface of the sea, but the nearest anchored boats were almost two hundred yards away – we had no craving for the company of other boats in harbour. At two hundred yards, in Torbay, we felt ourselves uncomfortably close: but the sea-bed shelved fairly steeply away from the little town and our present depth of twenty fathoms was the safe maximum for the sixty fathoms of chain we carried.

I heard the click as Hunslett's foot stepped on the deck-switch. 'She's up and down.'

'Put the pawl in for a moment. If that drum slips, I'll have no hands left.' I pulled the bags right for'ard, leaned out under the pulpit rail and used lengths of heaving line to secure them to the anchor chain. When the lines were secure I lifted the bags over the side and let them dangle from the chain.

'I'll take the weight,' I said. 'Lift the chain off the drum – we'll lower it by hand.'

Forty fathoms is 240 feet of chain and letting that lot down to the bottom didn't do my back or arms much good at all, and the rest of me was a long way below par before we started. I was pretty close to exhaustion from the night's work, my neck ached fiercely, my leg only badly and I was shivering violently. I know of various ways of achieving a warm rosy glow but wearing only a set of underclothes in the middle of a cold, wet and windy autumn night in the Western Isles is not one of them. But at last the job was done and we were able to go below. If anyone wanted to investigate what lay at the foot of our anchor chain he'd need a steel articulated diving suit.

Hunslett pulled the saloon door to behind us, moved around in the darkness adjusting the heavy velvet curtains then switched on a small table lamp. It didn't give much light but we knew from experience that it didn't show up through the velvet, and advertising the fact that we were up and around in the middle of the night was the last thing I wanted to do.

Hunslett had a dark narrow saturnine face, with a strong jaw, black bushy eyebrows and thick black hair – the kind of face which is so essentially an expression in itself that it rarely shows much else. It was expressionless now and very still.

'You'll have to buy another shirt,' he said. 'Your collar's too tight. Leaves marks.'

I stopped towelling myself and looked in a mirror. Even in that dim light my neck looked a mess. It was badly swollen and discoloured, with four wicked-looking bruises where the thumbs and forefinger joints had sunk deep into the flesh. Blue and green and purple they were, and they looked as if they would be there for a long time to come.

'He got me from behind. He's wasting his time being a criminal, he'd sweep the board at the Olympic weight-lifting. I was lucky. He also wears heavy boots.' I twisted around and looked down at my right calf. The bruise was bigger than my fist and if it missed out any of the colours of the rainbow I couldn't offhand think which one. There was a deep red gash across the middle of it and blood was ebbing slowly along its entire length. Hunslett gazed at it with interest.

'If you hadn't been wearing that tight scuba suit, you'd have most like bled to death. I'd better fix that for you.'

'I don't need bandages. What I need is a Scotch. Stop wasting your time. Oh, hell, sorry, yes, you'd better fix it, we can't have our guests sloshing about ankle deep in blood.'

'You're very sure we're going to have guests?'

'I half expected to have them waiting on the doorstep when I got back to the *Firecrest*. We're going to have guests, all right. Whatever our pals aboard the *Nantesville* may be, they're no fools. They'll have figured out by this time that I could have approached only by dinghy. They'll know damn' well that it was no nosey-parker local prowling about the ship – local lads in search of a bit of fun don't go aboard anchored ships in the first place. In the second place the locals wouldn't go near Beul nan Uamh – the mouth of the grave – in daylight, far less at night time. Even the *Pilot* says the place has an evil reputation. And in the third place no local lad would get aboard as I did, behave aboard as I did or leave as I did. The local lad would be dead.'

'I shouldn't wonder. And?'

'So we're not locals. We're visitors. We wouldn't be staying at any hotel or boarding-house – too restricted, couldn't move. Almost certainly we'll have a boat. Now, where would our boat be? Not to the north of Loch Houron for with a forecast promising a south-west Force 6 strengthening to Force 7, no boat is going to be daft enough to hang about a lee shore in that lot. The only holding ground and shallow enough sheltered anchorage in the other direction, down the Sound for forty miles, is in Torbay – and that's only four or five miles from where the *Nantesville* was lying at the mouth of Loch Houron. Where would you look for us?'

'I'd look for a boat anchored in Torbay. Which gun do you want?'

'I don't want any gun. You don't want any gun. People like us don't carry guns.'

'Marine biologists don't carry guns,' he nodded. 'Employees of the Ministry of Agriculture and Fisheries don't carry guns. Civil Servants are above reproach. So we play it clever. You're the boss.'

'I don't feel clever any more. And I'll take long odds that I'm not your boss any more. Not after Uncle Arthur hears what I have to tell him.'

'You haven't told *me* anything yet.' He finished tying the bandage round my leg and straightened. 'How's that feel?'

I tried it. 'Better. Thanks. Better still when you've taken the cork from that bottle. Get into pyjamas or something. People found fully dressed in the middle of the night cause eyebrows to go up.' I towelled my head as vigorously as my tired arms would let me. One wet hair on my head and eyebrows wouldn't just be lifting, they'd be disappearing into hairlines. 'There isn't much to tell and all of it is bad.'

He poured me a large drink, a smaller one for himself, and added water to both. It tasted the way Scotch always does after you've swum and rowed for hours and damn' near got yourself killed in the process.

'I got there without trouble. I hid behind Carrara Point till it was dusk and then paddled out to the Bogha Nuadh. I left the dinghy there and swam underwater as far as the stern of the ship. It was the *Nantesville* all right. Name and flag were different, a mast was gone and the white superstructure was now stone – but it was her all right. Near as dammit didn't make it – it was close to the turn of the tide but it took me thirty minutes against that current. Must be wicked at the full flood or ebb.'

'They say it's the worst on the West Coast – worse even than Coirebhreachan.'

'I'd rather not be the one to find out. I had to hang on to the stern post for ten minutes before I'd got enough strength back to shin up that rope.'

'You took a chance.'

'It was near enough dark. Besides,' I added bitterly, 'there are some precautions intelligent people don't think to take about crazy ones. There were only two or three people in the after accommodation. Just a skeleton crew aboard, seven or eight, no more. All the original crew have vanished completely.'

'No sign of them anywhere?'

'No sign. Dead or alive, no sign at all. I had a bit of bad luck. I was leaving the after accommodation to go to the bridge when I passed someone a few feet away. I gave a half wave and grunted something and he answered back, I don't know what. I followed him back to the quarters. He picked up a phone in the crew's mess and I heard him talking to someone, quick and urgent. Said that one of the original crew must have been hiding and was trying to get away. I couldn't stop him – he faced the door as he was talking and he had a gun in his hand. I had to move quickly. I walked to the bridge structure—'

'You what? When you knew they were on to you? Mr Calvert, you want your bloody head examined.'

'Uncle Arthur will put it less kindly. It was the only chance I'd ever have. Besides, if they thought it was only a terrified member of the original crew they wouldn't have been so worried: if this guy had seen me walking around dripping wet in a scuba suit he'd have turned me into a colander. He wasn't sure. On the way for'ard I passed another bloke without incident – he'd left the bridge superstructure before the alarm had been given, I suppose. I didn't stop at the bridge. I went right for'ard and hid behind the winchman's shelter. For about ten minutes there was a fair bit of commotion and a lot of flash-light work around the bridge island then I saw and heard them moving aft – must have thought I was still in the after accommodation.

'I went through all the officers' cabins in the bridge island. No one. One cabin, an engineer's, I think had smashed furniture and a carpet heavily stained with dry blood. Next door, the captain's bunk had been saturated with blood.'

'They'd been warned to offer no resistance.'

'I know. Then I found Baker and Delmont.'

'So you found them. Baker and Delmont.' Hunslett's eyes were hooded, gazing down at the glass in his hand. I wished to God he'd show some expression on that dark face of his.

'Delmont must have made a last-second attempt to send a call for help. They'd been warned not to, except in emergency, so they must have been discovered. He'd been stabbed in the back with a half-inch wood chisel and then dragged into the radio officer's cabin which adjoined the radio office. Some time later Baker had come in. He was wearing an officer's clothes – some desperate attempt to disguise himself, I suppose. He'd a gun in his hand, but he was looking the wrong way and the gun was pointing the wrong way. The same chisel in the back.'

Hunslett poured himself another drink. A much larger one. Hunslett hardly ever drank. He swallowed half of it in one gulp. He said: 'And they hadn't all gone aft. They'd left a reception committee.'

'They're very clever. They're very dangerous. Maybe we've moved out of our class. Or I have. A one-man reception committee, but when that one man was this man, two would have been superfluous. I know he killed Baker and Delmont. I'll never be so lucky again.'

'You got away. Your luck hadn't run out.'

And Baker's and Delmont's had. I knew he was blaming me. I knew London would blame me. I blamed myself. I hadn't much option. There was no one else to blame.

'Uncle Arthur,' Hunslett said. 'Don't you think—'

'The hell with Uncle Arthur. Who cares about Uncle Arthur? How in God's name do you think I feel?' I felt savage and I know I sounded it. For the first time a flicker of expression showed on Hunslett's face. I wasn't supposed to have any feelings.

'Not that,' he said. 'About the *Nantesville*. Now that she's been identified *as* the *Nantesville*, now we know her new name and flag – what were they, by the way?'

'*Alta Fjord*. Norwegian. It doesn't matter.'

'It does matter. We radio Uncle Arthur—'

'And have our guests find us in the engine-room with earphones round our heads. Are you mad?'

'You seem damned sure they'll come.'

'I *am* sure. You too. You said so.'

'I agreed this is where they would come. *If* they come.'

'If they come. *If* they come. Good God, man, for all that they know I was aboard that ship for hours. I may have the names and full descriptions of all of them. As it happens I couldn't identify any of them and their names may or may not mean anything. But they're not to know that. For all they know I'm on the blower right now bawling out descriptions to Interpol. The chances are at least even that some of them are on file. They're too good to be little men. Some must be known.'

'In that case they'd be too late anyway. The damage would be done.'

'Not without the sole witness who could testify against them?'

'I think we'd better have those guns out.'

'No.'

'You don't blame me for trying?'

'No.'

'Baker and Delmont. Think of them.'

'I'm thinking of nothing else but them. You don't have to stay.'

He set his glass down very carefully. He was really letting himself go tonight, he'd allowed that dark craggy face its second expression in ten minutes and it wasn't a very encouraging one. Then he picked up his glass and grinned.

'You don't know what you're saying,' he said kindly. 'Your neck – that's what comes from the blood supply to the brain being interrupted. You're not fit to fight off a teddy-bear. Who's going to look after you if they start playing games?'

'I'm sorry,' I said. I meant it. I'd worked with Hunslett maybe ten times in the ten years I'd known him and it had been a stupid thing for me to say. About the only thing Hunslett was incapable of was leaving your side in time of trouble. 'You were speaking of Uncle?'

'Yes. We know where the *Nantesville* is. Uncle could get a Navy boat to shadow her, by radar if—'

'I know where she was. She upped anchor as I left. By dawn she'll be a hundred miles away – in any direction.'

'She's gone? We've scared them off? They're going to love this.' He sat down heavily, then looked at me. 'But we have her new description—'

'I said that didn't matter. By to-morrow she'll have another description. The *Hokomaru* from Yokohama, with green topsides, Japanese flag, different masts—'

'An air search. We could—'

'By the time an air search could be organized they'd have twenty thousand square miles of sea to cover. You've heard the forecast. It's bad. Low cloud – and they'd have to fly under the low cloud. Cuts their effectiveness by ninety per cent. And poor visibility and rain. Not a chance in a hundred, not one in a thousand of positive identification. And if they do locate them – if – what then? A friendly wave from the pilot? Not much else he can do.'

'The Navy. They could call up the Navy—'

'Call up what Navy? From the Med? Or the Far East? The Navy has very few ships left and practically none in those parts. By the time any naval vessel could get to the scene it would be night again and the *Nantesville* to hell and gone. Even if a naval ship did catch up with it, what then? Sink it with gunfire – with maybe the twenty-five missing crew members of the *Nantesville* locked up in the hold?'

'A boarding party?'

'With the same twenty-five ex-crew members lined up on deck with pistols at their backs and Captain Imrie and his thugs politely asking the Navy boys what their next move was going to be?'

'I'll get into my pyjamas,' Hunslett said tiredly. At the doorway he paused and turned. 'If the *Nantesville* had gone, her crew – the new crew – have gone too and we'll be having no visitors after all. Had you thought of that?'

'No.'

'I don't really believe it either.'

They came at twenty past four in the morning. They came in a very calm and orderly and law-abiding and official fashion, they stayed for forty minutes and by the time they had left I still wasn't sure whether they were our men or not.

Hunslett came into my small cabin, starboard side forward, switched on the light and shook me. 'Wake up,' he said loudly. 'Come on. Wake up.'

I was wide awake. I hadn't closed an eye since I'd lain down. I groaned and yawned a bit without overdoing it then opened a bleary eye. There was no one behind him.

'What is it? What do you want?' A pause. 'What the hell's up? It's just after four in the morning.'

'Don't ask me what's up,' Hunslett said irritably. 'Police. Just come aboard. They say it's urgent.'

'Police? Did you say, "police"?'

'Yes. Come on, now. They're waiting.'

'Police? Aboard our boat? What—'

'Oh, for God's sake! How many more night-caps did you have last night after I went to bed? Police. Two of them and two customs. It's urgent, they say.'

'It better bloody well be urgent. In the middle of the bloody night. Who do they think we are – escaped train robbers? Haven't you told them who we are? Oh, all right, all right, all *right*! I'm coming.'

Hunslett left, and thirty seconds afterwards I joined him in the saloon. Four men sat there, two police officers and two customs officials. They didn't look a very villainous bunch to me. The older, bigger policeman got to his feet. A tall, burly, brown-faced sergeant in his late forties, he looked me over with a cold eye, looked at the near-empty whisky bottle with the two unwashed glassed on the table, then looked back at me. He didn't like wealthy yachtsmen. He didn't like wealthy yachtsmen who drank too much at night-time and were bleary-eyed, bloodshot and tousle-haired at the following crack of dawn. He didn't like wealthy effete yachtsmen who wore red silk dragon Chinese dressing-gowns with a Paisley scarf to match tied negligently round the neck. I didn't like them very much myself, especially the Paisley scarf, much in favour though it was with the yachting fraternity: but I had to have something to conceal those bruises on my neck.

'Are you the owner of this boat, sir?' the sergeant inquired. An unmistakable West Highland voice and a courteous one, but it took him all his time to get his tongue round the 'sir.'

'If you would tell me what makes it any of your damn' business,' I said unpleasantly, 'maybe I'll answer that and maybe I won't. A private boat is the same as a private house, Sergeant. You have to have a warrant before you shove your way in. Or don't you know the law?'

'He knows the law,' one of the customs men put in. A small dark character, smooth-shaven at four in the morning, with a persuasive voice, not West Highland. 'Be reasonable. This is not the sergeant's job. We got him out of bed almost three hours ago. He's just obliging us.'

I ignored him. I said to the sergeant: 'This is the middle of the night in a lonely Scottish bay. How would you feel if four unidentified men came aboard in the middle of the night?' I was taking a chance on that one, but a fair chance. If they were who I thought they might be and if I were who they thought I might be, then I'd never talk like that. But an innocent man would. 'Any means of identifying yourselves?'

'Identifying myself?' The sergeant stared coldly at me. 'I don't have to identify myself. Sergeant MacDonald. I've been in charge of the Torbay police station for eight years. Ask any man in Torbay. They all know me.' If he was who he claimed to be this was probably the first time in his life that anyone had asked him for identification. He nodded to the seated policeman. 'Police-Constable MacDonald.'

'Your son?' The resemblance was unmistakable. 'Nothing like keeping it in the family, eh, Sergeant?' I didn't know whether to believe him or not, but I felt I'd been an irate householder long enough. A degree less truculence was in order. 'And customs, eh? I know the law about you, too. No search warrants for you boys. I believe the police would like your powers. Go anywhere you like and ask no one's permission beforehand. That's it, isn't it?'

'Yes, sir.' It was the younger customs man who answered. Medium height, fair hair, running a little to fat, Belfast accent, dressed like the other in blue overcoat, peaked hat, brown gloves, smartly creased trousers. 'We hardly ever do, though. We prefer co-operation. We like to ask.'

'And you'd like to ask to search this boat, is that it?' Hunslett said.

'Yes, sir.'

'Why?' I asked. Puzzlement now in my voice. And in my mind. I just didn't know what I had on my hands. 'If we're all going to be so courteous and co-operative, could we have any explanation?'

'No reason in the world why not, sir.' The older customs man was almost apologetic. 'A truck with contents valued at £12,000 was hi-jacked on the Ayrshire coast last night – night before last, that is, now. In the news this evening. From information received, we know it was transferred to a small boat. We think it came north.'

'Why?'

'Sorry, sir. Confidential. This is the third port we've visited and the thirteenth boat – the fourth in Torbay – that we've been on in the past fifteen hours. We've been kept on the run, I can tell you.' An easy friendly voice, a voice that said: 'You don't really think we suspect you. We've a job to do, that's all.'

'And you're searching all boats that have come up from the south. Or you think have come from there. Fresh arrivals, anyway. Has it occurred to you that any boat with hi-jacked goods on board wouldn't dare pass through the Crinan canal? Once you're in there, you're trapped. For four hours. So he'd have to come round the Mull of Kintyre. We've been here since this afternoon. It would take a pretty fast boat to get up here in that time.'

'You've got a pretty fast boat here, sir,' Sergeant MacDonald said. I wondered how the hell they managed it, from the Western Isles to the East London docks every sergeant in the country had the same wooden voice, the same wooden face, the same cold eye. Must be something to do with the uniform. I ignored him.

'What are we – um – supposed to have stolen?'

'Chemicals. It was an I.C.I. truck.'

'Chemicals?' I looked at Hunslett, grinned, then turned back to the customs officer. 'Chemicals, eh? We're loaded with them. But not £12,000 worth, I'm afraid.'

There was a brief silence. MacDonald said: 'Would you mind explaining, sir?'

'Not at all.' I lit a cigarette, the little mind enjoying its big moment, and smiled. 'This is a government boat, Sergeant MacDonald. I thought you would have seen the flag. Ministry of Agriculture and Fisheries. We're marine biologists. Our after cabin is a floating laboratory. Look at our library here.' Two shelves loaded with technical tomes. 'And if you've still any doubt left I can give you two numbers, one in Glasgow, one in London, that will establish our *bona fides*. Or phone the lock-master in the Crinan sea-basin. We spent last night there.'

'Yes, sir.' The lack of impression I had made on the sergeant was total. 'Where did you go in your dinghy this evening?'

'I beg your pardon, Sergeant?'

'You were seen to leave this boat in a black rubber dinghy about five o'clock this evening.' I'd heard of icy fingers playing up and down one's spine but it wasn't fingers I felt then, it was a centipede with a hundred icy boots on. 'You went out into the Sound. Mr McIlroy, the postmaster, saw you.'

'I hate to impugn the character of a fellow civil servant but he must have been drunk.' Funny how an icy feeling could make you sweat. 'I haven't got a black rubber dinghy. I've never owned a black rubber dinghy. You just get out your little magnifying glass, Sergeant, and if you can find a black rubber dinghy I'll make you a present of the brown wooden dinghy, which is the only one we have on the *Firecrest.*'

The wooden expression cracked a little. He wasn't so certain now. 'So you weren't out?'

'I *was* out. In our own dinghy. I was just round the corner of Garve Island there, collecting some marine samples from the Sound. I can show them to you in the after cabin. We're not here on holiday, you know.'

'No offence, no offence.' I was a member of the working classes now, not a plutocrat, and he could afford to thaw a little. 'Mr McIlroy's eyesight isn't what it was and everything looks black against the setting sun. You don't *look* the type, I must say, who'd land on the shores of the Sound and bring down the telephone wires to the mainland.'

The centipede started up again and broke into a fast gallop. Cut off from the mainland. How very convenient for somebody. I didn't spend any time wondering who had brought the wires down – it had been no act of God, I was sure of that.

'Did you mean what I thought you to mean, Sergeant?' I said slowly. 'That you suspected me—'

'We can't take chances, sir.' He was almost apologetic now. Not only was I a working man, I was a man working for the Government. All men working for the Government are *ipso facto* respectable and trustworthy citizens.

'But you won't mind if we take a little look round?' The dark-haired customs officer was even more apologetic. 'The lines are down and, well, you know . . .' His voice trailed off and he smiled. 'If you were the hi-jackers – I appreciate now that it's a chance in a million, but still – and if we didn't search – well, we'd be out of a job to-morrow. Just a formality.'

'I wouldn't want to see that happen, Mr – ah—'

'Thomas. Thank you. Your ship's papers? Ah, thank you.' He handed them to the younger man. 'Let's see now. Ah, the wheelhouse. Could Mr Durran here use the wheelhouse to make copies? Won't take five minutes.'

'Certainly. Wouldn't he be more comfortable here?'

'We're modernized now, sir. Portable photo-copier. Standard on the job. Has to be dark. Won't take five minutes. Can we begin in this laboratory of yours?'

A formality, he'd said. Well, he was right there, as a search it was the least informal thing I'd ever come across. Five minutes after he'd gone to the wheelhouse Durran came aft to join us and he and Thomas went through the *Firecrest* as if they were looking for the Koh-i-noor. To begin with, at least. Every piece of mechanical and electrical equipment in the after cabin had to be explained to them. They looked in every locker and cupboard. They rummaged through the ropes and fenders in the large stern locker aft of the laboratory and I thanked God I hadn't followed my original idea of stowing the dinghy, motor and scuba gear in there. They even examined the after toilet. As if I'd be careless enough to drop the Koh-i-noor in there.

They spent most time of all in the engine-room. It was worth examining. Everything looked brand new, and gleamed. Two big 100 h.p. diesels, diesel generator, radio generator, hot and cold water pumps, central heating plant, big oil and water tanks and the two long rows of lead-acid batteries. Thomas seemed especially interested in the batteries.

'You carry a lot of reserve there, Mr Petersen,' he said. He'd learnt my name by now, even though it wasn't the one I'd been christened with. 'Why all the power?'

'We haven't even got enough. Care to start those two engines by hand? We have eight electric motors in the lab. – and the only time they're used, in harbour, we can't run either the engines or generators to supply juice. Too much interference. A constant drain.' I was ticking off my fingers. 'Then there's the central heating, hot and cold water pumps, radar, radio, automatic steering, windlass, power winch for the dinghy, echo-sounder, navigation lights—'

'You win, you win.' He'd become quite friendly by this time. 'Boats aren't really in my line. Let's move forward, shall we?'

The remainder of the inspection, curiously, didn't take long. In the saloon I found that Hunslett had persuaded the Torbay police force to accept the hospitality of the *Firecrest*. Sergeant MacDonald hadn't exactly become jovial, but he was much more human than when he'd come on board. Constable MacDonald, I noticed, didn't seem so relaxed. He looked positively glum. Maybe he didn't approve of his old man consorting with potential criminals.

If the examination of the saloon was cursory, that of the two forward cabins was positively perfunctory. Back in the saloon, I said:

'Sorry I was a bit short, gentleman. I like my sleep. A drink before you go?'

'Well.' Thomas smiled. 'We don't want to be rude either. Thank you.'

Five minutes and they were gone. Thomas didn't even glance at the wheelhouse – Durran had been there, of course. He had a quick look at one of the deck lockers but didn't bother about the others. We were in the clear. A civil good-bye on both sides and they were gone. Their boat, a big indeterminate shape in the darkness, seemed to have plenty of power.

'Odd,' I said.

'What's odd?'

'That boat. Any idea what it was like?'

'How could I?' Hunslett was testy. He was as short of sleep as I was. 'It was pitch dark.'

'That's just the point. A gentle glow in their wheelhouse – you couldn't even see what that was like – and no more. No deck lights, no interior lights, no nagivation lights even.'

'Sergeant MacDonald has been looking out over this harbour for eight years. Do you need light to find your way about your own living-room after dark?'

'I haven't got twenty yachts and cruisers in my living-room swinging all over the place with wind and tide. And wind and tide doesn't alter my own course when I'm crossing my living-room. There are only three boats in the harbour carrying anchor lights. He'll have to use something to see where he's going.'

And he did. From the direction of the receding sound of engines a light stabbed out into the darkness. A five-inch searchlight, I would have guessed. It picked up a small yacht riding at anchor less than a hundred yards ahead of it, altered to starboard, picked up another, altered to port, then swung back on course again.

' "Odd" was the word you used,' Hunslett murmured. 'Quite a good word, too, in the circumstances. And what are we to think of the alleged Torbay police force?'

'You talked to the sergeant longer than I did. When I was aft with Thomas and Durran.'

'I'd like to think otherwise,' Hunslett said inconsequentially. 'It would make things easier, in a way. But I can't. He's a genuine old-fashioned cop and a good one, too. I've met too many. So have you.'

'A good cop and an honest one,' I agreed. 'This is not his line of country and he was fooled. It is our line of country and we were fooled. Until now, that is.'

'Speak for yourself.'

'Thomas made one careless remark. An off-beat remark. You didn't hear it – we were in the engine-room.' I shivered, maybe it was the cold night wind. 'It meant nothing – not until I saw that they didn't want their boat recognized again. He said: "Boats aren't really in my line." Probably thought he'd been asking too many questions and wanted to reassure me. Boats not in his line – a customs officer and boats not in his line. They only spend their lives aboard boats, examining boats, that's all. They spend their lives looking and poking in so many odd corners and quarters that they know more about boats than the designers themselves. Another thing, did you notice how sharply dressed they were? A credit to Carnaby Street.'

'Customs officers don't usually go around in oil-stained overalls.'

'They've been living in those clothes for twenty-four hours. This is the what – the thirteenth boat they've searched in that time. Would you still have knife-edged creases to your pants after that lot? Or would you say they'd only just taken them from the hangers and put them on?'

'What else did they say? What else did they do?' Hunslett spoke so quietly that I could hear the note of the engines of the customs' boat fall away sharply as their searchlight lit up the low-water stone pier, half a mile away. 'Take an undue interest in anything?'

'They took an undue interest in everything. Wait a minute, though, wait a minute. Thomas seemed particularly intrigued by the batteries, by the large amount of reserve electrical power we had.'

'Did he now? Did he indeed? And did you notice how lightly our two customs friends swung aboard their launch when leaving?'

'They'll have done it a thousand times.'

'Both of them had their hands free. They weren't carrying anything. They should have been carrying something.'

'The photo-copier. I'm getting old.'

'The photo-copier. Standard equipment my ruddy foot. So if our fair-haired pal wasn't busy photo-copying he was busy doing something else.'

We moved inside the wheelhouse. Hunslett selected the larger screw-driver from the tool-rack beside the echo-sounder and had the face-plate off our RTD/DF set inside sixty seconds. He looked at the interior for five seconds, looked at me for the same length of time, then started screwing the face-plate back into position. One thing was certain, we wouldn't be using that transmitter for a long time to come.

I turned away and stared out through the wheelhouse windows into the darkness. The wind was still rising, the black sea gleamed palely as the whitecaps came marching in from the south-west, the *Firecrest* snubbed sharply on her anchor chain and, with the wind and the tide at variance, she was beginning to corkscrew quite noticeably now. I felt desperately tired. But my eyes were still working. Hunslett offered me a cigarette. I didn't want one, but I took one. Who knew, it might even help me to think. And then I had caught his wrist and was staring down at his palm.

'Well, well,' I said. 'The cobbler should stick to his last.'

'He what?'

'Wrong proverb. Can't think of the right one. A good workman uses only his own tools. Our pal with the penchant for smashing valves and condensers should have remembered that. No wonder my neck was twitching when Durran was around. How did you cut yourself?'

'I didn't cut myself.'

'I know. But there's a smear of blood on your palm. He's been taking lessons from Peter Sellers, I shouldn't wonder. Standard southern English on the *Nantesville*, northern Irish on the *Firecrest*. I wonder how many other accents he has up his sleeve – behind his larynx, I should say. And I thought he was running to a little fat. He's running to a great deal of muscle. You noticed he never took his gloves off, even when he had that drink?'

'I'm the best noticer you ever saw. Beat me over the head with a club and I'll notice anything.' He sounded bitter. 'Why didn't they clobber us? You, anyway? The star witness?'

'Maybe we *have* moved out of our class. Two reasons. They couldn't do anything with the cops there, genuine cops as we've both agreed, not unless they attended to the cops too. Only a madman would deliberately kill a cop and whatever those boys may lack it isn't sanity.'

'But why cops in the first place?'

'Aura of respectability. Cops are above suspicion. When a uniformed policeman shoves his uniformed cap above your gunwale in the dark watches of the night, you don't whack him over the head with a marline-spike. You invite him aboard. All others you might whack, especially if we had the bad consciences we might have been supposed to have.'

'Maybe. It's arguable. And the second point?'

'They took a big chance, a desperate chance, almost, with Durran. He was thrown to the wolves to see what the reaction would be, whether either of us recognized him.'

'Why Durran?'

'I didn't tell you. I shone a torch in his face. The face didn't register, just a white blur with screwed-up eyes half-hidden behind an upflung hand. I was really looking lower down, picking the right spot to kick him. But they weren't to know that. They wanted to find out if we would recognize him. We didn't. If we had done we'd either have started throwing the crockery at him or yelped for the cops to arrest them – if we're against them then we're with the cops. But we didn't. Not a flicker of recognition. Nobody's as good as that. I defy any man in the world to meet up again in the same night with a man who has murdered two other people and nearly murdered himself without at least twitching an eyebrow. So the immediate heat is off, the urgent necessity to do us in has become less urgent. It's a safe bet that if we didn't recognize Durran, then we recognized nobody on the *Nantesville* and so we won't be burning up the lines to Interpol.'

'We're in the clear?'

'I wish to God we were. They're on to us.'

'But you said—'

'I don't know how I know,' I said irritably. 'I know. They went through the after end of the *Firecrest* like a Treble Chance winner hunting for the coupon he's afraid he's forgotten to post. Then half-way through the engine-room search – click! – – just like that they weren't interested any more. At least Thomas wasn't. He'd found out something. You saw him afterwards in the saloon, the fore cabins and the upper deck. He couldn't have cared less.'

'The batteries?'

'No. He was satisfied with my explanation. I could tell. I don't know why, I only know I'm sure.'

'So they'll be back.'

'They'll be back.'

'I get the guns out now?'

'There's no hurry. Our friends will be sure we can't communicate with anyone. The mainland boat calls here only twice a week. It came to-day and won't be back for four days. The lines to the mainland are down and if I thought for a moment they would stay down I should be back in kindergarten. Our transmitter is out. Assuming there are no carrier pigeons in Torbay, what's the only remaining means of communication with the mainland?'

'There's the *Shangri-la.*' The *Shangri-la*, the nearest craft to ours, was white, gleaming, a hundred and twenty feet long and wouldn't have left her owner a handful of change from a quarter of a million pounds when he'd bought her. 'She'll have a couple of thousand quids' worth of radio equipment aboard. Then there are two, maybe three yachts big enough to carry transmitters. The rest will carry only receivers, if that.'

'And how many transmitters in Torbay harbour will still be in operating condition to-morrow?'

'One.'

'One. Our friends will attend to the rest. They'll have to. We can't warn anyone. We can't give ourselves away.'

'The insurance companies can stand it.' He glanced at his watch. 'This would be a nice time to wake up Uncle Arthur.'

'I can't put it off any longer.' I wasn't looking forward to talking to Uncle Arthur.

Hunslett reached for a heavy coat, pulled it on, made for the door and stopped. 'I thought I'd take a walk on the upper deck. While you're talking. Just in case. A second thought – I'd better have that gun now. Thomas said they'd already checked three boats in the harbour. MacDonald didn't contradict him, so it was probably true. Maybe there *are* no serviceable transmitters left in Torbay now. Maybe our friends just dumped the cops ashore and are coming straight back for us.'

'Maybe. But those yachts are smaller than the *Firecrest*. Apart from us, there's only one with a separate wheelhouse. The others will carry transmitters in the saloon cabin. Lots of them sleep in their saloon cabins. The owners would have to be banged on the head first before the radios could be attended to. They couldn't do that with MacDonald around.'

'You'd bet your pension on that? Maybe MacDonald didn't always go aboard.'

'I'll never live to collect my pension. But maybe you'd better have that gun.'

The *Firecrest* was just over three years old. The Southampton boatyard and marine-radio firm that had combined to build her had done so under conditions of sworn secrecy to a design provided by Uncle Arthur. Uncle Arthur had not designed her himself although he had never said so to the few people who knew of the existence of the boat. He'd pinched the idea from a Japanese-designed Indonesian-owned fishing craft that had been picked up with engine failure off the Malaysian coast. Only one engine had failed though two were installed, but still she had been not under command, an odd circumstance that had led the alert Engineer Lieutenant on the frigate that had picked her up to look pretty closely at her: the net result of his investigation, apart from giving this splendid inspiration to Uncle Arthur, was that the crew still languished in a Singapore prisoner of war camp.

The *Firecrest*'s career had been chequered and inglorious. She had cruised around the Eastern Baltic for some time, without achieving anything, until the authorities in Memel and Leningrad, getting tired of the sight of her, had declared the *Firecrest persona non grata* and sent her back to England. Uncle Arthur had been furious, especially as he had to account to a parsimonious Under-Secretary for the considerable expense involved. The Waterguard had tried their hand with it at catching smugglers and returned it without thanks. No smugglers. Now for the first time ever it was going to justify its existence and in other circumstances Uncle Arthur would have been delighted. When he heard what I had to tell him he would have no difficulty in restraining his joy.

What made the *Firecrest* unique was that while she had two screws and two propeller shafts, she had only one engine. Two engine casings, but only one engine, even although that one engine was a special job fitted with an underwater bypass exhaust valve. A simple matter of disengaging the fuel pump coupling and unscrewing four bolts on top – the rest were dummies – enabled the entire head of the diesel starboard engine to be lifted clear away, together with the fuel lines and injectors. With the assistance of the seventy foot telescopic radio mast housed inside our aluminium foremast, the huge gleaming transmitter that took up eighty per cent of the space inside the starboard engine casing could have sent a signal to the moon, if need be: as Thomas had observed, we had power and to spare. As it happened I didn't want to send a signal to the moon, just to Uncle Arthur's combinex office and home in Knightsbridge.

The other twenty per cent of space was taken up with a motley collection of material that even the Assistant Commissioner in New Scotland Yard wouldn't have regarded without a thoughtful expression on his face. There were some packages of pre-fabricated explosives with amatol, primer and chemical detonator combined in one neat unit with a miniature timing device that ranged from five seconds to five minutes, complete with sucker clamps. There was a fine range of burglar's house-breaking tools, bunches of skeleton keys, several highly sophisticated listening devices, including one that could be shot from a Very-type pistol, several tubes of various harmless-looking tablets which were alleged, when dropped in some unsuspecting character's drink, to induce unconsciousness for varying periods, four pistols and a box of ammunition. Anyone who was going to use that lot in one operation was in for a busy time indeed. Two of the pistols were Lugers, two were 4.25 German Lilliputs, the smallest really effective automatic pistol on the market. The Lilliput had the great advantage that it could be concealed practically anywhere on your person, even upside down in a spring-loaded clip in your lower left sleeve – if, that was, you didn't get your suits cut in Carnaby Street.

Hunslett lifted one of the Lugers from its clamp, checked the loading indicator and left at once. It wasn't that he was imagining that he could already hear stealthy footsteps on the upper deck, he just didn't want to be around when Uncle Arthur came on the air. I didn't blame him. I didn't really want to be around then either.

I pulled out the two insulated rubber cables, fitted the powerfully spring-loaded saw-toothed metal clamps on to the battery terminals, hung on a pair of earphones, turned on the set, pulled another switch that actuated the call-up and waited. I didn't have to tune in, the transmitter was permanently pre-set, and pre-set on a VHF frequency that would have cost the licence of any ham operator who dared wander anywhere near it for transmission purposes.

The red receiver warning light came on. I reached down and adjusted the magic eye control until the green fans met in the middle.

'This is station SPFX,' a voice came. 'Station SPFX.'

'Good morning. This is Caroline. May I speak to the manager, please?'

'Will you wait, please?' This meant that Uncle Arthur was in bed. Uncle Arthur was never at his best on rising. Three minutes passed and the earphones came to life again.

'Good morning, Caroline. This is Annabelle.

'Good morning. Location 481, 281.' You wouldn't find those references in any Ordnance Survey Map, there weren't a dozen maps in existence with them. But Uncle Arthur had one. And so had I.

'There was a pause, then: 'I have you, Caroline. Proceed.'

'I located the missing vessel this afternoon. Four or five miles north-west of here. I went on board to-night.'

'You did what, Caroline?'

'Went on board. The old crew has gone home. There's a new crew aboard. A smaller crew.'

'You located Betty and Dorothy?' Despite the fact that we both had scramblers fitted to our radio phones, making intelligible eavesdropping impossible, Uncle Arthur always insisted that we spoke in a roundabout riddle fashion and used code names for his employees and himself. Girls' names for our surnames, initials to match. An irritating foible, but one that we had to observe. He was Annabelle, I was Caroline, Baker was Betty, Delmont, Dorothy and Hunslett, Harriet. It sounded like a series of Caribbean hurricane warnings.

'I found them.' I took a deep breath. 'They won't be coming home again, Annabelle.'

'They won't be coming home again,' he repeated mechanically. He was silent for so long that I began to think that he had gone off the air. Then he came again, his voice empty, remote. 'I warned you of this, Caroline.'

'Yes, Annabelle, you warned me of this.'

'And the vessel?'

'Gone.'

'Gone where?'

'I don't know. Just gone. North, I suppose.'

'North, you suppose.' Uncle Arthur never raised his voice, when he went on it was as calm and impersonal as ever, but the sudden disregard of his own rules about circumlocution betrayed the savage anger in his mind. 'North where? Iceland? A Norwegian fjord? To effect a trans-shipment of cargo anywhere in a million square miles between the mid-Atlantic and the Barents Sea? And you lost her. After all the time, the trouble, the planning, the expense, you've lost her!' He might have spared me that bit about the planning, it had been mine all the way. 'And Betty and Dorothy.' The last words showed he'd taken control of himself again.

'Yes, Annabelle, I've lost her.' I could feel the slow anger in myself. 'And there's worse than that, if you want to listen to it.'

'I'm listening.'

I told him the rest and at the end of it he said: 'I see. You've lost the vessel. You've lost Betty and Dorothy. And now our friends know about you, the one vital element of secrecy is gone for ever and every usefulness and effectiveness you might ever have had is completely negated.' A pause. 'I shall expect you in my office at nine p.m. to-night. Instruct Harriet to take the boat back to base.'

'Yes, sir.' The hell with his Annabelle. 'I had expected that. I've failed. I've let you down. I'm being pulled off.'

'Nine o'clock to-night, Caroline. I'll be waiting.'

'You'll have a long wait, Annabelle.'

'And what might you mean by that?' If Uncle Arthur had had a low silky menacing voice then he'd have spoken those words in a low silky menacing voice. But he hadn't, he'd only this flat level monotone and it carried infinitely more weight and authority than any carefully modulated theatrical voice that had ever graced a stage.

'There are no planes to this place, Annabelle. The mailboat doesn't call for another four days. The weather's breaking down and I wouldn't risk our boat to try and get to the mainland. I'm stuck here for the time being, I'm afraid.'

'Do you take me for a nincompoop, sir?' Now he was at it. 'Go ashore this morning. An air-sea rescue helicopter will pick you up at noon. Nine p.m. at my office. Don't keep me waiting.'

This, then, was it. But one last try. 'Couldn't you give me another twenty-four-hours, Annabelle?'

'Now you're being ridiculous. And wasting my time. Good-bye.'

'I beg of you, sir.'

'I'd thought better of you than that. Good-bye.'

'Good-bye. We may meet again sometime. It's not likely. Good-bye.'

I switched the radio off, lit a cigarette and waited. The call-up came through in half a minute. I waited another half-minute and switched on. I was very calm. The die was cast and I didn't give a damn.

'Caroline? Is that you, Caroline?' I could have sworn to a note of agitation in his voice. This was something for the record books.

'Yes.'

'What did you say? At the end there?'

'Good-bye. You said good-bye. I said good-bye.'

'Don't quibble with me, sir! You said—'

'If you want me aboard that helicopter,' I said, 'you'll have to send a guard with the pilot. An armed guard. I hope they're good. I've got a Luger, and you know I'm good. And if I have to kill anyone and go into court, then you'll have to stand there beside me because there's no single civil action or criminal charge that even you, with all your connections, can bring against me that would justify the sending of armed men to apprehend me, an innocent man. Further, I am no longer in your employment. The terms of my civil service contract state clearly that I can resign at any moment, provided that I am not actively engaged on an operation at that moment. You've pulled me off, you've recalled me to London. My resignation will be on your desk as soon as the mail can get through. Baker and Delmont weren't your friends. They were my friends. They were my friends ever since I joined the service. You have the temerity to sit there and lay all the blame for their deaths on my shoulders when you know damn' well that every operation must have your final approval, and now you have the final temerity to deny me a one last chance to square accounts. I'm sick of your damned soulless service. Good-bye.'

'Now wait a moment, Caroline.' There was a cautious, almost placatory note to his voice. 'No need to go off half-cocked.' I was sure that no one had ever talked to Rear-Admiral Sir Arthur Arnford-Jason like that before but he didn't seem particularly upset about it. He had the cunning of a fox, that infinitely agile and shrewd mind would be examining and discarding possibilities with the speed of a computer, he'd be wondering whether I was playing a game and if so how far he could play it with me without making it impossible for me to retreat from the edge of the precipice. Finally he said quietly: 'You wouldn't want to hang around there just to shed tears. You're on to something.'

'Yes, sir, I'm on to something.' I wondered what in the name of God I was on to.

'I'll give you twenty-four hours, Caroline.'

'Forty-eight.'

'Forty-eight. And then you return to London. I have your word?'

'I promise.'

'And Caroline?'

'Sir?'

'I didn't care for your way of talking there. I trust we never have a repetition of it.'

'No, sir. I'm sorry, sir.'

'Forty-eight hours. Report to me at noon and midnight.' A click. Uncle Arthur was gone.

The false dawn was in the sky when I went on deck. Cold heavy slanting driving rain was churning up the foam-flecked sea. The *Firecrest,* pulling heavily on her anchor chain, was swinging slowly through an arc of forty degrees, cockscrewing quite heavily now on the outer arc of the swing, pitching in the centre of them. She was snubbing very heavily on the anchor and I wondered uneasily how long the lengths of heaving line securing the dinghy, outboard and scuba gear to the chain could stand up to this sort of treatment.

Hunslett was abaft the saloon, huddling in what little shelter it afforded. He looked up at my approach and said: 'What do you make of that?' He pointed to the palely gleaming shape of the *Shangri-la*, one moment on our quarter, the next dead astern as we swung on our anchor. Lights were burning brightly in the fore part of her superstructure, where the wheelhouse would be.

'Someone with insomnia,' I said. 'Or checking to see if the anchor is dragging. What do you think it is – our recent guests laying about the *Shangri-la* radio installation with crow-bars? Maybe they leave lights on all night.'

'Came on just ten minutes ago. And look, now – they're out. Funny. How did you get on with Uncle?'

'Badly. Fired me, then changed his mind. We have forty-eight hours.'

'Forty-eight hours? What are you going to do in forty-eight hours?'

'God knows. Have some sleep first. You too. Too much light in the sky for callers now.'

Passing through the saloon, Hunslett said, apropos of nothing: 'I've been wondering. What did you make of PC MacDonald? The young one.'

'What do you mean?'

'Well, glum, downcast. Heavy weight on his shoulders.'

'Maybe he's like me. Maybe he doesn't like getting up in the middle of the night. Maybe he has girl trouble and if he has I can tell you that PC MacDonald's love-life is the least of my concerns. Good night.'

I should have listened to Hunslett more. For Hunslett's sake.

Chapter Three

Tuesday: 10 a.m. – 10 p.m.

I need my sleep, just like anyone else. Ten hours, perhaps only eight, and I would have been my own man again. Maybe not exuding brightness, optimism and cheerfulness, the circumstances weren't right for that, but at least a going concern, alert, perceptive, my mind operating on what Uncle Arthur would be by now regarding as its customary abysmal level but still the best it could achieve. But I wasn't given that ten hours. Nor even the eight. Exactly three hours after dropping off I was wide awake again. Well, anyway, awake. I would have had to be stone deaf, drugged or dead to go on sleeping through the bawling and thumping that was currently assailing my left ear from what appeared to be a distance of not more than twelve inches.

'Ahoy, there, *Firecrest*! Ahoy there!' Thump, thump, thump on the boat's side. 'Can I come aboard? Ahoy, there! Ahoy, ahoy, ahoy!'

I cursed this nautical idiot from the depths of my sleep-ridden being, swung a pair of unsteady legs to the deck and levered myself out of the bunk. I almost fell down, I seemed to have only one leg left, and my neck ached fiercely. A glance at the mirror gave quick external confirmation of my internal decrepitude. A haggard unshaven face, unnaturally pale, and bleary bloodshot eyes with dark circles under them. I looked away hurriedly, there were lots of things I could put up with first thing in the morning, but not sights like that.

I opened the door across the passage. Hunslett was sound asleep and snoring. I returned to my own cabin and got busy with the dressing-gown and Paisley scarf again. The iron-lunged thumping character outside was still at it, if I didn't hurry he would be roaring out 'avast there' any moment. I combed my hair into some sort of order and made my way to the upper deck.

It was a cold, wet and windy world. A grey, dreary, unpleasant world, why the hell couldn't they have let me sleep on. The rain was coming down in slanting sheets, bouncing inches high on the decks, doubling the milkiness of the spume-flecked sea. The lonely wind mourned through the rigging and the lower registers of sound and the steep-sided wind-truncated waves, maybe three feet from tip to trough, were high enough to make passage difficult if not dangerous for the average yacht tender.

They didn't make things in the slightest difficult or dangerous for the yacht tender that now lay alongside us. It maybe wasn't as big – it looked it at first sight – as the *Firecrest,* but it was big enough to have a glassed-in cabin for'ard, a wheelhouse that bristled and gleamed with controls and instrumentation that would have been no disgrace to a VC-10 and, abaft that, a sunken cockpit that could have sunbathed a football team without overcrowding. There were three crewmen dressed in black oilskins and fancy French navy hats with black ribbons down the back, two of them each with a boat-hook round one of the *Firecrest*'s guardrail stanchions. Half a dozen big inflated spherical rubber fenders kept the *Firecrest* from rubbing its plebeian paintwork against the whitely-varnished spotlessness of the tender alongside and it didn't require the name on the bows or the crew's hats to let me know that this was the tender that normally took up most of the after-deck space on the *Shangri-la*.

Amidships a stocky figure, clad in a white vaguely naval brass-buttoned uniform and holding above his head a gold umbrella that would have had Joseph green with envy, stopped banging his gloved fist against the *Firecrest*'s planking and glared up at me.

'Ha!' I've never actually heard anyone snort out a word but this came pretty close to it. 'There you are at last. Took your time about it, didn't you? I'm soaked, man, soaked!' A few spots of rain did show up quite clearly on the white seersucker. 'May I come aboard?' He didn't wait for any permission, just leaped aboard with surprising nimbleness for a man of his build and years and nipped into the *Firecrest*'s wheelhouse ahead of me, which was pretty selfish of him as he still had his umbrella and all I had was my dressing-gown. I followed and closed the door behind me.

He was a short, powerfully built character, fifty-five I would have guessed, with a heavily-tanned jowled face, close-cropped iron-grey hair with tufted eyebrows to match, long straight nose and a mouth that looked as if it had been closed with a zip-fastener. A good-looking cove, if you liked that type of looks. The dark darting eyes looked me up and down and if he was impressed by what he saw he made a heroic effort to keep his admiration in check.

'Sorry for the delay,' I apologized. 'Short of sleep. We had the customs aboard in the middle of the night and I couldn't get off after that.' Always tell everyone the truth if there's an even chance of that truth coming out anyway, which in this case there was: gives one a reputation for forthright honesty.

'The customs?' He looked as if he intended to say 'pshaw' or 'fiddlesticks' or something of that order, then changed his mind and looked up sharply. 'An intolerable bunch of busybodies. And in the middle of the night. Shouldn't have let them aboard. Sent them packing. Intolerable. What the deuce did they want?' He gave the distinct impression of having himself had some trouble with the customs in the past.

'They were looking for stolen chemicals. Stolen from some place in Ayrshire. Wrong boat.'

'Idiots!' He thrust out a stubby hand, he'd passed his final judgment on the unfortunate customs and the subject was now closed. 'Skouras. Sir Anthony Skouras.'

'Petersen.' His grip made me wince, less from the sheer power of it than from the gouging effects of the large number of thickly encrusted rings that adorned his fingers. I wouldn't have been surprised to see some on his thumbs but he'd missed out on that. I looked at him with new interest. 'Sir Anthony Skouras. I've heard of you of course.'

'Nothing good. Columnists don't like me because they know I despise them. A Cypriot who made his shipping millions through sheer ruthlessness, they say. True. Asked by the Greek Government to leave Athens. True. Became a naturalized British citizen and bought a knighthood. Absolutely true. Charitable works and public services. Money can buy anything. A baronetcy next but the market's not right at the moment. Price is bound to fall. Can I use your radio transmitter? I see you have one.'

'What's that?' The abrupt switch had me off-balance, no great achievement the way I was feeling.

'Your radio transmitter, man! Don't you listen to the news? All those major defence projects cancelled by the Pentagon. Price of steel tumbling. Must get through to my New York broker at once!'

'Sorry. Certainly you may – but, but your own radio-telephone? Surely—'

'It's out of action.' His mouth became more tight-lipped than ever and the inevitable happened: it disappeared. 'It's urgent, Mr Petersen.'

'Immediately. You know how to operate this model?'

He smiled thinly, which was probably the only way he was capable of smiling. Compared to the cinema-organ job he'd have aboard the *Shangri-la*, asking him if he could operate this was like asking the captain of a transatlantic jet if he could fly a Tiger Moth. 'I think I can manage, Mr Petersen.'

'Call me when you're finished. I'll be in the saloon.' He'd be calling me before he'd finished, he'd be calling me before he'd even started. But I couldn't tell him. Word gets around. I went down to the saloon, contemplated a shave and decided against it. It wouldn't take that long.

It didn't. He appeared at the saloon door inside a minute, his face grim. 'Your radio is out of order, Mr Petersen.'

'They're tricky to operate, some of those older jobs,' I said tactfully. 'Maybe if I—'

'I say it's out of order. I mean it's out of order.'

'Damned odd. It was working—'

'Would you care to try it, please?'

I tried it. Nothing. I twiddled everything I could lay hands on. Nothing.

'A power failure, perhaps,' I suggested. 'I'll check—'

'Would you be so good as to remove the face-plate, please?'

I stared at him in perplexity, switching the expression, after a suitable interval, to shrewd thoughtfulness. 'What do you know, Sir Anthony, that I don't?'

'You'll find out.'

So I found out and went through all the proper motions of consternation, incredulity and tight-lipped indignation. Finally I said: 'You knew. How did you know?'

'Obvious, isn't it?'

'Your transmitter,' I said slowly. 'It's more than just out of order. You had the same midnight caller.'

'And the *Orion*.' The mouth vanished again. 'The big blue ketch lying close in. Only other craft in the harbour apart from us with a radio transmitter. Smashed. Just come from there.'

'Smashed? Theirs as well? But who in God's name – it must be the work of a madman.'

'Is it? Is it the work of a madman? I know something of those matters. My first wife—' He broke off abrupty and gave an odd shake of the head, then went on slowly: 'The mentally disturbed are irrational, haphazard, purposeless, aimless in their behaviour patterns. This seems an entirely irrational act, but an act with a method and a purpose to it. Not haphazard. It's planned. There's a reason. At first I thought the reason was to cut off my connection with the mainland. But it can't be that. By rendering me temporarily incommunicado nobody stands to gain, I don't stand to lose.'

'But you said the New York Stock—'

'A bagatelle,' he said contemptuously. 'Nobody likes to lose money.' Not more than a few millions anyway. 'No Mr Petersen, I am not the target. We have here an A and a B. A regards it as vital that he remains in constant communication with the mainland. B regards it as vital that A doesn't. So B takes steps. There's something damned funny going on in Torbay. And something big. I have a nose for such things.'

He was no fool but then not many morons have ended up as multi-millionaires. I couldn't have put it better myself. I said: 'Reported this to the police yet?'

'Going there now. After I've made a phone call or two.' The eyes suddenly became bleak and cold. 'Unless our friend has smashed up the two public call boxes in the main street.'

'He's done better than that. He's brought down the lines to the mainland. Somewhere down the Sound. No one knows where.'

He stared at me, wheeled to leave, then turned, his face empty of expression. 'How did you know that? The tone matched the face.

'Police told me. They were aboard with the customs last night.'

'The police? That's damned odd. What were the police doing here?' He paused and looked at me with his cold measuring eyes. 'A personal question, Mr Petersen. No impertinence intended. A question of elimination. What are *you* doing here? No offence.'

'No offence. My friend and I are marine biologists. A working trip. Not our boat – the Ministry of Agriculture and Fisheries.' I smiled. 'We have impeccable references, Sir Anthony.'

'Marine biology, eh? Hobby of mine, you might say. Layman, of course. Must have a talk sometime.' He was speaking absent-mindedly, his thoughts elsewhere. 'Could you describe the policeman, Mr Petersen?'

I did and he nodded. 'That's him all right. Odd, very odd. Must have a word with Archie about this.'

'Archie?'

'Sergeant MacDonald. This is my fifth consecutive season's cruising based on Torbay. The South of France and the Aegean can't hold a candle to these waters. Know quite a few of the locals pretty well by this time. He was alone?'

'No. A young constable. His son, he said. Melancholy sort of lad.'

'Peter MacDonald. He had reason for his melancholy, Mr Petersen. His two young brothers, sixteen years old, twins, died a few months back. At an Inverness school, lost in a late snow-storm in the Cairngorms. The father is tougher, doesn't show it so much. A great tragedy. I knew them both. Fine boys.'

I made some appropriate comment but he wasn't listening.

'I must be on my way, Mr Petersen. Put this damned strange affair in MacDonald's hand. Don't see that he can do much. Then off for a short cruise.'

I looked through the wheelhouse windows at the dark skies, the white-capped seas, the driving rain. 'You picked a day for it.'

'The rougher the better. No bravado. I like a mill-pond as well as any man. Just had new stabilizers fitted in the Clyde – we got back up here only two days ago – and it seems like a good day to try them out.' He smiled suddenly and put out his hand. 'Sorry to have barged in. Taken up far too much of your time. Seemed rude, I suppose. Some say I am. You and your colleague care to come aboard for a drink to-night? We eat early at sea. Eight o'clock, say? I'll send the tender.' That meant we didn't rate an invitation to dinner, which would have made a change from Hunslett and his damned baked beans, but even an invitation like this would have given rise to envious tooth-gnashing in some of the stateliest homes in the land: it was no secret that the bluest blood in England, from Royalty downwards, regarded a holiday invitation to the island Skouras owned off the Albanian coast as the conferment of the social cachet of the year or any year. Skouras didn't wait for an answer and didn't seem to expect one. I didn't blame him. It would have been many years since Skouras had discovered that it was an immutable law of human nature, human nature being what it is, that no one ever turned down one of his invitations,

'You'll be coming to tell me about your smashed transmitter and asking me what the devil I intend to do about it,' Sergeant MacDonald said tiredly. 'Well, Mr Petersen, I know all about it already. Sir Anthony Skouras was here half an hour ago; Sir Anthony had a lot to say. And Mr Campbell, the owner of the *Orion,* has just left. He'd a lot to say, too.'

'Not me, Sergeant. I'm a man of few words.' I gave him what I hoped looked like a self-deprecatory smile. 'Except, of course, when the police and customs drag me out of bed in the middle of the night. I take it our friends have left?'

'Just as soon as they'd put us ashore. Customs are just a damn' nuisance.' Like myself, he looked as if he could do with some hours' sleep. 'Frankly, Mr Petersen, I don't know what to do about the broken radio-transmitters. Why on earth – who on earth would want to do a daft vicious thing like that?'

'That's what I came to ask you.'

'I can go aboard your boat,' MacDonald said slowly. 'I can take out my note-book, look around and see if I can't find any clues. I wouldn't know what to look for. Maybe if I knew something about fingerprinting and analysis and microscopy I might just find out something. But I don't. I'm an island policeman, not a one-man Flying Squad. This is CID work and we'd have to call in Glasgow. I doubt if they'd send a couple of detectives to investigate a few smashed radio valves.'

'Old man Skouras draws a lot of water.'

'Sir?'

'He's powerful. He has influence. If Skouras wanted action I'm damned sure he could get it. If the need arose and the mood struck him I'm sure he could be a very unpleasant character indeed.'

'There's not a better man or a kinder man ever sailed into Torbay,' MacDonald said warmly. That hard brown face could conceal practically anything that MacDonald wanted it to conceal but this time he was hiding nothing. 'Maybe his ways aren't my ways. Maybe he's a hard, aye, a ruthless businessman. Maybe, as the papers hint, his private life wouldn't bear investigation. That's none of my business. But if you were to look for a man in Torbay to say a word against him, you'll have a busy time on your hands, Mr Petersen.'

'You've taken me up wrongly, Sergeant,' I said mildly. 'I don't even know the man.'

'No. But we do. See that?' He pointed through the side window of the police station to a large Swedish-style timber building beyond the pier. 'Our new village hall. Town hall, they call it. Sir Anthony gave us that. Those six wee chalets up the hill there? For old folks. Sir Anthony again – every penny from his own pocket. Who takes all the schoolchildren to the Oban Games – Sir Anthony on the *Shangri-la*. Contributes to every charity going and now he has plans to build a boatyard to give employment to the young men of Torbay – there's not much else going since the fishing-boats left.'

'Well, good for old Skouras,' I said. 'He seems to have adopted the place. Lucky Torbay. I wish he'd buy me a new radio-transmitter.'

'I'll keep my eyes and ears open, Mr Petersen. I can't do more. If anything turns up I'll let you know at once.'

I told him thanks, and left. I hadn't particularly wanted to go there, but it would have looked damned odd if I hadn't turned up to add my pennyworth to the chorus of bitter complaint.

I was very glad that I had turned up.

The midday reception from London was poor. This was due less to the fact that reception is always better after dark than to the fact that I couldn't use our telescopic radio mast: but it was fair enough and Uncle's voice was brisk and businesslike and clear.

'Well, Caroline, we've found our missing friends,' he said.

'How many?' I asked cautiously. Uncle Arthur's ambiguous references weren't always as clear as Uncle Arthur imagined them to be.

'All twenty-five.' That made it the former crew of the *Nantesville*. 'Two of them are pretty badly hurt but they'll be all right.' That accounted for the blood I had found in the captain's and one of the engineers' cabins.

'Where?' I asked.

He gave me a map reference. Just north of Wexford. The *Nantesville* had sailed from Bristol, she couldn't have been more than a few hours on her way before she'd run into trouble.

'Exactly the same procedure as on the previous occasions,' Uncle Arthur was saying. 'Held in a lonely farmhouse for a couple of nights. Plenty to eat and drink and blankets to keep the cold out. Then they woke up one morning and found their guards had gone.'

'But a different procedure in stopping the – *our* friend?' I'd almost said *Nantesville* and Uncle Arthur wouldn't have liked that at all.

'As always. We must concede them a certain ingenuity, Caroline. After having smuggled men aboard in port, then using the sinking fishing-boat routine, the police launch routine and the yacht with the appendicitis case aboard, I thought they would be starting to repeat themselves. But this time they came up with a new one – possibly because it's the first time they've hi-jacked a ship during the hours of darkness. Carley rafts, this time, with about ten survivors aboard, dead ahead of the vessel. Oil all over the sea. A weak distress flare that couldn't have been seen a mile away and probably was designed that way. You know the rest.'

'Yes, Annabelle.' I knew the rest. After that the routine was always the same. The rescued survivors, displaying a marked lack of gratitude, would whip out pistols, round up the crew, tie black muslin bags over their heads so that they couldn't identify the vessel that would appear within the hour to take them off, march them on board the unknown vessel, land them on some lonely beach during the dark then march them again, often a very long way indeed, till they arrived at their prison. A deserted farmhouse. Always a deserted farmhouse. And always in Ireland, three times in the north and now twice in the south. Meantime the prize crew sailed the hi-jacked vessel to God alone knew where and the first the world knew of the disappearance of the pirated vessel was when the original crew, released after two or three days' painless captivity, would turn up at some remote dwelling and start hollering for the nearest telephone.

'Betty and Dorothy,' I said. 'Were they still in safe concealment when the crew were taken off?'

'I imagine so. I don't know. Details are still coming in and I understand the doctors won't let anyone see the captain yet.' Only the captain had known of the presence aboard of Baker and Delmont. 'Forty-one hours now, Caroline. What have you done?'

For a moment I wondered irritably what the devil he was talking about. Then I remembered. He'd given me forty-eight hours. Seven were gone.

'I've had three hours' sleep.' He'd consider that an utter waste of time, his employees weren't considered to need sleep. 'I've talked to the constabulary ashore. And I've talked to a wealthy yachtsman, next boat to us here. We're paying him a social call to-night.'

There was a pause. 'You're doing *what* to-night, Caroline?'

'Visiting. We've been invited. Harriet and I. For drinks.'

This time the pause was markedly longer. Then he said: 'You have forty-one hours, Caroline.'

'Yes, Annabelle.'

'We assume you haven't taken leave of your senses.'

'I don't know how unanimous informed opinion might be about that. I don't think I have.'

'And you haven't given up? No, not that. You're too damn' stiff-necked and – and—'

'Stupid?'

'Who's the yachtsman?'

I told him. It took me some time, partly because I had to spell out names with the aid of his damned code-book, partly because I gave him a very full account of everything Skouras had said to me and everything Sergeant MacDonald had said about Skouras. When his voice came again it was cagey and wary. As Uncle Arthur couldn't see me I permitted myself a cynical grin. Even Cabinet Ministers found it difficult to make the grade as far as Skouras's dinner-table, but the Permanent Under-Secretaries, the men with whom the real power of government lies, practically had their own initialled napkin rings. Under-Secretaries were the bane of Uncle Arthur's life.

'You'll have to watch your step very carefully here, Caroline.'

'Betty and Dorothy aren't coming home any more, Annabelle. Someone has to pay. I want someone to pay. You want someone to pay. We all do.'

'But it's inconceivable that a man in his position, a man of his wealth—'

'I'm sorry, Annabelle. I don't understand.'

'A man like that. Dammit all, I know him well, Caroline. We dine together. First-name terms. Know his present wife even better. Ex-actress. A philanthropist like that. A man who's spent five consecutive seasons there. Would a man like that, a millionaire like that, spend all that time, all that money, just to build up a front—'

'Skouras?' I used the code name. Interrogatory, incredulous, as if it had just dawned upon me what Uncle Arthur was talking about. 'I never said I suspected him, Annabelle. I have no reason to suspect him.'

'Ah!' It's difficult to convey a sense of heartfelt gladness, profound satisfaction and brow-mopping relief in a single syllable, but Uncle Arthur managed it without any trouble. 'Then why go?' A casual eavesdropper might have thought he detected a note of pained jealousy in Uncle Arthur's voice, and the casual eavesdropper would have been right. Uncle Arthur had only one weakness in his make-up – he was a social snob of monumental proportions.

'I want aboard. I want to see this smashed transmitter of his.'

'Why?'

'A hunch, let me call it, Annabelle. No more.'

Uncle Arthur was going in for the long silences in a big way to-day. Then he said: 'A hunch? A *hunch*? You told me this morning you were on to something.'

'There's something else. I want you to contact the Post Office Savings Bank, Head Office, in Scotland. After that, the Records files of some Scottish newspapers. I suggest *The Glasgow Herald,* the *Scottish Daily Express* and, most particularly, the West Highland weekly, the *Oban Times*.'

'Ah!' No relief this time, just satisfaction. 'This is more like it, Caroline. What do you want and why?'

So I told him what I wanted and why, lots more of the fancy code work, and when I'd finished he said: 'I'll have my staff on to this straight away. I'll have all the information you want by midnight.'

'Then I don't want it, Annabelle. Midnight's too late for me. Midnight's no use to me.'

'Don't ask the impossible, Caroline.' He muttered something to himself, something I couldn't catch, then: 'I'll pull every string, Caroline. Nine o'clock.

'Four o'clock, Annabelle.'

'Four o'clock this afternoon?' When it came to incredulity he had me whacked to the wide. 'Four hours' time? You *have* taken leave of your senses.'

' You can have ten men on it in ten minutes. Twenty in twenty minutes. Where's the door that isn't open to you? Especially the door of the Assistant Commissioner. Professionals don't kill for the hell of it. They kill because they must. They kill to gain time. Every additional hour is vital to them. And if it's vital to them, how much more so is it to us? Or do you think we're dealing with amateurs, Annabelle?'

'Call me at four,' he said heavily. 'I'll see what I have for you. What's your next move, Caroline?'

'Bed,' I said. 'I'm going to get some sleep.'

'Of course. Time, as you said, is of the essence. You mustn't waste it, must you, Caroline?' He signed off. He sounded bitter. No doubt he was bitter. But then, insomnia apart, Uncle Arthur could rely on a full quota of sleep during the coming night. Which was more than I could. No certain foreknowledge, no second sight, just a hunch, but not a small one, the kind of hunch you couldn't have hidden behind the Empire State Building. Just like the one I had about the *Shangri-la.*

I only just managed to catch the last fading notes of the alarm as it went off at ten minutes to four. I felt worse than I had done when we'd lain down after a miserable lunch of corned beef and reconstituted powdered potatoes – if old Skouras had had a spark of human decency, he'd have made that invitation for dinner. I wasn't only growing old, I felt old. I'd been working too long for Uncle Arthur. The pay was good but the hours and working conditions – I'd have wagered that Uncle Arthur hadn't even set eyes on a tin of corned beef since World War II – were shocking. And all this constant worrying, chiefly about life expectancy, helped wear a man down.

Hunslett came out of his cabin as I came out of mine. He looked just as old as I did. If they had to rely on a couple of ageing crocks like us, I thought morosely, the rising generation must be a pretty sorry lot.

Passing through the saloon, I wondered bitterly about the identity of all those characters who wrote so glibly about the Western Isles in general and the Torbay area in particular as being a yachtsman's paradise without equal in Europe. Obviously, they'd never been there. Fleet Street was their home and home was a place they never left, not if they could help it. An ignorant bunch of travel and advertising copy writers who regarded King's Cross as the northern limits of civilization. Well, maybe not all that ignorant, at least they were smart enough to stay south of King's Cross.

Four o'clock on an autumn afternoon, but already it was more night than day. The sun wasn't down yet, not by a very long way, but it might as well have been for all the chance it had of penetrating the rolling masses of heavy dark cloud hurrying away to the eastwards to the inky blackness of the horizon beyond Torbay. The slanting sheeting rain that foamed whitely across the bay further reduced what little visibility there was to a limit of not more than four hundred yards. The village itself, half a mile distant and nestling in the dark shadow of the steeply-rising pine-covered hills behind, might never have existed. Off to the north-west I could see the navigation lights of a craft rounding the headland, Skouras returning from his stabilizer test run. Down in the *Shangri-la*'s gleaming galley a master chef would be preparing the sumptuous evening meal, the one to which we hadn't been invited. I tried to put the thought of that meal out of my mind, but I couldn't, so I just put it as far away as possible and followed Hunslett into the engine-room.

Hunslett took the spare earphones and squatted beside me on the deck, note-book on his knee. Hunslett was as competent in shorthand as he was in everything else. I hoped that Uncle Arthur would have something to tell us, that Hunslett's presence there would be necessary. It was.

'Congratulations, Caroline,' Uncle Arthur said without preamble. 'You really are on to something.' As far as it is possible for a dead flat monotone voice to assume an overtone of warmth, then Uncle Arthur's did just that. He sounded positively friendly. More likely it was some freak of transmission or reception but at least he hadn't started off by bawling me out.

'We've traced those Post Office Savings books,' he went on. He rattled off book numbers and details of times and amounts of deposits, things of no interest to me, then said: 'Last deposits were on December 27th. Ten pounds in each case. Present balance is £78 14s. 6d. Exactly the same in both. And those accounts have not been closed.'

He paused for a moment to let me congratulate him, which I did, then continued.

'That's nothing, Caroline. Listen. Your queries about any mysterious accidents, deaths, disappearances off the west coasts of Inverness-shire or Argyll, or anything happening to people from that area. We've struck oil, Caroline, we've really struck oil. My God, why did we never think of this before. Have your pencil handy?'

'Harriet has.'

'Here we go. This seems to have been the most disastrous sailing season for years in the west of Scotland. But first, one from last year. The *Pinto*, a well-found sea-worthy forty-five foot motor cruiser left Kyle of Lochalsh for Oban at eight a.m. September 4th. She should have arrived that afternoon. She never did. No trace of her has ever been found.'

'What was the weather at the time, Annabelle?'

'I thought you'd ask me that, Caroline.' Uncle Arthur's combination of modesty and quiet satisfaction could be very trying at times. 'I checked with the Met. office. Force one, variable. Flat calm, cloudless sky. Then we come to this year. April 6th and April 26th. The *Evening Star* and the *Jeannie Rose*. Two East Coast fishing boats – one from Buckie, the other from Fraserburgh.'

'But both based on the west coast?'

'I wish you wouldn't try to steal my thunder.' Uncle Arthur complained. 'Both were based on Oban. Both were lobster boats. The *Evening Star*, the first one to go, was found stranded on the rocks of Islay. The *Jeannie Rose* vanished without trace. No member of either crew was ever found. Then again on the 17th of May. This time a well-known racing yacht, the *Cap Gris Nez*, an English built and owned craft, despite her name, highly experienced skipper, navigator and crew, all of them long-time and often successful competitors in RORC races. That class. Left Londonderry for the north of Scotland in fine weather. Disappeared. She was found almost a month later – or what was left of her – washed up on the Isle of Skye.'

'And the crew?'

'Need you ask? Never found. Then the last case, a few weeks ago – August 8th. Husband, wife, two teenage children, son and daughter. Converted lifeboat, the *Kingfisher*. By all accounts a pretty competent sailor, been at it for years. But he'd never done any night navigation, so he set out one calm evening to do a night cruise. Vanished. Boat and crew.'

'Where did he set out from?'

'Torbay.'

That one word made his afternoon. It made mine, too. I said: 'And do you still think the *Nantesville* is hell and gone to Iceland or some remote fjord in northern Norway?'

'I never thought anything of the kind.' Uncle's human relationship barometer had suddenly swung back from friendly to normal, normal lying somewhere between cool and glacial. 'The significance of the dates will not have escaped you?'

'No, Annabelle, the significance had not escaped me.' The Buckie fishing-boat, the *Evening Star*, had been found washed up on Islay three days after the SS *Holmwood* had vanished off the south coast of Ireland. The *Jeannie Rose* had vanished exactly three days after the MV *Antara* had as mysteriously disappeared in the St George's Channel. The *Cap Gris Nez,* the RORC racer that had finally landed up on the rocks of the island of Skye had vanished the same day as the MV *Headley Pioneer* had disappeared somewhere, it was thought, off Northern Ireland. And the converted lifeboat, *Kingfisher*, had disappeared, never to be seen again, just two days after the SS *Hurricane Spray* had left the Clyde, also never to be seen again. Coincidence was coincidence and I classed those who denied its existence with intellectual giants like the twentieth-century South African president who stoutly maintained that the world was flat and that an incautious step would take you over the edge with results as permanent as they would be disastrous: but this was plain ridiculous. The odds against such a perfect matching of dates could be calculated only in astronomical terms: while the complete disappearance of the crews of four small boats that had come to grief in so very limited an area was the final nail in the coffin of coincidence. I said as much to Uncle.

'Let us not waste time by dwelling upon the obvious, Caroline,' Uncle said coldly, which was pretty ungracious of him as the idea had never even entered his head until I had put it there four hours previously. 'The point is – what is to be done? Islay to Skye is a pretty big area. Where does this get us?'

'How much weight can you bring to bear to secure the co-operation of the television and radio networks?'

There was a pause, then: 'What do you have in mind, Caroline?' Uncle at his most forbidding.

'An insertion of an item in their news bulletins.'

'Well.' An even longer pause. 'It was done daily during the war, of course. I believe it's been done once or twice since. Can't compel them, of course – they're a stuffy lot, both the BBC and the ITA.' His tone left little doubt as to his opinion of those diehard reactionaries who brooked no interference, an odd reaction from one who was himself a past-master of brookmanship of this nature. 'If they can be persuaded that it's completely apolitical and in the national interest there's a chance. What do you want?'

'An item that a distress signal has been received from a sinking yacht somewhere south of Skye. Exact position unknown. Signals ceased, the worst feared, an air-sea search to be mounted at first light to-morrow. That's all.'

'I may manage it. Your reason, Caroline?'

'I want to look around. I want an excuse to move around without raising eyebrows.'

'You're going to volunteer the *Firecrest* for this search and then poke around where you shouldn't?'

'We have our faults, Annabelle, Harriet and I, but we're not crazy. I wouldn't take this tub across the Serpentine without a favourable weather forecast. It's blowing a Force 7 outside. And a boat search would take a lifetime too long in those parts. What I had in mind was this. At the very eastern tip of Torbay Island, about five miles from the village, there's a small deserted sandy cove, semicircular and well protected by steep bluffs and pine trees. Will you please arrange to have a long-range helicopter there exactly at dawn.'

'And now it's your turn to think I am crazy,' Uncle Arthur said coldly. That remark about the sea-keeping qualities of his own brain-child, the *Firecrest*, would have rankled badly. 'I'm supposed to snap my fingers and hey presto! a helicopter will be there at dawn.'

'That's fourteen hours from now, Annabelle. At five o'clock this morning you were prepared to snap your fingers and have a helicopter here by noon. Seven hours. Exactly half the time. But that was for something important, like getting me down to London to give me the bawling out of a lifetime before firing me.'

'Call me at midnight, Caroline. I hope to God you know what you are doing.'

I said: 'Yes, sir,' and hung up. I didn't mean, Yes, sir, I knew what I was doing, I meant, Yes, sir, I hoped to God I knew what I was doing.

If the carpet in the *Shangri-la*'s saloon had cost a penny under five thousand pounds, then old Skouras must have picked it up second-hand somewhere. Twenty by thirty, bronze and russet and gold, but mainly gold, it flowed across the deck like a field of ripe corn, an illusion heightened both by its depth and the impediment if offered to progress. You had to wade through the damn' thing. I'd never seen an item of furnishing like it in my life except for the curtains that covered two-thirds of the bulkhead space. The curtains made the carpet look rather shoddy. Persian or Afghanistan, with a heavy gleaming weave that gave a shimmering shot-silk effect with every little movement of the *Shangri-la*, they stretched all the way from deckhead to deck. What little of the bulkheads that could be seen were sheathed in a satiny tropical hardwood, the same wood as was used for the magnificent bar that took up most of the after bulkhead of the saloon. The opulently upholstered settees and armchairs and bar-stools, dark green leather with gold piping, would have cost another fortune, even the trade-in value of the beaten copper tables scattered carelessly about the carpet would have fed a family of five for a year. At the Savoy Grill.

On the port bulkhead hung two Cézannes, on the starboard two Renoirs.

The pictures were a mistake. In that room they didn't have a chance. They'd have felt more at home in the galley.

So would I. So, I was pretty sure, would Hunslett. It wasn't merely that our sports coats and Paisley scarves clashed violently with the décor in general and the black ties and dinner jackets of our host and his other guests in particular. It wasn't even that the general run of conversation might have been specifically designed to reduce Hunslett and myself to our proper status of artisans and pretty inferior artisans at that. All this talk about debentures and mergers and cross-options and takeovers and millions and millions of dollars has a pretty demoralizing effect on the lower classes, but you didn't need to have the IQ of a genius to realize that this line of talk wasn't being aimed specifically at us; to the lads with the black ties, debentures and takeovers were the stuff and staff of life and so a principal staple of conversation. Besides, this wish to be somewhere else obviously didn't apply only to us: at least two others, a bald-headed, goatee-bearded merchant banker by the name of Henri Biscarte and a big bluff Scots lawyer by the name of MacCallum were just as uncomfortable as I felt, but showed it a great deal more.

A silent movie picture of the scene would have given no clue as to what was wrong. Everything was so very comfortable, so very civilized. The deep armchairs invited complete relaxation. A blazing if superfluous log-fire burned in the hearth. Skouras was the smiling and genial host to the life. The glasses were never empty – the press of an unheard bell brought a white-jacketed steward who silently refilled glasses and as silently departed again. All so urbane, so wealthy, so pleasantly peaceful. Until you cut in the movie sound-track, that was. That was when you wished you were in the galley.

Skouras had his glass refilled for the fourth time in the forty-five minutes we had been there, smiled at his wife sitting in the armchair across the fire from him, lifted his glass in a toast. 'To you, my dear. To your patience with putting up with us all so well. A most boring trip for you, most boring. I congratulate you.'

I looked at Charlotte Skouras. Everybody looked at Charlotte Skouras. There was nothing unusual in that, millions of people had looked at Charlotte Skouras when she had been the most sought-after actress in Europe. Even in those days she'd been neither particularly young nor beautiful, she didn't have to be because she'd been a great actress and not a beautiful but boneheaded movie star. Now she was even older and less good-looking and her figure was beginning to go. But men still looked at her. She was somewhere in her late thirties, but they would still be looking at her when she was in her bathchair. She had that kind of face. A worn face, a used face, a face that had been used for living and laughing and thinking and feeling and suffering, a face with brown tired wise-knowing eyes a thousand years old, a face that had more quality and character in every little line and wrinkle – and heaven only knew there was no shortage of these – than in a whole battalion of the fringe-haired darlings of contemporary society, the ones in the glossy magazines, the ones who week after week stared out at you with their smooth and beautiful faces, with their beautiful and empty eyes. Put them in the same room as Charlotte Skouras and no one would ever have seen them. Mass-produced carbon copies of chocolate boxes are no kind of competition at all for a great painter's original in oils.

'You are very kind, Anthony.' Charlotte Skouras had a deep slow slightly-foreign accented voice, and, just then, a tired strained smile that accorded well with the darkness under the brown eyes. 'But I am never bored. Truly. You know that.'

'With this lot as guests?' Skouras's smile was as broad as ever. 'A Skouras board meeting in the Western Isles instead of your blue-blooded favourites on a cruise in the Levant? Take Dollmann here.' He nodded to the man by his side, a tall thin bespectacled character with receding thin dark hair who looked as if he needed a shave but didn't. John Dollmann, the managing director of the Skouras shipping lines. 'Eh, John? How do you rate yourself as a substitute for young Viscount Horley? The one with sawdust in his head and fifteen million in the bank?'

'Poorly, I'm afraid, Sir Anthony.' Dollmann was as urbane as Skouras himself, as apparently unconscious of anything untoward in the atmosphere. 'Very poorly. I've a great deal more brains, a great deal less money and I've no pretensions to being a gay and witty conversationalist.'

'Young Horley *was* rather the life and soul of the party, wasn't he? Especially when I wasn't around,' Skouras added thoughtfully. He looked at me. 'You know him, Mr Petersen?'

'I've heard of him. I don't move in those circles, Sir Anthony.' Urbane as all hell, that was me.

'Um.' Skouras looked quizzically at the two men sitting close by myself. One, rejoicing in the good Anglo-Saxon name of Hermann Lavorski, a big jovial twinkling-eyed man with a great booming laugh and an inexhaustible supply of risqué stories, was, I'd been told, his accountant and financial adviser. I'd never seen anyone less like an accountant and finance wizard, so that probably made him the best in the business. The other, a middle-aged, balding, Sphinx-faced character with a drooping handle-bar moustache of the type once sported by Wild Bill Hickock and a head that cried out for a bowler hat, was Lord Charnley, who, in spite of his title, found it necessary to work as a broker in the City to make ends meet. 'And how would you rate our two good friends here, Charlotte?' This with another wide and friendly smile at his wife.

'I'm afraid I don't understand.' Charlotte Skouras looked at her husband steadily, not smiling.

'Come now, come now, of course you do understand. I'm still talking about the poor company I provide for so young and attractive a woman as you.' He looked at Hunslett. 'She *is* a young and attractive woman, don't you think, Mr Hunslett?'

'Well, now.' Hunslett leaned back in his armchair, fingers judiciously steepled, an urbanely sophisticated man entering into the spirit of things. 'What is youth, Sir Anthony? I don't know.' He smiled across at Charlotte Skouras. 'Mrs Skouras will never be old. As for attractive – well, it's a bit superfluous to ask that. For ten million European men – and for myself – Mrs Skouras was the most attractive actress of her time.'

'*Was*, Mr Hunslett? *Was*?' Old Skouras was leaning forward in his chair now, the smile a shadow of its former self. 'But now, Mr Hunslett?'

'Mrs Skouras's producers must have employed the worst cameramen in Europe.' Hunslett's dark, saturnine face gave nothing away. He smiled at Charlotte Skouras. 'If I may be pardoned so personal a remark.'

If I'd had a sword in my hand and the authority to use it, I'd have knighted Hunslett on the spot. After, of course, having first had a swipe at Skouras.

'The days of chivalry are not yet over,' Skouras smiled. I saw MacCallum and Biscarte, the bearded banker, stir uncomfortably in their seats. It was damnably awkward. Skouras went on: 'I only meant, my dear, that Charnley and Lavorski here are poor substitutes for sparkling young company like Welshblood, the young American oil man, or Domenico, that Spanish count with the passion for amateur astronomy. The one who used to take you on the afterdeck to point out the stars in the Ægean.' He looked again at Charnley and Lavorski. 'I'm sorry, gentlemen, you just wouldn't do at all.'

'I don't know if I'm all that insulted,' Lavorski said comfortably. 'Charnley and I have our points. Um – I haven't seen young Domenico around for quite some time.' He'd have made an excellent stage feed man, would Lavorski, trained to say his lines at exactly the right time.

'You won't see him around for a very much longer time,' Skouras said grimly. 'At least not in my yacht or in any of my houses.' A pause. 'Or near anything I own. I promised him I'd see the colour of his noble Castilian blood if I ever clapped eyes on him again.' He laughed suddenly. 'I must apologize for even bringing that nonentity's name into the conversation. Mr Hunslett. Mr Petersen. Your glasses are empty.'

'You've been very kind, Sir Anthony. We've enjoyed ourselves immensely.' Bluff old, stupid old Calvert, too obtuse to notice what was going on. 'But we'd like to get back. It's blowing up badly to-night and Hunslett and I would like to move the *Firecrest* into the shelter of Garve Island.' I rose to a window, pulling one of his Afghanistan or whatever curtains to one side. It felt as heavy as a stage fire curtain, no wonder he needed stabilizers with all that topweight on. 'That's why we left our riding and cabin lights on. To see if we'd moved. She dragged a fair bit earlier this evening.'

'So soon? So soon?' He sounded genuinely disappointed. 'But of course, if you're worried—' He pressed a button, not the one for the steward, and the saloon door opened. The man who entered was a small weatherbeaten character with two gold stripes on his sleeves. Captain Black, the *Shangri-la*'s captain. He'd accompanied Skouras when we'd been briefly shown around the *Shangri-la* after arriving aboard, a tour that had included an inspection of the smashed radio transmitter. No question about it, their radio was well and truly out of action.

'Ah, Captain Black. Have the tender brought alongside at once, will you. Mr Petersen and Mr Hunslett are anxious to get back to the *Firecrest* as soon as possible.'

'Yes, sir. I'm afraid there'll be a certain delay, Sir Anthony.'

'Delay?' Old Skouras could put a frown in his voice without putting one on his face.

'The old trouble, I'm afraid,' Captain Black said apologetically.

'Those bloody carburettors,' Skouras swore. 'You were right, Captain Black, you were right. Last tender I'll ever have with petrol engines fitted. Let me know as soon as she's all right. And detail one of the hands to keep an eye on the *Firecrest* to see that she doesn't lose position. Mr Petersen's afraid she'll drag.'

'Don't worry, sir.' I didn't know whether Black was speaking to Skouras or myself. 'She'll be all right.'

He left. Skouras spent some time in extolling diesel engines and cursing petrol ones, pressed some more whisky on Hunslett and myself and ignored my protests, which were based less on any dislike of whisky in general or Skouras in particular than on the fact that I didn't consider it very good preparation for the night that lay ahead of me. Just before nine o'clock he pressed a button by his arm rest and the doors of a cabinet automatically opened to reveal a 23-inch TV set.

Uncle Arthur hadn't let me down. The newscaster gave quite a dramatic account of the last message received from the TSDY *Moray Rose*, reported not under command and making water fast somewhere to the south of the Island of Skye. A full-scale air and sea search, starting at dawn the next day, was promised.

Skouras switched the set off. 'The sea's crowded with damn' fools who should never be allowed outside a canal basin. What's the latest on the weather? Anyone know?'

'There was a Hebrides Force 8 warning on the 1758 shipping forecast,' Charlotte Skouras said quietly. 'South-west, they said.'

'Since when did you start listening to forecasts?' Skouras demanded. 'Or to the radio at all? But of course, my dear, I'd forgotten. Not so much to occupy your time these days, have you? Force 8 and south-west, eh? And the yacht would be coming down from the Kyle of Lochalsh, straight into it. They must be mad. And they have a radio – they sent a message. That makes them stark staring lunatics. Whether they didn't listen to the forecast or whether they listened and still set out, they must have been lunatics. Get them everywhere.'

'Some of those lunatics may be dying, drowning now. Or already drowned,' Charlotte Skouras said. The shadows under the brown eyes seemed bigger and darker than ever, but there was still life in those brown eyes.

For perhaps five seconds Skouras, face set, stared at her and I felt that if I snapped my fingers there would be a loud tinkling or crashing sound, the atmosphere was as brittle as that. Then he turned away with a laugh and said to me: 'The little woman, eh, Petersen? The little mother – only she has no children. Tell me, Petersen, are you married?'

I smiled at him while debating the wisdom of throwing my whisky glass in his face or clobbering him with something heavy, then decided against it. Apart from the fact that it would only make matters worse, I didn't fancy the swim back to the *Firecrest*. So I smiled and smiled, feeling the knife under the cloak, and said: 'Afraid not, Sir Anthony.'

'Afraid not? Afraid not?' He laughed his hearty good-fellowship laugh, the kind I can't stand, and went on cryptically: 'You're not so young to be sufficiently naïve to talk that way, come now, are you, Mr Petersen?'

'Thirty-eight and never had a chance,' I said cheerfully, 'The old story, Sir Anthony. The ones I'd have wouldn't have me. And vice-versa.' Which wasn't quite true. The driver of a Bentley with, the doctors had estimated, certainly not less than a bottle of whisky inside him, had ended my marriage before it was two months old – and also accounted for the savagely scarred left side of my face. It was then that Uncle Arthur had prised me from my marine salvage business and since then no girl with any sense would ever have contemplated marrying me if she'd known what my job was. What made it even more difficult was the fact that I couldn't tell her in the first place. And the scars didn't help.

'You don't look a fool to me,' Skouras smiled. 'If I may say so without offence.' That was rich, old Skouras worrying about giving offence. The zip-fastener of a mouth softened into what, in view of his next words, I correctly interpreted in advance as being a nostalgic smile. 'I'm joking, of course. It's not all that bad. A man must have his fun. Charlotte?'

'Yes?' The brown eyes wary, watchful.

'There's something I want from our stateroom. Would you—?'

'The stewardess. Couldn't she—?'

'This is personal, my dear. And, as Mr Hunslett has pointed out, at least by inference, you're a good deal younger than I am.' He smiled at Hunslett to show that no offence was intended. 'The picture on my dressing-table.'

'What!' She suddenly sat forward in her armchair, hands reaching for the fronts of the arm rests as if about to pull herself to her feet. Something touched a switch inside Skouras and the smiling eyes went bleak and hard and cold, changing their direction of gaze fractionally. It lasted only a moment because his wife had caught it even before I did, because she sat forward abruptly, smoothing down the short sleeves of her dress over sun-tanned arms. Quick and smooth, but not quite quick enough. For a period of not more than two seconds the sleeves had ridden nearly all the way up to her shoulders – and nearly four inches below those shoulders each arm had been encircled by a ring of bluish-red bruises. A continuous ring. Not the kind of bruises that are made by blows or finger pressure. The kind that are made by a rope.

Skouras was smiling again, pressing the bell to summon the steward. Charlotte Skouras rose without a further word and hurried quickly from the room. I could have wondered if I'd only imagined this momentary tableau I'd seen, but I knew damned well I hadn't. I was paid not to have an imagination of that kind.

She was back inside a moment, a picture frame maybe six by eight in her hand. She handed it to Skouras and sat down quickly in her own chair. This time she was very careful with the sleeves, without seeming to be.

'My wife, gentlemen,' Skouras said. He rose from his armchair and handed round a photograph of a dark-eyed, dark-haired woman with a smiling face that emphasized the high Slavonic cheek-bones. 'My first wife. Anna. We were married for thirty years. Marriage isn't all that bad. That's Anna, gentlemen.'

If I'd a gramme of human decency left in me I should have knocked him down and trampled all over him. For a man to state openly in company that he kept the picture of his former wife by his bedside and then impose upon his present wife the final and utter humiliation and degradation of fetching it was beyond belief. That and the rope-burns on his present wife's arms made him almost too good for shooting. But I couldn't do it, I couldn't do anything about it. The old coot's heart was in his voice and his eyes. If this was acting, it was the most superb acting I had ever seen, the tear that trickled down from his right eye would have rated an Oscar any year since cinema had begun. And if it wasn't acting then it was just the picture of a sad and lonely man, no longer young, momentarily oblivious of this world, gazing desolately at the only thing in this world that he loved, that he ever had loved or ever would love, something gone beyond recall. And that was what it was.

If it hadn't been for the other picture, the picture of the still, proud, humiliated Charlotte Skouras staring sightlessly into the fire, I might have felt a lump in my own throat. As it happened, I'd no difficulty in restraining my emotion. One man couldn't, however, but it wasn't sympathy for Skouras that got the better of him. MacCallum, the Scots lawyer, pale-faced with outrage, rose to his feet, said something in a thick voice about not feeling well, wished us good night and left. The bearded banker left on his heels. Skouras didn't see them go, he'd fumbled his way back to his seat and was staring before him, his eyes as sightless as those of his wife. Like his wife, he was seeing something in the depths of the flames. The picture lay face down on his knee. He didn't even look up when Captain Black came in and told us the tender was ready to take us back to the *Firecrest*.

When the tender had left us aboard our own boat we waited till it was half-way back to the *Shangri-la*, closed the saloon door, unbuttoned the studded carpet and pulled it back. Carefully I lifted a sheet of newspaper and there, on the thin film of flour spread out on the paper below it, were four perfect sets of footprints. We tried our two for'ard cabins, the engine-room and the after cabin, and the silk threads we'd so laboriously fitted before our departure to the *Shangri-la* were all snapped.

Somebody, two at least to judge from the footprints, had been through the entire length of the *Firecrest*. They could have had at least a clear hour for the job, so Hunslett and I spent a clear hour trying to find out why they had been there. We found nothing, no reason at all.

'Well,' I said, 'at least we know now why they were so anxious to have us aboard the *Shangri-la*.'

'To give them a clear field here? That's why the tender wasn't ready – it was here.'

'What else?'

'There's something else. I can't put my finger on it. But there's something else.'

'Let me know in the morning. When you call Uncle at midnight, ask him to dig up what information he can on those characters on the *Shangri-la* and about the physician who attended the late Lady Skouras. There's a lot I want to know about the late Lady Skouras.' I told him what I wanted to know. 'Meantime, let's shift this boat over to Garve Island. I've got to be up at three-thirty – you've all the time for sleep in the world.'

I should have listened to Hunslett. Again I should have listened to Hunslett. And again for Hunslett's sake. But I didn't know then that Hunslett was to have time for all the sleep in the world.

Chapter Four

Wednesday: 5 a.m. – dusk

As the saying went in those parts, it was as black as the earl of hell's waistcoat. The sky was black, the woods were black, and the icy heavy driving rain reduced what little visibility there was to just nothing at all.

The only way to locate a tree was to walk straight into it, the only way to locate a dip in the ground was to fall into it. When Hunslett had woken me at three-thirty with a cup of tea he told me that when he'd been speaking to Uncle Arthur at midnight – I'd been asleep – he was left in no doubt that although the helicopter had been laid on Uncle had been most unenthusiastic and considered the whole thing a waste of time. It was a rare occasion indeed when I ever felt myself in total agreement with Uncle Arthur but this was one of those rare occasions.

It was beginning to look as if I'd never even find that damned helicopter anyway. I wouldn't have believed that it could have been so difficult to find one's way across five miles of wooded island at night-time. It wasn't even as if I had to contend with rivers or rushing torrents or cliffs or precipitous clefts in the ground or any kind of dense or tangled vegetation. Torbay was just a moderately wooded gently sloping island and crossing from one side to the other of it would have been only an easy Sunday afternoon stroll for a fairly active octogenarian. I was no octogenarian, though I felt like one, but then this wasn't a Sunday afternoon.

The trouble had started from the moment I'd landed on the Torbay shore opposite Garve Island. From the moment I'd tried to land. Wearing rubber-soled shoes and trying to haul a rubber dinghy over slippery seaweed-covered rocks, some as much as six feet in diameter, to a shore-line twenty interminable yards away is, even in broad daylight, a bone-breaking job: in pitch darkness it's almost as good a way as any for a potential suicide to finish off the job with efficiency and dispatch. The third time I fell I smashed my torch. Several bone-jarring bruises later my wrist-compass went the same way. The attached depth-gauge, almost inevitably, remained intact. A depth-gauge is a great help in finding your way through a trackless wood at night.

After deflating and caching the dinghy and pump I'd set off along the shore-line remote from the village of Torbay. It was logical that if I followed this long enough I'd be bound to come to the sandy cove at the far end of the island where I was to rendezvous with the helicopter. It was also logical that, if the tree line came right down to the shore, if that shore was heavily indented with little coves and if I couldn't see where I was going, I'd fall into the sea with a fair degree of regularity. After I'd hauled myself out for the third time I gave up and struck inland. It wasn't because I was afraid of getting wet – as I hadn't seen much point in wearing a scuba suit for walking through a wood and sitting in a helicopter I'd left it aboard and was already soaked to the skin. Nor was it because of the possibility that the hand distress flares I'd brought along for signalling the helicopter pilot, wrapped though they were in oilskin, might not stand up to this treatment indefinitely. The reason why I was now blundering my blind and painful way through the wood was that if I'd stuck to the shoreline my rate of progress there wouldn't have brought me to the rendezvous before midday.

My only guides were the wind-lashed rain and the lie of the land. The cove I was heading for lay to the east, the near-gale force wind was almost due west, so as long as I kept that cold stinging rain on the back of my neck I'd be heading in approximately the right direction: as a check on that, the Island of Torbay has a spinal hog's back, covered in pines to the top, running its east-west length and when I felt the land falling away to one side or the other it meant I was wandering. But the rain-laden wind swirled unpredictably as the wood alternately thinned and became dense again, the hog's back had offshoots and irregularities and as a result of the combination of the two I lost a great deal of time. Half an hour before dawn – by my watch, that was, it was still as black as the midnight hour – I was beginning to wonder if I could possibly make it in time.

And I was beginning to wonder if the helicopter could make it either. There was no doubt in my mind that it could land – that eastern cove was perfectly sheltered – but whether it could get there at all was another question. I had a vague idea that helicopters were unmanageable above certain wind speeds but had no idea what those wind speeds were. And if the helicopter didn't turn up, then I was faced with the long cold wet trudge back to where I had hidden the dinghy and then an even longer, colder and hungry wait until darkness fell at night and I could get out to the *Firecrest* unseen. Even now, I had only twenty-four hours left. By nightfall I would have only twelve. I began to run.

Fifteen minutes and God knows how many iron-hard tree trunks later I heard it, faint and intermittent at first, then gradually swelling in strength – the clattering roar of a helicopter engine. He was early, damn him, he was far too early, he'd land there, find the place deserted and take off for base again. It says much for my sudden desperate state of mind that it never occurred to me how he could even begin to locate, far less land in, that sandy cove in a condition of darkness that was still only a degree less than total. For a moment I even contemplated lighting a flare to let the pilot know that I was at least there or thereabouts and had the flare half-way out of my pocket before I shoved it back again. The arrangement had been that the flare would be lit only to show the landing strip in the sand: if I lit one there and then he might head for it, strike the tops of the pine trees and that would be the end of that.

I ran even faster. It had been years since I'd run more than a couple of hundred yards and my lungs were already wheezing and gasping like a fractured bellows in a blacksmith's shop. But I ran as hard as I could. I cannoned into trees, I tripped over roots, fell into gullies, had my face whipped time and again by low-spreading branches, but above all I cannoned into those damned trees. I stretched my arms before me but it did no good, I ran into them all the same. I picked up a broken branch I'd tripped over and held it in front of me but no matter how I pointed it the trees always seemed to come at me from another direction. I hit every tree in the Island of Torbay. I felt the way a bowling ball must feel after a hard season in a bowling alley, the only difference, and a notable one, being that whereas the ball knocked the skittles down, the trees knocked me down. Once, twice, three times I heard the sound of the helicopter engine disappearing away to the east, and the third time I was sure he was gone for good. But each time it came back. The sky was lightening to the east now, but still I couldn't see the helicopter: for the pilot, everything below would still be as black as night.

The ground gave way beneath my feet and I fell. I braced myself, arms outstretched, for the impact as I struck the other side of the gully. But my reaching hands found nothing. No impact. I kept on falling, rolling and twisting down a heathery slope, and for the first time that night I would have welcomed the appearance of a pine tree, any kind of tree, to stop my progress. I don't know how many trees there were on that slope, I missed the lot. If it was a gully, it was the biggest gully on the Island of Torbay. But it wasn't a gully at all, it was the end of Torbay. I rolled and bumped over a sudden horizontal grassy bank and landed on my back in soft wet sand. Even while I was whooping and gasping and trying to get my knocked-out breath back into my lungs I still had time to appreciate the fortunate fact that kindly providence and a few million years had changed the jagged rocks that must once have fringed that shore into a nice soft yielding sandy beach.

I got to my feet. This was the place, all right. There was only one such sandy bay, I'd been told, in the east of the Isle of Torbay and there was now enough light for me to see that this was indeed just that, though a lot smaller than it appeared on the chart. The helicopter was coming in again from the east, not, as far as I could judge, more than three or four hundred feet up. I ran half-way down to the water's edge, pulled a hand flare from my pocket, slid away the waterproof covering and tore off the ignition strip. It flared into life at once, a dazzling blue-white magnesium light so blinding that I had to clap my free hand over my eyes. It lasted for only thirty seconds, but that was enough. Even as it fizzled and sputtered its acrid and nostril-wrinkling way to extinction the helicopter was almost directly overhead. Two vertically-downward pointing searchlights, mounted fore and aft on the helicopter, switched on simultaneously, interlocking pools of brilliance on the pale white sand. Twenty seconds later the skids sank into the soft sand, the rackety clangour of the motor died away and the blades idled slowly to a stop. I'd never been in a helicopter in my life but I'd seen plenty: in the half-darkness this looked like the biggest one I'd ever seen.

The right-hand door opened and a torch shone in my face as I approached. A voice, Welsh as the Rhondda Valley, said: 'Morning. You Calvert?'

'Me. Can I come aboard?'

'How do I know you're Calvert?'

'I'm telling you. Don't come the hard man, laddie. You've no authority to make an identification check.'

'Have you no proof? No papers?'

'Have you no sense? Haven't you enough sense to know that there are some people who *never* carry any means of identification? Do you think I just happened to be standing here, five miles from nowhere, and that I just happened to be carrying flares in my pocket? You want to join the ranks of the unemployed before sunset?' A very auspicious beginning to our association.

'I was told to be careful.' He was worried and upset as a cat snoozing on a sun-warmed wall. Still a marked lack of cordiality. 'Lieutenant Scott Williams, Fleet Air Arm. Takes an admiral to sack me. Step up.'

I stepped up, closed the door and sat. He didn't offer to shake hands. He flicked on an overhead light and said: 'What the hell's happened to your face?'

'What's the matter with my face?'

'Blood. Hundreds of little scratches.'

'Pine needles.' I told him what had happened. 'Why a machine this size? You could ferry a battalion in this one.'

'Fourteen men, to be precise. I do lots of crazy things, Calvert, but I don't fly itsy-bitsy two-bit choppers in this kind of weather. Be blown out of the sky. With only two of us, the long-range tanks are full.'

'You can fly all day?'

'More or less. Depends how fast we go. What do you want from me?'

'Civility, for a start. Or don't you like early morning rising?'

'I'm an Air-Sea Rescue pilot, Calvert. This is the only machine on the base big enough to go out looking in this kind of weather. And I should be out looking, not out on some cloak-and-dagger joy-ride. I don't care how important it is, there's people maybe clinging to a life-raft fifty miles out in the Atlantic. That's my job. But I've got my orders. What do you want?'

'The *Moray Rose*?'

'You heard? Yes, that's her.'

'She doesn't exist. She never has existed.'

'What are you talking about? The news broadcasts—'

'I'll tell you as much as you need to know, Lieutenant. It's essential that I be able to search this area without arousing suspicion. The only way that can be done is by inventing an ironclad reason. The foundering *Moray Rose* is that reason. So we tell the tale.'

'Phoney?'

'Phoney.'

'You can fix it?' he said slowly. 'You can fix a news broadcast?'

'Yes.'

'Maybe you could get me fired at that.' He smiled for the first time. 'Sorry, sir. Lieutenant Williams – Scotty to you – is now his normal cheerful willing self. What's on?'

'Know the coast-lines and islands of this area well?'

'From the air?'

'Yes.'

'I've been here twenty months now. Air-Sea Rescue and in between army and navy exercises and hunting for lost climbers. Most of my work is with the Marine Commandos. I know this area at least as well as any man alive.'

'I'm looking for a place where a man could hide a boat. A fairly big boat. Forty feet – maybe fifty. Might be in a big boathouse, might be under overhanging trees up some creek, might even be in some tiny secluded harbour normally invisible from the sea. Between Islay and Skye.'

'Well, now, is that all. Have you any idea how many hundreds of miles of coastline there is in that lot, taking in all the islands? Maybe thousands? How long do I have for this job? A month?'

'By sunset to-day. Now, wait. We can cut out all centres of population, and by that I mean anything with more than two or three houses together. We can cut out known fishing grounds. We can cut out regular steamship routes. Does that help?'

'A lot. What are we really looking for?'

'I've told you.'

'Okay, okay, so mine is not to reason why. Any idea where you'd like to start, any ideas for limiting the search?'

'Let's go due east to the mainland. Twenty miles up the coast, then twenty south. Then we'll try Torbay Sound and the Isle of Torbay. Then the islands farther west and north.'

'Torbay Sound has a steamer service.'

'Sorry, I should have said a daily service. Torbay has a bi-weekly service.'

'Fasten your seat-belt and get on those earphones. We're going to get thrown around quite a bit to-day. I hope you're a good sailor.'

'And the earphones?' They were the biggest I'd ever seen, four inches wide with inch-thick linings of what looked like sorbo rubber. A spring loaded swing microphone was attached to the headband.

'For the ears,' the lieutenant said kindly. 'So that you don't get perforated drums. And so you won't be deaf for a week afterwards. If you can imagine yourself inside a steel drum in the middle of a boiler factory with a dozen pneumatic chisels hammering outside, you'll have some idea of what the rackct is likc oncc wc start up.'

Even with the earphone muffs on, it sounded exactly like being in a steel drum in a boiler factory with a dozen pneumatic chisels hammering on the outside. The earphones didn't seem to have the slightest effect at all, the noise came hammering and beating at you through every facial and cranial bone, but on the one and very brief occasion when I cautiously lifted one phone to find out what the noise was like without them and if they were really doing any good at all, I found out exactly what Lieutenant Williams meant about perforated drums. He hadn't been joking. But even with them on, after a couple of hours my head felt as if it were coming apart. I looked occasionally at the dark lean face of the young Welshman beside me, a man who had to stand this racket day in, day out, the year round. He looked quite sane to me. I'd have been in a padded cell in a week.

I didn't have to be in that helicopter a week. Altogether, I spent eight hours' flying time in it and it felt like a leap year.

Our first run northwards up the mainland coast produced what was to be the first of many false alarms that day. Twenty minutes after leaving Torbay we spotted a river, a small one but still a river, flowing into the sea. We followed it upstream for a mile, then suddenly the trees, crowding down close to the bank on both sides, met in the middle where the river seemed to run through some rocky gorge.

I shouted into the microphone: 'I want to see what's there.'

Williams nodded. 'We passed a place a quarter of a mile back. I'll set you down.'

'You've got a winch. Couldn't you lower me?'

'When you know as much as I do about the effect of forty to fifty miles an hour winds in a steep-sided valley,' he said, 'you'll never talk about such things. Not even in a joke. I want to take this kite home again.'

So he turned back and set me down without much difficulty in the shelter of a bluff. Five minutes later I'd reached the beginning of the overhanging stretch. Another five minutes and I was back in the helicopter.

'What luck?' the lieutenant asked.

'No luck. An ancient oak tree right across the river, just at the entrance to the overhang.'

'Could be shifted.'

'It weighs two or three tons, it's imbedded feet deep in the mud and it's been there for years.'

'Well, well, we can't be right first time, every time.'

A few more minutes and another river mouth. It hardly looked big enough to take a boat of any size, but we turned up anyway. Less than half a mile from its mouth the river foamed whitely as it passed through rapids. We turned back.

By the time it was fully daylight we had reached the northern limit of possibility in this area. Steep-sided mountains gave way to precipitous cliffs that plunged almost vertically into the sea.

'How far does this go north?' I asked.

'Ten, twelve miles to the head of Loch Lairg.'

'Know it?'

'Flown up there a score of times.'

'Caves?'

'Nary a cave.'

I hadn't really thought that there would be. 'How about the other side?' I pointed to the west where the mountainous shore-line, not five miles away yet barely visible through the driving rain and low scudding cloud, ran in an almost sheer drop from the head of Loch Lairg to the entrance to Torbay Sound.

'Even the gulls can't find a foothold there. Believe me.'

I believed him. We flew back the way we had come as far as our starting point on the coast, then continued southwards. From the Isle of Torbay to the mainland the sea was an almost unbroken mass of foaming white, big white-capped rollers marching eastwards across the darkened firth, long creamy lines of spume torn from the wave-tops veining the troughs between. There wasn't a single craft in sight, even the big drifters had stayed at home, it was as bad as that. In that buffeting gale-force wind our big helicopter was having a bad time of it now, violently shaking and swaying like an out-of-control express train in the last moments before it leaves the track: one hour's flying in those conditions had turned me against helicopters for life. But when I thought of what it would be like down there in a boat in that seething maelstrom of a firth I could feel a positive bond of attachment growing between me and that damned helicopter.

We flew twenty miles south – if the way we were being jarred and flung through the air could be called flying – but covered sixty miles in that southing. Every little sound between the islands and the mainland, every natural harbour, every sea-loch and inlet had to be investigated. We flew very low most of the time, not much above two hundred feet: sometimes we were forced down to a hundred feet – so heavy was the rain and so powerful the wind now battering against the streaming windscreen that the wipers were almost useless and we had to get as low as possible to see anything at all. As it was, I don't think we missed a yard of the coastline of the mainland or the close in-shore islands. We saw everything. And we saw nothing.

I looked at my watch. Nine-thirty. The day wearing on and nothing achieved. I said: 'How much more of this can the helicopter stand?'

'I've been 150 miles out over the Atlantic in weather a damn' sight worse than this.' Lieutenant Williams showed no signs of strain or anxiety or fatigue, if anything he seemed to be enjoying himself. 'The point is how much more can *you* stand?'

'Very little. But we'll have to. Back to where you picked me up and we'll make a circuit of the coast of Torbay. South coast first, then north up the west coast, then east past Torbay and down the southern shore of the Sound.'

'Yours to command.' Williams brought the helicopter round to the north-west in a swinging side-slipping movement that didn't do my stomach any good. 'You'll find coffee and sandwiches in that box there.' I left the sandwiches and coffee where they were.

It took us almost forty minutes to cover the twenty-five miles to the eastern tip of the Isle of Torbay, that wind took us two steps back for every three forward. Visibility was so bad that Williams flew on instruments the whole way and with that violent cross-wind blowing he should have missed our target by miles. Instead he hit that sandy cove right on the nose as if he'd been flying in on a radio beacon. I was beginning to have a very great deal of confidence in Williams, a man who knew exactly what he was doing: I was beginning to have no confidence at all in myself and to wonder if I had any idea in the world what I was doing. I thought about Uncle Arthur and quickly decided I'd rather think about something else.

'There,' Williams pointed. We were about half-way along the south coast of Torbay. 'A likely set-up, wouldn't you say?'

And a likely set-up it was. A large white three-story stone-built Georgian house, set in a clearing about a hundred yards back from and thirty yards above the shore. There are dozens of such houses scattered in the most unlikely positions in some of the most barren and desolate islands in the Hebrides. Heaven only knew who built them, why or how. But it wasn't the house that was the focal point of interest in this case, it was the big boathouse on the edge of a tiny land-locked harbour. Without a further word from me Williams brought the big machine down neatly in the shelter of the trees behind the house.

I unwrapped the polythene bag I'd been carrying under my shirt. Two guns. The Luger I stuck in my pocket, the little German Lilliput I fixed to the spring clip in my left sleeve. Williams stared unconcernedly ahead and began to whistle to himself.

Nobody had lived in that house for years. Part of the roof had fallen in, years of salt air erosion had removed all paintwork and the rooms, when I looked in through the cracked and broken windows, were bare and crumbling with long strips of wall-paper lying on the floor. The path down to the little harbour was completely overgrown with moss. Every time my heel sunk into the path a deep muddy mark was left behind, the first made there for a long long time. The boatshed was big enough, at least sixty by twenty, but that was all that could be said for it. The two big doors had three hinges apiece and two huge padlocks where they met in the middle. Padlocks and hinges alike were almost eaten through by rust. I could feel the heavy tug of the Luger in my pocket and the weight made me feel faintly ridiculous. I went back to the helicopter.

Twice more in the next twenty minutes we came across almost identical situations. Big white Georgian houses with big boathouses at their feet. I knew they would be false alarms but I had to check them both. False alarms they were. The last occupants of those houses had been dead before I'd been born. People had lived in those houses once, people with families, big families, people with money and ambition and confidence and no fear at all of the future. Not if they had built houses as big as those. And now the people were gone and all that was left were those crumbling, mouldering monuments to a misplaced faith in the future. Some years previously I'd seen houses in plantations in South Carolina and Georgia, houses widely dissimilar but exactly the same, white-porticoed ante-bellum houses hemmed in by evergreen live oaks and overgrown with long grey festoons of Spanish moss. Sadness and desolation and a world that was gone for ever.

The west coast of the Isle of Torbay yielded nothing. We gave the town of Torbay and Garve Island a wide berth and flew eastwards down the southern shore of the Sound with the gale behind us. Two small hamlets, each with its disintegrating pier. Beyond that, nothing.

We reached the sandy cove again, flew north till we reached the northern shore of the Sound, then westwards along this shore. We stopped twice, once to investigate a tree-overhung land-locked harbour less than forty yards in diameter, and again to investigate a small complex of industrial buildings which had once, so Williams said, produced a fine-quality sand that had been one of the ingredients in a famous brand of toothpaste. Again, nothing.

At the last place we stopped for five minutes. Lieutenant Williams said he was hungry. I wasn't. I'd become used to the helicopter by now but I wasn't hungry. It was midday. Half our time gone and nothing accomplished. And it was beginning to look very much as if nothing was going to be accomplished. Uncle Arthur would be pleased. I took the chart from Williams.

'We have to pick and choose,' I said. 'We'll have to take a chance. We'll go up the Sound to Dolman Head, opposite Garve Island, then go up Loch Hynart.' Loch Hynart was a seven-mile long loch, winding and many-islanded, that ran more or less due east, nowhere more than half a mile wide, deep into the heart of the mountain massif. 'Back to Dolman Point again then along the southern shore of the mainland peninsula again as far as Carrara Point. Then east along the southern shore of Loch Houron.'

'Loch Houron,' Williams nodded. 'The wildest waters and the worst place for boats in the West of Scotland. Last place I'd go looking, Mr Calvert, that's for sure. From all accounts you'll find nothing there but wrecks and skeletons. There are more reefs and skerries and underwater rocks and overfalls and whirlpools and tidal races in twenty miles there than in the whole of the rest of Scotland. Local fishermen won't go near the place.' He pointed at the chart. 'See this passage between Dubh Sgeir and Ballara Island, the two islands at the mouth of Loch Houron? That's the most feared spot of all. You should see the grip the fishermen get on their whisky glasses when they talk about it. Beul nan Uamh, it's called. The mouth of the grave.'

'They're a cheery lot, hereabouts. It's time we were gone.'

The wind blew as strongly as ever, the sea below looked as wicked as ever, but the rain had stopped and that made our search all that much easier. The stretch of the Sound from the sand quarry to Dolman Point yielded nothing. Neither did Loch Hynart. Between Loch Hynart and Carrara Point, eight miles to the west, there were only two tiny hamlets crouched against the water's edge, their backs to the barren hills behind, their inhabitants – if there were any inhabitants – subsisting on God alone knew what. Carrara Point was storm-torn desolation itself. Great jagged broken fissured cliffs, huge fanged rocks rising from the sea, massive Atlantic breakers smashing in hundred foot high spray against the cliffs, the rocks and the tiny-seeming lighthouse at the foot of the cliffs. If I were Sir Billy Butlin looking for the site of my latest holiday camp, I wouldn't have spent too much time on Carrara Point.

We turned north now, then north-east, then east, along the southern shore of Loch Houron.

Many places have evil reputations. Few, at first seeing, live up to those reputations. But there are a few. In Scotland, the Pass of Glencoe, the scene of the infamous massacre, is one of them. The Pass of Brander is another. And Loch Houron was beyond all doubt another.

It required no imagination at all to see this as a dark and deadly and dangerous place. It looked dark and deadly and dangerous. The shores were black and rocky and precipitous and devoid of any form of vegetation at all. The four islands strung out in a line to the east were a splendid match for the hospitable appearance of the shores. In the far distance the northern and the southern shores of the loch came close together and vanished in a towering vertical cleft in the sinister brooding mountains. In the lee of the islands the loch was black as midnight but elsewhere it was a seething boiling white, the waters wickedly swirling, churning, spinning in evil-looking whirlpools as it passed across overfalls or forced its way through the narrow channels between the islands or between the islands and the shore. Water in torment. In the Beul nan Uamh – the mouth of the grave – between the first two islands the rushing leaping milk-white waters looked like floodwater in the Mackenzie river rapids in springtime, when the snows melt. A yachtsman's paradise. Only a madman would take his boat into these waters.

Apparently there were still a few madmen around. We'd just left the first of the islands, Dubh Sgeir, to port, when I caught sight of a narrow break in the cliffs on the southern mainland. A small rock-girt bay, if bay it could be called, about the size of a couple of tennis courts, almost completely enclosed from the sea, the entrance couldn't have been more than ten yards wide. I glanced at the chart – Little Horseshoe Bay, it was called. Not original, but very apt. There was a boat in there, a fairly big one, a converted MFV by the looks of her, anchored fore and aft in the middle of the bay. Behind the bay was a little plateau, mossy or grass-covered, I couldn't tell which, and, behind that, what looked like a dried-up river bed rising steeply into the hills behind. On the little plateau were four khaki-coloured tents, with men working at them.

'This could be it?' Williams said.

'This could be it.'

This wasn't it. A glance at the thin, wispy-bearded, pebble-bespectacled lad who came hurrying forward to greet me when I stepped on to the ground was all the proof I required that this was indeed not it. Another glance at the seven or eight bearded, scarved and duffel-coated characters behind him who had not, as I'd thought, been working but were struggling to prevent their tents from being blown away by the wind, was almost superfluous proof. That lot couldn't have hi-jacked a rowing boat. The MFV, I could see now, was down by the stern and listing heavily to starboard.

'Hallo, hallo, hallo,' said the character with the wispy beard. 'Good afternoon, good afternoon. By Jove, are we glad to see you!'

I looked at him, shook the outstretched hand, glanced at the listing boat and said mildly: 'You may be shipwrecked, but those are hardly what I'd call desperate straits. You're not on a deserted island. You're on the mainland. Help is at hand!'

'Oh, we know where we are all right.' He waved a deprecating hand. 'We put in here three days ago but I'm afraid our boat was holed in a storm during the night. Most unfortunate, most inconvenient.'

'Holed as she lay there? Just as she's moored now?'

'Yes, indeed.'

'Bad luck. Oxford or Cambridge?'

'Oxford, of course.' He seemed a bit huffed at my ignorance. 'Combined geological and marine biological party.'

'No shortage of rocks and sea-water hereabouts,' I agreed. 'How bad is the damage?'

'A holed plank. Sprung. Too much for us, I'm afraid.'

'All right for food?'

'Of course.'

'No transmitter?'

'Receiver only.'

'The helicopter pilot will radio for a shipwright and engineer to be sent out as soon as the weather moderates. Good-bye.'

His jaw fell about a couple of inches. 'You're off? Just like that?'

'Air-Sea Rescue. Vessel reported sinking last night.'

'Ah, that. We heard.'

'Thought you might be it. Glad for your sakes you're not. We've a lot of ground to cover yet.'

We continued eastwards towards the head of Loch Houron. Half-way there I said: 'Far enough. Let's have a look at those four islands out in the loch. We'll start with the most easterly one first of all – what's it called, yes, Eilean Oran – then make our way back towards the mouth of Loch Houron again.'

'You said you wanted to go all the way to the top.'

'I've changed my mind.'

'You're the man who pays the piper,' he said equably. He was a singularly incurious character, was young Lieutenant Williams. 'Northward ho for Eilean Oran.'

We were over Eilean Oran in three minutes. Compared to Eilean Oran, Alcatraz was a green and lovely holiday resort. Half a square mile of solid rock and never a blade of grass in sight. But there was a house. A house with smoke coming from its chimney. And beside it a boatshed, but no boat. The smoke meant an inhabitant, at least one inhabitant, and however he earned his living he certainly didn't do it from tilling the good earth. So he would have a boat, a boat for fishing for his livelihood, a boat for transportation to the mainland, for one certain thing among the manifold uncertainties of this world was that no passenger vessel had called at Eilean Oran since Robert Fulton had invented the steamboat. Williams set me down not twenty yards from the shed.

I rounded the corner of the boathouse and stopped abruptly. I always stop abruptly when I'm struck in the stomach by a battering-ram. After a few minutes I managed to whoop enough air into my lungs to let me straighten up again.

He was tall, gaunt, grey, in his middle sixties. He hadn't shaved for a week or changed his collarless shirt in a month. It wasn't a battering-ram he'd used after all, it was a gun, none of your fancy pistols, just a good old-fashioned double-barrelled twelve-bore shotgun, the kind of gun that at close range – six inches in this case – can give points even to the Peacemaker Colt when it comes to blowing your head off. He had it aimed at my right eye. It was like staring down the Mersey tunnel. When he spoke I could see he'd missed out on all those books that laud the unfailing courtesy of the Highlander.

'And who the hell are you?' he snarled.

'My name's Johnson. Put that gun away. I—'

'And what the hell do you want here?'

'How about trying the "Ceud Mile Failte" approach?' I said. 'You see it everywhere in those parts. A hundred thousand welcomes—'

'I won't ask again, mister.'

'Air-Sea Rescue. There's a missing boat—'

'I haven't seen any boat. You can just get to hell off my island.' He lowered his gun till it pointed at my stomach, maybe because he thought it would be more effective there or make for a less messy job when it came to burying me. 'Now!'

I nodded to the gun. 'You could get prison for this.'

'Maybe I could and maybe I couldn't. All I know is that I don't like strangers on my island and that Donald MacEachern protects his own.'

'And a very good job you make of it, too, Donald,' I said approvingly. The gun moved and I said quickly: 'I'm off. And don't bother saying "haste ye back" for I won't be.'

As we rose from the island Williams said: 'I just caught a glimpse. That was a gun he had there?'

'It wasn't the outstretched hand of friendship they're always talking about in those parts,' I said bitterly.

'Who is he? What is he?'

'He's an undercover agent for the Scottish Tourist Board in secret training to be their goodwill ambassador abroad. He's not any of those I'm looking for, that I know. He's not a nut case, either – he's as sane as you are. He's a worried man and a desperate one.'

'You didn't look in the shed. You wanted to find out about a boat. Maybe there was someone pointing a gun at him.'

'That was one of the thoughts that accounted for my rapid departure. I could have taken the gun from him.'

'You could have got your head blown off.'

'Guns are my business. The safety catch was in the "On" position.'

'Sorry.' Williams's face showed how out of his depth he was, he wasn't as good at concealing his expression as I was. 'What now?'

'Island number two to the west here.' I glanced at the chart. 'Craigmore.'

'You'll be wasting your time going there.' He sounded very positive. 'I've been there. Flew out a badly injured man to a Glasgow hospital.'

'Injured how?'

'He'd cut himself to the thigh-bone with a flensing knife. Infection had set in.'

'A flensing knife? For whales? I'd never heard—'

'For sharks. Basking sharks. They're as common as mackerel hereabouts. Catch them for their livers – you can get a ton of liver oil from a good-size one.' He pointed to the chart, to a tiny mark on the north coast. 'Craigmore village. Been abandoned, they say, from before the First World War. We're coming up to it now. Some of those old boys built their homes in the damnedest places.'

Some of those old boys had indeed built their homes in the damnedest places. If I'd been compelled to build a home either there or at the North Pole I'd have been hard put to it to make a choice. A huddle of four small grey houses built out near the tip of a foreland, several wicked reefs that made a natural breakwater, an even more wicked-looking entrance through the reefs and two fishing boats swinging and rolling wildly at anchor inside the reefs. One of the houses, the one nearest the shore, had had its entire seaward wall cut away. On the twenty or thirty feet of sloping ground that separated the house from the sea I could see three unmistakable sharks. A handful of men appeared at the open end of the house and waved at us.

'That's one way of making a living. Can you put me down?'

'What do you think, Mr Calvert?'

'I don't think you can.' Not unless he set his helicopter down on top of one of the little houses, that was. 'You winched this sick man up?'

'Yes. And I'd rather not winch you down, if you don't mind. Not in this weather and not without a crewman to help me. Unless you're desperate.'

'Not all that desperate. Would you vouch for them?'

'I'd vouch for them. They're a good bunch. I've met the boss, Tim Hutchinson, an Aussie about the size of a house, several times. Most of the fishermen on the west coast would vouch for them.'

'Fair enough. The next island is Ballara.'

We circled Ballara once. Once was enough. Not even a barnacle would have made his home in Ballara.

We were over the channel between Ballara and Dubh Sgeir now and the Beul nan Uamh was a sight to daunt even the stoutest-hearted fish. It certainly daunted me, five minutes in that lot whether in a boat or scuba suit and that would have been that. The ebb-tide and the wind were in head-on collision and the result was the most spectacular witches' cauldron I'd ever seen. There were no waves as such, just a bubbling swirling seething maelstrom of whirlpools, overfalls and races, running no way and every way, gleaming boiling white in the overfalls and races, dark and smooth and evil in the hearts of the whirlpools. Not a place to take Aunty Gladys out in a row-boat for a gentle paddle in the quiet even fall.

Oddly enough, close in to the east and south coast of Dubh Sgeir, one *could* have taken Aunty Gladys out. In those tidal races between islands a common but not yet clearly understood phenomenon frequently leaves an undisturbed stretch of water close in to one or other of the shores, calm and smooth and flat, a millpond with a sharply outlined boundary between it and the foaming races beyond. So it was here. For almost a mile between the most southerly and easterly headlands of Dubh Sgeir, for a distance of two or three hundred yards out from the shore, the waters were black and still. It was uncanny.

'Sure you really want to land here?' Williams asked.

'Is it tricky?'

'Easy. Helicopters often land on Dubh Sgeir. Not mine – others. It's just that you're likely to get the same reception here as you got on Eilean Oran. There are dozens of privately owned islands off the West Coast and none of them like uninvited visitors. The owner of Dubh Sgeir hates them.'

'This world-famous Highland hospitality becomes positively embarrassing at times. The Scotsman's home is his castle, eh?'

'There *is* a castle here. The ancestral home of the Clan Dalwhinnie. I think.'

'Dalwhinnie's a town, not a clan.'

'Well, something unpronounceable.' That was good, considering that he like as not hailed from Rhosllanerchrugog or Pontrhydfendgaid. 'He's the clan chief. Lord Kirkside. Ex-Lord Lieutenant of the shire. Very important citizen but a bit of a recluse now. Seldom leaves the place except to attend

Highland Games or go south about once a month to flay the Archbishop of Canterbury in the Lords.'

'Must be difficult for him to tell which place he's at, at times. I've heard of him. Used to have a very low opinion of the Commons and made a long speech to that effect every other day.'

'That's him. But not any more. Lost his older son – and his future son-in-law – in an air accident some time ago. Took the heart from the old boy, so they say. People in these parts think the world of him.'

We were round to the south of Dubh Sgeir now and suddenly the castle was in sight. Despite its crenallated battlements, round towers and embrasures, it didn't begin to rank with the Windsors and Balmorals of this world. A pocket castle. But the side had the Windsors and Balmorals whacked to the wide. It grew straight out of the top of a hundred and fifty foot cliff and if you leaned too far out of your bedroom window the first thing to stop your fall would be the rocks a long long way down. You wouldn't even bounce once.

Below the castle and a fair way to the right of it a cliff-fall belonging to some bygone age had created an artificial foreshore some thirty yards wide. From this, obviously at the cost of immense labour, an artificial harbour had been scooped out, the boulders and rubble having been used for the construction of a horseshoe breakwater with an entrance of not more than six or seven yards in width. At the inner end of this harbour a boathouse, no wider than the harbour entrance and less than twenty feet in length, had been constructed against the cliff face. A boathouse to berth a good-sized row-boat, no more.

Williams took his machine up until we were two hundred feet above the castle. It was built in the form of a hollow square with the landward side missing. The seaward side was dominated by two crenellated towers, one topped by a twenty-foot flagpole and flag, the other by an even taller TV mast. Aesthetically, the flagpole had it every time. Surprisingly the island was not as barren as it had appeared from the sea. Beginning some distance from the castle and extending clear to the cliff-bound northern shore of the island ran a two hundred yard wide stretch of what seemed to be flat smooth turf, not the bowling green standard but undoubtedly grass of the genuine variety as testified by the heads down position of a handful of goats that browsed close to the castle. Williams tried to land on the grass but the wind was too strong to allow him to hold position: he finally put down in the eastern lee of the castle, close but not too close to the cliff edge.

I got out, keeping a wary eye on the goats, and was rounding the landward corner of the castle when I almost literally bumped into the girl.

I've always known what to look for in a suddenly-encountered girl in a remote Hebridean Island. A kilt, of course, a Hebridean girl without a kilt was unthinkable, a Shetland two-piece and brown brogues: and that she would be a raven-haired beauty with wild, green, fey eyes went without saying. Her name would be Deirdre. This one wasn't like that at all, except for the eyes, which were neither green nor fey but certainly looked wild enough. What little I could see of them, that was. Her blonde hair was cut in the uniform peekaboo scalloped style of the day, the one where the long side hair meets under the chin and the central fringe is hacked off at eyebrow level, a coiffure which in any wind above Force 1 allows no more than ten per cent of the face to be seen at any one time. Below hair level she wore a horizontally striped blue and white sailor's jersey and faded blue denim pants that must have been fixed on with a portable sewing machine as I didn't see how else she could have got into them. Her tanned feet were bare. It was comforting to see that the civilizing influence of television reached even the remoter outposts of empire.

I said: 'Good afternoon, Miss – um—'

'Engine failure?' she asked coldly.

'Well, no—'

'Mechanical failure? Of any kind? No? Then this is private property. I must ask you to leave. At once, please.'

There seemed to be little for me here. An outstretched hand and a warm smile of welcome and she'd have been on my list of suspects at once. But this was true to established form, the weary stranger at the gates receiving not the palm of the hand but the back of it. Apart from the fact that she lacked a blunderbuss and had a much better figure, she had a great deal in common with Mr MacEachern. I bent forward to peer through the windblown camouflage of blonde hair. She looked as if she had spent most of the night and half the morning down in the castle wine cellars. Pale face, pale lips, dark smudges under the blue-grey eyes. But clear blue-grey eyes.

'What the hell's the matter with you?' she demanded.

'Nothing. The end of a dream. Deirdre would never have talked like that. Where's your old man?'

'My old man?' The one eye I could see had the power turned up to its maximum shrivelling voltage. 'You mean my father?'

'Sorry. Lord Kirkside.' It was no feat to guess that she was Lord Kirkside's daughter, hired help are too ignorant to have the execrable manners of their aristocratic betters.

'I'm Lord Kirkside.' I turned round to see the owner of the deep voice behind me, a tall rugged-looking character in his fifties, hawk nose, jutting grey eyebrows and moustache, grey tweeds, grey deer-stalker, hawthorn stick in hand. 'What's the trouble, Sue?'

Sue. I might have known. Exit the last vestige of the Hebridean dream. I said: 'My name is Johnson. Air-Sea Rescue. There was a boat, the *Moray Rose*, in bad trouble somewhere south of Skye. If she'd been not under command but still afloat she might have come drifting this way. We wondered—'

'And Sue was going to fling you over the cliff before you had a chance to open your mouth?' He smiled down affectionately at his daughter. 'That's my Sue. I'm afraid she doesn't like newspapermen.'

'Some do and some don't. But why pick on me?'

'When you were twenty-one could you, as the saying goes, tell a newspaperman from a human being? I couldn't. But I can now, a mile away. I can also tell a genuine Air-Sea Rescue helicopter when I see one. And so should you too, young lady. I'm sorry, Mr Johnson, we can't help you. My men and I spent several hours last night patrolling the cliff-tops to see if we could see anything. Lights, flares, anything. Nothing, I'm afraid.'

'Thank you, sir. I wish we had more voluntary co-operation of this kind.' From where I stood I could see, due south, the gently rocking masts of the Oxford field expedition's boat in Little Horseshoe Bay. The boat itself and the tents beyond were hidden behind the rocky eastern arm of the bay. I said to Lord Kirkside: 'But why newspapermen, sir? Dubh Sgeir isn't quite as accessible as Westminster.'

'Indeed, Mr Johnson.' He smiled, not with his eyes. 'You may have heard of – well, of our family tragedy. My elder boy, Jonathan, and John Rollinson – Sue's fiancé.'

I knew what was coming. And after all those months she had those smudges under her eys. She must have loved him a lot. I could hardly believe it.

'I'm no newspaperman, sir. Prying isn't my business.' It wasn't my business, it was my life, the *raison d'être* for my existence. But now wasn't the time to tell him.

'The air accident. Jonathan had his own private Beechcraft.' He waved towards the stretch of green turf running to the Northern cliffs. 'He took off from here that morning. They – the reporters – wanted on-the-spot reporting. They came by helicopter and boat – there's a landing stage to the west.' Again the mirthless smile. 'They weren't well received. Care for a drink? You and your pilot?' Lord Kirkside, for all the reputation Williams had given him, seemed to be cast in a different mould from his daughter and Mr Donald MacEachern: on the other hand, as the Archbishop of Canterbury knew to his cost, Lord Kirkside was a very much tougher citizen than either his daughter or Mr MacEachern.

'Thank you, sir. I appreciate that. But we haven't many hours of daylight left.'

'Of course, of course. How thoughtless of me. But you can't have much hope left by this time.'

'Frankly, none. But, well, you know how it is, sir.'

'We'll cross our fingers for that one chance in a million. Good luck, Mr Johnson.' He shook my hand and turned away. His daughter hesitated then held out her hand and smiled. A fluke of the wind had blown the hair off her face, and when she smiled like that, sooty eyes or not, the end of Deirdre and the Hebridean dream didn't seem to be of so much account after all. I went back to the helicopter.

'We're getting low on both fuel and time,' Williams said. 'Another hour or so and we'll have the dark with us. Where now, Mr Calvert?'

'North. Follow this patch of grass – seems it used to be used as a light aircraft runway – out over the edge of the cliff. Take your time.'

So he did, taking his time as I'd asked him, then continued on a northward course for another ten minutes. After we were out of sight of watchers on any of the islands we came round in a great half circle to west and south and east and headed back for home.

The sun was down and the world below was more night than day as we came in to land on the sandy cove on the eastern side of the Isle of Torbay. I could just vaguely distinguish the blackness of the tree-clad island, the faint silvery gleam of the sand and the semicircular whiteness where the jagged reef of rocks fringed the seaward approach to the cove. It looked a very dicey approach indeed to me but Williams was as unworried as a mother at a baby-show who has already slipped the judge a five-pound note. Well, if he wasn't going to worry, neither was I: I knew nothing about helicopters but I knew enough about men to recognize a superb pilot when

I sat beside one. All I had to worry about was that damned walk back through those Stygian woods. One thing, I didn't have to run this time.

Williams reached up his hand to flick on the landing lights but the light came on a fraction of a second before his fingers touched the switch. Not from the helicopter but from the ground. A bright light, a dazzling light, at least a five-inch searchlight located between the high-water line of the cove and the tree-line beyond. For a moment the light wavered, then steadied on the cockpit of the helicopter, making the interior bright as the light from the noon-day sun. I twisted my head to one side to avoid the glare. I saw Williams throw up a hand to protect his eyes, then slump forward wearily, dead in his seat, as the white linen of his shirt turned to red and the centre of his chest disintegrated. I flung myself forwards and downwards to try to gain what illusory shelter I could from the cannonading sub-machine shells shattering the windscreen. The helicopter was out of control, dipping sharply forwards and spinning slowly on its axis. I reached out to grab the controls from the dead man's hands, but even as I did the trajectory of the bullets changed, either because the man with the machine-gun had altered his aim or because he'd been caught off-balance by the sudden dipping of the helicopter. An abruptly mad cacophony of sound, the iron clangour of steel-nosed bullets smashing into the engine casing mingled with the banshee ricochet of spent and mangled shells. The engine stopped, stopped as suddenly as if the ignition had been switched off. The helicopter was completely out of control, lifeless in the sky. It wasn't going to be in the sky much longer but there was nothing I could do about it. I braced myself for the jarring moment of impact when we struck the water, and when the impact came it was not just jarring, it was shattering to a degree I would never have anticipated. We'd landed not in the water but on the encircling reef of rocks.

I tried to get at the door but couldn't make it, we'd landed nose down and facing seawards on the outside of the reefs and from the position where I'd been hurled under the instrument panel the door was above and beyond my reach. I was too dazed, too weak, to make any real effort to get at it. Icy water poured in through the smashed windscreen and the fractured floor of the fuselage. For a moment everything was as silent as the grave, the hiss of the flooding waters seemed only to emphasize the silence then the machine-gun started again. The shells smashed through the lower after part of the fuselage behind me and went out through the top of the windscreen above me. Twice I felt angry tugs on the right shoulder of my coat and I tried to bury my head even more deeply into the freezing waters. Then, due probably to a combination of an accumulation of water in the nose and the effect of the fusillade of bullets aft, the helicopter lurched forwards, stopped momentarily, then slid off the face of the reef and fell like a stone, nose first, to the bottom of the sea.

Chapter Five

Wednesday: dusk – 8.40 p.m.

Among the more ridiculous and wholly unsubstantiated fictions perpetuated by people who don't know what they are talking about is the particularly half-witted one that death by drowning is peaceful, easy and, in fact, downright pleasant. It's not. It's a terrible way to die. I know, because I was drowning and I didn't like it one little bit. My ballooning head felt as if it were being pumped full of compressed air, my ears and eyes ached savagely, my nostrils, mouth and stomach were full of sea water and my bursting lungs felt as if someone had filled them with petrol and struck a match. Maybe if I opened my mouth, maybe if to relieve that flaming agony that was my lungs I took that one great gasping breath that would be the last I would ever take, maybe then it would be quiet and pleasant and peaceful. On the form to date, I couldn't believe it.

The damned door was jammed. After the beating the fuselage had taken, first of all in smashing into the reef and then into the sea-bed it would be a miracle if it hadn't jammed. I pushed the door, I pulled at it, I beat at it with my clenched fists. It stayed jammed. The blood roared and hissed in my ears, the flaming vice around my chest was crushing my ribs and lungs, crushing the life out of me. I braced both feet on the instrument panel, laid both hands on the door handle. I thrust with my legs and twisted with my hands, using the power and the leverage a man can use only when he knows he is dying. The door handle sheared, the thrust of my legs carried me backwards and upwards toward the after end of the fuselage and suddenly my lungs could take no more. Death couldn't be worse than this agony. The air rushed out through my water-filled mouth and nostrils and I sucked in this one great gasping breath, this lungful of sea-water, this last I would ever take.

It wasn't a lungful of water, it was a lungful of air. Noxious compressed air laden with the fumes of petrol and oil, but air for all that. Not the tangy salt-laden air of the Western Isles, not the wine-laden air of the Ægean, the pine-laden air of Norway or the sparkling champagne air of the high Alps. All those I'd tasted and all of them put together were a thin and anaemic substitute for this marvellous mixture of nitrogen and oxygen and petrol and oil that had been trapped in an air pocket under the undamaged upper rear part of the helicopter's fuselage, the only part of the plane that hadn't been riddled by machine-gun bullets. This was air as it ought to be.

The water level was around my neck. I took half a dozen deep whooping breaths, enough to ease the fire in my lungs and the roaring and hissing and dizziness in my head to tolerable levels, then pushed myself backwards and upwards to the extreme limit of the fuselage. The water was at chest level now. I moved a hand around in the blind darkness to try to estimate the amount of air available to me. Impossible to judge accurately, but enough, I guessed, compressed as it was, to last for ten to fifteen minutes.

I moved across to the left of the fuselage, took a deep breath and pushed myself forwards and downwards. Eight feet behind the pilot's seat was the passenger door, maybe I could force that. I found it right away, not the door but the opening where the door had been. The impact that had jammed the door on the righthand side where I'd been had burst this door open. I pushed myself back to the upper part of the fuselage again and helped myself to a few more deep breaths of that compressed air. It didn't taste quite so good as it had done the first time.

Now that I knew I could go at any time, I was in no hurry to leave. Up above, guns in hand, those men would be waiting and if there was one outstanding attribute that characterized their attitude to work on hand, it was a single-minded thoroughness. Where those lads were concerned, a job half done was no job at all. They could only have come there by boat and that boat would have been very nearby. By this time it would be even nearer by, it would be sitting directly over the spot where the helicopter had gone down and the crew wouldn't be sitting around with drinks in their hands congratulating themselves on their success, they'd be lining the side with searchlights or flashes and waiting to see if anyone would break surface. With their guns in their hands.

If I ever got back to the *Firecrest* again, if I ever got in touch with Uncle Arthur again, I wondered dully what I would say to him. Already I'd lost the *Nantesville*, already I'd been responsible for the deaths of Baker and Delmont, already I'd given away to the unknown enemy the secret of my identity – if that hadn't been obvious after the fake customs officers had smashed our transmitter it was bitterly obvious now – and now I'd lost Lieutenant Scott Williams his life and the Navy a valuable helicopter. Of Uncle Arthur's forty-eight hours only twelve were left now, and nothing could be more certain than when Uncle Arthur had finished with me, I wouldn't be allowed even those twelve hours. After Uncle Arthur had finished with me my days as an investigator would be finished, and finished for ever; with the kind of references he'd give me I wouldn't even qualify as a store detective in a street barrow. Not that it would make any difference what Uncle Arthur thought now. Baker and Delmont and Williams were gone. There was a heavy debt that had to be paid and the matter was out of Uncle Arthur's hands now. On the form to date, I thought bleakly, there wasn't one bookmaker in the land who would have given odds of one in a thousand of that debt ever being repaid. Only a fool bets against a certainty.

I wondered vaguely how long the men up top would wait – my conviction that they would be waiting was absolute. And then I felt a dry salty taste in my mouth that had nothing to do with the steadily deteriorating quality of air. It was pretty foul by this time, but a man can survive a surprisingly long time in foul air and there was enough oxygen left in that heavily tainted atmosphere to last me for a good few minutes yet.

The question was not how long they would wait but how long I could wait. Or had I already waited too long? I could feel the panic in my throat like some solid lump in my windpipe completely obstructing my breathing and had to make a conscious physical effort to force it down.

I tried to recall all I could from my marine salvage days. How long had

I been under water and how deep down was I? How long had that dive down from the surface of the sea to the bottom taken?

Under those conditions time loses all meaning. Say forty seconds. Just over half-way down I'd taken my last gulp of air before the water in the fuselage had flooded over my head. And then a minute, probably a minute and a half, fighting with that jammed door. Since then a minute to recover, half a minute to locate that open door, and then how long since? Six minutes, seven? Not less than seven. I couldn't reckon on a total of less than ten minutes. The lump was back in my throat again.

How deep was I? That was the life-or-death question. I could tell from the pressure that I was pretty deep. But how deep? Ten fathoms? Fifteen? Twenty? I tried to recall the chart of Torbay Sound. There were eighty fathoms in the deepest channel and the channel was pretty close to the southern shore at this point, so that the water was steep-to. God above, I might even be in twenty-five fathoms. If I was, well that was it. Finish. How did the decompression tables go again? At thirty fathoms a man who has been under water for ten minutes requires to spend eighteen minutes for decompression stops on the way up. When you breathe air under pressure, the excess nitrogen is stored in the tissues: when you begin to surface this nitrogen is carried by the blood-stream to the lungs and is eliminated in respiration: and if you rise too rapidly respiration can't cope with it and nitrogen bubbles form in the blood, causing the agonizing and crippling diver's bends. Even at twenty fathoms I'd require a six-minute halt for decompression on the way up and if there was one certain fact in life it was that decompression stops were out for me. I'd be a broken man. What I did know for certain was that every additional second I remained there would make the bends all the more agonizing and crippling when they finally struck. All at once the prospect of surfacing beneath the steady guns and the pitiless eyes of the men above seemed positively attractive compared to the alternative. I took several deep breaths to get as much oxygen as possible into my blood-stream, exhaled to the fullest extent, took a long final breath to fill every last cubic millimetre in every last nook and cranny in my lungs, dived under the water, pushed my way out through the doorway and made for the surface.

I'd lost count of time on the way down and I now lost all count of time on the way up. I swam slowly and steadily using enough power to assist my progress through the water, but not so much as prematurely to use up all the stored oxygen. Every few seconds I let a little air escape from my mouth, not much, just enough to ease the pressure in my lungs. I looked up but the waters above me were as black as ink, there could have been fifty fathoms above my head for any trace of light I could see. And then suddenly, quite some time before the air supply was exhausted and before my lungs had begun to hurt again, the water was a shade less than pitch black and my head struck something hard and unyielding. I grabbed it, held on, surfaced, sucked in some lungfuls of that cold, salt, wonderful air and waited for the decompression pains to start, those sharply agonizing twinges in the joints of the limbs. But none came. I couldn't have been more than fifteen fathoms down and even then I should have felt something. It had probably been something nearer ten.

During the past ten minutes my mind had taken as much a beating as any other part of me but it would have to have been in very much poorer shape than it was for me not to recognize what I was clinging to. A boat's rudder, and if any confirmation had been required the milkily phosphorescent water being turned up by the two slowly turning screws a couple of feet ahead of me would have been all that was required. I'd surfaced right under their boat. I was lucky. I might have surfaced right under one of their propellers and had my head cut in half. Even now, if the man at the wheel suddenly decided to go astern I'd be sucked into the vortex of one or other of the screws and end up like something that had passed through a turnip-cutting machine. But I'd been through too much to cross any bridges before I came to them.

Off to port I could see, sharply illuminated by a couple of powerful lights from the boat's deck, the reef where we'd crashed. We were about forty yards away and, relative to the reefs, stationary in the water, the engines turning just enough to maintain the boat's position against the effect of wind and tide. Now and again a searchlight patrolled the dark waters all around. I couldn't see anything of the men on deck, but I didn't have to be told what they were doing, they were waiting and watching and the safety catches would be off. Nor could I see anything of the boat itself but I made up my mind that, even though I couldn't recognize it, I'd know it if I ever came across it again. I took out the knife from the sheath behind my neck and cut a deep vee notch in the trailing edge of the rudder.

For the first time, I heard voices. I heard four voices and I had no difficulty in the world in identifying any of them. If I lived to make Methuselah look a teenager I'd never forget any one of them.

'Nothing on your side, Quinn?' Captain Imrie, the man who had organized the manhunt for me aboard the *Nantesville*.

'Nothing on my side, Captain.' I could feel the hairs rise on the nape of my neck. Quinn. Durran. The bogus customs officer. The man who had almost, but not quite, strangled me to death.

'Your side, Jacques?' Captain Imrie again.

'Nothing, sir.' The machine-pistol specialist. 'Eight minutes since we've been here, fifteen since they went under. A man would require pretty good lungs to stay down that long, Captain.'

'Enough,' Imrie said. 'There'll be a bonus for all of us for this night's work. Kramer?"

'Captain Imrie?' A voice as guttural as Imrie's own.

'Full ahead. Up the Sound.'

I thrust myself backwards and dived deep. The waters above my head boiled into turbulent, phosphorescent life. I stayed deep, maybe ten feet down, heading for the reef. How long I swam like that, I don't know. Certainly less than a minute, my lungs weren't what they used to be, not even what they had been fifteen minutes ago: but when I was forced to the surface, I'd my dark oilskin over my head.

I needn't have bothered. I could see the faintly shimmering outline of the disappearing wake, no more. The searchlights were extinguished; when Captain Imrie decided a job was finished, then that job was finished. Predictably, the boat was in complete darkness with neither interior nor navigation lights showing.

I turned and swam slowly towards the reef. I reached a rock and clung to it until a measure of strength returned to my aching muscles, to my exhausted body. I would not have believed that fifteen minutes could have taken so much out of a man. I stayed there for five minutes. I could have stayed there for an hour. But time was not on my side. I slipped into deep water again and made for the shore.

Three times I tried and three times I failed to pull myself up from the rubber dinghy over the gunwale of the *Firecrest*. Four feet, no more. Just four feet. A Matterhorn. A ten-year-old could have done it. But not Calvert. Calvert was an old, old man.

I called out for Hunslett, but Hunslett did not come. Three times I called, but he did not come. The *Firecrest* was dark and still and lifeless. Where the hell was he? Asleep? Ashore? No, not ashore, he'd promised to stay aboard in case word came through at any time from Uncle Arthur. Asleep, then, asleep in his cabin. I felt the blind unreasoning anger rise. This was too much, after what I had been through this was too much. Asleep. I shouted at the top of my voice and hammered feebly on the steel hull with the butt of my Luger. But he didn't come.

The fourth time I made it. It was touch and go, but I made it. For a few seconds, dinghy painter in hand, I teetered on my stomach on the edge of the gunwale then managed to drag myself aboard. I secured the painter and went in search of Hunslett. There were words I wished to have with Hunslett.

I never used them. He wasn't aboard. I searched the *Firecrest* from forepeak to the after storage locker, but no Hunslett. No signs of a hasty departure, no remnants of a meal on the saloon table or unwashed dishes in the galley, no signs of any struggle, everything neat and in good order. Everything as it ought to have been. Except that there was no Hunslett.

For a minute or two I sat slumped in the saloon settee trying to figure out a reason for his absence, but only for a minute or two. I was in no condition to figure out anything. Wearily I made my way out to the upper deck and brought dinghy and outboard over the side. No fancy tricks about securing them to the anchor chain this time: apart from the fact that it was, the way I felt, physically impossible, the time for that was past. I deflated the dinghy and stowed it, along with the outboard, in the after locker. And if someone came aboard and started looking? If someone came aboard and started looking he'd get a bullet through him. I didn't care if he claimed to be a police superintendent or an assistant commissioner or the top customs official in the country, he'd get a bullet through him, in the arm or leg, say, and I'd listen to his explanations afterwards. If it was one of my friends, one of my friends from *Nantesville* or the reef back there, he got it through the head.

I went below. I felt sick. The helicopter was at the bottom of the sea. The pilot was down there with it, half his chest shot away by machine-gun bullets. I'd every right to feel sick. I stripped off my clothes and towelled myself dry and the very action of towelling seemed to drain away what little strength was left to me. Sure I'd had a hard time in the last hour, all this running and slipping and stumbling through the dark woods, locating and blowing up the dinghy and dragging it over those damned seaweed covered boulders had taken it out of me, but I was supposed to be fit, it shouldn't have left me like this. I was sick, but the sickness was in the heart and mind, not in the body.

I went into my cabin and laboriously dressed myself in fresh clothes, not forgetting the Paisley scarf. The rainbow coloured bruises that Quinn had left on my neck had now swollen and spread to such an extent that I had to bring the scarf right up to the lobes of my ears to hide them. I looked in the mirror. It might have been my grandfather staring back at me. My grandfather on his deathbed. My face had that drawn and waxy look that one normally associates with approaching dissolution. Not an all-over waxiness though, there was no blood on my face now but the pine needles had left their mark, I looked like someone with galloping impetigo. I felt like someone with galloping bubonic plague.

I checked that the Luger and the little Lilliput – I'd put them both back in their waterproof covering after leaving Dubh Sgeir – were still in working order. They were. In the saloon I poured myself a stiff three fingers of whisky. It went down my throat like a ferret down a burrow after a rabbit, one moment there, the next vanished in the depths. The weary old red corpuscles hoisted themselves to their feet and started trudging around again. It seemed a reasonable assumption that if I encouraged them with some more of the same treatment they might even break into a slow gallop and I had just closed my hand around the bottle when I heard the sound of an approaching engine. I put the bottle back in the rack, switched out the saloon lights – although they would have been invisible from outside through the velvet curtains – and took up position behind the open saloon door.

I was pretty sure the precautions were unnecessary, ten to one this was Hunslett coming back from shore, but why hadn't he taken the dinghy, still slung on the davits aft? Probably someone, for what Hunslett had regarded as an excellent reason, had persuaded him to go ashore and was now bringing him back.

The motor-boat's engine slowed, went into neutral, astern, then neutral again. A slight bump, the murmur of voices, the sound of someone clambering aboard and then the engine opening up again.

The footfalls passed over my head as the visitor – there was only one set of footfalls – made his way towards the wheelhouse door. The springy confident step of a man who knew what he was about. There was only one thing wrong with that springy confident step. It didn't belong to Hunslett. I flattened myself against the bulkhead, took out the Luger, slid off the safety catch and prepared to receive my visitor in what I had now come to regard as the best traditions of the Highlands.

I heard the click as the wheelhouse door opened, the louder click as it was shut by a firm hand. A pool of light from a flashlamp preceded the visitor down the four steps from the wheelhouse to the saloon. He paused at the foot of the steps and the light moved away as he made to locate the lightswitch. I stepped round the door and did three things at once – I hooked an arm around his neck, brought up a far from gentle knee into the small of his back and ground the muzzle of the Luger into his right ear. Violent stuff, but not unnecessarily violent stuff, it might have been my old friend Quinn. The gasp of pain was enough to show that it wasn't.

'This isn't a hearing aid you feel, friend. It's a Luger pistol. You're one pound pressure from a better world. Don't make me nervous.'

The better world seemed to have no appeal for him. He didn't make me nervous. He made an odd gurgling noise in his throat, he was trying either to speak or breathe, but he stood motionless, head and back arched. I eased the pressure a little.

'Put that light switch on with your left hand. Slowly. Carefully.'

He was very slow, very careful. The saloon flooded with light.

'Raise your hands above your head. As high as you can reach.'

He was a model prisoner, this one, he did exactly as he was told. I turned him round, propelled him into the centre of the room and told him to face me.

He was of medium height, nattily dressed in an astrakhan coat and a fur Cossack hat. He had a beautifully trimmed white beard and moustache, with a perfectly symmetrical black streak in the centre of the beard, the only one of its kind I had ever seen. The tanned face was red, either from anger or near-suffocation. From both, I decided. He lowered his hands without permission, sat on the settee, pulled out a monocle, screwed it into his right eye and stared at me with cold fury. I gave him look for look, stare for stare, pocketed the Luger, poured a whisky and handed it to Uncle Arthur. Rear-Admiral Sir Arthur Arnford-Jason, KCB and all the rest of the alphabet.

'You should have knocked, sir,' I said reproachfully.

'I should have knocked.' His voice sounded half-strangled, maybe I had exerted more pressure than had been necessary. 'Do you always greet your guests this way?'

'I don't have guests, sir. I don't have friends, either. Not in the Western Isles. All I have is enemies. Anyone who comes through that door is an enemy. I didn't expect to see you here, sir.'

'I hope not. In view of that performance, I hope not.' He rubbed his throat, drank some whisky and coughed. 'Didn't expect to be here myself. Do you know how much bullion was aboard the *Nantesville*?'

'Close on a million, I understand.'

'That's what I understood. Eight millions! Think of it, eight million pounds' worth. All this gold that's being shovelled back from Europe into the vaults at Fort Knox usually goes in small lots, 108 lb. ingots at a time. For safety. For security. In case anything goes wrong. But the Bank knew that nothing could go wrong this time, they knew our agents were aboard, they were behind with their payments, so they cleverly loaded fourteen hundred and forty ingots without telling anyone. Eight million. The Bank is hopping mad. And everyone is taking it out on me.'

And he'd come up here to take it out on me. I said: 'You should have let me know. That you were coming.'

'I tried to. You failed to keep your noon-day schedule. The most elementary of crimes, Calvert, and the most serious. You failed to keep a schedule. You or Hunslett. Then I knew things were going from bad to worse. I knew I had to take over myself. So I came by plane and RAF rescue launch.' That would have been the high-speed launch I'd seen taking a bad battering in the Sound as we had headed down towards the cove. 'Where's Hunslett?'

'I don't know, sir.'

'You don't know?' He was using his quiet unemphatic tone, the one I didn't care for very much. 'You're out of your depth in this one, Calvert, aren't you?'

'Yes, sir. I'm afraid he's been removed by force. I'm not sure how. What have you been doing in the past two hours, sir?'

'Explain yourself.' I wished he'd stop screwing that damned monocle into his eye. It was no affectation, that monocle, he was nearly blind on that side, but it was an irritating mannerism. At that moment, anything would have irritated me.

'That RAF launch that dropped you off here just now. It should have been here at least two hours ago. Why didn't you come aboard then?'

'I did. We almost ran the *Firecrest* down in the darkness as we came round the headland. No one here. So I went and had some dinner. Nothing but baked beans aboard this damned boat as far as I could see.'

'The Columbia hotel wouldn't offer you much more. Toast below the beans, if you were lucky.' The Columbia was Torbay's only hotel.

'I had smoked trout, filet mignon and an excellent bottle of hock. I dined aboard the *Shangri-la*.' This with the slight hint of a smile. Uncle Arthur's Achilles' heel was showing again: Uncle Arthur loved a lord like nobody's business, and a knight with a seven-figure income was as good as a lord any day.

'The *Shangri-la*?' I stared at him, then remembered. 'Of course. You told me. You know Lady Skouras well. No, you said you knew her very well and her husband well. How is my old Sir Anthony?'

'Very well,' he said coldly. Uncle Arthur had as much humour as the next man, but discussing titled millionaires in tones of levity was not humorous.

'And Lady Skouras?'

He hesitated. 'Well—'

'Not so well. Pale, drawn, unhappy, with dark smudges under her eyes. Not unlike myself. Her husband mistreats her and mistreats her badly. Mentally and physically. He humiliated her in front of a group of men last night. And she had rope burns on her arms. Why would she have rope burns on her arms, Sir Arthur?'

'Impossible. Quite fantastic. I knew the former Lady Skouras, the one who died this year in hospital. She—'

'She was undergoing treatment in a mental hospital. Skouras as good as told me.'

'No matter. She adored him. He adored her. A man can't change like that. Sir Anthony – Sir Anthony's a gentleman.'

'Is he? Tell me how he made his last millions. You saw Lady Skouras, didn't you?'

'I saw her,' he said slowly. 'She was late. She arrived with the filet mignon.' He didn't seem to find anything funny in that. 'She didn't look very well and she's a bruise on her right temple. She'd fallen climbing aboard from the tender and hit her head against a guardrail.'

'Hit her head against her husband's fist, more like. To get back to the first time you boarded the *Firecrest* this evening. Did you search it?'

'I searched it. All except the after cabin. It was locked. I assumed there was something in there you didn't want chance callers to see.'

'There was something in there that callers, not chance, didn't want *you* to see,' I said slowly. 'Hunslett. Hunslett under guard. They were waiting for word of my death, then they'd have killed Hunslett or kept him prisoner. If word came through that I hadn't been killed, then they'd have waited until my return and taken me prisoner too. Or killed us both. For by then they would have known that I knew too much to be allowed to live. It takes time, a long time, to open up a strong-room and get all those tons of gold out and they know their time is running out. They're desperate now. But they still think of everything.'

'They were waiting for word of your death,' Uncle Arthur said mechanically. 'I don't understand.'

'That helicopter you laid on for me, sir. We were shot down to-night after sunset. The pilot's dead and the machine is at the bottom of the sea. They believe me to be dead also.'

'I see. You go from strength to strength, Calvert.' The absence of reaction was almost total, maybe he was getting punch-drunk by this time, more likely he was considering the precise phraseology that would return me to the ranks of the unemployed with economy and dispatch. He lit a long, thin and very black cheroot and puffed meditatively. 'When we get back to London remind me to show you my confidential report on you.'

'Yes, sir.' So this was how it was coming.

'I was having dinner with the Under-Secretary just forty-eight hours ago. One of the things he asked me was which country had the best agents in Europe. Told him I'd no idea. But I told him who I thought, on the balance of probabilities, was the best agent in Europe. Philip Calvert.'

'That was very kind of you, sir.' If I could remove that beard, whisky, cheroot and monocle, at least three of which were obscuring his face at any given moment, his expression might have given me some faint clue as to what was going on in that devious mind. 'You were going to fire me thirty-six hours ago.'

'If you believe that,' Uncle Arthur said calmly, 'You'll believe anything.' He puffed out a cloud of foul smoke and went on: 'one of the comments in your report states: "Unsuitable for routine investigation. Loses interest and becomes easily bored. Operates at his best only under extreme pressure. At this level he is unique." It's on the files, Calvert. I don't cut off my right hand.'

'No, sir. Do you know what your are, sir?'

'A Machiavellian old devil,' Uncle Arthur said with some satisfaction. 'You know what's going on?'

'Yes, sir.'

'Pour me another whisky, my boy, a large one, and tell me what's happened, what you know and what you think you know.'

So I poured him another whisky, a large one, and told him what had happened, what I knew and as much of what I thought I knew as seemed advisable to tell him.

He heard me out, then said: 'Loch Houron, you think?'

'Loch Houron it must be. I spoke to no one else, anywhere else, and to the best of my knowledge no one else saw me. Someone recognized me. Or someone transmitted my description. By radio. It must have been by radio. The boat that was waiting for Williams and myself came from Torbay or somewhere near Torbay, a boat from Loch Houron could never have made it to the eastern end of the Sound of Torbay in five times the time we took. Somewhere near here, on land or sea, is a transceiver set. Somewhere out on Loch Houron there's another.'

'This University expedition boat you saw on the south shore of Loch Houron. This alleged University expedition. It would have a radio transmitter aboard.'

'No, sir. Boys with beards.' I rose, pulled back the saloon curtains on both sides, then sat down again. 'I told you their boat was damaged and listing.

She'd been riding moored fore and aft in plenty of water. They didn't hole it themselves and it wasn't holed by any act of nature. Somebody kindly obliged. Another of those odd little boating incidents that occur with such profusion up and down the west coast.'

'Why did you pull those curtains back?'

'Another of those odd little boating incidents, sir. One that's about to happen. Some time to-night people will be coming aboard. Hunslett and I, those people think, are dead. At least, I'm dead and Hunslett is dead or a prisoner. But they can't leave an abandoned *Firecrest* at anchor to excite suspicion and invite investigation. So they'll come in a boat, up anchor, and take the *Firecrest* out into the Sound, followed by their own boat. Once there, they'll slice through the flexible salt-water cooling intake, open the salt-water cock, take to their own boat and lift their hats as the *Firecrest* goes down to join the helicopter. As far as the big wide innocent world is concerned, Hunslett and I will just have sailed off into the sunset.'

'And the gulfs will have washed you down,' Uncle Arthur nodded. 'You are very sure of this, Calvert?'

'You might say I'm absolutely certain.'

'Then why open those blasted curtains?'

'The scuttling party may be coming from anywhere and they may not come for hours. The best time to scuttle a boat in close waters is at slack tide, when you can be sure that it will settle exactly where you want it to settle, and slack tide is not until one o'clock this morning. But if someone comes panting hotfoot aboard soon after those curtains are opened, then that will be proof enough that the radio transmitter we're after, and our friends who are working the transmitter, are somewhere in this bay, ashore or afloat.'

'How will it be proof?' Uncle Arthur said irritably. 'Why should they come, as you say, panting hotfoot?'

'They know they have Hunslett. At least, I assume they have, I can't think of any other reason for his absence. They think they know I'm dead, but they can't be sure. Then they see the beckoning oil lamp in the window. What is this, they say to themselves, Calvert back from the dead? Or a third, or maybe even a third and a fourth colleague of Calvert and Hunslett that we wot not of? Whether it's me or my friends, they must be silenced. And silenced at once. Wouldn't you come panting hotfoot?'

'There's no need to treat the matter with levity,' Uncle Arthur complained.

'In your own words, sir, if you can believe that, you can believe anything.'

'You should have consulted me first, Calvert.' Uncle Arthur shifted in his seat, an almost imperceptible motion, though his expression didn't change. He was a brilliant administrator, but the more executive side of the business, the sand-bagging and pushing of people off high cliffs, wasn't exactly in his line. 'I've told you that I came to take charge.'

'Sorry, Sir Arthur. You'd better change that report, hadn't you? The bit about the best in Europe, I mean.'

'*Touché, touché, touché*,' he grumbled. 'And they're coming at us out of the dark, is that it? On their way now. Armed men. Killers. Shouldn't we – shouldn't we be preparing to defend ourselves? Dammit, man, I haven't even got a gun.'

'You won't need one. You may not agree with me.' I handed him the

Luger. He took it, checked the indicator and that the safety catch moved easily, then sat there holding it awkwardly in his hand.

'Shouldn't we move, Calvert? We're sitting targets here.'

'They won't be here for some time. The nearest house or boat is a mile away to the east. They'll be pushing wind and tide and they daren't use a motor. Whether they're rowing a boat or paddling a rubber dinghy they have a long haul ahead of them. Time's short, sir. We have a lot to do to-night. To get back to Loch Houron. The expedition's out, they couldn't pirate a dinghy, far less five ocean-going freighters. Our friend Donald MacEachern acts in a highly suspicious fashion, he's got the facilities there, he's dead worried and he might have had half a dozen guns at his back while he had his in my front. But it was all too good to be true, professionals wouldn't lay it on the line like that.'

'Maybe that's how professionals would expect a fellow-professional to react. And you said he's worried.'

'Maybe the fish aren't biting. Maybe he's involved, but not directly. Then there's the shark-fishers. They have the boats, the facilities and, heaven knows, they're tough enough. Against that, they've been based there for years, the place is littered with sharks – it should be easy enough to check if regular consignments of liver oil are sent to the mainland – and they're well known and well thought of along the coast. They'll bear investigating. Then there's Dubh Sgeir. Lord Kirkside and his lovely daughter Sue.'

'Lady Susan,' Uncle Arthur said. It's difficult to invest an impersonal, inflectionless voice with cool reproach, but he managed it without any trouble. 'I know Lord Kirkside, of course' – his tone implied that it would be remarkable if he didn't – 'and while I may or may not be right about Sir Anthony, and I will lay you a hundred to one, in pounds, that I am, I'm convinced that Lord Kirkside is wholly incapable of any dishonest or illegal action.'

'Me, too. He's a very tough citizen, I'd say, but on the side of the angels.'

'And his daughter? I haven't met her.'

'Very much a girl of to-day. Dressed in the modern idiom, speaks in the modern idiom, I'm tough and I'm competent and I can take care of myself, thank you. She's not tough at all, just a nice old-fashioned girl in new-fashioned clothes.'

'So that clears them.' Uncle Arthur sounded relieved. 'That leaves us the expedition, in spite of your sneers, or MacEachern's place, or the shark-fishers. I go for the sharkfishers myself.'

I let him go for wherever he wanted to. I thought it was time I went to the upper deck and told him so.

'It won't be long now?'

'I shouldn't think so, sir. We'll put out the lights in the saloon here – it would look very odd if they peered in the windows and saw no one here. We'll put on the two sleeping-cabin lights and the stern light. That will destroy their night-sight. The after deck will be bathed in light. For'ard of that, as far as they are concerned, it will be pitch dark. We hide in the dark.'

'Where in the dark?' Uncle Arthur didn't sound very confident.

'You stand inside the wheelhouse. All wheelhouse doors are hinged for'ard and open outwards. Keep your hand on the inside handle. Lightly. When you feel it begin to turn, a very slow and stealthy turn, you can bet your boots, wait till the door gives a fraction, then kick the rear edge, just below the handle, with the sole of your right foot and with all the weight you have. If you don't break his nose or knock him overboard you'll at least set him in line for a set of false teeth. I'll take care of the other or others.'

'How?'

'I'll be on the saloon roof. It's three feet lower than the loom of the stern light even if they approach from the wheelhouse roof so they can't see me silhouetted against the loom of the stern light even if they approach from the bows.'

'But what are you going to do?'

'Clobber him or them. A nice big Stilson from the engine-room with a rag round it will do nicely.'

'Why don't we just dazzle them with torches and tell them to put their hands up?' Uncle Arthur clearly didn't care for my proposed *modus operandi*.

'Three reasons. These are dangerous and deadly men and you never give them warning. Not the true sporting spirit, but it helps you survive. Then there will almost certainly be night-glasses trained on the *Firecrest* at this very moment. Finally, sound carries very clearly over water and the wind is blowing towards Torbay. Shots, I mean.'

He said no more. We took up position and waited. It was still raining heavily with the wind still from the west. For once the rain didn't bother me, I'd a full set of oilskins on. I just lay there, spread-eagled on the saloon coach-roof, occasionally easing the fingers of my hands, the right round the Stilson, the left round the little knife. After fifteen minutes they came. I heard the gentle scuff of rubber on our starboard side – the side of the wheelhouse door. I pulled on the cord which passed through the rear window of the wheelhouse. The cord was attached to Uncle Arthur's hand.

There were only two of them. My eyes were perfectly tuned to the dark by this time and I could easily distinguish the shape of the first man coming aboard just below where I lay. He secured a painter and waited for his mate. They moved forward together.

The leading man gave a cough of agony as the door smashed, fair and square, as we later established, into his face. I wasn't so successful, the second man had cat-like reactions and had started to drop to the deck as the Stilson came down. I caught him on back or shoulder, I didn't know which, and dropped on top of him. In one of his hands he'd have either a gun or a knife and if I'd wasted a fraction of a second trying to find out which hand and what he had in it, I'd have been a dead man. I brought down my left hand and he lay still.

I passed the other man lying moaning in agony in the scuppers, brushed by Uncle Arthur, pulled the saloon curtains to and switched on the lights. I then went out, half-pulled, half-lifted the moaning man through the wheelhouse door, down the saloon steps and dropped him on the carpet. I didn't recognize him. That wasn't surprising, his own mother or wife wouldn't have recognized him. Uncle Arthur was certainly a man who believed in working with a will and he'd left the plastic surgeon a very tricky job.

'Keep your gun on him, sir,' I said. Uncle Arthur was looking down at his handiwork with a slightly dazed expression. What one could see of his face behind the beard seemed slightly paler than normal. 'If he breathes, kill him.'

'But – but look at his face, man. We can't leave—'

'You look at this, sir.' I stooped and picked up the weapon that had fallen from the man's hand as I'd dropped him to the floor. 'This is what is technically known to the United States' police departments as a whippet. A shot-gun with two-thirds of the barrel and two-thirds of the stock sawn off. If he'd got you first, you wouldn't have any face left at all. I mean that literally. Do you still feel like playing Florence Nightingale to the fallen hero?' That wasn't at all the way one should talk to Uncle Arthur, there would be a few more entries in the confidential report when we got back. If we got back. But I couldn't help myself, not then. I passed by Uncle Arthur and went out.

In the wheelhouse I picked up a small torch, went outside and shone it down into the water, hooding it with my hand so that the beam couldn't have been seen fifty yards away. They had a rubber dinghy, all right – and an outboard motor attached. The conquering heroes, bathed in that warm and noble glow of satisfaction that comes from the comforting realization of a worthwhile job well done, had intended to make it home the easy way.

Looping a heaving line round the outboard's cylinder head and hauling alternately on the heaving line and painter, I had both dinghy and outboard up and over in two minutes. I unclamped the outboard, lugged the dinghy round to the other side of the superstructure, the side remote from the inner harbour, and examined it carefully in the light of the torch. Apart from the manufacturer's name there was no mark on it, nothing to indicate to which craft it belonged. I sliced it to ribbons and threw it over the side.

Back in the wheelhouse, I cut a twenty-foot length from a roll of PVC electric wiring cable, went outside again and lashed the outboard to the dead man's ankles. I searched his pockets. Nothing, I'd known there would be nothing, I was dealing with professionals. I hooded the torch and looked at his face. I'd never seen him before. I took from him the pistol still clutched in his right hand, undid the spring clips holding the guard-chains in place above the gunwale slots for our companionway ladder, then eased, first the outboard, and then the man, over the side. They vanished into the dark waters of Torbay harbour without the whisper of a splash. I went inside, closing wheelhouse and saloon doors behind me.

Uncle Arthur and the injured man had reversed positions by this time. The man was on his feet now, leaning drunkenly against the bulkhead, dabbing his face with a blood-stained towel Uncle Arthur must have found, and moaning from time to time. I didn't blame him, if I'd a broken nose, most of my front teeth displaced and a jaw that might or might not have been fractured, I'd have been moaning too. Uncle Arthur, gun in one hand and some more of my Scotch in the other, was sitting on the settee and contemplating his bloody handiwork with an odd mixture of satisfaction and distaste. He looked at me as I came in, nodded towards the prisoner.

'Making a fearful mess of the carpet,' he complained. 'What do we do with him?'

'Hand him over to the police.'

'The police? You had your reservations about the police, I thought.'

'Reservations is hardly the word. We have to make the break some time.'

'Our friend outside, as well?'

'Who?'

'This fellow's – ah – accomplice.'

'I threw him over the side.'

Uncle Arthur made the mess on the carpet even worse. He spilt whisky all over it. He said: 'You what?'

'There's no worry.' I pointed downwards. 'Twenty fathoms and thirty pounds of metal attached to his ankles.'

'At – at the bottom of the sea?'

'What did you expect me to do with him? Give him a state funeral? I'm sorry, I didn't tell you, he was dead. I had to kill him.'

'Had to? Had to?' He seemed upset. 'Why, Calvert?'

'There's no "why." There's no justification needed. I killed him or he killed me, and then you, and now we'd both be where he is. Do you have to justify killing men who have murdered at least three times, probably oftener? And if that particular character wasn't a murderer, he came to-night to murder. I killed him with as little thought and compunction and remorse as I'd have tramped on a black widow spider.'

'But you can't go around acting like a public executioner.'

'I can and I will. As long as it's a choice between them and me.'

'You're right, you're right.' He sighed. 'I must confess that reading your reports of an operation is quite different from being with you on one. But I must also confess that it's rather comforting having you around at times like this. Well, let's put this man in cells.'

'I'd like to go to the *Shangri-la* first, sir. To look for Hunslett.'

'I see. To look for Hunslett. Has it occurred to you, Calvert, that if they are hostile to us, as you admit is possible, that they may not let you look for Hunslett?'

'Yes, sir. It's not my intention to go through the *Shangri-la*, a gun in each hand, searching for him. I wouldn't get five feet. I'm just going to ask for him, if anyone has seen him. Assuming they really are the bandits, don't you think it might be most instructive, sir, to observe their reactions when they see a dead man walking aboard, especially a dead man coming alongside from a boat to which they'd shortly beforehand dispatched a couple of killers? And don't you think it will become more and more instructive to watch them as time passes by with no sign of First and Second Murderers entering left?'

'Assuming they are the bandits, of course.'

'I'll know before we say good-bye to them.'

'And how do we account for our knowing one another?'

'If they're white as the driven snow, we don't have to account to them. If they're not, they won't believe a damned word either of us say anyway.'

I collected the roll of flex from the wheelhouse and led our prisoner to the after cabin. I told him to sit down with his back to one of the bulkhead generators and he did. Resistance was the last thought in his mind. I passed a few turns of flex round his waist and secured him to the generator: his feet I secured to one of the stanchions. His hands I left free. He could move, he could use the towel and the bucket of cold fresh water I left to administer first aid to himself whenever he felt like it. But he was beyond reach of any glass or sharp instrument with which he could either free himself or do himself in. On the latter score I wasn't really worried one way or another.

I started the engines, weighed anchor, switched on the navigation lights and headed for the *Shangri-la*. Quite suddenly, I wasn't tired any more.

Chapter Six

Wednesday: 8.40 p.m. – 10.40 p.m.

Less than two hundred yards from the *Shangri-la* the anchor clattered down into fifteen fathoms of water. I switched off the navigation lights, switched on all the wheelhouse lights, passed into the saloon and closed the door behind me.

'How long do we sit here?' Uncle Arthur asked.

'Not long. Better get into your oilskins now, sir. Next really heavy shower of rain and we'll go.'

'They'll have had their night-glasses on us all the way across the bay, you think?'

'No question of that. They'll still have the glasses on us. They'll be worried stiff, wondering what the hell has gone wrong, what's happened to the two little playmates they sent to interview us. *If* they are the bandits.'

'They're bound to investigate again.'

'Not yet. Not for an hour or two. They'll wait for their two friends to turn up. They may think that it took them longer than expected to reach the *Firecrest* and that we'd upped anchor and left before they got there. Or they may think they'd trouble with their dinghy.' I heard the sudden drumming of heavy rain on the coach-roof. 'It's time to go.'

We left by the galley door, felt our way aft, quietly lowered the dinghy into the water and climbed down the transom ladder into it. I cast off. Wind and tide carried us in towards the harbour. Through the driving rain we could dimly see the *Shangri-la*'s riding light as we drifted by about a hundred yards from her port side. Half-way between the *Shangri-la* and the shore I started up the outboard motor and made back towards the *Shangri-la*.

The big tender was riding at the outer end of a boom which stretched out from the *Shangri-la*'s starboard side about ten feet for'ard of the bridge. The stern of the tender was about fifteen out from the illuminated gangway. I approached from astern, upwind, and closed in on the gangway. An oil-skinned figure wearing one of the *Shangri-la*'s crew's fancy French sailor hats came running down the gangway and took the painter.

'Ah, good-evening, my man,' Uncle Arthur said. He wasn't putting on the style, it was the way he talked to most people. 'Sir Anthony is aboard?'

'Yes, sir.'

'I wonder if I could see him for a moment?'

'If you could wait a—' The sailor broke off and peered at Sir Arthur. 'Oh, it's – it's the Admiral, sir.'

'Admiral Arnford-Jason. Of course – you're the fellow who ran me ashore to the Columba after dinner.'

'Yes, sir. I'll show you to the saloon, sir.'

'My boat will be all right here for a few moments.' The unspoken implication was that I was his chauffeur.

'Perfectly, sir.'

They climbed the gangway and went aft. I spent ten seconds examining the portable lead that served the gangway light, decided that it would offer much resistance to a good hefty tug, then followed the two men aft. I passed by the passage leading to the saloon and hid behind a ventilator. Almost at once the sailor emerged from the passage and made his way for'ard again. Another twenty seconds and he'd be yelling his head off about the mysteriously vanished chauffeur. I didn't care what he did in twenty seconds.

When I reached the partly open saloon door I heard Sir Arthur's voice.

'No, no, I really am most sorry to break in upon you like this. Well, yes, thank you, small one if you will. Yes, soda, please.' Uncle Arthur really was having a go at the whisky to-night. 'Thank you, thank you. Your health, Lady Skouras. Your health, gentlemen. Mustn't delay you. Fact is, I wonder if you can help us. My friend and I are most anxious, really most anxious. I wonder where he is, by the way? I thought he was right behind—'

Cue for Calvert. I turned down the oilskin collar that had been obscuring the lower part of my face, removed the sou'wester that had been obscuring most of the upper part of my face, knocked politely and entered. I said: 'Good evening, Lady Skouras. Good-evening, gentlemen. Please forgive the interruption, Sir Anthony.'

Apart from Uncle Arthur there were six of them gathered round the fire at the end of the saloon. Sir Anthony standing, the others seated. Charlotte Skouras, Dollmann, Skouras's managing director, Lavorski, his accountant, Lord Charnley, his broker and a fifth man I didn't recognize. All had glasses in their hands.

Their reaction to my sudden appearance, as expressed by their faces, was interesting. Old Skouras showed a half-frowning, half-speculative surprise. Charlotte Skouras gave me a strained smile of welcome: Uncle Arthur hadn't been exaggerating when he spoke of that bruise, it was a beauty. The stranger's face was noncommittal, Lavorski's inscrutable, Dollmann's rigid as if carved from marble and Lord Charnley's for a fleeting moment that of a man walking through a country churchyard at midnight when someone taps him on the shoulder. Or so I thought. I could have imagined it. But there was no imagination about the sudden tiny snapping sound as the stem of the glass fell soundlessly on to the carpet. A scene straight from Victorian melodrama. Our aristocratic broker friend had something on his mind. Whether the others had or not it was difficult to say. Dollmann, Lavorski and, I was pretty sure, Sir Anthony could make their faces say whatever they wanted them to say.

'Good lord, Petersen!' Skouras's tone held surprise but not the surprise of a person welcoming someone back from the grave. 'I didn't know you two knew each other.'

'My goodness, yes. Petersen and I have been colleagues for years, Tony. UNESCO, you know.' Uncle Arthur always gave out that he was a British delegate to UNESCO, a cover that gave him an excellent reason for his frequent trips abroad. 'Marine biology may not be very cultural, but it's scientific and educational enough. Petersen's one of my star performers. Lecturing, I mean. Done missions for me in Europe, Asia, Africa and South America.' Which was true, enough, only they weren't lecture missions. 'Didn't even know he was here until they told me at the hotel. But dear me, dear me, mustn't talk about ourselves. It's Hunslett. Petersen's colleague. And mine in a way. Can't find him anywhere. Hasn't been in the village. Yours is the nearest boat. Have you seen anything of him, anything at all?'

'Afraid I haven't,' Skouras said. 'Anybody here? No? Nobody?' He pressed a bell and a steward appeared. Skouras asked him to make inquiries aboard and the steward left. 'When did he disappear, Mr Petersen?'

'I've no idea. I left him carrying out experiments. I've been away all day collecting specimens. Jellyfish.' I laughed deprecatingly and rubbed my inflamed face. 'The poisonous type, I'm afraid. No sign of him when I returned.'

'Could your friend swim, Mr Petersen?' the stranger asked. I looked at him, a dark thickset character in his middle forties, with black snapping eyes deepset in a tanned face. Expressionless faces seemed to be the order of the day there, so I kept mine expressionless. It wasn't easy.

'I'm afraid not,' I said quietly. 'I'm afraid you're thinking along the same lines as myself. We've no guard rails aft. A careless step—' I broke off as the steward re-entered and reported that no one had seen a sign of Hunslett, then went on: 'I think I should report this to Sergeant MacDonald at once.'

Everybody else seemed to think so, too, so we left. The cold slanting rain was heavier than ever. At the head of the gangway I pretended to slip, flung my arms about wildly for a bit then toppled into the sea, taking the gangway wandering lead with me. What with the rain, the wind and the sudden darkness there was quite a bit of confusion and it was the better part of a minute before I was finally hauled on to the landing stage of the companionway. Old Skouras was commiseration itself and offered me a change of clothes at once but I declined politely and went back to the *Firecrest* with Uncle Arthur. Neither of us spoke on the way back.

As we secured the dinghy I said: 'When you were at dinner on the *Shangri-la* you must have given some story to account for your presence here, for your dramatic appearance in an RAF rescue launch.'

'Yes. It was a good one. I told them a vital UNESCO conference in Geneva was being dead-locked because of the absence of a certain Dr Spenser Freeman. It happens to be true. In all the papers to-day. Dr Freeman is not there because it suits us not to have him there. No one knows that, of course. I told them that it was of vital national importance that he should be there, that we'd received information that he was doing field research in Torbay and that the Government had sent me here to get him back.'

'Why send the launch away? That would seem odd.'

'No. If he's somewhere in the wilds of Torbay I couldn't locate him before daylight. There's a helicopter, I said, standing by to fly him out. I've only to lift the phone to have it here in fifty minutes.'

'And of course, you weren't to know that the telephone lines were out of order. It might have worked if you hadn't called at the *Firecrest* in the rescue launch *before* you went to the *Shangri-la*. You weren't to know that our friends who were locked in the after cabin when you went aboard would report back that they'd heard an RAF rescue launch here at such and such a time. They might have seen it through a porthole, but even that wouldn't be necessary, the engines are unmistakable. So now our friends know you're lying like a trooper. The chances are that they've now a very shrewd idea as to who exactly you are. Congratulations, sir. You've now joined the category I've been in for years – no insurance company in the world would issue you a life policy even on a ninety-nine per cent premium.'

'Our trip to the *Shangri-la* has removed your last doubts about our friends out there?'

'Yes, sir. You saw the reaction of our belted broker, Lord Charnley. And him an aristocrat to boot!'

'A small thing to base a big decision on, Calvert,' Uncle Arthur said coldly.

'Yes, sir.' I fished my scuba suit from the after locker and led the way below. 'I didn't fall into the water by accident. By accident on purpose. I didn't mention that when I was hanging on to the boat's rudder off the reef this evening I cut a notch in it. A deep vee notch. The *Shangri-la*'s tender has a deep vee notch in it. Same notch, in fact. Same boat.'

'I see. I see indeed.' Uncle Arthur sat on the settee and gave me the combination of the cold blue eye and the monocle. 'You forgot to give me advance notification of your intentions.'

'I didn't forget.' I started to change out of my soaking clothes. 'I'd no means of knowing how good an actor you are, sir.'

'I'll accept that. So that removed your last doubts.'

'No, sir. Superfluous confirmation, really. I knew before then. Remember that swarthy character sitting beside Lavorski who asked me if Hunslett could swim. I'll bet a fortune to a penny that he wasn't at the *Shangri-la*'s dinner table earlier on.'

'You would win. How do you know?'

'Because he was in command of the crew of the boat who shot down the helicopter and killed Williams and hung around afterwards waiting to have a go at me. His name is Captain Imrie. He was the captain of the prize crew of the *Nantesville*.'

Uncle Arthur nodded, but his mind was on something else. It was on the scuba suit I was pulling on.

'What the hell do you think you're going to do with that thing?' he demanded.

'Advance notification of intentions, sir. Won't be long. I'm taking a little trip to the *Shangri-la*. The *Shangri-la*'s tender, rather. With a little homing device and a bag of sugar. With your permission, sir.'

'Something else you forgot to tell me, hey, Calvert? Like that breaking off the *Shangri-la*'s gangway light was no accident?'

'I'd like to get there before they replace it, sir.'

'I can't believe it, I can't believe it.' Uncle Arthur shook his head. For a moment I thought he was referring to the dispatch with which I had made the uneventful return trip to the *Shangri-la*'s tender, but his next words showed that his mind was on higher and more important things. 'That Tony Skouras should be up to his neck in this. There's something far wrong. I just *can't* believe it. Good God, do you know he was up for a peerage in the next List?'

'So soon? He told me he was waiting for the price to come down.'

Uncle Arthur said nothing. Normally, he would have regarded such a statement as a mortal insult, as he himself automatically collected a life peerage on retirement. But nothing. He was as shaken as that.

'I'd like nothing better than to arrest the lot of them,' I said. 'But our hands are tied. We're helpless. But now that I know what we do know I wonder if you would do me a favour before we go ashore, sir. There are two things I want to know. One is whether Sir Anthony really was down at some Clyde shipyard a few days ago having stabilizers fitted – a big job few yards would tackle in a yacht that size. Should find out in a couple of hours. People tell silly and unnecessary lies. Also I'd like to find out if Lord Kirkside has taken the necessary steps to have his dead son's title – he was Viscount somebody or other – transferred to his younger son.'

'You get the set ready and I'll ask them anything you like,' Uncle Arthur said wearily. He wasn't really listening to me, he was still contemplating with stunned disbelief the possibility that his future fellow peer was up to the neck in skulduggery on a vast scale. 'And pass me that bottle before you go below.'

At the rate Uncle Arthur was going, I reflected, it was providential that the home of one of the most famous distilleries in the Highlands was less than half a mile from where we were anchored.

I lowered the false head of the starboard diesel to the engine-room deck as if it weighed a ton. I straightened and stood there for a full minute, without moving. Then I went to the engine-room door.

'Sir Arthur?'

'Coming, coming.' A few seconds and he was at the door-way, the glass of whisky in his hand. 'All connected up?'

'I've found Hunslett, sir.'

Uncle Arthur moved slowly forward like a man in a dream.

The transmitter was gone. All our explosives and listening devices and little portable transmitters were gone. That had left plenty of room. They'd had to double him up to get him in, his head was resting on his forearms and his arms on his knees, but there was plenty of room. I couldn't see his face. I could see no marks of violence. Half-sitting, half-lying there he seemed curiously peaceful, a man drowsing away a summer afternoon by a sun-warmed wall. A long summer afternoon because for ever was a long time. That's what I'd told him last night, he'd all the time in the world for sleep.

I touched his face. It wasn't cold yet. He'd been dead two to three hours, no more. I turned his face to see if I could find how he had died. His head lolled to one side like that of a broken rag doll. I turned and looked at Sir Arthur. The dream-like expression had gone, his eyes were cold and bitter and cruel. I thought vaguely of the tales I'd heard, and largely discounted, of Uncle Arthur's total ruthlessness. I wasn't so ready to discount them now. Uncle Arthur wasn't where he was now because he'd answered an advertisement in the *Daily Telegraph*, he'd have been hand-picked by two or three very clever men who would have scoured the country to find the one man with the extraordinary qualifications they required. And they had picked Uncle Arthur, the man with the extraordinary qualifications, and total ruthlessness must have been one of the prime requisites. I'd never really thought of it before.

He said: 'Murdered, of course.'

'Yes, sir.'

'How?'

'His neck is broken, sir.'

'His neck? A powerful man like Hunslett?'

'I know a man who could do it with one twist of his hands. Quinn. The man who killed Baker and Delmont. The man who almost killed me.'

'I see.' He paused, then went on, almost absently: 'You will, of course, seek out and destroy this man. By whatever means you choose. You can reconstruct this, Calvert?'

'Yes, sir.' When it came to reconstruction when it was too damn' late, I stood alone. 'Our friend or friends boarded the *Firecrest* very shortly after I had left this morning. That is, before daylight. They wouldn't have dared try it after it was light. They overpowered Hunslett and kept him prisoner. Confirmation that he was held prisoner all day comes from the fact that he failed to meet the noon-day schedule. They still held him prisoner when you came aboard. There was no reason why you should suspect that there was anyone aboard – the boat that put them aboard before dawn would have gone away at once. They couldn't leave one of the *Shangri-la*'s boats lying alongside the *Firecrest* all day.'

'There's no necessity to dot i's and cross t's.'

'No, sir. Maybe an hour or so after you departed the *Shangri-la*'s tender with Captain Imrie, Quinn and company aboard turns up: they report that I'm dead. That was Hunslett's death warrant. With me dead they couldn't let him live. So Quinn killed him. Why he was killed this way I don't know. They may have thought shots could be heard, they may not have wanted to use knives or blunt instruments in case they left blood all over the deck. They were intending to abandon the boat till they came back at night, at midnight, to take it out to the Sound and scuttle it and someone might have come aboard in the interim. My own belief is that he was killed this way because Quinn is a psychopath and compulsive killer and liked doing it this way.'

'I see. And then they said to themselves: "Where can we hide Hunslett till we come back at midnight? Just in case someone does come aboard." And then they said: "Ha! We know. We'll hide him in the dummy diesel." So they threw away the transmitter and all the rest of the stuff – or took it with them. It doesn't matter. And they put Hunslett inside.' Uncle Arthur had been speaking very quietly throughout and then suddenly, for the first time I'd ever known it, his voice became a shout. 'How in the name of God did they know this was a dummy diesel, Calvert? How *could* they have known?' His voice dropped to what was a comparative whisper. 'Someone talked, Calvert. Or someone was criminally careless.'

'No one talked, sir. Someone was criminally careless. I was. If I'd used my eyes Hunslett wouldn't be lying there now. The night the two bogus customs officers were aboard I knew that they had got on to something when we were in the engine-room here. Up to the time that they'd inspected the batteries they'd gone through the place with a tooth-comb. After that they didn't give a damn. Hunslett even suggested that it was something to do with the batteries but I was too clever to believe him.' I walked to the work-bench, picked up a torch and handed it to Uncle Arthur. 'Do you see anything about those batteries that would excite suspicion?'

He looked at me, that monocled eye still ice-cold and bitter, took the torch and examined the batteries carefully. He spent all of two minutes searching, then straightened.

'I see nothing,' he said curtly.

'Thomas – the customs man who called himself Thomas – did. He was on to us from the start. He knew what he was looking for. He was looking for a powerful radio transmitter. Not the tuppence ha'penny job we have up in the wheelhouse. He was looking for signs of a power take-off from those batteries. He was looking for the marks left by screw clamps or by a pair of saw-toothed, powerfully spring-loaded crocodile clips.'

Uncle Arthur swore, very quietly, and bent over the batteries again. This time his examination took only ten seconds.

'You make your point well, Calvert.' The eyes were still bitter, but no longer glacial.

'No wonder they knew exactly what I was doing to-day,' I said savagely. 'No wonder they knew that Hunslett would be alone before dawn, that I'd be landing at that cove this evening. All they required was radio confirmation from someone out in Loch Houron that Calvert had been snooping around there and the destruction of the helicopter was a foregone conclusion. All this damned fol-de-rol about smashing up radio transmitters and making us think that we were the only craft left with a transmitter. God, how blind can you be?'

'I assume that there's some logical thought behind this outburst,' Uncle Arthur said coldly.

'That night Hunslett and I were aboard the *Shangri-la* for drinks. I told you that when we returned we knew that we'd had visitors. We didn't know why, then. My God!'

'You've already been at pains to demonstrate the fact that I was no brighter than yourself about the battery. It's not necessary to repeat the process—'

'Let me finish,' I interrupted. Uncle Arthur didn't like being interrupted. 'They came down to the engine-room here. They knew there was a transmitter. They looked at that starboard cylinder head. Four bolts – the rest are dummies – with the paint well and truly scraped off. The port cylinder head bolts without a flake of paint missing. They take off this head, wire into the transceiver lines on the output side of the scrambler and lead out to a small radio transmitter hidden, like as not, behind the battery bank there. They'd have all the equipment with them for they knew exactly what they wanted to do. From then on they could listen in to our every word. They knew all our plans, everything we intended to do, and made their own plans accordingly. They figured – and how right they were – that it would be a damn' sight more advantageous for them to let Hunslett and I have our direct communication with you and so know exactly what was going on than to wreck this set and force us to find some other means of communication that they couldn't check on.'

'But why – but why destroy the advantage they held by – by—' He gestured at the empty engine casing.

'It wasn't an advantage any longer,' I said tiredly. 'When they ripped out that set Hunslett was dead and they thought Calvert was dead. They didn't need the advantage any more.'

'Of course, of course. My God, what a fiendish brew this is.' He took out his monocle and rubbed his eye with the knuckle of his hand. 'They're bound to know that we will find Hunslett the first time we attempt to use this radio. I am beginning to appreciate the weight of your remark in the saloon that we might find it difficult to insure ourselves. They cannot know how much we know, but they cannot afford to take chances. Not with, what is it now, a total of seventeen million pounds at stake. They will have to silence us.'

'Up and off is the only answer,' I agreed. 'We've been down here too long already, they might even be on their way across now. Don't let that Luger ever leave your hand, sir. We'll be safe enough under way. But first we must put Hunslett and our friend in the after cabin ashore.'

'Yes. Yes, we must put them ashore first.'

At the best of times, weighing anchor by electric windlass is not a job for a moron, even an alert moron. Even our small windlass had a pull of over 1,400 pounds. A carelessly placed hand or foot, a flapping trouser leg or the trailing skirts of an oilskin, any of those being caught up between chain and drum and you can be minus a hand or foot before you can cry out, far less reach the deck switch which is invariably placed abaft the windlass. Doing this on a wet slippery deck is twice as dangerous. Doing it on a wet slippery deck, in total darkness, heavy rain and with a very unstable boat beneath your feet, not to mention having the brake pawl off and the winch covered by a tarpaulin, is a highly dangerous practice indeed. But it wasn't as dangerous as attracting the attention of our friends on the *Shangri-la*.

Perhaps it was because of my total absorption in the job on hand, perhaps because of the muffled clank of the anchor coming inboard, that I didn't locate and identify the sound as quickly as I might. Twice I'd thought I'd heard the far-off sound of a woman's voice, twice I'd vaguely put it down to late-night revelry on one of the smaller yachts in the bay – it would require an IBM computer to work out the gallonage of gin consumed in British yacht harbours after the sun goes down. Then I heard the voice again, much nearer this time, and I put all thought of revelry afloat out of my mind. The only cry of desperation ever heard at a yacht party is when the gin runs out: this soft cry had a different quality of desperation altogether. I stamped on the deck switch, and all sound on the fo'c'sle ceased. The Lilliput was in my hand without my knowing how it had got there.

'Help me!' The voice was low and urgent and desperate. 'For God's sake, help me.'

The voice came from the water, amidships on the port side. I moved back silently to where I thought the voice had come from and stood motionless. I thought of Hunslett and I didn't move a muscle. I'd no intention of helping anyone until I'd made sure the voice didn't come from some dinghy – a dinghy with two other passengers, both carrying machine-guns. One word, one incautious flash of light, a seven pound pull on a trigger and Calvert would be among his ancestors if, that was, they would have anything to do with such a bloody fool of a descendant.

'Please! Please help me! Please!'

I helped her. Not so much because the desperation in the voice was unquestionably genuine as because of the fact that it as unquestionably belonged to Charlotte Skouras.

I pushed through between the scuppers and the lowest guard-rail, a rubber tyre fender that was permanently attached to one of the guard-rail stanchions and lowered it to water-level. I said: 'Lady Skouras?'

'Yes, yes, it's me. Thank God, thank God!' Her voice didn't come just as easily as that, she was gasping for breath and she'd water in her mouth.

'There's a fender at the boat's side. Catch it.'

A moment or two, then: 'I have it.'

'Can you pull yourself up?'

More splashing and gasping, then: 'No. No, I can't do it.'

'No matter. Wait.' I turned round to go for Uncle Arthur but he was already by my side. I said softly in his ear: 'Lady Skouras is down there in the water. It may be a trap. I don't think so. But if you see a light, shoot at it.'

He said nothing but I felt his arm move as he took the Luger from his pocket. I stepped over the guard-rail and lowered myself till my foot came to rest on the lower part of the tyre. I reached down and caught her arm. Charlotte Skouras was no slender sylph-like figure, she had some bulky package tied to her waist, and I wasn't as fit as I'd been a long, long time ago, say about forty-eight hours, but with a helping hand from Uncle Arthur I managed to get her up on deck. Between us, we half carried her to the curtained saloon and set her down on the settee. I propped a cushion behind her head and took a good look at her.

She'd never have made the front cover of Vogue. She looked terrible. Her dark slacks and shirt looked as if they had spent a month in the sea instead of probably only a few minutes. The long tangled auburn hair was plastered to her head and cheeks, her face was dead-white, the big brown eyes, with the dark half-circles, were wide open and frightened and both mascara and lipstick had begun to run. And she hadn't been beautiful to start with. I thought she was the most desirable woman I'd ever seen. I must be nuts.

'My dear Lady Skouras, my dear Lady Skouras!' Uncle Arthur was back among the aristocracy and showed it. He knelt by her side, ineffectually dabbing at her face with a handkerchief. 'What in God's name has happened? Brandy, Calvert, brandy! Don't just stand there, man. Brandy!'

Uncle Arthur seemed to think he was in a pub but, as it happened, I did have some brandy left. I handed him the glass and said: 'If you'll attend to Lady Skouras, sir, I'll finish getting the anchor up.'

'No, no!' She took a gulp of the brandy, choked on it and I had to wait until she had finished coughing before she went on. 'They're not coming for at least two hours yet. I know. I heard. There's something terrible going on, Sir Arthur. I had to come, I had to come.'

'Now, don't distress yourself, Lady Skouras, don't distress yourself,' Uncle Arthur said, as if she weren' distressed enough already. 'Just drink this down, Lady Skouras.'

'No, not that!' I got all set to take a poor view of this, it was damned good brandy, then I realized she was talking of something else. 'Not Lady Skouras. Never again! Charlotte. Charlotte Meiner. Charlotte.'

One thing about women, they always get their sense of priorities right. There they were on the *Shangri-la*, rigging up a home-made atom bomb to throw through our saloon windows and all she could think was to ask us to call her 'Charlotte.' I said: 'Why did you have to come?'

'Calvert!' Uncle Arthur's voice was sharp. 'Do you mind? Lady – I mean, Charlotte – has just suffered a severe shock. Let her take her time to—'

'No.' She struggled to an upright sitting position and forced a wan smile, half-scared, half-mocking. 'No, Mr Petersen, Mr Calvert, whatever your name, you're quite right. Actresses tend to over-indulge their emotions. I'm not an actress any longer.' She took another sip of the brandy and a little colour came back to her face. 'I've known for some time that something was very far wrong aboard the *Shangri-la*. Strange men have been aboard. Some of the old crew were changed for no reason. Several times I've been put ashore with the stewardess in hotels while the *Shangri-la* went off on mysterious journeys. My husband – Sir Anthony – would tell me nothing. He has changed terribly since our marriage – I think he takes drugs. I've seen guns. Whenever those strange men came aboard I was sent to my stateroom after dinner.' She smiled mirthlessly. 'It wasn't because of any jealousy on my husband's part, you may believe me. The last day or two I sensed that everything was coming to a climax. To-night, just after you were gone, I was sent to my stateroom. I left, but stayed out in the passage. Lavorski was talking. I heard him saying: "If your admiral pal is a UNESCO delegate, Skouras, then I'm King Neptune. I know who he is. We all know who he is. It's too late in the day now and they know too much. It's them or us." And then Captain Imrie – how I hate that man! – said: "I'll send Quinn and Jacques and Kramer at midnight. At one o'clock they'll open the sea-cocks in the Sound".'

'Charming friends your husband has,' I murmured.

She looked at me, half-uncertainly, half-speculatively and said: 'Mr Petersen or Mr Calvert – and I heard Lavorski call you Johnson—'

'It *is* confusing,' I admitted. 'Calvert. Philip Calvert.' 'Well, Philip,' – she pronounced it the French way and very nice it sounded too – 'you are one great bloody fool if you talk like that. You are in deadly danger.'

'Mr Calvert,' Uncle Arthur said sourly – it wasn't her language he disapproved of, it was this Christian name familiarity between the aristocracy and the peasants – 'is quite aware of the danger. He has unfortunate mannerisms of speech, that's all. You are a very brave woman, Charlotte.' Blue-bloods first-naming each other was a different thing altogether. 'You took a great risk in eavesdropping. You might have been caught.'

'I was caught, Sir Arthur.' The smile showed up the lines on either side of her mouth but didn't touch her eyes. 'That is another reason why I am here. Even without the knowledge of your danger, yes, I would have come. My husband caught me. He took me into my stateroom.' She stood up shakily, turned her back to us and pulled up the sodden dark shirt. Right across her back ran three great blue-red weals. Uncle Arthur stood stock-still, a man incapable of movement. I crossed the saloon and peered at her back. The weals were almost an inch wide and running half-way round her body. Here and there were tiny blood-spotted punctures. Lightly I tried a finger on one of the weals. The flesh was raised and puffy, a fresh weal, as lividly-genuine a weal as ever I'd clapped eyes on. She didn't move. I stepped back and she turned to face us.

'It is not nice, is it? It does not feel very nice.' She smiled and again that smile. 'I could show you worse than that.'

'No, no, no,' Uncle Arthur said hastily. 'That will not be necessary.' He was silent for a moment, then burst out: 'My dear Charlotte, what you must have suffered. It's fiendish, absolutely fiendish. He must be – he must be inhuman. A monster. A monster, perhaps under the influence of drugs. I would never have believed it!' His face was brick-red with outrage and his voice sounded as if Quinn had him by the throat. Strangled. 'No one would ever have believed it!'

'Except the late Lady Skouras,' she said quietly. 'I understand now why she was in and out of mental homes several times before she died.' She shrugged. 'I have no wish to go the same way. I am made of tougher stuff than Madeleine Skouras. So I pick up my bag and run away.' She nodded at the small polythene bag of clothes that had been tied to her waist. 'Like Dick Whittington, is it not?'

'They'll be here long before midnight when they discover you're gone,' I observed.

'It may be morning before they find out. Most nights I lock my cabin door. To-night I locked it from the outside.'

'That helps,' I said. 'Standing about in those sodden clothes doesn't. There's no point in running away only to die of pneumonia. You'll find towels in my cabin. Then we can get you a room in the Columba Hotel.'

'I had hoped for better than that.' The fractional slump of the shoulders was more imagined than seen, but the dull defeat in the eyes left nothing to the imagination. 'You would put me in the first place they would look for me. There is no safe place for me in Torbay. They will catch me and bring me back and my husband will take me into that stateroom again. My only hope is to run away. Your only hope is to run away. Please. Can we not run away together?'

'No.'

'A man not given to evasive answers, is that it?' There was a lonely dejection, a proud humiliation about her that did very little for my self-respect. She turned towards Uncle Arthur, took both his hands in hers and said in a low voice: 'Sir Arthur. I appeal to you as an English gentleman.' Thumbs down on Calvert, that foreign-born peasant. 'May I stay? Please?'

Uncle Arthur looked at me, hesitated, looked at Charlotte Skouras, looked into those big brown eyes and was a lost man.

'Of course you may stay, my dear Charlotte.' He gave a stiff old-fashioned bow which, I had to admit, went very well with the beard and the monocle. 'Yours to command, my dear lady.'

'Thank you, Sir Arthur.' She smiled at me, not with triumph or satisfaction, just an anxious-to-be-friendly smile. 'It would be nice, Philip, to have the consent – what do you say? – unanimous.'

'If Sir Arthur wishes to expose you to a vastly greater degree of risk aboard this boat than you would experience in Torbay, that is Sir Arthur's business. As for the rest, my consent is not required. I'm a well-trained civil servant and I obey orders.'

'You are gracious to a fault,' Uncle Arthur said acidly.

'Sorry, sir.' I'd suddenly seen the light and a pretty dazzling beam it was too. 'I should not have called your judgment in question. The lady is very welcome. But I think she should remain below while we are alongside the pier, sir.'

'A reasonable request and a wise precaution,' Uncle Arthur said mildly. He seemed pleased at my change of heart, my proper deference to the wishes of the aristocracy.

'It won't be for long.' I smiled at Charlotte Skouras. 'We leave Torbay within the hour.'

'What do I care what you charge him with?' I looked from Sergeant MacDonald to the broken-faced man with the wet blood-stained towel, then back to MacDonald again. 'Breaking and entering. Assault and battery.

Illegal possession of a dangerous weapon with intent to create a felony – murder. Anything you like.'

'Well, now. It's just not quite as easy as that.' Sergeant MacDonald spread his big brown hands across the counter of the tiny police station and looked at the prisoner and myself in turn. 'He didn't break and enter, you know, Mr Petersen. He boarded. No law against that. Assault and battery: It looks as if he has been the victim and not the perpetrator. And what kind of weapon was he carrying, Mr Petersen?'

'I don't know. It must have been knocked overboard.'

'I see. Knocked overboard, was it? So we have no real proof of any felonious intent.'

I was becoming a little tired of Sergeant MacDonald. He was fast enough to co-operate with bogus customs officers but with me he was just being deliberately obstructive. I said: 'You'll be telling me next that it's all a product of my fevered imagination. You'll be telling me next that I just stepped ashore, grabbed the first passer-by I saw, hit him in the face with a four-by-two then dragged him up here inventing this tale as I went. Even you can't be so stupid as to believe that.'

The brown face turned red and, on the counter, the brown knuckles turned ivory. He said softly: 'You'll kindly not talk to me like that.'

'If you insist on behaving like a fool I'll treat you as such. Are you going to lock him up?'

'It's only your word against his.'

'No. I had a witness. He's down at the old pier now, if you want to see him. Admiral Sir Arthur Arnford-Jason. A very senior civil servant.'

'You had a Mr Hunslett with you last time I was aboard your boat.'

'He's down there, too.' I nodded at the prisoner. 'Why don't you ask a few questions of our friend here?'

'I've sent for the doctor. He'll have to fix his face first. I can't understand a word he says.'

'The state of his face doesn't help,' I admitted. 'But the main trouble is that he speaks Italian.'

'Italian, is it? I'll soon fix that. The owner of the Western Isles café is an Italian.'

'That helps. There are four little questions he might put to our pal here. Where is his passport, how he arrived in this country, who is his employer and where does he live.'

The sergeant looked at me for a long moment then said slowly: 'It's a mighty queer marine biologist that you are, Mr Petersen.'

'And it's a mighty queer police sergeant that you are, Mr MacDonald. Good night.'

I crossed the dimly-lit street to the sea-wall and waited in the shadow of a phone booth. After two minutes a man with a small bag came hurrying up the street and turned into the police station. He was out again in five minutes, which wasn't surprising: there was little a GP could do for what was plainly a hospital job.

The station door opened again and Sergeant MacDonald came hurrying out, long black mackintosh buttoned to the neck. He walked quickly along the sea-wall, looking neither to left nor right, which made it very easy for me to follow him, and turned down the old stone pier. At the end of the pier he flashed a torch, went down a flight of steps and began to haul in a small boat. I leaned over the pier wall and switched on my own torch.

'Why don't they provide you with a telephone or radio for conveying urgent messages?' I asked. 'You could catch your death of cold rowing out to the *Shangri-la* on a night like this.'

He straightened slowly and let the rope fall from his hands. The boat drifted out into the darkness. He came up the steps with the slow heavy tread of an old man and said quietly: 'What did you say about the *Shangri-la?*'

'Don't let me keep you, Sergeant,' I said affably. 'Duty before the idle social chit-chat. Your first duty is to your masters. Off you go, now, tell them that one of their hirelings has been severely clobbered and that Petersen has very grave suspicions about Sergeant MacDonald.'

'I don't know what you are talking about,' he said emptily. 'The *Shangri-la* – I'm not going anywhere near the *Shangri-la.*'

'Where are you going, then? Do tell. Fishing? Kind of forgotten your tackle, haven't you?'

'And how would you like to mind your own damn' business?' MacDonald said heavily.

'That's what I'm doing. Come off it, Sergeant. Think I give a damn about our Italian pal? You can charge him with playing tiddley-winks in the High Street for all I care. I just threw him at you, together with a hint that you yourself were up to no good, to see what the reaction would be, to remove the last doubts in my mind. You reacted beautifully.'

'I'm maybe not the cleverest, Mr Petersen,' he said with dignity. 'Neither am I a complete idiot. I thought you were one of them or after the same thing as them.' He paused. 'You're not. You're a Government agent.'

'I'm a civil servant.' I nodded to where the *Firecrest* lay not twenty yards away. 'You'd better come to meet my boss.'

'I don't take orders from Civil Servants.'

'Suit yourself,' I said indifferently, turned away and looked out over the sea-wall. 'About your two sons, Sergeant MacDonald. The sixteen-year-old twins who, I'm told, died in the Cairngorms some time back.'

'What about my sons?' he said tonelessly.

'Just that I'm not looking forward to telling them that their own father wouldn't lift a finger to bring them back to life again.'

He just stood there in the darkness, quite still, saying nothing. He offered no resistance when I took his arm and led him towards the *Firecrest.*

Uncle Arthur was at his most intimidating and Uncle Arthur in full intimidating cry was a sight to behold. He'd made no move to rise when I'd brought MacDonald into the saloon and he hadn't asked him to sit. The blue basilisk stare, channelled and magnified by the glittering monocle, transfixed the unfortunate sergeant like a laser beam.

'So your foot slipped, Sergeant,' Uncle Arthur said without preamble. He was using his cold, flat, quite uninflected voice, the one that curled your hair. 'The fact that you stand here now indicates that. Mr Calvert went ashore with the prisoner and enough rope for you to hang yourself and you seized it with both hands. Not very clever of you, Sergeant. You should not have tried to contact your friends.'

'They are no friends of mine, sir,' MacDonald said bitterly.

'I'm going to tell you as much as you need to know about Calvert – Petersen was a pseudonym – and myself and what we are doing.' Uncle Arthur hadn't heard him. 'If you ever repeat any part of what I say to anyone, it will cost you your job, your pension, any hope that you will ever again, in whatever capacity, get another job in Britain and several years in prison for contravention of the Official Secrets Act. I myself will personally formulate the charges.' He paused then added in a masterpiece of superfluity: 'Do I make myself clear?'

'You make yourself very clear,' MacDonald said grimly. So Uncle Arthur told him all he thought MacDonald needed to know, which wasn't much, and finished by saying: 'I am sure we can now count on your hundred per cent co-operation, Sergeant.'

'Calvert is just guessing at my part in this,' he said dully.

'For God's sake!' I said. 'You *knew* those customs officers were bogus. You *knew* they had no photo-copier with them. You *knew* their only object in coming aboard was to locate and smash that set – and locate any other we might have. You *knew* they couldn't have gone back to the mainland in that launch – it was too rough. The launch, was, in fact, the *Shangri-la*'s tender – which is why you left without lights – and no launch left the harbour after your departure. We'd have heard it. The only life we saw after that was when they switched on their lights in the *Shangri-la*'s wheelhouse to smash up their own radio – *one* of their own radios, I should have said. And how did you *know* the telephone lines were down in the Sound? You knew they were down, but why did you say the Sound? Because you *knew* they had been cut there. Then, yesterday morning, when I asked you if there was any hope of the lines being repaired, you said no. Odd. One would have thought that you would have told the customs boys going back to the mainland to contact the GPO at once. But you *knew* they weren't going back there. And your two sons, Sergeant, the boys supposed to be dead, you forgot to close their accounts. Because you *knew* they weren't dead.'

'I forgot about the accounts,' MacDonald said slowly. 'And all the other points – I'm afraid I'm not good at this sort of thing.' He looked at Uncle Arthur. 'I know this is the end of the road for me. They said they would kill my boys, sir.'

'If you will extend us your full co-operation,' Uncle Arthur said precisely, 'I will personally see to it that you remain the Torbay police sergeant until you're falling over your beard. Who are "they"?'

'The only men I've seen is a fellow called Captain Imrie and the two customs men – Durran and Thomas. Durran's real name is Quinn. I don't know the others' names. I usually met them in my house, after dark. I've been out to the *Shangri-la* only twice. To see Imrie.'

'And Sir Anthony Skouras?'

'I don't know.' MacDonald shrugged helplessly. 'He's a good man, sir, he really is. Or I thought so. Maybe he is mixed up in this. Anyone can fall into bad company. It's very strange, sir.'

'Isn't it? And what's been your part in this?'

'There's been funny things happening in this area in the past months. Boats have vanished. People have vanished. Fishermen have had their nets torn, in harbour, and yacht engines have been mysteriously damaged, also in harbour. This is when Captain Imrie wants to prevent certain boats from going certain places at the wrong time.'

'And your part is to investigate with great diligence and a total lack of success,' Uncle Arthur nodded. 'You must be invaluable to them, Sergeant. A man with your record and character is above suspicion. Tell me, Sergeant, what are they up to?'

'Before God, sir, I have no idea.'

'You're totally in the dark?'

'Yes, sir.'

'I don't doubt it. This is the way the very top men operate. And you will have no idea where your boys are being held?'

'No sir.'

'How do you know they're alive?'

'I was taken out to the *Shangri-la* three weeks ago. My sons had been brought there from God only knows where. They were well.'

'And are you really so naïve as to believe that your sons will be well and will be returned alive when all this is over? Even although your boys will be bound to know who their captors are and would be available for testimony and identification if the time came for that?'

'Captain Imrie said they would come to no harm. If I co-operated. He said that only fools ever used unnecessary violence.'

'You are convinced, then, they wouldn't go to the length of murder?'

'Murder! What are you talking about, sir?'

'Calvert?'

'Sir?'

'A large whisky for the sergeant.'

'Yes, sir.' When it came to lashing out with my private supplies Uncle Arthur was generous to a fault. Uncle Arthur paid no entertainment allowance. So I poured the sergeant a large whisky and, seeing that bankruptcy was inevitable anyway, did the same for myself. Ten seconds later the sergeant's glass was empty. I took his arm and led him to the engine-room. When we came back to the saloon in a minute's time the sergeant needed no persuading to accept another glass. His face was pale.

'I told you that Calvert carried out a helicopter reconnaissance to-day,' Uncle Arthur said conversationally. 'What I didn't tell you was that his pilot was murdered this evening. I didn't tell you that two other of my best agents have been killed in the last sixty hours. And now, as you've just seen, Hunslett. Do you still believe, Sergeant, that we are dealing with a bunch of gentlemanly law-breakers to whom human life is sacrosanct?'

'What do you want me to do, sir?' Colour was back in the brown cheeks again and the eyes were cold and hard and a little desperate.

'You and Calvert will take Hunslett ashore to your office. You will call in the doctor and ask for an official post-mortem – we must have an official cause of death. For the trial. The other dead men are probably beyond recovery. You will then row out to the *Shangri-la* and tell Imrie that we brought Hunslett and the other man – the Italian – to your office. You will tell them that you heard us say that we must go to the mainland for new depth-sounding equipment and for armed help and that we can't be back for two days at least. Do you know where the telephone lines are cut in the Sound?'

'Yes, sir. I cut them myself.'

'When you get back from the *Shangri-la* get out there and fix them. Before dawn. Before dawn to-morrow you, your wife and son must disappear. For thirty-six hours. If you want to live. That is understood?'

'I understand what you want done. Not why you want it done.'

'Just do it. One last thing. Hunslett has no relations – few of my men have – so he may as well be buried in Torbay. Knock up your local undertaker during the night and make arrangements for the funeral on Friday. Calvert and I would like to be there.'

'But – but Friday? That's just the day after to-morrow.'

'The day after to-morrow. It will be all over then. You'll have your boys back home.'

MacDonald looked at him in long silence, then said slowly: 'How can you be sure?'

'I'm not sure at all.' Uncle Arthur passed a weary hand across his face and looked at me. 'Calvert is. It's a pity, Sergeant, that the Secrets Act will never permit you to tell your friends that you once knew Philip Calvert. If it can be done, Calvert can do it. I think he can. I certainly hope so.'

'I certainly hope so, too,' MacDonald said sombrely.

Me too, more than either of them, but there was already so much despondency around that it didn't seem right to deepen it, so I just put on my confident face and led MacDonald back down to the engine-room.

Chapter Seven

Wednesday: 10.40 p.m. – Thursday: 2 a.m.

Three of them came to kill us, not at midnight as promised, but at 10.40 p.m. that night. Had they come five minutes earlier then they would have got us because five minutes earlier we were still tied up to the old stone pier. And had they come and got us that five minutes earlier, then the fault would have been mine for, after leaving Hunslett in the police station I had insisted that Sergeant MacDonald accompany me to use his authority in knocking up and obtaining service from the proprietor of the only chemist's shop in Torbay. Neither of them had been too keen on giving me the illegal help I wanted and it had taken me a full five minutes and the best part of my extensive repertoire of threats to extract from the very elderly chemist the minimum of reluctant service and a small green-ribbed bottle informatively labelled, 'The Tablets.' But I was lucky and I was back aboard the *Firecrest* just after 10.30 p.m.

The west coast of Scotland doesn't go in much for golden Indian summers and that night was no exception. Apart from being cold and windy, which was standard, it was also black as sin and bucketing heavily, which if not quite standard was at least not so unusual as to excite comment. A minute after leaving the pier I had to switch on the searchlight mounted on the wheelhouse roof. The western entrance to the Sound from Torbay harbour, between Torbay and Garve Island, is a quarter of a mile wide and I could have found it easily on a compass course: but there were small yachts, I knew, between the pier and the entrance and if any of them was carrying a riding light it was invisible in that driving rain.

The searchlight control was on the wheelhouse deckhead. I moved it to point the beam down and ahead, then traversed it through a forty-degree arc on either side of the bows.

I picked up the first boat inside five seconds, not a yacht riding at its moorings but a rowing dinghy moving slowly through the water. It was fine on the port bow, maybe fifty yards away. I couldn't identify the man at the oars, the oars wrapped at their middle with some white cloth to muffle the sound of the rowlocks, because his back was towards me. A very broad back. Quinn. The man in the bows was sitting facing me. He wore oilskins and a dark beret and in his hand he held a gun. At fifty yards it's almost impossible to identify any weapon, but his looked like a German Schmeisser machine-pistol. Without a doubt Jacques, the machine-gun specialist. The man crouched low in the stern-sheets was quite unidentifiable, but I could see the gleam of a short gun in his hand. Messrs Quinn, Jacques and Kramer coming to pay their respects as Charlotte Skouras had said they would. But much ahead of schedule.

Charlotte Skouras was on my right in the darkened wheelhouse. She'd been there only three minutes, having spent all our time alongside in her darkened cabin with the door closed. Uncle Arthur was on my left, desecrating the clean night air with one of his cheroots. I reached up for a clipped torch and patted my right hand pocket to see if the Lilliput was still there. It was.

I said to Charlotte Skouras: 'Open the wheelhouse door. Put it back on the catch and stand clear.' Then I said to Uncle Arthur: 'Take the wheel, sir. Hard a-port when I call. Then back north on course again.'

He took the wheel without a word. I heard the starboard wheelhouse door click on its latch. We were doing no more than three knots through the water. The dinghy was twenty-five yards away, the men in the bows and stern holding up arms to shield their eyes from our searchlight. Quinn had stopped rowing. On our present course we'd leave them at least ten feet on our port beam. I kept the searchlight steady on the boat.

Twenty yards separated us and I could see Jacques lining up his machine-pistol on our light when I thrust the throttle lever right open. The note of the big diesel exhaust deepened and the *Firecrest* began to surge forward.

'Hard over now,' I said.

Uncle Arthur spun the wheel. The sudden thrust of our single port screw boiled back against the port-angled rudder, pushing the stern sharply starboard. Flame lanced from Jacques' machine-pistol, a silent flame, he'd a silencer on. Bullets ricocheted off our aluminium foremast but missed both light and wheelhouse. Quinn saw what was coming and dug his oars deep but he was too late. I shouted 'Midships, now,' pulled the throttle lever back to neutral and jumped out through the starboard doorway on to the deck.

We hit them just where Jacques was sitting, breaking off the dinghy's bows, capsizing it and throwing the three men into the water. The overturned remains of the boat and a couple of struggling figures came slowly down the starboard side of the *Firecrest*. My torch picked up the man closer in to our side. Jacques, with the machine-pistol held high above his head, instinctively trying to keep it dry though it must have been soaked when he had been catapulted into the water. I held gun-hand and torch-hand together, aiming down the bright narrow beam. I squeezed the Lilliput's trigger twice and a bright crimson flower bloomed where his face had been. He went down as if a shark had got him, the gun in the stiffly-upstretched arms. It was a Schmeisser machine-pistol all right. I shifted the torch. There was only one other to be seen in the water and it wasn't Quinn, he'd either dived under the *Firecrest* or was sheltering under the upturned wreck of the dinghy. I fired twice more at the second figure and he started to scream. The screaming went on for two or three seconds, then stopped in a shuddering gurgle. I heard the sound of someone beside me on the deck being violently sick over the side. Charlotte Skouras. But I'd no time to stay and comfort Charlotte Skouras, she'd no damned right to be out on deck anyway. I had urgent matters to attend to, such as preventing Uncle Arthur from cleaving Torbay's old stone pier in half. The townspeople would not have liked it. Uncle Arthur's idea of midships differed sharply from mine, he'd brought the *Firecrest* round in a three-quarter circle. He would have been the ideal man at the helm of one of those ram-headed Phoenician galleys that specialized in cutting the opposition in two, but as a helmsman in Torbay harbour he lacked something. I jumped into the wheelhouse, pulled the throttle all the way to astern and spun the wheel to port. I jumped out again and pulled Charlotte Skouras away before she got her head knocked off by one of the barnacle-encrusted piles that fronted the pier. Whether or not we grazed the pier was impossible to say but we sure as hell gave the barnacles a nasty turn.

I moved back into the wheelhouse, taking Charlotte Skouras with me. I was breathing heavily. All this jumping in and out through wheelhouse doors took it out of a man. I said: 'With all respects, sir, what the hell were you trying to do?'

'Me?' He was as perturbed as a hibernating bear in January. 'Is something up, then?'

I moved the throttle to slow ahead, took the wheel from him and brought the *Firecrest* round till we were due north on a compass bearing. I said: 'Keep it there, please,' and did some more traversing with the searchlight. The waters around were black and empty, there was no sign even of the dinghy. I'd expected to see every light in Torbay lit up like a naval review, those four shots, even the Lilliput's sharp, light-weighted cracks, should have had them all on their feet. But nothing, no sign, no movement at all. The gin bottle levels would be lower than ever. I looked at the compass: north-twenty-west. Like the honey-bee for the flower, the iron filing for the magnet, Uncle Arthur was determinedly heading straight for the shore again. I took the wheel from him, gently but firmly, and said: 'You came a bit close to the pier back there, sir.'

'I believe I did.' He took out a handkerchief and wiped his monocle. 'Damn' glass misted up just at the wrong moment. I trust, Calvert, that you weren't just firing at random out there.' Uncle Arthur had become a good deal more bellicose in the past hour or so: he'd had a high regard for Hunslett.

'I got Jacques and Kramer. Jacques was the handy one with the automatic arms. He's dead. I think Kramer is too. Quinn got away.' What a set-up, I thought bleakly, what a set-up. Alone with Uncle Arthur on the high seas in the darkness of the night. I'd always known that his eyesight, even in optimum conditions, was pretty poor: but I'd never suspected that, when the sun was down, he was virtually blind as a bat. But unfortunately, unlike the bat, Uncle Arthur wasn't equipped with a built-in radar which would enable him to shy clear of rocks, headlands, islands and such-like obstructions of a similarly permanent and final nature with which we might go bump in the dark. To all intents and purposes I was single-handed. This called for a radical revision in plans only I didn't see how I could radically revise anything.

'Not too bad,' Uncle Arthur said approvingly. 'Pity about Quinn, but otherwise not too bad at all. The ranks of the ungodly are being satisfactorily depleted. Do you think they'll come after us?'

'No. For four reasons. One, they won't know yet what has happened. Two, both their sorties this evening have gone badly and they won't be in a hurry to try any more boarding expeditions for some time. Three, they'd use the tender for this job, not the *Shangri-la* and if they get that tender a hundred yards I've lost all faith in demerara sugar. Four, there's mist or fog coming up. The lights of Torbay are obscured already. They can't follow us because they can't find us.'

Till that moment the only source of illumination we'd had in the wheelhouse had come from the reflected light of the compass lamp. Suddenly the overhead light came on. Charlotte Skouras's hand was on the switch. Her face was haggard and she was staring at me as if I were the thing from outer space. Not one of those admiring affectionate looks.

'What kind of man are you, Mr Calvert?' No 'Philip' this time. Her voice was lower and huskier than ever and it had a shake in it. 'You – you're not human. You kill two men and go on speaking calmly and reasonably as if nothing had happened. What in God's name are you, a hired killer? It's – it's unnatural. Have you no feelings, no emotions, no regrets?'

'Yes, I have. I'm sorry I didn't kill Quinn too.'

She stared at me with something like horror in her face, then switched her gaze to Uncle Arthur. She said to him and her voice was almost a whisper: 'I saw that man, Sir Arthur. I saw his face being blown apart by the bullets. Mr Calvert could have – could have arrested him, held him up and handed him over to the police. But he didn't. He killed him. And the other. It was slow and deliberate. Why, why, why?'

'There's no "why" about it, my dear Charlotte.' Sir Arthur sounded almost irritable. 'There's no justification needed. Calvert killed them or they killed us. They came to kill us. You told us that yourself. Would you feel any compunction at killing a poisonous snake? Those men were no better than that. As for arresting them!' Uncle Arthur paused, maybe for the short laugh he gave, maybe because he was trying to recall the rest of the homily I'd delivered to him earlier that evening. 'There's no intermediate stage in this game. It's kill or be killed. These are dangerous and deadly men and you never give them warning.' Good old Uncle Arthur, he'd remembered the whole lecture, practically word for word.

She looked at him for a long moment, her face uncomprehending, looked at me then slowly turned and left the wheelhouse.

I said to Uncle Arthur: 'You're just as bad as I am.'

She reappeared again exactly at midnight, switching on the light as she entered. Her hair was combed and neat, her face was less puffy and she was dressed in one of those synthetic fibre dresses, white, ribbed and totally failing to give the impression that she stood in need of a good meal. From the way she eased her shoulders I could see that her back hurt. She gave me a faint tentative smile. She got none in return.

I said: 'Half an hour ago, rounding Carrara Point, I near as dammit carried away the lighthouse. Now I hope I'm heading north of Dubh Sgeir but I may be heading straight into the middle of it. It couldn't be any blacker if you were a mile down in an abandoned coal mine, the fog is thickening, I'm a not very experienced sailor trying to navigate my way through the most dangerous waters in Britain and whatever hope we have of survival depends on the preservation of what night-sight I've slowly and painfully built up over the past hour or so. *Put out that damned light!*'

'I'm sorry.' The light went out. 'I didn't think.'

'And don't switch on any other lights either. Not even in your cabin. Rocks are the least of my worries in Loch Houron.'

'I'm sorry,' she repeated. 'And I'm sorry about earlier on. That's why I came up. To tell you that. About the way I spoke and leaving so abruptly, I mean. I've no right to sit on judgment on others – and I think my judgment was wrong. I was just – well, literally shocked. To see two men killed like that, no, not killed, there's always heat and anger about killing, to see two men executed like that, because it wasn't kill or be killed as Sir Arthur said, and then see the person who did it not care . . .' Her voice faded away uncertainly.

'You might as well get your facts and figures right, my dear,' Uncle Arthur said. 'Three men, not two. He killed one just before you came on board to-night. He had no option. But Philip Calvert is not what any reasonable man would call a killer. He doesn't care in the way you say, because if he did he would go mad. In another way, he cares very much. He doesn't do this job for money. He's miserably paid for a man of his unique talents.' I made a mental note to bring this up next time we were alone. 'He doesn't do it for excitement, for – what is the modern expression? – kicks: a man who devotes his spare time to music, astronomy and philosophy does not live for kicks. But he cares. He cares for the difference between right and wrong, between good and evil, and when that difference is great enough and the evil threatens to destroy the good then he does not hesitate to take steps to redress the balance. And maybe that makes him better than either you or me, my dear Charlotte.'

'And that's not all of it either,' I said. 'I'm also renowned for my kindness to little children.'

'I'm sorry, Calvert,' Uncle Arthur said. 'No offence and no embarrassment, I hope. But if Charlotte thought it important enought to come up here and apologize, I thought it important enough to set the record straight.'

'That's not all Charlotte came up for,' I said nastily. '*If* that's what she came up for in the first plase. She came up here because she's consumed with feminine curiosity. She wants to know where we are going.'

'Do you mind if I smoke?' she asked.

'Don't strike the match in front of my eyes.'

She lit the cigarette and said: 'Consumed with curiosity is right. What do you think? Not about where we're going, I know where we're going. You told me. Up Loch Houron. What I want to know is what is going on, what all this dreadful mystery is about, why all the comings and goings of strange men aboard the *Shangri-la*, what is so fantastically important to justify the deaths of three men in one evening, what you are doing here, what you are, who you are. I never really thought you were a UNESCO delegate, Sir Arthur. I know now you're not. Please. I have the right to know, I think.'

'Don't tell her,' I advised.

'Why ever not?' Uncle Arthur said huffily. 'As she says, she is deeply involved, whether she wants it or not. She does have the right to know. Besides, the whole thing will be public knowledge in a day or two.'

'You didn't think of that when you threatened Sergeant MacDonald with dismissal and imprisonment if he contravened the Official Secrets Act.'

'Merely because he could ruin things by talking out of turn,' he said stiffly. 'Lady – I mean, Charlotte – is in no position to do so. Not, of course,' he went on quickly, 'that she would ever dream of doing so. Preposterous. Charlotte is an old and dear friend, a *trusted* friend, Calvert. She *shall* know.'

Charlotte said quietly: 'I have the feeling that our friend Mr Calvert does not care for me overmuch. Or maybe he just does not care for women.'

'I care like anything,' I said. 'I was merely reminding the admiral of his own dictum: Never, never, never – I forget how many nevers, I think there were four or five – tell anyone anything unless it's necessary, essential and vital. In this case it's none of the three.'

Uncle Arthur lit another vile cheroot and ignored me. His dictum was not meant to refer to confidential exchanges between members of the aristocracy. He said: 'This is the case of the missing ships, my dear Charlotte. Five missing ships, to be precise. Not to mention a fair scattering of very much smaller vessels, also missing or destroyed.

'Five ships, I said. On 5th April of this year the S.S. *Holmwood* disappeared off the south coast of Ireland. It was an act of piracy. The crew was imprisoned ashore, kept under guard for two or three days, then released unharmed. The *Holmwood* was never heard of again. On 24th April, the M.V. *Antara* vanished in St George's Channel. On 17th May, the M.V. *Headley Pioneer* disappeared off Northern Ireland, on 6th August the S.S. *Hurricane Spray* disappeared after leaving the Clyde and finally, last Saturday, a vessel called the *Nantesville* vanished soon after leaving Bristol. In all cases the crews turned up unharmed.

'Apart from their disappearances and the safe reappearances of their crews, those five vessels all had one thing in common – they were carrying extremely valuable and virtually untraceable cargoes. The *Holmwood* had two and a half million pounds of South African gold aboard, the *Antara* had a million and a half pounds' worth of uncut Brazilian diamonds for industrial use, the *Headley Pioneer* had close on two million pounds' worth of mixed cut and uncut Andean emeralds from the Muzo mines in Columbia, the *Hurricane Spray*, which had called in at Glasgow *en route* from Rotterdam to New York, had just over three million pounds' worth of diamonds, nearly all cut, and the last one, the *Nantesville*,' – Uncle Arthur almost choked over this one – 'had eight million pounds in gold ingots, reserves being called in by the US Treasury.

'We had no idea where the people responsible for these disappearances were getting their information. Such arrangements as to the decision to ship, when, how and how much, are made in conditions of intense secrecy. They, whoever "they" are, had impeccable sources of information. Calvert says he knows those sources now. After the disappearance of the first three ships and about six million pounds' worth of specie it was obvious that a meticulously organized gang was at work.'

'Do you mean to say – do you mean to say that Captain Imrie is mixed up in this?' Charlotte asked.

'Mixed up is hardly the word,' Uncle Arthur said dryly. 'He may well be the directing mind behind it all.'

'And don't forget old man Skouras,' I advised. 'He's pretty deep in the mire, too – about up to his ears, I should say.'

'You've no right to say that,' Charlotte said quickly.

'No right? Why ever not? What's he to you and what's all this defence of the maestro of the bull-whip? How's your back now?'

She said nothing. Uncle Arthur said nothing, in a different kind of way, then went on:

'It was Calvert's idea to hide two of our men and a radio signal transmitter on most of the ships that sailed with cargoes of bullion or specie after the *Headley Pioneer* had vanished. We had no difficulty, as you can imagine, in securing the co-operation of the various exporting and shipping companies and governments concerned. Our agents – we had three pairs working – usually hid among the cargo or in some empty cabin or machinery space with a food supply. Only the masters of the vessels concerned knew they were aboard. They delivered a fifteen-second homing signal at fixed – very fixed – but highly irregular intervals. Those signals were picked up at selected receiving stations round the west coast – we limited our stations to that area for that was where the released crews had been picked up – and by a receiver aboard this very boat here. The *Firecrest*, my dear Charlotte, is a highly unusual craft in many respects.' I thought he was going to boast, quietly of course, of his own brilliance in designing the *Firecrest* but he remembered in time that I knew the truth.

'Between 17th May and 6th August nothing happened. No piracy. We believe they were deterred by the short, light nights. On 6th August, the *Hurricane Spray* disappeared. We had no one aboard that vessel – we couldn't cover them all. But we had two men aboard the *Nantesville*, the ship that sailed last Saturday. Delmont and Baker. Two of our best men. The *Nantesville* was forcibly taken just off the Bristol Channel. Baker and Delmont immediately began the scheduled transmissions. Cross-bearings gave us a completely accurate position at least every half-hour.

'Calvert and Hunslett were in Dublin, waiting. As soon—'

'That's right,' she interrupted. 'Mr Hunslet. Where is he? I haven't seen—'

'In a moment. The *Firecrest* moved out, not following the *Nantesville*, but moving ahead of its predicted course. They reached the Mull of Kintyre and had intended waiting till the *Nantesville* approached there but a south-westerly gale blew up out of nowhere and the *Firecrest* had to run for shelter. When the *Nantesville* reached the Mull of Kintyre area our radio beacon fixes indicated that she was still on a mainly northerly course and that it looked as if she might pass up the Mull of Kintyre on the outside – the western side. Calvert took a chance, ran up Loch Fyne and through the Crinan Canal. He spent the night in the Crinan sea-basin. The sea-lock is closed at night. Calvert could have obtained the authority to have it opened but he didn't want to: the wind had veered to westerly late that evening and small boats don't move out of Crinan through the Dorus Mor in a westerly gusting up to Force 9. Not if they have wives and families to support – and even if they haven't.

'During the night the *Nantesville* turned out west into the Atlantic. We thought we had lost her. We think we know now why she turned out: she wanted to arrive at a certain place at a certain state of the tide in the hours of darkness, and she had time to kill. She went west, we believe, firstly because it was the easiest way to ride out the westerly gale and, secondly, because she didn't want to be seen hanging around the coast all of the next day and preferred to make a direct approach from the sea as darkness was falling.

'The weather moderated a fair way overnight. Calvert left Crinan at dawn, almost at the very minute the *Nantesville* turned back east again. Radio transmissions were still coming in from Baker and Delmont exactly on schedule. The last transmission came at 1022 hours that morning: after that, nothing.'

Uncle Arthur stopped and the cheroot glowed fiercely in the darkness. He could have made a fortune contracting out to the cargo shipping compaines as a one-man fumigating service. Then he went on very quickly as if he didn't like what he had to say next, and I'm sure he didn't.

'We don't know what happened. They may have betrayed themselves by some careless action. I don't think so, they were too good for that. Some member of the prize crew may just have stumbled over their hiding-place. Again it's unlikely, and a man who stumbled over Baker and Delmont wouldn't be doing any more stumbling for some time to come. Calvert thinks, and I agree with him, that by the one unpredictable chance in ten thousand, the prize crew's radio-operator happened to be traversing Baker and Delmont's wave-band at the very moment they were sending their fifteen second transmission. At that range he'd about have his head blasted off and the rest was inevitable.

'A plot of the *Nantesville*'s fixes between dawn and the last transmission showed her course as 082° true. Predicted destination – Loch Houron. Estimated time of arrival – sunset. Calvert had less than a third of the *Nantesville*'s distance to cover. But he didn't take the *Firecrest* into Loch Houron because he was pretty sure that Captain Imrie would recognize a radio beacon transmitter when he saw one and would assume that we had his course. Calvert was also pretty sure that if the *Nantesville* elected to continue on that course – and he had a hunch that it would – any craft found in the entrance to Loch Houron would receive pretty short shrift, either by being run down or sunk by gunfire. So he parked the *Firecrest* in Torbay and was skulking around the entrance to Loch Houron in a frogman's suit and with a motorized rubber dinghy when the *Nantesville* turned up. He went aboard in darkness. The name was changed, the flag was changed, one mast was missing and the superstructure had been repainted. But it was the *Nantesville*.

'Next day Calvert and Hunslett were storm-bound in Torbay but on Wednesday Calvert organized an air search for the *Nantesville* or some place where she might have been hidden. He made a mistake. He considered it extremely unlikely that the *Nantesville* would still be in Loch Houron because Imrie knew that we knew that he had been headed there and therefore would not stay there indefinitely, because the chart showed Loch

Houron as being the last place in Scotland where anyone in their sane minds would consider hiding a vessel and because, after Calvert had left the *Nantesville* that evening, she'd got under way and started to move out to Carrara Point. Calvert thought she'd just stayed in Loch Houron till it was dark enough to pass undetected down the Sound of Torbay or round the south of Torbay Island to the mainland. So he concentrated most of his search on the mainland and on the Sound of Torbay and Torbay itself. He thinks now the *Nantesville* is in Loch Houron. We're going there to find out.' His cheroot glowed again. 'And that's it, my dear. Now, with your permission, I'd like to spend an hour on the saloon settee. Those nocturnal escapades . . ." He sighed, and finished: 'I'm not a boy any longer. I need my sleep.'

I liked that. I wasn't a boy any longer either and I didn't seem to have slept for months. Uncle Arthur, I knew, always went to bed on the stroke of midnight and the poor man had already lost fifteen minutes. But I didn't see what I could do about it. One of my few remaining ambitions in life was to reach pensionable age and I couldn't make a better start than by ensuring that Uncle Arthur never laid hands on the wheel of the *Firecrest*.

'But surely that's not it,' Charlotte protested. 'That's not all of it. Mr Hunslett, where's Mr Hunslett? And you said Mr Calvert was aboard the *Nantesville*. How on earth did he—?'

'There are some things you are better not knowing, my dear. Why distress yourself unnecessarily? Just leave this to us.'

'You haven't had a good look at me recently, have you, Sir Arthur?' she asked quietly.

'I don't understand.'

'It may have escaped your attention but I'm not a child any more. I'm not even young any more. Please don't treat me as a juvenile. And if you want to get to that settee to-night—'

'Very well. If you insist. The violence, I'm afraid, has not all been one-sided. Calvert, as I said, was about the *Nantesville*. He found my two operatives, Baker and Delmont.' Uncle Arthur had the impersonal emotionless voice of a man checking his laundry list. 'Both men had been stabbed to death. This evening the pilot of Calvert's helicopter was killed when the machine was shot down in the Sound of Torbay. An hour after that Hunslett was murdered. Calvert found him in the *Firecrest*'s engine-room with a broken neck.'

Uncle Arthur's cheroot glowed and faded at least half a dozen times before Charlotte spoke. The shake was back in her voice. 'They are fiends. Fiends.' A long pause, then: 'How can you cope with people like that?'

Uncle Arthur puffed a bit more then said candidly: 'I don't intend to try. You don't find generals slugging it out hand-to-hand in the trenches. Calvert will cope with them. Good night, my dear.'

He pushed off. I didn't contradict him. But I knew that Calvert couldn't cope with them. Not any more, he couldn't. Calvert had to have help. With a crew consisting of a myopic boss and a girl who, every time I looked at her, listened to her or thought of her, started the warning bells clanging away furiously in the back of my head, Calvert had to have a great deal of help. And he had to have it fast.

After Uncle Arthur had retired, Charlotte and I stood in silence in the darkened wheelhouse. But a companionable silence. You can always tell. The rain drummed on the wheelhouse roof. It was as dark as it ever becomes at sea and the patches of white fog were increasing in density and number. Because of them I had cut down to half speed and with the loss of steerage way and that heavy westerly sea coming up dead astern I'd normally have been hard put to it to control the direction of the *Firecrest*: but I had the auto-pilot on and switched to 'Fine' and we were doing famously. The auto-pilot was a much better helmsman than I was. And streets ahead of Uncle Arthur.

Charlotte said suddenly: 'What is it you intend to do to-night?'

'You *are* a gourmand for information. Don't you know that Uncle Arthur – sorry, Sir Arthur – and I are engaged upon a highly secret mission? Security is all.'

'And now you're laughing at me – and forgetting I'm along on this secret mission too.'

'I'm glad you're along and I'm not laughing at you, because I'll be leaving this boat once or twice to-night and I have to have somebody I can trust to look after it when I'm away.'

'You have Sir Arthur.'

'I have, as you say, Sir Arthur. There's no one alive for whose judgment and intelligence I have greater respect. But at the present moment I'd trade in all the judgment and intelligence in the world for a pair of sharp young eyes. Going by to-night's performance, Sir Arthur shouldn't be allowed out without a white stick. How are yours?'

'Well, they're not so young any more, but I think they're sharp enough.'

'So I can rely on you?'

'On me? I – well, I don't know anything about handling boats.'

'You and Sir Arthur should make a great team. I saw you star once in a French film about—'

'We never left the studio. Even in the studio pool I had a stand-in.'

'Well, there'll be no stand-in to-night.' I glanced out through the streaming windows. 'And no studio pool. This is the real stuff, the genuine Atlantic. A pair of eyes, Charlotte, that's all I require. A pair of eyes. Just cruising up and down till I come back and seeing that you don't go on the rocks. Can you do that?'

'Will I have any option?'

'Nary an option.'

'Then I'll try. Where are you going ashore?'

'Eilean Oran and Craigmore. The two innermost islands in Loch Houron. If,' I said thoughtfully, 'I can find them.'

'Eilean Oran and Craigmore.' I could have been wrong, but I thought the faint French accent a vast improvement on the original Gaelic pronunciation. 'It seems so wrong. So very wrong. In the middle of all this hate and avarice and killing. These names – they breathe the very spirit of romance.'

'A highly deceptive form of respiration, my dear.' I'd have to watch myself, I was getting as bad as Uncle Arthur. 'Those islands breathe the very spirit of bare, bleak and rocky desolation. But Eilean Oran and Craigmore hold the key to everything. Of that I'm very sure.'

She said nothing. I stared out through the high-speed Kent clear-view screen and wondered if I'd see Dubh Sgeir before it saw me. After a couple of minutes I felt a hand on my upper arm and she was very close to me. The hand was trembling. Wherever she'd come by her perfume it hadn't been bought in a supermarket or fallen out of a Christmas cracker. Momentarily and vaguely I wondered about the grievous impossibility of ever understanding the feminine mind: before fleeing for what she had thought to be her life and embarking upon a hazardous swim in the waters of Torbay harbour, she hadn't forgotten to pack a sachet of perfume in her polythene kit-bag. For nothing was ever surer than that any perfume she'd been wearing had been well and truly removed before I'd fished her out of Torbay harbour.

'Philip?'

Well, this was better than the Mr Calvert stuff. I was glad Uncle Arthur wasn't there to have his aristocratic feelings scandalized. I said: 'Uh-huh?'

'I'm sorry.' She said it as if she meant it and I supposed I should have tried to forget that she was once the best actress in Europe. 'I'm truly sorry. About what I said – about what I thought – earlier on. For thinking you were a monster. The men you killed, I mean. I – well, I didn't know about Hunslett and Baker and Delmont and the helicopter pilot. All your friends. I'm truly sorry, Philip. Truly.'

She was overdoing it. She was also too damn' close. Too damn' warm. You'd have required a pile-driver in top condition to get a cigarette card between us. And that perfume that hadn't fallen out of a cracker – intoxicating, the ad-boys in the glossies would have called it. And all the time the warning bells were clanging away like a burglar alarm with the St Vitus's dance. I made a manful effort to do something about it. I put my mind to higher things.

She said nothing. She just squeezed my arm a bit more and even the pile-driver would have gone on strike for piece-work rates. I could hear the big diesel exhaust thudding away behind us, a sound of desolate reassurance. The *Firecrest* swooped down the long overtaking combers then gently soared again. I was conscious for the first time of a curious meteorological freak in the Western Isles. A marked rise in temperature after midnight. And I'd have to speak to the Kent boys about their guarantee that their clearview screen wouldn't mist up under any conditions, but maybe that wasn't fair, maybe they'd never visualized conditions like this. I was just thinking of switching off the auto-pilot to give me something to do when she said: 'I think I'll go below soon. Would you like a cup of coffee first?'

'As long as you don't have to put on a light to do it. And as long as you don't trip over Uncle Arthur – I mean, Sir—'

'Uncle Arthur will do just fine,' she said. 'It suits him.' Another squeeze of the arm and she was gone.

The meteorological freak was of short duration. By and by the temperature dropped back to normal and the Kent guarantee became operative again. I took a chance, left the *Firecrest* to its own devices and nipped aft to the stern locker. I took out my scuba diving equipment, together with air-cylinders and mask, and brought them for'ard to the wheelhouse.

It took her twenty-five minutes to make the coffee. Calor gas has many times the calorific efficiency of standard domestic coal gas and, even allowing for the difficulties of operating in darkness, this was surely a world record for slowness in making coffee at sea. I heard the clatter of crockery as the coffee was brought through the saloon and smiled cynically to myself in the darkness. Then I thought of Hunslett and Baker and Delmont and Williams, and I wasn't smiling any more.

I still wasn't smiling when I dragged myself on to the rocks of Eilean Oran, removed the scuba equipment and set the big, rectangular-based, swivel-headed torch between a couple of stones with its beam staring out to sea. I wasn't smiling, but it wasn't for the same reason that I hadn't been smiling when Charlotte had brought the coffee to the wheelhouse just over half an hour ago, I wasn't smiling because I was in a state of high apprehension and I was in a state of high apprehension because for ten minutes before leaving the *Firecrest* I'd tried to instruct Sir Arthur and Charlotte in the technique of keeping a boat in a constant position relative to a fixed mark on the shore.

'Keep her on a due west compass heading,' I'd said, 'Keep her bows on to the sea and wind. With the engine at "Slow" that will give you enough steerage way to keep your head up. If you find yourselves creeping too far forwards, come round to the *south*' – if they'd come round to the north they'd have found themselves high and dry on the rock shores of Eilean Oran – 'head due east at half speed, because if you go any slower you'll broach to, come sharply round to the north then head west again at slow speed. You can see those breakers on the south shore there. Whatever you do, keep them at least two hundred yards away on the starboard hand when you're going west and a bit more when you're going east.'

They had solemnly assured me that they would do just that and seemed a bit chuffed because of what must have been my patent lack of faith in them both, but I'd reason for my lack of faith for neither had shown any marked ability to make a clear distinction between shore breakers and the north-south line of the foaming tops of the waves rolling eastwards towards the mainland. In desperation, I'd said I'd place a fixed light on the shore and that that would serve as a permanent guide. I just trusted to God that Uncle Arthur wouldn't emulate the part of an eighteenth-century French sloop's skipper vis-à-vis the smugglers' lamp on a rock-girt Cornish shore and run the damned boat aground under the impression that he was heading for a beacon of hope. He was a very clever man, was Uncle Arthur, but the sea was not his home.

The boatshed wasn't quite empty, but it wasn't far off it. I flashed my small torch around its interior and realized that MacEachern's boatshed wasn't the place I was after. There was nothing there but a weather-beaten, gunwale-splintered launch, with, amidships, an unboxed petrol engine that seemed to be a solid block of rust.

I came to the house. On its northern side, the side remote from the sea, a light shone through a small window. A light at half-past one in the morning. I crawled up to this and hitched a wary eye over the window-sill. A neat, clean, well-cared-for small room, with lime-washed walls, mat-covered stone floor and the embers of a drift-wood fire smouldering in an ingle-nook in the corner. Donald MacEachern was sitting in a cane-bottomed chair, still unshaven, still in his month-old shirt, his head bent, staring into the dull red heart of the fire. He had the look of a man who was staring into a dying fire because that was all that was left in the world for him to do. I moved round to the door, turned the handle and went inside.

He heard me and turned around, not quickly, just the way a man would turn who knows there is nothing left on earth that can hurt him. He looked at me, looked at the gun in my hand, looked at his own twelve-bore hanging on a couple of nails on the wall then sank back into his chair again.

He said tonelessly: 'Who in the name of God are you?'

'Calvert's my name. I was here yesterday.' I pulled off my rubber hood and he remembered all right. I nodded to the twelve-bore. 'You won't be needing that gun to-night, Mr MacEachern. Anyway, you had the safety catch on.'

'You don't miss much,' he said slowly. 'There were no cartridges in the gun.'

'And no one standing behind you, was there?'

'I don't know what you mean,' he said tiredly. 'Who are you, man? What do you want?'

'I want to know why you gave me the welcome you did yesterday.' I put the gun away. 'It was hardly friendly, Mr MacEachern.'

'Who are you, sir?' He looked even older than he had done yesterday, old and broken and done.

'Calvert. They told you to discourage visitors, didn't they, Mr MacEachern?' No answer. 'I asked some questions to-night of a friend of yours. Archie MacDonald. The Torbay police sergeant. He told me you were married. I don't see Mrs MacEachern.'

He half rose from his cane chair. The old bloodshot eyes had a gleam to them. He sank back again and the eyes dimmed.

'You were out in your boat one night, weren't you, Mr MacEachern? You were out in your boat and you saw too much. They caught you and they took you back here and they took Mrs MacEachern away and they told you that if you ever breathed a word to anyone alive you would never see your wife that way again. Alive, I mean. They told you to stay here in case any chance acquaintances or strangers should call by and wonder why you weren't here and raise the alarm, and just to make sure that you wouldn't be tempted to go to the mainland for help – although heaven knows I would have thought there would be no chance in the world of you being as mad as that – they immobilized your engine. Salt-water impregnated sacks, I shouldn't wonder, so that any chance caller would think it was due to neglect and disuse, not sabotage.'

'Aye, they did that.' He stared sightlessly into the fire, his voice the sunken whisper of a man who is just thinking aloud and hardly aware that he is speaking. 'They took her away and they ruined my boat. And I had my life savings in the back room there and they took that too. I wish I'd had a million pounds to give them. If only they had left my Mairi. She's five years older than myself.' He had no defences left.

'What in the name of God have you been living on?'

'Every other week they bring me tinned food, not much, and condensed milk. Tea I have, and I catch a fish now and then off the rocks.' He gazed into the fire, his forehead wrinkling as if he were suddenly realizing that I brought a new dimension into his life. 'Who are you, sir? Who are you? You're not one of them. And you're not a policeman, I know you're not a policeman. I've seen them. I've seen policemen. But you are a very different kettle of fish.' There were the stirrings of life in him now, life in his face and in his eyes. He stared at me for a full minute, and I was beginning to feel uncomfortable under the gaze of those faded eyes, when he said: 'I know who you are. I know who you must be. You are a Government man. You are an agent of the British Secret Service.'

Well, by God, I took off my hat to the old boy. There I was, looking nondescript as anything and buttoned to the chin in a scuba suit, and he had me nailed right away. So much for the inscrutable faces of the guardians of our country's secrets. I thought of what Uncle Arthur would have said to him, the automatic threats of dismissal and imprisonment if the old man breathed a word. But Donald MacEachern didn't have any job to be dismissed from and after a lifetime in Eilean Oran even a maximum security prison would have looked like a hostelry to which Egon Ronay would have lashed out six stars without a second thought, so as there didn't seem to be much point in threatening him I said instead, for the first time in my life: 'I am an agent of the Secret Service, Mr MacEachern. I am going to bring your wife back to you.'

He nodded very slowly, then said: 'You will be a very brave man, Mr Calvert, but you do not know the terrible men who will wait for you.'

'If I ever earn a medal, Mr MacEachern, it will be a case of mistaken identification, but, for the rest, I know very well what I am up against. Just try to believe me, Mr MacEachern. It will be all right. You were in the war, Mr MacEachern.'

'You know. You were told?'

I shook my head. 'Nobody had to tell me.'

'Thank you, sir,' The back was suddenly very straight. 'I was a soldier for twenty-two years. I was a sergeant in the 51st Highland Division.'

'You were a sergeant in the 51st Highland Division,' I repeated. 'There are many people, Mr MacEachern, and not all of them Scots, who maintain that there was no better in the world.'

'And it is not Donald MacEachern who would be disagreeing with you, sir.' For the first time the shadow of a smile touched the faded eyes. 'There were maybe one or two worse. You make your point, Mr Calvert. We were not namely for running away, for losing hope, for giving up too easily.' He rose abruptly to his feet. 'In the name of God, what am I talking about? I am coming with you, Mr Calvert.'

I rose to my feet and touched my hands to his shoulders. 'Thank you, Mr MacEachern, but no. You've done enough. Your fighting days are over. Leave this to me.'

He looked at me in silence, then nodded. Again the suggestion of a smile. 'Aye, maybe you're right. I would be getting in the way of a man like yourself. I can see that.' He sat down wearily in his chair.

I moved to the door. 'Good night, Mr MacEachern. She will soon be safe.'

'She will soon be safe,' he repeated. He looked up at me, his eyes moist, and when he spoke his voice held the same faint surprise as his face. 'You know, I believe she will.'

'She will. I'm going to bring her back here personally and that will give me more pleasure than anything I've ever done in my life. Friday morning, Mr MacEachern.'

'Friday morning? So soon? So soon?' He was looking at a spot about a billion light years away and seemed unaware that I was standing by the open door. He smiled, a genuine smile of delight, and the old eyes shone. 'I'll not sleep a wink to-night, Mr Calvert. Nor a wink to-morrow night either.'

'You'll sleep on Friday,' I promised. He couldn't see me any longer, the tears were running down his grey unshaven cheeks, so I closed the door with a quiet hand and left him alone with his dreams.

Chapter Eight

Thursday: 2 a.m. – 4.30 a.m.

I had exchanged Eilean Oran for the island of Craigmore and I still wasn't smiling. I wasn't smiling for all sorts of reasons. I wasn't smiling because Uncle Arthur and Charlotte Skouras together made a nautical combination that terrified the life out of me, because the northern tip of Craigmore was much more exposed and reef-haunted than the south shore of Eilean Oran had been, because the fog was thickening, because I was breathless and bruised from big combers hurling me on to unseen reefs on my swim ashore, because I was wondering whether I had any chance in the world of carrying out my rash promise to Donald MacEachern. If I thought a bit more I'd no doubt I could come up with all sorts of other and equally valid reasons why I wasn't smiling, but I hadn't the time to think any more about it, the night was wearing on and I'd much to do before the dawn.

The nearest of the two fishing boats in the little natural harbour was rolling quite heavily in the waves that curled round the reef forming the natural breakwater to the west so I didn't have to worry too much about any splashing sound I might make as I hauled myself up on deck. What I did have to worry about was that damned bright light in its sealed inverted glass by the flensing shed, it was powerful enough to enable me to be seen from the other houses on shore. . . . But my worry about it was a little thing compared to my gratitude for its existence. Out in the wild blue yonder Uncle Arthur could do with every beacon of hope he could find.

It was a typical MFV, about forty-five feet long and with the general look of a boat that could laugh at a hurricane. I went through it in two minutes. All in immaculate condition, not a thing aboard that shouldn't have been there. Just a genuine fishing boat. My hopes began to rise. There was no other direction they could go.

The second MFV was the mirror image of the first, down to the last innocuous inch. It wouldn't be true to say that my hopes were now soaring, but at least they were getting up off the ground where they'd been for a long time.

I swam ashore, parked my scuba equipment above the high-water mark and made my way to the flensing shed, keeping its bulk between the light and myself as I went. The shed contained winches, steel tubs and barrels, a variety of ferocious weapons doubtless used for flensing, rolling cranes, some unidentifiable but obviously harmless machinery, the remains of some sharks and the most fearful smell I'd ever come across in my life. I left, hurriedly.

The first of the cottages yielded nothing. I flashed a torch through a broken window. The room was bare, it looked as if no one had set foot there for half a century, it was only too easy to believe Williams's statement that this tiny hamlet had been abandoned before the First World War. Curiously, the wall-paper looked as if it had been applied the previous day – a curious and largely unexplained phenomenon in the Western Isles. Your grandmother – in those days grandpa would have signed the pledge sooner than lift a finger inside the house – slapped up some wall-paper at ninepence a yard and fifty years later it was still there, as fresh as the day it had been put up.

The second cottage was as deserted as the first.

The third cottage, the one most remote from the flensing shed, was where the shark-fishers lived. A logical and very understandable choice, one would have thought, the farther away from that olfactory horror the better. Had I the option, I'd have been living in a tent on the other side of the island. But that was a purely personal reaction. The stench of that flensing shed was probably to the shark-fishers, as is the ammonia-laden, nostril-wrinkling, wholly awful *mist* – liquid manure – to the Swiss farmers: the very breath of being. The symbol of success. One can pay too high a price for success.

I eased open the well-oiled – shark-liver oil, no doubt – door and passed inside. The torch came on again. Grandma wouldn't have gone very much on this front parlour but grandpa would cheerfully have sat there watching his beard turn white through the changing seasons without ever wanting to go down to the sea again. One entire wall was given up to food supplies, a miserable couple of dozen crates of whisky and score upon scores of crates of beer. Australians, Williams had said. I could well believe it. The other three walls – there was hardly a scrap of wall-paper to be seen – was devoted to a form of art, in uninhibited detail and glorious Technicolor, of a type not usually to be found in the better-class museums and art galleries. Not grandma's cup of tea at all.

I skirted the furniture which hadn't come out of Harrods and opened the interior door. A short corridor lay beyond. Two doors to the right, three to the left. Working on the theory that the boss of the outfit probably had the largest room to himself, I carefully opened the first door to the right.

The flash-light showed it to be a surprisingly comfortable room. A good carpet, heavy curtains, a couple of good armchairs, bedroom furniture in oak, a double bed and a bookcase. A shaded electric light hung above the bed. Those rugged Australians believed in their home comforts. There was a switch beside the door. I touched it and the overhead lamp came on.

There was only one person in the double bed but even at that he was cramped in it. It's hard to gauge a man's height when he's lying down but if this lad tried to stand up in a room with a ceiling height of less than six feet four inches, he'd finish up with concussion. His face was towards me but I couldn't see much of it, it was hidden by a head of thick black hair that had fallen over his brows and the most magnificently bushy black beard I'd ever clapped eyes on. He was sound asleep.

I crossed to the bed, prodded his ribs with the gun barrel and a pressure sufficient to wake a lad of his size and said: 'Wake up.'

He woke up. I moved a respectful distance away. He rubbed his eyes with one hairy forearm, got his hands under him and heaved himself to a sitting position. I wouldn't have been surprised to see him wearing a bearskin, but no, he was wearing a pair of pyjamas in excellent taste, I might have chosen the colour myself.

Law-abiding citizens woken in the dark watches of the night by a gun-pointing stranger react in all sorts of ways, varying from terror to apoplectically-purple outrage. The man in the beard didn't react in any of the standard ways at all. He just stared at me from under dark overhanging cliffs of eyebrows and the expression in the eyes was that of a Bengal tiger mentally tucking in his napkin before launching himself on the thirty-foot leap that is going to culminate in lunch. I stepped back another couple paces and said: 'Don't try it.'

'Put that gun away, sonny boy,' he said. The deep rumbling voice seemed to come from the innermost recesses of the Carlsbad cavern. 'Put it away or I'll have to get up and clobber you and take it from you.'

'Don't be like that,' I complained, then added politely: 'If I put it away, will you clobber me?'

He considered this for a moment, then said: 'No.' He reached out for a big black cigar and lit it, his eyes on me all the time. The acrid fumes reached across the room and as it isn't polite for a guest in another's house to rush to open the nearest window without permission I didn't but it was a near thing. No wonder he'd never notice the stench from the flensing shed: compared to this, Uncle Arthur's cheroots came into the same category as Charlotte's perfume.

'My apologies for the intrusion. Are you Tim Hutchinson?'

'Yeah. And you, sonny boy?'

'Philip Calvert. I want to use one of your boat's transmitters to contact London. I also need your help. How urgently you can't imagine. A good many lives and millions of pounds can be lost in the next twenty-four hours.'

He watched a particularly noxious cloud of this Vesuvian poison gas drift up to the cringing ceiling, then bent his eyes on me again. 'Ain't you the little kidder, now, sonny boy.'

'I'm not kidding, you big black ape. And, while we're at it, we'll dispense with the "sonny boy," Timothy.'

He bent forward, the deep-set, coal-black eyes, not at all as friendly as I would have liked, then relaxed with a laugh. '*Touché*, as my French governess used to say. Maybe you ain't kidding at that. What are you, Calvert?'

In for a penny, in for a pound. This man would grant his co-operation for nothing less than the truth. And he looked like a man whose co-operation would be very well worth having. So, for the second time that night and the second time in my life, I said: 'I'm an agent of the British Secret Service.' I was glad that Uncle Arthur was out there fighting for his life on the rolling deep, his blood pressure wasn't what it ought to have been and a thing like this, twice in one night, could have been enough to see him off.

He considered my reply for some time, then said: 'The Secret Service. I guess you have to be at that. Or a nut case. But you blokes never tell.'

'I had to. It would have been obvious anyway when I tell you what I have to tell you.'

'I'll get dressed. Join you in the front room in two minutes. Help yourself to a Scotch there.' The beard twitched and I deduced from this that he was grinning. 'You should find some, somewhere.'

I went out, found some somewhere and was conducting myself on the grand tour of the Craigmore art gallery when Tim Hutchinson came in. He was dressed all in black, trousers, sailor's jersey, mackinaw and seaboots. Beds were deceptive, he'd probably passed the six foot four mark when he was about twelve and had just stopped growing. He glanced at the collection and grinned.

'Who would have thought it?' he said. 'The Guggenheim and Craigmore. Hotbeds of culture, both of them. Don't you think the one with the ear-rings looks indecently overdressed?'

'You must have scoured the great galleries of the world,' I said reverently.

'I'm no connoisseur. Renoir and Matisse are my cup of tea.' It was so unlikely that it had to be true. 'You look like a man in a hurry. Just leave out all the inessentials.'

I left out the inessentials, but not one of the essentials. Unlike MacDonald and Charlotte, Hutchinson got not only the truth but the whole truth.

'Well, if that isn't the most goddamned story any man ever heard. And right under our bloody noses.' It was hard to tell at times whether Hutchinson was Australian or American – I learnt later that he'd spent many years tuna-fishing in Florida. 'So it was you in that chopper this afternoon. Brother, you've had a day and then some. I retract that "sonny boy" crack. One of my more ill-advised comments. What do you want, Calvert?'

So I told him what I wanted, his own personal assistance that night, the loan of his boats and crews for the next twenty-four hours and the use of a radio transmitter immediately. He nodded.

'Count on us. I'll tell the boys. You can start using that transmitter right away.'

'I'd rather go out with you to our boat right away,' I said, 'leave you there and come back in myself to transmit.'

'You lack a mite confidence in your crew, hey?'

'I'm expecting to see the bows of the *Firecrest* coming through that front door any minute.'

'I can do better than that. I'll roust out a couple of the boys, we'll take the *Charmaine* – that's the MFV nearest the flensing shed – out to the *Firecrest*, I'll go aboard, we'll cruise around till you get your message off, then you come aboard the *Firecrest* while the boys take the *Charmaine* back again.'

I thought of the maelstrom of white breakers outside the mouth of the alleged harbour. I said: 'It won't be too dangerous to take an MFV out on a night like this?'

'What's wrong with a night like this? It's a fine fresh night. You couldn't ask for better. This is nothing, I've seen the boys take a boat out there, six o'clock in a black December evening, into a full gale.'

'What kind of emergency was that?'

'A serious one, admittedly.' He grinned. 'We'd run out of supplies and the boys wanted to get to Torbay before the pubs shut. Straight up, Calvert.'

I said no more. It was obviously going to be a great comfort to have Hutchinson around with me for the rest of the night. He turned towards the corridor and hesitated: 'Two of the boys are married. I wonder—'

'There'll be no danger for them. Besides, they'll be well rewarded for their work.'

'Don't spoil it, Calvert.' For a man with such a deep rumbling voice he could make it very soft at times. 'We don't take money for this kind of work.'

'I'm not hiring you,' I said tiredly. I'd quite enough people fighting me already without Tim Hutchinson joining their ranks. 'There's an insurance reward. I have been instructed to offer you half.'

'Ah, now, that's very different indeed. I'll be delighted to relieve the insurance companies of their excess cash at any time. But not half, Calvert, not half. Not for a day's work, not after all you've done. Twenty-five per cent to us, seventy-five per cent to you and your friends.'

'Half is what you get. The other half will be used to pay compensation for those who have suffered hardship. There's an old couple on Eilean Oran, for instance, who are going to be wealthy beyond their dreams for the rest of their days.'

'You get nothing?'

'I get my salary, the size of which I'd rather not discuss, as it's a sore point. Civil Servants are not permitted to accept gratuities.'

'You mean to say you get beaten up, shot down, half-drowned and suffered another couple of murder attempts just for a lousy pay cheque? What makes you tick, Calvert? Why the hell do you do it?'

'That's not an original question. I ask myself the same question about twenty times a day, rather more often recently. It's time we were gone.'

'I'll get the boys up. They'll be tickled pink by those gold watches or whatever the insurance boys will be handing over. Engraved, of course. We insist on that.'

'The reward will be in cash, not kind. Depends how much of the stolen goods are recovered. We're pretty sure to recover all the *Nantesville*'s cargo. Chances are that we'll recover the lot. The award is ten per cent. Yours will be five. The minimum you and your boys will pick up will be four hundred thousand pounds: the maximum will be eight hundred and fifty. Thousand pounds, I mean.'

'Say that in English.' He looked as if the London Post Office Tower had fallen on top of him. So I said it again, and after a time he looked as if only a telegraph pole had fallen on him and said carefully: 'At rates like that, a man might expect a fair bit of co-operation. Say no more. Put right out of your head any thoughts you had of advertising in the *Telegraph*. Tim Hutchinson is your man.'

And Tim Hutchinson was undoubtedly my man. On a night like that, dark as doomsday, rain sluicing down and a thickening mist making it impossible – for me, at least – to tell the difference between a naturally breaking sea and a wave foaming over a reef, Tim Hutchinson was my man. Cheap at half a million.

He was one of that rare breed, that very rare breed, of naturals to whom the sea is truly home. Twenty years' daily polishing and refining in every conceivable condition a rarely-bestowed gift with which you must be born in the first place and anyone can be like this. Just as the great Grand Prix drivers, the Carraciolas and Nuvolaris and Clarks, operate on a level incomprehensible to highly competent drivers of very fast cars, so Hutchinson operated on a level incomprehensible to the finest of amateur yachtsmen. Search your ocean racing clubs and Olympic yachting teams the world over and you will not find men like this. They are to be found, and even then so very seldom, only in the ranks of the professional deep-sea fishermen.

Those huge hands on throttle and wheel had the delicacy of a moth. He had the night-sight of a barn owl and an ear which could infallibly distinguish between waves breaking in the open sea, on reefs or on shores: he could invariably tell the size and direction of seas coming at him out of the darkness and mist and touch wheel or throttle as need be: he had an inbuilt computer which provided instant correlation of wind, tide, current and our own speed and always let him know exactly where he was. And I'll swear he could smell land, even on a lee shore and with the rest of us suffering olfactory paralysis from the fumes of the big black cigars which seemed to be an inseparable part of the man. It required only ten minutes beside him to realize that one's ignorance of the sea and ships was almost total. A chastening discovery.

He took the *Charmaine* out through the Scylla and Charybdis of that evil alleged harbour entrance under full throttle. Foaming white-fanged reefs reached out at us, bare feet away, on either side. He didn't seem to notice them. He certainly didn't look at them. The two 'boys' he'd brought with him, a couple of stunted lads of about six foot two or thereabouts, yawned prodigiously. Hutchinson located the *Firecrest* a hundred yards before I could even begin to imagine I could see any shape at all and brought the *Charmaine* alongside as neatly as I could park my car by the kerb in broad daylight – on one of my better days, that was. I went aboard the *Firecrest* to the vast alarm of Uncle Arthur and Charlotte who'd heard no whisper of our arrival, explained the situation, introduced Hutchinson and went back aboard the *Charmaine*. Fifteen minutes later, the radio call over, I was back aboard the *Firecrest*.

Uncle Arthur and Tim Hutchinson were already thick as thieves. The bearded Australian giant was extremely courteous and respectful, calling Uncle Arthur 'Admiral' every other sentence while Uncle Arthur was plainly delighted and vastly relieved to have him on board. If I felt this was a slight on my own seaman-like qualities, I was undoubtedly correct.

'Where are we off to now?' Charlotte Skouras asked. I was disappointed to see that she was just as relieved as Uncle Arthur.

'Dubh Sgeir,' I said. 'To pay a call on Lord Kirkside and his charming daughter.'

'Dubh Sgeir!' She seemed taken aback. 'I thought you said the answer lay in Eilean Oran and Craigmore?'

'So I did. The answers to some essential preliminary questions. But the end of the road lies in Dubh Sgeir. And the foot of the rainbow.'

'You talk in riddles,' she said impatiently.

'Not to me, he doesn't,' Hutchinson said jovially. 'The foot of the rainbow, ma'am. That's where the pot of gold lies.'

'Here and now I'd settle for a pot of coffee,' I said. 'Coffee for four and I'll make it with my own fair hands.'

'I think I would rather go to bed,' Charlotte said. 'I am very tired.'

'You made me drink your coffee,' I said threateningly. 'Now you drink mine. Fair's fair.'

'If you are quick, then.'

I was quick. I'd four cups on a little tin tray in nothing flat, a powerful mixture of instant coffee, milk and sugar in all of them and a little something extra in one of them. There were no complaints about the coffee. Hutchinson drained his cup and said: 'Can't see why you three shouldn't get your heads down for a little. Unless you think I need help?'

No one thought he needed help. Charlotte Skouras was the first to go, saying she felt very sleepy, which I didn't doubt. She sounded it. Uncle Arthur and I left a moment later, Tim Hutchinson promising to call me when we neared the landing stage on the west side of Dubh Sgeir. Uncle Arthur wrapped himself in a rug on the saloon settee. I went to my own cabin and lay down.

I lay for three minutes then rose, picked up a three-cornered file, softly opened my cabin door and as softly knocked on Charlotte's door. There was no reply, so I opened the door, passed in, silently closed it and switched on the lights.

She was asleep all right, she was a million miles away. She hadn't even managed to make it to bed, she was lying on the carpet, still fully clothed. I put her on the bunk and pulled a couple of blankets over her. I pushed up a sleeve and examined the mark left by the rope burn.

It wasn't a very big cabin and it took me only a minute to find what I was looking for.

It made a pleasant change and a very refreshing one to transfer myself from the *Firecrest* to land without that damned clammy scuba suit impeding every stroke or step of way.

How Tim Hutchinson located that old stone pier in the rain, the fog and the darkness was something that would have been for ever beyond me – if he hadn't told me later that night. He sent me to the bows with a torch in my hand and damned if the thing didn't loom out of the darkness as if he'd gone in on a radio bearing. He went into reverse, brought the bows, plunging heavily in the deep troughs, to within two feet of the pier, waited till I picked my moment to jump off then went full astern and disappeared into the fog and darkness. I tried to imagine Uncle Arthur executing that lot, but my imagination wasn't up to it. It boggled. Uncle Arthur, thank heaven, slept the sleep of the just. Drake was in his hammock and a thousand miles away, dreaming all the time of WC1.

The path from the landing stage to the plateau above was steep and crumbling and someone had carelessly forgotten to equip it with a handrail on the seaward side. I was in no way heavily burdened. All I was carrying apart from the weight of my own years was a torch, gun and coil of rope – I'd neither the intention nor the expectation of doing a Douglas Fairbanks on the outer battlements of the Dubh Sgeir castle, but experience had taught me that a rope was the most essential piece of equipment to carry along on a jaunt on a precipitously walled island – but even so I was breathing pretty heavily by the time I reached the top.

I turned not towards the castle but north along the grass strip that led to the cliff at the northern end of the island. The strip that Lord Kirkside's elder son had taken off from in his Beechcraft on the day when he and his brother-in-law to be had died, the strip that Williams and I had flown along less than twelve hours previously after our talk with Lord Kirkside and his daughter, the strip at the abrupt northern end of which I'd imagined I'd seen what I'd wanted to see, but couldn't be sure. Now I was going to make sure.

The strip was smooth and flat and I made good time without having to use the big rubber torch I had with me. I didn't dare use it anyway, not so close to the castle. There was no light to be seen from there but that was no guarantee that the ungodly weren't maintaining a sleepless watch on the battlements. If I were the ungodly, I'd have been maintaining a sleepless watch on the battlements. I stumbled over something warm and soft and alive and hit the ground hard.

My nerves weren't what they had been forty-eight hours ago and my reactions were comparatively fast. I had the knife in my hand and was on to him before he could get to his feet. To his four feet. He had about him the pungent aroma of a refugee from Tim Hutchinson's flensing shed. Well might they say why stinks the goat on yonder hill who seems to dote on chlorophyll. I said a few conciliatory words to our four-footed friend and it seemed to work for he kept his horns to himself. I went on my way.

This humiliating sort of encounter, I'd noticed, never happened to the Errol Flynns of this world. Moreover, if Errol Flynn had been carrying a torch a little fall like that would not have smashed it. Had he been carrying only a candle it would still have kept burning brightly in the darkness. But not my torch. Not my rubber encased, rubber mounted bulb, plexi-glass guaranteed unbreakable torch. It was kaput. I fished out the little pencil torch and tried it inside my jacket. I could have spared myself the caution, a glow-worm would have sneered at it. I stuck it back in my pocket and kept going.

I didn't know how far I was from the precipitous end of the cliff and I'd no intention of finding out the hard way. I dropped to my hands and knees and crawled forward, the glow-worm leading the way. I reached the cliff edge in five minutes and found what I was looking for almost at once. The deep score on the cliff edge was almost eighteen inches in width and four in depth in the centre. The mark was fresh but not too fresh. The grass had grown in again in most places. The time factor would be just about right. It was the mark that had been left by the tail fuselage of the Beechcraft plane when, with no one aboard, it had been started up, throttle opened and then the chocks removed. It hadn't had enough speed to become airborne and had fallen over the cliff edge, ripping this score in the earth as it had gone. That was all I needed, that and the holed hull of the Oxford expedition boat and the dark circles under the blue eyes of Susan Kirkside. Here was certainty.

I heard a slight noise behind me. A moderately fit five-year-old grabbing me by the ankles could have had me over the edge with nothing I could to to prevent it. Or maybe it was Billy the Kid back to wreak vengeance for the rude interruption of his night's sleep. I swung round with torch and gun at the ready. It *was* Billy the Kid, his yellow eyes staring balefully out of the night. But his eyes belied him, he was just curious or friendly or both. I moved back slowly till I was out of butting range, patted him weakly on the head and left. At this rate I'd die of heart failure before the night was out.

The rain had eased by this time and the wind fallen away quite a bit, but to compensate for this the mist was worse than ever. It swirled clammily around me and I couldn't see four feet in front of my face. I wondered grimly how Hutchinson was getting on in this lot, but put him quickly out of my mind. I'd no doubt he was a damned sight better at his job than I was at mine. I kept the wind on my right cheek and continued towards the castle. Under my rubber-canvas raincoat my last suit was sodden. The Civil Service was going to be faced with a cleaner's bill of some note.

I near as a toucher walked into the castle wall but saw its loom just in time. I didn't know whether I was to the right or the left of the entrance gate on the landward side, so I felt my way cautiously to the left to find out. After about ten feet the wall fell away at right angles to another wall. That meant I'd arrived at the left or eastern side of the gate. I began to feel my way to the right.

It was as well I had come upon the castle wall where I had done: had I arrived at the right-hand side, I'd have been upwind of the central gate and would never have smelled the tobacco smoke. It wasn't much as tobacco went, nothing like as robust as Uncle Arthur's cheroots and positively anaemic as compared to Tim Hutchinson's portable poison-gas factories, but tobacco smoke for all that. Someone at the entrance gate was smoking a cigarette. It was axiomatic that sentries should never smoke cigarettes. This I could deal with. They'd never trained me on how to handle billy goats on the edge of a precipice but on this subject they had become boringly repetitive.

I held the gun by the barrel and moved quietly forwards. He was leaning against the corner of the entrance, a hardly-seen shape, but his position outlined clearly enough by the movement of his cigarette end. I waited till he brought it to his mouth for the third time, and when it was glowing at its brightest and his night vision consequently most affected I took one step forward and brought the butt down where by extension of the curve and subsequent glow of the cigarette end the back of the head of a normal man ought to have been. Fortunately, he was a normal man.

He fell back against me. I caught him and something jabbed painfully into my ribs. I let him finish the trip down on his own and removed this item that had become stuck in my coat. A bayonet, and, what was more, a bayonet with a very nasty point to it. Attached to the bayonet was a Lee Enfield .303. Very military. It seemed unlikely that this was just a routine precaution. Our friends were becoming worried and I had no means of knowing how much they knew or guessed. Time was running very short for them, almost as short as it was for me. In a few hours it would be dawn.

I took the rifle and moved cautiously towards the edge of the cliff, the bayonet prodding the earth ahead of me as I went. By this time I was becoming quite adept at not falling over the edges of precipices and, besides, with a rifle and bayonet stretched out in advance you have five-feet notification of where eternity begins. I found the edge, stepped back, reversed the rifle, made two parallel scores in the sodden turf about a foot apart and eighteen inches in length, terminating on the very edge. I wiped the butt clean and placed the rifle on the ground. When the dawn came, the sentry changed and a search made, I trusted the proper conclusions would be drawn.

I hadn't hit him as hard as I'd thought, he was beginning to stir and moan feebly by the time I got back to him. This was all to the good, the alternative would have been to carry him and I was in no fit state to carry anyone. I stuffed a handkerchief into his mouth and the moaning stopped. Bad practice, I knew, for a gagged man with a head cold or nasal obstruction can die of suffocation in four minutes, but I hadn't the facilities to carry out a sinus examination, and, more importantly, it was his health or mine.

He was up on his feet in two minutes. He didn't try to run away or offer resistance, for by this time he had his ankles on a short hobble, his hands tied securely behind his back and the barrel of an automatic pressing into the side of his neck. I told him to walk, and he walked. Two hundred yards away, at the head of the path leading down to the landing stage, I led him off to one side, tied his wrists and ankles together and left him there. He seemed to be breathing without too much difficulty.

There were no other sentries, at least not on the main gate. I crossed the hollow square of a courtyard and came to the main door. It was closed but not locked. I passed inside and said a few hard things to myself for not having searched that sentry for the torch he would almost certainly have been carrying. The window curtains must have been drawn and the darkness inside that hall was total. I didn't much fancy moving around a Scottish baronial hall in total darkness, the risk of bringing down a suit of armour with a resounding metallic crash or impaling oneself on targes, claymores or a royal set of antlers must be high. I took out my pencil flash but the glow-worm inside was breathing its last, even when hard-pressed against the face of my wrist-watch it was impossible to tell the time. It was impossible to see the wrist-watch.

From the air, yesterday, I'd seen that the castle had been built in perfect symmetry round three sides of a hollow square. It was a reasonable assumption then that if the main door was in the middle of the central or seaward-facing section then the main staircase would be directly opposite. It seemed likely that the middle of the hall would offer a passage unimpeded by either claymores or antlers.

It did. The stairs were where they should have been. Ten wide shallow steps and then the stairs branched both right and left. I chose the right-hand side because above me, on that side, I could see a faint loom of light. Six steps on the second flight of stairs, another right turn, eight more steps and then I was on the landing. Twenty-four steps and never a creak. I blessed the architect who had specified marble.

The light was much stronger now. I advanced towards its source, a door no more than an inch ajar, and applied a wary eye to the crack. All I could see was the corner of a wardrobe, a strip of carpet, the corner of the foot of a bed and, on the last, a muddy boot. A low-register cacophony of sound emerged, reminiscent of a boiler factory in the middle distance. I pushed the door and walked inside.

I'd come to see Lord Kirkside, and whoever this was it wasn't Lord Kirkside, for whatever Lord Kirkside was in the habit of doing I was fairly certain that he didn't go to bed in boots, braces and cloth cap, with a bayoneted rifle lying on the blankets beside him, which was what this character had done. I couldn't see his face, because the cloth cap reached as far as his nose. On the bedside table beside him lay a torch and a half-empty whisky bottle. No glass, but from what little I could see of him I would have judged that he was, anyhow, one of those characters whose direct and simple enjoyment of life has not been impaired by the effete conventions of modern civilization. The faithful watchman prudently preparing himself for the rigours of the West Highland night before taking his turn at sentry-go. But he wouldn't be making it at the appointed hour for there was no one now to call him. From the look of it, he'd be lucky to make it for lunch.

It was just possible that he might wake himself up, those stentorian snores wouldn't have gone unremarked in a mortuary. He had about him the look of a man who, on regaining consciousness, would find himself in need of thirst-quenching nourishment, so I unscrewed the bottle top, dropped in half a dozen of the tablets supplied by my pharmaceutical friend in Torbay, replaced the top, took the torch and left.

Behind the next door to the left lay a bathroom. A filthy basin with, above it, a water-stained mirror, two shaving brushes covered with lather, a jar of shaving cream with the top off, two unwashed razors and, on the floor, two towels that might just possibly have been white at some distant aeon in the past. The interior of the bath was immaculate. Here was where the watchman performed his rudimentary ablutions.

The next room was a bedroom as dirty and disorderly as the watchman's. It was a fair guess that this was the home of the man I'd left lying out among the gorse and stones on the hillside.

I moved across to the left-hand side of the central block – Lord Kirkside would have his room somewhere in that block. He did, but he wasn't at home. The first room beyond the sleeping warrior's was his all right, a glance at the contents of the nearest wardrobe confirmed this. But his bed hadn't been slept in.

Predictably in this symmetrically designed house, the next room was a bathroom. The watchman wouldn't have felt at all at home in here, this antiseptic cleanliness was the hallmark of an effete aristocracy. A medicine cabinet was fixed to the wall. I took out a tin of Elastoplast and covered the face of the torch till I was left with a hole no more than the size of sixpence. I put the tin in my pocket.

The next door was locked but locks, in the days when the Dubh Sgeir Castle had been built, were pretty rudimentary affairs. I took from my pocket the best skeleton key in the world – an oblong of stiff celluloid. I shoved it between door and jamb at bolt level, pulled the door handle back in the direction of the hinges, eased in the celluloid, released the handle, repeated the process and stood stock-still. That click might have wakened my watchman friend, it should certainly have wakened the person inside. But I heard no sound of movement.

I opened the door a fraction of an inch and went through the stock-still standing process once more. There was a light on inside the room. I changed the torch for the gun, went on my knees, crouched low and abruptly opened the door wide. I stood up, closed and locked the door and crossed over to the bed.

Susan Kirkside wasn't snoring but she was just as deep in sleep as the man I'd just left. She had a blue silk band round her hair, and all of her face was visible, a sight that must have been rare indeed during her waking hours. Twenty-one, her father had said she was, but lying there asleep, smudged eyes and all, she looked no older than seventeen. A magazine had slipped from her hands to the floor. On the bedside table was a half-empty glass of water and beside that a bottle containing a commercial brand of Nembutal tablets. Oblivion appeared to be a pretty hard thing to come by in Dubh Sgeir and I'd no doubt Susan Kirkside found it more difficult than most.

I picked up a towel from a basin in the corner of the room, removed the worst of the moisture and dirt from head and face, combed my hair into some semblance of order and gave my kindly reassuring smile a try-out in the mirror. I looked like someone from the pages of the *Police Gazette*.

It took almost two minutes to shake her awake or, at least, to pull her up from the dark depths of oblivion to a state of semi-awareness. Full consciousness took another minute, and it was probably this that saved me from a screaming match, she had time to adjust herself to the slow realization of the presence of a stranger in the middle of the night. Mind you, I had my kindly smile going full blast till my face ached, but I don't think it helped much.

'Who are you? Who *are* you?' Her voice was shaking, the blue eyes, still misted with sleep, wide open and scared. 'Don't you touch me! Don't you – I'll scream for help – I'll—'

I took her hands just to show her that there was touching and touching. 'I won't touch you, Sue Kirkside. And a fat lot of good screaming for help would do around these parts. Don't scream, there's a good girl. In fact, don't even talk above a whisper. I don't think it would be very wise or safe, do you?'

She stared at me for a few seconds, her lips moving as if she were about to speak, but the fear slowly leaving her eyes. Suddenly she sat bolt upright. 'You're Mr Johnson. The man from the helicopter.'

'You should be more careful,' I said reproachfully. 'They'd have you arrested for that in the Folies-Bergère.' Her free hand hauled the blankets up to her chin and I went on: 'My name is Calvert. I work for the Government. I'm a friend. I think you need a friend, don't you, Susan? You and your old man – Lord Kirkside, that is.'

'What do you want?' she whispered, 'What are you doing here?'

'I'm here to end your troubles,' I said. 'I'm here to cadge an invitation to your wedding to the Honourable John Rollinson. Make it about the end of next month, will you? I'm due some leave, then.'

'Go away from here.' Her voice was low and desperate. 'Go away from here or you'll ruin everything. Please, please, *please* go away. I'm begging you, I'm begging you. Go away. If you're a friend, go away. Please, oh please go away!'

It seemed that she wanted me to leave. I said: 'It appears that they have you pretty well brain-washed. If you believe their promise, you'll believe anything in the world. They won't let you go, they daren't let you go, they'll destroy every shred and trace of evidence that might ever point a finger at them. That includes anyone who has ever had anything to do with them.'

'They won't, they *won't*. I was with Mr Lavorski when he promised Daddy that no one would come to any harm. He said they were businessmen, and killing was no part of business. He meant it.'

'Lavorski, is it? It had to be.' I looked at the earnest scared face. 'He may have meant it when he said it. He wouldn't have mentioned that they've murdered four people in the last three days, or that they have tried to murder me four times in the last three days.'

'You're lying! You're making this up. Things like that – things like that don't happen any more. For pity's sake leave us alone!'

'There speaks the true daughter of the old Scottish clan chieftain.' I said roughly. 'You're no good to me. Where's your father?'

'I don't know. Mr Lavorski and Captain Imrie – he's another of them – came for him at eleven to-night. Daddy didn't say where he was going. He tells me nothing.' She paused and snatched her hands away. Faint red patches stained her cheeks. 'What do you mean, I'm no good to you?'

'Did he say when he would be back?'

'What do you mean I'm no good to you?'

'Because you're young and not very clever and you don't know too much about this world and you'll believe anything a hardened criminal will tell you. But most especially because you won't believe me. You won't believe the one person who can save you all. You're a stupid and pig-headed young fool, Miss Kirkside. If it wasn't that he was jumping from the frying-pan into the fire, I'd say the Honourable Rollinson has had a lucky escape.'

'What do you mean?' It is hard for a mobile young face to be expressionless, but hers was then.

'He can't marry you when he is dead,' I said brutally. 'And he is going to die. He's going to die because Sue Kirkside let him die. Because she was too blind to know truth when she saw it.' I had what was, for me, an inspiration. I turned down my collar and pulled my scarf away. 'Like it?' I asked.

She didn't like it at all. The red faded from her cheeks. I could see myself in her dressing-table mirror and I didn't like it either. Quinn's handiwork was in full bloom. The kaleidoscope of colour now made a complete ring round my neck.

'Quinn?' she whispered.

'You know his name. You know him?'

'I know them all. Most of them, anyway. Cook said that one night, after he'd too much to drink, he'd been boasting in the kitchen about how he'd once been the strong man in a stage act. He'd an argument one night with his partner. About a woman. He killed his partner. That way.' She had to make a physical effort to turn her eyes away from my neck. 'I thought – I thought it was just talk.'

'And do you still think our pals are unpaid missionaries for the Society for the Propagation of Christian Knowledge?' I sneered. 'Do you know Jacques and Kramer?'

She nodded.

'I killed them both to-night. After they had killed a friend of mine. They broke his neck. Then they tried to kill my boss and myself. And I killed another. He came out of the dark to murder us. I think his name was Henry. Do you believe me now? Or do you still think we're all dancing round the old maypole on the village green, singing ring-a-ring-o'-roses as we go?'

The shock treatment worked almost too well. Her face wasn't pale now, it was ashen. She said: 'I think I'm going to be sick.'

'Later,' I said coldly. What little self-regard I had was down among my shoe-laces, what I would have liked to do was to take her in my arms and say: 'There, there, now, don't you worry your pretty head, just you leave everything to your old Uncle Philip and all will be well at the end of the day.' In fact, it was damned hard not to do it. Instead, what I said, still in the same nasty voice, was: 'We've no time for those little fol-de-rols. You want to get married, don't you? Did your father say when he would be back?'

She looked at the wash-basin in the corner of the room as if she were still making up her mind whether to be sick or not then pulled her eyes back to me and whispered: 'You're just as bad as they are. You're a terrible man. You're a killer.'

I caught her shoulders and shook them. I said savagely: 'Did he say when he would be back?'

'No.' Her eyes were sick with revulsion. It was a long time since any woman had looked at me like that. I dropped my hands.

'Do you know what those men are doing here?'

'No.'

I believed her. Her old man would know, but he wouldn't have told her. Lord Kirkside was too astute to believe that their uninvited guests would just up and leave them unharmed. Maybe he was just desperately gambling that if he told his daughter nothing and if he could swear she knew nothing then they would leave her be. If that was what he thought, he was in urgent need of an alienist. But that was being unjust, if I stood in his shoes – or, more accurately, was swimming in the murky waters he was in – I'd have grabbed at any straw.

'It's obvious that you know that your fiancé is still alive,' I went on. 'And your elder brother. And others. They're being held here, aren't they?'

She nodded silently. I wished she wouldn't look at me like that.

'Do you know how many?'

'A dozen. More than that. And I know there are children there. Three boys and a girl.'

That would be right. Sergeant MacDonald's two sons and the boy and the girl that had been aboard the converted lifeboat that had disappeared after setting off on the night cruise from Torbay. I didn't believe a word that Lavorski had said to Susan about their reverence for human life. But I wasn't surprised that the people in the boats who had accidentally stumbled across his illegal operations were still alive. There was a very good reason for this.

'Do you know where they are kept? There should be any amount of handy dungeons in Dubh Sgeir castle.'

'There are cellars deep underground. I've never been allowed to go near them in the past four months.'

'This is your big chance come at last. Get your clothes on and take me there.'

'Go down to the cellars?' Aghast was the word for her expression. 'Are you mad? Daddy tells me there are at least three men on guard duty all night long.' There were only two men now, but her opinion of me was low enough already, so I kept quiet. 'They're armed. You *must* be mad. I'm not going!'

'I didn't think you would. You'll let your boy friend die just because you're a contemptible little coward.' I could almost taste the self-loathing in my mouth. 'Lord Kirkside and the Honourable Rollinson. What a lucky father. What a fortunate fiancé.'

She hit me, and I knew I had won. I said without touching my face: 'Don't do that. You'll waken up the guard. Get your clothes on.'

I rose, sat on the footboard of the bed and contemplated the door and higher things while she changed. I was becoming tired of women telling me what a horrible character I was.

'I'm ready,' she said.

She was back in her uniform of pirate's jersey and the denims she'd outgrown when she was about fifteen. Thirty seconds flat and nary a sound of a portable sewing machine. Baffling, that's what it was.

Chapter Nine

Thursday: 4.30 a.m. – dawn

We went down the stairs hand in hand. I may have been the last man in the world she would have elected to be alone with on a desert island, but she clung on pretty tightly all the same.

At the foot of the steps we turned right. I flicked on the torch every few yards but it wasn't really necessary, Susan knew every yard of the way. At the end of the hall we turned left along the eastern wing. Eight yards and we stopped at a door on the right-hand side.

'The pantry,' she whispered. 'The kitchen is beyond that.'

I stooped and looked through the keyhole. Beyond was darkness. We passed through the doorway, then into an archway giving on to the kitchen. I flashed the tiny beam around the room. Empty.

There were three guards, Susan had said. The outside man, for whom I had accounted. The lad who patrolled the battlements. No, she didn't know what he did, but it was a good guess that he wasn't studying astronomy or guarding against parachutists. He'd have night glasses to his eyes and he'd be watching for fishing vessels, naval craft or fishery cruisers that might happen by and interrupt honest men at their work. He wouldn't see much on a night like this. And the third man, she said, guarded the back kitchen premises, the only entrance to the castle apart from the main gate – and the unfortunates in their cellars down below.

He wasn't in the kitchen premises, so he would be in the cellars down below.

A flight of steps led from the scullery beyond the kitchen down to a stone-flagged floor. To the right of this floor I could see the loom of light. Susan raised a finger to her lips and we made our way soundlessly down to the foot of the steps. I slid a cautious eye round the corner of this passageway.

It wasn't passageway, it was the damnedest flight of steps I'd ever come across. They were lit by two or three far-spaced and very weak electric bulbs, the walls coming together towards the foot like a pair of railway lines disappearing into the distance. Maybe fifty feet – or seventy steps – down, where the first light was, another passageway branched off to the right. There was a stool at the corner of the small stone landing there, and sitting on the stool a man. Across his knees lay a rifle. They certainly went in for heavy artillery.

I drew back. I murmured to Susan: 'Where in hell's name do those steps lead to?'

'The boathouse, of course.' A surprised whisper. 'Where else?'

Where else, indeed. Brilliant work, Calvert, brilliant work. You'd skirted the south side of the Dubh Sgeir in the helicopter, you'd seen the castle, you'd seen the boathouse, you'd seen nary a handhold on the sheer cliff separating them, and you'd never raised an eyebrow at the glaring obviousness of the fact that ne'er the twain did meet.

'Those are the cellars in that passage going off to the right?' She nodded. 'Why so far down? It's a long walk to collect the bubbly.'

'They're not really wine-cellars. They used to be used as water reservoirs.'

'No other way of getting down there?'

'No. Only this way.'

'And if we take five steps down this way he shoots us full of holes with his Lee Enfield. Know who it is?'

'Harry. I don't know his other name. He's an Armenian, Daddy says. People can't pronounce his real name. He's young and smooth and greasy – and detestable.'

'He had the effrontery to make a pass at the chieftain's daughter?'

'Yes. It was horrible.' She touched her lips with the back of her hand. 'He stank of garlic.'

'I don't blame him. I'd do it myself if I didn't feel my pension creeping up on me. Call him up and make amends.'

'What?'

'Tell him you're sorry. Tell him you misjudged his noble character. Tell him your father is away and this is the first chance you've had of speaking to him. Tell him anything.'

'No!'

'Sue!'

'He'll never believe me,' she said wildly.

'When he gets within two feet of you, he'll forget all about the reasoning why. He's a man, isn't he?'

'You're a man. And you're only six inches away.' The eternal female illogic.

'I've told you how it is, it's my pension coming between us. Quickly!'

She nodded reluctantly and I disappeared into the shadows of the nearest cellar, reversed gun in hand. She called and he came a-running, his rifle at the ready. When he saw who it was, he forgot all bout his rifle. Susan started to speak her lines but she might have saved her breath. Harry, if nothing else, was an impetuous young man. That wild Armenian blood. I stepped forwards, arm swinging, and lowered him to the ground. I tied him up and, as I'd run out of handkerchiefs, ripped away part of his shirt-front and used it as a gag. Susan giggled, a giggle with a note of hysteria.

'What's up?' I asked.

'Harry. He's what they call a snappy dresser. That's a silk shirt. You're no respecter of persons, Mr Calvert.'

'Not persons like Harry. Congratulations. Wasn't so bad, was it?'

'It was still horrible.' Again the hand to the mouth. 'He's reeking of whisky.'

'Youngsters have odd tastes,' I said kindly. 'You'll grow out of it. At least it must have been an improvement on the garlic.'

The boathouse wasn't really a boathouse at all, it was a large vaulting cave formed in a cleft in a natural fault in the cliff strata. At the inner end of the cave longitudinal tunnels stretched away on either side paralleling the coastline, until they vanished beyond the reach of my torch. From the air, the boathouse in the small artificial harbour, a structure of about twenty feet by twenty, had seemed incapable of housing more than two or three fair-sized rowing boats. Inside it was big enough to berth a boat the size of the *Firecrest*, and then leave room to spare. Mooring bollards, four in number, lined the eastern side of the boathouse. There were signs of recent work where the inner end of the cave had been lengthened in the direction of the longitudinal tunnels to increase the berthing space and provide a bigger working platform, but otherwise it was as it must have been for hundreds of years. I picked up a boat-hook and tried to test the depth, but couldn't find bottom. Any vessel small enough to be accommodated inside could enter and leave at any state of the tide. The two big doors looked solid but not too solid. There was a small dry-land doorway on the eastern side.

The berth was empty, as I had expected to find it. Our friends were apprehensive and on piece-work rates. It wasn't difficult to guess what they were working at, the working platform was liberally stacked with the tools of their trade: an oil engine-driven air compressor with a steel reservoir with outlet valves, a manually-operated, two-cylinder double-acting air pump with two outlets, two helmets with attached corselets, flexible, non-collapsible air tubes with metal couplings, weighted boots, diving dresses, life-cum-telephone lines, lead weights and scuba equipment such as I had myself, with a stack of compressed air cylinders at the ready.

I felt neither surprise nor elation, I'd known this must exist for the past forty-eight hours although I'd become certain of the location only that night. I was faintly surprised perhaps, to see all this equipment here, for this would surely be only the spares. But I shouldn't have been even vaguely surprised. Whatever this bunch lacked, it wasn't a genius for organization.

I didn't see that night, nor did I ever see, the cellars where the prisoners were housed. After I'd huffed and puffed three-quarters of the way up that interminable flight of steps, I turned left along the passageway where we'd first seen Harry taking his ease. After a few yards the passageway broadened out into a low damp chamber containing a table made of beer-cases, some seats of the same and, in one corner, some furniture that hadn't yet been drunk. A bottle of whisky, nearly full, stood on the table: Harry's remedy for garlic halitosis.

Beyond this chamber was a massive wooden door secured by an equally massive-looking lock with the key missing. All the celluloid in the world wouldn't open this lot but a beehive plastic explosive would do a very efficient job indeed. I made another of the many mental notes I'd made that night and went up the stairs to rejoin Susan.

Harry had come to. He was saying something in his throat which fortunately couldn't get past his silk-shirted gag to the delicate ears of the chieftain's young daughter, his eyes, to mint a phrase, spoke volumes and he was trying as best he could to do a Houdini with the ropes round his legs and arms. Susan Kirkside was pointing a rifle in his general direction and looking very apprehensive. She needn't have bothered, Harry was trussed like a turkey.

'These people down in the cellars,' I said. 'They've been there for weeks, some for months. They'll be blind as bats and weak as kittens by the time they get out.'

She shook her head. 'I think they'll be all right. They're taken out on the landing strip there for an hour and a half every morning under guard. They can't be seen from the sea. We're not allowed to watch. Or not supposed to. I've seen them often. Daddy insisted on it. And Sir Anthony.'

'Well, good old Daddy.' I stared at her. 'Old man Skouras. He comes here?'

'Of course.' She seemed surprised at my surprise. 'He's one of them. Lavorski and this man Dollmann, the men that do all the arranging, they work for Sir Anthony. Didn't you know? Daddy and Sir Anthony are friends – were friends – before this. I've been in Sir Anthony's London home often.'

'But they're not friends now?' I probed keenly.

'Sir Anthony has gone off his head since his wife died,' Susan said confidently. I looked at her in wonder and tried to remember when I'd last been so authoritatively dogmatic on subjects I knew nothing about. I couldn't remember. 'He married again, you know. Some French actress or other. That wouldn't have helped. She's no good. She caught him on the rebound.'

'Susan,' I said reverently, 'you're really wonderful. I don't believe you'll ever understand what I mean by my pension coming between us. You know her well?'

'I've never met her.'

'You didn't have to tell me. And poor old Sir Anthony – he doesn't know what he's doing, is that it?'

'He's all mixed up,' she said defensively. 'He's sweet, really he is. Or was.'

'All mixed up with the deaths of four men, not to mention three of his own,' I said. Sergeant MacDonald thought him a good man. Susan thought him sweet. I wondered what she would say if she saw Charlotte Skouras's back. 'How do the prisoners do for food?'

'We have two cooks. They do it all. The food is brought down to them.'

'What other staff?'

'No other staff. Daddy was made to sack them all four months ago.'

That accounted for the state of the watchman's bathroom. I said: 'My arrival in the helicopter here yesterday afternoon was duly reported by radio to the *Shangri-la*. A man with a badly scarred face. Where's the radio transmitter?'

'You know everything, don't you?'

'Know-all Calvert. Where is it?'

'Off the hall. In the room behind the stairs. It's locked.'

'I have keys that'll open the Bank of England. Wait a minute.' I went down to the guard's room outside the prisoners' cellar, brought the whisky bottle back up to where Susan was standing and handed it to her. 'Hang on to this.'

She looked at me steadily. 'Do you really need this?'

'Oh my God, sweet youth,' I said nastily. 'Sure I need it. I'm an alcoholic.'

I untied the rope round Harry's ankles and helped him to his feet. He repaid this Samaritan gesture by swinging at me with his right foot, but fifteen minutes on the floor hadn't helped his circulation or reactions any and I forestalled him with the same manoeuvre. When I helped him up the second time there was no fight left in him.

'Did you – did you really have to do that?' The revulsion was back in her eyes.

'Did I – did you see what he tried to do to me?' I demanded.

'You men are all the same,' she said.

'Oh, shut up!' I snarled. I was old and sick and tired and I'd run right out of the last of my witty ripostes.

The transceiver was a beauty, a big gleaming metallic RCA, the latest model as used in the naval vessels of a dozen nationalities. I didn't waste any time wondering where they had obtained it, that lot were fit for anything. I sat down and started tuning the set, then looked up at Susan. 'Go and fetch me one of your father's razor blades.'

'You don't want me to hear, is that it?'

'Think what you like. Just get it.'

If she'd been wearing a skirt she's have flounced out of the room. With what she was wearing flouncing was out of the question. The set covered every transmission frequency from the bottom of the long wave to the top of the VHF. It took only two minutes to raise SPFX. It was manned night and day the year round. It really was most considerate of the ungodly to provide me with such a magnificent instrument.

Sue Kirkside was back before I started speaking. I was ten minutes on the microphone altogether. Apart from code-names and map references I used plain English throughout. I had to, I'd no book, and time was too short anyway. I spoke slowly and clearly, giving precise instructions about the movements of men, the alignment of radio frequencies, the minutest details of the layout of Dubh Sgeir castle and asking all-important questions about recent happenings on the Riviera. I didn't repeat myself once, and I asked for nothing to be repeated to me, because every word was being recorded. Before I was half-way through, Susan's eyebrows had disappeared up under the blonde fringe and Harry was looking as if he had been sandbagged. I signed off, reset the tuning band to its original position and stood up.

'That's it,' I said. 'I'm off.'

'You're *what*?' The grey-blue eyes were wide, the eyebrows still up under the fringe, but with alarm, this time, not astonishment. 'You're leaving? You're leaving me here?'

'I'm leaving. If you think I'd stay a minute longer in this damned castle than I have to, you must be nuts. I've played my hand far enough already. Do you think I want to be around here when the guards change over or when the toilers on the deep get back here?'

'Toilers on the deep? What do you mean?'

'Skip it.' I'd forgotten she knew nothing about what our friends were doing. 'It's Calvert for home.'

'You've got a gun,' she said wildly. 'You could – you could capture them, couldn't you?'

'Capture who?' The hell with the grammar.

'The guards. They're on the second floor. They'll be asleep.'

'How many?'

'Eight or nine. I'm not sure.'

'Eight or nine, she's not sure! Who do you think I am, Superman? Stand aside, do you want me to get killed? And, Susan, tell nothing to anybody. Not even Daddy. Not if you want to see Johnny-boy walk down that aisle. You understand?'

She put a hand on my arm and said quietly but with the fear still in her face: 'You could take me with you.'

'I could. I could take you with me and ruin everything. If I as much as fired a single shot at any of the sleeping warriors up top, I'd ruin everything. Everything depends on their never knowing that anybody was here to-night. If they suspected that, just had a hint of a suspicion of that, they'd pack their bags and take off into the night. To-night. And I can't possibly do anything until to-morrow night. You understand, of course, that they wouldn't leave until after they had killed everyone in the cellar. And your father, of course. And they'd stop off at Torbay and make sure that Sergeant MacDonald would never give evidence against them. Do you want that, Susan? God knows I'd love to take you out of here, I'm not made of Portland cement, but if I take you the alarm bells will ring and then they'll pull the plug. Can't you see that? If they come back and find you gone, they'll have one thought and one thought only in their minds: our little Sue has left the island. With, of course, one thought in mind. You must not be missing.'

'All right.' She was calm now. 'But you've overlooked something.'

'I'm a great old overlooker. What?'

'Harry. He'll be missing. He'll have to be. You can't leave him to talk.'

'He'll be missing. So will the keeper of the gate. I clobbered him on the way in.' She started to get all wide-eyed again but I held up my hand, stripped off coat and windbreaker, unwrapped the razor she'd brought me and nicked my forearm, not too deeply, the way I felt I needed all the blood I had, but enough to let me smear the bottom three inches of the bayonet on both sides. I handed her the tin of Elastoplast and without a word she stuck a strip across the incision. I dressed again and we left, Susan with the whisky bottle and torch, myself with the rifle, shepherding Harry in front of me. Once in the hall I relocked the door with the skeleton key I'd used to open it.

The rain had stopped and there was hardly any wind, but the mist was thicker than ever and the night had turned bitterly cold. The Highland Indian summer was in full swing. We made our way through the courtyard across to where I'd left the bayonet lying on the cliff edge, using the torch, now with the Elastoplast removed from its face, quite freely, but keeping our voices low. The lad maintaining his ceaseless vigil on the battlements couldn't have seen us five yards away with the finest night-glasses in the world, but sound in heavy mist has unpredictable qualities, it can be muffled, it can be distorted, or it can occasionally be heard with surprising clarity, and it was now too late in the day to take chances.

I located the bayonet and told Harry to lie face down in the grass; if I'd left him standing he just might have been tempted to kick me over the edge. I gouged the grass in assorted places with heel and toe, made a few more scores with the butt of a bayonet, stuck the blade of the gate-keeper's bayonet in the ground at a slight angle so that the rifle was just clear of the ground, laid Harry down so that the blood-stained bayonet tip was also just clear of the ground, so preventing the blood from running off among the wet grass, scattered most of the contents of the whisky bottle around and carefully placed the bottle, about a quarter full now, close to one of the bayonets. I said to Susan: 'And what happened here do you think?'

'It's obvious. They had a drunken fight and both of them slipped on the wet grass over the edge of the cliff.'

'And what did you hear?'

'Oh! I heard the sound of two men shouting in the hall. I went on to the landing and I heard them shouting at the tops of their voices. I heard the one tell Harry to get back to his post and Harry saying, no, by God, he was going to settle it now. I'll say both men were drunk, and I won't repeat the kind of language they were using. The last I heard they were crossing the courtyard together, still arguing.'

'Good girl. That's exactly what you heard.'

She came with us as far as the place where I'd left the gate-keeper. He was still breathing. I used most of what rope I'd left to tie them together at the waist, a few feet apart, and wrapped the end of it in my hand. With their arms lashed behind their backs they weren't going to have much balancing power and no holding power at all on the way down that steep and crumbling path to the landing stage. If either slipped or stumbled I might be able to pull them back to safety with a sharp tug. There was going to be none of this Alpine stuff with the rope around my waist also. If they were going to step out into the darkness they were going to do it without me.

I said: 'Thank you, Susan. You have been a great help. Don't take any more of those Nembutal tablets to-night. They'd think it damn' funny if you were still asleep at midday to-morrow.'

'I wish it were midday the next day. I won't let you down, Mr Calvert. Everything is going to be all right, isn't it?'

'Of course.'

There was a pause, then she said: 'You could have pushed these two over the edge if you wanted to, couldn't you. But you didn't. You could have cut Harry's arm, but you cut your own. I'm sorry for what I said, Mr Calvert. About you being horrible and terrible. You do what you have to do.' Another pause. 'I think you're rather wonderful.'

'They all come round in the end,' I said, but I was talking to myself, she'd vanished into the mist. I wished drearily that I could have agreed with her sentiments, I didn't feel wonderful at all, I just felt dead tired and worried stiff for with all the best planning in the world there were too many imponderables and I wouldn't have bet a brass farthing on the next twenty-four hours. I got some of the worry and frustration out of my system by kicking the two prisoners to their feet.

We went slowly down that crumbling treacherous path in single file, myself last, torch in my left hand, rope tightly – but not too tightly – in my right hand. I wondered vaguely as we went why I *hadn't* nicked Harry instead of myself. It would have been so much more fitting, Harry's blood on Harry's bayonet.

'You had a pleasant outing, I trust?' Hutchinson asked courteously.

'It wasn't dull. You would have enjoyed it.' I watched Hutchinson as he pushed the *Firecrest* into the fog and the darkness. 'Let me into a professional secret. How in the world did you find your way back into this pier to-night? The mist is twice as bad as when I left. You cruise up and down for hours, impossible to take any bearings, there's the waves, tide, fog, currents – and yet there you are, right on the nose, to the minute. It can't be done.'

'It was an extraordinary feat of navigation,' Hutchinson said solemnly. 'There are such things as charts, Calvert, and if you look at that large-scale one for this area you'll see an eight fathom bank, maybe a cable in length, lying a cable and a half out to the west of the old pier there. I just steamed out straight into wind and tide, waited till the depth-sounder showed I was over the bank and dropped the old hook. At the appointed hour the great navigator lifts his hook and lets wind and tide drift him ashore again. Not many men could have done it.'

'I'm bitterly disappointed,' I said. 'I'll never think the same of you again. I suppose you used the same technique on the way in?'

'More or less. Only I used a series of five banks and patches. My secrets are gone for ever. Where now?'

'Didn't Uncle Arthur say?'

'You misjudge Uncle Arthur. He says he never interferes with you in – what was it? – the execution of a field operation. "I plan," he said. "I co-ordinate. Calvert finishes the job".'

'He has his decent moments,' I admitted.

'He told me a few stories about you in the past hour. I guess it's a privilege to be along.'

'Apart from the four hundred thousand quid or whatever?'

'Apart, as you say, from the green men. Where to, Calvert?'

'Home. If you can find it in this lot.'

'Craigmore? I can find it.' He puffed at his cigar and held the end close to his eyes. 'I think I should put this out. It's getting so I can't even see the length of the wheelhouse windows, far less beyond them. Uncle Arthur's taking his time, isn't he?'

'Uncle Arthur is interrogating the prisoners.'

'I wouldn't say he'd get much out of that lot.'

'Neither would I. They're not too happy.'

'Well, it *was* a nasty jump from the pier to the foredeck. Especially with the bows plunging up and down as they were. And more especially with their arms tied behind their backs.'

'One broken ankle and one broken forearm,' I said. 'It could have been worse. They could have missed the foredeck altogether.'

'You have a point,' Hutchinson agreed. He stuck his head out the side window and withdrew it again. 'It's not the cigar,' he announced. 'No need to quit smoking. Visability is zero, and I mean zero. We're flying blind on instruments. You may as well switch on the wheelhouse lights. Makes it all that easier to read the charts, depth-sounder and compass and doesn't affect the radar worth a damn.' He stared at me as the light came on. 'What the hell are you doing in that flaming awful outfit?'

'This is a dressing-gown,' I explained. 'I've three suits and all three are soaked and ruined. Any luck, sir?' Uncle Arthur had just come into the wheelhouse.

'One of them passed out.' Uncle Arthur wasn't looking very pleased with himself. 'The other kept moaning so loudly that I couldn't make myself heard. Well, Calvert, the story.'

'The story, sir? I was just going to bed. I've told you the story.'

'Half a dozen quick sentences that I couldn't hear above their damned caterwauling,' he said coldly. 'The whole story, Calvert.'

'I'm feeling weak, sir.'

'I've rarely known a time when you weren't feeling weak, Calvert. You know where the whisky is.'

Hutchinson coughed respectfully. 'I wonder if the admiral would permit—'

'Certainly, certainly,' Uncle Arthur said in a quite different tone. 'Of course, my boy.' The boy was a clear foot taller than Uncle Arthur. 'And while you're at it, Calvert, you might bring one for me, too, a normal-sized one.' He had his nasty side to him, had Uncle Arthur.

I said 'good night' five minutes later. Uncle Arthur wasn't too pleased, I'd the feeling he thought I'd missed out on the suspense and fancy descriptions, but I was as tired as the old man with the scythe after Hiroshima. I looked in on Charlotte Skouras, she was sleeping like the dead. I wondered about that chemist back in Torbay, he'd been three parts asleep, myopic as a barn owl and crowding eighty. He could have made a mistake. He could have had only a minimal experience in the prescribing of sleep-inducing drugs for those who lived in the land of the Hebridean prayer: 'Would that the peats might cut themselves and the fish jump on the shore, that I upon my bed might lie, and sleep for ever more.'

But I'd done the old boy an injustice. After what was, to me, our miraculous arrival in Craigmore's apology for a harbour it had taken me no more than a minute to shake Charlotte into something resembling wakefulness. I told her to get dressed – a cunning move this to make her think I didn't know she was still dressed – and come ashore. Fifteen minutes after that we were all inside Hutchinson's house and fifteen minutes still later, when Uncle Arthur and I had roughly splinted the prisoners' fractures and locked them in a room illuminated only by a sky-light that would have taken Houdini all his time to wriggle though, I was in bed in another tiny box-room that was obviously the sleeping-quarters of the chairman of the Craigmore's art gallery selection committee, for he'd kept all the best exhibits to himself. I was just dropping off to sleep, thinking that if the universities ever got around to awarding Ph.D.s to house agents, the first degree would surely go to the first man who sold a Hebridean hut within sniffing distance of a flensing shed, when the door opened and the lights came on. I blinked open exhausted eyes and saw Charlotte Skouras softly closing the door behind her.

'Go away,' I said. 'I'm sleeping.'

'May I come in?' she asked. She gazed around the art gallery and her lips moved in what could have been the beginnings of a smile. 'I would have thought you would have gone to sleep with the lights on to-night.'

'You should see the ones behind the wardrobe doors,' I boasted. I slowly opened my eyes as far as I could without mechanical aid. 'Sorry, I'm tired. What can I do? I'm not at my best receiving lady callers in the middle of the night.'

'Uncle Arthur's next door. You can always scream for help if you want to.' She looked at a moth-eaten armchair. 'May I sit down?'

She sat down. She still wore that uncrushable white dress and her hair was neatly combed, but that was about all you could say for her. Attempts at humour there might have been in her voice, but there was none in her face and none in her eyes. Those brown, wise, knowing eyes, eyes that knew all about living and loving and laughter, the eyes that had once made her the most sought-after actress of her time now held only sadness and despair. And fear. Now that she had escaped from her husband and his accomplices, there should have been no need for fear. But it was there, half-buried in the tired brown eyes, but there. Fear was an expression I knew. The lines round the eyes and mouth that looked so right, so inevitable, when she smiled or laughed – in the days when she had smiled and laughed – looked as if they had been etched by time and suffering and sorrow and despair into a face that had never known laughter and love. Charlotte Skouras's face, without the Charlotte Meiner of old behind it, no longer looked as if it belonged to her. A worn, a weary and an alien face. She must have been about thirty-five, I guessed, but she looked a deal older. And yet when she sat in that chair, almost huddled in that chair, the Craigmore art gallery no longer existed.

She said flatly: 'You don't trust me, Philip.'

'What on earth makes you say that? Why shouldn't I?'

'You tell me. You are evasive, you will not answer questions. No, that is wrong, you will and you do answer questions, but I know enough of men to know that the answers you give me are the ones you want to give me and not the ones I should hear. Why should this be, Philip? What have I done that you should not trust me?'

'So the truth is not in me? Well, I suppose I do stretch it a bit at times, I may even occasionally tell a lie. Strictly in the line of business, of course. I wouldn't lie to a person like you.' I meant it and intended not to – unless I had to do it for her sake, which was different.

'Why should you not lie to a person like me?'

'I don't know how to say it. I could say I don't usually lie to lovely and attractive women for whom I have a high regard, and then you'd cynically say I was stretching the truth till it snapped, and you'd be wrong because it is the truth, if truth lies in the eye of the beholder. I don't know if that sounds like an insult, it's never meant to be. I could say it's because I hate to see you sitting there all washed up and with no place to go and no one to turn to at the one time in your life you need some place to go and someone to turn to, but I suppose again that might sound like an insult. I could say I don't lie to my friends, but that again would be an insult, the Charlotte Skourases of this world don't make friends with government hirelings who kill for their wages. It's no good. I don't know what to say, Charlotte, except that it doesn't matter whether you believe me or not as long as you believe that no harm will come to you from me and, as long as I'm near you, no harm will come to you from anyone else either. Maybe you don't believe that either, maybe your feminine intuition has stopped working.'

'It is working – what you say? – overtime. Very hard indeed.' The brown eyes were still and the face without expression. 'I do think I could place my life in your hands.'

'You might not get it back again.'

'It's not worth all that much. I might not want it back.'

She looked at me for a long moment when there was no fear in her eyes, then stared down at her folded hands. She gazed at them so long that I finally looked in the same direction myself, but there was nothing wrong with her hands that I could see. Finally she looked up with an almost timid half-smile that didn't belong to her at all.

'You are wondering why I came,' she asked.

'No. You've told me. You want me to tell you a story. Especially the beginning and end of the story.'

She nodded. 'When I began as a stage actress, I played very small parts, but I knew what the play was all about. In this real-life play, I'm still playing a very small part. Only, I no longer know what the play is all about. I come on for three minutes in Act 2, but I have no idea what has gone before. I'm back for another minute in Act 4, but I've no idea in the world what's happened between Acts 2 and 4. And I cannot begin to imagine how it will all end.' She half-lifted her arms, turning the palms upwards. 'You cannot imagine how frustrating this can be for a woman.'

'You really know nothing of what has gone before this?'

'I ask you to believe me.'

I believed her. I believed her because I knew it to be true.

'Go to the front room and bring me, as they say in these parts, a refreshment,' I said. 'I grow weaker by the hour.'

So she rose obediently and went to the front room and brought me the refreshment which gave me just enough strength to tell her what she wanted to know.

'They were a triumvirate,' I said, which if not strictly accurate, was close enough to the truth for my explanation. 'Sir Anthony, Lavorski, who, I gather, was not only his public and private accountant, but his overall financial director as well, and John Dollmann, the managing director of the shipping companies – they were split up for tax reasons – associated with your husband's oil companies. I thought that MacCallum, the Scots lawyer, and Jules Biscarte, the lad with the beard who owns one of the biggest merchant banks in Paris, was in with them too. But they weren't. At least not Biscarte. I think he was invited aboard ostensibly to discuss business but actually to provide our triumvirate with information that would have given them the basis for their next coup, but he didn't like the way the wind was blowing and shied off. I know nothing about MacCallum.'

'I know nothing about Biscarte,' Charlotte said. 'Neither he nor Mr MacCallum stayed aboard the *Shangri-la*, they were at the Columba Hotel for a few days and were invited out twice for dinner. They haven't been aboard since the night you were there.'

'Among other things they didn't care for your husband's treatment of you.'

'I didn't care for it myself. I know what Mr MacCallum was doing aboard. My husband was planning to build a refinery in the Clyde estuary this coming winter and MacCallum was negotiating the lease for him. My husband said that, by the end of the year, he expected to have a large account of uncommitted capital for investment.'

'I'll bet he did, that's as neat a phrase for the proceeds of grand larceny as ever I've come across. Lavorski, I think we'll find, was the instigator and guiding brain behind all this. Lavorski it would have been who discovered that the Skouras empire was badly in need of some new lifeblood in the way of hard cash and saw the way of putting matters right by using means they already had close to hand.'

'But – but my husband was never short of money,' Charlotte objected. 'He had the best of everything, yachts, cars, houses—'

'He was never short in that sense. Neither were half the millionaires who jumped off the New York skyscrapers at the time of the stock market crash. Do be quiet, there's a good girl, you know nothing about high finance.' Coming from a character who eked out a bare living from an inadequate salary, I reflected, that was very good indeed. 'Lavorski struck upon the happy idea of piracy on a grand scale – vessels carrying not less than a million pounds' worth of specie at a time.'

She stared at me, her lips parted. I wished I had teeth like that, instead of having had half of them knocked out by Uncle Arthur's enemies over the years. Uncle Arthur, I mused bitterly, was twenty-five years older than I was and was frequently heard to boast that he'd still to lose his first tooth. She whispered: 'You're making all this up.'

'Lavorski made it all up. I'm just telling you, I wouldn't have the brains to think of something like that. Having thought up this splendid scheme for making money, they found themselves with three problems to solve: how to discover when and where large quantities of specie were being shipped, how to seize those ships and how to hide them while they opened the strong-room – a process which in ships fitted with the most modern strong-rooms can take anything up to a day – and removed said specie.

'Problem number one was easy. I have no doubt that they may have suborned high-ranking banking officials – the fact that they tried it on with Biscarte is proof of that – but I don't think it will ever be possible to bring those men to justice. But it will be possible to arrest and very successfully indict their ace informant, their trump card, our good friend the belted broker, Lord Charnley. To make a real good-going success of piracy you require the co-operation of Lloyd's. Well, that's an actionable statement, the co-operation of someone in Lloyd's. Someone like Lord Charnley. He is, by profession, a marine underwriter at Lloyd's. Stop staring at me like that, you're putting me off.

'A large proportion of valuable marine cargoes are insured at Lloyd's. Charnley would know of at least a number of those. He would know the amount, the firm or bank of dispatch, and possibly the date of dispatch and vessel.'

'But Lord Charnley is a wealthy man,' she said.

'Lord Charnley gives the appearance of being a wealthy man,' I corrected. 'Granted, he had to prove that he was a man of substance to gain admission to the old club, but he may have backed the wrong insurance horses or played the stock market. He either needed money or wanted money. He *may* have plenty but money is like alcohol, some people can take it and some can't, and with those who can't the more money they have the more they require.

'Dollmann solved problem two – the hi-jacking of the specie. I shouldn't imagine this strained his resources too far. Your husband ships his oil into some very odd and very tough places indeed and it goes without saying that he employs some very odd and very tough people to do it. Dollmann wouldn't have recruited the hi-jacking crew himself, he probably singled out our good friend Captain Imrie, who will prove to have a very interesting history, and gave him the authority to go through the Skouras fleets and hand-pick suitable men for the job. Once the hi-jacking crew was assembled and ready, Messrs Skouras, Lavorski and Dollmann waited till the victim was on the high seas, dumped you and the stewardess in a hotel, embarked the lads on the *Shangri-la*, intercepted the specie-carrying vessel and by one of a series of ruses I'll tell you about later, succeeded in boarding it and taking over. Then the *Shangri-la* landed the captured crew under guard while the prize crew sailed the hi-jacked vessel to the appointed hiding-place.'

'It can't be true, it can't be true,' she murmured. It was a long time since I'd seen any woman wringing her hands but Charlotte Skouras was doing it then. Her face was quite drained of colour. She knew that what I was saying was true and she'd never heard of any of it before. 'Hiding place, Philip? What hiding place?'

'Where would you hide a ship, Charlotte?'

'How should I know?' She shrugged tiredly. 'My mind is not very clear to-night. Up in the Arctic perhaps, or in a lonely Norwegian fjord or some desert island. I can't think any more, Philip. There cannot be many places. A ship is a big thing.'

'There are millions of places. You can hide a ship practically anywhere in the world. All you have to do is to open the bilge-valves and engine-room non-return valves to the bilges and detonate a couple of scuttling charges.'

'You mean – you mean that—'

'I mean just that. You send it to the bottom. The west side of the Sound to the east of Dubh Sgeir island, a cheery stretch of water rejoicing in the name of Beul nan Uamh – the mouth of the grave – must be the most densely packed marine graveyard in Europe to-day. At dead slack water the valves were opened at a very carefully selected spot in the Beul nan Uamh and down they went, all five of them, gurgle, gurgle, gurgle. Tide tables show that, coincidentally, most of them were sunk at or near midnight. Cease upon the midnight, as the poet says, only in this case with a very great deal of pain, at least for the underwriters involved. Beul nan Uamh. Odd, I never thought of it before. A very apt name indeed. The mouth of the grave. Damn' place is printed far too large in the chart, it doesn't have to be very obvious to be too obvious for Calvert.'

She hadn't been listening to my meanderings. She said: 'Dubh Sgeir? But – but that's the home of Lord Kirkside.'

'It's not but, it's because. The hiding place was picked either by your husband, or, if someone else, then the arrangement was made through your husband. I never knew until recently that your husband was an old drinking pal of Lord Kirkside. I saw him yesterday, but he wouldn't talk. Nor would his charming daughter.'

'You do move around. I've never met the daughter.'

'You should. She thinks you're an old gold-digging hag. A nice kid really. But terrified, terrified for her life and those of others.'

'Why on earth should she be?'

'How do you think our triumvirate got Lord Kirkside to agree to their goings-on?'

'Money. Bribery.'

I shook my head. 'Lord Kirkside is a Highlander and a gentleman. It's a pretty fierce combination. Old Skouras could never lay hands on enough money to bribe Lord Kirkside to pass the uncollected fares box on a bus, if he hadn't paid. A poor illustration, Lord Kirkside wouldn't recognize a bus even if it ran over him, but what I mean is, the old boy is incorruptive. So your charming friends kidnapped old Kirkside's elder son – the younger lives in Australia – and just to make sure that Susan Kirkside wouldn't be tempted to do anything silly, they kidnapped her fiancé. A guess, but a damned good one. They're supposed to be dead.'

'No, no,' she whispered. Her hand was to her mouth and her voice was shaking. 'My God, no!'

'My God, yes. It's logical and tremendously effective. They also kidnapped Sergeant MacDonald's sons and Donald MacEachern's wife for the same reason. To buy silence and co-operation.'

'But – but people just can't disappear like that.'

'We're not dealing with street corner boys, we're dealing with criminal master-minds. Disappearances are rigged to look like accidental death. A few other people have disappeared also, people who had the misfortune to be hanging around in small private boats while our friends were waiting for the tide to be exactly right before opening the sea-cocks on the hi-jacked ships.'

'Didn't it arouse police suspicion? Having so many small boats disappear in the same place.'

'They sailed or towed two of those boats fifty or more miles away and ran them on the rocks. Another could have disappeared anywhere. The fourth did set sail from Torbay and disappeared, but the disappearance of one boat is not enough to arouse suspicion.'

'It must be true, I know it must be true.' She shook her head as if she didn't believe it was true at all. 'It all fits so well, it explains so many things and explains them perfectly. But – but what's the good of knowing all this now? They're on to you, they *know* you know that something is far wrong and that that something is in Loch Houron. They'll leave—'

'How do they know we suspect Loch Houron?'

'Uncle Arthur told me in the wheelhouse last night.' Surprise in her voice. 'Don't you remember?'

I hadn't remembered. I did now. I was half-dead from lack of sleep. A stupid remark. Perhaps even a give-away remark. I was glad Uncle Arthur hadn't heard that one.

'Calvert nears the sunset of his days,' I said. 'My mind's going. Sure they'll leave. But not for forty-eight hours yet. They will think they have plenty of time, it's less than eight hours since we instructed Sergeant MacDonald to tell them that we were going to the mainland for help.'

'I see,' she said dully. 'And what did you do on Dubh Sgeir to-night, Philip?'

'Not much. But enough.' Another little white lie. 'Enough to confirm my every last suspicion. I swam ashore to the little harbour and picked the side door of the boathouse. It's quite a boathouse. Not only is it three times as big on the inside as it is from the outside, but it's stacked with diving equipment.'

'Diving equipment?'

'Heaven help us all, you're almost as stupid as I am. How on earth do you think they recover the stuff from the sunken vessels? They use a diving-boat and the Dubh Sgeir boathouse is its home.'

'Was – was that all you found out?'

'There was nothing more to find out. I had intended taking a look round the castle – there's a long flight of steps leading up to it from the boatyard inside the cliff itself – but there was some character sitting about three parts of the way up with a rifle in his hand. A guard of some sort. He was drinking out of some sort of bottle, but he was doing his job for all that. I wouldn't have got within a hundred steps of him without being riddled. I left.'

'Dear God,' she murmured. 'What a mess, what a terrible mess. And you've no radio, we're cut off from help. What are we going to do? What *are* you going to do, Philip?'

'I'm going there in the *Firecrest* this coming night, that's what I'm going to do. I have a machine-gun under the settee of the saloon in the *Firecrest* and Uncle Arthur and Tim Hutchinson will have a gun apiece. We'll reconnoitre. Their time is running short and they'll want to be gone tomorrow at the latest. The boathouse doors are ill-fitting and if there's no light showing that will mean they still haven't finished their diving. So we wait till they have finished and come in. We'll see the light two miles away when they open the door to let the diving-boat in to load up all the stuff they've cached from the four other sunken ships. The front doors of the boathouse will be closed, of course, while they load up. So we go in through the front doors. On the deck of the *Firecrest*. The doors don't look all that strong to me. Surprise is everything. We'll catch them napping. A sub-machine-gun in a small enclosed space is a deadly weapon.'

'You'll be killed, you'll be killed!' She crossed to and sat on the bed-side, her eyes wide and scared. 'Please, Philip! Please, *please* don't. You'll be killed, I tell you. I beg of you, don't do it!' She seemed very sure that I would be killed.

'I have to, Charlotte. Time has run out. There's no other way.'

'Please.' The brown eyes were full of unshed tears. This I couldn't believe. 'Please, Philip. For my sake.'

'No.' A tear-drop fell at the corner of my mouth, it tasted as salt as the sea. 'Anything else in the world. But not this.'

She rose slowly to her feet and stood there, arms hanging limply by her side, tears trickling down her cheeks. She said dully: 'It's the maddest plan I've ever heard in my life,' turned and left the room, switching off the light as she went.

I lay there staring into the darkness. There was sense in what the lady said. It *was*, I thought, the maddest plan *I'd* ever heard in my life. I was damned glad I didn't have to use it.

Chapter Ten

Thursday: noon – Friday: dawn

'Let me sleep.' I said. I kept my eyes shut. 'I'm a dead man.'

'Come on, come on.' Another violent shake, a hand like a power shovel. 'Up!'

'Oh, God!' I opened the corner of one eye. 'What's the time?'

'Just after noon. I couldn't let you sleep any more.'

'Noon! I asked to be shaken at five. Do you know—'

'Come here.' He moved to the window, and I swung my legs stiffly out of bed and followed him. I'd been operated on during my sleep, no anaesthetic required in the condition I was in, and someone had removed the bones from my legs. I felt awful. Hutchinson nodded towards the window. 'What do you think of that?'

I peered out into the grey opaque world. I said irritably: 'What do you expect me to see in that damn' fog?'

'The fog.'

'I see,' I said stupidly. 'The fog.'

'The two a.m. shipping forecast,' Hutchinson said. He gave the impression of exercising a very great deal of patience. 'It said the fog would clear away in the early morning. Well, the goddamned fog hadn't cleared away in the early morning.'

The fog cleared away from my befuddled brain. I swore and jumped for my least sodden suit of clothing. It was damp and clammy and cold but I hardly noticed these things, except subconsciously, my conscious mind was frantically busy with something else. On Monday night they'd sunk the *Nantesville* at slack water but there wasn't a chance in a thousand that they would have been able to get something done that night or the Tuesday night, the weather had been bad enough in sheltered Torbay harbour, God alone knew what it would have been like in Beul nan Uamh. But they could have started last night, they *had* started last night for there had been no diving-boat in the Dubh Sgeir boathouse, and reports from the *Nantesville*'s owners had indicated that the strongroom was a fairly antiquated one, not of hardened steel, that could be cut open in a couple of hours with the proper equipment. Lavorski and company would have the proper equipment. The rest of last night, even had they three divers and reliefs working all the time, they could have brought up a fair proportion of the bullion but I'd been damn' sure they couldn't possibly bring up all eighteen tons of it. Marine salvage had been my business before Uncle Arthur had taken me away. They would have required another night or at least a good part of the night, because they only dared work when the sun was down. When no one could see them. But no one could see them in dense fog like this. This was as good as another night thrown in for free.

'Give Uncle Arthur a shake. Tell him we're on our way. In the *Firecrest*.'

'He'll want to come.'

'He'll have to stay. He'll know damn' well he'll have to stay. Beul nan Uamh, tell him.'

'Not Dubh Sgeir? Not the boathouse?'

'*You* know damn' well we can't move in against that until midnight.'

'I'd forgotten,' Hutchinson said slowly. 'We can't move in against it until midnight.'

The Beul nan Uamh wasn't living up to its fearsome reputation. At that time in the afternoon it was dead slack water and there was only the gentlest of swells running up from the south-west. We crossed over from Ballara to the extreme north of the eastern shore of Dubh Sgeir and inched our way southward with bare steerage way on. We'd cut the by-pass valve into the underwater exhaust and, even in the wheelhouse, we could barely hear the throb of the diesel. Even with both wheelhouse doors wide open, we could just hear it and no more. But we hadn't the wheelhouse doors open for the purpose of hearing our own engine.

By this time we were almost half-way down the eastern patch of miraculously calm water that bordered the normal mill-race of Beul nan Uamh, the one that Williams and I had observed from the helicopter the previous afternoon. For the first time, Hutchinson was showing something approaching worry. He never spared a glance through the wheelhouse windows, and only a very occasional one for the compass: he was navigating almost entirely by chart and depth-sounder.

'Are you sure it'll be this fourteen-fathom ledge, Calvert?'

'It has to be. It damn' well has to be. Out to the seven fathom mark there the sea-bottom is pretty flat, but there's not enough depth to hide superstructure and masts at low tide. From there to fourteen it's practically a cliff. And beyond the fourteen fathom ledge it goes down to thirty-five fathom, steep enough to roll a ship down there. You can't operate at those depths without very special equipment indeed.'

'It's a damn' narrow ledge,' he grumbled. 'Less than a cable. How could they be sure the scuttled ship would fetch up where they wanted it to?'

'They could be sure. In dead slack water, you can always be sure.'

Hutchinson put the engine in neutral and went outside. We drifted on quietly through the greyly opaque world. Visibility didn't extend beyond our bows. The muffled beat of the diesel served only to enhance the quality of ghostly silence. Hutchinson came back into the wheelhouse, his vast bulk moving as unhurriedly as always.

'I'm afraid you're right. I hear an engine.'

I listened, then I could hear it too, the unmistakable thudding of an air compressor. I said: 'What do you mean afraid?'

'You know damn' well.' He touched the throttle, gave the wheel a quarter turn to port and we began to move out gently into deeper water. 'You're going to go down.'

'Do you think I'm a nut case? Do you think I *want* to go down? I bloody well don't want to go down – and you bloody well know that I *have* to go down. And you know why. You want them to finish up here, load up in Dubh Sgeir and the whole lot to be hell and gone before midnight?'

'Half, Calvert. Take half of our share. God, man, we do nothing.'

'I'll settle for a pint in the Columba Hotel in Torbay. You just concentrate on putting this tub exactly where she ought to be. I don't want to spend the rest of my life swimming about the Atlantic when I come up from the *Nantesville*.'

He looked at me, the expression in his eyes saying 'if,' not 'when,' but kept quiet. He circled round to the south of the diving-boat – we could faintly hear the compressor all the way – then slightly to the west. He turned the *Firecrest* towards the source of the sound, manoeuvring with delicacy and precision. He said: 'About a cable length.'

'About that. Hard to judge in fog.'

'North twenty-two east true. Let go the anchor.'

I let go the anchor, not the normal heavy Admiralty type on the chain but a smaller CQR on the end of forty fathoms of rope. It disappeared silently over the side and the Terylene as silently slid down after it. I let out all forty fathoms and made fast. I went back to the wheelhouse and strapped the cylinders on my back.

'You won't forget, now,' Hutchinson said. 'When you come up, just let yourself drift. The ebb's just setting in from the nor'-nor'-east and will carry you back here. I'll keep the diesel ticking, you'll be able to hear the underwater exhaust twenty yards away. I hope to hell the mist doesn't clear. You'll just have to swim for Dubh Sgeir.'

'That *will* be ducky. What happens to you if it clears?'

'I'll cut the anchor rope and take off.'

'And if they come after you?'

'Come after me? Just like that? And leave two or three dead divers down inside the *Nantesville*?'

'I wish to God,' I said irritably, 'that you wouldn't talk about dead divers inside the *Nantesville*.'

There were three divers aboard the *Nantesville*, not dead but all working furiously, or as furiously as one can work in the pressurized slow-motion world of the undersea.

Getting down there had been no trouble. I'd swum on the surface towards the diving-boat, the compressor giving me a clear bearing all the time, and dived when only three yards away. My hands touched cables, life-lines and finally an unmistakable wire hawser. The wire hawser was the one for me.

I stopped my descent on the wire when I saw the dim glow of light beneath me. I swam some distance to one side then down until my feet touched something solid. The deck of the *Nantesville*. I moved cautiously towards the source of the light.

There were two of them, standing in their weighted boots at the edge of an open hatchway. As I'd expected, they were wearing not my self-contained apparatus, but regular helmet and corselet diving gear, with air-lines and life-lines, the life-lines almost certainly with telephone wires imbedded inside them. Self-contained diving equipment wouldn't have been much use down here, it was too deep for oxygen and compressed-air stores too limited. With those suits they could stay down an hour and a half, at least, although they'd have to spend thirty to forty minutes on decompression stops on the way up. I wanted to be gone in less than that, I wanted to be gone that very moment, my heart was banging away against my chest wall like a demented pop drummer with the ague but it was only the pressure of the water, I told myself, it couldn't be fear, I was far too brave for that.

The wire rope I'd used to guide me down to the *Nantesville*, terminated in a metal ring from which splayed out four chains to the corners of a rectangular steel mesh basket. The two divers were loading this basket with wire- and wood-handled steel boxes that they were hauling up from the hold at the rate of, I guessed about one every minute. The steel boxes were small but obviously heavy: each held four 28-lb ingots of gold. Each box held a fortune. There were three hundred and sixty such fortunes aboard the *Nantesville*.

I tried to calculate the overall rate of unloading. The steel basket held sixteen boxes. Sixteen minutes to load. Another ten minutes to winch up to the diving-boat, unload and lower again. Say forty an hour. In a ninety-minute stretch, about sixty. But after ninety minutes they would have to change divers. Forty minutes, including two decompression stops of, say, twelve and twenty-four minutes, to get to the surface, then twenty minutes to change over and get other divers down. An hour at least. So, in effect, they were clearing sixty boxes every two and a half hours, or twenty-four an hour. The only remaining question was, how many boxes were left in the *Nantesville*'s strongroom?

I had to find out and I had to find out at once. I'd had only the two compressed air-cylinders aboard the *Firecrest* and already their two hundred atmospheres were seriously depleted. The wire hawser jerked and the full basket started to rise, the divers guiding it clear of the superstructure with a trailing guide rope. I moved forward from the corner of the partially opened hatch remote from where they were standing and cautiously wriggled over and down. With excessive caution, I supposed: their lamp cast only a small pool of light and they couldn't possibly have seen me from where I was standing.

I felt my hands – already puffed and numbed by the icy water – touch a life-line and air-line and quickly withdrew them. Below and to my right I could see another faint pool of light. A few cautious strokes and I could see the source of the light.

The light was moving. It was moving because it was attached to the helmet of a diver, angled so as to point down at an angle of forty-five degrees. The diver was inside the strong-room.

They hadn't opened that strongroom with any Yale key. They'd opened it with underwater torches cutting out a roughly rectangular section in the strongroom's side, maybe six feet by four.

I moved up to this opening and pushed my head round the side. Beyond the now stooping diver was another light suspended from the deckhead. The bullion boxes were neatly stacked in racks round the side and it was a five-second job to estimate their number. Of the three hundred and sixty bullion boxes, there were about one hundred and twenty left.

Something brushed my arm, pulled past my arm. I glanced down and saw that it was a rope, a nylon line, that the diver was pulling in to attach to the handle of one of the boxes. I moved my arm quickly out of the way.

His back was towards me. He was having difficulty in fastening the rope but finally secured it with two half hitches, straightened and pulled a knife from his waist sheath. I wondered what the knife was for.

I found out what the knife was for. The knife was for me. Stooped over as he had been, he could just possibly have caught a glimpse of me from the corner of his eye: or he might have felt the sudden pressure, then release of pressure, on the nylon rope: or his sixth sense was in better working condition than mine. I won't say he whirled round, for in a heavy diving suit at that depth the tempo of movement becomes slowed down to that of a slow-motion film.

But he moved too quickly for me. It wasn't my body that was slowing down as much as my mind. He was completely round and facing me, not four feet away, and I was still where I'd been when he'd first moved, still displaying all the lightning reactions and co-ordinated activity of a bag of cement. The six-inch-bladed knife was held in his lowered hand with thumb and forefinger towards me, which is the way that only nasty people with lethal matters on their minds hold knives, and I could see his face clearly. God knows what he wanted the knife for, it must have been a reflex action, he didn't require a knife to deal with me, he wouldn't have required a knife to deal with two of me.

It was Quinn.

I watched his face with a strangely paralysed intentness. I watched his face to see if the head would jerk down to press the telephone call-up buzzer with his chin. But his head didn't move, Quinn had never required any help in his life and he didn't require any now. Instead his lips parted in a smile of almost beatific joy. My mask made it almost impossible for my face to be recognized but he knew whom he had, he knew whom he had without any doubt in the world. He had the face of a man in the moment of supreme religious ecstasy. He fell slowly forwards, his knees bending, till he was at an angle of almost forty-five degrees and launched himself forward, his right arm already swinging far behind his back.

The moment of thrall ended. I thrust off backwards from the strongroom's outer wall with my left foot, saw the air-hose come looping down towards me as Quinn came through the jagged hole, caught it and jerked down with all my strength to pull him off-balance. A sharp stinging pain burned its way upwards from my lower ribs to my right shoulder. I felt a sudden jerk in my right hand. I fell backwards on to the floor of the hold and then I couldn't see Quinn any more, not because the fall had dazed me nor because Quinn had moved, but because he had vanished in the heart of an opaque, boiling, mushrooming cloud of dense air-bubbles. A non-collapsible air-hose can, and often has to, stand up to some pretty savage treatment, but it can't stand up to the wickedly slicing power of a razor-sharp knife in the hands of the strongest man I'd ever known. Quinn had cut his own air-hose, had slashed it cleanly in two.

No power on earth could save Quinn now. With a pressure of forty pounds to the square inch on that severed air-line, he would be drowning already, his suit filling up with water and weighting him down so that he could never rise again. Almost without realizing what I was doing I advanced with the nylon rope still in my hands and coiled it any old way round the madly threshing legs, taking great care indeed to keep clear of those flailing arms, for Quinn could still have taken me with him, could have snapped my neck like a rotten stick. At the back of my mind I had the vague hope that when his comrades investigated, as they were bound to do immediately – those great clouds of bubbles must have already passed out through the hold on their way to the surface – they would think he'd become entangled and tried to cut himself free. I did not think it a callous action then nor do I now. I had no qualms about doing this to a dying man, and no compunction: he was doomed anyway, he was a psychopathic monster who killed for the love of it and, most of all, I had to think of the living who might die, the prisoners in the cellars of the Dubh Sgeir castle. I left him threshing there, dying there, and swam up and hid under the deck-head of the hold.

The two men who had been on deck were already on their way down, being slowly lowered on their life-lines. As soon as their helmets sunk below my level I came up through the hatchway, located the wire hawser and made my way up. I'd been down for just under ten minutes so when my wrist depth-gauge showed a depth of two fathoms I stopped for a three-minute decompression period. By now, Quinn would be dead.

I did as Hutchinson had told me, drifted my way back to the *Firecrest* – there was no hurry now – and located it without difficulty. Hutchinson was there to help me out of the water and I was glad of his help.

'Am I glad to see you, brother,' he said. 'Never thought the day would come when Tim Hutchinson would die a thousand deaths, but die a thousand deaths he did. How did it go?'

'All right. We've time. Five or six hours yet.'

'I'll get the hook up.' Three minutes later we were on our way and three minutes after that we were out near enough in the mid-channel of the Beul nan Uamh, heading north-north-east against the gathering ebb. I could hear the helm going on auto-pilot and then Hutchinson came through the door into the lit saloon, curtains tightly if, in that fog, unnecessarily drawn, where

I was rendering some first aid to myself, just beginning to tape up a patch of gauze over the ugly gash that stretched all the way from lowest rib to shoulder. I couldn't see the expression behind the darkly-luxuriant foliage of that beard, but his sudden immobility was expression enough. He said, quietly: 'What happened, Calvert?'

'Quinn. I met him in the strongroom of the *Nantesville*.'

He moved forward and in silence helped me to tape up the gauze. When it was finished, and not until then, he said: 'Quinn is dead.' It wasn't a question.

'Quinn is dead. He cut his own air-hose.' I told him what had happened and he said nothing. He didn't exchange a dozen words all the way back to Craigmore. I knew he didn't believe me. I knew he never would.

Neither did Uncle Arthur. He'd never believe me till the day he died. But his reaction was quite different, it was one of profound satisfaction. Uncle Arthur was, in his own avuncular fashion, possessed of an absolute ruthlessness. Indeed, he seemed to take half the credit for the alleged execution. 'It's not twenty-four hours,' he'd announced at the tea-table, 'since I told Calvert to seek out and destroy this man by whatever means that came to hand. I must confess that I never thought the means would consist of the blade of a sharp knife against an air-hose. A neat touch, my boy, a very neat touch indeed.'

Charlotte Skouras believed me. I don't know why, but she believed me. While she was stripping off my makeshift bandage, cleaning the wound and re-bandaging it very efficiently, a process I suffered with unflinching fortitude because I didn't want to destroy her image of a secret service agent by bellowing out loud at the top of my voice, I told her what had happened and there was no doubt that she believed me without question. I thanked her, for bandage and belief, and she smiled.

Six hours later, twenty minutes before our eleven p.m. deadline for taking off in the *Firecrest*, she was no longer smiling. She was looking at me the way women usually look at you when they have their minds set on something and can see that they are not going to get their own way: a rather less than affectionate look.

'I'm sorry, Charlotte,' I said. 'I'm genuinely sorry, but it's not on. You are not coming with us, and that's that.' She was dressed in dark slacks and sweater, like one who had – or had had – every intention of coming with us on a midnight jaunt. 'We're not going picnicking on the Thames. Remember what you said yourself this morning. There will be shooting. Do you think I want to see you killed?'

'I'll stay below,' she pleaded. 'I'll stay out of harm's way. Please, Philip, let me come.'

'No.'

'You said you'd do anything in the world for me. Remember?'

'That's unfair, and you know it. Anything to help you, I meant. Not anything to get you killed. Not you, of all people.'

'Of all people? You think so much of me?'

I nodded.

'I mean so much to you?'

I nodded again. She looked at me for a long time, her eyes wide and questioning, her lips moving as if about to speak and yet not speaking, then took a step forward, latched her arms around my neck and tried to break it. At least, that was the way it felt, the dead Quinn's handiwork was still with me, but it wasn't that at all, she was clinging to me as she might cling to a person who she knew she would never see again. Maybe she was fey, maybe she had second sight, maybe she could see old Calvert floating, face down, in the murky waters of the Dubh Sgeir boathouse. When I thought about it I could see it myself, and it wasn't an attractive sight at all. I was beginning to have some difficulty with my breathing when she suddenly let me go, half-led, half-pushed me from the room and closed the door behind me. I heard the key turn in the lock.

'Our friends are at home,' Tim Hutchinson said. We'd circled far to the south of Dubh Sgeir, close in to the southern shore of Loch Houron, and were now, drifting quickly on the flood tide, engines stopped, in an east by northerly direction past the little man-made harbour of Dubh Sgeir. 'You were right, Calvert. They're getting all ready for their moonlit flitting.'

'Calvert is usually right,' Uncle Arthur said in his best trained-him-myself voice. 'And now, my boy?'

The mist had thinned now, giving maybe a hundred yards' visibility. I looked at the T-shaped crack of light showing where the boathouse doors didn't quite meet each other in the middle and where the tops of the doors sagged away from the main structure.

'Now it is,' I said. I turned to Hutchinson. 'We've all of a fifteen foot beam. That entrance is not more than twenty wide. There's not a beacon or a mark on it. There's a four knot tide running. You really think it can be done – taking her through that entrance at four or five knots, fast enough to smash open those doors, without piling ourselves up on the rocks on the way in?'

'There's only one way to find out.' He pressed the starter button and the warm diesel caught fire at once, its underpass exhaust barely audible. He swung her round to the south on minimum revs, continued on this course for two cables, westwards for the same distance, curved round to the north, pushed the throttle wide open and lit a cigar. Tim Hutchinson preparing for action. In the flare of the match the dark face was quiet and thoughtful, no more.

For just over a minute there was nothing to be seen, just the darkness and patches of grey mist swirling past our bows. Hutchinson was heading a few degrees west of north, making allowance for the set of the tide. All at once we could see it, slightly off the starboard bow as it had to be to correct for the tide, that big T-shaped light in the darkness, fairly jumping at us. I picked up the sub-machine-guns, opened and latched back the port wheelhouse door and stood there, gun in left hand, door-jamb in right, with one foot on the outside deck and the other still in the wheelhouse. Uncle Arthur, I knew, was similarly positioned on the starboard side. We were as firmly braced as it was possible to be. When the *Firecrest* stopped, it would stop very suddenly indeed.

Forty yards away, Hutchinson eased the throttle and gave the wheel a touch to port. That bright T was even farther round on our starboard side now, but directly in line with us and the patch of dark water to the west of the almost phosphorescently foaming whiteness that marked the point where the flood tide ripped past the outer end of the eastern breakwater. Twenty yards away he pushed the throttle open again, we were heading straight for where the unseen west breakwater must be, we were far too far over to port, it was impossible now that we could avoid smashing bow first into it, then suddenly Hutchinson had the wheel spinning to starboard, the tide pushing him the same way, and we were through and not an inch of Uncle Arthur's precious paintwork had been removed. Hutchinson had the engine in neutral. I wondered briefly whether, if I practised for the rest of my life, I could effect a manoeuvre like that: I knew damned well that I couldn't.

I'd told Hutchinson that the bollards were on the starboard side of the boathouse, so that the diving-boat would be tied up on that side. He angled the boat across the tiny harbour towards the right-hand crack of light, spun the wheel to port till we were angling in towards the central crack of light and put the engine full astern. It was no part of the plan to telescope the *Firecrest*'s bows against the wall of the boathouse and send it – and us – to the bottom.

As an entrance it erred, if anything, on the spectacular side. The doors, instead of bursting open at their central hasps, broke off at the hinges and we carried the whole lot before us with a thunderous crash. This took a good knot off our speed. The aluminium foremast, with Uncle Arthur's fancy telescopic aerial inside, almost tore the tabernacle clear of the deck before it sheared off, just above wheelhouse level, with a most unpleasant metallic shrieking. That took another knot off. The screw, biting deep in maximum revs astern, took off yet another knot, but we still had a fair way on when, amid a crackling, splintering of wood, partly of our planking but mainly of the doors, and the screeching of the rubber tyres on our well-fendered bows, we stopped short with a jarring shock, firmly wedged between the port quarter of the diving-boat and the port wall of the boathouse. Uncle Arthur's feelings must have been almost as bruised and lacerated as the planking of his beloved *Firecrest*. Hutchinson moved the throttle to slow ahead to keep us wedged in position and switched on the five-inch searchlight, less to illuminate the already sufficiently well-lit shed than to dazzle bystanders ashore. I stepped out on the deck with the machine-pistol in my hands.

We were confronted, as the travel books put it, with a scene of bustling activity, or, more precisely, what had been a scene of bustling activity before our entrance had apparently paralysed them all in whatever positions they had been at the time. On the extreme right three faces stared at us over the edge of the hold of the diving-boat, a typical forty-five-foot MFV about the same size as the *Charmaine*. Two men on deck were frozen in the act of lifting a box across to the hold. Another two were standing upright, one with his hands stretched above his head, waiting for another box swinging gently from a rope suspended from a loading boom. That box was the only moving thing in the boathouse. The winchman himself, who bore an uncommon resemblance to Thomas, the bogus customs officer, one lever against his chest and another held in his outstretched right hand, looked as if the lavas of Vesuvius had washed over him twenty centuries ago and left him frozen for ever. The others, backs bent, were standing on the wall at the head of the boathouse, holding a rope attached to a very large box which two frogmen were helping to lift clear of the water. When it came to hiding specie, they had one-track minds. On the extreme left stood Captain Imrie, presumably there to supervise operations, and, beside him, his patrons, Lavorski and Dollmann. This was the big day, this was the culmination of all their dreams, and they weren't going to miss a moment of it.

Imrie, Lavorski and Dollmann were the ones for me. I moved forward until I could see the barrel of the machine-gun and until they could also see that it was pointing at them.

'Come close,' I said. 'Yes, you three. Captain Imrie, speak to your men. Tell them that if they move, if they try anything at all, I'll kill all three of you. I've killed four of you already. If I double the number, what then? Under the new laws you get only fifteen years. For murderous vermin, that is not enough. I'd rather you died here. Do you believe me, Captain Imrie?'

'I believe you.' The guttural voice was deep and sombre. 'You killed Quinn this afternoon.'

'He deserved to die.'

'He should have killed you that night on the *Nantesville*,' Imrie said. 'Then none of this would have happened.'

'You will come aboard our boat one at a time,' I said. 'In this situation, Captain Imrie, you are without question the most dangerous man. After you, Lavorski, then—'

'Please keep very still. Terribly still.' The voice behind me was totally lacking in inflection, but the gun pressed hard against my spine carried its own message, one not easily misunderstood. 'Good. Take a pace forward and take your right hand away from the gun.'

I took a pace forward and removed my right hand. This left me holding the machine-pistol by the barrel.

'Lay the gun on the deck.'

It obviously wasn't going to be much use to me as a club, so I laid it on the deck. I'd been caught like this before, once or twice, and just to show that I was a true professional I raised my hands high and turned slowly round.

'Why, Charlotte Skouras!' I said. Again I knew what to do, how to act, the correct tone for the circumvented agent, bantering but bitter. 'Fancy meeting you here. Thank you very much my dear.' She was still dressed in the dark sweater and slacks, only they weren't quite as spruce as the last time I'd seen them. They were soaking wet. Her face was dead white and without expression. The brown eyes were very still. 'And how in God's name did you get here?'

'I escaped through the bedroom window and swam out. I hid in the after cabin.'

'Did you indeed? Why don't you change out of those wet clothes?'

She ignored me. She said to Hutchinson: 'Turn off that searchlight.'

'Do as the lady says,' I advised.

He did as the lady said. The light went out and we were all now in full view of the men ashore. Imrie said: 'Throw that gun over the side, Admiral.'

'Do as the gentleman says,' I advised.

Uncle Arthur threw the gun over the side. Captain Imrie and Lavorski came walking confidently towards us. They could afford to walk confidently, the three men in the hold, the two men who had suddenly appeared from behind the diving-boat's wheelhouse and the winch-driver – a nice round total of six – had suddenly sprouted guns. I looked over this show of armed strength and said slowly: 'You were waiting for us.'

'Certainly we were waiting for you,' Lavorski said jovially. 'Our dear Charlotte announced the exact time of your arrival. Haven't you guessed that yet, Calvert?'

'How do you know my name?'

'Charlotte, you fool. By heavens, I believe we have been grievously guilty of over-estimating you.'

'Mrs Skouras was a plant,' I said.

'A bait,' Lavorski said cheerfully. I wasn't fooled by his cheerfulness, he'd have gone into hysterics of laughter when I came apart on the rack. 'Swallowed hook, line, and sinker. A bait with a highly effective if tiny transmitter and a gun in a polythene bag. We found the transmitter in your starboard engine.' He laughed again until he seemed in danger of going into convulsions. 'We've known of every move you've made since you left Torbay. And how do you like that, Mr Secret Agent Calvert?'

'I don't like it at all. What are you going to do with us?'

'Don't be childish. What are you going to do with us, asks he naïvely. I'm afraid you know all too well. How did you locate this place?'

'I don't talk to executioners.'

'I think we'll shoot the admiral through the foot, to begin with,' Lavorski beamed. 'A minute afterwards through the arm, then the thigh—'

'All right. We had a radio-transmitter aboard the *Nantesville*.'

'We know that. How did you pin-point Dubh Sgeir?'

'The boat belonging to the Oxford geological expedition. It is moored fore and aft in a little natural harbour south of here. It's well clear of any rock yet it's badly holed. It's impossible that it would be holed naturally where it lay. It was holed unnaturally, shall we say. Any other boat you could have seen coming from a long way off, but that boat had only to move out to be in full sight of the boathouse – and the anchored diving-boat. It was very clumsy.'

Lavorski looked at Imrie, who nodded. 'He would notice that. I advised against it at the time. Was there more, Calvert?'

'Donald MacEachern on Eilean Oran. You should have taken him, not his wife. Susan Kirkside – you shouldn't have allowed her out and about, when did you last see a fit young twenty-one-year-old with blue shadows that size under her eyes? A fit young twenty-one-year-old with nothing in the world to worry about, that is? And you should have disguised that mark made by the tail fuselage of the Beechcraft belonging to Lord Kirkside's elder son when you ran it over the edge of the north cliff. I saw it from the helicopter.'

'That's all?' Lavorski asked. I nodded, and he looked again at Imrie.

'I believe him,' Imrie said. 'No one talked. That's all we need to know. Calvert first, Mr Lavorski?' They were certainly a brisk and business-like outfit.

I said quickly: 'Two questions. The courtesy of two answers. I'm a professional. I'd like to know. I don't know if you understand.'

'And two minutes,' Lavorski smiled. 'Make it quick. We have business on hand.'

'Where is Sir Anthony Skouras? He should be here.'

'He is. He's up in the castle with Lord Kirkside and Lord Charnley. The *Shangri-la*'s tied up at the west landing stage.'

'Is it true that you and Dollmann engineered the whole plan, that you bribed Charnley to betray insurance secrets, that you – or Dollmann, rather – selected Captain Imrie to pick his crew of cut-throats, and that you were responsible for the capture and sinking of the ships and the subsequent salvaging of the cargoes. And, incidentally, the deaths, directly or indirectly, of our men?'

'It's late in the day to deny the obvious.' Again Lavorski's booming laugh. 'We think we did rather well, eh, John?'

'Very well indeed,' Dollmann said coldly. 'We're wasting time.'

I turned to Charlotte Skouras. The gun was still pointing at me. I said: 'I have to be killed, it seems. As you will be responsible for my death, you might as well finish the job.' I reached down, caught the hand with the gun in it and placed it against my chest, letting my own hand fall away. 'Please do it quickly.'

There was no sound to be heard other than the soft throb of the *Firecrest*'s diesel. Every pair of eyes in that boatshed was on us, my back was to them all, but I knew it beyond any question. I wanted every pair of eyes in that boatshed on us. Uncle Arthur took a step inside the starboard door and said urgently: 'Are you mad, Calvert? She'll kill you! She's one of them.'

The brown eyes were stricken, there was no other expression for it, the eyes of one who knows her world is coming to an end. The finger came off the trigger, the hand opened slowly and the gun fell to the deck with a clatter that seemed to echo through the boatshed and the tunnels leading off on either side. I took her left arm and said: 'It seems Mrs Skouras doesn't feel quite up to it. I'm afraid you'll have to find someone else to—'

Charlotte Skouras cried out in sharp pain as her legs caught the wheelhouse sill and maybe I did shove her through that doorway with unnecessary force, but it was too late in the day to take chances now. Hutchinson had been waiting and caught her as she fell, dropping to his knees at the same time. I went through that door after her like an international rugby three-quarter diving for the line with a dozen hands reaching out for him, but even so Uncle Arthur beat me to it. Uncle Arthur had a lively sense of self-preservation. Even as I fell, my hand reached out for the loudhailer that had been placed in position on the wheelhouse deck.

'Don't fire!' The amplified voice boomed cavernously against the rock-faces and the wooden walls of the boatshed. 'If you shoot, you'll die! One shot, and you may all die. There's a machine-gun lined up on the back of every man in this boathouse. Just turn round, very very slowly, and see for yourselves.'

I half rose to my feet, hoisted a wary eye over the lower edge of a wheelhouse window, got the rest of the way to my feet, went outside and picked up the machine-gun on the deck.

Picking up that machine-gun was the most superfluous and unnecessary action I had performed for many a long day. If there was one thing that boathouse was suffering from at the moment it was a plethora of machine-guns. There were twelve of them in all, shoulder-slung machine-pistols, in twelve of the most remarkably steady pairs of hands I'd ever seen. The twelve men were ranged in a rough semicircle round the inner end of the boathouse, big, quiet, purposeful-looking men dressed in woollen caps, grey-and-black camouflaged smocks and trousers and rubber boots. Their hands and faces were the colour of coal. Their eyes gleamed whitely, like performers in the Black and White Minstrel show, but with that every hint of light entertainment ended.

'Lower your hands to your sides and let your guns fall.' The order came from a figure in the middle of the group, a man indistinguishable from the others. 'Do please be very careful. Slowly down, drop the guns, utter stillness. My men are very highly trained commandos. They have been trained to shoot on suspicion. They know only how to kill. They have not been trained to wound or cripple.'

They believed him. I believed him. They dropped their guns and stood very still indeed.

'Now clasp your hands behind your necks.'

They did. All but one. Lavorski. He wasn't smiling any more and his language had little to recommend it.

That they were highly trained I could believe. No word or signal passed. The commando nearest Lavorski walked towards him on soundless soles, machine-pistol across his chest. The butt seemed to move no more than three inches. When Lavorski picked himself up the lower part of his face was covered in blood and I could see the hole where some teeth had been. He clasped his hands behind his neck.

'Mr Calvert?' the officer asked.

'Me,' I said.

'Captain Rawley, sir. Royal Marine Commandos.'

'The castle, Captain?'

'In our hands.'

'The *Shangri-la*?'

'In our hands.'

'The prisoners?'

'Two men are on their way up, sir.'

I said to Imrie: 'How many guards?'

He spat and said nothing. The commando who had dealt with Lavorski moved forward, machine-pistol high. Imrie said: 'Two.'

I said to Rawley: 'Two men enough?'

'I hope, sir, that the guards will not be so foolish as to offer resistance.'

Even as he finished speaking the flat rapid-fire chatter of a sub-machine-gun came echoing down the long flight of stone steps. Rawley shrugged.

'They'll never learn to be wise now. Robinson?' This to a man with a waterproof bag over his shoulder. 'Go up and open the cellar door. Sergeant Evans, line them up in two rows against the wall there, one standing, one sitting.'

Sergeant Evans did. Now that there was no danger of being caught in cross-fire we landed and I introduced Uncle Arthur, full military honours and all, to Captain Rawley. Captain Rawley's salute was something to see. Uncle Arthur beamed. Uncle Arthur took over.

'Capitally done, my boy!' he said to Rawley. 'Capitally. There'll be a little something for you in this New Year's List. Ah! Here come some friends.'

They weren't all exactly friends, this group that appeared at the bottom of the steps. There were four tough but dispirited looking characters whom I'd never seen before, but unquestionably Imrie's men, closely followed by Sir Anthony Skouras and Lord Charnley. They, in their turn, were closely followed by four commandos with the very steady hands that were a hallmark of Rawley's men. Behind them came Lord Kirkside and his daughter. It was impossible to tell what the black-faced commandos were thinking, but the other eight had the same expression on their faces, dazed and utter bewilderment.

'My dear Kirkside! My dear fellow!' Uncle Arthur hurried forward and shook him by the hand, I'd quite forgotten that they knew one another. 'Delighted to see you safe and sound, my dear chap. Absolutely delighted. It's all over now.'

'What in God's name is happening?' Lord Kirkside asked. 'You - you've got them? You have them all? Where is my boy? Where is Rollinson? What—?'

An explosive crack, curiously muffled, came down the flight of steps. Uncle Arthur looked at Rawley, who nodded. 'Plastic explosive, sir.'

'Excellent, excellent,' Uncle Arthur beamed. 'You'll see them any minute, Kirkside.' He crossed over to where old Skouras was lined up against the wall, hands clasped behind his neck, reached up both his own, pulled Skouras's arms down and shook his right hand as if he were attempting to tear it off.

'You're lined up with the wrong team, Tony, my boy.' This was one of the great moments of Uncle Arthur's life. He led him across to where Lord Kirkside was standing. 'It's been a frightful nightmare, my boy, a frightful nightmare. But it's all over now.'

'Why did you do it?' Skouras said dully. 'Why did you do it? God, oh God, you don't know what you've done.'

'Mrs Skouras? The *real* Mrs Skouras?' There is the ham actor in all of us, but more than most in Uncle Arthur. He pushed back his sleeve and studied his watch carefully. 'She arrived in London by air from Nice just over three hours ago. She is in the London Clinic.'

'What in God's name do you mean? You don't know what you are saying. My wife—'

'Your wife is in London. Charlotte here is Charlotte Meiner and always was.' I looked at Charlotte. A total incomprehension and the tentative beginnings of a dazed hope. 'Earlier this year, blazing the trail for many kidnappings that were to follow, your friends Lavorski and Dollmann had your wife seized and hidden away to force you to act with them, to put your resources at their disposal. I think they felt aggrieved, Tony, that you should be a millionaire while they were executives: they had it all worked out, even to having the effrontery of intending to invest the proceeds in your empire. However. Your wife managed to escape, so they seized her cousin and best friend, Charlotte - a friend upon whom, shall we say, your wife was emotionally very dependent - and threatened to kill her unless they got Mrs Skouras back again. Mrs Skouras surrendered immediately. This gave them the bright idea of having two swords of Damocles hanging over your head, so, being men of honour, they decided to keep Charlotte as well as your imprisoned wife. Then, they knew, you would do exactly as they wanted, when and as they wanted. To have a good excuse to keep both you and Charlotte under their surveillance at the same time, and to reinforce the idea that your wife was well and truly dead, they gave out that you had been secretly married.' Uncle Arthur was a kind man: no mention of the fact that it was common knowledge that, at the time of her alleged death, brain injuries sustained by Mrs Skouras in a car crash two years previously had become steadily worse and it was known that she would never leave hospital again.

'How on earth did you guess that?' Lord Kirkside asked.

'No guess. Must give my lieutenants their due,' Uncle Arthur said in his best magnanimous taught-'em-all-I-know voice. 'Hunslett radioed me at midnight on Tuesday. He gave me a list of names of people about whom Calvert wanted immediate and exhaustive inquiries made. That call was tapped by the *Shangri-la* but they didn't know what Hunslett was talking about because in our radio transmissions all proper names are invariably coded. Calvert told me later that when he'd seen Sir Anthony on Tuesday night he thought Sir Anthony was putting on a bit of an act. He said it wasn't all act. He said Sir Anthony was completely broken and desolated by the thought of his dead wife. He said he believed the original Mrs Skouras was still alive, that it was totally inconceivable that a man who so patently cherished the memory of his wife should have married again two or three months later, that he could only have pretended to marry again for the sake of the one person whom he ever and so obviously loved.

'I radioed France. Riviera police dug up the grave in Beaulieu where she had been buried near the nursing home where she'd died. They found a coffin full of logs. You knew this, Tony.'

Old Skouras nodded. He was a man in a dream.

'It took them half an hour to find out who had signed the death certificate and most of the rest of the day to find the doctor himself. They charged him with murder. This can be done in France on the basis of a missing body. The doctor wasted no time at all in taking them to his own private nursing home, where Mrs Skouras was in a locked room. The doctor, matron and a few others are in custody now. Why in God's name didn't you come to us before?'

'They had Charlotte and they said they would kill my wife out of hand. What – what would you have done?'

'God knows,' Uncle Arthur said frankly. 'She's in fair health, Tony. Calvert got radio confirmation at five a.m.' Uncle Arthur jerked a thumb upwards. 'On Lavorski's big transceiver in the castle.'

Both Skouras and Lord Kirkside had their mouths open. Lavorski, blood still flowing from his mouth, and Dollmann looked as if they had been sandbagged. Charlotte's eyes were the widest wide I'd ever seen. She was looking at me in a very peculiar way.

'It's true,' Susan Kirkside said. 'I was with him. He told me to tell nobody.' She crossed to take my arm and smiled up at me. 'I'm sorry again for what I said last night. I think you're the most wonderful man I've ever known. Except Rolly, of course.' She turned round at the sound of footsteps coming down the stairs and promptly forgot all about the second most wonderful man she'd ever known.

'Rolly!' she cried. 'Rolly!' I could see Rolly bracing himself.

They were all there, I counted them, Kirkside's son, the Hon. Rollinson, the policeman's sons, the missing members of the small boats and, behind them all, a small brown-faced old woman in a long dark dress with a black shawl over her head. I went forward and took her arm.

'Mrs MacEachern,' I said. 'I'll take you home soon. Your husband is waiting.'

'Thank you, young man,' she said calmly. 'That will be very nice.' She lifted her arm and held mine in a proprietorial fashion.

Charlotte Skouras came and held my other arm, not in quite so proprietorial a fashion, but there for everyone to see. I didn't mind. She said: 'You were on to me? You were on to me all the time?'

'He was,' Uncle Arthur said thoughtfully. 'He just said he knew. You never quite got round to explaining that bit, Calvert.'

'It wasn't difficult, sir – if you know all the facts, that is,' I added hastily. 'Sir Anthony put me on to you. That visit he paid me on the *Firecrest* to allay any suspicion we might have had about our smashed radio set only served, I'm afraid, to make me suspicious. You wouldn't have normally come to me, you'd have gone ashore immediately to the police or to a phone, sir. Then, in order to get me talking about the cut telephone wires, you wondered if the radio-wrecker, to complete our isolation from the mainland, had smashed the two public call boxes. From a man of your intelligence, such a suggestion was fatuous, there must be scores of houses in Torbay with their private phone. But you thought it might sound suspicious if you suggested cut lines, so you didn't. Then Sergeant MacDonald gave me a glowing report about you, said you were the most respected man in Torbay and your public reputation contrasted so sharply with your private behaviour in the *Shangri-la* on Tuesday night – well, I just couldn't buy it.

'That nineteenth-century late Victorian melodrama act that you and Charlotte put on in the saloon that night had me fooled for all of five seconds. It was inconceivable that any man so devoted to his wife could be vicious towards another obviously nice woman—'

'Thank you kindly, sir,' Charlotte murmured.

'It was inconceivable that he send her for his wife's photograph, unless he had been ordered to do so. And you had been ordered to do so, by Lavorski and Dollmann. And it was inconceivable that she would have gone – the Charlotte Meiner I knew would have clobbered you over the head with a marline spike. Ergo, if you weren't what you appeared to be, neither were you, Charlotte.

'The villains, they thought, were laying a foundation for an excellent reason for your flight from the wicked baron to the *Firecrest*, where you could become their eyes and ears and keep them informed of all our plans and moves, because they'd no idea how long their secret little transmitter in the engine-room would remain undetected. After they knew we'd found Hunslett – they'd removed the transmitter by that time – it was inevitable that they would try to get you aboard the *Firecrest*. So they laid a little more groundwork by giving you a bruised eye – the dye is nearly off already – and some wicked weals across your back and dumped you into the water with your little polythene kitbag with the micro-transmitter and gun inside it. Do this, they said, or Mrs Skouras will get it.'

She nodded. 'They said that.'

'I have twenty-twenty eyesight. Sir Arthur hasn't – his eyes were badly damaged in the war. I had a close look at those weals on your back. Genuine weals. Also genuine pinpricks where the hypodermic with the anaesthetic had been inserted before the lashes were inflicted. To that degree, at least, someone was humane.'

'I could stand most things,' Skouras said heavily. 'I couldn't stand the thought of – the thought of—'

'I guessed you had insisted on the anaesthetic, sir. No, I knew. The same way that I knew that you had insisted that the crews of all those small yachts be kept alive or the hell with the consequences. Charlotte, I ran a finger-nail down one of those weals. You should have jumped through the saloon roof. You never batted an eyelid. After submersion in salt water. After that, I knew.

'I have devious reasons for the things I do. You told us that you had come to warn us of our deadly danger – as if we didn't know. I told you we were leaving Torbay within the hour, so off you trotted to your little cabin and told them we were going to leave within the hour. So Quinn, Jacques and Kramer came paddling across well in advance of the time you'd told us they would be coming, trusting we would have been lulled into a sense of false security. You must love Mrs Skouras very much, Charlotte. A clear-cut choice, she or us, and you made your choice. But I was waiting for them, so Jacques and Kramer died. I told you we were going to Eilean Oran and Craigmore, so off you trotted down to your little cabin and told them we were going to Eilean Oran and Craigmore, which wouldn't have worried them at all. Later on I told you we were going to Dubh Sgeir. So off you trotted down to your little cabin again, but before you could tell them anything you passed out on your cabin deck, possibly as a result of a little night-cap I'd put in your coffee. I couldn't have you telling your friends here that I was going to Dubh Sgeir, could I now? They would have had a reception committee all nicely organized.'

'You – you were in my cabin? You said I was on the floor?'

'Don Juan has nothing on me. I flit in and out of ladies' bedrooms like anything. Ask Susan Kirkside. You were on the floor. I put you to bed. I looked at your arms, incidentally, and the rope marks were gone. They'd used rubber bands, twisted pretty tightly, just before Hunslett and I had arrived?'

She nodded. She looked dazed.

'I also, of course, found the transmitter and gun. Then, back in Craigmore, you came and pumped me for some more information. And you did try to warn me, you were about torn in half by that time. I gave you that information. It wasn't the whole truth, I regret, but it was what I wanted you to tell Lavorski and company, which,' I said approvingly, 'like a good little girl you did. Off you trotted to your little white-washed bedroom—'

'Philip Calvert,' she said slowly, 'you are the nastiest, sneakingest, most low-down double-crossing—'

'There are some of Lavorski's men aboard the *Shangri-la*,' old Skouras interrupted excitedly. He had rejoined the human race. 'They'll get away—'

'They'll get life,' I said. 'They're in irons, or whatever Captain Rawley's men here are in the habit of using.'

'But how did you – how did you know where the *Shangri-la* was? In the darkness, in the mist, it's impossible—'

'How's the *Shangri-la*'s tender working?' I asked.

'The what? The *Shangri-la*'s – what the devil—?' He calmed down. 'It's not working. Engines out of order.'

'Demerara sugar has that effect upon them,' I explained. 'Any sugar has, in fact, when dumped in the petrol tanks, but demerara was all I could lay hands on that Wednesday night after Sir Arthur and I had left you but before we took the *Firecrest* in to the pier. I went aboard the tender with a couple of pounds of the stuff. I'm afraid you'll find the valves are ruined. I also took with me a homing signal transmitter, a transistorized battery-powered job, which I attached to the inner after bulkhead of the anchor locker, a place that's not looked at once a year. So, when you hauled the incapacitated tender aboard the *Shangri-la* – well, we knew where the *Shangri-la* was.'

'I'm afraid I don't follow, Calvert.'

'Look at Messrs Dollmann, Lavorski and Imrie. They follow all right. I know the exact frequency that transmitter sends on – after all, it *was* my transmitter. One of Mr Hutchinson's skippers was given this frequency and tuned into it. Like all MFVs it has a loop aerial for direction finding, he just had to keep turning the loop till the signal was at full strength. He couldn't miss. He didn't miss.'

'Mr Hutchinson's skippers?' Skouras said carefully. 'MFVs you said?'

It was as well, I reflected, that I wasn't overly troubled with self-consciousness, what with Mrs MacEachern on one hand, Charlotte on the other, and every eye, a large proportion of them hostile to a degree, bent upon me, it could have been embarrassing to a degree. 'Mr Hutchinson has two shark-fishing boats. Before I came to Dubh Sgeir last night I radioed from one of his boats asking for help – the gentlemen you see here. They said they couldn't send boats or helicopters in this weather, in almost zero visibility. I told them the last thing I wanted was their damned noisy helicopters, secrecy was everything, and not to worry about the sea transport, I knew some men for whom the phrase "zero visibility" was only a joke. Mr Hutchinson's skippers. They went to the mainland and brought Captain Rawley and his men back here. I didn't think they'd arrive until late at night, that's why Sir Arthur and I were afraid to move before midnight. What time did you get here, Captain Rawley?'

'Nine-thirty.'

'So early? I must admit it was a bit awkward without a radio. Then ashore in your little rubber boats, through the side door, waited until the diving-boat came back – and waited and waited.'

'We were getting pretty stiff, sir.'

Lord Kirkside cleared his throat. Maybe he was thinking of my nocturnal assignation with his daughter.

'Tell me this, Mr Calvert. If you radioed from Mr Hutchinson's boat in Craigmore, why did you have to radio again from here later that night?'

'If I didn't, you'd be down among the dead men by this time. I spent the best part of fifteen minutes giving highly detailed descriptions, of Dubh Sgeir externally and of the castle and boathouse layout internally. Everything that Captain Rawley and his men have done had to be done in total darkness. You'll keep an eye on our friends, Captain Rawley? A fishery cruiser will be off Dubh Sgeir shortly after dawn.'

The Marines herded them off into the left-hand cave, set three powerful lights shining into the prisoners' faces and mounted a four-man guard with machine-pistols at the ready. Our friends would undoubtedly keep until the fishery cruiser came in the morning.

Charlotte said slowly: 'That was why Sir Arthur remained behind this afternoon when you and Mr Hutchinson went to the *Nantesville*? To see that I didn't talk to the guards and find out the truth?'

'Why else?'

She took her arm away and looked at me without affection. 'So you put me through the hoop,' she said quietly. 'You let me suffer like this for thirty hours while you knew all the time.'

'Fair's fair. You were doing me down, I was doing you down.'

'I'm very grateful to you,' she said bitterly.

'If you aren't you damn' well ought to be,' Uncle Arthur said coldly. This was one for the books, Uncle Arthur talking to the aristocracy, even if only the aristocracy by marriage, in this waspish tone. 'If Calvert won't speak for himself, I will.

'Point one: if you hadn't kept on sending your little radio messages, Lavorski would have thought that there was something damned fishy going on and might well have left the last ton or two of gold in the *Nantesville* and taken off before we got here. People like Lavorski have a highly attuned sixth sense of danger. Point two: they wouldn't have confessed to their crimes unless they thought we were finished. Point three: Calvert wanted to engineer a situation where all attention was on the *Firecrest* so that Captain Rawley and his men could move into position and so eliminate all fear of unnecessary bloodshed – maybe *your* blood, my dear Charlotte. Point four, and more important: if you hadn't been in constant radio contact with them, advising them of our impending arrival right up to the moment we came through those doors – we'd even left the saloon door open so that you could clearly overhear us and know all we were doing – there would have been a pitched battle, guns firing as soon as those doors were breached, and who knows how many lives would have been lost. But they *knew* they were in control, they *knew* the trap was set, they *knew* you were aboard with that gun to spring the trap. Point five, and most important of all: Captain Rawley here was hidden almost a hundred yards away along the cross tunnel and the detachment up above were concealed in a store-room in the castle. How do you think *they* knew when to move in and move in simultaneously? Because, like all commandos, they had portable radio sets and were listening into every word of your running commentary. Don't forget your transmitter was stolen from the *Firecrest*. It was *Calvert*'s transmitter, my dear. He knew the transmitting frequency to the mainland last night. That was after he had – um – given you a little something to drink and checked your transmitter before using the one up in the castle last night.'

Charlotte said to me: 'I think you are the most devious and detestable and untrustworthy man I've ever met.' Her eyes were shining, whether from tears or whatever I didn't know. I felt acutely embarrassed and uncomfortable. She put her hand on my arm and said in a low voice: 'You fool, oh, you fool! That gun might have gone off. I – I might have killed you, Philip!'

I patted her hand and said: 'You don't even begin to believe that yourself.' In the circumstances, I thought it better not to say if that gun had gone off I'd never have trusted a three-cornered file again.

The grey mist was slowly clearing away and the dawn coming up on the quiet dark sea when Tim Hutchinson eased the *Firecrest* in towards Eilean Oran.

There were only four of us on the boat, Hutchinson, myself, Mrs MacEachern and Charlotte. I'd told Charlotte to find a bed in Dubh Sgeir castle for the night, but she'd simply ignored me, helped Mrs MacEachern on to the *Firecrest* and had made no move to go ashore again. Very self-willed, she was, and I could see that this was going to cause a lot of trouble in the years to come.

Uncle Arthur wasn't with us, a team of wild horses couldn't have dragged Uncle Arthur aboard the *Firecrest* that night. Uncle Arthur was having his foretaste of Paradise, sitting in front of a log fire in the Dubh Sgeir castle drawing-room, knocking back old Kirkside's superlative whisky and retailing his exploits to a breathless and spell-bound aristocracy. If I were lucky, maybe he'd mention my name a couple of times in the course of his recounting of the epic. On the other hand, maybe he wouldn't.

Mrs MacEachern wasn't having her foretaste of Paradise, she was there already, a calm dark old lady with a wrinkled brown face who smiled and smiled all the way to her home on Eilean Oran. I hoped to God old Donald MacEachern had remembered to change his shirt.

THE GUNS OF NAVARONE

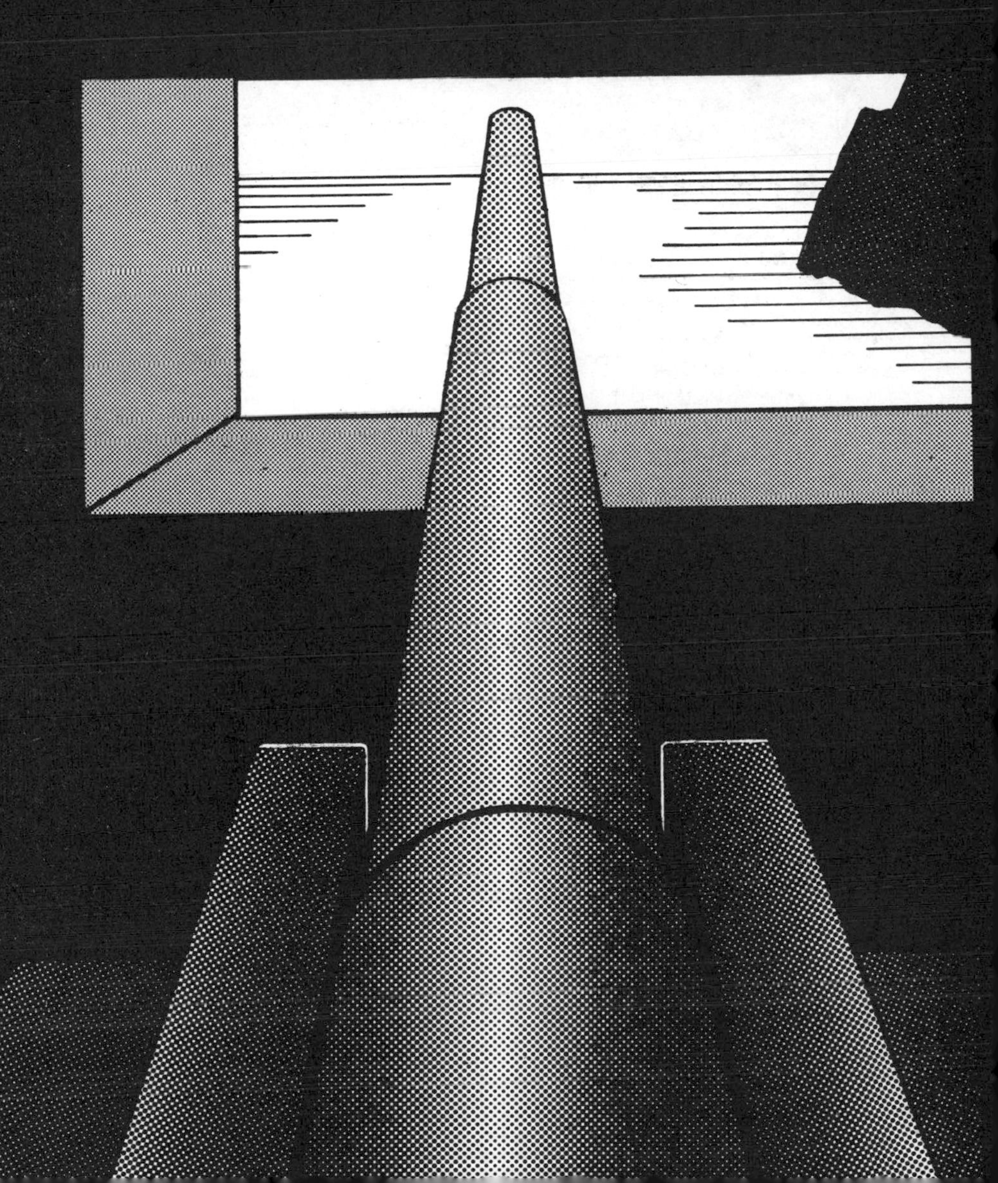

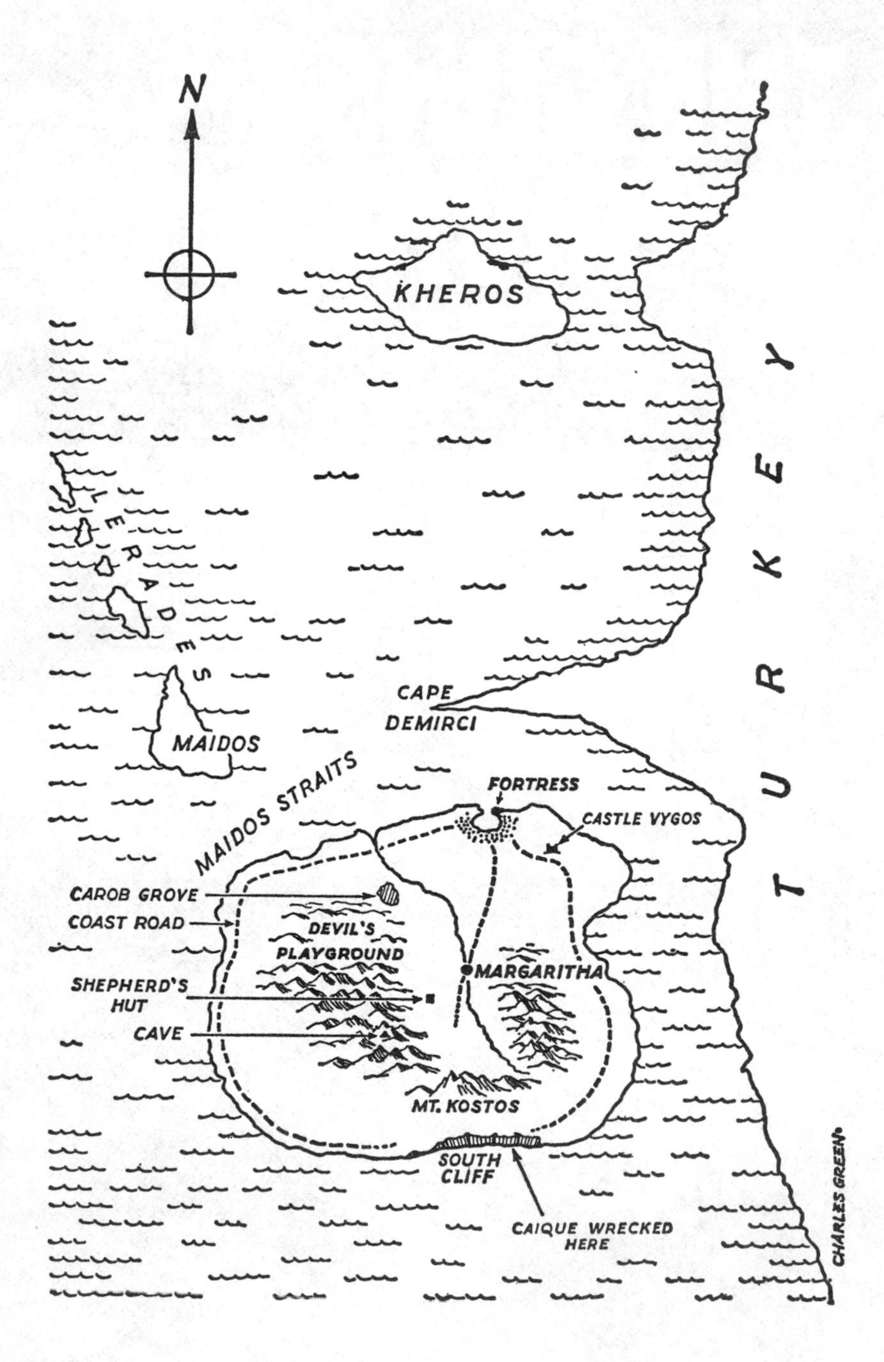
N
KHEROS
TURKEY
LERADES
MAIDOS
CAPE
DEMIRCI
MAIDOS STRAITS
FORTRESS
CASTLE VYGOS
CAROB GROVE
COAST ROAD
DEVIL'S
PLAYGROUND
SHEPHERD'S
HUT
CAVE
MARGARITHA
MT. KOSTOS
SOUTH
CLIFF
CAIQUE WRECKED
HERE
CHARLES GREEN

Chapter One

Prelude: Sunday 0100–0900

The match scratched noisily across the rusted metal of the corrugated iron shed, fizzled, then burst into a sputtering pool of light, the harsh sound and sudden brilliance alike strangely alien in the stillness of the desert night. Mechanically, Mallory's eyes followed the cupped sweep of the flaring match to the cigarette jutting out beneath the Group-Captain's clipped moustache, saw the light stop inches away from the face, saw too the sudden stillness of that face, the unfocused vacancy of the eyes of a man lost in listening. Then the match was gone, ground into the sand of the airfield perimeter.

'I can hear them,' the Group-Captain said softly. 'I can hear them coming in. Five minutes, no more. No wind tonight – they'll be coming in on Number Two. Come on, let's meet them in the interrogation room.' He paused, looked quizzically at Mallory and seemed to smile. But the darkness deceived, for there was no humour in his voice. 'Just curb your impatience, young man – just for a little longer. Things haven't gone too well tonight. You're going to have all your answers, I'm afraid, and have them all too soon.' He turned abruptly, strode off towards the squat buildings that loomed vaguely against the pale darkness that topped the level horizon.

Mallory shrugged, then followed on more slowly, step for step with the third member of the group, a broad, stocky figure with a very pronounced roll in his gait. Mallory wondered sourly just how much practice Jensen had required to achieve that sailorly effect. Thirty years at sea, of course – and Jensen had done exactly that – were sufficient warrant for a man to dance a hornpipe as he walked; but that wasn't the point. As the brilliantly successful Chief of Operations of the Subversive Operation Executive in Cairo, intrigue, deception, imitation and disguise were the breath of life to Captain James Jensen, DSO, RN. As a Levantine stevedore agitator, he had won the awed respect of the dock-labourers from Alexandretta to Alexandria: as a camel-driver, he had blasphemously out-camel-driven all available Bedouin competition: and no more pathetic beggar had ever exhibited such realistic sores in the bazaars and market-places of the East. Tonight, however, he was just the bluff and simple sailor. He was dressed in white from cap-cover to canvas shoes, the starlight glinted softly on the golden braid on epaulettes and cap peak.

Their footsteps crunched in companionable unison over the hard-packed sand, rang sharply as they moved on to the concrete of the runway. The hurrying figure of the Group-Captain was already almost lost to sight. Mallory took a deep breath and turned suddenly towards Jensen.

'Look, sir, just what *is* all this? What's all the flap, all the secrecy about? And why am *I* involved in it? Good lord, sir, it was only yesterday that I was pulled out of Crete, relieved at eight hours' notice. A month's leave, I was told. And what happens?'

'Well,' Jensen murmured, 'what did happen?'

'No leave,' Mallory said bitterly. 'Not even a night's sleep. Just hours and hours in the SOE Headquarters, answering a lot of silly, damnfool questions about climbing in the Southern Alps. Then hauled out of bed at midnight, told I was to meet you, and then driven for hours across the blasted desert by a mad Scotsman who sang drunken songs and asked hundreds of even more silly, damnfool questions!'

'One of my more effective disguises, I've always thought,' Jensen said smugly. 'Personally, I found the journey most entertaining!'

'One of your—' Mallory broke off, appalled at the memory of the things he had said to the elderly bewhiskered Scots captain who had driven the command vehicle. 'I – I'm terribly sorry, sir. I never realized—'

'Of course you didn't!' Jensen cut in briskly. 'You weren't supposed to. Just wanted to find out if you were the man for the job. I'm sure you are – I was pretty sure you were before I pulled you out of Crete. But where you got the idea about leave I don't know. The sanity of the SOE has often been questioned, but even *we* aren't given to sending a flying-boat for the sole purpose of enabling junior officers to spend a month wasting their substance among the flesh-pots of Cairo,' he finished dryly.

'I still don't know—'

'Patience, laddie, patience – as our worthy Group-Captain has just advocated. Time is endless. To wait, and to keep on waiting – that is to be of the East.'

'To total four hours' sleep in three days is not,' Mallory said feelingly. 'And that's all I've had. . . . Here they come!'

Both men screwed up their eyes in automatic reflex as the fierce glare of the landing light struck at them, the flare path arrowing off into the outer darkness. In less than a minute the first bomber was down, heavily, awkwardly, taxi-ing to a standstill just beside them. The grey camouflage paint of the after fuselage and tail-planes was riddled with bullet and cannon shells, an aileron was shredded and the port outer engine out of commission, saturated in oil. The cabin Perspex was shattered and starred in a dozen places.

For a long time Jensen stared at the holes and scars of the damaged machine, then shook his head and looked away.

'Four hours' sleep, Captain Mallory,' he said quietly. 'Four hours. I'm beginning to think that you can count yourself damn' lucky to have had even that much.'

The interrogation room, harshly lit by two powerful, unshaded lights, was uncomfortable and airless. The furniture consisted of some battered wall-maps and charts, a score or so of equally scuffed chairs and an unvarnished deal table. The Group-Captain, flanked by Jensen and Mallory, was sitting behind this when the door opened abruptly and the first of the flying crews entered, blinking rapidly in the fierceness of the unaccustomed light. They were led by a dark-haired, thick-set pilot, trailing helmet and flying-suit in his left hand. He had an Anzac bush helmet crushed on the back of his head, and the word 'Australia' emblazoned in white across each khaki shoulder. Scowling, wordlessly and without permission, he sat down in front of them, produced a pack of cigarettes and rasped a match across the surface of the table. Mallory looked furtively at the Group-Captain. The Group-Captain just looked resigned. He even sounded resigned.

'Gentlemen, this is Squadron Leader Torrance. Squadron Leader Torrance,' he added unnecessarily, 'is an Australian.' Mallory had the impression that the Group-Captain rather hoped this would explain some things, Squadron Leader Torrance among them. 'He led tonight's attack on Navarone. Bill, these gentlemen here – Captain Jensen of the Royal Navy, Captain Mallory of the Long Range Desert Group – have a very special interest in Navarone. How did things go tonight?'

Navarone! So that's why I'm here tonight, Mallory thought. Navarone. He knew it well, rather, knew of it. So did everyone who had served any time at all in the Eastern Mediterranean: a grim, impregnable iron fortress off the coast of Turkey, heavily defended by – it was thought – a mixed garrison of Germans and Italians, one of the few Ægean islands on which the Allies had been unable to establish a mission, far less recapture, at some period of the war. . . . He realized that Torrance was speaking, the slow drawl heavy with controlled anger.

'Bloody awful, sir. A fair cow, it was, a real suicide do.' He broke off abruptly, stared moodily with compressed lips through his own drifting tobacco smoke. 'But we'd like to go back again,' he went on. 'Me and the boys here. Just once. We were talking about it on the way home.' Mallory caught the deep murmur of voices in the background, a growl of agreement. 'We'd like to take with us the joker who thought this one up and shove him out at ten thousand over Navarone, without benefit of a parachute.'

'As bad as that, Bill?'

'As bad as that, sir. We hadn't a chance. Straight up, we really hadn't. First off, the weather was against us – the jokers in the Met. office were about as right as they usually are.'

'They gave you clear weather?'

'Yeah. Clear weather. It was ten-tenths over the target.' Torrance said bitterly. 'We had to go down to fifteen hundred. Not that it made any difference. We would have to have gone down lower than that anyway – about three thousand feet below sea-level then fly up the way: that cliff overhang shuts the target clean off. Might as well have dropped a shower of leaflets asking them to spike their own bloody guns. . . . Then they've got every second AA gun in the south of Europe concentrated along this narrow 50-degree vector – the only way you can approach the target, or anywhere near the target. Russ and Conroy were belted good and proper on the way in. Didn't even get half-way towards the harbour. . . . They never had a chance.'

'I know, I know.' The Group-Captain nodded heavily. 'We heard. W/T reception was good. . . . And McIlveen ditched just north of Alex?'

'Yeah. But he'll be all right. The old crate was still awash when we passed over, the big dinghy was out and it was as smooth as a millpond. He'll be all right,' Torrance repeated.

The Group-Captain nodded again, and Jensen touched his sleeve.

'May I have a word with the Squadron Leader?'

'Of course, Captain. You don't have to ask.'

'Thanks.' Jensen looked across at the burly Australian and smiled faintly.

'Just one little question, Squadron Leader. You don't fancy going back there again?'

'Too bloody right, I don't!' Torrance growled.

'Because?'

'Because I don't believe in suicide. Because I don't believe in sacrificing good blokes for nothing. Because I'm not God and I can't do the impossible.' There was a flat finality in Torrance's voice that carried conviction, that brooked no argument.

'It is impossible, you say?' Jensen persisted. 'This is terribly important.'

'So's my life. So are the lives of all these jokers.' Torrance jerked a big thumb over his shoulder. 'It's impossible, sir. At least, it's impossible for us.' He drew a weary hand down his face. 'Maybe a Dornier flying-boat with one of these new-fangled radio-controlled glider-bombs might do it and get off with it. I don't know. But I do know that nothing we've got has a snowball's chance in hell. Not,' he added bitterly, 'unless you cram a Mosquito full of TNT and order one of us to crash-dive it at four hundred into the mouth of the gun cave. That way there's always a chance.'

'Thank you, Squadron Leader – and all of you.' Jensen was on his feet. 'I know you've done your very best, no one could have done more. And I'm sorry. . . . Group-Captain?'

'Right with you, gentlemen.' He nodded to the bespectacled Intelligence officer who had been sitting behind them to take his place, led the way out through a side door and into his own quarters.

'Well, that is that, I suppose.' He broke the seal of a bottle of Talisker, brought out some glasses. 'You'll have to accept it as final, Jensen. Bill Torrance's is the senior, most experienced squadron left in Africa today. Used to pound the Ploesti oil well and think it a helluva skylark. If anyone could have done tonight's job it was Bill Torrance, and if he says it's impossible, believe me, Captain Jensen, it can't be done.'

'Yes.' Jensen looked down sombrely at the golden amber of the glass in his hand. 'Yes, I know now. I *almost* knew before, but I couldn't be sure, and I couldn't take the chance of being wrong. . . . A terrible pity that it took the lives of a dozen men to prove me right. . . . There's just the one way left, now.'

'There's just the one,' the Group-Captain echoed. He lifted his glass, shook his head. 'Here's luck to Kheros!'

'Here's luck to Kheros!' Jensen echoed in turn. His face was grim.

'Look!' Mallory begged. 'I'm completely lost. Would somebody please tell me—'

'Kheros,' Jensen interrupted. 'That was your cue call, young man. All the world's a stage, laddie, etc., and this is where you tread the boards in this particular little comedy.' Jensen's smile was quite mirthless. 'Sorry you've missed the first two acts, but don't lose any sleep over that. This is no bit part: you're going to be the star, whether you like it or not. This is it. Kheros, Act 3, Scene 1. Enter Captain Keith Mallory.'

Neither of them had spoken in the last ten minutes. Jensen drove the big Humber command car with the same sureness, the same relaxed efficiency that hall-marked everything he did: Mallory still sat hunched over the map on his knees, a large-scale Admiralty chart of the Southern Ægean illuminated by the hooded dashboard light, studying an area of the Sporades and

Northern Dodecanese heavily squared off in red pencil. Finally he straightened up and shivered. Even in Egypt these late November nights could be far too cold for comfort. He looked across at Jensen.

'I think I've got it now, sir.'

'Good!' Jensen gazed straight ahead along the winding grey ribbon of dusty road, along the white glare of the headlights that cleaved through the darkness of the desert. The beams lifted and dipped, constantly, hypnotically, to the cushioning of the springs on the rutted road. 'Good!' he repeated. 'Now, have another look at it and imagine yourself standing in the town of Navarone – that's on that almost circular bay on the north of the island. Tell me, what would you see from there?'

Mallory smiled.

'I don't have to look again, sir. Four miles or so away to the east I'd see the Turkish coast curving up north and west to a point almost due north of Navarone – a very sharp promontory, that, for the coastline above curves back almost due east. Then, about sixteen miles away, due north beyond this promontory – Cape Demirci, isn't it? – and practically in a line with it I'd see the island of Kheros. Finally, six miles to the west is the island of Maidos, the first of the Lerades group. They stretch away in a north-westerly direction, maybe fifty miles.'

'Sixty.' Jensen nodded. 'You have the eye, my boy. You've got the guts and the experience – a man doesn't survive eighteen months in Crete without both. You've got one or two special qualifications I'll mention by and by.' He paused for a moment, shook his head slowly. 'I only hope you have the luck – all the luck. God alone knows you're going to need it.'

Mallory waited expectantly, but Jensen had sunk into some private reverie. Three minutes passed, perhaps five, and there was only the swish of the tyres, the subdued hum of the powerful engine. Presently Jensen stirred and spoke again, quietly, still without taking his eyes off the road.

'This is Saturday – rather, it's Sunday morning now. There are one thousand two hundred men on the island of Kheros – one thousand two hundred British soldiers – who will be dead, wounded or prisoner by next Saturday. Mostly they'll be dead.' For the first time he looked at Mallory and smiled, a brief smile, a crooked smile, and then it was gone. 'How does it feel to hold a thousand lives in your hands, Captain Mallory?'

For long seconds Mallory looked at the impassive face beside him, then looked away again. He stared down at the chart. Twelve hundred men on Kheros, twelve hundred men waiting to die. Kheros and Navarone, Kheros and Navarone. What was that poem again, that little jingle that he'd learnt all these long years ago in that little upland village in the sheeplands outside Queenstown? Chimborazo – that was it. 'Chimborazo and Cotopaxi, you have stolen my heart away.' Kheros and Navarone – they had the same ring, the same indefinable glamour, the same wonder of romance that took hold of a man and stayed with him. Kheros and – angrily, almost, he shook his head, tried to concentrate. The pieces of the jigsaw were beginning to click into place, but slowly.

Jensen broke the silence.

'Eighteen months ago, you remember, after the fall of Greece, the Germans had taken over nearly all the islands of the Sporades: the Italians, of course, already held most of the Dodecanese. Then, gradually, we began to establish missions on these islands, usually spear-headed by your people, the Long

Range Desert Group or the Special Boat Service. By last September we had retaken nearly all the larger islands except Navarone – it was too damned hard a nut, so we just by-passed it – and brought some of the garrisons up to, and beyond, battalion strength.' He grinned at Mallory. 'You were lurking in your cave somewhere in the White Mountains at the time, but you'll remember how the Germans reacted?'

'Violently?'

Jensen nodded.

'Exactly. Very violently indeed. The political importance of Turkey in this part of the world is impossible to over-estimate – and she's always been a potential partner for either Axis or Allies. Most of these islands are only a few miles off the Turkish coast. The question of prestige, of restoring confidence in Germany, was urgent.'

'So?'

'So they flung in everything – paratroopers, airborne troops, crack mountain brigades, hordes of Stukas – I'm told they stripped the Italian front of dive-bombers for these operations. Anyway, they flung everything in – the lot. In a few weeks we'd lost over ten thousand troops and every island we'd ever recaptured – except Kheros.'

'And now it's the turn of Kheros?'

'Yes.' Jensen shook out a pair of cigarettes, sat silently until Mallory had lit them and sent the match spinning through the window towards the pale gleam of the Mediterranean lying north below the coast road. 'Yes, Kheros is for the hammer. Nothing that we can do can save it. The Germans have absolutely air superiority in the Ægean. . . .'

'But – but how can you be so sure that it's this week?'

Jensen sighed.

'Laddie, Greece is fairly hotching with Allied agents. We have over two hundred in the Athens-Piraeus area alone and—'

'Two hundred!' Mallory interrupted incredulously. 'Did you say—'

'I did.' Jensen grinned. 'A mere bagatelle, I assure you, compared to the vast hordes of spies that circulate freely among our noble hosts in Cairo and Alexandria.' He was suddenly serious again. 'Anyway our information is accurate. An armada of caiques will sail from the Piraeus on Thursday at dawn and island-hop across the Cyclades, holing up in the islands at night.' He smiled. 'An intriguing situation, don't you think? We daren't move in the Ægean in the daytime or we'd be bombed out of the water. The Germans don't dare move at night. Droves of our destroyers and MTBs and gunboats move into the Ægean at dusk: the destroyers retire to the south before dawn, the small boats usually lie up in isolated island creeks. But we can't stop them from getting across. They'll be there Saturday or Sunday – and synchronize their landings with the first of the airborne troops: they've scores of Junkers 52s waiting just outside Athens. Kheros won't last a couple of days.' No one could have listened to Jensen's carefully casual voice, his abnormal matter-of-factness and not have believed him.

Mallory believed him. For almost a minute he stared down at the sheen of the sea, at the faerie tracery of the stars shimmering across its darkly placid surface. Suddenly he swung round on Jensen.

'But the Navy, sir! Evacuation! Surely the Navy—'

'The Navy,' Jensen interrupted heavily, 'is not keen. The Navy is sick and tired of the Eastern Med. and the Ægean, sick and tired of sticking out its long-suffering neck and having it regularly chopped off – and all for sweet damn all. We've had two battleships wrecked, eight cruisers out of commission – four of them sunk – and over a dozen destroyers gone. . . . I couldn't even start to count the number of smaller vessels we've lost. And for what? I've told you – for sweet damn all! Just so's our High Command can play round-and-round-the-rugged-rocks and who's-the-king-of-the-castle with their opposite numbers in Berlin. Great fun for all concerned – except, of course, for the thousand or so sailors who've been drowned in the course of the game, the ten thousand or so Tommies and Anzacs and Indians who suffered and died on these same islands – and died without knowing why.'

Jensen's hands were whiteknuckled on the wheel, his mouth tight-drawn and bitter. Mallory was surprised, shocked almost, by the vehemence, the depth of feeling; it was so completely out of character. . . . Or perhaps it was in character, perhaps Jensen knew a very great deal indeed about what went on on the inside. . . .

'Twelve hundred men, you said, sir?' Mallory asked quietly. 'You said there were twelve hundred men on Kheros?'

Jensen flickered a glance at him, looked away again.

'Yes. Twelve hundred men.' Jensen sighed. 'You're right, laddie, of course you're right. I'm just talking off the top of my head. Of course we can't leave them there. The Navy will do its damnedest. What's two or three more destroyers – sorry, boy, sorry, there I go again. . . . Now listen, and listen carefully.

'Taking 'em off will have to be a night operation. There isn't a ghost of a chance in the daytime – not with two-three hundred Stukas just begging for a glimpse of a Royal Naval destroyer. It'll have to be destroyers – transports and tenders are too slow by half. And they can't possibly go north about the northern tip of the Lerades – they never get back to safety before daylight. It's too long a trip by hours.'

'But the Lerades is a pretty long string of islands,' Mallory ventured. 'Couldn't the destroyers go through—'

'Between a couple of them? Impossible.' Jensen shook his head. 'Mined to hell and back again. Every single channel. You couldn't take a dinghy through.'

'And the Maidos-Navarone channel. Stiff with mines also, I suppose?'

'No, that's a clear channel. Deep water – you can't moor mines in deep water.'

'So that's the route you've got to take, isn't it, sir? I mean, they're Turkish territorial waters on the other side and we—'

'We'd go through Turkish territorial waters tomorrow, and in broad daylight, if it would do any good,' Jensen said flatly. 'The Turks know it and so do the Germans. But all other things being equal, the Western channel is the one we're taking. It's a clearer channel, a shorter route – and it doesn't involve any unnecessary international complications.'

'All other things being equal?'

'The guns of Navarone.' Jensen paused for a long time, then repeated the words, slowly, expressionlessly, as one would repeat the name of some feared and ancient enemy. 'The guns of Navarone. They make everything equal. They cover the Northern entrances to both channels. We could take the twelve hundred men off Kheros tonight – if we could silence the guns of Navarone.'

Mallory sat silent, said nothing. He's coming to it now, he thought.

'These guns are no ordinary guns,' Jensen went on quietly. 'Our naval experts say they're about nine-inch rifle barrels. I think myself they're more likely a version of the 210 mm. "crunch" guns that the Germans are using in Italy – our soldiers up there hate and fear those guns more than anything on earth. A dreadful weapon – shell extremely slow in flight and damnably accurate. Anyway,' he went on grimly, 'whatever they were they were good enough to dispose of the *Sybaris* in five minutes flat.'

Mallory nodded slowly.

'The *Sybaris*? I think I heard—'

'An eight-inch cruiser we sent up there about four months ago to try conclusions with the Hun. Just a formality, a routine exercise, we thought. The *Sybaris* was blasted out of the water. There were seventeen survivors.'

'Good God!' Mallory was shocked. 'I didn't know—'

'Two months ago we mounted a large-scale amphibious attack on Navarone.' Jensen hadn't even heard the interruption. 'Commandos, Royal Marine Commandos and Jellicoe's Special Boat Service. Less than an even chance, we knew – Navarone's practically solid cliff all the way round. But then these were very special men, probably the finest assault troops in the world today.' Jensen paused for almost a minute, then went on very quietly. 'They were cut to ribbons. They were massacred almost to a man.

'Finally, twice in the past ten days – we've seen this attack on Kheros coming for a long time now – we sent in parachute saboteurs: Special Boat Service men.' He shrugged his shoulders helplessly. 'They just vanished.'

'Just like that?'

'Just like that. And then tonight – the last desperate fling of the gambler and what have you.' Jensen laughed, briefly and without humour. 'That interrogation hut – I kept pretty quiet in there tonight, I tell you. I was the "joker" that Torrance and his boys wanted to heave out over Navarone. I don't blame them. But I had to do it, I just had to do it. I knew it was hopeless – but it had to be done.'

The big Humber was beginning to slow down now, running silently between the tumble-down shacks and hovels that line the Western approach to Alexandria. The sky ahead was already beginning to streak in the first tenuous greys of the false dawn.

'I don't think I'd be much good with a parachute,' Mallory said doubtfully. 'In fact, quite frankly, I've never ever *seen* a parachute.'

'Don't worry,' Jensen said briefly. 'You won't have to use one. You're going into Navarone the hard way.'

Mallory waited for more, but Jensen had fallen silent, intent on avoiding the large potholes that were beginning to pock the roadway. After a time Mallory asked:

'Why me, Captain Jensen?'

Jensen's smile was barely visible in the greying darkness. He swerved violently to avoid a gaping hole and straightened up again.

'Scared?'

'Certainly I'm scared. No offence intended, sir, but the way you talk you'd scare anyone. . . . But that wasn't what I meant.'

'I know it wasn't. Just my twisted humour. . . . Why you? Special qualifications, laddie, just like I told you. You speak Greek like a Greek. You speak German like a German. Skilled saboteur, first-class organizer and eighteen unscathed months in the White Mountains of Crete – a convincing demonstration of your ability to survive in enemy-held territory.' Jensen chuckled. 'You'd be surprised to know just how complete a dossier I have on you!'

'No, I wouldn't.' Mallory spoke with some feeling. 'And,' he added, 'I know of at least three other officers with the same qualifications.'

'There are others,' Jensen agreed. 'But there are no other Keith Mallorys. Keith Mallory,' Jensen repeated rhetorically. 'Who hadn't heard of Keith Mallory in the palmy, balmy days before the war? The finest mountaineer, the greatest rock climber New Zealand has ever produced – and by that, of course, New Zealanders mean the world. The human fly, the climber of the unclimbable, the scaler of vertical cliffs and impossible precipices. The entire south coast of Navarone,' said Jensen cheerfully, 'consists of one vast, impossible precipice. Nary a hand or foot-hold in sight.'

'I see,' Mallory murmured. 'I see indeed. "Into Navarone the hard way." That was what you said.'

'That was,' Jensen acknowledged. 'You and your gang – just four others. Mallory's Merry Mountaineers. Hand-picked. Every man a specialist. You meet them all tomorrow – this afternoon, rather.'

They travelled in silence for the next ten minutes, turned up right from the dock area, jounced their uncomfortable way over the massive cobbles of the Rue Soeurs, slewed round into Mohammed Ali square, passed in front of the Bourse and turned right down the Sherif Pasha.

Mallory looked to the man behind the wheel. He could see his face quite clearly now in the gathering light.

'Where to, sir?'

'To see the only man in the Middle East who can give you any help now. Monsieur Eugene Vlachos of Navarone.'

'You are a brave man, Captain Mallory.' Nervously Eugene Vlachos twisted the long, pointed ends of his black moustache. 'A brave man and a foolish one, I would say – but I suppose we cannot call a man a fool when he only obeys his orders.' His eyes left the large drawing lying before him on the table and sought Jensen's impassive face.

'Is there no other way, Captain?' he pleaded.

Jensen shook his head slowly:

'There are. We've tried them all, sir. They all failed. This is the last.'

'He must go, then?'

'There are over a thousand men on Kheros, sir.'

Vlachos bowed his head in silent acceptance, then smiled faintly at Mallory.

'He calls me "sir." Me, a poor Greek hotel-keeper and Captain Jensen of the Royal Navy calls me "sir." It makes an old man feel good.' He stopped, gazed off vacantly into space, the faded eyes and tired, lined face soft with memory. 'An old man, Captain Mallory, an old man now, a poor man and a sad one. But I wasn't always, not always. Once I was just middle-aged, and rich and well content. Once I owned a lovely land, a hundred square miles of the most beautiful country God ever sent to delight the eyes of His creatures here below, and how well I loved that land!' He laughed self-consciously and ran a hand through his thick, greying hair. 'Ah, well, as you people say, I suppose it's all in the eye of the beholder. "A lovely land," I say. "That blasted rock," as Captain Jensen has been heard to describe it out of my hearing.' He smiled at Jensen's sudden discomfiture. 'But we both give it the same name – Navarone.'

Startled, Mallory looked at Jensen. Jensen nodded.

'The Vlachos family has owned Navarone for generations. We had to remove Monsieur Vlachos in a great hurry eighteen months ago. The Germans didn't care over-much for his kind of collaboration.'

'It was – how do you say – touch and go.' Vlachos nodded. 'They had reserved three very special places for my two sons and myself in the dungeons in Navarone. . . . But enough of the Vlachos family. I just wanted you to know, young man, that I spent forty years on Navarone and almost four days' – he gestured to the table – 'on that map. My information and that map you can trust absolutely. Many things will have changed, of course, but some things never change. The mountains, the bays, the passes, the caves, the roads, the houses and, above all, the fortress itself – these have remained unchanged for centuries, Captain Mallory.'

'I understand, sir.' Mallory folded the map carefully, stowed it away in his tunic. 'With this, there's always a chance. Thank you very much.'

'It is little enough, God knows.' Vlachos's fingers drummed on the table for a moment, then he looked up at Mallory. 'Captain Jensen informs me that most of you speak Greek fluently, that you will be dressed as Greek peasants and will carry forged papers. That is well. You will be – what is the word? – self-contained, will operate on your own.' He paused, then went on very earnestly.

'Please do not try to enlist the help of the people of Navarone. At all costs you must avoid that. The Germans are ruthless. I know. If a man helps you and is found out, they will destroy not only that man but his entire village – men, women and children. It has happened before. It will happen again.'

'It happened in Crete,' Mallory agreed quietly. 'I've seen it for myself.'

'Exactly.' Vlachos nodded. 'And the people of Navarone have neither the skill nor the experience for successful guerrilla operations. They have not had the chance – German surveillance has been especially severe in our island.'

'I promise you, sir—' Mallory began.

Vlachos held up his hand.

'Just a moment. If your need is desperate, really desperate, there are two men to whom you may turn. Under the first plane tree in the village square of Margaritha – at the mouth of the valley about three miles south of the fortress – you will find a man called Louki. He has been the steward of our family for many years. Louki has been of help to the British before – Captain Jensen will confirm that – and you can trust him with your life. He has a friend, Panayis: he, too, has been useful in the past.'

'Thank you, sir. I'll remember. Louki and Panayis and Margaritha – the first plane tree in the square.'

'And you will refuse all other aid, Captain?' Vlachos asked anxiously. 'Louki and Panayis – only these two,' he pleaded.

'You have my word, sir. Besides, the fewer the safer for us as well as your people.' Mallory was surprised at the old man's intensity.

'I hope so, I hope so.' Vlachos sighed heavily.

Mallory stood up, stretched out his hand to take his leave.

'You're worrying about nothing, sir. They'll never see us,' he promised confidently. 'Nobody will see us – and we'll see nobody. We're after only one thing – the guns.'

'Ay, the guns – those terrible guns.' Vlachos shook his head. 'But just suppose—'

'Please. It will be all right,' Mallory insisted quietly. 'We will bring harm to none – and least of all to your islanders.'

'God go with you tonight,' the old man whispered. 'God go with you tonight. I only wish I could go too.'

Chapter Two

Sunday Night 1900–0200

'Coffee, sir?'

Mallory stirred and groaned and fought his way up from the depths of exhausted sleep. Painfully he eased himself back on the metal-framed bucket-seat, wondering peevishly when the Air Force was going to get round to upholstering these fiendish contraptions. Then he was fully awake, tired, heavy eyes automatically focusing on the luminous dial of his wrist-watch. Seven o'clock. Just seven o'clock – he'd been asleep barely a couple of hours. Why hadn't they let him sleep on?

'Coffee, sir?' The young air-gunner was still standing patiently by his side, the inverted lid of an ammunition box serving as a tray for the cups he was carrying.

'Sorry, boy, sorry.' Mallory struggled upright in his seat, reached up for a cup of the steaming liquid, sniffed it appreciatively. 'Thank you. You know, this smells just like real coffee.'

'It is, sir.' The young gunner smiled proudly. 'We have a percolator in the galley.'

'He has a percolator in the galley.' Mallory shook his head in disbelief. 'Ye gods, the rigours of war in the Royal Air Force!' He leaned back, sipped the coffee luxuriously and sighed in contentment. Next moment he was on his feet, the hot coffee splashing unheeded on his bare knees as he stared out the window beside him. He looked at the gunner, gestured in disbelief at the mountainous landscape unrolling darkly beneath them.

'What the hell goes on here? We're not due till two hours after dark – and it's barely gone sunset! Has the pilot—?'

'That's Cyprus, sir.' The gunner grinned. 'You can just see Mount Olympus on the horizon. Nearly always, going to Castelrosso, we fly a big dog-leg over Cyprus. It's to escape observation, sir; and it takes us well clear of Rhodes.'

'To escape observation, he says!' The heavy transatlantic drawl came from the bucket-seat diagonally across the passage: the speaker was lying collapsed

– there was no other word for it – in his seat, the bony knees topping the level of one chin by several inches. 'My Gawd! To escape observation!' he repeated in awed wonder. 'Dog-legs over Cyprus. Twenty miles out from Alex by launch so that nobody ashore can see us takin' off by plane. And then what?' He raised himself painfully in his seat, eased an eyebrow over the bottom of the window, then fell back again, visibly exhausted by the effort. 'And then what? Then they pack us into an old crate that's painted the whitest white you ever saw guaranteed visible to a blind man at a hundred miles – 'specially now that it's gettin' dark.'

'It keeps the heat out,' the young gunner said defensively.

'The heat doesn't worry me, son.' The drawl was tireder, more lugubrious than ever. 'I like the heat. What I don't like are them nasty cannon shells and bullets that can ventilate a man in all the wrong places.' He slid his spine another impossible inch down the seat, closed his eyes wearily and seemed asleep in a moment.

The young gunner shook his head admiringly and smiled at Mallory.

'Worried to hell, isn't he, sir?'

Mallory laughed and watched the boy disappear for'ard into the control cabin. He sipped his coffee slowly, looked again at the sleeping figure across the passage. The blissful unconcern was magnificent: Corporal Dusty Miller of the United States, and more recently of the Long Range Desert Force, would be a good man to have around.

He looked round at the others and nodded to himself in satisfaction. They would all be good men to have around. Eighteen months in Crete had developed in him an unerring sense for assessing a man's capacity for survival in the peculiar kind of irregular warfare in which he himself had been so long engaged. Off-hand he'd have taken long odds on the capacity of these four to survive. In the matter of picking an outstanding team Captain Jensen, he reckoned, had done him proud. He didn't know them all yet – not personally. But he was intimately acquainted with the exhaustive dossier that Jensen held on each one of them. These were reassuring, to say the least.

Or was there perhaps a slight question mark against Stevens? Mallory wondered, looking across the passage at the fair-haired, boyish figure gazing out eagerly beneath the gleaming white wing of the Sunderland. Lieutenant Andy Stevens, RNVR, had been chosen for this assignment for three reasons. He would navigate the craft that was to take them to Navarone: he was a first-class Alpinist, with several outstanding climbs to his record: and, the product of the classical side of a red-brick university, he was an almost fanatical philhellene, fluent in both Ancient and Modern Greek, and had spent his last two long vacations before the war as a tourist courier in Athens. But he was young, absurdly young, Mallory thought as he looked at him, and youth could be dangerous. Too often, in that island guerrilla warfare, it had been fatal. The enthusiasm, the fire, the zeal of youth was not enough: rather, it was too much, a positive handicap. This was not a war of bugle calls and roaring engines and magnificent defiance in the clamour of battle: this was a war of patience and endurance and stability, of cunning and craft and stealth, and these were not commonly the attributes of youth. . . . But he looked as if he might learn fast.

Mallory stole another glance at Miller. Dusty Miller, he decided, had learnt it all a long, long time ago. Dusty Miller on a white charger, the bugle to his lips – no, his mind just refused to encompass the incongruity of it. He just didn't look like Sir Launcelot. He just looked as if he had been around for a long, long time and had no illusions left.

Corporal Miller had, in fact, been around for exactly forty years. By birth a Californian, by descent three parts Irish and one part Central European, he had lived and fought and adventured more in the previous quarter of a century than most men would in a dozen lifetimes. Silver-miner in Nevada, tunneller in Canada and oil-fire shooter all over the globe, he had been in Saudi Arabia when Hitler attacked Poland. One of his more remote maternal ancestors, some time around the turn of the century, had lived in Warsaw, but that had been affront enough for Miller's Irish blood. He had taken the first available plane to Britain and lied his way into the Air Force, where, to his immense disgust, and because of his age, he was relegated to the rear turret of a Wellington.

His first operational flight had been his last. Within ten minutes of taking off from the Menidi airfield outside Athens on a January night in 1941, engine failure had brought them to an ignominious though well-cushioned end in a paddy field some miles north-west of the city. The rest of the winter he had spent seething with rage in a cook-house back in Menidi. At the beginning of April he resigned from the Air Force without telling anyone and was making his way north towards the fighting and the Albanian frontier when he met the Germans coming south. As Miller afterwards told it, he reached Nauplion two blocks ahead of the nearest panzer division, was evacuated by the transport *Slamat*, sunk, picked up by the destroyer *Wryneck*, sunk, and finally arrived in Alexandria in an ancient Greek caique, with nothing left him in the world but a fixed determination never again to venture in the air or on the sea. Some months later he was operating with a long-range striking force behind the enemy lines in Libya.

He was, Mallory mused, the complete antithesis to Lieutenant Stevens. Stevens, young, fresh, enthusiastic, correct and immaculately dressed, and Miller, dried-up, lean, stringy, immensely tough and with an almost pathological aversion to spit and polish. How well the nickname 'Dusty' suited him: there could hardly have been a greater contrast. Again, unlike Stevens, Miller had never climbed a mountain in his life and the only Greek words he knew were invariably omitted from the dictionaries. And both these facts were of no importance at all. Miller had been picked for one reason only. A genius with explosives, resourceful and cool, precise and deadly in action, he was regarded by Middle East Intelligence in Cairo as the finest saboteur in southern Europe.

Behind Miller sat Casey Brown. Short, dark and compact, Petty Officer Telegraphist Brown was a Clydesider, in peace-time an installation and testing engineer in a famous yacht-builder's yard on the Gareloch. The fact that he was a born and ready-made engine-room artificer had been so blindingly obvious that the Navy had missed it altogether and stuck him in the Communications Branch. Brown's ill luck was Mallory's good fortune. Brown would act as the engineer of the boat taking them to Navarone and would maintain radio contact with base. He had also the further recommendation of being a first-class guerrilla fighter: a veteran of the Special Boat Service, he held the DCM and DSM for his exploits in the Ægean and off the coast of Libya.

The fifth and last member of the party sat directly behind Mallory.

Mallory did not have to turn round to look at him. He already knew him, knew him better than he knew anyone else in the world, better even than he knew his own mother. Andrea, who had been his lieutenant for all these eighteen interminable months in Crete. Andrea of the vast bulk, the continual rumbling laughter and tragic past, with whom he had eaten, lived and slept in caves, rock-shelters and abandoned shepherds' huts while constantly harried by German patrols and aircraft – that Andrea had become his *alter ego*, his *doppel-ganger*: to look at Andrea was to look in a mirror to remind himself what he was like. . . . There was no question as to why Andrea had come along. He wasn't there primarily because he was a Greek himself, with an intimate knowledge of the islanders' language, thought and customs, nor even because of his perfect understanding with Mallory, although all these things helped. He was, instead, there exclusively for the protection and safety he afforded. Endlessly patient, quiet and deadly, tremendously fast in spite of his bulk, and with a feline stealth that exploded into berserker action, Andrea was the complete fighting machine. Andrea was their insurance policy against failure.

Mallory turned back to look out the window again, then nodded to himself in imperceptible satisfaction. Jensen probably couldn't have picked a better team if he'd scoured the whole Mediterranean theatre. It suddenly occurred to Mallory that Jensen probably had done just that. Miller and Brown had been recalled to Alexandria almost a mongh ago. It was almost as long since Stevens's relief had arrived aboard his cruiser in Malta. And if their battery-charging engine hadn't slipped down that ravine in the White Mountains, and if the sorely harassed runner from the nearest listening post hadn't taken a week to cover fifty miles of snowbound, enemy patrolled mountains and another five days to find them, he and Andrea would have been in Alexandria almost a fortnight earlier. Mallory's opinion of Jensen, already high, rose another notch. A far-seeing man who planned accordingly, Jensen must have had all his preparations for this made even before the first of the two abortive parachute landings on Navarone.

It was eight o'clock and almost totally dark inside the plane when Mallory rose and made his way for'ard to the control cabin. The captain, face wreathed in tobacco smoke, was drinking coffee: the co-pilot waved a languid hand at his approach and resumed a bored scanning of the scene ahead.

'Good evening.' Mallory smiled. 'Mind if I come in?'

'Welcome in my office any time,' the pilot assured him. 'No need to ask.'

'I only thought you might be busy. . . .' Mallory stopped and looked again at the scene of masterly inactivity. 'Just who is flying this plane?' he asked.

'George. The automatic pilot.' He waved a coffee-cup in the direction of a black, squat box, its blurred outlines just visible in the near darkness. 'An industrious character, and makes a damn' sight fewer mistakes than that idle hound who's supposed to be on watch. . . . Anything on your mind, Captain?'

'Yes. What were your instructions for tonight?'

'Just to set you blokes down in Castelrosso when it was good and dark.' The pilot paused, then said frankly, 'I don't get it. A ship this size for only five men and a couple of hundred odd pounds of equipment. Especially to Castelrosso. Especially after dark. Last plane that came down here after dark just kept on going down. Underwater obstruction – dunno what it was. Two survivors.'

'I know. I heard. I'm sorry, but I'm under orders too. As for the rest, forget it – and I mean forget. Impress on your crew that they mustn't talk. They've never seen us.'

The pilot nodded glumly. 'We've all been threatened with court-martial already. You'd think there was a ruddy war on.'

'There is. . . . We'll be leaving a couple of cases behind. We're going ashore in different clothes. Somebody will be waiting for our old stuff when you get back.'

'Roger. And the best of luck, Captain. Official secrets, or no official secrets, I've got a hunch you're going to need it.'

'If we are, you can give us a good send-off.' Mallory grinned. 'Just set us down in one piece will you?'

'Reassure yourself, brother,' the pilot said firmly. 'Just set your mind at ease. Don't forget – I'm in this ruddy plane too.'

The clamour of the Sunderland's great engines was still echoing in their ears when the stubby little motor-boat chugged softly out of the darkness and nosed alongside the gleaming hull of the flying-boat. There was no time lost, there were no words spoken; within a minute the five men and all their gear had been embarked; within another the little boat was rubbing to a stop against the rough stone Navy jetty of Castelrosso. Two ropes were spinning up into the darkness, were caught and quickly secured by practised hands. Amidships, the rust-scaled iron ladder, recessed deep into the stone, stretched up into the star-dusted darkness above: as Mallory reached the top, a figure stepped forward out of the gloom.

'Captain Mallory?'

'Yes.'

'Captain Briggs, Army. Have your men wait here, will you? The colonel would like to see you.' The nasal voice peremptory in its clipped affectation, was far from cordial. Mallory stirred in slow anger, but said nothing. Briggs sounded like a man who might like his bed or his gin, and maybe their late visitation was keeping him from either or both. War was hell.

They were back in ten minutes, a third figure following behind them. Mallory peered at the three men standing on the edge of the jetty, identified them, then peered around again.

'Where's Miller got to?' he asked.

'Here, boss, here.' Miller groaned, eased his back off a big, wooden bollard, climbed wearily to his feet. 'Just restin', boss. Recuperatin', as you might say, from the nerve-rackin' rigours of the trip.'

'When you're all *quite* ready,' Briggs said acidly, 'Matthews here will take you to your quarters. You are to remain on call for the Captain, Matthews. Colonel's orders.' Briggs's tone left no doubt that he thought the colonel's orders a piece of arrant nonsense. 'And don't forget, Captain – two hours, the Colonel said.'

'I know, I know,' Mallory said wearily. 'I was there when he said it. It was to me he was talking. Remember? All right, boys, if you're ready.'

'Our gear, sir?' Stevens ventured.

'Just leave it there. Right, Matthews, lead the way, will you?'

Matthews led the way along the jetty and up interminable flights of steep, worn steps, the others followed in Indian file, rubber soles noiseless on the stone. He turned sharply right at the top, went down a narrow, winding alley, into a passage, climbed a flight of creaking, wooden stairs, opened the first door in the corridor above.

'Here you are, sir. I'll just wait in the corridor outside.'

'Better wait downstairs,' Mallory advised. 'No offence, Matthews, but the less you know of this the better.'

He followed the others into the room, closing the door behind him. It was a small, bleak room, heavily curtained. A table and half a dozen chairs took up most of the space. Over in the far corner the springs of the single bed creaked as Corporal Miller stretched himself out luxuriously, hands clasped behind his head.

'Gee!' he murmured admiringly. 'A hotel room. Just like home. Kinda bare, though.' A thought occurred to him. 'Where are all you other guys gonna sleep?'

'We aren't,' Mallory said briefly. 'Neither are you. We're pulling out in less than two hours.' Miller groaned. 'Come on, soldier,' Mallory went on relentlessly. 'On your feet.'

Miller groaned again, swung his legs over the edge of the bed and looked curiously at Andrea. The big Greek was quartering the room methodically, pulling out lockers, turning pictures, peering behind curtains and under the bed.

'What's he doin'?' Miller asked. 'Lookin' for dust?'

'Testing for listening devices,' Mallory said curtly. 'One of the reasons why Andrea and I have lasted so long.' He dug into the inside pocket of his tunic, a dark naval battledress with neither badge nor insignia, pulled out a chart and the map Vlachos had given him, unfolded and spread them out. 'Round the table, all of you. I know you've been bursting with curiosity for the past couple of weeks, asking yourselves a hundred questions. Well, here are all the answers. I hope you like them. . . . Let me introduce you to the island of Navarone.'

Mallory's watch showed exactly eleven o'clock when he finally sat back, folded away the map and chart. He looked quizzically at the four thoughtful faces round the table.

'Well, gentlemen, there you have it. A lovely set-up, isn't it?' He smiled wryly. 'If this was a film, my next line should be, "Any questions, men?" But we'll dispense with that because I just wouldn't have any of the answers. You all know as much as I do.'

'A quarter of a mile of sheer cliff, four hundred feet high, and he calls it the only break in the defences.' Miller, his head bent moodily over his tobacco tin, rolled a long, thin cigarette with one expert hand. 'This is just crazy, boss. Me, I can't even climb a bloody ladder without falling off.' He puffed strong, acrid clouds of smoke into the air. 'Suicidal. That's the word I was lookin' for. Suicidal. One buck gets a thousand we never get within five miles of them gawddamned guns!'

'One in a thousand, eh?' Mallory looked at him for a long time without speaking. 'Tell me, Miller, what odds are you offering on the boys on Kheros?'

'Yeah.' Miller nodded heavily. 'Yeah, the boys on Kheros. I'd forgotten about them. I just keep thinkin' about me and that damned cliff.' He looked hopefully across the table at the vast bulk of Andrea. 'Or maybe Andrea there would carry me up. He's big enough, anyway.'

Andrea made no reply. His eyes were half-closed, his thoughts could have been a thousand miles away.

'We'll tie you hand and foot and haul you up on the end of a rope,' Stevens said unkindly. 'We'll try to pick a fairly sound rope,' he added carelessly. The words, the tone, were jocular enough, but the worry on his face belied them. Mallory apart, only Stevens appreciated the almost insuperable technical difficulties of climbing a sheer, unknown cliff in the darkness. He looked at Mallory questioningly. 'Going up alone, sir or—'

'Excuse me, please.' Andrea suddenly sat forward, his deep rumble of a voice rapid in the clear, idiomatic English he had learnt during his long association with Mallory. He was scribbling quickly on a piece of paper. 'I have a plan for climbing this cliff. Here is a diagram. Does the Captain think this is possible?'

He passed the paper across to Mallory. Mallory looked at it, checked, recovered, all in one instant. There was no diagram on it. There were only two large, printed words: 'Keep talking.'

'I see,' Mallory said thoughtfully. 'Very good indeed, Andrea. This has distinct possibilities.' He reversed the paper, held it up before him so that they could all see the words. Andrea had already risen to his feet, was padding cat-footed towards the door. 'Ingenious, isn't it, Corporal Miller,' he went on conversationally. 'Might solve quite a lot of our difficulties.'

'Yeah.' The expression on Miller's face hadn't altered a fraction, the eyes were still half-closed against the smoke drifting up from the cigarette dangling between his lips. 'Reckon that might solve the problem, Andrea – and get me up in one piece, too.' He laughed easily, concentrated on screwing a curiously-shaped cylinder on to the barrel of an automatic that had magically appeared in his left hand. 'But I don't quite get that funny line and the dot at—'

It was all over in two seconds – literally. With a deceptive ease and nonchalance Andrea opened the door with one hand, reached out with the other, plucked a wildly-struggling figure through the gap, set him on the ground again and closed the door, all in one concerted movement. It had been as soundless as it had been swift. For a second the eavesdropper, a hatched-faced, swarthy Levantine in badly-fitting white shirt and blue trousers, stood there in shocked immobility, blinking rapidly in the unaccustomed light. Then his hand dived in under his shirt.

'Look out!' Miller's voice was sharp, the automatic lining up as Mallory's hand closed over his.

'Watch!' Mallory said softly.

The men at the table caught only a flicker of blued steel as the knife arm jerked convulsively back and plunged down with vicious speed. And then, incredibly, hand and knife were stopped dead in mid-air, the gleaming point only two inches from Andrea's chest. There was a sudden scream of agony, the ominous cracking of wrist bones as the giant Greek tightened his grip, and then Andrea had the blade between finger and thumb, had removed the knife with the tender, reproving care of a parent saving a well-loved but irresponsible child from himself. Then the knife was reversed, the point was at the Levantine's throat and Andrea was smiling down pleasantly into the dark and terror-stricken eyes.

Miller let out a long breath, half-sigh, half-whistle.

'Well, now,' he murmured. 'I guess mebbe Andrea has done that sort of thing before?'

'I guess maybe he has,' Mallory mimicked. 'Let's have a closer look at exhibit A, Andrea.'

Andrea brought his prisoner close up to the table, well within the circle of light. He stood there sullenly before them, a thin, ferret-faced man, black eyes dulled in pain and fear, left hand cradling his crushed wrist.

'How long do you reckon this fellow's been outside, Andrea?' Mallory asked.

Andrea ran a massive hand through his thick, dark, curling hair, heavily streaked with grey above the temples.

'I cannot be sure, Captain. I imagined I heard a noise – a kind of shuffle – about ten minutes ago, but I thought my ears were playing tricks. Then I heard the same sound a minute ago. So I am afraid—'

'Ten minutes, eh?' Mallory nodded thoughtfully, then looked at the prisoner. 'What's your name?' he asked sharply. 'What are you doing here?'

There was no reply. There were only the sullen eyes, the sullen silence – a silence that gave way to a sudden yelp of pain as Andrea cuffed the side of his head.

'The Captain is asking you a question,' Andrea said reproachfully. He cuffed him again, harder this time. 'Answer the Captain.'

The stranger broke into rapid, excitable speech, gesticulating wildly with both hands. The words were quite unintelligible. Andrea sighed, shut off the torrent by the simple expedient of almost encircling the scrawny throat with his left hand.

Mallory looked questioningly at Andrea. The giant shook his head.

'Kurdistan or Armenian, Captain, I think. But I don't understand it.'

'I certainly don't,' Mallory admitted. 'Do you speak English?' he asked suddenly.

Black, hate-filled eyes glared back at him in silence. Andrea cuffed him again.

'Do you speak English?' Mallory repeated relentlessly.

'Eenglish? Eenglish?' Shoulders and upturned palms lifted in the old-age gesture of incomprehension. 'Ka Eenglish!'

'He says he don't speak English,' Miller drawled.

'Maybe he doesn't and maybe he does,' Mallory said evenly. 'All we know is that he *has* been listening and that we can't take any chances. There are far too many lives at stake.' His voice suddenly hardened, the eyes were grim and pitiless. 'Andrea!'

'Captain?'

'You have the knife. Make it clean and quick. Between the shoulder blades!'

Stevens cried out in horror, sent his chair crashing back as he leapt to his feet.

'Good God, sir, you can't—'

He broke off and stared in amazement at the sight of the prisoner catapulting himself bodily across the room to crash into a distant corner, one arm up-curved in rigid defence, stark, unreasoning panic limned in every feature of his face. Slowly Stevens looked away, saw the triumphant grin on

Andrea's face, the dawning comprehension in Brown's and Miller's. Suddenly he felt a complete fool. Characteristically, Miller was the first to speak.

'Waal, waal, whaddya know! Mebbe he *does* speaka da Eenglish after all.'

'Maybe he does,' Mallory admitted. 'A man doesn't spend ten minutes with his ear glued to a keyhole if he doesn't understand a word that's being said. . . . Give Matthews a call, will you, Brown?'

The sentry appeared in the doorway a few seconds later.

'Get Captain Briggs here, will you, Matthews?' he asked. 'At once, please.'

The soldier hesitated.

'Captain Briggs has gone to bed, sir. He left strict orders that he wasn't to be disturbed.'

'My heart bleeds for Captain Briggs and his broken slumbers,' Mallory said acidly. 'He's had more sleep in a day than I've had in the past week.' He glanced at his watch and the heavy brows came down in a straight line over the tired, brown eyes. 'We've no time to waste. Get him here at once. Understand? At once!'

Matthews saluted and hurried away. Miller cleared his throat and clucked his tongue sadly.

'These hotels are all the same. The goin's-on – you'd never believe your eyes. Remember once I was at a convention in Cincinnati—'

Mallory shook his head wearily.

'You have a fixation about hotels, Corporal. This is a military establishment and these are army officers' billets.'

Miller made to speak but changed his mind. The American was a shrewd judge of people. There were those who could be ribbed and those who could not be ribbed. An almost hopeless mission, Miller was quietly aware, and as vital as it was, in his opinion, suicidal; but he was beginning to understand why they'd picked this tough, sunburnt New Zealander to lead it.

They sat in silence for the next five minutes, then looked up as the door opened. Captain Briggs was hatless and wore a white silk muffler round his throat in place of the usual collar and tie. The white contrasted oddly with the puffed red of the heavy neck and face above. These had been red enough when Mallory had first seen them in the colonel's office – high blood pressure and even higher living. Mallory had supposed: the extra deeper shades of red and purple now present probably sprang from a misplaced sense of righteous indignation. A glance at the choleric eyes, gleaming light-blue prawns afloat in a sea of vermilion, was quite enough to confirm the obvious.

'I think this is a bit much, Captain Mallory!' The voice was high pitched in anger, more nasal than ever. 'I'm not the duty errand-boy, you know. I've had a damned hard day and—'

'Save it for your biography,' Mallory said curtly, 'and take a gander at this character in the corner.'

Briggs's face turned an even deeper hue. He stepped into the room, fists balled in anger, then stopped in his tracks as his eye hit on the crumpled, dishevelled figure still crouched in the corner of the room.

'Good God!' he ejaculated. 'Nicolai!'

'You know him.' It was a statement, not a question.

'Of course I know him!' Briggs snorted. 'Everybody knows him. Nicolai. Our laundry-boy.'

'Your laundry-boy! Do his duties entail snooping around the corridors at night, listening at keyholes?'

'What do you mean?'

'What I say.' Mallory was very patient. 'We caught him listening outside the door.'

'Nicolai? I don't believe it—'

'Watch it, mister,' Miller growled. 'Careful who you call a liar. We all saw him.'

Briggs stared in fascination at the black muzzle of the automatic waving negligently in his direction, gulped, looked hastily away.

'Well, what if you did?' He forced a smile. 'Nicolai can't speak a word of English.'

'Maybe not,' Mallory agreed dryly. 'But he understands it well enough.' He raised his hand. 'I've no desire to argue all night and I certainly haven't the time. Will you please have this man placed under arrest, kept in solitary confinement and incommunicado for the next week at least. It's vital. Whether he's a spy or just too damned nosy, he knows far too much. After that, do what you like. My advice is to kick him out of Castelrosso.'

'*Your advice*, indeed!' Briggs's colour returned, and with it his courage. 'Who the hell are you to give me advice or to give me orders, Captain Mallory?' There was a heavy emphasis on the word 'captain.'

'Then I'm asking it as a favour,' Mallory pleaded wearily. 'I can't explain, but it's terribly important. There are hundreds of lives—'

'Hundreds of lives!' Briggs sneered. 'Melodramatic stuff and nonsense!' He smiled unpleasantly. 'I suggest you keep that for *your* cloak-and-dagger biography, Captain Mallory.'

Mallory rose, walked round the table, stopped a foot away from Briggs. The brown eyes were still and very cold.

'I could go and see your colonel, I suppose. But I'm tired of arguing. You'll do exactly as I say or I'll go straight to Naval HQ and get on the radio-telephone to Cairo. And if I do,' Mallory went on, 'I swear to you that you'll be on the next ship home to England – and on the troop-deck, at that.'

His last words seem to echo in the little room for an interminable time: the stillness was intense. And then, as suddenly as it had arisen, the tension was gone and Briggs's face, a now curiously mottled white and red, was slack and sullen in defeat.

'All right, all right,' he said. 'No need for all these damned stupid threats – not if it means all that much to you.' The attempt to bluster, to patch up the shredded rags of his dignity, was pathetic in its transparency. 'Matthews – call out the guard.'

The torpedo-boat, great aero engines throttled back half speed, pitched and lifted, pitched and lifted with monotonous regularity as it thrust its way into the long, gentle swell from the WNW. For the hundredth time that night Mallory looked at his watch.

'Running behind time, sir?' Stevens suggested.

Mallory nodded.

'We should have stepped straight into this thing from the Sunderland – there was a hold-up.'

Brown grunted. 'Engine trouble, for a fiver.' The Clydeside accent was very heavy.

'Yes, that's right.' Mallory looked up, surprised. 'How did you know?'

'Always the same with these blasted MTB engines,' Brown growled. 'Temperamental as a film star.'

There was silence for a time in the tiny blacked-out cabin, a silence broken only by the occasional clink of glass. The Navy was living up to its traditional hospitality.

'If we're late,' Miller observed at last, 'why doesn't the skipper open her up? They tell me these crates can do forty to fifty knots.'

'You look green enough already,' Stevens said tactlessly. 'Obviously, you've never been in an MTB full out in a heavy sea.'

Miller fell silent a moment. Clearly, he was trying to take his mind off his internal troubles. 'Captain?'

'Yes, what is it?' Mallory answered sleepily. He was stretched full length on a narrow settee, an almost empty glass in his fingers.

'None of my business, I know, boss, but – would you have carried out that threat you made to Captain Briggs?'

Mallory laughed.

'It *is* none of your business, but – well, no, Corporal, I wouldn't. I wouldn't because I couldn't. I haven't all that much authority invested in me – and I didn't even know whether there was a radio-telephone in Castelrosso.'

'Yeah. Yeah, do you know, I kinda suspected that.' Corporal Miller rubbed a stubbled chin. 'If he'd called your bluff, what would you have done, boss?'

'I'd have shot Nicolai,' Mallory said quietly. 'If the colonel had failed me. I'd have had no choice left.'

'I knew that too. I really believe you would. For the first time I'm beginning to believe we've got a chance. . . . But I kinda wish you *had* shot him – *and* little Lord Fauntleroy. I didn't like the expression on old Briggs's face when you went out that door. Mean wasn't the word. He coulda killed you then. You trampled right over his pride, boss – and to a phony like that nothin' else in the world matters.'

Mallory made no reply. He was already sound asleep, his empty glass fallen from his hand. Not even the banshee clamour of the great engines opening full out as they entered the sheltered calm of the Rhodes channel could plumb his bottomless abyss of sleep.

Chapter Three

Monday 0700–1700

'My dear fellow, you make me feel dreadfully embarrassed.' Moodily the officer switched his ivory-handled flyswat against an immaculately trousered leg, pointed a contemptuous but gleaming toe-cap at the ancient caique, broadbeamed and two-masted, moored stern on to the even older and more dilapidated wooden pier on which they were standing. 'I am positively ashamed. The clients of Rutledge and Company, I assure you, are accustomed only to the best.'

Mallory smothered a smile. Major Rutledge of the Buffs, Eton and Sandhurst as to intonation, millimetrically tooth-brushed as to moustache, Savile Row as to the quite dazzling sartorial perfection of his khaki drill, was so magnificently out of place in the wild beauty of the rocky, tree-lined bluffs of that winding creek that his presence there seemed inevitable. Such was the major's casual assurance, so dominating his majestic unconcern, that it was the creek, if anything, that seemed slightly out of place.

'It *does* look as if it had seen better days,' Mallory admitted. 'Nevertheless, sir, it's exactly what we want.'

'Can't understand it, I really can't understand it.' With an irritable but well-timed swipe the major brought down a harmless passing fly. 'I've been providing chaps with everything during the past eight or nine months – caiques, launches, yachts, fishing boats, everything – but no one has ever yet specified the oldest, most dilapidated derelict I could lay hands on. Quite a job laying hands on it, too, I tell you.' A pained expression crossed his face. 'The chaps know I don't usually deal in this line of stuff.'

'What chaps?' Mallory asked curiously.

'Oh, up the islands, you know.' Rutledge gestured vaguely to the north and west.

'But – but those are enemy held—'

'So's this one. Chap's got to have his HQ somewhere.' Rutledge explained patiently. Suddenly his expression brightened. 'I say, old boy, I know just the thing for you. A boat to escape observation and investigation – that was what Cairo insisted I get. How about a German E-boat, absolutely perfect condition, one careful owner. Could get ten thou. for her at home. Thirty-six hours. Pal of mine over in Bodrum—'

'Bodrum?' Mallory questioned. 'Bodrum? But – but that's in Turkey, isn't it?'

'Turkey? Well, yes, actually, I believe it is,' Rutledge admitted. 'Chap has to get his supplies from somewhere, you know,' he added defensively.

'Thanks all the same' – Mallory smiled – 'but this is exactly what we want. We can't wait, anyway.'

'On your own heads be it!' Rutledge threw up his hands in admission of defeat. 'I'll have a couple of my men shove your stuff aboard.'

'I'd rather we did it ourselves, sir. It's – well, it's a very special cargo.'

'Right you are,' the major acknowledged. 'No questions Rutledge, they call me. Leaving soon?'

Mallory looked at his watch.

'Half an hour, sir.'

'Bacon, eggs and coffee in ten minutes?'

'Thanks very much.' Mallory grinned. 'That's one offer we'll be very glad to accept.'

He turned away, walked slowly down to the end of the pier. He breathed deeply, savouring the heady, herb-scented air of an Ægean dawn. The salt tang of the sea, the drowsily sweet perfume of honeysuckle, the more delicate sharper fragrance of mint all subtly merged into an intoxicating whole, indefinable, unforgettable. On either side, the steep slopes, still brilliantly green with pine and walnut and holly, stretched far up to the moorland pastures above, and from these, faintly borne on the perfumed breeze, came the distant, melodic tinkling of goats' bells, a haunting, a nostalgic music, true symbol of the leisured peace the Ægean no longer knew.

Unconsciously almost, Mallory shook his head and walked more quickly to the end of the pier. The others were still sitting where the torpedo boat had landed them just before dawn. Miller, inevitably, was stretched his full length, hat tilted against the golden, level rays of the rising sun.

'Sorry to disturb you and all that, but we're leaving in half an hour; breakfast in ten minutes. Let's get the stuff aboard.' He turned to Brown. 'Maybe you'd like to have a look at the engine?' he suggested.

Brown heaved himself to his feet, looked down unenthusiastically at the weather-beaten, paint-peeled caique.

'Right you are, sir. But if the engine is on a par with this bloody wreck . . .' He shook his head in prophetic gloom and swung nimbly over the side of the pier.

Mallory and Andrea followed him, reaching up for the equipment as the other two passed it down. First they stowed away a sackful of old clothes, then the food, pressure stove and fuel, the heavy boots, spikes, mallets, rock axes and coils of wire-centred rope to be used for climbing, then, more carefully, the combined radio receiver and transmitter and the firing generator fitted with the old-fashioned plunge handle. Next came the guns - two Schmeissers, two Brens, a Mauser and a Colt - then a case containing a weird but carefully selected hodge-podge of torches, mirrors, two sets of identity papers and, incredibly, bottles of Hock, Moselle, *ouzo* and *retsima*.

Finally, and with exaggerated care, they stowed away for'ard in the forepeak two wooden boxes, one green in colour, medium sized and bound in brass, the other small and black. The green box held high explosive - TNT, amatol and a few standard sticks of dynamite, together with grenades, gun-cotton primers and canvas hosing; in one corner of the box was a bag of emery dust, another of ground glass, and a sealed jar of potassium, these last three items having been included against the possibility of Dusty Miller's finding an opportunity to exercise his unique talents as a saboteur. The black box held only detonators, percussion and electrical, detonators with fulminates so unstable that their exposed powder could be triggered off by the impact of a falling feather.

The last box had been stowed away when Casey Brown's head appeared above the engine hatch. Slowly he examined the main-mast reaching up above his head, as slowly turned for'ard to look at the foremast. His face carefully expressionless, he looked at Mallory.

'Have we got sails for these things, sir?'

'I suppose so. Why?'

'Because God only knows we're going to need them!' Brown said bitterly. 'Have a look at the engine-room, you said. This isn't an engine-room. It's a bloody scrap-yard. And the biggest, most rusted bit of scrap down there is attached to the propeller shaft. And what do you think it is? An old Kelvin two-cylinder job built more or less on my own doorstep - about thirty years ago.' Brown shook his head in despair, his face as stricken as only a Clydeside engineer's can be at the abuse of a beloved machine. 'And it's been falling to bits for years, sir. Place is littered with discarded bits and spares. I've seen junk heaps off the Gallowgate that were palaces compared to this.'

'Major Rutledge said it was running only yesterday,' Mallory said mildly.

'Anyway, come on ashore. Breakfast. Remind me we're to pick up a few heavy stones on the way back, will you?'

'Stones!' Miller looked at him in horror. 'Aboard that thing?'

Mallory nodded, smiling.

'But that gawddamned ship is sinkin' already!' Miller protested. 'What do you want stones for?'

'Wait and see.'

Three hours later Miller saw. The caique was chugging steadily north over a glassy, windless sea, less than a mile off the coast of Turkey, when he mournfully finished lashing his blue battle-dress into a tight ball and heaved it regretfully over the side. Weighted by the heavy stone he had carried aboard, it was gone from sight in a second.

Morosely he surveyed himself in the mirror propped up against the for'ard end of the wheelhouse. Apart from a deep violet sash wrapped round his lean middle and a fancifully embroidered waistcoat with its former glory mercifully faded, he was dressed entirely in black. Black lacing jackboots, black baggy trousers, black shirt and black jacket: even his sandy hair had been dyed to the same colour.

He shuddered and turned away.

'Thank Gawd the boys back home can't see me now!' he said feelingly. He looked critically at the others, dressed, with some minor variations, like himself. 'Waal, mebbe I ain't quite so bad after all. . . . Just what is all this quick-change business for, boss?'

'They tell me you've been behind the German lines twice, once as a peasant, once as a mechanic.' Mallory heaved his own ballasted uniform over the side. 'Well, now you see what the well-dressed Navaronian wears.'

'The double change, I meant. Once in the plane, and now.'

'Oh, I see. Army khaki and naval whites in Alex., blue battledress in Castelrosso and now Greek clothes? Could have been – almost certainly were – snoopers in Alex. or Castelrosso or Major Rutledge's island. And we've changed from launch to plane to MTB to caique. Covering our tracks, Corporal. We just can't take any chances.'

Miller nodded, looked down at the clothes sack at his feet, wrinkled his brows in puzzlement, stooped and dragged out the white clothing that had caught his eye. He held up the long, voluminous clothes for inspection.

'To be used when passing through the local cemeteries, I suppose.' He was heavily ironic. 'Disguised as ghosts.'

'Camouflage,' Mallory explained succinctly. 'Snow-smocks.'

'What!'

'Snow. That white stuff. There are some pretty high mountains in Navarone, and we may have to take to them. So – snow-smocks.'

Miller looked stunned. Wordlessly he stretched his length on the deck, pillowed his head and closed his eyes. Mallory grinned at Andrea.

'Picture of a man getting his full quota of sunshine before battling with the Arctic wastes. . . . Not a bad idea. Maybe you should get some sleep, too. I'll keep watch for a couple of hours.'

For five hours the caique continued on its course parallel to the Turkish coast, slightly west of north and rarely more than two miles off-shore. Relaxed and warm in the still kindly November sun, Mallory sat wedged between the bulwarks of the blunt bows, his eyes ceaselessly quartering sky and horizon. Amidships, Andrea and Miller lay asleep. Casey Brown still defied all attempts to remove him from the engine-room. Occasionally – very occasionally – he came up for a breath of fresh air, but the intervals between his appearances steadily lengthened as he concentrated more and more on the aged Kelvin engine, regulating the erratic drip-fed lubrication, constantly adjusting the air intake: an engineer to his fingertips, he was unhappy about that engine: he was drowsy, too, and headachy – the narrow hatchway gave hardly any ventilation at all.

Alone in the wheelhouse – an unusual feature in so tiny a caique – Lieutenant Andy Stevens watched the Turkish coast slide slowly by. Like Mallory's, his eyes moved ceaselessly, but not with the same controlled wandering. They shifted from the coast to the chart: from the chart to the islands up ahead off the port bow, islands whose position and relation to each other changed continually and deceptively, islands gradually lifting from the sea and hardening in definition through the haze of blue refraction: from the islands to the old alcohol compass swinging almost imperceptibly on corroded gimbals, and from the compass back to the coast again. Occasionally, he peered up into the sky, or swung a quick glance through a 180-degree sweep of the horizon. But one thing his eyes avoided all the time. The chipped, fly-blown mirror had been hung up in the wheelhouse again, but it was as if his eyes and the mirror were of opposite magnetic poles: he could not bring himself to look at it.

His forearms ached. He had been spelled at the wheel twice, but still they ached, abominably: his lean, tanned hands were ivory-knuckled on the cracked wheel. Repeatedly, consciously, he tried to relax, to ease the tension that was bunching up the muscles of his arms; but always, as if possessed of independent volition, his hands tightened their grip again. There was a funny taste in his mouth, too, a sour and salty taste in a dry, parched mouth, and no matter how often he swallowed, or drank from the sun-warmed pitcher at his side, the taste and the dryness remained. He could no more exorcise them than he could that twisting, cramping ball that was knotting up his insides, just above the solar plexus, or the queer, uncontrollable tremor that gripped his right leg from time to time.

Lieutenant Andy Stevens was afraid. He had never been in action before, but it wasn't that. This wasn't the first time he had been afraid. He had been afraid all his life, ever since he could remember: and he could remember a long way back, even to his early prep-school days when his famous father, Sir Cedric Stevens, the most celebrated explorer and mountaineer of his time, had thrown him bodily into the swimming pool at home, telling him that this was the only way he could learn to swim. He could remember still how he had fought and spluttered his way to the side of the pool, panic-stricken and desperate, his nose and mouth blocked with water, the pit of his stomach knotted and constricted in that nameless, terrifying ache he was to come to know so well: how his father and two elder brothers, big and jovial and nerveless like Sir Cedric himself, had wiped the tears of mirth from their eyes and pushed him in again. . . .

His father and brothers. . . . It had been like that all through his schooldays. Together, the three of them had made his life thoroughly miserable. Tough, hearty, open-air types who worshipped at the shrine of athleticism and physical fitness, they could not understand how anyone could fail to revel in diving from a five-metre springboard or setting a hunter at a five-barred gate or climbing the crags of the Peak district or sailing a boat in a storm. All these things they had made him do and often he had failed in the doing, and neither his father nor his brothers could ever have understood how he had come to dread those violent sports in which they excelled, for they were not cruel men, nor even unkind, but simply stupid. And so to the simple physical fear he sometimes and naturally felt was added the fear of failure, the fear that he was bound to fail in whatever he had to do next, the fear of the inevitable mockery and ridicule: and because he had been a sensitive boy and feared the ridicule above all else, he had come to fear these things that provoked the ridicule. Finally, he had come to fear fear itself, and it was in a desperate attempt to overcome this double fear that he had devoted himself – this in his late teens – to crag and mountain climbing: in this he had ultimately become so proficient, developed such a reputation, that father and brothers had come to treat him with respect and as an equal, and the ridicule had ceased. But the fear had not ceased; rather it had grown by what it fed on, and often, on a particularly difficult climb, he had all but fallen to his death, powerless in the grip of sheer unreasoning terror. But this terror he had always sought, successfully so far, to conceal. As now. He was trying to overcome, to conceal that fear now. He was afraid of failing – in what he wasn't quite sure – of not measuring up to expectation: he was afraid of being afraid: and he was desperately afraid, above all things, of being seen, of being known to be afraid . . .

The startling, incredible blue of the Ægean; the soft, hazy silhouette of the Anatolian mountains against the washed-out cerulean of the sky; the heart-catching, magical blending of the blues and violets and purples and indigoes of the sun-soaked islands drifting lazily by, almost on the beam now; the iridescent rippling of the water fanned by the gentle, scent-laden breeze newly sprung from the south-east; the peaceful scene on deck, the reassuring, interminable thump-thump thump-thump of the old Kelvin engine. . . . All was peace and quiet and contentment and warmth and languor, and it seemed impossible that anyone could be afraid. The world and the war were very far away that afternoon.

Or perhaps, after all, the war wasn't so far away. There were occasional pin-pricks – and constant reminders. Twice a German Arado seaplane had circled curiously overhead, and a Savoia and Fiat, flying in company, had altered course, dipped to have a look at them and flown off, apparently satisfied: Italian planes, these, and probably based on Rhodes, they were almost certainly piloted by Germans who had rounded up their erstwhile Rhodian allies and put them in prison camps after the surrender of the Italian Government. In the morning they had passed within half a mile of a big German caique – it flew a German flag and bristled with mounted machine-guns and a two-pounder far up in the bows; and in the early afternoon a high-speed German launch had roared by so closely that their caique had rolled wickedly in the wash of its passing: Mallory and Andrea had shaken their fists and cursed loudly and fluently at the grinning sailors on deck. But there had been no attempts to molest or detain them: neither British nor German hesitated at any time to violate the neutrality of Turkish territorial waters, but by the strange quixotry of a tacit gentlemen's agreement hostilities between passing vessels and planes were almost unknown. Like the envoys of warring countries in a neutral capital, their behaviour ranged from the impeccably and frigidly polite to a very pointed unawareness of one another's existence.

These, then, were the pin-pricks – the visitation and bygoings, harmless though they were, of the ships and planes of the enemy. The other reminders that this was no peace but an illusion, an ephemeral and a frangible thing, were more permanent. Slowly the minute hands of their watches circled, and every tick took them nearer to that great wall of cliff, barely eight hours away, that had to be climbed somehow: and almost dead ahead now, and less than fifty miles distant, they could see the grim, jagged peaks of Navarone topping the shimmering horizon and reaching up darkly against the sapphired sky, desolate and remote and strangely threatening.

At half-past two in the afternoon the engine stopped. There had been no warning coughs or splutters or missed strokes. One moment the regular, reassuring thump-thump: the next, sudden, completely unexpected silence, oppressive and foreboding in its absoluteness.

Mallory was the first to reach the engine hatch.

'What's up, Brown?' His voice was sharp with anxiety. 'Engine broken down?'

'Not quite, sir.' Brown was still bent over the engine, his voice muffled. 'I shut it off just now.' He straightened his back, hoisted himself wearily through the hatchway, sat on deck with his feet dangling, sucking in great draughts of fresh air. Beneath the heavy tan his face was very pale.

Mallory looked at him closely.

'You look as if you had the fright of your life.'

'Not that.' Brown shook his head. 'For the past two-three hours I've been slowly poisoned down that ruddy hole. Only now I realize it.' He passed a hand across his brow and groaned. 'Top of my blinkin' head just about lifting off, sir. Carbon monoxide ain't a very healthy thing.'

'Exhaust leak?'

'Aye. But it's more than a leak now.' He pointed down at the engine. 'See that stand-pipe supporting that big iron ball above the engine – the water-cooler? That pipe's as thin as paper, must have been leaking above the bottom flange for hours. Blew out a bloody great hole a minute ago. Sparks, smoke and flames six inches long. Had to shut the damned thing off at once, sir.'

Mallory nodded in slow understanding.

'And now what? Can you repair it, Brown?'

'Not a chance, sir.' The shake of the head was very definite. 'Would have to be brazed or welded. But there's a spare down there among the scrap. Rusted to hell and about as shaky as the one that's on . . . I'll have a go, sir.'

'I'll give him a hand,' Miller volunteered.

'Thanks, Corporal. How long, Brown, do you think?'

'Lord only knows, sir. Two hours, maybe four. Most of the nuts and bolts are locked solid with rust: have to shear or saw 'em – and then hunt for others.'

Mallory said nothing. He turned away heavily, brought up beside Stevens who had abandoned the wheelhouse and was now bent over the sail locker. He looked up questioningly as Mallory approached.

Mallory nodded. 'Just get them out and up. Maybe four hours, Brown says. Andrea and I will do our landlubbery best to help.'

Two hours later, with the engine still out of commission, they were well outside territorial waters, closing on a big island some eight miles away to the WNW. The wind, warm and oppressive now, had backed to a darkening and thundery east, and with only a lug and a jib – all the sails they had found – bent to the foremast, they could make no way at all into it. Mallory had decided to make for the island – the chances of being observed there were far less than in the open sea. Anxiously he looked at his watch then stared back moodily at the receding safety of the Turkish shore. Then he stiffened, peered closely at the dark line of sea, land and sky that lay to the east.

'Andrea! Do you see—'

'I see it, Captain.' Andrea was at his shoulder. 'Caique. Three miles. Coming straight towards us,' he added softly.

'Coming straight towards us.' Mallory acquiesced. 'Tell Miller and Brown. Have them come here.'

Mallory wasted no time when they were all assembled.

'We're going to be stopped and investigated,' he said quickly. 'Unless I'm much mistaken, it's that big caique that passed us this morning. Heaven only knows how, but they've been tipped off and they're going to be as suspicious as hell. This'll be no kid-glove, hands-in-the-pockets inspection. They'll be armed to the teeth and hunting trouble. There's going to be no half-measures. Let's be quite clear about that. Either they go under or we do: we can't possibly survive an inspection – not with all the gear *we've* got aboard. And,' he added softly, 'we're not going to dump that gear.' Rapidly he explained his plans. Stevens, leaning out from the wheelhouse window, felt the old sick ache in his stomach, felt the blood leaving his face. He was glad of the protection of the wheelhouse that hid the lower part of his body: that old familiar tremor in his leg was back again. Even his voice was unsteady.

'But, sir – sir—'

'Yes, yes, what is it, Stevens?' Even in his hurry Mallory paused at the sight of the pale, set face, the bloodless nails clenched over the sill of the window.

'You – you can't do *that*, sir!' The voice blurred harshly under the sharp edge of strain. For a moment his mouth worked soundlessly, then he rushed on. 'It's a massacre, sir, it's – it's just murder!'

'Shut up, kid!' Miller growled.

'That'll do, Corporal!' Mallory said sharply. He looked at the American for a long moment then turned to Stevens, his eyes cold. 'Lieutenant, the whole concept of directing a successful war is aimed at placing your enemy at a disadvantage, at *not* giving him an even chance. We kill them or they kill us. They go under or we do – and a thousand men on Kheros. It's just as simple as that, Lieutenant. It's not even a question of conscience.'

For several seconds Stevens stared at Mallory in complete silence. He was vaguely aware that everyone was looking at him. In that instant he hated Mallory, could have killed him. He hated him because – suddenly he was aware that he hated him only for the remorseless logic of what he said. He stared down at his clenched hands. Mallory, the idol of every young mountaineer and cragsman in pre-war England, whose fantastic climbing exploits had made world headlines, in '38 and '39: Mallory, who had twice been baulked by the most atrocious ill-fortune from surprising Rommel in his desert headquarters: Mallory, who had three times refused promotion in order to stay with his beloved Cretans who worshipped him the other side of idolatry. Confusedly these thoughts tumbled through his mind and he looked up slowly, looked at the lean, sunburnt face, the sensitive, chiselled mouth, the heavy, dark eyebrows bar-straight over the lined brown eyes that could be so cold or so compassionate, and suddenly he felt ashamed, knew that Captain Mallory lay beyond both his understanding and his judgment.

'I am very sorry, sir.' He smiled faintly. 'As Corporal Miller would say, I was talking out of turn.' He looked aft at the caique arrowing up from the south-east. Again he felt the sick fear, but his voice was steady enough as he spoke. 'I won't let you down, sir.'

'Good enough. I never thought you would.' Mallory smiled in turn, looked at Miller and Brown. 'Get the stuff ready and lay it out, will you? Casual, easy and keep it hidden. They'll have the glasses on you.'

He turned away, walked for'ard. Andrea followed him.

'You were very hard on the young man.' It was neither criticism nor reproach – merely statement of fact.

'I know.' Mallory shrugged. 'I didn't like it either . . . I had to do it.'

'I think you had,' Andrea said slowly. 'Yes, I think you had. But it was hard . . . Do you think they'll use the big guns in the bows to stop us?'

'Might – they haven't turned back after us unless they're pretty sure we're up to something fishy. But the warning shot across the bows – they don't go in for that Captain Teach stuff normally.'

Andrea wrinkled his brows.

'Captain Teach?'

'Never mind.' Mallory smiled. 'Time we were taking up position now. Remember, wait for me. You won't have any trouble in hearing my signal,' he finished dryly.

The creaming bow-wave died away to a gentle ripple, the throb of the heavy diesel muted to a distant murmur as the German boat slid alongside, barely six feet away. From where he sat on a fish-box on the port of the fo'c'sle, industriously sewing a button on to the old coat lying on the deck between his legs, Mallory could see six men, all dressed in the uniform of the regular German Navy – one crouched behind a belted Spandau mounted on its tripod just aft of the two-pounder, three others bunched amidships each armed with an automatic machine carbine – Schmeissers, he thought – the captain, a hard, cold-faced young lieutenant with the Iron Cross on his tunic, looking out the open door of the wheelhouse and, finally, a curious head peering over the edge of the engine-room hatch. From where he sat, Mallory couldn't see the poop-deck – the intermittent ballooning of the lug-sail in the uncertain wind blocked his vision; but from the restricted fore-and-aft lateral sweep of the Spandau, hungrily traversing only the for'ard half of their one caique, he was reasonably sure that there was another machine-gunner similarly engaged on the German's poop.

The hard-faced young lieutenant – a real product of the Hitler Jugend that one, Mallory thought – leaned out of the wheelhouse, cupped his hand to his mouth.

'Lower your sails!' he shouted.

Mallory stiffened, froze to immobility. The needle had jammed hard into the palm of his hand, but he didn't even notice it. The lieutenant had spoken in English! Stevens was so young, so inexperienced. He'd fall for it, Mallory thought with a sudden sick certainty, he's bound to fall for it.

But Stevens didn't fall for it. He opened the door, leaned out, cupped his hand to his ear and gazed vacantly up to the sky, his mouth wide open. It was so perfect an imitation of dull-witted failure to catch or comprehend a shouted message that it was almost a caricature. Mallory could have hugged him. Not in his actions alone, but in his dark, shabby clothes and hair as blackly counterfeit as Miller's, Stevens was the slow, suspicious island fisherman to the life.

'Eh?' he bawled.

'Lower your sails! We are coming aboard!' English again, Mallory noted; a persistent fellow this.

Stevens stared at him blankly, looked round helplessly at Andrea and Mallory: their faces registered a lack of comprehension as convincing as his own. He shrugged his shoulders in despair.

'I am sorry, I do not understand German,' he shouted. 'Can you not speak my language?' Stevens's Greek was perfect, fluent and idiomatic. It was also the Greek of Attica, not of the islands; but Mallory felt sure that the lieutenant wouldn't know the difference.

He didn't. He shook his head in exasperation, called in slow, halting Greek: 'Stop your boat at once. We are coming aboard.'

'Stop my boat!' The indignation was so genuine, the accompanying flood of furious oaths so authentic, that even the lieutenant was momentarily taken aback. 'And why should I stop my boat for you, you – you—'

'You have ten seconds,' the lieutenant interrupted. He was on balance again, cold, precise. 'Then we will shoot.'

Stevens gestured in admission of defeat and turned to Andrea and Mallory. 'Our conquerors have spoken,' he said bitterly. 'Lower the sails.'

Quickly they loosened the sheets from the cleats at the foot of the mast. Mallory pulled the jib down, gathered the sail in his arms and squatted sullenly on the deck – he knew a dozen hostile eyes were watching him – close by the fish-box. The sail covering his knees and the old coat, his forearms on his thighs, he sat with head bowed and hands dangling between his knees, the picture of heart-struck dejection. The lug-sail, weighted by the boom at the top, came down with a rush. Andrea stepped over it, walked a couple of uncertain paces aft, then stopped, huge hands hanging emptily by his sides.

A sudden deepening of the muted throbbing of the diesel, a spin of the wheel and the big German caique was rubbing alongside. Quickly, but carefully enough to keep out of the line of fire of the mounted Spandaus – there was a second clearly visible now on the poop – the three men armed with the Schmeissers leapt aboard. Immediately one ran forward, whirled round level with the foremast, his automatic carbine circling gently to cover all of the crew. All except Mallory – and he was leaving Mallory in the safe hands of the Spandau gunner in the bows. Detachedly, Mallory admired the precision, the timing, the clockwork inevitability of an old routine.

He raised his head, looked around him with a slow, peasant indifference. Casey Brown was squatting on the deck abreast the engine-room, working on the big ball-silencer on top of the hatch-cover. Dusty Miller, two paces farther for'ard and with his brows furrowed in concentration, was laboriously cutting a section of metal from a little tin box, presumably to help in the engine repairs. He was holding the wire-cutting pliers in his left hand – and Miller, Mallory knew, was right-handed. Neither Stevens nor Andrea had moved. The man beside the foremast still stood there, eyes unwinking. The other two were walking slowly aft, had just passed Andrea, their carriage relaxed and easy, the bearing of men who knew they have everything so completely under control that even the idea of trouble is ridiculous.

Carefully, coldly and precisely, at point-blank range and through the folds of both coat and sail. Mallory shot the Spandau machine-gunner through the heart, swung the still chattering Bren round and saw the guard by the mast crumple and die, half his chest torn away by the tearing slugs of the machine-gun. But the dead man was still on his feet, still had not hit the deck, when four things happened simultaneously. Casey Brown had had his hand on Miller's silenced automatic, lying concealed beneath the ball-silencer, for over a minute. Now he squeezed the trigger four times, for he wanted to mak' siccar; the after machine-gunner leaned forward tiredly over his tripod, lifeless fingers locked on the firing-guard. Miller crimped the three-second chemical fuse with the pliers, lobbed the tin box into the enemy engine-room, Stevens spun the armed stick-grenade into the opposite wheel-house and Andrea, his great arms reaching out with all the speed and precision of striking cobras, swept the Schmeisser gunners' heads together with sickening force. And then all five men had hurled themselves to the deck and the German caique was erupting in a roar of flame and smoke and dying débris: gradually the echoes faded away over the sea and there was left only the whining stammer of the Spandau, emptying itself uselessly skyward; and then the belt jammed and the Ægean was as silent as ever, more silent than it had been.

Slowly, painfully, dazed by the sheer physical shock and the ear-shattering proximity of the twin explosions, Mallory pushed himself off the wooden deck and stood shakily on his feet. His first conscious reaction was that of surprise, incredulity almost: the concussive blast of a grenade and a couple of lashed blocks of TNT, even at such close range, was far beyond anything he had expected.

The German boat was sinking, sinking fast. Miller's home-made bomb must have torn the bottom out of the engine-room. She was heavily on fire amidships, and for one dismayed instant Mallory had an apprehensive vision of towering black columns of smoke and enemy reconnaissance planes. But only for an instant: timbers and planking, tinder-dry and resinous, were burning furiously with hardly a trace of smoke, and the flaming, crumpling deck was already canted over sharply to port: she would be gone in seconds. His eyes wandered to the shattered skeleton of the wheelhouse, and he caught his breath suddenly when he saw the lieutenant impaled on the splintered wreck of the wheel, a ghastly, mangled caricature of what had once been a human being, decapitated and wholly horrible: vaguely, some part of Mallory's mind registered the harsh sound of retching, violent and convulsive, coming from the wheelhouse, and he knew Stevens must have seen it too. From deep within the sinking caique came the muffled roar of rupturing fuel tanks: a flame-veined gout of oily black smoke erupted from the engine-room and the caique miraculously struggled back on even keel, her gunwales almost awash, and then the hissing waters had overflowed and overcome the decks and the twisting flames, and the caique was gone, her slender masts sliding vertically down and vanishing in a turbulent welter of creaming foam and oil-filmed bubbles. And now the Ægean was calm and peaceful again, as placid as if the caique had never been, and almost as empty: a few charred planks and an inverted helmet drifted lazily on the surface of the shimmering sea.

With a conscious effort of will, Mallory turned slowly to look to his own ship and his own men. Brown and Miller were on their feet, staring down in fascination at where the caique had been, Stevens was standing at the wheelhouse door. He, too, was unhurt, but his face was ashen: during the brief action he had been a man above himself, but the aftermath, the brief glimpse he'd had of the dead lieutenant had hit him badly. Andrea, bleeding from a gash on the cheek, was looking down at the two Schmeisser gunners lying at his feet. His face was expressionless. For a long moment Mallory looked at him, looked in slow understanding.

'Dead?' he asked quietly.

Andrea inclined his head.

'Yes.' His voice was heavy. 'I hit them too hard.'

Mallory turned away. Of all the men he had ever known, Andrea, he thought, had the most call to hate and to kill his enemies. And kill them he did, with a ruthless efficiency appalling in its single-mindedness and thoroughness of execution. But he rarely killed without regret, without the most bitter self-condemnation, for he did not believe that the lives of his fellow-men were his to take. A destroyer of his fellow-man, he loved his fellow-man above all things. A simple man, a good man, a killer with a kindly heart, he was for ever troubled by his conscience, ill at ease with his inner self. But over and above the wonderings and the reproaches, he was informed by an honesty of thought, by a clear-sighted wisdom which sprang from and transcended his innate simplicity. Andrea killed neither for revenge, nor from hate, nor nationalism, nor for the sake of any of the other 'isms' which self-seekers and fools and knaves employ as beguilement to the battlefield and justification for the slaughter of millions too young and too unknowing to comprehend the dreadful futility of it all. Andrea killed simply that better men might live.

'Anybody else hurt?' Mallory's voice was deliberately brisk, cheerful. 'Nobody? Good! Right, let's get under way as fast as possible. The farther and the faster we leave this place behind, the better for all of us.' He looked at his watch. 'Almost four o'clock – time for our routine check with Cairo. Just leave that scrap-yard of yours for a couple of minutes, Chief. See if you can pick them up.' He looked at the sky to the east, a sky now purply livid and threatening, and shook his head. 'Could be that the weather forecast might be worth hearing.'

It was. Reception was very poor – Brown blamed the violent static on the dark, convoluted thunderheads steadily creeping up astern, now overspreading almost half the sky – but adequate. Adequate enough to hear information they had never expected to hear, information that left them silenced, eyes stilled in troubled speculation. The tiny loud-speaker boomed and faded, boomed and faded, against the scratchy background of static.

'Rhubarb calling Pimpernel! Rhubarb calling Pimpernel!' These were the respective code names for Cairo and Mallory. 'Are you receiving me?'

Brown tapped an acknowledgment. The speaker boomed again.

'Rhubarb calling Pimpernel. Now X minus one. Repeat, X minus one.' Mallory drew in his breath sharply. X – dawn on Saturday – had been the assumed date for the German attack on Kheros. It must have been advanced by one day – and Jensen was not the man to speak without certain knowledge. Friday, dawn – just over three days.

'Send "X minus one understood," ' Mallory said quietly.

'Forecast, East Anglia,' the impersonal voice went on: the Northern Sporades, Mallory knew. 'Severe electrical storms probable this evening, with heavy rainfall. Visibility poor. Temperature falling, continuing to fall next twenty-four hours. Winds east to south-east, force six, locally eight, moderating early tomorrow.'

Mallory turned away, ducked under the billowing lug-sail, walked slowly aft. What a set-up, he thought, what a bloody mess. Three days to go, engine u. s. and a first-class storm building up. He thought briefly, hopefully, of Squadron Leader Torrance's low opinion of the backroom boys of the Met. Office, but the hope was never really born. It couldn't be, not unless he was blind. The steep-piled buttresses of the thunderheads towered up darkly terrifying, now almost directly above.

'Looks pretty bad, huh?' The slow nasal drawl came from immediately behind him. There was something oddly reassuring about that measured voice, about the steadiness of the washed-out blue of the eyes, enmeshed in a spider's web of fine wrinkles.

'It's not so good,' Mallory admitted.

'What's all this force eight business, boss?'

'A wind scale,' Mallory explained. 'If you're in a boat this size and you're good and tired of life, you can't beat a force eight wind.'

Miller nodded dolefully.

'I knew it. I might have known. And me swearing they'd never get me on a gawddamned boat again.' He brooded a while, sighed, slid his legs over the engine-room hatchway, jerked his thumb in the direction of the nearest island, now less than three miles away. 'That doesn't look so hot, either.'

'Not from here,' Mallory agreed. 'But the chart shows a creek with a right-angle bend. It'll break the sea and the wind.'

'Inhabited?'

'Probably.'

'Germans?'

'Probably.'

Miller shook his head in despair and descended to help Brown. Forty minutes later, in the semi-darkness of the overcast evening and in torrential rain, lance-straight and strangely chill, the anchor of the caique rattled down between the green walls of the forest, a dank and dripping forest, hostile in its silent indifference.

Chapter Four

Monday Evening 1700–2330

'Brilliant!' said Mallory bitterly. 'Ruddy well brilliant! "Come into my parlour said the spider to the fly." ' He swore in chagrin and exasperated disgust, eased aside the edge of the tarpaulin that covered the for'ard hatchway, peered out through the slackening curtain of rain and took a second and longer look at the rocky bluff that elbowed out into the bend of the creek, shutting them off from the sea. There was no difficulty in seeing now, none at all: the drenching cloudburst had yielded to a gentle drizzle, and grey and white cloud streamers, shredding in the lifting wind, had already pursued the blackly towering cumulonimbus over the far horizon. In a clear band of sky far to the west, the sinking, flame-red sun was balanced on the rim of the sea. From the shadowed waters of the creek it was invisible, but its presence unmistakable from the gold-shot gauze of the falling rain, high above their heads.

The same golden rays highlighted the crumbling old watch-tower on the very point of the cliff, a hundred feet above the river. They burnished its fine-grained white Parian marble, mellowed it to a delicate rose: they gleamed on the glittering steel, the evil mouths of the Spandau machine-guns reaching out from the slotted embrasures in the massive walls, illumined the hooked cross of the swastika on the flag that streamed out stiffly from the staff above the parapet. Solid even in its decay, impregnable in its position, commanding in its lofty outlook, the tower completely dominated both waterborne approaches, from the sea and, upriver, down the narrow, winding channel that lay between the moored caique and the foot of the cliff.

Slowly, reluctantly almost. Mallory turned away and gently lowered the tarpaulin. His face was grim as he turned round to Andrea and Stevens, ill-defined shadows in the twilit gloom of the cabin.

'Brilliant!' he repeated. 'Sheer genius. Mastermind Mallory. Probably the only bloody creek within a hundred miles – and in a hundred islands – with a German guard post on it. And of course I had to go and pick it. Let's have another look at that chart, will you, Stevens?'

Stevens passed it across, watched Mallory study it in the pale light filtering in under the tarpaulin, leaned back against the bulkhead and drew heavily on his cigarette. It tasted foul, stale and acrid, but the tobacco was fresh enough, he knew. The old, sick fear was back again, as strongly as ever. He looked at the great bulk of Andrea across from him, felt an illogical resentment towards him for having spotted the emplacement a few minutes ago. They'll have cannon up there, he thought dully, they're bound to have cannon – couldn't control the creek otherwise. He gripped his thigh fiercely, just above the knee, but the tremor lay too deep to be controlled: he blessed the merciful darkness of the tiny cabin. But his voice was casual enough as he spoke.

'You're wasting your time, sir, looking at that chart and blaming yourself. This is the only possible anchorage within hours of sailing time from here. With that wind there was nowhere else we could have gone.'

'Exactly. That's just it.' Mallory folded the chart, handed it back. 'There was nowhere else we could have gone. There was nowhere else anyone could have gone. Must be a very popular port in a storm, this – a fact which must have become apparent to the Germans a long, long time ago. That's why I should have known they were almost bound to have a post here. However, spilt milk, as you say.' He raised his voice. 'Chief!'

'Hallo!' Brown's muffled voice carried faintly from the depths of the engine-room.

'How's it going?'

'Not too bad, sir. Assembling it now.'

Mallory nodded in relief.

'How long?' he called. 'An hour?'

'Aye, easy, sir.'

'An hour.' Again Mallory glanced through the tarpaulin, looked back at Andrea and Stevens. 'Just about right. We'll leave in an hour. Dark enough to give us some protection from our friends up top, but enough light left to navigate our way out of this damned corkscrew of a channel.'

'Do you think they'll try to stop us, sir?' Steven's voice was just too casual, too matter of fact. He was pretty sure Mallory would notice.

'It's unlikely they'll line the banks and give us three hearty cheers,' Mallory said dryly. 'How many men do you reckon they'll have up there, Andrea?'

'I've seen two moving around,' Andrea said thoughtfully. 'Maybe three or four altogether, Captain. A small post. The Germans don't waste men on these.'

'I think you're about right,' Mallory agreed. 'Most of them'll be in the garrison in the village – about seven miles from here, according to the chart, and due west. It's not likely—'

He broke off sharply, stiffened in rigid attention. Again the call came, louder this time, imperative in its tone. Cursing himself for his negligence in not posting a guard – such carelessness would have cost him his life in Crete – Mallory pulled the tarpaulin aside, clambered slowly on to the deck. He carried no arms, but a half-empty bottle of Moselle dangled from his left hand; as part of a plan prepared before they had left Alexandria, he'd snatched it from a locker at the foot of the tiny companionway.

He lurched convincingly across the deck, grabbed at a stay in time to save himself from falling overboard. Insolently he stared down at the figure on the bank, less than ten yards away – it hadn't mattered about a guard, Mallory realized, for the soldier carried his automatic carbine slung over his shoulder – insolently he tilted the wine to his mouth and swallowed deeply before condescending to talk to him.

He could see the mounting anger in the lean, tanned face of the young German below him. Mallory ignored it. Slowly, an inherent contempt in the gesture, he dragged the frayed sleeve of his black jacket across his lips, looked the soldier even more slowly up and down in a minutely provocative inspection as disdainful as it was prolonged.

'Well?' he asked truculently in the slow speech of the islands. 'What the hell do you want?'

Even in the deepening dusk he could see the knuckles whitening on the stock of the carbine, and for an instant Mallory thought he had gone too far. He knew he was in no danger – all noise in the engine-room had ceased, and Dusty Miller's hand was never far from his silenced automatic – but he didn't want trouble. Not just yet. Not while there were a couple of manned Spandaus in that watch-tower.

With an almost visible effort the young soldier regained his control. It needed little help from the imagination to see the draining anger, the first tentative stirrings of hesitation and bewilderment. It was the reaction Mallory had hoped for. Greeks – even half-drunk Greeks – didn't talk to their overlords like that – not unless they had an overpoweringly good reason.

'What vessel is this?' The Greek was slow and halting but passable. 'Where are you bound for?'

Mallory tilted the bottle again, smacked his lips in noisy satisfaction. He held the bottle at arm's length, regarded it with a loving respect.

'One thing about you Germans,' he confided loudly. 'You do know how to make a fine wine. I'll wager *you* can't lay your hands on this stuff, eh? And the swill they're making up above' – the island term for the mainland – 'is so full of resin that it's only good for lighting fires.' He thought for a moment. 'Of course, if you know the right people in the islands, they *might* let you have some ouzo. But some of us can get ouzo *and* the best Hocks *and* the best Moselles.'

The soldier wrinkled his face in disgust. Like almost every fighting man he despised Quislings, even when they were on his side: in Greece they were very few indeed.

'I asked you a question,' he said coldly. 'What vessel, and where bound?'

'The caique *Aigion*,' Mallory replied loftily. 'In ballast, for Samos. Under orders,' he said significantly.

'Whose orders?' the soldier demanded. Shrewdly Mallory judged the confidence as superficial only. The guard was impressed in spite of himself.

'Herr Commandant in Vathy. General Graebel,' Mallory said softly. 'You will have heard of the Herr General before, yes?' He was on safe ground here, Mallory knew, the reputation of Graebel, both as a paratroop commander and an iron disciplinarian, had spread far beyond these islands.

Even in the half-light Mallory could have sworn that the guard's complexion turned paler. But he was dogged enough.

'You have papers? Letters of authority?'

Mallory sighed wearily, looked over his shoulder.

'Andrea!' he bawled.

'What do you want?' Andrea's great bulk loomed through the hatchway. He had heard every word that passed, had taken his cue from Mallory: a newly-opened wine bottle was almost engulfed in one vast hand and he was scowling hugely. 'Can't you see I'm busy?' he asked surlily. He stopped short at the sight of the German and scowled again, irritably. 'And what does this halfling want?'

'Our passes and letters of authority from Herr General. They're down below.'

Andrea disappeared, grumbling deep in his throat. A rope was thrown ashore, the stern pulled in against the sluggish current and the papers passed over. The papers – a set different from those to be used if emergency arose in Navarone – proved to be satisfactory, eminently so. Mallory would have been surprised had they been anything else. The preparation of these, even down to the photostatic facsimile of General Graebel's signature, was all in the day's work for Jensen's bureau in Cairo.

The soldier folded the papers, handed them back with a muttered word of thanks. He was only a kid, Mallory could see now – if he was more than nineteen his looks belied him. A pleasant, open-faced kid – of a different stamp altogether from the young fanatics of the SS Panzer Division – and far too thin. Mallory's chief reaction was one of relief: he would have hated to have to kill a boy like this. But he had to find out all he could. He signalled to Stevens to hand him up the almost empty crate of Moselle. Jensen, he mused, had been very thorough indeed: the man had literally thought of everything . . . Mallory gestured in the direction of the watch-tower.

'How many of you are up there?' he asked.

The boy was instantly suspicious. His face had tightened up, stilled in hostile surmise.

'Why do you want to know?' he asked stiffly.

Mallory groaned, lifted his hands in despair, turned sadly to Andrea.

'You see what it is to be one of them?' he asked in mournful complaint. 'Trust nobody. Think everyone is as twisted as . . .' He broke of hurriedly, turned to the soldier again. 'It's just that we don't want to have the same trouble every time we come in here,' he explained. 'We'll be back in Samos in a couple of days, and we've still another case of Moselle to work through. General Graebel keeps his – ah – special envoys well supplied. . . . It must be thirsty work up there in the sun. Come on, now, a bottle each. How many bottles?'

The reassuring mention that they would be back again, the equally reassuring mention of Graebel's name, plus, probably, the attraction of the offer and his comrades' reaction if he told them he had refused it, tipped the balance, overcame scruples and suspicions.

'There are only three of us,' he said grudgingly.

'Three it is,' Mallory said cheerfully. 'We'll bring you some Hock next time we return.' He tilted his own bottle. '*Prosit!*' he said, an islander proud of airing his German, and then, more proudly still, '*Auf Wiedersehen!*'

The boy murmured something in return. He stood hesitating for a moment, slightly shame-faced, then wheeled abruptly, walked off slowly along the river bank, clutching his bottles of Moselle.

'So!' Mallory said thoughtfully. 'There are only three of them. That should make things easier—'

'Well done sir!' It was Stevens who interrupted, his voice warm, his face alive with admiration. 'Jolly good show!'

'Jolly good show!' Miller mimicked. He heaved his lanky length over the coaming of the engine hatchway. ' "Good" be damned! I couldn't understand a gawddamned word, but for my money that rates an Oscar. That was terrific, boss!'

'Thank you, one and all,' Mallory murmured. 'But I'm afraid the congratulations are a bit premature.' The sudden chill in his voice struck at them, so that their eyes aligned along his pointing finger even before he went on. 'Take a look,' he said quietly.

The young soldier had halted suddenly about two hundred yards along the bank, looked into the forest on his left in startled surprise, then dived in among the trees. For a moment the watchers on the boat could see another soldier, talking excitedly to the boy and gesticulating in the direction of their boat, and then both were gone, lost in the gloom of the forest.

'That's torn it!' Mallory said softly. He turned away. 'Right, that's enough. Back to where you were. It would look fishy if we ignored that incident altogether, but it would look a damned sight fishier if we paid too much attention to it. Don't let's appear to be holding a conference.'

Miller slipped down into the engine-room with Brown, and Stevens went back to the little for'ard cabin. Mallory and Andrea remained on deck, bottles in their hands. The rain had stopped now, completely, but the wind was still rising, climbing the scale with imperceptible steadiness, beginning to bend the tops of the tallest of the pines. Temporarily the bluff was affording them almost complete protection. Mallory deliberately shut his mind to what it must be like outside. They had to put out to sea – Spandaus permitting – and that was that.

'What do you think has happened, sir?' Steven's' voice carried up from the gloom of the cabin.

'Pretty obvious, isn't it?' Mallory asked. He spoke loudly enough for all to hear. 'They've been tipped off. Don't ask me how. This is the second time – and their suspicions are going to be considerably reinforced by the absence of a report from the caique that was sent to investigate us. She was carrying a wireless aerial, remember?'

'But why should they get so damned suspicious all of a sudden?' Miller asked. 'It doesn't make sense to me, boss.'

'Must be in radio contact with their HQ. Or a telephone – probably a telephone. They've just been given the old tic-tac. Consternation on all sides.'

'So mebbe they'll be sending a small army over from their HQ to deal with us,' Miller said lugubriously.

Mallory shook his head definitely. His mind was working quickly and well, and he felt oddly certain, confident of himself.

'No, not a chance. Seven miles as the crow flies. Ten, maybe twelve miles over rough hill and forest tracks – and in pitch darkness. They wouldn't think of it.' He waved his bottle in the direction of the watch-tower. 'Tonight's their big night.'

'So we can expect the Spandaus to open up any minute?' Again the abnormal matter-of-factness of Steven's voice.

Mallory shook his head a second time.

'They won't. I'm positive of that. No matter how suspicious they may be, how certain they are that we're the big bad wolf, they are going to be shaken to the core when that kid tells them we're carrying papers and letters of authority signed by General Graebel himself. For all they know, curtains for us may be the firing squad for them. Unlikely, but you get the general idea. So they're going to contact HQ, and the commandant on a small island like this isn't going to take a chance on rubbing out a bunch of characters who may be the special envoys of the Herr General himself. So what? So he codes a message and radios it to Vathy in Samos and bites his nails off to the elbow till a message comes back saying Graebel has never heard of us and why the hell haven't we all been shot dead?' Mallory looked at the luminous dial of his watch. 'I'd say we have at least half an hour.'

'And meantime we all sit around with our little bits of paper and pencil and write out our last wills and testaments.' Miller scowled. 'No percentage in that, boss. We gotta *do* somethin'.'

Mallory grinned.

'Don't worry, Corporal, we are going to do something. We're going to hold a nice little bottle party, right here on the poop.'

The last words of their song – a shockingly corrupted Grecian version of 'Lilli Marlene,' and their third song in the past few minutes – died away in the evening air. Mallory doubted whether more than faint snatches of the singing would be carried to the watch-tower against the wind, but the rhythmical stamping of feet and waving of bottles were in themselves sufficient evidence of drunken musical hilarity to all but the totally blind and deaf. Mallory grinned to himself as he thought of the complete confusion and uncertainty the Germans in the tower must have been feeling then. This was not the behaviour of enemy spies, especially enemy spies who know that suspicions had been aroused and that their time was running out.

Mallory tilted the bottle to his mouth, held it there for several seconds, then set it down again, the wine untasted. He looked round slowly at the three men squatting there with him on the poop, Miller, Stevens and Brown. Andrea was not there, but he didn't have to turn his head to look for him. Andrea, he knew, was crouched in the shelter of the wheelhouse, a waterproof bag with grenades and a revolver strapped to his back.

'Right!' Mallory said crisply. 'Now's your big chance for *your* Oscar. Let's make this as convincing as we can.' He bent forward, jabbed his finger into Miller's chest and shouted angrily at him.

Miller shouted back. For a few moments they sat there, gesticulating angrily and, to all appearances, quarrelling furiously with each other. Then Miller was on his feet, swaying in drunken imbalance as he leaned threateningly over Mallory, clenched fists ready to strike. He stood back as Mallory struggled to his feet, and in a moment they were fighting fiercely, raining apparently heavy blows on each other. Then a haymaker from the American sent Mallory reeling back to crash convincingly against the wheelhouse.

'Right, Andrea.' He spoke quietly, without looking round. 'This is it. Five seconds. Good luck.' He scrambled to his feet, picked up a bottle by the neck and rushed at Miller, upraised arm and bludgeon swinging fiercely down. Miller dodged, swung a vicious foot, and Mallory roared in pain as his shins caught on the edge of the bulwarks. Silhouetted against the pale gleam of the creek, he stood poised for a second, arms flailing wildly, then plunged heavily, with a loud splash, into the waters of the creek.

For the next half-minute – it would take about that time for Andrea to swim underwater round the next upstream corner of the creek – everything was a confusion and a bedlam of noise. Mallory trod water as he tried to pull himself aboard: Miller had seized a boathook and was trying to smash it down on his head: and the others, on their feet now, had flung their arms round Miller, trying to restrain him: finally they managed to knock him off his feet, pin him on the deck and help the dripping Mallory aboard. A minute later, after the immemorial fashion of drunken men, the two combatants had shaken hands with one another and were sitting on the engine-room hatch, arms round each other's shoulders and drinking in perfect amity from the same freshly-opened bottle of wine.

'Very nicely done,' Mallory said approvingly. 'Very nicely indeed. An Oscar, definitely, for Corporal Miller.'

Dusty Miller said nothing. Taciturn and depressed, he looked moodily at the bottle in his hand. At last he stirred.

'I don't like it, boss,' he muttered unhappily. 'I don't like the set-up one little bit. You shoulda let me go with Andrea. It's three to one up there, and they're waiting and ready.' He looked accusingly at Mallory. 'Dammit to hell, boss, you're always telling us how desperately important this mission is!'

'I know,' Mallory said quietly. 'That's why I didn't send you with him. That's why none of us has gone with him. We'd only be a liability to him, get in his way.' Mallory shook his head. 'You don't know Andrea, Dusty.' It was the first time Mallory had called him that: Miller was warmed by the unexpected familiarity, secretly pleased. 'None of you know him. But I know him.' He gestured towards the watch-tower, its square-cut lines in sharp silhouette against the darkening sky. 'Just a big, fat, good-natured chap, always laughing and joking.' Mallory paused, shook his head again, went on slowly. 'He's up there now, padding through that forest like a cat, the biggest and most dangerous cat you'll ever see. Unless they offer no resistance – Andrea never kills unnecessarily – when I send him up there after these three poor bastards I'm executing them just as surely as if they were in the electric chair and I was pulling the switch.'

In spite of himself Miller was impressed, profoundly so.

'Known him a long time, boss, huh?' It was half question, half statement.

'A long time. Andrea was in the Albanian war – he was in the regular army. They tell me the Italians went in terror of him – his long-range patrols against the Iulia division, the Wolves of Tuscany, did more to wreck the Italian morale in Albania than any other single factor. I've heard a good many stories about them – not from Andrea – and they're all incredible. And they're all true. But it was afterwards I met him, when we were trying to hold the Servia Pass. I was a very junior liaison lieutenant in the Anzac brigade at the time. Andrea' – he paused deliberately for effect – 'Andrea was a lieutenant-colonel in the 19th Greek Motorised Division.'

'A *what*?' Miller demanded in astonishment. Stevens and Brown were equally incredulous.

'You heard me. Lieutenant-colonel. Outranks me by a fairish bit, you might say.' He smiled at them, quizzically. 'Puts Andrea in rather a different light, doesn't it?'

They nodded silently but said nothing. The genial, hail-fellow Andrea – a good-natured, almost simple-minded buffoon – a senior army officer. The idea had come too suddenly, was too incongruous for easy assimilation and immediate comprehension. But, gradually, it began to make sense to them. It explained many things about Andrea to them – his repose, his confidence, the unerring sureness of his lightning reactions, and, above all, the implicit faith Mallory had in him, the respect he showed for Andrea's opinions whenever he consulted him, which was frequently. Without surprise now, Miller slowly recalled that he'd never yet heard Mallory give Andrea a direct order. And Mallory never hesitated to pull his rank when necessary.

'After Servia,' Mallory went on, 'everything was pretty confused. Andrea had heard that Trikkala – a small country town where his wife and three daughters lived – had been flattened by the Stukas and Heinkels. He reached there all right, but there was nothing he could do. A land-mine had landed in the front garden and there wasn't even rubble left.'

Mallory paused, lit a cigarette. He stared through the drifting smoke at the fading outlines of the tower.

'The only person he found there was his brother-in-law, George. George was with us in Crete – he's still there. From George he heard for the first time of the Bulgarian atrocities in Thrace and Macedonia – and his parents lived there. So they dressed in German uniforms – you can imagine how Andrea got those – commandeered a German army truck and drove to Protosami.' The cigarette in Mallory's hand snapped suddenly, was sent spinning over the side. Miller was vaguely surprised: emotion, or rather, emotional displays, were so completely foreign to that very tough New Zealander. But Mallory went on quietly enough.

'They arrived in the evening of the infamous Protosami massacre. George has told me how Andrea stood there, clad in his German uniform and laughing as he watched a party of nine or ten Bulgarian soldiers lash couples together and throw them into the river. The first couple in were his father and step-mother, both dead.'

'My Gawd above!' Even Miller was shocked out of his usual equanimity. 'It's just not possible—'

'You know nothing,' Mallory interrupted impatiently. 'Hundreds of Greeks in Macedonia died the same way – but usually alive when they were thrown in. Until you know how the Greeks hate the Bulgarians, you don't even begin to know what hate is. . . . Andrea shared a couple of bottles of wine with the soldiers, found out that they had killed his parents earlier in the afternoon – they had been foolish enough to resist. After dusk he followed them up to an old corrugated-iron shed where they were billeted for the night. All he had was a knife. They left a guard outside. Andrea broke his neck, went inside, locked the door and smashed the oil lamp. George doesn't know what happened except that Andrea went berserk. He was back outside in two minutes, completely sodden, his uniform soaked in blood from head to foot. There wasn't a sound, not even a groan to be heard from the hut when they left, George says.'

He paused again, but this time there was no interruption, nothing said. Stevens shivered, drew his shabby jacket closer round his shoulders: the air seemed to have become suddenly chill. Mallory lit another cigarette, smiled faintly at Miller, nodded towards the watch-tower.

'See what I mean by saying we'd only be a liability to Andrea up there?'

'Yeah. Yeah, I guess I do,' Miller admitted. 'I had no idea, I had no idea. . . . Not *all* of them, boss! He couldn't have killed—'

'He did,' Mallory interrupted flatly. 'After that he formed his own band, made life hell for the Bulgarian outposts in Thrace. At one time there was almost an entire division chasing him through the Rhodope mountains. Finally he was betrayed and captured, and he, George and four others were shipped to Stavros – they were to go on to Salonika for trial. They overpowered their guards – Andrea got loose among them on deck at night – and sailed the boat to Turkey. The Turks tried to intern him – they might as well have tried to intern an earthquake. Finally he arrived in Palestine, tried to join the Greek Commando Battalion that was being formed in the Middle East – mainly veterans of the Albanian campaign, like himself.' Mallory laughed mirthlessly. 'He was arrested as a deserter. He was released eventually, but there was no place for him in the new Greek Army. But Jensen's bureau heard about him, knew he was a natural for Subversive Operations . . . And so we went to Crete together.'

Five minutes passed, perhaps ten, but nobody broke the silence. Occasionally, for the benefit of any watchers, they went through the motions of drinking; but even the half-light was fading now and Mallory knew they could only be half-seen blurs, shadowy and indistinct, from the heights of the watch-tower. The caique was beginning to rock in the surge from the open sea round the bluff. The tall, reaching pines, black now as midnight cypress and looming impossibly high against the star-dusted cloud wrack that scudded palely overhead, were closing in on them from either side, sombre, watchful and vaguely threatening, the wind moaning in lost and mournful requiem through their swaying topmost branches. A bad night, an eerie and an ominous night, pregnant with that indefinable foreboding that reaches down and touches the well-springs of the nameless fears, the dim and haunting memories of a million years ago, the ancient racial superstitions of mankind: a night that sloughed off the tissue veneer of civilization and the shivering man complains that someone is walking over his grave.

Suddenly, incongruously, the spell was shattered and Andrea's cheerful hail from the bank had them all on their feet in a moment. They heard his booming laugh and even the forests seemed to shrink back in defeat. Without waiting for the stern to be pulled in, he plunged into the creek, reached the caique in half a dozen powerful strokes and hoisted himself easily aboard. Grinning down from his great height, he shook himself like some shaggy mastiff and reached out a hand for a convenient wine bottle.

'No need to ask how things went, eh?' Mallory asked, smiling.

'None at all. It was just too easy. They were only boys, and they never even saw me.' Andrea took another long swig from the bottle and grinned in sheer delight. 'And I didn't lay a finger on them,' he went on triumphantly. 'Well, maybe a couple of little taps. They were all looking down here, staring out over the parapet when I arrived. Held them up, took their guns off them and locked them in a cellar. And then I bent their Spandaus – just a little bit.'

This is it, Mallory thought dully, this is the end. This is the finish of everything, the strivings, the hopes, the fears, the loves and laughter of each one of us. This is what it all comes to. This is the end, the end for us, the end for a thousand boys on Kheros. In unconscious futility his hand came up, slowly wiped lips salt from the spray bulleting off the wind-flattened wave-tops, then lifted farther to shade bloodshot eyes that peered out hopelessly into the storm-filled darkness ahead. For a moment the dullness lifted, and an almost intolerable bitterness welled through his mind. All gone, everything – everything except the guns of Navarone. The guns of Navarone. They would live on, they were indestructible. Damn them, damn them, damn them! Dear God, the blind waste, the terrible uselessness of it all!

The caique was dying, coming away at the seams. She was literally being pounded to death, being shaken apart by the constant battering shocks of wind and sea. Time and time again the poop-deck dipped beneath the foam-streaked cauldron at the stern, the fo'c'sle rearing crazily into the air, dripping forefoot showing clear: then the plummetting drop, the shotgun, shuddering impact as broad-beamed bows crashed vertically down into the cliff-walled trough beyond, an explosive collision that threw so unendurable a strain on the ancient timbers and planks and gradually tore them apart.

It had been bad enough when they'd cleared the creek just as darkness fell, and plunged and wallowed their way through a quartering sea on a northward course for Navarone. Steering the unwieldly old caique had become difficult in the extreme: with the seas fine on the starboard quarter she had yawed wildly and unpredictably through a fifty degree arc, but at least her seams had been tight then, the rolling waves overtaking her in regular formation and the wind settled and steady somewhere east of south. But now all that was gone. With half a dozen planks sprung from the stem-post and working loose from the apron, and leaking heavily through the stuffing-gland of the propeller shaft, she was making water far faster than the ancient, vertical hand-pump could cope with: the wind-truncated seas were heavier, but broken and confused, sweeping down on them now from this quarter, now from that: and the wind itself, redoubled in its shrieking violence, veered and backed insanely from south-west to south-east. Just then it was steady from the south, driving the unmanageable craft blindly on to the closing iron cliffs of Navarone, cliffs that loomed invisibly ahead, somewhere in that all-encompassing darkness.

Momentarily Mallory straightened, tried to ease the agony of the pincers that were clawing into the muscles of the small of his back. For over two hours now he had been bending and straightening, bending and straightening, lifting a thousand buckets that Dusty Miller filled interminably from the well of the hold. God only knew how Miller felt. If anything, he had the harder job of the two and he had been violently and almost continuously seasick for hours on end. He looked ghastly, and he must have been feeling like death itself: the sustained effort, the sheer iron will-power to drive himself on in that condition reached beyond the limits of understanding. Mallory shook his head wonderingly. 'My God, but he's tough, that Yank.' Unbidden, the words framed themselves in his mind, and he shook his head in anger, vaguely conscious of the complete inadequacy of the words.

Fighting for his breath, he looked aft to see how the others were faring. Casey Brown, of course, he couldn't see. Bent double in the cramped confines of the engine-room, he, too, was constantly sick and suffering a blinding headache from the oil fumes and exhaust gases still filtering from the replacement stand-pipe, neither of which could find any escape in the unventilated engine-room: but, crouched over the engine, he had not once left his post since they had cleared the mouth of the creek, had nursed the straining, ancient Kelvin along with the loving care, the exquisite skill of a man born into a long and proud tradition of engineering. That engine had only to falter once, to break down for the time in which a man might draw a deep breath, and the end would be as immediate as it was violent. Their steerage way, their lives, depended entirely on the continuous thrust of that screw, the laboured thudding of that rusted old two-cylinder. It was the heart of the boat, and when that heart stopped beating the boat died too, slewed broadside on and foundering in the waiting chasms between the waves.

For'ard of the engine-room, straddle-legged and braced against the corner pillar of the splintered skeleton that was all that remained of the wheelhouse, Andrea laboured unceasingly at the pump, never once lifting his head, oblivious of the crazy lurching of the deck of the caique, oblivious, too, of the biting wind and stinging, sleet-cold spray that numbed bare arms and moulded the sodden shirt to the hunched and massive shoulders. Ceaselessly, tirelessly, his arm thrust up and down, up and down, with the metronomic regularity of a piston. He had been there for close on three hours now, and he looked as if he could go on for ever. Mallory, who had yielded him the pump in complete exhaustion after less than twenty minutes' cruel labour, wondered if there was any limit to the man's endurance.

He wondered, too, about Stevens. For four endless hours now Andy Stevens had fought and overcome a wheel that leapt and struggled in his hands as if possessed of a convulsive life and will of its own – the will to wrench itself out of exhausted hands and turn them into the troughs: he had done a superb job, Mallory thought, had handled the clumsy craft magnificently. He peered at him closely, but the spray lashed viciously across his eyes and blinded him with tears. All he could gather was a vague impression of a tightly-set mouth, sleepless, sunken eyes and little patches of skin unnaturally pale against the mask of blood that covered almost the entire face from hairline to throat. The twisting, towering comber that had stove in the planks of the wheelhouse and driven in the windows with such savage force had been completely unexpected: Stevens hadn't had a chance. The cut above the right temple was particularly bad, ugly and deep: the blood still pulsed over the ragged edge of the wound, dripped monotonously into the water that sloshed and gurgled about the floor of the wheelhouse.

Sick to his heart, Mallory turned away, reached down for another bucket of water. What a crew, he thought to himself, what a really terrific bunch of – of . . . He sought for words to describe them, even to himself, but he knew his mind was far too tired. It didn't matter anyway, for there were no words for men like that, nothing that could do them justice.

He could almost taste the bitterness in his mouth, the bitterness that washed in waves through his exhausted mind. God, how wrong it was, how terribly unfair! Why did such men have to die, he wondered savagely, why did they have to die so uselessly. Or maybe it wasn't necessary to justify dying, even dying ingloriously empty of achievement. Could one not die for intangibles, for the abstract and the ideal? What had the martyrs at the stake achieved? Or what was the old tag – *dulce et decorum est pro patria mori*. If one lives well, what matter how one dies. Unconsciously his lips tightened in quick revulsion and he thought of Jensen's remarks about the High Command playing who's-the-king-of-the-castle. Well, they were right bang in the middle of their playground now, just a few more pawns sliding into the limbo. Not that it mattered – they had thousands more left to play with.

For the first time Mallory thought of himself. Not with bitterness or self-pity or regret that it was all over. He thought of himself only as the leader of this party, his responsibility for the present situation. It's my fault, he told himself over and over again, it's all my fault. I brought them here, I made them come. Even while one part of his mind was telling him that he'd had no option, that his hand had been forced, that if they had remained in the creek they would have been wiped out long before the dawn, irrationally he still blamed himself the more. Shackleton, of all the men that ever lived, maybe Ernest Shackleton could have helped them now. But not Keith Mallory. There was nothing he could do, no more than the others were doing, and they were just waiting for the end. But he was the leader, he thought dully, he should be planning something, he should be doing something. . . . But there was nothing he could do. There was nothing anyone on God's earth could do. The sense of guilt, of utter inadequacy, settled and deepened with every shudder of the ancient timbers.

He dropped his bucket, grabbed for the security of the mast as a heavy wave swept over the deck, the breaking foam quicksilver in its seething phosphorescence. The waters swirled hungrily round his legs and feet, but he ignored them, stared out into the darkness. The darkness – that was the devil of it. The old caique rolled and pitched and staggered and plunged, but as if disembodied, in a vacuum. They could see nothing – not where the last wave had gone, nor where the next was coming from. A sea invisible and strangely remote, doubly frightening in its palpable immediacy.

Mallory stared down into the hold, was vaguely conscious of the white blur of Miller's face: he had swallowed some sea-water and was retching painfully, salt water laced with blood. But Mallory ignored it, involuntarily: all his mind was concentrated elsewhere, trying to reduce some fleeting impression, as vague as it had been evanescent, to a coherent realization. It seemed desperately urgent that he should do so. Then another and still heavier wave broke over the side and all at once he had it.

The wind! The wind had dropped away, was lessening with every second that passed. Even as he stood there, arms locked round the mast as the second wave fought to carry him away, he remembered how often in the high hills at home he had stood at the foot of a precipice as an onrushing wind, seeking the path of least resistance, had curved and lifted up the sheer face, leaving him standing in a pocket of relative immunity. It was a common enough mountaineering phenomenon. And these two freak waves – the surging backwash! The significance struck at him like a blow. The cliffs! They were on the cliffs of Navarone!

With a hoarse, wordless cry of warning, reckless of his own safety, he flung himself aft, dived full length through the swirling waters for the engine-room hatchway.

'Full astern!' he shouted. The startled white smudge that was Casey Brown's face twisted up to his. 'For God's sake, man, full astern! We're heading for the cliffs!'

He scrambled to his feet, reached the wheelhouse in two strides, hand pawing frantically for the flare pocket.

'The cliffs, Stevens! We're almost on them! Andrea – Miller's still down below!'

He flicked a glance at Stevens, caught the slow nod of the set, blood-masked face, followed the line of sight of the expressionless eyes, saw the whitely phosphorescent line ahead, irregular but almost continuous, blooming and fading, blooming and fading, as the pounding seas smashed against and fell back from cliffs still invisible in the darkness. Desperately his hands fumbled with the flare.

And then, abruptly, it was gone, hissing and spluttering along the near-horizontal trajectory of its flight. For a moment, Mallory thought it had gone out, and he clenched his fists in impotent bitterness. Then it smashed against the rock face, fell back on to a ledge about a dozen feet above the water, and lay there smoking and intermittently burning in the driving rain, in the heavy spray that cascaded from the booming breakers.

The light was feeble, but it was enough. The cliffs were barely fifty yards away, black and wetly shining in the fitful radiance of the flare – a flare that illuminated a vertical circle of less than five yards in radius, and left the cliff below the ledge shrouded in the treacherous dark. And straight ahead, twenty, maybe fifteen yards from the shore, stretched the evil length of a reef, gap-toothed and needle-pointed, vanishing at either end into the outer darkness.

'Can you take her through?' he yelled at Stevens.

'God knows! I'll try!' He shouted something else about 'steerage way,' but Mallory was already half-way to the for'ard cabin. As always in an emergency, his mind was racing ahead with that abnormal sureness and clarity of thought for which he could never afterwards account.

Grasping spikes, mallet and a wire-cored rope, he was back on deck in seconds. He stood stock still, rooted in the almost intolerable tension as he saw the towering, jagged rock bearing down upon them, fine on the starboard bow, a rock that reached half way to the wheelhouse. It struck the boat with a crash that sent him to his knees, rasped and grated along half the length of the buckled, splintered gunwales: and then the caique had rolled over to port and she was through, Stevens frantically spinning the wheel and shouting for full astern.

Mallory's breath escaped in a long, heavy sigh of relief – he had been quite unaware that he had stopped breathing – and he hurriedly looped the coil of rope round his neck and under his left shoulder and stuck spikes and hammer in his belt. The caique was slewing heavily round now, port side to, plunging and corkscrewing violently as she began to fall broadside into the troughs of the waves, waves shorter and steeper than ever under the double thrust of the wind and the waves and the backwash recoiling from the cliffs: but she was still in the grip of the sea and her own momentum, and the distance was closing with frightening speed. It's a chance I have to take, Mallory repeated to himself over and over again; it's a chance I have to take. But that little ledge remote and just inaccessible, was fate's last refinement of cruelty, the salt in the wound of extinction, and he knew in his heart of hearts that it wasn't a chance at all, but just a suicidal gesture. And then Andrea had heaved the last of the fenders – worn truck tyres – outboard, and was towering above him, grinning down hugely into his face: and suddenly Mallory wasn't so sure any more.

'The ledge?' Andrea's vast, reassuring hand was on his shoulder.

Mallory nodded, knees bent in readiness, feet braced on the plunging, slippery deck.

'Jump for it,' Andrea boomed. 'Then keep your legs stiff.'

There was no time for any more. The caique was swinging in broadside to, teetering on the crest of a wave, as high up the cliff as she would ever be, and Mallory knew it was now or never. His hands swung back behind his body, his knees bent farther, and then, in one convulsive leap he had flung himself upwards, fingers scrabbling on the wet rock of the cliff, then hooking over the rim of the ledge. For an instant he hung there at the length of his arms, unable to move, wincing as he heard the foremast crash against the ledge and snap in two, then his fingers left the ledge without their own volition, and he was almost half-way over, propelled by one gigantic heave from below.

He was not up yet. He was held only by the buckle of his belt, caught on the edge of the rock, a buckle now dragged up to his breastbone by the weight of his body. But he did not paw frantically for a handhold, or wriggle his body or flail his legs in the air – and any of these actions would have sent him crashing down again. At last, and once again, he was a man utterly at home in his own element. The greatest rock climber of his time, men called him, and this was what he had been born for.

Slowly, methodically, he felt the surface of the ledge, and almost at once he discovered a crack running back from the face. It would have been better had it been parallel to the face – and more than the width of a matchstick. But it was enough for Mallory. With infinite care he eased the hammer and a couple of spikes from his belt, worked a spike into the crack to obtain a minimal purchase, slid the other in some inches nearer, hooked his left wrist round the first, held the second spike with the fingers of the same hand and brought up the hammer in his free hand. Fifteen seconds later he was standing on the ledge.

Working quickly and surely, catlike in his balance on the slippery, shelving rock, he hammered a spike into the face of the cliff, securely and at a downward angle, about three feet above the ledge, dropped a clove hitch over the top and kicked the rest of the coil over the ledge. Then, and only then, he turned round and looked below him.

Less than a minute had passed since the caique had struck, but already she was a broken-masted, splintered shambles, sides caving in and visibly disintegrating as he watched. Every seven or eight seconds a giant comber would pick her up and fling her bodily against the cliff, the heavy truck tyres taking up only a fraction of the impact that followed, the sickening, rending crash that reduced the gunwales to matchwood, holed and split the sides and cracked the oaken timbers: and then she would roll clear, port side showing, the hungry sea pouring in through the torn and ruptured planking.

Three men were standing by what was left of the wheelhouse. *Three* men – suddenly, he realized that Casey Brown was missing, realized, too, that the engine was still running, its clamour rising and falling then rising again, at irregular intervals. Brown was edging the caique backwards and forwards along the cliff, keeping her as nearly as humanly possible in the same position, for he knew their lives depended on Mallory – and on himself. 'The fool!' Mallory swore. 'The crazy fool!'

The caique surged back in a receding trough, steadied, then swept in against the cliff again, heeling over so wildly that the roof of the wheelhouse smashed and telescoped against the wall of the cliff. The impact was so fierce, the shock so sudden, that Stevens lost both hand-grip and footing and was catapulted into the rock face, upflung arms raised for protection. For a moment he hung there, as if pinned against the wall, then fell back into the sea, limbs and head relaxed, lifeless in his limp acquiescence. He should have died then, drowned under the hammer-blows of the sea or crushed by the next battering-ram collision of caique and cliff. He should have died and he would have died but for the great arm that hooked down and plucked him out of the water like a limp and sodden rag doll and heaved him inboard a bare second before the next bludgeoning impact of the boat against the rock would have crushed the life out of him.

'Come on, for God's sake!' Mallory shouted desperately. 'She'll be gone in a minute! The rope – use the rope!' He saw Andrea and Miller exchange a few quick words, saw them shake and pummel Stevens and stand him on his feet, dazed and retching sea-water, but conscious. Andrea was speaking in his ear, emphasizing something and guiding the rope into his hands, and then the caique was swinging in again. Stevens automatically shortening his grip on the rope. A tremendous boost from below by Andrea, Mallory's long arm reaching out and Stevens was on the ledge, sitting with his back to the cliff and hanging on to the spike, dazed still and shaking a muzzy head, but safe.

'You're next, Miller!' Mallory called. 'Hurry up, man – jump for it!'

Miller looked at him and Mallory could have sworn that he was grinning. Instead of taking the rope from Andrea, he ran for'ard to the cabin.

'Just a minute, boss!' he bawled. 'I've forgotten my toothbrush.'

He reappeared in a few seconds, but without the toothbrush. He was carrying the big, green box of explosives, and before Mallory had appreciated what was happening the box, all fifty pounds of it, was curving up into the air, upthrust by the Greek's tireless arms. Automatically Mallory's hands reached for and caught it. He over-balanced, stumbled and toppled forward, still clutching the box, then was brought up with a jerk. Stevens, still clutching the spike, was on his feet now, free hand hooked in Mallory's belt: he was shivering violently, with cold and exhaustion and an oddly fear-laced excitement. But, like Mallory, he was a hillman at home again.

Mallory was just straightening up when the waterproofed radio set came soaring up. He caught it, placed it down, looked over the side.

'Leave that bloody stuff alone!' he shouted furiously. 'Get up here yourself – now!'

Two coils of rope landed on the ledge beside him, then the first of the rucksacks with the food and clothing. He was vaguely aware that Stevens was trying to stack the equipment in some sort of order.

'Do you hear me?' Mallory roared. 'Get up here at once! That's an order. The boat's sinking, you bloody idiots!'

The caique *was* sinking. She was filling up quickly and Casey Brown had abandoned the flooded Kelvin. But she was a far steadier platform now, rolling through a much shorter arc, less violent in her soggy, yielding collisions with the cliff wall. For a moment Mallory thought the sea was dropping away, then he realized that the tons of water in the caique's hold had drastically lowered her centre of gravity, were acting as a counter-balancing weight.

Miller cupped a hand to his ear. Even in the near darkness of the sinking flare his face had an oddly greenish pallor.

'Can't hear a word you say, boss. Besides, she ain't sinkin' yet.' Once again he disappeared into the for'ard cabin.

Within thirty seconds, with all five men working furiously, the remainder of the equipment was on the ledge. The caique was down by the stern, the poop-deck covered and water pouring down the engine-room hatchway as Brown struggled up the rope, the fo'c'sle awash as Miller grabbed the rope and started after him, and as Andrea reached up and swung in against the cliff his legs dangled over an empty sea. The caique had foundered, completely gone from sight: no drifting flotsam, not even an air bubble marked where she had so lately been.

The ledge was narrow, not three feet wide at its broadest, tapering off into the gloom on either side. Worse still, apart from the few square feet where Stevens had piled the gear, it shelved sharply outwards, the rock underfoot treacherous and slippery. Backs to the wall, Andrea and Miller had to stand on their heels, hands outspread and palms inward against the cliff, pressing in to it as closely as possible to maintain their balance. But in less than a minute Mallory had another two spikes hammered in about twenty inches above the ledge, ten feet apart and joined with a rope, a secure lifeline for all of them.

Wearily Miller slid down to a sitting position, leaned his chest in heartfelt thankfulness against the safe barrier of the rope. He fumbled in his breast pocket, produced a pack of cigarettes and handed them round, oblivious to the rain that soaked them in an instant. He was soaking wet from the waist downwards and both his knees had been badly bruised against the cliff wall: he was bitterly cold, drenched by heavy rain and the sheets of spray that broke continually over the ledge: the sharp edge of the rock bit cruelly into the calves of his legs, the tight rope constricted his breathing and he was still ashen-faced and exhausted from long hours of labour and seasickness: but when he spoke, it was with a voice of utter sincerity.

'My Gawd!' he said reverently. 'Ain't this wonderful!'

Chapter Five

Monday Night 0100–0200

Ninety minutes later Mallory wedged himself into a natural rock chimney on the cliff face, drove in a spike beneath his feet and tried to rest his aching, exhausted body. Two minutes' rest, he told himself, only two minutes while Andrea comes up: the rope was quivering and he could just hear, above the shrieking of the wind that fought to pluck him off the cliff face, the metallic scraping as Andrea's boots struggled for a foothold on that wicked overhang immediately beneath him, the overhang that had all but defeated him, the obstacle that he had impossibly overcome only at the expense of torn hands and body completely spent, of shoulder muscles afire with agony and breath that rasped in great gulping inhalations into his starving lungs. Deliberately he forced his mind away from the pains that racked his body, from its insistent demands for rest, and listened again to the ringing of steel against rock, louder this time, carrying clearly even in the gale. . . . He would have to tell Andrea to be more careful on the remaining twenty feet or so that separated them from the top.

At least, Mallory thought wryly, no one would have to tell him to be quiet. He couldn't have made any noise with his feet if he'd tried – not with only a pair of torn socks as cover for his bruised and bleeding feet. He'd hardly covered the first twenty feet of the climb when he'd discovered that his climbing boots were quite useless, had robbed his feet of all sensitivity, the ability to locate and engage the tiny toe-holds which afforded the only sources of purchase. He had removed them with great difficulty, tied them to his belt by the laces – and lost them, had them torn off, when forcing his way under a projecting spur of rock.

The climb itself had been a nightmare, a brutal, gasping agony in the wind and the rain and the darkness, an agony that had eventually dulled the danger and masked the suicidal risks in climbing that sheer unknown face, in interminable agony of hanging on by fingertips and toes, of driving in a hundred spikes, of securing ropes then inching on again up into the darkness. It was a climb such as he had not ever made before, such as he knew he would not ever make again, for this was insanity. It was a climb that had extended him to the utmost of his great skill, his courage and his strength, and then far beyond that again, and he had not known that such reserves, such limitless resources, lay within him or any man. Nor did he know the well-spring, the source of that power that had driven him to where he was, within easy climbing reach of the top. The challenge to a mountaineer, personal danger, pride in the fact that he was probably the only man in southern Europe who could have made the climb, even the sure knowledge that time was running out for the men on Kheros – it was none of these things, he knew that: in the last twenty minutes it had taken him to negotiate that overhang beneath his feet his mind had been drained of all thought and all emotion, and he had climbed only as a machine.

Hand over hand up the rope, easily, powerfully, Andrea hauled himself over the smoothly swelling convexity of the overhang, legs dangling in mid-air. He was festooned with heavy coils of rope, girdled with spikes that protruded from his belt at every angle and lent him the incongruous appearance of a comic-opera Corsican bandit. Quickly he hauled himself up beside Mallory, wedged himself in the chimney and mopped his sweating forehead. As always, he was grinning hugely.

Mallory looked at him, smiled back. Andrea, he reflected, had no right to be there. It was Stevens's place, but Stevens had still been suffering from shock, had lost much blood: besides, it required a first-class climber to bring up the rear, to coil up the ropes as he came and to remove the spikes – there must be no trace left of the ascent: or so Mallory had told him, and Stevens had reluctantly agreed, although the hurt in his face had been easy to see. More than ever now Mallory was glad he had resisted the quiet plea in Stevens's place: Stevens was undoubtedly a fine climber, but what Mallory had required that night was not another mountaineer but a human ladder. Time and time again during the ascent he had stood on Andrea's back, his shoulders, his upturned palm and once – for at least ten seconds and while he was still wearing his steel-shod boots – on his head. And not once had Andrea protested or stumbled or yielded an inch. The man was indestructible, as tough and enduring as the rock on which he stood. Since dusk had fallen that evening, Andrea had laboured unceasingly, done enough work to kill two ordinary men, and, looking at him then, Mallory realized, almost with despair, that even now he didn't look particularly tired.

Mallory gestured at the rock chimney, then upwards at its shadowy mouth limned in blurred rectangular outline against the pale glimmer of the sky. He leant forward, mouth close to Andrea's ear.

'Twenty feet, Andrea,' he said softly. His breath was still coming in painful gasps. 'It'll be no bother – it's fissured on my side and the chances are that it goes up to the top.'

Andrea looked up the chimney speculatively, nodded in silence.

'Better with your boots off,' Mallory went on. 'And any spikes we use we'll work in by hand.'

'Even on a night like this – high winds and rain, cold and black as a pig's inside – and on a cliff like this?' There was neither doubt nor question in Andrea's voice: rather it was acquiescence, unspoken confirmation of an unspoken thought. They had been so long together, had reached such a depth of understanding that words between them were largely superfluous.

Mallory nodded, waited while Andrea worked home a spike, looped his ropes over it and secured what was left of the long ball of twine that stretched four hundred feet below to the ledge where the others waited. Andrea then removed boots and spikes, fastening them to the ropes, eased the slender, double-edged throwing-knife in its leather shoulder scabbard, looked across at Mallory and nodded in turn.

The first ten feet were easy. Palms and back against one side of the chimney and stocking-soled feet against the other, Mallory jack-knifed his way upwards until the widening sheer of the walls defeated him. Legs braced against the far wall, he worked in a spike as far up as he could reach, grasped it with both hands, dropped his legs across and found a toe-hold in the crevice. Two minutes later his hands hooked over the crumbling edge of the precipice.

Noiselessly and with an infinite caution he fingered aside earth and grass and tiny pebbles until his hands were locked on the solid rock itself, bent his knee to seek lodgment for the final toe-hold, then eased a wary head above the cliff-top, a movement imperceptible in its slow-motion, millimetric stealth. He stopped moving altogether as soon as his eyes had cleared the level of the cliff, stared out into the unfamiliar darkness, his whole being, the entire field of consciousness, concentrated into his eyes and his ears. Illogically, and for the first time in all that terrifying ascent, he became acutely aware of his own danger and helplessness, and he cursed himself for his folly in not borrowing Miller's silenced automatic.

The darkness below the high horizon of the lifting hills beyond was just one degree less than absolute: shapes and angles, heights and depressions were resolving themselves in nebulous silhouette, contours and shadowy profiles emerging reluctantly from the darkness, a darkness suddenly no longer vague and unfamiliar but disturbingly reminiscent in what it revealed, clamouring for recognition. And then abruptly, almost with a sense of shock, Mallory had it. The cliff-top before his eyes was exactly as Monsieur Vlachos had drawn and described it – the narrow, bare strip of ground running parallel to the cliff, the jumble of huge boulders behind them and then, beyond these, the steep scree-strewn lower slopes of the mountains. The first break they'd had yet, Mallory thought exultantly – but what a break! The sketchiest navigation but the most incredible luck, right bang on the nose of the target – the highest point of the highest, most precipitous cliffs in Navarone: the one place where the Germans never mounted a guard, because the climb was impossible! Mallory felt the relief, the high elation wash through him in waves. Jubilantly he straightened his leg, hoisted himself half-way over the edge, arms straight, palms down on the top of the cliff. And then he froze into immobility, petrified as the solid rock beneath his hands, his heart thudding painfully in his throat.

One of the boulders had moved. Seven, maybe eight yards away, a shadow had gradually straightened, detached itself stealthily from the surrounding rock, was advancing slowly towards the edge of the cliff. And then the shadow was no longer 'it'. There could be no mistake now – the long jackboots, the long greatcoat beneath the waterproof cape, the close-fitting helmet were all too familiar. Damn Vlachos! Damn Jensen! Damn all the know-alls who sat at home, the pundits of Intelligence who gave a man wrong information and sent him out to die. And in the same instant Mallory damned himself for his own carelessness, for he had been expecting this all along.

For the first two or three seconds Mallory had lain rigid and unmoving, temporarily paralysed in mind and body: already the guard had advanced four or five steps, carbine held in readiness before him, head turned sideways as he listened into the high, thin whine of the wind and the deep and distant booming of the surf below, trying to isolate the sound that had aroused his suspicions. But now the first shock was over and Mallory's mind was working again. To go up on to the top of the cliff would be suicidal: ten to one the guard would hear him scrambling over the edge and shoot him out of hand: and if he did get up he had neither the weapons nor, after that exhausting climb, the strength to tackle an armed, fresh man. He would have to go back down. But he would have to slide down slowly, an inch at a time. At night, Mallory knew, side vision is even more acute than direct, and the guard might catch a sudden movement out of the corner of his eye. And then he would only have to turn his head and that would be the end: even in that darkness, Mallory realized, there could be no mistaking the bulk of his silhouette against the sharp line of the edge of the cliff.

Gradually, every movement as smooth and controlled as possible, every soft and soundless breath a silent prayer, Mallory slipped gradually back over the edge of the cliff. Still the guard advanced, making for a point about five yards to Mallory's left, but still he looked away, his ear turned into the wind. And then Mallory was down, only his finger-tips over the top, and Andrea's great bulk was beside him, his mouth to his ear.

'What is it? Somebody there?'

'A sentry,' Mallory whispered back. His arms were beginning to ache from the strain. 'He's heard something and he's looking for us.'

Suddenly he shrank away from Andrea, pressed himself as closely as possible to the face of the cliff, was vaguely aware of Andrea doing the same thing. A beam of light, hurtful and dazzling to eyes so long accustomed to the dark, had suddenly stabbed out at an angle over the edge of the cliff, was moving slowly along towards them. The German had his torch out, was methodically examining the rim of the cliff. From the angle of the beam, Mallory judged that he was walking along a couple of feet from the edge. On that wild and gusty night he was taking no chances on the crumbly, teacherous top-soil of the cliff: even more likely, he was taking no chances on a pair of sudden hands reaching out for his ankles and jerking him to a mangled death on the rocks and reefs four hundred feet below.

Slowly, inexorably, the beam approached. Even at that slant, it was bound to catch them. With a sudden sick certainty Mallory realized that the German wasn't just suspicious: he *knew* there was someone there, and he wouldn't stop looking until he found them. And there was nothing they could do, just nothing at all. . . . Then Andrea's head was close to his again.

'A stone,' Andrea whispered. 'Over there, behind him.'

Cautiously at first, then frantically, Mallory pawed the cliff-top with his right hand. Earth, only earth, grass roots and tiny pebbles – there was nothing even half the size of a marble. And then Andrea was thrusting something against him and his hand closed over the metallic smoothness of a spike: even in that moment of desperate urgency, with the slender, searching beam only a few feet away, Mallory was conscious of a sudden brief anger with himself – he had still a couple of spikes stuck in his belt and had forgotten all about them.

His arm swung back, jerked convulsively forward, sent the spike spinning away into the darkness. One second passed, then another, he knew he had missed, the beam was only inches from Andrea's shoulders, and then the metallic clatter of the spike striking a boulder fell upon his ear like a benison. The beam wavered for a second, stabbed out aimlessly into the darkness and then whipped round, probing into the boulders to the left. And then the sentry was running towards them, slipping and stumbling in his haste, the barrel of the carbine gleaming in the light of the torch held clamped to it. He'd gone less than ten yards when Andrea was over the top of the cliff like a great, black cat, was padding noiselessly across the ground to the shelter of the nearest boulder. Wraith-like, he fitted in behind it and was gone, a shadow long among shadows.

The sentry was about twenty yards away now, the beam of his torch darting fearfully from boulder to boulder when Andrea struck the haft of his knife against a rock, twice. The sentry whirled round, torch shining along the line of the boulders, then started to run clumsily back again, the skirts of the greatcoat fluttering grotesquely in the wind. The torch was swinging wildly now, and Mallory caught a glimpse of a white, straining face, wide-eyed and fearful, incongruously at variance with the gladiatorial strength of the steel helmet above. God only knew, Mallory thought, what wild and panic-stricken thoughts were passing through his confused mind: noises from the cliff-top, metallic sound from either side among the boulders, the long, eerie vigil, afraid and companionless, on a deserted cliff edge on a dark and tempest-filled night in a hostile land – suddenly Mallory felt a deep stab of compassion for this man, a man like himself, someone's well-loved husband or brother or son who was only doing a dirty and dangerous job as best he could and because he was told to, compassion for his loneliness and his anxieties and his fears, for the sure knowledge that before he had drawn breath another three times he would be dead. . . . Slowly, gauging his time and distance, Mallory raised his head.

'Help!' he shouted. 'Help me! I'm falling!'

The soldier checked in mid-stride and spun round, less than five feet from the rock that hid Andrea. For a second the beam of his torch waved wildly around, then settled on Mallory's head. For another moment he stood stock still, then the carbine in his right hand swung up, the left hand reached down for the barrel. Then he grunted once, a violent and convulsive exhalation of breath, and the thud of the hilt of Andrea's knife striking home against the ribs carried clearly to Mallory's ears, even against the wind. . . .

Mallory stared down at the dead man, at Andrea's impassive face as he wiped the blade of his knife on the greatcoat, rose slowly to his feet, sighed and slid the knife back in its scabbard.

'So, my Keith!' Andrea reserved the punctilious 'Captain' for company only. 'This is why our young lieutenant eats his heart out down below.'

'That is why,' Mallory acknowledged. 'I knew it – or I almost knew it. So did you. Too many coincidences – the German caique investigating, the trouble at the watch-tower – and now this.' Mallory swore, softly and bitterly. 'This is the end of our little friend Captain Briggs of Castelrosso. He'll be cashiered within the month. Jensen will make certain of that.'

Andrea nodded.

'He let Nicolai go?'

'Who else could have known that we were to have landed here, tipped off everyone all along the line?' Mallory paused, dismissed the thought, caught Andrea by the arm. 'The Germans are thorough. Even although they must know it's almost an impossibility to land on a night like this, they'll have a dozen sentries scattered along the cliffs.' Unconsciously Mallory had lowered his voice. 'But they wouldn't depend on one man to cope with five. So—'

'Signals,' Andrea finished for him. 'They must have some way of letting the others know. Perhaps flares—'

'No, not that,' Mallory disagreed. 'Give their position away. Telephone. It has to be that. Remember how they were in Crete – miles of field telephone wire all over the shop?'

Andrea nodded, picked up the dead man's torch, hooded it in his huge hand and started searching. He returned in less than a minute.

'Telephone it is,' he announced softly. 'Over there, under the rocks.'

'Nothing we can do about it,' Mallory said. 'If it does ring, I'll have to answer or they'll come hot-footing along. I only hope to heaven they haven't got a bloody password. It would be just like them.'

He turned away, stopped suddenly.

'But someone's got to come sometime – a relief, sergeant of the guard, something like that. Probably he's supposed to make an hourly report. Someone's bound to come – and come soon. My God, Andrea, we'll have to make it fast!'

'And this poor devil?' Andrea gestured to the huddled shadow at his feet.

'Over the side with him.' Mallory grimaced in distaste. 'Won't make any difference to the poor bastard now, and we can't leave any traces. The odds are they'll think he's gone over the edge – this top soil's as crumbly and treacherous as hell. . . . You might see if he's any papers on him – never know how useful they might be.'

'Not half as useful as these boots on his feet.' Andrea waved a large hand towards the scree-strewn slopes. 'You are not going to walk very far there in your stocking soles.'

Five minutes later Mallory tugged three times on the string that stretched down into the darkness below. Three answering tugs came from the ledge, and then the cord vanished rapidly down over the edge of the overhang, drawing with it the long, steel-cored rope that Mallory paid out from the coil on the top of the cliff.

The box of explosives was the first of the gear to come up. The weighted rope plummetted straight down from the point of the overhang, and padded though the box was on every side with lashed rucksacks and sleeping-bags it still crashed terrifyingly against the cliff on the inner arc of every wind-driven swing of the pendulum. But there was no time for finesse, to wait for the diminishing swing of the pendulum after each tug. Securely anchored to a rope that stretched around the base of a great boulder, Andrea leaned far out over the edge of the precipice and reeled in the seventy-pound deadweight as another man would a trout. In less than three minutes the ammunition box lay beside him on the cliff-top; five minutes later the firing generator, guns and pistols, wrapped in a couple of other sleeping-bags and their lightweight, reversible tent – white on one side, brown and green camouflage on the other – lay beside the explosives.

A third time the rope went down into the rain and the darkness, a third time the tireless Andrea hauled it in, hand over hand. Mallory was behind him, coiling in the slack of the rope, when he heard Andrea's sudden exclamation: two quick strides and he was at the edge of the cliff, his hand on the big Greek's arm.

'What's up, Andrea? Why have you stopped—?'

He broke off, peered through the gloom at the rope in Andrea's hand, saw that it was being held between only finger and thumb. Twice Andrea jerked the rope up a foot or two, let it fall again: the weightless rope swayed wildly in the wind.

'Gone?' Mallory asked quietly.

Andrea nodded without speaking.

'Broken?' Mallory was incredulous. 'A wire-cored rope?'

'I don't think so.' Quickly Andrea reeled in the remaining forty feet. The twine was still attached to the same place, about a fathom from the end. The rope was intact.

'Somebody tied a knot.' Just for a moment the giant's voice sounded tired. 'They didn't tie it too well.'

Mallory made to speak, then flung up an instinctive arm as a great, forked tongue of flame streaked between the cliff-top and unseen clouds above. Their cringing eyes were still screwed tight shut, their nostrils full of the acrid, sulphurous smell of burning, when the first volley of thunder crashed in Titan fury almost overhead, a deafening artillery to mock the pitiful efforts of embattled man, doubly terrifying in the total darkness that followed that searing flash. Gradually the echoes pealed and faded inland in diminishing reverberations, were lost among the valleys of the hills.

'My God!' Mallory murmured. 'That was close. We'd better make it fast, Andrea – this cliff is liable to be lit up like a fairground any minute. . . What was in that last load you were bringing up?' He didn't really have to ask – he himself had arranged for the breaking up of the equipment into three separate loads before he'd left the ledge. It wasn't even that he suspected his tired mind of playing tricks on him; but it was tired enough, too tired, to probe the hidden compulsion, the nameless hope that prompted him to grasp at nameless straws that didn't even exist.

'The food,' Andrea said gently. '*All* the food, the stove, the fuel – and the compasses.'

For five, perhaps ten seconds, Mallory stood motionless. One half of his mind, conscious of the urgency, the desperate need for haste, was jabbing him mercilessly: the other half held him momentarily in a vast irresolution, an irresolution of coldness and numbness that came not from the lashing wind and sleety rain but from his own mind, from the bleak and comfortless imaginings of lost wanderings on that harsh and hostile island, with neither food nor fire. . . . And then Andrea's great hand was on his shoulder, and he was laughing softly.

'Just so much less to carry, my Keith. Think how grateful our tired friend Corporal Miller is going to be. . . . This is only a little thing.'

'Yes,' Mallory said. 'Yes, of course. A little thing.' He turned abruptly, tugged the cord, watched the rope disappear over the edge.

Fifteen minutes later, in drenching, torrential rain, a great, sheeting downpour almost constantly illuminated by the jagged, branching stilettos of the forked lightning, Casey Brown's bedraggled head came into view over the edge of the cliff. The thunder, too, emptily cavernous in that flat and explosive intensity of sound that lies at the heart of a thunderstorm, was almost continuous: but in the brief intervals, Casey's voice, rich in his native Clydeside accent, carried clearly. He was expressing himself fluently in basic Anglo-Saxon, and with cause. He had had the assistance of two ropes on the way up – the one stretched from spike to spike and the one used for raising supplies, which Andrea had kept pulling in as he made the ascent. Casey Brown had secured the end of this round his waist with a bowline, but the bowline had proved to be nothing of the sort but a slip-knot, and Andrea's enthusiastic help had almost cut him in half. He was still sitting on the cliff-top, exhausted head between his knees, the radio still strapped to his back, when two tugs on Andrea's rope announced that Dusty Miller was on his way up.

Another quarter of an hour elapsed, an interminable fifteen minutes when, in the lulls between the thunderclaps, every slightest sound was an approaching enemy patrol, before Miller materialized slowly out of the darkness, half-way down the rock chimney. He was climbing steadily and methodically, then checked abruptly at the cliff-top, groping hands pawing uncertainly on the top-soil of the cliff. Puzzled, Mallory bent down, peered into the lean face: both the eyes were clamped tightly shut.

'Relax, Corporal,' Mallory advised kindly. 'You have arrived.'

Dusty Miller slowly opened his eyes, peered round at the edge of the cliff, shuddered and crawled quickly on hands and knees to the shelter of the nearest boulders. Mallory followed and looked down at him curiously.

'What was the idea of closing your eyes coming over the top?'

'I did not,' Miller protested.

Mallory said nothing.

'I closed them at the bottom,' Miller explained wearily. 'I opened them at the top.'

Mallory looked at him incredulously.

'What! All the way?'

'It's like I told you, boss,' Miller complained. 'Back in Castelrosso. When I cross a street and step up on to the sidewalk I gotta hang on to the nearest lamp-post. More or less.' He broke off, looked at Andrea leaning far out over the side of the cliff, and shivered again. 'Brother! Oh, brother! Was I scared!'

Fear. Terror. Panic. Do the thing you fear and the death of fear is certain. Do the thing you fear and the death of fear is certain. Once, twice, a hundred times, Andy Stevens repeated the words to himself, over and over again, like a litany. A psychiatrist had told him that once and he'd read it a dozen times since. Do the thing you fear and the death of fear is certain. The mind is a limited thing, they had said. It can only hold one thought at a time, one impulse to action. Say to yourself, I am brave, I am overcoming this fear, this stupid, unreasoning panic which has no origin except in my own mind, and because the mind *can* only hold one thought at a time, and because thinking and feeling are one, then you *will* be brave, you *will* overcome and the fear will vanish like a shadow in the night. And so Andy Stevens said these things to himself, and the shadows only lengthened and deepened, lengthened and deepened, and the icy claws of fear dug ever more savagely into his dull exhausted mind, into his twisted, knotted stomach.

His stomach. That knotted ball of jangled, writhing nerve-ends beneath the solar plexus. No one could ever know how it was, how it felt, except those whose shredded minds were going, collapsing into complete and final breakdown. The waves of panic and nausea and faintness that flooded up through a suffocating throat to a mind dark and spent and sinewless, a mind fighting with woollen fingers to cling on to the edge of the abyss, a tired and lacerated mind, only momentarily in control, wildly rejecting the clamorous demands of a nervous system, which had already taken far too much, that he should let go, open the torn fingers that were clenched so tightly round the rope. It was just that easy. 'Rest after toil, port after stormy seas.' What was that famous stanza of Spenser's? Sobbing aloud, Stevens wrenched out another spike, sent it spinning into the waiting sea three hundred long feet below, pressed himself closely into the face and inched his way despairingly upwards.

Fear. Fear had been at his elbow all his life, his constant companion, his *alter ego*, at his elbow, or in close prospect or immediate recall. He had become accustomed to that fear, at times almost reconciled, but the sick agony of this night lay far beyond either tolerance or familiarity. He had never known anything like this before, and even in his terror and confusion he was dimly aware that the fear did not spring from the climb itself. True, the cliff was sheer and almost vertical, and the lightning, the ice-cold rain, the darkness and the bellowing thunder was a waking nightmare. But the climb, technically, was simple: the rope stretched all the way to the top and all he had to do was to follow it and dispose of the spikes as he went. He was sick and bruised and terribly tired, his head ached abominably and he had lost a great deal of blood: but then, more often than not, it is in the darkness of agony and exhaustion that the spirit of man burns most brightly.

Andy Stevens was afraid because his self-respect was gone. Always before, that had been his sheet anchor, had tipped the balance against his ancient enemy – the respect in which other men had held him, the respect he had had for himself. But now these were gone, for his two greatest fears had been realized – he was known to be afraid, he had failed his fellow-man. Both in the fight with the German caique and when anchored above the watch-tower in the creek, he had known that Mallory and Andrea knew. He had never met such men before, and he had known all along that he could never hide his secrets from such men. He should have gone up that cliff with Mallory, but Mallory had made excuses and taken Andrea instead – Mallory *knew* he was afraid. And twice before, in Castelrosso and when the German boat had closed in on them, he had almost failed his friends – and tonight he had failed them terribly. He had not been thought fit to lead the way with Mallory – and it was he, the sailor of the party, who had made such a botch of tying that last knot, had lost all the food and the fuel that had plummetted into the sea a bare ten feet from where he had stood on the ledge . . . and a thousand men on Kheros were depending on a failure so abject as himself. Sick and spent, spent in mind and body and spirit, moaning aloud in his anguish of fear and self-loathing, and not knowing where one finished and the other began, Andy Stevens climbed blindly on.

The sharp, high-pitched call-up buzz of the telephone cut abruptly through the darkness on the cliff-top. Mallory stiffened and half-turned, hands clenching involuntarily. Again it buzzed, the jarring stridency carrying clearly above the bass rumble of the thunder, fell silent again. And then it buzzed again and kept on buzzing, peremptory in its harsh insistence.

Mallory was half-way towards it when he checked in mid-step, turned slowly round and walked back towards Andrea. The big Greek looked at him curiously.

'You have changed your mind?'

Mallory nodded but said nothing.

'They will keep on ringing until they get an answer,' Andrea murmured. 'And when they get no answer, they will come. They will come quickly and soon.'

'I know, I know.' Mallory shrugged. 'We have to take that chance – certainty rather. The question is – how long will it be before anyone turns up.' Instinctively he looked both ways along the windswept cliff-top: Miller and Brown were posted one on either side about fifty yards away, lost in the darkness. 'It's not worth the risk. The more I think of it, the poorer I think my chances would be of getting away with it. In matters of routine the old Hun tends to be an inflexible sort of character. There's probably a set way of answering the phone, or the sentry has to identify himself by name, or there's a password – or maybe my voice would give me away. On the other hand the sentry's gone without trace, all our gear is up and so's everyone except Stevens. In other words, we've practically made it. We've landed – and nobody knows we're here.'

'Yes.' Andrea nodded slowly. 'Yes, you are right – and Stevens should be up in two or three minutes. It would be foolish to throw away everything we've gained.' He paused, then went on quietly: 'But they are going to come running.' The phone stopped ringing as suddenly as it had started. 'They are going to come now.'

'I know. I hope to hell Stevens . . .' Mallory broke off, spun on his heel, said over his shoulder, 'Keep your eye open for him, will you? I'll warn the others we're expecting company.'

Mallory moved quickly along the cliff-top, keeping well away from the edge. He hobbled rather than walked – the sentry's boots were too small for him and chafed his toes cruelly. Deliberately he closed his mind to the thought of how his feet would be after a few hours' walking over rough territory in these boots: time enough for the reality, he thought grimly, without the added burden of anticipation. . . . He stopped abruptly as something hard and metallic pushed into the small of his back.

'Surrender or die!' The drawling, nasal voice was positively cheerful: after what he had been through on the caique and the cliff face, just to set feet on solid ground again was heaven enough for Dusty Miller.

'Very funny,' Mallory growled. 'Very funny indeed.' He looked curiously at Miller. The American had removed his oilskin cape – the rain had ceased as abruptly as it had come – to reveal a jacket and braided waistcoat even more sodden and saturated than his trousers. It didn't make sense. But there was no time for questions.

'Did you hear the phone ringing just now?' he asked.

'Was that what it was? Yeah, I heard it.'

'The sentry's phone. His hourly report, or whatever it was, must have been overdue. We didn't answer it. They'll be hotfooting along any minute now, suspicious as hell and looking for trouble. Maybe your side, maybe Brown's. Can't approach any other way unless they break their necks climbing over these boulders.' Mallory gestured at the shapeless jumble of rocks behind them. 'So keep your eyes skinned.'

'I'll do that, boss. No shootin', huh?'

'No shooting. Just get back as quickly and quietly as you can and let us know. Come back in five minutes anyway.'

Mallory hurried away, retracing his steps. Andrea was stretched full length on the cliff-top, peering over the edge. He twisted his head round as Mallory approached.

'I can hear him. He's just at the overhang.'

'Good.' Mallory moved on without breaking step. 'Tell him to hurry, please.'

Ten yards farther on Mallory checked, peered into the gloom ahead. Somebody was coming along the cliff-top at a dead run, stumbling and slipping on the loose gravelly soil.

'Brown?' Mallory called softly.

'Yes, sir. It's me.' Brown was up to him now, breathing heavily, pointing back in the direction he had just come. 'Somebody's coming, and coming fast! Torches waving and jumping all over the place – must be running.'

'How many?' Mallory asked quickly.

'Four or five at least.' Brown was still gasping for breath. 'Maybe more – four or five torches anyway. You can see them for yourself.' Again he pointed backwards, then blinked in puzzlement. 'That's bloody funny! They're all gone.' He turned back swiftly to Mallory. 'But I can swear—'

'Don't worry,' Mallory said grimly. 'You saw them all right. I've been expecting visitors. They're getting close now and taking no chances. . . . How far away?'

'Hundred yards – not more than a hundred and fifty.'

'Go and get Miller. Tell him to get back here fast.'

Mallory ran back along the cliff edge and knelt beside the huge length of Andrea.

'They're coming, Andrea,' he said quickly. 'From the left. At least five, probably more. Two minutes at the most. Where's Stevens? Can you see him?'

'I can see him.' Andrea was magnificently unperturbed. 'He is just passing the overhang . . .' The rest of his words were lost, drowned in a sudden, violent thunderclap, but there was no need for more. Mallory could see Stevens now, climbing up the rope, strangely old and enfeebled in action, hand over hand in paralysing slowness, half-way now between the overhang and the foot of the chimney.

'Good God!' Mallory swore. 'What's the matter with him? He's going to take all day . . .' He checked himself, cupped his hands to his mouth. 'Stevens! Stevens!' But there was no sign that Stevens had heard. He still kept climbing with the same unnatural over-deliberation, a robot in slow motion.

'He is very near the end,' Andrea said quietly. 'You see he does not even lift his head. When a climber does not lift his head, he is finished.' He stirred. 'I will go down for him.'

'No.' Mallory's hand was on his shoulder. 'Stay here. I can't risk you both. . . . Yes, what is it?' He was aware that Brown was back, bending over him, his breath coming in great heaving gasps.

'Hurry, sir; hurry, for God's sake!' A few brief words but he had to suck in two huge gulps of air to get them out. 'They're on top of us!'

'Get back to the rocks with Miller,' Mallory said urgently. 'Cover us. . . . Stevens! Stevens!' But again the wind swept up the face of the cliff, carried his words away.

'Stevens! For God's sake, man! Stevens!' His voice was low-pitched, desperate, but this time some quality in it must have reached through Stevens's fog of exhaustion and touched his consciousness, for he stopped climbing and lifted his head, hand cupped to his ear.

'Some Germans coming!' Mallory called through funnelled hands, as loudly as he dared. 'Get to the foot of the chimney and stay there. Don't make a sound. Understand?'

Stevens lifted his hand, gestured in tired acknowledgment, lowered his head, started to climb up again. He was going even more slowly now, his movements fumbling and clumsy.

'Do you think he understands?' Andrea was troubled.

'I think so. I don't know.' Mallory stiffened and caught Andrea's arm. It was beginning to rain again, not heavily yet, and through the drizzle he'd caught sight of a hooded torch beam probing among the rocks thirty yards away to his left. 'Over the edge with the rope,' he whispered. 'The spike at the bottom of the chimney will hold it. Come on – let's get out of here!'

Gradually, meticulous in their care not to dislodge the smallest pebble, Mallory and Andrea inched back from the edge, squirmed round and headed back for the rocks, pulling themselves along on their elbows and knees. The few yards were interminable and without even a gun in his hand Mallory felt defenceless, completely exposed. An illogical feeling, he knew, for the first beam of light to fall on them meant the end not for them but for the man who held the torch. Mallory had complete faith in Brown and Miller. . . . That wasn't important. What mattered was the complete escape from detection. Twice during the last endless few feet a wandering beam reached out towards them, the second a bare arm's length away: both times they pressed their faces into the sodden earth, lest the pale blur of their faces betray them, and lay very still. And then, all at once it seemed, they were among the rocks and safe.

In a moment Miller was beside them, a half-seen shadow against the darker dusk of the rocks around them.

'Plenty of time, plenty of time,' he whispered sarcastically. 'Why didn't you wait another half-hour?' He gestured to the left, where the flickering of torches, the now clearly audible murmur of guttural voices, were scarcely twenty yards away. 'We'd better move farther back. They're looking for him among the rocks.'

'For him or for his telephone,' Mallory murmured in agreement. 'You're right anyway. Watch your guns on these rocks. Take the gear with you. . . . And if they look over and find Stevens we'll have to take the lot. No time for fancy work and to hell with the noise. Use the automatic carbines.'

Andy Stevens had heard, but he had not understood. It was not that he panicked, was too terrified to understand, for he was no longer afraid. Fear is of the mind, but his mind had ceased to function, drugged by the last stages of exhaustion, crushed by the utter, damnable tiredness that held his limbs, his whole body, in leaden thrall. He did not know it, but fifty feet below he had struck his head against a spur of rock, a sharp, wicked projection that had torn his gaping temple wound open to the bone. His strength drained out with the pulsing blood.

He had heard Mallory, had heard something about the chimney he had now reached, but his mind had failed to register the meaning of the words. All that Stevens knew was that he was climbing, and that one always kept on climbing until one reached the top. That was what his father had always impressed upon him, his brothers too. You must reach the top.

He was half-way up the chimney now, resting on the spike that Mallory had driven into the fissure. He hooked his fingers in the crack, bent back his head and stared up towards the mouth of the chimney. Ten feet away, no more. He was conscious of neither surprise nor elation. It was just there: he had to reach it. He could hear voices, carrying clearly from the top. He was vaguely surprised that his friends were making no attempt to help him, that they had thrown away the rope that would have made those last few feet so easy, but he felt no bitterness, no emotion at all: perhaps they were trying to test him. What did it matter anyway – he had to reach the top.

He reached the top. Carefully, as Mallory had done before him, he pushed aside the earth and tiny pebbles, hooked his fingers over the edge, found the same toe-hold as Mallory had and levered himself upwards. He saw the flickering torches, heard the excited voices, and then for an instant the curtain of fog in his mind lifted and a last tidal wave of fear washed over him and he knew that the voices were the voices of the enemy and that they had destroyed his friends. He knew now that he was alone, that he had failed, that this was the end, one way or another, and that it had all been for nothing. And then the fog closed over him again, and there was nothing but the emptiness of it all, the emptiness and the futility, the overwhelming lassitude and despair and his body slowly sinking down the face of the cliff. And then the hooked fingers – they, too, were slipping away, opening gradually, reluctantly as the fingers of a drowning man releasing their final hold on a spar of wood. There was no fear now, only a vast and heedless indifference as his hands slipped away and he fell like a stone, twenty vertical feet into the cradling bottle-neck at the foot of the chimney.

He himself made no sound, none at all: the soundless scream of agony never passed his lips, for the blackness came with the pain: but the straining ears of the men crouching in the rocks above caught clearly the dull sickening crack as his right leg fractured cleanly in two, snapping like a rotten bough.

Chapter Six

Monday Night 0200–0600

The German patrol was everything that Mallory had feared – efficient, thorough and very, very painstaking. It even had imagination, in the person of its young and competent sergeant, and that was more dangerous still.

There were only four of them, in high boots, helmets and green, grey and brown mottled capes. First of all they located the telephone and reported to base. Then the young sergeant sent two men to search another hundred yards or so along the cliff, while he and the fourth soldier probed among the rocks that paralleled the cliff. The search was slow and careful, but the two men did not penetrate very far into the rocks. To Mallory, the sergeant's reasoning was obvious and logical. If the sentry had gone to sleep or taken ill, it was unlikely that he would have gone far in among that confused jumble of boulders. Mallory and the others were safely back beyond their reach.

And then came what Mallory had feared – an organized, methodical inspection of the cliff-top itself: worse still, it began with a search along the very edge. Securely held by his three men with interlinked arms – the last with a hand hooked round his belt – the sergeant walked slowly along the rim, probing every inch with the spot-lit beam of a powerful torch. Suddenly he stopped short, exclaimed suddenly and stooped, torch and face only inches from the ground. There was no question as to what he had found – the deep gouge made in the soft, crumbling soil by the climbing rope that had been belayed round the boulder and gone over the edge of the cliff. . . . Softly, silently, Mallory and his three companions straightened to their knees or to their feet, gun barrels lining along the tops of boulders or peering out between cracks in the rocks. There was no doubt in any of their minds that Stevens was lying there helplessly in the crutch of the chimney, seriously injured or dead. It needed only one German carbine to point down that cliff face, however carelessly, and these four men would die. They would have to die.

The sergeant was stretched out his length now, two men holding his legs. His head and shoulders were over the edge of the cliff, the beam from his torch stabbing down the chimney. For ten, perhaps fifteen seconds, there was no sound on the cliff-top, no sound at all, only the high, keening moan of the wind and the swish of the rain in the stunted grass. And then the sergeant had wriggled back and risen to his feet, slowly shaking his head. Mallory gestured to the others to sink down behind the boulders again, but even so the sergeant's soft Bavarian voice carried clearly in the wind.

'It's Ehrich all right, poor fellow.' Compassion and anger blended curiously in the voice. 'I warned him often enough about his carelessness, about going too near the edge of that cliff. It is very treacherous.' Instinctively the sergeant stepped back a couple of feet and looked again at the gouge in the soft earth. 'That's where his heel slipped – or maybe the butt of his carbine. Not that it matters now.'

'Is he dead, do you think, Sergeant?' The speaker was only a boy, nervous and unhappy.

'It's hard to say. . . . Look for yourself.'

Gingerly the youth lay down on the cliff-top, peering cautiously over the lip of the rock. The other soldiers were talking among themselves, in short staccato sentences when Mallory turned to Miller, cupped his hands to his mouth and the American's ear. He could contain his puzzlement no longer.

'Was Stevens wearing his dark suit when you left him?' he whispered.

'Yeah,' Miller whispered back. 'Yeah, I think he was.' A pause. 'No, dammit, I'm wrong. We both put on our rubber camouflage capes about the same time.'

Mallory nodded. The waterproofs of the Germans were almost identical with their own: and the sentry's hair, Mallory remembered, had been jet black – the same colour as Stevens's dyed hair. Probably all that was visible from above was a crumpled, cape-shrouded figure and a dark head. The sergeant's mistake in identity was more than understandable: it was inevitable.

The young soldier eased himself back from the edge of the cliff and hoisted himself carefully to his feet.

'You're right, Sergeant. It *is* Ehrich.' The boy's voice was unsteady. 'He's alive, I think. I saw his cape move, just a little. It wasn't the wind, I'm sure of that.'

Mallory felt Andrea's massive hand squeezing his arm, felt the quick surge of relief, then elation, wash through him. So Stevens *was* alive! Thank God for that! They'd save the boy yet. He heard Andrea whispering the news to the others, then grinned wryly to himself, ironic at his own gladness. Jensen definitely would not have approved of this jubilation. Stevens had already done his part, navigated the boat to Navarone, and climbed the cliff: and now he was only a crippled liability, would be a drag on the whole party, reduce what pitiful chances of success remained to them. For a High Command who pushed the counters around crippled pawns slowed up the whole game, made the board so damnably untidy. It was most inconsiderate of Stevens not to have killed himself so that they could have disposed of him neatly and without trace in the deep and hungry waters that boomed around the foot of the cliff. . . . Mallory clenched his hands in the darkness and swore to himself that the boy would live, come home again, and to hell with total war and all its inhuman demands. . . . Just a kid, that was all, a scared and broken kid and the bravest of them all.

The young sergeant was issuing a string of orders to his men, his voice was quick, crisp and confident. A doctor, splints, rescue stretcher, anchored sheer-legs, ropes, spikes – the trained, well-ordered mind missed nothing. Mallory waited tensely, wondering how many men, if any, would be left on guard, for the guards would have to go and that would inevitably betray them. The question of their quick and silent disposal never entered his mind – a whisper in Andrea's ear and the guards would have no more chance than penned lambs against a marauding wolf. Less chance even than that – the lambs could always run and cry out before the darkness closed over them.

The sergeant solved the problem for them. The assured competence, the tough, unsentimental ruthlessness that made the German NCO the best in the world gave Mallory the chance he never expected to have. He had just finished giving his orders when the young soldier touched him on the arm, then pointed over the edge.

'How about poor Ehrich, Sergeant?' he asked uncertainly. 'Shouldn't – don't you think one of us ought to stay with him?'

'And what could you do if you did stay – hold his hand?' the sergeant asked acidly. 'If he stirs and falls, then he falls, that's all, and it doesn't matter then if a hundred of us are standing up here watching him. Off you go, and don't forget the mallets and pegs to stay the sheer-legs.'

The three men turned and went off quickly to the east without another word. The sergeant walked over to the phone, reported briefly to someone, then set off in the opposite direction – to check the next guard post, Mallory guessed. He was still in sight, a dwindling blur in the darkness, when Mallory whispered to Brown and Miller to post themselves on guard again: and they could still hear the measured crunch of his firm footfalls on a patch of distant gravel as their belayed rope went snaking over the edge of the cliff, Andrea and Mallory sliding swiftly down even before it had stopped quivering.

Stevens, a huddled, twisted heap with a gashed and bleeding cheek lying cruelly along a razor-sharp spur of rock, was still unconscious, breathing stertorously through his open mouth. Below the knee his right leg twisted upwards and outwards against the rock at an impossible angle. As gently as he could, braced against either side of the chimney and supported by Andrea, Mallory lifted and straightened the twisted limb. Twice, from the depths of the dark stupor of his unconsciousness, Stevens moaned in agony, but Mallory had no option but to carry on, his teeth clenched tight until his jaws ached. Then slowly, with infinite care, he rolled up the trouser leg, winced and screwed his eyes shut in momentary horror and nausea as he saw the dim whiteness of the shattered tibia sticking out through the torn and purply swollen flesh.

'Compound fracture, Andrea.' Gently his exploring fingers slid down the mangled leg, beneath the lip of the jackboot, stopped suddenly as something gave way beneath his feather touch. 'Oh, my God! he murmured. 'Another break, just above the ankle. This boy is in a bad way, Andrea.'

'He is indeed,' Andrea said gravely. 'We can do nothing for him here?'

'Nothing. Just nothing. We'll have to get him up first.' Mallory straightened, gazed up bleakly at the perpendicular face of the chimney. 'Although how in the name of heaven—'

'I will take him up.' There was no suggestion in Andrea's voice either of desperate resolve or consciousness of the almost incredible effort involved. It was simply a statement of intention, the voice of a man who never questioned his ability to do what he said he would. 'If you will help me to raise him, to tie him to my back. . . .'

'With his broken leg loose, dangling from a piece of skin and torn muscle?' Mallory protested. 'Stevens can't take much more. He'll die if we do this.'

'He'll die if we don't,' Andrea murmured.

Mallory stared down at Stevens for a long moment, then nodded heavily in the darkness.

'He'll die if we don't,' he echoed tiredly. 'Yes, we have to do this.' He pushed outwards from the rock, slid half a dozen feet down the rope and jammed a foot in the crutch of the chimney just below Stevens's body. He took a couple of turns of rope round his waist and looked up.

'Ready, Andrea?' he called softly.

'Ready.' Andrea stooped, hooked his great hands under Stevens's armpits and lifted slowly, powerfully, as Mallory pushed from below. Twice, three times before they had him up, the boy moaned deep down in his tortured throat, the long, quivering 'Aahs' of agony setting Mallory's teeth on edge: and then his dangling, twisted leg had passed from Mallory's reach and he was held close and cradled in Andrea's encircling arm, the rain-lashed, bleeding mask of a face lolling grotesquely backwards, forlorn and lifeless with the dead pathos of a broken doll. Seconds later Mallory was up beside them, expertly lashing Stevens's wrists together. He was swearing softly, as his numbed hands looped and tightened the rope, softly, bitterly, continuously, but he was quite unaware of this: he was aware only of the broken head that lolled stupidly against his shoulder, of the welling, rain-thinned blood that filmed the upturned face, of the hair above the gashed temple emerging darkly fair as the dye washed slowly out. Inferior bloody boot-blacking, Mallory thought savagely: Jensen shall know of this – it could cost a man's life. And then he became aware of his own thoughts and swore again, still more savagely and at himself this time, for the utter triviality of what he was thinking.

With both hands free – Stevens's bound arms were looped round his neck, his body lashed to his own – Andrea took less than thirty seconds to reach the top; if the dragging, one hundred and sixty pound deadweight on his back made any difference to Andrea's climbing speed and power, Mallory couldn't detect it. The man's endurance was fantastic. Once, just once, as Andrea scrambled over the edge of the cliff, the broken leg caught on the rock, and the crucifying torture of it seared through the merciful shell of insensibility, forced a brief shriek of pain from his lips, a hoarse, bubbling whisper of sound all the more horrible for its muted agony. And then Andrea was standing upright and Mallory was behind him, cutting swiftly at the ropes that bound the two together.

'Straight into the rocks with him, Andrea, will you?' Mallory whispered. 'Wait for us at the first open space you come to.' Andrea nodded slowly and without raising his head, his hooded eyes bent over the boy in his arms, like a man sunk in thought. Sunk in thought or listening, and all unawares Mallory, too, found himself looking and listening into the thin, lost moaning of the wind, and there was nothing there, only the lifting, dying threnody and the chill of the rain hardening to an ice-cold sleet. He shivered, without knowing why, and listened again; then he shook himself angrily, turned abruptly towards the cliff face and started reeling in the rope. He had it all up, lying round his feet in a limp and rain-sodden tangle when he remembered about the spike still secured to the foot of the chimney, the hundreds of feet of rope suspended from it.

He was too tired and cold and depressed even to feel exasperated with himself. The sight of Stevens and the knowledge of how it was with the boy had affected him more than he knew. Moodily, almost, he kicked the rope over the side again, slid down the chimney, untied the second rope and sent the spike spinning out into the darkness. Less than ten minutes later, the wetly-coiled ropes over his shoulder, he led Miller and Brown into the dark confusion of the rocks.

They found Stevens lying under the lee of a huge boulder, less than a hundred yards inland, in a tiny, cleared space barely the size of a billiard table. An oilskin was spread beneath him on the sodden, gravelly earth, a camouflage cape covered most of his body: it was bitterly cold now, but the rock broke the force of the wind, sheltered the boy from the driving sleet. Andrea looked up as the three men dropped into the hollow and lowered their gear to the ground; already, Mallory could see, Andrea had rolled the trouser up beyond the knee and cut the heavy jackboot away from the mangled leg.

'Sufferin' Christ!' The words, half-oath, half-prayer, were torn involuntarily from Miller: even in the deep gloom the shattered leg looked ghastly. Now he dropped on one knee and stooped low over it. 'What a mess!' he murmured slowly. He looked up over his shoulder. 'We've gotta do something about that leg, boss, and we've no damned time to lose. This kid's a good canditate for the mortuary.'

'I know. We've got to save him, Dusty, we've just *got* to.' All at once this had become terribly important to Mallory. He dropped down on his knees. 'Let's have a look at him.'

Impatiently Miller waved him away.

'Leave this to me, boss.' There was a sureness, a sudden authority in his voice that held Mallory silent. 'The medicine pack, quick – and undo that tent.'

'You sure you can handle this?' God knew, Mallory thought, he didn't really doubt him – he was conscious only of gratitude, of a profound relief, but he felt he had to say something. 'How are you going—'

'Look, boss,' Miller said quietly. 'All my life I've worked with just three things – mines, tunnels and explosives. They're kinda tricky things, boss. I've seen hundreds of busted arms and legs – and fixed most of them myself.' He grinned wryly in the darkness. 'I was boss myself, then – just one of my privileges, I reckon.'

'Good enough!' Mallory clapped him on the shoulder. 'He's all yours, Dusty. But the tent!' Involuntarily he looked over his shoulder in the direction of the cliff. 'I mean—'

'You got me wrong, boss.' Miller's hands, steady and precise with the delicate certainty of a man who has spent a lifetime with high explosive, were busy with a swab and disinfectant. 'I wasn't fixin' on settin' up a base hospital. But we need tent-poles – splints for his legs.'

'Of course, of course. The poles. Never occurred to me for splints – and I've been thinking of nothing else for—'

'They're not too important, boss.' Miller had the medicine pack open now, rapidly selecting the items he wanted with the aid of a hooded torch. 'Morphine – that's the first thing, or this kid's goin' to die of shock. And then shelter, warmth, dry clothin'—'

'Warmth! Dry clothing!' Mallory interrupted incredulously. He looked down at the unconscious boy, remembering how Stevens had lost them the stove and all the fuel, and his mouth twisted in bitterness. His own executioner. . . . 'Where in God's name are we going to find them?'

'I don't know, boss,' Miller said simply. 'But we gotta find them. And not just to lessen shock. With a leg like this and soaked to the skin, he's bound to get pneumonia. And then as much sulfa as that bloody great hole in his leg will take – one touch of sepsis in the state this kid's in . . .' His voice trailed away into silence.

Mallory rose to his feet.

'I reckon you're the boss.' It was a very creditable imitation of the American's drawl, and Miller looked up quickly, surprise melting into a tired smile, then looked away again. Mallory could hear the chatter of his teeth as he bent over Stevens, and sensed rather than saw that he was shivering violently, continuously, but oblivious to it all in his complete concentration on the job in hand. Miller's clothes, Mallory remembered again, were completely saturated: not for the first time, Mallory wondered how he had managed to get himself into such a state with a waterproof covering him.

'You fix him up. I'll find a place.' Mallory wasn't as confident as he felt: still, on the scree-strewn, volcanic slopes of these hills behind, there ought to be a fair chance of finding a rock shelter, if not a cave. Or there would have been in day-light: as it was they would just have to trust to luck to stumble on one. . . . He saw that Casey Brown, grey-faced with exhaustion and illness – the after-effects of carbon monoxide poisoning are slow to disappear – had risen unsteadily to his feet and was making for a gap between the rocks.

'Where are you going, Chief?'

'Back for the rest of the stuff, sir.'

'Are you sure you can manage?' Mallory peered at him closely. 'You don't look any too fit to me.'

'I don't feel it either,' Brown said frankly. He looked at Mallory. 'But with all respects, sir, I don't think you've seen yourself recently.'

'You have a point,' Mallory acknowledged. 'All right then, come on. I'll go with you.'

For the next ten minutes there was silence in the tiny clearing, a silence broken only by the murmurs of Miller and Andrea working over the shattered leg, and the moans of the injured man as he twisted and struggled feebly in his dark abyss of pain: then gradually the morphine took effect and the struggling lessened and died away altogether, and Miller was able to work rapidly, without fear of interruption. Andrea had an oilskin outstretched above them. It served a double purpose – it curtained off the sleet that swept round them from time to time and blanketed the pinpoint light of the rubber torch he held in his free hand. And then the leg was set and bandaged and as heavily splinted as possible and Miller was on his feet, straightening his aching back.

'Thank Gawd that's done,' he said wearily. He gestured at Stevens. 'I feel just the way that kid looks.' Suddenly he stiffened, stretched out a warning arm. 'I can hear something, Andrea,' he whispered.

Andrea laughed. 'It's only Brown coming back, my friend. He's been coming this way for over a minute now.'

'How do you know it's Brown?' Miller challenged. He felt vaguely annoyed with himself and unobtrusively shoved his ready automatic back into his pocket.

'Brown is a good man among rocks,' Andrea said gently; 'but he is tired. But Captain Mallory . . .' He shrugged. 'People call me "the big cat" I know, but among the mountains and rocks the captain is more than a cat.

He is a ghost, and that was how men called him in Crete. You will know he is here when he touches you on the shoulder.'

Miller shivered in a sudden icy gust of sleet.

'I wish you people wouldn't creep around so much,' he complained. He looked up as Brown came round the corner of a boulder, slow with the shambling, stumbling gait of an exhausted man. 'Hi, there, Casey. How are things goin'?'

'Not too bad.' Brown murmured his thanks as Andrea took the box of explosives off his shoulder and lowered it easily to the ground. 'This is the last of the gear. Captain sent me back with it. We heard voices some way along the cliff. He's staying behind to see what they say when they find Stevens gone.' Wearily he sat down on top of the box. 'Maybe he'll get some idea of what they're going to do next, if anything.'

'Seems to me he could have left you there and carried that damned box back himself,' Miller growled. Disappointment in Mallory made him more outspoken than he'd meant to be. 'He's much better off than you are right now, and I think it's a bit bloody much . . .' He broke off and gasped in pain as Andrea's finger caught his arm like giant steel pincers.

'It is not fair to talk like that, my friend,' Andrea said reproachfully. 'You forget, perhaps, that Brown here cannot talk or understand a word of German?'

Miller rubbed his bruised arm tenderly, shaking his head in slow self-anger and condemnation.

'Me and my big mouth,' he said ruefully. 'Always talkin' outa turn Miller, they call me. Your pardon, one and all. . . . And what is next on the agenda, gentlemen?'

'Captain says we're to go straight on into the rocks and up the right shoulder of this hill here.' Brown jerked a thumb in the direction of the vague mass, dark and strangely foreboding, that towered above and beyond them. 'He'll catch us up within fifteen minutes or so.' He grinned tiredly at Miller. 'And we're to leave this box and a rucksack for him to carry.'

'Spare me,' Miller pleaded. 'I feel only six inches tall as it is.' He looked down at Stevens, lying quietly under the darkly gleaming wetness of the oilskins, then up at Andrea. 'I'm afraid, Andrea—'

'Of course, of course!' Andrea stooped quickly, wrapped the oilskins round the unconscious boy and rose to his feet, as effortlessly as if the oilskins had been empty.

'I'll lead the way,' Miller volunteered. 'Mebbe I can pick an easy path for you and young Stevens.' He swung generator and rucksacks on to his shoulder, staggering under the sudden weight; he hadn't realized he was so weak. 'At first, that is,' he amended. 'Later on, you'll have to carry us both.'

Mallory had badly miscalculated the time it would require to overtake the others; over an hour had elapsed since Brown had left him, and still there were no signs of the others. And with seventy pounds on his back, he wasn't making such good time himself.

It wasn't all his fault. The returning German patrol, after the first shock of discovery, had searched the cliff-top again, methodically and with exasperating slowness. Mallory had waited tensely for someone to suggest descending and examining the chimney – the gouge-marks of the spikes on the rock would have been a dead giveaway – but nobody even mentioned it.

With the guard obviously fallen to his death, it would have been a pointless thing to do anyway. After an unrewarding search, they had debated for an unconscionable time as to what they should do next. Finally they had done nothing. A replacement guard was left, and the rest made off along the cliff, carrying their rescue equipment with them.

The three men ahead had made surprisingly good time, although the conditions, admittedly, were now much easier. The heavy fall of boulders at the foot of the slope had petered out after another fifty yards, giving way to broken scree and rain-washed rubble. Possibly he had passed them, but it seemed unlikely: in the intervals between these driving sleet showers – it was more like hail now – he was able to scan the bare shoulder of the hill, and nothing moved. Besides, he knew that Andrea wouldn't stop until he reached what promised at least a bare minimum of shelter, and as yet these exposed windswept slopes had offered nothing that even remotely approached that.

In the end, Mallory almost literally stumbled upon both men and shelter. He was negotiating a narrow, longitudinal spine of rock, had just crossed its razor-back, when he heard the murmur of voices beneath him and saw a tiny glimmer of light behind the canvas stretching down from the overhang of the far wall of the tiny ravine at his feet.

Miller started violently and swung round as he felt the hand on his shoulder; the automatic was half-way out of his pocket before he saw who it was and sunk back heavily on the rock behind him.

'Come, come, now! Trigger-happy.' Thankfully Mallory slid his burden from his aching shoulders and looked across at the softly laughing Andrea. 'What's so funny?'

'Our friend here.' Andrea grinned again. 'I told him that the first thing he would know of your arrival would be when you touched him on the shoulder. I don't think he believed me.'

'You might have coughed or somethin',' Miller said defensively. 'It's my nerves, boss,' he added plaintively. 'They're not what they were forty-eight hours ago.'

Mallory looked at him disbelievingly, made to speak, then stopped short as he caught sight of the pale blur of a face propped up against a rucksack. Beneath the white swathe of a bandaged forehead the eyes were open, looking steadily at him. Mallory took a step forward, sank down on one knee.

'So you've come round at last!' He smiled into the sunken parchment face and Stevens smiled back, the bloodless lips whiter than the face itself. He looked ghastly. 'How do you feel, Andy?'

'Not too bad, sir. Really I'm not.' The bloodshot eyes were dark and filled with pain. His gaze fell and he looked down vacantly at his bandaged leg, looked up again, smiled uncertainly at Mallory. 'I'm terribly sorry about all this, sir. What a bloody stupid thing to do.'

'It wasn't a stupid thing.' Mallory spoke with slow, heavy emphasis. 'It was criminal folly.' He knew everyone was watching them, but knew, also, that Stevens had eyes for him alone. 'Criminal, unforgivable folly,' he went on quietly, '– and I'm the man in the dock. I'd suspected you'd lost a lot of blood on the boat, but I didn't know you had these big gashes on your forehead. I should have made it my business to find out.' He smiled wryly. 'You should have heard what these two insubordinate characters had to say to me about it when they got to the top. . . . And they were right. You should never have been asked to bring up the rear in the state you were in. It was madness.' He grinned again. 'You should have been hauled up like a sack of coals like the intrepid mountaineering team of Miller and Brown. . . . God knows how you ever made it – I'm sure you'll never know.' He leaned forward, touched Stevens's sound knee. 'Forgive me, Andy. I honestly didn't realize how far through you were.'

Stevens stirred uncomfortably, but the dead pallor of the high-boned cheeks was stained with embarrassed pleasure.

'Please, sir,' he pleaded. 'Don't talk like that. It was just one of these things.' He paused, eyes screwed shut and indrawn breath hissing sharply through his teeth as a wave of pain washed up from his shattered leg. Then he looked at Mallory again. 'And there's no credit due to me for the climb,' he went on quietly. 'I hardly remember a thing about it.'

Mallory looked at him without speaking, eyebrows arched in mild interrogation.

'I was scared to death every step of the way up,' Stevens said simply. He was conscious of no surprise, no wonder that he was saying the thing he would have died rather than say. 'I've never been so scared in all my life.'

Mallory shook his head slowly from side to side, stubbled chin rasping in his cupped palm. He seemed genuinely puzzled. Then he looked down at Stevens and smiled quizzically.

'Now I know you *are* new to this game, Andy.' He smiled again. 'Maybe you think I was laughing and singing all the way up that cliff? Maybe you think *I* wasn't scared?' He lit a cigarette and gazed at Stevens through a cloud of drifting smoke. 'Well, I wasn't. "Scared" isn't the word – I was bloody well terrified. So was Andrea here. We knew too much not to be scared.'

'Andrea!' Stevens laughed, then cried out as the movement triggered off a crepitant agony in his bone-shattered leg. For a moment Mallory thought he had lost consciousness, but almost at once he spoke again, his voice husky with pain. 'Andrea!' he whispered. 'Scared! I don't believe it.'

'Andrea *was* afraid.' The big Greek's voice was very gentle. 'Andrea *is* afraid. Andrea is always afraid. That is why I have lived so long.' He stared down at his great hands. 'And why so many have died. They were not so afraid as I. They were not afraid of everything a man could be afraid of, there was always something they forgot to fear, to guard against. But Andrea was afraid of everything – and he forgot nothing. It is as simple as that.'

He looked across at Stevens and smiled.

'There are no brave men and cowardly men in the world, my son. There are only brave men. To be born, to live, to die – that takes courage enough in itself, and more than enough. We are all brave men and we are all afraid, and what the world calls a brave man, he, too, is brave and afraid like all the rest of us. Only he is brave for five minutes longer. Or sometimes ten minutes, or twenty minutes – or the time it takes a man sick and bleeding and afraid to climb a cliff.'

Stevens said nothing. His head was sunk on his chest, and his face was hidden. He had seldom felt so happy, seldom so at peace with himself. He had known that he could not hide things from men like Andrea and Mallory, but he had not known that it would not matter. He felt he should say something, but he could not think what and he was deathly tired. He knew, deep down, that Andrea was speaking the truth, but not the whole truth; but he was too tired to care, to try to work things out.

Miller cleared his throat noisily.

'No more talkin', Lieutenant,' he said firmly. 'You gotta lie down, get yourself some sleep.'

Stevens looked at him, then at Mallory in puzzled inquiry.

'Better do what you're told, Andy,' Mallory smiled. 'Your surgeon and medical adviser talking. He fixed your leg.'

'Oh! I didn't know. Thanks, Dusty. Was it very – difficult?'

Miller waved a deprecatory hand.

'Not for a man of my experience. Just a simple break,' he lied easily. 'Almost let one of the others do it. . . . Give him a hand to lie down, will you, Andrea?' He jerked his head towards Mallory. 'Boss?'

The two men moved outside, turning their backs to the icy wind.

'We gotta get a fire, dry clothing, for that kid,' Miller said urgently. 'His pulse is about 140, temperature 103. He's runnin' a fever, and he's losin' ground all the time.'

'I know, I know,' Mallory said worriedly. 'And there's not a hope of getting any fuel on this damned mountain. Let's go in and see how much dried clothing we can muster between us.'

He lifted the edge of the canvas and stepped inside. Stevens was still awake. Brown and Andrea on either side of him. Miller was on his heels.

'We're going to stay here for the night,' Mallory announced, 'so let's make things as snug as possible. Mind you,' he admitted, 'We're a bit too near the cliff for comfort, but old Jerry hasn't a clue we're on the island, and we're out of sight of the coast. Might as well make ourselves comfortable.'

'Boss . . .' Miller made to speak, then fell silent again. Mallory looked at him in surprise, saw that he, Brown and Stevens were looking at one another, uncertainty, then doubt and a dawning, sick comprehension in their eyes. A sudden anxiety, the sure knowledge that something was far wrong, struck at Mallory like a blow.

'What's up?' he demanded, sharply. 'What is it?'

'We have bad news for you, boss,' Miller said carefully. 'We should have told you right away. Guess we all thought that one of the others would have told you. . . . Remember that sentry you and Andrea shoved over the side?'

Mallory nodded, sombrely. He knew what was coming.

'He fell on top of that reef twenty-thirty feet or so from the cliff,' Miller went on. 'Wasn't much of him left, I guess, but what was was jammed between two rocks. He was really stuck good and fast.'

'I see,' Mallory murmured. 'I've been wondering all night how you managed to get so wet under your rubber cape.'

'I tried four times, boss,' Miller said quietly. 'The others had a rope round me.' He shrugged his shoulders. 'Not a chance. Them gawddamned waves just flung me back against the cliff every time.'

'It will be light in three or four hours,' Mallory murmured. 'In four hours they will know we are on the island. They will see him as soon as it's dawn and send a boat to investigate.'

'Does it really matter, sir,' Stevens suggested. 'He could still have fallen.'

Mallory eased the canvas aside and looked out into the night. It was bitterly cold and the snow was beginning to fall all around them. He dropped the canvas again.

'Five minutes,' he said absently. 'We will leave in five minutes.' He looked at Stevens and smiled faintly. 'We are forgetful too. We should have told you. Andrea stabbed the sentry through the heart.'

The hours that followed were hours plucked from the darkest nightmare, endless, numbing hours of stumbling and tripping and falling and getting up again, of racked bodies and aching, tortured muscles, of dropped loads and frantic pawing around in the deepening snow, of hunger and thirst and all-encompassing exhaustion.

They had retraced their steps now, were heading WNW back across the shoulder of the mountain – almost certainly the Germans would think they had gone due north, heading for the centre of the island. Without compass, stars or moon to guide, Mallory had nothing to orientate them but the feel of the slope of the mountain and the memory of the map Vlachos had shown them in Alexandria. But by and by he was reasonably certain that they had rounded the mountain and were pushing up some narrow gorge into the interior.

The snow was the deadly enemy. Heavy, wet and feathery, it swirled all around them in a blanketing curtain of grey, sifted down their necks and jackboots, worked its insidious way under their clothes and up their sleeves, blocked their eyes and ears and mouths, pierced and then anaesthetized exposed faces, and turned gloveless hands into leaden lumps of ice, benumbed and all but powerless. All suffered, and suffered badly, but Stevens most of all. He had lost consciousness again within minutes of leaving the cave and clad in clinging, sodden clothes as he was, he now lacked even the saving warmth generated by physical activity. Twice Andrea had stopped and felt for the beating of the heart, for he thought that the boy had died: but he could feel nothing for there was no feeling left in his hands, and he could only wonder and stumble on again.

About five in the morning, as they were climbing up the steep valley head above the gorge, a treacherous, slippery slope with only a few stunted carob trees for anchor in the sliding scree, Mallory decided that they must rope up for safety's sake. In single file they scrambled and struggled up the ever-steepening slope for the next twenty minutes: Mallory, in the lead, did not even dare to think how Andrea was getting on behind him. Suddenly the slope eased, flattened out completely, and almost before they realized what was happening they had crossed the high divide, still roped together and in driving, blinding snow with zero visibility, and were sliding down the valley on the other side.

They came to the cave at dawn, just as the first grey stirrings of a bleak and cheerless day struggled palely through the lowering, snow-filled sky to the east. Monsieur Vlachos had told them that the south of Navarone was honey-combed with caves, but this was the first they had seen, and even then it was no cave but a dark, narrow tunnel in a great heap of piled volcanic slabs, huge, twisted layers of rock precariously poised in a gully that threaded down the slope towards some broad and unknown valley a thousand, two thousand feet, beneath them, a valley still shrouded in the gloom of night.

It was no cave, but it was enough. For frozen, exhausted, sleep-haunted men, it was more than enough, it was more than they had ever hoped for. There was room for them all, the few cracks were quickly blocked against the drifting snow, the entrance curtained off by the boulder-weighted tent.

Somehow, impossibly almost in the cramped darkness, they stripped Stevens of his sea- and rain-soaked clothes, eased him into a providentially zipped sleeping-bag, forced some brandy down his throat and cushioned the blood-stained head on some dry clothing. And then the four men, even the tireless Andrea, slumped down to the sodden, snow-chilled floor of the cave and slept like men already dead, oblivious alike of the rocks on the floor, the cold, their hunger and their clammy, saturated clothing, oblivious even to the agony of returning circulation in their frozen hands and faces.

Chapter Seven

Tuesday 1500–1900

The sun, rime-ringed and palely luminous behind the drifting cloud-wrack, was far beyond its zenith and dipping swiftly westwards to the snowlimned shoulder of the mountain when Andrea lifted the edge of the tent, pushed it gently aside and peered out warily down the smooth sweep of the mountainside. For a few moments he remained almost motionless behind the canvas, automatically easing cramped and aching leg muscles, narrowed, roving eyes gradually accustoming themselves to the white glare of the glistening, crystalline snow. And then he had flitted noiselessly out of the mouth of the tunnel and reached far up the bank of the gully in half a dozen steps; stretched full length against the snow, he eased himself smoothly up the slope, lifted a cautious eye over the top.

Far below him stretched the great, curved sweep of an almost perfectly symmetrical valley – a valley born abruptly in the cradling embrace of steep-walled mountains and falling away gently to the north. That towering, buttressed giant on his right that brooded darkly over the head of the valley, its peak hidden in the snow clouds – there could be no doubt about that, Andrea thought. Mt Kostos, the highest mountain in Navarone: they had crossed its western flank during the darkness of the night. Due east and facing his own at perhaps five miles' distance, the third mountain was barely less high: but its northern flank fell away more quickly, debouching on to the plains that lay to the north-east of Navarone. And about four miles away to the north-north-east, far beneath the snowline and the isolated shepherds' huts, a tiny, flat-roofed township lay in a fold in the hills, along the bank of the little stream that wound its way through the valley. That could only be the village of Margaritha.

Even as he absorbed the topography of the valley, his eyes probing every dip and cranny in the hills for a possible source of danger, Andrea's mind was racing back over the last two minutes of time, trying to isolate, to remember the nature of the alien sound that had cut through the cocoon of sleep and brought him instantly to his feet, alert and completely awake, even before his conscious mind had time to register the memory of the sound. And then he heard it again, three times in as many seconds, the high-pitched, lonely wheep of a whistle, shrill peremptory blasts that echoed briefly and died along the lower slopes of Mt Kostos: the final echo still hung faintly on the air as Andrea pushed himself backwards and slid down to the floor of the gully.

He was back on the bank within thirty seconds, cheek muscles contracting involuntarily as the ice-chill eyepieces of Mallory's Zeiss-Ikon binoculars screwed into his face. There was no mistaking them now, he thought grimly, his first, fleeting impression had been all too accurate. Twenty-five, perhaps thirty soldiers in all, strung out in a long, irregular line, they were advancing slowly across the flank of Kostos, combing every gully, each jumbled confusion of boulders that lay in their path. Every man was clad in a snow-suit, but even at a distance of two miles they were easy to locate: the arrow-heads of their strapped skis angled up above shoulders and hooded heads: startlingly black against the sheer whiteness of the snow, the skis bobbed and weaved in disembodied drunkenness as the men slipped and stumbled along the scree-strewn slopes of the mountain. From time to time a man near the centre of the line pointed and gestured with an alpenstock, as if co-ordinating the efforts of the search party. The man with the whistle, Andrea guessed.

'Andrea!' The call from the cave mouth was very soft. 'Anything wrong?'

Finger to his lips, Andrea twisted round in the snow. Mallory was standing by the canvas screen. Dark-jowled and crumple-clothed, he held up one hand against the glare of the snow while the other rubbed the sleep from his blood-shot eyes. And then he was limping forward in obedience to the crooking of Andrea's finger, wincing in pain at every step he took. His toes were swollen and skinned, gummed together with congealed blood. He had not had his boots off since he had taken them from the feet of the dead German sentry: and now he was almost afraid to remove them, afraid of what he would find. . . . He clambered slowly up the bank of the gully and sank down in the snow beside Andrea.

'Company?'

'The very worst of company,' Andrea murmured. 'Take a look, my Keith.' He handed over the binoculars, pointed down to the lower slopes of Mt Kostos. 'Your friend Jensen never told us that they were here.'

Slowly, Mallory quartered the slopes with the binoculars. Suddenly the line of searchers moved into his field of vision. He raised his head, adjusted the focus impatiently, looked briefly once more, then lowered the binoculars with a restrained deliberation of gesture that held a wealth of bitter comment.

'The WGB,' he said softly.

'A Jaeger battalion,' Andrea conceded. 'Alpine Corps – their finest mountain troops. This is most inconvenient, my Keith.'

Mallory nodded, rubbed his stubbled chin.

'If anyone can find us, they can. And they'll find us.' He lifted the glasses to look again at the line of advancing men. The painstaking thoroughness of the search was disturbing enough: but even more threatening, more frightening, was the snail-like relentlessness, the inevitability of the approach of these tiny figures. 'God knows what the Alpenkorps is doing here,' Mallory went on. 'It's enough that they are here. They must know that we've landed and spent the morning searching the eastern saddle of Kostos – that was the obvious route for us to break into the interior. They've drawn a blank there, so now they're working their way over to the other saddle. They must be pretty nearly certain that we're carrying a wounded man with us and that we can't have got very far. It's only going to be a matter of time, Andrea.'

'A matter of time,' Andrea echoed. He glanced up at the sun, a sun all but invisible in a darkening sky. 'An hour, an hour and a half at the most. They'll be here before the sun goes down. And we'll still be here.' He glanced quizzically at Mallory. 'We cannot leave the boy. And we cannot get away if we take the boy – and then he would die anyway.'

'We will not be here,' Mallory said flatly. 'If we stay we all die. Or finish up in one of those nice little dungeons that Monsieur Vlachos told us about.'

'The greatest good of the greatest number,' Andrea nodded slowly. 'That's how it has to be, has it not, my Keith? The greatest number. That is what Captain Jensen would say.' Mallory stirred uncomfortably, but his voice was steady enough when he spoke.

'That's how I see it, too, Andrea. Simple proportion – twelve hundred to one. You know it has to be this way.' Mallory sounded tired.

'Yes, I know. But you are worrying about nothing.' Andrea smiled. 'Come, my friend. Let us tell the others the good news.' Miller looked up as the two men came in, letting the canvas screen fall shut behind them. He had unzipped the side of Stevens's sleeping-bag and was working on the mangled leg. A pencil flashlight was propped on a rucksack beside him.

'When are we goin' to do somethin' about this kid, boss?' The voice was abrupt, angry, like his gesture towards the sleep-drugged boy beside him. 'This damned waterproof sleeping-bag is soaked right through. So's the kid – and he's about frozen stiff: his leg feels like a side of chilled beef. He's gotta have heat, boss, a warm room and hot drinks – or he's finished. Twenty-four hours.' Miller shivered and looked slowly round the broken walls of the rock-shelter. 'I reckon he'd have less than an even chance in a first-class general hospital. . . . He's just wastin' his time keepin' on breathin' in this gawddamned ice-box.'

Miller hardly exaggerated. Water from the melting snow above trickled continuously down the clammy, green-lichened walls of the cave or dripped directly on to the half-frozen gravelly slush on the floor of the cave. With no through ventilation and no escape for the water accumulating at the sides of the shelter, the whole place was dank and airless and terribly chill.

'Maybe he'll be hospitalized sooner than you think,' Mallory said dryly. 'How's his leg?'

'Worse.' Miller was blunt. 'A helluva sight worse. I've just chucked in another handful of sulpha and tied things up again. That's all I can do, boss, and it's just a waste of time anyway. . . . What was that crack about a hospital?' he added suspiciously.

'That was no crack,' Mallory said soberly, 'but one of the more unpleasant facts of life. There's a German search party heading this way. They mean business. They'll find us, all right.'

Miller swore. 'That's handy, that's just wonderful,' he said bitterly. 'How far away, boss?'

'An hour, maybe a little more.'

'And what are we goin' to do with Junior, here? Leave him? It's his only chance, I reckon.'

'Stevens comes with us.' There was a flat finality in Mallory's voice. Miller looked at him for a long time in silence: his face was very cold.

'Stevens comes with us,' Miller repeated. 'We drag him along with us until he's dead – that won't take long – and then we leave him in the snow. Just like that, huh?'

'Just like that, Dusty.' Absently Mallory brushed some snow off his clothes, and looked up again at Miller. 'Stevens knows too much. The Germans will have guessed why we're on the island, but they won't know how we propose to get inside the fortress – and they don't know when the Navy's coming through. But Stevens does. They'll make him talk. Scopolamine will make anyone talk.'

'Scopolamine! On a dying man?' Miller was openly incredulous.

'Why not? I'd do the same myself. If you were the German commandant and you knew that your big guns and half the men in your fortress were liable to be blown to hell any moment, you'd do the same.'

Miller looked at him, grinned wryly, shook his head.

'Me and my—'

'I know. You and your big mouth.' Mallory smiled and clapped him on the shoulder. 'I don't like it one little bit more than you do, Dusty.' He turned away and crossed to the other side of the cave. 'How are you feeling, Chief?'

'Not too bad, sir.' Casey Brown was only just awake, numbed and shivering in sodden clothes. 'Anything wrong?'

'Plenty,' Mallory assured him. 'Search party moving this way. We'll have to pull out inside half an hour.' He looked at his watch. 'Just on four o'clock. Do you think you could raise Cairo on the set?'

'Lord only knows,' Brown said frankly. He rose stiffly to his feet. 'The radio didn't get just the best of treatment yesterday. I'll have a go.'

'Thanks, Chief. See that your aerial doesn't stick up above the sides of the gully.' Mallory turned to leave the cave, but halted abruptly at the sight of Andrea squatting on a boulder just beside the entrance. His head bent in concentration, the big Greek had just finished screwing telescopic sights on to the barrel of his 7.92 mm Mauser and was now deftly wrapping a sleeping-bag lining round its barrel and butt until the entire rifle was wrapped in a white cocoon.

Mallory watched him in silence. Andrea glanced up at him, smiled, rose to his feet and reached out for his rucksack. Within thirty seconds he was clad from head to toe in his mountain camouflage suit, was drawing tight the purse-strings of his snowhood and easing his feet into the rucked elastic anklets of his canvas boots. Then he picked up the Mauser and smiled slightly.

'I thought I might be taking a little walk, Captain,' he said apologetically. 'With your permission, of course.'

Mallory nodded his head several times in slow recollection.

'You said I was worrying about nothing,' he murmured. 'I should have known. You might have told me, Andrea.' But the protest was automatic, without significance. Mallory felt neither anger nor even annoyance at this tacit arrogation of his authority. The habit of command died hard in Andrea: on such occasions as he ostensibly sought approval for or consulted about a proposed course of action it was generally as a matter of courtesy and to give information as to his intentions. Instead of resentment, Mallory could feel only an overwhelming relief and gratitude to the smiling giant who towered above him: he had talked casually to Miller about driving Stevens till he died and then abandoning him, talked with an indifference that masked a mind sombre with bitterness at what he must do, but even so he had not known how depressed, how sick at heart this decision had left him until he knew it was no longer necessary.

'I am sorry.' Andrea was half-contrite, half-smiling. 'I should have told you. I thought you understood. . . . It is the best thing to do, yes?'

'It is the only thing to do,' Mallory said frankly. 'You're going to draw them off up the saddle?'

'There is no other way. With their skis they would overtake me in minutes if I went down into the valley. I cannot come back, of course, until it is dark. You will be here?'

'Some of us will.' Mallory glanced across the shelter where a waking Stevens was trying to sit up, heels of his palms screwing into his exhausted eyes. 'We must have food and fuel, Andrea,' he said softly. 'I am going down into the valley tonight.'

'Of course, of course. We must do what we can.' Andrea's face was grave, his voice only a murmur. 'As long as we can. He is only a boy, a child almost. . . . Perhaps it will not be long.' He pulled back the curtain, looked out at the evening sky. 'I will be back by seven o'clock.'

'Seven o'clock,' Mallory repeated. The sky, he could see, was darkening already, darkening with the gloom of coming snow, and the lifting wind was beginning to puff little clouds of air-spun, flossy white into the little gully. Mallory shivered and caught hold of the massive arm. 'For God's sake, Andrea,' he urged quietly, 'look after yourself!'

'Myself?' Andrea smiled gently, no mirth in his eyes, and as gently he disengaged his arm. 'Do not think about me.' The voice was very quiet, with an utter lack of arrogance. 'If you must speak to God, speak to Him about these poor devils who are looking for us.' The canvas dropped behind him and he was gone.

For some moments Mallory stood irresolutely at the mouth of the cave, gazing out sightlessly through the gap in the curtain. Then he wheeled abruptly, crossed the floor of the shelter and knelt in front of Stevens. The boy was propped up against Miller's anxious arm, the eyes lack-lustre and expressionless, bloodless cheeks deep-sunken in a grey and parchment face. Mallory smiled at him: he hoped the shock didn't show in his face.

'Well, well, well. The sleeper awakes at last. Better late then never.' He opened his waterproof cigarette case, proffered it to Stevens. 'How are you feeling now, Andy?'

'Frozen, sir.' Stevens shook his head at the case and tried to grin back at Mallory, a feeble travesty of a smile that made Mallory wince.

'And the leg?'

'I think it must be frozen, too.' Stevens looked down incuriously at the sheathed whiteness of his shattered leg. 'Anyway, I can't feel a thing.'

'Frozen!' Miller's sniff was a masterpiece of injured pride. 'Frozen, he says! Gawddamned ingratitude. It's the first-class medical care, if I do say so myself!'

Stevens smiled, a fleeting, absent smile that flickered over his face and was gone. For long moments he kept staring down at his leg, then suddenly lifted his head and looked directly at Mallory.

'Look, sir, there's no good kidding ourselves.' The voice was soft, quite toneless. 'I don't want to seem ungrateful and I hate even the idea of cheap heroics, but – well, I'm just a damned great millstone round your necks and—'

'Leave you, eh?' Mallory interrupted. 'Leave you to die of the cold or be captured by the Germans. Forget it, laddie. We can look after you – and these ruddy guns – at the same time.'

'But, sir—'

'You insult us, Lootenant.' Miller sniffed again. 'Our feelings are hurt. Besides, as a professional man I gotta see my case through to convalescence, and if you think I'm goin' to do that in any gawddamned dripping German dungeon, you can—'

'Enough!' Mallory held up his hand. 'The subject is closed.' He saw the stain high up on the thin cheeks, the glad light that touched the dulled eyes, and felt the self-loathing and the shame well up inside him, shame for the gratitude of a sick man who did not know that their concern stemmed not from solicitude but from fear that he might betray them. . . . Mallory bent forward and began to unlace his high jackboots. He spoke without looking up.

'Dusty.'

'Yeah?'

'When you're finished boasting about your medical prowess, maybe you'd care to use some of it. Come and have a look at these feet of mine, will you? I'm afraid the sentry's boots haven't done them a great deal of good.'

Fifteen painful minutes later Miller snipped off the rough edges of the adhesive bandage that bound Mallory's right foot, straightened up stiffly and contemplated his handiwork with pride.

'Beautiful, Miller, beautiful,' he murmured complacently. 'Not even in Johns Hopkins in the city of Baltimore . . .' He broke off suddenly, frowned down at the thickly bandaged feet and coughed apologetically. 'A small point has just occurred to me, boss.'

'I thought it might eventually,' Mallory said grimly. 'Just how do you propose to get my feet into these damned boots again?' He shivered involuntarily as he pulled on a pair of thick woollen socks, matted and sodden with melted snow, picked up the German sentry's boots, held them at arm's length and examined them in disgust. 'Sevens, at the most – and a darned small sevens at that!'

'Nines,' Stevens said laconically. He handed over his own jackboots, one of them slit neatly down the sides where Andrea had cut it open. 'You can fix that tear easily enough, and they're no damned good to me now. No arguments, sir, please.' He began to laugh softly, broke off in a sharply indrawn hiss of pain as the movement jarred the broken bones, took a couple of deep, quivering breaths, then smiled whitely. 'My first – and probably my last – contribution to the expedition. What sort of medal do you reckon they'll give me for that, sir?'

Mallory took the boots, looked at Stevens a long moment in silence, then turned as the tarpaulin was pushed aside. Brown stumbled in, lowered the transmitter and telescopic aerial to the floor of the cave and pulled out a tin of cigarettes. They slipped from his frozen fingers, fell into the icy mud at his feet, became brown and sodden on the instant. He swore, briefly, and without enthusiasm, beat his numbed hands across his chest, gave it up and sat down heavily on a convenient boulder. He looked tired and cold and thoroughly miserable.

Mallory lit a cigarette and passed it across to him.

'How did it go, Casey? Manage to raise them at all?'

'They managed to raise me – more or less. Reception was lousy.' Brown drew the grateful tobacco smoke deep down into his lungs. 'And I couldn't get through at all. Must be that damned great hill to the south there.'

'Probably,' Mallory nodded. 'And what news from our friends in Cairo? Exhorting us to greater efforts? Telling us to get on with the job?'

'No news at all. Too damn' worried about the silence at this end. Said that from now on they were going to come through every four hours, acknowledgments or no. Repeated that about ten times, then signed off.'

'That'll be a great help,' Miller said acidly. 'Nice to know they're on our side. Nothin' like moral support.' He jerked his thumb towards the mouth of the cave. 'Reckon them bloodhounds would be scared to death if they knew. . . . Did you take a gander at them before you came in?'

'I didn't have to,' Brown said morosely. 'I could hear them – sounded like the officer in charge shouting directions.' Mechanically, almost, he picked up his automatic rifle, eased the clip in the magazine. 'Must be less than a mile away now.'

The search party, more closely bunched by this time, was less than a mile, was barely half a mile distant from the cave when the Oberleutnant in charge saw that the right wing of his line, on the steeper slopes to the south, was lagging behind once more. Impatiently he lifted his whistle to his mouth for the three sharp peremptory blasts that would bring his weary men stumbling into line again. Twice the whistle shrilled out its imperative urgency, the piercing notes echoing flatly along the snowbound slopes and dying away in the valley below: but the third *wheep* died at birth, caught up again and tailed off in a wailing, eldritch diminuendo that merged with dreadful harmony into a long bubbling scream of agony. For two or three seconds the Oberleutnant stood motionless in his tracks, his face shocked and contorted: then he jack-knifed violently forward and pitched down into the crusted snow. The burly sergeant beside him stared down at the fallen officer, looked up in sudden horrified understanding, opened his mouth to shout, sighed and toppled wearily over the body at his feet, the evil, whip-lash crack of the Mauser in his ears as he died.

High up on the western slopes of Mount Kostos, wedged in the V between two great boulders, Andrea gazed down the darkening mountainside over the depressed telescopic sights of his rifle and pumped another three rounds into the wavering, disorganized line of searchers. His face was quite still, as immobile as the eyelids that never flickered to the regular crashing of his Mauser, and drained of all feeling. Even his eyes reflected the face, eyes neither hard nor pitiless, but simply empty and almost frighteningly remote, a remoteness that mirrored his mind, a mind armoured for the moment against all thought and sensation, for Andrea knew that he must not think about this thing. To kill, to take the life of his fellows, that was the supreme evil, for life was a gift that it was not his to take away. Not even in fair fight. And this was murder.

Slowly Andrea lowered the Mauser, peered through the drifting gun-smoke that hung heavily in the frosty evening air. The enemy had vanished, completely, rolled behind scattered boulders or burrowed frantically into the blanketing anonymity of the snow. But they were still there, still potentially as dangerous as ever. Andrea knew that they would recover fast from the death of their officer – there were no finer, no more tenacious fighters in Europe than the ski-troops of the Jaeger mountain battalion – and would come after him, catch him and kill him if humanly possible. That was why Andrea's first case had been to kill their officer – he might not have come after him, might have stopped to puzzle out the reason for this unprovoked flank attack.

Andrea ducked low in reflex instinct as a sudden burst of automatic fire whined in murderous ricochet off the boulders before him. He had expected this. It was the old classic infantry attack pattern – advance under covering fire, drop, cover your mate and come again. Swiftly Andrea rammed home another charge into the magazine of his Mauser, dropped flat on his face and inched his way along behind the low line of broken rock that extended fifteen or twenty yards to his right – he had chosen his ambush point with care – and then petered out. At the far end he pulled his snow hood down to the level of his brows and edged a wary eye round the corner of the rock.

Another heavy burst of automatic fire smashed into the boulders he had just left, and half a dozen men – three from either side of the line – broke cover, scurried along the slope in a stumbling, crouching run, then pitched forward into the snow again. *Along* the slope – the two parties had run in opposite directions. Andrea lowered his head and rubbed the back of a massive hand across the stubbled grizzle of his chin. Awkward, damned awkward. No frontal attack for the foxes of the WGB. They were extending their lines on either side, the points hooking round in a great, encircling half-moon. Bad enough for himself, but he could have coped with that – a carefully reconnoitred escape gully wound up the slope behind him. But he hadn't forseen what was obviously going to happen: the curving crescent of line to the west was going to sweep across the rock-shelter where the others lay hidden.

Andrea twisted over on his back and looked up at the evening sky. It was darkening by the moment, darkening with the gloom of coming snow, and daylight was beginning to fail. He twisted again and looked across the great swelling shoulder of Mount Kostos, looked at the few scattered rocks and shallow depressions that barely dimpled the smooth convexity of the slope. He took a second quick look round the rock as the rifles of the WGB opened up once more, saw the same encircling manoeuvre being executed again, and waited no longer. Firing blindly downhill, he half-rose to his feet and flung himself out into the open, finger squeezing on the trigger, feet driving desperately into the frozen snow as he launched himself towards the nearest rock-cover, forty yards away if an inch. Thirty-five yards to go, thirty, twenty and still not a shot fired, a slip, a stumble on the sliding scree a catlike recovery, ten yards, still miraculously immune, and then he had dived into shelter to land on chest and stomach with a sickening impact that struck cruelly into his ribs and emptied his lungs with an explosive gasp.

Fighting for breath, he struck the magazine cover, rammed home another charge, risked a quick peep over the top of the rock and catapulted himself to his feet again, all inside ten seconds. The Mauser held across his body opened up again, firing downhill at vicious random, for Andrea had eyes only for the smoothly-treacherous ground at his feet, for the scree-lined depression so impossibly far ahead. And then the Mauser was empty, useless in his hand, and every gun far below had opened up, the shells whistling above his head or blinding him with spurting gouts of snow as they ricocheted off the solid rock. But twilight was touching the hills, Andrea was only a blur, a swiftly-flitting blur against a ghostly background, and uphill accuracy was notoriously difficult at any time. Even so, the massed fire from below was steadying and converging, and Andrea waited no longer. Unseen hands plucking wickedly at the flying tails of his snow-smock, he flung himself almost horizontally forward and slid the last ten feet face down into the waiting depression.

Stretched full length on his back in the hollow, Andrea fished out a steel mirror from his breast pocket and held it gingerly above his head. At first he could see nothing, for the darkness was deeper below and the mirror misted from the warmth of his body. And then the film vanished in the chill mountain air and he could see two, three and then half a dozen men breaking cover, heading at a clumsy run straight up the face of the hill – and two of them had come from the extreme right of the line. Andrea lowered the mirror and relaxed with a long sigh of relief, eyes crinkling in a smile. He looked up at the sky, blinked as the first feathery flakes of falling snow melted on his eyelids and smiled again. Almost lazily he brought out another charger for the Mauser, fed more shells into the magazine.

'Boss?' Miller's voice was plaintive.

'Yes? What is it?' Mallory brushed some snow off his face and the collar of his smock and peered into the white darkness ahead.

'Boss, when you were in school did you ever read any stories about folks gettin' lost in a snowstorm and wanderin' round and round in circles for days?'

'We had exactly the same book in Queenstown,' Mallory conceded.

'Wanderin' round and round until they died?' Miller persisted.

'Oh, for heaven's sake!' Mallory said impatiently. His feet, even in Stevens's roomy boots, hurt abominably. 'How can we be wandering in circles if we're going downhill all the time? What do you think we're on – a bloody spiral staircase?'

Miller walked on in hurt silence, Mallory beside him, both men ankle-deep in the wet, clinging snow that had been falling so silently, so persistently, for the past three hours since Andrea had drawn off the Jaeger search party. Even in mid-winter in the White Mountains in Crete Mallory could recall no snowfall so heavy and continuous. So much for the Isles of Greece and the eternal sunshine that gilds them yet, he thought bitterly. He hadn't reckoned on this when he'd planned on going down to Margaritha for food and fuel, but even so it wouldn't have made any difference to his decision. Although in less pain now, Stevens was becoming steadily weaker, and the need was desperate.

With moon and stars blanketed by the heavy snow-clouds – visibility, indeed, was hardly more than ten feet in any direction – the loss of their compasses had assumed a crippling importance. He didn't doubt his ability to find the village – it was simply a matter of walking downhill till they came to the stream that ran through the valley, then following that north till they came to Margaritha – but if the snow didn't let up their chances of locating that tiny cave again in the vast sweep of the hillsides . . .

Mallory smothered an exclamation as Miller's hand closed round his upper arm, dragged him down to his knees in the snow. Even in that moment of unknown danger he could feel a slow stirring of anger against himself, for his attention had been wandering along with his thoughts. . . . He lifted his hand as vizor against the snow, peered out narrowly through the wet, velvety curtain of white that swirled and eddied out of the darkness before him. Suddenly he had it – a dark, squat shape only feet away. They had all but walked straight into it.

'It's the hut,' he said softly in Miller's ear. He had seen it early in the afternoon, half-way between their cave and Margaritha, and almost in a line with both. He was conscious of relief, an increase in confidence: they would be in the village in less than half an hour. 'Elementary navigation, my dear Corporal,' he murmured. 'Lost and wandering in circles, my foot! Just put your faith . . .'

He broke off as Miller's fingers dug viciously into his arm, as Miller's head came close to his own.

'I heard voices, boss.' The words were a mere breath of sound.

'Are you sure?' Miller's silenced gun, Mallory noticed, was still in his pocket.

Miller hesitated.

'Dammit to hell, boss. I'm sure of nothin',' he whispered irritably. 'I've been imaginin' every damn' thing possible in the past hour!' He pulled the snow hood off his head, the better to listen, bent forward for a few seconds then sank back again. 'Anyway, I'm sure I *thought* I heard somethin'.'

'Come on. Let's take a look-see.' Mallory was on his feet again. 'I think you're mistaken. Can't be the Jaeger boys – they were half-way back across Mount Kostos when we saw them. And the shepherds only use these places in the summer months.' He slipped the safety catch of his Colt .455, walked slowly, at a half-crouch, towards the nearest wall of the hut, Miller at his shoulder.

They reached the hut, put their ears against the frail, tar-paper walls. Ten seconds passed, twenty, half a minute, then Mallory relaxed.

'Nobody at home. Or if they are, they're keeping mighty quiet. But no chances, Dusty. You go that way. I'll go this. Meet at the door – that'll be on the opposite side, facing into the valley. . . . Walk wide at the corners – never fails to baffle the unwary.'

A minute later both men were inside the hut, the door shut behind them. The hooded beam of Mallory's torch probed into every corner of the ramshackle cabin. It was quite empty – an earthen floor, a rough wooden bunk, a dilapidated stove with a rusty lantern standing on it, and that was all. No table, no chair, no chimney, not even a window.

Mallory walked over to the stove, picked up the lamp and sniffed it.

'Hasn't been used for weeks. Still full of kerosene, though. Very useful in that damn' dungeon up there – if we can ever find the place. . . .'

He froze into a sudden listening immobility, eyes unfocused and head cocked slightly to one side. Gently, ever so gently, he set the lamp down, walked leisurely across to Miller.

'Remind me to apologize at some future date,' he murmured. 'We have company. Give me your gun and keep talking.'

'Castelrosso again,' Miller complained loudly. He hadn't even raised an eyebrow. 'This is downright monotonous. A Chinaman – I'll bet it's a Chinaman this time.' But he was already talking to himself.

The silenced automatic balanced at his waist, Mallory walked noiselessly round the hut, four feet out from the walls. He had passed two corners, was just rounding the third when, out of the corner of his eye, he saw a vague figure behind him rising up swiftly from the ground and lunging out with upraised arm. Mallory stepped back quickly under the blow, spun round, swung his balled fist viciously and backwards into the stomach of his attacker. There was a sudden explosive gasp of agony as the man doubled up, moaned and crumpled silently to the ground. Barely in time Mallory arrested the downward, clubbing swipe of his reversed automatic.

Gun reversed again, the butt settled securely in his palm, Mallory stared down unblinkingly at the huddled figure, at the primitive wooden baton still clutched in the gloved right hand, at the unmilitary looking knapsack strapped to his back. He kept his gun lined up on the fallen body, waiting: this had been just too easy, too suspicious. Thirty seconds passed and still the figure on the ground hadn't stirred. Mallory took a short step forward and carefully, deliberately and none too gently kicked the man on the outside of the right knee. It was an old trick, and he'd never known it to fail – the pain was brief, but agonizing. But there was no movement, no sound at all.

Quickly Mallory stooped, hooked his free hand round the knapsack shoulder straps, straightened and made for the door, half-carrying, half-dragging his captive. The man was no weight at all. With a proportionately much heavier garrison than ever in Crete, there would be that much less food for the islanders, Mallory mused compassionately. There would be very little indeed. He wished he hadn't hit him so hard.

Miller met him at the open door, stooped wordlessly, caught the unconscious man by the ankles and helped Mallory dump him unceremoniously on the bunk in the far corner of the hut.

'Nice goin', boss,' he complimented. 'Never heard a thing. Who's the heavyweight champ?'

'No idea.' Mallory shook his head in the darkness. 'Just skin and bones, that's all, just skin and bones. Shut the door, Dusty, and let's have a look at what we've got.'

Chapter Eight

Tuesday 1900–0015

A minute passed, two, then the little man stirred, moaned and pushed himself to a sitting position. Mallory held his arm to steady him, while he shook his bent head, eyes screwed tightly shut as he concentrated on clearing the muzziness away. Finally he looked up slowly, glanced from Mallory to Miller and back at Mallory again in the feeble light of the newly-lit shuttered lantern. Even as the men watched, they could see the colour returning to the swarthy cheeks, the indignant bristling of the heavy, dark moustache, the darkening anger in the eyes. Suddenly the man reached up, tore Mallory's hand away from his arm.

'Who are you?' He spoke in English, clear, precise, with hardly a trace of accent.

'Sorry, but the less you know the better.' Mallory smiled, deliberately to rob the words of offence. 'I mean that for your own sake. How are you feeling now?'

Tenderly the little man massaged his midriff, flexed his leg with a grimace of pain.

'You hit me very hard.'

'I had to.' Mallory reached behind him and picked up the cudgel the man had been carrying. 'You tried to hit me with this. What did you expect me to do – take my hat off so you could have a better swipe at me?'

'You are very amusing.' Again he bent his leg, experimentally, looking up at Mallory in hostile suspicion. 'My knee hurts me,' he said accusingly.

'First things first. Why the club?'

'I meant to knock you down and have a look at you,' he explained impatiently. 'It was the only safe way. You might have been one of the WGB. . . . Why is my knee—?'

'You had an awkward fall,' Mallory said shamelessly. 'What are you doing here?'

'Who are you?' the little man countered.

Miller coughed, looked ostentatiously at his watch.

'This is all very entertainin', boss—'

'True for you, Dusty. We haven't all night.' Quickly Mallory reached behind him, picked up the man's rucksack, tossed it across to Miller. 'See what's in there, will you?' Strangely, the little man made no move to protest.

'Food!' Miller said reverently. 'Wonderful, wonderful food. Cooked meat, bread, cheese – and wine.' Reluctantly Miller closed the bag and looked curiously at their prisoner. 'Helluva funny time for a picnic.'

'So! An American, a Yankee.' The little man smiled to himself. 'Better and better!'

'What do you mean?' Miller asked suspiciously.

'See for yourself,' the man said pleasantly. He nodded casually to the far corner of the room. 'Look there.'

Mallory spun round, realized in a moment that he had been tricked, jerked back again. Carefully he leaned forward and touched Miller's arm.

'Don't look round too quickly, Dusty. And don't touch your gun. It seems our friend was not alone.' Mallory tightened his lips, mentally cursed himself for his obtuseness. Voices – Dusty had said there had been voices. Must be even more tired than he had thought. . . .

A tall, lean man blocked the entrance to the doorway. His face was shadowed under an enveloping snow-hood, but there was no mistaking the gun in his hand. A short Lee Enfield rifle, Mallory noted dispassionately.

'Do not shoot!' The little man spoke rapidly in Greek. 'I am almost sure that they are those whom we seek, Panayis.'

Panayis! Mallory felt the wave of relief wash over him. That was one of the names Eugene Vlachos had given him, back in Alexandria.

'The tables turned, are they not?' The little man smiled at Mallory, the tired eyes crinkling, the heavy black moustache lifting engagingly at one corner. 'I ask you again, who are you?'

'SOE,' Mallory answered unhesitatingly.

The man nodded in satisfaction. 'Captain Jensen sent you?'

Mallory sank back on the bunk and sighed in long relief.

'We are among friends, Dusty.' He looked at the little man before him. 'You must be Louki – the first plane tree in the square in Margaritha?'

The little man beamed. He bowed, stretched out his hand.

'Louki. At your service, sir.'

'And this of course, is Panayis?'

The tall man in the doorway, dark, saturnine, unsmiling, inclined his head briefly but said nothing.

'You have us right!' The little man was beaming with delight. 'Louki and Panayis. They know about us in Alexandria and Cairo, then?' he asked proudly.

'Of course!' Mallory smothered a smile. 'They spoke highly of you. You have been of great help to the Allies before.'

'And we will again,' Louki said briskly. 'Come, we are wasting time. The Germans are on the hills. What help can we give you?'

'Food, Louki. We need food – we need it badly.'

'We have it!' Proudly, Louki gestured at the rucksacks. 'We were on our way up with it.'

'You were on your way. . . .' Mallory was astonished. 'How did you know where we were – or even that we were on the island?'

Louki waved a deprecating hand.

'It was easy. Since first light German troops have been moving south through Margaritha up into the hills. All morning they combed the east col of Kostos. We knew someone must have landed, and that the Germans were looking for them. We heard, too, that the Germans had blocked the cliff path on the south coast, at both ends. So you must have come over the west col. They would not expect that – you fooled them. So we came to find you.'

'But you would never have found us—'

'We would have found you.' There was complete certainty in the voice. 'Panayis and I – we know every stone, every blade of grass in Navarone.' Louki shivered suddenly, stared out bleakly through the swirling snow. 'You couldn't have picked worse weather.'

'We couldn't have picked better,' Mallory said grimly.

'Last night, yes,' Louki agreed. 'No one would expect you in that wind and rain. No one would hear the aircraft or even dream that you would try to jump—'

'We came by sea,' Miller interrupted. He waved a negligent hand. 'We climbed the south cliff.'

'What? The south cliff!' Louki was frankly disbelieving. 'No one could climb the south cliff. It is impossible!'

'That's the way we felt when we were about half-way up,' Mallory said candidly. 'But Dusty, here, is right. That's how it was.'

Louki had taken a step back: his face was expressionless.

'I say it is impossible,' he repeated flatly.

'He is telling the truth, Louki,' Miller cut in quietly. 'Do you never read newspapers?'

'Of course I read newspapers!' Louki bristled with indignation. 'Do you think I am – how you say – illiterate?'

'Then think back to just before the war,' Miller advised. 'Think of mountaineerin' – and the Himalayas. You must have seen his picture in the papers – once, twice, a hundred times.' He looked at Mallory consideringly.

'Only he was a little prettier in those days. You must remember. This is Mallory, Keith Mallory of New Zealand.'

Mallory said nothing. He was watching Louki, the puzzlement, the comical screwing up of the eyes, head cocked to one side: then, all at once, something clicked in the little man's memory and his face lit up in a great, crinkling smile that swamped every last trace of suspicion. He stepped forward, hand outstretched in welcome.

'By heaven, you are right! Mallory! Of course I know Mallory!' He grabbed Mallory's hand, pumped it up and down with great enthusiasm. 'It is indeed as the American says. You need a shave. . . . And you look older.'

'I feel older,' Mallory said gloomily. He nodded at Miller. 'This is Corporal Miller, an American citizen.'

'Another famous climber?' Louki asked eagerly. 'Another tiger of the hills, yes?'

'He climbed the south cliff as it has never been climbed before,' Mallory answered truthfully. He glanced at his watch, then looked directly at Louki. 'There are others up in the hills. We need help, Louki. We need it badly and we need it at once. You know the danger if you are caught helping us?'

'Danger?' Louki waved a contemptuous hand. 'Danger to Louki and Panayis, the foxes of Navarone? Impossible! We are the ghosts of the night.' He hitched his pack higher up on his shoulders. 'Come. Let us take this food to your friends.'

'Just a minute.' Mallory's restraining hand was on his arm. 'There are two other things. We need heat – a stove and fuel, and we need—'

'Heat! A stove!' Louki was incredulous. 'Your friends in the hills – what are they? A band of old women?'

'And we also need bandages and medicine,' Mallory went on patiently. 'One of our friends has been terribly injured. We are not sure, but we do not think he will live.'

'Panayis!' Louki barked. 'Back to the village.' Louki was speaking in Greek now. Rapidly he issued his orders, had Mallory describe where the rock-shelter was, made sure that Panayis understood, then stood a moment in indecision, pulling at an end of his moustache. At length he looked up at Mallory.

'Could you find this cave again by yourself?'

'Lord only knows,' Mallory said frankly. 'I honestly don't think so.'

'Then I must come with you. I had hoped – you see, it will be a heavy load for Panayis – I have told him to bring bedding as well – and I don't think—'

'I'll go along with him,' Miller volunteered. He thought of his back-breaking labours on the caique, the climb up the cliff, their forced march through the mountains. 'The exercise will do me good.'

Louki translated his offer to Panayis – taciturn, apparently, only because of his complete lack of English – and was met by what appeared to be a torrent of protest. Miller looked at him in astonishment.

'What's the matter with old sunshine here?' he asked Mallory. 'Doesn't seem any too happy to me.'

'Says he can manage OK and wants to go by himself,' Mallory interpreted. 'Thinks you'll slow him up on the hills.' He shook his head in mock wonder. 'As if any man could slow Dusty Miller up!'

'Exactly!' Louki was bristling with anger. Again he turned to Panayis, fingers stabbing the empty air to emphasize his words. Miller turned, looked apprehensively at Mallory.

'What's he tellin' him now, boss?'

'Only the truth,' Mallory said solemnly. 'Saying he ought to be honoured at being given the opportunity of marching with Monsieur Miller, the world-famous American climber.' Mallory grinned. 'Panayis will be on his mettle tonight – determined to prove that a Navaronian can climb as well and as fast as any man.'

'Oh, my Gawd!' Miller moaned.

'And on the way back, don't forget to give Panayis a hand up the steeper bits.'

Miller's reply was luckily lost in a sudden flurry of snow-laden wind.

That wind was rising steadily now, a bitter wind that whipped the heavy snow into their bent faces and stung the tears from their blinking eyes. A heavy, wet snow that melted as it touched, and trickled down through every gap and ching in their clothing until they were wet and chilled and thoroughly miserable. A clammy, sticky snow that built up layer after energy-sapping layer under their leaden-footed boots, until they stumbled along inches above the ground, leg muscles aching from the sheer accumulated weight of snow. There was no visibility worthy of the name, not even of a matter of feet, they were blanketed, swallowed up by an impenetrable cocoon of swirling grey and white, unchanging, featureless: Louki strode on diagonally upwards across the slope with the untroubled certainty of a man walking up his own garden path.

Louki seemed as agile as a mountain goat, and as tireless. Nor was his tongue less nimble, less unwearied than his legs. He talked incessantly, a man overjoyed to be in action again, no matter what action so long as it was against the enemy. He told Mallory of the last three attacks on the island and how they had so bloodily failed – the Germans had been somehow forewarned of the seaborne assault, had been waiting for the Special Boat Service and the Commandos with everything they had and had cut them to pieces, while the two airborne groups had had the most evil luck, been delivered up to the enemy by misjudgment, by a series of unforeseeable coincidences; or how Panayis and himself had on both occasions narrowly escaped with their lives – Panayis had actually been captured the last time, had killed both his guards and escaped unrecognized; of the disposition of the German troops and check-points throughout the island, the location of the road blocks on the only two roads; and finally, of what little he himself knew of the layout of the fortress of Navarone itself. Panayis, the dark one, could tell him more of that, Louki said: twice Panayis had been inside the fortress, once for an entire night: the guns, the control rooms, the barracks, the officers' quarters, the magazine, the turbo rooms, the sentry points – he knew where each one lay, to the inch.

Mallory whistled softly to himself. This was more than he had ever dared hope for. They had still to escape the net of searchers, still to reach the fortress, still to get inside it. But once inside – and Panayis must know how to get inside. . . . Unconsciously Mallory lengthened his stride, bent his back to the slope.

'Your friend Panayis must be quite something,' he said slowly. 'Tell me more about him, Louki.'

'What can I tell you?' Louki shook his head in a little flurry of snowflakes. 'What do I know of Panayis? What does anyone know of Panayis? That he has the luck of the devil, the courage of a madman and that sooner the lion will lie down with the lamb, the starving wolf spare the flock, than Panayis breathe the same air as the Germans? We all know that, and we knew nothing of Panayis. All I know is that I thank God I am no German, with Panayis on the island. He strikes by stealth, by night, by knife and in the back.' Louki crossed himself. 'His hands are full of blood.'

Mallory shivered involuntarily. The dark, sombre figure of Panayis, the memory of the expressionless face, the hooded eyes, were beginning to fascinate him.

'There's more to him than that, surely,' Mallory argued. 'After all, you are both Navaronians—'

'Yes, yes, that is so.'

'This is a small island, you've lived together all your lives—'

'Ah, but that is where the Major is wrong!' Mallory's promotion in rank was entirely Louki's own idea: despite Mallory's protests and explanations he seemed determined to stick to it. 'I, Louki, was for many years in foreign lands, helping Monsieur Vlachos. Monsieur Vlachos,' Louki said with pride, 'is a very important Government official.'

'I know,' Mallory nodded. 'A consul. I've met him. He is a very fine man.'

'You have met him! Monsieur Vlachos?' There was no mistaking the gladness, the delight in Louki's voice. 'That is good! That is wonderful! Later you must tell me more. He is a great man. Did I ever tell you—'

'We were speaking about Panayis,' Mallory reminded him gently.

'Ah, yes, Panayis. As I was saying, I was away for a long time. When I came back, Panayis was gone. His father had died, his mother had married again and Panayis had gone to live with his stepfather and two little stepsisters in Crete. His stepfather, half-fisherman, half-farmer, was killed in fighting the Germans near Candia – this was in the beginning. Panayis took over the boat of his father, helped many of the Allies to escape until he was caught by the Germans, strung up by his wrists in the village square – where his family lived – not far from Casteli. He was flogged till the white of his ribs, of his backbone, was there for all to see, and left for dead. Then they burnt the village and Panayis's family – disappeared. You understand, Major?'

'I understand,' Mallory said grimly. 'But Panayis—'

'He should have died. But he is tough, that one, tougher than a knot in an old carob tree. Friends cut him down during the night, took him away into the hills till he was well again. And then he arrived back in Navarone, God knows how. I think he came from island to island in a small rowing-boat. He never says why he came back – I think it gives him greater pleasure to kill on his own native island. I do not know, Major. All I know is that food and sleep, the sunshine, women and wine – all these are nothing and less than nothing to the dark one.' Again Louki crossed himself. 'He obeys me, for I am the steward of the Vlachos family, but even I am afraid of him. To kill, to keep on killing, then kill again – that is the very breath of his being.' Louki stopped momentarily, sniffed the air like a hound seeking some fugitive scent, then kicked the snow off his boots and struck off up the hill at a tangent. The little man's unhesitating sureness of direction was uncanny.

'How far to go now, Louki?'

'Two hundred yards, Major. No more.' Louki blew some snow off his heavy, dark moustache and swore. 'I shall not be sorry to arrive.'

'Nor I.' Mallory thought of the miserable, draughty shelter in the dripping rocks almost with affection. It was becoming steadily colder as they climbed out of the valley, and the wind was rising, climbing up the register with a steady, moaning whine: they had to lean into it now, push hard against it, to make any progress. Suddenly both men stopped, listened, looked at each other, heads bent against the driving snow. Around them there was only the white emptiness and the silence: there was no sign of what had caused the sudden sound.

'You heard something, too?' Mallory murmured.

'It is only I.' Mallory spun round as the deep voice boomed out behind him and the bulky, white-smocked figure loomed out of the snow. 'A milk wagon on a cobbled street is as nothing compared to yourself and your friend here. But the snow muffled your voices and I could not be sure.'

Mallory looked at him curiously. 'How come you're here, Andrea?'.

'Wood,' Andrea explained. 'I was looking for firewood. I was high up on Kostos at sunset when the snow lifted for a moment. I could have sworn I saw an old hut in a gully not far from here – it was dark and square against the snow. So I left—'

'You are right,' Louki interrupted. 'The hut of old Leri, the mad one. Leri was a goatherd. We all warned him, but Leri would listen and speak to no man, only to his goats. He died in his hut, in a landslide.'

'It is an ill wind ...' Andrea murmured. 'Old Leri will keep us warm tonight.' He checked abruptly as the gully opened up at his feet, then dropped quickly to the bottom, sure-footed as a mountain sheep. He whistled twice, a double high-pitched note, listening intently into the snow for the answering whistle, walked swiftly up the gully. Casey Brown, gun lowered, met them at the entrance to the cave and held back the canvas screen to let them pass inside.

The smoking tallow candle, guttering heavily to one side in the icy draught, filled every corner of the cave with dark and flickering shadows from its erratic flame. The candle itself was almost gone, the dripping wick bending over tiredly till it touched the rock, and Louki, snow-suit cast aside, was lighting another stump of candle from the dying flame. For a moment, both candles flared up together, and Mallory saw Louki clearly for the first time – a small, compact figure in a dark-blue jacket black-braided at the seams and flamboyantly frogged at the breast, the jacket tightly bound to his body by the crimson *tsanta* or cummerbund and, above, the swarthy, smiling face, the magnificent moustache that he flaunted like a banner. A Laughing Cavalier of a man, a miniature d'Artagnan splendidly behung with weapons. And then Mallory's gaze travelled up to the lined, liquid eyes, eyes dark and sad and permanently tired, and his shock, a slow, uncomprehending shock had barely time to register before the stub of the candle had flared up and died and Louki had sunk back into the shadows.

Stevens was stretched in a sleeping-bag, his breathing harsh and shallow and quick. He had been awake when they had arrived but had refused all food and drink, and turned away and drifted off into an uneasy jerky sleep. He seemed to be suffering no pain at all now: a bad sign, Mallory thought bleakly, the worst possible. He wished Miller would return. . . .

Casey Brown washed down the last few crumbs of bread with a mouthful of wine, rose stiffly to his feet, pulled the screen aside and peered out mournfully at the falling snow. He shuddered, let the canvas fall, lifted up his transmitter and shrugged into the shoulder straps, gathered up a coil of rope, a torch and a groundsheet. Mallory looked at his watch: it was fifteen minutes to midnight. The routine call from Cairo was almost due.

'Going to have another go, Casey? I wouldn't send a dog out on a night like this.'

'Neither would I,' Brown said morosely. 'But I think I'd better sir. Reception is far better at night and I'm going to climb uphill a bit to get a clearance from that damned mountain there: I'd be spotted right away if I tried to do that in daylight.'

'Right you are, Casey. You know best.' Mallory looked at him curiously. 'What's all the extra gear for?'

'Putting the set under the groundsheet then getting below it myself with the torch,' Brown explained. 'And I'm pegging the rope here, going to pay it out on my way up. I'd like to be able to get back some time.'

'Good enough,' Mallory approved. 'Just watch it a bit higher up. This gully narrows and deepens into a regular ravine.'

'Don't you worry about me, sir,' Brown said firmly. 'Nothing's going to happen to Casey Brown.' A snow-laden gust of wind, the flap of the canvas and Brown was gone.

'Well, if Brown can do it . . .' Mallory was on his feet now, pulling his snow-smock over his head. 'Fuel, gentlemen – old Leri's hut. Who's for a midnight stroll?'

Andrea and Louki were on their feet together, but Mallory shook his head.

'One's enough. I think someone should stay to look after Stevens.'

'He's sound asleep,' Andrea murmured. 'He can come to no harm in the short time we are away.'

'I wasn't thinking of that. It's just that we can't take the chance of him falling into German hands. They'd make him talk, one way or another. It would be no fault of his – but they'd make him talk. It's too much of a risk.'

'Pouf!' Louki snapped his fingers. 'You worry about nothing, Major. There isn't a German within miles of here. You have my word.'

Mallory hesitated, then grinned. 'You're right. I'm getting the jumps.' He bent over Stevens, shook him gently. The boy stirred and moaned, opened his eyes slowly.

'We're going out for some firewood,' Mallory said. 'Back in a few minutes. You be OK?'

'Of course, sir. What can happen? Just leave a gun by my side – and blow out the candle.' He smiled. 'Be sure to call out before you come in!'

Mallory stooped, blew out the candle. For an instant the flame flared then died and every feature, every person in the cave was swallowed up in the thick darkness of a winter midnight. Abruptly Mallory turned on his heel and pushed out through the canvas into the drifting, wind-blown snow already filling up the floor of the gully. Andrea and Louki close behind.

It took them ten minutes to find the ruined hut of the old goatherd, another five for Andrea to wrench the door off its shattered hinges and smash it up to manageable lengths, along with the wood from the bunk and table, another ten to carry back with them to the rock-shelter as much wood as they could conveniently rope together and carry. The wind, blowing straight north off Kostos, was in their faces now – faces numbed with the chill, wet lash of the driving snow, and blowing almost at gale force: they were not sorry to reach the gully again, drop down gratefully between the sheltering walls.

Mallory called softly at the mouth of the cave. There was no reply, no movement from inside. He called again, listened intently as the silent seconds went by, turned his head and looked briefly at Andrea and Louki. Carefully, he laid his bundle of wood in the snow, pulled out his Colt and torch, eased aside the curtain, lamp switch and Colt safety-catch clicking as one.

The spotlight beam lit up the floor at the mouth of the cave, passed on, settled, wavered, probed into the farthest corner of the shelter, returned again to the middle of the cave and steadied there as if the torch were clamped in a vice. On the floor there was only a crumpled, empty sleeping-bag. Andy Stevens was gone.

Chapter Nine

Tuesday Night 0015–0200

'So I was wrong,' Andrea murmured. 'He wasn't asleep.'

'He certainly wasn't,' Mallory agreed firmly. 'He fooled me too – *and* he heard what I said.' His mouth twisted. 'He knows now why we're so anxious to look after him. He knows now that he was right when he spoke about a mill-stone. I should hate to feel the way he must be feeling right now.'

Andrea nodded. 'It is not difficult to guess why he has gone.'

Mallory looked quickly at his watch, pushed his way out of the cave.

'Twenty minutes – he can't have been gone more than twenty minutes. Probably a bit less to make sure we were well clear. He can only drag himself – fifty yards at the most. We'll find him in four minutes. Use your torches and take the hoods off – nobody will see us in this damn' blizzard. Fan out uphill – I'll take the gully in the middle.'

'Uphill?' Louki's hand was on his arm, his voice puzzled. 'But his leg—'

'Uphill, I said,' Mallory broke in impatiently. 'Stevens has brains – and a damn' sight more guts than he thinks we credit him with. He'll figure we'll think he's taken the easy way.' Mallory paused a moment then went on sombrely: 'Any dying man who drags himself out in this lot is going to do nothing the easy way. Come on!'

They found him in exactly three minutes. He must have suspected that Mallory wouldn't fall for the obvious, or he had heard them stumbling up the slope, for he had managed to burrow his way in behind the overhanging snowdrift that sealed off the space beneath a projecting ledge just above the rim of the gully. An almost perfect place of concealment, but his leg betrayed him: in the probing light of his torch Andrea's sharp eyes caught the tiny trickle of blood seeping darkly through the surface of the snow. He was already unconscious when they uncovered him, from cold or exhaustion or the agony of his shattered leg: probably from all three.

Back in the cave again, Mallory tried to pour some ouzo – the fiery, breath-catching local spirit – down Stevens's throat. He had a vague suspicion that this might be dangerous – or perhaps it was only dangerous in cases of shock, his memory was confused on that point – but it seemed better than nothing. Stevens gagged, spluttered and coughed most of it up again, but some at least stayed down. With Andrea's help Mallory tightened the loosened splints on the leg, staunched the oozing blood, and spread below and above the boy every dry covering he could find in the cave. Then he sat back tiredly and fished out a cigarette from his waterproof case. There was nothing more he could do until Dusty Miller returned with Panayis from the village. He was pretty sure there was nothing that Dusty could do for Stevens either. There was nothing anybody could do for him.

Already Louki had a fire burning near the mouth of the cave, the old tinder-dry wood blazing up in a fierce crackling blaze with hardly a wisp of smoke. Almost at once its warmth began to spread throughout the cave, and the three men edged gratefully nearer. From half a dozen points in the roof thin, steadily-increasing streams of water from the melting snows above began to splash down on the gravelly floor beneath: with these and with the heat of the blaze the ground was soon a quagmire. But, especially to Mallory and Andrea, these discomforts were a small price to pay for the privilege of being warm for the first time in over thirty hours. Mallory felt the glow seep through him like a benison, felt his entire body relax, his eyelids grow heavy and drowsy.

Back propped against the wall, he was just drifting off to sleep, still smoking that first cigarette, when there was a gust of wind, a sudden chilling flurry of snow and Brown was inside the cave, wearily slipping the transmitter straps from his shoulders. Lugubrious as ever, his tired eyes lit up momentarily at the sight of the fire. Blue-faced and shuddering with cold – no joke, Mallory thought grimly, squatting motionless for half an hour on that bleak and frozen hillside – he hunched down silently by the fire, dragged out the inevitable cigarette and gazed moodily into the flames, oblivious alike of the clouds of steam that almost immediately enveloped him, of the acrid smell of his singeing clothes. He looked utterly despondent. Mallory reached for a bottle, poured out some of the heated *retsimo* – mainland wine heavily reinforced with resin – and passed it across to Brown.

'Chuck it straight down the hatch,' Mallory advised. 'That way you won't taste it.' He prodded the transmitter with his foot and looked up at Brown again. 'No dice this time either?'

'Raised them no bother, sir.' Brown grimaced at the sticky sweetness of the wine. 'Reception was first class – both here and in Cairo.'

'You got through!' Mallory sat up, leaned forward eagerly. 'And were they pleased to hear from their wandering boys tonight?'

'They didn't say. The first thing they told me was to shut up and stay that way.' Brown poked moodily at the fire with a steaming boot. 'Don't ask me how, sir, but they've been tipped off that enough equipment for two or three small monitoring stations has been sent here in the past fortnight.'

Mallory swore.

'Monitoring stations! That's damned handy, that is!' He thought briefly of the fugitive, nomad existence these same monitoring stations had compelled Andrea and himself to lead in the White Mountains of Crete. 'Dammit, Casey, on an island like this, the size of a soup plate, they can pin-point us with their eyes shut!'

'Aye, they can that, sir,' Brown nodded heavily.

'Have you heard anything of these stations, Louki?' Mallory asked.

'Nothing, Major; nothing.' Louki shrugged. 'I am afraid I do not even know what you are talking about.'

'I don't suppose so. Not that it matters – it's too late now. Let's have the rest of the good news, Casey.'

'That's about it, sir. No sending for me – by order. Restricted to code abbreviations – affirmative, negative, repetitive, wilco and such-like. Continuous sending only in emergency or when concealment's impossible anyway.'

'Like from the condemned cell in these ducky little dungeons in Navarone,' Mallory murmured. ' "I died with my boots on, ma." '

'With all respects, sir, that's not funny,' Brown said morosely. 'Their invasion fleet – mainly caiques and E-boats – sailed this morning from the Piraeus,' he went on. 'About four o'clock this morning. Cairo expects they'll be holding up in the Cyclades somewhere tonight.'

'That's very clever of Cairo. Where the hell else could they hole up?' Mallory lit a fresh cigarette and looked bleakly into the fire. 'Anyway, it's nice to know they're on the way. That the lot, Casey?'

Brown nodded silently.

'Good enough, then. Thanks a lot for going out. Better turn in, catch up with some sleep while you can. . . . Louki reckons we should be down in Margaritha before dawn, hole up there for the day – he's got some sort of abandoned well all lined up for us – and push on to the town of Navarone tomorrow night.'

'My God!' Brown moaned. 'Tonight a leaking cave. Tomorrow night an abandoned well – half-full of water, probably. Where are we staying in Navarone, sir. The crypt in the local cemetery?'

'A singularly apt lodging, the way things are going,' Mallory said dryly. 'We'll hope for the best. We're leaving before five.' He watched Brown lie down beside Stevens and transferred his attention to Louki. The little man was seated on a box on the opposite side of the fire, occasionally turning a heavy stone to be wrapped in cloth and put to Stevens's numbed feet, and blissfully hugging the flames. By and by he became aware of Mallory's close scrutiny and looked up.

'You look worried, Major.' Louki seemed vexed. 'You look – what is the word? – concerned. You do not like my plan, no? I thought we had agreed—'

'I'm not worried about your plan,' Mallory said frankly. 'I'm not even worried about you. It's that box you're sitting on. Enough HE in it to blow up a battleship – and you're only three feet from that fire. It's not just too healthy, Louki.'

Louki shifted uneasily on his seat, tugged at one end of his moustache.

'I have heard that you can throw this TNT into a fire and that it just burns up nicely, like a pine full of sap.'

'True enough,' Mallory acquiesced. 'You can also bend it, break it, file it, saw it, jump on it and hit it with a sledge-hammer, and all you'll get is the benefit of the exercise. But if it starts to sweat in a hot, humid atmosphere – and then the exudation crystallizes. Oh, brother! And it's getting far too hot and sticky in this hole.'

'Outside with it!' Louki was on his feet, backing farther into the cave. 'Outside with it!' He hesitated. 'Unless the snow, the moisture—'

'You can also leave it immersed in salt water for ten years without doing it any harm,' Mallory interrupted didactically. 'But there are some primers there that might come to grief – not to mention that box of detonators beside Andrea. We'll just stick the lot outside, under a cape.'

'Pouf! Louki has a far better idea!' The little man was already slipping into his cloak. 'Old Leri's hut! The very place. Exactly! We can pick it up there whenever we want – and if you have to leave here in a hurry you do not have to worry about it.' Before Mallory could protest, Louki had bent over the box lifted it with an effort, half-walked, half-staggered round the fire, making for the screen. He had hardly taken three steps when Andrea was by his side, had relieved him firmly of the box and tucked it under one arm.

'If you will permit me—'

'No, no!' Louki was affronted. 'I can manage easily. It is nothing.'

'I know, I know,' Andrea said pacifically. 'But these explosives – they must be carried a certain way. I have been trained,' he explained.

'So? I did not realize. Of course it must be as you say! I, then, will bring the detonators.' Honour satisfied, Louki thankfully gave up the argument, lifted the little box and scuttled out of the cave close on Andrea's heels.

Mallory looked at his watch. One o'clock exactly. Miller and Panayis should be back soon, he thought. The wind had passed its peak and the snow was almost gone: the going would be all that easier, but there would be tracks in the snow. Awkward, these tracks, but not fatal – they themselves would be gone before light, cutting straight downhill for the foot of the valley. The snow wouldn't lie there – and even if there were patches they could take to the stream that wound through the valley, leaving no trace behind.

The fire was sinking and the cold creeping in on them again. Mallory shivered in his still wet clothes, threw some more wood on the fire, watched it blaze up, and flood the cave with light. Brown, huddled on a groundsheet, was already asleep. Stevens, his back to him, was lying motionless, his breathing short and quick. God only knew how long the boy would stay alive: he was dying, Miller said, but 'dying' was a very indefinite term: when a man, a terribly injured, dying man, made up his mind not to die he became the toughest, most enduring creature on earth. Mallory had seen it happen before. But maybe Stevens didn't want to live. To live, to overcome these desperate injuries – that would be to prove himself to himself, and to others, and he was young enough, and sensitive enough and had been hurt and had suffered so much in the past that that could easily be the most important thing in the world to him: on the other hand, he knew what an appalling handicap he had become – he had heard Mallory say so; he knew, too, that Mallory's primary concern was not for his welfare but the fear that he would be captured, crack under pressure and tell everything – he had heard Mallory say so; and he knew that he had failed his friends. It was all very difficult, impossible to say how the balance of contending forces would work out eventually. Mallory shook his head, sighed, lit a fresh cigarette and moved closer to the fire.

Andrea and Louki returned less than five minutes later, and Miller and Panayis were almost at their heels. They could hear Miller coming some distance away, slipping, falling and swearing almost continuously as he struggled up the gully under a large and awkward load. He practically fell across the threshold of the cave and collapsed wearily by the fire. He gave the impression of a man who had been through a very great deal indeed. Mallory grinned sympathetically at him.

'Well, Dusty, how did it go? Hope Panayis here didn't slow you up too much.'

Miller didn't seem to hear him. He was gazing incredulously at the fire, lantern jaw drooping open as its significance slowly dawned on him.

'Hell's teeth! Would you look at that!' He swore bitterly. 'Here I spend half the gawddamned night climbing up a gawddamned mountain with a stove and enough kerosene to bath a bloody elephant. And what do I find?' He took a deep breath to tell them what he found, then subsided into a strangled, seething silence.

'A man your age should watch his blood pressure,' Mallory advised him. 'How did the rest of it go?'

'Okay, I guess.' Miller had a mug of ouzo in his hand and was beginning to brighten up again. 'We got the beddin', the medicine kit—'

'If you'll give me the bedding I will get our young friend into it now,' Andrea interrupted.

'And food?' Mallory asked.

'Yeah. We got the grub, boss. Stacks of it. This guy Panayis is a wonder. Bread, wine, goat-cheese, garlic sausages, rice – everything.'

'Rice?' It was Mallory's turn to be incredulous. 'But you can't get the stuff in the islands nowadays, Dusty.'

'Panayis can.' Miller was enjoying himself hugely now. 'He got it from the German commandant's kitchen. Guy by the name of Skoda.'

'The German commandant's – you're joking!'

'So help me, boss, that's Gospel truth.' Miller drained half the ouzo at a gulp and expelled his breath in a long, gusty sigh of satisfaction. 'Little ol' Miller hangs around the back door, knees knockin' like Carmen Miranda's castanets, ready for a smart take off in any direction while Junior here goes in and cracks the joint. Back home in the States he'd make a fortune as a cat-burglar. Comes back in about ten minutes, luggin' that damned suitcase there.' Miller indicated it with a casual wave of his hand. 'Not only cleans out the commandant's pantry, but also borrows his satchel to carry the stuff in. I tell you, boss, associatin' with this character gives me heart attacks.'

'But – but how about guards, about sentries?'

'Taken the night off, I guess, boss. Old Panayis is like a clam – never says a word, and even then I can't understand him. My guess is that everybody's out lookin' for us.'

'There and back and you didn't meet a soul.' Mallory filled him a mug of wine. 'Nice going, Dusty.'

'Panayis's doin', not mine. I just tagged along. Besides, we did run into a couple of Panayis's pals – he hunted them up rather. Musta given him the tip-off about somethin'. He was hoppin' with excitement just afterwards, tried to tell me all about it.' Miller shrugged his shoulders sadly. 'We weren't operatin' on the same wave-length, boss.'

Mallory nodded across the cave. Louki and Panayis were close together, Louki doing all the listening, while Panayis talked rapidly in a low voice, gesticulating with both hands.

'He's still pretty worked up about something,' Mallory said thoughtfully. He raised his voice. 'What's the matter, Louki?'

'Matter enough, Major.' Louki tugged ferociously at the end of his moustache. 'We will have to be leaving soon – Panayis wants to go right away. He has heard that the German garrison is going to make a house-to-house check in our village during the night – about four o'clock, Panayis was told.'

'Not a routine check, I take it?' Mallory asked.

'This has not happened for many months. They must think that you have slipped their patrols and are hiding in the village.' Louki chuckled. 'If you ask me, I don't think they know *what* to think. It is nothing to you, of course. You will not be there – and even if you were they would not find you: and it will make it all the safer for you to come to Margaritha afterwards. But Panayis and I – we must not be found out of our beds. Things would go hard with us.'

'Of course, of course. We must take no risks. But there is plenty of time. You will go down in an hour. But first, the fortress.' He dug into his breast pocket, brought out the map Eugene Vlachos had drawn for him, turned to Panayis and slipped easily into the island Greek. 'Come, Panayis. I hear you know the fortress as Louki here knows his own vegetable patch. I already know much, but I want you to tell me everything about it – the layout, guns, magazines, power rooms, barracks, sentries, guard routine, exits, alarm systems, even where the shadows are deep and the others less deep – just everything. No matter how tiny and insignificant the details may seem to you, nevertheless you must tell me. If a door opens outwards instead of inwards, you must tell me: that could save a thousand lives.'

'And how does the Major mean to get inside?' Louki asked.

'I don't know yet. I cannot decide until I have seen the fortress.' Mallory was aware of Andrea looking sharply at him, then looking away. They had made their plans on the MTB for entering the fortress. But it was the keystone upon which everything depended, and Mallory felt that this knowledge should be confined to the fewest number possible.

For almost half an hour Mallory and the three Greeks huddled over the chart in the light of the flames, Mallory checking on what he had been told, meticulously pencilling in all the fresh information that Panayis had to give him – and Panayis had a very great deal to tell. It seemed almost impossible that a man could have assimilated so much in two brief visits to the fortress – and clandestine visits in the darkness, at that. He had an incredible eye and capacity for detail; and it was a burning hatred of the Germans, Mallory felt certain, that had imprinted these details on an all but photographic memory. Mallory could feel his hopes rising with every second that passed.

Casey Brown was awake again. Tired though he was, the babble of voices had cut through an uneasy sleep. He crossed over to where Andy Stevens, half-awake now, lay propped against the wall, talking rationally at times, incoherently at others. There was nothing for him to do there, Brown saw: Miller, cleaning, dusting and rebandaging the wounds had had all the help he needed – and very efficient help at that – from Andrea. He moved over to the mouth of the cave, listened blankly to the four men talking in Greek, moved out past the screen for a breath of the cold, clean night air. With seven people inside the cave and the fire burning continuously, the lack of almost all ventilation had made it uncomfortably warm.

He was back in the cave in thirty seconds, drawing the screen tightly shut behind him.

'Quiet, everybody!' he whispered softly. He gestured behind him. 'There's something moving out there, down the slope a bit. I heard it twice, sir.'

Panayis swore softly, twisted to his feet like a wild cat. A foot-long, two-edged throwing knife gleamed evilly in his hand and he had vanished through the canvas screen before anyone could speak. Andrea made to follow him, but Mallory stretched out his hand.

'Stay where you are, Andrea. Our friend Panayis is just that little bit too precipitate,' he said softly. 'There may be nothing – or it might be some diversionary move. . . . Oh, damn!' Stevens had just started babbling to himself in a loud voice. 'He would start talking now. Can't you do something . . .'

But Andrea was already bent over the sick boy, holding his hand in his own, smoothing the hot forehead and hair with his free hand and talking to him soothingly, softly, continuously. At first he paid no attention, kept on talking in a rambling, inconsequential fashion about nothing in particular; gradually, however, the hypnotic effect of the stroking hand, the gentle caressing murmur took effect, and the babbling died away to a barely audible muttering and ceased altogether. Suddenly his eyes opened and he was awake and quite rational.

'What is it, Andrea? Why are you—'

'Shh!' Mallory held up his hand. 'I can hear someone—'

'It's Panayis, sir.' Brown had his eye at a crack in the curtain. 'Just moving up the gully.'

Seconds later, Panayis was inside the cave, squatting down by the fire. He looked thoroughly disgusted.

'There is no one there,' he reported. 'Some goats I saw, down the hill, but that was all.' Mallory translated to the others.

'Didn't sound like goats to me.' Brown said doggedly. 'Different kind of sound altogether.'

'I will take a look,' Andrea volunteered. 'Just to make sure. But I do not think the dark one would make a mistake.' Before Mallory could say anything he was gone, as quickly and silently as Panayis. He was back in three minutes, shaking his head. 'Panayis is right. There is no one. I did not even see the goats.'

'And that's what it must have been, Casey,' Mallory said. 'Still, I don't like it. Snow almost dropped, wind dropping and the valley probably swarming with German patrols – I think it's time you two were away. For God's sake, be careful. If anyone tries to stop you, shoot to kill. They'll blame it on us anyway.'

'Shoot to kill!' Louki laughed dryly. 'Unnecessary advice, Major, when the dark one is with us. He never shoots any other way.'

'Right, away you go. Damned sorry you've got yourselves mixed up in all this – but now that you are, a thousand thanks for all you've done. See you at half-past six.'

'Half-past six,' Louki echoed. 'The olive grove on the bank of the stream, south of the village. We will be waiting there.'

Two minutes later they were lost to sight and sound and all was still inside the cave again, except for the faint crackling of the embers of the dying fire. Brown had moved out on guard, and Stevens had already fallen into a restless, pain-filled sleep. Miller bent over him for a moment or two, then moved softly across the cave to Mallory. His right hand held a crumpled heap of bloodstained bandages. He held them out towards Mallory.

'Take a sniff at that, boss,' he asked quietly. 'Easy does it.'

Mallory bent forward, drew away sharply, his nose wrinkled in immediate disgust.

'Good lord, Dusty! That's vile!' He paused, paused in sure, sick certainty. He knew the answer before he spoke. 'What on earth is it?'

'Gangrene.' Miller sat down heavily by his side, threw the bandages into the fire. All at once he sounded tired, defeated. 'Gas gangrene. Spreadin' like a forest fire – and he would have died anyway. I'm just wastin' my time.'

Chapter Ten

Tuesday Night 0400–0600

The Germans took them just after four o'clock in the morning, while they were still asleep. Bone-tired and deep-drugged with this sleep as they were, they had no chance, not the slightest hope of offering any resistance. The conception, timing and execution of the coup were immaculate. Surprise was complete.

Andrea was the first awake. Some alien whisper of sound had reached deep down to that part of him that never slept, and he twisted round and elbowed himself off the ground with the same noiseless speed as his hand reached out for his ready-cocked and loaded Mauser. But the white beam of the powerful torch lancing through the blackness of the cave had blinded him, frozen his stretching hand even before the clipped bite of command from the man who held the torch.

'Still! All of you!' Faultless English, with barely a trace of accent, and the voice glacial in its menace. 'You move, and you die!' Another torch switched on, a third, and the cave was flooded with light. Wide awake, now, and motionless, Mallory squinted painfully into the dazzling beams: in the backwash of reflected light, he could just discern the vague, formless shapes crouched in the mouth of the cave, bent over the dulled barrels of automatic rifles.

'Hands clasped above the heads and back to the wall!' A certainty, an assured competence in the voice that made for instant obedience. 'Take a good look at them, Sergeant.' Almost conversational now, the tone, but neither torch nor gun barrel had wavered a fraction. 'No shadow of expression in their faces, not even a flicker of the eyes. Dangerous men, Sergeant. The English choose their killers well!'

Mallory felt the grey bitterness of defeat wash through him in an almost tangible wave, he could taste the sourness of it in the back of his mouth. For a brief, heart-sickening second he allowed himself to think of what must now inevitably happen and as soon as the thought had come he thrust it savagely away. Everything, every action, every thought, every breath must be on the present. Hope was gone, but not irrecoverably gone: not so long as Andrea lived. He wondered if Casey Brown had seen or heard them coming, and what had happened to him: he made to ask, checked himself just in time. Maybe he was still at large.

'How did you manage to find us.' Mallory asked quietly.

'Only fools burn juniper wood,' the officer said contemptuously. 'We have been on Kostos all day and most of the night. A dead man could have smelt it.'

'On Kostos?' Miller shook his head. 'How could—?'

'Enough!' The officer turned to someone behind him. 'Tear down that screen,' he ordered in German, 'and keep us covered on either side.' He looked back into the cave, gestured almost imperceptibly with his torch. 'All right, you three. Outside – and you had better be careful. Please believe me that my men are praying for an excuse to shoot you down, you murdering swine!' The venomous hatred in his voice carried utter conviction.

Slowly, hands still clasped above their heads, the three men stumbled to their feet. Mallory had taken only one step when the whip-lash of the German's voice brought him up short.

'Stop!' He stabbed the beam of his torch down at the unconscious Stevens, gestured abruptly at Andrea. 'One side, you! Who is this?'

'You need not fear from him,' Mallory said quietly. 'He is one of us but he is terribly injured. He is dying.'

'We will see,' the officer said tightly. 'Move to the back of the cave!' He waited until the three men had stepped over Stevens, changed his automatic rifle for a pistol, dropped to his knees and advanced slowly, torch in one hand, gun in the other, well below the line of fire of the two soldiers who advanced unbidden at his heels. There was no inevitability, a cold professionalism about it all that made Mallory's heart sink.

Abruptly the officer reached out his gun-hand, tore the covers off the boy. A shuddering tremor shook the whole body, his head rolled from side to side as he moaned in unconscious agony. The officer bent quickly over him, the hard, clean lines of the face, the fair hair beneath the hood high-lit in the beam of his own torch. A quick look at Stevens's pain-twisted, emaciated features, a glance at the shattered leg, a brief, distasteful wrinkling of the nose as he caught the foul stench of the gangrene, and he had hunched back on his heels, gently replacing the covers over the sick boy.

'You speak the truth,' he said softly. 'We are not barbarians. I have no quarrel with a dying man. Leave him there.' He rose to his feet, walked slowly backwards. 'The rest of you outside.'

The snow had stopped altogether, Mallory saw, and stars were beginning to twinkle in the clearing sky. The wind, too, had fallen away and was perceptibly warmer. Most of the snow would be gone by midday, Mallory guessed.

Carelessly, incuriously, he looked around him. There was no sign of

Casey Brown. Inevitably Mallory's hopes began to rise. Petty Officer Brown's recommendation for this operation had come from the very top. Two rows of ribbons to which he was entitled but never wore bespoke his gallantry, he had a formidable reputation as a guerrilla fighter – and he had had an automatic rifle in his hand. If he were somewhere out there. . . . Almost as if he had divined his hopes, the German smashed them at a word.

'You wonder where your sentry is, perhaps?' he asked mockingly. 'Never fear, Englishman, he is not far from here, asleep at his post. Very sound asleep, I'm afraid.'

'You've killed him?' Mallory's hands clenched until his palms ached.

The other shrugged his shoulder in vast indifference.

'I really couldn't say. It was all too easy. One of my men lay in the gully and moaned. A masterly performance – really pitiable – he almost had me convinced. Like a fool your man came to investigate. I had another man waiting above, the barrel of his rifle in his hand. A very effective club, I assure you. . . .'

Slowly Mallory unclenched his fists and stared bleakly down the gully. Of course Casey would fall for that, he was bound to after what had happened earlier in the night. He wasn't going to make a fool of himself again, cry 'wolf' twice in succession: inevitably, he had gone to check first. Suddenly the thought occurred to Mallory that maybe Casey Brown *had* heard something earlier on, but the thought vanished as soon as it had come. Panayis did not look like the man to make a mistake: and Andrea never made a mistake; Mallory turned back to the officer again.

'Well, where do we go from here?'

'Margaritha, and very shortly. But one thing first.' The German, his own height to an inch, stood squarely in front of him, levelled revolver at waist height, switched-off torch dangling loosely from his right hand. 'Just a little thing, Englishman. Where are the explosives?' He almost spat the words out.

'Explosives?' Mallory furrowed his brows in perplexity. 'What explosives?' he asked blankly, then staggered and fell to the ground as the heavy torch swept round in a vicious half-circle, caught him flush on the side of the face. Dizzily he shook his head and climbed slowly to his feet again.

'The explosives.' The torch was balanced in the hand again, the voice silky and gentle. 'I asked you where they were.'

'I don't know what you are talking about.' Mallory spat out a broken tooth, wiped some blood off his smashed lips. 'Is this the way the Germans treat their prisoners?' he asked contemptuously.

'Shut up!'

Again the torch lashed out. Mallory was waiting for it, rode the blow as best he could: even so the torch caught him heavily high up on the cheekbone, just below the temple, stunning him with its jarring impact. Seconds passed, then he pushed himself slowly off the snow, the whole side of his face afire with agony, his vision blurred and unfocused.

'We fight a clean war!' The officer was breathing heavily, in barely controlled fury. 'We fight by the Geneva Conventions. But these are for soldiers, not for murdering spies—'

'We are no spies!' Mallory interrupted. He felt as if his head was coming apart.

'Then where are your uniforms?' the officer demanded. 'Spies, I say –

murdering spies who stab in the back and cut men's throats!' The voice was trembling with anger. Mallory was at a loss – nothing spurious about this indignation.

'Cut men's throats?' He shook his head in bewilderment. 'What the hell are you talking about?'

'My own batman. A harmless messenger, a boy only – and he wasn't even armed. We found him only an hour ago. Ach, I waste my time!' He broke off as he turned to watch two men coming up the gully. Mallory stood motionless for a moment, cursing the ill luck that had led the dead man across the path of Panayis – it could have been no one else – then turned to see what had caught the officers attention. He focused his aching eyes with difficulty, looked at the bent figure struggling up the slope, urged on by the ungentle prodding of a bayoneted rifle. Mallory let go a long, silent breath of relief. The left side of Brown's face was caked with blood from a gash above the temple, but he was otherwise unharmed.

'Right! Sit down in the snow, all of you!' He gestured to several of his men. 'Bind their hands!'

'You are going to shoot us now, perhaps?' Mallory asked quietly. It was suddenly, desperately urgent that he should know: there was nothing they could do but die, but at least they could die on their feet, fighting; but if they weren't to die just yet, almost any later opportunity for resistance would be less suicidal than this.

'Not yet, unfortunately. My section commander in Margaritha, Hauptmann Skoda, wishes to see you first – maybe it would be better for you if I *did* shoot you now. Then the Herr Commandant in Navarone – Officer Commanding of the whole island.' The German smiled thinly. 'But only a postponement, Englishman. You will be kicking your heels before the sun sets. We have a short way with spies in Navarone.'

'But, sir! Captain!' Hands raised in appeal, Andrea took a step forward, brought up short as two rifle muzzles ground into his chest.

'Not Captain – Lieutenant,' the officer corrected him. 'Oberleutnant Turzig, at your service. What is it you want, fat one?' he asked contemptuously.

'Spies! You said spies! I am no spy!' The words rushed and tumbled over one another, as if he could not get them out fast enough. 'Before God, I am no spy! I am not one of them.' The eyes were wide and staring, the mouth working soundlessly between the gasped-out sentences. 'I am only a Greek, a poor Greek. They forced me to come along as an interpreter. I swear it, Lieutenant Turzig, I swear it!'

'You yellow bastard!' Miller ground out viciously, then grunted in agony as a rifle butt drove into the small of his back, just above the kidney. He stumbled, fell forward on his hands and knees, realized even as he fell that Andrea was only playing a part, that Mallory had only to speak half a dozen words in Greek to expose Andrea's lie. Miller twisted on his side in the snow, shook his fist weakly and hoped that the contorted pain on his face might be mistaken for fury. 'You two-faced, double-crossing dago! You gawddamned swine, I'll get you . . .' There was a hollow, sickening thud and Miller collapsed in the snow: the heavy ski-boot had caught him just behind the ear.

Mallory said nothing. He did not even glance at Miller. Fists balled helplessly at his sides and mouth compressed, he glared steadily at Andrea through narrowed slits of eyes. He knew the lieutenant was watching him, felt he must back Andrea up all the way. What Andrea intended he could not even begin to guess – but he would back him to the end of the world.

'So!' Turzig murmured thoughtfully. 'Thieves fall out, eh?' Mallory thought he detected the faintest overtones of doubt, of hesitancy, in his voice, but the lieutenant was taking no chances. 'No matter, fat one. You have cast your lot with these assassins. What is it the English say? "You have made your bed, you must lie on it." ' He looked at Andrea's vast bulk dispassionately. 'We may need to strengthen a special gallows for you.'

'No, no, no!' Andrea's voice rose sharply, fearfully, on the last word. 'It is true what I tell you! I am not one of them, Lieutenant Turzig, before God I am not one of them!' He wrung his hands in distress, his great moon-face contorted in anguish. 'Why must I die for no fault of my own? I didn't want to come. I am no fighting man, Lieutenant Turzig!'

'I can see that,' Turzig said dryly. 'A monstrous deal of skin to cover a quivering jelly-bag your size – and every inch of it precious to you.' He looked at Mallory, and at Miller, still lying face down in the snow. 'I cannot congratulate your friends on their choice of companion.'

'I can tell you everything, Lieutenant, I can tell you everything!' Andrea pressed forward excitedly, eager to consolidate his advantage, to reinforce the beginnings of doubt. 'I am no friend of the Allies – I will prove it to you – and then perhaps—'

'You damned Judas!' Mallory made to fling himself forward, but two burly soldiers caught him and pinioned his arms from behind. He struggled briefly, then relaxed, looked balefully at Andrea. 'If you dare to open your mouth, I promise you you'll never live to—'

'Be quiet!' Turzig's voice was very cold. 'I have had enough of recrimination, of cheap melodrama. Another word and you join your friend in the snow there.' He looked at him a moment in silence, then swung back to Andrea. 'I promise nothing. I will hear what you have to say.' He made no attempt to disguise the repugnance in his voice.

'You must judge for yourself.' A nice mixture of relief, earnestness and the dawn of hope, of returning confidence. Andrea paused a minute and gestured dramatically at Mallory, Miller and Brown. 'These are no ordinary soldiers – they are Jellicoe's men, of the Special Boat Service!'

'Tell me something I couldn't have guessed myself,' Turzig growled. 'The English Earl has been a thorn in our flesh these many months past. If that is all you have to tell me, fat one—'

'Wait!' Andrea held up his hand. 'They are still no ordinary men but a specially picked force – an assault unit, they call themselves – flown last Sunday night from Alexandria to Castelrosso. They left that same night from Castelrosso in a motorboat.'

'A torpedo boat,' Turzig nodded. 'So much we know already. Go on.'

'You know already! But how—'

'Never mind how. Hurry up!'

'Of course, Lieutenant, of course.' Not a twitch in his face betrayed Andrea's relief. This had been the only dangerous point in his story. Nicolai, of course, had warned the Germans, but never thought it worth while mentioning the presence of a giant Greek in the party. No reason, of course, why he should have selected him for special mention – but if he had done, it would have been the end.

'The torpedo boat landed them somewhere in the islands, north of Rhodes. I do not know where. There they stole a caique, sailed it up through Turkish waters, met a big German patrol boat – and sunk it.' Andrea paused for effect. 'I was less than half a mile away at the time in my fishing boat.'

Turzig leaned forward. 'How did they manage to sink so big a boat?' Strangely, he didn't doubt that it had been sunk.

'They pretended to be harmless fishermen like myself. I had just been stopped, investigated and cleared,' Andrea said virtuously. 'Anyway, your patrol boat came alongside this old caique. Close alongside. Suddenly there were guns firing on both sides, two boxes went flying through the air – into the engine-room of your boat, I think. Pouf!' Andrea threw up his hands dramatically. 'That was the end of that!'

'We wondered . . .' Turzig said softly. 'Well, go on.'

'You wondered what, Lieutenant?' Turzig's eyes narrowed and Andrea hurried on.

'Their interpreter had been killed in the fight. They tricked me into speaking English – I spent many years in Cyprus – kidnapped me, let my sons sail the boat—'

'Why should they want an interpreter?' Turzig demanded suspiciously. 'There are many British officers who speak Greek.'

'I am coming to that,' Andrea said impatiently. 'How in God's name do you expect me to finish my story if you keep interrupting all the time? Where was I? Ah, yes. They forced me to come along, and their engine broke down. I don't know what happened – I was kept below. I think we were in a creek somewhere, repairing the engine, and then there was a wild bout of drinking – you will not believe this, Lieutenant Turzig, that men on so desperate a mission should get drunk – and then we sailed again.'

'On the contrary, I do believe you.' Turzig was nodding his head slowly, as if in secret understanding. 'I believe you indeed.'

'You do?' Andrea contrived to look disappointed. 'Well, we ran into a fearful storm, wrecked the boat on the south cliff of this island and climbed—'

'Stop!' Turzig had drawn back sharply, suspicion flaring in his eyes. 'Almost I believed you! I believed you because we know more than you think, and so far you have told the truth. But not now. You are clever, fat one, but not so clever as you think. One thing you have forgotten – or maybe you do not know. We are of the *Wurttembergische Gebirgsbataillon* – we *know* mountains, my friend, better than any troops in the world. I myself am a Prussian, but I have climbed everything worth climbing in the Alps and Transylvania – and I tell you that the south cliff cannot be climbed. It is impossible!'

'Impossible perhaps for you.' Andrea shook his head sadly. 'These cursed Allies will beat you yet. They are clever, Lieutenant Turzig, damnably clever!'

'Explain yourself,' Turzig ordered curtly.

'Just this. They knew men thought the south cliff could not be climbed. So they determined to climb it. You would never dream that this could be done, that an expedition could land on Navarone that way. But the Allies took a gamble, found a man to lead the expedition. He could not speak Greek, but that did not matter, for what they wanted was a man who could climb – and so they picked the greatest rock-climber in the world today.' Andrea paused for effect, flung out his arm dramatically. 'And this is the man they picked, Lieutenant Turzig! You are a mountaineer yourself and you are bound to know him. His name is Mallory – Keith Mallory of New Zealand!'

There was a sharp exclamation, the click of a switch, and Turzig had taken a couple of steps forward, thrust the torch almost into Mallory's eyes. For almost ten seconds he stared into the New Zealander's averted, screwed-up face, then slowly lowered his arm, the harsh spotlight limning a dazzling white circle in the snow at his feet. Once, twice, half a dozen times Turzig nodded his head in slow understanding.

'Of course!' he murmured. 'Mallory – Keith Mallory! Of course I know him. There's not a man in my *Abteilung* but has heard of Keith Mallory.' He shook his head. 'I should have known him, I should have known him at once.' He stood for some time with his head bent, aimlessly screwing the toe of his right boot into the soft snow, then looked up abruptly. 'Before the war, even during it, I would have been proud to have known you, glad to have met you. But not here, not now. Not any more. I wish to God they had sent someone else.' He hesitated, made to carry on, then changed his mind, turned wearily to Andrea. 'My apologies, fat one. Indeed you speak the truth. Go on.'

'Certainly!' Andrea's round moon face was one vast smirk of satisfaction. 'We climbed the cliff as I said – although the boy in the cave there was badly hurt – and silenced the guard. Mallory killed him,' Andrea added unblushingly. 'It was a fair fight. We spent most of the night crossing the divide and found this cave before dawn. We were almost dead with hunger and cold. We have been here since.'

'And nothing has happened since?'

'On the contrary.' Andrea seemed to be enjoying himself hugely, revelling in being the focus of attention. 'Two people came up to see us. Who they were I do not know – they kept their faces hidden all the time – nor do I know where they came from.'

'It is as well that you admitted that,' Turzig said grimly. 'I knew someone had been here. I recognized the stove – it belongs to Hauptmann Skoda!'

'Indeed?' Andrea raised his eyebrows in polite surprise. 'I did not know. Well, they talked for some time and—'

'Did you manage to overhear anything they were talking about?' Turzig interrupted. The question came so naturally, so spontaneously, that Mallory held his breath. It was beautifully done. Andrea would walk into it – he couldn't help it. But Andrea was a man inspired that night.

'Overhear them!' Andrea clamped his lips shut in sorely-tried forbearance, gazed heavenwards in exasperated appeal. 'Lieutenant Turzig, how often must I tell you that I am the interpreter? They *could* only talk through me. Of course I know what they were talking about. They are going to blow up the big guns in the harbour.'

'I didn't think they had come here for their health!' Turzig said acidly.

'Ah, but you don't know that they have the plans of the fortress. You don't know that Kheros is to be invaded on Saturday morning. You don't know that they are in radio contact with Cairo all the time. You don't know that destroyers of the British Navy are coming through the Maidos Straits on Friday night as soon as the big guns have been silenced. You don't know—'

'Enough!' Turzig clapped his hands together, his face alight with excitement. 'The Royal Navy, eh? Wonderful, wonderful! *That* is what we want to hear. But enough! Keep it for Hauptmann Skoda and the Kommandant in the fortress. We must be off. But first – one more thing. The explosives – where are they?'

Andrea's shoulders slumped in dejection. He spread out his arms, palms upward.

'Alas, Lieutenant Turzig, I do not know. They took them out and hid them – some talk about the cave being too hot.' He waved a hand towards the western col, in the diametrically opposite direction to Leri's hut. 'That way, I think. But I cannot be sure, for they would not tell me.' He looked bitterly at Mallory. 'These Britishers are all the same. They trust nobody.'

'Heaven only knows that I don't blame them for that!' Turzig said feelingly. He looked at Andrea in disgust. 'More than ever I would like to see you dangling from the highest scaffold in Navarone. But Herr Kommandant in the town is a kindly man and rewards informers. You may yet live to betray some more comrades.'

'Thank you, thank you, thank you! I knew you were fair and just. I promise you, Lieutenant Turzig—'

'Shut up!' Turzig said contemptuously. He switched into German. 'Sergeant, have these men bound. And don't forget the fat one! Later we can untie him, and he can carry the sick man back to the post. Leave a man on guard. The rest of you come with me – we must find those explosives.'

'Could we not make one of them tell us, sir?' the sergeant ventured.

'The only man who would tell us, can't. He's already told us all he knows. As for the rest – well, I was mistaken about them, Sergeant.' He turned to Mallory, inclined his head briefly, spoke in English. 'An error of judgment, Herr Mallory. We are all very tired. I am almost sorry I struck you.' He wheeled abruptly, climbed swiftly up the bank. Two minutes later only a solitary soldier was left on guard.

For the tenth time Mallory shifted his position uncomfortably, strained at the cord that bound his hands together behind his back, for the tenth time recognized the futility of both these actions. No matter how he twisted and turned, the wet snow soaked icily through his clothes until he was chilled to the bone and shaking continually with the cold; and the man who had tied these knots had known his job all too well. Mallory wondered irritably if Turzig and his men meant to spend all night searching for the explosives: they had been gone for more than half an hour already.

He relaxed, lay back on his side in the cushioning snow of the gully bank, and looked thoughtfully at Andrea who was sitting upright just in front of him. He had watched Andrea, with bowed head and hunched and lifting shoulders, making one single, titanic effort to free himself seconds after the guard had gestured them to sit down, had seen the cords bite and gouge until they had almost disappeared in his flesh, the fractional slump of his shoulders as he gave up. Since then the giant Greek had sat quite still and contented himself with scowling at the sentry in the injured fashion of one who has been grievously wronged. That solitary test of the strength of his bonds had been enough. Oberleutnant Turzig had keen eyes, and swollen, chafed and bleeding wrists would have accorded ill with the character Andrea had created for himself.

A masterly creation, Mallory mused, all the more remarkable for its spontaneity, its improvization. Andrea had told so much of the truth, so much that was verifiable or could be verified, that belief in the rest of his story followed almost automatically. And at the same time he had told Turzig nothing of importance, nothing the Germans could not have found out for themselves – except the proposed evacuation of Kheros by the Navy. Wryly Mallory remembered his dismay, his shocked unbelief when he heard Andrea telling of it – but Andrea had been far ahead of him. There was a fair chance that the Germans might have guessed anyway – they would reason, perhaps, that an assault by the British on the guns of Navarone at the same time as the German assault on Kheros would be just that little bit too coincidental: again, escape for them all quite clearly depended upon how thoroughly Andrea managed to convince his captors that he was all he claimed, and the relative freedom of action that he could thereby gain – and there was no doubt at all that it was the news of the proposed evacuation that had tipped the scales with Turzig: and the fact that Andrea had given Saturday as the invasion date would only carry all the more weight, as that had been Jensen's original date – obviously false information fed to his agents by German counter-Intelligence, who had known it impossible to conceal the invasion preparations themselves; and finally, if Andrea hadn't told Turzig of the destroyers, he might have failed to carry conviction, they might all yet finish on the waiting gallows in the fortress, the guns would remain intact and destroy the naval ships anyway.

It was all very complicated, too complicated for the state his head was in. Mallory sighed and looked away from Andrea towards the other two. Brown and a now conscious Miller were both sitting upright, hands bound behind their backs, staring down into the snow, occasionally shaking muzzy heads from side to side. Mallory could appreciate all too easily how they felt – the whole right-hand side of his face ached cruelly, continuously. Nothing but aching, broken heads everywhere. Mallory thought bitterly. He wondered how Andy Stevens was feeling, glanced idly past the sentry towards the dark mouth of the cave, stiffened in sudden, almost uncomprehending shock.

Slowly, with an infinitely careful carelessness, he let his eyes wander away from the cave, let them light indifferently on the sentry who sat on Brown's transmitter, hunched watchfully over the Schmeisser cradled on his knees, finger crooked on the trigger. Pray God he doesn't turn round, Mallory said to himself over and over again, pray God he doesn't turn round. Let him sit like that just for a little while longer, only a little while longer. . . . In spite of himself, Mallory felt his gaze shifting, being dragged back again towards that cave-mouth.

Andy Stevens was coming out of the cave. Even in the dim starlight every movement was terribly plain as he inched forward agonizingly on chest and belly, dragging his shattered leg behind him. He was placing his hands beneath his shoulders, levering himself upwards and forwards while his head dropped below his shoulders with pain and the exhaustion of the effort, lowering himself slowly on the soft and sodden snow, then repeating the same heart-sapping process over and over again. Exhausted and pain-filled as the boy might be, Mallory thought, his mind was still working: he had a white sheet over his shoulders and back as camouflage against the snow, and he carried a climbing spike in his right hand. He must have heard at least some of Turzig's conversation: there were two or three guns in the cave, he could easily have shot the guard without coming out at all – but he must have known that the sound of a shot would have brought the Germans running, had them back at the cave long before he could have crawled across the gully, far less cut loose any of his friends.

Five yards Stevens had to go, Mallory estimated, five yards at the most. Deep down in the gully where they were, the south wind passed them by, was no more than a muted whisper in the night; that apart, there was no sound at all, nothing but their own breathing, the occasional stirring as someone stretched a cramped or frozen leg. He's bound to hear him if he comes any closer, Mallory thought desperately, even in that soft snow he's bound to hear him.

Mallory bent his head, began to cough loudly, almost continuously. The sentry looked at him in surprise first, then in irritation as the coughing continued.

'Be quiet!' the sentry ordered in German. 'Stop that coughing at once!'

'*Hüsten? Hüsten?* Coughing, is it? I can't help it,' Mallory protested in English. He coughed again, louder, more persistently than before. 'It is your Oberleutnant's fault,' he gasped. 'He has knocked out some of my teeth.' Mallory broke into a fresh paroxysm of coughing, recovered himself with an effort. 'Is it my fault that I'm choking on my own blood?' he demanded.

Stevens was less than ten feet away now, but his tiny reserves of strength were almost gone. He could no longer raise himself to the full stretch of his arms, was advancing only a few pitiful inches at a time. At length he stopped altogether, lay still for half a minute. Mallory thought he had lost consciousness, but by and by he raised himself up again, to the full stretch this time, had just begun to pivot himself forward when he collapsed, fell heavily in the snow. Mallory began to cough again, but he was too late. The sentry leapt off his box and whirled round all in one movement, the evil mouth of the Schmeisser lined up on the body almost at his feet. Then he relaxed as he realized who it was, lowered the barrel of his gun.

'So!' he said softly. 'The fledgling has left its nest. Poor little fledgling!' Mallory winced as he saw the backswing of the gun ready to smash down on Stevens's defenceless head, but the sentry was a kindly enough man, his reaction had been purely automatic. He arrested the swinging butt inches above the tortured face, bent down and almost gently removed the spike from the feebly threatening hand, sent it spinning over the edge of the gully. Then he lifted Stevens carefully by the shoulders, slid in the bunched-up sheet as pillow for the unconscious head against the bitter cold of the snow, shook his head wonderingly, sadly, went back to his seat on the ammunition box.

Hauptmann Skoda was a small, thin man in his late thirties, neat, dapper, debonair and wholly evil. There was something innately evil about the long, corded neck that stretched up scrawnily above his padded shoulders, something repellent about the incongruously small bullet head perched above. When the thin, bloodless lips parted in a smile, which was often, they revealed a perfect set of teeth: far from lighting his face, the smile only emphasized the sallow skin stretched abnormally taut across the sharp nose and high cheek-bones, puckered up the sabre scar that bisected the left cheek from eyebrow to chin: and whether he smiled or not, the pupils of the deep-set eyes remained always the same, still and black and empty. Even at that early hour – as it was not yet six o'clock – he was immaculately dressed, freshly shaven, the wetly-gleaming hair – thin, dark, heavily indented above the temples – brushed straight back across his head. Seated behind a flat-topped table, the sole article of furniture in the bench-lined guardroom, only the upper half of his body was visible: even so, one instinctively knew that the crease of the trousers, the polish of the jackboots, would be beyond reproach.

He smiled often, and he was smiling now as Oberleutnant Turzig finished his report. Leaning far back in his chair, elbows on the arm-rests, Skoda steepled his lean fingers under his chin, smiled benignly round the guardroom. The lazy, empty eyes missed nothing – the guard at the door, the two guards behind the bound prisoners, Andrea sitting on the bench where he had just laid Stevens – one lazy sweep of those eyes encompassed them all.

'Excellently done, Oberleutnant Turzig!' he purred. 'Most efficient, really most efficient!' He looked speculatively at the three men standing before him, at their bruised and blood-caked faces, switched his glance to Stevens, lying barely conscious on the bench, smiled again and permitted himself a fractional lift of his eyebrows. 'A little trouble, perhaps, Turzig? The prisoners were not too – ah – co-operative?'

'They offered no resistance, sir, no resistance at all,' Turzig said stiffly. The tone, the manner, were punctilious, correct, but the distaste, the latent hostility were mirrored in his eyes. 'My men were maybe a little enthusiastic. We wanted to make no mistake.'

'Quite right, Lieutenant, quite right,' Skoda murmured approvingly. 'These are dangerous men and one cannot take chances with dangerous men.' He pushed back his chair, rose easily to his feet, strolled round the table and stopped in front of Andrea. 'Except maybe this one, Lieutenant?'

'He is dangerous only to his friends,' Turzig said shortly. 'It is as I told you, sir. He would betray his mother to save his own skin.'

'And claiming friendship with us, eh?' Skoda asked musingly. 'One of our gallant allies, Lieutenant.' Skoda reached out a gentle hand, brought it viciously down and across Andrea's cheek, the heavy signet ring on his middle finger tearing skin and flesh. Andrea cried out in pain, clapped one hand to his bleeding face and cowered away, his right arm raised above his head in blind defence.

'A notable addition to the armed forces of the Third Reich,' Skoda murmured. 'You were not mistaken, Lieutenant. A poltroon – the instinctive reaction of a hurt man is an infallible guide. It is curious,' he mused, 'how often very big men are thus. Part of nature's compensatory process, I suppose. . . . What is your name, my brave friend?'

'Papagos.' Andrea muttered sullenly. 'Peter Papagos.' He took his hand away from his cheek, looked at it with eyes slowly widening with horror, began to rub it across his trouser leg with jerky, hurried movements, the repugnance of his face plain for every man to see. Skoda watched him with amusement.

'You do not like to see blood, Papagos, eh?' he suggested. 'Especially your own blood?'

A few seconds passed in silence, then Andrea lifted his head suddenly, his fat face screwed up in misery. He looked as if he were going to cry.

'I am only a poor fisherman, your Honour!' he burst out. 'You laugh at me and say I do not like blood, and it is true. Nor do I like suffering and war. I want no part of any of these things!' His great fists were clenched in futile appeal, his face puckered in woe, his voice risen an octave. It was a masterly exhibition of despair, and even Mallory found himself almost believing in it. 'Why wasn't I left alone?' he went on pathetically. 'God only knows I am no fighting man—'

'A highly inaccurate statement,' Skoda interrupted dryly. 'That fact must be patently obvious to every person in the room by this time.' He tapped his teeth with a jade cigarette-holder. 'A fisherman you call yourself—'

'He's a damned traitor!' Mallory interrupted. The commandant was becoming just that little bit too interested in Andrea. At once Skoda wheeled round, stood in front of Mallory with his hands clasped behind his back, teetering on heels and toes, and looked him up and down in mocking inspection.

'So!' he said thoughtfully. 'The great Keith Mallory! A rather different proposition from our fat and fearful friend on the bench there, eh, Lieutenant?' He did not wait for an answer. 'What rank are you, Mallory?'

'Captain,' Mallory answered briefly.

'Captain Mallory, eh? Captain Keith Mallory, the greatest mountaineer of our time, the idol of pre-war Europe, the conqueror of the world's most impossible climbs.' Skoda shook his head sadly. 'And to think that it should all end like this. . . . I doubt whether posterity will rank your last climb as among your greatest: there are only ten steps leading to the gallows in the fortress of Navarone.' Skoda smiled. 'Hardly a cheerful thought, is it, Captain Mallory?'

'I wasn't even thinking about it,' the New Zealander answered pleasantly. 'What worries me is your face.' He frowned. 'Somewhere or other I'm sure I've seen it or something like it before.' His voice trailed off into silence.

'Indeed?' Skoda was interested. 'In the Bernese Alps, perhaps? Often before the war—'

'I have it now!' Mallory's face cleared. He knew the risk he was taking, but anything that concentrated attention on himself to the exclusion of Andrea was justified. He beamed at Skoda. 'Three months ago, it was, in the zoo in Cairo. A plains buzzard that had been captured in the Sudan. A rather old and mangy buzzard, I'm afraid,' Mallory went on apologetically, 'but exactly the same scrawny neck, the same beaky face and bald head—'

Mallory broke off abruptly, swayed back out of reach as Skoda, his face livid and gleaming teeth bared in rage, swung at him with his fist. The blow carried with it all Skoda's wiry strength, but anger blurred his timing and the fist swung harmlessly by: he stumbled, recovered, then fell to the floor with a shout of pain as Mallory's heavy boot caught him flush on the thigh, just above the knee. He had barely touched the floor when he was up like a cat, took a pace forward and collapsed heavily again as his injured leg gave way under him.

There was a moment's shocked stillness throughout the room, then Skoda rose painfully, supporting himself on the edge of the heavy table. He was breathing quickly, the thin mouth a hard, white line, the great sabre scar flaming redly in the sallow face drained now of all colour. He looked neither at Mallory nor anyone else, but slowly, deliberately, in an almost frightening silence, began to work his way round to the back of the table, the scuffling of his sliding palms on the leather top rasping edgily across over-tautened nerves.

Mallory stood quite still, watching him with expressionless face, cursing himself for his folly. He had overplayed his hand. There was no doubt in his mind – there could be no doubt in the mind of anyone in that room – that Skoda meant to kill him; and he, Mallory would not die. Only Skoda and Andrea would die: Skoda from Andrea's throwing knife – Andrea was rubbing blood from his face with the inside of his sleeve, fingertips only inches from the sheath – and Andrea from the guns of the guards, for the knife was all he had. You fool, you fool, you bloody stupid fool. Mallory repeated to himself over and over again. He turned his head slightly and glanced out of the corner of his eye at the sentry nearest him. Nearest him – but still six or seven feet away. The sentry would get him, Mallory knew, the blast of the slugs from the Schmeisser would tear him in half before he could cover the distance. But he would try. He must try. It was the least he owed to Andrea.

Skoda reached the back of the table, opened a drawer and lifted out a gun. An automatic, Mallory noted with detachment – a little, blue-metal, snub-nosed toy – but a murderous toy, the kind of gun he would have expected Skoda to have. Unhurriedly Skoda pressed the release button, checked the magazine, snapped it home with the palm of his hand, flicked off the safety catch and looked at Mallory. The eyes hadn't altered in the slightest – they were cold, dark and empty as ever. Mallory flicked a glance at Andrea and tensed himself for one convulsive fling backwards. Here it comes, he thought savagely, this is how bloody fools like Keith Mallory die – and then all of a sudden, and unknowingly, he relaxed, for his eyes were still on Andrea and he had seen Andrea doing the same, the huge hand slipping down unconcernedly from the neck, empty of any sign of knife.

There was a scuffle at the table and Mallory was just in time to see Turzig pin Skoda's gun-hand to the table-top.

'Not that, sir!' Turzig begged. 'For God's sake, not that way!'

'Take your hands away,' Skoda whispered. The staring, empty eyes never left Mallory's face. 'Take your hands away, I say – unless you want to go the same way as Captain Mallory.'

'You can't kill him, sir!' Turzig persisted doggedly. 'You just can't. Herr Kommandant's orders were very clear, Hauptmann Skoda. The leader must be brought to him alive.'

'He was shot while trying to escape,' Skoda said thickly.

'It's no good.' Turzig shook his head. 'We can't kill them all – and the other prisoners would talk.' He released his grip on Skoda's hands. 'Alive, Herr Kommandant said, but he didn't say how much alive.' He lowered his voice confidentially. 'Perhaps we may have some difficulty in making Captain Mallory talk,' he suggested.

'What? What did you say?' Abruptly the death's head smile flashed once more, and Skoda was completely on balance again. 'You are over-zealous, Lieutenant. Remind me to speak to you about it some time. You underestimate me: that was exactly what I was trying to do – frighten Mallory into talking. And now you've spoilt it all.' The smile was still on his face, the voice light, almost bantering, but Mallory was under no illusions. He owed his life to the young WGB lieutenant – how easily one could respect, form a friendship with a man like Turzig if it weren't for this damned, crazy war. . . . Skoda was standing in front of him again: he had left his gun on the table.'

'But enough of this fooling, eh, Captain Mallory?' The German's teeth fairly gleamed in the bright light from the naked lamps overhead. 'We haven't all night, have we?'

Mallory looked at him, then turned away in silence. It was warm enough, stuffy almost, in that little guardroom, but he was conscious of a sudden, nameless chill; he knew all at once, without knowing why, but with complete certainty, that this little man before him was utterly evil.

'Well, well, well, we are not quite so talkative now, are we, my friend?' He hummed a little to himself, looked up abruptly, the smile broader than ever. 'Where are the explosives, Captain Mallory?'

'Explosives?' Mallory lifted an interrogatory eyebrow. 'I don't know what you are talking about.'

'You don't remember, eh?'

'I don't know what you are talking about.'

'So.' Skoda hummed to himself again and walked over in front of Miller. 'And what about you, my friend?'

'Sure I remember,' Miller said easily. 'The captain's got it all wrong.'

'A sensible man!' Skoda purred – but Mallory could have sworn to an undertone of disappointment in the voice. 'Proceed, my friend.'

'Captain Mallory has no eye for detail,' Miller drawled. 'I was with him that day. He is malignin' a noble bird. It was a vulture, not a buzzard.'

Just for a second Skoda's smile slipped, then it was back again, as rigidly fixed and lifeless as if it had been painted on.

'Very, very witty men, don't you think, Turzig? What the British would call music-hall comedians. Let them laugh while they may, until the hangman's noose begins to tighten. . . .' He looked at Casey Brown. 'Perhaps you—'

'Why don't you go and take a running jump to yourself?' Brown growled.

'A running jump? The idiom escapes me, but I fear it is hardly complimentary.' Skoda selected a cigarette from a thin case, tapped it thoughtfully on a thumb nail. 'Hmm. Not just what one might call too co-operative, Lieutenant Turzig.'

'You won't get these men to talk, sir.' There was a quiet finality in Turzig's voice.

'Possibly not, possibly not.' Skoda was quite unruffled. 'Nevertheless, I shall have the information I want, and within five minutes.' He walked unhurriedly across to his desk, pressed a button, screwed his cigarette into its jade holder, and leaned against the table, an arrogance, a careless contempt in every action, even to the leisurely crossing of the gleaming jackboots.

Suddenly a side door was flung open and two men stumbled into the room, prodded by a rifle barrel. Mallory caught his breath, felt his nails dig savagely into the palms of his hands. Louki and Panayis! Louki and Panayis, bound and bleeding, Louki from a cut above the eye, Panayis from a scalp wound. So they'd got them too, and in spite of his warnings. Both men were shirt-sleeved; Louki, minus his magnificently frogged jacket, scarlet *stanta* and the small arsenal of weapons that he carried stuck beneath it, looked strangely pathetic and woebegone – strangely, for he was red-faced with anger, the moustache bristling more ferociously than ever. Mallory looked at him with eyes empty of all recognition, his face expressionless.

'Come now, Captain Mallory,' Skoda said reproachfully. 'Have you no word of greeting for two old friends? No? Or perhaps you are just overwhelmed?' he suggested smoothly. 'You had not expected to see them so soon again, eh, Captain Mallory?'

'What cheap trick is this?' Mallory asked contemptuously. 'I've never seen these men before in my life.' His eyes caught those of Panayis, held there involuntarily: the black hate that stared out of those eyes, the feral malevolence – there was something appalling about it.

'Of course not,' Skoda sighed wearily. 'Oh, of course not. Human memory is so short, is it not, Captain Mallory.' The sigh was pure theatre – Skoda was enjoying himself immensely, the cat playing with the mouse. 'However, we will try again.' He swung round, crossed over to the bench where Stevens lay, pulled off the blanket and, before anyone could guess his intentions, chopped the outside of his right hand against Stevens's smashed leg, just below the knee. . . . Stevens's entire body leapt in a convulsive spasm, but without even the whisper of a moan: he was still fully conscious, smiling at Skoda, blood trickling down his chin from where his teeth had gashed his lower lip.

'You shouldn't have done that, Hauptmann Skoda,' Mallory said. His voice was barely a whisper, but unnaturally loud in the frozen silence of the room. 'You are going to die for that, Hauptmann Skoda.'

'So? I am going to die, am I?' Again he chopped his hand against the fractured leg, again without reaction. 'Then I may as well die twice over – eh, Captain Mallory? This young man is very, very tough – but the British have soft hearts, have they not, my dear Captain?' Gently his hand slid down Stevens's leg, closed round the stockinged ankle. 'You have exactly five seconds to tell me the truth, Captain Mallory, and then I fear I will be compelled to re-arrange these splints – *Gott in Himmel!* What's the matter with that great oaf?'

Andrea had taken a couple of steps forward, was standing only a yard away, swaying on his feet.

'Outside! Let me outside!' His breath came in short, fast gasps. He bowed his head, one hand to his throat, one over his stomach. 'I cannot stand it! Air! Air! I must have air!'

'Ah, no, my dear Papagos, you shall remain here and enjoy – Corporal! Quickly!' He had seen Andrea's eyes roll upwards until only the whites showed. 'The fool is going to faint! Take him away before he falls on top of us!'

Mallory had one fleeting glimpse of the two guards hurrying forwards, of the incredulous contempt on Louki's face, then he flicked a glance at Miller and Brown, caught the lazy droop of the American's eyelid in return, the millimetric inclination of Brown's head. Even as the two guards came up behind Andrea and lifted the flaccid arms across their shoulders, Mallory glanced half-left, saw the nearest sentry less than four feet away now, absorbed in the spectacle of the toppling giant. Easy, dead easy – the gun dangling by his side: he could hit him between wind and water before he knew what was happening. . . .

Fascinated, Mallory watched Andrea's forearms slipping nervelessly down the shoulders of the supporting guards till his wrists rested loosely beside their necks, palms facing inwards. And then there was the sudden leap of the great shoulder muscles and Mallory had hurled himself convulsively sidewards and back, his shoulder socketing with vicious force into the guard's stomach, inches below the breast-bone: an explosive *ouf*! of agony, the crash against the wooden walls of the room and Mallory knew the guard would be out of action for some time to come.

Even as he dived. Mallory had heard the sickening thud of heads being swept together. Now, as he twisted round on his side, he had a fleeting glimpse of another guard thrashing feebly on the floor under the combined weights of Miller and Brown, and then of Andrea tearing an automatic rifle from the guard who had been standing at his right shoulder: the Schmeisser was cradled in his great hands, lined up on Skoda's chest even before the unconscious man had hit the floor.

For one second, maybe two, all movement in the room ceased, every sound sheared off by a knife edge: the silence was abrupt, absolute – and infinitely more clamorous than the clamour that had gone before. No one moved, no one spoke, no one even breathed: the shock, the utter unexpectedness of what had happened held them all in thrall.

And then the silence erupted in a staccato crashing of sound, deafening in that confined space. Once, twice, three times, wordlessly, and with great care, Andrea shot Hauptmann Skoda through the heart. The blast of the shells lifted the little man off his feet, smashed him against the wall of the hut, pinned him there for one incredible second, arms outflung as though nailed against the rough planks in spreadeagle crucifixion; and then he collapsed, fell limply to the ground a grotesque and broken doll that struck its heedless head against the edge of the bench before coming to rest on its back on the floor. The eyes were still wide open, as cold, as dark, as empty in death as they had been in life.

His Schmeisser waving in a gentle arc that covered Turzig and the sergeant, Andrea picked up Skoda's sheath knife, sliced through the ropes that bound Mallory's wrists.

'Can you hold this gun, my Captain?'

Mallory flexed his stiffened hands once or twice, nodded, took the gun in silence. In three steps Andrea was behind the blind side of the door leading to the ante-room, pressed to the wall, waiting, gesturing to Mallory to move as far back as possible out of the line of sight.

Suddenly the door was flung open. Andrea could just see the tip of the rifle barrel projecting beyond it.

'Oberleutnant Turzig! *Was ist los? Wer schoss . . .*' The voice broke off in a coughing grunt of agony as Andrea smashed the sole of his foot against the door. He was round the outside of the door in a moment, caught the man as he fell, pulled him clear of the doorway and peered into the adjacent hut. A brief inspection, then he closed the door, bolted it from the inside.

'Nobody else there, my Captain,' Andrea reported. 'Just the one gaoler, it seems.'

'Fine! Cut the others loose, will you, Andrea?' He wheeled round towards Louki, smiled at the comical expression on the little man's face, the tentative, spreading, finally ear-to-ear grin that cut through the baffled incredulity.

'Where do the men sleep, Louki – the soldiers, I mean?'

'In a hut in the middle of the compound, Major. This is the officers' quarters.'

'Compound? You mean—?'

'Barbed wire,' Louki said succinctly. 'Ten feet high – and all the way round.'

'Exits?'

'One and one only. Two guards.'

'Good! Andrea – everybody into the side room. No, not you, Lieutenant. You sit down here.' He gestured to the chair behind the big desk. 'Somebody's bound to come. Tell him you killed one of us – trying to escape. Then send for the guards at the gate.'

For a moment Turzig didn't answer. He watched unseeingly as Andrea walked past him, dragging two unconscious soldiers by their collars. Then he smiled. It was a wry sort of smile.

'I am sorry to disappoint you, Captain Mallory. Too much has been lost already through my blind stupidity. I won't do it.'

'Andrea!' Mallory called softly.

'Yes?' Andrea stood in the ante-room doorway.

'I think I hear someone coming. Is there a way out of that side room?'

Andrea nodded silently.

'Outside! The front door. Take your knife. If the Lieutenant . . .' But he was talking to himself. Andrea was already gone, slipping out through the back door, soundless as a ghost.

'You will do exactly as I say,' Mallory said softly. He took position himself in the doorway to the side room, where he could see the front entrance between door and jamb: his automatic rifle was trained on Turzig. 'If you don't, Andrea will kill the man at the door. Then we will kill you and the guards inside. Then we will knife the sentries at the gate. Nine dead men – and all for nothing, for we will escape anyway. . . . Here he is now.' Mallory's voice was barely a whisper, eyes pitiless in a pitiless face. 'Nine dead men, Lieutenant – and just because your pride is hurt.' Deliberately, the last sentence was in German, fluent, colloquial, and Mallory's mouth twisted as he saw the almost imperceptible sag of Turzig's shoulders. He knew he had won, that Turzig had been going to take a last gamble on his ignorance of German, that this last hope was gone.

The door burst open and a soldier stood on the threshold, breathing heavily. He was armed, but clad only in a singlet and trousers, oblivious of the cold.

'Lieutenant! Lieutenant!' He spoke in German. 'We heard the shots—'

'It is nothing, Sergeant.' Turzig bent his head over an open drawer, pretended to be searching for something to account for his solitary presence in the room. 'One of our prisoners tried to escape. . . . We stopped him.'

'Perhaps the medical orderly—'

'I'm afraid we stopped him rather permanently.' Turzig smiled tiredly. 'You can organize a burial detail in the morning. Meantime, you might tell the guards at the gate to come here for a minute. Then get to bed yourself – you'll catch your death of cold!'

'Shall I detail a relief guard—'

'Of course not!' Turzig said impatiently. 'It's just for a minute. Besides, the only people to guard against are already in here.' His lips tightened for a second as he realized what he had said, the unconscious irony of the words. 'Hurry up, man! We haven't got all night!' He waited till the sound of the running footsteps died away, then looked steadily at Mallory. 'Satisfied?'

'Perfectly. And my very sincere apologies,' Mallory said quietly. 'I hate to do a thing like this to a man like you.' He looked round the door as Andrea came into the room. 'Andrea, ask Louki and Panayis if there's a telephone switchboard in this block of huts. Tell them to smash it up and any receivers they can find.' He grinned. 'Then hurry back for our visitors from the gate. I'd be lost without you on the reception committee.'

Turzig's gaze followed the broad retreating back.

'Captain Skoda was right. I still have much to learn.' There was neither bitterness nor rancour in his voice. 'He fooled me completely, that big one.'

'You're not the first,' Mallory reassured him. 'He's fooled more people than I'll ever know. . . . You're not the first,' he repeated. 'But I think you must be just about the luckiest.'

'Because I'm still alive?'

'Because you're still alive,' Mallory echoed.

Less than ten minutes later the two guards at the gate had joined their comrades in the back room, captured, disarmed, bound and gagged with a speed and noiseless efficiency that excited Turzig's professional admiration, chagrined though he was. Securely tied hand and foot, he lay in a corner of the room, not yet gagged.

'I think I understand now why your High Command chose you for this task, Captain Mallory. If anyone could succeed, you would – but you must fail. The impossible must always remain so. Nevertheless, you have a great team.'

'We get by,' Mallory said modestly. He took a last look round the room, then grinned down at Stevens.

'Ready to take off on your travels again, young man, or do you find this becoming rather monotonous?'

'Ready when you are, sir.' Lying on a stretcher which Louki had miraculously procured, he sighed in bliss. 'First-class travel, this time, as befits an officer. Sheer luxury. I don't mind how far we go!'

'Speak for yourself,' Miller growled morosely. He had been allocated first stint at the front or heavy end of the stretcher. But the quirk of his eyebrows robbed the words of all offence.

'Right, then, we're off. One last thing. Where is the camp radio, Lieutenant Turzig?'

'So you can smash it, I suppose?'

'Precisely.'

'I have no idea.'

'What if I threaten to blow your head off?'

'You won't.' Turzig smiled, though the smile was a trifle lopsided. 'Given certain circumstances, you would kill me as you would a fly. But you wouldn't kill a man for refusing such information.'

'You haven't as much to learn as your late and unlamented captain thought,' Mallory admitted. 'It's not all that important. . . . I regret we have to do all this. I trust we do not meet again – not at least, until the war is over. Who knows, some day we might even go climbing together.' He signed to Louki to fix Turzig's gag and walked quickly out of the room. Two minutes later they had cleared the barracks and were safely lost in the darkness and the olive groves that stretched to the south of Margaritha.

When they cleared the groves, a long time later, it was almost dawn. Already the black silhouette of Kostos was softening in the first feathery greyness of the coming day. The wind was from the south, and warm, and the snow was beginning to melt on the hills.

Chapter Eleven

Wednesday 1400–1600

All day long they lay hidden in the carob grove, a thick clump of stunted, gnarled trees that clung grimly to the treacherous, scree-strewn slope abutting what Louki called the 'Devil's Playground.' A poor shelter and an uncomfortable one, but in every other way all they could wish for: it offered concealment, a first-class defensive position immediately behind, a gentle breeze drawn up from the sea by the sun-baked rocks to the south, shade from the sun that rode from dawn to dusk in a cloudless sky – and an incomparable view of a sun-drenched, shimmering Ægean.

Away to their left, fading through diminishing shades of blue and indigo and violet into faraway nothingness, stretched the islands of the Lerades, the nearest of them, Maidos, so close that they could see isolated fisher cottages sparkling whitely in the sun: through that narrow, intervening gap of water would pass the ships of the Royal Navy in just over a day's time. To the right, and even farther away, remote, featureless, back-dropped by the towering Anatolian mountains, the coast of Turkey hooked north and west in a great curving scimitar: to the north itself, the thrusting spear of Cape Demirci, rock-rimmed but dimpled with sandy coves of white, reached far out into the placid blue of the Ægean: and north again beyond the Cape, haze-blurred in the purple distance, the island of Kheros lay dreaming on the surface of the sea.

It was a breath-taking panorama, a heart-catching beauty sweeping majestically through a great semi-circle over the sunlit sea. But Mallory had no eyes for it, had spared it only a passing glance when he had come on guard less than half an hour previously, just after two o'clock. He had dismissed it with one quick glance, settled by the bole of a tree, gazed for endless minutes, gazed until his eyes ached with strain at what he had so long waited to see. Had waited to see and come to destroy – the guns of the fortress of Navarone.

The town of Navarone – a town of from four to five thousand people, Mallory judged – lay sprawled round the deep, volcanic crescent of the harbour, a crescent so deep, so embracing, that it was almost a complete circle with only a narrow bottleneck of an entrance to the north-west, a gateway dominated by searchlights and mortar and machine-gun batteries on either side. Less than three miles distant to the north-east from the carob grove, every detail, every street, every building, every caique and launch in the harbour were clearly visible to Mallory and he studied them over and over again until he knew them by heart: the way the land to the west of the harbour sloped up gently to the olive groves, the dusty streets running down to the water's edge: the way the ground rose more sharply to the south, the streets now running parallel to the water down to the old town: the way the cliffs to the east – cliffs pockmarked by the bombs of Torrance's Liberator

Squadron – stretched a hundred and fifty sheer feet above the water, then curved dizzily out over and above the harbour, and the great mound of volcanic rock towering above that again, a mound barricaded off from the town below by the high wall that ended flush with the cliff itself: and finally, the way the twin rows of AA guns, the great radar scanners and the barracks of the fortress, squat, narrow-embrasured, built of big blocks of masonry, dominated everything in sight – including that great, black gash in the rock, below the fantastic overhang of the cliff.

Unconsciously, almost, Mallory nodded to himself in slow understanding. This was the fortress that had defied the Allies for eighteen long months, that had dominated the entire naval strategy in the Sporades since the Germans had reached out from the mainland into the isles, that had blocked all naval activity in that 2000 square mile triangle between the Lerades and the Turkish coast. And now, when he saw it, it all made sense. Impregnable to land attack – the commanding fortress saw to that: impregnable to air attack – Mallory realized just how suicidal it had been to send out Torrance's squadron against the great guns protected by that jutting cliff, against those bristling rows of anti-aircraft guns: and impregnable to sea attack – the waiting squadrons of the Luftwaffe on Samos saw to that. Jensen had been right – only a guerrilla sabotage mission stood any chance at all: a remote chance, an all but suicidal chance, but still a chance, and Mallory knew he couldn't ask for more.

Thoughtfully he lowered the binoculars and rubbed the back of his hand across his aching eyes. At last he felt he knew exactly what he was up against, was grateful for the knowledge, for the opportunity he'd been given of this long-range reconnaissance, this familiarizing of himself with the terrain, the geography of the town. This was probably the one vantage point in the whole island that offered such an opportunity together with concealment and near immunity. No credit to himself, the leader of the mission, he reflected wryly, that they had found such a place: it had been Louki's idea entirely.

And he owed a great deal more than that to the sad-eyed little Greek. It had been Louki's idea that they first move up-valley from Margaritha, to give Andrea time to recover the explosives from old Leri's hut, and to make certain there was no immediate hue and cry and pursuit – they could have fought a rearguard action up through the olive groves, until they had lost themselves in the foothills of Kostos: it was he who had guided them back past Margaritha when they had doubled on their tracks, had halted them opposite the village while he and Panayis had slipped wraith-like through the lifting twilight, picked up outdoor clothes for themselves, and, on the return journey, slipped into the *Abteilung* garage, torn away the coil ignitions of the German command car and truck – the only transport in Margaritha – and smashed their distributors for good measure; it was Louki who had led them by a sunken ditch right up to the road-block guard post at the mouth of the valley – it had been almost ludicrously simple to disarm the sentries, only one of whom had been awake – and, finally, it was Louki who had insisted that they walk down the muddy centre of the valley track till they came to the metalled road, less than two miles from the town itself. A hundred yards down this they had branched off to the left across a long, sloping field of lava that left no trace behind, arrived in the carob copse just on sunrise.

And it had worked. All these carefully engineered pointers, pointers that not even the most sceptical could have ignored and denied, had worked magnificently. Miller and Andrea, who had shared the forenoon watch, had seen the Navarone garrison spending long hours making the most intensive house-to-house search of the town. That should make it doubly, trebly safe for them the following day, Mallory reckoned: it was unlikely that the search would be repeated, still more unlikely that, if it were, it would be carried out with a fraction of the same enthusiasm. Louki had done his work well.

Mallory turned his head to look at him. The little man was still asleep – wedged on the slope behind a couple of tree-trunks, he hadn't stirred for five hours. Still dead tired himself, his legs aching and eyes smarting with sleeplessness. Mallory could not find it in him to grudge Louki a moment of his rest. He'd earned it all – and he'd been awake all through the previous night. So had Panayis, but Panayis was already awakening, Mallory saw, pushing the long, black hair out of his eyes: awake, rather, for his transition from sleep to full awareness was immediate, as fleeting and as complete as a cat's. A dangerous man, Mallory knew, a desperate man, almost, and a bitter enemy, but he knew nothing of Panayis, nothing at all. He doubted if he ever would.

Farther up on the slope, almost in the centre of the grove, Andrea had built a high platform of broken branches and twigs against a couple of carob poles maybe five feet apart, gradually filling up the space between slope and trees until he had a platform four feet in width, as nearly level as he could make it. Andy Stevens lay on this, still on his stretcher, still conscious. As far as Mallory could tell, Stevens hadn't closed his eyes since they had been marched away by Turzig from their cave in the mountains. He seemed to have passed beyond the need for sleep, or had crushed all desire for it. The stench from the gangrenous leg was nauseating, appalling, poisoned all the air around. Mallory and Miller had had a look at the leg shortly after their arrival in the copse, uncovered it, examined it, smiled at one another, tied it up again and assured Stevens that the wound was closing. Below the knee, the leg had turned almost completely black.

Mallory lifted his binoculars to have another look at the town, but lowered them almost at once as someone came sliding down the slope, touched him on the arm. It was Panayis, upset, anxious, almost angry looking. He gesticulated towards the westering sun.

'The time, Captain Mallory?' He spoke in Greek, his voice low, sibilant, urgent – an inevitable voice, Mallory thought, for the lean, dark mysteriousness of the man. 'What is the time?' he repeated.

'Half-past two, or thereabouts.' Mallory lifted an interrogatory eyebrow. 'You are concerned, Panayis. Why?'

'You should have wakened me. You should have wakened me hours ago!' He *was* angry, Mallory decided. 'It is my turn to keep watch.'

'But you had no sleep last night,' Mallory pointed out reasonably. 'It just didn't seem fair—'

'It is my turn to keep watch, I tell you!' Panayis insisted stubbornly.

'Very well, then. If you insist.' Mallory knew the high, fierce pride of the islanders too well to attempt to argue. 'Heaven only knows what we would have done without Louki and yourself. . . . I'll stay and keep you company for a while.'

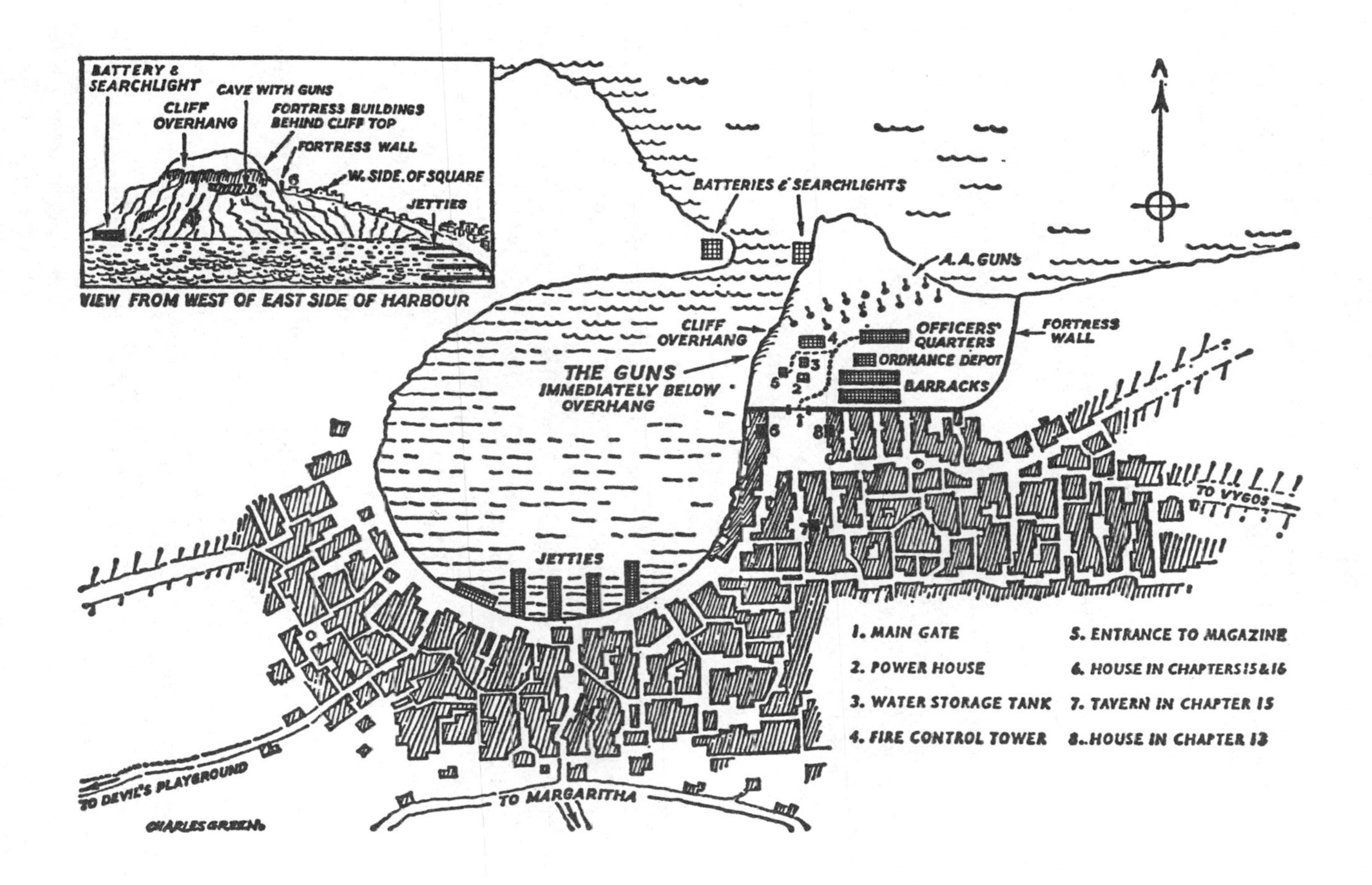
BATTERY & SEARCHLIGHT
CLIFF OVERHANG
CAVE WITH GUNS
FORTRESS BUILDINGS BEHIND CLIFF TOP
FORTRESS WALL
W. SIDE. OF SQUARE
JETTIES
VIEW FROM WEST OF EAST SIDE OF HARBOUR
BATTERIES & SEARCHLIGHTS
A.A. GUNS
CLIFF OVERHANG
THE GUNS IMMEDIATELY BELOW OVERHANG
OFFICERS' QUARTERS
ORDNANCE DEPOT
BARRACKS
FORTRESS WALL
JETTIES
TO VYGOS
TO DEVIL'S PLAYGROUND
TO MARGARITHA
1. MAIN GATE
2. POWER HOUSE
3. WATER STORAGE TANK
4. FIRE CONTROL TOWER
5. ENTRANCE TO MAGAZINE
6. HOUSE IN CHAPTERS 15 & 16
7. TAVERN IN CHAPTER 15
8. HOUSE IN CHAPTER 13
CHARLES GREEN

'Ah, so that is why you let me sleep on!' There was no disguising the hurt in the eyes, the voice. 'You do not trust Panayis—'

'Oh, for heaven's sake!' Mallory began in exasperation, checked himself and smiled. 'Of course we trust you. Maybe I should go and get some more sleep anyway; you are kind to give me the chance. You will shake me in two hours' time?'

'Certainly, certainly!' Panayis was almost beaming. 'I shall not fail.'

Mallory scrambled up to the centre of the grove and stretched out lazily along the ledge he had levelled out for himself. For a few idle moments he watched Panayis pacing restlessly to and fro just inside the perimeter of the grove, lost interest when he saw him climbing swiftly up among the branches of a tree, seeking a high lookout vantage point and decided he might as well follow his advice and get some sleep while he could.

'Captain Mallory! Captain Mallory!' An urgent, heavy hand was shaking his shoulder. 'Wake up! Wake up!'

Mallory stirred, rolled over on his back, sat up quickly, opening his eyes as he did so. Panayis was stooped over him, the dark, saturnine face alive with anxiety. Mallory shook his head to clear away the mists of sleep and was on his feet in one swift, easy movement.

'What's the matter, Panayis?'

'Planes!' he said quickly. 'There is a squadron of planes coming our way!'

'Planes? What planes? Whose planes?'

'I do not know, Captain. They are yet far away. But—'

'What direction?' Mallory snapped.

'They come from the north.'

Together they ran down to the edge of the grove. Panayis gestured to the north, and Mallory caught sight of them at once, the afternoon sun glinting off the sharp dihedral of the wings. Stukas, all right, he thought grimly. Seven – no, eight of them – less than three miles away, flying in two echelons of four, two thousand, certainly not more than twenty-five hundred feet. . . . He became aware that Panayis was tugging urgently at his arm.

'Come, Captain Mallory!' he said excitedly. 'We have no time to lose!' He pulled Mallory round, pointed with outstretched arm at the gaunt, shattered cliffs that rose steeply behind them, cliffs crazily riven by rock-jumbled ravines that wound their aimless way back into the interior – or stopped as abruptly as they had begun. 'The Devil's Playground! We must get in there at once! At once, Captain Mallory!'

'Why on earth should we?' Mallory looked at him in astonishment. 'There's no reason to suppose that they're after us. How can they be? No one knows we're here.'

'I do not care!' Panayis was stubborn in his conviction. 'I know. Do not ask me how I know, for I do not know that myself. Louki will tell you – Panayis knows these things. I know, Captain Mallory, I *know*!'

Just for a second Mallory stared at him, uncomprehending. There was no questioning the earnestness, the utter sincerity – but it was the machine-gun staccato of the words that tipped the balance of instinct against reason. Almost without realizing it, certainly without realizing why, Mallory found himself running uphill, slipping and stumbling in the scree. He found the others already on their feet, tense, expectant, shrugging on their packs, the guns already in their hands.

'Get to the edge of the trees up there!' Mallory shouted. 'Quickly! Stay there and stay under cover – we're going to have to break for that gap in the rocks.' He gestured through the trees at a jagged fissure in the cliff-side, barely forty yards from where he stood, blessed Louki for his foresight in choosing a hideout with so convenient a bolt-hole. 'Wait till I give the word. Andrea!' He turned round, then broke off, the words unneeded. Andrea had already scooped up the dying boy in his arms, just as he lay in stretcher and blankets and was weaving his way uphill in and out among the trees.

'What's up, boss?' Miller was by Mallory's side as he plunged up the slope. 'I don't see nothin'.'

'You can hear something if you'd just stop talking for a moment,' Mallory said grimly. 'Or just take a look up there.'

Miller, flat on his stomach, now and less than a dozen feet from the edge of the grove, twisted round and craned his neck upwards. He picked up the planes immediately.

'Stukas!' he said incredulously. 'A squadron of gawddamned Stukas! It can't be, boss!'

'It can and it is,' Mallory said grimly. 'Jensen told me that Jerry has stripped the Italian front of them – over two hundred pulled out in the last few weeks.' Mallory squinted up at the squadron, less than half a mile away now. 'And he's brought the whole damn' issue down to the Ægean.'

'But they're not lookin' for us,' Miller protested.

'I'm afraid they are,' Mallory said grimly. The two bomber echelons had just dove-tailed into line ahead formation. 'I'm afraid Panayis was right.'

'But – but they're passin' us by—'

'They aren't.' Mallory said flatly. 'They're here to stay. Just keep your eyes on that leading plane.'

Even as he spoke, the flight-commander tilted his gull-winged Junkers 87 sharply over to port, half-turned, fell straight out of the sky in a screaming power-dive, plummeting straight for the carob grove.

'Leave him alone!' Mallory shouted. 'Don't fire!' The Stuka's, airbrakes at maximum depression, had steadied on the centre of the grove. Nothing could stop him now – but a chance shot might bring him down directly on top of them: the chances were poor enough as it was. . . . 'Keep your hands over your heads – and your heads down!'

He ignored his own advice, his gaze following the bomber every foot of the way down. Five hundred, four hundred, three, the rising crescendo of the heavy engine was beginning to hurt his ears, and the Stuka was pulling sharply out of its plunging fall, its bomb gone.

Bomb! Mallory sat up sharply, screwing up his eyes against the blue of the sky. Not one bomb but dozens of them, clustered so thickly that they appeared to be jostling each other as they arrowed into the centre of the grove, striking the gnarled and stunted trees, breaking off branches and burying themselves to their fins in the soft and shingled slope. Incendiaries! Mallory had barely time to realize that they had been spared the horror of a 500-kilo HE bomb when the incendiaries erupted into hissing, guttering life, into an incandescent magnesium whiteness that reached out and completely destroyed the shadowed gloom of the carob grove. Within a matter of seconds the dazzling coruscation had given way to thick, evil-smelling clouds of acrid black smoke, smoke laced with flickering tongues of red, small at first then licking and twisting resinously upwards until entire trees were enveloped in a cocoon of flame. The Stuka was still pulling upwards out of its dive, had not yet levelled off when the heart of the grove, old and dry and tindery, was fiercely ablaze.

Miller twisted up and round, nudging Mallory to catch his attention through the crackling roar of the flames.

'Incendiaries, boss,' he announced.

'What did you think they were using?' Mallory asked shortly. 'Matches? They're trying to smoke us out, to burn us out, get us in the open. High explosive's not so good among trees. Ninety-nine times out of a hundred this would have worked.' He coughed as the acrid smoke bit into his lungs, peered up with watering eyes through the tree-tops. 'But not this time. Not if we're lucky. Not if they hold off another half-minute or so. Just look at that smoke!'

Miller looked. Thick, convoluted, shot through with fiery sparks, the rolling cloud was already a third of the way across the gap between grove and cliff, borne uphill by the wandering catspaws from the sea. It was the complete, the perfect smoke-screen. Miller nodded.

'Gonna make a break for it, huh, boss?'

'There's no choice – we either go, or we stay and get fried or blown into very little bits. Probably both.' He raised his voice. 'Anybody see what's happening up top?'

'Queuing up for another go at us, sir,' Brown said lugubriously. 'The first bloke's still circling around.'

'Waiting to see how we break cover. They won't wait long. This is where we take off.' He peered uphill through the rolling smoke, but it was too thick, laced his watering eyes until everything was blurred through a misted sheen of tears. There was no saying how far uphill the smoke-bank had reached, and they couldn't afford to wait until they were sure. Stuka pilots had never been renowned for their patience.

'Right, everybody!' he shouted. 'Fifteen yards along the treeline to that wash, then straight up into the gorge. Don't stop till you're at least a hundred yards inside. Andrea, you lead the way. Off you go!' He peered through the blinding smoke. 'Where's Panayis?'

There was no reply.

'Panayis!' Mallory called. 'Panayis!'

'Perhaps he went back for somethin'.' Miller had stopped, half-turned. 'Shall I go—'

'Get on your way!' Mallory said savagely. 'And if anything happens to young Stevens I'll hold you . . .' But Miller, wisely, was already gone, Andrea stumbling and coughing by his side.

For a couple of seconds Mallory stood irresolute, then plunged back downhill towards the centre of the grove. Maybe Panayis had gone back for something – and he couldn't understand English. Mallory had hardly gone five yards when he was forced to halt and fling his arm up before his face: the heat was searing. Panayis couldn't be down there; no one could have been down there, could have lived for seconds in that furnace. Gasping for air, hair singeing and clothes smoldering with fire, Mallory clawed his way back up the slope, colliding with trees, slipping, falling, then stumbling desperately to his feet again.

He ran along to the east end of the wood. No one there. Back to the other end again, towards the wash, almost completely blind now, the super-heated air searing viciously through throat and lungs till he was suffocating, till his breath was coming in great, whooping, agonized breaths. No sense in waiting longer, nothing he could do, nothing anyone could do except save himself. There was a noise in his ears, the roaring of the flames, the roaring of his own blood – and the screaming, heart-stopping roar of a Stuka in a power-dive. Desperately he flung himself forward over the sliding scree, stumbled and pitched headlong down to the floor of the wash.

Hurt or not, he did not know and he did not care. Sobbing aloud for breath, he rose to his feet, forced his aching legs to drive him somehow up the hill. The air was full of the thunder of engines, he knew the entire squadron was coming in to the attack, and then he had flung himself uncaringly to the ground as the first of the high explosive bombs erupted in its concussive blast of smoke and flame – erupted not forty yards away, to his left and ahead of him. *Ahead* of him! Even as he struggled upright again, lurched forward and upward once more, Mallory cursed himself again and again and again. You madman, he thought bitterly, confusedly, you damned crazy madman. Sending the others out to be killed. He should have thought of it – oh, God, he should have thought of it, a five-year-old could have thought of it. Of course Jerry wasn't going to bomb the grove: they had seen the obvious, the inevitable, as quickly as he had, were dive-bombing the pall of smoke between the grove and the cliff! A five-year-old – the earth exploded beneath his feet, a giant hand plucked him up and smashed him to the ground and the darkness closed over him.

Chapter Twelve

Wednesday 1600–1800

Once, twice, half a dozen times, Mallory struggled up from the depths of a black, trance-like stupor and momentarily touched the surface of consciousness only to slide back into the darkness again. Desperately, each time, he tried to hang on to these fleeting moments of awareness, but his mind was like the void, dark and sinewless, and even as he knew that his mind was slipping backwards again, loosing its grip on reality, the knowledge was gone, and there was only the void once more. Nightmare, he thought vaguely during one of the longer glimmerings of comprehension, I'm having a nightmare, like when you know you are having a nightmare and that if you could open your eyes it would be gone, but you can't open your eyes. He tried it now, tried to open his eyes, but it was no good, it was still as dark as ever and he was still sunk in this evil dream, for the sun had been shining brightly in the sky. He shook his head in slow despair.

'Aha! Observe! Signs of life at last!' There was no mistaking the slow, nasal drawl. 'Ol' Medicine Man Miller triumphs again!' There was a moment's silence, a moment in which Mallory was increasingly aware of the diminishing thunder of aero engines, the acrid, resinous smoke that stung his nostrils and eyes, and then an arm had passed under his shoulders and Miller's persuasive voice was in his ear. 'Just try a little of this, boss. Ye olde vintage brandy. Nothin' like it anywhere.'

Mallory felt the cold neck of the bottle, tilted his head back, took a long pull. Almost immediately he had jerked himself upright and forward to a sitting position, gagging, spluttering and fighting for breath as the raw, fiery ouzo bit into the mucous membrane of cheeks and throat. He tried to speak but could do no more than croak, gasp for fresh air and stare indignantly at the shadowy figure that knelt by his side. Miller, for his part, looked at him with unconcealed admiration.

'See, boss? Just like I said – nothin' like it.' He shook his head admiringly. 'Wide awake in an instant, as the literary boys would say. Never saw a shock and concussion victim recover so fast!'

'What the hell are you trying to do?' Mallory demanded. The fire had died down in his throat, and he could breathe again. 'Poison me?' Angrily he shook his head, fighting off the pounding ache, the fog that still swirled round the fringes of his mind. 'Bloody fine physician you are! Shock, you say, yet the first thing you do is administer a dose of spirits—'

'Take your pick,' Miller interrupted grimly. 'Either that or a damned sight bigger shock in about fifteen minutes or so when brother Jerry gets here.'

'But they've gone away. I can't hear the Stukas any more.'

'This lot's comin' up from the town,' Miller said morosely. 'Louki's just reported them. Half a dozen armoured cars and a couple of trucks with field guns the length of a telegraph pole.'

'I see.' Mallory twisted round, saw a gleam of light at a bend in the wall. A cave – a tunnel, almost. Little Cyprus, Louki had said some of the older people had called it – the Devil's Playground was riddled with a honeycomb of caves. He grinned wryly at the memory of his momentary panic when he thought his eyes had gone and turned again to Miller. 'Trouble again, Dusty, nothing but trouble. Thanks for bringing me round.'

'Had to,' Miller said briefly. 'I guess we couldn't have carried you very far, boss.'

Mallory nodded. 'Not just the flattest of country hereabouts.'

'There's that, too.' Miller agreed. 'What I really meant is that there's hardly anyone left to carry you. Casey Brown and Panayis have both been hurt, boss.'

'What! Both of them?' Mallory screwed his eyes shut, shook his head in slow anger. 'My God, Dusty, I'd forgotten all about the bomb – the bombs.' He reached out his hand, caught Miller by the arm. 'How – how bad are they?' There was so little time left, so much to do.

'How bad?' Miller shook out a pack of cigarettes and offered one to Mallory. 'Not bad at all – if we could get them into hospital. But hellish painful and cripplin' if they gotta start hikin' up and down those gawddamned ravines hereabouts. First time I've seen canyon floors more nearly vertical than the walls themselves.'

'You still haven't told me—'

'Sorry, boss, sorry. Shrapnel wounds, both of them, in exactly the same place – left thigh, just above the knee. No bones gone, no tendons cut. I've just finished tying up Casey's leg – it's a pretty wicked-lookin' gash. He's gonna know all about it when he starts walkin'.'

'And Panayis?'

'Fixed his own leg.' Miller said briefly. 'A queer character. Wouldn't even let me look at it, far less bandage it. I reckon he'd have knifed me if I'd tried.'

'Better to leave him alone anyway,' Mallory advised. 'Some of these islanders have strange taboos and superstitions. Just as long as he's alive. Though I still don't see how the hell he managed to get here.'

'He was the first to leave,' Miller explained. 'Along with Casey. You must have missed him in the smoke. They were climbin' together when they got hit.'

'And how did I get here?'

'No prizes for the first correct answer.' Miller jerked a thumb over his shoulder at the huge form that blocked half the width of the cave. 'Junior here did his St Bernard act once again. I wanted to go with him, but he wasn't keen. Said he reckoned it would be difficult to carry both of us up the hill. My feelin's were hurt considerable.' Miller sighed. 'I guess I just wasn't born to be a hero, that's all.'

Mallory smiled. 'Thanks again, Andrea.'

'Thanks!' Miller was indignant. 'A guy saves your life and all you can say is "thanks"!'

'After the first dozen times or so you run out of suitable speeches,' Mallory said dryly. 'How's Stevens?'

'Breathin'.'

Mallory nodded forward towards the source of light, wrinkled his nose. 'Just round the corner, isn't he?'

'Yeah, it's pretty grim,' Miller admitted. 'The gangrene's spread up beyond the knee.'

Mallory rose groggily to his feet, picked up his gun. 'How is he really, Dusty?'

'He's dead, but he just won't die. He'll be gone by sundown. Gawd only knows what's kept him goin' so far.'

'It may sound presumptuous,' Mallory murmured; 'but I think I know too.'

'The first-class medical attention?' Miller said hopefully.

'Looks that way, doesn't it?' Mallory smiled down at the still kneeling Miller. 'But that wasn't what I meant at all. Come, gentlemen, we have some business to attend to.'

'Me, all I'm good for is blowin' up bridges and droppin' a handful of sand in engine bearin's,' Miller announced. 'Strategy and tactics are far beyond my simple mind. But I still think those characters down there are pickin' a very stupid way of committin' suicide. It would be a damned sight easier for all concerned if they just shot themselves.'

'I'm inclined to agree with you.' Mallory settled himself more firmly behind the jumbled rocks in the mouth of the ravine that opened on the charred and smoking remains of the carob grove directly below and took another look at the Alpenkorps troops advancing in extended order up the steep, shelterless slopes. 'They're no children at this game. I bet they don't like it one little bit, either.'

'Then why the hell are they doin' it, boss?'

'No option, probably. First off, this place can only be attacked frontally.'

Mallory smiled down at the little Greek lying between himself and Andrea. 'Louki here chose the place well. It would require a long detour to attack from the rear – and it would take them a week to advance through that devil's scrapheap behind us. Secondly, it'll be sunset in a couple of hours, and they know they haven't a hope of getting us after it's dark. And finally – and I think this is more important than the other two reasons put together – it's a hundred to one that the commandant in the town is being pretty severely prodded by his High Command. There's too much at stake, even in the one in a thousand chance of us getting at the guns. They can't afford to have Kheros evacuated under their noses, to lose—'

'Why not?' Miller interrupted. He gestured largely with his hands. 'Just a lot of useless rocks—'

'They can't afford to lose face with the Turks,' Mallory went on patiently. 'The strategic importance of these islands in the Sporades is negligible, but their political importance is tremendous. Adolph badly needs another ally in these parts. So he flies in Alpenkorps troops by the thousand and the Stukas by the hundred, the best he has – and he needs them desperately on the Italian front. But you've got to convince your potential ally that you're a pretty safe bet before you can persuade him to give up his nice, safe seat on the fence and jump down on your side.'

'Very interestin',' Miller observed. 'So?'

'So the Germans are going to have no compunction about thirty or forty of their best troops being cut into little pieces. It's no trouble at all when you're sitting behind a desk a thousand miles away. . . . Let 'em come another hundred yards or so closer. Louki and I will start from the middle and work out: you and Andrea start from the outside.'

'I don't like it, boss.' Miller complained.

'Don't think that I do either,' Mallory said quietly. 'Slaughtering men forced to do a suicidal job like this is not my idea of fun – or even of war. But if we don't get them, they get us.' He broke off and pointed across the burnished sea to where Kheros lay peacefully on the hazed horizon, striking golden glints off the western sun. 'What do you think they would have us do, Dusty?'

'I know, I know, boss.' Miller stirred uncomfortably. 'Don't rub it in.' He pulled his woollen cap low over his forehead and stared bleakly down the slope. 'How soon do the mass executions begin?'

'Another hundred yards, I said.' Mallory looked down the slope towards the coast road and grinned suddenly, glad to change the topic. 'Never saw telegraph poles shrink so suddenly before, Dusty.'

Miller studied the guns drawn up on the roads behind the two trucks and cleared his throat.

'I was only sayin' what Louki told me,' he said defensively

'What Louki told you!' The little Greek was indignant. 'Before God, Major, the Americano is full of lies!'

'Ah, well, mebbe I was mistaken,' Miller said magnanimously. He squinted again at the guns, forehead lined in puzzlement. 'That first one's a mortar, I reckon. But what in the universe that other weird-looking contraption can be—'

'Also a mortar,' Mallory explained. 'A five-barrelled job, and very nasty. The *Nebelwerfer* or Moanin' Minnie. Howls like all the lost souls in hell. Guaranteed to turn the knees to jelly, especially after nightfall – but it's still the other one you have to watch. A six-inch mortar, almost certainly using fragmentation bombs – you use a brush and shovel for clearing up afterwards.'

'That's right,' Miller growled. 'Cheer us all up.' But he was grateful to the New Zealander for trying to take their minds off what they had to do. 'Why don't they use them?'

'They will,' Mallory assured him. 'Just as soon as we fire and they find out where we are.'

'Gawd help us,' Miller muttered. 'Fragmentation bombs, you said!' He lapsed into gloomy silence.

'Any second now,' Mallory said softly. 'I only hope that our friend Turzig isn't among this lot.' He reached out for his field-glasses but stopped in surprise as Andrea leaned across Louki and caught him by the wrist before he could lift the binoculars. 'What's the matter, Andrea?'

'I would not be using these, my Captain. They have betrayed us once already. I have been thinking, and it can be nothing else. The sunlight reflecting from the lenses . . .'

Mallory stared at him, slowly released his grip on the glasses, nodded several times in succession.

'Of course, of course! I had been wondering. . . . Someone has been careless. There was no other way, there *could* have been no other way. It would only require a single flash to tip them off.' He paused, remembering, then grinned wryly. 'It could have been myself. All this started just after I had been on watch – and Panayis didn't have the glasses.' He shook his head in mortification. 'It *must* have been me, Andrea.'

'I do not believe it,' Andrea said flatly. 'You couldn't make a mistake like that, my Captain.'

'Not only could, but did, I'm afraid. But we'll worry about that afterwards.' The middle of the ragged line of advancing soldiers, slipping and stumbling on the treacherous scree, had almost reached the lower limits of the blackened, stunted remains of the copse. 'They've come far enough. I'll take the white helmet in the middle, Louki.' Even as he spoke he could hear the soft scrape as the three others slid their automatic barrels across and between the protective rocks in front of them, could feel the wave of revulsion that washed through his mind. But his voice was steady enough as he spoke, relaxed and almost casual. 'Right. Let them have it now!'

His last words were caught up and drowned in the tearing, rapid-fire crash of the automatic carbines. With four machine-guns in their hands – two Brens and two 9 mm. Schmeissers – it was no war, as he had said, but sheer, pitiful massacre, with the defenceless figures on the slope below, figures still stunned and uncomprehending, jerking, spinning round and collapsing like marionettes in the hands of a mad puppeteer, some to die where they fell, others to roll down the steep slope, legs and arms flailing in the grotesque disjointedness of death. Only a couple stood still where they had been hit, vacant surprise mirrored in their lifeless faces, then slipped down tiredly to the stony ground at their feet. Almost three seconds had passed before the handful of those who still lived – about a quarter of the way in from either end of the line where the converging streams of fire had not yet met – realized what was happening and flung themselves desperately to the ground in search of the cover that didn't exist.

The phrenetic stammering of the machine-guns stopped abruptly and in unison, the sound sheared off as by a guillotine. The sudden silence was curiously oppressive, louder, more obtrusive than the clamour that had gone before. The gravelly earth beneath his elbows grated harshly as Mallory shifted his weight slightly, looked at the two men to his right, Andrea with his impassive face empty of all expression, Louki with the sheen of tears in his eyes. Then he became aware of the low murmuring to his left, shifted round again. Bitter-mouthed, savage, the American was swearing softly and continuously, oblivious to the pain as he pounded his fist time and again into the sharp-edged gravel before him.

'Just one more, Gawd.' The quiet voice was almost a prayer. 'That's all I ask. Just one more.'

Mallory touched his arm. 'What is it, Dusty?'

Miller looked round at him, eyes cold and still and empty of all recognition, then he blinked several times and grinned, a cut and bruised hand automatically reaching for his cigarettes.

'Jus' daydreamin', boss,' he said easily. 'Jus' daydreamin'.' He shook out his pack of cigarettes. 'Have one?'

'That inhuman bastard that sent these poor devils up that hill,' Mallory said quietly. 'Make a wonderful picture seen over the sights of your rifle, wouldn't he?'

Abruptly Miller's smile vanished and he nodded.

'It would be all of that.' He risked a quick peep round one of the boulders, eased himself back again. 'Eight, mebbe ten of them still down there, boss,' he reported. 'The poor bastards are like ostriches – trying to take cover behind stones the size of an orange. . . . We leave them be?'

'We leave them be!' Mallory echoed emphatically. The thought of any more slaughter made him feel almost physically sick. 'They won't try again.' He broke off suddenly, flattened himself in reflex instinct as a burst of machine-gun bullets struck the steep-walled rock above their heads and whined up the gorge in vicious ricochet.

'Won't try again, huh?' Miller was already sliding his gun around the rock in front of him when Mallory caught his arm and pulled him back.

'Not them? Listen!' Another burst of fire, then another, and now they could hear the savage chatter of the machine-gun, a chatter rhythmically interrupted by a weird, half-human sighing as its belt passed through the breech. Mallory could feel the prickling of the hairs on the nape of his neck.

'A Spandau. Once you've heard a Spandau you can never forget it. Leave it alone – it's probably fixed on the back of one of the trucks and can't do us any harm. . . . I'm more worried about these damned mortars down there.'

'I'm not,' Miller said promptly. 'They're not firing at us.'

'That's why I'm worried. . . . What do you think, Andrea?'

'The same as you, my Captain. They are waiting. This Devil's Playground, as Louki calls it, is a madman's maze, and they can only fire as blind men—'

'They won't be waiting much longer,' Mallory interrupted grimly. He pointed to the north. 'Here come their eyes.'

At first only specks above the promontory of Cape Demirci, the planes were soon recognizable for what they were, droning in slowly over the Ægean at about fifteen hundred feet. Mallory looked at them in astonishment, then turned to Andrea.

'Am I seeing things, Andrea?' He gestured at the first of the two planes, a high-winged little monoplane fighter. 'That can't be a PZL?'

'It can be and it is,' Andrea murmured. 'An old Polish plane we had before the war,' he explained to Miller. 'And the other is an old Belgian plane – Breguets, we called them.' Andrea shaded his eyes to look again at the two planes, now almost directly overhead. 'I thought they had all been lost during the invasion.'

'Me too,' Mallory said. 'Must have patched up some bits and pieces. Ah, they've seen us – beginning to circle. But why on earth they use these obsolete death traps—'

'I don't know and I don't care,' Miller said rapidly. He had just taken a quick look round the boulder in front of him. 'These damned guns down there are just linin' up on us, and muzzle-on they look a considerable sight bigger than telegraph poles. Fragmentation bombs, you said! Come on, boss, lets get the hell outa here!'

Thus the pattern was set for the remainder of that brief November afternoon, for the grim game of tip-and-run, hide-and-seek among the ravines and shattered rocks of the Devil's Playground. The planes held the key to the game, cruised high overhead observing every move of the hunted group below, relaying the information to the guns on the coast road and the company of Alpenkorps that had moved up through the ravine above the carob grove soon after the planes reported that the positions there had been abandoned. The two ancient planes were soon replaced by a couple of modern Henschels – Andrea said that the PZL couldn't remain airborne for more than an hour anyway.

Mallory was between the devil and the deep sea. Inaccurate though the mortars were, some of the deadly fragmentation bombs found their way into the deep ravines where they took temporary shelter, the blast of metal lethal in the confined space between the sheering walls. Occasionally they came so close that Mallory was forced to take refuge in some of the deep caves that honeycombed the walls of the canyons. In these they were safe enough, but the safety was an illusion that could lead only to ultimate defeat and capture; in the lulls, the Alpenkorps, whom they had fought off in a series of brief, skirmishing rearguard actions during the afternoon, could approach closely enough to trap them inside. Time and time again Mallory and his men were forced to move on to widen the gap between themselves and their pursuers, following the indomitable Louki wherever he chose to lead them, and taking their chance, often a very slender and desperate chance, with the mortar bombs. One bomb arced into a ravine that led into the interior, burying itself in the gravelly ground not twenty yards ahead of them, by far the nearest anything had come during the afternoon. By one chance in a thousand, it didn't explode. They gave it as wide a berth as possible, almost holding their breaths until they were safely beyond.

About half an hour before sunset they struggled up the last few boulder-strewn yards of a steeply-shelving ravine floor, halted just beyond the shelter of the projecting wall where the ravine dipped again and turned sharply to the right and the north. There had been no more mortar bombs since the one that had failed to explode. The six-inch and the weirdly-howling *Nebelwerfer* had only a limited range, Mallory knew, and though the planes still cruised overhead, they cruised uselessly: the sun was dipping towards the horizon and the floors of the ravines were already deep-sunk in shadowed gloom, invisible from above. But the Alpenkorps, tough, dogged, skilful soldiers, soldiers living only for the revenge of their massacred comrades, were very close behind. And they were highly-trained mountain troops, fresh, resilient, the reservoir of their energies barely tapped: whereas his own tiny band, worn out from continuous days and sleepless nights of labour and action. . . .

Mallory sank to the ground near the angled turn of the ravine where he could keep lookout, glanced at the others with a deceptive casualness that marked his cheerless assessment of what he saw. As a fighting unit they were in a pretty bad way. Both Panayis and Brown were badly crippled, the latter's face grey with pain. For the first time since leaving Alexandria, Casey Brown was apathetic, listless and quite indifferent to everything: this Mallory took as a very bad sign. Nor was Brown helped by the heavy transmitter still strapped to his back – with point-blank truculence he had ignored Mallory's categorical order to abandon it. Louki was tired, and looked it: his physique, Mallory realized now, was no match for his spirit, for the infectious smile that never left his face, for the panache of that magnificently upswept moustache that contrasted so oddly with the sad, tired eyes above. Miller, like himself, was tired, but, like himself, could keep on being tired for a long time yet. And Stevens was still conscious but even in the twilit gloom of the canyon floor his face looked curiously transparent, while the nails, lips and eyelids were drained of blood. And Andrea, who had carried him up and down all these killing canyon tracks – where there had been tracks – for almost two interminable hours, looked as he always did: immutable, indestructible.

Mallory shook his head, fished out a cigarette, made to strike a light, remembered the planes still cruising overhead and threw the match away. Idly his gaze travelled north along the canyon and he slowly stiffened, the unlit cigarette crumpling and shredding between his fingers. This ravine bore no resemblance to any of the others through which they had so far passed – it was broader, dead straight, at least three times as long – and, as far as he could see in the twilight, the far end was blocked off by an almost vertical wall.

'Louki!' Mallory was on his feet now, all weariness forgotten. 'Do you know where you are? Do you know this place?'

'But certainly, Major!' Louki was hurt. 'Have I not told you that Panayis and I, in the days of our youth—'

'But this is a cul-de-sac, a dead-end!' Mallory protested. 'We're boxed in, man, we're trapped!'

Louki grinned impudently and twirled a corner of his moustache. The little man was enjoying himself.

'So? The Major does not trust Louki, is that it?' He grinned again, relented, patted the wall by his side. 'Panayis and I, we have been working this way all afternoon. Along this wall there are many caves. One of them leads through to another valley that leads down to the coast road.'

'I see, I see.' Relief washing through his mind, Mallory sank down on the ground again. 'And where does this other valley come out?'

'Just across the strait from Maidos.'

'How far from the town?'

'About five miles, Major, maybe six. Not more.'

'Fine, fine! And you're sure you can find this cave?'

'A hundred years from now and my head in a goat-skin bag!' Louki boasted.

'Fair enough!' Even as he spoke, Mallory catapulted himself violently to one side, twisted in mid-air to avoid falling across Stevens and crashed heavily into the wall between Andrea and Miller. In a moment of unthinking carelessness he had exposed himself to view from the ravine they had just climbed: the burst of machine-gun fire from its lower end – a hundred and fifty yards away at the most – had almost blown his head off. Even as it was, the left shoulder of his jacket had been torn away, the shell just grazing his shoulder. Miller was already kneeling by his side, fingering the gash, running a gently exploratory hand across his back.

'Careless, damn' careless,' Mallory murmured. 'But I didn't think they were so close.' He didn't feel as calm as he sounded. If the mouth of that Schmeisser had been another sixteenth of an inch to the right, he'd have had no head left now.

'Are you all right, boss?' Miller was puzzled. 'Did they—'

'Terrible shots,' Mallory assured him cheerfully. 'Couldn't hit a barn.' He twisted round to look at his shoulder. 'I hate to sound heroic, but this really is just a scratch. . . .' He rose easily to his feet, and picked up his gun. 'Sorry and all that, gentlemen, but it's time we were on our way again. How far along is this cave, Louki?'

Louki rubbed his bristly chin, the smile suddenly gone. He looked quickly at Mallory, then away again.

'Louki!'

'Yes, yes, Major. The cave.' Louki rubbed his chin again. 'Well, it is a good way along. In fact, it is at the end,' he finished uncomfortably.

'The *very* end?' asked Mallory quietly.

Louki nodded miserably, stared down at the ground at his feet. Even the ends of his moustache seemed to droop.

'That's handy,' Mallory said heavily. 'Oh, that's very handy!' He sank down to the ground again. 'Helps us no end, that does.'

He bowed his head in thought and didn't even lift it as Andrea poked a Bren round the angle of the rock, and fired a short downhill burst more in token of discouragement than in any hope of hitting anything. Another ten seconds passed, then Louki spoke again, his voice barely audible.

'I am very, very sorry. This is a terrible thing. Before God, Major, I would not have done it but that I thought they were still far behind.'

'It's not your fault, Louki.' Mallory was touched by the little man's obvious distress. He touched his ripped shoulder jacket. 'I thought the same thing.'

'Please!' Stevens put his hand on Mallory's arm. 'What's wrong? I don't understand.'

'Everybody else does, I'm afraid, Andy. It's very, very simple. We have half a mile to go along this valley here – and not a shred of cover. The Alpenkorps have less than two hundred yards to come up that ravine we've just left.' He paused while Andrea fired another retaliatory short burst, then continued. 'They'll do what they're doing now – keep probing to see if we're still here. The minute they judge we're gone, they'll be up here in a flash. They'll nail us before we're half-way, quarter way to the cave – you know we can't travel fast. And they're carrying a couple of Spandaus – they'll cut us to ribbons.'

'I see,' Stevens murmured. 'You put it all so nicely, sir.'

'Sorry, Andy, but that's how it is.'

'But could you not leave two men as a rear-guard, while the rest—'

'And what happens to the rear-guard?' Mallory interrupted dryly.

'I see what you mean,' he said in a low voice. 'I hadn't thought of that.'

'No, but the rear-guard would. Quite a problem, isn't it?'

'There is no problem at all,' Louki announced. 'The Major is kind, but this is all my fault. I will—'

'You'll do damn all of the kind!' Miller said savagely. He tore Louki's Bren from his hand and laid it on the ground. 'You heard what the boss said – it wasn't your fault.' For a moment Louki stared at him in anger, then turned dejectedly away. He looked as if he were going to cry. Mallory, too, stared at the American, astonished at the sudden vehemence, so completely out of character. Now that he came to think of it. Dusty had been strangely taciturn and thoughtful during the past hour or so – Mallory couldn't recall his saying a word during all that time. But time enough to worry about that later on. . . .

Casey Brown eased his injured leg, looked hopefully at Mallory. 'Couldn't we stay here till it's dark – real dark – then make our way—'

'No good. The moon's almost full tonight – and not a cloud in the sky. They'd get us. Even more important, we have to get into the town between sunset and curfew tonight. Our last chance. Sorry, Casey, but it's no go.'

Fifteen seconds, half a minute passed, and passed in silence, then they all started abruptly as Andy Stevens spoke.

'Louki *was* right, you know,' he said pleasantly. The voice was weak, but filled with a calm certainty that jerked every eye towards him. He was propped up on one elbow, Louki's Bren cradled in his hands. It was a measure of their concentration on the problem on hand that no one had heard or seen him reach out for the machine-gun. 'It's all very simple,' Stevens went on quietly. 'Just let's use our heads, that's all. . . . The gangrene's right up past the knee, isn't it, sir?'

Mallory said nothing: he didn't know what to say, the complete unexpectedness had knocked him off balance. He was vaguely aware that Miller was looking at him, his eyes begging him to say 'No.'

'Is it or isn't it?' There was a patience, a curious understanding in the voice, and all of a sudden Mallory knew what to say.

'Yes,' he nodded. 'It is.' Miller was looking at him in horror.

'Thank you, sir.' Stevens was smiling in satisfaction. 'Thank you very much indeed. There's no need to point out all the advantages of my staying here.' There was an assurance in his voice no one had ever heard before, the unthinking authority of a man completely in charge of a situation. 'Time I did something for my living anyway. No fond farewells, please. Just leave me a couple of boxes of ammo, two or three thirty-six grenades and away you go.'

'I'll be damned if we will!' Miller was up on his feet, making for the boy, then brought up abruptly as the Bren centred on his chest.

'One step nearer and I'll shoot you,' Stevens said calmly. Miller looked at him in long silence, sank slowly back to the ground.

'I would, you know,' Stevens assured him. 'Well, goodbye, gentlemen. Thank you for all you've done for me.'

Twenty seconds, thirty, a whole minute passed in a queer, trance-like silence, then Miller heaved himself to his feet again, a tall, rangy figure with tattered clothes and a face curiously haggard in the gathering gloom.

'So long, kid. I guess – waal, mebbe I'm not so smart after all.' He took Stevens's hand, looked down at the wasted face for a long moment, made to say something else, then changed his mind. 'Be seein' you,' he said abruptly, turned and walked off heavily down the valley. One by one the others followed him, wordlessly, except for Andrea who stooped and whispered in the boy's ear, a whisper that brought a smile and a nod of complete understanding, and then there was only Mallory left. Stevens grinned up at him.

'Thank you, sir. Thanks for not letting me down. You and Andrea – you understand. You always did understand.'

'You'll – you'll be all right, Andy?' God, Mallory thought, what a stupid, what an insane thing, to say.

'Honest, sir, I'm OK.' Stevens smiled contentedly. 'No pain left – I can't feel a thing. It's wonderful!'

'Andy, I don't—'

'It's time you were gone, sir. The others will be waiting. Now if you'll just light me a gasper and fire a few random shots down that ravine . . .'

Within five minutes Mallory had overtaken the others, and inside fifteen they had all reached the cave that led to the coast. For a moment they stood in the entrance, listening to the intermittent firing from the other end of the valley, then turned wordlessly and plunged into the cave. Back where they had left him, Andy Stevens was lying on his stomach, peering down into the now almost dark ravine. There was no pain left in his body, none at all. He drew deeply on a cupped cigarette, smiled as he pushed another clip home into the magazine of the Bren. For the first time in his life Andy Stevens was happy and content beyond his understanding, a man at last at peace with himself. He was no longer afraid.

Chapter Thirteen

Wednesday Evening 1800–1915

Exactly forty minutes later they were safely in the heart of the town of Navarone, within fifty yards of the great gates of the fortress itself.

Mallory, gazing out at the gates and the still more massive arch of stone that encased them, shook his head for the tenth time and tried to fight off the feeling of disbelief and wonder that they should have reached their goal at last – or as nearly as made no difference. They had been due a break some time, he thought, the law of averages had been overwhelmingly against the continuation of the evil fortune that had dogged them so incessantly since they had arrived on the island. It was only right, he kept telling himself, it was only just that this should be so: but even so, the transition from that dark valley where they had left Andy Stevens to die to this tumbledown old house on the east side of the town square of Navarone had been so quick, so easy, that it still lay beyond immediate understanding or unthinking acceptance.

Not that it had been too easy in the first fifteen minutes or so, he remembered. Panayis's wounded leg had given out on him immediately after they had entered the cave, and he had collapsed; he must have been in agony, Mallory had thought, with his torn, roughly-bandaged leg, but the failing light and the dark, bitter impassive face had masked the pain. He had begged Mallory to be allowed to remain where he was, to hold off the Alpenkorps when they had overcome Stevens and reached the end of the valley, but Mallory had roughly refused him permission. Brutally he had told Panayis that he was far too valuable to be left there – and that the chances of the Alpenkorps picking that cave out of a score of others were pretty remote. Mallory had hated having to talk to him like that, but there had been no time for gentle blandishments, and Panayis must have seen his point for he had made neither protest nor struggle when Miller and Andrea picked him up and helped him to limp through the cave. The limp, Mallory had noticed, had been much less noticeable then, perhaps because of the assistance, perhaps because now that he had been baulked of the chance of killing a few more Germans it had been pointless to exaggerate his hurt.

They had barely cleared the mouth of the cave on the other side and were making their way down the tree-tufted, sloping valley side towards the sea, the dark sheen of the Ægean clearly visible in the gloom, when Louki, hearing something, had gestured them all to silence. Almost immediately Mallory, too, heard it, a soft guttural voice occasionally lost in the crunch of approaching feet on gravel, had seen that they were providentially screened by some stunted trees, given the order to stop and sworn in quick anger as he had heard the soft thud and barely muffled cry behind them. He had gone back to investigate and found Panayis stretched on the ground unconscious. Miller, who had been helping him along, had explained that Mallory had halted them so suddenly that he'd bumped into Panayis, that the Greek's bad leg had given beneath him, throwing him heavily, his head striking a stone as he had fallen. Mallory had stooped down in instantly renewed suspicion – Panayis was a throw-back, a natural-born killer, and he was quite capable of faking an accident if he thought he could turn it to his advantage, line a few more of the enemy up on the sights of his rifle . . . but there had been no fake about that: the bruised and bloodied gash above the temple was all too real.

The German patrol, having had no inkling of their presence, moved noisily up the valley till they had finally gone out of earshot. Louki had thought that the commandant in Navarone was becoming desperate, trying to seal off every available exit from the Devil's Playground. Mallory had thought it unlikely, but had not stayed to argue the point. Five minutes later they had cleared the mouth of the valley, and in another five had not only reached the coast road but silenced and bound two sentries – the drivers, probably – who had been guarding a truck and command car parked by the roadside, stripped them of denims and helmets and bundled them out of sight behind some bushes.

The trip into Navarone had been ridiculously simple, but the entire lack of opposition was easily understandable, because of the complete unexpectedness of it all. Seated beside Mallory on the front seat, clad, like Mallory, in captured clothes. Louki had driven the big car, and driven it magnificently, an accomplishment so unusual to find in a remote Ægean island that Mallory had been completely mystified until Louki had reminded him that he had been Eugene Vlachos's Consulate chaffeur for many years. The drive into town had taken less than twelve minutes – not only did the little man handle the car superbly, but he knew the road so well that he got the utmost possible out of the big machine, most of the time without benefit of any lights at all.

Not only a simple journey, but quite uneventful. They had passed several parked trucks at intervals along the road, and less than two miles from the town itself had met a group of about twenty soldiers marching in the opposite direction in column of twos. Louki had slowed down – it would have been highly suspicious had he accelerated, endangering the lives of the marching men – but had switched on the powerful headlights, blinding them, and blown raucously on the horn, while Mallory had leaned out of the right-hand window, sworn at them in perfect German and told them to get out of his damned way. This they had done, while the junior officer in charge had come smartly to attention, throwing up his hand in punctilious salute.

Immediately afterwards they had run through an area of high-walled, terraced market gardens, passed between a decaying Byzantine church and a whitewashed orthodox monastery that faced each other incongruously across the same dusty road, then almost at once were running through the lower part of the old town. Mallory had had a vague impression of narrow, winding, dim-lit streets only inches wider than the car itself, hugely cobbled and with almost knee-high pavements, then Louki was making his way up an arched lane, the car climbing steeply all the time. He had stopped abruptly, and Mallory had followed his quick survey of the darkened lane: completely deserted though over an hour yet to curfew. Beside them had been a flight of white stone steps innocent of any hand-rail, running up parallel to the wall of a house, with a highly ornamented lattice-work grill protecting the outside landing at the top. A still groggy Panayis had led them up these stairs, through to a house – he had known exactly where he was – across a shallow roof, down some more steps, through a dark courtyard and into this ancient house where they were now. Louki had driven the car away even before they reached the top of the stairs; it was only now that Mallory remembered that Louki hadn't thought it worth while to say what he intended to do with the car.

Still gazing out of the windowless hole in the wall at the fortress gate, Mallory found himself hoping intensely that nothing would happen to the sad-eyed little Greek, and not only because in his infinite resource and local knowledge he had been invaluable to them and was likely to prove so again; all these considerations apart, Mallory had formed the deepest affection for him, for his unvarying cheerfulness, his enthusiasm, his eagerness to help and to please, above all for his complete disregard of self. A thoroughly lovable little man, and Mallory's heart warmed to him. More than he could say for Panayis, he thought sourly, and then immediately regretted the thought: it was no fault of Panayis's that he was what he was, and in his own dark and bitter way he had done as much for them as Louki. But the fact remained that he was sadly lacking in Louki's warm humanity.

He lacked also Louki's quick intelligence, the calculated opportunism that amounted almost to genius. It had been a brilliant idea on Louki's part, Mallory mused, that they should take over this abandoned house: not that there had been any difficulty in finding an empty house – since the Germans had taken over the old castle the inhabitants of the town had left in their scores for Margaritha and other outlying villages, none more quickly than those who had lived in the town square itself; the nearness of the fortress wall that formed the north side of the square had been more than many of them could stomach, with the constant coming and going of their conquerors through the fortress gates, the sentries marching to and fro, the never ceasing reminders that their freedom was a vanished thing. So many gone that more than half the houses on the west side of the square – those nearest the fortress – were now occupied by German officers. But this same enforced close observation of the fortress's activities had been exactly what Mallory had wanted. When the time came to strike they had only yards to go. And although any competent garrison commander would always be prepared against the unexpected. Mallory considered it unlikely indeed that any reasonable man could conceive of a sabotage group so suicidally minded as to spend an entire day within a literal stones' throw of the fortress wall.

Not that the house as such had much to recommend it. As a home, a dwelling place, it was just about as uncomfortable as possible, as dilapidated as it could be without actually falling down. The west side of the square – the side perched precariously on the cliff-top – and the south side were made up of fairly modern buildings of whitewashed stone and Parian granite, huddled together in the invariable fashion of houses in these island towns, flat-roofed to catch as much as possible of the winter rains. But the east side of the square, where they were, was made up of antiquated timber and turf houses, of the kind much more often found in remote mountain villages.

The beaten earth floor beneath his feet was hummocky, uneven, and the previous occupants had used one corner of it – obviously – for a variety of purposes, not least as a refuse dump. The ceiling was of rough-hewn, blackened beams, more or less covered with planks, these in turn being covered with a thick layer of trodden earth: from previous experience of such houses in the White Mountains, Mallory knew that the roof would leak like a sieve whenever the rain came on. Across one end of the room was a solid ledge some thirty inches high, a ledge that served, after the fashion of similar structures in Eskimo igloos, as bed, tables or settee as the occasion demanded. The room was completely bare of furniture.

Mallory started as someone touched him on the shoulder and turned round. Miller was behind him, munching away steadily, the remains of a bottle of wine in his hand.

'Better get some chow, boss,' he advised. 'I'll take a gander through this hole from time to time.'

'Right you are, Dusty. Thanks.' Mallory moved gingerly towards the back of the room – it was almost pitch dark inside and they dared not risk a light – and felt his way till he brought up against the ledge. The tireless Andrea had gone through their provisions and prepared a meal of sorts – dried figs, honey, cheese, garlic sausages and pounded roast chestnuts. A horrible mixture, Mallory thought, but the best Andrea could do: besides he was too hungry, ravenously so, to worry about such niceties as the pleasing of his palate. And by the time he had washed it down with some of the local wine that Louki and Panayis had provided the previous day, the sweetly-resinous rawness of the drink had obliterated every other taste.

Carefully, shielding the match with his hand, Mallory lit a cigarette and began to explain for the first time his plan for entering the fortress. He did not have to bother lowering his voice – a couple of looms in the next house, one of the few occupied ones left on that side of the square, clacked incessantly throughout the evening. Mallory had a shrewd suspicion that this was more of Louki's doing, although it was difficult to see how he could have got word through to any of his friends. But Mallory was content to accept the situation as it was, to concentrate on making sure that the others understood his instructions.

Apparently they did, for there were no questions. For a few minutes the talk became general, the usually taciturn Casey Brown having the most to say, complaining bitterly about the food, the drink, his injured leg and the hardness of the bench where he wouldn't be able to sleep a wink all night long. Mallory grinned to himself but said nothing; Casey Brown was definitely on the mend.

'I reckon we've talked enough, gentlemen.' Mallory slid off the bench and stretched himself. God, he was tired! 'Our first and last chance to get a decent night's sleep. Two hour watches – I'll take the first.'

'By yourself?' It was Miller calling softly from the other end of the room. 'Don't you think we should share watches, boss? One for the front, one for the back. Besides, you know we're all pretty well done up. One man by himself might fall asleep.' He sounded so anxious that Mallory laughed.

'Not a chance, Dusty. Each man will keep watch by the window there and if he falls asleep he'll damn' soon wake up when he hits the floor. And it's because we're so darned bushed that we can't afford to have anyone lose sleep unnecessarily. Myself first, then you, then Panayis, then Casey, then Andrea.'

'Yeah, I suppose that'll be OK,' Miller conceded grudgingly.

He put something hard and cold into his hand. Mallory recognized it at once – it was Miller's most cherished possession, his silenced automatic.

'Just so's you can fill any nosy customers full of little holes without wakin' the whole town.' He ambled off to the back of the room, lit a cigarette, smoked it quietly for a few moments, then swung his legs up on the bench. Within five minutes everyone except the silently watchful man at the window was sound asleep.

Two or three minutes later Mallory jerked to unmoving attention as he heard a stealthy sound outside – from the back of the house, he thought. The clacking of the looms next door had stopped, and the house was very still. Again there came the noise, unmistakable this time, a gentle tapping at the door at the end of the passage that led from the back of the room.

'Remain there, my Captain.' It was Andrea's soft murmur, and Mallory marvelled for the hundredth time at Andrea's ability to rouse himself from the deepest of sleeps at the slightest alien sound: the violence of a thunderstorm would have left him undisturbed. 'I will see to it. It must be Louki.'

It was Louki. The little man was panting, near exhaustion, but extraordinarily pleased with himself. Gratefully he drank the cup of wine that Andrea poured for him.

'Damned glad to see you back again!' Mallory said sincerely. 'How did it go? Someone after you?'

Mallory could almost see him drawing himself up to his full height in the darkness.

'As if any of these clumsy fools could see Louki, even on a moonlit night, far less catch him,' he said indignantly. He paused to draw some deep breaths. 'No, no, Major, I knew you would be worried about me so I ran back all the way. Well, nearly all the way,' he amended. 'I am not so young as I was, Major Mallory.'

'All the way from where?' Mallory asked. He was glad of the darkness that hid his smile.

'From Vygos. It is an old castle that the Franks built there many generations ago, about two miles from here along the coast road to the east.' He paused to drink another mouthful of wine. 'More than two miles, I would say – and I only walked twice, a minute at a time, on the way back.' Mallory had the impression that Louki already regretted his momentary weakness in admitting that he was no longer a young man.

'And what did you do there?' Mallory asked.

'I was thinking, after I left you,' Louki answered indirectly. 'Me, I am always thinking,' he explained. 'It is a habit of mine. I was thinking that when the soldiers who are looking for us out in the Devil's Playground find out that the car is gone, they will know that we are no longer in that accursed place.'

'Yes.' Mallory agreed carefully. 'Yes, they will know that.'

'Then they will say to themselves, "Ha, those *verdammt Englanders* have little time left." They will know that we will know that they have little hope of catching us in the island – Panayis and I, we know every rock and tree and path and cave. So all they can do is to make sure that we do not get into the town – they will block every road leading in, and tonight is our last chance to get in. You follow me?' he asked anxiously.

'I am trying very hard.'

'But first' – Louki spread his hands dramatically – 'but first they will make sure we are not in the town. They would be fools to block the roads if we were already in the town. They *must* make sure we are not in the town. And so – the search. The very great search. With – how do you say? – the teeth-comb!'

Mallory nodded his head in slow understanding.

'I'm afraid he's right, Andrea.'

'I, too, fear so,' Andrea said unhappily. 'We should have thought of this. But perhaps we could hide – the roof-tops or—'

'With a teeth-comb, I said!' Louki interrupted impatiently. 'But all is well. I, Louki, have thought it all out. I can smell rain. There will be clouds over the moon before long, and it will be safe to move. . . . You do not want to know what I have done with the car, Major Mallory?' Louki was enjoying himself immensely.

'Forgotten all about it,' Mallory confessed. 'What *did* you do with the car?'

'I left it in the courtyard of Vygos castle. Then I emptied all the petrol from the tank and poured it over the car. Then I struck a match.'

'You did *what*?' Mallory was incredulous.

'I struck a match. I think I was standing too near the car, for I do not seem to have any eyebrows left.' Louki sighed. 'A pity – it was such a splendid machine.' Then he brightened. 'But before God, Major, it burned magnificently.'

Mallory stared at him.

'Why on earth—?'

'It is simple,' Louki explained patiently. 'By this time the men out in the Devil's Playground must know that their car has been stolen. They see the fire. They hurry back to – how do you say?'

'Investigate?'

'So. Investigate. They wait till the fire dies down. They investigate again. No bodies, no bones in the car, so they search the castle. And what do they find?'

There was silence in the room.

'Nothing!' Louki said impatiently. 'They find nothing. And then they search the countryside for half a mile around. And what do they find? Again nothing. So then they know that they have been fooled, and that we are in the town, and will come to search the town.'

'With the teeth-comb,' Mallory murmured.

'With the teeth-comb. And what do they find?' Louki paused, then hurried on before anyone could steal his thunder. 'Once again, they will find nothing,' he said triumphantly. 'And why? For by then the rain will have come, the moon will have vanished, the explosives will be hidden – and we will be gone!'

'Gone where?' Mallory felt dazed.

'Where but to Vygos castle, Major Mallory. Never while night follows day will they think to look for us there!'

Mallory looked at him in silence for long seconds without speaking, then turned to Andrea.

'Captain Jensen's only made one mistake so far,' he murmured. 'He picked the wrong man to lead this expedition. Not that it matters anyway. With Louki here on our side, how can we lose?'

Mallory lowered his rucksack gently to the earthen roof, straightened and peered up into the darkness, both hands shielding his eyes from the first drizzle of rain. Even from where they stood – on the crumbling roof of the house nearest the fortress on the east side of the square – the walls stretched fifteen, perhaps twenty feet above their heads; the wickedly out- and down-curving spikes that topped the wall were all but lost in the darkness.

'There she is, Dusty,' Mallory murmured. 'Nothing to it.'

'Nothin' to it!' Miller was horrified. 'I've – I've gotta get over *that*?'

'You'd have a ruddy hard time going through it,' Mallory answered briefly. He grinned, clapped Miller on the back and prodded the rucksack at his feet. 'We chuck this rope up, the hook catches, you shin smartly up—'

'And bleed to death on those six strands of barbed wire,' Miller interrupted. 'Louki says they're the biggest barbs he's ever seen.'

'We'll use the tent for padding,' Mallory said soothingly.

'I have a very delicate skin, boss,' Miller complained. 'Nothin' short of a spring mattress—'

'Well, you've only an hour to find one,' Mallory said indifferently. Louki had estimated that it would be at least an hour before the search party would clear the northern part of the town, give himself and Andrea a chance to begin a diversion. 'Come on, let's cache this stuff and get out of here. We'll shove the rucksacks in this corner and cover 'em with earth. Take the rope out first, though; we'll have no time to start undoing the packs when we get here.'

Miller dropped to his knees, hands fumbling with straps, then exclaimed in sudden annoyance.

'This can't be the pack' he muttered in disgust. Abruptly his voice changed. 'Here, wait a minute, though.'

'What's up, Dusty?'

Miller didn't answer immediately. For a few seconds his hands explored the contents of the pack, then he straightened.

'The slow-burnin' fuse, boss.' His voice was blurred with anger, with a vicious anger that astonished Mallory. 'It's gone!'

'What!' Mallory stooped, began to search through the pack. 'It can't be, Dusty, it just *can't*! Dammit to hell, man, you packed the stuff yourself!'

'Sure, I did, boss,' Miller grated, 'And then some crawlin' bastard comes along behind my back and unpacks it again.'

'Impossible!' Mallory protested. 'It's just downright impossible, Dusty. *You* closed that rucksack – I saw you do it in the grove this morning – and Louki has had it all the time. And I'd trust Louki with my life.'

'So would I, boss.'

'Maybe we're both wrong,' Mallory went on quietly. 'Maybe you did miss it out. We're both helluva tired, Dusty.'

Miller looked at him queerly, said nothing for a moment then began to swear again. 'It's my own fault, boss, my own gawddamned fault.'

'What do you mean, your own fault? Heavens above, man, I was there when . . .' Mallory broke off, rose quickly to his feet and stared through the darkness at the south side of the square. A single shot had rung out there, the whiplash crack of a carbine followed the thin, high whine of a ricochet, and then silence.

Mallory stood quite still, hands clenched by his sides. Over ten minutes had passed since he and Miller had left Panayis to guide Andrea and Brown to the Castle Vygos – they should have been well away from the square by this time. And almost certainly Louki wouldn't be down there. Mallory's instructions to him had been explicit – to hide the remainder of the TNT blocks in the roof and then wait there to lead himself and Miller to the keep. But something could have gone wrong, something could always go wrong. Or a trap, maybe a ruse. But what kind of trap?

The sudden off-beat stammering of a heavy machine-gun stilled his thoughts, and for a moment or two he was all eyes and straining ears. And then another, and lighter machine-gun, cut in, just for a few seconds: as abruptly as they had started, both guns died away, together. Mallory waited no longer.

'Get the stuff together again,' he whispered urgently. 'We're taking it with us. Something's gone wrong.' Within thirty seconds they had ropes and explosives back in their knapsacks, had strapped them on their backs and were on their way.

Bent almost double, careful to make no noise whatsoever, they ran across the roof-tops towards the old house where they had hidden earlier in the evening, where they were now to rendezvous with Louki. Still running, they were only feet away from the house when they saw his shadowy figure rise up, only it wasn't Louki, Mallory realized at once, for it was too tall for

Louki and without breaking step he catapulted the horizontal driving weight of his 180 pounds at the unknown figure in a homicidal tackle, his shoulder catching the man just below the breast-bone, emptying every last particle of air from the man's lungs with an explosive, agonized *whoosh*. A second later both of Miller's sinewy hands were clamped round the man's neck, slowly choking him to death.

And he would have choked to death, neither of the two men were in any mind for half-measures, had not Mallory, prompted by some fugitive intuition, stooped low over the contorted face, the staring, protruding eyes, choked back a cry of sudden horror.

'Dusty!' he whispered hoarsely. 'For God's sake stop! Let him go! It's Panayis!'

Miller didn't hear him. In the gloom his face was like stone, his head sunk farther and farther between hunching shoulders as he tightened his grip, strangling the Greek in a weird savage silence.

'It's Panayis, you bloody fool, Panayis!' Mallory's mouth was at the American's ear, his hands clamped round the other's wrists as he tried to drag him off Panayis's throat. He could hear the muffled drumming of Panayis's heels on the turf of the roof, tore at Miller's wrists with all his strength: twice before he had heard that sound as a man had died under Andrea's great hands, and he knew with sudden certainty that Panayis would go the same way, and soon, if he didn't make Miller understand. But all at once Miller understood, relaxed heavily, straightened up still kneeling, hands hanging limply by his sides. Breathing deeply he stared down in silence at the man at his feet.

'What the hell's the matter with you?' Mallory demanded softly. 'Deaf or blind or both?'

'Just one of these things, I guess.' Miller rubbed the back of a hand across his forehead, his face empty of expression. 'Sorry, boss, sorry.'

'Why the hell apologize to me?' Mallory looked away from him, looked down at Panayis: the Greek was sitting up now, hands massaging his bruised throat, sucking in long draughts of air in great, whooping gasps. 'But maybe Panayis here might appreciate—'

'Apologies can wait,' Miller interrupted brusquely. 'Ask him what's happened to Louki.'

Mallory looked at him for a moment, made no reply, changed his mind, translated the question. He listened to Panayis's halting answer – it obviously hurt him even to try to speak – and his mouth tightened in a hard, bitter line. Miller watched the fractional slump of the New Zealander's shoulders, felt he could wait no longer.

'Well, what is it, boss? Somethin's happened to Louki, is that it?'

'Yes,' Mallory said tonelessly. 'They'd only got as far as the lane at the back when they found a small German patrol blocking their way. Louki tried to draw them off and the machine-gunner got him through the chest. Andrea got the machine-gunner and took Louki away. Panayis says he'll die for sure.'

Chapter Fourteen

Wednesday Night 1915–2000

The three men cleared the town without any difficulty, striking out directly across country for the castle Vygos and avoiding the main road. It was beginning to rain now, heavily, persistently, and the ground was mired and sodden, the few ploughed fields they crossed almost impassable. They had just struggled their way through one of these and could just see the dim outline of the keep – less than a cross-country mile from the town instead of Louki's exaggerated estimate – when they passed by an abandoned earthen house and Miller spoke for the first time since they had left the town square of Navarone.

'I'm bushed, boss.' His head was sunk on his chest, and his breathing was laboured. 'Ol' man Miller's on the downward path, I reckon, and the legs are gone. Couldn't we squat inside here for a couple of minutes, boss, and have a smoke?'

Mallory looked at him in surprise thought how desperately weary his own legs felt and nodded in reluctant agreement. Miller wasn't the man to complain unless he was near exhaustion.

'Okay, Dusty, I don't suppose a minute or two will harm.' He translated quickly into Greek and led the way inside, Miller at his heels complaining at length about his advancing age. Once inside, Mallory felt his way across to the inevitable wooden bunk, sat down gratefully, lit a cigarette then looked up in puzzlement. Miller was still on his feet, walking slowly round the hut, tapping the walls as he went.

'Why don't you sit down?' Mallory asked irritably. 'That was why you came in here in the first place, wasn't it?'

'No, boss, not really.' The drawl was very pronounced. 'Just a low-down trick to get us inside. Two-three very special things I want to show you.'

'Very special? What the devil are you trying to tell me?'

'Bear with me, Captain Mallory,' Miller requested formally. 'Bear with me just a few minutes. I'm not wastin' your time. You have my word, Captain Mallory.'

'Very well.' Mallory was mystified, but his confidence in Miller remained unshaken. 'As you wish. Only don't be too long about it.'

'Thanks, boss.' The strain of formality was too much for Miller. 'It won't take long. There'll be a lamp or candles in here – you said the islanders never leave an abandoned house without 'em?'

'And a very useful superstition it's been to us, too.' Mallory reached under the bunk with his torch, straightened his back. 'Two or three candles here.'

'I want a light, boss. No windows – I checked. OK?'

'Light one and I'll go outside to see if there's anything showing.' Mallory was completely in the dark about the American's intentions. He felt Miller didn't want him to say anything, and there was a calm surety about him that precluded questioning. Mallory was back in less than a minute. 'Not a chink to be seen from the outside,' he reported.

'Fair enough. Thanks, boss.' Miller lit a second candle, then slipped the rucksack straps from his shoulders, laid the pack on the bunk and stood in silence for a moment.

Mallory looked at his watch, looked back at Miller.

'You were going to show me something,' he prompted.

'Yeah, that's right. Three things, I said.' He dug into the pack, brought out a little black box hardly bigger than a matchbox. 'Exhibit A, boss.'

Mallory looked at it curiously. 'What's that?'

'Clockwork fuse.' Miller began to unscrew the back panel. 'Hate the damned things. Always make me feel like one of those Bolshevik characters with a dark cloak, a moustache like Louki's and carryin' one of those black cannon-ball things with a sputterin' fuse stickin' outa it. But it works.' He had the back off the box now, examining the mechanism in the light of his torch. 'But this one doesn't, not any more,' he added softly. 'Clock's OK, but the contact arm's been bent right back. This thing could tick till Kingdom Come and it couldn't even set off a firework.'

'But how on earth—?'

'Exhibit B.' Miller didn't seem to hear him. He opened the detonator box, gingerly lifted a fuse from its felt and cottonwool bed and examined it closely under his torch. Then he looked at Mallory again. 'Fulminate of mercury, boss. Only seventy-five grains, but enough to blow your fingers off. Unstable as hell, too – the littlest tap will set it off.' He let it fall to the ground, and Mallory winced and drew back involuntarily as the American smashed a heavy heel down on top of it. But there was no explosion, nothing at all.

'Ain't workin' so good either, is it, boss? A hundred to one the rest are all empty, too.' He fished out a pack of cigarettes, lit one, and watched the smoke eddy and whirl about the heat of the candles. He slid the cigarettes into his pocket.

'There was a third thing you were going to show me,' Mallory said quietly.

'Yeah, I was goin' to show you somethin' else.' The voice was very gentle, and Mallory felt suddenly cold. 'I was goin' to show you a spy, a traitor, the most vicious, twistin', murderin', double-crossin' bastard I've ever known.' The American had his hand in his pocket now, the silenced automatic sitting snugly against his palm, the muzzle trained over Panayis's heart. He went on, more gently than ever. 'Judas Iscariot had nothin' on the boy-friend here, boss . . . Take your coat off, Panayis.'

'What the devil are you doing? Are you crazy?' Mallory started forward, half-angry, half-amazed, but brought up sharply against Miller's extended arm, rigid as a bar of iron. 'What bloody nonsense is this? He doesn't understand English!'

'Don't he, though? Then why was he out of the cave like a flash when Casey reported hearin' sounds outside . . . and why was he the first to leave the carob grove this afternoon if he didn't understand your order? Take your coat off, Judas, or I'll shoot you through the arm. I'll give you two seconds.'

Mallory made to throw his arms round Miller and bring him to the ground, but halted in mid-step as he caught the look on Panayis's face –

teeth bared, murder glaring out from the coal-black eyes. Never before had Mallory seen such malignity in a human face, a malignity that yielded abruptly to shocked pain and disbelief as the .32 bullet smashed into his upper arm, just below the shoulder.

'Two seconds and then the other arm,' Miller said woodenly. But Panayis was already tearing off his jacket, the dark, bestial eyes never leaving Miller's face. Mallory looked at him, shivered involuntarily, looked at Miller. Indifference, he thought, that was the only word to describe the look on the American's face. Indifference. Unaccountably, Mallory felt colder than ever.

'Turn round!' The automatic never wavered.

Slowly Panayis turned round. Miller stepped forward, caught the black shirt by the collar, ripped it off his back with one convulsive jerk.

'Waal, waal, now, whoever woulda thought it?' Miller drawled. 'Surprise, surprise, surprise! Remember, boss, this was the character that was publicly flogged by the Germans in Crete, flogged until the white of his ribs showed through. His back's in a helluva state, isn't it?'

Mallory looked but said nothing. Completely off balance, his mind was in a kaleidescopic whirl, his thoughts struggling to adjust themselves to a new set of circumstances, a complete reversal of all his previous thinking. Not a scar, not a single blemish, marked the dark smoothness of that skin.

'Just a natural quick healer,' Miller murmured. 'Only a nasty, twisted mind like mine would think that he had been a German agent in Crete, became known to the Allies as a fifth columnist, lost his usefulness to the Germans and was shipped back to Navarone by fast motor-launch under cover of night. Floggin'! Island-hoppin' his way back here in a row-boat! Just a lot of bloody eyewash!' Miller paused, and his mouth twisted. 'I wonder how many pieces of silver he made in Crete before they got wise to him?'

'But heavens above, man, you're not going to condemn someone just for shooting a line!' Mallory protested. Strangely, he didn't feel nearly as vehement as he sounded. 'How many survivors would there be among the Allies if—?'

'Not convinced yet, huh?' Miller waved his automatic negligently at Panayis. 'Roll up the left trouser leg, Iscariot. Two seconds again.'

Panayis did as he was told. The black venomous eyes never looked away from Miller's. He rolled the dark cloth up to the knee.

'Farther yet? That's my little boy,' Miller encouraged him. 'And now take that bandage off – right off.' A few seconds passed, then Miller shook his head sadly. 'A ghastly wound, boss, a ghastly wound!'

'I'm beginning to see your point,' Mallory said thoughtfully. The dark sinewy leg wasn't even scratched. 'But why on earth—?'

'Simple. Four reasons at least. Junior here is a treacherous, slimy bastard – no self-respectin' rattlesnake would come within a mile of him – but he's a clever bastard. He faked his leg so he could stay in the cave in the Devil's Playground when the four of us went back to stop the Alpenkorps from comin' up the slope below the carob grove.'

'Why? Frightened he'd stop something?'

Miller shook his head impatiently.

'Junior here's scared o' nothin'. He stayed behind to write a note. Later on he used his leg to drop behind us some place, and leave the note where it could be seen. Early on, this must have been. Note probably said that we would come out at such and such a place, and would they kindly send a welcomin' committee to meet us there. They sent it, remember: it was their car we swiped to get to town. . . . That was the first time I got real suspicious of the boy-friend: after he'd dropped behind he made up on us again quick – too damn' quick for a man with a game leg. But it wasn't till I opened that rucksack in the square this evenin' that I really knew.'

'You only mentioned two reasons,' Mallory prompted.

'Comin' to the others. Number three – he could fall behind when the welcomin' committee opened up in front – Iscariot here wasn't goin' to get himself knocked off before he collected his salary. And number four – remember that real touchin' scene when he begged you to let him stay at the far end of the cave that led into the valley we came out? Goin' to do his Horatio-on-the-bridge act?'

'Going to show them the right cave to pick, you mean.'

'Check. After that he was gettin' pretty desperate. I still wasn't sure, but I was awful suspicious, boss. Didn't know what he might try next. So I clouted him good and hard when that last patrol came up the valley.'

'I see,' Mallory said quietly. 'I see indeed.' He looked sharply at Miller. 'You should have told me. You had no right—'

'I was goin' to, boss. But I hadn't a chance – Junior here was around all the time. I was just startin' to tell you half an hour back, when the guns started up.'

Mallory nodded in understanding. 'How did you happen on all this in the first place, Dusty?'

'Juniper,' Miller said succinctly. 'Remember that's how Turzig said he came to find us? He smelt the juniper.'

'That's right. We *were* burning juniper.'

'Sure we were. But he said he smelt it on Kostos – and the wind was blowin' off Kostos all day long.'

'My God,' Mallory whispered. 'Of course, of course! And I missed it completely.'

'But Jerry knew we were there. How? Waal, he ain't got second sight no more than I have. So he was tipped off – he was tipped off by the boy-friend here. Remember I said he'd talked to some of his pals in Margaritha when we went down there for the supplies?' Miller spat in disgust. 'Fooled me all along the line. Pals? I didn't know how right I was. Sure they were his pals – his German pals! And that food he said he got from the commandant's kitchen – he got it from the kitchen all right. Almost certainly he goes in and asks for it – and old Skoda hands him his own suitcase to stow it in.'

'But the German he killed on the way back to the village? Surely to God—'

'Panayis killed him.' There was a tired certainty in Miller's voice. 'What's another corpse to sunshine here. Probably stumbled on the poor bastard in the dark and had to kill him. Local colour. Louki was there, remember, and he couldn't have Louki gettin' suspicious. He would have blamed it on Louki anyway. The guy ain't human. . . . And remember when he was flung into Skoda's room in Margaritha along with Louki, blood pourin' from a wound in his head?'

Mallory nodded.

'High-grade ketchup. Probably also from the commandant's kitchen,' Miller said bitterly. 'If Skoda had failed by every other means, there would still have been the boy-friend here as a stool-pigeon. Why he never asked Louki where the explosives were I don't know.'

'Obviously he didn't know Louki knew.'

'Mebbe. But one thing the bastard did know – how to use a mirror. Musta heliographed the garrison from the carob grove and given our position. No other way, boss. Then sometime this morning he must have got hold of my rucksack, whipped out all the slow fuse and fixed the clock fuse and detonators. He should have had his hands blown off tamperin' with them fulminates. Lord only knows where he learnt to handle the damn' things.'

'Crete,' Mallory said positively. 'The Germans would see to that. A spy who can't also double as a saboteur is no good to them.'

'And he was very good to them,' Miller said softly. 'Very, very good. They're gonna miss their little pal. Iscariot here was a very smart baby indeed.'

'He was. Except tonight. He should have been smart enough to know that at least one of us would be suspicious—'

'He probably was,' Miller interrupted. 'But he was misinformed. I think Louki's unhurt. I think Junior here talked Louki into letting him stay in his place – Louki was always a bit scared of him – then he strolled across to his pals at the gate, told 'em to send a strong-arm squad out to Vygos to pick up the others, asked them to fire a few shots – he was very strong on local colour, was our loyal little pal – then strolls back across the square, hoists himself up on the roof and waits to tip off his pals as soon as we came in the back door. But Louki forgot to tell him just one thing – that we were goin' to rendezvous on the roof of the house, not inside. So the boy-friend here lurks away for all he's worth up top, waiting to signal his friends. Ten to one that he's got a torch in his pocket.'

Mallory picked up Panayis's coat and examined it briefly. 'He has.'

'That's it, then.' Miller lit another cigarette, watched the match burn down slowly to his fingers, then looked up at Panayis. 'How does it feel to know that you're goin' to die, Panayis, to feel like all them poor bastards who've felt just as you're feeling now, just before they died – all the men in Crete, all the guys in the sea-borne and air landings on Navarone who died because they thought you were on their side? How does it feel, Panayis?'

Panayis said nothing. His left hand clutching his torn right arm, trying to stem the blood, he stood there motionless, the dark, evil face masked in hate, the lips still drawn back in that less than human snarl. There was no fear in him, none at all, and Mallory tensed himself for the last, despairing attempt for life that Panayis must surely make, and then he had looked at Miller and knew there would be no attempt, because there was a strange sureness and inevitability about the American, an utter immobility of hand and eye that somehow precluded even the thought, far less the possibility, of escape.

'The prisoner has nothin' to say.' Miller sounded very tired. 'I suppose I should say somethin'. I suppose I should give out with a long spiel about me bein' the judge, the jury and the executioner, but I don't think I'll bother myself. Dead men make poor witnesses. . . . Mebbe it's not your fault, Panayis, mebbe there's an awful good reason why you came to be what you are. Gawd only knows. I don't, and I don't much care. There are too many dead men. I'm goin' to kill you, Panayis, and I'm goin' to kill you now.'

Miller dropped his cigarette, ground it into the floor of the hut. 'Nothin' at all to say?'

And he had nothing at all to say, the hate, the malignity of the black eyes said it all for him and Miller nodded, just once, as if in secret understanding. Carefully, accurately, he shot Panayis through the heart, twice, blew out the candles, turned his back and was half-way towards the door before the dead man had crashed to the ground.

'I am afraid I cannot do it, Andrea.' Louki sat back wearily, shook his head in despair. 'I am very sorry, Andrea. The knots are too tight.'

'No matter.' Andrea rolled over from his side to a sitting position, tried to ease his tightly-bound legs and wrists. 'They are cunning, these Germans, and wet cords can only be cut.' Characteristically, he made no mention of the fact that only a couple of minutes previously he had twisted round to reach the cords on Louki's wrists and undone them with half a dozen tugs of his steel-trap fingers. 'We will think of something else.'

He looked away from Louki, glanced across the room in the faint light of the smoking oil-lamp that stood by the grille door, a light so yellow, so dim that Casey Brown, trussed like a barnyard fowl and loosely secured, like himself, by a length of rope to the iron hooks suspended from the roof, was no more than a shapeless blur in the opposite corner of the stone-flagged room. Andrea smiled to himself, without mirth. Taken prisoner again, and for the second time that day – and with the same ease and surprise that gave no chance at all of resistance: completely unsuspecting, they had been captured in an upper room, seconds after Casey had finished talking to Cairo. The patrol had known exactly where to find them – and with their leader's assurance that it was all over, with his gloating explanation of the part Panayis had played, the unexpectedness, the success of the coup was all too easy to understand. And it was difficult not to believe his assurance that neither Mallory nor Miller had a chance. But the thought of ultimate defeat never occurred to Andrea.

His gaze left Casey Brown, wandered round the room, took in what he could see of the stone walls and floor, the hooks, the ventilation ducts, the heavy grille door. A dungeon, a torture dungeon, one would have thought, but Andrea had seen such places before. A castle, they called this place, but it was really only an old keep, no more than a manor house built round the crenellated towers. And the long-dead Frankish nobles who had built these keeps had lived well. No dungeon this, Andrea knew, but simply the larder where they had hung their meat and game, and done without windows and light for the sake of . . .

The light! Andrea twisted round, looking at the smoking oil-lamp, his eyes narrowing.

'Louki!' he called softly. The little Greek turned round to look at him.

'Can you reach the lamp?'

'I think so. . . . Yes, I can.'

'Take the glass off.' Andrea whispered. 'Use a cloth – it will be hot. Then wrap it in the cloth, hit it on the floor – gently. The glass is thick – you can cut me loose in a minute or two.'

Louki stared at him for an uncomprehending moment, then nodded in understanding. He shuffled across the floor – his legs were still bound – reached out, then halted his hand abruptly, only inches from the glass. The peremptory, metallic clang had been only feet away, and he raised his head slowly to see what had caused it.

He could have stretched out his hand, touched the barrel of the Mauser that protruded threateningly through the bars of the grille door. Again the guard rattled the rifle angrily between the bars, shouted something he didn't understand.

'Leave it alone, Louki,' Andrea said quietly. His voice was tranquil, unshadowed by disappointment. 'Come back here. Our friend outside is not too pleased.' Obediently Louki moved back, heard the guttural voice again, rapid and alarmed this time, the rattle as the guard withdrew his rifle quickly from the stones outside as he raced up the passage.

'What's the matter with our little friend?' Casey Brown was as lugubrious, as weary as ever. 'He seems upset.'

'He is upset.' Andrea smiled. 'He's just realized that Louki's hands are untied.'

'Well, why doesn't he tie them up again?'

'Slow in the head he may be, but he is no fool,' Andrea explained. 'This could be a trap and he's gone for his friends.'

Almost at once they heard a thud, like the closing of a distant door, the sound of more than one pair of feet running down the passage, the tinny rattling of keys on a ring, the rasp of a key against the lock, a sharp click, the squeal of rusty hinges and then two soldiers were in the room, dark and menacing with their jackboots and ready guns. Two or three seconds elapsed while they looked around them, accustoming their eyes to the gloom, then the man nearest the door spoke.

'A terrible thing, boss, nothin' short of deplorable! Leave 'em alone for a couple of minutes and see what happens? The whole damn' bunch is tied up like Houdini on an off night!'

There was a brief, incredulous silence, then all three were sitting upright, staring at them. Brown recovered first.

'High time, too,' he complained. 'Thought you were never going to get here.'

'What he means is that he thought we were never going to see you again,' Andrea said quietly. 'Neither did I. But here you are, safe and sound.'

'Yes,' Mallory nodded. 'Thanks to Dusty and his nasty suspicious mind that cottoned on to Panayis while all the rest of us were asleep.'

'Where is he?' Louki asked.

'Panayis?' Miller waved a negligent hand. 'We left him behind – he met with a sorta accident.' He was across at the other side of the door now, carefully cutting the cords that pinioned Brown's injured leg, whistling tunelessly as he sawed away with his sheath knife. Mallory, too, was busy, slicing through Andrea's bonds, explaining rapidly what had happened, listening to the big Greek's equally concise account of what had befallen the other in the keep. And then Andrea was on his feet, massaging his numbed hands, looking across at Miller.

'That whistling, my Captain. It sounds terrible and, what is worse, it is very loud. The guards—'

'No worry there,' Mallory said grimly. 'They never expected to see Dusty and myself again. . . . They kept a poor watch.' He turned round to look at Brown, now hobbling across the floor.

'How's the leg, Casey?'

'Fine, sir.' Brown brushed it aside as of no importance. 'I got through to Cairo, tonight, sir. The report—'

'It'll have to wait, Casey. We must get out as fast as we can. You all right, Louki?'

'I am heart-broken, Major Mallory. That a countryman of mine – a trusted friend—'

'That too, will have to wait. Come on!'

'You are in a great hurry,' Andrea protested mildly. They were already out in the passage, stepping over the cell guard lying in a crumpled heap on the floor. 'Surely if they're all like our friend here—'

'No danger from this quarter,' Mallory interrupted impatiently. 'The soldiers in the town – they're bound to know by now that we've either missed Panayis or disposed of him. In either case they'll know that we're certain to come hot-footing out here. Work it out for yourself. They're probably half-way here already, and if they do come . . .' He broke off, stared at the smashed generator and the ruins of Casey Brown's transmitter set lying in one corner of the entrance hall. 'Done a pretty good job on these, haven't they?' he said bitterly.

'Thank the lord,' Miller said piously. 'All the less to tote around, is what I say. If you could only see the state of my back with that damned generator—'

'Sir!' Brown had caught Mallory's arm, an action so foreign to the usually punctilious petty officer that Mallory halted in surprise. 'Sir, it's terribly important – the report, I mean. You *must* listen, sir!'

The action, the deadly earnestness, caught and held Mallory's full attention. He turned to face Brown with a smile.

'OK, Casey, let's have it,' he said quietly. 'Things can't possibly be any worse than they are now.'

'They can, sir.' There was something tired, defeated about Casey Brown, and the great, stone hall seemed strangely chill. 'I'm afraid they can, sir. I got through tonight. First-class reception. Captain Jensen himself, and he was hopping mad. Been waiting all day for us to come on the air. Asked how things were, and I told him that you were outside the fortress just then, and hoped to be inside the magazine in an hour or so.'

'Go on.'

'He said that was the best news he'd ever had. He said his information had been wrong, he'd been fooled, that the invasion fleet didn't hole up overnight in the Cyclades, that they had come straight through under the heaviest air and E-boat escort ever seen in the Med., and are due to hit the beaches on Kheros some time before dawn tomorrow. He said our destroyers had been waiting to the south all day, moved up at dusk and were waiting word from him to see whether they would attempt the passage of the Maidos Straits. I told him maybe something could go wrong, but he said not with Captain Mallory and Miller inside and besides he wasn't – he couldn't risk the lives of twelve hundred men on Kheros just on the off chance that he might be wrong.' Brown broke off suddenly and looked down miserably at his feet. No one else in the hall moved or made any sound at all.

'Go on,' Mallory repeated in a whisper. His face was very pale.

'That's all, sir. That's all there is. The destroyers are coming through the Straits at midnight.' Brown looked down at his luminous watch. 'Midnight. Four hours to go.'

'Oh, God! Midnight!' Mallory was stricken, his eyes for the moment unseeing, ivory-knuckled hands clenched in futility and despair. 'They're coming through at midnight! God help them! God help them all now!'

Chapter Fifteen

Wednesday Night 2000–2115

Eight-thirty, his watch said. Eight-thirty. Exactly half an hour to curfew. Mallory flattened himself on the roof, pressed himself as closely as possible against the low retaining wall that almost touched the great, sheering sides of the fortress, swore softly to himself. It only required one man with a torch in his hand to look over the top of the fortress wall – a cat-walk ran the whole length of the inside of the wall, four feet from the top – and it would be the end of them all. The wandering beam of a torch and they were bound to be seen, it was impossible not to be seen: he and Dusty Miller – the American was stretched out behind him clutching the big truck battery in his arms – were wide open to the view of anyone who happened to glance down that way. Perhaps they should have stayed with the others a couple of roofs away, with Casey and Louki, the one busy tying spaced knots in a rope, the other busy splicing a bent wire hook on to a long bamboo they had torn from a bamboo hedge just outside the town, where they had hurriedly taken shelter as a convoy of three trucks had roared past them heading for the castle Vygos.

Eight thirty-two. What the devil was Andrea doing down there, Mallory wondered irritably and at once regretted his irritation. Andrea wouldn't waste an unnecessary second. Speed was vital, haste fatal. It seemed unlikely that there would be any officers inside – from what they had seen, practically half the garrison were combing either the town or the countryside out in the direction of Vygos – but if there were and even one gave a cry it would be the end.

Mallory stared down at the burn on the back of his hand, thought of the truck they had set on fire and grinned wryly to himself. Setting the truck on fire had been his only contribution to the night's performance so far. All the other credit went to either Andrea or Miller. It was Andrea who had seen in this house on the west side of the square – one of several adjoining houses used as officer's billets – the only possible answer to their problem. It was Miller, now lacking all time-fuses, clockwork, generator and every other source of electric power who had suddenly stated that he must have a battery, and again it was Andrea, hearing the distant approach of a truck, who had blocked the entrance to the long driveway to the keep with heavy stones from the flanking pillars, forcing the soldiers to abandon their truck at the gates and run up the drive towards their house. To overcome the driver and his mate and bundle them senseless into a ditch had taken seconds only, scarcely more time than it had taken Miller to unscrew the terminals of the heavy battery, find the inevitable jerri-can below the tail-board and pour the contents over engine, cab and body. The truck had gone up in a roar and *whoosh* of flames: as Louki had said earlier in the night, setting petrol-soaked vehicles on fire was not without its dangers – the charred patch on his hand stung painfully – but, again as Louki had said it had burned magnificently. A pity, in a way – it had attracted attention to their escape sooner than was necessary – but it had been vital to destroy the evidence, the fact that a battery was missing. Mallory had too much experience of and respect for the Germans ever to underrate them: they could put two and two together better than most.

He felt Miller tug at his ankle, started, twisted round quickly. The American was pointing beyond him, and he turned again and saw Andrea signalling to him from the raised trap in the far corner: he had been so engrossed in his thinking, the giant Greek so catlike in his silence, that he had completely failed to notice his arrival. Mallory shook his head, momentarily angered at his own abstraction, took the battery from Miller, whispered to him to get the others, then edged slowly across the roof, as noiselessly as possible. The sheer deadweight of the battery was astonishing, it felt as if it weighed a ton, but Andrea plucked it from his hands, lifted it over the trap coaming, tucked it under one arm and nimbly descended the stairs to the tiny hall-way as if it weighed nothing at all.

Andrea moved out through the open doorway to the covered balcony that overlooked the darkened harbour, almost a hundred vertical feet beneath. Mallory, following close behind, touched him on the shoulder as he lowered the battery gently to the ground.

'Any trouble?' he asked softly.

'None at all, my Keith.' Andrea straightened. 'The house is empty. I was so surprised that I went over it all, twice, just to make sure.'

'Fine! Wonderful! I suppose the whole bunch of them are out scouring the country for us – interesting to know what they would say if they were told we were sitting in their front parlour?'

'They would never believe it,' Andrea said without hesitation. 'This is the last place they would ever think to look for us.'

'I've never hoped so much that you're right!' Mallory murmured fervently. He moved across to the latticed railing that enclosed the balcony, gazed down into the blackness beneath his feet and shivered. A long, long drop and it was very cold; that sluicing, vertical rain chilled one to the bone. . . . He stepped back, shook the railing.

'This thing strong enough, do you think?' he whispered.

'I don't know, my Keith. I don't know at all.' Andrea shrugged. 'I hope so.'

'I hope so,' Mallory echoed. 'It doesn't really matter. This is how it has to be.' Again he leaned far out over the railing, twisted his head to the right and upwards. In the rain-filled gloom of the night he could just faintly make out the still darker gloom of the mouth of the cave housing the two great guns, perhaps forty feet away from where he stood, at least thirty feet higher – and all vertical cliff-face between. As far as accessibility went, the cave mouth could have been on the moon.

He drew back, turned round as he heard Brown limping on to the balcony.

'Go to the front of the house and stay there, Casey, will you? Stay by the window. Leave the front door unlocked. If we have any visitors let them in.'

'Club 'em, knife 'em, no guns,' Brown murmured. 'Is that it, sir?'

'That's it, Casey.'

'Just leave this little thing to me,' Brown said grimly. He hobbled away through the doorway.

Mallory turned to Andrea. 'I make it twenty-three minutes.'

'I, too. Twenty-three minutes to nine.'

'Good luck,' Mallory murmured. He grinned at Miller. 'Come on, Dusty. Opening time.'

Five minutes later, Mallory and Miller were seated in a *taverna* just off the south side of the town square. Despite the garish blue paint with which the *tavernaris* had covered everything in sight, walls, tables, chairs, shelves all in the same execrably vivid colour (blue and red for the wine shops, green for the sweetmeat shops was the almost invariable rule throughout the islands) – it was a gloomy, ill-lit place, as gloomy almost as the stern, righteous, magnificently-moustached heroes of the Wars of Independence whose dark, burning eyes glared down at them from a dozen faded prints scattered at eye-level along the walls. Between each pair of portraits was a brightly-coloured wall advertisement for Fix's beer: the effect of the décor, taken as a whole, was indescribable, and Mallory shuddered to think what it would have been like had the *tavernaris* had at his disposal any illumination more powerful than the two smoking oil-lamps placed on the counter before him.

As it was, the gloom suited him well. Their dark clothes, braided jackets, *tsantas* and jackboots looked genuine enough. Mallory knew, and the black-fringed turbans Louki had mysteriously obtained for them looked as they ought to look in a tavern where every islander there – about eight of them – wore nothing else on their heads. Their clothes had been good enough to pass muster with the *tavernaris* – but then even the keeper of a wine shop could hardly be expected to know every man in a town of five thousand, and a patriotic Greek, as Louki had declared this man to be, wasn't going to lift even a faintly suspicious eyebrow as long as there were German soldiers present. And there were Germans present – four of them, sitting round a table near the counter. Which was why Mallory had been been glad of the semi-darkness. Not, he was certain, that he and Dusty Miller, had any reason to be physically afraid of these men. Louki had dismissed them contemptuously as a bunch of old women – headquarters clerks, Mallory guessed – who came to this tavern every night of the week. But there was no point in sticking out their necks unnecessarily.

Miller lit one of the pungent, evil-smelling local cigarettes, wrinkling his nose in distaste.

'Damn' funny smell in this joint, boss.'

'Put your cigarette out,' Mallory suggested.

'You wouldn't believe it, but the smell I'm smelling is a damn' sight worse than that.'

'Hashish,' Mallory said briefly. 'The curse of these island ports.' He nodded over towards a dark corner. 'The lads of the village over there will be at it every night in life. It's all they live for.'

'Do they have to make that gawddamned awful racket when they're at it?' Miller asked peevishly. 'Toscanini should see this lot!'

Mallory looked at the small group in the corner, clustered round the young man playing a *bouzouko* – a long-necked mandolin – and singing the haunting, nostalgic *rembetika* songs of the hashish smokers of the Piraeus. He supposed the music did have a certain melancholy, lotus-land attraction, but right then it jarred on him. One had to be in a certain twilit, untroubled mood to appreciate that sort of thing; and he had never felt less untroubled in his life.

'I suppose it *is* a bit grim,' he admitted. 'But at least it lets us talk together, which we couldn't do if they all packed up and went home.'

'I wish to hell they would,' Miller said morosely. 'I'd gladly keep my mouth shut.' He picked distastefully at the *meze* – a mixture of chopped olives, liver, cheese and apples – on the plate before him: as a good American and a bourbon drinker of long standing he disapproved strongly of the invariable Greek custom of eating when drinking. Suddenly he looked up and crushed his cigarette against the table top. 'For Gawd's sake, boss, how much longer?'

Mallory looked at him, then looked away. He knew exactly how Dusty Miller felt, for he felt that way himself – tense, keyed-up, every nerve strung to the tautest pitch of efficiency. So much depended on the next few minutes; whether all their labour and their suffering had been necessary, whether the men on Kheros would live or die, whether Andy Stevens had lived and died in vain. Mallory looked at Miller again, saw the nervous hands, the deepened wrinkles round the eyes, the tightly compressed mouth, white at the outer corners, saw all these signs of strain, noted them and discounted them. Excepting Andrea alone, of all the men he had ever known he would have picked the lean, morose American to be his companion that night. Or maybe even including Andrea. 'The finest saboteur in southern Europe' Captain Jensen had called him back in Alexandria. Miller had come a long way from Alexandria, and he had come for this alone. Tonight was Miller's night.

Mallory looked at his watch.

'Curfew in fifteen minutes,' he said quietly. 'The balloon goes up in twelve minutes. For us, another four minutes to go.'

Miller nodded, but said nothing. He filled his glass again from the beaker in the middle of the table, lit a cigarette. Mallory could see a nerve twitching high up in his temple and wondered dryly how many twitching nerves Miller could see in his own face. He wondered, too, how the crippled Casey Brown was getting on in the house they had just left. In many ways he had the most responsible job of all – and at the critical moment he would have to leave the door unguarded, move back to the balcony. One slip up there. . . . He saw Miller look strangely at him and grinned crookedly. This had to come off, it just had to: he thought of what must surely happen if he failed, then shied away from the thought. It wasn't good to think of these things, not now not at this time.

He wondered if the other two were at their posts, unmolested; they should be, the search party had long passed through the upper part of the town; but you never knew what could go wrong, there was so much that could go wrong, and so easily. Mallory looked at his watch again: he had never seen a second hand move so slowly. He lit a last cigarette, poured a final glass of wine, listened without really hearing to the weird, keening threnody of the *rembetika* song in the corner. And then the song of the hashish singers died plaintively away, the glasses were empty and Mallory was on his feet.

'Time bringeth all things,' he murmured. 'Here we go again.'

He sauntered easily towards the door, calling good night to the *tavernaris*. Just at the doorway he paused, began to search impatiently through his pockets as if he had lost something: it was a windless night, and it was raining, he saw, raining heavily, the lances of rain bouncing inches off the cobbled street – and the street itself was deserted as far as he could see in either direction. Satisfied Mallory swung round with a curse, forehead furrowed in exasperation, started to walk back towards the table he had just left, right hand now delving into the capacious inner pocket of his jacket. He saw without seeming to that Dusty Miller was pushing his chair back, rising to his feet. And then Mallory had halted, his face clearing and his hands no longer searching. He was exactly three feet from the table where the four Germans were sitting.

'Keep quite still!' He spoke in German, his voice low but as steady, as menacing, as the Navy Colt .455 balanced in his right hand. 'We are desperate men. If you move we will kill you.'

For a full three seconds the soldiers sat immobile, expressionless except for the shocked widening of their eyes. And then there was a quick flicker of the eyelids from the man sitting nearest the counter, a twitching of the shoulder and then a grunt of agony as the .32 bullet smashed into his upper arm. The soft thud of Miller's silenced automatic couldn't have been heard beyond the doorway.

'Sorry, boss,' Miller apologized. 'Mebbe he's only sufferin' from St Vitus' Dance.' He looked with interest at the pain-twisted face, the blood welling darkly between the fingers clasped tightly over the wound. 'But he looks kinda cured to me.'

'He is cured,' Mallory said grimly. He turned to the inn-keeper, a tall, melancholy man with a thin face and mandarin moustache that drooped forlornly over either corner of his mouth, spoke to him in the quick, colloquial speech of the islands. 'Do these men speak Greek?'

The *tavernaris* shook his head. Completely unruffled and unimpressed, he seemed to regard armed hold-ups in his tavern as the rule rather than the exception.

'Not them!' he said contemptuously. 'English a little, I think – I am sure. But not our language. That I do know.'

'Good. I am a British Intelligence officer. Have you a place where I can hide these men?'

'You shouldn't have done this,' the *tavernaris* protested mildly. 'I will surely die for this.'

'Oh, no, you won't.' Mallory had slid across the counter, his pistol boring into the man's midriff. No one could doubt that the man was being threatened – and violently threatened – no one, that is, who couldn't see the broad wink that Mallory had given the inn-keeper. 'I'm going to tie you up with them. All right?'

'All right. There is a trap-door at the end of the counter here. Steps lead down to the cellar.'

'Good enough. I'll find it by accident.' Mallory gave him a vicious and all too convincing shove that sent the man staggering, vaulted back across the counter, walked over to the *rembetika* singers at the far corner of the room.

'Go home,' he said quickly. 'It is almost curfew time anyway. Go out the back way, and remember – you have seen nothing, no one. You understand?'

'We understand.' It was the young *bouzouko* player who spoke. He jerked his thumb at his companions and grinned. 'Bad men – but good Greeks. Can we help you?'

'No!' Mallory was emphatic. 'Think of your families – these soldiers have recognized you. They must know you well – you and they are here most nights, is that not so?'

The young man nodded.

'Off you go, then. Thank you all the same.'

A minute later, in the dim, candle-lit cellar, Miller prodded the soldier nearest him – the one most like himself in height and build. 'Take your clothes off!' he ordered.

'English pig!' the German snarled.

'Not *English*,' Miller protested. 'I'll give you thirty seconds to get your coat and pants off.'

The man swore at him, viciously, but made no move to obey. Miller sighed. The German had guts, but time was running out. He took a careful bead on the soldier's hand and pulled the trigger. Again the soft *plop* and the man was staring down stupidly at the hole torn in the heel of his left hand.

'Mustn't spoil the nice uniforms, must we?' Miller asked conversationally. He lifted the automatic until the soldier was staring down the barrel of the gun. 'The next goes between the eyes.' The casual drawl carried complete conviction. 'It won't take me long to undress you, I guess.' But the man had already started to tear his uniform off, sobbing with anger and the pain of his wounded hand.

Less than another five minutes had passed when Mallory, clad like Miller in German uniform, unlocked the front door of the tavern and peered cautiously out. The rain, if anything, was heavier than ever – and there wasn't a soul in sight. Mallory beckoned Miller to follow and locked the door behind him. Together the two men walked up the middle of the street, making no attempt to seek either shelter or shadows. Fifty yards took them into the town square, where they turned right along the south side of the square, then left along the east side, not breaking step as they passed the old house where they had hidden earlier in the evening, not even as Louki's hand appeared mysteriously behind the partly opened door, a hand weighted down with two German Army rucksacks – rucksacks packed with rope, fuses, wire and high explosive. A few yards farther on they stopped suddenly, crouched down behind a couple of huge wine barrels outside a barber's shop, gazed at the two armed guards in the arched gateway, less than a hundred feet away, as they shrugged into their packs and waited for their cue.

They had only moments to wait – the timing had been split-second throughout. Mallory was just tightening the waist-belt of his rucksack when a series of explosions shook the centre of the town, not three hundred yards away, explosions followed by the vicious rattle of a machine-gun, then by further explosions. Andrea was doing his stuff magnificently with his grenades and home-made bombs.

Both men suddenly shrank back as a broad, white beam of light stabbed out from a platform high above the gateway, a beam that paralleled the top of the wall to the east, showed up every hooked spike and strand of barbed wire as clearly as sunlight. Mallory and Miller looked at each other for a fleeting moment, their faces grim. Panayis hadn't missed a thing: they would have been pinned on these strands like flies on fly-paper and cut to ribbons by machine-guns.

Mallory waited another half-minute, touched Miller's arm, rose to his feet and started running madly across the square, the long hooked bamboo pressed close to his side, the American pounding behind him. In a few seconds they had reached the gates of the fortress, the startled guards running the last few feet to meet them.

'Every man to the Street of Steps!' Mallory shouted. 'Those damned English saboteurs are trapped in a house down there! We've got to have some mortars. Hurry, man, hurry, in the name of God!'

'But the gate!' one of the two guards protested. 'We cannot leave the gate!' The man had no suspicions, none at all: in the circumstances – the near darkness, the pouring rain, the German-clad soldier speaking perfect German, the obvious truth that there was a gun-battle being fought near-hand – it would have been remarkable had he shown any signs of doubt.

'Idiot!' Mallory screamed at him. '*Dummkopf*! What is there to guard against here? The English swine are in the Street of Steps. They must be destroyed! For God's sake, hurry!' he shouted desperately. 'If they escape again it'll be the Russian Front for all of us!'

Mallory had his hand on the man's shoulder now, ready to push him on his way, but his hand fell to his side unneeded. The two men were already gone, running pell-mell across the square, had vanished into the rain and the darkness already. Seconds later Mallory and Miller were deep inside the fortress of Navarone.

Everywhere there was complete confusion – a bustling, purposeful confusion as one would expect with the seasoned troops of the Alpenkorps, but confusion nevertheless, with much shouting of orders, blowing of whistles, starting of truck engines, sergeants running to and fro chivvying their men into marching order or into the waiting transports. Mallory and Miller ran too, once or twice through groups of men milling round the tailboard of a truck. Not that they were in any desperate hurry for themselves, but nothing could have been more conspicuous – and suspicious – that the sight of a couple of men walking calmly along in the middle of all than urgent activity. And so they ran, heads down or averted whenever they passed through a pool of light, Miller cursing feelingly and often at the unaccustomed exercise.

They skirted two barrack blocks on their right, then the power-house on their left, then an ordnance depot on their right and then the *Abteilung* garage on their left. They were climbing, now, almost in darkness, but Mallory knew where he was to the inch: he had so thoroughly memorized the closely tallying descriptions given him by Vlachos and Panayis that he would have been confident of finding his way with complete accuracy, even if the darkness had been absolute.

'What's that, boss?' Miller had caught Mallory by the arm, was pointing to a large, uncompromisingly rectangular building that loomed gauntly against the horizon. 'The local hoosegow?'

'Water storage tank,' Mallory said briefly. 'Panayis estimates there's half a million gallons in there – magazine flooding in an emergency. The magazines are directly below.' He pointed to a squat, box-like, concrete structure a little farther on. 'The only entrance to the magazine. Locked and guarded.'

They were approaching the senior officers' quarters now – the commandant had his own flat on the second storey, directly overlooking the massive reinforced ferro-concrete control tower that controlled the two great guns below. Mallory suddenly stopped, picked up a handful of dirt, rubbed it on his face and told Miller to do the same.

'Disguise,' he explained. 'The experts would consider it a bit on the elementary side, but it'll have to do. The lighting's apt to be a bit brighter inside this place.'

He went up the steps to the officers' quarters at a dead run, crashed through the swing doors with a force that almost took them off their hinges. The sentry at the keyboard looked at him in astonishment, the barrel of his submachine-gun lining up on the New Zealander's chest.

'Put that thing down, you damned idiot!' Mallory snapped furiously. 'Where's the commandant? Quickly, you oaf! It's life or death!'

'Herr – Herr Kommandant?' the sentry stuttered. 'He's left – they are all gone, just a minute ago.'

'What? All gone?' Mallory was staring at him with narrowed, dangerous eyes. 'Did you say "all gone"?' he asked softly.

'Yes. I – I'm sure they're . . . ' He broke off abruptly as Mallory's eyes shifted to a point behind his shoulder.

'Then who the hell is that?' Mallory demanded savagely.

The sentry would have been less than human not to fall for it. Even as he was swinging round to look, the vicious judo cut took him just below the left ear. Mallory had smashed open the glass of the keyboard before the unfortunate guard had hit the floor, swept all the keys – about a dozen in all – off their rings and into his pocket. It took them another twenty seconds to tape the man's mouth and hands and lock him in a convenient cupboard; then they were on their way again, still running.

One more obstacle to overcome, Mallory thought as they pounded along in the darkness, the last of the triple defences. He did not know how many men would be guarding the locked door to the magazine, and in that moment of fierce exaltation he didn't particularly care. Neither, he felt sure, did Miller. There were no worries now, no taut-nerved tensions or nameless anxieties. Mallory would have been the last man in the world to admit it, or even believe it, but this was what men like Miller and himself had been born for.

They had their hand-torches out now, the powerful beams swinging in wide arcs as they plunged along, skirting the massed batteries of AA guns. To anyone observing their approach from the front, there could have been nothing more calculated to disarm suspicion than the sight and sound of the two men running towards them without any attempt at concealment, one of them shouting to the other in German, both with lit torches whose beams lifted and fell, lifted and fell as the men's arms windmilled by their sides. But these same torches were deeply hooded, and only a very alert observer indeed would have noticed that the downward arc of the light never passed backwards beyond the runners' feet.

Suddenly Mallory saw two shadows detaching themselves from the darker shadow of the magazine entrance, steadied his torch for a brief second to check. He slackened speed.

'Right!' he said softly. 'Here they come – only two of them. One each – get as close as possible first. Quick and quiet – a shout, a shot, and we're finished. And for God's sake don't start clubbing 'em with your torch. There'll be no lights on in that magazine and I'm not going to start crawling around there with a box of bloody matches in my hand!' He transferred his torch to his left hand, pulled out his Navy Colt, reversed it, caught it by the barrel, brought up sharply only inches away from the guards now running to meet them.

'Are you all right?' Mallory gasped. 'Anyone been here? Quickly, man, *quickly*!'

'Yes, yes, we're all right.' The man was off guard, apprehensive. 'What in the name of God is all that noise—'

'Those damned English saboteurs!' Mallory swore viciously. 'They've killed the guards and they're inside! Are you sure no one's been here? Come, let me see.'

He pushed his way past the guard, probed his torch at the massive padlock, then straightened his back.

'Thank heaven for that anyway!' He turned round, let the dazzling beam of his torch catch the man square in the eyes, muttered an apology and switched off the light, the sound of the sharp click lost in the hollow, soggy thud of the heel of his Colt catching the man behind the ear, just below the helmet. The sentry was still on his feet, just beginning to crumple, when Mallory staggered as the second guard reeled into him, staggered, recovered, clouted him with the colt for good measure, then stiffened in sudden dismay as he heard the vicious hissing *plop* of Miller's automatic, twice in rapid succession.

'What the hell—'

'Wily birds, boss,' Miller murmured. 'Very wily indeed. There was a third character in the shadows at the side. Only way to stop him.' Automatic cocked in his ready hand, he stooped over the man for a moment, then straightened. 'Afraid he's been stopped kinda permanent, boss.' There was no expression in his voice.

'Tie up the others.' Mallory had only half heard him, he was already busy at the magazine door, trying a succession of keys in the lock. The third key fitted, the lock opened and the heavy steel door gave easily to his touch. He took a last swift look round, but there was no one in sight, no sound but the revving engine of the last of the trucks clearing the fortress gates, the distant rattle of machine-gun fire. Andrea was doing a magnificent job – if only he didn't overdo it, leave his withdrawal till it was too late. . . . Mallory turned quickly, switched on his torch, stepped inside the door. Miller would follow when he was ready.

A vertical steel ladder fixed to the rock led down to the floor of the cave. On either side of the ladder were hollow lift-shafts, unprotected even by a cage, oiled wire ropes glistening in the middle, a polished metal runner at each side of the square to guide and steady the spring-loaded side-wheels of the lift itself. Spartan in their simplicity but wholly adequate, there was no mistaking these for anything but what they were – the shell hoist shafts going down to the magazine.

Mallory reached the solid floor of the cave and swept his torch round through a 180-degree arc. This was the very end of that great cave that opened out beneath the towering overhang of rock that dominated the entire harbour. Not the natural end, he saw after a moment's inspection, but a man-made addition: the volcanic rock around him had been drilled and blasted out. There was nothing here but the two shafts descending into the pitchy darkness and another steel ladder, also leading to the magazine. But the magazine could wait: to check that there were no more guards down here and to ensure an emergency escape route – these were the two vital needs of the moment.

Quickly Mallory ran along the tunnel, flipping his torch on and off. The Germans were past-masters of booby traps – explosive booby traps – for the protection of important installations, but the chances were that they had none in that tunnel – not with several hundred tons of high explosive stored only feet away.

The tunnel itself, dripping-damp and duck-board floored, was about seven feet high and even wider, but the central passage was very narrow – most of the space was taken up by the roller conveyors, one on either side, for the great cartridge and shells. Suddenly the conveyors curved away sharply to the left and right, the sharply-sheering tunnel roof climbed steeply up into the near-darkness of the vaulted dome above, and, almost at his feet, their burnished steel caught in the beam from his torch, twin sets of parallel rails, imbedded in the solid stone and twenty feet apart, stretched forward into the lightened gloom ahead, the great, gaping mouth of the cave. And just before he switched off the torch – searchers returning from the Devil's Playground might easily catch the pinpoint of light in the darkness – Mallory had a brief glimpse of the turn-tables that crowned the far end of these shining rails and, crouched massively above, like some nightmare monsters from an ancient and other world, the evil, the sinister silhouettes of the two great guns of Navarone.

Torch and revolver dangling loosely in his hands, only dimly aware of the curious tingling in the tips of his fingers, Mallory walked slowly forward. Slowly, but not with the stealthy slowness, the razor-drawn expectancy of a man momentarily anticipating trouble – there was no guard in the cave, Mallory was quite sure of that now – but with that strange, dream-like slowness, the half-belief of a man who has accomplished something he had known all along he could never accomplish, with the slowness of a man at last face to face with a feared but long-sought enemy. I'm here at last, Mallory said to himself over and over again. I'm here at last, I've made it, and these are the guns of Navarone: these are the guns I came to destroy, the guns of Navarone, and I have come at last. But somehow he couldn't quite believe it. . . .

Slowly still Mallory approached the guns, walked half-way round the perimeter of the turn-table of the gun on the left, examined it as well as he could in the gloom. He was staggered by the sheer size of it, the tremendous girth and reach of the barrel that stretched far out into the night. He told himself that the experts thought it was only a nine-inch crunch gun, that the crowding confines of the caves were bound to exaggerate its size. He told himself these things, discounted them: twelve-inch bore if an inch, that gun was the biggest thing he had ever seen. Big? Heavens above, it was gigantic! The fools, the blind crazy fools who had sent the *Sybaris* out against these . . .

The train of thought was lost, abruptly. Mallory stood quite still, one hand resting against the massive gun carriage and tried to recall the sound that had jerked him back to the present. Immobile, he listened for it again, eyes closed the better to hear, but the sound did not come again, and suddenly he knew that it was no sound at all but the absence of sound that had cut through his thoughts, triggered off some unconscious warning bell. The night was suddenly very silent, very still: down in the heart of the town the guns had stopped firing.

Mallory swore softly to himself. He had already spent far too much time day-dreaming, and time was running short. It *must* be running short – Andrea had withdrawn, it was only a matter of time until the Germans discovered that they had been duped. And then they would come running – and there was no doubt where they would come. Swiftly Mallory shrugged out of his rucksack, pulled out the hundred-foot wire-cored rope coiled inside. Their emergency escape route – whatever else he did he must make sure of that.

The rope looped round his arm, he moved forward cautiously, seeking a belay, but had only taken three steps when his right knee-cap struck something hard and unyielding. He checked the exclamation of pain, investigated the obstacle with his free hand, realized immediately what it was – an iron railing stretched waist-high across the mouth of the cave. Of course! There had been bound to be something like that, some barrier to prevent people from falling over the edge, especially in the darkness of the night. He hadn't been able to pick it up with the binoculars from the carob grove that afternoon – close though it was to the entrance, it had been concealed in the gloom of the cave. But he should have thought of it.

Quickly Mallory felt his way along to the left, to the very end of the railing, crossed it, tied the rope securely to the base of the vertical stanchion next to the wall, paid out the rope as he moved gingerly to the lip of the cave mouth. And then, almost at once, he was there and there was nothing below his probing foot but a hundred and twenty feet of sheer drop to the land-locked harbour of Navarone.

Away to his right was a dark, formless blur lying on the water, a blur that might have been Cape Demirci: straight ahead, across the darkly velvet sheen of the Maidos Straits, he could see the twinkle of far-away lights – it was a measure of the enemy's confidence that they permitted these lights at all, or, more likely, these fisher cottages were useful as a bearing marker for the guns at night: and to the left, surprisingly near, barely thirty feet away in a horizontal plane, but far below the level where he was standing, he could see the jutting end of the outside wall of the fortress where it abutted on the cliff, the roofs of the houses on the west side of the square beyond that, and, beyond that again, the town itself curving sharply downwards and outwards, to the south first, then to the west, close-girdling and matching the curve of the crescent harbour. Above – but there was nothing to be seen above, that fantastic overhang above blotted out more than half the sky; and below, the darkness was equally impenetrable, the surface of the harbour inky and black as night. There were vessels down there, he knew, Grecian caiques and German launches, but they might have been a thousand miles away for any sign he could see of them.

The brief, all encompassing glance had taken barely ten seconds, but Mallory waited no longer. Swiftly he bent down, tied a double bowline in the end of the rope and left it lying on the edge. In an emergency they could kick it out into the darkness. It would be thirty feet short of the water, he estimated – enough to clear any launch or masted caique that might be moving about the harbour. They could drop the rest of the way, maybe a bone-breaking fall on to the deck of a ship, but they would have to risk it. Mallory took one last look down into the Stygian blackness and shivered: he hoped to God that he and Miller wouldn't have to take that way out.

Dusty Miller was kneeling on the duck-boards by the top of the ladder leading down to the magazine as Mallory came running back up the tunnel, his hands busy with wires, fuses, detonators and explosives. He straightened up as Mallory approached.

'I reckon this stuff should keep 'em happy, boss.' He set the hands of the clockwork fuse, listened appreciatively to the barely audible hum, then eased himself down the ladder. 'In here among the top two rows of cartridges, I thought.'

'Wherever you say,' Mallory acquiesced. 'Only don't make it too obvious – or too difficult to find. Sure there's no chance of them suspecting that we knew the clock and fuses were dud?'

'None in the world,' Miller said confidently. 'When they find this here contraption they'll knock holes in each other's back congratulatin' themselves – and they'll never look any further.'

'Fair enough.' Mallory was satisfied. 'Lock the door up top?'

'Certainly I locked the door!' Miller looked at him reproachfully. 'Boss, sometimes I think . . .'

But Mallory never heard what he thought. A metallic reverberating clangour echoed cavernously through the cave and magazine, blotting out Miller's words, then died away over the harbour. Again the sound came, while the two men stared bleakly at one another, then again and again, then escaped for a moment of time.

'Company,' Mallory murmured. 'Complete with sledgehammers. Dear God, I only hope that door holds.' He was already running along the passage towards the guns, Miller close behind him.

'Company!' Miller was shaking his head as he ran. 'How in the hell did they get here so soon?'

'Our late lamented little pal,' Mallory said savagely. He vaulted over the railing, edged back to the mouth of the cave. 'And we were suckers enough to believe he told the whole truth. But he never told us that opening that door up top triggered off an alarm bell in the guard-room.'

Chapter Sixteen

Wednesday Night 2115–2345

Smoothly, skilfully, Miller paid out the wire-cored rope – double-turned round the top rail – as Mallory sank out of sight into the darkness. Fifty feet had gone, he estimated, fifty-five, sixty, then there came the awaited sharp double tug on the signal cord looped round his wrist and he at once checked the rope, stooped and tied it securely to the foot of the stanchion.

And then he had straightened again, belayed himself to the rail with the

the rope's end, leaned far out over the edge, caught hold of the rope with both hands as far down as he could reach and began slowly, almost imperceptibly at first, then with gradually increasing momentum, to swing man and rope from side to side, pendulum-wise. As the swings of the pendulum grew wider, the rope started to twist and jump in his hands, and Miller knew that Mallory must be striking outcrops of rock, spinning uncontrollably as he bounced off them. But Miller knew that he couldn't stop now, the clanging of the sledges behind him was almost continuous: he only stooped the lower over the rope, flung all the strength of his sinewy arms and shoulders into the effort of bringing Mallory nearer and still nearer to the rope that Brown would by now have thrown down from the balcony of the house where they had left him.

Far below, half-way between the cave mouth and the invisible waters of the harbour, Mallory swung in a great arc through the rain-filled darkness of the sky, forty rushing, bone-bruising feet between the extremities of the swings. Earlier he had struck his head heavily on an outcrop of rock, all but losing consciousness and his grip on the rope. But he knew where to expect that projection now and pushed himself clear each time as he approached it, even although this made him spin in a complete circle every time. It was as well, he thought, that it was dark, that he was independent of sight anyway: the blow had reopened an old wound Turzig had given him, his whole upper face was masked with blood, both eyes completely gummed.

But he wasn't worried about the wound, about the blood in his eyes. The rope – that was all that mattered. Was the rope there? Had anything happened to Casey Brown? Had he been jumped before he could get the rope over the side? If he had, then all hope was gone and there was nothing they could do, no other way they could span the forty sheer feet between house and cave. It just *had* to be there. But if it were there, why couldn't he find it? Three times now, at the right extremity of a swing, he had reached out with his bamboo pole, heard the hook scrape emptily, frustratingly, against the bare rock.

And then, the fourth time, stretched out to the straining limit of both arms, he felt the hook catch on! Immediately he jerked the pole in, caught the rope before he dropped back on the downward swing, jerked the signal cord urgently, checked himself gradually as he fell back. Two minutes later, near exhaustion from the sixty-foot climb up the wet, slippery rope, he crawled blindly over the lip of the cave and flung himself to the ground, sobbing for breath.

Swiftly, without speaking, Miller bent down, slipped the twin loops of the double bowline from Mallory's legs, undid the knot, tied it to Brown's rope, gave the latter a tug and watched the joined ropes disappear into the darkness. Within two minutes the heavy battery was across, underslung from the two ropes, lowered so far by Casey Brown then hauled up by Mallory and Miller. Within another two minutes, but with infinitely more caution, this time, the canvas bag with the nitro, primers and detonators, had been pulled across, lay on the stone floor beside the battery.

All noise had ceased, the hammering of the sledges against the steel door had stopped completely. There was something threatening, foreboding about the stillness, the silence was more menacing than all the clamour that had gone before. Was the door down, the lock smashed, the Germans waiting for them in the gloom of the tunnel, waiting with cradled machine-carbines that would tear the life out of them? But there was no time to wonder, no time to wait, no time now to stop to weigh the chances. The time for caution was past, and whether they lived or died was of no account any more.

The heavy Colt .455 balanced at his waist, Mallory climbed over the safety barrier, padded silently past the great guns and through the passage, his torch clicking on half-way down its length. The place was deserted, the door above still intact. He climbed swiftly up the ladder, listened at the top. A subdued murmur of voices, he thought he heard, and a faint hissing sound on the other side of the heavy steel door, but he couldn't be sure. He leaned forward to hear better, the palm of his hand against the door, drew back with a muffled exclamation of pain. Just above the lock, the door was almost red-hot. Mallory dropped down to the floor of the tunnel just as Miller came staggering up with the battery.

'That door's as hot as blazes. They must be burning—'

'Did you hear anything?' Miller interrupted.

'There was a kind of hissing—'

'Oxy-acetylene torch,' Miller said briefly. 'They'll be burnin' out the lock. It'll take time – that door's made of armoured steel.'

'Why don't they blow it in – gelignite or whatever you use for that job?'

'Perish the thought,' Miller said hastily. 'Don't even *talk* about it, boss. Sympathetic detonation's a funny thing – there's an even chance that the whole damned lot would go up. Give me a hand with this thing, boss, will you?'

Within seconds Dusty Miller was again a man absorbed in his own element, the danger outside, the return trip he had yet to make across the face of the cliff, completely forgotten for the moment. The task took him four minutes from beginning to end. While Mallory was sliding the battery below the floored well of the lift, Miller squeezed in between the shining steel runners of the lift shaft itself, stopped to examine the rear one with his torch and establish, by the abrupt transition from polished to dull metal, exactly where the spring-loaded wheel of the shell-hoist came to rest. Satisfied, he pulled out a roll of sticky black tape, wound it a dozen times round the shaft, stepped back to look at it: it was quite invisible.

Quickly he taped the ends of two rubber-covered wires on the insulated strip, one at either side, taped these down also until nothing was visible but the bared steel cores at the tips, joined these to two four-inch strips of bared wire, taped these also, top and bottom, to the insulated shaft, vertically and less than half an inch apart. From the canvas bag he removed the TNT, the primer and the detonator – a bridge mercury detonator lugged and screwed to his own specification – fitted them together and connected one of the wires from the steel shaft to a lug on the detonator, screwing it firmly home. The other wire from the shaft he led to the positive terminal on the battery, and a third wire from the negative terminal to the detonator. It only required the ammunition hoist to sink down into the magazine – as it would do as soon as they began firing – and the spring-loaded wheel would short out the bare wires, completing the circuit and triggering off the detonator. A last check on the position of the bared vertical wires and he sat back satisfied. Mallory had just descended the ladder from the tunnel. Miller tapped him on the leg to draw his attention, negligently waving the steel blade of his knife within an inch of the exposed wires.

'Are you aware, boss,' he said conversationally, 'that if I touched this here blade across those terminals, the whole gawddamned place would go up in smithereens.' He shook his head musingly. 'Just one little slip of the hand, just one teeny little touch and Mallory and Miller are among the angels.'

'For God's sake put that thing away!' Mallory snapped nervously. 'And let's get the hell out of here. They've got a complete half-circle cut through that door already!'

Five minutes later Miller was safe – it had been a simple matter of sliding down a 45-degree tautened rope to where Brown waited. Mallory took a last look back into the cave, and his mouth twisted. He wondered how many soldiers manned the guns and magazine during action stations. One thing, he thought, they'll never know anything about it, the poor bastards. And then he thought, for the hundredth time, of all the men on Kheros and the destroyers, and his lips tightened and he looked away. Without another backward glance he slipped over the edge, dropped down into the night. He was half-way there, at the very lowest point of the curve and about to start climbing again, when he heard the vicious, staccato rattle of machine-gun fire directly overhead.

It was Miller who helped him over the balcony rail, an apprehensive-looking Miller who glanced often over his shoulder in the direction of the gun-fire – and the heaviest concentration of fire, Mallory realized with sudden dismay, was coming from their own, the west side of the square, only three or four houses away. Their escape route was cut off.

'Come on, boss!' Miller said urgently. 'Let's get away from this joint. Gettin' downright unhealthy round these parts.'

Mallory jerked his head in the direction of the fire. 'Who's down there?' he asked quickly.

'A German patrol.'

'Then how in the hell can we get away?' Mallory demanded. 'And where's Andrea?'

'Across the other side of the square, boss. That's who those birds along there are firing at.'

'The other side of the square!' He glanced at his watch. 'Heavens above, man, what's he doing there?' He was moving through the house now, speaking over his shoulder. 'Why did you let him go?'

'I didn't let him go, boss,' Miller said carefully. 'He was gone when I came. Seems that Brown here saw a big patrol start a house to house search of the square. Started on the other side and were doin' two or three houses at a time. Andrea – he'd come back by this time – thought it a sure bet that they'd work right round the square and get here in two or three minutes, so he took off like a bat across the roofs.'

'Going to draw them off?' Mallory was at Louki's side staring out of the window. 'The crazy fool! He'll get himself killed this time – get himself killed for sure! There are soldiers everywhere. Besides, they won't fall for it again. He tricked them once up in the hills, and the Germans—'

'I'm not so sure, sir,' Brown interrupted excitedly. 'Andrea's just shot out the searchlight on his side. They'll think for certain that we're going to break out over the wall and – look, sir, look! There they go!' Brown was almost dancing with excitement, the pain of his injured leg forgotten. 'He's done it, sir, he's done it!'

Sure enough, Mallory saw, the patrol had broken away from their shelter in the house to their right and were running across the square in extended formation, their heavy boots clattering on the cobbles, stumbling, falling, recovering again as they lost footing on the slippery wetness of the uneven stones. At the same time Mallory could see torches flickering on the roofs of the houses opposite, the vague forms of men crouching low to escape observation and making swiftly for the spot where Andrea had been when he had shot out the great Cyclops eye of the searchlight.

'They'll be on him from every side.' Mallory spoke quietly enough, but his fists clenched until the nails cut into the palms of his hands. He stood stock-still for some seconds, stooped quickly and gathered a Schmeisser up from the floor. 'He hasn't a chance. I'm going after him.' He turned abruptly, brought up with equal suddenness: Miller was blocking his way to the door.

'Andrea left word that we were to leave him be, that he'd find his own way out.' Miller was very calm, very respectful. 'Said that no one was to help him, not on any account.'

'Don't try to stop me, Dusty.' Mallory spoke evenly, mechanically almost. He was hardly aware that Dusty Miller was there. He only knew that he must get out at once, get to Andrea's side, give him what help he could. They had been together too long, he owed too much to the smiling giant to let him go so easily. He couldn't remember how often Andrea had come after *him*, more than once when he had thought hope was gone. . . . He put his hand against Miller's chest.

'You'll only be in his way, boss.' Miller said urgently. 'That's what you said . . .'

Mallory pushed him aside, strode for the door, brought up his fist to strike as hands closed round his upper arm. He stopped just in time, looked down into Louki's worried face.

'The American is right,' Louki said insistently. 'You must not go. Andrea said you were to take us down to the harbour.'

'Go down yourselves,' Mallory said brusquely. 'You know the way, you know the plans.'

'You would let us all go, let us all—'

'I'd let the whole damn' world go if I could help him.' There was an utter sincerity in the New Zealander's voice. 'Andrea would never let me down.'

'But you would let him down,' Louki said quietly. 'Is that it, Major Mallory?'

'What the devil do you mean?'

'By not doing as he wishes. He may be hurt, killed even, and if you go after him and are killed too, that makes it all useless. He would die for nothing. Is it thus you would repay your friend?'

'All right, all right, you win,' Mallory said irritably.

'That is how Andrea would want it,' Louki murmured. 'Any other way you would be—'

'Stop preaching at me! Right, gentlemen, let's be on our way.' He was back on balance again, easy, relaxed, the primeval urge to go out and kill well under control. 'We'll take the high road – over the roofs. Dig into that kitchen stove there, rub the ashes all over your hands and faces. See that there's nothing white on you anywhere. And no talking!'

The five-minute journey down to the harbour wall – a journey made in soft-footed silence with Mallory hushing even the beginnings of a whisper – was quite uneventful. Not only did they see no soldiers, they saw no one at all. The inhabitants of Navarone were wisely obeying the curfew, and the streets were completely deserted. Andrea had drawn off pursuit with a vengeance. Mallory began to fear that the Germans had taken him, but just as they reached the water's edge he heard the gunfire again, a good deal farther away this time, in the very north-east corner of the town, round the back of the fortress.

Mallory stood on the low wall above the harbour, looked at his companions, gazed out over the dark oiliness of the water. Through the heavy rain he could just distinguish, to his right and left, the vague blurs of caiques moored stern on to the wall. Beyond that he could see nothing.

'Well, I don't suppose we can get much wetter than we are right now,' he observed. He turned to Louki, checked something the little man was trying to say about Andrea. 'You sure you can find it all right in the darkness?' It was the commandant's personal launch, a thirty-six foot ten-tonner always kept moored to a buoy a hundred feet off-shore. The engineer, who doubled as guard, slept aboard, Louki had said.

'I am already there,' Louki boasted. 'Blindfold me as you will and I—'

'All right, all right,' Mallory said hastily. 'I'll take your word for it. Lend me your hat, will you, Casey?' He jammed the automatic into the crown of the hat, pulled it firmly on to his head, slid gently into the water and struck out by Louki's side.

'The engineer,' Louki said softly. 'I think he will be awake, Major.'

'I think so, too,' Mallory said grimly. Again there came the chatter of machine-carbines, the deeper whiplash of a Mauser. 'So will everyone else in Navarone,unless they're deaf or dead. Drop behind as soon as we see the boat. Come when I call.'

Ten seconds, fifteen passed, then Louki touched Mallory on the arm.

'I see it,' Mallory whispered. The blurred silhouette was less than fifteen yards away. He approached silently, neither legs nor arms breaking water, until he saw the vague shape of a man standing on the poop, just aft of the engine-room hatchway. He was immobile, staring out in the direction of the fortress and the upper town: Mallory slowly circled round the stern of the boat and came up behind him, on the other side. Carefully he removed his hat, took out the gun, caught the low gunwale with his left hand. At the range of seven feet he knew he couldn't possibly miss, but he couldn't shoot the man, not then. The guard-rails were token affairs only, eighteen inches high at the most, and the splash of the man falling into the water would almost certainly alert the guards at the harbour mouth emplacements.

'If you move I will kill you!' Mallory said softly in German. The man stiffened. He had a carbine in his hand, Mallory saw.

'Put the gun down. Don't turn round.' Again the man obeyed, and Mallory was out of the water and on to the deck, in seconds, neither eye nor automatic straying from the man's back. He stepped softly forward, reversed the automatic, struck, caught the man before he could fall overboard and lowered him quietly to the deck. Three minutes later all the others were safely aboard.

Mallory followed the limping Brown down to the engine-room, watched him as he switched on his hooded torch, looked around with a professional eye, looked at the big, gleaming, six-cylinder in line Diesel engine.

'This,' said Brown reverently, 'is an engine. What a beauty! Operates any number of cylinders you like. I know the type, sir.'

'I never doubted but you would. Can you start her up, Casey?'

'Just a minute till I have a look round, sir.' Brown had all the unhurried patience of the born engineer. Slowly, methodically, he played the spotlight round the immaculate interior of the engine-room, switched on the fuel and turned to Mallory. 'A dual control job, sir. We can take her from up top.'

He carried out the same painstaking inspection in the wheelhouse, while Mallory waited impatiently. The rain was easing off now, not much, but sufficiently to let him see the vague outlines of the harbour entrance. He wondered for the tenth time if the guards there had been alerted against the possibility of an attempted escape by boat. It seemed unlikely – from the racket Andrea was making, the Germans would think that escape was the last thing in their minds. . . . He leaned forward, touched Brown on the shoulder.

'Twenty past eleven, Casey,' he murmured. 'If these destroyers come through early we're apt to have a thousand tons of rock falling on our heads.'

'Ready now, sir,' Brown announced. He gestured at the crowded dashboard beneath the screen. 'Nothing to it really.'

'I'm glad you think so,' Mallory murmured fervently. 'Start her moving, will you? Just keep it slow and easy.'

Brown coughed apologetically. 'We're still moored to the buoy. And it might be a good thing, sir, if we checked on the fixed guns, searchlights, signalling lamps. life-jackets and buoys. It's useful to know where these things are,' he finished deprecatingly.

Mallory laughed softly, clapped him on the shoulder.

'You'd make a great diplomat, Chief. We'll do that.' A landsman first and last, Mallory was none the less aware of the gulf that stretched between him and a man like Brown, made no bones about acknowledging it to himself. 'Will you take her out, Casey?'

'Right, sir. Would you ask Louki to come here – I think it's steep to both sides, but there may be snags or reefs. You never know.'

Three minutes later the launch was half-way to the harbour mouth, purring along softly on two cylinders, Mallory and Miller, still clad in German uniform, standing on the deck for'ard of the wheelhouse, Louki crouched low inside the wheelhouse itself. Suddenly, about sixty yards away, a signal lamp began to flash at them, its urgent clacking quite audible in the stillness of the night.

'Dan'l Boone Miller will now show how it's done,' Miller muttered. He edged closer to the machine-gun on the starboard bow. 'With my little gun I shall . . .'

He broke off sharply, his voice lost in the sudden clacking from the wheelhouse behind him, the staccato off-beat chattering of a signal shutter triggered by professional fingers. Brown had handed the wheel over to Louki, was morsing back to the harbour entrance, the cold rain lancing palely through the flickering beams of the lamp. The enemy lamp had stopped but now began again.

'My, they got a lot to say to each other,' Miller said admiringly. 'How long do the exchange of courtesies last, boss?'

'I should say they are just about finished.' Mallory moved back quickly to the wheelhouse. They were less than a hundred feet from the harbour entrance. Brown had confused the enemy, gained precious seconds, more time than Mallory had ever thought they could gain. But it couldn't last. He touched Brown on the arm.

'Give her everything you've got when the balloon goes up.' Two seconds later he was back in position in the bows, Schmeisser ready in his hands. 'Your big chance, Dan'l Boone. Don't give the searchlights a chance to line up – they'll blind you.'

Even as he spoke, the light from the signal lamp at the harbour mouth cut off abruptly and two dazzling white beams, one from either side of the harbour entrance, stabbed blindingly through the darkness, bathing the whole harbour in their savage glare – a glare that lasted for only a fleeting second of time, yielded to a contrastingly Stygian darkness as two brief bursts of machine-gun fire smashed them into uselessness. From such short range it had been almost impossible to miss.

'Get down, everyone!' Mallory shouted. 'Flat on the deck!'

The echoes of the gunfire were dying away, the reverberations fading along the great sea wall of the fortress when Casey Brown cut in all six cylinders of the engine and opened the throttle wide, the surging roar of the big Diesel blotting out all other sounds in the night. Five seconds, ten seconds, they were passing through the entrance, fifteen, twenty, still not a shot fired, half a minute and they were well clear, bows lifting high out of the water, the deep-dipped stern trailing its long, seething ribbon of phosphorescent white as the engine crescendoed to its clamorous maximum power and Brown pulled the heeling craft sharply round to starboard, seeking the protection of the steep-walled cliffs.

'A desperate battle, boss, but the better men won.' Miller was on his feet now, clinging to a mounted gun for support as the deck canted away beneath his feet. 'My grandchildren shall hear of this.'

'Guards probably all up searching the town. Or maybe there *were* some poor blokes behind these searchlights. Or maybe we just took 'em all by surprise.' Mallory shook his head. 'Anyway you take it, we're just plain damn' lucky.'

He moved aft, into the wheelhouse. Brown was at the wheel, Louki almost crowing with delight.

'That was magnificent, Casey,' Mallory said sincerely. 'A first-class job of work. Cut the engine when we come to the end of the cliffs. Our job's done. I'm going ashore.'

'You don't have to, Major.'

Mallory turned. 'What's that?'

'You don't have to. I tried to tell you on the way down, but you kept telling me to be quiet.' Louki sounded injured, turned to Casey. 'Slow down, please. The last thing Andrea told me, Major, was that we were to come this way. Why do you think he let himself be trapped against the cliffs to the north instead of going out into the country, where he could have hidden easily?'

'Is this true, Casey?' Mallory asked.

'Don't ask me, sir. Those two – they always talk in Greek.'

'Of course, of course.' Mallory looked at the low cliffs close off the starboard beam, barely moving now with the engine shut right down, looked back at Louki. 'Are you quite sure . . .'

He stopped in mid-sentence, jumped out through the wheelhouse door. The splash – there had been no mistaking the noise – had come from almost directly ahead. Mallory, Miller by his side, peered into the darkness, saw a dark head surfacing above the water less than twenty feet away, leaned far over with outstretched arm as the launch slid slowly by. Five seconds later Andrea stood on the deck, dripping mightily and beaming all over his great moon face. Mallory led him straight into the wheelhouse, switched on the soft light of the shaded chart-lamp.

'By all that's wonderful, Andrea, I never thought to see you again. How did it go?'

'I will soon tell you,' Andrea laughed. 'Just after—'

'You've been wounded!' Miller interrupted. 'Your shoulder's kinda perforated.' He pointed to the red stain spreading down the sea-soaked jacket.

'Well, now, I believe I have.' Andrea affected vast surprise. 'Just a scratch, my friend.'

'Oh, sure, sure, just a scratch! It would be the same if your arm had been blown off. Come on down to the cabin – this is just a kindergarten exercise for a man of my medical skill.'

'But the captain—'

'Will have to wait. And your story. Ol' Medicine Man Miller permits no interference with his patients. Come on!'

'Very well, very well,' Andrea said docilely. He shook his head in mock resignation, followed Miller out of the cabin.

Brown opened up to full throttle again, took the launch north almost to Cape Demirci to avoid any hundred to one chance the harbour batteries might make, turned due east for a few miles then headed south into the Maidos Straits. Mallory stood by his side in the wheelhouse, gazing out over the dark, still waters. Suddenly he caught a gleam of white in the distance, touched Brown's arm and pointed for'ard.

'Breakers ahead, Casey, I think. Reefs perhaps?'

Casey looked in long silence, finally shook his head.

'Bow-wave,' he said unemotionally. 'It's the destroyers coming through.'

Chapter Seventeen

Wednesday Night Midnight

Commander Vincent Ryan, RN, Captain (Destroyers) and Commanding Officer of His Majesty's latest S-class destroyer *Sirdar*, looked round the cramped chart-room and tugged thoughtfully at his magnificent Captain Kettle beard. A scruffier, a more villainous, a more cut and battered-looking bunch of hard cases he had never seen, he reflected, with the possible exception of a Bias Bay pirate crew he had helped round up when a very junior officer on the China Station. He looked at them more closely, tugged his beard again, thought there was more to it than mere scruffiness. He wouldn't care to be given the task of rounding this lot up. Dangerous, highly dangerous, he mused, but impossible to say why, there was only this quietness, this relaxed watchfulness that made him feel vaguely uncomfortable. His 'hatchet-men,' Jensen had called them: Captain Jensen picked his killers well.

'Any of you gentlemen care to go below,' he suggested. 'Plenty of hot water, dry clothes – and warm bunks. We won't be using them tonight.'

'Thank you very much, sir.' Mallory hesitated. 'But we'd like to see this through.'

'Right then, the bridge it is,' Ryan said cheerfully. The *Sirdar* was beginning to pick up speed again, the deck throbbing beneath their feet. 'It is at your own risk, of course.'

'We lead charmed lives,' Miller drawled. 'Nothin' ever happens to us.'

The rain had stopped and they could see the cold twinkling of stars through broadening rifts in the clouds. Mallory looked around him, could see Maidos broad off the port bow and the great bulk of Navarone slipping by to starboard. Aft, about a cable length away, he could just distinguish two other ships, high-curving bow-waves piled whitely against tenebrious silhouettes. Mallory turned to the captain.

'No transports, sir?'

'No transports.' Ryan felt a vague mixture of pleasure and embarrassment that this man should call him 'sir'. 'Destroyers only. This is going to be a smash-and-grab job. No time for dawdlers tonight – and we're behind schedule already.'

'How long to clear the beaches?'

'Half an hour.'

'What! Twelve hundred men?' Mallory was incredulous.

'More.' Ryan sighed. 'Half the ruddy inhabitants want to come with us, too. We could still do it in half an hour, but we'll probably take a bit longer. We'll embark all the mobile equipment we can.'

Mallory nodded, let his eye travel along the slender outlines of the *Sirdar*. 'Where are you going to put 'em all, sir.'

'A fair question,' Ryan admitted. 'Five p.m. on the London Underground will be nothing compared to this little lot. But we'll pack them in somehow.'

Mallory nodded again and looked across the dark waters at Navarone. Two minutes, now, three at the most, and the fortress would open behind that headland. He felt a hand touch his arm, half-turned and smiled down at the sad-eyed little Greek by his side.

'Not long now, Louki,' he said quietly.

'The people, Major,' he murmured. 'The people in the town. Will they be all right?'

'They'll be all right. Dusty says the roof of the cave will go straight up. Most of the stuff will fall into the harbour.'

'Yes, but the boats—?'

'Will you stop worrying! There's nobody aboard them – you know they have to leave at curfew time.' He looked round as someone touched his arm.

'Captain Mallory, this is Lieutenant Beeston, my gunnery officer.' There was a slight coolness in Ryan's voice that made Mallory think that he wasn't overfond of his gunnery officer. 'Lieutenant Beeston is worried.'

'I *am* worried!' The tone was cold, aloof, with an indefinable hint of condescension. 'I understand that you have advised the captain not to offer any resistance?'

'You sound like a BBC communiqué,' Mallory said shortly. 'But you're right. I did say that. You couldn't locate the guns except by searchlight and that would be fatal. Similarly with gunfire.'

'I'm afraid I don't understand.' One could almost see the lift of the eyebrows in the darkness.

'You'd give away your position,' Mallory said patiently. 'They'd nail you first time. Give 'em two minutes and they'd nail you anyway. I have good reason to believe that the accuracy of their gunners is quite fantastic.'

'So has the Navy,' Ryan interjected quietly. 'Their third shell got the *Sybaris*'s B magazine.'

'Have you got any idea why this should be, Captain Mallory?' Beeston was quite unconvinced.

'Radar-controlled guns,' Mallory said briefly. 'They have two huge scanners atop the fortress.'

'The *Sirdar* had radar installed last month,' Beeston said stiffly. 'I imagine we could register some hits ourselves if—'

'You could hardly miss.' Miller drawled out the words, the tone dry and provocative. 'It's a helluva big island, Mac.'

'Who – who are you?' Beeston was rattled. 'What the devil do you mean?'

'Corporal Miller.' The American was unperturbed. 'Must be a very selective instrument, Lootenant, that can pick out a cave in a hundred square miles of rock.'

There was a moment's silence, then Beeston muttered something and turned away.

'You've hurt Guns's feelings, Corporal,' Ryan murmured. 'He's very keen to have a go – but we'll hold our fire. . . . How long till we clear that point, Captain?'

'I'm not sure.' He turned. 'What do you say, Casey?'

'A minute, sir. No more.'

Ryan nodded, said nothing. There was a silence on the bridge, a silence only intensified by the sibilant rushing of the waters, the weird, lonesome pinging of the Asdic. Above, the sky was steadily clearing, and the moon, palely luminous, was struggling to appear through a patch of thinning cloud. Nobody spoke, nobody moved. Mallory was conscious of the great bulk of Andrea beside him, of Miller, Brown and Louki behind. Born in the heart of the country, brought up on the foothills of the Southern Alps, Mallory knew himself as a landsman first and last, an alien to the sea and ships: but he had never felt so much at home in his life, never really known till now what it was to belong. He was more than happy, Mallory thought vaguely to himself, he was content. Andrea and his new friends and the impossible well done – how could a man be but content? They weren't all going home, Andy Stevens wasn't coming with them, but strangely he could feel no sorrow, only a gentle melancholy. . . . Almost as if he had divined what Mallory was thinking, Andrea leaned towards him, towering over him in the darkness.

'He should be here,' he murmured. 'Andy Stevens should be here. That is what you are thinking, is it not?'

Mallory nodded and smiled, and said nothing.

'It doesn't really matter, does it, my Keith?' No anxiety, no questioning, just a statement of fact. 'It doesn't really matter.'

'It doesn't matter at all.'

Even as he spoke, he looked up quickly. A light, a bright orange flame had lanced out from the sheering wall of the fortress; they had rounded the headland and he hadn't even noticed it. There was a whistling roar – Mallory thought incongruously of an express train emerging from a tunnel – directly overhead, and the great shell had crashed into the sea just beyond them. Mallory compressed his lips, unconsciously tightened his clenched fists. It was easy now to see how the *Sybaris* had died.

He could hear the gunnery officer saying something to the captain, but the words failed to register. They were looking at him and he at them and he did not see them. His mind was strangely detached. Another shell, would that be next? Or would the roar of the gunfire of that first shell come echoing across the sea? Or perhaps . . . Once again, he was back in that dark magazine entombed in the rocks, only now he could see men down there, doomed, unknowing men, could see the overhead pulleys swinging the great shells and cartridges towards the well of the lift, could see the shell hoist ascending slowly, the bared, waiting wires less than half an inch apart, the shining, spring-loaded wheel running smoothly down the gleaming rail, the gentle bump as the hoist . . .

A white pillar of flame streaked up hundreds of feet into the night sky as the tremendous detonation tore the heart out of the great fortress of Navarone. No after-fire of any kind, no dark, billowing clouds of smoke, only that one blinding white column that lit up the entire town for a single instant of time, reached up incredibly till it touched the clouds, vanished as if it had never been. And then, by and by, came the shock waves, the solitary thunderclap of the explosion, staggering even at that distance, and finally the deep-throated rumbling as thousands of tons of rock toppled majestically into the harbour – thousands of tons of rock and the two great guns of Navarone.

The rumbling was still in their ears, the echoes fading away far out across the Ægean, when the clouds parted and the moon broke through, a full moon silvering the darkly-rippling waters to starboard, shining iridescently through the spun phosphorescence of the *Sirdar*'s boiling wake. And dead ahead, bathed in the white moonlight, mysterious, remote, the island of Kheros lay sleeping on the surface of the sea.

LISTAIR MACLEAN ALISTAIR MACLEAN ALISTAIR
STAIR MACLEAN ALISTAIR MACLEAN ALISTAIR M
LISTAIR MACLEAN ALISTAIR MACLEAN ALISTAIR
STAIR MACLEAN ALISTAIR MACLEAN ALISTAIR M
LISTAIR MACLEAN ALISTAIR MACLEAN ALISTAIR
STAIR MACLEAN ALISTAIR MACLEAN ALISTAIR M
LISTAIR MACLEAN ALISTAIR MACLEAN ALISTAIR
STAIR MACLEAN ALISTAIR MACLEAN ALISTAIR M
LISTAIR MACLEAN ALISTAIR MACLEAN ALISTAIR
STAIR MACLEAN ALISTAIR MACLEAN ALISTAIR M
LISTAIR MACLEAN ALISTAIR MACLEAN ALISTAIR
STAIR MACLEAN ALISTAIR MACLEAN ALISTAIR M
LISTAIR MACLEAN ALISTAIR MACLEAN ALISTAIR
STAIR MACLEAN ALISTAIR MACLEAN ALISTAIR M
LISTAIR MACLEAN ALISTAIR MACLEAN ALISTAIR
STAIR MACLEAN ALISTAIR MACLEAN ALISTAIR M
LISTAIR MACLEAN ALISTAIR MACLEAN ALISTAIR
STAIR MACLEAN ALISTAIR MACLEAN ALISTAIR M
LISTAIR MACLEAN ALISTAIR MACLEAN ALISTAIR
STAIR MACLEAN ALISTAIR MACLEAN ALISTAIR M
LISTAIR MACLEAN ALISTAIR MACLEAN ALISTAIR
STAIR MACLEAN ALISTAIR MACLEAN ALISTAIR M
LISTAIR MACLEAN ALISTAIR MACLEAN ALISTAIR
STAIR MACLEAN ALISTAIR MACLEAN ALISTAIR M
LISTAIR MACLEAN ALISTAIR MACLEAN ALISTAIR
STAIR MACLEAN ALISTAIR MACLEAN ALISTAIR M
LISTAIR MACLEAN ALISTAIR MACLEAN ALISTAIR
STAIR MACLEAN ALISTAIR MACLEAN ALISTAIR M
LISTAIR MACLEAN ALISTAIR MACLEAN ALISTAIR
STAIR MACLEAN ALISTAIR MACLEAN ALISTAIR M
LISTAIR MACLEAN ALISTAIR MACLEAN ALISTAIR
STAIR MACLEAN ALISTAIR MACLEAN ALISTAIR M
LISTAIR MACLEAN ALISTAIR MACLEAN ALISTAIR
STAIR MACLEAN ALISTAIR MACLEAN ALISTAIR M
LISTAIR MACLEAN ALISTAIR MACLEAN ALISTAIR
STAIR MACLEAN ALISTAIR MACLEAN ALISTAIR M